A Plain Commentary on the Four Holy Gospels

Vol. II

Anatiposi

John William Burgon

A Plain Commentary on the Four Holy Gospels

Vol. II

Reprint of the original.

1st Edition 2023 | ISBN: 978-3-38230-270-2

Anatiposi Verlag is an imprint of Outlook Verlagsgesellschaft mbH.

Verlag (Publisher): Outlook Verlag GmbH, Zeilweg 44, 60439 Frankfurt, Deutschland
Vertretungsberechtigt (Authorized to represent): E. Roepke, Zeilweg 44, 60439 Frankfurt, Deutschland
Druck (Print): Books on Demand GmbH, In de Tarpen 42, 22848 Norderstedt, Deutschland

A

PLAIN COMMENTARY

ON

THE FOUR HOLY GOSPELS.

𝔍𝔫𝔱𝔢𝔫𝔡𝔢𝔡 ℭ𝔥𝔦𝔢𝔣𝔩𝔶 𝔣𝔬𝔯 𝔇𝔢𝔳𝔬𝔱𝔦𝔬𝔫𝔞𝔩 𝔥𝔢𝔞𝔡𝔦𝔫𝔤.

ASK FOR THE OLD PATHS, WHERE IS THE GOOD WAY, AND WALK THEREIN; AND YE SHALL FIND
REST FOR YOUR SOULS.—*JEREMIAH* vi. 16.

GRANT, O LORD, THAT IN READING THY WORD, I MAY NEVER PREFER MY OWN SENTIMENTS BEFORE
THOSE OF THE CHURCH IN THE PURELY ANCIENT TIMES OF CHRISTIANITY.—*Bp. WILSON.*

IN TWO VOLUMES.

VOL. II.
ST. LUKE.—ST. JOHN.

SECOND AMERICAN EDITION, COMPLETE FROM THE LONDON EDITION.

PHILADELPHIA:
PUBLISHED BY HERMAN HOOKER,
S.W. CORNER CHESTNUT AND EIGHTH STREETS.
1859.

A PLAIN COMMENTARY

ON

THE FOUR HOLY GOSPELS.

ST. LUKE.

CHAPTER I.

ST. LUKE, who wrote his Gospel after those of St. Matthew and St. Mark had been published, will be found to supply many particulars of our LORD's life which the two earlier Evangelists omit. He was divinely guided to begin his Narrative from a much earlier period than they; and to "set forth in order" the history of the Birth, not only of our Blessed SAVIOUR, but of His Forerunner likewise. It has been piously, and reasonably thought, that he derived some of his information as to these events, (subject to the suggestions and guidance of the HOLY GHOST,) from the Virgin Mother herself. In the course of this portion of his Gospel, occur the three Inspired Hymns which make part of our Daily Service.

St. Luke then proceeds to relate the same events, generally, as are found in St. Matthew and St. Mark; but always with important differences, in matters of detail. Five consecutive chapters, however, (ch. xiii. to ch. xvii.,) contain information peculiar to the present Gospel.

Though not actually one of the Apostolic body, he seems to have been an eye-witness of many of the events which he describes. (See below, the note on verse 3.) And there are places in his Gospel where he has been permitted to come wonderfully near his LORD; as when he describes the mysterious hour of His Agony in the Garden:—xxii. 41 to 46.

He begins his Narrative with relating something about himself; his qualification for the work of an Evangelist, and the purpose with which he wrote his Gospel:—where every word is full of wonder, and even of difficulty. The Reader will also, (it is trusted,) find that every statement may be turned to edification and delight, as well. St. Paul relates(a) that St. Luke was a Physician of the Body. "The Brother, whose praise is in the Gospel throughout all the Churches,"(b) is found to have been also a skillful Physician of the Soul.

1, 2 FORASMUCH as many have taken in hand to set forth in order a declaration of those things which are most surely believed among us,

(a) Colossians iv. 14. (b) 2 Cor. viii. 18.

even as they delivered them unto us, which from the beginning were eye-witnesses, and ministers of the Word:

These four verses are called the "Preface" to St. Luke's Gospel: from which, we learn many things of importance; as, first, that there was a time when, from the report of eye-witnesses, many narratives of our LORD's Life, besides the four which we now possess, had been committed to writing. But observe,—their Authors had "*taken in hand*" a task which they were not divinely commissioned to perform. It may be inferred, from what is here said, that to be in possession of the personal notices of eye-witnesses even, was not a sufficient qualification to enable a man to become an Evangelist; inasmuch as all the narratives here alluded to, have perished. St. Luke did not so "take in hand" to write a Gospel. The HOLY SPIRIT moved him;—whereupon it seemed good to him;—and he wrote.

3 it seemed good to me also, having had perfect understanding of all things from the very first, to write unto thee in order, most excellent Theophilus,

You observe that St. Luke contrasts the way in which *he* had obtained his information, with that in which the "many" who had "taken in hand" to write a History of our LORD's Life, had obtained theirs. *They* wrote from tradition: St. Luke had enjoyed "perfect understanding of all things from the very first,"—probably as an eye-witness. The Church has indeed always inclined to the belief that he was one of the Seventy Disciples,—whose sending out, he alone describes in his tenth Chapter. *That* portion of Scripture is therefore appointed to be read on St. Luke's Day.

4 that thou mightest know the certainty of those things, wherein thou hast been instructed.

This, then, was the object with which this Gospel was written. The Evangelist seems to have bestowed all his labour in building up one Gentile heart in the Christian faith. And GOD blessed him in the deed; for thereby the whole Church of CHRIST hath been, and will be, edified forever. Shall *we* sometimes disdain a narrow field for labour, and be discontented at having to minister (if need be) to a single soul?

About Theophilus, whom St. Luke addresses, we know nothing: but his name signifies "Beloved of GOD;" and (O Reader!) be sure of this, that if *thou* art beloved of GOD, St. Luke's Gospel is specially addressed to *thee*.

5 There was in the days of Herod, the king of Judæa, a certain priest named Zacharias, of the course of Abia:

David distributed the priests into twenty-four courses ;(c) when "the eighth" lot came forth "to Abijah." (ver. 10.) Zacharias was descended from one of the priests who belonged to *his* "course."

and his wife *was* of the daughters of Aaron, and her name *was* Elisabeth.

The Old Testament names immediately meet us. "Elisabeth" is the same word as "Elisheba,"(d) and "Mary" as "Miriam."(e)

6, 7 And they were both righteous before GOD, walking in all the commandments and ordinances of the LORD, blameless. And they had no child, because that Elisabeth was barren, and they both were *now* well stricken in years.

The expression in the original is,—"they were both *far advanced in their days:*" as if implying that this holy pair had wellnigh reached the end of their earthly race.

(c) 1 Chron. xxiv. 1–18.   (d) Exodus vi. 23.   (e) Exodus xv. 20.

8, 9 And it came to pass, that while he executed the Priest's office before GOD in the order of his course, according to the custom of the Priest's office, his lot was to burn incense when he went into the Temple of the LORD.

10 And the whole multitude of the people were praying without, at the time of incense.

Refer, here, to Leviticus xvi. 17.

11 And there appeared unto him an Angel of the LORD standing on the right side of the altar of incense.

The dawn of the Gospel takes place in the Temple of GOD.
Concerning the Altar of incense, see Exodus xxx. 1 to 9. It stood "before the veil that is by the ark of the testimony." Incense was symbolical of Prayer; whence it is said in the Book of Revelation that the "odours" in the golden vials, are "*the prayers of Saints*,"—chap. v. 8. See also Revelation viii. 3, 4; and the note on St. Matthew ii. 11 may be consulted.
We are reminded by this description of where the Angel stood, not only of the place of Session of the Eternal SON.(*f*)—but also that it was on *the right side* of the Holy Sepulchre that a heavenly Messenger was seen after the Resurrection of our LORD;(*g*) and on *the right side* of the ship that the net was lowered on the capturing of the second miraculous draught of fishes.(*h*)

12, 13 And when Zacharias saw *him*, he was troubled, and fear fell upon him. But the Angel said unto him, Fear not, Zacharias: for thy prayer is heard; and thy wife Elisabeth shall bear thee a son,

So that, in former years, Zacharias had prayed earnestly for children; but he had long since made up his mind that GOD had refused his petition. The Angel informs him that it was far otherwise.
Until this time, only two cases of conception, predicted by an Angel, are recorded to have occurred: namely, the prediction respecting Isaac, made to Abraham;(*i*) and the prediction respecting Samson, made to Manoah's wife.(*k*) See the note on St. Luke ii. 21.

and thou shalt call his name John.

See the note on the latter part of St. Luke ii. 21.

14, 15 And thou shalt have joy and gladness; and many shall rejoice at his birth. For he shall be great in the sight of the LORD, and shall drink neither wine nor strong drink: and he shall be filled with the HOLY GHOST, even from his Mother's womb.

That is to say, the vow of the Nazarite should be upon him, (as it had been upon Samson,)(*l*) from the time of his birth. Concerning that vow, see Numbers vi. 2, 3.

16, 17 And many of the children of Israel shall he turn to the LORD their GOD. And he shall go before Him in the spirit and power of Elias, to turn the hearts of the fathers to the children, and the disobedient to the wisdom of the just; to make ready a people prepared for the LORD.

This is best explained by a reference to the actual prophecy of Malachi, (iv. 5, 6,) alluded to by the Angel. "Behold, I will send you Elijah the prophet before the coming of the great and dreadful day of the LORD: and he shall turn the heart of the Fathers to the Children, and the heart of the Children to their Fathers." The Baptist came "in the spirit and power of Elias," inasmuch as he was one who

(*f*) St. Mark xvi. 19.   (*g*) St. Mark xvi. 5.   (*h*) St. John xxi. 6.
(*i*) Genesis xvii. 21, &c.   (*k*) Judges xiii. 3.   (*l*) Judges xiii. 4, 5.

"constantly spoke the truth, boldly rebuked vice, and patiently suffered for the Truth's sake."*(m)*

18, 19 And Zacharias said unto the Angel, Whereby shall I know this? for I am an old man, and my wife well stricken in years. And the Angel answering said unto him, I am Gabriel, that stand in the presence of God; and am sent to speak unto thee, and to show thee these glad tidings.

An awful, yet most calm rebuke, truly; and worthy of an Angel from Heaven.*(n)* He that speaks to thee is Gabriel, (that is, "the Man of God,") whose office in Heaven it is to stand in the presence of the Most High. I, who in the days of old was sent to Daniel,*(o)* behold am now sent with heavenly tidings *unto thee!* . . . . How must the heart, which a moment before wavered, have been overcome by the solemn recollections which every word of the glorious Speaker awakened!

20 And, behold, thou shalt be dumb, and not able to speak, until the day that these things shall be performed; because thou believest not my words, which shall be fulfilled in their season.

So that Zacharias received a sign, though a very different one from what he had expected: and an appropriate sign it was; for behold, the faculty of speech, which he had misused to express mistrust in God's promises, was for a fixed time withdrawn. He became *deaf* moreover, as well as dumb; for, when the Baptist was to be circumcised, we shall find that the neighbours "*made signs* to his Father, how he would have him called." ver. 62.

In the words actually employed by Zacharias, and the Blessed Virgin Mary, respectively,*(p)* there does not seem to be much difference; but the Speakers were very diversely affected. While *hers* was the hesitation of *Faith*,*(q)* which timidly asked for *explanation*,—*his* was the reluctance of *Unbelief*, which required a *sign*. Hence, *her* doubt was solved,—*his*, punished.

21 And the people waited for Zacharias, and marvelled that he tarried so long in the Temple.

They were waiting for him to come out and bless them. "How was he honoured in the midst of the people in his coming out of the sanctuary!"—as it is said by the son of Sirach. "He went down, and lifted up his hands over the whole congregation of the children of Israel, to give the blessing of the Lord with his lips."*(r)*

22 And when he came out, he could not speak unto them: and they perceived that he had seen a vision in the Temple: for he beckoned unto them, and remained speechless.

He could not pronounce the accustomed words of Blessing. Surely it was a highly significant circumstance that at the moment when the good tidings of the Gospel had been proclaimed, and an event had been announced by which the Law was to cease, the Priest should come forth from the Sanctuary of God with dumb lips! Consider St. Luke xvi. 16; and St. Matthew xi. 13.

23 And it came to pass, that, as soon as the days of his ministration were accomplished, he departed to his own house.

24, 25 And after those days his wife Elisabeth conceived, and hid herself five months, saying, Thus hath the Lord dealt with me in the days wherein He looked on *me*, to take away my reproach among men.

She speaks after the manner of the daughters of Abraham,—with whom, to go childless was accounted a reproach.

The case of Elisabeth more nearly resembles that of Sarah, than of any other

---

(m) Collect for St. John Baptist's Day.
(o) Daniel viii. 16: ix. 21.
(q) See verse 45.
(n) Compare Jude ver. 9.
(p) See ver. iv. 34.
(r) Ecclesiasticus l. 5, 20.

pious Matron whose history is given in the Bible:(s) but Rebekah, Rachel, Manoah's wife, and Hannah, are all additional instances of that mysterious economy which from the beginning had been preparing the minds of faithful men for a Birth in "the latter days" which should be out of the course of Nature: the Birth of One whose name should be called "Wonderful." Accordingly, in ver. 36, we shall find the Angel Gabriel bringing forward this very case of Elisabeth, in order to reconcile the Mind of the Blessed Virgin to the mysterious destiny which was in store for herself.

26 And in the sixth month, the Angel Gabriel was sent from GOD unto a city of Galilee, named Nazareth,

No common Angel, but one of the highest order; as was meet, at the sending down from Heaven of the most Blessed message which had ever yet reached this suffering Earth.

That message was to exalt Human Nature above the Cherubim, by proclaiming the Incarnation of the WORD. Yet the Archangel Gabriel hastens with love and obedience to fulfill his embassy. "And," to quote the pious words of Bishop Taylor, "if we were to reduce our prayers to action, and do GOD's will on earth as the Angels in Heaven do it, we should promptly execute every part of the Divine Will; though it were to be instrumental in the exaltation of a brother above ourselves."

27 to a virgin espoused to a man whose name was Joseph, of the house of David; and the virgin's name *was* Mary.

Something has been already said (in the Commentary on St. Matthew's Gospel) concerning the Divine Economy by which it was overruled that Mary should have been "espoused" to Joseph, at the time of the Annunciation; and immediately afterwards have become his Wife. See notes on St. Matth. i. 16, 18, 24. It was needful in this manner, at first, to shroud the mighty mystery of our LORD's Birth from the eyes of carnal men: and (what is more) it was seen fit by this master-piece of divine contrivance, to defeat the vigilance of the Powers of Darkness also.

Do but note with what amazing simplicity, the most wonderful event which had happened in all the ages, is described! *This* was the hour for which Creation had groaned, ever since the Fall. The eyes of Patriarchs and Prophets had ever been turned in wonder and adoration towards *this* event. Faith and Hope had supported themselves "since the world began," in sure belief that the day for the disclosure of the great mystery here revealed, must at last arrive. When it came, how unlike did the manner of its coming prove, to what men had expected! The House was David's House indeed; yet, reduced to what a low condition! In the secrecy of her private chamber,—to a Virgin,—dwelling in a despised city,—far from Bethlehem of Judæa, the scene of the promises,—the Angel Gabriel brings the wondrous tidings which were destined to make all the ends of the Earth rejoice!

See the second note on St. Luke ii. 38.

28 And the Angel came in unto her,

The Angel came *in* unto her,—so that the Blessed Virgin was *within* when she heard the heavenly tidings. Sarah, in like manner, was "in the tent," when she heard the promise.(t) In connection with this subject, consider the following texts,—St. John xi. 20; 1 Tim. v. 13; Titus ii. 5.

and said, Hail, *thou that art* highly favoured, the LORD *is* with thee: blessed *art* thou among women.

The Angel is instructed to bid Mary "Hail;" that is, to bring her a message of *Peace* and *Joy:* whereby GOD revokes the sentence which He had pronounced on our first Mother,—"*In sorrow* thou shalt bring forth children."(u)

29 And when she saw *him*, she was troubled at his saying, and cast in her mind what manner of salutation this should be.

(s) See note on ver. 37.   (t) Genesis xviii. 9, 10.   (u) Genesis iii. 16.

30 And the Angel said unto her, Fear not, Mary: for thou hast found favour with GOD.

He calls her by her name,—as if to inspire confidence, and show that he knew her.

31 And, behold, thou shalt conceive in thy womb, and bring forth a Son, and shalt call His Name JESUS.

It should not escape notice that these words are formed exactly upon those of the prophet Isaiah vii. 14:(x) and what follows (ver. 32) is a distinct allusion to another passage in the same prophet, namely ix. 6, 7.

32 He shall be great, and shall be called the Son of the Highest: and the LORD GOD shall give unto Him the throne of His Father David.

Reminding her thereby of many an ancient prophecy which had gone before; and teaching her that the Offspring of her body was to be none other than the CHRIST.

33 And He shall reign over the house of Jacob forever; and of His Kingdom there shall be no end.

34 Then said Mary unto the Angel, How shall this be, seeing I know not a man?

The Blessed Virgin clearly understood that this promise was made to her in her Virgin estate

35 And the Angel answered and said unto her, The HOLY GHOST shall come upon thee, and the Power of the Highest shall overshadow thee: therefore also that Holy Thing which shall be born of thee shall be called the SON of GOD.

By which words, it is worth observing that the Angel Gabriel declared to the Virgin the mystery of the Blessed Trinity.

There was this contrast between the Old and the New Creation; that whereas, in the first, GOD "*spake* and it was done, He commanded and it stood fast;"—in the second, He wrought secretly and silently,—"coming down," as the Psalmist speaks,(y) with reference to the days of MESSIAH, "like the rain into a fleece of wool, even as the drops that water the Earth."

One of the very earliest of the Fathers, (Ignatius, second Bishop of Antioch,) says of this,—that it was "a crying mystery wrought in the silence of GOD:" a memorable saying, which the Church has never been able to forget.

36 And, behold, thy cousin Elisabeth, she hath also conceived a son in her old age: and this is the sixth month with her, who was called barren.

Mary asked for no sign, yet a sign (the most fitting imaginable!) is given her;—given in love, not in anger as in the case of Zacharias.

Elisabeth was the Blessed Virgin's "cousin." Hence her wondrous son also was the Kinsman of CHRIST.

37 For with GOD nothing shall be impossible.

There is an allusion here to the words of Genesis xviii. 14. The case of Elisabeth resembled that of Sarah. See the note on ver. 25.

38 And Mary said, Behold the handmaid of the LORD; be it unto me according to thy word.

And the Angel departed from her.

(x) Compare St. Matthew i. 21 and 23. (y) Psalm lxxii. 6.

She submits to it, rather as a mysterious dispensation which she could not tell
how to comprehend, than glories in it as a privilege. Her answer befits the Mother
of One who was declared to be "meek and lowly;" owning herself but the Handmaid of Him who was to be her Son.

Observe the wondrous contrast with what took place "in the beginning." At
the Fall of Man, that old serpent, Satan, held parley with a Woman, and deceived
her by the Spirit of Pride. In order to the Restoration of our Nature, an Archangel discourses with another Woman, and persuades her through her Humility.

And here, it may be well worth remarking (with Bishop Taylor) that "the holy
Virgin came to her great perfection and height of piety, by a few, and those,
modest and unattractive, exercises and actions. St. Paul travelled over the world;
preached to the Gentiles and disputed against the Jews; wrote Epistles; suffered
dangers, injuries, affronts, and persecutions to the height of wonder; whereby he
won for himself a crown. But the holy Virgin attained perfection by the means of
a quiet and silent piety, by internal actions of love, devotion, and contemplation:
and instructs us that silent affections, the splendours of an internal devotion, the
union of love, humility, and obedience, the daily offices of prayer and praises sung
to God, acts of faith and fear, of patience and meekness, of hope and reverence,
repentance and charity, and those graces which walk in a veil and silence; make
great ascents to God, and as sure progress to favour and a crown, as the more
ostentatious and laborious exercises of a more public religion."

**39 And Mary arose in those days, and went into the hill country
with haste, into a city of Juda;**

Thirty-eight cities of Judah "in the mountains," are enumerated in the Book of
Joshua, (xv. 48 to 60:) but Tradition has always pointed out "Kirjath-Arba, which
is Hebron,"(z) as the dwelling-place of the venerable pair to whom Mary hastened.

40 and entered into the house of Zacharias, and saluted Elisabeth.

She seems to have taken the holy pair by surprise, through the fervent haste
with which she performed her journey. (The grace of the Holy Spirit knows
nothing of slow endeavours!) Surely the mountains of that "hill country,"—the
forest, and every tree therein,—broke forth into singing, and Earth was joyful; for
the Lord had redeemed Jacob, and comforted His people.(a) "How beautiful upon
the mountains are the feet of him that bringeth good tidings!"(b)

**41 And it came to pass, that, when Elisabeth heard the salutation
of Mary, the Babe leaped in her womb; and Elisabeth was filled with
the HOLY GHOST.**

These holy women, meeting to compare and unite their joys, and then made prophetic and inspired, must needs have discoursed like Angels; for (as a pious Bishop
has remarked) all the faculties of Nature were turned into Grace. It is not easy
to imagine the rapture of this blessed meeting. Never, but in Heaven, was there
more joy and ecstasy!

**42 And she spake out with a loud voice, and said, Blessed *art* thou
among women, and blessed *is* the Fruit of thy womb.**

Observe the "*loud* voice." Verily, if she had not spoken as she did, the very
stones must have cried out!

Notice also, that she repeats the Angel's salutation; see ver. 28.

Rightly does Elisabeth call our SAVIOUR CHRIST, "the fruit of thy womb:" for
she spake of One "who took Man's nature in the womb of the Blessed Virgin, of
her substance."(c)

**43, 44 And whence *is* this to me, that the Mother of My LORD should
come to me? For, lo, as soon as the voice of thy salutation sounded
in mine ears, the Babe leaped in my womb for joy.**

(z) Joshua xv. 54.   (a) Isaiah xliv. 23, and xlix. 13.   (b) Isaiah liii. 7.
                            (c) Article II.

It has been said,—"Grace introduces things to which Nature is a stranger." The Forerunner, yet unborn, bears testimony to his yet unborn Lord:—a significant circumstance, surely; as indicative of the coming of a Kingdom where mysteries are hidden from the wise and prudent, but revealed unto Babes!(d)

We shall behold our Saviour in like manner coming to His servant, (the Greater to the Less!) for Holy Baptism. See note on St. Matth. iii. 13.

45 And blessed is she that believed: for there shall be a performance of those things which were told her from the Lord.

Every word of this address(e) is clearly prophetical,—for which the declaration in ver. 41 prepares us. Elisabeth sees the whole extent of the mystery. Not only does she declare the present wonder, that Mary is the Mother of the Redeemer; and the future issue, that all things shall be fulfilled which have been foretold her; but she is able also to declare the state of heart in which her kinswoman received the Angel Gabriel's message: Past, and Present, and Future open to her prophetic sight.

Thereupon was poured forth the Divine "Magnificat,"—whose echoes yet fill the Churches of Christendom. The Hymn of the Blessed Virgin is manifestly constructed upon the same model as that strain of thankfulness which Hannah gave utterance to, on a similar occasion;(f) and with which indeed it should be compared throughout. The germ of both heavenly compositions is to be found in a yet more ancient Song,—namely, that of Sarah, contained in Genesis xxi. 6.

46, 47 And Mary said, My soul doth magnify the Lord, and my spirit hath rejoiced in God my Saviour.

Now, "the fruit of the Spirit is Love, Joy, Peace."(g)
Observe how she drops, in her exceeding exultation, the thought of self. Her joy is not in herself, but in GOD her SAVIOUR.

48 For He hath regarded the low estate of His handmaiden: for, behold, from henceforth all generations shall call me blessed.

She speaks not of her poverty,—and yet, she was very poor; but (after the manner of a Hebrew mother) her words have reference to the reproach of childlessness which God had removed from her. Compare ver. 25. What a profound and glorious meaning do the common words of rejoicing among the Mothers of Israel,(h) assume on the lips of the Virgin Mother of our Lord!—the "Blessed Virgin" let us call her,—and so, fulfill her prophecy.

49 For He that is mighty hath done to me great things; and holy is His Name.

"That Soul," as Bede remarks, "can alone duly magnify the Lord, for whom He deigns to do mighty things."

50 And His Mercy is on them that fear Him from generation to generation.

To quote the same writer, once more,—"As if she had said, Not only for me hath He that is mighty done great things; but in every nation, he that feareth God is accepted of Him."
This is almost a quotation from Psalm ciii. 17.

51 He hath showed strength with His arm; He hath scattered the proud in the imagination of their hearts.

That is, Those who, in the imagination of their hearts, are proud,—He hath scattered.

52, 53 He hath put down the mighty from their seats, and exalted

(d) St. Matth. xi. 26.   (e) Ver. 42 to 45.   (f) 1 Samuel ii. 1 to 10.
(g) Galat. v. 22.   (h) See Leah's words,—Genesis xxix. 32: and Hannah's,—1 Sam. i. 11.

them of low degree. He hath filled the hungry with good things; and the rich He hath sent empty away.

With verses 51, 52, 53, compare the corresponding parts of Hannah's Song,—namely, 1 Sam. ii. 4, 5, 6, 7, 8.

The following places of Scripture will also be found worth referring to, in illustration of the three last verses, viz., Job v. 11: Psalm cxiii. 7: Ezekiel xvii. 24: xxi. 26.

Some of the wonders to be achieved by the Introduction of the Gospel are here glanced at. First, is described the dethronement and casting down of the Devil, and of all his evil host,(i)—together with the exaltation of "the poor of this world, rich in faith," to be "heirs of the Kingdom."(k)   Next, it is prophesied how they who hunger after Eternal Life with their whole soul,(l) shall be filled, when Christ shall appear in glory; while they who, rejoicing in their self-righteousness, think themselves rich, shall in the end be sent empty away.

54 He hath holpen His servant Israel, in remembrance of *His* Mercy;

This verse seems intended to recall Psalm xcviii. 3.

55 as He spake to our Fathers, to Abraham and to his seed forever.

The allusion in this verse to the last words of the prophet Micah (vii. 20) seems unmistakable.

The Blessed Virgin speaks, of course, of the true spiritual Israel. "For," as St. Paul explains, "they are not all Israel, which are of Israel:"(m) but "the Israel of God"(n) are "such as are of a clean heart."(o)   "*They which are of Faith*, the same are *the children of Abraham.*"(p)   And this promise is not narrowed by any limits; but to the very end of time there shall never lack believers,—whereby Abraham shall have a "seed, *forever.*"

It is a divine thing that the Blessed Virgin should have thus glanced back to the beginning, from the end; and by this allusion to God's promise made to Abraham,(q) should have virtually admitted, and in the very highest sense, "that there had not failed aught of any good thing which the Lord had spoken unto the house of Israel. All had come to pass."(r)

If any do inquire how it happens that this Hymn, poured forth in expression of the Blessed Virgin's Joy and Thankfulness, should have become a portion of the Church's Daily Service,—let them know that it does not contain one word of exultation but what every humble Christian may make his own. When the Eternal Word was made flesh, it was not, of course, the Blessed Virgin in particular, but mankind in general, which He designed to honour. The purpose of the Son of God, when He honoured the Blessed Virgin so far as in, and from, her to become Man, was to advance Human Nature by assuming it into the Unity of His Divine Person; so that, being born of her, He might procure not only hers, but our common Salvation.   Every member of the great human family may therefore sing the "Magnificat;" and when he bears his part in that divine Anthem, should learn to make the Blessed Virgin's raptures a private and a personal concern:—"My soul doth magnify the Lord, and my Spirit rejoiceth in God my Saviour; because He did regard the low estate of us poor mortal men,—His afflicted servants. For behold, in consequence of the Incarnation of the Son of God, all generations of mankind, ay, and every order of the Angelic Host, shall for evermore pronounce us 'Blessed:' for the Mighty One did mighty things for us, when He united Himself to our fallen Nature: wherefore Holy is He; and Blessed for evermore be His Holy Name!"

56 And Mary abode with her about three months, and returned to her own house.

During those three months Prayer and Meditation rather than converse, was surely the resource of this pair of holy Matrons: for unspeakable was the blessed-

---

(i) Compare St. Luke x. 18.   (k) St. James ii. 5.
(l) Compare St. Luke xv. 16, 17, 23, (the case of the Gentile world:) St. Matthew xv. 26, 27, &c.   (m) Romans ix. 6.
(n) Galat. vi. 16.   (o) Psalm lxxiii. 1.   (p) Galat. iii. 7.
(q) Genesis xii. 3, xvii. 7, &c.   (r) Joshua xxi. 45, and xxiii. 14.

ness to which they had been respectively called. And now, when Elisabeth was about to become a Mother, they parted; and we are not informed that they ever met again.

57, 58, 59 Now Elisabeth's full time came that she should be delivered; and she brought forth a son. And her neighbours and her cousins heard how the LORD had showed great mercy upon her; and they rejoiced with her. And it came to pass, that on the eighth day they came to circumcise the child; and they called him Zacharias, after the name of his father.

Rather, "they were for calling him,"—"They wanted to call him." Compare St. Matthew iii. 14.

60, 61, 62 And his Mother answered and said, Not *so;* but he shall be called John. And they said unto her, There is none of thy kindred that is called by this name. And they made signs to his Father, how he would have him called.

They "made signs" to Zacharias, because he was now *deaf* as well as dumb. See the note on verse 20.

63, 64 And he asked for a writing-table, and wrote, saying, His name is John. And they marvelled all. And his mouth was opened immediately, and his tongue *loosed,* and he spake, and praised God.

As Unbelief had bound him, so Faith now set him free. And, as an ancient writer remarks, it was but reasonable that when the voice of the WORD came forth, —see St. John i. 23,—the tongue of his Father should have been loosed likewise.

65, 66 And fear came on all that dwelt round about them: and all these sayings were noised abroad throughout all the hill country of Judæa. And all they that heard *them* laid *them* up in their hearts, saying, What manner of child shall this be! And the Hand of the LORD was with him.

67 And his father Zacharias was filled with the HOLY GHOST, and prophesied, saying,

The first purpose in which he employed the recovered gift of speech seems to have been the pouring out of that Inspired Hymn,—the "Benedictus,"—which Holy Church has since adopted as a part of her daily utterance. Well may she have done so! for every word here, prophetically spoken, has reference to the Spiritual Reign of MESSIAH; and the blessings commemorated, belong not to the nation of the Jews only, but, in the full extent of their signification, to all the people of GOD.

68 Blessed *be* the LORD GOD of Israel; for He hath visited and redeemed His people,

See how his prophetic speech glances on to the last page of the Gospel! And yet, it is not to be supposed that the inspired speaker had any conception of the sublime mystery which his words enfolded. He opened his lips to praise the GOD of Israel for having at last "visited,"—that is, "looked graciously upon,"—His people; and wrought for them the long-promised deliverance from their enemies: but he knew not the true nature of that deliverance, though he was divinely guided to call it by its proper name,—*Redemption.* See Ephes. i. 7: Coloss. i. 14: Rev. v. 9.

69 and hath raised up an Horn of Salvation for us in the house of His servant David;

Or, as it stands in the Prayer-book, "a *mighty* Salvation;" for "a horn" is the emblem—because, with certain animals, it is the instrument—of strength. Hence such expressions as are found in Jeremiah xlviii. 25, Psalm lxxv. 4, 10, cxii. 9, &c. Compare 1 Sam. ii. 10, and Psalm xviii. 2: but especially Psalm cxxxii. 17.

Note also, that here and elsewhere, *Kingly* power is chiefly intended; whence "horns" actually stand for "Kings" in the Book of Daniel, and other parts of Scripture.(s)

70 (as He spake by the mouth of His holy Prophets, which have been since the World began:)

For the whole volume of the Old Testament is but one long prophecy of CHRIST; "Yea, and all the Prophets, from Samuel, and those that follow after, as many as have spoken, have likewise foretold of these days."(t)

To speak more truly, it was GOD, (as we learn from this place,) who spoke *by their mouth*. Compare the language of Acts i. 16, and see the note on St. Matth. i. 22. Our own Hooker has said on this subject,—"They neither spake nor wrote any word of their own, but uttered syllable by syllable as the SPIRIT put it into their mouths; no otherwise than as the harp or the lute doth give a sound according to the discretion of *his* hands that holdeth and striketh it with skill." . . . . It is remarkable that the very word for a Prophet, in Hebrew, is thought by the learned to imply *one who speaks as another moves him*.

This appeal to GOD's "holy Prophets of old" is introduced parenthetically: verses 69 and 71 must be taken together.

71, 72 that we should be saved from our enemies, and from the hand of all that hate us; to perform the Mercy *promised* to our Fathers, and to remember His holy covenant;

According to the mind of the SPIRIT, the reference in this place is, of course, to ghostly, not to bodily, enemies. CHRIST,—the Horn spoken of in ver. 69,—is declared, in ver. 71, to be "*Salvation from our enemies*," &c. And thereby, in the verse which follows, it is prophetically foretold that the LORD GOD of Israel was about "*to show mercy to our Fathers*, and to remember His holy covenant" with them.

73, 74, 75 the oath which He sware to our Father Abraham, that He would grant unto us, that we being delivered out of the hand of our enemies might serve Him without fear, in holiness and righteousness before Him, all the days of our life.

Here, the HOLY SPIRIT is His own interpreter. The reference is to GOD's great oath to Abraham, contained in Genesis xxii. 16 to 18,—and alluded to in Hebrews vi. 13, 14. Compare the language of Psalm cv. 8 to 10.

It seems then, that those famous words,—"I will *bless* thee, and . . . . multiply thy seed as the stars of Heaven,"(u)—were fulfilled, in their highest sense, when it was "granted unto" men, that is, *Power was given them*,(x) to serve GOD in Holiness and Righteousness(y) all the days of their life. For consider, that this was brought about by the outpouring and gift of the HOLY GHOST; whereby GOD procured to the Father of the Faithful, in CHRIST, a spiritual seed, numerous as the stars of Heaven, and as the sand which is upon the sea-shore. Compare Galatians iii. 14.

It appears further, that the words,—"Thy seed shall possess the gate of his enemies,"—besides their obvious, historical sense, which was fulfilled in the days of King David,—received their perfect fulfillment in the days of the Gospel; when, by our SAVIOUR's Advent, the Human Race were "delivered out of the hand of their enemies,"—Sin and Death. See Rom. vi. 18, 22. 1 Cor. xv. 24 to 26; also 55 to 57. Titus ii. 14. 2 St. Peter i. 4. 1 St. John v. 4, 5.—Take notice, by the way, that *these*, (which Zacharias mentions,) were the two great heads of Blessing which Eliezer seems to have recounted to Laban and Bethuel, when they sent away Rebekah to become Isaac's wife. See Genesis xxiv. 60.

And thus, it is declared that the entire fulfillment of all the glorious promises which GOD had once made to the Fathers, was now at length about to be performed *to them;*—for, as it is elsewhere said by CHRIST Himself,—"all," (that is, all the

---

(s) Daniel vii. 7, 8. Zech. i. 18. Rev. xiii. 1.　　(t) Acts iii. 24. Compare Acts x. 43.
(u) Gen. xxii. 17.　　　　(x) Compare Rev. xi. 3.　　　(y) Compare Eph. iv. 24.

Fathers,—for He was speaking of *them*,—Abraham, Isaac, and Jacob,) "live unto Him."(z)

"Blessed be the LORD, that hath given rest unto His people Israel, according to all that He promised. *There hath not failed one word of all His good promise* which He promised by the hand of Moses His Servant."(a) In such terms could the wise King of Israel express his sense of GOD's Faithfulness, Constancy, and Love. Where shall *we* find language adequate to the expression of ours,—we, "on whom the ends of the World are come?"(b)

76 And thou, child, shalt be called the Prophet of the Highest: for thou shalt go before the face of the LORD to prepare His ways;

The Father turns, in his prophetic rapture, to address his infant child; foretelling that he should "be," (for *that* is the meaning of "being *called*,") "the prophet of the Most High" GOD.(c) We have here, besides, an allusion to Isaiah xl. 3; so that the Gospel itself is briefly summed up in this inspired Hymn.

77, 78, 79 to give knowledge of Salvation unto His people by the remission of their sins, through the tender mercy of our GOD; whereby the Dayspring from on high hath visited us, to give light to them that sit in Darkness and *in* the shadow of Death, to guide our feet into the way of Peace.

"Dayspring" is here a name of CHRIST; whether it should be translated the "East,"—or the "Sun-rising,"(d)—or the "Branch," as in Zech. iii. 8. There is here an evident allusion to Isaiah ix. 1, (quoted in St. Matth. iv. 16:) but the *reason* of the expression "the shadow of Death" will best appear by a comparison with Psalm xxiii. 4; where, as Hammond beautifully points out, it is implied that the sunlight lingers longest on the hills,—the valleys being all the while veiled in gloom, and wearing soonest a funereal shadow.

80 And the child grew, and waxed strong in the spirit, and was in the deserts till the day of his showing unto Israel.

The former of these two statements, we shall presently find repeated with respect to the MESSIAS. See ch. ii. 40.—The "deserts" here spoken of do not necessarily imply such a howling wilderness as that of Jordan. In Judæa every tract of waste, uncultivated country was called *a desert;* whether its barren surface produced nothing but "reeds shaken by the wind,"(e) or whether there happened to be "much grass in the place."(f) What is meant therefore probably, is, that the youthful Nazarite was brought up in solitude and retirement,—remote from all the influences of the Town. There, he increased in stature, and waxed strong in spirit; and, by "enduring hardness,"(g) prepared himself for the wondrous office to which the good Providence of GOD had designed him from his Mother's womb.

For, instead of raiment, he wore a hairy garment and a leathern girdle. Moreover, GOD fed him with locusts; and "satisfied" him, from day to day, "with honey out of the stony rock."(h) And thus, the Baptist grew to manhood; (for we hear no more of him until he had attained the age of thirty years;) an Orphan, doubtless, from his earliest youth. But be sure that "when his Father and his Mother had forsaken him, then the LORD took him up."(i)

THE PRAYER.

We beseech Thee, O LORD, pour Thy Grace into our hearts; that, as we have known the Incarnation of Thy Son JESUS CHRIST by the message of an Angel, so, by His Cross and Passion, we may be brought unto the Glory of His Resurrection; through the same JESUS CHRIST our LORD. Amen.

(z) St. Luke xx. 38.   (a) 1 Kings viii. 56.   (b) 1 Cor. x. 11.
(c) Compare verse 32.   (d) Compare Malachi iv. 2.   (e) St. Matth. xi. 7.
(f) Compare St. Matth. xiv. 13, 15, with St. John vi. 10.   (g) 2 Tim. ii. 3.
(h) Psalm lxxxi. 16. Compare St. Matth. iii. 4.   (i) Psalm xxvii. 10.

CHAPTER II.

1 *Augustus taxeth all the Roman empire.* 6 *The nativity of* CHRIST. 8 *One Angel relateth it to the Shepherds.* 13 *Many sing praises to* GOD *for it.* 21 CHRIST *is Circumcised.* 22 *Mary purified.* 28 *Simeon and Anna prophesy of* CHRIST. 40 *Who increaseth in wisdom.* 46 *Questioneth in the Temple with the Doctors.* 51 *And is obedient to His parents.*

1 AND it came to pass in those days, that there went out a decree from Cæsar Augustus, that all the world should be taxed.

A decree for a general enrolment and numbering of names, rather than for a Census of property, seems to be here spoken of. And the expression, "all the world," probably does not mean all the Roman Empire, but only the whole of Palestine.

2 (*And* this taxing was first made when Cyrenius was governor of Syria.)

Volumes have been written on this verse of Scripture. A person named *Varus* was President of Syria at the time here spoken of. Cyrenius (or Quirinus) did not succeed to the office till about eleven years after; but, (what is remarkable,) on coming to his Presidentship, he certainly did conduct a census. To reconcile the statement of the Evangelist with the known history of the period, has been felt to be a task of great difficulty.

But, it is to be observed, that St. Luke *does not say* that Cyrenius was *President* of Syria at the time of the "taxing." He merely says that he was, then, *governor* of the province; and this, Cyrenius may very well have been, although the Presidentship was in other hands. St. Luke's authority on a point of history is, of course, more trustworthy than that of any uninspired writer; and when he asserts, (as here he seems to do,) that "the taxing" at the time of the Nativity proved the first [of two] taxings which were made while Cyrenius governed Syria,—what difficulty need we feel in accepting the blessed Writer's assurance on the subject?—These remarks shall suffice; but the Reader is referred to the note on St. Luke iii. 1: also to the notes on St. Matthew i. 16, and St. Luke iii. 36.

3 And all went to be taxed, every one into his own city.

This seems to imply the careful record which every Jewish family preserved of its descent; whereby they were enabled, on an occasion like the present, to repair to the city from which the founder of their line had originally come.

4 And Joseph also went up from Galilee, out of the city of Nazareth, into Judea, unto the city of David, which is called Bethlehem;

Bethlehem was the true "City of David:" for his father, Jesse, was of that city.(a) It appears also from a comparison of verses 11 and 15, that the Shepherds knew it by that name. But Jerusalem, as the Seat of David's Royalty, was now almost exclusively so called.

(because he was of the house and lineage of David:)

As St. Luke himself shows in the next chapter,—making use, it may be, of the

(a) 1 Sam. xvi. 1 and 4. Compare St. John vii. 42.

genealogy which the records of Bethlehem furnished.   See also St. Matthew's first chapter.

5 to be taxed with Mary his espoused wife, being great with child.

The Blessed Virgin went up to be taxed, as well as her wedded husband.   She was, therefore, herself "of the house and lineage of David."   See the note on St. Matthew i. 16.

6 And so it was, that, while they were there, the days were accomplished that she should be delivered.

The Bible may be regarded as a Book which removes the veil from History, and reveals *the reason* of it.   The Providence of God is there discovered to us, overruling the actions of mankind, and adapting them to ends and purposes of which their authors were little conscious.   Thus, the present "taxing," whether dictated by the ambition, or the curiosity, or the avarice of the Roman Emperor,—is shown to have furnished an occasion for drawing this holy pair from their remote home in Nazareth of Galilee, to Bethlehem of Judæa; the village which the finger of Prophecy had long before pointed out as destined to be the place of Messiah's birth. The season of the taxing is found, moreover, to have corresponded exactly with the date of the Nativity.   Thus, the official return of the Bethlehemites, stored up among the Roman Archives, will have become documentary evidence of the most unquestionable kind, concerning the very foundation of the Faith.   So entirely was Augustus ministering to the Divine pleasure, while, in the exercise of Imperial power, he followed the dictates of his own unfettered will.

7 And she brought forth her first-born Son,

"First-born,"—because none had been born before Him.   The word is not used to imply that any were born *after*.   See the first note on St. Matthew i. 25.

and wrapped Him in swaddling clothes, and laid Him in a manger:

It has been said,—"No man will have cause to complain of his coarse robe, if he remembers the swaddling-clothes of this Holy Child: nor to be disquieted at his hard bed, when he considers Jesus laid in a manger."
Since this blessed Mother, after she had brought forth her first-born Son, swathed Him herself, and with her own hands deposited His infant limbs in a manger, as St. Luke seems clearly to imply;—it is reasonable to infer that His Nativity was, as His sinless Conception had been,—out of the course of Nature, and miraculous; and that the holy Mother, by a painless birth, had experienced the reversal of the sorrowful sentence passed on our Mother Eve,—recorded in Genesis iii. 16.
What is, at least, quite certain,—hereby was reversed the calamity which our first Mother had brought upon the Human Race.   As, by a woman, Death had been conveyed to all mankind,—so was a woman now made the blessed Instrument whereby He who is our Life came into the world.

because there was no room for them in the Inn.

"*No room* for them in the Inn!"   No room found for *Him* who filleth all things. And is it not so still?   Do we not find room for all other things; yet no room is found for Christ?

8 And there were in the same country Shepherds, abiding in the field, keeping watch over their flock by night.

By the invitation of these poor shepherds to Bethlehem, we are taught that none are fit to come to Christ but those who are poor in spirit, despisers of the world, guileless, simple-hearted.   And with reference to the pastoral Office, a pious writer has said concerning those who watch their flock as well by night as by day,— "these are Shepherds who first converse with Angels, and finally shall enter into the presence of the Lord."

9 And, lo, the Angel of the LORD came upon them, and the glory of the LORD shone round about them: and they were sore afraid.

"Came upon them," here means stood suddenly before them,—as in St. Luke ix. 1. Acts iv. 1: xii. 7, &c.

10, 11 And the Angel said unto them, Fear not: for, behold, I bring you good tidings of great joy, which shall be to all people. For unto you is born this day in the city of David, a SAVIOUR, which is CHRIST the LORD.

The first persons in the world who are apprized of the actual Advent of the MES-SIAH, are the Shepherds of Bethlehem, who keep watch over their flock by night. A singularly honoured occupation, truly; to have numbered of old among those who pursued it. Jacob,(b) Moses,(c) and David;(d) all eminent types of CHRIST:—to have furnished our LORD, moreover, with an appellation in which He delighted;(e) and an image under which He conveyed some of His most solemn and impressive teaching!(ƒ)

12 And this *shall* be a sign unto you; ye shall find the Babe wrapped in swaddling clothes, lying in a manger.

Compare verses 7 and 16. This seems to show that on the day, or rather, *on the very night* of the Nativity, this wondrous vision of Angels was vouchsafed to the Shepherds.

13, 14 And suddenly there was with the Angel a multitude of the Heavenly Host praising GOD, and saying, Glory to GOD in the highest, and on Earth Peace, good will toward Men.

This, then, was the first "Christmas-Carol;"—where Angels were the Choristers, and Salvation was the theme, and Heaven and Earth bowed down to listen. What a jubilant Hymn must this have been, on the redemption of the whole Human Race, if one sinner's repentance can suffice to fill the courts of Heaven with joy!
A single glorious Angel having communicated the joyous tidings,—and so, in a measure, prepared the minds of these simple swains for what might follow,—"a multitude of the heavenly host"(g) are suddenly revealed to their wondering sight; and the heavenly strain which follows, breaks on their ravished ears. It was the birthday of the New Creation.(h) A new corner-stone was being laid. Well, therefore, may the Morning-Stars have sung together, and all the Sons of GOD have shouted for joy!(i)
How much is left in Holy Scripture for the heart of man to realize! How brief and simple are its sublimest statements! How calm and unadorned its most wonderful descriptions! Consider such places as the following:—St. Matthew iv. 23, xvii. 2: St. Mark i. 13, xvi. 19. St. Luke ii. 51, 52, x. 18, xxii. 43, xxiv. 27 and 51, &c. &c. &c. See the note on St. Matthew iii. 5, 6.

15 And it came to pass, as the Angels were gone away from them into Heaven, the Shepherds said one to another, Let us now go even unto Bethlehem, and see this thing which is come to pass, which the LORD hath made known unto us.

16 And they came with haste, and found Mary, and Joseph, and the Babe lying in a manger.

Yet, even there, as He lay,—wrapped in swaddling bands, and reclining in that

(b) Gen. xxx. 31: xxxi. 38–41. Such also was the occupation of Jacob's sons;—see Gen. xxxvii. 13 and xlvii. 3.   (c) Exod. iii. 1.   (d) 1 Sam. xvi. 11: xvii. 15.
(e) St. John x. 11–16.   (ƒ) St. Matth. xxv. 32, 33: xviii. 12: St. Luke xv. 3–7, &c.
(g) See Daniel vii. 10. Hebrews xii. 22. Rev. v. 11, &c.
(h) See the end of the note on St. Matth. iii. 17.   (i) Job xxxviii. 7.

manger,—as God, He filled Creation. For "the Son of Man" which "came down from Heaven," was "*in* Heaven."(*k*) So Cowper, in a well-known Hymn:

> As much, when in the manger laid,
> Almighty Ruler of the sky,
> As when the six days' work He made,
> And filled the morning-stars with joy.

But the remark had been made 1450 years before, by Cyril, Bishop of Alexandria. In consequence of the repeated statement that *a manger* cradled the Infant Saviour,(*l*) painters have loved to represent Him as reclining between the ox and the ass: and the prophecy in Isaiah i. 3, has been (somewhat fancifully, perhaps,) connected with the circumstance. "*The* Manger," (for so it should be rendered,) does in fact here denote that part of the homestead which was set apart for the cattle; and it seems a fitting thing that the second Adam should thus have been among the dumb creatures in the hour of His Nativity, no less than during the hour of His Temptation. See St. Mark i. 13.

17 And when they had seen *it*, they made known abroad the saying which was told them concerning this Child.

They could not contain their rapture, for God had filled their hearts to overflowing. "My cup *runneth over*," saith the Psalmist.(*m*)

18, 19 And all they that heard *it*, wondered at those things which were told them by the shepherds. But Mary kept all these things, and pondered *them* in her heart.

The indications afforded in the Gospel of this Blessed Woman's character, are exceedingly few. The present statement, (which is found partly to recur in ver. 51,) is one of the most remarkable,—namely, that she possessed "the ornament of a meek and *quiet* spirit;" which treasured up every intimation of God's Love, and brooded over the recollection of His many and unspeakable mercies, in the recesses of her own pure heart.

20 And the shepherds returned, glorifying and praising God for all the things that they had heard and seen, as it was told unto them.

These "holy and humble Men of heart,"—Shepherds of Bethlehem,—were therefore the foremost who were chosen to do homage to the Infant Saviour; therein taking precedence even of the Royal and the Wise!(*n*) To "bless the Lord,"—to "praise Him and magnify Him forever," is found to have been instinctively their occupation, on their return.

21 And when eight days were accomplished for the circumcising of the Child,

He who came to fulfill the Law,(*o*) submits like every other descendant of Abraham to be "circumcised on the eighth day;" "so teaching us to be strict in our duties, and sparing in the right of privilege and dispensation." "He sheds His blood now, in drops; giving an earnest of those rivers which He did afterwards pour out for the cleansing all Human Nature, and extinguishing the wrath of God." And thereupon was bestowed that Holy Name at which "every knee should bow, of things in Heaven, and things in Earth, and things under the Earth."(*p*)

His name was called JESUS, which was so named of the Angel before He was conceived in the womb.

To have a name bestowed by God before the birth, is recorded to have occurred altogether in only four cases; that of Ishmael and Isaac, in the Old Testament,(*q*) —that of John Baptist and our Blessed Lord in the New. Of these persons, Ishmael was named *after* conception; Isaac and St. John, like our Saviour, were named *before*.

(*k*) St. John iii. 13.   (*l*) verses 7, 12, 16.   (*m*) Psalm xxiii. 5.
(*n*) See St. Matth. ii. 1, &c.   (*o*) St. Matth. v. 17.
(*p*) Philippians ii. 10.   (*q*) Genesis xvi. 11, and xvii. 19.

22 And when the days of her Purification according to the Law of Moses were accomplished, they brought Him to Jerusalem, to present *Him* to the LORD:

This was at the end of forty days;(r) whence the Feast of "the Purification of St. Mary the Virgin," (which our Church wisely prefers to call "the Presentation of CHRIST in the Temple,")(s) is celebrated on the 2d of February.

The incident which follows, occupies sixteen verses of the Gospel; and is encompassed, as a great writer points out, "with a greater variety of circumstance and detail than any other of the recorded events of our SAVIOUR'S Infancy."

23 (as it is written in the Law of the LORD, Every male that openeth the womb shall be called holy to the LORD;)

Reference is made to Exodus xxxiv. 19.

24 and to offer a sacrifice according to that which is said in the Law of the LORD, A pair of turtle doves, or two young pigeons.

The Blessed Mother made the offering appointed in Leviticus xii. 8, for a poor person, unable to attain to the more costly offering which the Law prescribed to those who could afford it,—namely, a lamb of the first year.(t)

25 And, behold, there was a man in Jerusalem, whose name *was* Simeon; and the same man *was* just and devout, waiting for the Consolation of Israel: and the HOLY GHOST was upon him.

"The Consolation of Israel" denotes the personal Advent of our SAVIOUR CHRIST, —to which many among the Jews were at this time looking anxiously forward. Compare the language of ver. 38. St. Mark xv. 43. St. Matth. xi. 3. St. John i. 19, 20. St. Luke iii. 15.

26 And it was revealed unto him by the HOLY GHOST, that he should not see death, before he had seen the LORD'S CHRIST.

Before he *saw* Death, it was promised to Holy Simeon that he should *see* the LORD'S Anointed.—whom an Apostolic Father calls "Life in Death." This announcement to Simeon may be regarded as the earliest streak of dawn,—the first harbinger of the coming day of the Gospel.

27, 28 And he came by the SPIRIT into the Temple: and when the parents brought in the child JESUS, to do for Him after the custom of the law, then took he Him up in his arms, and blessed GOD, and said,

29, 30 LORD, now lettest Thou Thy servant depart in peace, according to Thy Word: For mine eyes have seen Thy salvation,

How like to those words of Israel to Joseph,—"Now let me die, since I have seen thy face."(u)

Not only had Simeon's eyes "seen," but "his hands had handled," yea, he had embraced and circumscribed in his arms, Him that filled all the World. Simeon, however, is bent on bearing testimony to GOD'S faithfulness in keeping His promise: and so well satisfied is he with it, "that straightway he desires to live no longer: foreseeing that he should never more find comfort in any other object this world could minister."

31, 32 which Thou hast prepared before the face of all people; a light to lighten the Gentiles, and the glory of Thy people Israel.

The prophetic intimation, contained in this last verse, of the scope and purpose of MESSIAH'S coming,(x) is what has so endeared this brief, burning Hymn of holy

---

(r) Leviticus xii. 2, 4.   (s) See the Collect in the Book of Common Prayer.
(t) Leviticus xii. 6.   (u) Genesis xlvi. 30.
(x) With which compare Isaiah xliii. 6: xlix. 6 and lx. 1–3.

Simeon to the heart of all Christendom. Holy Church, by the eye of faith, sees daily, in her second Lesson, *that* Salvation which Simeon beheld with his bodily eyes; and she pours out her thanksgiving in his own prophetic words.

We have repeated this inspired Song so often, that our Spirits are scarcely stirred any longer by its sublimity: but with what ecstatic fervour must it have flowed from the lips of that favoured Servant of God,—conscious, while he uttered it, that he embraced in his arms the Desire of all nations,—Him whom all Creation groaned for,—the Incarnate JEHOVAH!

33 And Joseph and His Mother marvelled at those things which were spoken of Him.

34 And Simeon blessed them, and said unto Mary His Mother, Behold, this *Child* is set for the fall and rising again of many in Israel; and for a sign which shall be spoken against;

CHRIST was to prove the occasion of *falling* to as many of the Jewish nation as should reject Him: but of *rising* "*to become the Sons of God*," to as many as should "believe on His name."(y) The Prophet Isaiah had declared as much, when he said of MESSIAH,—"He shall be for *a Sanctuary;*" (adding in the same breath,)—"but for *a stone of stumbling*, and for *a rock of offence*."(z)

35 (yea, a sword shall pierce through thy own soul also,)

Simeon is supposed to allude to the day of the Crucifixion; when the Mother, pierced with many sorrows, was a witness of the Cross and Passion, and precious Death of her Divine Son.(a)

that the thoughts of many hearts may be revealed.

It seems to be implied that the doctrine of CHRIST, no less than CHRIST Himself, —who had been likened, on this very occasion of His appearance, to *a Refiner's fire*,(b)—was destined to prove a great test of individual character; a wondrous means of revealing what was in the hearts of mankind. "For the preaching of the Cross," says St. Paul, "is to them that perish foolishness; but unto us which are saved, it is the power of God."(c) So St. Peter,(d)—"Unto you, therefore, which believe, He is precious; but unto them which be disobedient . . . . . a stone of stumbling and a rock of offence; even to them which stumble at the word, being disobedient." St. Paul describes the Gospel, as, "a discerner of the thoughts and intents of the heart."(e) While our LORD says plainly,—"He that rejecteth Me, and receiveth not My words, hath one that judgeth him: the word that I have spoken, the same shall judge him in the last day."(f)

36 And there was one Anna, a prophetess, the daughter of Phanuel, of the tribe of Aser:

St. Paul, in like manner, declares of himself that he was of the tribe of Benjamin;(g) which shows how carefully, even to a late period, individuals of the Jewish nation preserved the record of their descent. But the case of Anna is the more extraordinary; since Aser (that is "Asher") was one of the ten tribes which the King of Assyria led away captive into Assyria,—and which had never returned. See 2 Kings xvii. 6.

37 she was of a great age, and had lived with an husband seven years from her virginity; and she was a Widow of about fourscore and four years, which departed not from the Temple, but served GOD with Fastings and Prayers night and day.

(y) St. John i. 12.   (z) Isaiah viii. 14.   (a) St. John xix. 25.
(b) Malachi iii. 2. See below, the note on ver. 38.
(c) 1 Cor. i. 18: and see all the rest of the chapter; also ii. 14. Compare 2 Cor. ii. 15, and St. John iii. 39.
(d) 1 St. Peter ii. 7, 8.   (e) Hebrews iv. 12.   (f) St. John xii. 48.
(g) Rom. xi. 1, and Phil. iii. 5.

She had been a widow for 84 years,—and was therefore upwards of a hundred years old. Her wedded life had been of but seven years' duration, and she had ever since dedicated herself to the service of God. She was therefore one of those "widows indeed," (as St. Paul speaks,) who are entitled to honour; and, as such, she won for herself this glorious mention in the Book of Life. "Now, she that is a widow indeed, and desolate, trusteth in God, and continueth in supplications and prayers night and day."(*h*)

38 And she coming in that instant gave thanks likewise unto the LORD,

"The returns of prayer, and the blessings of piety," says an old writer, "are certain; and though not dispensed according to our narrow expectations, yet shall they so come,—at such times and in such measures,—as shall crown the piety, and satisfy the desires, and reward the expectation. It was in the Temple, the same place where she had for so many years poured out her heart to God, that God poured forth His heart to her; sent His Son from His bosom; and there she received His benediction."

Contemptuous things are sometimes said of a congregation consisting of an old man and woman,—a poor man and his wife. Yet *this* was the very Congregation here assembled,—and CHRIST was among them!

and spake of Him to all them that looked for Redemption in Jerusalem.

It was thus then that the LORD, even the Messenger of the Covenant, suddenly came to His Temple,—as the prophecy of Malachi had foretold, (iii. 1.) How secretly and silently it was done! Consider in like manner the singular fulfillment of Hosea xi. 1, (in St. Matthew ii. 15,) of Jerem. xxxi. 15: (in St. Matt. ii. 18:) of Isaiah xi. 1, &c. (in St. Matt. ii. 23:) of Isaiah liii. 4, (in St. Matt. viii. 17.) Consider even the unlooked-for completion of Zechariah ix. 9, (in St. Matt. xxi. 5,) and of Malachi iv. 5, (in St. Luke i. 13 to 17.) Surely these unexpected fulfillments of ancient prophecies should make *us* very thoughtful. How know we but what unfulfilled prophecy may take *us* equally by surprise, and find *us* equally unprepared? See for example St. Matt. xxiv. 42,—a prophetic warning which is repeated in xxv. 13, &c. &c.

See the note on St. Matthew iv. 14.

39 And when they had performed all things according to the Law of the LORD, they returned into Galilee, to their own city Nazareth.

But first they went down into Egypt,—as St. Matthew had before explained.(*i*) It is the manner of the sacred writers, when they pass over an event in silence, thus to supply no hint of their omission.

40 And the Child grew, and waxed strong in Spirit, filled with Wisdom: and the Grace of GOD was upon Him.

See the note on ver. 52.

41 Now His parents went to Jerusalem every year at the Feast of the Passover.

According to the requirement of the Jewish Law,—Exodus xxiii. 15, 17: xxxiv. 18, 23. Deut. xvi. 1, 16.

42 And when He was twelve years old, they went up to Jerusalem after the custom of the Feast.

43 And when they fulfilled the days, as they returned, the Child JESUS tarried behind in Jerusalem; and Joseph and His Mother knew not *of it*.

44, 45 But they, supposing Him to have been in the company, went a

(*h*) 1 Tim. v. 5.   (*i*) St. Matthew ii. 13–15.

day's journey; and they sought Him among *their* kinsfolk and acquaintance.　And when they found Him not,

For whosoever seeks JESUS, (says a pious Bishop,) must seek Him in the offices of Religion, in the Temple: not amongst the engagement and pursuits of worldly interests.

46 they turned back again to Jerusalem, seeking Him.　And it came to pass, that after three days they found Him in the Temple,

They had gone one day's journey, and had to return: on the third day they found Him.

It has been piously and beautifully suggested by the author last quoted, that Joseph and the Blessed Virgin, after a long and fruitless search,—"almost despairing, faint and sick with travel and fear, with desire and tedious expectations, at last came into the Temple *to pray to* GOD *for conduct and success;* knowing and believing assuredly that if they could find GOD, they should not long miss to find the Holy JESUS.　And their faith," he adds, "deceived them not; for they sought GOD, and found Him that was GOD and man, in the midst and circle of the Doctors." . . . .
Certain it is that *we* also, if we would find CHRIST, must seek Him where He is ever to be found,—in His Holy Temple.

sitting in the midst of the Doctors, both hearing them, and asking them questions.

Whereby, as the same writer has piously remarked, He consigned this truth to His Disciples: that they who mean to be doctors, and teach others, must first learn of those whom GOD and public order hath set over us, in the mysteries of Religion.

47 And all that heard Him were astonished at His understanding and answers.

This mention of "His *answers*" proved that the learned Rabbies were not slow to question *Him* in turn: while the amazement which they testified at the proofs He gave of His understanding, seems to imply that He was induced to discourse to them likewise.　So "filled with Wisdom," was He,—as we read in ver. 40: such "increase" had there already been.　See ver. 52.

It is written in a certain place,—"I have more understanding than My teachers, for Thy testimonies are My study."(*k*)

48 And when they saw Him, they were amazed: and His Mother said unto Him, Son, why hast Thou thus dealt with us? behold, Thy Father and I have sought Thee sorrowing.

49 And He said unto Them, How is it that ye sought Me? wist ye not that I must be about My FATHER's business?

Our Blessed LORD's reply to His Mother's mournful remonstrance is clearly directed against the language in which that remonstrance was conveyed.　She had said,—"*Thy Father* and I have sought Thee."　The Eternal SON makes answer that He had been where He ought to be,—*in His FATHER'S House;* (for so the words should be translated:) and therefore asks, How it came to pass that they had *sought* Him? . . . Which, by the way, are the first words recorded to have been spoken by our Saviour CHRIST.

50, 51 And they understood not the saying which He spake unto them.　And He went down with them, and came to Nazareth, and was subject unto them:

From this time forward, we hear no more of Joseph.　He is thought to have been an old man; and to have died soon after.　Observe, that he is not mentioned in St. Mark vi. 3, or in St. John ii. 12.—For a few words about Nazareth, the scene of our LORD's Infancy and Youth, see the note on St. Luke iv. 16.

(*k*) Psalm cxix. 99.

but His Mother kept all these sayings in her heart.

See the note on ver. 19.

52 And JESUS increased in wisdom and stature, and in favour with GOD and Man.

We are indebted to St. Luke's Gospel, for the only glimpse of the sacred person of our LORD with which we are favoured, from the time of the return to Nazareth, (recorded in ver. 39,) until the period of His Baptism. What is first said of Him, generally, (in ver. 43,) is found to have been equally applicable to the Baptist, at the same time of his life. Compare chap. i. 80. But, of our Blessed LORD it is added, that He was "filled with Wisdom;" and it is specially noted, in the present verse, that He *increased* in wisdom as He increased in stature. St. Luke also mentions (in ver. 51) that our SAVIOUR lived in subjection to His reputed Parents. To these slight intimations, must be added what is suggested, if it be not implied, by the inquiry in St. Mark vi. 3,—"Is not this *the Carpenter?*"—and we have been presented with the sum of all that has been expressly revealed concerning the early years of the Son of Man.

THE PRAYER.

ALMIGHTY and everliving GOD, we humbly beseech Thy Majesty, that, as Thy only-begotten SON was this day presented in the Temple in substance of our flesh, so we may be presented unto Thee with pure and clean hearts by the same Thy SON JESUS CHRIST our LORD. Amen.

CHAPTER III.

---

1 *The preaching and baptism of* John. 15 *His testimony of* CHRIST. 20 *Herod imprisoneth* John. 21 CHRIST *baptized, receiveth testimony from Heaven.* 23 *The age and genealogy of* CHRIST, *from Joseph upwards.*

1, 2 Now in the fifteenth year of the reign of Tiberius Cæsar, Pontius Pilate being governor of Judæa, and Herod being tetrarch of Galilee, and his brother Philip tetrarch of Ituræa and of the region of Trachonitis, and Lysanius the tetrarch of Abilene, Annas and Caiaphas being the high-priests,

By all these conspiring notes of time does the Holy Evangelist guide us to the date of John's preaching: a mighty event, truly, to be fixed by so many concurrent circumstances. Learned men, however, in modern days, have perceived a difficulty here, which seems never to have struck our Fathers in the Faith as any difficulty at all. "The fifteenth year of the reign of Tiberius Cæsar," dates from August, A.D. 28, to the same month in A.D. 29. But there is good reason for fixing the

Birth of CHRIST to an earlier period than the spring of B.C. 4.(*a*) Thus our LORD would have been *more* than 32 years of age at His Baptism: whereas St. Luke says that He then "began to be *about thirty;*" and the inspired Writer doubtless *meant* to say what he *said;* and no other thing.

This certainly occasions a difficulty: for it does not seem a very likely thing that St. Luke should be here fixing *the year of the Crucifixion*—as pious men were once contented to believe. On the other hand, it is ten thousand times more improbable, or rather it is simply incredible, that this Blessed Writer, (to whom so many events beyond mortal ken were revealed,) should have fallen into a mistake(!!!) concerning one of the most ordinary facts in the History of his own time. What remains then, but to suggest that, as St. John reckoned the hours of the day in a peculiar manner, so St. Luke reckoned the regnal years of Tiberius from some unusual epoch—two years earlier than the period commonly assigned to the beginning of his reign? There is nothing at all *improbable* in this suggestion. The years of Augustus Cæsar are variously counted from *five* different epochs. But it certainly is a strange thing that St. Luke should have reckoned the reign of Tiberius, from an epoch (as far as we yet know) *peculiar to himself*. And this shall suffice on a subject concerning which volumes have been written.

It is humbly suggested that a few difficulties of this class may have been suffered to find place in Holy Writ, in order to exercise the faith of persons who, while they feel such intellectual trials very keenly, are but little affected by those which imperil the salvation of the ordinary class of mankind. This remark seems applicable, besides, to such texts as St. Luke ii. 2, and ver. 36 of the present chapter.

And does it not appear as if the HOLY SPIRIT would by this means humble our pride, and convince us of our own ignorance? Some Heavenly doctrine is propounded; and we declare, "It is high: I cannot attain unto it."(*b*) This is only reasonable. But a plain historical fact—a fact of the dryest and most ordinary kind—is next stated; and the result is just the same. It is found to defy all the ingenuity, and all the learning, and all the experience, of all the world! . . . . See the note on St. Matthew i. 16: especially the remarks at the end.

Concerning the Herod and the Philip here mentioned, see the note on St. Mark vi. 17. Upon the deposition of Archelaus, (their brother—mentioned in St. Matthew ii. 22,) Pontius Pilate was sent from Rome as Governor (or *Procurator*) of Judæa. It may be right, however, to state in this place, that the Philip here mentioned is not the Philip we read of below, in ver. 19, (where see the note:) but another brother of the Herod there mentioned. Herod [Antipas] and Philip were sons of Herod the Great by the same wife—Cleopatra of Jerusalem.

the Word of GOD came unto John the son of Zacharias in the Wilderness.

The same mode of expression is found in the Old Testament. "The Word of GOD came to Shemaiah,"(*c*) and "to Nathan."(*d*) We also read of "the Word of the LORD that came unto Hosea,"(*e*) and "to Micah."(*f*) Compare also Jeremiah i. 2, 4, 11, 13: ii. 1, &c. But *the manner* of these communications is one of "the secret things which belong unto the LORD our GOD."(*g*)

Yet, if you would know the substance of *the message* which the Word of GOD brought to the Baptist, you may in part gather it from the subsequent statements of the Baptist himself. See for example, St. John i. 33: also ver. 31.

3, 4, 5, 6 And he came into all the country about Jordan, preaching the Baptism of Repentance for the remission of sins; as it is written in the book of the words of Esaias the Prophet, saying, The voice of one crying in the wilderness, Prepare ye the way of the LORD, make His paths straight. Every valley shall be filled, and every mountain and hill shall be brought low: and the crooked shall be made straight, and the rough ways *shall be* made smooth; and all flesh shall see the Salvation of GOD.

(*a*) See the end of the note on St. Matth. ii. 20.
(*c*) 1 Kings xii. 22.   (*d*) 1 Chron. xvii. 3.
(*f*) Micah i. 1.   (*g*) Deut. xxix. 29.

(*b*) Psalm cxxxix. 6.
(*e*) Hosea i. 1.

This citation from "the book of the words of Isaiah,"—xl. 3 to 5,—is, in part, common to all the four Evangelists:(*h*) but it is given most fully by St. Luke,—to whose Gospel the words "Every Valley," &c., to the end, are peculiar. They are beautifully descriptive of the progress and effects of the Gospel in the world. What so effectually lifts up the lowly and meek, and abases the proud:—casting down the swelling imaginations of the heart, and every high thing which exalteth itself against God? By this, "straight paths are made for our feet,"(*i*) and the rugged way is made plain for us to walk in.

7 Then said he to the multitude that came forth to be baptized of him, O generation of vipers,

That is, "Offspring of vipers,"—implying that they inherited the wickedness of their sires. See the first note on St. Matthew xii. 34.

who hath warned you to flee from the wrath to come?

That is, to seek, by applying to me for Baptism, to escape the righteous vengeance of God. Wherefore he proceeds:

8 Bring forth therefore fruits worthy of Repentance,

Prove your repentance sincere, by a change of life: for "every good tree bringeth forth *good fruit*."(*k*) See the notes on St. Matthew xii. 33, 34.

and begin not to say within yourselves, We have Abraham to *our* Father: for I say unto you, That God is able of these stones to raise up children unto Abraham.

Presume not upon God's promises made to Abraham, and to his seed: overlooking the power of the Almighty to fulfill His words in more than one mysterious way. See the note on St. Matth. iii. 9; and take notice that he had already called them the "offspring" (or seed) "*of vipers*,"—in ver. 7.

The tendency of the heart to rely on the promises of God, as if they were unconditional; instead of conforming the life to His precepts, which really are absolute, has been pointed out in a note on St. Luke iv. 12.

In connection with this subject, read Jeremiah vii.

9 And now also the axe is laid unto the root of the trees; every tree therefore which bringeth not forth good fruit is hewn down, and cast into the fire.

See the note on St. Matthew iii. 10.

10, 11 And the people asked him, saying, What shall we do then? He answereth and saith unto them, He that hath two coats, let him impart to him that hath none; and he that hath meat, let him do likewise.

This amounts to an exhortation to Brotherly Love; or, as it is commonly called in Holy Scripture, *Charity*. "But whoso hath this world's good, and seeth his brother have need, and shutteth up his bowels of compassion from him—how dwelleth the Love of God in *him?*"(*l*)

12, 13 Then came also publicans to be baptized, and said unto him, Master, what shall we do? And he said unto them, Exact no more than that which is appointed you.

These were the *tax-gatherers*, or persons whose business it was to collect *tribute*. The lawless rapacity of this class of officials is revealed by the reply which the Baptist makes to them. Concerning the lesson taught by that reply, see the following note.

(*h*) St. Matth. iii. 3: St. Mark i. 3: St. John i. 23.　　(*i*) Prov. iv. 26, as quoted in Heb. xii. 13.
(*k*) St. Matth. vii. 17.　　(*l*) St. John iii. 17.

14 And the soldiers likewise demanded of him, saying, And what shall we do? And he said unto them, Do violence to no man, neither accuse *any* falsely; and be content with your wages.

This reply of the Baptist to the soldiers surely supplies a sufficient answer to those well-intentioned, but misguided persons, who maintain the unlawfulness of bearing arms. In reply to the question—"And what shall we do?" he does not bid the men abandon their profession; but merely requires of them the performance of "their duty in that state of life to which it had pleased GOD to call them." See the last note on St. Luke vii. 9. The same remark applies equally to what was said to the publicans—in ver. 13.

The men who asked this question were probably not regular soldiery; but an armed force, bound on one of those military expeditions which the feuds of Herod's successors made so common: and the answer they obtained shows, plainly enough, the sins to which they were most addicted.

15, 16 And as the people were in expectation, and all men mused in their hearts of John, whether he were the CHRIST, or not; John answered, saying unto *them* all, I indeed baptize you with water; but One mightier than I cometh, the latchet of whose shoes I am not worthy to unloose; He shall baptize you with the HOLY GHOST and with fire:

He contrasts his Baptism with *that* which CHRIST should hereafter bestow: not a mere outward washing of the body with water, but an inward purifying,—a searching spiritual influence, like that of fire. But his words had a *literal* fulfillment and intention also: see the note on St. Matthew iii. 11.

17 whose fan *is* in His hand, and He will thoroughly purge His floor, and will gather the wheat into His garner; but the chaff He will burn with fire unquenchable.

To make a separation between the righteous and the wicked,—even as a winnowing-fan separates the chaff from the wheat,—is the office constantly claimed to Himself, under different figures, by our Blessed LORD. See, for example, St. Matth. xiii. 30; also 47, 48. Again, see St. Matth. xxv. 32, 33,—where the sheep and the goats supply our LORD with a familiar image.

Delightful it is to discover Almighty GOD employing *the same* figures in the Old Testament as in the New. Thus, the threshing-floor and the fan obtain notice in Isaiah xli. 15, 16,—and Jerem. xv. 7, and li. 2:—while the sheep and the goats are found to recur in Ezek. xxxiv. 17. And what wonder? Was not the same Inspiring SPIRIT the Divine Author of both Testaments?

Take notice, therefore, that the Heavenly "Husbandman," (for so He is styled by the Eternal SON in St. John xv. 1,) has His Vineyard and His Corn-fields:—His flocks and His herds:—His wine-press, and His barns, and His threshing-floor:—His Labourers, and His Servants, and His Shepherds:—all of which, in turn, supply Him with materials for His Heavenly teaching. See the note on St. Matthew iii. 12.

18, 19, 20 And many other things in his exhortation preached he unto the people. But Herod the Tetrarch, being reproved by him for Herodias, his brother Philip's wife, and for all the evils which Herod had done, added yet this above all, that he shut up John in prison.

The scene of his captivity was the castle of Machærus,—a fortress at the very borders of Herod's dominions.

But the whole narrative is an anticipation; for, as will be seen from a comparison of St. John ii. 13 with iii. 24, the Baptist was not cast into prison until a period subsequent to the First Passover. It would seem as if St. Luke were anxious to exhibit the history of John at one view, and to connect his bold preaching with the imprisonment in which it issued.

And probably this, which is a very favourite method with the HOLY SPIRIT, is not without its teaching. By coupling the remote cause with its ultimate consequence;—the course pursued, with the results it eventually led to;—(dropping every intermediate fact, and all irrelevant circumstances;)—the Inspired Writers forcibly remind us how *He* must regard our Lives and Actions and Characters, who seeth, as well as "declareth, *the end from the beginning.*"(*m*)

Concerning the incident here alluded to, rather than described, see the notes on St. Mark vi. 17–20. It shall suffice, in this place, to mention that the Herod spoken of, was Herod Antipas,—son of *that* Herod who murdered the Holy Innocents. His lawful wife was a daughter of Aretas, king of Petra in Arabia: Herodias, (a grand-daughter of Herod the Great, and therefore niece to Herod Antipas,) had married Philip,—another of her uncles; whom she forsook in order to live in adultery with the person here mentioned. The history of the Herods is one long history of adultery, incest, and murder.

21, 22 Now when all the people were baptized, it came to pass, that JESUS also being baptized, and praying, the Heaven was opened, and the HOLY GHOST descended in a bodily shape like a dove upon Him; and a Voice came from Heaven, which said, Thou art My beloved SON; in Thee I am well pleased.

St. Luke notices the Baptism of our LORD with brevity; but he mentions two circumstances of exceeding interest and preciousness. He is the only Evangelist who relates that our LORD was "*praying,*" after His Baptism, when the visible descent of the SPIRIT took place,—and the Voice was heard from Heaven, proclaiming His Divine SONSHIP: and it is worthy of observation that our SAVIOUR is stated to have been in the act of prayer on all the three occasions when the same Heavenly Voice was heard. Besides the present, see the account of the Transfiguration,—when, "*as He prayed,* the fashion of His countenance was altered;"(*n*) and that third occasion recorded by St. John, (xii. 28,) when the request of the SON was audibly answered from Heaven.

Further,—St. Luke alone it also is, who marks with precision that the "HOLY GHOST descended *in the bodily shape* like a dove upon Him." *But* for these express words, it might have been pretended, with some show of reason, that no bodily form was seen; whereby a most instructive circumstance would have been lost. See the note on St. Matth. iii. 16, 17.

So many remarks on this wondrous incident have been already offered in the notes on St. Matthew's Gospel, (iii. 13 to 17,) and St. Mark, (i. 9 to 11,) that the Reader is referred to those places for further information.

23 And JESUS Himself began to be about thirty years of age,

Our LORD, at this time, may have completed twenty-nine years of His earthly life. He therefore "began to be about *thirty* years of age;"—which was the age of Joseph, when he stood before Pharaoh;(*o*) and of David, "when he began to reign."(*p*) These were eminent types of CHRIST.

being (as was supposed) the Son of Joseph,

Men supposed Him to be naturally sprung from Joseph of Nazareth,—who was indeed *legally* His Father, being the Blessed Virgin's wedded Husband. See the note on St. Matth. i. 16.

The genealogy which follows, is manifestly that of *Joseph;* and may have been actually obtained by the Evangelist from the archives of the census itself.

which was *the son* of Heli,

But in St. Matthew's Gospel, (i. 16.) it is said,—"*Jacob* begat Joseph." These two statements are reconciled by a venerable tradition derived from the descendants of the holy family. It declares Heli to have been *legally* the Father of the Blessed Virgin's husband;—while his *natural* parent was Jacob. The two lines of descent, given respectively by St. Matthew and St. Luke, converge in the persons of Matthan, (who is mentioned in St. Matth. i. 15;) and Matthat, (whose name will be found in the next ensuing verse of the present chapter of St. Luke's Gospel.) These

(*m*) Isaiah xlvi. 10.   (*n*) St. Luke ix. 29.
(*o*) Gen. xli. 46.   (*p*) 2 Sam. v. 4.

men became successively the husbands of the same heiress (Estha,)—by whom each had issue: whereby the first became naturally,—the second, legally,—the grandfather of Joseph.

24, 25, 26, 27 which was *the son* of Matthat, which was *the son* of Levi, which was *the son* of Melchi, which was *the son* of Janna, which was *the son* of Joseph, which was *the son* of Mattathias, which was *the son* of Amos, which was *the son* of Naum, which was *the son* of Esli, which was *the son* of Nagge, which was *the son* of Maath, which was *the son* of Mattathias, which was *the son* of Simei, which was *the son* of Joseph, which was *the son* of Juda, which was *the son* of Joanna, which was *the son* of Rhesa, which was *the son* of Zorobabel,

All the eighteen names from Heli (in ver. 23) to Rhesa, inclusive, are recorded nowhere but in this place. *How,* or in what sense, Rhesa "was *the son* of Zorobabel," does not appear. His name is not found in 1 Chron. iii. 19, 20,—where the children of Zorobabel are enumerated.

which was *the son* of Salathiel,

The same statement occurs in Ezra, (iii. 2; v. 2,) and in Haggai, (i. 1, 12; ii. 2.) Moreover, it is found repeated in St. Matthew's Gospel,—i. 12, where see the second note. But, from 1 Chron. iii. 17 to 24, it would appear that, in strictness, Zorobabel was the son of *Pedaia,*—Salathiel's brother. Naturally, therefore, Salathiel will have been his uncle; and only legally, his parent.

The two genealogies according to St. Matthew and St. Luke, having met at this place,—and having both exhibited the glorious names of Salathiel and Zorobabel among the ancestors of our Blessed LORD, again diverge,—to meet again in the person of David the King.

which was *the son* of Neri,

Neri was his actual Father. Compare the statement in St. Matth. i. 12, and see the note there.

28, 29, 30, 31 which was *the son* of Melchi, which was *the son* of Addi, which was *the son* of Cosam, which was *the son* of Elmodam, which was *the son* of Er, which was *the son* of Jose, which was *the son* of Eliezer, which was *the son* of Jorim, which was *the son* of Matthat, which was *the son* of Levi, which was *the son* of Simeon, which was *the son* of Juda, which was *the son* of Joseph, which was *the son* of Jonan, which was *the son* of Eliakim, which was *the son* of Melea, which was *the son* of Menan, which was *the son* of Mattatha, which was *the son* of Nathan, which was *the son* of David,

Here the two genealogies again converge,—see the last note but one. The "Nathan" here mentioned is, obviously, a person wholly distinct from the prophet mentioned in 2 Sam. xii. He was the elder brother of Solomon,—whose descendants St. Matthew has recorded. See 2 Sam. v. 14, and 1 Chron. iii. 5.

32, 33, 34 which was *the son* of Jesse, which was *the son* of Obed, which was *the son* of Booz, which was *the son* of Salmon, which was *the son* of Naason, which was *the son* of Aminadab, which was *the son* of Aram, which was *the son* of Esrom, which was *the son* of Phares, which was *the son* of Juda, which was *the son* of Jacob, which was *the son* of Isaac, which was *the son* of Abraham,

These well-known names are common to both the genealogies. With that of "Abraham," St. Matthew's genealogy begins.

Twenty worthies remain, of which only *one* is found to occasion the least difficulty.

35, 36 which was *the son* of Thara, which was *the son* of Nachor, which was *the son* of Saruch, which was *the son* of Ragau, which was *the son* of Phalec, which was *the son* of Heber, which was *the son* of Sala, which was *the son* of Cainan,

This insertion of the name of a second Cainan, (besides the Cainan in verse 37,) is one of the hardest things to explain and account for, in the Holy Gospels; for for the name does not occur in Genesis xi. 12, between the names of Arphaxad and Salah, where we should, of course, expect to find it: nor indeed elsewhere in the Hebrew Bible. It is found, however, in a Greek Translation of the Pentateuch, which was made before the time of our LORD; and which (because it was commonly read in the Synagogues, and therefore familiarly known to the people) the Evangelists and Apostles are found to have freely used and quoted.

The humble student of the Gospels will do well to believe, on the testimony of St. Luke, that there actually *was* such a person as Cainan,—the son of Arphaxad and father of Sala; while, at the same time, he may cheerfully admit that, as yet, he sees not how the fact is to be reconciled in a satisfactory manner with the particulars (of age and of descent) which Moses was divinely moved to record. It does not, of course, prove, that when he has occasion to reason concerning the early generations of mankind, he need in the least degree distrust the statements which the Hebrew text supplies. The "Spirit of Truth,"(*q*) by whom Moses and St. Luke were alike inspired, may well be deemed his sufficient guarantee on this head.

The case, after all, admits of easy illustration. Two things are indeed stated which seem to be inconsistent; but the same might be said, with at least equal truth, of the assertion in St. Matthew i. 8, that "Joram begat Ozias,"—and the circumstantial statement in 2 Kings xiv. 21, that Azariah (that is, Ozias or Uzziah) was the son of Amaziah. These two statements *seem* wholly incompatible, and inconsistent; but they are proved *not to be so.* Thus again, as we have already seen, Ezra the priest and Haggai the prophet concur with St. Luke, (see above ver. 27,) in describing Zorobabel, their contemporary. as the son of Salathiel; and, St. Matthew even says, "Salathiel *begat Zorobabel,*" (i. 12:) but the same Ezra explains that Zorobabel was *the son of Padaiah.*(*r*) These statements appear to be contradictory, but they are not really so. They only seem contradictory, at first, because we do not at first understand them. . . . . Let us remember, when difficulties of this kind try us to the uttermost, (and they were doubtless *intended* to be a trial,) that they are not nearly so serious as those which must have assailed the faithful in Israel when they reasoned on the prophecies which had gone before concerning the Advent of CHRIST. See also the note on another difficult text,—namely, chap. ii. 2.

It will appear, therefore, that either Evangelist, in his respective genealogy, has displayed *in one particular* his acquaintance with the else-unrevealed details of Old Testament History:—St. Matthew, by recording Talmon marriage with Rahab:—St. Luke, by vindicating for the second Cainan a place among the ancestors of the Messiah.

37, 38 which was *the son* of Arphaxad, which was *the son* of Sem, which was *the son* of Noe, which was *the son* of Lamech, which was *the son* of Mathusala, which was *the son* of Enoch, which was *the son* of Jared, which was *the son* of Maleleel, which was *the son* of Cainan, which was *the son* of Enos, which was *the son* of Seth, which was *the son* of Adam, which was *the son* of GOD.

While St. Matthew, therefore, contents himself with deriving the descent of MESSIAH from *Abraham,*—the Father of the Jewish people,(*s*) and the patriarch to whom the promises were originally given; St. Luke traces back MESSIAH's line to Adam,—the Father of the whole human race. The former Evangelist wrote his Gospel especially for the use of his own nation: it was sufficient, therefore, that he should show that the SAVIOUR was "Abraham's seed."(*t*) But the latter Evangelist, like the great Apostle whom he accompanied, addressed himself to Jew and

(*q*) St. John xvi. 13.   (*r*) 1 Chron. iii. 19.   (*s*) St. John viii. 33, 39, &c.
                                 (*t*) St. Matth. i. 1, 2.

Gentile, alike. Accordingly, he exhibits the SAVIOUR as the promised "Seed of the Woman," who should hereafter bruise the Serpent's head;(u) and in whom all the great human family has an equal interest,—as children (by adoption) of the same Almighty FATHER, and heirs (by promise) of the same eternal Kingdom.

Seth was the son *of Adam;*—for Adam "begat a son *in his own likeness*, after his image; and called his name Seth."(x)   But Adam was the son *of* GOD;—for "in the day that GOD created man,—*in the likeness of* GOD *made He him.*"(y)

It cannot be by accident that the number of the names in this genealogy,—first and last,—should be exactly *seventy-seven.*

THE PRAYER.

ALMIGHTY GOD, who hast given us Thy only-begotten SON to take our nature upon Him, and as at this time to be born of a pure Virgin; grant that we being regenerate, and made Thy children by Adoption and Grace, may daily be renewed by Thy HOLY SPIRIT; through the same our LORD JESUS CHRIST, Who liveth and reigneth with Thee and the same SPIRIT, ever one GOD, world without end.   Amen.

CHAPTER IV.

1 *The Temptation and Fasting of* CHRIST. 13 *He overcometh the Devil.* 14 *Beginneth to preach.* 16 *The people of Nazareth admire His gracious words.* 33 *He cureth one possessed of a devil,* 38 *Peter's mother-in-law,* 40 *and divers other sick persons.* 41 *The devils acknowledge* CHRIST, *and are reproved for it.* 43 *He preacheth through the Cities.*

CONCERNING the Temptation of CHRIST,—the great event with which the present chapter commences,—the Reader is referred to a long note at the beginning of St. Matthew iv.—What has been there said, shall not be repeated in this place.

"Behold," says one of the ancients, "He is among the wrestlers, who, as GOD, awards the prizes. He is among the crowned, who crowns the heads of the Saints."

1 And JESUS being full of the HOLY GHOST returned from Jordan.

It is necessary to bear in mind that the last event which obtained notice, was the Baptism of our LORD in the river Jordan: with obvious reference to which, He is now described as "being *full of the HOLY GHOST.*"(a)   His Temptation follows. "And thus," says Leighton, "shalt *thou* be sure to be assaulted, when thou hast received the greatest enlargements from Heaven: either at the Sacrament,— or in Prayer,—or in any other way. *Then* look for an onset. This arch-pirate lets the empty ships pass, but lays wait for them when they return richest laden." See the notes on the last half of St. Mark i. 12: also the notes on St. Matthew iv. 1.

and was led by the SPIRIT into the Wilderness,

Concerning our LORD's conflict with the Powers of Darkness, much has been

(u) Gen. iii. 15.   (x) Gen. v. 3.
(y) Gen. v. 1.   Compare i. 26, 27.   (a) See St. Luke iii. 22.

already remarked in the notes on St. Matthew, chap. iv: and something more will
be found in the note on St. Mark i. 13. This great event lies on the very threshold of the sacred History in the three first Gospels; and in each our LORD's approach to it is described in terms of the same import. "Sweet is it," says Leighton, "in all things, to be carried: not to go of ourselves any way; but that, of each
step, it may be said,—He was *led by the SPIRIT!* led to be tempted, on purpose
that he might return with the glory of the victory."

"The Apostle doth fitly style our LORD JESUS 'the Captain' or Leader 'of our
Salvation.'(b) It was meet He should be made 'perfect by sufferings.'(c) He
therefore leads the way; putting on us nothing that He hath not first encountered."

2 Being forty days tempted of the Devil.

For the space of forty days was our Blessed LORD tempted : but the three marvellous scenes which St. Matthew and St. Luke describe, belong to *the last* day :
and these, because they are the only part of the Temptation which concerns us,
are the only part recorded. Over all the rest, a veil of mysterious silence has been
drawn. See the first note on St. Mark i. 13.

And in those days He did eat nothing: and when they were ended, He afterward hungered.

It has been already pointed out, (in the note on St. Matthew iv. 2,) that Moses
and Elijah had observed a similar miraculous fast, before Him. Those two mighty
personages, who appeared together in Glory on the Mount of Transfiguration,(d)
—symbolize respectively the Law and the Prophets: between which, and the Gospel, this forty days' fast of their great Antitype, served to show that there was an
harmonious correspondence and agreement.

And it must be obvious to remark, that in imitation of this mighty transaction,
the Church of CHRIST observes her Lent-fast of forty days: not straining her weak
powers therein, as if in rivalry of her LORD ; but maintaining an humble distance,
and seeking only to tread faithfully in His footsteps,—although planting a weak
and most uncertain foot.

3 And the Devil said unto Him, If Thou be the SON of GOD, command this stone that it be made bread.

Upon this Temptation, see the notes on St. Matthew iv. 3.

It was all his object to discover whether, in the disguise of the frail and fainting
form before him, there might be concealed the MESSIAH, the Desire of all nations,—
his own foretold Vanquisher. Hence, his repeated address,—"*If thou be* the SON
of GOD."

Take notice how the Devil treats those whom he is permitted to tempt. He sees
that they want *Bread:* he offers them *a Stone!*

4 And JESUS answered him, saying, It is written, That man shall not live by bread alone, but by every word of GOD.

It was out of mere condescension and love towards us, that our SAVIOUR thus
answered the Tempter: for He met his suggestion in language which any one of
ourselves might equally make use of under the like circumstances. And marvellous
it is to contemplate the wisdom which thus knew how to select out of the heavenly
Armory a weapon which should suffice at once for the mysterious requirements of
the Incarnate GOD, and for those of creatures weak and sinful as ourselves. The
quotation is from Deut. viii. 3.

This place of Scripture, upon our SAVIOUR's lips, informs us that for all our
needs,—for those alike of our higher, and those of our lower nature,—"we are to
hold ourselves dependent entirely on the promised protection and providence of
GOD; a protection," to use the words of a great writer, "which is ever to be sought
agreeably to His revealed Word and Will. It is a reply therefore to every infernal
suggestion that we should either despair of GOD's goodness, or distrust His power,
—that we should seek the satisfaction of our lower wants by unlawful or unhallowed
means, or impatiently refuse to abide the issue of our honest endeavours,—thus,

---

(b) Hebrews ii. 10.   (c) Hebrews ii. 10.   (d) St. Matth. xvii 3.

with the SAVIOUR of Mankind, to make answer to the Tempter,—It is written, *Man shall not live by bread alone.*"
It is obvious to notice the breadth which is thus given to that petition in the LORD's Prayer,—"Give us this day *our daily bread.*" See note on St. Matth. vi. 11. On the present verse, more will be found in the note on St. Matth. iv. 4.

5 And the Devil, taking Him up into an high mountain, showed unto Him all the Kingdoms of the World in a moment of time.

Foiled in his attempt to seduce the Second Adam by the snare of carnal appetite, —the Enemy tries next the lure of Worldly ambition. Satan "takes" our LORD "up into an high mountain,"—bearing Him, it may be, through the air, by the permission of Him with whom he had to do. See the note on St. Matthew iv. 5.
He there discovers to the Incarnate SON a most wondrous sight,—namely, "all the Kingdoms of the World," and, (as St. Matthew adds,) "*the glory* of them." Moreover, the better to dazzle human imagination, and overset the judgment, he performs this act of Temptation "*in a moment of time:*" like a warrior who collects the force of many strokes into a single mighty blow. All the majesty of the four great Empires,—their united strength and splendour,—their fame and glory,—and whatever else it is unsafe for Man to set his heart on, or even to behold; but which, nevertheless, he loves and longs for;—*all* is made to sweep before the calm gaze of the second Adam, in unspeakable magnificence and beauty! See a few words more on the subject in the note to St. Matthew iv. 8.
It has been finely pointed out, by an ancient Bishop, how fitting it is that all the Kingdoms of the World, and the glory of them, should be displayed "*in a moment of time.*" "For here it is not so much the rapid glance of sight which is signified, as the frailty of mortal power which is declared. For in a moment all this passes away; and oftentimes the glory of this World has vanished before it has arrived." Another says,—"A moment of Time! For the Present is but a moment in comparison of Eternity."

6 And the Devil said unto Him, All this power will I give Thee, and the glory of them:

That is,—of these Kingdoms. See the place in St. Matthew iv. 8.

for that is delivered unto me: and to whomsoever I will, I give it.

Was this, in *any* respect, a true boast? For instance,—Has GOD *really* delivered Earthly Power and Glory into the hands of Satan?
Certainly *not altogether;* for "there is no power but of GOD: the powers that be, are ordained of GOD."(e) Again,—Pomp, and State, and Magnificence,—*Glory*, as it may be called,—dwells chiefly in King's Courts. Now, Kings are the LORD's Anointed: clothed with His authority; and, (doubt it not!) regarded by Him with special favour,—as images of Himself. In what limited sense, then, did Satan speak truly, when he said, "All this power . . . . . and glory . . . . is delivered unto *me?*" For the falsity of the words which follow, shall be pointed out in the next note.
That Satan had been permitted by GOD to take up his abode in this part of GOD's Creation, which we inhabit,—we know. The marvellous extent to which he had usurped dominion over the bodies of men,—is frequently set before us.(f) St. Paul speaks of him, in one place, as "the Prince of the power of the Air."(g) In another, he calls him *the god*,(h)—and our SAVIOUR styles him *the Prince*,—*of this World :*(i) seems to say that the Earth is *his House :*(k) or rather, (being a Prince,) his *Palace :*(l) that he occupied it, once, like *a strong man armed :*(m) and that he required *binding*, before his goods could be spoiled. St. John (probably) says that "the whole World lieth in the hands," or "under the power, of the Wicked One :"(n) and our LORD Himself scarcely says less, in Acts xxvi. 18. Now, when to all this, is added the well-known fact that GOD permits Satan to tempt His ser-

(e) Rom. xiii. 1.   (f) St. Luke xiii. 16, in particular, may be consulted.
(g) Ephes. ii. 2.   (h) 2 Cor. iv. 4.   (i) St. John xii. 31 : xiv. 30 : xvi. 11.
(k) St. Matth. xii. 29.   (l) St. Luke xi. 21.
(m) For his employment here below, see Job i. 7 : ii. 2. Also 1 St. Peter v. 8.
(n) 1 St. John v. 19.

wants(o) in order thereby to make proof of their faithfulness ; and when it is remembered that the splendours of this World,—riches, and honour, and glory,—the very things, remember, against which our SAVIOUR so earnestly and so faithfully cautions us,—are the lures with which the Enemy of souls most successfully baits his hook :—may we not presume that we have discovered his meaning? ascertained the limited sense in which he could dare to say that all the good things of Earth had been delivered over to *him ?*

7 If Thou therefore wilt worship me, all shall be Thine.

Yes,—*If CHRIST would worship him :* but not else.
The boast which goes before, was worthy of the Father of Lies ; a splendid Lie, —yet full of weakness. "That is delivered unto me." By *whom* "delivered ?" Thou confessest, then, that there is a Greater One than thyself in Creation, —whose vassal thou art ! . . . . And "To whomsoever I will, I give it." *That* is false,— as the words which follow prove. See the note on St. Matthew iv. 9.
An old African Bishop asks.—" And dost thou, whose lot is the unquenchable fire, dare to promise to the LORD of all, that which is *His own ?* Dost thou think to have *Him* for thy worshipper, from dread of whom the whole Creation trembles ?" He might have added.—And dost thou offer *earthly* "Kingdoms," "power," and "glory," to Him whose "is *the* Kingdom, and *the* Power, and *the* Glory ?"(*p*)

8 And JESUS answered and said unto him, Get thee behind Me, Satan :

"Thus, when anything moves to debauch, and draw off the heart from GOD, it is to be beat away with indignation. And thus, in all conflicts, continue fighting in thy LORD's strength : give not over, resist still, and the Enemy shall flee, as here."

for it is written, Thou shalt worship the LORD thy GOD, and Him only shalt thou serve.

Written—in Deuteronomy vi. 13. See the note on St. Matthew iv. 10. Our LORD *might* have said to the Tempter,—Thou shalt worship *Me :* but then, how would his example have availed *us ?* He used words which, under similar circumstances of Temptation, might be used by the humblest of His servants. See the note on St. Matthew iv. 7.
This Temptation was the last of the three, in actual order ; and accordingly, it stands third in St. Matthew's Gospel. "Our SAVIOUR was pleased thus to bear many assaults," says a good man, "and thus to force and beat off the Tempter by the Word, both for our Instruction and our Comfort : who otherwise, for Himself, could immediately have repelled him, and sent him back at first. But indeed ' He pleased not Himself (*q*) in anything : had an eye to *us*, in all He did and suffered ; and did all in reference to *our* advantage. O how should we love Him !"

9 And he brought Him to Jerusalem, and set Him on a pinnacle of the Temple,

See the note on St. Matthew iv. 5.

and said unto Him, If Thou be the SON of GOD, cast Thyself down from hence :

The Tempter next assails our LORD on the side of *Vain-glory,* or *Spiritual Pride.* He will find himself powerless as before against the Holy One. "The Prince of this World cometh," said our SAVIOUR once to His Disciples, "and *hath nothing in Me.*"(*r*) See the first note on St. Matthew iv. 6.

10, 11 for it is written, He shall give His Angels charge over Thee, to keep Thee : and in *their* hands they shall bear Thee up, lest at any time Thou dash Thy foot against a stone.

(o) Job I. 12 : ii. 6.   1 Cor. x. 13.   2 St. Peter ii. 9, &c.   (p) St. Matthew vi. 13.
(q) Romans xv. 3.   (r) St. John xiv. 30.

The Devil can quote Scripture in support of his foulest purposes. It is no sufficient recommendation therefore,—either of counsel, suggested from without; or of doubts, arising from within,—that of *this* thing, or *that* thing, it may be said, with some show of truth, " It is written."

Better, however, in all such cases, to follow our SAVIOUR's method. He contests not the place of Scripture quoted ; but He meets it with another. He *might* have disputed the text,—exposing the subtlety of its misapplication ; and condemning the wickedness which could misquote,—(see the second note on St. Matthew iv. 6,) in order to mislead : but He teaches us "a more excellent way." " And this downright, sure method," says Leighton, "beats off the sophister with another quotation, —clearly and plainly carrying that truth which *he* opposes and *we* adhere to. So, though thou canst not clear the sense of an obscure Scripture, thou shalt always find a sufficient guard in another that is clearer."

12 And JESUS answering said unto him, It is said, Thou shalt not tempt the LORD thy GOD.

Not that our SAVIOUR takes to Himself (as He might have done,) the awful title, —" The LORD thy GOD." He simply quotes the command which Satan was tempting Him to transgress. See the notes on St. Matthew iv. 7.

You perceive that, whereas the Adversary quoted *a Promise;* (which, moreover, he exhibited disjoined from its context, and in a garbled form :)(*s*) our SAVIOUR opposes him with *a Precept.* The *Promise,* absolutely stated, is gratifying, because it involves no duties. The *Precept,* on the contrary, points to continued obedience, and prescribes a long, and therefore painful course of virtuous action.—Thereby a great lesson is unmistakably conveyed to us all. True indeed it is that GOD's promises to His creatures, when attentively examined, are all found to be conditional: equally true is it that His precepts are all, as delivered by Him, absolute :—yet is it the nature of blind spiritual Presumption to rely on GOD's Promises as if no condition were annexed to their fulfillment ; to substitute Reliance for Obedience ; and to represent to itself GOD's decrees respecting Man, as absolute and unconditional, —rather than as dependent wholly upon the foreseen decisions of that human Will which the same Almighty Being created free to choose between good and evil.

This temptation of our SAVIOUR therefore, which in St. Luke's Gospel occupies the third place, may be regarded as the great type of Religious Presumption, and Spiritual Pride. Satan seeks to persuade the Incarnate SON that the Divine support is absolutely certain ; is wholly unconditional, and stands pledged to Him irrevocably. . . . . Of how many proud souls, (who yet fancied themselves humble and meek,) has the same insinuation proved the downfall ! How many persons among ourselves, at the present day, are the dupes of a Religious system which, by thus exhibiting only a partial and distorted view of the Truth, favours the same pernicious error, and most unscriptural view !

13 And when the Devil had ended all the Temptation, he departed from Him for a season.

When the Devil had ended all the Temptation, or rather *" every kind of Temptation,"*—(for *that* is what the Evangelist says,)—he "departed" from the Holy One. Yet, not as he came. He began the conflict *strong;* he departed from it, *weak :* he assailed his Enemy, *free ;* he departed from Him, *bound.*(*t*) And this is much to be noted.

Further,—even from the Holy One, Satan departed only "for a season !" We must therefore always be prepared for new onsets ; never supposing ourselves safe from them, so long as these, the days of our warfare, last. See however the comfortable words quoted on this subject in the note on St. Matthew iv. 11.

St. Luke, who will hereafter give us the fullest account of the Agony in the Garden,(*u*) is the only Evangelist who hints that the Tempter departed from our LORD but *"for a season :"* or, (as the words should properly be translated,) *"until* a season." Satan's next assault was reserved for the close of that Ministry which was now about to begin. Refer to, and by all means consider, St. Luke xxii. 53 : St. John xiv. 30: together with that hint of approaching triumph,—St. John xii.

(*s*) See the note on St. Matthew iv. 6.   (*t*) See St. Matthew xii. 29.
(*u*) St. Luke xxii. 43, 44.

31. As, in the Wilderness, by every allurement of *Pleasure*, —so, in the Garden, and on the Cross, by every avenue of *Pain*,—did the Devil seek to shake the second Adam from His steadfastness. And *this* also may teach us what we have to expect; at one time, the seductions,—at another, the threats,—of an evil World. "And who is sufficient for these things?"(z)

14 And JESUS returned in the power of the SPIRIT into Galilee:

He came "*in the power* of the SPIRIT:" for is He not the Great Captain of our Salvation? and had He not just vanquished the Enemy of our Race? The phrase just quoted, recalls the language of verse 1, and is said with manifest reference to His Baptism,—when He was once more "anointed" (as St. Peter speaks,) "with the HOLY GHOST and *with power*."(y)—Read verse 18; and notice how aptly the prophecy and its fulfillment suit each other.
Take notice that *the occasion* of this departure into Galilee is recorded in St. Matthew iv. 12, and St. Mark i. 14,—where see the notes.

15 and there went out a fame of Him through all the region round about.   And He taught in their synagogues, being glorified of all.

16 And He came to Nazareth, where He had been brought up:

He is desirous to communicate the knowledge of Himself to those among whom He had been brought up,—the inhabitants of the city in which the first twenty-nine years of His earthly life had been passed.—Good men, in ancient days, who delighted to find living counsel in every line of the Book of Life, suggest that CHRIST thereby taught us to benefit and instruct first, our brethren,—then, to extend our kindness to the rest of our friends.
A modern Traveller describes the scenery about the home of our SAVIOUR as very wonderful.   Having walked to the top of the hill over Nazareth,—"Here," he says, "quite unexpectedly, a glorious prospect opened to the view. The air was perfectly clear and serene; and I shall never forget the impression I received, as the enchanting panorama burst suddenly upon me. There lay the magnificent plain of Esdraelon ; on the left was seen the round top of Tabor over the intervening hills, with portions of the Little Hermon and Gilboa, and the opposite mountains of Samaria.   Then came the long line of Carmel itself. In the west, lay the Mediterranean gleaming in the morning sun: seen, first, far in the south on the left of Carmel; then, interrupted by that mountain; and again appearing on its right. Below, on the north, was spread out another of the beautiful plains of Northern Palestine. . . .
"In the Village below, the SAVIOUR of the World had passed His Childhood: and there are certain features of Nature which meet our eyes now, just as they once met His. He must often have visited the fountain near which we had pitched our tent: His feet must frequently have wandered over the adjacent hills: and His eyes doubtless have gazed on the splendid prospect from this very spot. Here the Prince of Peace looked down upon the great plain where the din of battles so oft had rolled, and the garments of the warrior been dyed in blood : and He looked out, too, upon that Sea, over which the swift ships were to bear the tidings of His Salvation to Nations and to Continents then unknown!"

and, as His custom was, He went into the Synagogue on the Sabbath day, and stood up for to read.

We know, from Acts xiii. 15, that other persons were allowed to address the people in the Synagogue, besides the Priest.   From this place we learn that other persons might "read" publicly, also. Observe the hint in the text as to what the "custom" of the SAVIOUR of the World was, in the days of His humiliation.
It appears from the Acts of the Holy Apostles, that the Law(z) and the Prophets(a) were read in the Synagogues every Sabbath-day: at the end of which, "a word of exhortation" to the people, was delivered. See Acts xiii. 15.

17, 18, 19 And there was delivered unto Him the Book of the Pro-

(z) 2 Cor. ii. 16.   (y) Acts x. 38. See Acts iv. 27 : and compare St. Luke i. 35.
(s) Acts xv. 21.   (a) Acts xiii. 27.

phet Esaias. And when He had opened the Book, He found the place
where it was written, The SPIRIT of the LORD *is* upon Me, because He
hath anointed Me to preach the Gospel to the poor; He hath sent Me
to heal the broken-hearted, to preach deliverance to the captives, and
recovering of sight to the blind, to set at liberty them that are bruised,
to preach the acceptable year of the LORD.

Our LORD, unrolling the Book of His Prophet, (a roll, like those which are used
in the Jewish Synagogues at this day,) fixed upon the words which are found in the
beginning of the 61st chapter; either making choice of that passage because He
designed to preach from it; or, (what seems more likely,) because it was the portion of Scripture appointed to be read, in regular course, on that day. But there
was a divine Providence in the matter, be sure. See above the note on verse 14.
Observe, that, instead of "the poor,"—it is in the original, "*the meek:*" a beautiful comment on St. Matthew v. 3. as compared with St. Luke vi. 20. See St. Matthew xi. 5.—Observe also, that instead of "recovery of sight to the blind," the Hebrew, (as our Bibles show us,) has "the opening of the prison to them that are
bound." A remarkable comment of the SPIRIT! Compare Psalm cxlvi. 7, 8.—See
also Acts xxvi. 18.

20 And He closed the Book, and He gave *it* again to the Minister,
and sat down. And the eyes of all them that were in the Synagogue
were fastened on Him.

How minute is all this, and exactly descriptive of the Scene:—the closing of the
Book,—the giving it to the Attendant or Servant,—the resuming of His seat; and
then, the fixed gaze of all within the Synagogue. Doubt not that there was something unearthly in His manner: that His Divinity flashed through the poor fleshly
garment in which it was enshrined, and "could not be hid!"—Consider verse 22,
below; and see the last note on St. Matthew vii.

21 And He began to say unto them, This day is this Scripture fulfilled in your ears.

That is,—the Prophet spake in *My* Person, and by *My* SPIRIT, when he committed these words to writing, more than seven hundred years ago: and behold, at
last, I am come into the World,—I of whom Isaiah wrote; and the words which
you have been listening to, find their fulfillment, *at this present day,*—and they are
fulfilled *in Me.*—See above, the note on verse 14.
Oh to have heard the Discourse which followed!—"the gracious words," in order
to drink the sound of which, Angels must have thronged the place, unseen.

22 And all bare Him witness, and wondered at the gracious words
which proceeded out of His mouth. And they said, Is not this Joseph's
Son?

They spoke as men who remembered His "manner of life from His youth;"—
remembered Joseph the Carpenter, (see St. John i. 4, 5;) and the lowly Maiden, our
LORD's Mother, whom they looked upon as Joseph's wife; together with many
others of their kindred. Compare what was said on another similar occasion:—
St. Mark vi. 2, 3.
It has been already pointed out, (in the note on ver. 20,) that there must have
been something wondrous heavenly in the manner of our SAVIOUR, to account for
passages like the present, which so frequently recur in the Gospels. But *who* so
dull as not to perceive that, on the occasion here recorded, there was more than
usual wonder in His sayings? They beheld,—to all appearance,—their humble
townsman suddenly claiming to be the subject of a well-known prophecy! But, in
reality, it was the Eternal SON, emptied of His Glory indeed, yet still the same Almighty One, by whose Spirit the Prophets had spoken,—turning to the written
record of *His* Servant's words, (words which had proceeded from *Himself,*) and
condescending to become their Interpreter! How must the heart of every one have
burned within him at so wondrous a spectacle!

23 And He said unto them, Ye will surely say unto Me this proverb, Physician, heal thyself; whatsoever we have heard done in Capernaum, do also here in Thy country.

Our LORD spake this, knowing the secret thoughts of His auditory. From His word we learn that, notwithstanding the admiration and delight which His Discourse had occasioned, the people were reasoning within themselves as follows:— "He has wrought wonders at Capernaum. Why does He not work them here? Is not this Joseph's son? Why does He not improve His own lowly condition, and that of all His family? 'Physician, heal thyself!' We demand this thing of Thee, as a sign; and then, we will believe Thee."
Note however, by the way, that as yet we have heard of only *one* miracle which had been wrought in Capernaum; namely, the healing of the nobleman's son.(*b*)

24 And He said, Verily I say unto you, No Prophet is accepted in his own country.

In *this* way, then, our SAVIOUR answers the thoughts of His auditory. It is observable that, first, He meets the proverb which they were thinking of, with another; the tendency of *theirs* having been to require miracles at His hands, the proverb which *He* cites assigns the reason why He will not work any; namely, because by no display of miraculous power could He win credit with the men of Nazareth, among whom He had been brought up.
He appeals, next, to Holy Scripture; and proceeds to vindicate the strict conformity of His present conduct with that which GOD had observed towards His chosen people of old. For He shows that miracles were not vouchsafed anciently to the persons by whom—or at the seasons in which—they might have been most expected: but simply according to the good will and pleasure of ALMIGHTY GOD.

25 But I tell you of a truth, many widows were in Israel in the days of Elias, when the heaven was shut up three years and six months, when great famine was throughout all the land;

Observe, by the way, that the "six months" are not noticed in the Old Testament History of the event here referred to. See 1 Kings xvii. 1, and xviii. 1. St. James, however,—verse 17,—mentions the time with the same exactness as our LORD.

26 but unto none of them was Elias sent, save unto Sarepta, *a city* of Sidon, unto a woman *that was* a widow.

See the affecting History of Elijah and the Widow of Zarephath, in 1 Kings xvii. 8, &c.
What awful interest, by the way, attaches to every passage in the Old Testament thus appealed to, by our LORD! The Finger of Him, by whose inspiring Spirit the Bible was given, laid upon a particular History, surely invests it evermore with special delight and wonder!

27 And many lepers were in Israel in the time of Eliseus the prophet; and none of them was cleansed, saving Naaman the Syrian.

For the history of Naaman's cure, by Elisha the prophet, see 2 Kings v.
The teaching of these two narratives, on the present occasion, was clearly this: As Elijah was not sent to one of the widows of Israel—but to a Gentile woman, the lone widow of Sarepta; and as Elisha was commissioned to work no cures on the lepers of Israel, but on a Gentile soldier—Naaman the Syrian: so should it create no surprise in the men of Nazareth if a preference were shown to Strangers, on the present occasion also; if our SAVIOUR wrought wonders in Capernaum, and refused to work any among *them*.

28 And all they in the Synagogue, when they heard these things, were filled with wrath,

(*b*) St. John iv. 46 to 54.

The very men who so lately "bare Him witness, and wondered at His gracious words!" (ver. 22.) They were filled with wrath at the hint which the latter part of His discourse conveyed. Such language always inflamed the Jews to madness, —as in Acts xxii. 21, 22. This Jealousy had been set forth in Prophecy,—see Deuteronomy xxxii. 21; and was displayed by our Lord, in Parable,—see St. Luke xv. 28.

29 and rose up and thrust Him out of the city; and led Him unto the brow of the hill whereon their city was built, that they might cast Him down headlong.

On the south-west part of the town of Nazareth, the hill breaks off in a perpendicular wall,—forty or fifty feet in height. *That* must have been the spot to which these murderers sought to conduct their Fellow-townsman.

How wondrous an illustration, by the way, was thus afforded to the aptness of the proverb which our Lord had just before cited against them! What evidence could prevail with hearts which were thus evilly disposed? See the note on verse 24.

30 But He, passing through the midst of them, went His way;

Compare the other occasions when the Holy One was obliged to do the like:— St. John viii. 59: x. 39: xii. 36. And notice, that we are again reminded of the union of the Divine and Human Nature, in the person of our Lord. He had been speaking, as God, in the Synagogue—verses 18 to 21. As Man, He here saves His life by flight. Not but what He must be thought to have saved His life by miracle: but the act of escape was human—like that which He afterward enjoined on His disciples. See St. Matthew x. 23.

31, 32 and came down to Capernaum, a city of Galilee, and taught them on the Sabbath days. And they were astonished at His doctrine: for His Word was with power.

See the last note on St. Matthew vii.—and observe that not only was the Saviour's *Word* with power; but He proceeded to confirm it "by signs following." A mighty *work* ensues, which is related also by St. Mark—i. 23 to 26: where see the notes.

33, 34 And in the Synagogue there was a man which had a spirit of an unclean devil, and cried out with a loud voice, saying, Let *us* alone;

For aught that appears to the contrary, the afflicted man was at first a silent and orderly member of the congregation. At the presence of the Holy Jesus, however, the unclean spirit within him cannot contain his trouble. The very presence of Christ is torture to devils. See all the notes on St. Matthew viii. 29.

The Reader is referred to the notes on St. Mark i. 24, for many observations on the present verse, which cannot be here repeated.

what have we to do with Thee, *Thou* Jesus of Nazareth? art Thou come to destroy us? I know Thee who Thou art: the Holy One of God.

Ever after the Temptation of our Saviour in the Wilderness by Satan, (the chief of the fallen Angels,) the devils are found to have known Christ. It was no longer, "*If Thou be* the Son of God," (as in verses 3 and 9,) but "*I know Thee who Thou art!*" . . . Compare verse 41. . . . The tidings that their great Enemy had, in some mysterious way, at last appeared, must have spread like lightning through all the host of fallen Spirits.

Not that it is to be supposed that they knew the *real Nature* of Him with whom they had to do; "for," as we are expressly told, "had they known, they would not have crucified the Lord of Glory:"(c) but they were convinced that, in *some*

(c) 1 Cor. ii. 8.

sense, He was the Son of God. Of the Reality of His Humanity, there could be no doubt.

"*JESUS of Nazareth*," was the title by which, afterwards, the Saviour of the World became commonly called, and was best known. It is a strange thing, that this name, (which fulfilled prophecy, and showed how effectually the mystery of the Nativity had been hid from the ken of evil spirits,) should be so soon found in the mouth of a devil. We have met with the appellation only once before; namely, in St. John i. 45.

35 And Jesus rebuked him, saying, Hold thy peace, and come out of him.

Our Lord rejects his testimony. Doubt not but what the confession in the former verse was either the cry of abject fear; or (what seems more likely) the subtle device of Satan to terrify mankind: to mar the progressive character of our Saviour's teaching; and cast suspicion and discredit on the Truth itself. See the note on St. Mark i. 25.

And when the devil had thrown him in the midst, he came out of him, and hurt him not.

But by "throwing him in the midst," and "*tearing* him," (as St. Mark records,) the unclean Spirit did the man all the harm he could. See the note on St. Mark i. 26.

There may be a comfortable message to man, concealed under these repeated notices of the violence of the Evil Spirit in the hour of its ejectment. See particularly St. Mark ix. 25 to 27. It has been remarked by a thoughtful writer, that "something similar is evermore finding place; and Satan vexes with temptations and with buffetings none so much as those who are in the act of being delivered from his dominion forever."

36 And they were all amazed, and spake among themselves, saying, What a word *is* this! for with authority and power He commandeth the unclean spirits, and they come out.

Take notice, then, that this miracle of healing was wrought on the Sabbath-day. An ancient bishop discourses as follows on the subject;—"The work of Divine healing commenced on the Sabbath: Christ signifying thereby that He *began anew* where the Old Creation *ceased*—in order that He might declare at the very beginning that the Son of God was not under the Law, but above the Law. Rightly, also, He began on the Sabbath, that He might show Himself the Creator, who interweaves His works one with another, and follows up that which He had before begun. Just as a builder, determining to reconstruct a house, begins to pull down the old one, not from the foundation, but from the top, so as to apply His hand first to that part where He had before left off."

37 And the fame of Him went out into every place of the country round about.

38 And He arose out of the Synagogue, and entered into Simon's house. And Simon's wife's mother was taken with a great fever; and they besought Him for her.

See the note on St. Mark i. 30.—Concerning "Simon's wife's Mother," see the note on St. Matthew viii. 14.

39 And He stood over her, and rebuked the fever; and it left her:

"*Rebuked* the fever:"—just as, before, He had rebuked the unclean Spirit;(*d*) and as, on a later occasion, "He rebuked the winds and the sea."(*e*) Speaking words to it, doubtless,—as to a subject creature. See the note on St. Matthew viii. 9.

and immediately she arose, and ministered unto them.

(*d*) See verse 35. (*e*) St. Mark iv. 39.

The first use she made of her recovered strength, was to employ it in her Master's service. And does she not become a pattern therein to Christians, who, on their restoration to spiritual health, should employ their powers in ministering to CHRIST, in the person of their poorest members of his mystical body? See the note on St. Mark v. 32.

The Reader is referred to St. Mark's rather fuller account of this miracle; and to the notes upon St. Mark i. 31.

40 Now when the sun was setting, all they that had any sick with divers diseases brought them unto Him; and He laid His hands on every one of them, and healed them.

See the note on St. Mark i. 32. "Observe His Divine power and goodness," writes Leighton, "shining forth in the miraculous cure of *all* diseases. And whatsoever be thy spiritual maladies, though never so many and so desperate, yet come. Never any came to Him, and went away uncured."

41 And devils also came out of many, crying out, and saying, Thou art CHRIST the SON of GOD. And He rebuking *them* suffered them not to speak: for they knew that He was CHRIST.

See above, the note on verse 34.

42 And when it was day, He departed and went into a desert place:

He withdrew at this early hour into a lonely place, *for the purpose of Prayer*,— as St. Mark is careful to inform us. See St. Mark i. 35.

43 and the people sought Him, and came unto Him, and stayed Him, that He should not depart from them. And He said unto them, I must preach the Kingdom of GOD to other cities also; for therefore am I sent.

Simon Peter, and the others, came in quest of their Great Benefactor. See how St. Mark notices this same circumstance:—i. 36 to 38.

44 And He preached in the Synagogues of Galilee.

This was our LORD's first great Ministerial Journey. How briefly described! And should not this very circumstance induce us to dwell upon it, in thought, the longer? The humble endeavour to do so, will be rendered easier by a reference to the parallel places,—namely, St. Matthew iv. 23 to 25; and St. Mark i. 39.

The SAVIOUR of the World might, indeed, by abiding in the same place, have drawn all men unto Himself,—as an ancient Bishop remarks: but He did not do so; because He would give *us* an example to go about, and seek those who are perishing; as the Shepherd, his lost sheep.

THE PRAYER.

LORD, we beseech Thee, grant Thy people grace to withstand the temptations of the World, the Flesh, and the Devil, and with pure hearts and minds to follow Thee the only GOD; through JESUS CHRIST our LORD. Amen.

CHAPTER V.

1 CHRIST *teacheth the people out of Peter's ship.* 4 *In a miraculous taking of fishes, showeth how He will make him and his partners fishers of men.* 12 *Cleanseth the Leper.* 16 *Prayeth in the Wilderness.* 18 *Healeth one sick of the palsy.* 27 *Calleth Matthew the publican.* 29 *Eateth with sinners, as being the Physician of souls.* 34 *Foretelleth the fastings and afflictions of the Apostles after His Ascension.* 36 *And likeneth faint-hearted and weak Disciples to old bottles and worn garments.*

1 AND it came to pass, that, as the people pressed upon Him to hear the Word of GOD, He stood by the Lake of Gennesaret:

Otherwise called the "Sea of Galilee," and the "Lake of Tiberias." See the note on St. Mark i. 16.—One of the ancients remarks,—"When the LORD had performed many and various kinds of cures, the multitude began to heed neither time nor place in their desire to be healed. The evening came,—they followed; a lake is before them,—they still press on."

2 and saw two ships standing by the Lake: but the fishermen were gone out of them, and were washing *their* nets.

The miracle which follows, and which our LORD wrought on the occasion of the call of Simon and Andrew, James and John, to their Apostleship, is peculiar to the present Gospel: but the call of those Disciples is found also in St. Matthew iv. 18 to 22, and St. Mark i. 16 to 20. The accounts should, of course, be carefully compared. The result will be, surprise to find the same incident so very diversely narrated: but, in fact, St. Luke supplies everything which the two earlier Evangelists had omitted; and repeats scarcely anything which they had said.
See the notes on St. Matthew iv. 18.

3 And He entered into one of the ships, which was Simon's, and prayed him that he would thrust out a little from the land. And He sat down, and taught the people out of the ship.

A convenient position,—in which our LORD is found to have delivered the parables contained in St. Matthew xiii. See the note on St. Mark iv. 1. He entered the Ship and was upon the Sea, in order the better to fish for the men upon the shore: but He had His eye, specially, on the two noble pair of Brethren—whom He had already drawn to His side indeed, but not yet called to Apostleship.

4 Now when He had left speaking, He said unto Simon, Launch out into the deep, and let down your nets for a draught.

The Divine Speaker, "when He had left speaking," proceeded to confirm the Word *by signs following.* Compare what is said in the note prefixed to St. Matthew viii. Observe, that the Second Adam was now about to exercise "dominion *over the fish of the Sea*,"—which was the first grant of empire which GOD gave to Man.(a) "Thou hast put all things under His feet," says the Psalmist: (divinely applying to the Second Adam what was originally spoken of the First:)—"the fish of the sea, and whatsoever passeth through the paths of the sea."(b)

(a) See Genesis i. 26.   (b) Psalm viii. 6, 8: quoted in Hebrews ii. 6 to 8.

5 And Simon answering said unto Him, Master, we have toiled all
the night, and have taken nothing: nevertheless, at Thy word I will
let down the net.

It is written,—"Sorrow may endure for a night, but Joy cometh in the morning."(c)
Compare what is said concerning these same Fishermen on another similar occasion,—St. John xxi. 3 and 5, when *the second* miraculous draught of fishes took
place: and doubt not, that on both occasions, the net was lowered in perfect faith.

6 And when they had this done, they inclosed a great multitude of
fishes:

The net was lowered "at CHRIST's Word:" and see the result! Obedience ever
inherits a blessing.
Consider further, the mere worldly advantage of having *Him* for a guest and in-
mate! The Holy One who so multiplied the store at Cana, where He had been
kindly entertained,—now showers down plenty upon the man from whose boat He
had been teaching. The net breaks,—the ship sinks,—beneath the largeness of
His bounty.
Was it not so with Obed-Edom, in whose house the Ark (the Symbol of His presence,) continued three months?(d)   Fared it not so with the Widow of Zarephath,(e) and the Shunammite,(f)—with whom Elijah and Elisha, (His chosen servants,) respectively, sojourned?   Doubt not that so it ever is!   Laban was blessed
for his son-in-law Jacob's sake;(g) and Potiphar, for his servant Joseph's;(h) while
GOD gave St. Paul all the two hundred and seventy-six souls which sailed with him.(i)
A cup of cold water given, for the love of CHRIST, to the meanest of CHRIST's Servants, shall in no wise lose its reward.

and their net brake.

Contrast this with what is said in St. John xxi. 11,—"and for all there was so
many, *yet was not the net broken:*" in which words of "the Disciple whom JESUS
loved," there seems to be a reference to the present place in St. Luke's Gospel.

"Their net *brake;*" yet the fish escaped not.   Here was a double miracle,—as
will be found pointed out in the latter part of the note on St. Mark i. 31.
Observe the last words of St. Matthew iv. 21,—and see the note there.

7 And they beckoned unto *their* partners, which were in the other
ship, that they should come and help them.

"*They* beckoned unto *their* partners;" for Andrew was in the ship, as well as
Simon,—although his name is not mentioned.
Why did they *beckon* and not *call?*   An ancient writer was of opinion that Peter
used a sign, being unable to speak for astonishment.   See ver. 9.   They had doubtless never taken such a draught before.

And they came, and filled both the ships, so that they began to sink.

Every part of this miracle is *full* of wonder,—*full* of prophetic meaning.   The
entire incident may be regarded as a parable, or a prophecy, in action: so particularly related,—only because every particular has a deep symbolic import.   There
were "two ships," as there were two Churches, the Gentile and the Jewish; pursuing with one mind the same occupation; and both, we read, were filled.   A great
draught of fishes was, however, only *then* captured, when the Net was let down at
CHRIST's Word:—the toil of the long dark night had been fruitless.   And did it
not fare so in the Church's history?   The net was broken in consequence,—as at
this day the Church is rent and torn by reason of our unhappy divisions: whereby,
not only her Discipline gives way, but her unity is destroyed, and the safety of the

(c) Psalm xxx. 5.   (d) 2 Samuel vi. 10 to 12.   (e) 1 Kings xvii. 9 to 2
(f) 2 Kings iv. 8 to 17.   (g) Gen. xxx. 27.   (h) Gen. xxxix. 5.
                                  (i) Acts xxvii. 24 and 37.

souls within her is endangered; and yet they are not therefore lost. The ships moreover begin to sink; but they sink not,—for CHRIST is in them.

In all these respects, this miracle is to be compared with another prophetic incident,—namely, *the second* miraculous draught of fishes, related by St. John in the last chapter of his Gospel; and having obvious reference to the final destiny of the same Church, whose earthly progress is here depicted. On *this* occasion CHRIST sits on the unquiet waters;—on *that*, He is found, after His Resurrection, standing on the fixed, motionless shore. *Here*, the net is cast on either side; is drawn up into the ships; and is found to have taken fishes of every kind,—good and bad, large and small:—*there*, the net is cast "*on the right side;*" is drawn to *land;* and is found to be "full of *great* fishes" only. The number of them is moreover specified,—an hundred and fifty and three; as if in allusion to *the number* of GOD's elect.(*k*)   *Here*, again, the net breaks; but *there*,—"for all there were so many, yet *was not* the net broken." Observe, lastly, that on this first occasion, it was promised to St. Peter that he should "catch men;" that is, win Disciples, make converts, to CHRIST. On the second, he is commanded to "feed the sheep" of GOD;—that is, to tend the people already gathered into His pasture,—those who have already become "the sheep of His hand." . . . . . It is wrong,—at least it is dangerous and unwise,—to indulge in fanciful expositions of Holy Scripture; but how so many and such striking points of contrast can be overlooked or disregarded, it is hard to understand. We may not be able to trace out the analogy of an incident like the present, in perfect detail: but shall we therefore fail to follow it out as far as we are able? Consider whether it is likely,—or rather, whether it is credible,—that so many minute particulars should be recorded without an object. Consider, next, the symbolic meaning attached by the SPIRIT to other events, in themselves strictly historical: as the history of Hagar and Sarah, in Galatians iv. 21 to 31. Lastly, compare these two miracles with the parable of the draw-net in St. Matthew xiii. 47 to 50: and *then*,—dull indeed must he be, and slow of heart, who can read the present narrative without the deepest conviction that it teems with hidden, symbolic teaching of the loftiest kind. Such, at least, has been the belief of the wisest and holiest in every age.

8 When Simon Peter saw *it*, he fell down at JESUS' knees, saying, Depart from me; for I am a sinful man, O LORD.

Thus Peter, while spreading his own net for fish, is himself taken in the net which a Greater Fisherman has spread invisibly for *him*.
Compare the exclamation of the Widow of Zarephath to Elijah. "What have I to do with thee, O thou man of GOD? art thou come unto me *to call my sin to remembrance?*"(*l*)   Simon Peter, in like manner, becomes conscious of his sinfulness when he finds himself in the presence of GOD. Consider that saying of holy Job:—"I have heard of Thee by the hearing of the ear; but now mine eye seeth Thee. *Wherefore I abhor myself.*"(*m*)   Consider also the following texts:—Judges vi. 22, 23: xiii. 22. Isaiah vi. 5. Daniel x. 16, 17.
Take notice, however, that the present miracle was, in a singular manner, an appeal to the Disciples' *Faith. Some* fish they *expected* to catch; even *many* fish, they *hoped* for. But the draught was excessive,—and "their hearts burned within them,"(*n*)—and something whispered Simon Peter, "*It is the* LORD!"(*o*)

9 For he was astonished, and all that were with him, at the draught of the fishes which they had taken:

Andrew, namely; and probably "hired servants,"—as in the boat which belonged to the sons of Zebedee. See St. Mark i. 20, where the note may be consulted.

10 and so *was* also James, and John, the sons of Zebedee, which were partners with Simon.

And JESUS said unto Simon, Fear not; from henceforth thou shalt catch men.

(*k*) See the Burial Service: and consider Rev. vii. 4 to 8, and xiv. 1.   (*l*) 1 Kings xvii. 10.
(*m*) Job xlii. 5, 6.   (*n*) St. Luke xxiv. 32.   (*o*) Compare St. John xxi. 7.

Rather,—From henceforth thou shalt take in thy net [not fishes, but] men, alive! Capture them, that is, not for death, but *for life.* Thou shalt draw men by the net of the Gospel, out of the gloomy and troubled waters of this Life, into the Region of Eternal Day; (for CHRIST calls men "out of Darkness," as the same St. Peter elsewhere says, "into His Marvellous Light:")(*p*) where Angels shall gather the good into vessels,—Angels, who are already expecting their arrival on the shore! See St. Matthew xiii. 48, 49.

The prophecy here delivered, began to be fulfilled on the first Christian Day of Pentecost,—when, after St. Peter's sermon, "the same day, there were added unto them about *three thousand souls.*"(*q*)   See the note on St. Matthew iv. 19.

But notwithstanding the prominence given to the fisher's craft, on the present and other occasions, by our LORD Himself; notwithstanding, also, its aptness to represent the great object of ministerial desire,—namely, to win many souls to CHRIST; (for which the servant toils patiently and long, yet knows not what success His Master will give him!)—the heart of Christendom has yet preferred another figure, almost to the exclusion of *this:* pronouncing with one mouth that she loves best to behold in him who has the cure of souls, an image "of the Good *Shepherd,*"—who gave His Life for the sheep!   It is the charge which Simon Peter received after the *second* miraculous draught of fishes,—(to "feed the flock of GOD,"(*r*)—His "sheep" and His "lambs,")—which has thrown this earlier promise and appellation into the shade.(*s*)   The Elder Covenant, like the Gospel, recognises *both* images.   See Ezekiel xxxiv. and xlvii. 9, 10.

11 And when they had brought their ships to land, they forsook all, and followed Him.

He knows nothing of Human Nature who thinks that these men forsook little, when they followed CHRIST.   They forsook all they had,—all they loved and cared for.   They even forsook *themselves.*

12 And it came to pass, when He was in a certain city, behold a man full of leprosy: who, seeing JESUS, fell on *his* face, and besought Him, saying, LORD, if Thou wilt, Thou canst make me clean.

The Reader is referred to the notes on St. Matthew viii. 2, and St. Mark i. 40.

13 And He put forth *His* hand, and touched him, saying, I will: be thou clean.

Contrast the manner of this cure with that performed on Miriam.   "Moses cried unto the LORD, saying, *Heal her now,* O GOD, I beseech Thee."(*t*)   But our SAVIOUR "spake,—and it was done."   Contrast also the manner of Elijah's miracles:—1 Kings xvii. 21: xviii. 36, 37: St. James v. 17, 18, (which it is instructive to compare with 1 Kings xvii. 1, and xviii. 42 to 45:) &c.

"I will;"—*that* is the saying of GOD,—and GOD only; the saying of Him, whose Almighty *Will* is the cause of all things.   When His servants wrought Miracles, far different was the phrase they used.   See Genesis xli. 16, where Joseph says, "It is not *in me: GOD* shall give Pharaoh an answer of peace."   Compare also Daniel ii. 30; and above all, Acts iii. 6 and 12.

And immediately the leprosy departed from him.

Leprosy,—the most hideous of all disorders, and by man's art known to be incurable,—was the type of Sin.   To touch a leper was to incur pollution:(*u*) not because the malady was in itself contagious; but to convince men of the deep defilement of that more terrible malady of the soul, of which Leprosy was the type. Observe, however, that when our LORD would cleanse one who was "*full* of leprosy," He did it by His *touch;* and it was to teach men that as Sin had no place in

(*p*) 1 St. Peter ii. 9.   (*q*) Acts ii. 41.
(*r*) Compare 1 St. Peter v. 2, with St. John xxi. 15, 16, 17.
(*s*) St. Paul himself set the example of this preference.   See Acts xx. 28.   The early Christians however seem to have been very fond of the symbol of a *fish,*—using it oftener perhaps than any other, on their signets.   (*t*) Numb. xii. 13.   (*u*) Leviticus v. 3.

Him, so could no defilement pass upon Him either. Disease could not vex the
second Adam; who had taken upon Himself our Human Nature, indeed, but *not
our fallen Human Nature.* He came into the world to "take our Infirmities and
bear our Sicknesses," as an Evangelist,(x)—interpreting, not quoting, the words of
a Prophet,(y)—has declared: but He bore them like a burthen,—without participation, and without pollution; because "in Him," as in a Fountain, "was LIFE."(z)
See the first note on St. Mark i. 41.

"This King's *Touch*," says Leighton, "cures all sorts of Diseases. It did so
while He walked in a low, despised condition on Earth; and it does so still by that
virtual Divine Power, now that He is in Heaven. And although His Glory there
is greater, His Compassion is not less than when He was here; and His compassion
always was, and is, directed much more to souls diseased, than to bodies, as they
are better and more valuable."

**14 And He charged him to tell no man: but Go, and show thyself
to the priest, and offer for thy cleansing, according as Moses commanded, for a testimony unto them.**

This seems to mean that when the priests had admitted the cleansing to be complete, and accepted the offerings prescribed on such occasions by the Law,(a) those
offerings would remain forever an abiding witness or testimony against them, if
they presumed still to deny the claims of JESUS of Nazareth to be the promised
MESSIAH.

Or it may mean that the offerings would be a testimony of our SAVIOUR's observance of the Law.

**15, 16 But so much the more went there a fame abroad of Him:
and great multitudes came together to hear, and to be healed by Him
of their infirmities. And He withdrew Himself into the Wilderness,
and prayed.**

On this, an ancient Bishop remarks,—"Our REDEEMER performed His Miracles
by day, and passed the night in Prayer: hinting to perfect preachers that as they
should not entirely desert the active Life from love of contemplation, so neither
should they despise the joys of contemplation from an excess of activity; but, in
silent thought, imbibe that which they might afterwards give back in words to their
neighbours."

**17 And it came to pass on a certain day, as He was teaching, that
there were Pharisees and Doctors of the Law sitting by, which were
come out of every town of Galilee, and Judæa, and Jerusalem: and the
Power of the LORD was *present* to heal them.**

To heal *whom?* The Pharisees and Doctors of the Law? Clearly not. The
truth is, the whole scene rose up before the Evangelist, while he wrote; so that he
used the word "*them*" with reference to the many sick persons who (as he knew)
had been brought to our SAVIOUR on this occasion, and were waiting for an opportunity of being healed. Concerning the cures which He may have now wrought on
those other persons, we hear nothing. Our attention is called, in the next and following verses, to the case of a poor suffering Paralytic: who, because he came late,
was debarred the usual mode of access to the Great Physician. He doubtless
thought himself singularly unfortunate, in consequence. He little knew the blessedness which awaited him: little suspected, that his obstacle was to turn out the
very occasion and instrument of GOD's Glory, and his own greatest good! See the
note on St. Matthew ii. 16; and the second note on St. Mark v. 24 and 35.

On that expression, "the Power of the LORD was present to heal,"—see chap.
vi. 19.

18 And, behold, men brought in a bed a man which was taken with

(x) St. Matth. viii. 17.　　　　　　　　　　(y) Isaiah liii. 4.
(z) St. John i. 4.　　　　　　　　　　　　　(a) Leviticus xiv. 10, 21, 22.

a palsy: and they sought *means* to bring him in, and to lay *him* before Him.

The Reader is referred to the notes on St. Mark ii. 3.

19 And when they could not find by what *way* they might bring him in because of the multitude, they went upon the house-top,

Which was easily done, in a country like Palestine, where there is commonly a flight of steps *outside* the House; and where the roof (or house-top) is usually flat, —so as to be a convenient place for discourse,(*b*) for walking,(*c*) or for prayer;(*d*) and furnished with a battlement or parapet,(*e*) at the extremity.

But *how* exactly the four men(*f*) who bore the paralytic, performed the act next described,—see St. Mark ii. 4,—the present writer has never seen quite accounted for: nor do recent travellers in Palestine explain it satisfactorily. There seems to have been something peculiar in the construction of this particular house.

and let him down through the tiling with *his* couch into the midst before JESUS.

Truly, "the Kingdom of Heaven suffereth violence, and the violent take it by force."(*g*)

Our Countryman, Bede, says beautifully,—"Oftentimes, amid the very sweetnesses of secret prayer, and, as it may be called, the pleasant converse with GOD, a crowd of thoughts, disturbing the clear vision of the mind, shuts out CHRIST from its sight. Let us not, then, remain in the lowest ground, where the crowds are bustling; but aim at the roof of the House,—that is, the sublimity of the Holy Scriptures, and meditate on the Law of the LORD!"

20 And when He saw their faith, He said unto him, Man, thy sins are forgiven thee.

What is required of persons to receive Forgiveness of sins? Repentance, whereby they forsake Sin; and Faith, whereby they steadfastly believe the promises of GOD.—Why then was this man forgiven, since, by reason of his helplessness and infirmity, he could give no signs of either Faith or Repentance? Because he promised them both, by his four sureties,—see St. Mark ii. 3;—which promise, as soon as he was able, himself was bound to perform.

The Reader is referred to the notes on St. Mark ii. 3 and 5: also on St. John v. 7.

Take notice that this man had put up no petition: but his palsied body told his need; while his action was a loud and earnest prayer.

21 And the Scribes and the Pharisees began to reason, saying, Who is this which speaketh blasphemies? Who can forgive sins, but GOD alone?

See the note on St. Mark ii. 7.

They wanted "an outward and visible sign of the inward and spiritual grace given;" and our LORD was prepared to grant them all they wanted. Theirs, however, was not the weak Faith, which timidly asks for a sign; but the obdurate temper which resists every appeal. These men were secretly charging our LORD with Blasphemy, and sneering at His prudence in setting up a claim to powers spiritual and unseen. Whence it follows,—

22, 23 But when JESUS perceived their thoughts, He answering said unto them, What reason ye in your hearts? Whether is easier, to say, Thy sins be forgiven thee; or to say, Rise up and walk?

That is,—to utter words which lead to *no* visible consequences, or to utter words

---

(*b*) 1 Sam. ix. 25. (*c*) 2 Sam. xi. 2. (*d*) Acts x. 9.
(*e*) Deut. xxii. 8. (*f*) See St. Mark ii. 3. (*g*) St. Matth. xi. 12.

which are meant to disturb the visible course of Nature?—Our LORD does not compare *the acts* themselves: but the safety of claiming the power to perform them. The Reader is referred to the notes on St. Mark's Gospel,—ii. 8 and 9.

24 But that ye may know that the Son of Man hath power upon Earth to forgive sins, (He said unto the sick of the palsy,) I say unto thee, Arise, and take up thy couch, and go into thine house.

Because it is easier to deliver a saying, than to perform a miracle, our LORD proceeds to exhibit a stupendous act of Almighty Power. See the notes on St. Mark ii. 10 and 11.

25 And immediately he rose up before them, and took up that whereon he lay, and departed to his own house, glorifying GOD.

Well had it been prophesied of the days of MESSIAH,—"Strengthen ye the weak hands, and confirm the feeble knees!"(*h*) . . . . See the note on St. Mark ii. 12.
"That whereon he lay:"—for it was a poor couch, or pallet, and could hardly be called "a bed."—He departed in the direction of his home; but the crowd was excessive,—see ver. 19. The wondering assembly must therefore have fallen back, and made way for the man: *fear* helping to do what amazement would hardly have effected. For the Evangelist proceeds,—

26 And they were all amazed, and they glorified GOD, and were filled with fear, saying, We have seen strange things to-day.

27, 28 And after these things He went forth, and saw a publican, named Levi, sitting at the receipt of custom: and He said unto him, Follow Me. And he left all, rose up, and followed Him.

The remarks which have been already made on the call of Levi, (that is, of St. Matthew,) in St. Mark's Gospel,—chap. ii. 14.—are so entirely applicable to this place, that the Reader may be simply referred thither.
Like St. Mark, the present Evangelist hastens on to give an account of the great feast which St. Matthew made, long after, to his Divine Master. See the note above referred to; and compare the note on St. Matthew ix. 9.

29 And Levi made Him a great feast in his own house: and there was a great company of Publicans and of others that sat down with them.

30 But their Scribes and Pharisees murmured against His Disciples, saying, Why do ye eat and drink with Publicans and Sinners?

Concerning the Scribes, see the note on St. Mark iii. 22: and concerning the "Publicans and Sinners," see the note on St. Mark ii. 15.

31, 32 And JESUS answering said unto them, They that are whole need not a Physician; but they that are sick. I came not to call the righteous, but sinners to repentance.

See the notes on St. Mark ii. 17.
"A great encouragement to *sinners*," writes Leighton, "but no encouragement at all to *sin*. He came to call sinners; but it was to call them *to Repentance*. If thou bring thy sins to JESUS CHRIST, as thy malady and misery, to be cured of them, and delivered from them,—it is well: but to come with them as thy beloved darlings and delight, thinking still to retain *them*, and to receive *Him*, thou mistakest Him grossly, and miserably deludest thyself. The great Redemption He wrought, was, to separate our hearts and Sin. We know Him not, if we take it otherwise. And this says clearly, that though He hath come to us, and stretched forth His hands long among us,—few of us are come to Him. Oh, how few have trod on the neck of their beloved sin to come to JESUS CHRIST!"

(*h*) Isaiah xxxv. 3.

33 And they said unto Him, Why do the disciples of John fast often, and make prayers, and likewise *the disciples* of the Pharisees; but Thine eat and drink?

See the notes on St. Mark ii. 18.

34, 35 And He said unto them, Can ye make the children of the bride-chamber fast, while the Bridegroom is with them? But the days will come, when the Bridegroom shall be taken away from them, and then shall they fast in those days.

The Reader is referred to the notes on St. Mark ii. 19, 20; and should take notice that these words of the "Bridegroom" himself, explain why Holy Church directs her children to interrupt their Lent Fast on Sundays; and to regard all Sundays and Saints' Days in the year, as Feasts. "The children of the Bride-chamber" cannot fast when the Bridegroom is presented to their notice; either in His own Person, or glorified in the persons of His Saints.

36 And He spake also a parable unto them; No man putteth a piece of a new garment upon an old; if otherwise, then both the new maketh a rent, and the piece that was *taken* out of the new agreeth not with the old.

On these words, some remarks have been already offered in the note on St. Mark ii. 21.

Two inconveniences are specified: the new piece causeth a rent in the old garment; and the old garment disliketh the new piece. Having thus briefly pointed out the twofold evil which would have resulted from the course which the Scribes and Pharisees recommended, our Blessed LORD proceeds to discourse of that evil, more in detail: showing, by two several examples, the mischief of imparting a body of new Doctrines to men who had been brought up in an entirely different system. First, He shows the fatal consequence of such a proceeding.

37, 38 And no man putteth new wine into old bottles; else the new wine will burst the bottles, and be spilled, and the bottles shall perish. But new wine must be put into new bottles; and both are preserved.

The Reader is again referred to the notes on St. Mark's Gospel—ii. 22. By a further striking saying, which is peculiar to St. Luke, our LORD shows the reluctance with which men, accustomed to the Ceremonial Law, would receive the Gospel of the Kingdom.

39 No man also having drunk old *wine* straightway desireth new: for he saith, The old is better.

Our LORD's Discourse may be said to conclude with three short *Parables.* See the first words of verse 36. It is worth observing that *Doctrine* is here again compared to *Wine:* but whereas, in the former instance, *the danger* of hastily imparting new Truths to persons not duly prepared to receive them, was spoken of— a danger which arises out of the nature of the thing imparted; in this place, allusion is made to *the obstacle* presented by the Receiver himself. Men, by the very law of their constitution, prefer that which is old to that which is new. And to this natural disposition of His creatures, He who "knew what was in Man," is content to make this solemn and instructive appeal.

This, therefore, furnishes another reason for the progressive course which our LORD was pursuing towards His disciples; and of which we have so many notices in the Gospels. Thus, in the last days of His ministry, He could say, "I have yet many things to say unto you, but ye cannot bear them now."(i) He had discoursed of "earthly things," and men "believed not:" how should they believe if He told them of "heavenly things?"(k) He spake the Word to the people, therefore, at all times, "*as they were able to bear it.*"(l)

(i) St. John xvi. 12.   (k) St. John iii. 12.   (l) St. Mark iv. 33.

As the Master had acted, so did the Disciple. St. Paul was careful to feed the Christians of Corinth "with milk, and not with meat,"—because he found them "not able to bear it."(m)   Towards his Hebrew converts, he was content to pursue the like course; remarking that "strong meat belongeth to them that are of full age."(n)   And doubtless these hints have been set on eternal record for our guidance in the communication of Divine Truth.

THE PRAYER.

ALMIGHTY and everlasting GOD, give unto us the increase of Faith, Hope, and Charity; and, that we may obtain that which Thou dost promise, make us to love that which Thou dost command; through JESUS CHRIST our LORD. Amen.

CHAPTER VI.

---

1 CHRIST *reproveth the Pharisees' blindness about the observation of the Sabbath, by Scripture, Reason, and Miracle. 13 Chooseth Twelve Apostles. 17 Healeth the diseased. 20 Preacheth to His Disciples before the people, of blessings and curses. 27 How we must love our enemies. 46 And join the obedience of good works to the hearing of the Word: lest in the evil day of temptation we fall, like an house built upon the face of the earth, without any foundation.*

1 AND it came to pass on the second Sabbath after the first,

The particular Sabbath which St. Luke here speaks of, is not known: but it was one which fell somewhere about the Passover season—for, (as we see,) the corn was ripe. See the note on St. Mark ii. 23.   It came to pass at such a time,

2 that He went through the corn-fields ; and His Disciples plucked the ears of corn, and did eat, rubbing *them* in *their* hands.   And certain of the Pharisees said unto them, Why do ye that which is not lawful to do on the Sabbath days ?
3 And JESUS answering them said,

See how kindly He takes their part—answering their enemies for them ! He is ever thus towards those who put their trust in Him: "hiding them privily *by His presence* from the provoking of all men ; keeping them secretly in His Tabernacle from the strife of tongues."(a)   He said,—

4, 5 Have ye not read so much as this, what David did, when him-

(m) 1 Cor. iii. 12.   (n) Heb. v. 12, 13, 14.   (a) Psalm xxxi. 22.

self was an hungered, and they which were with him; how he went into the House of God, and did take and eat the show-bread, and gave also to them that were with him; which it is not lawful to eat but for the Priests alone? And He said unto them, that The Son of Man is Lord also of the Sabbath.

The Reader is referred to the notes on St. Mark ii. 23 to 28, concerning this entire transaction. A few more notes will be found in the corresponding place of St. Matthew's Gospel—xii. 1 to 8. A mighty miracle next comes before us.

6, 7 And it came to pass also on another Sabbath, that He entered into the Synagogue and taught: and there was a man whose right hand was withered. And the Scribes and Pharisees watched Him, whether He would heal on the Sabbath day; that they might find an accusation against Him.

See the notes on St. Mark iii. 1 and 2.—St. Matthew here supplies what St. Luke omits. See St. Matthew xii. 11 and 12, with the notes thereon.

8, 9, 10, 11 But He knew their thoughts, and said to the man which had the withered hand, Rise up, and stand forth in the midst. And he arose and stood forth. Then said Jesus unto them, I will ask you one thing; Is it lawful on the Sabbath days to do good, or to do evil? to save life, or to destroy it? And looking round about upon them all, He said unto the man, Stretch forth thy hand. And he did so: and his hand was restored whole as the other. And they were filled with madness; and communed one with another what they might do to Jesus.

It must suffice once more to refer the Reader to the notes on St. Mark iii. 3, 4, 5, 6.

12 And it came to pass in those days, that He went out into a mountain to pray; and continued all night in prayer to God.

Compare this remarkable disclosure with what St. Mark says—chap. i. ver. 35; and take notice that on *that* occasion, our Divine Master prepared himself by prolonged Prayer for His First great Ministerial Journey:(*b*) on *this*, for the solemn Call of His Twelve Apostles, which was to take place on the morrow—as it is said in the next verse. . . . . . How are we taught hereby, in what manner to commence any work of piety—to prepare ourselves for any great undertaking! And how severe a rebuke is it to our short and lifeless devotions, thus to read of *Him* who "continued *all night* in prayer to God!" . . . . . Compare also St. Matthew xiv. 23, or St. Mark vi. 46.

But did the Son of God *require* the aid and support of Prayer? This form of putting the question is apt to mislead us: for thereby the attention is called away from the *whole Person of* Christ, to His *Divine Nature*—in respect of which, He was One with the Father; and therefore, Himself the Source of all Spiritual Strength. But doubtless, as the *Son of Man*,—as the Word "made flesh,"—our Saviour prayed for supplies of Grace, and obtained them in answer to His prayers. Consider St. Luke xxii. 42, 44; and St. Matthew xxvii. 46. We may never overlook the entire reality of our Lord's Human Nature: never so maintain the Truth of His Godhead, as to show ourselves forgetful of the Truth of His Manhood. When we think of His Humanity, let us conceive of it as of the sinless Humanity of Adam *before the Fall;* and we shall not err.

If any do prefer, in the prayers of Christ, the Head, chiefly to behold a living Pattern, and perpetual Reproof to ourselves, His Members—we object not. For our imitation, doubtless, in great part, these mysterious scenes were set on eternal record. But our Lord's prayers may not be regarded as an *unreal* thing; offered up, as well as recorded, for *Man's* sake—rather than for *His own*.

(*b*) Recorded in St. Mark i. 39,—St. Matthew iv. 23,—St. Luke iv. 44.

13 And when it was day, He called *unto Him* His Disciples : and of them He chose Twelve, whom also He named Apostles :

"*He* chose:"—but in Acts x. 41, the Apostles are said to have been "*chosen by* GOD." And,—"*He* called:"—but in St. John xvii. 6, 9, 12, they are said to have been *given to Him by the FATHER.* Is it not true, that after Guidance has been effectually sought by earnest Prayer to GOD, the work on which we are about to engage becomes not *ours*, but *His?*

"*Twelve*,"—for the reason mentioned in the first note on St. Mark iii. 14. These "He ordained," (St. Mark says,) "that He might *send them forth* to preach."(c) Hence their title of "Apostle,"—a word which denotes "One sent forth;" and is translated *Messenger* in Philippians ii. 25.—Compare Haggai i. 13, and Malachi ii. 7.

The successors of the *Apostles* are called *Bishops;* and those titles were at first indifferently used, as appears by a comparison of Philippians ii. 25 with 1 Timothy iii. 1; but, in process of time, the term "Apostles" became restricted to the Twelve. Let it be noted however that these great Ambassadors of CHRIST had a special dignity of their own:—(1st) as being *immediately called* by CHRIST Himself:—(2dly) as being *infallibly guided:*—(3dly) as being *universally charged;* (that is, having a general commission to do all things pertaining to the Ministry of Salvation, in all places, and towards all persons:)—(4thly) as being *miraculously gifted* with the skill of speaking all languages,—with the knowledge of all secrets,—with the power of confirming their doctrine by signs and miracles,—and of imparting the like spiritual gifts to others by the Imposition of their hands. In all these respects, they had not, and could not have, Successors. Descent, (or, as it is called, *Succession*,) supplies in the present day the place of the first; *their own Writings*, of the second: *a several See*, of the third: *Schools and Universities*, of the last.

But then, besides these special and peculiar *Gifts*, they had a solemn *Office;* namely, they were Church Governors, appointed to order and settle the affairs of CHRIST's Spiritual Kingdom; and therein, (beside the preaching of the Gospel and baptizing, common to them with other Ministers,) to ordain a succession of the great Governors of the Church. In *this* respect, (in respect of their *Office*, namely,) they had,—they must needs have had,—Successors; and to those Successors we give the name of *Bishops*.

14, 15, 16 Simon, (whom He also named Peter,) and Andrew his brother, James and John, Philip and Bartholomew, Matthew and Thomas, James the *son* of Alphæus, and Simon called Zelotes, and Judas *the brother* of James, and Judas Iscariot, which also was the traitor.

These twelve great names will be found remarked upon, at some length, in the notes on St. Mark's Gospel,—iii. 16 to 19: whither the Reader is referred.— "Surely," (says Leighton,) "of all that ever lived on earth, the most blessed was this handful and small company which our LORD chose for His constant attendants, —to see His Divine Miracles,—to enjoy His sweetest society,—and to hear His Divine Doctrine. What a holy flame of Love must have burned in their hearts,— who were always so near the Sun of Righteousness!"

17 And He came down with them, and stood in the plain,

Not "*the* plain," but "a plain (that is, *a level*) *spot:*" for our LORD was upon a Mountain. What follows, is St. Luke's shorter version of the "Sermon on the Mount," (as the Discourse in St. Matthew v. vi. and vii. is called:) and this is much to be noted, for it reminds us that the statements in St. Matthew and St. Luke are to be attentively compared throughout.

18, 19 and the company of His Disciples, and a great multitude of people out of all Judæa and Jerusalem, and from the sea coast of Tyre and Sidon, which came to hear Him, and to be healed of their diseases; and they that were vexed with unclean spirits: and they were healed.

(c) St. Mark iii. 14.

And the whole multitude sought to touch Him: for there went virtue out of Him, and healed *them* all.

Concerning the places enumerated above, in verse 17, the Reader may consult the notes on St. Matthew iv. 24, 25; and St. Mark iii. 8.—On the statement in ver. 19, he is requested to read the notes on St. Mark v. 31. The Sermon on the Mount begins at this place.

20 And He lifted up His eyes on His Disciples, and said, Blessed *be ye* poor: for yours is the Kingdom of GOD.

We have sometimes seen it pointed out that since, in St. Matthew, (v. 3,) we find "Blessed are the poor *in spirit*,"—not Poverty of Estate, but Lowliness of Heart, has here the promise of a Blessing.

But let no one be so cruel as to rob the poor man of his Inheritance, (as this most precious promise may be called,) by seeking thus to explain it away. "I hold it for a most infallible rule, in Expositions of Sacred Scripture," (says Hooker,) "that where a literal construction will stand, the farthest from the letter is commonly the worst." Now, "a literal construction will stand" *here;*—is in strict keeping with our LORD's other recorded sayings; (as, St. Luke xviii. 24, 25: St. Matthew xix. 23, 24;)—and is *required* by what follows in ver. 24. It is not hard to see how conducive to Holiness is a lowly Estate; how many helps it affords to the practice of Piety; from how many snares it defends a man. *Then* only are the "poor" in their possessions not "blessed," when they are covetous in their dispositions: *not* "rich in Faith." But Poverty cheerfully submitted to and patiently endured, is doubtless full of Blessedness,—will certainly inherit a blessing. Consider, by all means, 2 Cor. vi. 10: and St. James ii. 5,—where there seems to be a reference to the present place. See also the note on St. Matthew v. 3.

21 Blessed *are ye* that hunger now: for ye shall be filled.

An excellent living Writer supposes that among the multitude addressed by our LORD, there may have been many who were actually suffering Hunger, in consequence of their long attendance on His footsteps: and he refers to St. Matthew xiv. 15, and xv. 32. So that the paraphrase of our LORD's words would run thus:— "Blessed are ye, whose Hunger and Thirst after Righteousness leads you patiently to endure bodily Hunger, while you follow Me: for ye shall be filled with Bread from Heaven."(*d*)

Blessed *are ye* that weep now: for ye shall laugh.

"In the eye of Heaven," says an ancient Bishop, "Blessedness begins at the point which, in human estimation, is reckoned the extreme of Misery." See St. John xvi. 20 to 22. Of our Blessed LORD it is stated twice, that He hungered;(*e*) and twice, that He thirsted:(*f*) three times it is said that He "wept."(*g*) It is not once recorded that He *smiled*.

22 Blessed are ye, when men shall hate you, and when they shall separate you *from their company*, and shall reproach *you*, and cast out your name as evil, for the Son of Man's sake.

"*Separate* you;"—that is, from their Religious Assemblies; as in St. John ix. 22, 34: xii. 42. See especially St. John xvi. 2.

"*Your name:*"—that is, the name of "*Christian.*"(*h*) See St. Matthew xxiv. 9. —St. Peter,—(who heard our LORD pronounce the words in the text,)—alludes to them in his first Epistle:—iv. 14 and 16. So also may St. James be thought to do, in ver. 7 of his second chapter; when his previous allusion to St. Luke vi. 20, (already noticed,)(*i*) is considered.

23 Rejoice ye in that day, and leap for joy: for, behold, your

(*d*) St. John vi. 32 to 35.   (*e*) St. Matthew iv. 2: xxi. 18.
(*f*) St. John iv. 6, 7: xix. 28.   (*g*) St. Luke xix. 41.   St. John xi. 35.   Hebrews v. 7.
(*h*) Which was a *very* early appellation. See Acts xi. 26: xxvi. 28.
(*i*) See above, the end of the note on ver. 20.

reward *is* great in Heaven: for in the like manner did their fathers unto the Prophets.

24 But woe unto you that are rich!

It is obvious that Poverty and Riches, in the literal sense of those words, are here spoken of: see above, on ver. 20. And consider St. Mark x. 23, 24: and St. James v. 1. But our LORD does not, of course, denounce "Woe" on persons simply because they are rich, (as He denounces it on the Pharisees, in St. Matthew xxiii. 13 to 16.) Nor does He denounce *woe*, at all; but rather says, "*Alas!* for you that are rich:" (which is the force of "Woe" in St. Matthew xxiv. 19;)

for ye have received your consolation.

"For ye that, trusting in your riches, and accounting them sufficient for your Happiness, neglect the spiritual treasures which I offer you,—may be assured that you have received all your enjoyment in this world, and have no ground for expecting any in the world to come." Verses 22 and 23 may be compared with St. Matthew v. 11, 12; where see the notes. In connection with verse 24, recollect the words of Abraham addressed to Lazarus,—St. Luke xvi. 25.

25 Woe unto you that are full! for ye shall hunger.

"For ye that are full of earthly good things, are in imminent peril of not desiring anything better. And all such shall one day find the want of both heavenly and earthly goods."

The Parable of Lazarus is again brought to our remembrance by these solemn sayings. Consider how the Rich Man, who had "fared sumptuously every day," being in torments, prayed that a drop of water might be sent to "cool his tongue!"(k)

Woe unto you that laugh now! for ye shall mourn and weep.

"Alas! for as many of you as spend all your lives in careless and ungodly mirth. For the portion of all such is the place of torment."

26 Woe unto you, when all men shall speak well of you! for so did their fathers to the false prophets.

Thus "Woe" has been four times denounced,—corresponding with the four proclamations of "Blessed" which preceded. What was "said to them of old time," —and which St. Matthew gives next, (v. 21 to 43,)—is in a great measure suppressed by St. Luke: with reference however to all that he omits, he proceeds with the word "But:"

27, 28 But I say unto you which hear, Love your enemies, do good to them which hate you, bless them that curse you, and pray for them which despitefully use you.

In conformity with which precept of her LORD, the Church, in her liturgy, directs us to pray for "our enemies, persecutors, and slanderers." Compare the words of the text, with St. Matthew v. 44, and see the note there.

We are not to think that the Prophets,—as David, throughout the Book of Psalms, —violate the spirit of this precept. Their imprecations are against *GOD'S* enemies; not against their own. Those awful words in Psalm cix., for instance, which shock the carnal ear, (verses 6 to 13,) prove to have been words "*which the* HOLY GHOST, *by the mouth of David, spake concerning Judas, which was guide to them that took* JESUS."(l) If, therefore, David "devoteth his enemies to destruction," (as it is said in the heading of Psalm lxix.)—he is found, throughout, to speak prophetically, in the person of CHRIST.(m) Or again, they are his own enemies, only because they are the enemies of GOD, and His Church: whether "flesh and blood,"(n) —(as when David prays to be delivered "out of the hand of the *wicked*, out of the

---

(k) St. Luke xvi. 24.   (l) Acts i. 16: and see ver. 20.
(m) Compare verse 4 of that Psalm, with St. John xv. 25:—verse 9, with St. John ii. 17, and Romans xv. 3:—ver. 21, with St. John xix. 29:—ver. 25, with Acts i. 20.
                              (n) Ephes. vi. 12.

hand of the *unrighteous* and *cruel man:*"(o) or the *Spiritual* Enemies of Man's Salvation.

29, 30, 31 And unto him that smiteth thee on the *one* cheek, offer also the other; and him that taketh away thy cloak, forbid not *to take thy* coat also. Give to every man that asketh of thee; and of him that taketh away thy goods ask *them* not again. And as ye would that men should do to you, do ye also to them likewise.

Concerning verses 29 and 30, the reader is referred to the notes on St. Matthew v. 41 and 42. Compare verse 31 with St. Matthew vii. 12, and see the note there.

32, 33, 34 For if ye love them which love you, what thank have ye? for sinners also love those that love them. And if ye do good to them which do good to you, what thank have ye? for sinners also do even the same. And if ye lend *to them* of whom ye hope to receive, what thank have ye? for sinners also lend to sinners, to receive as much again.

Verses 32 to 34 should be compared with St. Matthew v. 46, 47,—where see the notes. St. Matthew, instead of "sinners," says "Publicans;" concerning whom see the note on St. Mark ii. 15.—"What thank have ye?" (for which St. Matthew(p) gives "What *reward* have ye?") signifies—What favour can ye expect at the hands of GOD?

35, 36 But love ye your enemies, and do good, and lend, hoping for nothing again; and your reward shall be great, and ye shall be the Children of the Highest; for He is kind unto the unthankful and *to* the evil. Be ye therefore merciful, as your Father also is merciful.

These verses are illustrated by St. Matthew v. 44, 45 and 48; and should be compared with them.
It will be perceived that the entire contents of St. Matthew vi. are omitted in this part of St. Luke's Gospel. It is because St. Luke intended to supply the sayings which St. Matthew there records, later,—when the same Divine Speaker repeated the self-same sayings, or the like of them. This method of the Evangelists tends to the enriching of the Gospel Treasury, and is full of instruction and delight.

37, 38 Judge not, and ye shall not be judged: condemn not, and ye shall not be condemned: forgive, and ye shall be forgiven: give, and it shall be given unto you: good measure, pressed down, and shaken together, and running over, shall men give into your bosom. For with the same measure that ye mete withal, it shall be measured to you again.

Compare verses 37 and 38 with St. Matthew vii. 1 and 2; (where see the notes;) and observe how useful the later Gospel is in completing the sense of the earlier one. But our LORD does not say "*shall men give.*" His words "[they] shall give," probably signify only "shall be given:" just as "[they] require," in St. Luke xii. 20, is Englished,—"*shall be required.*" . . . Where the vest is large and loose, as in the East it is, corn may be carried in the bosom. See Psalm lxxix. 12, and xxxv. 13.

39, 40 And He spake a parable unto them, Can the blind lead the blind? shall they not both fall into the ditch? The Disciple is not above his Master: but every one that is perfect shall be as his Master.

That is,—Greater Virtue cannot be expected in the Disciple than was displayed by the Master. Strictly to resemble his Master, is the praise of a perfect Disciple.

(o) Psalm lxxi. 4.   (p) St. Matth. v. 46.

But besides this,—No keenness of spiritual discernment can be looked for in the blind. Whence it follows,—

41 And why beholdest thou the mote that is in thy Brother's eye, but perceivest not the beam that is in thine own eye?

Consider the conduct of Judah, when he passed sentence on Tamar,—Genesis xxxviii. 24: and, still more remarkably, of David, when "Nathan's parable of the ewe lamb caused him to be his own judge."(q) How many men come under the censure of the present passage!

Take notice in how marked a manner Sin is here (verses 39 to 42) spoken of as something which blinds the eye; and blocks up the door at which Knowledge chiefly enters. Surely an apt figure! since *To see GOD*, is the blessing promised to "the pure in heart:"(r) while correct *spiritual discernment* is often spoken of as the privilege of the Just.(s) Little sins are *motes*,—which slightly impair the faculty of vision: great sins are *beams*,—which entirely destroy it. He therefore that lives in Sin walks in Darkness. Consider the constancy of the Sacred Imagery, by a reference to such places as the following.—St. Matthew vi. 22, 23, (where see the notes;) xv. 14: St. John iii. 19, 20: ix. 39 to 41: 2 Cor. iv. 4: 2 St. Peter i. 9: 1 St. John ii. 9 and 11, &c.

42 Either how canst thou say to thy Brother, Brother, let me pull out the mote that is in thine eye, when thou thyself beholdest not the beam that is in thine own eye? Thou hypocrite, cast out first the beam out of thine own eye, and then shalt thou see clearly to pull out the mote that is in thy brother's eye.

The Reader is requested to read the remarks already offered on this verse, in the notes on St. Matthew vii. 5. Our LORD is showing that he "is not a good man who, although he reproves others for their faults, does bad actions himself." He proceeds, therefore, to say,—"For there is no good tree which bringeth forth bad fruit:" or, as it is here rendered,—

43, 44, 45 For a good tree bringeth not forth corrupt fruit; neither doth a corrupt tree bring forth good fruit. For every tree is known by his own fruit. For of thorns men do not gather figs, nor of bramble-bush gather they grapes. A good man out of the good treasure of his heart bringeth forth that which is good; and an evil man out of the evil treasure of his heart bringeth forth that which is evil: for of the abundance of the heart his mouth speaketh.

46 And why call ye Me, LORD, LORD, and do not the things which I say?

For if GOD be our absolute LORD,—we, His vassals,—He has a right to require our service: *we* are bound to do what He commands. To cry, "LORD, LORD,"—and not "to do the things which He says,"—is to deny, even while we confess Him.

Concerning verses 43 and 44, see the notes on St. Matthew vii. 18 and 19. Verse 45 recurs in St. Matthew xii. 35. Compare verse 46 with St. Matthew vii. 21,—and see the notes there.

47, 48 Whosoever cometh to Me, and heareth My sayings, and doeth them, I will show you to whom he is like: he is like a man which built an house, and digged deep, and laid the foundation on a rock: and when the flood arose, the stream beat vehemently upon that house, and could not shake it: for it was founded upon a rock.

49 But he that heareth, and doeth not, is like a man that without

(q) 2 Sam. xii. See the heading of that Chapter.
(r) St. Matth. v. 8,—with which compare 1 St. John iii. 2, 3.
(s) St. John vii. 17. Psalm xix. 8. Ecclesiasticus xxi. 11.

a foundation built an house upon the earth; against which the stream did beat vehemently, and immediately it fell; and the ruin of that house was great.

Take notice that there was nothing to distinguish these two houses outwardly. Both were fair to view. The difference lay entirely in the foundation on which they were respectively built;—the one, piled up on the soft and yielding earth, or rather on the shifting and unsteady sand; (which was no foundation at all;) the other, based on the solid rock.

The three preceding verses have been discussed at such length in the notes on St. Matthew,—vii. 24 to 27,—that it shall suffice to refer the Reader back to the earlier Gospel. But it may be worth pointing out that the short clause in verse 48, peculiar to St. Luke,—"and digged deep,"—derives singular illustration from what is the practice to this day, in Palestine. A recent traveller, describing the house of stone in which he lodged, at Nazareth, says, that the owner, "in order to lay the foundations, had dug down to the solid rock,—as is usual throughout the country,—on this occasion, to the depth of thirty feet."

And thus ends the "Sermon on the Mount:"—for a short review of which, the Reader is referred to the notes on St. Matthew vii. 27. "Others may grow stale," exclaims pious Leighton, "but this Sermon, never so often read over, is always new. Oh, how full of Divine Doctrine! How plain, and yet how high and excellent; delighting the soul, as a bright day,—clear all along! Our SAVIOUR begins with that great point which all are concerned in, and all naturally someway desirous to know,—the Doctrine of Blessedness: and the rest of His Discourse follows out the same argument, directing the way to Happiness in the graces of Purity, Meekness, Mercy."

THE PRAYER.

LORD, we pray Thee that Thy Grace may always prevent and follow us, and make us continually to be given to all good works; through JESUS CHRIST our LORD. Amen.

CHAPTER VII.

1 CHRIST findeth a greater Faith in the Centurion, a Gentile, than in any of the Jews. 10 Healeth his Servant being absent. 11 Raiseth from Death the Widow's Son at Nain. 19 Answereth John's messengers with the declaration of His miracles. 24 Testifieth to the people what opinion He held of John. 30 Inveigheth against the Jews, who, with neither the manners of John nor of JESUS, could be won. 36 And showeth by occasion of Mary Magdalene, how He is a friend to sinners, not to maintain them in sins, but to forgive them their sins, upon their Faith and Repentance.

1 Now when He had ended all His sayings in the audience of the people, He entered into Capernaum.

This was after the "Sermon in the Mount," contained in the preceding Chapter.

The Reader is referred to the note on St. Matthew viii. 1, and the beginning of the note on verse 2.

2 And a certain Centurion's servant, who was dear unto him, was sick, and ready to die.

The narrative which follows, is to be compared carefully, throughout, with the corresponding narrative in St. Matthew's Gospel,—viii. 5 to 13. It will be seen, first of all, that the notice of the love which the Roman Soldier bore towards his Slave is peculiar to this Gospel.

The Centurion was a Proselyte to the Jewish Religion. The Religion of Heathen Rome had failed (as well it might!) to supply the wants of such a spirit as his. He had been guided to embrace the purest system of all which existed in his day; and "the Father of Mercies and God of all comfort"(a) left him not without further light; but first guided him to the knowledge, and now brought him into the very presence, of Him who is the LIGHT Itself.

The Centurion's Servant was "ready to die;" the daughter of Jairus was just dead:(b) the widow of Nain's Son was on the way to burial:(c) Lazarus had been lying in the grave four days.(d)   Almighty Power is no less required to dispel the beginnings of Illness, than to raise a dead corpse to life.

3 And when he heard of JESUS, he sent unto Him the Elders of the Jews, beseeching Him that He would come and heal his Servant.

The Roman Centurion sent *Jewish* Elders to CHRIST, probably because he conceived that it would be more acceptable to Him to be addressed by persons of His own Nation; as well as a more respectful proceeding to approach One of such surpassing sanctity through the Ministers of Religion. As for coming in person,—he stood so low in his own estimation, that he thought himself unworthy to draw near. A further explanation why his choice may have fallen on these particular persons is supplied by the circumstance stated in the 5th verse; namely, because he had himself built the Synagogue of Capernaum, in which they probably ministered.

4, 5 And when they came to JESUS, they besought Him instantly, saying, That he was worthy for whom He should do this: For he loveth our Nation, and he hath built us a Synagogue.

It is marvellous how much of individual *character* is revealed by these short Bible narratives. Not only had the Centurion a "*Faith* which could move mountains," but a burning *Love* was his also. It was not to obtain his own, but his Servant's ūre,—the cure of *a sick Slave*,—that he had laboriously contrived this solemn embassy of Jewish Elders; and in the next verse, we shall find that he further sent to CHRIST a deputation of his "friends." We scarcely need the assurance (in ver. 2) that the Centurion *loved* the servant for whom he was prepared to do so much! It further appears that he had proved the strength of his love towards the Jewish people by the munificent act recorded in verse 5. And these two incidents put together, remind us that the Centurion was one of those noble hearts which look out beyond themselves, for opportunities of Liberality: or, (if you will,) one of those consistent characters, which, in their zeal to confer a public benefit, do not overlook the more sacred claims of their own household.

Observe, then, that here was no dead principle, but a living Faith. This man was not one of those who delight in watching *their own feelings*, and in *describing* and *talking about* them. His whole care was *to act* up to the light which he enjoyed. He showed his Faith *by his Works:* and take notice, that "Faith, if it have not Works, is dead, being alone."(e)

He was, besides, a man of most deep *Humility:* see the first note on verse 6; and observe the language of that, as well as the ensuing verse.

6 Then JESUS went with them. And when He was now not far from the house, the Centurion sent friends to Him, saying unto Him, LORD, trouble not Thyself:

(a) 2 Cor. i. 3.   (b) St. Matthew ix. 18.   (c) See below, ver. 12.
(d) St. John xi. 39.   (e) St. James ii. 17, 18.

This, then, was the message which the Soldier sent to CHRIST, when he beheld those blessed footsteps "not far from the house." St. Matthew further reveals the beautiful circumstance that the Centurion could not endure the doubt of what might be the issue of this second deputation; but hastened forth from his door to deliver the message with his own lips! . . . . At first he sent "the Elders of the Jews:" presently, he "sent friends:" at last, he came himself. A sense of undesert,—a deep feeling of his own unworthiness, ("neither thought I myself worthy to come unto Thee!")—was what had delayed his personal approach so long. But the coldness of his self-distrust thawed away at last, under the ardour of his mingled Zeal and Love: for his Faith, (which burned the brighter as the Object of it approached his dwelling,) had long since reminded him that he had asked an unnecessary favour in requesting that our LORD would "*come* and heal his servant."(*f*) "Trouble not Thyself," he therefore says:

7 for I am not worthy that Thou shouldest enter under my roof: wherefore neither thought I myself worthy to come unto Thee: but say in a word, and my Servant shall be healed.

The Centurion desired to hear words like those which the same Great Physician had addressed some time before to the father of a child who lay sick in the same city, "Go thy way; thy son liveth."(*g*) See the first note on St. Matthew viii. 8. Himself a soldier, he did but wish to hear "the word of command," as it were, uttered: *certain* as to what must be the consequence.

8 For I also am a man set under authority, having under me soldiers, and I say unto one, Go, and he goeth; and to another, Come, and he cometh; and to my Servant, Do this, and he doeth *it*.

For the correct understanding of these words, see the note on St. Matthew viii. 9. The Centurion knew that Diseases were all, in like manner, subject to the command of Him with whom He spoke. So indeed they are: and "so also," says Leighton, "He rebukes the diseases of the Soul, and they are gone. Oh, if we did but believe this, and put Him to it! For Faith doth, in a manner, command Him,—as He doth all other things."

Contrast this Centurion's Faith, with that of another Gentile Soldier,—Naaman the Syrian: 2 Kings v. 11, 12.

9 When JESUS heard these things, He marvelled at him, and turned Him about, and said unto the people that followed Him,

In this way the Evangelists, every now and then, lift the curtain slightly from the scenes they describe. You discover, from these last words, what it was which the Centurion saw "not far from the house,"—and which induced him to leave the chamber where his servant lay a-dying:—our SAVIOUR drew near, attended, not only by the Elders of the Jews, but also by *a multitude of persons*. It was, in fact, a part of that mighty company, which, after the Sermon on the Mount, followed our LORD down the mountain side. See St. Matthew viii. 1.

Concerning the statement that our SAVIOUR "marvelled," see the first note on St. Matth. viii. 10. See also St. Mark iii. 5, and St. Luke viii. 23.

I say unto you, I have not found so great Faith, no, not in Israel.

A Roman *soldier*, then, was the first-fruits of the Gentile world!—Consider that Moses,(*h*) Joshua, and David were warrior-saints in the Old Testament: two Centurions,—(for Cornelius of Cæsarea was also a Centurion,)(*i*)—are patterns of Faith and Prayer, in the New. And observe that our LORD does not require the Centurion of Capernaum to forsake his calling. The profession of arms is honourable in GOD's sight; and "a devout soldier"(*k*) may be not so rare a character as some suppose. See the note on St. Luke iii. 14.

(*f*) St. Luke vii. 3.   (*g*) St. John iv. 50.
(*h*) Compare Exod. ii. 12, with Acts vii. 22, 24 and 25. See also Exod. ii. 17 and 19.
(*i*) Acts x. 1.   (*k*) Acts x. 7.

10 And they that were sent, returning to the house, found the Servant whole that had been sick.

Our LORD had said to the Centurion—"Go thy way; and as thou hast believed, so be it done unto thee!" This we learn from St. Matthew viii. 13. But observe, —the Centurion *did not go.* He needed not "the evidence of his senses," (as the phrase is,) that *as* CHRIST had spoken, *so* had it been done. He left that pitiful method of conviction for others. *"They that were sent,* returned; and found the servant whole."

11 And it came to pass the day after,

"The day after" the healing of the Centurion's Servant; which probably took place on the same day as the Delivery of the Sermon on the Mount. See St. Matth. viii. 5. Our SAVIOUR will therefore have been journeying southward; and when on the confines of Galilee and Samaria, a little to the south of Mount Tabor, it will have come to pass,—

that He went into a City called Nain; and many of His Disciples went with Him, and much people.

"Many of His Disciples,"—*"much* people." It was pointed out above, (in one of the notes on verse 9,) *what* multitude this was. The "Sermon on the Mount" had been pronounced, probably, only yesterday: the concourse of persons who had listened to it, had not therefore yet dispersed. Take notice, further, that the crowd here described, encountered another lesser crowd, (as it is said in the next verse,) emerging from the city-gate. It was in the presence of that vast assembly, therefore, that the second recorded miracle of raising the Dead took place.
The MS. Journal of a friend—recently from the Holy Land—furnishes the following extract.—"A few interesting spots retain names very similar to those by which they are mentioned in Scripture. On descending the northern slope of the little hill of Hermon, we came to a village; and, on inquiring its name from one of the natives who met us, were told it was *Nein*. Oh! how the word sounded on our ears! We knew it was *Nain;* but to hear it so called by one living there, was inexpressibly delightful. . . . . A few poor, and for the most part roofless, houses, and a spring of clear and living water, is all that we found there.
"Here then it was that the ever Blessed One met a poor sorrowing widow, who was following her only son to the grave. *There* is the road, down which no doubt he sad and mournful company were passing. Beyond, too, may be easily traced he path along which the Divine SAVIOUR approached. A few graves at the lower art of the hill still mark an ancient burying-place. . . . On this exact spot, I felt was, that the Lord of Life vanquished Death. . . . . Could I do other than wonr and adore?"
It is interesting to find that on this little village, the Christian pilgrim has had eye fixed from the earliest time. It was duly recognized by the Crusaders also, en they visited the Holy Land.
'ake notice how miracle is here linked on to miracle. The stupendous act of 'er which follows, was wrought unsolicited—unlike the former miracle, which in answer to prayer. And we are thereby reminded of the mighty blessings th many a time have overtaken ourselves, unsought—exceeding not only our e, but even our very desires.
ie Reader will find a remark on the verse next ensuing, in the note on St. Luke 42; and in the last note on St. Matthew ix. 25. It shall be only further ed out in explanation of what follows, that the ancients buried their dead 'e the walls of their cities.

Now when He came nigh to the gate of the city, behold, there dead man carried out, the only son of his mother, and she was)w: and much people of the city was with her.

t a picture of desolation is here given in a few words; "A dead man—the —of a widowed mother." Consider Jeremiah vi. 26: Zechariah xii. 10: iii. 10: and the many places in Scripture where a widow's sorrow is made type of grief.

As an ancient Bishop of Nyssa, in Cappadocia, feelingly remarks: "St. Luke has told us the sum of her misery in a few words. The mother was a widow: with no further hope of having children; nor with any upon whom she might look in the place of Him that was dead. To him alone she had given suck. He alone made her home cheerful. All that is sweet and precious to a mother, was he alone to her! . . . . A *young man*," (as it is said in ver. 14:) "that is, in the flower of his age; just ripening into manhood; just entering upon the time of marriage: the scion of his race; the branch of succession; the sight of his mother's eyes; the staff of her declining years!" . . . . Doubtless, it was a case singularly calculated to excite compassion. Not only was "much people of the city" with her: but, as it follows,—

13 And when the LORD saw her, He had compassion on her,

Take notice how the *Human* feeling of compassion attends the exercise of *Divine* power, which is to follow. See the note on St. Luke viii. 23.

and said unto her, Weep not.

By those words teaching *us* also (be sure) not to be sorry, as men without hope, for them "which sleep in JESUS."(*l*)   For what was He who spake, but "the Resurrection and the Life?"(*m*) Of whom it has been said that He shall hereafter "wipe away all tears?"(*n*)

14 And He came and touched the bier: and they that bare him stood still.

"Life had met Death: wherefore the bier stopped." So says an old Arabian bishop: adding—"It was not thus Elijah raised the widow's son—'*stretching himself upon the dead three times:*'(*o*) nor Elisha—when he applied mouth, eyes, and hands, to the same parts of the dead:(*p*) nor Peter, when he prayed for Tabitha.(*q*) But this was none other but 'GOD, who quickeneth the dead, and calleth those things which be not, as though they were.'(*r*) Whence it follows,"—

And He said, Young man, I say unto thee, Arise.

Which was also His word to the daughter of Jairus: St. Mark v. 41. The youth was lying decked for burial—enclosed in no coffin, but exposed; as is usual in the East. Starting into life therefore, at the Divine summons, it is added,—

15 And he that was dead sat up, and began to speak. And He delivered him to his mother.

What words can describe such a scene as followed? . . . Well may it be said of our LORD that "*He delivered* him to his mother:"(*s*) for the young man had been snatched, like a captive, from the hand of Death; rescued from the power of the Grave. "The last Enemy that shall be destroyed,"(*t*) already receives a death-blow, therefore; and the Conqueror hath a right to divide the spoil with whom He will.

16 And there came a fear on all; and they glorified GOD, saying, That a great Prophet is risen up among us; and, That GOD hath visited His People.

Which words are almost a quotation from the Hymn called *Benedictus:* St. Luke i. 68, 69. Take notice that "there came *a fear* on all:" traces of which feeling are often discoverable in the accounts of our SAVIOUR's miracles. See St. Luke v. 26: viii. 37. St. Mark iv. 41.

· 17 And this rumour of Him went forth throughout all Judæa, and throughout all the regions round about.

(*l*) 1 Thess. iv. 13, 14.   (*m*) St. John xii. 25.   (*n*) Rev. vii. 17: xxi. 4.
(*o*) 1 Kings xvii. 21.   (*p*) 2 Kings iv. 34.   (*q*) Acts ix. 40.
(*r*) Romans iv. 17.   (*s*) Compare 1 Kings xvii. 23. 2 Kings iv. 36.   St. Luke ix. 42.
                             (*t*) 1 Cor. xv. 26.

18, 19 And the disciples of John showed him of all these things. And John calling *unto him* two of his disciples sent *them* to JESUS, saying, Art Thou He that should come? or look we for another?

The memorable transaction here described has been already discussed, at considerable length, in the notes on St. Matthew's Gospel—xi. 3: whither the Reader is referred. The Baptist was at this time a prisoner in Herod's castle of Machærus.

20 When the men were come unto Him, they said, John Baptist hath sent us unto Thee, saying, Art Thou He that should come? or look we for another?

21, 22, 23 And in the same hour He cured many of *their* infirmities and plagues, and of evil spirits; and unto many *that were* blind He gave sight. Then JESUS answering said unto them, Go your way, and tell John what things ye have seen and heard; how that the blind see, the lame walk, the lepers are cleansed, the deaf hear, the dead are raised, to the poor the Gospel is preached. And blessed is *he*, whosoever shall not be offended in me.

Concerning these last words, see the note on St. Matthew xi. 6.

As our LORD so often declared of men, that they should be *"known by their fruits,"*(u)—so does He, in the preceding verses, and in many other places,(x) appeal to his own works as the evidence of His being the MESSIAH.

For, "in that day," (it had been foretold by the prophet,) "shall the deaf hear *the words of the Book*, and the eyes of the blind shall see out of obscurity, and out of darkness. The meek also," (it was added,) "shall increase their joy in the LORD, *and the poor among men shall rejoice in the Holy One of Israel.*"(y) Accordingly, it was now the crowning work of all, that, "*to the poor* the Gospel is preached." And, as we know, *they* at least, "heard Him *gladly.*"(z) Compare what St. James says on this subject—ii. 5. That which made this feature in our LORD's ministry so remarkable, was the contemptuous manner in which the Jewish Doctors had been wont to treat the humbler sort of people—as appears from St. John vii. 49: ix. 34. By "*Poverty,*" however, doubtless the same thing is intended, in this, as in other places of the Gospel; namely, *that* condition of heart which is usually found to belong to persons endued with a very slender portion of this World's goods.

The Reader will find more on this subject in the note on St. Matthew xi. 5.

24, 25, 26, 27, 28 And when the messengers of John were departed, He began to speak unto the people concerning John: What went ye out into the wilderness for to see? A reed shaken with the wind? But what went ye out for to see? A man clothed in soft raiment? Behold, they which are gorgeously apparelled, and live delicately, are in kings' courts. But what went ye out for to see? A Prophet? Yea, I say unto you, and much more than a Prophet. This is *he*, of whom it is written, Behold, I send My Messenger before Thy face, which shall prepare Thy way before Thee. For I say unto you, Among those that are born of women there is not a greater Prophet than John the Baptist: but he that is least in the Kingdom of GOD is greater than he.

These verses will be found to recur in St. Matthew xi. 7 to 11; where they have been discussed at some length. The Reader is therefore referred to the notes on the earlier Gospel. Our SAVIOUR is here reminding the people of the reverence in which they once held the man whose inquiry had been just recited in their ears. It was no familiar sight which had drawn so many thousands of them into the Wilderness: no spectacle to be found in the courts of kings, which had led them

(u) St. Matth. vii. 16, 20, &c.   (x) St. John v. 36: x. 25, 38: xiv. 11: xv. 24, &c.
(y) Isaiah xxix. 18, 19.   (z) St. Mark xii. 37.

into the Waste. But they had gone to behold a mighty Prophet; and such an one our LORD assures them they had actually seen: for a greater (He declares) had never been born of woman.

Take notice, that He who spake the words recorded by the Prophet Malachi—iii. 1, (quoted above in ver. 27,) was certainly JEHOVAH, the LORD of Hosts. Just as certain is it, from St. Matthew iii. 3, that CHRIST is the LORD before whose face John Baptist prepared the way. CHRIST is therefore JEHOVAH.

29 And all·the people that heard *Him*, and the Publicans, justified GOD, being baptized with the Baptism of John.

They "*justified* GOD," that is, acknowledged His Justice, Mercy, Truth, and Goodness:—with reference to which, as it seems, our LORD declares, (in ver. 35,) that "Wisdom *is justified* of all her Children." This verse and the next are peculiar to St. Luke. They have been thought by some to contain the sayings of CHRIST; but it is more likely that these are the words of the Evangelist. For the historical fact here alluded to, see St. Luke iii. 12.

30 But the Pharisees and Lawyers rejected the counsel of GOD against themselves, being not baptized of him.

That is,—"they *frustrated* the Counsel of GOD *towards* themselves: made His merciful intentions and gracious purpose, manifested in the ministry of John, of no effect, through their Pride and Obstinacy." This is spoken only generally, however. Many of the Pharisees *had* come to John for Baptism,—as appears from St. Matthew iii. 7.

31, 32, 33, 34 And the LORD said, Whereunto then shall I liken the men of this generation? and to what are they like? They are like unto children sitting in the market-place, and calling one to another, and saying, We have piped unto you, and ye have not danced; we have mourned to you, and ye have not wept. For John the Baptist came neither eating bread nor drinking wine; and ye say, He hath a devil. The Son of Man is come eating and drinking; and ye say, Behold a gluttonous man, and a wine-bibber, a friend of publicans and sinners!

Our LORD merely means that He did not observe such fasts as St. John observed, and imposed upon his Disciples. The foul imputations to which He thereby exposed Himself, are discovered from no other place of Holy Scripture, besides the present.

Again,—that the SAVIOUR Himself was repeatedly charged with "having a devil," we know from St. John vii. 20: viii. 48, 52: x. 20. But in this place only is it also recorded that the same thing was said of His Forerunner.

For some observations on the last four verses, the Reader is referred to the notes on St. Matthew xi. 16 to 19. John Baptist is regarded as a type of the Law, which brought men to CHRIST, and prepared His way accordingly. There were natures which neither the Severity of the Law, nor the Graciousness of the Gospel, could win over. Yet had CHRIST His faithful children,—His true Disciples,—under either Dispensation. As it follows,—(speaking of Himself,—under the name of WISDOM,)—

35 But Wisdom is justified of all Her Children.

See above, on ver. 29: also, the note on St. Matthew xi. 19.

The Reader is requested further, to take notice, that our LORD's Discourse did not end with these words. To know what He added, see St. Matthew xi. 20 to the end of the chapter. It will be perceived that He concluded with a gracious invitation to all "that labour and are heavy laden: and I," saith He, "will give you rest. Take My yoke upon you, and learn of Me; for I am meek and lowly in heart: and ye shall find rest unto your souls. For My yoke is easy, and My burden is light."(a)

(a) St. Matthew xi. 28 to 30.

The effect of this blessed address on at least *one* among the multitude,—will be discovered from the narrative which follows.

36 And one of the Pharisees desired Him that He would eat with him. And He went into the Pharisee's house, and sat down to meat.

"One of the Pharisees"—mentioned in ver. 30, perhaps. And he may have proffered this act of Hospitality in consequence of the intimation in ver. 34, that the Son of Man had "come eating and drinking." His name is given in ver. 40.

A memorable transaction follows, full of affecting interest and beauty; and concerning which, not a little of a controversial character has been written. Some persons have thought that the Woman who is here related to have anointed our LORD, was Mary the Sister of Lazarus. But this is a pure assumption; and the conjecture is an unfair one; for there is not the least ground for supposing that the blessed creature of whom the SAVIOUR declared that she had "chosen that good part which should not be taken away from her,"(b)—was at any time such an one as is here meant by "a sinner." Others have even thought that St. Luke in this place describes the incident which took place at Bethany, and which is described by the other three Evangelists:(c) but *that* is simply *impossible*. Our Translators, (as the heading of the present Chapter shows,) were of opinion that "Mary Magdalene," who is mentioned in the beginning of the next Chapter, was the Woman here spoken of: concerning which conjecture, (for it is no more than a conjecture,) all that can be said is, that it is *possibly* correct.

37, 38 And, behold, a Woman in the city, which was a sinner, when she knew that JESUS sat at meat in the Pharisee's house, brought an alabaster box of ointment, and stood at His feet behind *him* weeping,

To understand how this was done, it must be borne in mind that, anciently, persons *reclined* at meals.—Placed in a recumbent posture,—their feet also resting upon the couch or sofa whereon themselves lay,—any one desirous of approaching them closely, would perforce stand behind them; and might easily perform the act of Love and Humility which is next described.

and began to wash His feet with tears, and did wipe *them* with the hairs of her head, and kissed His feet, and anointed *them* with the ointment.

The singular resemblance of the present transaction to *that* recorded in connection with the Supper at Bethany, immediately before the Last Passover,(d) cannot fail to strike every Reader. Let us beware, however, of inquiring concerning it, (with the Traitor,)—"To what purpose is this waste?"(e) but rather rejoice in the repeated record of an incident which cannot but be full of divine teaching, and deep significancy.

It is well said by an excellent living writer, (contrasting the two incidents,)— "what brought *this* Woman with the alabaster box of ointment to JESUS, was the earnest yearning after the forgiveness of her sin; and she, in her deep shame and abasement of soul before Him, presumed not to approach Him nearer than to anoint His feet only, standing the while behind. Kissing those feet with her lips, and wiping them with the hair of her head, she realized, as it were in an outward act, the bidding of St. Paul,—'as ye have yielded your members servants to Uncleanness, and to Iniquity unto Iniquity; even so now yield your members servants to Righteousness unto Holiness.'"(f) She used the "long hair," which was "a glory to her," in order to wipe her LORD's feet; as if confessing that our best gifts "only find their true place, when acknowledging their subjection and doing service to Him."

39 Now when the Pharisee which had bidden Him saw *it*, he spake within himself, saying, This Man, if He were a Prophet, would have

(b) St. Luke x. 42.   (c) St. Matth. xxvi. 6, 7.   St. Mark xiv. 3.   St. John xii. 3.
(d) See the references above, in note (c).   (e) St. Matth. xxvi. 8.   (f) Romans vi. 19.

known who and what manner of woman *this is* that toucheth Him: for she is a sinner.

The discernment of spirits was accounted the mark of a true Prophet;(g) and such knowledge was recognized as the very note of MESSIAH,(h)—as the Confession of Nathanael,(i) and of the Woman of Samaria,(k) show. Consider also the blasphemy of the soldiers, whon they had blindfolded our LORD,—St. Matthew xxvi. 67, 68.

This Pharisee was murmuring against the Great Physician, for conveying Life and Health;—and against one diseased, yea, at the point to die, for coming to Him for cure. Little did he advert to the fact that here was a Physician standing between *two* diseased persons: differing, however, chiefly in *this*,—that the Pharisee's was the more dangerous case of the two!

Our SAVIOUR proceeds forthwith to convince His entertainer that He *is* a Prophet,—by showing him that He knows *"what manner of man is this"* that entertaineth Him. "The Pharisee . . . . *spake within himself*," and yet was *answered*; —for it follows:—

40 And JESUS answering said unto him, Simon, I have somewhat to say unto thee And he saith, Master, say on.

41, 42 There was a certain Creditor which had two Debtors: the one owed five hundred pence, and the other fifty. And when they had nothing to pay, He frankly forgave them both. Tell me therefore, which of them will love Him most?

43 Simon answered and said, I suppose that *he*, to whom He forgave most. And He said unto him, Thou hast rightly judged.

In this parable, (says a grave and learned Bishop,)—*"We* are the debtors; and our debts are sins; and the creditor is GOD. The Remission of our sins is the frank forgiving of our debts: and for *that*, we are obliged to return our love." *Frankly* to forgive, is "to forgive out of mere grace and favour."

Simon had "rightly judged,"—not that he who sins most largely will, when forgiven, love the most; but that he who most keenly feels the burden of his guilt, —and who therefore has the liveliest sense of his need of *Forgiveness*,—will repay with most love the Being who removes his burden. For it has been truly pointed out that he "to whom little is forgiven," "is not necessarily he who has sinned little; but he who is lacking in any strong conviction of the exceeding sinfulness of Sin;" he who is unconscious of his need of a SAVIOUR. The warning therefore becomes personal, to Simon: reveals him to himself. And here, he who reads these blessed pages in the right spirit, will pause to consider on how many other occasions our LORD did the like; showed that He was yearning after a human soul, by the practical and personal turn which He gave to His Discourse. Consider, for example, the answer which the Lawyer obtained to his memorable question,—"And who is my neighbour?"(l)

In this place, accordingly, our LORD goes on to apply the parable which He had just delivered, to the case of His entertainer and the sinful Woman;—who even now, it would appear, was hiding her shame by bending over His feet to kiss them. The proportion of fifty to five hundred, doubtless, in the ears of the Pharisee, expressed the relative position in which himself and that poor creature actually stood towards GOD. But on the lips of the Divine Speaker, those numbers rather represented their respective *sense of undesert*: their respective *consciousness of Sin*.

44, 45, 46 And He turned to the Woman, and said unto Simon, Seest thou this Woman? I entered into thine house, thou gavest me no water for My feet: but she hath washed My feet with tears, and wiped *them* with the hairs of her head. Thou gavest Me no kiss: but this woman since the time I came in hath not ceased to kiss My feet.

(g) Consider 1 Kings xiv. 6: 2 Kings i. 3: v. 26.
(h) Isaiah xi. 3, 4. Compare St. John ii. 25.   (i) St. John i. 49.
(k) St. John iv. 29.   (l) St. Luke x. 29. See verses 36 and 37.

head with oil thou didst not anoint: but this woman hath anointed feet with ointment.

Take notice how He is pleased thus graciously to enumerate and dwell upon every rticular of her homage. She may have thought herself unnoticed; certainly, heeded. But no expression of her love had escaped the eyes of Him with whom e had to do!

And the next thing which strikes us, is the want of respectful consideration with hich the SAVIOUR had evidently been treated by this Pharisee. Water for the set was, (and to this day is,) a common Oriental attention:(m) while a Salutation rith the lips,(n) and wherewithal to anoint the head,(o)—would, (as it seems,) have been only becoming courtesies on an occasion like the present. All these, however easily procurable, had been withheld: whereas the feet, washed at the fountain of tears, had been made, by this guilty woman, the object of extraordinary honour. On them, also, (instead of on the forehead,) had she bestowed her many kisses: and fragrant ointment, instead of common oil, had been employed to testify the depth of *her* joy at His presence!

47 Wherefore I say unto thee, Her sins, which are many, are forgiven; for she loved much: but to whom little is forgiven, *the same* loveth little.

This seems to mean,—It is clear, from her conduct, that she has been forgiven many sins: for you see that she loves *much*. Whereas, he to whom little is forgiven.—that is, "to whom, according to his own views of himself, little is forgiven, because he regards his sins as few,—the same loveth little." . . . The sentence is certainly a hard one: but it must be explained by the light of the foregoing Parable: which shows that Forgiveness comes first, and Love follows after.

48 And He said unto her, Thy sins are forgiven.

An act of Absolution which cannot be regarded as any encouragement to *Sin*, yet, as the strongest encouragement imaginable to Sinners: and so it is remarked in the heading of the present Chapter. Here was one sunk very deep in pollution. Her history, indeed, we know not: but we know concerning her that Sin had been her choice, and Shame her portion, until the present hour. We know further, that in the end, there was sincere Repentance on her side: entire Forgiveness on the part of GOD. Which things are "written for our learning: that we, through patience and comfort of the Scriptures, might have hope."(p)

49 And they that sat at meat with Him began to say within themselves, Who is this that forgiveth sins also?

Which reminds us of what had occurred in the case of the cure of the Paralytic, —borne of four. See St. Luke v. 20, 21. See also the note on St. Mark ii. 7. They regarded Him as a mere Man; and, What Man, (say they,) can pretend to forgive Sin? Take notice, therefore, that while *they* murmured in Unbelief,—*she*, in the fullness of her Faith, came to Him *as GOD*, to obtain forgiveness of her sins. Whence it follows,—

50 And He said to the Woman, Thy faith hath saved thee; go in Peace.

See the note on St. Mark v. 34.
Faith, then, had been the root,—and *Love*, (as our LORD Himself has just reminded us,) the Flower; or rather, *the Fruit:* "Faith *which worketh by Love*."(q) And this corresponds with the beautiful picture of spiritual growth which St. Peter has drawn, in the first chapter of his second Epistle,—verse 5 to 7.
Compare the words which our LORD addressed to the Woman of Canaan,—St.

(m) Genesis xviii. 4: xix. 2: xxiv. 32: xliii. 24, &c.
(n) Gen. xxix. 13: xxxiii. 4: xlv. 15. Exodus xviii. 7. St. Matthew xxvi. 49.
(o) Ruth iii. 3. Psalm xxxiii. 5. Daniel x. 3. St. Matthew vi. 17.
(p) Romans xv. 4.
                                 (q) Galat. v. 6.

Matthew xv. 28; and take notice that as *there* it was Earnestness and Humility, so *here* it is Penitence and Love which meet the eye; but our Saviour, in both cases, commends *the Faith* of the applicant. *We see only the Branches: He,—the Root.*

THE PRAYER.

O God, Who hast prepared for them that love Thee such good things as pass man's understanding; pour into our hearts such love toward Thee, that we, loving Thee above all things, may obtain Thy promises, which exceed all that we can desire; through Jesus Christ our Lord. Amen.

CHAPTER VIII.

3 *Women minister unto* Christ *of their substance.* 4 Christ, *after He had preached from place to place, attended with His Apostles, propoundeth the Parable of the Sower,* 16 *and of the candle.* 21 *Declareth who are His Mother, and Brethren.* 22 *Rebuketh the winds.* 26 *Casteth the legion of Devils out of the man into the herd of swine.* 37 *Is rejected of the Gadarenes.* 43 *Healeth the woman of her bloody issue.* 49 *And raiseth from death Jairus' Daughter.*

1 And it came to pass afterward, that He went throughout every city and village, preaching and showing the glad tidings of the Kingdom of God: and the Twelve *were* with Him,

One of the ancients, who was also a Countryman of our own, remarks on this, that—"like the Eagle enticing its young ones to fly, our Lord, step by step, raises up His Disciples to heavenly things. He first of all teaches in the synagogues, and performs Miracles. Next, He chooses twelve, whom He names Apostles; He afterwards takes them with Him, as He preaches throughout the cities and villages." Lastly,—He sends them forth alone, as we read in St. Matthew x. 1 to 5.

2 and certain Women, which had been healed of evil spirits and infirmities, Mary called Magdalene, out of whom went seven devils,

The same statement is repeated in St. Mark xvi. 9. This Mary came from Magdala,—the city mentioned in St. Matthew xv. 39; and it is probably meant that she had been a person of most unholy life, in whom *many* evil spirits had once taken up their habitation. Consider St. Luke xi. 26.

3 and Joanna the wife of Chuza Herod's steward, and Susanna, and many others, which ministered unto Him of their substance.

These holy women enjoyed the blessed privilege of waiting on our Saviour's footsteps, and supplying His earthly needs. One connected even with Herod's Court was among them. Compare St. Matthew xxvii. 55, 56.

4 And when much people were gathered together, and were come to Him out of every city, He spake by a Parable:

The parable of "the Sower" follows,—which is found related in all the three Gospels. The Reader is referred chiefly to the notes on the same parable in St. Mark's Gospel, (chap. iv. 3 to 9, and 14 to 20,)—for many remarks, which could not be repeated in this place. See also St. Matthew's Gospel,—xiii. 1 to 9, and 18 to 23 ; and the notes there: especially the note on ver. 2.

This parable was delivered to a multitude standing on the shore, by our SAVIOUR as He sat in a boat on the Sea of Galilee. See the note on St. Mark iv. 1.

5 A Sower went out to sow his seed:

A familiar image, truly; yet, how ennobled by the use which our SAVIOUR here makes of it!

To know how large an amount of teaching lies concealed in that word,—"seed," see the note on St. Mark iv. 14: also on St. Matthew xiii. 8.   Take notice further, that as by the image of a corn of wheat, our LORD here teaches us *how to live;* so does His great Apostle, from the same source, instruct us *how to die.*   Consider 1 Corinthians xv. 35 to 49.

Observe that the Sower goes forth to sow "*his* seed." Now, the Sower is our SAVIOUR CHRIST: "who receives not the word, as borrowed," (says an Arabian Bishop,) "for He is by nature the WORD of the living GOD." If the term be extended to the Ministers of CHRIST, then let them beware how they sow any other seed than *His!*

See more in the note on St. Mark iv. 3.

and as he sowed, some fell by the way-side; and it was trodden down,

The certain fate of seed cast upon the highway ! Yet St. Luke alone it is, who notices this circumstance.   We learn from the language of all the three Gospels that the seed is less endangered by carelessness from within, than by hostility from without.   It is less the chance tread of passenger thoughts coming and going, than the active malice of the Devil, which is to be dreaded.

One of the ancients points out that our LORD says not,—"He sowed some by the way-side;" but that "some *fell*" there.   For he who soweth, soweth with good intent.   It depends upon the hearer, where the seed shall *fall.*

6 and the fowls of the air devoured it. And some fell upon a rock ; and as soon as it was sprung up, it withered away, because it lacked moisture.

"An unchanged, unsoftened heart, like an evil soil, disappoints the fruit. Though sown by a weak hand, yea, possibly a foul one, yet, if received into a clean and honest heart, it will fructify much."

The *way-side* is interpreted to mean a heart trodden and hardened by the continual passage of evil thoughts.   The *rock* denotes the hardness of *self-will:* a nature unsubdued, unyielding, unbroken.

Venerable Bede observes, that "the *moisture* at the root of the seed is the same as what is called in another parable the oil, to trim the lamps of the Virgins ;(a) that is, Love and steadfastness in Virtue."

See more in the note on St. Mark iv. 6.

7 And some fell among thorns; and the thorns sprang up with it, and choked it.

The seed did not fall so much among thorns that were full grown, as in ground where the roots of these had not been carefully weeded out.   Hence, as a thoughtful modern writer continues, "they grew together,—only the thorns overtopped the good seed; shut them out from the air and light; and drew away the moisture which should have nourished them. . . . . It is not here, as in the first case, that

(a) St. Matthew xxv. 3, 5, 8.
30

there was no soil; nor yet, as in the second case, that there was a shallow soil. What was deficient was *careful husbandry*.

See more in the note on St. Mark iv. 7.

8 And other fell on good ground, and sprang up, and bare fruit an hundredfold.

"Whence then is the difference? Not from the seed. *That* is the same to all. Not from the Sower, neither; for though these be divers, and of different abilities, yet, it depends little or nothing on *that*. Indeed, he is the fittest to preach who is himself most like his message; and comes forth, not only with a handful of seed in his hand, but with store of it in his heart,—the word *dwelling richly in him.*(b) Yet, the seed he sows, being this Word of Life, depends not on his qualifications in any kind; either of common gifts, or special grace. People mistake this greatly; and it is a carnal conceit to hang on the advantages of the Minister, or to eye that much." . . . The words are Archbishop Leighton's.

"A hundredfold!" Such increase attends a good man's sowing. Thus it fared with Isaac when he sowed in the land of the Philistines, "and the LORD blessed him,"—as we read in Genesis xxvi. 12.

See more in the note on St. Mark iv. 8.

And when He had said these things, He cried, He that hath ears to hear, let him hear.

9 And His Disciples asked Him, saying, What might this Parable be?

Some remarks will be found on what precedes in the notes on St. Mark iv. 9 and 10, to which the Reader is referred.

10 And He said, Unto you it is given to know the mysteries of the Kingdom of GOD:

See the note on St. Matthew xiii. 11; and observe what follows in that Gospel, with the notes thereon.

but to others in Parables: that seeing they might not see, and hearing they might not understand.

Observe *the reason* assigned for this in St. Matthew xiii. 13. St. Luke omits the quotation from Isaiah which is found in St. Matthew xiii. 14, 15, and St. Mark iv. 12.

11 Now the Parable is this: The Seed is the Word of GOD.

12 Those by the way-side are they that hear; then cometh the Devil, and taketh away the Word out of their hearts, lest they should believe and be saved.

Concerning this portion of the Divine exposition of the Parable of the Sower, the Reader is referred to what has been already offered in the notes on St. Mark iv. 14 and 15.

13 They on the rock *are they*, which, when they hear, receive the word with joy; and these have no root, which for a while believe, and in time of temptation fall away.

"O rocky hearts!" exclaims pious Leighton, "how shallow, shallow are the impressions of Divine things upon you! Religion goes never further than the upper surface of your hearts. You have but few deep thoughts of GOD, and of JESUS CHRIST, and of the things of the world to come. All are but slight and transient glances!

"The seed goes not deep. It springs up indeed, but any thing blasts and withers it. There is little room in some. If trials arise, either the heat of *perse-*

(b) Coloss. iii. 16.

cution without, or of *temptation* within, this sudden spring-seed can stand before neither."

See more in the note on St. Mark iv. 16, 17.

14 And that which fell among thorns are they, which, when they have heard, go forth, and are choked with cares and riches and pleasures of *this* life, and bring no fruit to perfection.

This parable, as St. Luke gives it, abounds in singular touches which are peculiar to his Gospel. See the notes on verse 15. In this place, it will be seen that he alone preserves the statement that characters of a certain class, "when they have heard, *go forth*, and are choked with cares," &c. The expression seems to indicate the restlessness of such characters; as contrasted with "the *patient abiding* of the meek."

What a lively picture is here presented to us of those thickening cares, which at first interfere with growth in Holiness,—and at last, unless they be cut away, destroy the spiritual life altogether!

Some hearts, then, are a highway; some, a rock; some, thorny ground. By such terms, at least, the reception which men give to the Word, when, like seed, it is sown in their ears,—may be fitly represented. "*Take heed, therefore, how ye hear*,"(c) saith the SPIRIT. And, verily, it cannot be so easy a matter to hear aright! . . . . See more in the note on St. Mark iv. 19.

15 But that on the good ground are they, which in an honest and good heart, having heard the Word, keep *it*,

"In an honest and good heart:" the words are found only in the present Gospel, and are highly expressive of the character which becomes fruitful in good works. As for captious inquiries concerning Human Goodness, we know indeed that "there is none good but one, that is GOD:"(d) and yet Scripture, Reason, and Experience, convince us that some natures afford a better soil for the growth of Spiritual seed, than others.

St. Luke also alone it is who says that these persons "*keep*" the Word: that is, they *hold it fast*. Our LORD declares of such that they shall "never see Death."(e) In the language of our Advent Collect, they "inwardly digest" the Word; and by patience and comfort of it, they "embrace, *and ever hold fast*, the blessed Hope of Everlasting Life."(f)

See more in the note on St. Mark iv. 20.

and bring forth fruit with patience.

"*With patience:*"—a memorable word! There must be "*patient continuance* in well-doing:"(g) perseverance unto the end. Consider the places referred to on the subject of the great Christian grace of *Patience*, in the note on St. Matthew iv. 7.

"'He that hath ears to hear,' as our SAVIOUR closes, 'let him hear.' The LORD apply our hearts to this work: and though discouragements should arise without, or within, and little present fruit appear, but corruption is rather stronger and greater, yet, watch and pray. Wait on; it shall be better. This fruit is to be brought forth '*with patience.*' And this Seed, this Word, the LORD calls by that very name, the 'Word *of His Patience*.'(h) Keep it, hide it in thy heart, and in due time it shall spring up. And this Patience shall be but for a little while. The day of Harvest is at hand, when all who have been in any measure fruitful in Grace, shall be gathered into Glory."

16 No man, when he hath lighted a Candle, covereth it with a vessel, or putteth *it* under a bed; but setteth *it* on a Candlestick, that they which enter in may see the light.

"Having spoken of the effect of the Word upon *the hearers*, He now tells His Disciples what they must do as *teachers* of the Word." See the note on St. Mark iv. 21, and on St. Matthew v. 15.

(c) St. Luke viii. 18.　　　　(d) St. Matth. xix. 17.　　　　(e) St. John viii. 51.
(f) Collect for the Second Sunday in Advent.　　(g) Romans ii. 7.　　(h) Rev. iii. 10.

17, 18 For nothing is secret, that shall not be made manifest; neither *any thing* hid, that shall not be known and come abroad. Take heed therefore how ye hear: for whosoever hath, to him shall be given; and whosoever hath not, from him shall be taken even that which he seemeth to have.

"*How* ye hear." In St. Mark iv. 24, it is—"*What* ye hear." . . . . "Even that which he *seemeth to have*,"—is peculiar to this Gospel. The phrase marks the unreality of the possession so neglected: and may be compared, or rather, contrasted, with the language of St. Luke xvi. 12.

19 Then came to Him *His* Mother and His Brethren, and could not come at Him for the press.

Concerning the "Brethren of our LORD," see the note on St. Matthew xiii. 55. How mighty must the crowd have been to have occasioned such an incident as this!

20, 21 And it was told Him *by certain* which said, Thy Mother and Thy Brethren stand without, desiring to see Thee. And He answered and said unto them, My Mother and My Brethren are these which hear the Word of GOD, and do it.

This was surely said for the comfort of as many as should come after: and it is well worthy of remark how our Blessed LORD, in countless ways, contrived that "as many as are afar off,"(*i*)—even we, at this distant day,—should be made to feel that advantages of the highest order are ours; privileges, equal to any which were enjoyed by Kinsmen and Disciples in the Days of the Son of Man. . . . . . . These verses occur in St. Mark's Gospel,—iii. 31 to 35; where see the notes.

22 Now it came to pass on a certain day, that He went into a ship with His Disciples: and He said unto them, Let us go over unto the other side of the Lake. And they launched forth.

This was done, as St. Matthew relates, (viii. 18,) "when JESUS saw great multitudes about Him." The blessed company were about to cross over from the Western to the Eastern side of the Lake, in the direction of Decapolis.

23 But as they sailed He fell asleep:

Jonah was a memorable type of CHRIST: and we read of *him* also, that in the midst of the mighty storm, "he was fast asleep."(*k*)

As *man*, our SAVIOUR slept: as *GOD*, He stilled the storm. In some such manner we are often reminded at once, of the Divine and Human nature of our LORD. Thus, immediately after cleansing the leper, He is related to have "withdrawn Himself into the Wilderness, and *prayed:*"(*l*) when He performed the stupendous miracle at Capernaum, on the Centurion's servant, He is said to have "*marvelled:*"(*m*) and when He was about to call Lazarus out of the grave, it is stated that "JESUS *wept.*"(*n*)
See the notes on St. Mark iii. 5: vii. 34: St. Luke iv. 30: vii. 13.

and there came down a storm of wind on the lake; and they were filled *with water*, and were in jeopardy.

"There *came down* a storm of wind." This is what happens in the case of mountain-lakes: and is observed to take place to this day on the Sea of Galilee. See the note on St. Mark i. 16.

24 And they came to Him, and awoke Him, saying, Master, master, we perish. Then He arose, and rebuked the Wind and the raging of the Water: and they ceased, and there was a calm.

(*i*) Acts ii. 39.   (*k*) Jonah i. 5.   (*l*) St. Luke v. 16.
(*m*) St. Luke vii. 9.   (*n*) St. John xi. 35.

Our LORD rebuked both the Wind and the Sea;(o) accordingly, the one ceased, the other grew calm. *First,* the Wind was silenced; *then,* the Sea: because *that was a cause,* this, an *effect.* Even from so minute a circumstance as this, one may gather a lesson!

"The floods have lifted up, O LORD, the floods have lifted up their voice, the floods have lifted up their waves. The LORD on high is mightier than the noise of many waters: yea, than the mighty waves of the sea."(p)

25 And He said unto them, Where is your Faith? And they being afraid wondered, saying one to another, What manner of Man is this! for He commandeth even the winds and water, and they obey Him.

They forgot that this was He of whom the Psalmist had said, "Thy way is in the sea, and Thy path in the great waters, and Thy footsteps are not known!"(q)

26 And they arrived at the country of the Gadarenes, which is over against Galilee.

Our LORD had now reached the Eastern shore of the Lake. We are about to behold Him performing a mighty act, illustrative of the very purpose of His coming: for, "For this purpose the SON OF GOD was manifested, *that He might destroy the works of the Devil.*"(r)

27 And when He went forth to land, there met Him out of the City a certain man,

So St. Mark says,(s) but we learn from St. Matthew viii. 28, that there were *two* persons: of whom it seems that *one* was so exceedingly fierce, and proved so very conspicuous, that St. Mark and St. Luke have confined themselves *to his* history.

which had Devils long time, and wore no clothes, neither abode in any house, but in the tombs.

Concerning this, see the last note on the second half of St. Matthew viii. 28.

28 When he saw JESUS, he cried out, and fell down before Him, and with a loud voice said, What have I to do with Thee, JESUS, *thou* SON of GOD Most High? I beseech Thee, torment me not.

The very presence of CHRIST is torture to the evil Spirits. Compare what happened in the Synagogue of Capernaum, St. Luke iv. 33, 34: and note the behaviour of the deaf and dumb Spirit when "*he saw* CHRIST."(t) This reminds us that Heaven *would not be Heaven* to the unholy.

29 (For He had commanded the unclean spirit to come out of the man.

It is called an "*unclean* spirit." Is it possible that such possession was the result of sensual indulgence and unclean living? that unbridled lust laid men open to these incursions of the Powers of Darkness? See the notes on St. Mark v. 1.

For oftentimes it had caught him: and he was kept bound with chains and in fetters; and he brake the bands, and was driven of the Devil into the wilderness.)

This is even more particularly described by St. Mark v. 4, 5.—The result of this violence is mentioned by St. Matthew, namely, "that *no man might pass by that way.*"(u)

30 And JESUS asked him, saying, What is thy name? And he said, Legion: because many devils were entered into him.

(o) St. Mark iv. 39.   (p) Psalm xciii. 3, 4.   (q) Psalm lxxvii. 19.
(r) 1 St. John iii. 8.   (s) St. Mark v. 2.   (t) St. Mark ix. 20.
(u) St. Matthew viii. 28.

"Legion!" a name suggestive not only of numbers, but of organized strength, tried courage; distinction of ranks, and unity of purpose. As there was "a multitude of the *heavenly host*;"(x) as also there were more than "twelve *legions* of Angels"(y) ready to do the bidding of the Incarnate Son;—so does Satan's Kingdom discover military resources also. Himself "the Prince of the devils:"(z) under him, "Principalities and Powers,"(a) and other ranks of inferior spirits; which have different degrees of strength,(b) depending perhaps on their different degrees of wickedness.(c) Our Lord describes the Enemy as "a strong man *armed*," and speaks of his "*armour*."(d) Hence, the Christian, who has to contend with him, or his agents, is furnished with "weapons of warfare,"(e) also; "the whole armour of God;" girdle, and breast-plate,—shield, and helmet, and sword.(f) See the notes on St. Luke xi. 22.

The Reader is referred to the notes on St. Matthew xii. 43 to 45.

31 And they besought Him that He would not command them to go out into the Deep.

Rather, into the "bottomless pit;" for the word here used is "the *abyss*,"—which probably in this place denotes the pit of Hell.

St. John the Divine beheld (in the Spirit) "an Angel come down from Heaven, having the key of the bottomless pit and a great chain in his hand. And he laid hold on the Dragon, that old Serpent, which is the Devil, and Satan; and bound him a thousand years, and cast him into the bottomless pit, and set a seal upon him that he should deceive the nations no more."(g) These are mysterious words, which we cannot presume to explain: but, taken in connection with the text, they seem to imply that the bottomless pit is reserved for the Apostate Angels; and that it was the prayer of this Legion of Spirits that Christ would not anticipate their sentence, by sending them thither "before the time."(h) Compare St. Jude, verse 6.

32 And there was there an herd of many swine feeding on the mountain: and they besought Him that He would suffer them to enter into them.

See the notes on St. Mark v. 12.

33 And He suffered them. Then went the devils out of the man, and entered into the swine: and the herd ran violently down a steep place into the Lake, and were choked.

See the note on St. Mark v. 13.

34, 35 When they that fed *them* saw what was done, they fled, and went and told *it* in the city and in the country. Then they went out to see what was done; and came to Jesus, and found the man, out of whom the devils were departed, sitting at the feet of Jesus, clothed, and in his right mind; and they were afraid.

Take notice, then, how complete the recovery had been; that he who, an hour ago, had been a frantic demoniac, was already converted into a meek disciple of the Lamb. All this is implied by the statement, that he was now to be seen "sitting at the feet of Jesus;" for this was the attitude of a Disciple. It was thus that Scholars received the instructions of their Master. See Deut. xxxiii. 3. 2 Kings iv. 38. St. Luke x. 39. Acts xxii. 3. Compare Ezekiel viii. 1: xiv. 1: xx. 1: xxxiii. 31.

36, 37 They also which saw *it* told them by what means he that was possessed of the devils was healed. Then the whole multitude of the

---

(x) St. Luke ii. 13.   (y) St. Matth. xxvi. 53.   (z) St. Matth. ix. 34.
(a) Eph. i. 21, and vi. 12: Rom. viii. 38: Col. ii. 15.   (b) St. Matth. xvii. 21.
(c) St. Matth. xii. 45.   (d) St. Luke xi. 21, 22.   (e) 2 Cor. x. 4.
(f) Ephes. vi. 14 to 17.   (g) Rev. xx. 1 to 3.   (h) St. Matth. viii. 20.

country of the Gadarenes round about besought Him to depart from them ;

They forgot that they had been delivered from a scourge which had rendered it unsafe for any man "to pass by that way."(i)　They overlooked the blessing which had befallen two(k) of their own most afflicted citizens; whereby they had been restored to their families and to themselves.　Above all, they gave no heed to the actual presence of CHRIST their SAVIOUR.　They could think only of the swine that had been lost.　They were confounded at the amazing history they had heard; and wished for nothing so much as the departure of One who had, in reality, shown Himself their Friend, and greatest Benefactor.

How hard it is to recognize the Hand of GOD in anything which interrupts our present enjoyment; brings us loss; and, in any way, interferes with our worldly prosperity!　We overlook the actual blessings which mingle with the most afflicting dispensation.　We do not consider how near we may have been brought, by chastisement, to the sacred person of our LORD.　We simply are impatient and afraid.　We desire nothing so much as to be as, and what, we were.

for they were taken with great fear: and He went up into a Ship, and returned back again.

He took them at their word.　He granted their prayer: yet, surely, in wrath, or in sorrow, rather than in mercy!　See the note on St. Matthew vii. 8.

38 Now the man out of whom the devils were departed, besought Him that he might be with Him;

See the notes on St. Mark v. 18.

39 but JESUS sent him away, saying, Return to thine own house, and show how great things GOD hath done unto thee.

Sometimes our LORD invited men to follow Him, and they resisted His invitation.(l)　Here, when one expressed a wish to follow, he is not allowed to do so.—In like manner, the SAVIOUR sometimes enjoined silence on those whom He healed.(m) Here, He commands the very opposite course. . . . Doubtless, He makes trial of each in a peculiar way; has different demands for different persons; and shows to every one the path which will conduct *him* most safely to the Land of Everlasting Rest.　See the note on St. Matthew xi. 5, and on St. Mark v. 19.

And he went his way, and published throughout the whole city how great things JESUS had done unto him.

40 And it came to pass, that, when JESUS was returned, the people *gladly* received Him : for they were all waiting for Him.

He beheld them, as He approached the Western shore of the Lake, drawn up to receive Him.　Compare St. Mark v. 21, and the note there.

41 And, behold, there came a man named Jairus, and he was a Ruler of the Synagogue :

The Reader is referred to the notes on St. Mark v. 22.

42 And he fell down at JESUS' feet, and besought Him that He would come into his house: for he had one only daughter, about twelve years of age, and she lay a-dying.

"One *only* Daughter."—So, at Nain, and after the Transfiguration, it was an *only* Son:(n) and at Bethany, an *only* Brother.　The Great Physician knows who stand in the greatest need!

(i) St. Matthew viii. 28.　　　　(k) See above, the first note on verse 27.
(l) St. Luke ix. 59 : xviii. 22.　　(m) St. Matth. viii. 4 : ix. 30 : xii. 16.　St. Luke viii. 56.
　　　　　　　　(n) St. Luke vii. 12, and St. Luke ix. 38.

43 But as He went, the people thronged Him. And a Woman having an issue of blood twelve years, which had spent all her living upon physicians, neither could be healed of any,   .

St. Luke "the Physician"(*o*) does not add, (as St. Mark does, in this place,)(*p*)— "*but rather grew worse.*"
Concerning the words of the text, see the note on St. Mark v. 26.

44 came behind *Him*, and touched the border of His garment: and immediately her issue of blood stanched.

"The *garment* of CHRIST," says an ancient writer, "represented the mystery of His *Incarnation*." It is probable that he meant thereby to imply, that "he that will be saved" "must believe rightly the Incarnation of our LORD JESUS CHRIST."(*q*) See the notes on St. Mark v. 27.
Concerning "*the border* of His Garment," see the note on St. Matthew viii. 20.

45 And JESUS said, Who touched Me?

Not as though He *needed* the information; for this was He who said to Nathanael,—"Before that Philip called thee, when thou wast under the fig tree, *I saw thee*."(*r*) . . . Compare the language of Elisha to Gehazi,—2 Kings v. 26.—See the note on the latter part of St. Mark v. 30.
This was not an *encouraging* reception, as men speak. Consider the following texts:—St. Matthew xv. 23 to 26: and St. John i. 38.

46 When all denied, Peter and they that were with Him said, Master, the multitude throng Thee, and press *Thee*, and sayest Thou, Who touched Me? And JESUS said, Somebody hath touched Me: for I perceive that virtue is gone out of Me.

The poor woman had approached His Sacred garments as men are said to touch relics; with a blind faith in their mysterious virtue and efficacy. Even *thus*, she obtained a blessing; for it *was*—Faith. But CHRIST would not so be touched. He will have us know that the Fountain of grace is the living GOD,—who beholdeth all things in Heaven and Earth; and who claims of His rational creatures a reasonable worship.
Do but think how full, to overflowing, must have been the house of clay wherein the SAVIOUR of the World condescended to make His habitation; that the virtue of His Divinity,—like the precious ointment on Aaron's head,—should have thus gone down to the very skirts of His clothing!(*s*) Consider St. John v. 26.
Compare St. Luke vi. 19; and see the notes on St. Mark v. 31, 32.

47 And when the woman saw that she was not hid, she came trembling; and falling down before Him, she declared unto Him before all the people for what cause she had touched Him, and how she was healed immediately.

Take notice, that in *this* miracle the cure came first. This was vouchsafed as a help and encouragement; that so, the open confession which the SAVIOUR requires, and which must follow,—see Acts viii. 37,—might prove the easier.—It is further remarkable as having been a miracle within a miracle;—and one, wherein CHRIST wrought without a word, or sign.

48 And He said unto her, Daughter, be of good comfort: thy Faith hath made thee whole: go in peace.

Our LORD had used the self-same form of address, in the former Chapter, to the "woman which was a sinner;"—vii. 50. Faith is the hand which lays hold on the Blessing.

(*o*) Coloss. iv. 14.   (*p*) St. Mark v. 26.
(*q*) See that most precious part of our whole Church Service,—the Athanasian Creed.
(*r*) St. John i. 48.   (*s*) Psalm cxxxiii. 2.

49 While He yet spake, there cometh one from the Ruler of the Synagogue's *house,* **saying to him, Thy Daughter is dead; trouble not the Master.**

For the fatigue to which our Blessed SAVIOUR was being exposed must have been apparent to all. See the note on St. Mark v. 24.

To raise the dead seemed impossible. Such a wonder had been recorded once of Elijah,(t) twice of Elisha.(u) But how could such a thing be expected on the present occasion? When the damsel drew her parting breath, the last ray of Hope became extinct also.

50 But when JESUS heard *it,* **He answered him, saying, Fear not: believe only, and she shall be made whole.**

And had not our LORD supplied him with a mighty ground of confidence by the miracle which he had wrought on the way? The note on St. Mark v. 36 may be referred to.

51, 52 And when He came into the house, He suffered no man to go in, save Peter, and James, and John, and the father and the mother of the maiden. And all wept, and bewailed her: but He said, Weep not, she is not dead, but sleepeth.

In the eyes of "the Father of Spirits" she did but sleep; did but wait till He, (who is the Resurrection and the Life,) should come to waken her.

See the notes on St. Mark v. 37, 38, 39.

53, 54 And they laughed Him to scorn, knowing that she was dead. And He put them all out,

The scorner is not suffered to be a witness of CHRIST's miracles. Thus our LORD illustrated one of His own sayings, by His own example. See St. Matthew vii. 6. Elijah in like manner,(x) and Elisha,(y) are found to have been even *alone* when they raised the dead.

55 and took her by the hand, and called, saying, Maid, arise. And her spirit came again, and she arose straightway:

The first few words of verse 55 are found also in 1 Kings xvii. 22. The Reader is referred to the notes on St. Mark v. 40, 41, 42.

and He commanded to give her meat.

The King of Heaven and Earth, cares, therefore, for the meal of a little child!— See the notes on St. Mark v. 43.

56 And her parents were astonished: but He charged them that they should tell no man what was done.

The three examples above specified,(z) were so many confirmations under the Law, of a Resurrection to Life after Death; and we have three to equal them under the Gospel.(a) One, we have been already considering. Another took place at Nain. "Thus CHRIST raised the dead in the chamber, and in the street; from the bed, and from the bier:" and, not content with this, He proceeded to the grave of Lazarus.—These three miracles under the Gospel were so many proofs, and preludes, of the Last and General Resurrection.

The present miracle seems to have been attended with some features of exceeding solemnity, for three only of the Apostles were deemed worthy to behold it,—the same three who were the chosen witnesses of CHRIST's greatest Glory,(b) as well as

(t) 1 Kings xvii. 22.   (u) 2 Kings iv. 35 and xiii. 21.
(x) 1 Kings xvii. 19,—compared with ver. 23.   (y) 2 Kings iv. 33.
(z) In the note on ver. 49.   (a) Concerning which, see the note on St. Matth. ix. 25.
                                     (b) St. Matthew xvii. 1, 2.

of His lowest Humiliation.(c) The injunction to "tell no man what was done," is fully explained by the temper of mind of the assembled company, recorded in verse 53.

THE PRAYER.

ALMIGHTY GOD, with Whom do live the spirits of them that depart hence in the LORD, and with Whom the souls of the faithful, after they are delivered from the burden of the flesh, are in joy and felicity; we beseech Thee, that it may please Thee, of Thy gracious goodness, shortly to accomplish the number of Thine elect, and to hasten Thy Kingdom; that we, with all those that are departed in the true faith of Thy Holy Name, may have our perfect consummation and bliss, both in body and soul, in Thy eternal and everlasting Glory; through JESUS CHRIST our LORD. Amen.

CHAPTER IX.

1 CHRIST *sendeth His Apostles to work miracles, and to preach.* 7 *Herod desired to see* CHRIST. 17 CHRIST *feedeth five thousand.* 18 *Enquireth what opinion the world had of Him: foretelleth His Passion.* 23 *Proposeth to all the pattern of His patience.* 28 *Transfiguration.* 37 *He healeth the lunatic.* 43 *Again forewarneth His Disciples of His Passion.* 46 *Commendeth Humility.* 51 *Biddeth them to show mildness towards all, without desire of revenge.* 57 *Divers would follow Him, but upon conditions.*

1 THEN He called His twelve Disciples together, and gave them power and authority over all devils, and to cure diseases.

St. Luke is speaking of the Twelve Apostles, whose names he gave in chap. vi. 14 to 16. Concerning the several catalogues of the Apostles, see the note on St. Mark iii. 15: and, for some remarks on each of those great Saints, the Reader is referred to the Commentary on St. Mark iii. 16 to 19.

2 And He sent them to preach the Kingdom of GOD, and to heal the sick.

Hitherto, "as an Eagle . . . . fluttereth over her young, spreadeth abroad her wings, taketh them, beareth them on her wings,"(a)—so had the LORD dealt with His Apostles. But it is now time that they should make their first Ministerial Journey alone; and He proceeds to deliver to them His parting Charge and Commission. Concerning the four ensuing verses, enough has been already offered in the notes on St. Matthew x. 1 to 15,—to which the Reader is accordingly here referred.

(c) St. Matthew xxvi. 37.   (a) Deut. xxxii. 11.

3, 4, 5 And He said unto them, Take nothing for *your* journey, neither staves, nor scrip, neither bread, neither money; neither have two coats apiece. And whatsoever house ye enter into, there abide, and thence depart. And whosoever will not receive you, when ye go out of the city, shake off the very dust from your feet for a testimony against them.

6 And they departed, and went through the towns, preaching the Gospel, and healing everywhere.

St. Mark,—vi. 12, 13,—relates this incident in a very interesting manner; but we must refer to St. Matthew's narrative if we would understand the words which follow. The last-named Evangelist relates that "when Jesus had made an end of commanding His Twelve Disciples, He departed thence to teach and to preach in their cities."(b) In other words, He took His third Great Ministerial Journey, and He took it *alone.*

7, 8 Now Herod the Tetrarch heard of all that was done by Him: and he was perplexed, because that it was said of some, that John was risen from the dead; and of some, that Elias had appeared; and of others, that one of the old Prophets was risen again.

"John" was said to have "*risen from the dead;*" because the Baptist had been killed and was buried: "Elias," to have "*appeared,*"—for Elijah was translated, and had never seen death. Elijah, we know, was *expected* to appear before the Advent of CHRIST. Hence the inquiry in St. John i. 21, and in St. Matthew xvii. 11:—hence also the suspicion which we shall find expressed lower down, in verse 19;—and hence the scoff of the populace as our SAVIOUR hung upon the Cross,— "Let be, let us see whether Elias will come to save Him."(c)

9 And Herod said, John have I beheaded: but who is this, of whom I hear such things? And he desired to see Him.

With which remarkable words St. Luke dismisses one of the most striking and instructive histories in the Bible. He will be found, in an earlier part of his Gospel, (namely, in chap. iii. 19, 20,) to have narrated the imprisonment of the Baptist. In this place therefore he passes over what St. Matthew,(d) and especially St. Mark,(e) have described so much in detail.

From the combined narrative of the three Evangelists we obtain a striking picture of the downward progress of one who has entered on a career of crime. At first, sensible of the beauty of Holiness, though recommended by its very sternest preacher, and conscious of the power and authority with which John spoke, Herod had not only gladly listened, but even largely obeyed him. Next, influenced by a criminal passion, he shuts up the Saint in prison. Even so, however, he is careful to secure the personal safety of his captive; and he makes provision that the disciples of John may have free access to their Master. At last, "when a convenient day was come," Herod is found capable of giving orders that the Baptist should be put to death. He would surely have recoiled with horror, could he but have seen the end from the beginning!

A tortured conscience is the consequence; and the murderer can discern nothing less than the Baptist restored to life in the wondrous histories which at this time reached him concerning our LORD. "And he desired to see Him." But it was the curiosity not of Faith, but of Unbelief; of a heart hardening, if not already hardened, against holy impressions. The report of our SAVIOUR's heavenly Discourses,—His Acts of Love,—His Miracles of Mercy,—wrought none of those blessed effects on Herod, which they produced on guileless and innocent hearts. He longed to see CHRIST, "because he had heard many things of Him; and *he hoped to have seen some miracle done by Him.*"(f) His interview with the SAVIOUR accordingly set the seal upon his iniquity; and became the means of handing down

(b) St. Matth. xi. 1.   (c) 1 St. Matth. xxvii. 49.   (d) St. Matth. xiv. 3 to 12.
(e) St. Mark vi. 17 to 29.   (f) St. Luke xxiii. 8.

his name to the latest age of the Church, in connection with that of Pontius Pilate, as the murderer of "the Prince of Life."(g)

The Reader who desires more on this subject, may be referred to the notes on St. Matthew xiv. 1 to 10: and on St. Mark vi. 17 to 29.

10 And the Apostles, when they were returned, told Him all that they had done. And He took them, and went aside privately into a desert place belonging to the city called Bethsaida.

This will be found more particularly related in St. Mark's Gospel,—chap. vi. 30 to 32; where see the note. Travellers describe such "a desert place,"—that is, a barren tract of uncultivated ground, at the north-eastern extremity of the Lake, not far from which stood Bethsaida-Julias.

11, 12 And the people, when they knew *it*, followed Him: and He received them, and spake unto them of the Kingdom of God, and healed them that had need of healing. And when the day began to wear away, then came the Twelve, and said unto Him, Send the multitude away, that they may go into the towns and country round about, and lodge, and get victuals: for we are here in a desert place.

The Reader is again referred to the notes on St. Mark's Gospel,—vi. 33 to 36. The second Evangelist will be found, as before, to be more full and particular in this place than either St. Matthew or St. Luke.

Did not the Disciples, in effect, doubt their LORD's power, when they made the request here recorded? " Yea, they spake against GOD. They said, Can GOD furnish a table in the wilderness? Behold," He hath done many mighty works: "can He give bread also, or provide flesh for His people?"(h)

13, 14 But He said unto them, Give ye them to eat. And they said, We have no more but five loaves and two fishes; except we should go and buy meat for all this people. For they were about five thousand men.

So large is ever the Divine requirement; so slender, and (as it often seems) so wholly inadequate, the human means of satisfying it! Yet will GOD assuredly enable His servants to perform whatever He has Himself commanded, if there be but obedience and a willing mind,—the fruit of Faith.

The Reader is referred to the notes on St. Matthew xiv. 17,—St. Mark vi. 37,—and St. John vi. 5 to 10.

And He said to His Disciples, Make them sit down by fifties in a company.

According to St. Mark, they were distributed in groups of fifty and of a hundred persons: "in which subordinate circumstance," remarks a thoughtful writer, " we behold His wisdom, who is the LORD and lover of order. Thus all confusion was avoided. There was no danger that the weaker, the women and the children, should be passed over; while the stronger and ruder unduly put themselves forward. The Apostles were thus able to pass easily up and down among the multitude; and to minister in orderly succession to the needs of every part."

Take notice, here, how our LORD condescends to *minute details*: making them a matter of express direction. Many such intimations of the Divine Method occur in the Book of Life. *One* is found in the Sermon on the Mount,—St. Matthew vi. 6, where see the note. The History of this very Miracle supplies another: see St. John vi. 12. A remark which was made at the end of the Commentary on St. Mark v. also, here presents itself.

15 And they did so, and made them all sit down.

The ancients, who gathered wisdom from every word of Scripture, point out that

(g) See Acts iii. 15, and consider Acts iv. 27.   (h) Psalm lxxviii. 19, 20.

these men were made to sit down *before* the supply of food appeared; in order to teach us that, with GOD, "things which be not" are "as though they were."(*i*)

Refer here to the first note on St. Matthew xiv. 19; and the note on St. Mark vi. 40.

16 Then He took the five loaves and two fishes, and looking up to Heaven, He blessed them, and brake, and gave to the Disciples to set before the multitude.

Thus, after He had suffered the multitude to feel the pang of hunger, He waited till His Apostles applied to Him concerning their relief;—then, He took the bread at their hands; next, He restored it, fraught with the power of miraculous increase, back to the Apostles again: and all, in order that they might have the fullest testimony concerning what was done, and continue the more mindful of it. . . . . A marvellous miracle, truly! Very different from instantaneous *growth*, was the phenomenon it revealed; for, by growth, we mean an unfolding, and progress to maturity, (whether slow or sudden,) according to a certain law: but here was growth without progress; or rather, increase without development.

The act of *taking the bread* into His hands, seems to have been one of weighty import; for it is distinctly noticed by all the four Evangelists.(*k*) By three of them, also, the *looking up to Heaven* is recorded. The Reader is referred to the second note on St. Matthew xiv. 19; and to the notes on St. Mark vi. 41.

17 And they did eat, and were all filled: and there was taken up of fragments that remained to them twelve baskets.

See the notes on St. Matthew xiv. 20, and on St. Mark vi. 42, 43, 44.

There remained "*twelve* baskets," because, in conformity with our LORD's injunction, the Twelve Apostles gathered up the fragments that remained.(*l*) Take notice that to eat, and to "leave thereof," was a sure sign that there had been abundance.(*m*)

He who reads the Gospel with attention, will be amazed to notice in how many respects, and on how many occasions, the Incarnate SON was engaged in acts strictly symbolical of, or rather closely corresponding with, what had been "in the beginning;" thereby indirectly proclaiming His Divine power and Godhead. Besides the five loaves, we here behold Him "*blessing*" the "*two fishes*," and so feeding many thousands of persons. And what is this but the act of Him who, on the fifth day, "*blessed them*," saying, Be fruitful, and *multiply*, and fill the waters in the seas?"(*n*) . . . . The same verse proceeds—"And let the *fowl* multiply in the Earth:" reminding us, that, besides *bread* from Heaven, the same Almighty hand had rained upon His people in the wilderness "feathered *fowls*," "as thick as dust."(*o*)

St. Luke, having thus brought his narrative down to the eve of the third Passover, omits several incidents, (which are nevertheless set down in due order by St. Matthew and St. Mark:)(*p*) resuming his history with the account of a transaction which took place, also on the eastern side of the Jordan, in the course of the following year. The method is surely a very marvellous one. Who would suspect that between the 17th and 18th verses of this Gospel so many great events had been omitted; and that the transition is suddenly made to the neighbourhood of Cæsarea Philippi, whither our LORD had conducted His Twelve Apostles?

The Reader who would study this part of the sacred narrative with advantage, is referred to St. Matthew xvi. 1 to 12, or St. Mark viii. 10 to 26; where he is requested to read the notes.

18 And it came to pass, as He was alone praying, His Disciples were with Him: and He asked them, saying, Whom say the people that I am?

St. Mark declares that our SAVIOUR made this inquiry "by the way;"(*q*) so that there might seem to be some contradiction here. But, as an ancient Father gravely

(i) Romans iv. 17.   (k) St. Matth. xiv. 19. St. Mark vi. 41. St. Luke ix. 16. St. John vi. 11.
(l) St. John vi. 12.   (m) Consider Ruth ii. 14, 18, and 2 Kings iv. 43, 44.
(n) Gen. i. 22.   (o) Psalm lxxviii. 25, 28.
(p) St. Matth. xiv. 22 to xvi. 12, and St. Mark vi. 45 to viii. 26.   (q) St. Mark viii. 27.

remarks—"This can only be a difficulty *to him who has never prayed by the way.*" . . . The Blessed Company were now in the neighbourhood of the city once called Laish, (afterwards Dan,) near the sources of the Jordan; having journeyed thither from Bethsaida-Julias. In answer to our LORD's inquiry—

19, 20, 21, 22 They answering said, John the Baptist; but some *say*, Elias; and others *say*, that one of the old prophets is risen again. He said unto them, But whom say ye that I am? Peter answering said, The CHRIST of GOD. And He straitly charged them, and commanded *them* to tell no man that thing; saying, The Son of Man must suffer many things, and be rejected of the Elders and Chief Priests and Scribes, and be slain, and be raised the third day.

Concerning this important portion of Scripture,—the Confession, namely, of St. Peter, and the wondrous promise which it immediately drew from the SAVIOUR of the World—so much has been already said, that it shall suffice in this place to refer the Reader to the notes on St. Matthew's Gospel—xvi. 13 to 21; and on St. Mark viii. 27 to 31. St. Luke, who omits the promise to St. Peter, omits also the rebuke which he addressed to CHRIST, as well as the terrible rebuke which was addressed to him in turn: after which the Evangelist adds—

23 And He said to *them* all, If any *man* will come after Me, let him deny himself, and take up his cross daily, and follow Me.

The connection of this verse with what precedes would never have been suspected from the present Gospel; but (as already hinted) from the two earlier Gospels it is found that St. Peter, immediately after hearing the prophecy of his Divine Master's sufferings—His approaching Passion and Death—"took Him, and began to rebuke Him."(*r*) *Therefore* it was that our LORD spake the words here recorded; words, which will be perceived to contain a covert allusion to the manner of His own death. Whereas St. Peter had said, "Be it far from Thee, LORD: this shall not be unto Thee"—our SAVIOUR makes answer,—"So far removed shall this be from the fact, that if any one of yourselves is willing to come after Me, and become My Disciple, let him know that he must share My Humiliation: must deny himself, as I have also done: must take up his Cross daily, and follow Me." . . . The Cross to be borne "*daily*," is a remarkable addition of the present Evangelist. The meaning of the phrase will be best understood by those to whom some "thorn in the flesh,"(*s*) —some abiding grief—hath been allotted as their constant portion.

And this leads one to remark on the difference between "self-denial" and "bearing the Cross." The first is a man's own act, and requires the strenuous exercise of the will: the second implies patient submission to the will of another.

24, 25, 26 For whosoever will save his life shall lose it: but whosoever will lose his life for My sake, the same shall save it. For what is a man advantaged, if he gain the whole World, and lose himself, or be cast away? For whosoever shall be ashamed of Me and of My words, of Him shall the Son of Man be ashamed, when He shall come in His own Glory, and *in His* FATHER'S, and of the holy Angels.

"Such a necessity there is of Confession of Faith," says Bishop Pearson, "in respect of GOD—who commanded it, and is glorified by it: in respect of ourselves, —who shall be rewarded for it; and in respect of our brethren—who are edified and confirmed by it."

CHRIST "will appear," says Patrick, "not only in 'His own glory,' but 'in the glory of His FATHER' also: as if there were something more than He hath already received at His Right Hand; that is, He will come from thence to judge the quick and the dead—to appear as the supreme LORD and Governor of the World, to whom Men and Angels are accountable for their actions. This then is a thing still behind; and there are, it seems, some Royal Majestic Robes belonging to this high office, which He hath not yet put on."

(*r*) St. Matth. xvi. 22.   St. Mark viii. 32.   (*s*) 2 Cor. xii. 7,

Take notice that our LORD will come in the glory "of the Holy Angels" also. They will be present "to bear witness how much they, by the mission of GOD, have administered to the Salvation of Mankind."

27 But I tell you of a truth, there be some standing here, which shall not taste of death, till they see the Kingdom of GOD.

This is expressed differently by St. Matthew and St. Mark. The former says— "till they see the Son of Man coming in His Kingdom:"(t) the latter—"till they have seen the Kingdom of GOD come with power."(u) We must explain this, the shortest statement of all, by those fuller ones: and it will appear that some great event is here alluded to, which certain of the Twelve were to witness before they died; and which might be described as CHRIST's coming with power in His own and His FATHER's Kingdom. This has been thought by some learned men to be the Destruction of Jerusalem, which took place about forty years later: but there can be little doubt, (as already explained in the note on St. Matthew xvi. 28,) that the allusion is to the Transfiguration—an event which immediately follows, in all the three Gospels.(x)

The connection of the mysterious announcement in verse 27, with what goes before, has been already pointed out in the note on St. Matthew xvi. 27. The beginning of CHRIST's Glorious Kingdom has been already set up: not visibly, indeed, (for "the Kingdom of GOD cometh not with observation:")(y) nor was its hidden brightness such as mortal eyes could behold, and live. But it had really begun— begun here on earth; and in its *true* nature it was *glorious*. "The Glory which Thou gavest Me," said our LORD, praying to the FATHER, "I have given them: that they may be one, even as We are One."(z) On which an excellent living writer remarks—"It follows that 'the Glory of the Only-Begotten of the FATHER' belongs also, in its degree, to the Church on Earth—to the Church in its days of waiting, of warfare, and of trial."(a) The great Apostle proclaims no less when he declares that "the brightness of the Law which shone on Moses' face was no brightness at all in comparison of the Glory of the LORD, which shone upon every baptized Corinthian." For, contrasting the privileges of every Christian man with those of the Lawgiver of Israel,(b) he says—"We all, with unveiled face, reflecting like mirrors the glory of the LORD, are being transfigured into the same likeness"—that is, "into CHRIST's image: going on from Glory to Glory;"(c)—that is, from one degree of glory to another. From the Glory of Baptism to the Glory of Salvation: "from the Glory of Faith' (as one of the Ancients expresses it,) 'to the Glory of sight:' from the dim Glory of Regeneration, to the 'Exceeding and Eternal weight of Glory'(d) of the Resurrection."

Of those glories therefore which will be hereafter beheld by every eye, the Son of Man is about to give His three most highly favoured Disciples a blessed foretaste and earnest; for He was willing, says an Ancient Father, "to assure their very sight, and to show what kind of Glory that is wherewith He is to come, so far as it was possible for them to learn." They were to behold "the Kingdom of GOD," not as it seems to mortal eyes, but in its true nature, and as it appears *in GOD'S sight*. CHRIST Himself they were also to behold at the same time: not meanly clad, and "marred" in countenance, as to common eyes He appeared during the days of His Humiliation; but with shining raiment, "white as the Light," and a face that "did shine as the Sun." They beheld Him, in short, as it is promised that the just shall behold Him when He shall finally appear,(e)—namely, "*as He is.*"(f)

28 And it came to pass about an eight days after these sayings, He took Peter and John and James, and went up into a mountain to pray.

(t) St. Matth. xvi. 28.   (u) St. Mark ix. 1.
(x) St. Matth. xvii. 1: St. Mark ix. 2: and St. Luke ix. 28.
(y) St. Luke xvii. 20.   (z) St. John xvii. 22.
(a) Rev. George Moberly—in a valuable Sermon, called "The Transfiguration of Christians."
(b) Exodus xxxiv. 34.
(c) 2 Cor. iii. 18: the true meaning of which Scripture, it is believed, is given above. The same doctrine may be established from Coloss. i. 27: 1 Thess. ii. 12: and 2 St. Peter i. 3. See Rom. viii. 30: ix. 23: xv. 7. 1 Cor. ii. 7. 2 Cor. iv. 4, 6. Ephes. i. 18. Col. i. 27. 2 Thess. ii. 14. Heb. ii. 10. 1 St. Peter iv. 14: v. 10.   (d) 2 Cor. iv. 17.
(e) Does not St. Peter allude to the Transfiguration in his First Epistle—v. 1?
(f) St. John iii. 2.

What mountain this was, is not known. Tradition points out Mount Tabor in Galilee, as the scene of the Transfiguration; but there is no other reason for supposing that our SAVIOUR had yet left the Eastern side of the Jordan. It is worth observing that all three Evangelists who have described this great Transaction conspire in mentioning that it took place exactly one week after the former sayings.

It would seem as if, having selected the highly favoured Sons of Zebedee and St. Peter out of the whole body of the Apostles, our SAVIOUR took them apart,—as He is found to have done on another great occasion,(*g*)—to be with Him while He prayed: conducted them up an adjoining mountain; and there occupied Himself in mysterious prayer. It may have been the Evening of the Day; and deep slumber (as on the other occasion alluded to) is found to have overcome the three weary Apostles. They were "heavy with sleep," as the present Evangelist relates.(*h*) Presently they awoke, and beheld their Divine Master engaged in solemn intercourse with the FATHER.

29 And as He prayed, the fashion of His countenance was altered, and His raiment *was* white *and* glistering.

This was done "*as He prayed:*" which reminds us that at His Baptism also,(*i*) and in the Garden,(*k*) He prayed previously to the coming forth of the glories of the unseen World. . . . . "Prayer," says a good man, "is the Key to Divine Mysteries; to the discerning of CHRIST in the Law and the Prophets." By Prayer, we also gather glory; and become changed; and hold communion with Him who is invisible.

"*The fashion of His Countenance was altered,*"—answers to St. Matthew and St. Mark's phrase, "*He was transfigured* before them:"(*l*) for the change which passed upon the form and features of the Son of Man is the circumstance from which the entire Event derives its name—"The Transfiguration." What was the nature of this change, has not been revealed. St. Matthew indeed says that "His Face did shine as the Sun:"(*m*) but more than *that* seems to be implied by the statement of the text. We are reminded rather of St. Paul's repeated assurance that *a change* will pass upon us,—(and doubtless upon our forms and features, no less than upon the constitution of our mortal bodies,)—at our Resurrection from Death.(*n*) St. Mark's statement that our LORD, after His Resurrection appeared to two of His Disciples "*in another form,*"(*o*) is also brought to our remembrance: and the belief is suggested that while the three Apostles who witnessed the Transfiguration of the Son of Man remained fully aware that it was *He* whom they beheld, and none other, (for indeed His features remained the same,) yet that the foretaste of Future Glory with which He was now revealed to their mortal eyes, conveyed to His Divine Countenance also a foretaste of the mighty Change which was to pass upon it hereafter: that St. John beheld Him *now*, in short, as afterwards by Revelation he beheld Him,—"His Head and Hair, white as wool, as white as snow; and His Eyes as a flame of fire; and His Feet, like unto fine brass, as if they burned in a furnace; . . . . and His Countenance—*as the Sun shineth in his strength.*"(*p*) An old Writer remarks that "in *His* Transfiguration, we have a most exact pattern of *our* Resurrection." But this statement probably falls short of the Truth. There seems rather to have been as close an exhibition as human eyes could bear of the LORD as He will come in the Day of Judgment,—that is, "in the Glory of His Father with the Holy Angels:"(*q*) a partial revelation of that Glory in which even now He dwells,—"above the brightness of the Sun."(*r*)

The raiment which became "*white and glistering,*"—or, as St. Mark expresses it "shining, exceeding white as snow; so as no fuller on Earth can white them,"(*s*)— no less than the dazzling lustre of the Face, is an attribute of glorious visitors from the other World: an attribute derived doubtless from their nearness to Him "who only hath Immortality, dwelling in the Light which no man can approach unto."(*t*) Thus, of the Angel who rolled away the stone from the Holy Sepulchre, it is declared that "His countenance was like lightning, and His raiment white as

(*g*) St. Matth. xxvi. 37, 38.   (*h*) See below, verse 32.   (*i*) St. Luke iii. 21, 22.
(*k*) St. Luke xxii. 41 to 43.   (*l*) St. Matth. xvii. 2.   St. Mark ix. 2.   (*m*) St. Matth. xvii. 2
(*n*) 1 Cor. xv. 51, 52.   Phil. iii. 21.   Consider 1 St. John iii. 2.   Rom. viii. 18.   2 Cor. iv. 17 Coloss. iii. 4.
(*o*) St. Mark xvi. 12.   (*p*) Rev. i. 14 to 16.   (*q*) St. Mark viii. 38.
(*r*) Acts xxvi. 13.   (*s*) St. Mark ix. 3.   (*t*) 1 Tim. vi. 16.

snow."(*u*) "The Spouse in the Canticles," remarks pious Bishop Andrewes, "being asked concerning her Beloved's colours, saith of Him, 'My Beloved is *white* and *red*.'(*x*) 'White' of Himself, as when He was transfigured on the Mount. How comes the 'red' then? Not of Himself, but for *us*. That is our natural colour: for we are polluted in our own blood;(*y*) red is the colour of sin.(*z*) He, in Mount Golgotha, like unto us; that we, in Mount Tabor, might be like unto Him!"

30 And, behold, there talked with Him two men, which were Moses and Elias :

As our SAVIOUR was attended by two when He visited Abraham at Mamre:(*a*) as two Angels guarded His Sepulchre, when He had risen;(*b*) and two were His Messengers to the Eleven, at the time of His Ascension;(*c*) so, at His Transfiguration, "behold, there talked with Him *two* men, which were Moses and Elias:"

31 who appeared in glory, and spake of His decease which He should accomplish at Jerusalem.

Every part of this wondrous narrative is exceedingly important and striking. Moses and Elijah, (as if to represent the Law and the Prophets, and to show the consent of the Gospel with both,) "appear *in glory:*" an attribute, as already remarked, of Beings from the unseen World. And they are seen "*talking* with JESUS,"—as St. Matthew and St. Mark relate.(*d*) How remarkable a statement! These two mighty Saints, who by Faith had seen the Day of CHRIST afar off, and had been made glad thereby,—Moses and Elijah, are selected out of the whole "goodly company" which had gone before, thus to "talk" with the SAVIOUR of the World; and to behold, not so much His Glory as His Humiliation. O joy unspeakable, no less than privilege beyond all price! How does it exceed our powers, reasoning as living men, even to conceive the amount of their blessedness! How may the types and shadows of the Law be presumed to have fled away before their brightening spiritual vision: the allegorical parts of true History,(*e*) to have teemed with hidden meanings: the dark places of Prophecy, to have grown bright and obvious! . . . . . But the Sacred Narrative, as usual, is severely brief. It does but inform us that the approaching Sacrifice of CHRIST's *Death* formed the subject of this discourse; leaving us to infer from the word which St. Luke here employs, *how* "His decease which He should accomplish at Jerusalem" may have been conversed about by these mysterious Speakers. "*His Exodus*" is the expression of the Evangelist; a hint which a pious Writer has thus expanded:—"May we not imagine the Deliverer of Israel addressed by the World's REDEEMER in some such words as these?—'By thy hand I did once vouchsafe to bring forth My people from the afflicting bondage of Egypt; but lo, I am about to turn the multitude of the Gentiles from the Power of Satan unto GOD. Of old time, I made a path through the Red Sea for My redeemed ones to pass over; but I am about to make a more wonderful way through the waves of Death, whereby to guide them. Yea, though the floods shall compass Me about, yet shall My Life be brought up from corruption. Thou rememberest how the chariots and horsemen of Pharaoh, and the mighty host of Egypt, were seen overthrown in the midst of the Sea when the morning appeared: but I am about to triumph over principalities and powers, and overwhelm them in the Lake of Fire. Thou didst lead My people through the Wilderness, and gavest them the Law which had "the shadow of good things to come;" but now will I Myself be their Guide, and write a new Law in their hearts,(*f*) and teach them to worship Me in Spirit and in Truth. Thou indeed didst bring Israel to the borders of the Promised Land; but *I* am Israel's true Shepherd, and they who follow Me shall pass even from Death unto Life.'"(*g*)

(*u*) St. Matth. xxviii. 3. Compare St. Luke xxiv. 4.
(*y*) Lam. iv. 14. Ezek. xvi. 6.
(*b*) St. Luke xxiv. 4.
(*d*) St. Matth. xvii. 3, and St. Mark ix. 4.
(*f*) Heb. viii. 10. See Jer. xxxi. 31 to 33.

(*x*) Song of Solomon v. 10.
(*z*) Isaiah i. 18.
(*a*) Gen. xviii. 2.
(*c*) Acts i. 10.
(*e*) Alluding to Gal. iv. 21 to 31.

(*g*) Altered from Bishop Horne.—If the Reader is offended at this, or any other attempt in these pages, to supply the omissions of Scripture, he is welcome to reject them. They are always hazardous attempts, and are never put forth without great hesitation. It is thought, however, that they may sometimes be found useful.

32, 33 But Peter and they that were with him were heavy with sleep: and when they were awake, they saw His Glory, and the two men that stood with Him. And it came to pass, as they departed from Him, Peter said unto JESUS, Master, it is good for us to be here:

So then the three Apostles did not awake till this mysterious transaction was ended. *Then* indeed they aroused themselves; and it was to behold such a spectacle as men will not look upon until they awake to the glories of the Everlasting Morning. "Perhaps they were oppressed with sleep," (says an Ancient Father,) "that after their rest they might behold the Resurrection." Terrified and astonished at the sight,(*h*) (as may well have been the case,) only one of their number is found to have ventured to break the solemn silence: moved thereto, as it would appear, by the departure of the Heavenly visitants, whom he would gladly have detained. Simon Peter, foremost on every occasion in speech or action, proceeds:

and let us make three tabernacles; one for Thee, and one for Moses, and one for Elias : not knowing what he said.

It has been excellently remarked that "although St. Peter knew not what he said, yet the solemn record of his words intimates that they were not to fall to the ground, but were spoken divinely."(*i*)
"If," (says Venerable Bede,) "the society of but two Saints seen for a moment with the LORD in glory could confer such a degree of delight that St. Peter wished to stay their departure even by doing them service,—how great a happiness will it be to enjoy the vision of GOD, amid choirs of Angels, for ever!"—See more, on these words of St. Peter, in the note on St. Matthew xvii. 4.

34 While he thus spake, there came a cloud, and overshadowed them: and they feared as they entered into the cloud.

For this was He of whom it was said, "Behold, He cometh with clouds."(*k*) Take notice that this was not a cloud which, while it overshadows, darkens the face of the sky; but it was "a *bright* cloud;"(*l*) the token of the Divine Presence;(*m*) a cloud whose very shadow was glory. St. Peter, in a certain place, calls this cloud "the Excellent Glory."(*n*)

35 And there came a Voice out of the cloud, saying, This is My beloved SON : hear Him.

St. Matthew adds,—"And when the Disciples heard it, they fell on their face, and were sore afraid. And JESUS came and touched them, and said, Arise, and be not afraid."(*o*)

36 And when the voice was past, JESUS was found alone.

Refer here to the notes on St. Matthew xvii. 8.
All this, then, took place at night. On the next morning, St. Matthew relates that "as they came down from the Mountain, JESUS charged them, saying, Tell the vision to no man until the Son of Man be risen again from the dead."(*p*) It follows,—

And they kept *it* close, and told no man in those days any of those things which they had seen.

"Questioning one with another what the rising from the dead should mean."(*q*) To know how the conversation of this blessed Company proceeded as they came down "the Holy Mount," the Reader must refer to the two earlier Gospels.(*r*) St. Luke proceeds to show that a night had been passed on the Mountain, and that it was now the following day:

(*h*) St. Mark ix. 6.　　(*i*) Rev. I. Williams.　　(*k*) Rev. i. 7.
(*l*) St. Matth. xvii. 5.　　(*m*) Exod. xl. 34, 35.　1 Kings viii. 10, 11.
(*n*) 2 St. Pet. i. 17.　　　　　　　　　　　(*o*) St. Matth. xvii. 6, 7.
(*p*) St. Matth. xvii. 9.　Compare St. Mark ix. 9.　　(*q*) St. Mark ix. 10.
(*r*) St. Matth. xvii. 10 to 13, and St. Mark ix. 11 to 13:—where see the notes.

37 And it came to pass, that on the next day, when they were come down from the hill, much people met Him.

St. Luke does not explain that they came "running to Him," drawn by the heavenly lustre which had not yet quite faded away from His Divine Features!—Concerning this, see the note on St. Mark ix. 15. Indeed, the Gospel of St. Mark is so full and particular on the subject of the lunatic child, that it should be continually referred to by him who desires to be reminded of all the details of the stupendous miracle which follows.(s)

38 And, behold, a man of the company cried out, saying, Master, I beseech Thee, look upon my son : for he is mine only child.

"Mine *only* child ;"—how powerful a plea ! . . . So was the daughter of Jairus, whom our SAVIOUR raised from the bed of Death, an *only Daughter* ;(t) and the Widow of Nain's son, whom He raised on the way to Burial, an *only son.*(u) Lazarus, too,—who had lain four days in the grave,—was an *only Brother.* Such things are written for the special consolation of mourners ; whose tears are all noted by GOD, and who lays upon none a heavier burden than He will also enable them to bear. Nay, He has relief in store for those who need it most, as these examples were doubtless meant to teach us.

39, 40 And, lo, a Spirit taketh him, and he suddenly crieth out ; and it teareth him that he foameth again, and bruising him, hardly departeth from him. And I besought Thy Disciples to cast him out ; and they could not.

41, 42 And JESUS answering said, O faithless and perverse generation, how long shall I be with you, and suffer you ? Bring thy Son hither. And as he was yet a coming, the Devil threw him down, and tare *him.* And JESUS rebuked the unclean Spirit, and healed the child ; and delivered him again to his father.

These verses have been already the subject of ample comment in the notes on St. Mark ix. 18, 19, 20 ; and 25, 26, 27.

43, 44, 45 And they were all amazed at the mighty power of GOD. But while they wondered every one at all things which JESUS did, He said unto His Disciples, Let these sayings sink down into your ears ; for the Son of Man shall be delivered into the hands of men. But they understood not this saying, and it was hid from them, that they perceived it not ; and they feared to ask Him of that saying.

From a comparison of this, with St. Matthew and St. Mark's account of the same conversation, it will appear that the saying which the Disciples "understood not," and "feared to ask of," was a further prophecy which our LORD now delivered ; namely, that the Jews should " kill Him," and that on the third day He should "be raised again."(x)

The Reader will find some remarks on the foregoing verses in the notes on St. Mark's Gospel.(y) St. Luke is briefest, St. Mark fullest of all, in this place : so that the latter should be constantly referred to, down to verse 50 of the present Chapter. It will be seen that the Blessed Company were passing through Galilee, privately, at the time that our LORD delivered these sayings to the Twelve.(z)—They finally reached Capernaum, which was the scene of the following incident.(a)

46 Then there arose a reasoning among them, which of them should be greatest.

(s) St. Mark ix. 14 to 29.　　　　(t) St. Luke viii. 42.　　　　(u) St. Luke vii. 12.
(x) St. Matth. xvii. 23. Compare St. Mark ix. 31.　　　　(y) St. Mark ix. 31, 32.
(z) St. Matth. xvii. 22 : St. Mark ix. 30.
(a) St. Matth. xvii. 24, and St. Mark ix. 33.

Not *hereafter*, but *now*. They disputed "which of themselves *was* the greatest."(*b*)

47, 48 And JESUS, perceiving the thought of their heart, took a child, and set him by Him, and said unto them, Whosoever shall receive this child in My Name receiveth Me: and whosoever shall receive Me receiveth Him that sent Me: for He that is least among you all, the same shall be great.

This entire incident, related far more in detail both by St. Matthew and St. Mark, has been already fully remarked upon elsewhere.(*c*)

49, 50 And John answered and said, Master, we saw one casting out Devils in Thy Name; and we forbad him, because he followeth not with us. And JESUS said unto him, Forbid *him* not: for he that is not against us is for us.

Concerning this incident also, which seems to have been an interruption of the divine discourse on the part of St. John, see the notes on St. Mark's Gospel.(*d*) The earlier Evangelists will be found to relate how the Discourse proceeded, after our SAVIOUR had replied to the beloved Disciple. St. Luke here breaks off the narrative,—to introduce an incident of somewhat similar character, but which belongs to an altogether subsequent period.

51, 52 And it came to pass, when the time was come that He should be received up, He steadfastly set His Face to go to Jerusalem, and sent messengers before His Face; and they went, and entered into a Village of the Samaritans, to make ready for Him.

The time alluded to is that solemn season, a few months before the last Passover, when our SAVIOUR is found to have made the circuit of Samaria. The time had then come, (or rather, was approaching to its fulfillment,) "that He should be received up" into Heaven: and accordingly He set His face like a flint(*e*) to repair to the scene of His approaching sufferings. The messengers which He sent before, gave additional solemnity to His act.

53 And they did not receive Him, because His Face was as though He would go to Jerusalem.

The enmity between the Jews and Samaritans was excessive,—as many a passage in the Gospel reminds us,(*f*) and as the present place sufficiently shows. This enmity was considerably aggravated at the Season of the great Jewish festivals; when, not on Mount Gerizim, but at Jerusalem, the whole nation testified their determination to worship. Our LORD even "sends messengers before His face," openly "to make ready" for His approach. This explains why they "did not receive Him."

54 And when His Disciples James and John saw *this*, they said, LORD, wilt Thou that we command fire to come down from Heaven, and consume them, even as Elias did?

They allude to the repeated act of Elijah, on a well-known occasion, when Ahaziah, King of Israel, sent soldiers to apprehend him.(*g*) Their inquiry gives a lively notion of the sense they entertained of their LORD's importance, as well as of their own burning zeal and jealousy on His behalf.

55, 56 But He turned, and rebuked them, and said, Ye know not what manner of spirit ye are of. For the Son of Man is not come to destroy men's lives, but to save *them*.

(*b*) Compare the language of St. John xiii. 24.
(*c*) See St. Matthew xviii. 1 to 5, and the notes there: also St. Mark ix. 33 to 37, and the notes there.
(*d*) See St. Mark ix. 38 to 40.　　　(*e*) Isaiah l. 7.　　　(*f*) St. John iv. 9: viii. 48.
(*g*) 2 Kings i. 9 to 12.

And they went to another village.

57, 58 And it came to pass, that, as they went in the way, a certain *man* said unto Him, LORD, I will follow Thee whithersoever Thou goest. And JESUS said unto him, Foxes have holes, and birds of the air *have* nests; but the Son of Man hath not where to lay *His* head.

59, 60 And He said unto another, Follow Me. But he said, LORD, suffer me first to go and bury my Father. JESUS said unto him, Let the dead bury their dead: but go thou and preach the Kingdom of GOD.

It is surprising to discover that both these incidents are related in succession by St. Matthew, as having occurred on quite a distinct occasion. The Reader is therefore referred to the remarks which he will find in the earlier Gospel.(*h*)

61, 62 And another also said, LORD, I will follow Thee; but let me first go bid them farewell, which are at home at my house. And JESUS said unto him, No man having put his hand to the plough, and looking back, is fit for the Kingdom of GOD.

In the proverbial saying thus employed by our LORD, there seems to be an allusion to the call of Elisha,—"who was ploughing with twelve yoke of oxen before him, and he with the twelfth," when "Elijah passed by him, and cast his mantle upon him." Whereupon "he left the oxen, and ran after Elijah, and said, Let me, I pray thee, kiss my Father and my Mother, and then I will follow thee."(*i*)

Our SAVIOUR's answer implies that he who enters into the service of the Great "Husbandman,"(*k*) and undertakes to "preach the Kingdom of GOD,"(*l*) must not look wistfully back to that World which he professes to have renounced and forsaken. His hand is upon the plough; and his eyes should look straight forward. He should give his whole heart to his Master's work.

CHAPTER X.

---

1 CHRIST *sendeth out at once Seventy Disciples to work miracles and to preach.* 17 *Admonisheth them to be humble, and wherein to rejoice.* 21 *Thanketh his* FATHER *for his grace.* 23 *Magnifieth the happy estate of His Church.* 25 *Teacheth the lawyer how to attain eternal Life, and to take every one for his neighbour that needeth his mercy.* 41 *Reprehendeth Martha, and commendeth Mary her sister.*

"AFTER these things"—that is, after making the circuit of Samaria—our SAVIOUR, journeying towards Jerusalem, proceeded to make the circuit of Galilee also. Preparatory to this, He is found to have sent forth seventy disciples to prepare His way. This sending forth of the Seventy, which is recorded by St. Luke alone, (who is thought to have been one of their number,)(*a*) occupies the first sixteen verses of the present chapter. The parting charge which they received resembles in many respects, and forcibly recalls, the charge which our LORD had already

(*h*) St. Matth. viii. 19 to 22.
(*k*) See the note on St. Luke iii. 17.
(*a*) See the note on St. Luke i. 3.

(*i*) 1 Kings xix. 19, 20.
(*l*) See above, ver. 60.

given to the Twelve Apostles, on sending them forth. On both occasions it will be observed that He sent His Ambassadors " by two and two."

1 After these things the LORD appointed other Seventy also, and sent them two and two before His face into every city and place, whither He himself would come.

As the number of the Twelve Apostles appears to have reference to the number of the Patriarchs, so do these Seventy Disciples recall the number of the Elders who were called up into Mount Sinai to behold the wondrous vision of GOD, and to eat and drink in his presence;(b) who moreover assisted MOSES to govern the people. " An outline of the present ordinance," remarks one of the Fathers, "was set forth in the words of Moses; who, at the command of GOD, chose out Seventy upon whom GOD poured out His Spirit."(c) How is it possible to avoid recalling, in connection with the mission of the *Twelve* and the *Seventy*, that interesting record, twice found in the Books of Moses, that at Elim the children of Israel found "twelve wells of water and threescore and ten palm trees?"(d)

2, 3, 4, 5, 6, 7 Therefore said He unto them, The harvest truly *is* great, but the labourers *are* few: pray ye therefore the LORD of the harvest, that he would send forth labourers into His harvest. Go your ways: behold, I send you forth as lambs among wolves. Carry neither purse, nor scrip, nor shoes: and salute no man by the way. And into whatsoever house ye enter, first say, Peace *be* to this house. And if the son of peace be there, your peace shall rest upon it: if not, it shall turn to you again. And in the same house remain, eating and drinking such things as they give: for the labourer is worthy of his hire. Go not from house to house.

It will be perceived that the same words which our LORD addresses to the Seventy, in ver. 2, are found in His charge to the Twelve, in St. Matthew ix. 37, 38 : where see the note. Verse 3, in like manner, recurs in St. Matthew x. 16: where also the note may be consulted. The injunction in ver. 4 is found in St. Matthew x. 9, 10, with which compare St. Mark vi. 8, 9, and St. Luke ix. 3.

The language of verses 5 and 6 is more full than in the corresponding passage of our LORD's Charge to the Twelve—St. Matthew x. 12, 13, where see the notes;— and helps to explain the concise record of the earlier Evangelist. Verse 7 should be compared with St. Matthew x. 11,—where the Commentary may be also referred to.

8, 9, 10, 11, 12 And into whatsoever city ye enter, and they receive you, eat such things as are set before you: and heal the sick that are therein, and say unto them, The Kingdom of GOD is come nigh unto you. But in whatsoever city ye enter, and they receive you not, go your ways out into the streets of the same, and say, Even the very dust of your city, which cleaveth on us, we do wipe off against you: notwithstanding be ye sure of this, that the Kingdom of GOD is come nigh unto you. But I say unto you, that it shall be more tolerable in that day for Sodom, than for that city.

"*That* Day" is the great and terrible Day of the LORD—the Day of Days, which, by reason of its momentous import, is often spoken of in Scripture simply as "*the* day."(e) . . . . Compare these three last verses with St. Matthew x. 14, 15—and see the note there. See also the note on St. Mark vi. 11.

13, 14, 15 Woe unto thee, Chorazin! woe unto thee, Bethsaida! for if the mighty works had been done in Tyre and Sidon which have been

---

(b) Exod. xxiv. 1, 9 to 11.   (c) Cyril, referring to Numb. xi. 16, 24, 25.
(d) Exod. xv. 27, and Numb. xxxiii. 9.
(e) As in St. Matthew vii. 22. 1 Cor. iii. 13. 1 Thess. v. 4. 2 Tim. i. 12, 18: iv. 8, &c.

done in you, they had a great while ago repented, sitting in sackcloth
and ashes.   But it shall be more tolerable for Tyre and Sidon at the
Judgment, than for you.   And thou, Capernaum, which art exalted to
Heaven, shall be thrust down to Hell.

The Reader is requested to refer to the notes on St. Matthew xi. 21, 22, 24, (where
the same language is found,) for some observations on this striking passage.   The
precious assurance contained in the verse which follows,(ƒ) will be found already
remarked upon in the Commentary on St. Matthew x. 40, where it recurs.

16 He that heareth you heareth Me; and he that despiseth you despiseth Me; and he that despiseth Me despiseth Him that sent Me.

Before proceeding to read the ensuing portion of the History, we are to remember that an interval must have elapsed: whether short or long, cannot be declared
with certainty.   The Seventy had had time, at least, to make the discovery that
the powers of the unseen world were subject to them, through the prevailing Name
of Him who had sent them forth.

17 And the Seventy returned again with joy, saying, LORD, even the
devils are subject unto us through Thy Name.

"They seemed indeed to rejoice rather that they were made workers of miracles,
than that they had become ministers of preaching."(g)   Accordingly, in ver. 20,
our LORD reminds them of the much higher ground of rejoicing which was theirs.
But first, He replies to their address.

18 And He said unto them, I beheld Satan as lightning fall from
Heaven.

A very striking saying, surely; and (to speak in the manner of men) one which
conveys a notion of exceeding grandeur concerning the sudden and utter fall which
Satan had sustained by the coming of CHRIST.   It has been thought, indeed, that
the fall of the Angels " which kept not their first estate,"(h) is alluded to in the
words before us.   But when it is remembered that Capernaum is said(i) to have
been "exalted to Heaven," (which can only mean in respect of its mighty privileges,) and especially when it is considered that, at the time of our LORD's Advent,
Satan had usurped dominion to a surprising extent over the souls and bodies of
men—of which dominion, (as already observed,) he had now been most unexpectedly, as well as most completely, despoiled; it seems more reasonable to suppose
that by this vivid comparison our SAVIOUR did but intend to convey the sudden and
amazing overthrow which His great enemy had sustained at His hands—an overthrow which had been shared by the rest of the evil angels, as their subjection to
the Seventy clearly proved.   To the All-seeing Eye of the Incarnate SON, the downfall of Satan was a thing which might be *gazed upon*.   Accordingly, He says,—"I
beheld Satan as lightning fall from Heaven."   The expression, (which was doubtless intended to recall the language of Isaiah, with reference to Lucifer,)(k) further
derives awful interest from the name by which St. Paul denotes the chief of the
fallen angels—namely, "*the Prince of the Power of the Air.*"(l)

Our LORD proceeds to confirm the powers which he had already conveyed to the
Seventy; supplying at the same time a marvellous hint of some secret connection
subsisting between Evil Spirits and the noxious part of the Animal Creation.

19 Behold, I give unto you power to tread on serpents and scorpions,
and over all the power of the Enemy: and nothing shall by any means
hurt you.

Consider how serpents and scorpions are ever connected in Holy Scripture with
what is noxious to man.(m)   Remember also, the parting promise of our SAVIOUR
CHRIST to His Church.(n)

(ƒ) Verse 16.   (g) Cyril.   (h) St. Jude verse 6.
(i) In verse 15.   (k) Isaiah xiv. 12.   (l) Ephes. ii. 2.
(m) Genesis iii. 1.   Rev. xii. 9: xx. 2.   Numbers xxi. 6.   Acts xxviii. 8.   Psalm xci. 13.
Rev. ix. 3 to 10, &c.   (n) St. Mark xvi. 18.

20 Notwithstanding, in this rejoice not, that the spirits are subject unto you; but rather rejoice, because your names are written in Heaven.

They are not forbidden to rejoice at finding the powers of Satan subject unto them; but a higher ground of rejoicing is pointed out.(o)

When Gregory the Great sent Augustine the monk into Britain, A.D. 597, (to plant Christianity afresh in these islands, (he reminded him of this text, and cautioned him against being too much elated by any success with which GOD might have blessed his endeavours; bidding him keep his eye turned inwardly, in strict self-examination. "And," said he, "if ever thou rememberest having offended against thy CREATOR, in word or deed, be thou mindful to call the same constantly to mind; that so the memory of thine offence may keep down the proud swelling thoughts of thine heart. Whatever signs thou mayest have been enabled to perform, consider them less as gifts made to thyself than to them, for whose sakes the power was conferred upon thee."

"Names written in Heaven," and the like mode of speech, is not unusual with the SPIRIT. So He speaks by Moses, in the Law:(p) by David, in the Psalms:(q) by His Prophets Isaiah(r) and Daniel:(s) by His Apostles St. Paul(t) and St. John:(u) and so, on many occasions, (as in this place,) speaks the Ancient of Days in His own person.(x)

There is an obvious connection between what goes before and what follows. "Our LORD knew that through the operation of the HOLY SPIRIT, which He had given to His Apostles, many would be brought over to the faith;"(y) and the prospect is here declared to have filled His human soul with mysterious joy; as it follows—

21, 22 In that hour JESUS rejoiced in Spirit, and said, I thank Thee, O FATHER, LORD of Heaven and Earth, that Thou hast hid these things from the wise and prudent, and hast revealed them unto babes: even so, FATHER: for so it seemed good in Thy sight. All things are delivered to Me of My FATHER: and no man knoweth who the SON is, but the FATHER; and who the FATHER is, but the SON, and *he* to whom the SON will reveal *Him*.

These two verses have been already met with, although in quite a different connection, in St. Matthew's Gospel,—whither the Reader is referred for some remarks concerning them.(z) The Son of Man here rejoices not that the mysteries of the Gospel were *hid* from any; but that what had been hid from the proud had been revealed to the humble,—to those child-like hearts which are ever found in CHRIST's little ones.

23, 24 And He turned Him unto *His* Disciples, and said privately, Blessed *are* the eyes which see the things that ye see: for I tell you, that many prophets and kings have desired to see those things which ye see, and have not seen *them;* and to hear those things which ye hear, and have not heard *them.*

How striking are these words, which are *twice*(a) found on the lips of CHRIST Himself,—"the Desire of all Nations!"(b) . . . He,—"unto whom all hearts are open, all desires known, and from whom no secrets are hid,"—was fully aware of all those passionate yearnings which had been felt by His ancient Prophets,—"unto whom it was revealed that not unto themselves, but unto *us*, they did minister;" who saw the Day of CHRIST indeed,(c) but only afar off, and very darkly; of which, therefore, they "inquired and searched diligently:" for, (as St. Peter informs us in a most precious passage,) they earnestly desired to know "what, or what manner of time *the Spirit of* CHRIST *which was in them* did signify, when it testified

(o) See the notes on St. Matthew ix. 13, and St. John v. 30.   (p) Exod. xxxii. 32.
(q) Psalm lxix. 28.   (r) Isaiah iv. 3.   (s) Dan. xii. 1.
(t) Phil. iv. 3: Heb. xii. 23.   (u) Rev. xiii. 8: xvii. 8: xx. 12: xxi. 27.
(x) Exod. xxxii. 33: Rev. iii. 5.   (y) Cyril.   (z) St. Matth. xi. 25 to 27.
(a) See St. Matth. xiii. 16, 17,—and the note there.   (b) Haggai ii. 7.
                    (c) St. John viii. 56.

⌐foreband the sufferings of CHRIST, and the glory that shall follow."(d) . . . .
Wherefore, they are not to be heard, which feign that the old Fathers did look
only for transitory promises."(e)
It is easy to discover a connection between what goes before, and what follows,
in verse 25. Our LORD has been speaking of the names "written in Heaven." It
follows, accordingly,—

25 And, behold, a certain Lawyer stood up, and tempted Him, saying, Master, what shall I do to inherit eternal life?

The same question was afterwards addressed to our LORD by "a certain
Ruler;"(f) and in reply, He rehearsed to him the precepts of the Second Table.
At a yet later period of His Ministry, a Scribe or Lawyer inquired, "Which is the
great commandment in the Law?" Our LORD made answer in the words which
will be presently found in verse 27.(g)

26, 27 He said unto him, What is written in the Law? how readest
thou? And he answering said, Thou shalt love the LORD thy GOD
with all thy heart, and with all thy soul, and with all thy strength,
and with all thy mind; and thy neighbour as thyself.

This Scribe or Lawyer quotes from Deuteronomy vi. 4, 5, and Leviticus xix. 18.
The first impression, on reading his reply, is, that he must have been an unusually
attentive Student of the Books of Moses, to pick out for himself such a summary
of their entire teaching; but from the circumstance already noticed,—namely, that
our SAVIOUR, on a certain occasion, used the same blended quotations,—it may be
thought that this had become an approved method, in the Jewish Schools, of
declaring the *essence* of the Law.

28 And He said unto him, Thou hast answered right: this do, and
thou shalt live.

"That is to say,—Fulfil My Commandments, keep thyself upright and perfect
in them according to My will; then thou shalt live and not die. Eternal Life is
promised with this condition. But such is the frailty of man since the Fall; such
his weakness and imbecility, that he cannot walk uprightly in GOD'S Commandments; but daily and hourly falls from his bounden duty, offending the LORD his
GOD divers ways."(h) All this, however, the Lawyer understood not. Still less
did he suppose that in the parable which he was about to hear, the helplessness of
human nature was, in effect, set before him; that *he* was, in truth, the man who
fell among thieves, and that the good Samaritan was none other than the Blessed
Speaker Himself! . . . It follows:—

29 But he, willing to justify himself, said unto JESUS, And who is
my neighbour?

30 And JESUS answering said, A certain *man* went down from Jerusalem to Jericho, and fell among thieves, which stripped him of his
raiment, and wounded *him*, and departed, leaving *him* half dead.

The Traveller in this Parable, who "went," (or rather, "was going") down from
Jerusalem, had to traverse the wild, rocky road which leads to Jericho, and which
preserves to this day its ancient dangerous character, as well as its ancient glowing
aspect,—being, in some places, a savage mountain pass, well fitted for deeds of
violence, such as our LORD here describes.

31, 32 And by chance there came down a certain Priest that way:
and when he saw him, he passed by on the other side. And likewise a
Levite, when he was at the place, came and looked *on him*, and passed
by on the other side.

(d) 1 St. Peter i. 10 to 12.　　　　　　　　　　　　　　(e) Article vii.
(f) St. Matth. xix. 16,—St. Mark x. 17,—St. Luke xviii. 18.
(g) St. Matth. xxii. 35, 40. St. Mark xii. 28 to 31,—where see the notes.
(h) Second Homily of the Passion.

Take notice, that these persons *looked* upon the misery which they yet did not even attempt to relieve. The wounded man was doubtless a Jew: one of their own nation, therefore; and thus, in the highest degree, entitled to some display of active sympathy. And yet they showed him *none*. It seems as if the Levite had even gone a little out of his way, in order to look upon the wounded Traveller.

33, 34, 35 But a certain Samaritan, as he journeyed, came where he was: and when he saw him, he had compassion *on him*, and went to *him*, and bound up his wounds, pouring in oil and wine, and set him on his own beast and brought him to an inn, and took care of him. And on the morrow when he departed, he took out two pence, and gave *them* to the host, and said unto him, Take care of him; and whatsoever thou spendest more, when I come again, I will repay thee.

It should be observed that all this tenderness towards the wounded man proceeded from a *Samaritan*. He belonged to a people with whom the Jews had no dealings;(i) whose name was a very by-word of reproach and infamy;(k) and who were regarded by them as aliens and strangers,(l)—almost reckoned with the very heathen.(m) On such an one, therefore, the bleeding Traveller had no claim whatever. A reason might, on the contrary, have been easily invented by the Samaritan for passing on, and leaving him to his fate.

But this man had studied in a better school than the great bulk of either nation. He is found to have left no effort untried to mitigate the wounded man's sufferings. Regardless alike of the danger and fatigue, he conveys him to an Inn,—spares from his slender supply of money, as much as the stranger can require for two days,(n)—consigns him to the care of the host,—and departs with a loving injunction and a most generous promise.

36 Which now of these three, thinkest thou, was neighbour unto him that fell among the thieves?

The obvious answer would be,—"The *Samaritan:*" but it seems as if the Lawyer, being a Jew, could not bring himself to admit that a member of that hateful nation was entitled to such praise. He describes *the character* of the man in the Parable, instead:—

37 And He said, He that showed mercy on him. Then said JESUS unto him, Go, and do thou likewise.

Rather,—"Go, and show thou [mercy] likewise." In reading which words, (and they are the conclusion of the whole matter,) we cannot but be struck with the remarkable turn which our Blessed LORD had by this time given to the entire discourse. In the beginning, the Lawyer had asked to be informed who was his "neighbour?" Which class of persons ought he to regard as standing to him in that relation? Instead of satisfying the man's curiosity in this respect, our LORD has related to him a Parable, which sets before his eyes a touching picture of active humanity on the part of the Samaritan towards a Jew. Now, that the wounded man was *not* looked upon as a "neighbour" by the Priest or the Levite; but that he *was* so regarded, and rightly, by the Samaritan, is obvious. The lesson derived from the Parable of our LORD Himself is not, however, that "every one who needs our mercy is to be taken for our neighbour."(o) Nothing of the kind. But the Blessed Speaker, after drawing from the Lawyer a free admission that, of the three persons concerned with the wounded man, the "*neighbour*" was "he that *showed mercy* on him," closes the conversation by proposing the conduct of the Samaritan,—the active benevolence which he displayed even towards an enemy,—as a model for imitation. Thus, *the practice* of Religion is revealed as the best help to *the understanding* of it. The attention is diverted from considering who is the fit *object* of Love, and guided instead to the *exercise* of Love itself. As in every other part of the Bible, the object proposed is to school *the heart*,—not to inform *the understanding*.

(i) St. John iv. 9.   (k) St. John viii. 48.   (l) St. Luke xvii. 18.
(m) See the note on St. Matth. x. 6.   (n) See St. Matth. xx. 2.
(o) See the heading of the Chapter.

Such a lesson, then, of Love and Mercy,—and nothing more,—must the parable of "The Good Samaritan" have conveyed to the Lawyer to whom it was addressed. Well would it be for us, indeed, were we careful to profit by this, its practical teaching. "But indeed there are very few of us who have yet learned to exert themselves as they might do for the relief of the general misery and destitution which they cannot but see about them. The World is full of it; but is not full of that Heavenly Compassion which it was meant to call forth."(p) It is however the high privilege of the Christian who studies the written record of his LORD's Discourses, to see a prophetic meaning beneath the veil of the letter; and however exquisite, however sufficient, the literal sense of the words spoken, it is not to be doubted that *he* only can be said to profit duly by the divine narrative, who has been guided to a part, at least, of its mystical meaning also.

Human Nature, therefore, is the "man" in this parable:—Human Nature, which having forsaken the seat of Innocence and Holiness,—(the "Dwelling of Peace," as the name of Jerusalem is explained to mean,)—is going down to the city of the curse.(q) The Enemy of our souls, (who "was a murderer from the beginning,")(r) and his evil angels, are those murderous ones under whose power our Nature is represented as having fallen. Stripped of that robe of Original Righteousness,(s) by the loss of which our First Parents became aware that they were "naked,"(t)—and grievously wounded besides, in the most vital part,—*what* but a state almost of Death was ours when the Law came to us, and passed us by? It looked upon Man indeed, (as the Priest and the Levite in the Parable looked upon the wounded Traveller:) but the Law, having looked, could do no more than "pass by on the other side:" for a law had not as yet been given, "which could give Life."(u)

It was reserved for CHRIST.(x) (the good Samaritan of the Parable,) to look upon us, and to feel *compassion:*"(y) to *draw near,* (as He did by "the mystery of His Holy Incarnation:")—to heal the wounds of our Nature with the blessed medicine of His Word and Sacraments,(z)—(that "oil and wine" wherewith the great Physician "binds up that which was broken, and strengthens that which was sick:")(a)—"for our sakes to become poor, that we through His poverty might be rich,"(b)—(which was aptly represented when the Traveller set the wounded man on his own beast, and was content to perform the weary journey by his side, on foot:)—to convey Man, thus rescued from Death, to the Church,—(that Inn provided for the reception of all "strangers and pilgrims," travelling towards "a better country, that is, an heavenly:")(c)—and *there* to "take care of him." . . . . All this, it was reserved for CHRIST (the Good Samaritan) to perform for Man.

Indeed, "it was natural and proper, in answer to the question, 'And who is my neighbour?' that our LORD should speak of one whom the Jew would not acknowledge as his neighbour; and should represent such an one as doing, towards a Jew, something like what He was doing Himself towards the Jews, and towards mankind. In fact, our blessed LORD, though Himself a Jew, and of the Royal Tribe and Family, was an 'alien to His Mother's children.'(d) He was called a Samaritan, and treated like an alien and an enemy by His own people the Children of the Jewish Church, in which He had vouchsafed to be born."(e)

"Behold," (said our Blessed LORD,) "I do cures to-day and to-morrow, and the third day I shall be perfected."(f) Accordingly, it is said in the parable that "on the morrow, when He departed, He took out two pence, and gave them to the host, and said unto him, Take care of him;"—(that is, Continue to deal with the objects of My Love as *I* have dealt with them:)(g) "and whatsoever thou spendest more, when I come again, I will repay thee." And what is this, but a mysterious hint, first,—that CHRIST, at His departing, bequeathed to His Church great gifts, (and chiefly the Two Sacraments,)—gifts and graces which were to be exercised for the relief of sick souls, until His coming again? Next,—that when He "shall come

---

(p) Rev. C. Marriott.   (q) See Joshua vi. 26.   (r) St. John viii. 44.
(s) The Reader is requested to consider the following places of Scripture:—St. Luke xv. 22: 2 Cor. v. 3: Gal. iii. 27: Rev. iii. 17, 18: xvi. 15: xix. 8.
(t) Genesis iii. 7.   (u) Consider Gal. iii. 21.   (x) See Rom. viii. 3.
(y) Consider the following texts:—St. Matth. ix. 36: xiv. 14: xv. 32: xx. 34. St. Mark i. 41: v. 19: ix. 22. St. Luke vii. 13. Also consider St. Matth. xviii. 27, 33: and St. Luke xv. 20,—remembering *who* is there spoken of.   (z) Rev. xxii. 2.
(a) Ezek. xxxiv. 16. Compare Isa. lxi. 1.   (b) 2 Cor. viii. 9.   (c) Heb. xi. 13 and 16.
(d) Psalm lxix. 8.   (e) Rev. C. Marriott.   (f) St. Luke xiii. 32.
(g) See the last words of verse 34. Consider St. John xxi. 15, 16, 17.

again in His glorious Majesty to judge both the quick and dead," He will not only graciously allow what Love and Zeal have done in His blessed Service, but will give it His mighty sanction also; and, (in the language of the Parable,) "repay" it?

An interesting, and highly suggestive incident follows:—"A servant receives her LORD,—the sick her SAVIOUR,—the creature her Creator. But if any should say, 'Blessed are they who have been thought worthy to receive CHRIST into their houses,'—grieve not thou: for He says, "Inasmuch as ye have done it unto the least of these My brethren, ye have done it unto Me.'"(*h*)

38 Now it came to pass, as they went, that He entered into a certain village : and a certain woman named Martha received Him into her house.

This must have been at "Bethany,—the town of Mary and her sister Martha."(*i*) On the other occasion when our LORD is said to have been entertained at Bethany, it was "in the house of Simon the leper" that "they made Him a supper."(*k*) Here, the house was Martha's.

39, 40 And she had a sister called Mary, which also sat at JESUS' feet, and heard His Word. But Martha was encumbered about much serving,

In the language of GOD's ancient people, disciples were said to "sit at the feet" of their Teachers.(*l*) Thus, St. Paul was brought up "*at the feet* of Gamaliel."(*m*) But the phrase doubtless represents what was the habitual posture of the body. Consider what is said of the demoniac of Gadara, in St. Luke viii. 35.—The "serving" alluded to,(*n*) implies attendance at the table.

The character of these two sisters reappears on the other occasion already alluded to, when they again come before us. It is there recorded that "Martha served:" but of Mary, that she "anointed the feet of JESUS, and wiped His feet with her hair."(*o*)

Very expressive is the language of the original in this place. St. Paul may be thought to have alluded to the entire incident when he declared, in similar language, that it was the object of his precepts to the other sex,—"that they might *attend upon the* LORD *without distraction*."(*p*) While Mary was thus blessedly engaged, Martha "came suddenly upon" the Teacher and His disciple,—

and came to Him, and said, LORD, dost Thou not care that my sister hath left me to serve alone? bid her therefore that she help me.

Observe, by the way, the smallness of the household, and the very humble nature of what is passing. She who provides the entertainment, has to prepare it likewise; and she must prepare it *alone!* Yet, who is the guest? The LORD of Heaven and Earth! . . . . How should proud hearts bow down before such a spectacle, and forget their pride! Poverty surely inherits a blessing!

"Mary commits her cause to *the Judge*," remarks an ancient Father,(*q*) "and He becomes her *Advocate*." How many examples there are in the Gospel, of CHRIST thus *taking the part* of them who trust their cause to *Him!*(*r*)

41, 42 And JESUS answered and said unto her, Martha, Martha, thou art careful and troubled about many things : but one thing is needful : and Mary hath chosen that good part, which shall not be taken away from her.

(*h*) Augustine, quoting St. Matth. xxv. 40.
(*k*) St. Matth. xxvi. 6, compared with St. John xii. 1, 2.
(*l*) Deut. xxxiii. 3. 2 Kings iv. 38.
(*n*) As in St. Luke iv. 39: xii. 37: xvii. 8: St. John xii. 2: Acts vi. 2, and elsewhere.
(*o*) St. John xii. 2, 3. (*p*) 1 Cor. vii. 35.
(*r*) As St. Luke vi. 3, (see the note there:) vii. 39, 40. St. Matth. xxvi. 10, &c. Consider Psalm xxxviii. 15, (margin,) and x. 14, (16 in Prayer Book.)

(*i*) St. John xi. 1.

(*m*) Acts xxii. 3.

(*q*) Augustine.

Mary had chosen *one* thing: Martha was troubled about *many*. The double repetition of her name is a note of special earnestness.(s)

He reads the Gospel to little purpose who finds here nothing beyond the account of two sisters,—one engrossed with worldly business, the other devoted to Religion; of whom one incurs rebuke, and the other commendation. Martha is a great saint, no less than her sister; and St. John's record is express, that "JESUS *loved Martha.*"(t) She is here engaged in the active service of CHRIST; and doubtless had chosen for herself a very blessed portion when she determined to minister to the human wants of her LORD. Behold, He has journeyed, and is weary, and "hath not where to lay His head."(u) She has invited Him to her dwelling, and He has come to bless "her house" with His presence. Shall she not exert herself in an hour like this? and by the pains she takes to entertain Him well, seek to testify the largeness of her gratitude, and love, and joy? If Hospitality be ever honourable,(x) how much more on an occasion like the present!

Not until she seeks to draw her sister away from CHRIST, therefore, is a syllable addressed to her in the way of reproof. The act of hospitality which so occupies her, cannot but be most acceptable in the eyes of her Divine guest: who says not that she has chosen a *bad* part; but only that Mary has chosen a *better*.

"*Why* better?" asks Augustine; "Because *it shall not be taken away from her.* From thee, the burden of business shall one time be taken away; for when thou comest into the heavenly country, thou wilt find no stranger to receive with hospitality. But for thy good it shall be taken away; that what is better may be given thee. Trouble shall be taken away, that rest may be given thee. But in the mean time *thou* art yet at sea; *thy sister* is in port."

These words prepare us for another remark of the same great writer; namely, that Martha was occupied, as the Church of CHRIST is occupied here below,—in the active service of CHRIST: Mary, as the same Church will be engaged hereafter in Heaven,—in devout adoration of His perfections. Our Fathers in the Faith delighted in taking a somewhat similar view of the entire transaction,—when they pointed out that these two sisters respectively symbolize the active and the contemplative side of the religious life: both excellent,—yet the contemplative the more excellent of the two; for it is "that good part, which shall not be taken away,"—but rather endure throughout the ages of Eternity, and become perfected by the presence of Him who is its object.(y) The practical life has its own honours and its own rewards. Those who pursue it, are only *then* to be checked when they would cast blame on the conduct of such as have chosen the Word of GOD for their study,(z) and CHRIST Himself for their portion.(a)

THE PRAYER.

O ALMIGHTY GOD, who alone canst order the unruly wills and affections of sinful men; Grant unto Thy people, that they may love the thing which Thou commandest, and desire that which Thou dost promise; that so, among the sundry and manifold changes of the world, our hearts may surely there be fixed, where true joys are to be found; through JESUS CHRIST our LORD. Amen.

(s) Compare St. Luke xxii. 31.   (t) St. John xi. 5.
(u) St. Matth. viii. 20, and St. Luke ix. 58.
(x) Romans xii. 13. 1 Tim. iii. 2. Titus i. 8. Heb. xiii. 2. 1 St. Peter iv. 9.
(y) Compare St. John xvi. 22.   (z) Psa. cxix. 18, 24, 54, 72, 97, 103, 105, 127, 162, &c.
(a) Psa. xvi. 5: lxxiii. 26: cxix. 57: cxlii. 5, &c.

CHAPTER XI.

1 CHRIST *teacheth to pray, and that instantly.* 11 *Assuring that* GOD *so will give us good things.* 14 *He, casting out a dumb devil, rebuketh the blasphemous Phari-sees.* 28 *And showeth who are blessed.* 29 *Preacheth to the people.* 37 *And reprehendeth the outward show of holiness in the Pharisees, Scribes, and Lawyers.*

1 AND it came to pass, that as He was praying in a certain place, when He ceased, one of His Disciples said unto Him, LORD, teach us to pray, as John also taught his Disciples.

It was usual, among the Jews, for Masters to give their Scholars a Form of Prayer. St. John Baptist had given his Disciples such a Form,—which would have been preserved to this day, had it concerned us to know what it was.

2 And He said unto them, When ye pray, say,

The Prayer which follows, had been already delivered by our SAVIOUR to His Disciples, in the Sermon on the Mount: then, unasked; now, in compliance with the request of a Disciple. See St. Matthew's Gospel, vi. 9 to 13,—and the note there. This repeated delivery of the LORD's Prayer, reminds us of the twofold delivery of His Commandments.(*a*) Very significant, surely, is the circumstance that *the same* Prayer was delivered on both occasions. Well may the Church make such frequent use of it in her Daily Service!

Our FATHER

We are not taught to say "My Father," but "*Our* Father;" partly, to remind us of our *Brotherhood* in CHRIST,—partly, to remind us of the duty of *Common* Prayer. To say "My FATHER," was the peculiar prerogative of the Only-Begotten SON. See St. John v. 18; and the note which immediately goes before it.

GOD is "our Father," because He is our Creator:(*b*)—because, by His Power our life is sustained; by His Providence all our wants are supplied:(*c*)—and because lastly, we are His adopted Children by Faith in CHRIST JESUS.(*d*)

Which art in Heaven,

These words, at the very beginning of the LORD's Prayer, are intended, (like the summons, "Lift up your hearts,") to carry our thoughts from Earth to Heaven, and to remind us where our conversation, as "the Sons of GOD,"(*e*) should be.

Hallowed be Thy Name.

This first petition of the LORD's Prayer, by the form it assumes, seems to testify anxiety on behalf of ALMIGHTY GOD: but, in reality, it is only a supplication offered up for ourselves,—a prayer that GOD's Name, (which is thrice Holy,) may be sancti-fied *in us.*

And when, both in ourselves and others, *that* Holy Name is hallowed,—what will delay the fulfilment of the petition which stands in the second place?

Thy Kingdom come.

By this petition, "the Church militant here in Earth" anticipates those "great voices in Heaven," which St. John heard, triumphantly "saying, The Kingdom

(*a*) See Deut. ix. 10, and x. 4.   (*b*) Deut. xxxii. 6.   (*c*) St. Matth. vii. 9 to 11.
(*d*) Gal. iii. 26.   (*e*) St. John i. 12, and 1 St. John iii. 1, 2.

of this World are become the Kingdoms of our LORD, and of His CHRIST; and He shall reign for ever and ever."(f)

But it is, in effect, a prayer for growth in Grace; for the increase of Holiness, both in ourselves and others: "for, behold, the Kingdom of GOD is within you."(g) The Kingdom, moreover, has been visibly set up on Earth: and "no doubt is come upon us:"(h) but as the Blind see not the Light, (in which they nevertheless "live, and move, and have their being,") so may it be with ourselves! We have need continually to pray that GOD would bring us sensibly to the Knowledge of His Kingdom: and convince us of its "coming."

Thy Will be done, as in Heaven, so in Earth.

If men sought to do GOD's Will on Earth, as constantly and faithfully as the holy Angels do His Will in Heaven,—(for they alway "do His commandments, hearkening unto the voice of His Word,")(i)—the coming of His Kingdom would be delayed no longer. Faithfully to do His Will, is indeed to make Heaven begin here on Earth. Heartily to will what He willeth, is the nearest imaginable approach to perfection.

The three former petitions are expressive of our solicitude for GOD's Glory. On our parts, they are petitions for grace "to worship Him, serve Him, and obey Him as we ought to do." The four which follow, have Man for their subject: and in them, we severally enumerate, and pray for the supply of, our own greatest needs.

3 Give us day by day our daily bread.

By which words, we "pray unto GOD that He will send us all things that be needful both for our souls and bodies." Thus, besides being a prayer for food and raiment,—(with which possessions, we are reminded that we ought to be content:(k) and for which, we are warned against being over careful;)(l)—this petition has an obvious reference to the "true Bread which came down from Heaven:" even to "the strengthening and refreshing of our souls by the Body and Blood of CHRIST." "For," as our LORD Himself speaks, "My Flesh is Meat indeed, and My Blood is Drink indeed."(m) And this is, of course, the loftiest meaning of the prayer.

Yet more generally,—for our LORD's use of Deut. viii. 3, (concerning which, see the note on St. Luke iv. 4,) forbids any such limited application of that place of Scripture;—we are hereby taught to place our entire dependence, to repose all our hopes and anxieties, on GOD: to refer all our needs, to commit all our schemes, as well as to resign the issue of every thing we undertake, to the disposition of His good Providence.

Lastly, to do the Will of GOD the FATHER,—as we learn from St. John iv. 32 and 34, is to "have meat to eat" which the World knows not of. That is, spiritual strength and sustenance is derived to the Church from this source. Moreover,— "It is written, Man shall not live by Bread alone, but by every Word that proceedeth out of the mouth of GOD."(n) There is therefore an allusion here to the commands and sanctions contained in the Book of Life; concerning which, the Christian prays that he may find therein his daily strength and sustentation.

And thus, although it would seem that, in this petition, our Blessed LORD, out of His great compassion toward our infirmities, had simply given the foremost place to a supplication in behalf of the temporal wants of His creatures,—it will be felt that even here, abundant provision has been made for the more spiritually-minded; enabling them to lift up their hearts above this earthly scene; and to feel, with the Psalmist, even while they use the language of mere bodily craving;—"My soul thirsteth for Thee: my flesh longeth for Thee!"(o) "My flesh and my heart faileth: but GOD is the strength of my heart, and my portion forever."(p)

4 And forgive us our Sins; for we also forgive every one that is indebted to us.

On this petition, and the memorable plea on which it rests, see the note in St. Matthew's Gospel,—vi. 12: also the note on verses 14 and 15 of the same chapter.

(f) Rev. xi. 15.   (g) St. Luke xvii. 21.
(h) St. Luke xi. 20; and St. Matth. xii. 28.   (i) Psalm ciii. 20.
(k) 1 Tim. vi. 8.   (l) St. Matth. vi. 24 to 34.   (m) St. John vi. 55.
(n) St. Matthew iv. 4,—where our LORD quotes Deut. viii. 3.
(o) Ps. lxiii. 1.   Compare Psalm lxxxiv. 2.   (p) Psalm lxxiii. 26.

To enforce the duty of forgiveness of Injuries, our LORD delivered a Parable of the King that took account of his Servants; and punished him who showed no mercy to his fellow."(q) We learn also from St. Matthew's Gospel, that the Blessed Speaker recurred to the present petition immediately after the former delivery of the LORD's Prayer:(r) and He is related by St. Mark to have used exactly similar language concerning this great duty, on a subsequent occasion.(s)

And lead us not into Temptation.

We are hereby reminded of the comfortable truth that the Adversary has no power, even to tempt us,—unless GOD permit him. When the Eternal SON was led into the Wilderness to be tempted by the Devil, He was led by the SPIRIT.(t) All our Fear, and all our Devotion, ought therefore to be addressed to GOD.

A connection may be perceived between this petition, and the last. *There*, we prayed to be forgiven for our past transgressions. *Here*, we pray to be saved from the commission of more.

See the note on this petition in St. Matthew vi. 13; where the difference is pointed out between God's *Trial of our Constancy*, and Satan's *Solicitation to Sin*,—which, in the language of Scripture, are alike called "Temptation."

But deliver us from Evil.

This may well be the concluding petition of the LORD's Prayer,—being the Creature's cry to the CREATOR for final deliverance from all that stands in the way of his Eternal Salvation: Evil,—whether from without, or from within. That deliverance from *the Evil One* is implied, cannot, of course, be doubted; and probably this is the thing *chiefly* meant: in illustration of which hint, the Reader is particularly referred to the notes on St. Luke iv. 6. But more than *that*, if possible, is meant by these words. They are a prayer that GOD would deliver us, as St. Paul speaks, "from this body of death."(u) By such language, (in the words of the same Apostle,) showing that "we ourselves groan within ourselves; waiting for the Adoption, to wit, the Redemption of the Body."(x)

This petition, which is the largest in extent of any, may be regarded as summing up, and comprehending, all our desires. It enables the Christian, into whatever tribulation he may happen to be cast, to vent the fulness of his grief; and, in the fewest possible words, to pray to GOD for effectual deliverance,—in Time and in Eternity.

When our LORD first delivered His pattern Prayer, He added a few words enforcing the duty of Forgiveness of Injuries.(y) On this occasion, He delivers a Parable enforcing *earnestness*, or rather *importunity*, in prayer. It is as if the Divine Speaker had said,—"You ask me for a form of words. It is well. Learn, however, that *that* form must be poured forth heartily; as the expression of the needs of each individual heart. Nor suppose, because your requests are not immediately granted, that therefore they will be denied altogether. Hearken to a parable."

5 And He said unto them, Which of you shall have a friend, and shall go unto him at midnight,

GOD is that Friend.(z) "*At midnight* I will rise to give thanks unto Thee," saith the Psalmist.(a) We learn from this place, that GOD is to be addressed with midnight prayers, as well as midnight praises; and the example of Paul and Silas teaches us the same thing. See Acts xvi. 25.

and say unto him, Friend, lend me three loaves;

The request, you observe, is for *Bread;* concerning the meaning of which term, see above, the notes on verse 3. Consider, in connection with these two places, the language of ver. 11; and see the note there.

(q) St. Matthew xviii. 23 to the end.　　　(r) St. Matthew vi. 14, 15.
(s) St. Mark xi. 25, 26. See also Ephes. iv. 32: Coloss. iii. 13: and Ecclesiasticus xxviii. 1 to 7.
(t) St. Matthew iv. 1.　　　(u) Romans vii. 24.　　　(x) Romans viii. 23.
(y) St. Matthew vi. 14, 15.　　　(z) St. John xv. 14.　　　(a) Psalm cxix. 62.

But why "*three* loaves?" It seems reasonable on more accounts than one, to compare this place with Genesis xviii. 6.

6 for a friend of mine in his journey is come to me, and I have nothing to set before him?

The type, it may be presumed, of a sudden requirement—an unexpected want. Thus, in Nathan's "parable of the Ewe Lamb," the supposed occasion when the Rich man spared to take of his own flock and of his own herd, was when "*there came a traveller* unto the rich man."(b) . . . Or does the present parable perhaps exhibit the efficacy of *intercessory* prayer?

An ancient bishop beautifully puts the case of a stranger seeking Divine Knowledge, *a reason*, at the hands of one who has it not to give. "Not having wherewith to satisfy his hunger, you are compelled to seek in the LORD's Book: for perhaps what he asks is contained there, but obscure. You are not permitted to ask St. Paul himself, or St. Peter, or any Prophet; for all that family is now resting with their LORD; and the ignorance of the world is very great—that is, it is midnight; and your friend is urgent from hunger, and not contented with a simple faith. Must he then be abandoned? Go to the LORD himself, with whom the family is sleeping; 'Knock and Pray.' If He delays to give, it is because he wishes that you should the more earnestly desire what is delayed; lest, by being given at once, it should grow common."

Take notice, in passing, of the *very* humble sphere of life from which our LORD draws His illustration. It is because—"*To the poor* the Gospel is preached."(c) Well might the Psalmist exclaim, "Who is like unto the LORD, our GOD, who dwelleth on high; who humbleth Himself to behold the things that are in Heaven and in the Earth!"(d)

7 And he from within shall answer and say, Trouble me not: the door is now shut, and my children are with me in bed: I cannot rise and give thee.

Rather—"My children, as well as myself, are gone to rest." He says, "Trouble me not," and delays, only to kindle the greater desire—to occasion redoubled earnestness. See the note on the next verse.

An ancient Father refers all this to these latter days, when there is "a famine of the Word; and those who once dealt the Gospel throughout the world, as it were Bread, are now in their secret rest with the LORD." Doubtless the Saints are GOD's "children;"(e) and "the dead in CHRIST,"—those "which sleep in JESUS,"(f)—may well be spoken of as "in their beds."(g) "Let the Saints be joyful with glory," says the Psalmist, "Let them rejoice *in their beds*."(h)

Consider, how it is only when "an open door"(i) is set before us, that we can hope for access to GOD. Hence our SAVIOUR CHRIST calls Himself "the door,"(k)—because He presents our petitions; and because, offered in His most Holy Name, they become prevailing.(l) Hence, too, such expressions as we meet with in Acts xiv. 27: 1 Cor. xvi. 9: 2 Cor. ii. 12: and Coloss. iv. 3.—Take notice that "the door" is more than "*shut;*" it is (in the original) "*locked:*" and so in St. Matthew vi. 6. The thoughtful Reader will recollect a short but striking clause in St. Matthew xxv. 10.

8 I say unto you, Though he will not rise and give him, because he is his Friend, yet because of his importunity he will rise and give him as many as he needeth.

Whether "three" or more.

What a marvellous lesson is here set before us—even by the very Being who answereth Prayer! He may see fit to delay granting our petitions: but He would have us persevere; and He will grant them in the end. "The Kingdom of Heaven suffereth violence; and the violent take it by force."(m) The present warning is

---

(b) 2 Samuel xii. 4. (c) St. Luke vii. 22. (d) Psalm cxiii. 6.
(e) 1 St. John iii. 1, 2, &c. (f) 1 Thess. iv. 14, 16.
(g) Compare Job xvii. 13 Isaiah lvii. 2. 2 Chron. xvi. 14. (h) Psalm cxlix. 5.
(i) Rev. iii. 8. (k) St. John x. 9. (l) St. John xiv. 13: xv. 16: xvi. 23.
(m) St. Matthew xi. 12.
33

by no means singular and solitary. Our LORD caused two blind men, on a certain occasion, thus to cry after Him, and follow Him into the house:(n) the two blind men at Jericho, He healed not, in like manner, until after they had called upon Him so as to incur the displeasure of the multitude:(o) but above all, to the Woman of Canaan, He thus acted—"answering her not a word," in reply to her prolonged and repeated cries—even repulsing her when at last she came and worshipped.(p) And what other lesson than one of earnestness in Prayer, is taught us by Jacob's wrestling with an Angel until the breaking of the day? Jacob said, "I will not let Thee go, except Thou bless me. . . . And He said, . . . As a Prince hast thou power with GOD and with men, and hast prevailed. . . . And He blessed him there."(q) Whence his name, "Israel;" that is, a Prince of GOD.

Observe, that the friend's compliance is not from friendship, but in consequence of the other's importunity; or rather "shamelessness,"—for so it stands in the original: so that the argument strictly resembles that in the parable of "The Unjust Judge;" or rather of "The importunate Widow;" which was spoken "to this end, that men ought always to pray and not to faint."(r) Consider, by all means St. Luke xviii. 1 to 8.

Now, "GOD is Love."(s) Moreover, "Behold, He that keepeth Israel shall neither slumber nor sleep."(t) Consider therefore with how much greater certainty of success we shall knock at Heaven's Gate! "He would not so encourage us to ask were He not willing to bestow. He is more willing to give than we to receive." There is no overcoming of reluctance here; the reluctance, on the contrary, is all our own.

The Divine Speaker proceeds to add a few words without any parable: "no longer in a figure, but plainly."

9 And I say unto you, Ask, and it shall be given you; seek, and ye shall find; knock, and it shall be opened unto you.

This, and the four following verses, (ver. 9 to ver. 13,) recur, with some small varieties of expression, in our LORD's Sermon on the Mount—St. Matthew vii. 7 to 11: where the Reader is requested to consult the notes. To "ask,"—to "seek,"—to "knock,"—seem to imply different degrees of earnestness.

10 For every one that asketh receiveth; and he that seeketh findeth and to him that knocketh it shall be opened.

"Receiveth,"—not perhaps the very thing he asked for; but "that which is most expedient for him;" and therefore a better thing than he knew how to ask. He "findeth"—something: a treasure, doubtless; though perhaps not the very thing he sought. And "the door" is "opened,"—whereby he may "go in and out, and find pasture."(u) See the note on St. Matthew vii. 8.

11 If a Son shall ask bread of any of you that is a Father, will he give him a stone? or if he ask a fish, will he for a fish give him a serpent?

The connection of this with what goes before is obvious. Notice in the prayer beginning "Our Father," the petition for "Bread;" and the subject of the midnight request in verse 5—where see the note. See what has been already written on St. Matthew vii. 9.

12, 13 Or if he shall ask an egg, will he offer him a scorpion? If ye then, being evil, know how to give good gifts unto your children how much more shall your Heavenly FATHER give the HOLY SPIRIT to them that ask Him?

These words have already come before us in the "Sermon on the Mount,"—St. Matthew vii. 10, 11; where see the notes. A similar argument to that used above is here repeated. There, it was,—If a common Friend, to escape molestation; here

---

(n) St. Matth. ix. 27, 28.   (o) St. Matth. xx. 30 to 34.   (p) St. Matth. xv. 22 to 26.
(q) Gen. xxxii. 24 to 29.   (r) St. Luke xviii. 1.   (s) 1 St. John iv. 16.
(t) Psalm cxxi. 4.   (u) St. John x. 9.

If a human Father, because bound by natural ties, grants the favour required of him—how much more shall *He* who never sleepeth,(z) and whose Mercy is over all His works;(y) how much more shall thy Heavenly Father, "grant thee thy heart's desire, and fulfil all thy mind!"(z)

14 And He was casting out a devil, and it was dumb. And it came to pass, when the devil was gone out, the dumb spake; and the people wondered.

Compare the account of this miracle in St. Matthew's Gospel—xii. 22, 23; where see the notes.

15 But some of them said, He casteth out devils through Beelzebub the chief of the devils.

The Reader is referred to the note on St. Matthew xii. 24. Also, to a long note on St. Mark iii. 22.

16 And others, tempting *Him*, sought of Him a sign from Heaven.

This pretended desire of a sign less equivocal,—a sign *from Heaven*, such as Moses exhibited before the Israelites,(a)—could only proceed from minds corrupted, as were those of the Pharisees, by the dangerous habit of trifling with the divine Oracles; and making that accurate knowledge they possessed of the external means of Salvation, a mere instrument of pride and worldly advancement. Compare St. Matthew xii. 38, and the note there.

17, 18, 19 But He, knowing their thoughts, said unto them, Every Kingdom divided against itself is brought to desolation; and a House *divided* against a House falleth. If Satan also be divided against himself, how shall his Kingdom stand? because ye say that I cast out devils through Beelzebub. And if I by Beelzebub cast out devils, by whom do your sons cast *them* out? therefore shall they be your judges.

The Reader is referred to all the notes on St. Matthew xii. 25, 26, 27—where the three preceding verses will be found discussed at some length. Some remarks on the first two, (verses 17 and 18,) will be also found in the Commentary on St. Mark iii. 26.

20 But if I with the Finger of GOD cast out devils, no doubt the Kingdom of GOD is come upon you.

In St. Matthew xii. 28, instead of "The *Finger* of GOD," it is "The *Spirit* of GOD:" a most precious circumstance, since we are thereby reminded of the meaning of the former phrase when it occurs in Scripture. But *why* is the Spirit of GOD spoken of as His *Finger?* Probably, first, because that little member possesses such wondrous activity, and is mainly employed in all the operations of the hands: wherefore, when the Magicians of Pharaoh would ascribe a miracle to the power of GOD's *Spirit*, they exclaim, "This is the *Finger* of GOD."(b)—To the finger, again, chiefly belong all works of Creative energy and skill: wherefore, the Heavens, (concerning which it is said in the Book of Job, "By His *Spirit* He hath garnished" them,)(c) are described in Psalm viii. 3, as "the work of His *Fingers*."—Next, it may be because with this member words are consigned to writing: whence the Ten Commandments on two tables of stone, are said to have been "written with the *Finger* of GOD;"(d) with manifest reference to which, St. Paul speaks of an Epistle written "with the *Spirit* of the living GOD; not in tables of stone, but in fleshly tables of the heart."(e)—We speak of the Bible, in like manner, as written with the *Finger* of GOD; by which we do but mean that it is inspired throughout by GOD's HOLY SPIRIT. Consider Daniel v. 5, which de-

---

(x) Psalm cxxi. 3, 4.　　(y) Psalm cxlv. 9.　　(z) Psalm xx. 4.
(a) Exodus xvi. 4, 15; referred to in Psalm lxxviii. 24, and in St. John vi. 30 to 32.
(b) Exodus viii. 19.
(d) Exodus xxxi. 18: Deut. ix. 10.
(c) Job xxvi. 13.
(e) 2 Cor. iii. 3.

scribes how there "came forth *fingers of a man's hand and wrote*" upon the wall; and "the part of the hand," (as we read in verse 24,) *was sent from GOD.* Remember also how, on a certain occasion, the Incarnate WORD Himself "stooped down, and *with His finger wrote* on the ground."(*f*)

When acts of stupendous Power are attributed to *the Finger* of GOD, there seems further to be an allusion to the *ease* and *despatch* with which He performs His works.

But the Reader is referred to the note on St. Matthew xii. 28, for some remarks upon the present verse.

21, 22 When a Strong Man armed keepeth his palace, his goods are in peace: but when a Stronger than he shall come upon him, and overcome him, He taketh from him all his armour wherein he trusted, and divideth his spoils.

Our SAVIOUR CHRIST Himself is that "Stronger than the Strong,"—one of whose types in the Old Testament was *Samson.* He is a *Warrior.* Consider the following places of Scripture,—Psalm xlv. 3, and 5, (with which compare Rev. vi. 2: also xix. 15 and 21:) Ephes. iv. 8, (quoting Psalm lxviii. 18:) Coloss. ii. 15: 1 Cor. xv. 25, 26. To "divide spoils" is the act of victorious soldiers,—compare Numb. xxxi. 27: Joshua xxii. 8: Judges v. 30: 1 Samuel xxx. 24: Psalm lxviii. 12: Isaiah xxxiii. 23. Even thus it had been foretold of CHRIST Himself that He should "*divide the spoil with the strong.*"(*g*)

See the note on St. Matthew xii. 29: also on St. Mark iii. 27, and the places there referred to. The Reader is also referred to the note on St. Luke viii. 30.

"All his armour:" rather, "his *complete suit of armour.*"(*h*)—"*Wherein he trusted:*"—how much of dismay and disappointment is revealed in those few words!

23 He that is not with Me is against Me; and He that gathereth not with Me scattereth.

The Reader is referred to the note on St. Matthew xii. 30.

24, 25 When the unclean Spirit is gone out of a man, he walketh through dry places, seeking rest: and finding none, he saith, I will return unto my house whence I came out. And when he cometh, he findeth *it* swept and garnished.

These wonderful words will be found remarked upon, at great length, in the notes on St. Matthew xii. 43.

26 Then goeth he, and taketh *to him* seven other spirits more wicked than himself;

"As if answering to the sevenfold graces of the HOLY SPIRIT, by which the faithful Christian is confirmed and sealed." See the Hymn in the Ordination Service, beginning "Come, HOLY GHOST," &c.; and consider the following places of Scripture: Rev. i. 4: iii. 1: iv. 5: v. 6. Compare Isaiah xi. 2.

For, in the case before us, "that most Holy Inhabitant has been quenched,(*i*) and grieved,(*k*) and thrust away."

Consider, in connection with this, St. John v. 14.

and they enter in, and dwell there: and the last *state* of that man is worse than the first.

For "it is impossible," says the Apostle, addressing the Hebrews, "to renew again such unto repentance:"(*l*) that is, such as "were once enlightened, and have tasted of the heavenly gift, and were made partakers of the HOLY GHOST, and have tasted the good Word of GOD, and the powers of the World to come," and yet have fallen away to apostasy. Most true it is that GOD gives pardon ever to the truly

(*f*) St. John viii. 6.   (*g*) Isaiah liii. 12.
(*h*) Compare Ephes. vi. 11, 13; where it is rendered "the whole armour."
(*i*) 1 Thess. v. 19.   (*k*) Ephes. iv. 30.   (*l*) Hebrews vi. 4 to 6.

repenting Sinner. But *who* will give Repentance itself to him who has put it far
from him,—when the HOLY SPIRIT, the only Author and Giver of Repentance, is
grieved, and provoked to become an Enemy? What if every feeling on which con-
trition can be fastened has ceased to exist,—and every breath of devout affection
as stopped,—and baptismal grace has been abused, and wasted, and lost,—and the
Blood of the Covenant, wherewith the man was sanctified, hath become to him as
an unholy thing, and a lasting despite is done to "the Spirit of Grace?"(*m*)

 The entire contents of the present verse will be found remarked upon, at great
length, in the note on St. Matthew xii. 45,—to which the Reader is referred.

 **27, 28 And it came to pass, as He spake these things, a certain
Woman of the company lifted up her voice and said unto Him, Blessed
is the womb that bare Thee, and the paps which Thou hast sucked.
But He said, Yea rather, blessed *are* they that hear the Word of GOD,
and keep it.**

 The Reader is referred to the note on St. Luke viii. 21.—It is obvious to remark
in these words that nothing derogatory to the unspeakable honour of the Blessed
Virgin Mary was intended. The very thought were ridiculous. An Archangel
from Heaven had proclaimed her blessedness. The HOLY SPIRIT, (by her own lips,)
had pronounced her blessed eternally.(*n*) That no Woman since the Creation was
ever so honoured,—nor till the end of the World *will* be,—is too evident to require
asserting. In the words of grave Bishop Pearson,—"We cannot bear too reverend
regard unto 'the Mother of our LORD,' so long as we give her not that worship
which is due unto the LORD Himself."

 And yet, he must be blind indeed who sees not in such passages as the present,—
St. Luke viii. 20, 21,—St. Matth. xii. 48 to 50,—the clear condemnation of all those
who would unduly exalt our LORD's Mother.(*o*) There are parts of the Church
where the Blessed Virgin is even worshipped; and *that*, openly. But the blasphemous practice is of only modern date; and could never have arisen where the Word
of GOD was held in due honour.

 **29 And when the people were gathered thick together, He began
to say,**

 In reply to the Pharisees, who had said,—"Master, we would see a sign from
Thee." See St. Matthew xii. 38, and the note there.

 **30 This is an evil generation: they seek a sign; and there shall no
sign be given it, but the sign of Jonas the Prophet. For as Jonas
was a sign unto the Ninevites, so shall also the Son of Man be to this
generation.**

 Take notice, that one of the unrecorded facts in Old Testament History is here
revealed to us, from the lips of CHRIST Himself.

 **31, 32 The Queen of the South shall rise up in the Judgment with
the men of this generation, and condemn them: for she came from the
utmost parts of the Earth to hear the wisdom of Solomon; and, behold,
. Greater than Solomon *is* here. The men of Nineveh shall rise up in
the Judgment with this generation, and shall condemn it: for they
repented at the preaching of Jonas; and, behold, a Greater than Jonas
is here.**

 The Reader will find this entire passage fully remarked upon in the notes on St.
Matthew xii. 39, 40, 41, 42. It is very easy to point out one of the meanings of the
words which follow: easy, also, to invent *some* connection with what goes before.
But how hard is it to declare with certainty what the SPIRIT intended! . . . It *seems*
as if our LORD were here proclaiming the openness of His teaching; and declaring

that, just as openly should His Church, (the "Candlestick,") bear witness concern ing Him, to the end: for He says:—

33 No man, when he hath lighted a candle, putteth *it* in a secre place, neither under a bushel; but on a candlestick, that they whicl come in may see the light.

Almost the same words are found in the "Sermon on the Mount." See the not on St. Matthew v. 15. They also recur (in quite a different connection) in St. Mar iv. 21,—where see the note. In what follows, our LORD seems to declare tha "whether men should be enlightened by His Doctrine, or not, would depend upo the state of their own minds; according as they should be clear from prejudices o darkened by evil passions." See below, on ver. 36; and consider St. John v. 44.

34 The light of the body is the eye: therefore when thine eye i single, thy whole body is also full of light; but when *thine eye* is evil thy body also *is* full of darkness.

These words also occurred in the "Sermon on the Mount," and will be found dis cussed in the notes on St. Matthew vi. 22, 23.

35, 36 Take heed therefore that the light which is in thee be ne darkness. If thy whole body therefore *be* full of light, having no par dark, the whole shall be full of light, as when the bright shining of ı candle doth give thee light.

"What is here said of the body, is to be applied to the soul. The sense is: Iı in consequence of the singleness of thy heart, thy whole mind be enlightened, ther will be Light all around thee, to direct thee in all thy ways."

37, 38 And as He spake, a certain Pharisee besought Him to din with him: and He went in, and sat down to meat. And when the Pha risee saw *it*, he marvelled that He had not first washed before dinner.

The reason is given in St. Mark vii. 3 and 4.

39 And the LORD said unto him, Now do ye Pharisees make clea the outside of the cup and the platter;

—"but within, they are full of extortion and excess:"(*p*) even so ye are carefu to cultivate a fair outside,—

40 but your inward part is full of ravening and wickedness. Yı fools, did not He that made that which is without make that which is within also?

This means,—You ascribe to Divine Tradition those outward cleansings which you extend even to cup and platter. But you do not consider that He who formed the outside, fashioned the inward part also; and must require purity in respect of *both*—Soul as well as Body. "Behold, Thou desirest Truth *in the inward parts*," says the Psalmist. "Make me *a clean heart*, O God."

41 But rather gives alms of such things as ye have; and, behold, all things are clean unto you.

This should be translated,—"But rather bestow in alms the things which are inside" the cup and the platter: (corresponding with the Baptist's directions, in St. Luke iii. 11.) "*Alms*" are specified, because the Pharisees were "full of Rav ening,"—that is, of *Extortion*. On the doctrine here taught, consider the following places of Scripture: Isaiah lviii. 7. Daniel iv. 27. St. Luke xii. 33. And com pare the two preceding verses with St. Matthew xxiii. 25, 26,—where see the notes.

(*p*) St. Matthew xxiii. 25.

Take notice, that Woe is next three times denounced on the Pharisees,—verses 2, 43, and 44: and as often on the Lawyers, verses 46, 47, and 52.

42 But woe unto you, Pharisees! for ye tithe mint and rue and all manner of herbs, and pass over Judgment and the Love of GOD: these ught ye to have done, and not to leave the other undone.

That is,—And *yet* not to leave the other undone. See the note on St. Matthew xiii. 23.

The Pharisees *did* give tithe to GOD, even of "all manner of herbs,"—which the aw did not require: but *as* they gave it, it was not Alms. Consider St. Matthew i. 1 to 4, and the notes there.

43 Woe unto you, Pharisees! for ye love the uppermost seats in the ynagogues, and greetings in the markets.

Our LORD reproached them for their pride and ambition in these respects, on nother occasion. Compare St. Matthew xxiii. 6, which answers to St. Mark xii. 3, 39: St. Luke xx. 46.

44 Woe unto you, Scribes and Pharisees, hypocrites! for ye are as raves which appear not, and the men that walk over *them* are not ware *of them.*

This should be compared with St. Matthew xxiii. 27: but the sense of the two laces is different. *There*, the Pharisees are compared to "whited sepulchres," d are reproached for their inward impurity, combined with a fair exterior. *Here*, e skill with which they succeeded in hiding their internal corruption,—so that en suspected not the pollution with which they were in contact, (q)—is the subject ' rebuke. See the note on the last half of St. Matthew viii. 28.

45 Then answered one of the Lawyers, and said unto Him, Master, us saying, Thou reproachest us also.

Our countryman Bede remarks on this,—"In what a grievous state is that con- ience, which, hearing the Word of GOD, thinks it a reproach against itself; and, the account of the punishment of the wicked, perceives its own condemnation!" ake notice, that when our LORD couples the "Scribes" with the "Pharisees," one the *Lawyers* speaks. The reason may be gathered from the note on St. Mark i. 22, which see. The learned do not know whether there was *any* difference etween a Lawyer and a Scribe; but they suggest that the former may have ex- ounded the Law privately, in Schools: the latter, publicly, in the Synagogues.

The three Woes denounced against the Lawyers follow,—as was pointed out in e note which immediately precedes verse 42.

46 And He said, Woe unto you also, *ye* Lawyers! for ye lade men ith burdens grievous to be borne, and ye yourselves touch not the urdens with one of your fingers.

To "lade men with burdens," in the language of Scripture, is, so to interpret he Law that its fulfillment shall prove intolerable. Thus, St. Peter describes the ircumcision of Christians, as "*a yoke upon the neck* of the Disciples:"(r) and, in the ecree of the Council of Jerusalem, it is said to have "seemed good to the HOLY HOST, and to us, *to lay upon you no greater burden* than these necessary things."(s) These false Teachers, as our LORD elsewhere declares, "*said*, but *did not*:"(t) or, as it is here expressed, "touched not the burdens with one of their fingers." See on St. Matthew xxiii. 4.

47 Woe unto you! for ye build the sepulchres of the Prophets, and your Fathers killed them.

(q) See Numbers xix. 16.   (r) Acts xv. 10.   (s) Acts xv. 28.
                           (t) St. Matthew xxiii. 3.

Our LORD does not, of course, denounce woe against them for building the Sepulchres of the Prophets; but for their *hypocrisy:* as appears from St. Matthew xxiii. 29.

48 Truly ye bear witness that ye allow the deeds of your Fathers;

Rather,—"Thereby ye bear witness to the deeds of your Fathers, and are consenting thereto;"

for they indeed killed them, and ye build their sepulchres.

That is,—For, by building the Sepulchres of the Prophets, ye bear witness publicly to the guilt of those who slew them; while, by busying yourselves with the graves of the murdered men, ye are perceived by Him who seeth in secret, to inherit the disposition of those, their murderers. The whole passage, however, is to be compared with St. Matthew xxiii. 29 to 33, where the language is more full;—and see the notes there. Yet, who that reads all that ever was written in explanation of the words of CHRIST, feels not that there still remains something to be explained? that it is *indeed* "the voice of GOD" to which he has been listening, "and not of a Man?" . . . He proceeds:—

49 Therefore also said the Wisdom of GOD,

In St. Matthew xxiii. 34, instead of "The Wisdom of GOD," it is simply "I." CHRIST therefore is,—(as St. Paul *says* that He is,)—"the Wisdom of GOD."(u) This must be because in Him "are hid all the treasures of Wisdom and Knowledge."(x) Accordingly, by this name of WISDOM is the Eternal SON discoursed of throughout the Book of Proverbs. Consider particularly, Proverbs iii. 19: viii. 22 to 31, &c.

50, 51 I will send them Prophets and Apostles, and *some* of them they shall slay and persecute: that the blood of all the Prophets, which was shed from the foundation of the World, may be required of this generation; from the blood of Abel unto the blood of Zacharias, which perished between the Altar and the Temple: verily I say unto you, It shall be required of this generation.

The Reader should compare this with St. Matthew xxiii. 34 to 36; where some remarks on these verses will be found.

52 Woe unto you, Lawyers! for ye have taken away the key of Knowledge; ye entered not in yourselves, and them that were entering in ye hindered.

This also recurs, though in a somewhat different form, in St. Matthew xxiii. 13,—where see the note. "The Key of Knowledge,"—because it was their business to unlock the hard places of Scripture: in token of which, it was usual to present them with a key, on appointing them to their office. Concerning the Lawyers, see the note on St. Mark iii. 22.

53, 54 And as He said these things unto them, the Scribes and the Pharisees began to urge Him vehemently, and to provoke Him to speak of many things: laying wait for Him and seeking to catch something out of His mouth, that they might accuse Him.

They harassed Him with questions, as their manner was; of which we have so singular an example in St. Matthew xxii. 15, 23, 34, 46. And this was done in order to provoke Him to "*the multitude of words;*" in which, (says the Wise Man,) "*there wanteth not sin.*"(y) They forgot with whom they had to do: even with Him who spake as "never man spake,"(z) and of whom it had been said,—"Full of Grace are Thy Lips!"(a)

(u) 1 Cor. i. 24.   (x) Coloss. ii. 3.   (y) Proverbs x. 19.
(z) St. John vii. 46.   (a) Psalm xlv. 3.

THE PRAYER.

O Merciful God, who hast made all men, and hatest nothing that Thou hast made, nor wouldest the death of a sinner, but rather that he should be converted and live; have mercy upon all Jews, Turks, Infidels, and Heretics, and take from them all ignorance, hardness of heart, and contempt of Thy Word; and so fetch them home, Blessed Lord, to Thy flock, that they may be saved among the remnant of the true Israelites, and be made one fold under one Shepherd, Jesus Christ our Lord, who liveth and reigneth with Thee and the Holy Spirit, one God, World without end. Amen.

CHAPTER XII.

1 Christ *preacheth to His Disciples to avoid hypocrisy, and fearfulness in publishing His doctrine.* 13 *Warneth the people to beware of covetousness, by the parable of the rich man who set up greater barns.* 22 *We must not be over-careful of earthly things,* 31 *but seek the Kingdom of God,* 33 *give alms,* 36 *be ready at a knock to open to our Lord whensoever He cometh.* 41 Christ's *ministers are to see to their charge,* 49 *and look for persecution.* 54 *The people must take this time of grace,* 58 *because it is a fearful thing to die without reconciliation.*

1 In the mean time, when there were gathered together an innumerable multitude of people, insomuch that they trode one upon another, He began to say unto His Disciples first of all, Beware ye of the leaven of the Pharisees, which is hypocrisy.

Take notice of the immense concourse of persons thus hinted at, in whose presence our Blessed Lord denounced the wickedness of the most powerful of the Jewish sects. The striking saying here recorded, (which will be found remarked upon in the notes on St. Mark viii. 15, and St. Matth. xvi. 6,) is discovered to have been employed by Him on more than one occasion. The reason of the warning, as it seems, follows:

2 For there is nothing covered, that shall not be revealed; neither hid, that shall not be known.

This striking saying, like the last, is found to have been of repeated occurrence.(a) It has been commented upon in the note on St. Matthew x. 26,—which is the first of eight verses closely resembling the second, and seven following verses, of the present chapter. The entire passage, although very like the present, occurs in quite a different connection in the earlier Gospel; being part of the Charge which our Lord delivered to the Twelve.

(a) Namely, St. Matth. x. 26, St. Mark iv. 22, (which is St. Luke viii. 17,) and here.

And here, let it be remarked in passing, that the attentive student of the Gospels, on making such a discovery, instead of thinking himself at liberty to proceed at once to what follows, will feel it incumbent upon him to pause rather, and to inquire humbly and carefully into the nature of the strange circumstance before him. For a strange circumstance it certainly is, that of the fifty-nine verses which compose the present chapter, no less than thirty-five should prove to have been delivered on *quite distinct occasions;* and not in single verses either, but by seven, eight, and even ten verses at a time.

He must have a very unworthy notion of the dignity of the Gospel who can make light of a fact like this. There have been found persons, indeed, capable of supposing that the later Evangelists made an unskilful use of the materials provided for them by those who wrote first. Some have even thought that they saw traces of error in these Divine narratives. Far be from us such miserable delusions! "O my soul, come not thou into their secret!" Rather, let us be well persuaded that over and above the advantage to be derived from every passage so repeated, considered in and by itself, there is a further use provided by its repetition; discoverable, however, only by him who will diligently seek for it by minute comparison exceeding watchfulness, and patient thought. Consider whether these may not be some of the "hid treasures" of which the SPIRIT speaks in Prov. ii. 4,—and which to be found, must be "sought" and "searched for."(b)

And it may be pointed out, while we are on this subject, first, that although a given expression may seem to be simply repeated on two distinct occasions, yet, on closer inspection, it will be often found that there are minute but important differences between the first and second wording of the place: whereby it is, in fact made new. Thus St. Luke xii. 2 to 9 might be thought to be quite the same as St. Matth. x. 26 to 33; and yet the two passages are full of small, but striking differences. St. Luke xii. 2 and St. Matth. x. 26 will be found noticed below. Compare further St. Luke xii. 3 with St. Matth. x. 27. Next, the great depth and fulness of the Divine sayings is forcibly suggested, as well as the variety of their intention, when we make the discovery that words in substance the same, are found sometimes to recur in a wholly different connection. Thus, although the saying in St. Luke xii. 2 is the same which is found in St. Matth. x. 26, and again in St. Mark iv. 22,(c)—how diverse does its purpose seem in those places! In St. Luke, it follows a warning against hypocrisy: in St. Matthew, a warning against fear. In St. Mark, the openness of the Gospel-message seems to be chiefly declared.

And then, lastly, when two passages appear to be in all respects similar, as St. Luke xii. 22 to 31, and St. Matth. vi. 25 to 33, it is surely, in itself, a circumstance full of edification that the HOLY SPIRIT should have seen fit thus to inform us that our SAVIOUR repeated the self-same teaching on two distinct occasions; and almost in the self-same words. By some, this will be felt to be a rebuke of such curiosity as was indulged by those polite heathens who "spent their time in nothing else but either to tell or to hear *some new thing.*"(d) While to others, it will seem an indication of the peculiar weight and importance which belong to certain of the sayings of Him, "in whom are hid all the treasures of Wisdom and Knowledge."(e)

3 Therefore whatsoever ye have spoken in darkness shall be heard in the light; and that which ye have spoken in the ear in closets shall be proclaimed upon the house-tops.

As in St. Matthew's Gospel, so here, an exhortation not to fear Man but God follows. For this, the presence of the Pharisees may be thought to supply a sufficient reason.(f) Take notice that the Blessed Speaker addresses the multitude about Him, as His "friends,"(g)—"*My* friends."

4, 5 And I say unto you My friends, Be not afraid of them that kill the body, and after that have no more that they can do. But I will forewarn you whom ye shall fear: Fear Him, which after He hath killed hath power to cast into Hell; yea, I say unto you, Fear Him.

(b) See the notes on St. Matth. xiii. 44.
(d) Acts xvii. 21.
(f) Consider St. John ix. 22, 34: xii. 42: xix. 38.

(c) Or St. Luke viii. 17.
(e) Col. ii. 3.
(g) Compare St. John xv. 14, 15

"Three times we are commanded to fear, and only one reason is given, but sufficient for a thousand fears,—the power of Him who is able eternally to punish us."(h)

6, 7 Are not five sparrows sold for two farthings, and not one of them is forgotten before GOD? But even the very hairs of your head are all numbered. Fear not therefore: ye are of more value than many sparrows.

8, 9 Also I say unto you, Whosoever shall confess Me before men, him shall the Son of Man also confess before the angels of GOD: but he that denieth Me before men shall be denied before the angels of GOD.

Words very like those contained in these seven verses, as already pointed out, are found in St. Matth. x. 27 to 33,—whither the Reader is referred for several remarks concerning them. His attention is called, in the mean time, to the suggestions which have been offered above, in the long note which precedes verse 3. He will perceive that verses 2 and 3 are to be read in close connection with the warning at the end of verse 1.

10 And whosoever shall speak a word against the Son of Man, it shall be forgiven him: but unto him that blasphemeth against the HOLY GHOST, it shall not be forgiven.

Words very like the present also, our LORD is found to have used on quite a different occasion. The Reader is referred to the Commentary on St. Mark iii. 28, 29, 30, and on St. Matth. xii. 32.

11, 12 And when they bring you unto the synagogues and *unto* magistrates, and powers, take ye no thought how or what thing ye shall answer, or what ye shall say: for the HOLY GHOST shall teach you in the same hour what ye ought to say.

These words, like the preceding, recur in our LORD's Commission to the Twelve, —where some remarks will be found concerning them.(i) The same saying is also met with in St. Mark xiii. 11,—in quite a different connection. Lastly, it will be found almost to recur in chap. xxi. 14, 15 of the present Gospel, where see the note. Sayings of repeated occurrence, like these, are surely entitled to particular attention at our hands!
In this place, verses 11, 12 evidently continue the words of caution and encouragement which are found in verses 4 to 7: while verses 8 to 10, (which go together,) arise naturally out of what went before.
An unseasonable interruption follows, which introduces a parable peculiar to St. Luke's Gospel.

13 And one of the company said unto Him, Master, speak to my brother, that he divide the inheritance with me.

If the Reader will refer to the three places referred to, in the preceding note, he will perceive that they are immediately followed by a prophecy concerning the treatment which one *Brother* was to experience at the hand of another.(k) Now, since nothing which our LORD is *related* to have said on the present occasion can have suggested the interruption of "one of the Company," here recorded,—may it not be suspected that He went on now to deliver the same prophetic intimation as on other occasions, and that it was *this* which in some way suggested the request before us?

14 And He said unto him, Man, who made Me a judge or a divider over you?

(h) Bp. Pearson.   (i) See the note on St. Matth. x. 19, 20.
(k) St. Matth. x. 21: St. Mark xiii. 12: St. Luke xxi. 16.

It will be perceived that our LORD's words are moulded on those which are foun in Exodus ii. 14: "and *there* Moses was, by anticipation, assuming his office as th lawgiver of a temporal kingdom; which CHRIST disclaims, because His Kingdom was not of this world."(*l*) Or, He may be understood to say,—"I will not be liabl to such objections from men, as were then ungratefully made against Moses,— 'Who made thee a prince and a judge over us?'"(*m*)

"Between brothers," says Ambrose, "no judge should intervene, but natura affection should be the umpire to divide the inheritance. And yet, Eternal Life not riches, is the inheritance which men should wait for." Our LORD proceeds t point out *the root* from which this request had sprung; and to warn His hearer against it.

15 And He said unto them, Take heed, and beware of covetousness for a man's life consisteth not in the abundance of the things which h possesseth.

That is,—"A man's life does not depend upon his possessions, however abundan they may be." . . . . Here then, we have another of those many warnings again the sin of Judas, which are found in the Gospel. This will be found pointed o elsewhere;(*n*) but it deserves to be repeated.

16, 17, 18 And He spake a Parable unto them, saying, The groun of a certain rich man brought forth plentifully : and he thought withi himself, saying, What shall I do, because I have no room where to be stow my fruits? And he said, This will I do: I will pull down m barns, and build greater; and there will I bestow all my fruits and m goods.

This was a miserable scheme, indeed! He has "no room where to bestow h fruits." "The Author and Giver of all good things," ("sending rain on the ju and on the unjust,")(*o*) has so blessed him, that he is even perplexed and encun bered with the largeness of the Divine Bounty. "What shall I do?" he ask Was it not time to think of giving to him that needeth?(*p*) Would not the empt stomachs of the poor have supplied him with "barns large enough?"—as one o the ancients strikingly asks. But the case of his poor neighbour enters not at a into his thoughts. He is engrossed with greedy schemes about himself:—"M barns—*my* fruits—*my* goods."

19 And I will say to my soul, Soul, thou hast much goods laid u for many years ; take thine ease, eat, drink, *and* be merry.

In Greek, it is,—"many goods for many years: rest, eat, drink, feast!" H calls his possessions his "*goods*," observe. Such were the "good things" whic Abraham in the Parable reminds the rich man that he had "received in his life time."(*q*) Basil remarks of this man that "he was permitted to *deliberate* in ever thing, and to manifest his purpose, in order that he might receive a sentence suc as his inclinations deserved." As he had "*thought* within himself, *saying*;"(*r*) the counsel of GOD towards him is represented by what "GOD *said* unto him." A it follows:—

20 But GOD said unto him, *Thou* fool, this night thy soul shall b required of thee :

Every word here is terrible. What folly must be his, whom GOD Himself ad dresses as—"Fool!" . . . Instead of "Thy soul shall be required of thee," in th original it is, "*They shall require* thy soul of thee." Either way, the sense is ob viously the same; but there seems to be a mysterious hint thrown out by th Speaker that His unseen messengers will be sent to the miserable man, to "require

---

(*l*) Williams.   (*m*) Hammond : and so, Tertullian.
(*n*) See the latter part of the note on St. Mark xiv. 25.   (*o*) St. Matth. vi. 45.
(*p*) Ephes. iv. 28.   (*q*) St. Luke xvi. 25.   (*r*) See above, ver. 17.

the surrender of that life which he counted on enjoying for "many years."(s) Moreover, it is in the stillness and darkness of *the night* that he will receive the unwelcome summons. . . . . "Then," (asks the same Divine Speaker,)—

then whose shall those things be, which thou hast provided?

Not *thine*, surely: "nor can anything be called ours which we cannot take away with us."(t)

21 So *is* he that layeth up treasure for himself, and is not rich toward GOD.

Consider St. Matthew vi. 19 to 21, and the notes on the place, as a commentary on these words. See also, 1 Tim. vi. 17 to 19. The blessed Speaker turns His discourse next to the Disciples.

22, 23, 24 And He said unto His Disciples, Therefore, I say unto you, Take no' thought for your life, what ye shall eat; neither for the body, what ye shall put on. The life is more than meat, and the body is *more* than raiment. Consider the ravens; for they neither sow nor reap; which neither have storehouse nor barn; and GOD feedeth them: how much more are ye better than the fowls?

25, 26 And which of you with taking thought can add to his stature one cubit? If ye then be not able to do that thing which is least, why take ye thought for the rest?

27, 28 Consider the lilies, how they grow: they toil not, they spin not; and yet I say unto you, that Solomon in all his glory was not arrayed like one of these. If then GOD so clothe the grass, which is to-day in the field, and to-morrow is cast into the oven; how much more *will He clothe* you, O ye of little faith?

29, 30, 31 And seek not ye what ye shall eat, or what ye shall drink, neither be ye of doubtful mind. For all these things do the nations of the world seek after: and your Father knoweth that ye have need of these things. But rather seek ye the Kingdom of GOD; and all these things shall be added unto you.

These ten verses are found, with slight verbal differences, in our LORD'S "Sermon on the Mount."(u) The circumstance has been already pointed out, and commented upon at some length, in the note on verse 2 of the present chapter. See particularly towards the end of the note.

As, in the Old Testament, men are sent to the ant for a lesson of wisdom,(x) so in the New are they sent to the ravens for a lesson of reliance on GOD.(y) "*Doubtful* mind," in ver. 29, means "distracted," "over-anxious."

Take notice that, in ver. 30, it is not said "GOD knoweth,"—but "*your Father* knoweth."

32 Fear not, little flock; for it is your Father's good pleasure to give you the Kingdom.

The Good Shepherd calls His flock "little,"—partly, perhaps, because though "many be called, few are chosen." Partly, because "the poor in spirit," to whom belongs "the Kingdom of Heaven,"(z) are as "little ones" in His sight.(a)

33, 34 Sell that ye have, and give alms; provide yourselves bags which wax not old, a treasure in the Heavens that faileth not, where

(s) Compare the sense of "they" in St. Matthew xiii. 48, 49, and St. Mark ix. 44, and St. Luke xvi. 9. Consider also that mysterious "he" in Deut. xxxiv. 6.
(t) Ambrose.   (u) St. Matth. vi. 25 to 33.   (x) Prov. vi. 6.
(y) Compare Job xxxviii. 41: Ps. cxlvii. 9.   (z) St. Matth. v. 2.
(a) Consider St. Matth. x. 42, and the note there. See 1 Cor. i. 26.

no thief approacheth, neither moth corrupteth.   For where your trea
sure is, there will your heart be also.

The plain and frequent Exhortations to Alms-giving in the Gospel are much t
be noted. This duty occupies a prominent position in the Sermon on the Mount.(*b*
"Go, and sell that thou hast, and give to the poor, and thou shalt have treasure i
Heaven," was what our LORD required of the rich young Ruler.(*c*)—"Bag" her
means "purse."

The two preceding verses may be usefully compared with St. Matthew vi. 19, 2(
and 21; where several remarks will be found which apply entirely to the verse
before us. It is observable that in St. Matthew's Gospel, as well as in this place
our LORD goes on to speak of "Light."—The four verses which follow are the Go
pel which is read at the Ordination of Deacons. In their actual form, they ar
peculiar to St. Luke's Gospel: but St. Matthew gives us instead the Parable of th
wise and foolish Virgins.(*d*)

85 Let your loins be girded about, and *your* lights burning ;

The loins are "girded about" for activity,—and the lamp is kept "burning," b
him who expects another's return. The mystical meaning of the passage seem
therefore to be that men should be prompt and eager in working out their ow
Salvation,—always ready to do the work of the LORD; and further that they shoul
set a bright example,—the inner life being sustained by the influence of GOD's Hol
Spirit. For consider what follows the exhortation, "Let your Light shine befor
men,"—namely, "*that they may see your good works.*"(*e*)
"But if a man has both of these, whosoever he be, nothing remains for him bu
that he should place his whole expectation on the Coming of the REDEEMER. There
fore it is added,"(*f*)

36 and ye yourselves like unto men that wait for their lord, when he
will return from the wedding; that when he cometh and knocketh, they
may open unto him immediately.

"CHRIST returns to all from the heavenly Wedding at the end of the World
when He has taken to Himself His Bride, the Church: to each individual He comes
when He stands suddenly before a man at the hour of Death."(*g*) He "knocketh,"
by pain and sickness; and those who are watching for their LORD are found to ope
the door.   "Even so, come LORD JESUS,"(*h*) say they.   And these are blessed; a
it follows,—

37 Blessed *are* those servants, whom the lord when he cometh shal
find watching: verily I say unto you, that he shall gird himself, and
make them to sit down to meat, and will come forth and serve them.

He will "gird Himself," as one who serveth. He will "make them sit down,"—
for it will be the land of Everlasting Rest.
It is written in another place,—"Behold, I stand at the door and knock: if an
man hear My voice, and open the door, I will come in to him and *will sup with him
and he with Me.*"(*i*)   Thus, both in St. Luke's Gospel and in the Book of Revela
tion the joys of the Life to come are likened to a Feast,—where those blessed one
who "hunger and thirst after Righteousness"(*k*) "shall hunger no more, neithe
thirst any more;"(*l*) but "be filled."

38 And if he shall come in the second watch, or come in the thir
watch, and find *them* so, blessed are those servants.

39, 40 And this know, that if the goodman of the house had know
what hour the thief would come, he would have watched, and not hav
suffered his house to be broken through. Be ye therefore ready also
for the Son of Man cometh at an hour when ye think not.

(*b*) St. Matth. vi. 1 to 4.   (*c*) St. Matth. xix. 21.   (*d*) St. Matth. xxv. 1 to 13.
(*e*) St. Matth. v. 16.   (*f*) Gregory.   (*g*) Theophylact.
(*h*) Rev. xxii. 20.   (*i*) Rev. iii. 20.   (*k*) St. Matth. v. 6.   (*l*) Rev. vii. 16.

"For yourselves know perfectly," writes St. Paul to the Thessalonians, "that the Day of the LORD so cometh as a thief in the night."(m) St. Peter in like manner says,—"the Day of the LORD will come as a thief in the night." This latter allusion to the present (or St. Matthew's parallel)(n) passage is of peculiar interest, since the saying recorded in ver. 41 shows that the man who made it was deeply impressed by the entire discourse to which we also are permitted here to listen.

41 Then Peter said unto Him, LORD, speakest Thou this parable unto us, or even to all?

42, 43, 44, 45, 46 And the LORD said, Who then is that faithful and wise steward, whom *his* LORD shall make ruler over His Household, to give *them their* portion of meat in due season? Blessed *is* that servant, whom his LORD when He cometh shall find so doing. Of a truth I say unto you, that He will make him ruler over all that He hath. But if that servant say in his heart, My LORD delayeth His coming; and shall begin to beat the men-servants and maidens, and to eat and drink, and to be drunken; the LORD of that servant will come in a day when he looketh not for *Him*, and at an hour when he is not aware, and will cut him in sunder, and will appoint him his portion with the unbelievers.

There is some doubt among learned men, about the meaning of "cut him asunder," here and in St. Matthew.(o) The margin suggests "cut him off,"—that is, sever or sunder him from his office. Others remark that a double or deceitful man is fairly punished if he be "cut in twain." Perhaps the true meaning is, "will terribly scourge:"— a sense which is supported by the words which follow, and which are an allusion to the law contained in Deut. xxv. 2.

47, 48 And that servant, which knew his LORD'S will, and prepared not *himself*, neither did according to His will, shall be beaten with many *stripes*. But he that knew not, and did commit things worthy of stripes, shall be beaten with few *stripes*. For unto whomsoever much is given, of him shall be much required: and to whom men have committed much, of him they will ask the more.

On a comparison of what precedes, (ver. 39 to 46.) with the place in St. Matthew's Gospel, where, on a subsequent occasion, similar words are found to have been used, (chap. xxiv. 43 to 51,) the difficulty of the passage becomes apparent. It would be safer to pass by in silence language the true force of which we seem to understand so imperfectly. But the Reader will expect a few words of comment. It seems then that St. Peter, who (with the rest of the Apostles) had been attentively drinking in every word of our LORD's discourse, on perceiving that the parabolic language of verses 35 to 38 had ceased, inquired (in ver. 41) on behalf of his fellow-Apostles, whether the warning which those verses contain had been addressed to themselves specially, or whether it was of general application? To this question, however, our LORD returns no *direct* answer. He proceeds with what He was before saying, and does not seem so much to ask in turn, as to exclaim,—How rare are the qualities required in that servant whom his lord sets as a steward over his household! Blessed is the man who proves faithful to such a trust; and miserable he who is found to abuse it!

Thus, St. Peter's question, though not formally answered, was virtually replied to: for it is manifest that what St. Paul said of himself, (with reference perhaps to this very place,) might with at least equal truth have been asserted by Simon Peter and the rest of the Twelve, of themselves: "Let a man so account of *us* as of . . . stewards of the mysteries of GOD."(p) A famous ancient Bishop remarks accordingly, that "although unwearied watchfulness is required of all men, yet does

(m) 1 Thess. v. 2.　　　　(n) St. Matth. xxiv. 43, 44.　　　　(o) St. Matth. xxiv. 51.
(p) 1 Cor. iv. 1,—and see the next verse. See also Titus i. 7. Consider further whether there is not an allusion to St. Luke xii. 42 and 48 in 1 St. Peter iv. 10.

CHRIST here enjoin upon His *Bishops* specially the expectation of His Coming: for *this* is what is meant by the faithful and wise servant set over the Household, to whom is intrusted the care of providing for the people committed to him."(q)

But, (as our LORD proceeds to show,) *all* are stewards in their degree: some indeed have been intrusted with five talents, and some with two; but *all* have received their *one* talent. It is remarkable that the Parable of "the Talents" follows in St. Matthew's Gospel,—chap. xxv. That is,—all men know *something* of their Divine Master's will,—though some know less, some more. And corresponding thereto will be the penalty incurred by the disobedient. See above, ver. 47 and 48

Such seems to be the general purport of what is here delivered. The entire discourse is remarkable, as usual, for its *practical* bearing. Simon Peter seems to ask whether the singular blessedness of the servant whom his Lord shall find watching applies to the chief Pastor alone, or to the flock at large? He is reminded in reply that unto chief Pastors *most is committed*: but he is also warned that "unto whom soever much is given, of him shall much be required: and to whom men have committed much, of him they will ask the more."(r) This seems to be the force of ver 47, 48.

In conclusion, the Reader is earnestly implored not to accept the clumsy suggestion that St. Luke is here stringing together sayings of our LORD which were delivered on different occasions, but which have no actual connection. Do not men when they say such things, "therefore err because they know not the Scriptures neither the Power of GOD?" Doubtless on this occasion, our SAVIOUR said all the He is on this occasion recorded to have said; and at the close of His Ministry when sayings very like these recur,(s) doubtless He delivered sayings very like these over again.

For take notice that when, sitting on the Mount of Olives, our SAVIOUR repeated in the audience of St. Peter, the very words which are here found from ver. 39 to ver. 46, (*with the exception of St. Peter's question in ver.* 41,—"LORD, speakest Thou this parable unto us, or even to all?") the Blessed Speaker, as if with reference to the occasion we are now considering, adds the very answer which St. Peter had once wished for, which the Apostle no longer presumed to ask,—"*And what I say unto you, I say unto all, Watch.*"(t)

There seems to be a change of subject in what follows next.

49 I am come to send fire on the earth; and what will I, if it be already kindled?

Rather,—"And what will I?" (that is, "What is My desire?") "Would that it were already kindled!". . . . It seems to be here declared that the consequence of CHRIST'S Coming into the world would be to kindle the fire of persecution,—"not Peace," (as He goes on to say,) "but Division."

Is it not singular that St. Peter, the attentive hearer of this discourse, after alluding to CHRIST'S speedy coming to Judgment,(u) and men's duty as *Stewards*,(x) —should proceed in his Epistle to speak of "*the fiery trial*" which was to try the Church?(y)

50 But I have a Baptism to be baptized with: and how am I straitened till it be accomplished!

He speaks of that Baptism *of Blood* which was in reserve for Him, and to which He also alluded when addressing the sons of Zebedee.(z) He looks forward to that tremendous hour with eagerness,—yet does the anticipation fill His human soul with distress. For the sense of "straitened," in this place, compare Phil. i. 23.

51, 52, 53 Suppose ye that I am come to give peace on earth? I tell you, Nay; but rather division: for from henceforth there shall be

---

(q) Hilary. Consider the language of the Ordination Service,—"Ye are called . . . . . to be . . . Stewards of the LORD; to teach, and to premonish, to feed and provide for the LORD's family," &c.   (r) St. Luke xii. 48.
(s) See St. Matth. xxiv. 42 to 44: St. Mark xiii. 33 to 35: St. Luke xxi. 34 to 36.
(t) St. Mark xiii. 37.   (u) Compare 1 St. Peter iv. 5 and 7 with ver. 35 to 40, above
(x) Compare 1 St. Peter iv. 10, with ver. 42 and 48, above.
(y) Compare 1 St. Pet. iv. 12 with ver. 49 to 53, above. See also 1 Pet. i. 7.
(z) St. Matth. xx. 22, 23: St. Mark x. 38, 39, where see the notes.

five in one house divided, three against two, and two against three.
The father shall be divided against the son, and the son against the
father; the mother against the daughter, and the daughter against the
mother; the mother-in-law against her daughter-in-law, and the daughter-in-law against her mother-in-law.

See above, on ver. 49; and compare this place with St. Matth. x. 33 to 36,—
where the note should be consulted. The prophet Micah, who is there actually
quoted, is here very clearly referred to.(a) It has been ingeniously pointed out(b)
that only *five* persons are mentioned in ver. 53,—since the "mother" and the
"mother-in-law" are one and the same person.
The Blessed Speaker is found next to turn His Discourse to the people.

54, 55, 56 And He said also to the people, When ye see a cloud rise
out of the west, straightway ye say, There cometh a shower; and so it
is. And when *ye see* the south wind blow, ye say, There will be heat;
and it cometh to pass. *Ye* hypocrites, ye can discern the face of the
sky and of the earth; but how *is* it that ye do not discern this Time?

He reminds them of the skill and shrewdness with which they were enabled to
foretell natural phenomena:(c) and declares that it required no greater discernment
to recognize His Advent, which the Prophets by so many signs had foretold. He
said the same thing to the Pharisees and Sadducees, when they came desiring of
Him "a sign from Heaven."(d) But, (as He declared on another occasion,) "the
children of this World are in their generation wiser than the children of Light."(e)
He proceeds to show them that they might learn wisdom in so vital a matter even
from the prudence with which they conducted themselves in the concerns of daily
life:—

57 Yea, and why even of yourselves judge ye not what is right?

That is, "what is right to be done,"—"the right thing to do." A saying follows
which we have already met with at the end of the Sermon on the Mount:(f) and
which was there introduced in order to enforce the duty of speedy reconciliation
with one's neighbour. Here, the injunction is clearly of a different tendency; and
the remark which was offered above, on verse 2; again presents itself. In the
original, what follows is connected with what went before.

58, 59 When thou goest with thine adversary to the magistrate, *as
thou art* in the way, give diligence that thou mayest be delivered from
him; lest he hale thee to the judge, and the judge deliver thee to the
officer, and the officer cast thee into prison. I tell thee, thou shalt not
depart thence, till thou hast paid the very last mite.

Our SAVIOUR seems to say,—in a merely temporal manner, you are careful to
act thus prudently. While the Day of Mercy yet lasts, should you not discover
the like anxiety to avail yourselves of it? through Me, to obtain deliverance from
the wrath of GOD, before it be too late?

(a) Micah vii. 6.   (b) By Ambrose.
(c) Compare St. Matth. xvi. 2, 3: xxiv. 32: St. John iv. 34.
(d) See St. Matth. xvi. 1 to 3, and the last part of the note on the latter verse.
(e) St. Luke xvi. 8.   (f) See St. Matth. v. 25, 26, and the note.
                                34

CHAPTER XIII.

1 CHRIST *preacheth repentance upon the punishment of the Galilæans, and othe*
6 *The fruitless fig-tree may not stand.* 11 *He healeth the crooked woman.*
Showeth the powerful working of the Word in the hearts of His chosen, by t
parable of the grain of Mustard-seed, and of Leaven. 24 *Exhorteth to enter in*
the strait gate. 31 *And reproveth Herod and Jerusalem.*

1 THERE were present at that season some that told Him of th
Galilæans, whose blood Pilate had mingled with their sacrifices.

Where our Blessed LORD was, when these tidings were brought to Him, does n
appear: neither is the event known to which allusion is here made. But it accor
very well with what we' elsewhere read of the merciless disposition of Pilate, th
he should have butchered certain Galilæans, (whether followers of Judas of Ga
lee,(a) or not,) while they were in the very act of doing sacrifice at Jerusalem;
that the hideous spectacle was presented of human blood mingling with that
"bulls and goats," and polluting the Holy Place.

Our SAVIOUR's reply to the persons who brought Him this report, discloses wh
was the secret thought of their hearts. They had put their own interpretation
the occurrence, and made up their minds that it was GOD's just punishment i
Sin.(b)

2, 3 And JESUS answering said unto them, Suppose ye that thes
Galilæans were sinners above all the Galilæans, because they suffere
such things? I tell you, Nay: but, except ye repent, ye shall all lik
wise perish.

Our SAVIOUR does not say that the calamity which had overtaken these Galilæa
was *not* a punishment for Sin. He "contests not about *that;* but rather seems
agree to them so far, and draws that warning out of it. He only corrects the mi
conceit it seems they were in, in thrusting it too far off from themselves, and thro
ing it too heavy upon them that sacrificed."(c) Doubtless, the connection betwe
Sin and Suffering is of the closest kind; but it is not in Man's power to trace th
connection in every particular instance: nor can he scarcely ever pretend to do
without presumption. Our LORD proceeds,—

4 Or those eighteen, upon whom the tower in Siloam fell, and sle
them, think ye that they were sinners above all men that dwelt i
Jerusalem?

Rather, "*debtors* above all men,"—for the word is not the same as in verse
The expression is a remarkable one, implying that men are *debtors* to fulfil Go
Law. The word seems to have been used with reference to the two concludi
verses of the foregoing chapter.(d)

(a) See Acts v. 37.—The massacre here recorded may also have been either the cause or
consequence of the quarrel recorded in St. Luke xxiii. 12.
(b) Consider St. John ix. 1 to 3: also Acts xxviii. 4.   (c) Leighton.
(d) See St. Luke xii. 58, 59. Consider also the following places,—St. Matth. vi. 12: xv
23, 24. St. Luke vii. 21.

5 I tell you, Nay: but, except ye repent, ye shall all likewise perish.

The people whom our SAVIOUR was addressing had described to Him a calamity where *Man* was the immediate agent. He reminds them of another fatal event of recent occurrence, which they would have called *an accident*—namely, the unexpected falling of a tower in Jerusalem, (somewhere near the Pool of Siloam, (a) probably,) whereby eighteen lives were lost. "Shall there be evil in the city," asks the Prophet, "and the LORD hath not done it?"(b) Both events, alike, had proceeded from GOD. He asks them therefore if they supposed that *this* also was a proof of greater wickedness in those eighteen "above all men that dwelt in Jerusalem?" "I tell you, Nay;" He repeats. And thereby He reproves as many of ourselves as are guilty of hasty judgments concerning our neighbours, and rashly presume to interpret the misfortunes which befall others.

Leighton well says—"Be it a judgment: be the persons great sinners in a sinful course: yet they are not always the greatest of all because they suffer, and others escape. GOD is to be adored, who useth His own freedom in *this*—He does injustice to none, yet chooses them whom He will make examples of His justice, and whom He will let pass; and gives not account of this to any. Some, less wicked, have been made examples to them who were much more wicked than they. . . . Why am not *I* made an example to others, as well as so many have been made examples to me? Now, let me fall down at His feet, and beg of Him that as He hath not made me an example of justice all this while, He may now make me an example of mercy and free grace to all that shall look on me."

And in this beautiful spirit, doubtless, Holy Scripture should always be read,— namely, as having a direct *personal* teaching: thus shall we escape the censure which our LORD in this very place bestows on the disposition which prefers barren speculation about Divine things to the living practice of them.(c) And yet the historical and national bearing of our SAVIOUR's words, in this and the 5th verse, is very striking. Except the Jews repented, He here prophesies to them that they should all perish,—(not "*likewise*," in the common sense of the word, but,)—"*in like manner*." And so it signally came to pass; for Josephus relates that, at the destruction of Jerusalem, multitudes of the inhabitants were crushed beneath its ruins; while numbers were slain in the very act of sacrificing within the Temple.

"Except ye repent, ye shall all likewise perish." *Repentance* then, was the end of the preaching of the Great Shepherd and Bishop of Souls:(d) and on this text, doubtless, should we ever preach not only to others, but to ourselves. For, as pious Leighton reminds us, "the far more dismal perishing of unrepenting sinners, is *that* death which lies unseen on the other side of the death which we see and are so afraid to look on. Oh, saw we the other, this would appear nothing: *that* would be the only terrible thing. And how terrible soever, it is the unfailing attendant on impenitence. These, GOD hath linked together; and no creature can sever them,—continuance in sin, and perishing; Repentance and Life. It is Faith indeed that lays hold on our pardon, and life in CHRIST, and by that we are justified and saved; yet, so as this is still true, that there is no *Life* without *Repentance*."

The connection of the parable which follows with what goes before, is of the closest kind. "All" should perish like those Galilæans, and like these eighteen, except they repented. To what then were they indebted for their actual preservation? To nothing but the long-suffering patience of ALMIGHTY GOD. This is accordingly set forth in the parable of "the barren fig-tree;" which enforces the same doctrine of Repentance, upon the motive of GOD's Forbearance.

6 He spake also this parable; A certain *man* had a fig-tree planted in his vineyard; and he came and sought fruit thereon, and found none.

Elsewhere, "the Vineyard of the LORD of Hosts is the House of Israel;"(e) but it is not so here. Among the nations of the earth, (the "Vineyard" here spoken of,) ALMIGHTY GOD, (the "certain man" in the parable,) had the Jewish people, for "His pleasant plant,"—or, as it is here said, His "fig-tree." The fruit of good

---

(a) Nehem. iii. 15.　St. John ix. 7, 11.　Compare Isa. viii. 6.　　　(b) Amos iii. 6.
(c) The Reader is referred to the note on St. Luke xiii. 23.
(d) Consider the following places: St. Matth. iv. 17: ix. 13.　St. Mark i. 15.　(e) Isa. v. 7.

works, He had come seeking thereon, for many years, in vain.(a) He had found
none. Whereupon, He requires of "the Dresser of His Vineyard," that this
unprofitable tree be at once removed. As it follows:

**7 Then said he unto the dresser of his vineyard, Behold, these three
years I come seeking fruit on this fig-tree, and find none: cut it down;
why cumbereth it the ground?**

Rather, "Why doth it *even*,"—"Why doth it *so much as* cumber the ground?"
But, in the original, something more than "cumber" is implied. Gregory the
Great brings out the meaning very well when he remarks that wherever the un-
fruitful man is placed, "he there denies to another the opportunity of working."
What is even better worth our notice,—We have here set before us a picture of
God's merciful manner of dealing with His creatures. For three years had the
owner of this Vineyard come seeking fruit of a barren tree which grew within it.
"The axe is laid to the root of the tree,"(b) in warning, before the fatal blow is
suffered to fall. For, (as an ancient writer remarks,) God does not bring punishment silently or secretly ; but, by His threatenings, first proclaims them to be at
hand,—thus inviting the sinner to repentance.(c) "Let us not then strike sud
denly," (says another,) "but overcome by gentleness ; lest we cut down the fig-tree
still able to bear fruit, which the care of a skilful dresser will perhaps restore."(d)
Next, the Intercession of the Eternal Son is set before us,—pleading with the
Father in behalf of the sinful race. Not, however, (be it observed,) in order that
they may be spared in their barrenness, does He plead : but that time may be
allowed them wherein to become fruitful.

**8, 9 And he answering said unto him, LORD, let it alone this year
also, till I shall dig about it, and dung *it* : and if it bear fruit, *well* :
and if not, *then* after that thou shalt cut it down.**

And this is the end of the Parable. Every means and appliance was to be used;
—the loosening of the soil in which the tree grew,—and a supply of that which is
found to be most congenial to the life of plants, and has the effect of rendering
them productive. God is found to have thus dealt with His people,—God thus
deals now with us. He offers large measures of His Grace,—He multiplies opportunities. What is all the remainder of the Gospel, from this place onward, but the
History of One who had said in behalf of the Jewish nation,—"LORD, let it alone
this year also, till I shall dig about it, and dung it?" The object of His preaching,
His parables, and His miracles, was to break the stubborn soil ;—His precious
blood-shedding was intended to bring forth a plenteous Harvest.
This then, is at once a Prophecy and a Parable,—a Prophecy which found *typical*
fulfilment in the cursing of the barren fig-tree ;(e) *actual* fulfilment in the destruc-
tion of Jerusalem, and final overthrow of the Jewish-nation.
The simplest and most obvious interpretation of the Parable seems the best.
Since for three years God came seeking fruit of His chosen people, and found none,
—it is reasonable to take the "three years" of the parable *literally:* especially
since the third year of our LORD's Ministry had also just come to a close. "The
Dresser of His Vineyard," who pleads for prolonged patience and mercy, (saying,
"Let it alone this year also!") as already observed, is CHRIST Himself,—who was
cut off. in the midst of the fourth year of His Ministry.
But the Parable has clearly a personal application,(f) as well as a national one.
Year after year, to lead an unprofitable life ; to resist God's visitations "in boy-
hood, in manhood, in old age,"(g)—putting forth much leafy promise, but producing no fruit,—what is this but to stand like a barren fig-tree in the LORD's Vine
yard? such a one does more than "cumber the ground." His presence does
actual mischief. In the mean time, He who "ever liveth to make intercession,"(h)
is still the merciful Advocate, who pleads for one more year of grace ; and during
that year spares no pains to make the man fruitful. The parallel here in the case

(a) Consider Isa. v. 1 to 4 : and the notes on St. Matth. vii. 16, &c.
(b) St. Matth. iii. 10,—where see the note.
(c) Pseudo-Basil. Consider Gen. vi. 3 : xviii. 24, &c.   (d) Gregory of Nazianzum.
(e) St. Matth. xxi. 18, 19, or St. Mark xi. 12 to 14, 20, 21.
(f) Consider St. Matth. iii. 10.   (g) Theophylact.   (h) Heb. vii. 25.

of individuals is obvious. Pharaoh, Balaam, Saul, Herod, Judas,—no less than the Old World, Sodom, Nineveh, Jerusalem,—every individual, however obdurate, has his warnings, and his prolonged season of probation; during which, the alternative is still admitted as possible,—"*If* he bear fruit," . . for the door of repentance is left open to all.

10 And He was teaching in one of the synagogues on the Sabbath.

Consider the places referred to at foot.(*s*)

11 And, behold, there was a woman which had a spirit of infirmity eighteen years, and was bowed together, and could in no wise lift up *herself*.

She therefore aptly represented the condition of those who have become so bowed down by sin or sorrow that they look not up to Heaven, but fix all their grovelling regards on Earth. St. Luke says that she "had a spirit of infirmity." What this means we should not have known but for our LORD's express statement that she was one whom *Satan had bound*.

12, 13 And when JESUS saw her, He called *her to Him*, and said unto her, Woman, thou art loosed from thine infirmity. And He laid *His* hands upon her: and immediately she was made straight, and glorified GOD.

This then seems to have been one of those miracles of healing which were wrought without solicitation. But the very presence of such a sufferer, in the Synagogue, was a prayer. It may even be suspected, from the words of the Ruler which follow, that this afflicted creature had "come" purposely "to be healed."

Our SAVIOUR seems to have proclaimed her release from captivity, first; and then to have removed the physical consequence of the chain by which she had been so long held. It does not appear that He spoke, and laid His Divine hands upon her, at one and the same time.

14 And the Ruler of the synagogue answered with indignation, because that JESUS had healed on the Sabbath day; and said unto the people, There are six days in which men ought to work: in them therefore come and be healed, and not on the Sabbath day.

He addresses *the people*,—not *CHRIST*. Hypocrite as he was, the Ruler did not dare to look the Holy One in the face while he brought forward a complaint which, though spoken to *them*, was evidently levelled against *Him*. "He preferred that this woman should, like a beast, look upon the earth, rather than that CHRIST should be magnified."(*t*)

15, 16 The LORD then answered him, and said, *Thou* hypocrite, doth not each one of you on the Sabbath loose his ox or *his* ass from the stall, and lead *him* away to watering? and ought not this woman, being a daughter of Abraham, whom Satan hath bound, lo, these eighteen years, be loosed from this bond on the Sabbath day?

Our SAVIOUR, though hitherto carefully shunned by the other, begins by addressing *him*. But after one withering word, He turns to the people, and makes them the umpires between Himself and the Ruler of the Synagogue. Every word of His Discourse is here emphatic. If any of *you* (He says) are at liberty on the Sabbath day to loose certain of the brute creation, as an ox or ass which yourselves had bound, and to lead these away to watering, an act requiring time and trouble, —ought not this *woman*, being not only a creature made in the image of GOD, but also one who enjoys that proudest of titles, "*a daughter of Abraham*,"(*u*)—ought not *she*, who has been bound by *the Enemy of Man*, not for a few hours only, but

(*s*) St. Luke iv. 16. St. Matth. iv. 23: xiii. 54. St. Mark i. 21. St. John vi. 59: iii. 20, &c.
(*t*) Cyril.   (*u*) St. Matth. iii. 9: St. Luke xix. 9: St. John viii. 33, 39: Acts xiii. 26.

for *eighteen years,*—ought not *she* to enjoy the benefit of release which had been effected by a word from these Lips, and a touch of these Hands, in a moment of time?

Observe how plainly it is here stated that this woman's infirmity was the work *of Satan,*—who kept her bound, as a prisoner. The same thing is implied of diseases generally, in many other places,—as in St. Matthew x. 1, Acts x. 38, 2 Cor xii. 7, 1 St. John iii. 8: and it may be worth pointing out that the words translated "recovery of sight to the blind," (in St. Luke iv. 18,) are, in the Hebrew, "opening the prison *to them that are bound.*"(x) Take notice that our SAVIOUR had "first *bound the strong man;*" and now was He "spoiling his house."(y)

17 And when He had said these things, all His adversaries were ashamed : and all the people rejoiced for all the glorious things that were done by Him.

From which it is found that the Ruler of the Synagogue had not been alone in his wickedness; but, (like Judas Iscariot, when he complained of the waste of the precious ointment,)(z) had carried others along with him, in his hypocrisy.

The foregoing miracle should be compared with that performed on the withered hand, in St. Matthew xii. 9 to 13,—as well as with that on the dropsy, in St. Luke xiv. 2 to 6.   All three miracles were wrought on the Sabbath day; but in this instance, and that which St. Matthew records, the cure was effected in the Synagogue itself.

Our LORD proceeds to show "the powerful working of the Word in the hearts of His chosen, by the Parable of the Grain of Mustard Seed, and of Leaven."(a)

18, 19 Then said He, Unto what is the Kingdom of GOD like ? and whereunto shall I resemble it ?   It is like a grain of mustard seed, which a man took, and cast into his garden; and it grew, and waxed a great tree ? and the fowls of the air lodged in the branches of it.

This parable recurs in the Gospels of St. Matthew and St. Mark,—where it has been already so fully considered in the notes, that it shall suffice on the present occasion to refer the Reader thither.(b)   But it is worthy of remark that the grain of mustard seed which, according to St. Matthew, "a Man took and sowed in His field," the same Man *here* is said to have cast into "His *Garden:*" for who can fail to call to mind that of CHRIST Himself it is recorded that "in the place where He was crucified there was a Garden, and in the Garden a new Sepulchre:" and that "*there laid they JESUS?*"(c)   Was not *this* the true germ of that Kingdom which from a very small beginning, has become so supremely great?   "Except a corn of wheat fall into the ground and die," said He of Himself, "it abideth alone: but if it die, it bringeth forth much fruit."(d)   There is nothing new in this remark Gregory the Great made it almost 1300 years ago; and Ambrose 200 years before him.

20, 21 And again He said, Whereunto shall I liken the Kingdom of GOD?   It is like leaven, which a woman took and hid in three measures of meal, till the whole was leavened.

A parable which is also a prophecy!   It is here foretold that, in the end, the Religion of CHRIST shall prevail over all obstacles; imparting to all society its own ennobling nature, and conforming whatever it encounters, to itself.—And what is true of nations, is here true of individuals also.   "The Gospel," says Hammond "has such a secret invisible influence on the hearts of men,—to change them and affect them, and all the actions that flow from them,—that it is fitly resembled to Leaven; so mixed thoroughly with the whole, that although it appeareth not in any part visibly, yet every part hath a tincture from it."

The discovery is surely a very interesting one, that these two Parables, here re

(x) Isaiah lxi. 2.   (y) St. Matth. xii. 29.   Consider Isaiah xlix. 24 to 26.
(z) St. John xii. 3 to 6.   Compared with St. Matth. xxvi. 8, &c.
(a) See the heading of the Chapter.
(b) See St. Matthew xiii. 31 to 32, and St. Mark iv. 30 to 32.
(c) St. John xix. 41, 42.   (d) St. John xii. 24.   Consider 1 Cor. xv. 35 to 44.

corded together, were delivered by our Blessed LORD in the same order, and almost in the same words, more than a year before, to the multitudes assembled on the shore of the Sea of Galilee. For the knowledge of this fact, we are indebted to the first of the four Gospels. The present Parable has been already met with in St. Matthew xiii. 33,—whither the Reader is referred for several remarks upon it.

22, 23 And He went through the cities and villages, teaching, and journeying towards Jerusalem. Then said one unto Him, Lord, are there few that be saved?

Who may this "one" have been? Was it one of the Apostles? And what led him to ask the question? Did it grow naturally out of some unrecorded discourse which our LORD had been delivering? It is impossible to offer more than a conjecture in reply to these inquiries. But it is reasonable to suspect that it was one of the Twelve,—such an one as St. Peter; for observe, our LORD was on a journey; and the question having been put by *one*, the answer is made to *several*.

On one occasion our SAVIOUR had said, "Many are called, but few are chosen:"(e) and on another,—"Few there be that find" the strait gate and narrow way "that leadeth unto Life."(f) But He says not so on the present occasion:—

24 And He said unto them, Strive to enter in at the strait gate:

Consider on how many occasions our SAVIOUR answered in this manner, questions of the kind here recorded,—if *that* may be called answering, which does not give the information desired, and which is not addressed to the person who asked the question. Inquiries purely speculative, and which are simply the growth of carnal curiosity, are always discouraged: and the attention is guided instead to the *practice* of piety and virtue.(g)

Our LORD here uses a stronger word than "strive." "*Agonize*," He says,(h)—a term indicative of the greatness of the effort, (more literally, of *the struggle*,) required. Blessed be GOD, however, that this very expression, denoting the earnestness required in those who would obtain an entrance into Life, shows also that Salvation is within the reach of *all*. . . . . "The strait gate" recalls the solemn doctrine concerning the avenues of Life and Destruction, respectively, which are discoursed of in the Sermon on the Mount.(i)

It is piously remarked by Leighton,—"What bustle is there made, by sea and land, for scraps of this earth; and Heaven alone is so cheap in our eyes, as if it were worth no diligence, scarce even a serious thought! Surely, either Heaven is but a fancy, or the world is mad." . . . . For this, then, men must toil,—

for many, I say unto you, will seek to enter in, and shall not be able.

Take notice that their "seeking" will be like that of the foolish Virgins,—of the Rich man in torments,—of Esau, when it was too late, "earnestly seeking" that blessing(k) which he had before, by his own deliberate act, forfeited.

25, 26, 27 When once the Master of the House is risen up, and hath shut to the door, and ye begin to stand without, and to knock at the door, saying, LORD, LORD, open unto us; and He shall answer and say unto you, I know you not whence ye are: then shall ye begin to say, We have eaten and drunk in Thy presence, and Thou hast taught in our streets. But He shall say, I tell you, I know you not whence ye are; depart from Me, all ye workers of iniquity.

This is a terrible prophecy, truly; and its most alarming feature seems to be the hint conveyed of the *self-delusion* in which some men will be found to have lived— and died.(l) Not only will they plead passionately for admission into that blissful

---

(e) St. Matth. xxii. 14.　　　　　　　　　　　(f) St. Matth. vii. 14.
(g) See the latter part of the note on St. Matth. vii. 5.　See also St. Luke x. 29, 36: xii. 42: Acts i. 7, &c.　　　　　　　　(h) St. Paul uses the same word,—Col. i. 29.
(i) St. Matth. vii. 13, 14,—where see the notes.　Consider St. John x. 9.
(k) Hebrews xii. 17.　Observe, it was "*the blessing*" which he "sought,"—not "place of repentance."　　　　　　　　(l) See the latter part of the note on St. Matth. vii. 23.

abode whither the Saints will have already entered,(m) but they will remonstrat
with "the Master of the House," and remind Him of all their past privileges,—
forgetting that these have but increased the measure of their guilt!

"We have eaten and drunk in Thy presence," they will say,—("as the Israelite
who partook of the sacrifices; or, as they with whom CHRIST lived; or, as they wh
are admitted to His Sacraments: for in all these cases is *that* fulfilled which wa
declared of the Seventy Elders,—namely, that ' they saw GOD, and did eat an
drink;'")(n) but they will be reminded that "he that eateth and drinketh unwo
thily, eateth and drinketh damnation to himself."(o) . . . . "Thou hast taught i
our streets," they will say: but they will be reminded that "not *the hearers* of th
law are just before GOD, but *the doers* of the law shall be justified."(p)   As it
written,—"Be ye doers of the Word, and not hearers only, deceiving your ow
selves."(q) . . . . No splendour of outward advantages,—neither the daily walk i
GOD'S House, nor Sacraments received, nor Sermons listened to,—will be of an
avail in and by themselves.

Take notice that, in contrast with the scene here described,—(the "door" hop
lessly closed,—"the Master of the House" deaf to entreaty,)—concerning our pr
sent Day of Grace it is more than once said,—"knock, and *it shall be opened* un
you." Nay more,—CHRIST saith of Himself, "behold *I* stand at the door an
knock. If any man hear My voice, and open the door, I will come in to him."(r
He now invites us freely to receive Himself,—who will then refuse to receive us.

On those solemn words of denial,—"*I know ye not* whence ye are," see the not
on St. Matth. xxv. 12.   The resemblance of the entire passage to two verses i
"the Sermon on the Mount,"(s) is very striking. Scarcely less remarkable are th
points of difference. *There*, the warning seemed chiefly addressed to the teacher
of religion,—*here*, to the taught.

28, 29 There shall be weeping and gnashing of teeth, when ye shal
see Abraham, and Isaac, and Jacob, and all the prophets, in the King
dom of GOD, and you *yourselves* thrust out. And they shall come from
the East, and *from* the West, and from the North, and *from* the South
and shall sit down in the Kingdom of GOD.

These remarkable expressions should be compared with the language which ou
LORD is found to have used after the healing of the Centurion's servant, in St. Mat
thew viii. 11, 12,—where the notes may be referred to.(t) The admission of th
Gentiles to the Kingdom is hereby clearly foretold. Observe the mysterious hin
here conveyed that it will be an aggravation of the misery of those whom Go
finally rejects, *to behold* others in the enjoyment of the bliss from which they wil
be themselves excluded.(u) And notice, by the way, the Love which declares, (i
verse 28 and elsewhere,) the acceptance of *many;* but has nowhere set on recor
the final rejection of more than *one.*(x)

30 And, behold, there are last which shall be first, and there ar
first which shall be last.

This saying, which occurs three times in the Gospel, has been already made th
subject of remark in a long note on St. Matthew xix. 30,—to which the Reader i
referred.

31 The same day there came certain of the Pharisees, saying unt
Him, Get Thee out, and depart hence: for Herod will kill Thee.

Rather, "*wishes,*" "*desires* to kill Thee." This must have happened somewher
in Galilee, or in the district east of the Jordan, called Peræa, for Herod's dominio
extended no farther. That there were many of the sect of the Pharisees in th
region, we know from chap. v. 17.

It has been thought that the crafty king, ("that fox," as our LORD styles him i

(m) Consider St. Matth. xxv. 10.   (n) Williams, quoting Exod. xxiv. 11.
(o) 1 Cor. xi. 29.   (p) Rom. ii. 13.   (q) St. James i. 22.   (r) Rev. iii. 2
(s) St. Matth. vii. 22, 23.   Consider also ver. 21.
(t) See also the notes on St. Luke xiv. 15.   (u) Compare St. Luke xvi. 2
(x) St. Matth. xxvi. 24.

the next verse,) himself sent these messengers to our SAVIOUR in order to induce Him to withdraw from a neighbourhood where His presence must perforce have been a source of disquiet to the man who had murdered the Baptist, and who was now living in open adultery with his brother's wife.　For this purpose, though himself a Sadducee,(y) Herod is thought to have availed himself of the services of some of the opposite sect, in order to convey to our LORD a feigned tale of the danger that awaited Him, if He remained where He was.

But others have supposed, with perhaps more of reason, that the whole was a mere device of the Pharisees to procure our LORD's prompt withdrawal towards Jerusalem,—where snares were laid against His Life;(z) and that when He said in reply, "Tell *this* fox,"(a) he aimed his message, in reality, as much at the crafty speaker, as at the King.

32 And He said unto them, Go ye, and tell that fox, Behold, I cast out devils, and I do cures to-day and to-morrow, and the third *day* I shall be perfected.

There is some difficulty here: but perhaps the obvious sense of the passage, as it stands in our translation, is the true one.　Our LORD gives His pretended friends to understand that the duration of His Ministry is fixed, and settled,—and that the season of His Death, in like manner, is determined in GOD's deep counsels; not to be hastened or delayed by any act on the part either of Herod or of themselves. The period of His Ministry is noticed, after the Hebrew method,—as for "to-day and to-morrow:"(b) on "the third day," He will " be perfected,"—that is, will finish His course,(c) and fulfil His work,(d) and receive His complete reward. *Three* days are thus specified,—perhaps in order to intimate a definite predetermined period.　"But our LORD's answer is doubtless for our instruction under similar circumstances; teaching us that times and seasons are with GOD.　It is ours to do our duty, and leave the event with Him."(e)　He proceeds,—

33 Nevertheless I must walk to-day, and to-morrow, and the *day* following: for it cannot be that a prophet perish out of Jerusalem.

That is, "'Nevertheless I must indeed *depart home*,' as ye counsel Me, while the time appointed for My Ministry—['to-day, and to-morrow, and the day following'—] continues, and go on My way to Jerusalem; for that City is the place where the prophets of GOD must perish.'　The word here translated 'walk,' is the same with that translated 'depart,' in verse 31."(f)　Away from Jerusalem, (our SAVIOUR says,) is no danger.　*There* is the seat of iniquity.　All type and prophecy requires that I, the great Prophet, should suffer where all my goodly fellowship of Prophets have suffered before Me.(g) . . . . The pathetic lamentation which follows, grows naturally out of our LORD's recent mention of the City.

34, 35 O Jerusalem, Jerusalem, which killest the prophets, and stonest them that are sent unto thee; how often would I have gathered thy children together, as a hen *doth gather* her brood under *her* wings, and ye would not!　Behold, your house is left unto you desolate: and verily I say unto you, Ye shall not see Me, until *the time* come when ye shall say, Blessed *is* He that cometh in the Name of the LORD.

The self-same words are heard from our LORD's lips on a quite different occasion, —namely, some months later, when He was crossing the threshold of the Temple, and leaving it for the last time.　He repeats the name of the city *twice*, to denote earnestness and affection.(h)　So much has been already offered concerning this affecting address, that it shall suffice to refer the Reader to the notes on St. Matthew xxiii. 37 to 39.　It has been thought indeed, by some of the very greatest writers,

(y) See the note on St. Mark viii. 19.　　(z) St. John vii. 25.　　(a) So in the original.
(b) Compare Hos. vi. 2.　Lonsdale and Hale supply the following valuable references to the margin of the Bible:—Gen. xxxi. 2.　Exod. iv. 10.　Deut. xix. 6.　Josh. iii. 4.　1 Sam. xix. 7.　1 Chron. xi. 2.　　(c) Compare Phil. iii. 12.　Also Acts xx. 24.
(d) See St. John iv. 34: v. 36: xvii. 4.　　　　　　　　(e) Williams.
(f) Bp. Lonsdale and Archd. Hale.　　　　　　(g) Consider St. Luke ix. 51.
(h) So Chrysostom.　Consider St. Luke x. 41, and the note there.

ancient as well as modern, that our LORD so spoke on only one occasion; and that St. Luke here introduces the address out of its proper place. Surely, an improbable, not to say a monstrous, supposition!

THE PRAYER.

O GOD, whose never-failing providence ordereth all things both in heaven and earth; We humbly beseech Thee to put away from us all hurtful things, and to give us those things which be profitable for us; through JESUS CHRIST our LORD. Amen.

CHAPTER XIV.

2 CHRIST *healeth the dropsy on the Sabbath.* 7 *Teacheth humility.* 12 *To feast the poor.* 15 *Under the parable of the Great Supper, showeth how worldly-minded men, who contemn the Word of* GOD, *shall be shut out of Heaven.* 25 *Those who will be His Disciples, to bear their cross must make their accounts aforehand, lest with shame they revolt from Him afterward,* 34 *and become altogether unprofitable, like salt that hath lost his savour.*

IT will be perceived that in this part of the Gospel the hostility of the Pharisees comes prominently before us. Their crafty address was noticed at the close of chap. xiii.: (*a*) Pharisees are found hanging about our SAVIOUR's footsteps in the next chapter: (*b*) and they are found to be still among His hearers, when He delivers the parable of "the Unjust Steward," in chap. xvi. (*c*) Here, a Pharisee of note, (he seems to have been "a Ruler,") invites the Holy One to a Feast, (*d*)—and many of the same hostile sect are present. (*e*) All this should be noticed, for a reason which will be found suggested below, in the note on ver. 7. We are reminded of those other occasions when our LORD was entertained by a Pharisee, (*f*) and when the motive on the part of the host was anything but a desire to show hospitality. What, therefore, but words of reproof are to be expected from the lips of our great Example?

1, 2 AND it came to pass, as He went into the house of one of the chief Pharisees to eat bread on the Sabbath day, that they watched Him. And, behold, there was a certain man before Him which had the dropsy.

(*a*) See St. Luke xiii. 31.   (*b*) See St. Luke xv. 2.   (*c*) See St. Luke xvi. 14.
(*d*) See ver. 12, below.   (*e*) See ver. 3, below.
(*f*) See St. Luke vii. 36, 39: -i. 37, and all that follows.

That is, "the Lawyers and Pharisees"—(mentioned in ver. 3)—"watched Him," as they are related to have done on a former occasion,(g) to see whether He would heal this person on the Sabbath day. Indeed, our Blessed LORD, on more than one occasion, had made choice of the Sabbath for performing His works of Mercy:(h) and this was done in order to show the true meaning of the Divine Institution, and to teach men that certain works are a fulfilment, not a violation, of the Law. From works of Love, GOD never rests; but "worketh hitherto," as our SAVIOUR Himself declares.(i) The miracle which follows seems to have happened the instant He entered "the House of one of the chief Pharisees:" for we saw in ver. 1, that "it came to pass as He went into the House." It is reasonable to believe that the dropsical man spoken of as standing "before" CHRIST, had so stationed himself in faith.(k) But the supposition is no less probable that it was the result of malicious contrivance on the part of our LORD's hypocritical entertainer, or some of his guests, that one so urgently in need of the Great Physician's help was present on this occasion at all.—Let it be remembered that Dropsy was one of the diseases accounted incurable.

3 And JESUS answering spake unto the lawyers and Pharisees, saying, Is it lawful to heal on the Sabbath day?

He answered to their wicked thoughts,—as on so many other occasions.(l) Once before, in the synagogue, when "there was a man" present "which had his hand withered," "they" had "asked Him, saying, Is it lawful to heal on the Sabbath days? that they might accuse him."(m) The same question they now hear addressed to themselves.

4 And they held their peace. And He took him, and healed him, and let him go;

"Took hold of him," rather: that is to say, CHRIST laid His Almighty hands upon the afflicted man, and so healed him,—"letting him go," or rather "dismissing him," afterwards; by which expression, it is implied that He took leave of the man with a solemn form of blessing.—Our attention is called from the object of CHRIST's mercy to the Pharisees whom He had just put to silence:

5 and answered them, saying, Which of you shall have an ass or an ox fallen into a pit, and will not straightway pull him out on the Sabbath day?

Again He "answers them," although they have "held their peace." That is because their minds were full of fierce rebellious thoughts; and thoughts are words in the ears of Him with whom we have to do.(n)

It is impossible to forget that, in the former chapter, we met with an instance very closely resembling the present,—(the healing, namely, of "the crooked woman,")(o) —as well in respect of the general course of the narrative, as of the reasoning whereby our LORD defended His gracious act. On both occasions, a severe bodily ailment was remedied, and both cures were wrought upon a Sunday. Ox and ass, on both occasions, supplied the Divine Speaker with an argument; and on both occasions His enemies were confounded and put to silence. The form of argument is moreover the same,—contrasting the worth of the creatures; the severity of their respective misfortunes; and the amount of labour involved by the effort to relieve them. But the most striking parallel is supplied by the cure of the withered hand in the synagogue, to which allusion has already been made; for there our LORD

(g) St. Luke vi. 8.   See also the note on St. Mark iii. 2.
(h) Thus, in St. Mark i. 21 to 26, we have the casting out of an unclean spirit:—in St. Matth. xii. 9 to 13, compared with St. Luke vi. 6 to 11, the healing of the withered hand:—in St. Luke xiii. 10 to 17, the woman with a spirit of infirmity; and all these occurred in the synagogue itself. The gift of sight to the man born blind, (St. John ix. 14,) and the present miracle performed on one who had the dropsy, also took place on the Sabbath.
(i) St. John v. 17.   (k) Compare what was said on chap. xiii. 13.
(l) For example, St. Luke vi. 8.   (m) St. Matth. xii. 10.
(n) The ancient Prayer at the beginning of our Communion Service runs very strikingly in the original :—" unto whom all hearts be open, all desires speak."
(o) See the heading of chap. xiii.

reasoned exactly as here, in the Pharisee's house;—"What man shall there be among you, that shall have one sheep, and if it fall into a pit on the Sabbath day, will he not lay hold on it, and lift it out? How much then is a man better than a sheep! Wherefore it is lawful for a man to do well on the Sabbath day."(*p*)

6 And they could not answer Him again to these things.

The remark may be worth the making that the recorded discourses of our LORD often meet with the issue here described: that is, they have the effect of putting His enemies to silence. This deserves attention; because it must be allowed that the arguments of the Divine Speaker are often unexpected and extraordinary; while they may be sometimes thought even to admit of refutation, or at least to afford to an adversary some loophole for escape. The inference to be gathered from the statement, (in this or any other place,) that the men whom He addressed "could not answer Him again to these things,"—is, however, obvious. We perceive that His arguments were felt *to be* unanswerable,—or they would have been answered:(*q*) for He is represented as engaged in controversy with the most learned of the nation.

It will be found therefore that the recorded discourses of our SAVIOUR possess an extraordinary interest and value, beyond what might at first be suspected.—Perhaps, had the blessed Speaker been addressing the men of our own day, He would have sometimes reasoned differently. It may, at least, be suspected that He would have silenced *us* with arguments the force of which we should have more readily felt and admitted. But He was reasoning with the learned Jewish Doctors. Much of the traditional meaning of Holy Scripture, they certainly retained; and He was therefore able to meet them on common ground,—appeal to their own familiar teaching,—adopt their own method,—and slay them with their own weapons. Can we doubt moreover that those weapons, that method, and that teaching, as often as *He* condescended to employ them, were divine? Thus, it may well be suspected that the Law contained in Exod. xxiii. 5, and Deut. xxii. 4, was here alluded to by our LORD; and that the spiritual intention of that precept was present to the mind of all who heard. "Doth GOD take care of oxen?" (as the great Apostle exclaims;) "or saith He [not] it altogether for our own sakes? *For our sakes, no doubt, this is written.*"(*r*)

Our LORD may now be supposed to have reached the scene of the entertainment. It follows:—

7 And He put forth a Parable to those which were bidden, when He marked how they chose out the chief rooms;

In some sense, then, what follows is a *parable*. The words have a clear and obvious meaning, doubtless; but there lies beneath them a deeper lesson; and in order to draw attention to this, the Evangelist calls our LORD's discourse "a parable."

It is evident, by the way, that the present entertainment was no ordinary meal,—for here were many guests assembled,—who had all been bidden, (that is, formally "invited,")—and they appear to have been persons of importance; for we find that there was some rivalry among them for the chief places at table. Doubtless, if our LORD's remarks which follow appear to us unduly harsh or unseasonable, it is a proof that we are utterly mistaken in our conception of the circumstances and the scene. The Reader is referred to some remarks which were offered at the commencement of the present chapter; where it was suggested that the hostility of all assembled, to the Divine Being who had been invited to partake of the festivity, affords a clue to the severity of His language. We seem to hear One who is Himself sitting in the lowest room,—that is, who reclines on the couch farthest removed from the place of honour,—

8 saying unto them, When thou art bidden of any *man* to a wedding,

Mark, by the way, the nature of the "parable" which our LORD is delivering. The present is no wedding entertainment. Why then this allusion to a wedding? Doubtless to imply that He is covertly speaking of the "marriage" which "a cer-

(*p*) St. Matth. xii. 11, 12,—where see the notes. The Commentary on St. Mark iii. 1 to 5 may be also consulted with advantage.
(*q*) See the note on St. Matthew xxii. 46.   (*r*) 1 Cor. ix. 9, 10.

ain King made for His Son,(s)—"the Marriage of the Lamb."(t)   At this wedding then,—

9, 10 sit not down in the highest room: lest a more honourable man han thou be bidden of him: and he that bade thee and him come nd say to thee, Give this man place; and thou begin with shame to ake the lowest room.   But when thou art bidden, go and sit down in he lowest room; that when he that bade thee cometh, he may say unto hee, Friend, go up higher.   Then shalt thou have worship in the presence of them that sit at meat with thee.

Our LORD's words do more than recall,—they are even a quotation from the Book of Proverbs: "Put not forth thyself in the presence of the King, and stand not in the place of great men; for better it is that it be said unto thee, Come up hither, than that thou shouldest be put lower in the presence of the Prince whom thine eyes have seen."(u) . . . . . "This shows that the proverbial teaching of the Old Testament, in like manner with that of the New, contains parables of Evangelical Wisdom, wherein more is intended than meets the outward ear."(x)

But what is the present Parable? The Christian Church is the "wedding," and the guests are we. All are bidden who are Christians. How then do we behave? Do we covet high places for ourselves? do we desire to take precedence of our fellow-men,—those guests who sit down with us in GOD's visible Kingdom, here on earth,—presuming upon our wealth or influence, birth or station? If so, we have here our warning. At the end of the World, the Bridegroom will come in to see the guests,(y) and then verily will it be found that "there are last which shall be first, and there are first which shall be last."(z) It will no longer be possible for the base man to lord it over his humbler brother, nor for the meek man, overlooked, to occupy the lowest seat. The standard of honour and merit will be entirely changed the instant the Bridegroom enters. "He that bade thee and him" alike, will feel Himself aggrieved if ambition and self-conceit have at all been the cause why the guests are so misplaced at His Table. He will come to the less honourable who occupies the higher seat, and, bringing forward the virtuous brother of low degree, will say to the former, "Give this man place." Shame will be the portion of him who shall then begin to occupy, as his abiding portion,(a) the lowest room: just as he will enjoy great honour, to whom, in the presence of admiring men and angels, those blessed words shall be spoken, "Friend, go up higher!" . . . . This will be the man who in his lifetime chose CHRIST for his pattern, and was content daily to tread in the footsteps of the Crucified. These are the meek ones of the earth. They are found in every class of society, in every calling, doubtless; in the most exalted, as well as in the very humblest of all: yet surely if we were to go in search of such, we should seek them among the despised and afflicted,—among the very poor!

Consider how, both in the Old and New Testaments, it is intimated that *Shame* will befall the wicked in the Day of Judgment,(b)—shame, at detection and exposure before all. In the Book of Proverbs, a striking hint is given that it will be a terrible thing in that hour "to be put lower in the presence of THE PRINCE, *whom their eyes have seen.*"(c) Here, the wonder and indignation of our fellow-men is the thing appealed to. And "the great Proverb of the Gospel"(d) follows:—

11 For whosoever exalteth himself shall be abased: and he that humbleth himself shall be exalted.

Enough has been offered concerning these memorable words in other parts of the Commentary, to which it must suffice to refer the Reader.(e)

12 Then said He also to him that bade Him, When thou makest a dinner or a supper, call not thy friends, nor thy brethren, neither thy

---

(s) St. Matth. xxii. 2.   (t) Rev. xix. 9.   (u) Prov. xxv. 6, 7.
(x) Williams.   (y) St. Matth. xxii. 11.   (z) St. Luke xiii. 30.
(a) That is the meaning of "*taking* the lowest room," in ver. 9.
(b) Dan. xii. 2.   (c) Prov. xxv. 7: and see Job xlii. 5.   (d) Williams.
(e) See the note on the latter part of St. Luke xviii. 14: also on St. Matthew xxiii. 12.

kinsmen, nor *thy* rich neighbours; lest they also bid thee again, and recompense be made thee.

That which is so often sought after, is therefore the very thing we are taught t shun and dread. Consider St. Luke vi. 32 to 35. It can scarcely be needful t point out that our LORD does not here *prohibit* hospitality to "rich neighbours; but, (according to His well-known method on other occasions,)(*f*) He declares wh are *rather* to be entertained. Hospitality towards "friends, brethren," and th like, is good; it is even one of the graces of the Gospel.(*g*) Yet does our SAVIOU show unto us "a more excellent way:" as it follows,—

13, 14 But when thou makest a feast, call the poor, the maimed, th lame, the blind: and thou shalt be blessed; for they cannot recompens thee: for thou shalt be recompensed at the Resurrection of the just.

The needy, and halt, and lame, and blind, have not the means to make thee an return; but thou shalt be blessed, for a return shall be made thee at the Resurrec tion of the Just. "Come, ye blessed of My FATHER," (will then be said by the So of Man to as many as "have done it unto one of the least of these His Brethren,' "inherit the Kingdom prepared for you from the beginning of the World: for was an-hungered, and ye gave Me meat: I was thirsty, and ye gave Me drink."(*k* Wherefore, (as it is said in another place,) I appoint unto you a Kingdom, ... that ye may eat and drink at My Table."(*i*)

15 And when one of them that sat at meat with Him heard thes things, he said unto Him, Blessed *is* he that shall eat bread in th Kingdom of GOD.

On the speaker's lips, this saying was probably nothing more than a devout ex clamation on hearing our LORD allude to the recompense which should attend th Resurrection of the Just. As if he had said,—Blessed will he be who shall shar in that recompense of which Thou speakest so persuasively and well! Or, (t borrow the language of the SPIRIT to St. John the Divine,) "Blessed are the which are called to the Marriage-Supper of the LAMB!"(*k*) The words probabl meant no more; for they appear to have been suggested by what our SAVIOUR ha said,(*l*)—and we discover from His practice on other occasions that it was th manner of GOD's ancient people to speak of "the Resurrection of the Just," as "*sitting down* with Abraham, Isaac, and Jacob *in the Kingdom of GOD*."(*m*)

But our SAVIOUR takes the human words as they fall from the unconsciou speaker, and straightway moulds them to a higher purpose by imparting to thes a divine meaning. He denies not what the other had said,—namely, "Blessed i he that shall eat bread in the Kingdom of GOD!" Far from it! But He proceed to show by a parable that "the Kingdom" spoken of, hath its beginning *here o Earth;* and He foretells, darkly indeed, yet in wondrous detail, how different woul be its reception from what the Speaker supposed. Those "that were bidden. (namely, GOD's chosen people,—the "heirs of the Kingdom,") would reject th gracious invitation to come, when all things were ready. Nay, the very Gentile (heirs by adoption,) so far from accounting it their supreme blessedness to "eat brea in the Kingdom of GOD," would invent all manner of pretexts for staying away.

This latter is at least one chief meaning of the Parable; and it is the bett worth our attention, inasmuch as the Church, in her second Exhortation in th Communion Service, is found so to apply our LORD's teaching. The Parable fo lows:—

16, 17 Then said He unto him, A certain Man made a great suppe and bade many: and sent His servant at supper time to say to thes that were bidden, Come; for all things are now ready.

(*f*) See the note on St. Luke x. 20, and the place there referred to.
(*g*) See Rom. xii. 13.　Heb. xvii. 2.　1 St. Pet. iv. 9.　　　(*h*) St. Matth. xxv. 34, 35, 40.
(*i*) St. Luke xxii. 29, 30.　　　　　　(*k*) Rev. xix. 9.　Compare St. Matth. xxii. 2, 3.
(*l*) St. Matth. viii. 11.　St. Luke xiii. 29.　　　　　　(*m*) Gal. iv. 4.

God is this "certain man,"—God, who "when the fulness of the time was come, sent forth His Son."(n) Christ Himself therefore, who took upon Him the form of a servant, or any one whom Christ sendeth, is the servant in the parable;—His Church and Kingdom "is the Great Supper;"—the "things now ready," are His Word and Sacraments; "the Vision of God, the society of Angels, the fellowship with the Saints." Heavenly joys are even spoken of in Holy Scripture under this image of a Feast,—a feast where plenty, instead of cloying, does but add keenness to the appetite; and where fulness, instead of producing satiety, awakens only delight. How strong the call of appetite for earthly food! how soon appeased! when appeased, how small seems the joy! But the reverse is true of the heavenly banquet. We hunger for it but little; yet will the ages of Eternity not suffice to satisfy the soul's desire: and when experienced how will the joys of Heaven surpass all that the heart has ever imagined of bliss!(o) Now, because this Heavenly Banquet begins here on earth, Christ's visible Kingdom is likened to a great supper. "Come; for all things are now ready." . . . . Surely in this, the evening of the World, we hear that invitation daily! What are opportunities of obedience,—occasions for the exercise of the graces of the Gospel,—invitations to prayer,—the return of sacred seasons,—the music of Sabbath-bells,—what is each of these but a summons to "come, for all things are now ready?"—Mark next the conduct of those invited:

18 And they all with one *consent* began to make excuse.

Hitherto, the parable of "the Great Supper" reminds us forcibly of the parable of "the marriage of the King's Son."(p) When all is ready, the Servants are sent out to call the guests,—but no guests are willing to come. In the case of the Marriage, however, the summons is refused and disregarded,—the field(q) and the merchandise still furnishing the greater attraction. But civil excuses are offered by those who were invited to the Great Supper.

19 The first said unto him, I have bought a piece of ground, and I must needs go and see it: I pray thee have me excused. And another said, I have bought five yoke of oxen, and I go to prove them: I pray thee have me excused.

Thus, "one goes to his farm, another to his merchandise."(r) The piece of ground and the five yoke of oxen (for ploughing)(s) have been bought subject to approval. Hence the first must be inspected, and trial must be made of the second.

20 And another said, I have married a wife, and therefore I cannot come.

"Yet this Feast is that invisible Kingdom of Grace into which men must press with violence!"(t) Land,—oxen,—a wife: "all innocent; perhaps all needful: all certainly fatal. They loved them too much, or the Gospel too little. Their love for them was perhaps not excessive; it might have been but little: but, at all events, their love for the Gospel was less. Or their love for the Gospel might have been great, very great; but their love of the world was greater. Still, it all came to one and the same end; for God will not have a divided heart. It is the choice of the two which is presented at all times. To have married a wife was provided for in the Law as a sufficient plea not to go forth to war;(u) but the Gospel is higher in its requirements. 'He that loveth wife or children more than Me, is not worthy of Me.'"(x)

It may be observed that, in describing the reception which the Gospel would meet with, our Lord mentions the very things which He notices in speaking of the old World and of Sodom. "He omits all mention of their great crimes, but chooses

<hr>

(n) Gregory.
(o) See St. Matth. xxii. 1, &c.
(p) The word translated "a piece of ground" in St. Luke xiv. 18, is translated a "farm" in St. Matth. xxii. 5.
(q) St. Matth. xxii. 5.
(r) See 1 Kings xix. 19.
(s) St. Matth. xi. 12; St. Luke xvi. 16.
(t) Deut. xxiv. 5.
(u) Williams, quoting St. Matth. x. 37.
(x) St. Luke xvii. 28.

out, for their resemblance to the last day, points innocent in themselves, but of a absorbing worldly nature. In the days of Lot, which are likened to the end of th world, 'they bought and sold,'(y)—as here the excuse is 'I have bought oxen, an I go to prove them.' In the former, 'they planted, they builded,'—as here th plea is 'I have bought a field, and must needs go and see it.' Again, in the day of Noah and of Lot, 'they married and gave in marriage,'(z)—and the Gospel in th parable is rejected, because, 'I have married a wife, and therefore I cannot com The same things, therefore, are true of the days of the Son of Man, as appears fra Scripture; whether we speak of CHRIST's final Coming, or of the Christian dispe sation generally."(a) And can it be needful to point out that for the same caus which are daily seen to be in operation, the Gospel is practically rejected? or th "a wife" here stands for all earthly ties, because Marriage is the closest and mo sacred: oxen to be proved, and land which must be visited, for all worldly good and possessions whatsoever?

21 So that servant came, and showed his Lord these things. The the Master of the house being angry, said to his servant, Go ou quickly into the streets and lanes of the city, and bring in hither th poor, and the maimed, and the halt, and the blind.

"When thou makest a feast," (our LORD had said in ver. 13) "call the poor, th maimed, the lame, the blind:" and these are precisely the classes of persons whic the servant is ordered in the parable to "bring in," to be partakers of the Gre Supper. But of the heavenly banquet here spoken of, it is of course "the poor i spirit," who are desired; and such as, because their hand offended them, cut it of and so became maimed: because their foot offended them, cut it off, and so becam lame: because their eye offended them, plucked it out, and so became blind.(b)

22, 23 And the Servant said, Lord, it is done as Thou hast com manded, and yet there is room. And the Lord said unto the Servant Go out into the highways and hedges, and compel them to come in that My House may be filled.

As usual, a prophecy of what was to be hereafter, is here set before us. Th fulfilment was obvious. The Jews rejected the Gospel. The Publicans and harlo were straightway brought in from the streets and lanes of the Holy City; and ye there was room. Whereupon the offer was freely made to the Gentiles. Consid Acts xiii. 46.

24 For I say unto you, That none of those men which were bidde shall taste of My Supper.

The Parable being brought to a close, our Blessed LORD, by a single word, giv His auditors to understand that He is Himself the Giver of the Supper, and th He is discoursing to them concerning the decrees of His own Providence: "For say unto you." The words are no longer those of the Lord of the Feast addressir a single messenger. They are the words of GOD Himself!

Many of the Jewish nation did indeed, afterwards, embrace the Gospel: but was no longer as Jews that they tasted of God's Mercy. They came in with th other nations of the earth. But surely these terrible words have a yet broad meaning, and are addressed to as many as shall come after, to the end of the work Those who, when bidden, refuse the Feast, shall afterwards find themselves e cluded. See the last part of St. Luke xiii. 24, and the note there.

Consider, finally, what an instructive specimen is here afforded us of our Bless LORD's method, and His untiring zeal in the shepherding of souls. It is the Sa bath-day, and the Service of the Synagogue over, (where doubtless He has be delivering a divine discourse,)(c) He proceeds to eat bread at a certain House. person afflicted with dropsy stands before Him. He heals him. Sinful men a by; and for their sakes, He defends His action, and by His comment upon it, brin the Gospel into harmony with the Law. He enters,—and takes occasion from wh

(y) St. Luke xvii. 28.   (z) St. Luke xvii. 26, 27.   (a) Williams.
(b) Consider St. Mark ix. 43, (hand,)—45, (foot,)—47, (eye.)
(c) Consider St. Luke iv. 15, 16, &c.

He sees, to "teach Humility;"(*d*) conveying at the same time a parable of marvellous value and secret beauty. To the giver of the entertainment, He delivers precious counsel concerning "feasting the poor."(*e*) A guest, in reply to what our SAVIOUR had been saying, ventures an ordinary remark; and our SAVIOUR forthwith addresses to him the parable of "the Great Supper.". . . . It may all have been the work of half an hour!

25, 26 And there went great multitudes with Him: and He turned and said unto them, If any *man* come to Me, and hate not his Father, and Mother, and Wife, and Children, and Brethren, and Sisters, yea, and his own life also, he cannot be My disciple.

Our SAVIOUR had been prophetically declaring that worldly possessions or earthly ties would prove the things to prevent a man from freely embracing the Gospel. But the scene of His discourse is changed. Instead of the festive chamber, it is now the weary highway; and among the "great crowds" which "journeyed with Him," there may or may not have been those who listened to the parable of the Great Supper which was delivered at the banquet. It does not follow, however, because the scene is changed, that the subject of our LORD's discourse is unconnected with what went before. On the contrary, the Evangelist seems to have been divinely guided to select from what our LORD proceeded to deliver, such sayings as bore directly on His previous teaching. All things, therefore, (it is here declared,) must be relinquished for the Gospel: or, (as our LORD will be found to re-word the matter below, in verse 33,)—"Whosoever he be of you that forsaketh not all that he hath, he cannot be My disciple." Moreover, the temper requisite in one who would follow the Crucified, is further insisted upon in a saying which is itself almost a prophecy.(*f*)

27 And whosoever doth not bear his cross, and come after Me, cannot be My disciple.

Verses 26 and 27 will be found very nearly repeated in our SAVIOUR's Charge delivered to the Twelve.(*g*) The saying in the latter verse may be considered to recur three times in the Gospel,—being found besides in the discourse which He delivered after His Transfiguration; as all the three Evangelists conspire in recording.(*h*)

28, 29, 30 For which of you, intending to build a tower, sitteth not down first, and counteth the cost, whether he have *sufficient* to finish *it?* Lest haply, after he hath laid the foundation, and is not able to finish *it*, all that behold *it* begin to mock him, saying, This man began to build, and was not able to finish.

Take notice how He who created Man such as he is, here, for the second time,(*i*) appeals to Man's sense of *Shame*,—as above (in ver. 10) He appealed to Man's sense of *Pride*.

So difficult, then, and so formidable a thing is the work of Salvation!—"The foundation" must indeed be laid in Faith in CHRIST,—for "other foundation can no man lay."(*k*) But, besides this, it is a work of labour and difficulty; demanding, as our LORD specially notes, great sacrifices,—and to be accomplished only at a large cost of time, and skill, and labour,—even as the building of a tower. Then, besides a great work to accomplish, we have also a powerful King to encounter. And take notice, that the hostile sovereign spoken of in the next verse, is none other than CHRIST Himself. It follows,—

31, 32 Or what king, going to make war against another King, sitteth not down first, and consulteth whether he be able with ten thou-

---

(*d*) See the heading of the chapter.   (*e*) See the heading.
(*f*) See the note on St. Matth. x. 38.   (*g*) St. Matth. x. 37, 38.
(*h*) St. Matth. xvi. 24, St. Mark viii. 34, St. Luke ix. 23,—on each of which places the notes may be consulted.
(*i*) See above, ver. 9.   (*k*) 1 Cor. iii. 11.

sand to meet Him that cometh against him with twenty thousand? or
else, while the Other is yet a great way off, he sendeth an ambassage
and desireth conditions of peace.

So that our LORD's counsel on this occasion closely resembles that other word of
His, which has already twice come before us,—"Agree with thine Adversary
quickly, while thou art in the way with Him."(*l*) He comes against us with Might
and with Majesty which none may presume to resist. "Behold," (saith Enoch)
"the LORD cometh with ten thousands of His Saints,"(*m*)—yea, with "ten thousand
times ten thousand."(*n*) "But who may abide the day of His coming? and who
shall stand when He appeareth?"(*o*) Wholly unable are we to meet Him in Judgment, when He shall appear with all His hosts. What remains, then, but to make
our peace with Him while He "is yet a great way off," (being not yet seen coming
in Judgment:) to send Him an ambassage of prayers and tears, and earnestly to
desire of Him "conditions of Peace!"

33 So likewise, whomsoever he be of you that forsaketh not all that
he hath, he cannot be My Disciple.

Thus does our LORD gather up into a single sentence the teaching of the seven
verses which go before.(*p*) So slow and laborious is the work of Salvation,—so
formidable is He with whom we have to do,—that unless there be a forsaking of all
things, a man is not fit to be CHRIST's disciple. A remark already twice met with
follows:

34, 35 Salt *is* good: but if the salt have lost his savour, wherewith
shall it be seasoned? It is neither fit for the land, nor yet for the
dunghill; *but* men cast it out.

These words have been explained already.(*q*) They mean here,—To be a Christian is a good thing: but let the Christian character once lose that which gives
all its savour, and it becomes nothing worth. Men are hereby taught the consequence of falling away from CHRIST in the hour of trial, from not having well considered beforehand what it would cost them to be His followers. There must be
perseverance—*to the end;* and this is the doctrine of all Scripture, to an extent
which few persons imagine. "He who after the knowledge of the Truth falls back
(our LORD says,) "is neither able to bring forth the fruit of good works himself
nor to instruct others. He must therefore be cast out."(*r*) And lest this application of His words might be overlooked, He added His well-known saying,—

He that hath ears to hear, let him hear.

(*l*) St. Matth. v. 25, and St. Luke xii. 58,—on which last place, see the note.
(*m*) St. Jude ver 14.   (*n*) Dan. vii. 10.   (*o*) Mal. iii. 2.
(*p*) See above, the note on ver. 26.
(*q*) See the notes on St. Matth. v. 13: St. Mark ix. 50.   (*r*) Bede.

CHAPTER XV.

1 *The Parable of the Lost Sheep:* 8 *of the Piece of Silver:* 11 *of the Prodigal Son.*

1 THEN drew near unto Him all the Publicans and Sinners for to hear Him.

Concerning "Publicans and Sinners,"—of whom such frequent mention is made in the Gospel,—see the note on St. Mark ii. 15. The former were persons who, both from their odious calling, and their sinful manner of life, were deemed infamous, by the rest of the nation. But, among their number, was found the Saint, and Apostle, and Evangelist.(*a*) They supplied, moreover, patterns of Faith,(*b*) of Prayer,(*c*) and of Zeal.(*d*) At their table the SAVIOUR of the world, homeless Himself, and despised of men, was many a time the welcome and the honoured Guest. . . . How unspeakably precious in the ears of all such must have been the gracious words which follow !

2 And the Pharisees and Scribes murmured, saying, This man receiveth sinners, and eateth with them.

There is much of gracious meaning in this intimation that our LORD "*received* Sinners." Consider such places as St. Luke ix. 11;—where, (as in St. Luke viii. 40: xix. 6; St. John i. 11, 12: iv. 45, &c.,) a kind and hearty welcome is evidently implied.

"To *eat*" with Publicans was evidently deemed a pollution. See St. Matthew ix. 11, and St. Luke xix. 7. This was because the Publicans belonged to a class which was reckoned among *the heathen*,—with whom to eat was to be polluted: see Acts xi. 3; Gal. ii. 12, &c. Compare St. Matthew xviii. 17, and the note St. Mark ii. 15.

3 And He spake this parable unto them, saying,

The parable of the Lost Sheep follows: in studying which we are to remember that our SAVIOUR CHRIST is "the Good Shepherd,"—as He Himself declared.(*e*) Here, then, we have explained to us the object and purpose with which He "received sinners, and ate with them." He was "*going after that which was lost.*" . . . The same parable, somewhat more briefly given, is found in St. Matthew's Gospel, xviii. 12–14,—where it stands actually prefaced by the words,—"The Son of Man is come to save that which was lost."

4 What man of you, having an hundred sheep, if he lose one of them, doth not leave the ninety and nine in the wilderness, and go after that which is lost, until he find it ?

Our Blessed LORD appeals to one of the instincts of the human heart. The ninety and nine, which are in safety, are left; for the sake of the *one* which is lost. But the Heavenly Shepherd's care for "the people of His pasture and the sheep of His hand"(*f*) is such, that He rests not "*until He find.*"

Concerning "the wilderness," see the note on St. Luke i. 80.

Who, that reads, exclaims not,—"*I* have gone astray like a sheep that is lost. O seek Thy servant ?"

(*a*) St. Matth. x. 3.   (*b*) St. Matth. xxi. 32.   (*c*) St. Luke xviii. 10–14.
(*d*) St. Luke xix. 2–4.   (*e*) St. John x. 11.   (*f*) Ps. xcv. 7.

5 And when he hath found *it*, he layeth *it* on his shoulders, rejoi
ing.

He who "gathereth the lambs with His arm, and carrieth them in His bosom,"(*g*
"layeth" the lost sheep "on His shoulders," also: for "all we like sheep hai
gone astray; we have turned every one to his own way; and the LORD hath laid o
Him the iniquity of us all." "Surely He hath borne our griefs, and carried ou
sorrows!"(*h*) And beneath this heavy burden, "the Shepherd and Bishop of ou
Souls"(*i*) is found to walk "*rejoicing*."
Observe, therefore, that the purpose with which the Good Shepherd goes afte
His lost sheep, is not to *drive* it back to the fold; much less to *punish* it. He wil
convey it back, on His shoulders. He will *carry it* all the way.

6 And when he cometh home, he calleth together *his* friends and
neighbours, saying unto them, Rejoice with me; for I have found my
sheep which was lost.

We shall be reminded in the next verse, that *Heaven* is the Good Shepherd'
"home:" and from verse 10 we learn that the "friends and neighbours" are non
other than *the Angels of* GOD. "Friends,"—because they do the FATHER'S will;(*k*
"Neighbours,"—because they stand in His presence,(*l*) behold His face,(*m*) an
gather brightness from His glory.
The Heavenly Shepherd having come after us that were lost, until He found us
—after He had taken our Nature upon Him, and borne our sins,—straightway r
turned home. "I came forth from the FATHER," He said, "and am come into th
World: again, I leave the World, and go to the FATHER."(*n*)

7 I say unto you, that likewise joy shall be in Heaven over one sin
ner that repenteth, more than over ninety and nine just persons whic
need no repentance.

Take notice, that it is not said that those who have sinned and repented, are o
jects of greater *Love* than the righteous. Not Love but *Joy*, is the emotion excite
by the Penitent's return. *Love* is for those who have *never wandered away* fro
the Shepherd's side.
The phrase,—"Just persons, which need no repentance," admits of an obvious ex
planation. "There is *none* that doeth good; no, *not one*."(*o*) But, compared wit
the "lost;" compared with those who "were dead, and are alive again:" man
are "just,"—and "need no repentance."
On "Joy shall be *in Heaven*,"—see the note on verses 6 and 10.

8 Either what woman

The SAVIOUR of the World reappears, but it is now under another form. (
this may represent Him, in the person of His Church, seeking for one, possess
before; but since, accidentally, let slip. The Woman knows that she shall find tl
lost part of her treasure *within* her house. By the aid of "a burning and a shi
ing light,"(*p*) she therefore commences an anxious search.

having ten pieces of silver, if she lose one piece, doth not light
candle, and sweep the house, and seek diligently till she find *it*?

Under this domestic image, then,—the humble figure of a Woman with a light
candle, sweeping the house, in anxious search of a lost piece of money,—does th
SAVIOUR of the World here set forth to us His zeal for the souls of men. The lo
piece of money was precious because it bore the image and likeness(*q*) of the Gre
King. Compare the language of St. Luke xx. 24, and of 1 Cor. xv. 49.

9 And when she hath found *it*, she calleth *her* friends and *her* neigl

(*g*) Isaiah xl. 11.   (*h*) Isaiah liii. 6, 4.   (*i*) 1 St. Peter ii. 25.
(*k*) St. Matth. vi. 10, compared with St. John xv. 14.   (*l*) St. Luke i. 19.
(*m*) St. Matth. xviii. 10.   (*n*) St. John xvi. 28.   (*o*) Ps. xiv. 1, 3.
(*p*) St. John v. 35, compared with St. Matth. v. 14, 15.   (*q*) Gen. i. 26.

bours together, saying, Rejoice with me; for I have found the piece which I had lost.

The powers of Heaven are once more made partakers of the SAVIOUR's joy. See the next note.

10 Likewise, I say unto you, there is joy in the presence of the Angels of GOD over one sinner that repenteth.

How wonderful a view is here opened to us of the sympathy of the Holy Angels with this part of GOD's Creation! They love us with more than a brother's love. With what intense interest must they behold us! with what assiduity and care must they minister and watch for us;(r) that the tidings of "one Sinner that repenteth," should fill the courts of Heaven with joy!

Most affecting of all, however, is the joy of CHRIST—the Good Shepherd. "Rejoice *with Me*,"—He says. His friends and neighbours are but invited to be partakers of *His* mysterious joy! See the note on verse 7. Also, the note on verse 6.

Can we doubt, by the way, that when "the Holy Church throughout all the World" keeps Christmas, or Easter,—celebrates Good-Friday, Ascension-Day, or Whitsuntide;—there must be a corresponding strain of sympathy among the Angels in Heaven, likewise: if the welfare of *one* can fill the skies with joy?

The Parable of the Prodigal Son follows.

11 And He said, A certain Man had two Sons:

About the "certain Man," in the parable, there can be no difference of opinion. The "two Sons" set forth, as well the Jew and the Gentile, as two opposite characters;—the "sinner that repenteth," and the "just person that needeth no repentance." We shall do well to seek our likeness in the former character,—*that*, namely, of the poor prodigal; where we shall assuredly be most likely to find it.

12 and the younger of them said to *his* father, Father, give me the portion of goods that falleth *to me*. And he divided unto them *his* living.

If this be understood nationally,—then, we have here a picture of the portion which the nations of the Gentile world chose for themselves when they wandered forth from the haunts of Shem.

If individually,—then, behold here the impatience of one who cannot brook the restraints of his Heavenly Father's home; but claims his portion and receives it:—health and strength,—youthful spirits and intellectual vigour,—the portion of good things, whatever it may happen to be, which falleth to him. In both cases the gifts *of Nature* are implied, as contrasted with the gifts *of Grace*.

13 And not many days after, the younger son gathered all together, and took his journey into a far country,

Behold the Youth's impatience! He sets out "*not many days*" after. He goes, in fact, whenever, and whithersoever he pleases; for *the will* of man is left perfectly *free*.

And he travels "into a far country;" for this is the fate of all those who forsake GOD. To be deprived of the light of *His* countenance, is to be in a very "far country" indeed.

"Not many days"—seems to mark the impatience of the natural man to break away from GOD.

and there wasted his substance with riotous living.

He "wasted his substance," for he made a prodigal and a reckless use of the gifts of Nature: in consequence whereof, (as St. Paul says of the Gentile world,) "he became vain in his imaginations, and his foolish heart was darkened." "Professing himself to be wise, he became as a fool."(s)

(r) See the Collect for "St. Michael and all Angels."   (s) Rom. i. 21, 22.

His high endowments all turned to his shame. His very moral sense was darkened. The candle of the LORD had gone out within him.

14 And when he had spent all, there arose a mighty famine in that land; and he began to be in want.

Spiritual needs are set forth to us in Scripture under the image of *hunger and thirst*.(*t*) "Behold the days come, saith the LORD GOD, that I will send a famine in the land; not a famine of bread, nor a thirst for water, but of hearing the word of the LORD."(*u*)

Surely, there was a mighty Famine in *all* lands, (typically set forth in the history of Joseph,)(*x*) at the time of the Advent of our SAVIOUR CHRIST; and the younger Brother had been made to *feel* the want of which he had long before "begun" to be aware! There was nothing to satisfy the soul's cravings in those systems with which men had beguiled themselves so long; and Faith had departed from them.

Then, besides its national bearing, this part of the Parable sets forth the spiritual misery of an individual who is seeking to live "without GOD in the World."(*y*) A mighty Famine arises, and it reaches also unto him. He himself, (for so it is in the original,) begins to be in want. Too often, however, *the beginnings* of distress fail to recall such an one to a sense of his true position and of his duty. When he only "*begins*" to suffer, his proud heart remains unsubdued. He probably acts in the manner described in the following verse.

15 And he went and joined himself to a citizen of that country, and he sent him into his fields to feed swine.

Under such a degrading image is the hard service which the younger Son had engaged in exhibited. The "Citizen of that country" is the Devil,—who is "a citizen" and therefore *at home*, where the Prodigal Son is but an outcast and stranger. Here then, we trace the downward course of one who has fled from the presence, and forsaken the service of GOD. He straightway enters into the service of the Devil.

The "swine" represent those "filthy dreamers,† (as St. Jude speaks,)(*z*) who belong to the Evil One; and in pandering to whose lusts, he employs any miserable being whom he gets into his power. They are fitly called *swine:* those being the unclean creatures with which the devils love most to be,—as we learn from St. Matt viii. 31. The animal, moreover, was among those which the nation were forbidden to eat, and which they held in peculiar abhorrence.

St. Paul further helps us to the *national* application of this part of the Parable for, (describing the consequences to the Gentiles, "when they knew GOD," of "not glorifying Him as GOD,") he adds,—"Wherefore GOD also *gave them up to uncleanness.*" "And even as they did not like to retain GOD in their knowledge, GOD gave *them over to a reprobate mind.*"(*a*)

In its individual application,—this part of the Parable reminds us of those who nourish foul desires and unclean thoughts in their soul: despising "Angels' food;"(*b*) and "serving divers lusts and pleasures,"(*c*) as the Apostle speaks.

16 And he would fain have filled his belly with the husks that the swine did eat: and no man gave unto him.

There is in the East a peculiar kind of bean-shaped fruit, here called "husks," which is given to swine, and which may be eaten by men also. But the degree of misery here described must be very great: to be reduced so low as to crave a portion for one's self of the food one is dispensing to the herd; yet no one found to pity one's necessity, and supply a more wholesome diet! . . . The Prodigal Son seemed before, reduced to the lowest depth of misery; but here, a still lower depth discovers itself. His soul was fainting within him; and yet to "fill *his belly,*"—to gratify his lower appetites,—is the utmost object of his desire!

17 And when he came to himself,

(*t*) St. John iv. 10–14; Isaiah xlix. 10: Rev. vii. 16, 17; Psalm xxiii. 2, &c. &c.
(*u*) Amos viii. 2.   (*x*) Gen. xli. 57, &c.   (*y*) Eph. ii. 12.
(*z*) St. Jude, ver. 8.   (*a*) Rom. i. 21, 24, and 28.   (*b*) Ps. lxxviii. 25.
                            (*c*) Titus iii. 3.

For one who could so act,—forsake such a Father, and desert such a home, to incur nothing but misery, insult, and the pangs of hunger,—can only be spoken of as one not in his right mind.

He "came to himself," and forthwith came *home*. From which we may rightly infer that when he "took his journey into a far country," (ver. 13,) he altogether *departed from himself*.

he said, How many hired servants of my father's have bread enough and to spare, and I perish with hunger!

How pregnant here is every word with meaning! The "*hired* servants;"—those labourers, namely, whom the Heavenly Father had hired for a penny a day, according to the Parable,(d) and sent to work in His Vineyard. . . . . "*Bread enough*:"—for under that image, God's Word(e) and Sacraments(f) are spoken of in the Gospel. All Christian privileges, it may be, are "briefly comprehended in that one saying,"(g) "the children's *Bread*."(h) . . . . "And *to spare;*"—whence arises the duty of imparting and distributing to others.

He who lacks the "Bread" here spoken of, does more than suffer want. He even "*perishes with hunger.*"

18 I will arise and go to my Father,

He will "arise,"—for he has been till now grovelling in the dust. He will "go,"—for he is a very long way off. To his "Father,"—for at present he dwells among swine.

And that he shall be able to "say—*Father!*" is the ground of all his confidence; the foundation of all his hope.

and will say unto him, Father, I have sinned against Heaven, and before thee,

This is the language of true Repentance, "I have sinned—*against Heaven*." Compare that of David,—"Against *Thee, Thee only*, have I sinned."(i) Compare also 2 Sam. xii. 13; and two earlier instances, in Gen. xx. 6, and xxxix. 9.

19 and am no more worthy to be called thy son:

Such words do we make our own, as often as we draw near to the Divine presence, in the public services of the Church. Thereby, not only interpreting the Parable, but identifying ourselves with the most conspicuous character in it.

make me as one of thy hired servants.

The entrance into the courts of Glory is by the gate of Humility.

A very ancient writer, (who was also an Archbishop,) commenting on these words, piously exclaims,—"O Lord Jesus! Preserve us from such husks as the swine did eat, and instead thereof, give unto us the true Bread; for Thou art Steward in Thy Father's House. As Labourers, vouchsafe to hire us also, although arriving late; for Thou dost hire men, even at the eleventh hour,—and givest to all alike the same reward of Life eternal."

20 And he arose, and came to his Father.

In this, lies one of the most instructive lessons which the Parable conveys. The Father was yearning towards the Prodigal with tenderness unspeakable; the robe and the ring, the shoes and the banquet, were all in store; but the Prodigal must first *arise and go*. He was, as yet, "*dead*" in the Father's sight; ver. 24: "wherefore He saith, Awake, thou that sleepest, and *arise from the dead*, and Christ shall give thee light."(k) *We* must first "draw nigh to God," and then He will "draw nigh" to us.(l) When the Son *has* risen, mark all that follows:—

But when he was yet a great way off, his Father saw him, and had compassion, and ran, and fell on his neck, and kissed him.

(d) St. Matth. xx.　　　(e) St. Matth. iv. 4.　　　(f) St. John vi. 35–58.
(g) Rom. xiii. 9.　　　(h) St. Matth. xv. 26.　　　(i) Ps. li. 4.
(k) Ephes. v. 14.　　　　　　　　　　　　　　　　(l) St. James iv. 8.

What can be imagined more affecting? The returning wretch recognized, whil "he was yet *a great way off:*" the prevailing feeling of "*compassion,*" which hi return excites: the impatience, which must "*run*" to meet him, half way: the love which "*falls upon his neck;*" the tenderness, which "*kisses him!*" . . . In the running, says an Ancient, there is Foreknowledge: in the embrace, Mercy.

We do not read that *the Son,*—tied and bound with the chain, and burdened with the weight, of his many sins,—ran to meet the Father. It was *the Father,* on the contrary, who ran to meet *him.* We cannot "run," (as the Psalmist in a certain place declares,) till GOD has "set our hearts at liberty:"(*m*) sore let and hindered else, in running the race that is set before us. We *feel after* GOD,—the heavenly FATHER *finds* us: running to meet us, while we are "yet a great way off!"

When CHRIST so falls upon the neck of the returning Penitent, He removes thence from the weary and heavy-laden, the yoke of slavery,—and instead thereof, bestows there His own light Burden, and easy Yoke. For this, He invites all men to "come unto Him."(*n*)

21 And the Son said unto him, Father, I have sinned against Heaven, and in thy sight, and am no more worthy to be called thy Son.

The Father does not give him time to say the rest of what he intended to say see verses 18, 19. He would have almost spared him the pain of Confession altogether,—for he has already embraced; and, in act, has forgiven him. Observe how he proceeds to heap blessing upon blessing:—

22 But the Father said to his Servants, Bring forth the best robe and put *it* on him; and put a ring on his hand, and shoes on *his* feet

"The best robe" was the robe of honour, and the special property of the elder son: see Genesis xxvii. 15. The ring was a mark of dignity,—a badge of rank, as well as an ornament; as may be inferred from Genesis xxxviii. 18: xli. 42: and St James ii. 2. Lastly, *he* wore "shoes on his feet," who was invited to "draw nigh,' —not to a terrific presence, as in Exodus iii. 5, and Joshua v. 15; but to the tender embrace of a most loving Father.

But we have to look for some far loftier meaning than this: for the merciful CREATOR, and the repenting Creature, are here spoken of. Whether we shall succeed in finding what we perceive that we must search after, is another question.

The Father replies not directly, *to the Son,* (for our prayers are not answered by a voice from Heaven;) but He addresses His answer "to His Servants;"—those heavenly, or those earthly ministers of His, "that do His pleasure," and "fulfil His commandment, and hearken unto the voice of His words."(*o*) "The best robe,' then, may denote Holy Baptism, for which Repentance is the fitting preparation;— "for," in the Apostle's words,—"as many as have been baptized into CHRIST, have *put on* CHRIST."(*p*) It is *that* recovered robe of innocence, which, when Adam lost he "knew that he was naked."(*q*) Compare 2 Cor. v. 3; Rev. iii. 17, 18 and xvi. 15.

But the meaning of the Ring and the Shoes, is less clear: and it is better to confess ignorance than to venture on merely fanciful and unfounded conjecture. Some have thought that the Ring is a badge of that union with CHRIST, which every member of CHRIST's Church, (which is the Spouse of CHRIST,) should carry. (Compare the language of 2 Cor. xi. 2; Eph. v. 32; Rev. xxi. 2, &c. See also, Hosea ii. 19, 20.) And it is easy to connect the notion of Shoes, with that Christian walk or race,(*r*) which directs attention so constantly to *the feet* of the believer,—as seeking "the path of life:"(*s*) requiring "a light," and "a lantern:"(*t*) being "shod with the preparation of the Gospel:"(*u*) and the like. But of such things, we can only speak conjecturally.—The Father continues,

23 and bring hither the fatted calf, and kill *it;* and let us eat, and be merry:

(*m*) Ps. cxix. 32.   (*n*) St. Matth. xi. 28–30.   (*o*) Psalm ciii. 20.
(*p*) Gal. iii. 27.   (*q*) Gen. iii. 7.
(*r*) Gen. v. 22; and places in the margin: 1 Cor. ix. 24: Heb. xii. 1, &c.
(*s*) Psalm xvi. 11: compare xvii. 5, and xxvii. 11; Proverbs iv. 18, 26, &c.
(*t*) Psalm cxix. 105.   (*u*) Eph. vi. 15.

This can be none other than the heavenly banquet of *His* Body,—whose Sacrifice is set forth throughout the whole of the Bible:—the pledge of the reconciliation of us Gentiles to an offended GOD. *That* banquet is now celebrated throughout the whole World,—feeds the whole House,—and fills the hearts of all with joy and gladness.

24 for this my Son was dead, and is alive again; he was lost, and is found. And they began to be merry.

He who lives in sin, is *dead* in GOD's sight, even while he liveth. See Eph. ii. 1; 1 Timothy v. 6; 1 St. John iii. 14; and compare with the phrase,—"he was lost and is found," St. Peter's words,—"Ye were as sheep *gone astray*, but are now *returned* unto the Shepherd and Bishop of your souls:" by which, the first and last of these Parables are connected together. See 1 St. Pet. ii. 25.

25 Now his elder Son was in the field: and as he came and drew nigh to the house, he heard music and dancing.

Here begins the second part of the Parable,—by which the history is carried on beyond the point which was reached in the two former Parables.(*z*) The elder Brother now appears; just in time to witness the merriment and rejoicing which, in each of the three Parables, obtains such prominent notice.

As before, (see verses 7 and 10,) Angels are the harpers; and the Christian Church swells their Songs of Triumph with her own Hymns of Praise.

26, 27, 28 And he called one of the servants, and asked what these things meant. And he said unto him, Thy Brother is come; and thy Father hath killed the fatted calf, because he hath received him safe and sound. And he was angry, and would not go in.

Even as the Pharisees and Scribes, in ver. 2, "murmured, saying, This man receiveth sinners, and eateth with them." As *their* Father, also, (although they knew Him not,) had come out, and was even now entreating them. It is the same to this day. The Jew is still standing without, and "will not come in."

But to return from the national, to the individual interpretation of the Parable, —we have here represented to us the envious displeasure of the wicked, at every advance in holiness on the part of the just. For the world does not, by any means, rejoice at the sight of goodness in others: rather the reverse.

Therefore came his Father out, and entreated him.

It has been thought that this indicates what will take place hereafter, when "the fulness of the Gentiles" shall have come in; that so, "all Israel may be saved."(*y*)

29 And he answering said to *his* Father, Lo, these many years do I serve thee, neither transgressed I at any time thy commandment:

This boastful speech is an apt exhibition of the remonstrance of the Scribes and Pharisees, already alluded to. *They* were the elder Brother. In ver. 2, they had, in effect, been saying of themselves the very thing which is here attributed to the self-righteous man, in the Parable. Our LORD Himself, certainly, gave them a very different character. See St. Matthew xxiii. 13, and what follows, especially verse 33.

and yet thou never gavest me a kid, that I might make merry with my friends:

There is a double emphasis at the end of this verse: "Thou never gavest *me*," so much as "*a kid*." Which may perhaps mean, that no effectual deliverance had been wrought for the Jewish people;—whereas the return of the Gentiles had been celebrated, as well as effected, by the sacrifice of the greatest Victim of all.

The elder Brother will not see that *he* is invited to be a partaker of the same banquet. He contemplates a scene of merriment, apart "with his friends." And

(*z*) See the end of the note on St. Matth. xxii. 10.   (*y*) Romans xi. 25, 26.

yet he is aware that "the fatted Calf,"—the great Victim which had been so lo
promised,—has been killed! . . . . He proceeds,

30 but as soon as this thy Son was come, which hath devoured t!
living with harlots, thou hast killed for him the fatted calf.

Observe how wickedly he, who in the former verse exaggerated his own obe
ence, in the present verse magnifies the offence of his Brother! Compare what
here said with what was stated in verse 13.

Also,—"As soon as this *thy Son*"(!) he says, "was *come.*"(!)   And why i
"*my Brother,*"—"*was returned?*"

31 And he said unto him, Son, thou art ever with me, and all th
I have is thine.

The Father, who received back the younger Son without reproaches, forbears an
to rebuke His elder Son; far less does He charge him with untruth,—remindi
him, as He might have done, of countless acts of unfaithfulness and disobedien
He proceeds calmly,—

32 It was meet that we should make merry, and be glad: for th
thy Brother was dead, and is alive again; and was lost, and is found

It was the one thought which filled the Father's heart.   See ver. 24.

Notice here the delicacy of the implied reproof.   "This *thy Son*," had been t
language of the elder Brother, in ver. 30.   But the Father, entreating with hi
says not, "For this my Son was dead and is alive again;" but,—"*This thy Brothe*
reminding him, thereby, of the claim which the poor Prodigal had upon *him*.

The frequent preference given to the younger Son over the elder, in Holy Scr
ture,—had prepared men's minds for that great national dispensation, which,
the present Parable also, is traced prophetically: namely, the ultimate accepta
of the Gentiles.   Even where no marked contrast is established, or preferer
avowed,—as when GOD said, "I loved Jacob, and I hated Esau,"(z)—the place
favour is again and again assigned to the younger Son.   Seth, Shem, Peleg, Ab
ham: then Jacob, who has been already noticed: Joseph and Ephraim: Jud
and Pharez:(a) Moses and David,—are all examples prefiguring what was to hap
long after.   Consider also the language of Judges vi. 15, and 1 Samuel ix. 21.

Three Parables, so nearly of one tendency, delivered in succession, call for co
parison.   Each sets forth the concern of ALMIGHTY GOD for every individual so
We are reminded, in all three, that it is not His will that *any* should perish.   A
they correspond in noticing the Heavenly rejoicing which attends one sinner's
covery.

On the other hand, they exhibit some points of contrast.   The first Parable
scribes the case of one who has simply gone astray, and wandered from the Fo
the second,—*that* of one who has been lost through neglect: the last, and longe
is the history of a wilfully disobedient man.   And the methods adopted for the
covery of each, are found to differ likewise.   No pains are spared for the recove
of the first,—who is followed after, until he is found.   For the recovery of the s
ond, a patient heart and a vigilant eye are alone required.   But the last is left
obey, or to disregard, the motions of the HOLY SPIRIT,—urging him to return.
this last case, the first step towards reconciliation must be taken by the offender.

And the recovery of one *in a hundred*,—of one *in ten*,—and of the other *of two*,
seems intended to repress all curious inquiries into a subject with which we ha
no practical concern: namely, the spiritual condition of *our neighbours;* and Go
dealings with them; and whether few persons, or many, stand in need of the Re
very here spoken of.   Our SAVIOUR'S words on a recent occasion, when He soug
to discourage unprofitable speculations of a similar class, are strictly applicable
this place:—"*Except ye repent*, ye shall all likewise perish."

The following remarks, by a good and thoughtful man, are too apposite and bea
tiful to be omitted here,—where GOD'S *Love* is so strikingly shown in three succe

(z) Mal. i. 2, 3; quoted Rom. ix. 13.   (a) Gen. xxxviii. 29.

ive Parables. "There is nothing more worthy of observation" (he says) "than the way in which the natural habits and affections of men are used in Scripture, to illustrate the dealings and dispositions of the Invisible GOD; nor can anything be imagined more likely to bring the Truth and Love of GOD home to our hearts, than when we are thus made to feel an image of it in ourselves. It is to be observed, however, that the habits and affections of mankind, thus taken and made use of, are purely natural,—as GOD made and willed them; and noways connected with the degeneracy of the sinful state. We may then feel the justness of their use in this way, to make known to us the things of GOD. For GOD not only made man upright, but He made him in His own image: and if so, then in the Human Nature, (that is, our own,) we may see as in a glass the truth of GOD's. For an image is but the resemblance of something original, which only is the reality, the substance,—of which the other is a shadow. We may understand, moreover, that there is in the Creature a natural capacity and fitness, given it no doubt by its CREATOR from the first, for setting forth His own Love, and Goodness, and Glory. For otherwise, how could the SON of GOD have taken upon Himself the form,—and been made in the likeness,—of Man ?"(b)

CHAPTER XVI.

THE Parables of our SAVIOUR here succeed each other with marvellous rapidity. We met with three in the former chapter. In the present, two more are recorded. The parable of "the Unjust Steward," which comes first, is certainly one of the most difficult of our LORD's parables; partly, because after bringing forward, and stating in detail, a case of great dishonesty, the Divine Speaker not only withholds His censure, but even *seems* to dismiss it with words of commendation: partly also, because of the doctrinal application of the Parable, which is certainly far from obvious. Much of this difficulty will be found to disappear, on a careful study of the narrative: but there will remain much to make us thoughtful; and to impress us with the strangeness, even in its minutest details, of a Revelation which comes from GOD.

The three last Parables were addressed to the Pharisees and Scribes. Not so the Parable of "the Unjust Steward,"—though the Pharisees are found still standing by. It was spoken to the Disciples:—

1 AND He said also unto His Disciples, There was a certain rich Man, which had a Steward; and the same was accused unto Him that he had wasted His goods.

So far, all seems plain. The "Rich Man" is GOD; the "Steward" is one of ourselves: and this reveals to us one very important relation in which we all stand towards our MAKER, namely, that of *stewards*,—stewards of the opportunities with

(b) From a MS. Sermon by the Rev. W. J. Palmer.

which His Providence hath intrusted us. Now, "it is required in stewards that a man be found *faithful.*"(a) Elsewhere, we are taught to regard ourselves as Traders: but in either case, our opportunities are His "goods;" the *ownership* rests with *Him*, not *us;* and terrible is the responsibility of those who "*waste* His goods." Verily there is one that ever accuseth us unto Him,—even Satan, who from that very circumstance is called *the Accuser of the Brethren.*(b)

2 And He called him, and said unto him, How is it that I hear this of thee? give an account of thy stewardship; for thou mayest be no longer Steward.

And GOD calls us in many ways:—by afflictions, by illness, by the signs of decay in ourselves or others, by the sight of Death. Whatever speaks to us of departure, and of Judgment to come, is a call from GOD. Of course, the actual requirement to give up our stewardship, comes with the Day of our Departure,—when GOD will call us to our Great Account. But it is plain that Death itself is not what is referred to in the Parable, but rather a warning that Death is at hand; else would the Steward have found it impossible to act as he acted: and it is clearly unfair to press the Parable, so as to make its details applicable to what may take place upon a death-bed.

3, 4 Then the Steward said within himself, What shall I do? for my Lord taketh away from me the stewardship: I cannot dig; to beg I am ashamed.   I am resolved what to do, that, when I am put out of the stewardship, they may receive me into their houses.

Hitherto, he who reads the Parable readily admits that under the names of "a certain Rich man," and "a Steward," he is hearing about GOD and Man. The transactions which follow, beginning with the last words in ver. 4, seem to show that this is a mistake: that we are, in fact, hearing of a purely human transaction the conduct of a shrewd, but wholly unprincipled servant with respect to a confiding employer. And yet, our LORD's comment recalls our original conviction. Indeed it proves that it was correct. The difficulty consists, (as we at once discover,) in deciding on the *extent* to which the details of the Parable are capable of being applied to ourselves.

Now, the Steward's perplexity we can readily apply and explain. He has no strength of his own,—("I cannot dig:") he is ashamed to seek help of his fellows, —("to beg I am ashamed.") Neither from within nor from without does he find security. He resolves on a proceeding, therefore, which, when he becomes houseless, may prove the means of providing him with a refuge.

5, 6, 7 So he called every one of his Lord's debtors *unto him*, and said unto the first, How much owest thou unto my Lord? And he said, An hundred measures of oil. And he said unto him, Take thy bill, and sit down quickly, and write fifty. Then said he to another, And how much owest thou? And he said, An hundred measures of wheat. And he said unto him, Take thy bill, and write fourscore.

The lord of the Steward had evidently great possessions,—olive-yards and harvest-fields,—which were farmed by tenants, on condition of their paying him a fixed proportion of the produce. One of these tenants had yet a hundred measures of oil to send in; another still owed his lord as many measures of wheat. The Steward bids them both "sit down quickly," (for no time must be lost,)—gives them back their "bill," (the written acknowledgment of their respective debts,)—and bids them alter the amount to a far less sum.

8 And the *lord* commended the unjust Steward, because he had done wisely; for the children of this world are in their generation wiser than the children of Light.

"*The* lord,"—namely, *of the Steward.* Not *our* LORD, observe. This is often

(a) 1 Cor. iv. 2.   (b) Rev. xii. 10.

verlooked, but is much to be noted. *Our* LORD does not commend the servant; nay, He calls him *"unjust."* But the man's master, on hearing the history of what ne had done, praised him *for his shrewdness,*—commended *the prudence* he had shown in providing for his own temporal interest. The Steward had, in fact, so availed himself of his position,—so improved his remaining opportunities,—that though displaced from his office and driven from his home, he found himself provided at once with a place of refuge, and with friends.

Next, let *our* LORD's comment on what precedes, be carefully noted. He has told us nothing about the Steward,—except that he was "unjust." Concerning the entire transaction, however, He has this remarkable observation,—that "the children of this world are in their generation wiser than the children of Light."

Let it be observed, therefore, that these words supply the true clew to the Parable; and that it is at our peril that we seek to draw our SAVIOUR's words aside from their declared intention, in order to elicit from them teaching which they were never meant to convey. He is discoursing of the Use and Abuse of Riches,—or, (as He calls them in the next verse,) "the Mammon of Unrighteousness:" and He has shown how a man of shrewd foresight would act with respect to the unrighteous Mammon, in the prospect of dismissal from his stewardship. That he would act *unrighteously,* was to be expected. He was an unrighteous man,—one who had wasted his lord's goods. But the man's *character* is not the question. He acted *providently,*—and that was all. As in the Parable of "the Unjust Judge," so here, our attention is invited to a single circumstance. Since *here,* the Steward,—as *there,* the Judge,—is "unjust," the argument may be considered to stand in this case, somewhat as in the other:—"See how the unjust Steward acted, in order to secure for himself mere temporal comfort. And shall not the children of Light display the same anxiety to provide for themselves an eternal home?"(c) Our LORD's declaration, in the verse before us, is in fact little else than this question, thrown into a different shape. The Prudence displayed by worldly persons, so far surpassing *that* of many Christian men,—is the thing we are called upon to notice; and a striking thing it certainly is.—Our LORD proceeds.

9 And I say unto you, Make to yourselves friends of the mammon of unrighteousness; that when ye fail, they may receive you into everlasting habitations.

On this, it may be observed first, that "when ye *fail,*" means nothing else than "when ye *die:*" but it is an uncommon, as well as a very beautiful expression, implying a peaceful and happy end,(d) like that of Abraham, and Isaac, and Jacob:(e) —a mere "failing" in respect of bodily strength, and passing out of this visible world. "Whosoever liveth and believeth in Me," (saith our SAVIOUR,) *"shall never die."*(f) But the next words present graver difficulty, and more require explanation.

"Mammon," though a word of foreign origin, was a familiar term, in the language of the ancient Jews, for *"riches."* On our LORD's lips, therefore, it denotes worldly wealth generally.(g) And because the goods of this world are so often obtained by unfair, unholy means,—so often expended in a selfish, unholy manner, —He here calls Riches "the Mammon of unrighteousness," or "the unrighteous Mammon."(h) "They are so frequently and so generally *misused,*" (says a good man,) "as from that to have acquired a name."(i) But it is of Money, nevertheless, unrighteous though it be, that our LORD here bids us "make to ourselves friends;" and the mysterious reason is added,—"that when ye fail, they may receive you into everlasting habitations:"—concerning which striking mode of expression the reader is referred to the note on St. Luke xii. 20. This counsel, in fact, it is, which is so pregnant with difficulty: for we are actually required to do something with respect to *money* which, in its result, shall so resemble the proceeding of "the unjust steward," "that, when we are put out of the stewardship, they may receive us,— not indeed into their houses, but,—into everlasting habitations."(k)

It is useless therefore to overlook this difficulty. It might be truly remarked, for example, that since our LORD's debtors are sinful men, and their *debts, sins;* he who

---

(c) Compare the language of St. Luke xviii. 6.   (d) So Bp. Pearson.
(e) See the ancient Greek version of Gen. xxv. 8: xxxv. 29: xlix. 33,—where we render the word "give up the ghost."
(f) St. John xi. 26.   (g) Compare St. Matth. vi. 24.
(h) See below, ver. 11.   (i) Rev. W. J. Palmer.   (k) Compare ver. 4.

turns the sinner from the error of his way, causes him who in reality owes an hun dred to write fifty or fourscore,—and makes for himself friends who will becom powerful intercessors for him with GOD.(*l*) But then, how is this a making "frienc with the *mammon of unrighteousness?*" Our business is clearly to ascertain wha this means, and how this is to be done.

The inference from our LORD's words, then, is unavoidable. It is possible so t exercise the stewardship of our opportunities,—so to conduct ourselves in the mai agement of our wealth,—that the great Work of our Salvation, (so far as it is to l wrought out with fear and trembling by ourselves,)(*m*) shall be forwarded thereby Let each one consider this matter for himself, and apply to his own particular cas the principles by our LORD here so emphatically laid down. By *Faith*, doubtless are men saved ; not by *Works:* yet is Faith, if it hath not Works, dead,(*n*) or rathe it is *not* Faith. "What doth it profit, my brethren, though a man say he hath Faith and have not Works?   Can Faith save him?"(*o*)   "Faith which worketh b Love"(*p*) is what GOD requires: and doubtless great signs of Love towards man ma be displayed by the distribution we make of our worldly wealth. "Now, we hav by some means become very jealous of such statements, and very unwilling to adm that any reward hereafter is promised to good works and alms-deeds; but we cann shut our eyes to the fact that such promises are made in Holy Scripture; and it not our business to set them aside, but to interpret them rightly."(*q*)

Can we then do exactly as the Steward did in the Parable? Certainly not: an it is obvious that if, by any strictly similar proceeding, we *could* secure to ourselv the good will of any order of beings in the great and terrible Day, it would be crime to do so. It may be thought, in fact, that the analogy fails altogether in th respect: since it will be the holy Angels who will receive the just into everlastin habitations.(*r*)

And yet,—(for the sayings of CHRIST may not be disposed of as if they were con mon sayings, of which we are sure that we understand entirely the meaning,) what if it should prove that "*friends*" is the word to be supplied before—"recei you?" and what if it were our LORD's actual intention in this place to set befo the rich the affecting warning that they will be themselves hereafter welcomed the bowers of Bliss by those very persons whom their bounty had in life sustaine —the poor of this world, rich in Faith, whom He expressly describes as the hei of the Kingdom? "Make friends of the poor," (the meaning will therefore be "by ministering to their wants; for to them belong those everlasting tabernack into which thou wilt hereafter desire to be thyself admitted." It must be allowe that the Parable of Lazarus, which comes next, strongly supports this view. O " if we were to interpret these by other words of our LORD, we might say that sinc He graciously considers what is done for His poor as done for Himself,(*s*) we ar making *Him* our Friend when we devote our means to their relief; and that H will receive us into everlasting habitations."(*t*)

Enough has perhaps now been offered concerning this very difficult Parable What is most dark, we must be content to leave so. The suggestions alread offered concerning what is doubtful, we forbear to press. It remains that we hol fast the great lesson which the Parable was meant to convey,—and clearly appre hend its *undoubted* point. The steward was wondrous *prudent* in his conduct, di playing a great amount of worldly wisdom. How is it that Christian men display a little of that better wisdom which they have been taught in the School of CHRIST Again, it was in respect of the unrighteous Mammon that he showed his wisdom How does it happen that we, the Stewards of a LORD dividing to every man seve rally as He will,(*u*)—whence is it that *we* overlook the similar result with which th same unrighteous Mammon may also be dispensed by ourselves: namely, so tha when "flesh and heart faileth,"(*x*) we may be received into an everlasting home?(*j*

The strangeness of the history adduced by our Blessed LORD, in order to esta blish this lesson, was freely admitted at the outset. In taking leave of it, the piou suggestion of a living writer well deserves attention; namely, that it may be o

(*l*) Williams.   (*m*) Phil. ii. 12.   (*n*) St. James ii. 17.
(*o*) St. James ii. 14.   (*p*) Gal. v. 6.
(*q*) From a MS. Sermon by the Rev. C. Marriott.   (*r*) See St. Matth. xiii. 48, 49
(*s*) St. Matth. xxv. 40.   (*t*) From a MS. Sermon by the Rev. C. Marriott.
(*u*) 1 Cor. xii. 11.   (*x*) Psalm lxxiii. 26.
(*y*) Consider the following places,—St. Matthew vi. 19 to 21: xix. 21. St. Luke xii. 21, 3
1 Tim. vi. 17 to 19, &c.

ɔbject of the narrative, (which, like the next, has been supposed to be a true history,) "to show that all the occurrences of the world, however bad and unworthy in themselves, yet should minister to the spiritual edification and wisdom of GOD's children; that whatever language they may speak to others, they contain within them another better language which they speak to these, . . . Here was an instance ɔf great iniquity, crowned with success, and admired by the world for its wisdom; and which might, therefore, have been supposed to serve as a stumbling-block to the good: yet, on the contrary, it comes forth with the greater force and beauty as bearing witness to the transient nature of things below, and of eternal habitations with GOD. There is a peculiar sweetness and power in such teaching. It seems to show the world as GOD's world: all things as working for good to His elect. It corrects the error of looking upon the things of the world in any way as apart from GOD; as if, because iniquity abounded, it were not His world. Thus Love itself is instructed, and need not wax cold, nor be stifled, but burn the brighter; while the very evils of the world are made to minister to the divine flame of Charity, and the wisdom of the just."(z)

Our SAVIOUR proceeds "to lay down a rule upon which GOD's judgment will be justified in withholding the enjoyment of the greater good in Heaven from those who have not used aright the things intrusted to them on Earth:"(a)

10 He that is faithful in that which is least, is faithful also in much: and he that is unjust in the least is unjust also in much.

"Which is as much as if He had said,—The use which men make of the goods of this present world, which are comparatively of small value, shows the use they would make of such as are far greater, were the same committed to them, and which belong to the children of GOD in Heaven. If they have used these aright, so would they use those; and if they have abused these, they would abuse those likewise. *Faithfulness* and *Injustice* are properly applied to the use and abuse of things not our own, but committed to us for the honour and purposes of the owner. For to apply them to our *own* uses and purposes, and not *His*, would be a breach of trust, and therefore unfaithful and unjust in a very high degree."(b)

This, then, supplies the answer to any doubt which may arise concerning the dignity of the little concerns of daily life. The Saints of GOD will hereafter "judge angels."(c) Can then the petty concerns of an earthly stewardship be worthy of their attention? "It is in these small matters that the fidelity is to be proved which shall be found meet to inherit eternal treasures; in these shadows of good is to be shown worthiness for the Divine realities."(d) Hence it follows,—

11 If therefore ye have not been faithful in the unrighteous mammon, who will commit to your trust the true *riches?*

"Assuredly, no wise person will; and therefore neither in this case will GOD commit to your power the riches of the world to come.

"But," proceeds the pious man just now mentioned at the foot of the page, "the very nature of the possession of present and future good is different. The present is not our own: the future, by GOD's gift, will be. The present belongs to another: it is only committed in trust to those who enjoy it for a season. To GOD and CHRIST present things belong: to us, they are only committed in trust, being lent; graciously lent, that by them we may work out an inestimable reward. If we have not been faithful in these,—if we have not done the works for the doing of which they were intrusted to our care, and concerning which we know that we shall have to render an account,—never must we expect to be put in possession of those better things, which at a future day, and if we have used these aright, we may hope to call *our own*." As it follows:

12 And if ye have not been faithful in that which is another man's, who shall give you that which is your own?

(z) Williams.   (a) Rev. W. J. Palmer.
(b) From a Sermon by the Rev. W. J. Palmer,—late Rector of Mixbury and Finmere: a man of truly primitive piety and exemplary goodness; who gave in the account of a most blessed stewardship, on the 28th September, 1853.
(c) 1 Cor. vi. 3.   (d) Williams.

"*Our own*,"—because "no account will be required concerning them; and in respect of them our will, will be as GOD's. The force of the argument is clear to the apprehension of those who bear in mind what is revealed of the conditions of that glorious state where GOD shall be 'all in all,'(*e*) and where we shall be as Kings and Priests before GOD and the FATHER of our LORD?"(*f*)

So far, a good and faithful man, but lately gone to his reward. Let us not fail to notice the singular light thrown by the preceding words of Scripture on the life to come,—concerning which so little has been revealed, that every fresh communication on the subject from the lips of CHRIST Himself is unspeakably precious. The *social* character of the future Life,—the bliss which will spring out of the preservation and the perfection of human ties,—St. Paul distinctly notices.(*g*) The promotion to a loftier trust and a more splendid stewardship is further declared by our SAVIOUR in other places of the Gospel besides the present.(*h*) And we may not fail to observe that, on more than one occasion, a difference in *the nature* of the Tenure is proclaimed. No longer Service, but *Rule*,(*i*)—no longer another's goods, but *our own*,—will occupy as many as are greeted with the blessed salutation,—"Well done, good and faithful servant!"

It only remains to notice the sayings with which our SAVIOUR takes leave of the subject.

13 No servant can serve two masters: for either he will hate the one, and love the other; or else he will hold to the one, and despise the other. Ye cannot serve GOD and Mammon.

"Mammon," in this place, denotes the pleasures of this life generally; because money is the means of procuring them. And the intention of these words seems to be, to convey to our LORD's hearers a solemn warning against any attempt to effect a compromise between the service of GOD and the service of the World: that is, to declare the impossibility of doing GOD's pleasure here, and our own pleasure after the flesh, at the same time. In the Sermon on the Mount we have met with this saying already:(*k*) but take notice that, instead of "no *man* can serve two masters," (as there,) it is here, "no *servant*,"—in allusion to the Steward in the parable which goes before.

14 And the Pharisees also, who were covetous, heard all these things: and they derided Him.

They perceived that the Parable of "the Unjust Steward" was directed against *the sin of Judas*.(*l*) The Pharisees were themselves largely infected by the same vice. Accordingly, they seek to turn into derision what the Holy One has spoken.

15 And He said unto them, Ye are they which justify yourselves before men; but GOD knoweth your hearts: for that which is highly esteemed among men is an abomination in the sight of GOD.

These last few words seem to contain an awful foretaste of the parable which is to follow;—if *that* may be called a parable which has every appearance of being a true history. Our LORD's meaning is probably very well represented by the expression "highly esteemed;" but what He actually said, was—"that which is *lofty*." He was addressing a dominant sect among the Jews, notorious for nothing so much as for their ambition, self-righteousness, and vain-glorious pride;(*m*) and who fenced themselves within the sanctions of the Law,—of which they may have meant to imply that our SAVIOUR was an authorized Teacher. He therefore informs them that,

16 The Law and the Prophets *were* until John: since that time, the Kingdom of GOD is preached, and every man presseth into it.

In other words, the entire fabric of the Law had already effected its purpose; and the predictions of the Prophets, having now found fulfilment, both "the Law and the

(*e*) 1 Cor. xv. 28.   (*f*) Rev. i. 6.   (*g*) 1 Thess. ii. 19, 20.
(*h*) Consider St. Luke xix. 17, 19.   (*i*) See the note on St. Luke xix. 17.
(*k*) St. Matth. vi. 24, where see the notes.   (*l*) See the notes on St. Mark xiv. 25.
(*m*) Consider St. Matth. xxiii. (the whole chapter): St. Luke xi. 37 to 44: xiv. 7.

Prophets" belonged in a manner to the past. "The preaching of John," as it was the birthday of the Gospel,(n) so was it also the day of departure for the Law and the Prophets.(o) "Thenceforward, the good tidings of GOD's Kingdom are proclaimed; and every one forceth his way in;" that is, the Kingdom is being taken by violence, like Canaan of old, from you its ancient possessors,—who "dwell careless, after the manner of the Zidonians."(p)

Not that the Law had *indeed* failed by the bringing in of the Gospel. Its deeper meanings had but thereby been discovered, and its true intention seen. Hence the words which follow:

17 And it is easier for Heaven and Earth to pass, than one tittle of the Law to fail.

CHRIST therefore was not about to destroy the Law. He came not to destroy but to fulfil,—and to convict them of their wickedness in making that Law of none effect by their lax interpretation of it. Adverting to their wicked teaching on the subject of divorce, He proceeds to give one instance of the inviolability of the Law: saying,—

18 Whosoever putteth away his wife, and marrieth another, committeth adultery: and whosoever marrieth her that is put away from *her* husband, committeth adultery.

Full of instruction it surely is to find the sanctity of Marriage, and the indissoluble nature of the Marriage bond, so often insisted upon by our SAVIOUR; and here, singled out of the whole Law, to be a sample of it. Consider St. Matthew v. 31, 32: also xix. 9, and the notes on both places. The Reader is also requested to read what has been offered on St. Matthew xix. 10. He is further requested to take notice that the four verses we have just been considering are but costly samples of our LORD's teaching on this occasion,—precious fragments of a long, and lost, Discourse.

Hitherto, our SAVIOUR "has been showing how by a certain right use, Riches may be made available even to our being received into everlasting Happiness when we die. In what follows, He inverts the picture: showing the loss of one who uses the good things with which his life may have been blessed, upon himself alone,— namely, in advancing his state and condition in the world, serving in various ways his own ease, pleasure, and gratification."(q) The Parable of Lazarus is in fact a most astonishing Revelation. Whereas all the other parables of our LORD refer either to the Life present or to the Life to come, this parable refers to that mysterious Life which lies between the two. It follows the soul of man beyond the limits of the Grave, uncovers the unseen World, and tells us many things concerning that hereafter concerning which we cannot but feel such deep and awful interest. The constant belief of the Church that what follows is a true history, adds to the sense of wonder with which we read it.

19, 20 There was a certain rich man, which was clothed in purple and fine linen, and fared sumptuously every day: and there was a certain beggar named Lazarus,

The name of the "certain rich man" is not mentioned; but the beggar bore the name of our SAVIOUR's friend,(r)—and that, for a mysterious reason which will be found suggested below, in the note on ver. 31. It is the *only* proper name which occurs in any of our LORD's parables. "Does He not seem to have been quoting," (asks Augustine,) "from that book where He found the name of the poor man written, but where the name of the rich man was blotted out?"(s)

What is said concerning these two persons must be carefully noticed. No sins are laid to the rich man's charge. It is only related of him that his outer and his inner garments were habitually of the most costly and luxurious kind; and that he "fared sumptuously"—(literally, "feasted(t) splendidly")—"every day." From

(n) Acts i. 22.
(p) Judges xviii. 7,—quoted by Williams.
(r) St. John xi. 5.
(t) See the note on St. Luke xii. 19,—where the same word is found.

(o) See the note on St. Matth. xvii. 8.
(q) Rev. W. J. Palmer.
(s) Consider Exod. xxxiii. 12: also the note on St. Luke x. 28.

this last circumstance, he is styled in the heading of the Chapter(*u*) "*the rich glutton;*" and without pretending to defend such an interpretation of our LORD's words, we may yet remark that the man is a glutton whose fare is sumptuous *every day.*(*x*)

As the rich man is charged with no single crime, so neither does the beggar obtain a word of praise. It is simply said that,—so far from sharing the luxurious life of the rich man,—he was one

21 which was laid at his gate full of sores, and desiring to be fed with the crumbs which fell from the rich man's table: moreover the dogs came and licked his sores.

Words, few indeed; yet conspiring to exhibit a case of truly abject misery. The picture of the dogs approaching to lick the beggar's sores, is surely more than affecting—on the lips of such a Speaker! Take notice, however, that it is not implied that the beggar was *habitually* laid at the rich man's gate. It is only said that on a certain occasion he "had been laid" there. On the other hand, it *does* seem to be implied that he wished, but *wished in vain,* to be fed with the crumbs which fell from the other's table; and further, that his bodily ailments were as little regarded as his bodily needs. The poor sufferer, it may be, having been once laid near the rich man's threshold, remained there till he died; having had the sense of his own misery heightened by the sight of the other's enjoyment,—whose selfish hardness of heart was also thus left without excuse.

22 And it came to pass, that the beggar died, and was carried by the Angels into Abraham's bosom:

Let us notice, one by one, the several points which are here revealed to us concerning the state of the soul after death: and first, the statement that the souls of the just are "carried by the Angels into Abraham's bosom,"—that is, into the place where Abraham is; a region of Peace and Joy, where, (as it is said in ver. 25,) the souls of the just are "comforted." The beggar died; and oh, blessed change! He who knew no friend on earth, finds that "the sons of GOD"(*y*) are appointed to minister to his bliss. Yesterday, dogs licked his sores: to-day,—"not one Angel carries him, but many; for many are eager to bear:"(*z*) "each rejoicing to touch such a burthen."(*a*) "Are they not all ministering Spirits, sent forth to minister for them who shall be heirs of Salvation?"(*b*) It follows,

the rich man also died, and was buried;

Note the contrast. After a time, "the rich man also died,—*and was buried.*" Nothing more is related. His end was marked by a splendid funeral, and that was all. (Weeping friends, of whom the rich man was unconscious,—instead of rejoicing Angels, whose embracing arms the beggar felt!) Whether Lazarus was buried or not we are not told; neither do we care to inquire. . . . . And all this is set down for the comfort of the poor, who have but humble funerals. The rich man, then, was buried; "but he carried nothing away: his glory did not descend after him."(*c*) Far from it:

23 and in Hell he lifted up his eyes, being in torments, and seeth Abraham afar off, and Lazarus in his bosom.

Further, and yet more wondrous disclosures are here made. A state of torment, in the case of the wicked, is found to *precede* their final condemnation,—"a certain fearful looking-for of judgment,"(*d*) as the Apostle speaks. Their souls are gathered into the chambers of the departed, and they are "tormented." Is it not also implied that they *behold* the Saints afar off in bliss? It would indeed seem so, from another place in Scripture as well as the present:(*e*) and, in such case, the remark would be as true as it is striking, that "as the poor man, while he lived, had his sufferings heightened by beholding the other's abundance; so does it now add

---

(*u*) From the Vulgate.
(*x*) Consider St. Matth. vi. 16, and the note there. See also the note on St. Luke xviii. 12.
(*y*) Job i. 6.   (*z*) Williams.   (*a*) Ludolphus.   (*b*) Heb. i. 14.
(*c*) See Ps. xlix. 17.   (*d*) Heb. x. 27.
(*e*) See St. Luke xiii. 28. Compare Isaiah lxv. 13.

to the torment of the rich man to behold Lazarus in bliss."(*f*) But it may be unsafe to take our LORD's words concerning this matter quite literally. What is certain, the regions occupied by the wicked and the just are not only different, but they are so entirely distinct that there is no longer any possibility of passing from the one to the other. This is made plainer by the words which follow, in ver. 26.

24 And he cried and said, Father Abraham, have mercy on me, and send Lazarus, that he may dip the tip of his finger in water, and cool my tongue: for I am tormented in this flame.

Truly *that* was "a great and exceeding bitter cry!"(*g*) The rich man is now the beggar; and see how piteously he pleads! Release, he knows to be impossible: some relief, he thinks he *may* obtain. Moreover, he can apprehend no channel of mercy so obvious as the hands of the very beggar whom in life he had slighted! Consider this in connection with what was offered above in the note on ver. 9,—fourth paragraph from the end.

Many of the Fathers observe that "he who had refused crumbs of bread, now asks for a drop of water:" but, (as a thoughtful writer observes,) "it is more than this. Lazarus desired to be filled with the crumbs: the rich man prayed for but one drop of water on the tip of his finger; and that for his tongue only."(*h*) And this is a safer remark than the other; for it is not *stated* that the rich man refused crumbs to the beggar.

The suffering wretch addresses himself to Abraham; and calls him his "Father," because, being a Jew, he was himself a son of Abraham:(*i*) but our LORD's warning in this matter had been very emphatic,—"Think not to say within yourselves, We have Abraham to our Father!"(*k*) . . . . Moreover, the rich man knows that he is addressing one who was hospitable to strangers;(*l*) and surely (he thinks) Abraham will not turn a deaf ear to such a small request from himself! But in this respect also, he has to be undeceived.

Gregory the Great, in his Commentary on the Book of Job, has a striking remark on the rich man's complaint that *his tongue* was the seat of his suffering. "Almost always," he observes, "is unbridled speech the attendant of banqueting. Hence, the man who used to 'fare sumptuously every day,' in the end is declared to have coveted a drop of water to cool *his tongue*. The punishment is a hint as to what had been his sin." But the force of this remark would not be diminished if it should be thought that in respect to *gluttony* also the rich man had greatly offended. The narrative, however, is severely brief. Not one of the rich man's sins are recorded.

The mention of "eyes," "finger," "tongue," in this place, is, of course, figurative. So we speak of the eyes, the finger, the mouth of GOD. But it has been well remarked that "as, in this latter case, there may be some secret reference to the Incarnation, so there may be, in the former, *to the Resurrection of the Body*."(*m*) To proceed:

25 But Abraham said, Son, remember that thou in thy lifetime receivedst thy good things, and likewise Lazarus evil things: but now he is comforted, and thou art tormented.

The discourse of Abraham reminds us of the discourse of Him whose day "Abraham saw, and was glad."(*n*) "Woe unto you that are rich,"—"that are full,"—"that laugh now;"—"for ye have received your consolation!"(*o*) Indeed, the two places should be compared; for we are thereby guided to a right understanding of the case before us.

It is sometimes pointed out concerning the present parable, not only that the rich man is not related to have been guilty of any heinous offence, but that he appears to have gone to the place of torment less for sins of commission, than for sins of omission:—that he had failed to *do* anything in order to serve and please GOD;—and the like.

But we must be very careful as to the inferences we draw from Holy Scripture.

(*f*) Chrysostom.   (*g*) Gen. xxvii. 34.   (*h*) Williams.
(*i*) Consider St. Luke xiii. 16.   (*k*) St. Matth. iii. 9.
(*l*) Heb. xiii. 2, alluding partly to Gen. xviii. 3.   (*m*) Williams.
(*n*) St. John viii. 56.   (*o*) St. Luke vi. 24, 25.

True indeed it is that nothing actually sinful is distinctly recorded concerning the Rich Man; but then, (as already observed,) neither is there a syllable spoken concerning *the Beggar*, in the way of *praise*. We must reason backward concerning them therefore: and since the one was finally accepted,—the other, miserable,—their lives must have been such and such. The one certainly was not rewarded *because* he had been poor, any more than the other was punished *because* he was rich. Of Abraham, with whom the beggar had his eternal portion, it is even expressly recorded that he was "*very rich*."(o) The reason, therefore, of their respective fates is to be sought in some unrelated cause: and it is not difficult to see of what nature that cause must have been. Indeed, the rich man's sin is contained and all-but formally stated, in the reproof addressed to him by Abraham: "Son remember that *thou*," (the word is emphatic,) "didst in thy lifetime *have out*," or "fully take, *thy* good things." The things spoken of were not *really* good: true. But the rich man in this parable, (like the rich fool, in another,)(p) had made them his "good" things, all the same. He had lived for this world only: and had no treasure, no hope, no concern in the world to come. "*Thou*," (says Abraham, "in *thy lifetime*,"—for the rich man had cared for no life but *that*.

But the Beggar had received "evil things" only, all his days: that is, he had suffered poverty, disease, hunger, abject misery,—all those things which the world accounts "evil." It is to be supposed further, that he had hungered and thirsted after heavenly consolation, even more than earthly: had been patient in suffering and become perfected by the discipline of pain. His loathsome condition will have bred in him the most abject sense of his own vileness: whereby it came to pass that he found favour with Him who "raiseth up the poor out of the dust, and lifteth up the beggar from the dunghill."(q) How plainly, at all events, are we taught hereby that such an estate is a favourable condition to future Blessedness;—but that the possessor of Riches, on the contrary, because he is in danger of *trusting* in his Riches,(r) incurs the further peril of forgetting his GOD! It seems to be the object of our LORD's discourse to show the fatal tendency of a luxurious life to close the heart against want and misery; and to set forth, in solemn warning, the contrast which may exist between the conditions of men in Time and in Eternity. . . Such, then, seems to be the general tendency of the parable,—severe in its brevity and wondrous sparing, (as the manner of Scripture is,) in its details. "It is setting forth, in living representation, of the concluding maxim of the foregoing parable,—namely, 'Make to yourselves friends' of the poor, by the use of riches for here the rich man is shown as having failed to make Lazarus his friend. 'The poor,' says Augustine, 'have no habitation here on earth into which they can receive us; but they have habitations which are Eternal.'"(s)—Abraham continues

26 And besides all this, between us and you there is a great gulf fixed: so that they which would pass from hence to you cannot; neither can they pass to us, that *would come* from thence.

The gulf is "great,"—because it sunders the evil from the just, as the West is severed from the East: "fixed,"—because GOD hath separated good from evil by an everlasting barrier which can never be disturbed. And this seems as express statement as an honest mind can desire against the doctrine that after a season of purgatorial suffering the souls of the departed may be transferred from the place of torment to the place of rest. *Life*, it is implied, is the season for Repentance:—whence it follows,—

27, 28 Then he said, I pray thee therefore, Father, that thou wouldest send him to my father's house: for I have five brethren; that he may testify unto them, lest they also come into this place of torment.

We are thus presented with another striking disclosure: namely, that in the state of departed souls, not only consciousness remains, but "the recollection of what was done on earth, and of the persons of those with whom the dead formerly conversed."(t) "The rich man's knowledge and memory are preserved for his punishment; for he knew Lazarus whom he had despised, and he remembered his brethren whom he had left."(u)

(o) Gen. xiii. 2.   (p) See St. Luke xii. 19.
(q) 1 Sam. ii. 8,—which must be compared with St. Luke i. 52, 53.
(r) St. Mark x. 23, 24.   (s) Williams.   (t) Rev. W. J. Palmer.   (u) Gregory the Great

Take notice, that whatever the sins of the rich man may have been, (and they were doubtless great,) *a kindly disposition* seems yet to have been his. Very little is revealed concerning him: but the anxiety he displays to provide for the safety of his "five brethren" is an affecting indication of feelings not yet wholly blunted,—a heart by no means callous to the claims of family and kindred.

It is even better worth our observation, however, that we behold here, as in so many other places of Scripture, the strivings of fruitless remorse. As the foolish go in search of oil when it is too late,—as the wicked begin to knock "when once the Master of the house hath shut to the door,"(x)—as Judas brings back the price of blood, and seeks to make a miserable restitution, after his LORD had been condemned,(y)—as Esau, with "a great and exceeding bitter cry," demands of his father the blessing which he has already forfeited,—so here does the rich man, when it is too late, begin to think of sending a preacher to those brethren with whom, in life, he had so often made a mock of Heaven and Hell,—of the unseen World,—of Religion itself! Unavailing sorrow becomes henceforth part of his torment; and probably its most bitter ingredient.

29 Abraham saith unto him, They have Moses and the prophets; let them hear them.

"As if he said, Thy brethren are not so much thy care as *His* who created them, and appointed them teachers."(z) "They have sufficient means of grace afforded them: let them act up to their own light."(a)

30 And he said, Nay, father Abraham: but if one went unto them from the dead, they will repent.

It is ever thus with sinners: they fancy that had they but greater opportunities they must surely become saints. This man supposed that clearer *evidences* of religion would have made of himself and all his brethren, true believers. In the meanwhile, his perseverance in the argument is no less affecting than it is striking. But Abraham is unmoved:

31 And he said unto him, If they hear not Moses and the prophets, neither will they be persuaded, though one rose from the dead.

He does not *say* that he will not grant the thing asked for; but that it will be unavailing. Thus, a Lazarus *was* actually sent from the dead, at the end of four days, to the Jewish people; but without effect. And it may be thought that it was in order to draw the attention of the nation towards this circumstance, that our SAVIOUR assigned to the beggar beforehand the name of him whom He would hereafter awake out of sleep.(b)

"This part of the Parable," writes a good man,—"prophetic as it was of the continued unbelief of the Jews, who, refusing to hear the law and the testimony of the Prophets, and to believe the miracles which JESUS our LORD had done before their eyes, failed to be converted by that greatest miracle of all, His own Resurrection from the Grave,—teaches us this lesson,—that it is of the very last moment immediately to set about performing the will of GOD in such things as it hath been once revealed: for, by the example of the Jews, we may understand that otherwise no reason can render intelligible a dispensation which we do not like; no evidence can persuade us of truths which we are not willing to receive."(c)

This, in truth, is the sum of the matter. There is not,—there never hath been, —any lack of evidence. A change of heart, not a more impressive teacher, is the one thing needed. Concerning all impenitent sinners of these latter days, Abraham's words declare thus much:—If the Old and New Testaments,—the Gospel of JESUS CHRIST,—the means of Grace by GOD Himself provided,—Sacraments, and the services of the Sanctuary, and the teaching of the Prayer-Book,—CHRIST pleading with us, invisibly, by His HOLY SPIRIT,—and the countless helps afforded to Christian men in a Christian country;—if all *these* prove unavailing to produce repentance, and to awaken to a life of holiness,—*nothing* could achieve that blessed end! Men will not repent,—men will not be persuaded,—no, not though one rose from the Dead!

(x) St. Luke xiii. 25.   (y) St. Matth. xxvii. 3 to 5.   (z) Chrysostom.
(a) Williams.   (b) St. John xi. 11, &c.   (c) Rev. W. J. Palmer.

CHAPTER XVII.

1 CHRIST *teacheth to avoid occasions of offence.* 3 *One to forgive another.* 6 *The power of Faith.* 7 *How we are bound to* GOD, *and not He to us.* 11 *He healeth ten lepers.* 22 *Of the Kingdom of* GOD, *and the Coming of the Son of Man.*

IT is obvious to suppose that some interval elapsed between the delivery of the Parable of Lazarus, with which the former chapter ended, and the discourse which follows. The first word ("then") has no relation, in this place, to Time.

1, 2, 3 THEN said He unto the Disciples, It is impossible but the offences will come: but woe *unto him*, through whom they come It were better for him that a millstone were hanged about his neck and he cast into the sea, than that he should offend one of these little ones. Take heed to yourselves.

Whether our LORD is here speaking particularly of children in age,(a) or of men with childlike hearts,(b) does not appear.

We have already met with these sayings, in St. Matthew's Gospel ;(c) but the clauses are there found in a contrary order. Moreover, they were then delivered in quite a different connection.

But it will be asked,—What connection have our SAVIOUR's words in this place with the words which follow? And it must be freely admitted that they do no appear, at first sight, to have any connection at all. The same thing may be said of verses 3 and 4, and of verse 6,—in all of which places, sayings of our LORD are recorded which are found more or less exactly given in different parts of St. Matthew's Gospel.(d) We are not, however, on that account at liberty to assume that these sayings are scraps of those other discourses, selected at random by St. Luke and here set down by him, in utter disregard of Time and Place. And yet, this is so frequently assumed by writers of good repute, and the suspicion seems so likely to cross the mind of an ordinary reader, that a few remarks shall here be offered on the subject. They will not be out of place, and certainly they are not uncalled for

It may be regarded as quite certain, then, that the recorded Discourses of our Blessed SAVIOUR, are *only partially* set down in the Gospels. *Perfect* indeed, those discourses are, as they stand recorded: (that is, there is nothing in them to change or add, or take away: there has not been one word set down which it concerns us not to possess; nor has there been one word withheld which it would concern us to recover:) yet have those Discourses been *not entirely* given. This is obvious. The World itself would not contain the record of our LORD's actions:(e) and is it to be supposed that Four short Gospels contain more than a sample of His oral Teaching That those Divine Discourses have been seldom, *if ever*, given *entire*, is surely ob vious. This then will explain why it is often so difficult to trace the connection between one sentence and another; and to detect the nature of every transition. A link often seems,—doubtless often *is*,—wanting: so that what must once have been beautifully connected in all its parts, is often presented to us in a state which, for want of a better word, we must term *fragmentary.*

But we are not at liberty to assume that there *never was* any connection, because there does not appear *to be* any connection *now*. The beads are unstrung. True

(a) As in St. Matth. xviii. 2, 6.   (b) As in St. Matth. x. 40, 42.
(c) St. Matth. xviii. 6, 7; where see the notes.
(d) With St. Luke xvii. 3, 4, compare St. Matth. xviii. 15, 21. With St. Luke xvii. 6, com pare St. Matth. xvii. 20: xxi. 21, (St. Mark xi. 23.)   (e) St. John xxi. 25.

But it does not follow that nothing ever held them together. And if, (as not seldom happens,) the fragmentary sayings in question are found to recur in a different part of another Gospel, it is surely a mark of singular impatience, or uncommon weakness, that the suspicion should be so readily admitted that those sayings were uttered only once; and that the Evangelists had been putting together, at random, sayings which were uttered at a different time, and on a widely different occasion. The jewels may exactly resemble each other, and yet the threads on which they were once strung may surely be wholly distinct. How much worthier, (as well as more obvious,) is the belief that those words were more than once delivered; and that, out of a long discourse, for some good reason, they alone have been preserved on this, the second time of their delivery! In *such* cases, it will often be useless to seek to recover the lost links of thought or expression. They are perhaps hopelessly gone. And the sayings must be studied, (like those in the Book of Proverbs,) each by itself.

It has, indeed, many times been the reward of Piety and Learning to supply the wished-for clew; and great is the gratification which results from the discovery that the members of a discourse which at first seemed unconnected, do, on the contrary, marvellously cohere. Yet, frequent variety of opinion reminds us that there is seldom any real *certainty* in such criticism. It is the effort of a human artist to supply what the Divine Artificer has purposely left incomplete. Hence the difficulty, and indeed the danger, of attempting to supply absent words, and to recover the missing link of thought.

The remarks thus made, once for all, shall not be repeated: but they will be called to mind with advantage by those who love to ponder over the sayings of their LORD; and who desire to entertain worthy notions of the Book wherein those sayings stand recorded.—In a case like the present, it seems to be the safer plan gratefully to recognise the fragments of one of His many long and lost Discourses: and carefully to gather them up, that nothing, through neglect of ours, be lost. Surely, the fact that the same sayings have already been met with elsewhere, should only serve the more to awaken our attention,—suggesting as it does their uncommon weight, dignity, and importance.

Our LORD proceeds to speak of forgiveness of injuries. What follows should begin with the word " Moreover,"—

4 If thy brother trespass against thee, rebuke him; and if he repent, forgive him. And if he trespass against thee seven times in a day, and seven times in a day turn again to thee, saying, I repent; thou shalt forgive him.

Sayings very closely resembling these, (as already explained,) yet clearly *not* the same, are found in St. Matthew's Gospel.(*f*) It is interesting to discover that in St. Matthew also, they are preceded by a discourse concerning the "little ones." Can it require stating that "seven" in this place is indefinite(*g*) and stands for an unlimited number? There are to be no bounds to our forgiveness. "Not until seven times, but until seventy times seven."(*h*)

5 And the Apostles said unto the LORD, Increase our Faith.

How beautiful a prayer! and in itself, how strong a proof of Faith in the blessed speakers! They knew therefore that their hearts and minds were in their Master's Hands: and He could mould and fashion them according to His own sovereign will. As Williams truly says,—"For Faith they ask: and by asking, show their Faith. Thus Prayer ever increases Faith, and Faith ever inclines to Prayer." The Reader is referred to the latter part of the note on St. Luke xviii. 8.

6 And the LORD said, If ye had Faith as a grain of mustard-seed, ye might say unto this sycamine tree, Be thou plucked up by the root, and be thou planted in the sea; and it should obey you.

Though this precise saying occurs nowhere but here, its resemblance to the words which our LORD delivered on two other occasions,—namely, after His Transfigura-

(*f*) St. Matth. xviii. 15, 21.   (*g*) Compare Prov. xxiv. 16.   (*h*) St. Matth. xviii. 22.

tion,(i) and during the last Week of His Ministry,(k)—is too striking
notice. The points of difference, however, are both numerous and consid₁
the first occasion, our LORD was speaking of the Faith required to worl
and He mentioned mustard-seed, and the removing of a mountain, but n₁
said of the sea.—On the present occasion, He has been speaking of the F
of Injuries; and He mentions mustard-seed, and the sea, but nothing is
mountain. A tree, (one of the *fig* species,) to be plucked up by the ro
coursed of instead.—On the third and last occasion, we shall find Him spe
of Forgiveness of Injuries(l) and the working of miracles; and though-z
is made of mustard-seed, both the moving of a mountain, and the drying
tree "from the roots,"(m) obtain notice. So much likeness with so mu
deserves attention.

It has been already freely admitted(n) that the six preceding verses app
sight to have no manner of connection either with what goes before, or w
after them; and in the long note at the beginning of the present Chapter,
ble reason of this was suggested, as well as the risk encountered by hi
deavors to furnish the missing links of thought. It is only right, howe
dismissing the passage, to point out that a bond of connection,—neither i
nor far-fetched,—between the several parts may be easily supplied. Thu
of the rich man (in the parable of Lazarus) is one of the most striking
(that is, *stumbling-blocks*) with which we are acquainted. The prospe
wicked "offended" the prophet Jeremiah:(o) and the Psalmist declared ₁
himself, that the sight of it had so "offended" him, that his "steps ha₁
slipped."(p)—The transition from "offending" little ones, to the duty of
ness of injuries," in verses 2, 3, finds a striking precedent in St. Matth.
14, and 15 to 35. It may be that "offences" of a certain class cause me
in need of forgiveness at the hands of their fellow-men. The Disciples
deeply conscious that so large a measure of Forgiveness as their Divine
quired could proceed only from a large measure of Faith,(q) apply to H
the Fountain of all Goodness, for this great gift: and their request gives
remarkable saying which we have just been considering.

What follows, takes the same form as certain Parables,—that of "the l
for example:(r) and it is therefore sometimes called a Parable. But, b₁
rule, ought not St. Luke xi. 11: xiii. 15: xiv. 5 and 28, to be called P
Our LORD asks:

7, 8 But which of you, having a servant ploughing or feedir
will say unto him by and by, when he is come from the field, G
down to meat? and will not rather say unto him, Make ready w
I may sup, and gird thyself, and serve me, till I have e₁
drunken; and afterward thou shalt eat and drink?

Now, what does this mean? and above all, how is it connected with w
diately goes before? The meaning and the connection may possibly
nature.

The Apostles had asked for a large measure of Faith. They knew d₁
the *moral* wonders which Faith can work: their request in fact *shows*
knew it. They knew also that they were asking for a gift which wo₁
them to perform *miracles*. Of this their Divine Master had assured the₁
mer occasion;(s) and He reminds them of it now. But was this request
—(the request that a double portion, as it were, of their Master's Spirit
upon them,)(t)—a reasonable request at this time? Such gifts "had no₁
given, because CHRIST had not yet been glorified."(u) "It was expedie
Disciples that He should go away: for if He went not away, the COMFOR
not come unto them; but if He departed, He would send Him unto
"Greater works than those which they had seen Him do, would then I

(i) St. Matth. xvii. 20.   (k) St. Matth. xxi. 21.   (l) St. Mar₁
(m) St. Mark xi. 20.   (n) See the beginning of the note on verse 3.
(o) Jer. xii. 1.   (p) Ps. lxxiii. 2, 3.
(q) The connection is established by St. Mark xi. 22, 25, 26.
(r) St. Luke xv. 4. Compare xv. 8: xi. 5: xvii. 7.
(s) St. Matth. xvii. 19, 20.   (t) 2 Kings ii. 9.   (u) St. Jo₁
(z) St. John xvi. 7.

selves: but not now,—because He had not yet gone to the **Father**."(y) Their rest was therefore ill timed; and not more reasonable, (our **Lord** seems to say,) that a servant should be directed to sit down and refresh himself before his ... It is implied therefore that the Apostles must wait,—(perhaps until the ... of Pentecost.)—and in the mean while be content to minister unto their **Lord**. ... indeed, as yet, had been their labour at the plough,(z)—slight indeed had ... their shepherding,(a)—and they were not to claim at once the rewards of pro... iged service; nor anticipate the hour when their **Lord** would "gird Himself, and ake them sit down to meat, and come forth, and serve them."(b) In the mean ... He proceeds to remind them that they had no *claims* upon Himself whatever; ... shows, (in the words of the heading of the Chapter,) "how we are bound to Joe, and not He to us." When a master has been duly waited upon by his servant, (our **Lord** asks,)—

9 Doth he thank that servant because he did the things that were commanded him? I trow not.

Rather,—Doth he *feel obliged to* that servant? (for *thank* him he doth doubtless.)

10 So likewise ye, when ye shall have done all those things which are commanded you, say, We are unprofitable servants: we have done that which was our duty to do.

Thus ends this mysterious and difficult Parable; which we have read so often, that its strangeness no longer strikes us. The general purport of the first half was explained above, in the note on ver. 8. In this latter portion, (namely, verses 9 and 10,) it is no longer the duty of patiently serving our Divine Master until the appointed time of refreshment,—which is enjoined; but the duty of forming a lowly estimate of the relation in which we stand towards God. And this was necessary; because impatience of reward can only spring from a mistaken view of the relation in which we stand towards Him who deigns to employ us, and from an over-estimation of our service.

We are therefore "unprofitable servants," at best; but if this is to be said by those who have "*done all*," what should be the language of those who have offended by thought, word, and deed, against God's Divine Majesty; and that grievously? what should be *our* language? . . . . The Church embodies the text in her XIVth Article against the Romish Doctrine of "voluntary works besides, over and above, God's Commandments."

11, 12 And it came to pass, as He went to Jerusalem, that He passed through the midst of Samaria and Galilee. And as He entered into a certain village, there met Him ten men that were lepers, which stood afar off:

Because their touch would have brought pollution. As companions in misfortune, they consort together;(c) yet do they hold themselves aloof from all. "They were obliged to keep without the city;"(d) in type of those unclean ones who shall be shut out from the City of God, by Him who bears the keys of the House of David.(e)
The Reader is referred to the notes on the cure of the Leper in the eighth chapter of St. Matthew's Gospel.(f) "There has been already occasion to speak of the nature and meaning of Leprosy in the Law of Moses;(g) that it was the outward symbol of Sin in its deepest malignity,—of Sin therefore as involving entire separation from God. Not of spiritual sickness only, but spiritual Death; since absolute separation from the one fountain of Life must be no life."(h)

(y) St. John xiv. 12.
(z) St. Luke ix. 62. Consider 1 Kings xix. 19, 1 Cor. ix. 10: and see the note on St. Luke iii. 17.
(a) There is nothing said about "feeding *cattle*" in the original. The word (and it is presumed the allegorical meaning) is the same as in St. John xxi. 16: Acts xx. 28: 1 St. Pet. v. 2.
(b) St. Luke xii. 37.　　　　(c) Compare 2 Kings vii. 3.　　　　(d) Lev. xiii. 46.
(e) Rev. iii. 7. Compare Isa. xxii. 22.　　　　(f) St. Matth. viii. 2.
(g) See the second note of St. Luke v. 13. Also the notes on St. Matth. viii. 2, and St. Mark i. 41.　　　　(h) Trench.

13, 14 And they lifted up *their* voices, and said, JESUS, Master, hav mercy on us. And when He saw *them*, He said unto them, Go sho yourselves unto the priests. And it came to pass, that, as they wen they were cleansed.

On the sanction of the Law of Moses implied by the command "Go show you selves unto the priests,"—see the last note on St. Matthew viii. 4.

Take notice therefore that it was not by the Priests, but by CHRIST Himself th these men were released from that malady which is the great type of Sin. Neith were they commanded to "show themselves" to the Priests with any view to the *cleansing.* The office of the Priest was (and is) merely to pronounce with authori on the sufferer's state: for who can forgive sins save GOD only? Enough has be already offered on this subject in the second note on St. Matthew viii. 4.

"MOST instructive is it," (observes Mr. Trench,) "to observe the differences our LORD's dealing with the different sufferers and mourners who are brought contact with Him; how the Physician who is all wisdom and tenderness varies E treatment according to the varying needs of His patients:(*i*) how He seems resist a strong Faith, that He may make it stronger yet;(*k*) how he meets a we Faith, lest it should prove altogether too weak in the trial:(*l*) how one, He forgiv first and heals after;(*m*) and another, whose heart could only be softened by rece ing an earthly benefit, He first heals and then pardons.(*n*) There is here, too, doubt a reason why these ten are dismissed as yet uncleansed, and bidden to show themselves to the priests; while that other, whose healing was before 1 corded, is first cleansed, and not till afterwards bidden to present himself in tl Temple. Doubtless there was here a heavier trial of Faith:" for, while yet in the uncleanness, they were bidden to do that which implied they were clean,—"to tal a journey which would have been ridiculous, unless CHRIST's implied promi proved true. They could not have thought that they were sent to the priests i order to be cured: for they must have well known that this was no part of tl Priest's office,—but only to declare cured."

15 And one of them, when he saw that he was healed, turned bacl and with a loud voice glorified GOD,

As he had been loud in Prayer,(*o*) so is he now loud in Praise. But the Pray had been uttered in impurity, and therefore at a distance: the Praise, because was spoken after cleansing, was poured forth by the Leper at our SAVIOUS feet. How far the party had got on their way, when the blessing overtook ther does not appear: but they were probably out of sight of their Benefactor: at once removed from His presence, they were unmindful of His benefits also. On one returned; but *this* man pressed up to the very feet of the Holy One, whom E had discovered to be "mighty to save."(*p*) As it follows,—

16, 17 and fell down on *his* face at His feet, giving Him thanks: as he was a Samaritan. And JESUS answering said, Were there not te cleansed? but where *are* the nine?

Rather,—"Were not *the ten* cleansed?" . . . How striking an expression of su prise on the lips of our SAVIOUR! He adds,—

18 There are not found that returned to give glory to GOD, save th stranger.

For the Samaritans were looked upon as strangers and "aliens from the Co monwealth of Israel."(*q*) Thus was it typically shown that "the Gentiles we not excluded from the Kingdom of GOD; nay, rather might find a place in it bef others who by birth were children of the Kingdom;—that the ingratitude of the

(*i*) See notes on St. Luke viii. 39: St. Matth. xi. 5: St. Mark v. 19.
(*k*) As in St. Matth. xv. 24 to 27,—where see notes.
(*l*) As in St. Mark v. 36,—where see notes.
(*m*) As in St. Mark ii. 5,—where see notes.   (*n*) As in the present instance.
(*o*) See above, ver. 13.   (*p*) Isa. lxiii. 1.
(*q*) Eph. ii. 12. See the note on St. Matth. x. 6.

might exclude them, while the Faith of those might give them an abundant entrance into all its blessings."(r)

"The nine others were already healed and hastening to the Priest,—that they might be restored to the society of men, and their life in the world: but the first thoughts of the Samaritan are turned to his Deliverer. He had forgotten all, in the sense of God's mercy, and of his own unworthiness."(s) Like Naaman the Syrian, when recovered from the same terrible disorder, he had come back to his Benefactor, saying,—"I pray thee, take a blessing of thy servant!"(t)

19 And He said unto him, Arise, go thy way: thy Faith hath made thee whole.

From which words it is obvious to suspect that some higher good had befallen this man than his nine companions in suffering. All had been made clean; but nine ungrateful ones were hastening back to the World. Only one was found eager to remain with his SAVIOUR. It seems to have been the design of that blessed assurance, "Thy Faith hath saved thee," to imply that the Samaritan had experienced an inward as well as outward cleansing: that, in *his* case, the soul as well as the body had been the object of saving Love.

How strikingly was the history of Israel itself displayed in the conduct of those nine men! "When He slew them they sought Him, and they returned and inquired after God. . . . Nevertheless . . . their heart was not right with Him. . . . Yea, they turned back, and . . . remembered not His Hand, nor the day when He delivered them from the enemy."(u) And is it not the way with every one of ourselves? Under the pressure of calamity,—under disease, and in the near prospect of Death,—all are prone to lift up their voices from afar, and cry aloud to God for mercy: but when His heavy Hand has been removed, what man can say that he has remembered to be duly thankful for the release? "We open our mouths wide," (says Sanderson,) "till He opens His Hand; but after, as if the filling of our mouths were the stopping of our throats, so are we speechless and heartless."

Not only a joyful,(x) but a *thankful* spirit also, is of great price in God's sight. Hence that pious outbreak of the Psalmist,—"Bless the LORD, O my soul; and all that is within me, bless His Holy Name. Bless the LORD, O my soul, *and forget not all His benefits.*"(y) What follows might have been fitly spoken by the Samaritan himself.

Our LORD was at this time on the way to Jerusalem:(z) and it is reasonable to think that either from the eager anticipations of His Followers, or from something which He may Himself have said, a suspicion had arisen that the Kingdom of MESSIAH was at hand.(a) This may have suggested the inquiry which follows.

20 And when He was demanded of the Pharisees, when the Kingdom of God should come, He answered them and said, The Kingdom of God cometh not with observation:

The Pharisees knew not what they asked. If the Apostles themselves put forth a similar question in ignorance,(b) how much more the enemies of our SAVIOUR! These men in fact were inquiring after the visible Advent of that MESSIAH whom they had not eyes to discern, nor the hearts to desire, when they saw Him.(c) How then was it possible to satisfy their question? The answer which our SAVIOUR returned was one which contained as large a measure of the truth as they were able to bear. "In another place indeed we are told that both Comings of the Kingdom, the first and the last, are with observation; and may be known by the signs of the times:(d) but it is here meant that it was not with such signs as the Pharisees intended,—of which the bodily eye and ear could be witnesses; but with such indications as Faith alone could perceive."(e) Our LORD's reply suggested to them that the Kingdom after which they inquired had begun *already; that it was secret in its nature, and silent in its progress; that it was not only above and around them, but within them likewise. As it follows,

---

(r) Trench. (s) Williams. (t) 2 Kings v. 15. (u) Ps. lxxviii. 34 to 42.
(x) See the note on St. Matth. xi. 30. (y) Ps. ciii. 1, 2.
(z) See above, ver. 11. (a) Consider and compare St. Luke xix. 11.
(b) See the note on St. Matth. xxiv. 3. (c) Isaiah liii. 2.
(d) See St. Mark xiii. 29, and the notes there. (e) Williams.

21 Neither shall they say, Lo here! or, lo there! for, behold, the
Kingdom of God is within you.

That is,—"Not a Kingdom seen, material, and temporal ; but invisible, spiritual,
and eternal: an unseen Kingdom, whose door is opened by Faith, which has its
seat in the soul itself."(*f*)   "The kingdom of God," says the Apostle, "is Righteousness, and Peace, and Joy in the Holy Ghost."(*g*)
But having returned this general answer to the Pharisees, our Saviour proceeds
to give to His Disciples a more particular account of the great mystery after which
the others had inquired.   His discourse, which partakes of the prophetic character
of that delivered as He sat on the Mount of Olives, begins with the near Future;
and straightway stretches on to the end of the World,—embracing the terrors of the
second Advent, in its span.

22 And He said unto the Disciples, The days will come, when ye
shall desire to see one of the days of the Son of Man, and ye shall not
see *it*.

He speaks of the season, now close at hand, when He should be taken from them;
and prophesies (how truly, what heart does not *feel?*) that they would then wish
for one of those days back, of which as yet they so little knew the value.   He proceeds to warn them of what would prove to them a source of especial danger:

23, 24 And they shall say to you, See here; or, see there: go not
after *them*, nor follow *them*.   For as the lightning, that lighteneth out
of the one *part* under Heaven, shineth unto the other *part* under Heaven; so shall also the Son of Man be in His day.

These words have been already discussed, and at length, in the Commentary on
St. Matthew's Gospel,—to which it must suffice to refer the Reader.(*h*)   It shall
only be repeated that as "false Christs" arose both before and after(*i*) the Fall of
Jerusalem, so it is evident from Prophecy that Pretenders will attend the second
Advent of Messiah.   Of *both* sets of Deceivers, therefore, our Lord here speaks:
although it is plain that His words point chiefly to what will happen in *the end of
the World*,—that tremendous Day when the glorious Advent of Messiah will be no
matter of private opinion, and vague rumour, but a thing patent as the lightning
which fills the air with brightness, and makes itself seen in an instant from one
extremity of Heaven to the other.

25 But first must He suffer many things, and be rejected of this
generation.

Thus does He ever check the ardour and impatience of His Disciples, by some
allusion to His Passion,—some assurance that of Himself, no less than of the
humblest of His followers, it holds true that He must endure the Cross, before He
wears the Crown.   Very brief, however, is the allusion to His own coming humiliation;—after which, He at once resumes His Prophecy concerning the end of all
things,—as a comparison of what follows, with St. Matthew xxiv. 36 to 39, is
enough to prove.   The direct connection in which our Saviour thus presents to
our view His own lowest depth of Humiliation and loftiest height of Glory,—departing as a despised criminal, and returning as a triumphant Judge,—is surely very
striking!

26, 27 And as it was in the days of Noe, so shall it be also in the
days of the Son of Man.   They did eat, they drank, they married
wives, they were given in marriage, until the day that Noe entered into
the Ark, and the flood came, and destroyed them all.

The sudden destruction of mankind by the waters of the Flood is cited by our

(*f*) Williams.   (*g*) Rom. xiv. 17.
(*h*) See the notes on St. Matth. xxiv. 23 to 27.
(*i*) As St. John expressly informs us.   See 1 St. John ii. 18, &c., and iv. 3,—where the allusion is clearly to the present place, or to St. Matth. xxiv. 5, 24.

LORD in another place as a great type of the sudden destruction which will come upon the World in the Last Day.(k) In this place, besides the vengeance which was taken on mankind by the Element of Water, "in the days of Noe,"—the overthrow of Sodom, "in the days of Lot," by Fire, is adduced (in respect of its sudden and unexpected nature) as typical of the great and terrible Day.—It will be remembered that St. Peter in like manner connects these two tremendous Judgments, in his Second Epistle.(l)

28, 29, 30 Likewise also as it was in the days of Lot; they did eat, they drank, they bought, they sold, they planted, they builded; but the same day that Lot went out of Sodom it rained fire and brimstone from heaven, and destroyed *them* all. Even thus shall it be in the Day when the Son of Man is revealed.

"What is here said of the end of the World is fulfilled and multiplied in little images in the life of each: in every case these are, by Divine appointment, preceding judgments which warn of the suddenness and surprise with which Eternity overtakes each man. And for the same reason that from each, the day of his Death is hidden, in order that he may be always living in expectation of it,—so is it also with the End of the World, that by every generation it may be expected. 'Behold,' says Chrysostom, 'we know *the signs* of old age, but we know not *the Day* of Death; so we know not the End of the World, though we know the signs of its approaching.'"(m)

31 In that Day, he which shall be upon the housetop, and his stuff in the house, let him not come down to take it away; and he that is in the field, let him likewise not return back.

This striking warning also forms part of the Prophecy which our SAVIOUR delivered on the Mount of Olives; but, (what is remarkable,) in *that* place it as unmistakably forms part of the predictions relative to the Destruction of Jerusalem, as in *this* place it must be considered to relate to the Destruction of the World: for, to suppose that the Divine Speaker discourses of the Day of Judgment from ver. 26 to ver. 30, and again from ver. 34 to the end of the chapter,—and yet, that He interposes some remarks (in ver. 31 to ver. 33) relative only to *the Fall of Jerusalem*, —is absurd. In the Commentary on the first two Gospels, perfect order and method were shown to exist in the Prophecy on the Mount;(n) and we are loath to believe, or rather we cannot for a moment admit the suspicion, that there exists any want of order and method here.—What, then, is to be thought of the words before us? We are compelled to inquire in what sense the warning which was to be *literally* understood by those Christians who were alive at the Destruction of Jerusalem, will be capable of being acted upon by the Church of CHRIST in the great and terrible Day: and our first impulse is to point it out as manifest that since, in the Day of Judgment, there can be no "turning back,"—only in a figurative sense can the present precept be intended for the Church's guidance *then*. But he who revolves the matter maturely, will perhaps be led at last to adopt a more diffident mode of expression. We know absolutely *nothing* concerning the nature of the End, and the manner of our Blessed LORD's second Coming,—*except what He has been pleased to reveal*. Should we not therefore reverse the process of remark; and rather occupy ourselves in silence with the strangeness of the Revelation here made to us?—the assurance, namely, that a trial resembling that of Lot and his family, in the Day of Sodom; a trial resembling that of the early Christians, in the Day of Jerusalem; will befall the Church of CHRIST in the latter Days: when delay will be Danger, and return—Death?—Something more will be found on this subject in the notes on verse 33.

But in the mean time, does not one great object with which the words are here introduced seem to be, to suggest to us that the Fall of Jerusalem, no less than the overthrow of Sodom, was typical of the Destruction of the World? "Then, let them which be in Judæa flee into the mountains," said our LORD concerning the first event. "Let him which is on the housetop not come down to take anything

(k) St. Matth. xxiv. 37 to 39.   (l) 2 St. Peter ii. 5 to 7.
(m) Williams.   (n) See the notes on St. Matth. xxiv. 3, 35, &c.

out of his house: neither let him which is in the field return back to take h
clothes. And woe unto them that are with child, and to them that give suck
those days!"(o) What our SAVIOUR here says is clearly connected with the end
Sodom, and carries on what He has been saying in ver. 29. "The same express
of warning, therefore, comes down to us with the force of an additional ty
wherein the figure has been twice already fulfilled,—both in Sodom and in Je
salem."(p) That our LORD, in ver. 31, is carrying on the allusion contained
verses 28, 29, is proved by the very striking words which follow,—

32 Remember Lot's wife.

Referring to Genesis xix. 17 to 26.—"This allusion to Lot's wife is remarkab
as showing how every incident in the Old Testament is replete with 'instructi
in Righteousness:'(q) for it deduces a type from what appears to be nothing mo
than one of the miraculous incidents of history; and leaves it as a proverbi
warning unto the end of the World."(r) Compare St. Luke ix. 62: also Phili
pians iii. 13, 14.

33 Whosoever shall seek to save his life shall lose it; and whosoev shall lose his life shall preserve it.

This is one of those sayings, so full of deep Evangelical meaning, the exact bea
ing of which on the matter in hand it is often (as in this place) very difficult to d
termine. This difficulty arises probably from our entire ignorance of what will tak
place at the Last Day. It may be that during that terrible overthrow,—the
destruction of the Earth and the works that be therein,—the heavenly-minded wil
be able to give signal proof of their heavenly-mindedness; and the worldly, of thei
hankering after the things of this World. Regardless of the warning of "Lot'
wife," the men who refused to be seasoned with the salt of her sad history wi
"return back" at the last,—and be involved in the tremendous fate of which he
was but the type or shadow. Then will he who thought to save his life, lose it
while he whose obedience caused him to pursue the path of apparent danger, wi
in the end be saved. All this, however, is a subject which nothing but the eve
will make intelligible. We do well to meditate on unfulfilled Prophecy. It is ot
bounden duty so to do.(s) But we have no right to understand it.

Our SAVIOUR proceeds to foretell "some extraordinary interpositions of a di
criminating Providence, which will preserve the righteous in situations of t
greatest danger from certain public calamities which in the last ages of the Wor
will fall upon wicked nations."(t). His first example, (the two men asleep on o
couch,) is peculiar to the present Gospel; and seems to be added to the other tw
in order to increase the doubt and uncertainty in which "that Day and Hour"
involved. Will CHRIST come during the hours of Light? Nay, but it will be in tl
season "when men sleep"(u) that He will come. Will it be in the Night, the
Nay, but the hind will be in the field, and maid-servant at the mill.

34, 35, 36 I tell you, in that night there shall be two men in o bed; the one shall be taken, and the other shall be left. Two wom shall be grinding together; the one shall be taken and the other le Two men shall be in the field; the one shall be taken and the other le

Compare St. Matthew xxiv. 40 and 41. It seems to be implied that the great
discrimination will be used in distinguishing between the righteous and the wick
at the Last Day. And it is worth observing, that both the examples here giv
are selected from very humble life. One, of two labouring men in the field,—o
of two female slaves grinding at the mill,—are mentioned as samples of those w
shall be heirs of future Glory.(x) They will be "taken" at the last Day, ("caug
up," as it is elsewhere said,)(y) "to meet the LORD in the air." The wicked w
be "left," to incur their tremendous sentence.

37 And they answered and said unto Him, Where, LORD? And I

(o) St. Matth. xxiv. 16 to 19.   (p) Williams.   (q) 2 Tim. iii. 16.
(r) Williams.   (s) See Rev. i. 3: xxii. 7.   (t) Bishop Horsley.
(u) St. Matth. xxiii. 25. Compare St. Matth. xxv. 6.
(x) Consider 1 Cor. i. 26 to 29.   (y) 1 Thess. iv. 17.

said unto them, Wheresoever the Body *is*, thither will the eagles be gathered together.

That is,—No doubt will exist as to *where* all this shall be. As the eagles about the slain,(z) so will the saints of God(a) be seen in that Day gathered about "the Lamb that was slain from the foundation of the World."(b) Wheresoever "in the clouds"(c) the Human Body of the Incarnate Son is, thither will His thousand thousands be gathered together! See more on the note in St. Matthew xxiv. 28; and take notice that what *there* is called "*the Carcass*," is here called "*the Body.*" The reason is perhaps that in that place, (as already suggested,) the Divine language is so shaped as to have indirect reference to the slaughter which attended the Destruction of Jerusalem; whereas here, the reference is to the Day of Judgment only.

In terms purposely dark, rather than vague, did our Saviour return this reply to the curious inquiry of His Disciples. They cannot have understood all that He intended: perhaps they understood Him not at all. Yet was it doubtless more edifying to them thus to have their doubts resolved, than to be favoured with any more explicit statement. The interpretation of our Saviour's saying afforded above, we hold to be the true one: yet would we by no means deny that such wondrous words as His may embrace within their scope a yet wider meaning, and convey a message of comfort, as well as a note of warning, to all. "It is probable that the eagle and the carcass was a proverbial image among the people of the East, expressing things inseparably connected by natural affinities and sympathies." So that it may be a true, although only a partial, paraphrase of our Lord's words, to understand Him to say,—"Wheresoever sinners shall dwell, there shall My vengeance overtake them; and there will I interpose to protect My faithful servants."(d)

CHAPTER XVIII.

The Parable of "The Importunate Widow,"(e) which follows, "is addressed to the Disciples; and stands in closest relation with what has gone immediately before, with the description of the sufferings and distress of the last times, when even the Disciples 'shall desire to see one of the Days of the Son of Man, and shall not see it.'"(f) "Watch *and pray*" is the injunction which our Saviour delivers in connection with every prophecy of the suddenness of His second Coming: and the same

---

(z) "Her eyes behold afar off; . . . *and where the slain are, there is she.*" Job xxxix. 29, 30.

(a) "They that wait upon the Lord shall renew their strength. *They shall mount up with wings as eagles:* they shall run and not be weary; and they shall walk and not faint." Isaiah xl. 31. Compare Ps. ciii. 5.

(b) Rev. xiii. 8.   (c) 1 Thess. iv. 17.   (d) Bp. Horsley.
(e) Sometimes less happily called "The Unjust Judge;" but see the heading of the Chapter.
(f) Trench.

lesson is here taught by a Parable,—the last words of which contain express mention of the great events alluded to.—It follows,

1 AND He spake a parable unto them *to this end*, that men ought always to pray, and not to faint:

Rather,—"that *they* ought always to pray." The precept is addressed to *the Disciples*.

Such a statement as is found here, and in verse 9, seems to demand our gratitude; for, in both places, the Author of the Gospel becomes His own Interpreter, and directs us to the scope and intention of the parable which follows, by Himself openly declaring it. Deprived of such assistance, the Parable of "the Labourers in the Vineyard"(c) may convince us of our real helplessness in the Interpretation of GOD'S Word.

"Men ought *always* to pray." The duty is urged, in the same language, in other parts of the New Testament:(d) from which it will appear that the Christian Life should be one continuous Prayer,—one long reaching out of the heart to GOD. For "the soul which is accustomed to direct itself to GOD upon every occasion,—which, whatever chord be struck, is ever turned towards *Him*,—that soul prays sometimes when it does not know that it is praying."(e) The knee cannot indeed be bent for-ever; but the desire and longing of the soul should never cease.

Our LORD adds, "and not *to faint;*" knowing how prone is the heart of man to weary, despond, and grow slack, if it does not at once obtain the thing it prayed for. This precept will also be found urged in countless places of Scripture. See below, the second note on verse 5.

2 saying, There was in a city a Judge, which feared not GOD, neither regarded Man:

A fearful character is drawn in two words. Here was one who was neither restrained from crime by the fear of GOD'S anger; nor deterred by regard for the good opinion of mankind. He was recklessly wicked. And this man was *a Judge!*

3 and there was a widow in that city; and she came unto him, say-ing, Avenge me of mine adversary.

"A widow,"—the very type of weakness, poverty, and affliction throughout GOD'S Word!(f) Surely, hers was a hopeless case, having to do with such a one as the former verse describes. However, she did what she could: St. Luke says "she kept *continually* coming to him," with the petition that he would "do her justice" against her Adversary.

4 And he would not for a while: but afterwards he said within himself,

That is, "he *thought* within himself:" but "*said*" is better, for it sets forth the close connection between evil thoughts and evil words. The voice of the heart is a loud cry in the ears of GOD. He said at last,

5 Though I fear not GOD, nor regard Man; yet because this Widow troubleth me, I will avenge her, lest by her continual coming she weary me.

He used a much stronger word than "*weary* me." He was a bold, bad man,—unscrupulous in language as in conduct; and his impatience here finds vent in a metaphor which transforms the poor, helpless, persevering widow into a spiteful pugilist.

GOD, (as will be presently more fully shown,) is not *like* the Unjust Judge; but the course He pursues towards His elect "which cry day and night unto Him," is so far like that of the man described in the Parable, that "*He bears long with*

(c) St. Matth. xx. 1 to 16.   (d) See Ephes. vi. 18, and 1 Thess. v. 17.   (e) Donne.
(f) See the note on St. Luke vii. 12: and consider such places as Exod. xxii. 22. Deut. x. 18: xxiv. 17. Job xxix. 13. 1 Kings xvii. 9 to 12. St. Mark xii. 42. 1 Tim. v. 5, &c. See also the note (and reference) on St. Matth. xxiii. 14.

them."(*g*) This truth He set forth by a Miracle, when He caused the blind to follow Him into a house,(*h*)—and when He heeded not at first the cry of the blind at Jericho,(*i*)—and when He suffered the waves wellnigh to engulf the ship, in which He sailed the Lake.(*k*) Above all, He set forth this way of His Providence in His dealings with the woman of Canaan,(*l*)—whom He not only neglected for a while, but even repulsed. Nor may we doubt that what our LORD enforced twice by a Parable, so often by a Miracle, and on countless occasions by precept, it especially concerns every Christian man to carry in his constant remembrance. The Reader is referred to the notes on St. Luke xi. 8,—St. Matthew vii. 7, 8, and xv. 24, 27, 28.

6, 7 And the LORD said, Hear what the unjust Judge saith. And shall not GOD

"The *unjust* Judge;"—not touched with *pity*, but *weary* of molestation; not mindful of *the widow's* wrongs, but careful for *his own* case and quiet; not desirous of drawing her to himself, but of being rid of her importunity!

"Hear what *the unjust* Judge saith:" and shall not the "LORD, *the Righteous Judge,*"(*m*)

avenge His own elect, which cry day and night unto Him, though He bear long with them?

Our LORD often reasons in this manner. "Which of you, *though he be but a man,*" &c.(*n*) "If a son shall ask bread of any *of you* that is a Father," &c.(*o*) GOD is not therefore *like* the unjust Judge in this Parable; neither is He like the churlish neighbour of whom we read in the Parable of "the Friend at midnight."(*p*) The argument is,—If the unfriendly and the unrighteous can thus be moved by persevering prayer and entreaty, how much more "the Holy One and the Just;"(*q*) who "*tires only when we are silent,*"—as one of the Fathers beautifully remarks.(*r*)

But it is time to advert to the intention of the Parable; which doubtless sets forth to us the Church in these the days of her Widowhood,—"when the Bridegroom is taken from her."(*s*) She cries to GOD "the Righteous Judge," "Avenge me of mine Adversary,"—that is, the Devil,(*t*) and all those powers of the World which she finds continually arrayed against her. "O GOD, how long shall the Adversary do this dishonour?"(*u*)

For, in the words of a thoughtful Writer,—"The World is *always*, whether consciously or unconsciously, whether by unwholesome patronage or by hostile violence, oppressing the Church; and Satan is evermore seeking to hinder the life of GOD in every one of her members. Prayer is the cry 'out of the deep' which the elect utter, the calling in of a mightier to aid, when they feel the danger to be earnest, lest the enemy should prevail against them."(*x*)

And like other parables, the present has also its personal and private application. What is true of the Body is true of each of the members. "Every soul," (says a great Father,) "conscious of its loneliness, conscious that it has no help save in GOD only, is a widow."(*y*) What do we else day by day, than repeat the Widow's prayer, when we exclaim, "Deliver us from Evil," or rather "from *the Evil One?*"(*z*) We may not doubt that as many as are conscious of a conflict with the powers of Darkness and the World, find here their lesson; are taught what must be their own special course.

But to return to the precious assurance of the text:—If the *unjust* Judge could act thus towards the *despised widow*, who made a feeble wail at his gate, during the short period when causes might come before him,—shall not the *Righteous* Judge attend to the desire of *His own elect*, (His "jewels,")(*a*) whose great and exceeding bitter cry resounds in His ears all day and all night?—"Though He *bear long* with them," may perhaps mean, "Though He be *patient* with respect to *them*;" that is, although He displays, even towards those who oppress *them*, that long-suffering

---

(*g*) See below, verse 7.　　(*h*) St. Matth. ix. 27, 28.　　(*i*) St. Matth. xx. 30 to 34.
(*k*) See St. Mark iv. 38, and the note there.　　　　　　　　(*l*) St. Matth. xv. 22 to 26.
(*m*) 2 Tim. iv. 8.　　　　(*n*) St. Matth. vii. 9,—where see the note. See also verses 10, 11.
(*o*) St. Luke xi. 11 to 13.　　　　(*p*) St. Luke xi. 5 to 8, where see the notes.
(*q*) Acts iii. 14.　　　　　　　　　　　　　　　　　　　　　(*r*) Chrysostom.
(*s*) St. Matth. ix. 15, and St. Mark ii. 20,—where see note.　　(*t*) 1 St. Peter v. 8.
(*u*) Ps. lxxiv. 10.　　　　　　(*x*) Trench.　　　　　　　　(*y*) Augustine.
(*z*) See St. Matth. vi. 13, St. Luke xi. 4,—and the notes there.　(*a*) Mal. iii. 17.

37

Patience whereby He seeks to lead men to Repentance.(b)   For, (as St. Peter explains,) "The LORD is not slack concerning His promise, as some men count slackness: but is long-suffering," or, "patient toward us; not willing that any should perish, but that all should come to Repentance."(c) . . . . "How long, O LORD, holy and true, dost Thou not judge and avenge our blood on them that dwell on the Earth?"(d)—is the cry of the souls of GOD's martyred Saints beneath the altar. And we hear GOD's answer in the words which follow:

8 I tell you that He will avenge them speedily. Nevertheless, when the Son of Man cometh, shall He find Faith on the Earth?

This entire passage will be found to derive singular illustration from that part of St. Peter's second Epistle, where he speaks of CHRIST's second Advent,—delayed indeed, yet certain: delayed, moreover, only because of that very *long-suffering patience* of GOD which has been already noticed.(e) . . . "I tell you," (the Righteous Judge Himself here declares,) "He will avenge them speedily."   And these, which are the concluding words of the Parable, are the concluding words of the Volume of Revelation also,—"Surely I come quickly!"(f)   "For He cometh," (says the Psalmist,) "for He cometh to judge the Earth."(g)   "Nevertheless," (it is mournfully added,)—"*when* the Son of Man cometh, shall He find Faith on the Earth?" Or rather, "*the* faith:" that is, "the faith which cries and prays to GOD continually."   For we know that, in the last days, "false Christs and false prophets shall arise,"—showing signs, and working miracles enough to "deceive, if it were possible, the very elect."(h)   The faithful will then be reduced to a very little band; for, "because Iniquity shall abound, the Love of the many will wax cold;"(i) and doubtless their *Faith* also. Nay, even *their* Faith, (as our LORD Himself here assures us,) will have wellnigh died away.

One of the Fathers remarks that our LORD spoke these words "to show that when Faith fails, Prayer dies. In order to pray, then, we must have Faith; and that our Faith fail not, we must pray. Faith pours forth Prayer; and the pouring forth of the heart in Prayer, gives steadfastness to Faith."(k)   See the note on St. Luke xvii. 5.

9 And He spake this Parable unto certain which trusted in themselves that they were righteous, and despised others:

It was the object of the foregoing Parable, then, to set forth the duty of praying *earnestly*. The Parable which follows teaches the duty of praying *humbly*. Or, the one may be regarded as setting forth the duty of Prayer: the other, as teaching in what spirit that duty is to be performed.

10 Two men went up into the Temple to pray;

We shall be told in the next words who and what these "two *men*" were. "They are as yet called by that name only, in which all of every degree stand equal before their common LORD." They "went *up*,"—for the Temple stood on Mount Sion;(l) and to *pray*,—for the Temple was a "House of *Prayer*." "They entered severally the Court of the Israelites out of the hours of stated worship, in order to perform this excellent duty."(m)   They went up *really* to pray. The difference between them was great indeed; yet should it be noticed how much they had in common. And these men were,

the one a Pharisee, and the other a Publican.

Concerning the Publicans, that is, the Jews who collected the taxes for the Roman conquerors of Judæa, something has been said already.(n)   "The persuasion was most popular and general that for the free-born children of Abraham, it was unlawful to pay tribute to Cæsar, or any heathen government; and the Jews who could so far forget their sacred character as to be the collectors of such tribute, or

(b) Rom. ii. 4.   (c) 2 St. Peter iii. 9.   (d) Rev. vi. 10.
(e) See 2 St. Peter iii. 9 and 15. (f) Rev. xxii. 20.   (g) Ps. xcvi. 13.
(h) St. Matth. xxiv. 24.   (i) St. Matth. xxiv. 12.   (k) Augustine.
(l) Ps. xxiv. 3.—Accordingly, in verse 14, below, it is said that the Publican "went down to his house."
(m) Dr. W. H. Mill.   (n) See the note on St. Mark ii. 15.

to inform against their countrymen who paid it not, hence came to be regarded with horror as sinful men,—apostates from the character and profession of true Israelites. The Pharisees, on the other hand, were men whose exactness in the observance of the Law was proverbial among the people; indicated by their very name, which denoted their *separation* from all others. . . . Hence, therefore, to say of these two men that the one was a Publican, the other a Pharisee, is to say that one passed among the people necessarily for a *sinner*,—the other, necessarily for a *saint*. How they were viewed in this respect by the ALMIGHTY, who sees the heart,"(*o*) the rest of the Parable sufficiently shows.

11, 12 The Pharisee stood and prayed thus with himself,

They *both* stood to pray. Standing was anciently a more usual attitude of prayer than now.(*p*)

GOD, I thank Thee, that I am not as other men *are*, extortioners, unjust, adulterers, or even as this Publican. I fast twice in the week, I give tithes of all that I possess.

Although a single fast-day in the year was all that was *required* by the Divine Law,(*q*) GOD's ancient people, (like some branches of the Christian Church,) observed *two* weekly fasts; not *one* only, as our Church directs. These were kept on Monday and Thursday: and these, the Pharisee faithfully kept. By his profession of giving a tithe of all he possessed, or rather, "of all his *gains*," he means,—"Not only the portion which the Law exacts for Religion, and its ministers; but from everything, however minute, which at any time becomes my property,—from mint and anise and cummin,—I scrupulously measure off and lay aside a tenth part for the same purpose."(*r*)

And here, the character of the Pharisee's thanksgiving and profession must be noticed; for it cannot be called *a Prayer*. "If you look into his words," (says Augustine,) "you will find that he asked nothing of GOD. He goes up indeed to pray; but instead of praying, he praises himself." In thanking GOD for having kept him from the commission of heinous sin, he was, however, undoubtedly right. His practice of fasting was sanctioned both by the example and the precept of our LORD;(*s*) and his strictness in this behalf was a commendable thing. All will allow that his dedication of a part of his substance to pious uses, was religious and praiseworthy: while it is but fair to suppose that he imputes to GOD's grace no less what he had actually *done* of good, than what he had *avoided* of evil; and therefore that he "thanks" Him for *all*. There was no "self-righteousness" here.

But all that can be said in his favour, has now been said. His utter absence of Humility comes out forcibly in the form which his profession takes,—"GOD, I thank Thee that I am not *as other men:*" for, "by what right does he introduce the consideration of *other men*, as objects of comparison with himself, when he is approaching the presence of GOD?"(*t*) Consider too, above all, the uncharitableness of that clause,—"*or even* as this Publican." "To despise the whole race of man was not enough for him: he must yet attack the Publican."(*u*) Surely, the very sight of one who pursued an infamous calling, coming into the Temple for the mere purpose of approaching GOD, and engaged in the manner which the next verse describes, should have inspired a good man with cheerful hopes concerning him. "When thou returnest thanks to GOD," (says an excellent preacher,) "let Him be all in all to thee. Turn not thy thoughts to men, nor condemn thy neighbour."(*x*) A pious Writer has said,—"If we desire that GOD should not enter into judgment with us, two great rules are given us in Holy Scripture, for each of which this Parable furnishes an example. 'Judge not, that ye be not judged;"(*y*) and, 'If we would judge ourselves, we should not be judged'(*z*) of the LORD."

(*o*) Dr. W. H. Mill.
(*p*) Hannah *stood* (1 Sam. i. 26,) while she poured forth her passionate prayer,—1 Sam. i. 9 to 13. See also St. Matth. vi. 5, and St. Mark xi. 25.—*Kneeling*, however, has ever been the approved attitude of addressing GOD. Notice how 2 Chron. vi. 13 supplies what 1 Kings viii. 22 omits. See also Dan. vi. 10, &c. &c.
(*q*) Levit. xvi. 29: xxiii. 27: Numb. xxix. 7,—alluded to in Acts xxvii. 9.
(*r*) Dr. W. H. Mill.   (*s*) St. Matth. vi. 16 to 18.   (*t*) Dr. W. H. Mill.
(*u*) Chrysostom.   (*x*) Chrysostom.   (*y*) St. Matth. vii. 1.
(*z*) 1 Cor. xi. 31. The quotation is from a Sermon by the Rev. C. Marriott.

13 And the Publican, standing afar off, would not lift up so much as *his* eyes unto Heaven,

He stood *afar off*, because he thought himself unworthy to join the rest of GOD's worshippers: yet was he "not afar off from GOD; for the LORD is '*nigh* unto them that 'are of a contrite heart.'"(*a*) He would not "so much as lift up his eyes unto Heaven," being self-abased before the Majesty of Him whom he was approaching. He felt as Ezra felt, of old,—"O my GOD, I am ashamed and blush to lift up my face to Thee, my GOD."(*b*)

but smote upon his breast, saying, GOD be merciful to me a sinner.

He smote his breast again and again, as a sign of the grief of his Spirit.(*c*) "He not only felt himself unworthy to draw near to GOD, but had a strong sense of his deserving punishment; and a desire to condemn and chastise Sin in himself, which he expressed by beating on his breast. We must take the action for what it naturally means, because our LORD bears witness to him."(*d*)

The language which he used is moreover highly remarkable; for it is found not only to express his desire of mercy, and of reconciliation with GOD, but to contain the notion of a propitiatory offering as being needed also. "Besides, he meant more in calling himself a *sinner* than we do, who have learned to call ourselves *sinners*. It is rather what we should mean by 'a wicked man,' or 'a guilty man;' and is what a man would not say of himself unless he were under a very deep conviction of his own faults."(*e*)

His words of Confession and Prayer were of course "inaudible to the Pharisee, as they were meant to be: yet the Publican's attitude and gesture, might have been marked by him. They must have been seen, as the Publican is so present to the mind of the Pharisee in his prayer: yet, instead of inspiring the kind interest which a just man should ever take in a sincere penitent, these marks of humiliation seem to him only evidences of the guilt of his fellow-worshipper. . . . . . . Far different from this vain estimate is the decision of Him to whom he thus presumed to address himself. The man whose prayer was so remarkable for all the features which the other's wanted,—the man who realized the Divine presence, and spread his full wretchedness before Him without a word or thought of extenuation,—who never compares himself with others more guilty, or pleads their evil example in arrest of judgment, but asks of mere mercy what it is for Divine Mercy alone to bestow,"—

14 I tell you, this man went down to his house justified *rather* than the other :

The one found acceptance with GOD. The other stands on record, as a warning to mankind forever. For it is not by any means implied that the Pharisee was justified *a little*, and the Publican *much*. Nothing of the kind. The one was accepted; (that is, his prayer had been heard, and GOD had had mercy on him) the other was rejected.

And let us be well persuaded that "the spiritual pride which was the characteristic of the Pharisee, may lurk under the humblest theory of Religion; supposing even, (which is not always the case,) that the view, presumed to be humble, is such in reality. The Religion, whatever be its theory, of which the main effect is to establish in the mind a persuasion that there is something in ourselves which belongs not to others of CHRIST'S Brotherhood and Family,—which makes the ruling feeling of any to be to think GOD that he is not as other men,—is in great danger of producing also the worst points of Pharisaism."(*f*)

He "went *down* to his house," because he was returning from Mount Sion.(*g*) The remark is obvious. Of how different a character is the following observation, which a pious and thoughtful Writer has made on the text! "The words of our LORD," he says, "clearly point to the truth, that our several actions pass under His judgment. For He says that '*this man went down to his house* justified rather than

(*a*) Trench from Augustine, quoting Ps. xxxiv. 18.
(*b*) Ezra ix. 6.
(*c*) Consider St. Luke xxiii. 48.
(*d*) Rev. C. Marriott.
(*e*) Rev. C. Marriott, referring to St. Luke v. 8.
(*f*) Dr. W. H. Mill.
(*g*) See above, on verse 10

ie other;' clearly meaning that the very act of worship he had been performing
t the Temple was approved, as well as that his person was accepted.   And we
hould do well to bear this in mind in every action, that judgment is passed on it;
nd that we go from it justified in it or not, in respect of what we have done."(h)

It were, of course, a mere abuse of this parable to infer that external observances,
—as Fasting and Almsgiving,—are worthless forms, because in the Pharisee's case
hey happen to be united with a self-righteous spirit; or, that the essence of Religion consists in an occasional abject cry to GOD for mercy, however careless the life
may be of external helps.   This were indeed to trifle with Divine Truth.   The
uncharitable Pharisee was wanting in Humility; the Publican stands forth the
very model of that great virtue.   Hence, alone, the sentence passed upon either by
our SAVIOUR.

for every one that exalteth himself shall be abased; and he that
humbleth himself shall be exalted.

Rather, "he that *abaseth* himself shall be exalted."

The present Parable, therefore, is not only prefaced, like the last, by a sentence
declaring its general scope and purpose, but it also concludes with a proverbial
saying,—which, in the way of inference, as it were, gathers up its heavenly teaching. The same thing was also observed in the case of the parable of "the Labourers
in the Vineyard."(i)

The words alluded to may be regarded almost as the very motto and moral of the
Gospel itself.   They are found in many shapes; but they still embody one and the
same great truth, or rather solemn warning;—whether they occur in the Blessed
Virgin's Hymn of Praise, where mention is made of the proud and the humble;(k)
or in the Sermon on the Mount, where the fate of the rich and the poor, the hungry
and the full, is contrasted;(l) or whether they be spoken of first and last;(m) or,
(as here,) of those who humble and those who exalt themselves.(n)

Wondrous anticipations of this, as of so many other great Gospel truths, exist in
the Old Testament.(o)   The words of Proverbs iii. 34, in particular, are found to
have supplied St. Peter(p) and St. James(q) with all they required, when they
wished to remind the Church that "GOD resisteth the proud, but giveth grace unto
the humble."

Our LORD's last saying forms a beautiful transition to the incident which follows.

15, 16, 17 And they brought unto Him also Infants, that He would
touch them: but when *His* Disciples saw *it*, they rebuked them.   But
JESUS called them *unto Him*, and said, Suffer little Children to come
unto Me, and forbid them not: for of such is the Kingdom of GOD.
Verily I say unto you, Whosoever shall not receive the Kingdom of
GOD as a little Child, shall in no wise enter therein.

Concerning this precious incident, which is related also by St. Matthew and St.
Mark, the Reader is referred to the notes on the earlier Gospels.(r)

18, 19, 20, 21, 22, 23 And a certain Ruler asked Him, saying, Good
Master, what shall I do to inherit Eternal Life?   And JESUS said unto
him, Why callest thou Me good? none *is* good, save one, *that is*, GOD.
Thou knowest the commandments: Do not commit adultery, Do not
kill, Do not steal, Do not bear false witness, Honour thy father and
thy mother.   And he said, All these have I kept from my youth up.
Now when JESUS heard these things, He said unto him, Yet lackest
thou one thing: sell all that thou hast, and distribute unto the poor,

(h) Rev. C. Marriott.   (i) See St. Matth. xx. 16.   (k) St. Luke i. 52, 53.
(l) St. Luke vi. 20, 21, and 24, 25.   (m) St. Matth. xix. 30: where see the note.
(n) See also St. Matth. xxiii. 12, and St. Luke xiv. 11: where the saying will be found to
recur.
(o) It is obvious to refer to 1 Sam. ii. 4 to 9.   (p) 1 St. Peter v. 5.
(q) St. James iv. 6.   (r) See on St. Matth. xix. 13 to 15: and St. Mark x. 13 to 16.

and thou shalt have treasure in Heaven : and come, follow Me.   An
when he heard this he was very sorrowful : for he was very rich.

24, 25, 26 And when JESUS saw that he was very sorrowful, H
said, How hardly shall they that have riches enter into the Kingdom o
GOD!   For it is easier for a camel to go through a needle's eye, tha
for a rich man to enter into the Kingdom of GOD.   And they tha
heard it said, Who then can be saved?

These verses have been commented on elsewhere.(s)

27 And He said, the things which are impossible with men are po
sible with GOD.

That which unassisted man finds impossible, (namely, this making of himss
"poor in spirit,") GOD's grace can accomplish : for the Kingdom of Grace knows (
greater marvels than the Kingdom of Nature.   "The impossible thing, which y
is possible with GOD, is not the saving of the Rich man, but the making of the Ric
man poor."

28 Then PETER said, Lo, we have left all, and followed Thee.

"What shall we have therefore?" he added : to which our LORD returned a won
drous answer.   See St. Matthew xix. 27, 28, and the notes there.

29, 30 And He said unto them, Verily I say unto you, There is n
man that hath left House, or Parents, or Brethren, or Wife, or Chil
dren, for the Kingdom of GOD's sake, who shall not receive manifold
more in this present time, and in the World to come, Life Everlasting.

Not only ye, but every one, to the end of the World, who shall forsake the thin
which he loves best, when called upon to do so "for My sake and the Gospel's,"(t
shall "in this present time" be recompensed a hundredfold ; and in the world t
come, shall be everlastingly rewarded.
This portion of St. Luke's Gospel is also found in the two earlier Gospels.   Th
Reader is therefore again referred thither.(u)

31 Then He took unto Him the Twelve, and said unto them, Be
hold, we go up to Jerusalem, and all things that are written by th
Prophets concerning the Son of Man shall be accomplished.

Take notice how He guides them to that sure word of Prophecy which He ha
prepared concerning Himself.   In the writings of Moses and of the Prophets, an
in the Psalms, all that was to befall the Son of Man might be found written o
Him.(x)

32, 33 For He shall be delivered unto the Gentiles, and shall b
mocked, and spitefully entreated, and spitted on : and they sha
scourge Him and put Him to death : and the third day He shall ris
again.

34 And they understood none of these things : and this saying wa
hid from them, neither knew they the things which were spoken.

But they understood it afterwards, and called to mind everything which the
LORD had so spoken ; as we are often reminded in the later pages of the Gospel.(y
These verses have been already made the subject of Comment ; to which it sha
suffice, in this place, to refer the Reader.(z)

(s) In the notes on St. Matth. xix. 16 to 26, and St. Mark x. 17 to 26.
(t) St. Mark x. 29, where see the note.
(u) See on St. Matth. xix. 25 to 30 ; and St. Mark x. 27 to 31.
(x) Consider St. Luke xxiv. 25, 26.   (y) St. Luke xxiv. 8.   St. John ii. 22, 4
(z) See on St. Matth. xx. 17 to 19, and St. Mark x. 32 to 34.

35, 36, 37, 38, 39 And it came to pass, that as He was come nigh unto Jericho, a certain blind man sat by the way-side begging: and hearing the multitude pass by, he asked what it meant. And they told him, that JESUS of Nazareth passeth by. And he cried, saying, JESUS, *Thou* Son of David, have mercy on me. And they which went before rebuked him, that he should hold his peace: but he cried so much the more, *Thou* Son of David, have mercy on me.

This rebuke then is found to have proceeded from them "that went before." Doubtless there was much of majesty in the common events of our LORD's daily life, notwithstanding the depth of Humiliation to which He submitted Himself. Here was a crowded thoroughfare,—the close of a weary day's journey,—an impatient multitude. Yet are there found persons to walk in advance, as if to herald His august coming; and when a beggar begins to cry out, "Thou Son of David, have mercy on me,"—"many" are heard rebuking him, and charging him to hold his peace while the "Prince of Peace" passes by. It has been piously suggested that CHRIST "was teaching as He went, and they would not have Him interrupted."(a)

Viewed as conveying a lesson to ourselves, we are reminded of what may sometimes befall those who are most earnest in the matter of their Salvation. Their conduct procures for them the rebuke not only of the enemies of CHRIST, but even of those who walk with Him and profess zeal for His Honour.—Observe, however, what follows:

40 And JESUS stood, and commanded him to be brought unto Him:

Whereupon, "they call the blind man, saying unto him, Be of good comfort, rise; He calleth thee."(b)

This, too, observes an ancient Father, "repeats itself often in the spiritual history of men's lives. If a man will only despise these obstacles from a World which calls itself Christian; if, despite of them all, he will go on until CHRIST is plainly with him; then, they who began by blaming, will finish by applauding: they who said first, He is mad, will end with saying, He is a saint."(c)

41, 42 And when he was come near, He asked him, saying, What wilt thou that I shall do unto thee? And he said, LORD, that I may receive my sight. And JESUS said unto him, Receive thy sight: thy Faith hath saved thee.

Thus, the Chapter ends as it begun,—by showing the fruits of importunity in Prayer!

And immediately he received his sight, and followed Him, glorifying GOD: and all the people, when they saw *it*, gave praise unto GOD.

The miracle performed by our LORD on the *two* blind men of Jericho, will be also found fully related by St. Matthew and St. Mark. The Reader is therefore referred to the notes in the earlier Gospels.(d) But it is well worth observing how these blessed Writers, when describing one and the same transaction, although, to a careless observer, they may seem to have employed nearly the same terms, will yet be found, by countless minute touches, to have achieved immense variety; and by consequence to have supplied a large amount of unsuspected information, as well as of most precious teaching. Without dwelling further on this remark, it shall suffice to point out that St. Luke, in this place, is the only Evangelist who preserves the beautiful circumstance of *the gratitude* manifested by this object of our SAVIOUR's mercy. St. Matthew informed us that he "followed" CHRIST;(e) and St. Mark explains that he "followed JESUS *in the way*."(f) But St. Luke declares that he followed Him, with praises on his tongue; and not only so, but that his example was followed by the people, who, "*all*, when they saw it, *gave praise unto GOD*."

(a) Trench.   (b) St. Mark x. 49.   (c) Augustine, quoted by Trench.
(d) See on St. Matth. xx. 29 to 34: and St. Mark x. 46 to 52.
(e) St. Matth. xx. 34.   (f) St. Mark x. 52.

CHAPTER XIX.

1 *Of Zacchæus a publican.* 11 *The ten pieces of Money.* 28 CHRIST *rideth into Jerusalem with triumph:* 41 *weepeth over it:* 45 *driveth the Buyers and Sellers out of the Temple:* 47 *teaching daily in it. The Rulers would have destroyed Him, but for fear of the people.*

1 AND JESUS entered and passed through Jericho.

The narratives of the two earlier Evangelists transport us at once from Jericho, the scene of the miracle performed on the two Blind men, to Jerusalem; or rather to the Mount of Olives, which stands on the Eastern side of the City.(a) St. Luke interposes an incident, full of the deepest interest and beauty, and subjoins a Parable: taking up the narrative of the other Evangelists, at verse 29. What follows is the history of what took place as our LORD "was passing through Jericho."

2 And, behold, *there was* a man named Zacchæus, which was the chief among the Publicans, and he was rich.

Enough has been said elsewhere, concerning the class of men to which Zacchæus belonged.(b) The farmers of the Revenue were probably all wealthy men: we may "*the chief* among the Publicans," (or rather, "*a chief* Publican,") have been "rich!"

After the interview in which we beheld our LORD so recently engaged with young Ruler having great possessions, and the Discourse concerning Riches which followed,(c) it becomes a matter of special interest to notice what took place on the present occasion, when the SAVIOUR is brought into direct contact with another rich man. Nor should it escape us that here was one, not only rich, but who had acquired riches in a disreputable, even in a dishonest, way. It will be observed that CHRIST does not bid *him* go and sell all that he has and give to the poor. He simply commends him for his virtuous resolution to give up *half.* Cornelius, in like manner, was assured that his alms had gone up "for a memorial before GOD;"(d) without any hint that GOD required larger sacrifices at his hand. Then further, instead of an intimation that the needle's eye would prove too narrow for His present Entertainer, we shall find our LORD graciously declaring that this day is Salvation come to the House of Zacchæus. Bede accordingly remarks, "See how the camel disencumbered of his hunch," and of his burden!

3 And he sought to see JESUS who He was; and could not for the press, because he was little of stature.

Zacchæus, like Herod Antipas, desired to see CHRIST:(e) but in how different spirit did they entertain this desire! Mere carnal curiosity was the motive in the case of the King: in the case of the despised publican, it was the result of sincere piety; the act of one who desired "to *see* what sort of person JESUS was," in order that he might the better *love*(f) the Being of whom he had heard so much, and whose Disciple he was already so well prepared to become.

Hastening therefore along the road whereby our LORD was travelling, and getting

(a) St. Matth. xx. 34: xxi. 1, and St. Mark x. 52: xi. 1.
(b) See the note on St. Mark ii. 15, and the second note on St. Luke xviii. 10.
(c) See St. Luke xviii. 18 to 30.   (d) Acts x. 4.
(e) See St. Luke ix. 9.   (f) See 1 St. John iv. 20.

in advance of the crowd, (from among(g) which he had found it impossible, on account of his smallness of stature, to behold the person of CHRIST,) he availed himself of one of the fruit trees which grew by the wayside to obtain a view of the Holy One who must needs presently approach the spot. As it follows,

4 And he ran before, and climbed up into a sycamore tree to see Him: for He was to pass that *way.*

Much has been written on the subject of the tree into which Zacchæus climbed. Its name is here literally translated "Sycamore,"—a word which denotes "Fig-mulberry."   Accordingly, some have thought it was a Fig, some, a Mulberry tree. A great botanist thus settles the question:—Out of two hundred known species of the Fig, only two are eatable, *that* in common use, (*Ficus Carica,*) and the inferior kind here noticed, (*Ficus Sycomorus,*) which, as its name denotes, has leaves resembling those of the mulberry.   "'I was no prophet, neither was I a prophet's son;' says the Prophet Amos,(h) 'but I was an herdman, and a gatherer *of Syca-more fruit:*' from which, and from other passages of Scripture, it may be inferred that this tree was of very great importance among the Jews."(i)
Screened by the foliage of such a tree, Zacchæus may well have expected that he should remain unseen.   But he had to do with the same All-seeing Eye which had spied Nathanael beneath the fig-tree, "before that Philip called" him.(k)   Of this, he was soon made conscious; for it follows,

5 And when JESUS came to the place, He looked up, and saw him, and said unto him, Zacchæus,

(For "the LORD knoweth them that are His:"(l) "He calleth them all by their names.")(m)

make haste and come down; for to-day I must abide at thy house.

Zacchæus desired no more than to *see* CHRIST; but He who does for us more than we can either ask or think, was prepared to grant him a much greater favour, and one for which he was little prepared.   "Our SAVIOUR comes uninvited to his house; for though He had not heard the word of invitation, He had already seen the will to ask Him."(n)   Nothing but humility, like that of the Centurion,(o) had kept Zacchæus silent.

6 And he made haste, and came down, and received Him joyfully.

Such verses as this are for the Reader to pause at, and for his imagination to picture.   The astonishment of the man, detected through his leafy screen, when the Mighty Stranger halted on "coming to the place,"—looked up,—spied him out,—kindly called him by his name,—and even expressed impatience that he should come down; with the gracious announcement that He "must needs pass this day in his house:" then, the haste and joy with which the other obeyed the welcome summons,—the wonder of the populace, who, a moment ago, had witnessed the vain efforts of the man, as he stood among them, to obtain even a glimpse of our LORD's person,—and the final withdrawing of the Blessed One and His Disciples to the house of the delighted host:—all this is matter for *the heart* rather than for *the pen.*   If the Gospel were indeed sweet to our taste,—"sweeter than honey and the honey-comb,"—we should read it more slowly; and be made sensible that the purely narrative portions, in their literal sense, yield abundant delight, as well as instruction.

7 And when they saw *it,* they all murmured, saying, That He was gone to be guest with a man that is a sinner.

They called him a "sinner" only because he was "a publican."   The Reader is requested to refer to the second note on St. Luke xviii. 10, for some remarks on

(g) Instead of "*for* the press," it should be "*from among* the crowd."
(h) Amos vii. 14: where see the margin.
(i) Sir W. Hooker's "Guide to Kew Gardens."—See the note on St. Luke xvii. 6.
(k) St. John i. 48.   (l) 2 Tim. ii. 19.
(m) Ps. cxlviii. 4: compare St. John x. 3.   Consider also Gen. xvi. 8.
(n) Ambrose.   (o) See St. Matth. viii. 8.

this subject. There is no reason whatever for doubting that Zacchæus was a Jew.

An entertainment must have followed; after which we are perhaps to fancy much of lofty teaching. What need to say *who* will have been the most attentive listener? At last, we read,—

8 And Zacchæus stood, and said unto the LORD; Behold, LORD, the half of my goods I give to the poor; and if I have taken anything from any man by false accusation, I restore *him* fourfold.

He seems to have come forward in presence of the assembled guests, and standing before his LORD and ours, to have made this declaration of what henceforth he was resolved to do, in testimony of the sincerity of his belief and repentance; as well as of his hearty acceptance of the sublime precepts to which he had been listening. He may have heard our SAVIOUR declare that the Estate of Poverty is holy and precious in GOD's sight; that Riches are an encumbrance to him who would enter by the "strait gate;" and that "it is more blessed to give than to receive."(p) Then, as St. John Baptist was asked by the Pharisees for a rule, bade them "exact no more than that which was appointed them,"(q) it is obvious to suppose that our SAVIOUR will have discoursed to this man of Truthfulness and Mercy. "Behold, LORD," he therefore replies, "half of every thing I have, I this day give up to the poor; and if I retain the other half of my property, it is chiefly in order that I may have wherewith to fulfil the further resolution which I have made, to give back fourfold to every one whom I have ever wronged by false accusation." ... On this, Williams remarks kindly,—"The expression seems to indicate that his gains had been comparatively innocent, in an occupation proverbial for extortion: else, how could he restore fourfold out of the remainder?"

Concerning the proposed measure of restitution, it is to be observed that Zacchæus imposed upon himself the severest measure enjoined by the Law concerning any one *convicted of theft;* (as it is written, "he shall restore four sheep for a sheep":)(r) but this was exacted only of him who had made away with the property he had stolen. "If the theft be certainly *found in his hand alive,*" whether "ox, or ass, or sheep," he was only to "restore *double.*"(s) Whereas, with respect to him who *confessed* his crime, it is but said, "he shall recompense his trespass with the principal thereof, and add unto it *the fifth part thereof,* and give it unto him against whom he hath trespassed."(t) Zacchæus therefore judged himself, and *that* severely: a pattern surely to us all! "for if we would judge ourselves, we should not be judged."(u)

9 And JESUS said unto him, This day is salvation come to this house, forasmuch as he also is a son of Abraham.

It seems likely that St. Luke means that our SAVIOUR spake thus "*concerning,*" "*with reference to,*" Zacchæus: not actually *to* him. He may have turned and addressed the company. His words imply, that the Gospel message had come to the wealthy publican's doors; and that he had closed at once with the offer of Mercy. Salvation had therefore come to him, on that day; for that *he* also, by that day's conduct, had recovered his birthright, heretofore forfeited, and shown himself a true descendant of "faithful Abraham."

CHRIST "well says, 'He also;' to declare that not only those who have lived justly, but those who are raised up from a life of injustice, belong to the sons of promise."(x) "He says not that he 'was,' but that he now 'is.' For before, when he was chief among the publicans, and bore no likeness to righteous Abraham, he was *not* his son."(y) Hence, the fitness of the words which follow:

10 For the Son of Man is come to seek and to save that which was lost.

That is, "the lost sheep of the house of Israel."(z) Take notice then, that CHRIST the Good Shepherd was "seeking" this one lost sheep, as He prepared to

---

(p) Acts xx. 35.   (q) St. Luke iii. 12, 13.   (r) Exod. xxii. 1.   Consider 2 Samuel xii. 6.
(s) Exod. xxii. 4.   (t) Numbers v. 7.   (u) 1 Cor. xi. 31.
(x) Bede.   (y) Theophylact.   (z) St. Matth. x. 6.

depart from Jericho. . . . . The saying is found to recur, with the exception of one affecting word, in St. Matthew xviii. 11. But observe, that a parable immediately follows, (in St. Matthew,) which more than supplies the omission of that word.(a)

How great a consolation to many a burdened conscience, may this entire portion of Scripture well prove! Dishonest gains do not exclude a man hopelessly from the Kingdom. The door of Repentance yet remains open,—while there is life. But then, the offer of Mercy may not be trifled with. Zacchæus acted promptly. It is worth observing that he acted *openly* also.

11 And as they heard these things, He added and spake a parable, because He was nigh to Jerusalem, and because they thought that the Kingdom of God should immediately appear.

That is, "the Kingdom *of Israel;*" for compare Acts i. 6. That the Kingdom of Messiah could not be far away, the Jews knew from prophecy; but they had formed a wrong notion of its nature.

Is it perhaps implied that our Saviour's announcement of the purpose of His coming, (in verse 10,) and the allusion to Abraham which is found in verse 9, had already awakened proud hopes in the breasts of His hearers? as if He had declared that it was His intention *now* to "gather together in one the children of God that were scattered abroad,"(b) "and to perform the oath which He sware to their father Abraham?"(c)

The parable of "the Pounds," which follows, and which St. Luke alone relates, resembles in many respects the parable of "the Talents," which is peculiar to St. Matthew's Gospel.(d) Yet are the two parables strikingly contrasted. Both, however, are prophecies; and the present parable opens with the express mention of "a Kingdom" yet future.

12 He said therefore, A certain Nobleman went into a far country to receive for Himself a Kingdom, and to return.

He "went into *a far country,*"(!) in order to obtain for Himself the right and title to that Kingdom which, on His return, He should "receive:" for consider the language of verse 15.—This is that "far country,"(e) from which the "good news" is "as cold waters to a thirsty soul."

13 And He called His ten servants, and delivered them ten pounds, and said unto them, Occupy till I come.

It matters nothing what is the particular sum here spoken of.(f) The thing to be observed is, that calling "ten of His servants," this Nobleman intrusted each of them with *the same* amount,—bidding them "employ," or "trade with" it, till His return. The knowledge of the way of Salvation, ("one Faith, one Baptism,")(g) seems to be the "pound" given to all alike. And here, one of the points of contrast between the Parable of "the Talents," and of "the Pounds," presents itself. See St. Matthew xxv. 15, and the note there.

Take notice, that there are *Ten* Servants, as there were Ten Virgins.(h) This was a favourite number with God's people. It seems not unlikely, however, that the number of servants, so nearly corresponding with the number of the Apostolic body, was meant to quicken the Twelve to strenuous exertion after their Master's departure. *Can* we be mistaken in seeing a warning addressed to the Traitor, in every hint which fell from the lips of Christ, of *one* who had proved faithless, and who alone acted in a manner unworthy of his lofty calling? See the note on St. Mark xiv. 25.

14 But His citizens hated Him, and sent a message after Him, saying, We will not have this *man* to reign over us.

We shall hear more of them, and of what befell them, in verse 27.—Was it perhaps especially the victims of persecution,—St. Stephens, St. James, and the rest,—

(a) See St. Matthew xviii. 12. (b) St. John xi. 52. (c) St. Luke i. 72, 73.

(d) St. Matthew xxv. 14 to 30. (e) Proverbs xxv. 25.

(f) It is called a *mina*, which is rather more than 3l. See the margin of a reference Bible.

(g) Ephes. iv. 5. (h) St. Matthew xxv. 1.

whose blood cried to Heaven, and whose souls carried into the unseen world the message from those "of whom, as concerning the flesh, CHRIST came,"(i) and w were, therefore, "His citizens?" When the Jews exclaimed, "We have no Ki but Cæsar;" and "Write not, The King of the Jews,"(k) they did nothing else effect but say, "We will not have this Man to rule over us," even before His parture.

But the Parable may not be thus limited in its application. The disobedient all ages find here their picture; and, in verse 27, they read their final doom. A many as refuse subjection to the yoke of CHRIST, send the same message after Him and this will continue to the end. See Psalm ii. 2, 3.

15 And it came to pass, that when He was returned, having received the Kingdom, then He commanded these servants to be called unt Him, to whom He had given the money, that He might know how much every man had gained by trading.

And thus we are transported at once to the end of the World, and to the great Day of Accounts. Then will "the Kingdom" have "come;" for CHRIST will have "received" of the FATHER "the heathen for His inheritance, and the uttermost parts of the earth for His possession."(l) Then will be "given Him Dominion and Glory, and a Kingdom, that all people, nations, and languages, shall serve Him: His Dominion is an Everlasting Dominion, which shall not pass away, and His Kingdom that which shall not be destroyed."(m)

16 Then came the first, saying, LORD, Thy pound hath gained ten pounds.

Spoken as becomes a Servant of CHRIST: "Thy pound hath gained:" as co scious that it was GOD who had "given the increase."(n) So, after saying, ' laboured more abundantly than they all," St. Paul suddenly checks himself, a adds,—"Yet not I, but the Grace of GOD which was with me."(o)

17 And He said unto him, Well, thou good servant: because thou hast been faithful in a very little, have thou authority over ten citie

How mighty a reward is here hinted at! The man who before had to toil, as servant, with a single piece of money, now reigns, like a King, over ten cities.(Verily, now was "judgment given to the Saints of the Most High; and the ti came that the Saints possessed the Kingdom!"(q)
And we may notice that the riches and magnificent resources of CHRIST's Kin dom are here not obscurely hinted at, although in figurative language: a spu surely, to increased exertion while yet our LORD "delays His coming!"

18 And the second came, saying, LORD, Thy pound hath gained fiv pounds.

Observe, he uses the same pious language as the former "good servant." They seem to have been of one mind, and to have said day by day as they toiled,—"No unto us, O LORD, not unto us, but unto Thy Name give the praise!"(r)

19 And He said likewise to him, Be thou also over five cities.

The reward, we find, was proportioned to the work.—Only one other servant i told of. The remaining seven may have gained some more, some less. But these three represent classes,—the very faithful, the very faithless, and those who hav simply done well. The Reader is requested to read the note on St. Matthew xxv. 17
The third servant next comes forward, "with that self-confidence ever found i the rejected:"(s)

20, 21 And another came, saying, LORD, behold, here is Thy pound

(i) Romans ix. 5.
(k) St. John xix. 15 and 21.
(l) Psalm ii. 8.
(m) Dan. vii. 14.
(n) 1 Cor. iii. 6.
(o) 1 Cor. xv. 10.
(p) See notes on St. Luke xvi. 12, and xx. 38.
(q) Dan. vii. 22.
(r) Ps. cxv. 1.
(s) See the note on St. Matth. xxv. 44.

which I have kept laid up in a napkin: for I feared Thee, because Thou art an austere man: Thou takest up that Thou layedst not down, and reapest that Thou didst not sow.

22, 23, 24 And He saith unto him, Out of thine own mouth will I judge thee, *thou* wicked servant. Thou knewest that I was an austere man, taking up that I laid not down, and reaping that I did not sow: wherefore then gavest not thou My money into the bank, that at My coming I might have required Mine own with usury? And He said unto them that stood by, Take from him the pound, and give *it* to him that hath ten pounds.

The resemblance of these five verses to as many in the parable of "the Talents" in St. Matthew's Gospel, (xxv. 24 to 28,) is very striking. The Reader is referred to the notes on St. Matthew xxv. 24 and 27.—A Talent is too large a sum, (being nearly 200*l.*) to be "laid up in a napkin;" it must needs be buried in the Earth. Hence the variety of circumstance between the two Parables.

25 (And they said unto Him, LORD, he hath ten pounds.)

The meaning of these words, it is hard to discover. Do the Angels, then, (for it is *they* who "stand by," and execute the LORD's commands,) testify surprise at the directions given them? They seem to say,—Nay, but he hath already *ten* of these, and hath been set over as many cities. He therefore hath no need of more. . . But it is hard to see *why* such a saying was introduced into the Parable. Indeed there are several points in the Parables of "the Pounds" and "the Talents" which have never yet been satisfactorily explained.

26, 27 For I say unto you, That unto every one which hath, shall be given; and from him that hath not, even that he hath shall be taken away from him.(*t*) But those Mine enemies, which would not that I should reign over them, bring hither, and slay *them* before Me.

This recalls what went before, in verse 14; and reminds us that the present Parable is a complex one. It will be observed that nothing is said of any punishment which awaited the unprofitable servant, as in the other Parable.(*u*) His punishment here seems only to have been the forfeiture of that which he had. Attention is directed instead to the doom of those rebellious citizens, who sent the message of defiance recorded in verse 14.

28, 29 And when He had thus spoken, He went before, ascending up to Jerusalem.

30 And it came to pass, when He was come nigh to Bethphage and Bethany, at the Mount called *the mount* of Olives, He sent two of His Disciples, saying, Go ye into the village over against *you;* in the which at your entering ye shall find a colt tied, whereon yet never man sat: loose him, and bring *him hither.*

St. Mark and St. Luke are careful to notice that on this ass's colt, "never man sat." The mystical meaning of this statement will be found fully noticed in the note on St. Mark xi. 2.

31 And if any man ask you, Why do ye loose *him?* thus shall ye say unto him, Because the LORD hath need of him.

32, 33, 34, 35, 36 And they that were sent went their way, and found even as He had said unto them. And as they were loosing the colt, the owners thereof said unto them, Why loose ye that colt? And they said, The LORD hath need of him. And they brought him to

(*t*) See the note on St. Matth. xxv. 29.　　　　(*u*) See St. Matth. xxv. 30.

JESUS: and they cast their garments upon the colt, and they set JESUS thereon. And as He went, they spread their clothes in the way.

37, 38, 39, 40 And when He was come nigh, even now at the descent of the Mount of Olives, the whole multitude of the Disciples began to rejoice and praise GOD with a loud voice for all the mighty works that they had seen, saying, Blessed *be* the King that cometh in the Name of the LORD: Peace in Heaven and Glory in the highest. And some of the Pharisees from among the multitude said unto Him, Master, rebuke Thy Disciples. And He answered and said unto them, I tell you that if these should hold their peace, the stones would immediately cry out.

What a soul-stirring declaration! proceeding, as it does, from the very Author of Creation! How are we reminded of the mysterious pangs which soon after shook the Earth; when the Sun underwent an eclipse, and the whole framework of Nature became convulsed with portentous anguish! "Surely, if the LORD of Angels, amid His Humiliation, was not to receive even this acknowledgment from the poor, the very lifeless stones must re-echo back the Voice of Prophecy which had sounded from the beginning of the World!"

41 And when He was come near, He beheld the City,

Which lay beautifully spread before Him, covering the whole of the rising ground on the other side of the valley. The Temple crowned the sacred height and the everlasting hills stood round about,—an emblem of His own undying Love.(x) How mysterious is the sorrow which we are permitted next to witness "He beheld the City,"—

42 and wept over·it, saying, If thou hadst known, even thou, at least in this thy day, the things *which belong* unto thy peace! but now they are hid from thine eyes.

That is, "Oh that thou hadst known!" "This thy Day,"—that is, the day foretold in Prophecy, as that on which thy King should visit thee.(y)

43 For the days shall come upon thee, that thine enemies shall cast a trench about thee, and compass thee round, and keep thee in on every side,

There is more on this subject in St. Luke xxi. 20.

44 and shall lay thee even with the ground, and thy children within thee; and they shall not leave in thee one stone upon another; because thou knowest not the time of thy visitation.

The allusion in our Blessed LORD's words to the language in which the prophet Isaiah denounced "Woe to Ariel, to Ariel, the City where David dwelt,"(z) seems unmistakable. But what is principally brought to mind, is our SAVIOUR's own passionate lamentation over the Holy City, recorded in a former chapter; (a) and which, like the present place, intimates that the Day of Grace and Probation had at last closed upon Jerusalem forever. Many a time would He have gathered her children together, even as a hen gathereth her chickens under her wings,—and she "would not!" Judicial blindness had therefore overtaken the City. The things which belonged unto her peace were now hid from her eyes.

Take notice that the SAVIOUR *weeps*, even while foretelling the utter destruction of Jerusalem: somewhat as Joseph, (His type,) wept, even while he bound Simeon before the eyes of his brethren.(b) He does not, however, withdraw his threatened judgments, tremendous though they be, on *that* account. Very terrible is His wrath, although it be "the wrath *of the LAMB*."(c) And *who* so blind as not to

(x) Ps. cxxv. 2.　　　　　(y) See St. Matth. xxi. 4, 5.　　　　　(z) Isaiah xxix. 1 to 8.
(a) St. Luke xiii. 34, and St. Matth. xxiii. 37 to 39.　　　　　(b) Gen. xlii. 24.
(c) Rev. vi. 16.

see the private and personal teaching of the text? To the spiritual Jerusalem, as well as to the very least of "her children within her," doubtless GOD declares His Almighty Power most chiefly in showing *Mercy and Pity:* but does He therefore cease to be a GOD of *Justice* also? And have not *they* the time of their Visitation?

45, 46 And He went into the Temple, and began to cast out them that sold therein, and them that bought; saying unto them, It is written, My house is the House of Prayer: but ye have made it a den of thieves.

Several remarks will be found on this incident and these sayings, in the notes on St. Matth. xxi. 12, 13; and especially on St. Mark xi. 16, 17.

47, 48 And He taught daily in the Temple. But the Chief Priests and the Scribes, and the chief of the people sought to destroy Him, and could not find what they might do: for all the people were very attentive to hear Him.

The expression in the original is striking. It denotes that the people *"hung upon"* the words of CHRIST. See the last note on St. Matthew vii.

CHAPTER XX.

1 CHRIST *avoucheth His authority by a question of John's Baptism.* 9 *The Parable of the Vineyard.* 19 *Of giving tribute to Cæsar.* 27 *He convinceth the Sadducees that denied the Resurrection.* 41 *How* CHRIST *is the Son of David.* 45 *He warneth His Disciples to beware of the Scribes.*

1, 2 AND it came to pass, *that* on one of those days, as He taught the people in the Temple, and preached the Gospel, the chief Priests and the Scribes came upon *Him* with the elders, and spake unto Him, saying, Tell us, by what authority doest Thou these things? or who is he that gave Thee this authority?

The expression used in verse 1, denotes that these assailants of the Holy One came *suddenly* into His presence with their imperious demand. Our LORD's reply has already been the subject of sufficient comment in the notes on the two earlier Gospels,—as will be presently indicated.

3, 4 And He answered and said unto them, I will also ask you one thing; and answer Me: The Baptism of John, was it from Heaven, or of men?

5, 6, 7 And they reasoned with themselves, saying, If we shall say, From Heaven; He will say, Why then believed ye him not? but and if we say, Of men; all the people will stone us: for they be persuaded that John was a Prophet. And they answered, that they could not tell whence *it was*.

8 And JESUS said unto them, Neither tell I you by what authority I do these things.

Concerning all this, the Reader is referred to what has been already offered in the Commentary on St. Matthew and St. Mark.(a)—The parable of "the Vineyard let out to Husbandmen" follows, which is found in all the three Gospels.

9, 10, 11, 12, 13, 14, 15 Then began He to speak to the people this parable: A certain man planted a Vineyard, and let it forth to husbandmen, and went into a far Country for a long time. And at the season He sent a servant to the husbandmen, that they should give Him of the fruit of the Vineyard: but the husbandmen beat him, and sent *him* away empty. And again He sent another servant: and they beat him also, and entreated *him* shamefully, and sent *him* away empty. And again He sent a third: and they wounded him also, and cast *him* out. Then said the Lord of the Vineyard, What shall I do? I will send My beloved Son: it may be they will reverence *Him* when they see Him. But when the husbandmen saw Him, they reasoned among themselves, saying, This is the Heir: come, let us kill Him, that the inheritance may be ours. So they cast Him out of the Vineyard, and killed *Him*.

16 What therefore shall the Lord of the Vineyard do unto them? He shall come and destroy these husbandmen, and shall give the Vineyard to others.

And when they heard *it*, they said, GOD forbid.

Concerning this remarkable Parable, which is none other than a Prophecy, so much has been already said, that it must suffice to refer the Reader to the notes on St. Matthew,—xxi. 33 to 41; and on St. Mark xii. 1 to 9. "GOD, the great Householder, was pleased to mark off, as it were, one part of the Earth to be more particularly His own; He 'planted a Vineyard,' when 'He chose Jacob unto Himself, and Israel for His own possession.'(b) This Vineyard was kept separate from the rest of the world. The rite of Circumcision, the whole of the Ceremonial Law, was the 'hedge' round about it, which shut out the Gentiles. It had its 'wine-press' in the altar of burnt-offerings, and its 'tower' in the Temple. But what fruit did the Vineyard produce to Him that planted it?(c) The rest of the Parable is Prophecy.

The only circumstantial difference to which the Reader's attention shall be directed is, that *here* the Parable is represented as spoken "to the people,"(d) rather than, (as in the former instance,) to their teachers.

17 And He beheld them,

That is, He looked them steadily in the face; as His Divine manner seems to have been when He was about to deliver any saying of unusual solemnity,—

and said, What is this then that is written, The stone which the builders rejected, the same is become the Head of the corner? Whosoever shall fall upon that stone shall be broken; but on whomsoever it shall fall, it will grind him to powder.

The Reader is referred to the notes on St. Matthew xxi. 44, and on St. Mark xii. 11.

(a) See the notes on St. Matth. xxi. 27, and St. Mark xi. 28, 30, 31, and 33.
(b) Ps. cxxxv. 4.   (c) Dr. Jacobson's Sermons.   (d) See above, verses 9 and 1.

19 And the chief Priests and the Scribes the same hour sought to ~~l~~y hands on Him; and they feared the people: for they perceived ~~th~~at He had spoken this Parable against them.

20 And they watched *Him*, and sent forth spies, which should feign ~~th~~emselves just men, that they might take hold of His words, that so ~~th~~ey might deliver Him unto the power and authority of the Governor.

21, 22 And they asked Him, saying, Master, we know that Thou ~~s~~ayest and teachest rightly, neither acceptest Thou the person *of any*, ~~b~~ut teachest the way of GOD truly: is it lawful for us to give tribute unto Cæsar, or no?

They felt sure that He would return a negative answer to their question: for they had, with perfect truth, set forth the fearless character of our LORD's teaching; and they knew that He was influenced solely by regard for GOD's Honour, without any admixture of worldly considerations. They cared not, however, which way His answer might incline. For if He allowed the payment of Tribute to their Roman Masters, they foresaw that His reputation with the people would be at an end; if, on the contrary, He forbade the practice, they would have a valid charge to bring against Him before Pilate, the Roman Governor of the Province.—Concerning the character of these assailants of CHRIST, whom both St. Matthew and St. Mark describe as "Pharisees and Herodians," the Reader is referred to the note on St. Matthew xxii. 17.

23 But He perceived their craftiness, and said unto them, Why tempt ye Me?

"Ye hypocrites!" adds St. Matthew;(*e*) and such they truly were; seeking, as "a ground of accusation against Him, that which of all things they most desired themselves, namely, the exemption of their nation from Tribute." Here, again, were men who sought to "procure His condemnation by the Romans as a rebel against Cæsar; whereas, if He had possessed that character, and sustained it with vigour, they would themselves have flocked eagerly to His standard. He found means, however, so to answer their inquiry as at the same time to display their hypocrisy and to elicit the Truth, in sight of that very multitude"(*f*) whose indignation they sought to draw down upon Him: saying,

24 Show Me a penny. Whose image and superscription hath it? They answered and said, Cæsar's.

They brought him a piece of money, called *denarius*,—a Roman coin, of silver, (worth about 7*d*. or 8*d*.)—which bore upon it the name and portrait of Tiberius Cæsar.

"The coin which they affected to scruple about paying into the Roman Treasury, itself bore the Emperor's effigy and legend,—the mark of *his* sovereignty, and *their* subjection. This money they hesitated not to circulate among themselves in all matters of traffic and exchange; and they well knew the import of its image and superscription. The absurdity of scrupling to withhold from a sovereignty thus acknowledged, the necessary homage of obeying its import; as well as the consistency of such a payment with the higher claims of the one supreme and unchangeable LORD of all,"(*g*)—our SAVIOUR proceeds to make manifest in the famous words which follow.

25 And He said unto them, Render therefore unto Cæsar the things which be Cæsar's, and unto GOD the things which be GOD's.

"This sentence, which confounded and baffled those blind guides of the people, extends further in its application than to the mere question in reply to which it was given. Since Tribute here represents the whole of that allegiance of which it is an essential part and symbol, we may view our LORD's sentence as embracing these two propositions:—First, that there are certain duties which we owe to Cæsar,

(*e*) St. Matth. xxii. 18.   (*f*) Dr. W. H. Mill.   (*g*) Abridged from Dr. W. H. Mill.

the sovereign power of the State, as such; Secondly, that these duties, rightly comprehended, cannot interfere with those to which they should ever be united, the duties which we owe directly and immediately to GOD."(*h*)

26 And they could not take hold of His words before the people: and they marvelled at His answer, and held their peace.

27, 28 Then came to *Him* certain of the Sadducees, which deny that there is any Resurrection; and they asked Him, saying, Master, Moses wrote unto us, If any man's brother die, having a wife, and he die without children, that his brother should take his wife, and raise up seed unto his brother.

They allude to the Law found in Deuteronomy xxv. 5; which prescribed that the next of kin should marry the widow of a deceased kinsman, under the circumstances spoken of. "And it shall be," (so ran the law,) "that the first-born which she beareth shall succeed in the name of his brother which is dead, that his name be not put out of Israel." It was a remarkable enactment, truly; the mystical intention of which was to shadow forth the Doctrine of the Resurrection of the Dead. This has been more fully shown in the note on St. Mark xii. 19.

29, 30, 31, 32, 33 There were therefore seven brethren: and the first took a wife, and died without children. And the second took her to wife, and he died childless. And the third took her; and in like manner the seven also: and they left no children, and died. Last of all, the woman died also. Therefore in the Resurrection whose wife of them is she? for seven had her to wife.

34, 35, 36 And JESUS answering said unto them, The children of this World marry, and are given in marriage: but they which shall be accounted worthy to obtain that World, and the Resurrection from the dead, neither marry, nor are given in marriage: neither can they die any more:

Rather "*for* neither can they die any more:" by which words our SAVIOUR assigns the object of Holy Matrimony,—which chiefly is the procreation of children, in order to supply the losses which Death occasions. And of this, the Church is faithful to remind us, in the Marriage service.

for they are equal unto the Angels; and are the children of GOD, being the children of the Resurrection.

"CHRIST is 'the first-born from the dead;'(*i*) and we, 'the children of the Resurrection.' The Spirit of CHRIST abiding in us maketh us the members of CHRIST; and by the same SPIRIT, we have a full right and title to rise with our Head."(*k*)

37, 38 Now, that the dead are raised, even Moses showed at the bush, when he calleth the LORD the GOD of Abraham, and the GOD of Isaac, and the GOD of Jacob. For He is not a GOD of the dead, but of the living: for all live unto Him.

"Our LORD's answer seems to imply that the Patriarchs had not, and needed not any express declaration of this doctrine; for that an affectionate piety, and a due apprehension of GOD's power, had in these words the fullest assurance that it was capable of receiving."(*l*)
"At the bush," denotes that section of Scripture which contains the history of the burning bush. Moses, because he wrote that history, is here said to have "*called* the LORD, the GOD of Abraham," &c.: but GOD was, of course, the Speaker. Our SAVIOUR is, in fact, explaining now the words which He spoke *then*.
The Reader is referred to the notes on St. Mark's Gospel,—xii. 18 to 27, for a

(*h*) Dr. W. H. Mill.   (*i*) Col. i. 18.
(*k*) Bp. Pearson.   (*l*) Williams.

exposition of the preceding most precious portion of the Gospel. It shall suffice, in addition, to call attention to the fact that many more hints are supplied in Holy Scripture of the Future Life than is commonly supposed. How often are we reminded of its joyous character;(*m*)—of its social aspect,(*n*) (if the expression be allowable;)—of the perfection to which every earth relation, (as *that* which subsists between a Pastor and his flock,)(*o*) will then attain! In the former chapter, the enlarged sphere of stewardship then to be revealed, was not obscurely indicated.(*p*) In this place, the ennobled and exalted nature of the Body, is as plainly declared.

39 Then certain of the Scribes answering, said, Master, Thou hast well said.

By comparing the present Gospel with those of St. Matthew and St. Mark, it will be found that the saying of the Scribes here recorded has reference to a portion of narrative which St. Luke omits,—namely, our LORD's reply to a Scribe who had asked Him which is the first, or great commandment?(*q*) All the three Evangelists concur in the statement that, "from that day forth," the Holy One was never more molested with questions by His adversaries. As it follows,—

40 And after that, they durst not ask Him any *question at all*.

We next behold our LORD,—who has already put to silence the chief Priests, Scribes, and Elders,(*r*) the Pharisees and the Herodians, the Sadducees, and last of all the Scribes, or expounders of the Law,—Himself addressing a question to the most conspicuous of His enemies. They have hitherto assailed *Him*. It is now *His* turn to be the assailant.

And surely, we have grown *too* familiar with the contents of the Gospel, if we can approach the words which He employed on an occasion like this, without the deepest reverence and attention. Before Him lay the whole volume of Inspiration. He knew its manifold resources, for His Divine Spirit had inspired it in every part; and out of all that various store, He was about to select somewhat which might at once silence His opponents, and edify the bystanders.

We find that, "when the Pharisees had heard that He had put the Sadducees to silence, they were gathered together:"(*s*) and, while they were yet "gathered together, JESUS asked them, saying, What think ye of CHRIST? whose Son is He?" (This quotation from St. Matthew's Gospel is made here, in order to render the more concise narrative of St. Luke which follows, fully intelligible.) "They say unto Him, The Son of David."(*t*)

There is nothing unexpected in the reply; which, in fact, expressed the general belief of all the nation.(*u*) At the same time, the words were used in a *merely human* sense. Our SAVIOUR does not blame the Pharisees therefore because they confess Him to be the Son of David; but because they did not believe Him to be the Son of GOD. Now, it seems to have been His design, in this brief dialogue, to "lift up their hearts;" and to suggest to as many as had "ears to hear," that far more is implied in Scripture concerning the nature of MESSIAH than they supposed. It has been truly pointed out that one "great source of the unbelief which filled these Pharisees, was a low sense of the MESSIAH; and pride in a literal but very superficial knowledge of the Scriptures."(*x*) Still addressing the Pharisees, therefore, our SAVIOUR turns Himself to the populace, (who may be supposed to have watched the progress of His recent dialogue with wonder, and marked its close with admiration,)—

41, 42, 43 And He said unto them, How say they that CHRIST is David's Son? and David himself saith in the Book of Psalms, The LORD said unto my Lord, Sit Thou on My right hand, till I make Thine enemies Thy footstool.

(GOD the FATHER is addressing GOD the SON.)

(*m*) St. Matth. xxv. 21,—where see the note.   (*n*) St. Matth. viii. 11,—where see the note.
(*o*) 1 Thess. ii. 19.   (*p*) St. Luke xix. 17, 19: also the notes on St. Luke xvi. 12.
(*q*) See St. Matthew xxii. 36.   St. Mark xii. 28 and 32.   (*r*) St. Luke xx. 1.
(*s*) St. Matth. xxii. 34.   (*t*) St. Matth. xxii. 41, 42.
(*u*) St. Matth. ix. 27: xii. 23: xv. 22: xx. 30, 31: xxi. 9, 15, &c.   (*x*) Williams.

44 David therefore calleth Him Lord, how is He then his Son?

Our Lord here quotes the first words of the 110th Psalm, which prophesies of "The Kingdom, the Priesthood, the Conquest, and the Passion of Christ;"(y) and declares both that David was the author of that Psalm, and that the Psalmist was inspired by the Holy Ghost while he wrote it.(z)   The present text is, in fact, three times quoted,(a) (besides the present place,) and once referred to, in the course of the New Testament,(b) as descriptive of our Lord's subsequent exaltation.(c)—Does there not seem to be a peculiar adaptation of the text quoted, to the circumstances under which it was now uttered?   Surrounded by enemies whom He had even now subdued with "the sword of His mouth,"(d) does not the Divine Speaker seem to imply that what had been that day witnessed was but the prelude to Victories and a Dominion yet future; when He who was now enthroned only in the hearts of a few Disciples, (for St. Mark declares that the people "heard Him gladly,")(e) should occupy the Right Hand of the Majesty on High?

But the suggestion which has been already offered, (in a note on St. Mark xii. 27,) here recurs; namely, that there is reason to suspect that we ourselves "know not the Scriptures," nor indeed that we thoroughly understand our Lord's interpretation of them.   For it is easy to see what answer a captious carnal reasoner of the modern school would have returned to our Lord's inquiry.   David, (it might be said,) does indeed speak of his illustrious Descendant, as his "Lord;" but is not *that* only because Christ was to be so much greater a King than David?   Christ is still David's *Son*, because He is David's *Descendant*.

And indeed it must be admitted that our Lord's question "does not, by the passage referred to, solve any difficulty: but rather throws out a difficulty which might arrest the attention of a Scribe desirous to know the Truth, such as would lead him to see there was something far higher and more mysterious about the Messiah than he supposed. . . . . Our Lord's words were a clew, by which Faith might apprehend the secret nature of the Kingdom.   To Reason, they proved nothing: but to Faith, they opened lofty views of the Divine Economy in the Gospel; as far surpassing anything which Reason could have inferred, or imagination could conceive, as Heaven is above Earth."(f)

"And I think," adds the excellent Writer hitherto quoted, "it may be stated generally, that they who expect clear and express warrant in the words of Scripture as concerning the Doctrine of the Trinity, and the like, will find nothing of this kind promised in our Lord's Teaching: but, on the contrary, hints and allusions thrown out, which He, by and by, in His Church, or in the ways of a particular Providence, will solve to those who will obey Him; and to those alone."

45, 46, 47 Then in the audience of all the people, He said unto His Disciples, Beware of the Scribes, which desire to walk in long robes, and love greetings in the markets, and the highest seats in the synagogues, and the chief rooms at feasts; which devour widows' houses, and for a show make long prayers: the same shall receive greater damnation.

These sayings form but a part of the long Discourse which our Lord proceeded to deliver at this time,—the weighty denunciations which occupy an entire chapter in St. Matthew's Gospel, and which will be found fully commented upon elsewhere. See particularly St. Matth. xxiii. 5, 6, and 14.

Thus ends this remarkable portion of the sacred narrative; remarkable, as presenting a succession of assaults made by carnally-minded men against the Saviour of the World, and which were all attended with the same result.   Not only "in the same net which they hid privily, is their foot taken,"(g) but some fresh aspect of Divine Truth is vindicated at every step.   A thoughtful writer has said,—"One circumstance arises accidentally out of another; and new inquiries take place with various spirit and temper.   But whatever the nature of the question may be, it i

---

(y) See the heading of the Psalm.
(z) See St. Mark xii. 36: also St. Matth. xxii. 43: and consider Acts i. 16: ii. 30.
(a) Acts ii. 34, 35.   Heb. i. 13: x. 12, 13.   (b) 1 Cor. xv. 25.
(c) See the last note on St. Matthew xxii.   (d) Rev. i. 16: ii. 16: xix. 15, 21.
(e) St. Mark xii. 37.   (f) Williams.   (g) Psalm ix. 15.

the occasion at the same time of answering what is in the heart of the Speaker, of instructing the promiscuous crowd, and of putting forth to all ages the highest truths of God.   And perhaps what here takes place in the Temple is a type of God's Providence generally in His Church, to be shown forth in its History:—that by disputes and discussions and questionings among those that engage in them under various feelings and motives, (and these sometimes not the most pure,) others, of a temper more meek and teachable, are instructed; and the Church of all ages is furnished with great and saving Doctrines."(k)

CHAPTER XXI.

1 CHRIST commendeth the poor Widow.   5 He foretelleth the destruction of the Temple, and of the city of Jerusalem.   25 The signs also which shall be before the last Day.   34 He exhorteth them to be watchful.

THE truly affecting incident with which the present chapter commences, is found only in the Gospels of St. Mark(a) and St. Luke.   The place where the History of "the poor" (or, as she may fairly be termed, "the munificent") "widow," occurs, is highly remarkable; for take notice that it stands midway between the weighty discourses of the former chapter, and the tremendous prophecies contained in the present: so that it occupies the little halting-place between our LORD's leave-taking of His enemies, and His anticipation of the vengeance which was to be wrought upon them,—first, by His avenging armies; next, by His legions of Angels.   It immediately follows His refutation of chief Priests, Scribes, and Elders,(b)—of Pharisees and Herodians, Sadducees and Lawyers;(c) together with His eight withering denunciations of Woe against those "Scribes and Pharisees, hypocrites," whose enmity He had borne with so long;(d) and it immediately precedes His prophecies concerning the Destruction of Jerusalem and the End of the World.   But before entering upon that far-sighted prophecy, the whole tenor of which shows that the Blessed Speaker's eye was already filled with images of magnificence and grandeur unspeakable,—the destinies of the whole Human Race, and the consummation of all things,—being now about to leave the Temple, St. Mark says that He took His seat "over against the Treasury;" (that is, opposite to the great money-chest of the Temple, which stood "on the right side as one cometh into the House of the LORD,"—the work of Jehoiada the priest, in the reign of King Jehoash:)(e)

1 AND He looked up, and saw the rich men casting their gifts into the treasury.

Are we perhaps to understand from this expression, (which also occurs in many other places of the Gospel,) that our SAVIOUR had been sitting till now with downcast eyes?   Be this as it may,—Looking up, He "beheld how the people cast money into the Treasury; and many that were rich, cast in much:"(f)

(k) Williams.   (a) St. Mark xii. 41 to 44.   (b) St. Luke xx. 1.
(c) St. Matth. xxii. 16, 23, 25.   (d) St. Matth. xxiii.
(e) 2 Kings xii. 9.   (f) St. Mark xii. 41.

2 And He saw also a certain poor Widow casting in thither t mites.

So then, amid all the weariness of His Human Body, and the anguish of H Human Soul,—amid griefs unrevealed and bitterness of Spirit inscrutable,— LORD of Heaven and Earth was at leisure to sit down and watch the ways of c of the humblest of His creatures! He saw before Him the Destruction of the Te ple, and the fall of Jerusalem; the wreck of Nature, and the crash of Worlds, a the setting up of the great White Throne, and the gathering together of all t Tribes of the Earth: all this, He saw. But "He saw also *a certain poor Widow* and it was His Divine pleasure to scrutinize her act, and weigh it in a balance, a to pronounce upon it, calmly and at length, as if Life and Death hung upon t issue. "He called unto Him His Disciples,"(g)—

3, 4 And He said, Of a truth I say unto you, that this poor Wide hath cast in more than they all; for all these have of their abundan cast in unto the offerings of GOD: but she of her penury hath cast all the living that she had.

The language of our LORD is even stronger. *They* had given of what they h over and above: *she*, of her short supply.
So carefully then are the little things noted by GOD! So true also is it that I seeth not as Man seeth! What is remarkable, the days of the Temple were nu bered. The offerings, even of "the rich men," were therefore no longer of a avail. But the sum cast in by this very poor Widow, could not, under any circu stances, from its exceeding smallness, have been of any real use. It was bu *farthing!* And yet we find it attracted the notice of the LORD of all Creati and drew from Him words of loftiest praise. Learn from this, to mistrust t reasoning, (however plausible it may sound,) of those who would discourage of ings intended for GOD's Honour. Learn also, (and from His own lips,) the ma ner in which He who weighs acts of munificence in a heavenly balance, forms I estimate of their importance and value. . . . For a few words more on this su ject, see the last note on St. Mark xii.
The present Evangelist is not careful, like St. Mark,(h) and still more St. M thew,(i) to point out that the conversation which follows took place when the Bles Company *had left* the Temple: when our SAVIOUR indeed had "departed" from —never to enter its courts again. The Disciples appear to have directed th LORD's attention to the huge stones of which the Temple was built,(k) and to t royal offerings which it contained,—such as are alluded to in Judith xvi. 19, a 2 Maccabees v. 16: ix. 16.

5, 6 And as some spake of the Temple, how it was adorned wi goodly stones and gifts, He said, *As for* these things which ye behol the days will come, in which there shall not be left one stone up another, that shall not be thrown down.

"This prophecy of the total overthrow of buildings which at the time when t prophecy was uttered seemed to defy assault, was fulfilled to the very letter for years from that very time. Titus, who conducted the siege, had given orders th the Temple should be preserved; but one of the soldiers, moved, (as the Jewi Historian Josephus relates,) by a divine impulse, set it on fire, and every effo to extinguish the flames was ineffectual." The Reader is referred to the notes St. Matthew xxiv. 2, and St. Mark xiii. 2.

7 And they asked Him, saying, Master, but when shall these thin be? and what sign *will there be* when these things shall come to pass

Four of their number are found to have approached our LORD with this questio as He sat on the Mount of Olives:(l) and to them, apart from the rest of the Twel our LORD delivered the stupendous predictions which ensue. St. Andrew on th

(g) St. Mark xii. 43.   (h) St. Mark xiii. 1.   (i) St. Matth. xxiv. 1.
(k) See the note in St. Mark xiii. 1.   (l) St. Mark xiii. 3.

great occasion is admitted to share the privilege of those other three most favoured of our Lord's Disciples,—St. Peter, St. James, and St. John. Well may the whole company of the Disciples have been disquieted by the sentence of desolation which they had just heard their Lord pronounce upon the beautiful structure which lay full in view before them,—covered with plates of gold, and of a dazzling whiteness. "It had been so sanctified by the Almighty in ancient days, and their Religion was so bound up with that spot, that they looked upon it with an awful reverence beyond what we can understand."(m) They are found to have asked Him *two* questions. (1st,) *When* these great buildings should be overthrown; and *what sign* there should be when these things should come to pass? (2dly,)—What sign there should be of Christ's Coming, and of the end of the World? St. Luke only records the former of these inquiries,—as will be found fully explained in the note on St. Matthew xxiv. 3.

8, 9 And He said, Take heed that ye be not deceived: for many shall come in My Name, saying, I am *CHRIST;* and the time draweth near: go ye not therefore after them. But when ye shall hear of wars and commotions, be not terrified: for these things must first come to pass: but the end *is* not by and by.

That is,—"But not immediately [cometh] the end: *for* nation shall rise against nation," &c., as in the two earlier Gospels; where see the notes.(n)

10, 11 Then said he unto them, Nation shall rise against nation, and kingdom against kingdom: and great earthquakes shall be in divers places, and famines, and pestilences: and fearful sights and great signs shall there be from Heaven.

"These are the beginnings of birth-pangs,"—as it is elsewhere added.(o) And all these things actually happened before the Destruction of the City and Temple of Jerusalem. Civil dissensions and hostile movements abounded; the famine foretold by Agabus, "which came to pass in the days of Claudius Cæsar,"(p) made itself severely felt in Judea;(q) while in Jerusalem, many actually perished for want of food. Pestilence is known ever to follow at the heels of Famine. During the extremities of the siege, these two scourges prevailed to an extent which was altogether appalling. Many earthquakes are recorded to have taken place throughout the East; while the portents and prodigies which are described by an eye-witness, (who knew nothing of the Gospel, nor would have believed it had he known it,) were regarded by the people themselves as unmistakable signs of something tremendous which was to follow. A flaming meteor, like a fiery sword, hung over the city by the space of a year; one night, a radiance like the light of noon, shone about the Temple and altar, for half an hour's space: a heifer, as it was being led to sacrifice, brought forth a lamb in the Temple: the eastern gate, which was of brass, and so heavy that twenty men could scarcely shut it, although secured by deep bolts, swung open at midnight of its own accord. Josephus mentions one more prodigy, which he admits would be thought a fable, but for the evidence on which it rests. Chariots and troops of armed soldiers were seen at sunset, careering in the clouds, and besieging cities in the air. The Roman Historian, Tacitus, records the same thing.

12, 13 But before all these, they shall lay their hands on you, and persecute *you,* delivering *you* up to the synagogues, and into prisons, being brought before Kings and Rulers for My Name's sake. And it shall turn to you for a testimony.

That is, "It will afford you an opportunity of bearing witness to your Religion."(r)

14, 15 Settle *it* therefore in your hearts, not to meditate before what

(m) Williams.   (n) On St. Matth. xxiv. 5, and St. Mark xiii. 6.
(o) St. Mark xiii. 8. Compare St. Matth. xxiv. 8.   (p) Acts xi. 28.
(q) Consider Rom. xv. 25, &c.   (r) Burton. See St. Mark xiii. 9, and note.

ye shall answer: for I will give you a mouth and wisdom, which all your adversaries shall not be able to gainsay nor resist.

And so it came to pass; for, as it is said in the case of St. Stephen, "They were not able to resist the wisdom and the spirit by which He spake."(s)   These four verses should be compared with four others which are found in a much earlier part of St. Matthew's Gospel; namely, in our LORD's charge to His Twelve Apostles.(f More briefly, the substance of the prophecy, the injunction, and the promise here delivered, may be also seen in St. Luke;—but in quite a different connection.(u Take notice that on all the three occasions where this solemn subject recurs, it is expressly promised that the HOLY GHOST shall speak by the mouth of the Apostles.(u)

16, 17, 18 And ye shall be betrayed both by parents, and brethren, and kinsfolk, and friends; and *some* of you shall they cause to be put to death. And ye shall be hated of all *men* for My Name's sake. But there shall not an hair of your head perish.

The substance of these verses also will be found in our LORD's Charge to the Twelve;(y) including the precious assurance that the very hairs of the head are all numbered in His sight.(z)   "The truth contained in these words is the foundation of all Christian courage; which consists in an entire dependence on GOD, as taking the most watchful and particular care over the very minutest circumstance that can appertain to us. And yet it is very remarkable, and most important to observe, that this the strongest description of a particular and protecting Providence, implies no relief from temporal evils, while at the same time it promises the most assured safety."(a) We are nowhere encouraged to expect or hope that Christian men shall pass their days without danger and distress. The pledge is but given that they shall *be safe* under the shadow of the Almighty wings,—that *no real harm* shall befall those who put their trust in GOD.

Having thus assured the Disciples of their safety, our SAVIOUR adds:

19 In your patience possess ye your souls.

These words, however, do not at all give the meaning of our LORD's saying; which should rather be translated,—"Save your lives by your patience."   The injunction, in fact, corresponds to the promise which is found in the two earlier Gospels,—"He that shall endure unto the end, the same shall be saved."(b) And thus the grace of *Patience*, which is so often singled out for Divine commendation,(c) is held up to the Church's notice, as of prime importance, to secure her safety in the coming strife.

The passage answering to this, in St. Mark's Gospel, is found to be transcribed, word for word, from our LORD's Charge to the Twelve, in St. Matthew.(d)—The Blessed Speaker continues:

20, 21 And when ye shall see Jerusalem compassed with armies, then know that the destruction thereof is nigh.   Then let them which are in Judæa flee to the mountains; and let them which are in the midst of it depart out; and let not them that are in the countries enter thereinto.

By "the midst of *it*," and "*thereinto*," the Evangelist means Jerusalem,—which he mentioned in verse 20. These, then, are the directions which our SAVIOUR gave to the faithful for their guidance, when "the end"(e) should come.   The remoter signs of coming danger He specifies from verse 8 to verse 11. "But before all

(s) Acts vi. 10.   Consider Exod. xiv. 14.
(t) St. Matth. x. 17, 18, 19, 20; where see the notes.   See also below, the note on verses 18 and 19.   (u) St. Luke xii. 11, 12.
(x) See St. Matth. x. 20; St. Luke xii. 12: and St. Mark xiii. 11, which answers to the present place.
(y) See St. Matth. x. 21, 22, 30.   (z) St. Matth. x. 30: St. Luke xii. 7.   (a) Williams
(b) St. Matth. xxiv. 13, (compare x. 22:) and St. Mark xiii. 13.
(c) See the note on St. Matth. iv. 7.
(d) See St. Mark xiii. 12, 13:—compare with St. Matth. x. 21, 22.
(e) St. Matth. xxiv. 14.

these" things, (He said,) His followers must be prepared for the hardships and persecutions, which He enumerates from verse 12 to verse 19. Next follow (in verse 20) the signs of danger, no longer remote, but at the very doors; and from which, safety must be procured by flight. And the reason follows:

22 For these be the days of vengeance, that all things which are written may be fulfilled.

Very instructive it is, and full of delight, to turn from this prophecy to the pages of the Jewish Historian Josephus; who little thought that, in writing the History of the siege of Jerusalem, he was recording the fulfilment of our SAVIOUR's predictions, and a wondrous illustration of His words.

It is found that thirty-seven years after this discourse was delivered, Cestius Gallio, the president of Syria, with a large army, marched against Jerusalem at the time of the Feast of Tabernacles, and encamped within a mile of the city. At the end of four days, he advanced to the very walls; and for five days assailed them from every quarter. Next day the attack was formally begun; the walls were undermined, and the enemy were about to set fire to the gates of the Temple, when, contrary to all expectation, and without any apparent reason, the Commander, ("*most unaccountably,*" says Josephus, A.D. 66,) "*retired from the City!*" A fierce sally of the inhabitants, and a successful onslaught, was the consequence. The Romans fled, and the Jewish army returned in triumph; whereupon it is recorded that a large number of the inhabitants "swam away from the city, as from a ship about to sink." This took place in the beginning of October.

Unaccountable indeed, in the eyes of the impatient soldiery, as well as of the terrified inhabitants of Jerusalem, must the withdrawal of the enemy at such a moment have appeared: but the Christians who were immured within its walls, mindful of their SAVIOUR's words, must have known very well how to account for the opportunity of a departure thus unexpectedly afforded them. They had the sure promise of the Eternal GOD, that "not a hair of their heads should perish."(*f*) They had received directions to flee from the city when they should see it "compassed with armies." Hath He then said, and shall He not do it? Hath He counselled flight, and shall He not also provide *a way* to escape? Doubtless, if it was not "a blast" and "a rumour," (as in the days of Sennacherib,)(*g*) it was that the heart of the Roman "melted, neither was there spirit in him any more," and the terror of the Jews fell upon him:(*h*) but, for whatever reason, the enemy withdrew; and the Christians suddenly found themselves at liberty to follow their LORD's direction, and to escape.

Those, however, within the city, who missed the sign alluded to, cannot have mistaken the indications of danger three years later, when Titus came in person against Jerusalem and formally besieged it. After wasting some time before the walls, the Roman resolved to encircle the city with a fortification, five miles in extent; and the work was conducted with such spirit, that *in three days* it was completed. *This* may well have been the special sign of danger, to which our LORD alluded; for the inhabitants from the walls must then have beheld their City literally "compassed with armies,"(*i*)—("compassed round, and kept in on every side," as it is elsewhere said:)(*k*) and it is worth remarking that to cut off from them further opportunities of egress and escape was one of the special objects which the enemy had in view. At the critical moment when this work was first being undertaken, it is obvious to suppose that as many as were resolved to save their lives by flight, availed themselves of the opportunity to retire from the devoted City. Our SAVIOUR continues:

23 But woe unto them that are with child, and to them that give suck, in those days! for there shall be great distress in the land, and wrath upon this people.

The sufferings which, in the time of the siege, should befall the wife and the mother in her hour of greatest need, are twice alluded to by our LORD. "Behold, the days are coming," (He prophesied as He was being led to Crucifixion,) "in the

(*f*) See above, verse 18.   (*g*) See 2 Kings xix. 7.   (*h*) See Josh. ii. 9: v. 1.
(*i*) See above, verse 20.   (*k*) St. Luke xix. 43.

which they shall say, Blessed are the barren, and the wombs that never bare, the paps which never gave suck."(*l*)—See the note on St. Mark xiii. 17.

24 And they shall fall by the edge of the sword, and shall be away captive into all nations:

And so indeed it came to pass: for the entire number of the slain in the was reckoned at upwards of a million; while ninety-seven thousand are sai have been carried away captive. "Spread as it were on the surface of the Oc but not blended with its waters; scattered through the mass of mankind, but preserved distinct,"(*m*)—they remain a living witness of the Sacred Narrativ are here considering. GOD hath set a mark upon the members of that nation which they are at once known; and there is no land where their name is not a word and a reproach; no land where they are not identified with transaction money,—through the lust of which Judas fell. "The children of Israel," (i was foretold concerning them,) "abide without a King, and without a Prince, without a sacrifice;"(*n*) sifted and dispersed "among all nations, like as ot sifted in a sieve."(*o*)

Take notice, that as forty years elapsed between the institution of the Pass and the entering of the Promised land, so between the sacrifice of the true Pas Lamb and the loss of that Land, did forty years elapse also. The men of Nin had forty days of warning, and they repented at the preaching of Jonah: but unbelieving Jews, though they had forty *years* of warning, (and behold, a gre than Jonas was there,) yet repented not.—Our LORD proceeds:

and Jerusalem shall be trodden down of the Gentiles, until the ti of the Gentiles be fulfilled.

So trodden under foot is she at this day; but her restoration is promised, glorious things are spoken of it, and of her.(*p*) "If the casting away of the exclaims the Apostle, "be the reconciling of the world, what shall the receiving them be, but life from the dead?"(*q*) In the mean while, a fixed period of t known only in the deep counsels of GOD, ("the times of the Gentiles," as it is l called,) must elapse: concerning which remarkable expression, consider such pl as the following:—St. John ii. 4: vii. 6, 8: xiii. 1: xvii. 1. Acts i. 7: xvii. Gal. iv. 4. Eph. i. 9. 1 Tim. ii. 6: vi. 15. Rev. ix. 15.

The dew of Heaven, which at first was on the fleece alone, (the little floc Israel,) while it was "dry upon all the earth," hath been transferred, in turn, to nations of the Earth. GOD hath said, in Gideon's words, "Let it now be dry o upon the fleece, and upon all the ground let there be dew:"(*r*) and it is so. "Bli ness in part is happened to Israel, until the fulness of the Gentiles be come in; but when "the times of the Gentiles be fulfilled," the dew of Heaven shall ref all the Earth, "and there shall be one fold, and One Shepherd."(*t*)

But our attention is invited to "the signs" which shall precede the coming the great Day.

25, 26, 27 And there shall be signs in the Sun, and in the Mo and in the Stars; and upon the Earth distress of nations, with perpl ity; the sea and the waves roaring; men's hearts failing them for fe and for looking after those things which are coming on the Earth: the powers of Heaven shall be shaken. And then shall they see Son of Man coming in a cloud, with power and great glory.

St. Luke is more full and particular in the two former verses, than either of other Evangelists. Concerning what precedes, see the notes on St. Matthew x 29, 30: and observe how parallel are not only the two great events which form subject of our LORD's prophecy,(*u*) but also the signs which were to precede

(*l*) St. Luke xxiii. 29.   (*m*) Churton.   (*n*) Hosea iii.
(*o*) Amos ix. 9.   (*p*) Isaiah lx. 15 to 20.   (*q*) Rom. xi. 1
(*r*) Judges vi. 37 to 40.   (*s*) Romans xi. 25.
(*t*) St. John x. 16. The thought in the text is borrowed from Churton.
(*u*) See the latter part of the note on St. Matth. xxiv. 26.

other. The remoter tokens, in both cases, are declared to be false Christs and false prophets:(x) the nearer tokens,—fearful sights, and signs in Heaven.(y)

28 And when these things begin to come to pass, then look up, and lift up your heads: for your Redemption draweth nigh.

Consider this place, and St. Matthew xxiv. 8, (where see the note,) in connection with the following: "We know that the whole Creation groaneth and travaileth in pain together until now. And not only they, but . . . . even we ourselves groan within ourselves, waiting for the adoption, to wit *the Redemption* of our body."(z)

29, 30, 31, 32, 33 And He spake to them a parable: Behold the fig tree, and all the trees; when they now shoot forth, ye see and know of your own selves that summer is now nigh at hand. So likewise ye, when ye see these things come to pass, know ye that the Kingdom of God is nigh at hand. Verily I say unto you, this generation shall not pass away, till all be fulfilled. Heaven and Earth shall pass away: but My Words shall not pass away.

With these verses, which are found very closely repeated in all the three Gospels,(a)—(but notice that St. Luke adds, "*and all the trees,*")—St. Luke takes leave of our LORD's reply to the twofold question with which the chapter commences;(b) adding only certain words of general caution. There was the less need why this Evangelist should say anything about the "day and hour" of CHRIST's final Coming,(c) since he had not recorded the Disciples' inquiry concerning that event. See the notes on St. Matth. xxiv. 33 and 35, and especially on St. Mark xiii. 29, for some remarks on these verses.

34, 35 And take heed to yourselves, lest at any time your hearts be overcharged with surfeiting, and drunkenness, and cares of this life, and so that Day come upon you unawares. For as a snare shall it come on all them that dwell on the face of the whole earth.

Rather, "that *sit* on the face:" implying a state of carelessness and ease, unconscious of its misery and unsuspicious of its danger.(d)
The Reader is referred to some remarks in the latter part of the note on St. Mark xiii. 29. He will observe that what, in St. Matthew's Gospel, takes the form of a warning, derived from the conduct of the men before the Flood,—("eating and drinking, marrying and giving in marriage,")(e)—is here delivered as an exhortation. "Lest," (says our LORD,) "your hearts be overcharged with surfeiting, and drunkenness, and cares of this life."

36 Watch ye therefore, and pray always, that ye may be accounted worthy to escape all these things that shall come to pass, and to stand before the Son of Man.

For "who may abide the Day of His coming? or who shall *stand* when He appeareth?"(f) "Wherefore," (says the Apostle,) "take unto you the whole armour of GOD, that ye may be able to withstand in the evil day; and, having done all, *to stand:*"(g) that is, to appear as those who are acquitted by their Judge.
"The one great point to which our LORD is attracting notice throughout the whole of these warnings, is in some sense true of all generations of Christians, as well as it will be of the last: that their final day overtakes them unawares, not

(x) Compare St. Matth. xxiv. 5 with ver. 24 of the same Chapter.
(y) Compare ver. 11 with verses 25 and 26 of the present Chapter.
(z) Rom. viii. 22, 23: see also verses 18 to 21.
(a) St. Matth. xxiv. 32 to 35: St. Mark xiii. 28 to 31.
(b) See the note on St. Matth. xxiv. 3. See also above,—the note on verse 7.
(c) See St. Matth. xxiv. 36, and St. Mark xiii. 32.
(d) Consider Isa. ix. 2, as quoted in St. Matth. iv. 16.   (e) St. Matth. xxiv. 38.
(f) Mal. iii. 2. Compare Nahum i. 6. Also Ezra ix. 15. Ps. i. 5, cxxx. 3.
(g) Eph. vi. 13.

from want of warnings, of which they have had great abundance; but from want of attention,—their minds being occupied by worldly pursuits."(*h*)

Having thus finished his narrative of our LORD's great Prophecy, the Evangelist adds:

37, 38 And in the day time He was teaching in the Temple; and at night He went out, and abode in the mount that is called *the mount of Olives.*

And all the people came early in the morning to Him in the Temple, for to hear Him.

Such is the Evangelist's brief record, and summary, of the manner in which these solemn days were spent! At night, our LORD's habit was to repair to the village of Bethany,—(the village of Lazarus and his sisters,)—which was about two miles from Jerusalem: but first, He seems to have frequented the Garden of Gethsemane, situate at the foot of the Mount of Olives; where, lighted by the Paschal moon, He spent the earlier hours of the night in the company of His Disciples.(*i*)

CHAPTER XXII.

1 *The Jews conspire against* CHRIST. 3 *Satan prepareth Judas to betray Him.* 7 *The Apostles prepare the Passover.* 19 CHRIST *instituteth His Holy Supper,* 21 *covertly foretelleth of the Traitor,* 24 *dehorteth the rest of His Apostles from ambition,* 31 *assureth Peter his faith should not fail:* 34 *and yet he should deny Him thrice.* 39 *He prayeth in the mount, and sweateth blood,* 47 *is betrayed with a kiss:* 59 *He healeth Malchus' ear.* 54 *He is thrice denied of Peter,* 63 *shamefully abused,* 66 *and confesseth Himself to be the* SON *of* GOD.

1, 2 Now the Feast of unleavened bread drew nigh, which is called the Passover. And the chief Priests and Scribes sought how they might kill Him; for they feared the people.

It was now the Wednesday in Passover week. It therefore wanted "two days" of the Feast, as we learn from the earlier Gospels,—where some remarks have been offered on the preceding verses, to which it must suffice to refer the reader.(*a*) Our LORD had withdrawn from Jerusalem to Bethany on the evening of this day, and a brief period of rest is thus interposed between the terrible events which are immediately to follow. In the mean time, His enemies are intent on nothing less than His death; and are seeking for some means of effecting their wicked purpose "by craft,"(*b*)—not daring to apprehend Him openly, and on the Feast Day. All this,

---

(*h*) Williams.   (*i*) See the note on St. Matth. xxi. 17.
(*a*) See the notes on St. Matth. xxvi. 1 to 5. Also St. Mark xiv. 1, 2, with the note prefixed to those verses.   (*b*) St. Matth. xxvi. 4: St. Mark xiv. 1.

hich St. Matthew and St. Mark explain at length, St. Luke omits; contenting imself with assigning *the reason* of their conduct,—namely, "*for they feared the people.*" It is clear from verse 6, below, that this is the meaning of the present Evangelist's briefer record.

. 3 Then entered Satan into Judas, surnamed Iscariot, being of the number of the Twelve.

The word "then," in this place, does not relate to time. In fact, the period when "Satan entered into Judas," is not specified by St. Luke, at all; but it is carefully marked by the two Evangelists who wrote before him, (especially by St. Matthew,)(c) is the period of the Supper at Bethany, on the evening of the Sabbath previous.(d) Take notice, however, that St. Luke supplies what the others omit,—namely, the remarkable statement that it was "*Satan*" who "*entered into*" the Traitor, before the commission of his crime.

And this circumstance suggests the remark, that among the points of difference between the Bible and every other Book, not least striking is the fact that *here*, and *here only*, is the veil removed from Creation, and the true cause of an event assigned. Does a dumb creature refuse to proceed on its journey? It was because it "saw the Angel of the LORD standing in the way, and his sword drawn in his hand."(e) Is Elisha secure amid the hosts of Syria? The LORD opened the eyes of his servant, "and he saw: and, behold, the mountain was full of horses and chariots of fire round about."(f) Does Zedekiah the son of Chenaanah prophesy falsely? A lying Spirit had gone forth from the LORD, and spoke by his lips.(g) Does David offend GOD by numbering the people? It was at Satan's suggestion that he offended.(h) And does Disease in consequence ravage Jerusalem? It was the work of the Angel of the LORD.(i) So again,—Has a woman been bowed together for eighteen years? Lo, Satan hath bound her throughout all that long period.(k) Is the surface of a pool ruffled, and a healing virtue straightway communicated to its waters? It was once more the work of an Angel, "which went down at a certain season into the pool, and troubled the water."(l) The agent on the present occasion was none other than Satan himself,—the chief of the fallen Angels, and the great Enemy of the Second Adam. Judas was possessed by *him*.

4, 5, 6 And he went his way, and communed with the chief Priests and Captains, how he might betray Him unto them. And they were glad, and covenanted to give him money. And he promised, and sought opportunity to betray Him unto them in the absence of the multitude.

Such then was the accursed work of Judas on the Wednesday of Holy Week,— and Wednesday has evermore preserved the impress of his crime, and partaken in the solemn observance of Friday. For some remarks on this subject, see the notes on St. Matth. xxvi. 15, 16, and St. Mark xiv. 11.

7, 8 Then came the day of unleavened bread, when the Passover must be killed. And He sent Peter and John, saying, Go and prepare us the Passover, that we may eat.

The beginning of the 14th day of the month Nisan, is spoken of. This may have been either the evening of Wednesday or the morning of Thursday; but it was most probably the former. St. Luke alone it is who mentions the names of the favoured pair of Disciples who were sent from Bethany to Jerusalem, on this great errand,—the same, it may well be thought, whom our SAVIOUR had sent on a former occasion to bring Him the ass and the ass-colt on which He made His triumphant entry into His Capital.(m)

(c) St. Matth. xxvi. 14.   (d) See the note on St. Matth. xxvi. 5.
(e) Numb. xxii. 23.   (f) 2 Kings vi. 17.   (g) 1 Kings xxii. 21, 22.
(h) 1 Chron. xxi. 1.   Compare 2 Sam. xxiv. 1.   (i) 1 Chron. xxi. 15, 16.
(k) St. Luke xiii. 16.   (l) St. John v. 4.
(m) See St. Matth. xxi. 1 to 3, &c. St. Mark xi. 1 to 6, &c. (where see the notes,) St. Luke xix. 29 to 34.

9 And they said unto Him, Where wilt Thou that we prepare?

10, 11, 12 And He said unto them, Behold, when ye are entered into the City, there shall a man meet you, bearing a pitcher of water; follow him into the house where he entereth in. And ye shall say unto the goodman of the house, The Master saith unto thee, Where is the guest-chamber, where I shall eat the passover with My Disciples? And he shall show you a large upper room furnished: there make ready.

All this has a most mysterious air; and the suspicion is unavoidable that there must be more in the narrative than meets the eye. Why did our LORD give the Disciples *a sign* whereby they should know the House in which it was His Divine pleasure to eat His last Passover; instead of telling them the name of the owner of the House? and further,—What meaning may be supposed to attach to the peculiar sign He gave them, of one bearing water? Our reply to both of these questions may well be brief, since conjecture on such a subject is all that can be offered.

It seems not unlikely, then, that one great purpose of the Divine directions which St. Peter and St. John now received, was to impress the minds of those Disciples, (and through them, the minds of all the rest,) with the dignity and solemnity of the errand on which they were now sent: to awaken the attention of all to this Paschal Supper, as unlike those former three of which they had been partakers with their LORD,—not only in its actual progress, but also in the very circumstances of its preparation. Next, to convince them at once of His own Divine Foreknowledge, and Almighty Power: Foreknowledge,—since He was able to describe what should befall them; and Power,—since He was about to show them how mysteriously, (according to His ancient Name,)(n) He could "provide." The hearts of men are in His Hands, and the Human Will becomes obedient at His bidding; while the "large upper room" proves furnished and prepared, when His mysterious necessity makes itself felt.

As for the particular sign,—it shall suffice to remind the Reader of the many occasions when singular mercies are described in Scripture as having befallen men in connection with that element which our SAVIOUR consecrated to the mystical washing away of Sin. Thus an Angel found Hagar at the well Lahai-roi,(o) (the first instance of Angelic ministration on record;)—and near the same well, Rebekah met Isaac.(p) For the second time, at a well of water, the Angel found Hagar;(q) and Eliezer met Rebekah;(r) and Jacob met Rachel;(s) and Moses met Zipporah.(t) By a well, also, our LORD revealed Himself to the Woman of Samaria.(u)—

Whether we are right in connecting these many incidents with the event recorded in the text, can only be matter of conjecture: but it is hard to resist the suspicion that there exists some secret affinity between them; and it shall suffice to have thrown out the hint, in this place.—The Reader may further be reminded how, almost 1900 years before, one bearing a pitcher of water proved a sign to the servant of Isaac;(x) at a time also, when that eminent type of CHRIST was about to take to himself his Bride,—as in truth our SAVIOUR CHRIST was now.—On the preceding verses the Reader is requested further to refer to the commentary on St. Matthew xxvi. 17 and 19.

13 And they went, and found as He had said unto them: and they made ready the Passover.

14 And when the hour was come, He sat down, and the Twelve Apostles with Him.

When the hour of evening had arrived, the Son of Man, attended by the Twelve, proceeded from Bethany to the place of entertainment so mysteriously provided for their reception. What first occurred is related by St. Luke alone, in the four verses which follow:—

(n) Gen. xxii. 14,—see the margin.   (o) Gen. xvi. 7, 14.
(p) Gen. xxiv. 62, 63.   (q) Gen. xxi. 19.
(r) Gen. xxiv. 11 to 20.   (t) Exod. ii. 15 to 17.
(u) St. John iv. 6.   (s) Gen. xxix. 2 to 10.
(x) Gen. xxiv. 14, 15, and 43 to 45.

15 And He said unto them, With desire I have desired to eat this 'assover with you before I suffer:

"Very vehement desire is on no other occasion attributed to our LORD, either by Himself or others. So great was this occasion, when, before He left His Disciples, Is had to give to them the New Covenant of His Body and Blood."(y)

16 for I say unto you, I will not any more eat thereof, until it be fulfilled in the Kingdom of GOD.

The Passover was "fulfilled in the Kingdom of GOD" when He, the true Paschal Lamb, was offered on the bitter Cross.(z)   "The Kingdom of GOD,"—which in one sense had come already,(a) and which, in the highest sense of all, is yet to come,(b) —that Kingdom would then in a special manner have arrived; for the Veil of the Temple having been rent in twain, the shadows of the Law would have departed, and the substance would have been at length revealed. CHRIST "came not to destroy, but to fulfil,"—as He Himself declared;(c) and the fulfilment of the Passover, which was to take place on the morrow, was the prime end of His Coming.

"Until," in this place, has the same meaning as in St. Matthew i. 25, and elsewhere.(d)   Our SAVIOUR'S words obviously imply that He will *never* partake of the Paschal Supper any more.

17, 18 And He took the cup, and gave thanks, and said, Take this, and divide *it* among yourselves: for I say unto you, I will not drink of the fruit of the Vine, until the Kingdom of GOD shall come.

Rather,—"And He took *a cup:*" for this cup of wine mingled with water was one which was drunk by the ancient Jews before the celebration of the Paschal Supper. It has been called "the Cup of the Old Testament;" and is evidently a thing apart from that "cup *after* Supper" which our SAVIOUR converted into the Sacrament of His most precious Blood. See what has been already offered on this subject, and on the method observed at the Paschal Supper generally, in the note on St. Mark xiv. 21.

Two things are here to be noticed: first, that from the language of our Blessed LORD in verses 17, 18, it would appear that He denied Himself the refreshment of the Cup on the occasion of this, His last Supper. And next, it will be perceived that our SAVIOUR, (in verse 18,) varies the phrase which he used above, in verse 16. The reason is obvious. The Wine which was drunk at the Paschal Supper, symbolized no spiritual Blessing: there could be no "fulfilment" therefore, here, as in the case of the Paschal Lamb. The words—"I will drink no more of the fruit of the Vine, till the Kingdom of GOD shall come,"—may be compared, and their meaning safely gathered, from our LORD'S declaration with respect to "the Cup of Blessing;" namely, that He "would drink no more of the fruit of the Vine, until the day when He should drink it new with His Disciples in the Kingdom of GOD:"(e) concerning which words, the Reader is referred to an earlier part of the present Commentary.(f)

And now, the Paschal Supper was actually proceeding, as St. Matthew and St. Mark are careful to inform us.(g)

19 And He took Bread, and gave thanks, and brake *it*, and gave unto them, saying, This is My Body which is given for you: this do in remembrance of Me.

Which loving command, "to continue a perpetual memory of that His precious Death until His coming again,"—the Church pleads evermore at the celebration of the LORD's Supper.

(y) Williams.   (z) See the note on St. John i. 29. Also on St. Matth. v. 17.
  (a) See the note on St. Matth. xvi. 28, and especially the note on St. Luke ix. 27: also, on St. Luke xvii. 20, 21. Consider St. Matth. xi. 12, St. Luke xi. 20, &c.
  (b) See St. Matthew vi. 10: St. Luke xiii. 28, &c.   (c) St. Matth. v. 17.
  (d) Besides the note on St. Matthew i. 25, see on St. Matthew xviii. 34; and the last paragraph of the Commentary on St. Matthew.
  (e) St. Matth. xxvi. 29: St. Mark xiv. 25.   (f) See the note on St. Matth. xxvi. 29.
  (g) St. Matth. xxvi. 26: St. Mark xiv. 22.

St. Luke, in his account of the Institution of this great Sacrament, is thought to have followed closely in the footsteps of St. Paul,—who declares that he received his account of the first LORD's Supper from the LORD Himself. "For I have received of the LORD that which also I delivered unto you, that the LORD JESUS, the same night in which He was betrayed, took bread: and when He had given thanks, He brake it, and said, Take, eat: this is My Body, which is broken for you: this do in remembrance of Me."(h) Here was "not a typical or prefigurative rite, therefore, but commemorative, as St. Paul himself explains it: 'for as often as ye eat this Bread, and drink this Cup, ye do show the LORD's Death till He come.'"(i) —But the Reader must be requested to examine what has been already offered on this great subject in the Commentary on the two earlier Gospels.(k)

What interval of time may have elapsed between the appointment of the Bread in the Holy Eucharist, and the consecration of the Wine to the same great mystery, does not appear. But that the Paschal Supper was now ended, is clear from the form of words in which both St. Paul and his companion in travel, St. Luke, describes that part of the Institution. As it follows:

20 Likewise also the Cup after Supper, saying, This Cup is the New Testament in My Blood, which is shed for you.

"'Likewise,'—for if these two were not connected together by the time of their appointment, yet there was something, either in the marked and emphatic manner of our LORD, or some other circumstance, that distinguished these two actions beyond all the other transactions of that memorable evening; drawing them out, and putting them forth together, as the two cardinal ordinances of which the Old Dispensation spoke in type and figure."(l) Once more, however, it must suffice to refer to what has been already offered on this subject.(m)

"The New Testament" (or "Covenant") "in My blood,"—is said with reference to the words used by Moses concerning the Elder Covenant: "This is the Blood of the Testament which GOD hath enjoined unto you,"(n)—as St. Paul quotes the language of Exodus xxiv. 8. "For where a Testament is, there must also of necessity be the death of the testator. . . . . Whereupon neither the first testament was dedicated without blood; . . . . . and without shedding of blood is no remission." . . . . Now, "if the blood of bulls and of goats . . . . sanctifieth to the purifying of the flesh; how much more shall the Blood of CHRIST, who through the Eternal SPIRIT offered Himself without spot to GOD, purge your conscience from dead works to serve the living GOD!"(o)—See more, in the first note on St. Matthew xxvi. 28.

Thus then hath "Wisdom builded her House," and "mingled her Wine," and "furnished her Table." "Come," saith she, "Eat of My Bread, and drink of the Wine which I have mingled."(p)—Thus was the great Sacrament of CHRIST's Body and Blood instituted; and who can fail to be struck with the brevity of the record? How many words do we waste on trifles; and on this, the grandest of all occasions, how few and simple are the words spoken!—words which have nevertheless filled the Church with divisions, and occasioned endless strife and debate, although conveying the most precious legacy of Love. Yet has not this, in great measure, proceeded from carnal curiosity; which seeks to reason and dispute, where GOD has rather willed that men should believe and adore? The Reader is referred on this subject to the famous language of Hooker quoted in the Commentary on the latter part of St. Matthew xxvi. 28.

The Divine Author of this blessed mystery is straightway found to renew the awful declaration which He had made while the Paschal Supper was yet proceeding.(q)

21, 22 But, behold, the hand of him that betrayeth Me is with Me on the table. And truly the Son of Man goeth, as it was determined: but woe unto that man by whom He is betrayed!

On this terrible announcement, see the note on St. Matthew xxvi. 24. Some

(h) 1 Cor. xi. 23, 24.   (i) Williams, quoting 1 Cor. xi. 26.
(k) See all the notes on St. Matth. xxvi. 26, and on St. Mark xiv. 22.   (l) Williams.
(m) See all the notes on St. Matth. xxvi. 27, 28, and on St. Mark xiv. 23, 24.
(n) Heb. ix. 20.   (o) Heb. ix. 16, 18, 22, 13, 14.
(p) Prov. ix. 1 to 5.   (q) St. Matth. xxvi. 21 to 25, and St. Mark xiv. 18 to 21.

remarks will be found elsewhere offered on the extraordinary circumstance that although our SAVIOUR, at an earlier stage of the Last Supper, not only announced the presence of the Traitor with Him at the Table, but even gave a sign whereby it might be known which was he; nor only so, but in reply to a question addressed to Him by Judas, further proceeded to reveal the Traitor to himself;(r) it should be found that by no one of those present, except Judas himself, was this last intimation understood.(s)   Our SAVIOUR therefore repeats, but in a more solemn manner, His former warning: whereupon, strange to say, it is added concerning the Twelve Apostles,—

23 And they began to inquire among themselves, which of them it was that should do this thing.

The remarks which have been already offered on a similar passage of St. Matthew's Gospel are so applicable here, that the Reader is requested to refer to the Commentary on the earlier Evangelist.(t)—Strange as to us it may appear, eleven of the Apostles, in their guileless love, and simplicity of character, find it impossible to realize the notion of such villany as our LORD foretold, and as one of their number was actually contemplating.—To know what happened next, we should probably read St. John xiii. 22 to 30,—from which it will be perceived that at this juncture, Judas Iscariot ("Mine own familiar friend, in whom I trusted, *which did eat of My Bread!*")(u) left the table and went forth on his accursed errand. It follows:

24 And there was also a strife among them, which of them should be accounted the greatest.

A sufficient proof, by the way, that no superiority over the other Apostles had been yet bestowed upon Simon.   Consider what has been said on the subject in the note on St. Matthew xvi. 19.   It is not very evident what should have led to contention on such a subject at such a time; and perhaps this is one of those places where the connecting link has been withheld by the Evangelist.   The train of thought may be other than can be gathered from the perusal of a single Gospel.

25 And He said unto them, The Kings of the Gentiles exercise lordship over them; and they that exercise authority upon them are called Benefactors.

As if He had said,—"You are right in supposing that you are on the point of being established in My Spiritual Kingdom over the World, in order to do good to Mankind: but think not that from the benefits you shall confer on the World, you are to bring any honour or credit upon yourselves; for My Kingdom is of a far different character."(x)—"The Kings of the Gentiles," (says our SAVIOUR,) "lord it over them; and their oppressors are called 'Benefactors:'" alluding at once to the well-known course followed, and to the well-known title assumed, by many of the heathen Sovereigns of Antiquity; who, while laying claim to an appellation which implied that they enjoyed the love of a grateful people, were observed to be guilty of a tyrannical exercise of an absolute power.

26 But ye *shall* not *be* so: but he that is greatest among you, let him be as the younger; and he that is chief, as he that doth serve.

"The Nobles, and Princes, and Judges of CHRIST's Kingdom, were to be formed on the type and model of Him, who being in the form of GOD took on Him the form of a servant."(y)

27 For whether *is* greater, he that sitteth at meat, or he that serveth? *is* not he that sitteth at meat? but I am among you as he that serveth.

(r) St. Matth. xxvi. 25.
(s) See the note on St. John xiii. 29. See, also, on St. Matth. xxvi. 22.
(t) See the note on St. Matth. xxvi. 22.
(x) Williams.   (u) Ps. xli. 9.
                                          (y) Dr. W. H. Mill,—quoting Phil. ii. 6, 7.

Words, of which we should not have suspected the full force and significancy, but for the express record which St. John's Gospel supplies of our SAVIOUR's gracious condescension in washing the Disciples' feet on this occasion.(z)

It will be remembered that sayings very much resembling these, have been met with already. It was with such measured language of reproof that our SAVIOUR addressed the Ten, when He beheld them "moved with indignation" against James and John, at the request of those two brethren that they might be permitted to occupy the two places of highest honour in His Kingdom.(a) "But on this occasion, He takes pains not only to repeat the words, but by that expressive action to engrave,—as it were by the finger of the HOLY GHOST,—that lesson on their heart: for those expressions in St. Matthew and St. Mark, as well as these now in St. Luke, seem like comments on that which had just before taken place."(b)

28, 29, 30 Ye are they which have continued with Me in My temptations. And I appoint unto you a Kingdom, as My FATHER hath appointed unto Me; that ye may eat and drink at My Table in My Kingdom, and sit on thrones, judging the Twelve Tribes of Israel.

"In this sentence," (says Dr. Mill,) "our LORD describes the highest honours of that Kingdom which, in the verses preceding, He had distinguished from all others founded by man."(c) "There is hardly any passage in the Scriptures," (observes an excellent living writer,)(d) "in which the high and glorious estate of the Church, the personal feebleness and insufficiency of those who are called its pillars, and the true secret of its strength and glory, are more strikingly exhibited," than in the seven preceding verses.

"Ye which have followed Me," (said our LORD to Simon Peter, on a previous occasion,)—"in the Regeneration, when the Son of Man shall sit in the Throne of His Glory, ye also shall sit upon Twelve Thrones, judging the Twelve Tribes of Israel."(e) The two places closely resemble each other; but the points of difference are very significant and striking. Thus, the nearer approach of CHRIST's Kingdom may have suggested the distinct allusion to it by name, in this place; while it seems impossible not to connect the promise that the Disciples should "eat and drink at the LORD's Table, in His Kingdom," with the recent institution of the Blessed Sacrament of CHRIST's Body and Blood.(f) It will be observed, further, that there is no mention here of *Twelve* Thrones,—as in the other place referred to.

31, 32 And the LORD said, Simon, Simon, behold, Satan hath desired *to have* you, that he may sift *you* as wheat: but I have prayed for thee, that thy faith fail not:

Satan had earnestly desired to get *them* into his power: ("*you*," not "*thee:*") he was "seeking to devour" them *all:* (that phrase, observe, is St. Peter's own:) but especially did the Enemy of Souls desire to have St. Peter. Hence, our LORD adds.—"But I have prayed *for thee.*" And who may describe the power of that prayer? It was not, however, a prayer that Simon might not *fall;* (for fall he did, and that grievously:) but that his faith might not eventually *fail* him.

How striking a revelation, by the way, of what had been taking place in that darkest place of the Realm of Darkness, (the heart of Satan,) for the last three years! He had longed beyond all things to deal with the Twelve violently and mercilessly,—exposing them to sharp and sudden trials, (even as when he had to do with the patriarch Job;)(g)—so, in short, to deal with them, as the husbandman

(z) St. John xiii. 1 to 15.
(a) St. Matth. xx. 25 to 28, and St. Mark x. 42 to 45,—where see the notes.
(b) Williams.
(c) Contrast this, with the four Empires which had gone before it: Dan. ii. 31 to 35, and 38 to 40: also 44, 45.
(d) Dr. Moberly.   (e) St. Matth. xix. 28,—where see the notes.
(f) Compare and consider St. Luke xiii. 26.
(g) See Job i. 15, 16, 17, 18,—while one messenger "*was yet speaking,*" the bearer of fresh evil tidings coming in.

deals with a sieve of mingled wheat and chaff! For Satan is at once a Serpent and a Lion; a Serpent in craft,—a Lion in assault.(*k*)

And let not the beauty of the present saying be overlooked: still less let it be suspected that since the object of "sifting" is the purification of the good, the image which our SAVIOUR has here employed is inappropriate. Satan does indeed sift in order to destroy,—in order that nothing may be preserved which can possibly be scattered and caused to perish. On the other hand, he does no more harm than GOD is graciously pleased to permit: nor, (what is especially to be noted,) when he rages most fiercely, can he do more than *sift* the Disciples. The chaff is indeed reserved for the burning; and that which is chaff, Satan causes straightway to appear: but the wheat will the Heavenly Husbandman gather into His garner,(*i*) —purified by affliction, and rendered more precious by the fiery trial through which it has been made to pass. These words are therefore found to convey a message of comfort and assurance to all.—Our SAVIOUR adds:

and when thou art converted, strengthen thy brethren.

The phrase "when thou art converted," is apt to convey a very wrong impression to an English reader; and yet it cannot perhaps be mended. The popular sense of the term "Conversion," be it however observed, is as much excluded here, as in chap. xvii. 4,—where the same word recurs; though it is there translated "turn," instead of "be converted." Our LORD is in fact here giving St. Peter an indirect hint of that desertion and denial, which, in ver. 34, He foretells more distinctly.

"Strengthen thy brethren." What is this but the command,—"Feed My Sheep!"(*k*) Now, this was to be when St. Peter was "converted:" which seems to mean after his fall, and subsequent recovery,—when it is to be supposed that he became an altered man.(*l*) And such, in truth, his Epistles prove him to have become: for, contrast the impetuous protestations of ver. 33, and again of St. Mark xiv. 29, 31, with those words of counsel which he afterwards delivered to the Church, —"Give an answer . . . with Meekness and Fear;" and—"Be clothed with Humility."(*m*)—Notice, lastly, that the Divine purpose with which strength is imparted, is the confirmation of the weak brother: according to that of the Psalmist, —"O give me the comfort of Thy help again, and establish me with Thy free Spirit; *then shall I teach Thy ways unto the wicked.*"(n)

The resemblance of part of the verse under consideration, and that which follows, to the Greek version of 2 Samuel xv. 20, 21, is extraordinary.

33, 34 And he said unto Him, LORD, I am ready to go with Thee, both into prison, and to death. And He said, I tell thee, Peter, the cock shall not crow this day, before that thou shalt thrice deny that thou knowest Me.

Thus does the Holy One for the first time predict that Simon will deny Him.(*o*) It is remarkable that on this occasion, (*and on no other,*) our SAVIOUR should be related to have addressed Simon by his name of Strength,—*Peter.*(*p*)

35 And He said unto them, When I sent you without purse, and scrip, and shoes, lacked ye any thing? And they said, Nothing.

He alludes to the mysterious charge which He had given to the Twelve,(*q*) and again repeated to the Seventy:(*r*) as if He had said,—When I bade you provide yourselves with no human aids, did ye not find My words come true that neither would ye require any?

36 Then said He unto them, But now, he that hath a purse, let him

---

(*k*) This was a favourite remark of Augustine. It occurs five times in the course of his writings. Hence the language of our Litany,—"From Sin, *from the crafts and assaults of the Devil,*" &c.

(*i*) St. Matth. iii. 12, where see the notes.   (*k*) St. John xxi. 15, 16, 17.

(*l*) See the note on St. Matth. xxvi. 75.   (*m*) 1 St. Peter iii. 15 : v. 5.

(*n*) Ps. li. 12, 13. Compare also the language of 2 Cor. i. 3, 4.

(*o*) For the second prophecy, see St. Matth. xxvi. 33, 34,—and the note there.

(*p*) See St. Matth. xvi. 18.   (*q*) St. Matth. x. 9, 10.   (*r*) St. Luke x. 4.

take *it*, and likewise *his* scrip: and he that hath no sword, let him sell his garment, and buy one.

Rather,—"and he that hath not [a purse,] let him sell his garment, and [therewith] buy a sword." Words which it is obvious *to us* are purely symbolical, as will admit of none but an allegorical interpretation. They do but imply that a season of exceeding trial was at hand; when the lives of the Apostles would be endangered, and when every other personal concern would be swallowed up by the need of providing for the preservation of life.

The Blessed Speaker proceeds to give the reason why every means, at once of support and defence, would henceforth be needed by His Disciples. The time was at hand when He, whose presence had so long been their protection, would be withdrawn from them; nor only so, but by the Death He should die, He would leave them a legacy of shame and reproach. As it follows:

37 For I say unto you, that this that is written must yet be accomplished in Me. And He was reckoned among the transgressors: for the things concerning Me have an end.

Our SAVIOUR quotes certain well-known words of Prophecy,(*s*) as still requiring fulfilment; (for *that* is the meaning of the expression "have an end;") and take notice that St. Mark points out how, on the morrow, "*the Scripture was fulfilled,* which saith, 'And He was numbered with the transgressors.'"(*t*)

The citation of such a prophecy at such a time may, to some readers, seem strange: and it may be well that readers of every class should be reminded how frequent are the appeals to ancient prophecy,—(whether in the way of direct quotation, or indirect allusion,)—throughout this, the concluding scene of our LORD's earthly Ministry.(*u*) The reason of those references is obvious. Like a wise Master-Builder, the Author of our most holy Faith was careful, before He departed out of the World, to neglect no part of that foundation on which the Spiritual fabric of His Church was presently to rise. For take notice that *the fulfilment of Prophecy* in our LORD's person,—not *the reality of His Miracles,*—was the evidence on which the Apostles rested their proof that Christianity was a Revelation sent from GOD. "The invariable purport of all their arguments, the end which they kept before them, in whatever they said or wrote, was to prove that the subject of all the various prophecies with which the Old Testament Scriptures were filled, was the Gospel which they preached; and, so far as appears, this only it was which the Jews denied."(*x*)

Our LORD had been warning His Disciples therefore of the need they would experience of every means of defence:

38 And they said, LORD, behold here *are* two swords. And He said unto them, It is enough.

Observe how literally these holy men understood our SAVIOUR's words.(*y*) Two of their number (St. Peter was certainly one;(*z*) and what if St. John were the other?) show that they have provided themselves each with a weapon; but of what avail would "*two swords*" have been, had a contest ensued? Clearly of none. "I

(*s*) Isaiah liii. 12.   (*t*) St. Mark xv. 28.

(*u*) The Reader will do well to verify the following references:—St. Matth. xxvi. 28, (alluding to Exod. xxiv. 8:)—31, (quoting Zech. xiii. 7:)—38, (alluding to Ps. xlii. 5:—54, (alluding to same places as Isa. liii. 7, &c.:)—56, (referring generally to all that now took place:)—64, (alluding Dan. vii. 13:)—xxvii. 9, (quoting Zech. xii. 12:)—34, (alluding to Ps. lxix. 21:)—43, (quoting Ps. xxii. 8:)—46, (quoting Ps. xxii. 1:)—St. Mark xv. 28, (quoting Isa. liii. 12:) St. Luke xx 37, (quoting the same prophecy:)—69, (alluding to Dan. vii. 13:) xxiii. 30, (quoting Hos. x. 8:) 34, 35, (alluding to Ps. xxii. 7:)—46, (quoting Ps. xxxi. 5:) St. John xiii. 18, 19, (quoting Ps. xli. 9:) xix. 24, (quoting Ps. xxii. 18:)—28, (alluding to Ps. lxix. 21:)—36, (quoting Exod. xii. 46, or Numb. ix. 12, and Ps. xxxiv. 20:)—37, (quoting Zech. xii. 10:) and there may be a few more places.

(*x*) Dean Lyall,—"*To Him give all the Prophets witness,*" said St. Peter, when "he preached CHRIST to Cornelius and his company." Acts x. 43. See St. Luke xxiv. 25, 26; and the rest there.

(*y*) Consider the evidences of this disposition on the part of the Apostles supplied by Matth. xvi. 5 to 12. St. John xl. 13: xxi. 23, &c.

(*z*) For see St. John xviii. 10.

is enough," however, says our LORD! thereby plainly showing how different a meaning from what they supposed, His divine words were intended to convey. By that exclamation He simply puts the subject aside for the moment; leaving to the events of that terrible night, to discover His real meaning.(a)

The Paschal Supper having been concluded with the customary Hymn,(b) there followed that long and affecting discourse which "the disciple whom JESUS loved" has alone recorded;(c) and the blessed company, eleven Apostles and their LORD, (for Judas, after receiving the Holy Eucharist, had left the Table,)(d) moving slowly through the moon-lit streets of Jerusalem, at last left the city by the gate which led to the Mount of Olives.

39 And He came out, and went, as He was wont, to the Mount of Olives; and His Disciples also followed Him.

After descending a slight declivity, they crossed the brook Kidron, and, again ascending, made their way towards the retired spot which was to be the scene of our SAVIOUR's mysterious Agony: but as they went, He is found to have prophesied St. Peter's denial, and the cowardice of all.(e)

"Then cometh JESUS with them unto a place called Gethsemane:(f) where was a Garden, into the which He entered, and His Disciples."(g) Thus was a Garden made the scene of our SAVIOUR's Passion, as it was the place where He made His Grave:(h) and thus, the curse which was entailed on our race in a Garden, by the first Adam, was there also, by the second Adam, undone.

40 And when He was at the place, He said unto them, Pray that ye enter not into temptation.

These words do not seem to have been addressed to all the Eleven: but only to those three Disciples,—("Peter and James and John,")—whom our SAVIOUR selected out of the entire number to be the witnesses, or rather to be the companions, of His greatest Agony. To the rest He said on first entering the Garden, "Sit ye here, while I go and pray yonder:"(i) but to these, He appears to have spoken the words of the text, after withdrawing with them to a more retired part of the Garden. There,—"sore amazed and very heavy,"—He is found to have added, "My soul is exceeding sorrowful, even unto death; tarry ye here, and watch with Me."(k)— Concerning such passages, we know not how to speak. The Reader is, however, referred to the notes on the earlier Gospels.(l)

41, 42 And He was withdrawn from them about a stone's cast, and kneeled down, and prayed, saying, FATHER, if Thou be willing, remove this cup from Me: nevertheless not My will, but Thine, be done.

The two earlier Gospels here discover to us our Blessed REDEEMER as "fallen on His face" "to the ground,"(m) while He poured forth these mysterious words of resignation to the FATHER's Will.—"I seek not Mine own Will," (said He on another occasion,) "but the Will of the FATHER which hath sent Me."(n)

And here, it is obvious to remark how completely the text establishes the existence of a Human, as distinct from a Divine Will, in the one Person of our SAVIOUR CHRIST,—"Very GOD, and Very Man." Not that it is here implied that His own "Will" was at variance with the Will of the Eternal FATHER: but the very instincts of Humanity cause us to shrink from Agony; and here was Agony the sharpest that had ever been endured by any of the sons of Adam. See the note on St. Matthew xxvi. 42.

"The expression 'Not My Will, but Thine, be done,' uttered with respect to that which would then only become sinful if followed in preference to the Divine Will,

(a) Consider below, ver. 49 to 51. St. Matth. xxvi. 51 to 53. St. John xviii. 10, 11; and, not least of all, 36.
(b) See St. Matth. xxvi. 30, and the note there.   (c) St. John xv., xvi., xvii.
(d) See the conclusion of the note on ver. 23, above.
(e) See St. Matth. xxvi. 31 to 35.   (f) St. Matth. xxvi. 36.   (g) St. John xviii. 1.
(h) St. John xix. 41.   (i) St. Matth. xxvi. 36.
(k) St. Matth. xxvi. 38: St. Mark xiv. 33.
(l) See the notes on St. Matth. xxvi. 37 and 38. Also on St. Mark xiv. 34.
(m) St. Matth. xxvi. 39: St. Mark xiv. 35.   (n) St. John v. 30.

may inform us where mere Temptation ends, and where Sin (which in our Lo had not the remotest place) begins. And may we not conceive also that the mo acute apprehension of things which the perfect contexture of His Humanity brou with it,—the keener sense of pain and distress, as well as of others' ingratitude a treachery, which His sinless soul entertained,—might give a sharper edge to t description of trial in Him, and far more than counterbalance, in respect of h ness of endurance, that which less holy and duller spirits have to encounter fr what in Him had no place,—the remnants of native corruption, and ill desires i perfectly mortified?"(o)—These valuable remarks prepare us for the memoral statement which follows, and which exhibits to us the LORD of Angels sustained His hour of mysterious extremity by one of His own creatures.

43 And there appeared an Angel unto Him from Heaven, strengt ening Him.

"In such infinite condescension did He deign as Man to suffer agony, and in t suffering to receive support from one of His own creatures, who was made and w lived by the breath of His mouth."(p)

Consider the comment of the SPIRIT on this mysterious transaction. After m tioning our REDEEMER's "strong crying,"—and noticing a circumstance nowh else recorded, namely the precious "tears" of CHRIST,—St. Paul, (who derived l Gospel by immediate revelation from GOD,)(q) declares,—He "was heard,—in t He feared."(r) . . . . It seems to be implied that He was "heard" by this sendi of the Angel; whose appearance, (says Theophylact,) is recorded for our sake, teach us the efficacy of Prayer.(s) But the precise occasion of "Fear," in the ca of our Blessed LORD, seems too awful a matter for the speculations of such as v are. It may suffice to remind the Reader of a place in the Psalms where this arti of the Passion finds express prophetic notice:—"My heart is sore pained with Me; and the terrors of Death are fallen upon Me. Fearfulness and trembling a come upon Me, and horror hath overwhelmed Me. And I said, Oh that I h wings like a dove! for then would I fly away and be at rest."(t)

A living writer remarks,—"When our LORD was tempted in the Wilderness, was not till after His Temptation was ended, that 'Angels came and minister unto Him.'(u) Here, an Angel comes from Heaven to strengthen Him duri His trial: from which we may infer that this was a far more severe struggle th the former. The same inference may be drawn from the accounts of the Evang lists, and from our LORD's own language and demeanour, on this latter occasion."(This was, in fact, that "season," darkly hinted at in St. Luke iv. 13, (where the note,) until which, Satan had departed from the Holy One; and for which, l had doubtless gathered up all his strength, in order to make one tremendous assau "The Prince of this World cometh,"(y)—our LORD had said a few hours befo He had now, doubtless, come.(z) It follows:

44 And being in an Agony He prayed more earnestly: and H Sweat was as it were great drops of blood falling down to the grou

Every word here is full of dignity, awe, and wonder. By that "Agony a Bloody Sweat," the Church evermore prays to her Good LORD for deliverance. W it not, in a manner, the undoing of a part of the ancient curse, that the seco Adam should have thus watered the earth, (which was cursed for the transgress of the first Adam,) with the Sweat, not only of His sinless Brow, but of all E Divine Person? Surely CHRIST bore that curse now in its fulness; not in a figu but literally: even as when, on the morrow, He submitted to wear a crown thorns. Consider the first note on St. Matthew xxvii. 29.

The heavy burden of our SAVIOUR's Suffering on this tremendous Night noticed by all the four Evangelists, and confessed by Himself.(a) "Yes, that E

(o) Dr. W. H. Mill. (p) Williams. (q) Gal. i. 12. (r) Heb. v. 7.
(s) Thus it fared with Hagar, (Gen. xxi. 17,) with Daniel, (Dan. ix. 20 to 23,) and with C nelius, (Acts x. 3, 4.) (t) Ps. lv. 4, 5, 6. (u) St. Matth. iv. 11.
(x) Bishop Lonsdale and Archd. Hale. (y) St. John xiv. 30.
(z) See ver. 53, below, and the note thereon.
(a) St. Matth. xxvi. 37, 38: St. Mark xiv. 33, 34: St. John xii. 27.

strange and never else heard-of Sweat,—drops of blood plenteously issuing from
Him all over His Body, no man then touching Him, none being near Him;—*that*
Blood came certainly from some great Sorrow, wherewith His soul was pierced."
So, Bishop Andrewes, who dwells on the circumstance with pious wonder; remarking that "when no manner of violence was offered Him in Body,—no man touching
Him, or being near Him,—in a cold Night, (for they were fain to have a fire within
doors,)—lying abroad in the air,—and upon the cold Earth,—to be all of a Sweat!
and that Sweat to be Blood! and not a thin faint Sweat, but of great drops; and
those, so many, so plenteous, as they went through His apparel and all; and
through all, streamed to the ground, and *that* in great abundance! Read, inquire,
and consider if ever there were sweat like this Sweat of His! Never the like
Sweat certainly, and therefore never like Sorrow. . . . That hour, what His feelings were, it is dangerous to define. We know them not; we may be too bold to
determine of them. To very good purpose it is that the ancient Fathers of the
Greek Church, in their Liturgy, after they have recounted all the particular pains
as they are set down in His Passion,—and by all, and by every one of them, called
for Mercy,—do, after all, shut up all with this: '*By Thine unknown Sorrows and
Sufferings*, [felt by Thee, but not distinctly known by us,] Have mercy upon us
and save us!'"(b)

**45, 46 And when He rose up from Prayer, and, was come to His
Disciples, He found them sleeping for sorrow, and said unto them, Why
sleep ye? rise and pray, lest ye enter into temptation.**

Allestree has some striking remarks on this. "Truly" (he says) "of two visions
which our SAVIOUR gave to His most intimate Apostles, Peter, James, and John,—
the one of Glory on Mount Tabor, the other of sufferings in Gethsemane: showing
in the one, Heaven and Himself transfigured, a glimpse of beatific vision; and in
the other Hell transfigured, and a sad scene of all its agonies.—He thought this a
more concerning sight: for when they fell asleep at both, at His Transfiguration,
'Peter and they that were with him were heavy with sleep;'(c) yet does He not
rouse them up to behold His glory. When they did awake indeed, they saw a
glimpse of it, but straight 'there came a cloud, and overshadowed them.'(d) But
at His Passion, He bids them 'watch with Him:'(e) and when He findeth them
asleep, He says, 'What, could ye not watch with Me one hour?'(f) and bids them
'watch' again,(g) and comes again a third time and upbraids their drowsiness.(h)
So much more necessary was it to behold His Agonies, than to see His felicities!
Glory does not discover or invite to Heaven, so much as sufferings drive to it; and
we are more concerned to take a view of that Garden of Gethsemane, than that of
Paradise; and the going down from the Mount of Olives does more advantage us
in climbing the Eternal Hills, than all Mount Tabor's height."
The narratives of St. Matthew and St. Mark, which are somewhat fuller in this
place, should here be consulted.(i) Little or nothing will be found in the way of
Commentary, however, on the verses in question. In truth, the entire History of
our SAVIOUR's Passion is a subject for Meditation and Prayer; not for criticism and
dry discussion. Solemn and affecting, past all words, we pass by the most striking
passages, not knowing how to speak of them as we should. . . . "Rise," (said
our REDEEMER, at last, to His slumbering Disciples,) "let us be going; behold, he
is at hand that doth betray Me."(k)

**47 And while He yet spake, behold a multitude, and he that was
called Judas, one of the Twelve, went before them, and drew near
unto JESUS to kiss Him.**

For this was the concerted "sign" or "token" by which the traitor had promised
to indicate the Divine Person of his LORD to his partners in crime.(l) St. Luke
alone of the Evangelists remarks that Judas walked *in advance* of the rabble and
soldiery who came to apprehend our Blessed LORD. It will be remembered that
St. Peter in another place notices the same circumstance, when he proposes that a

(b) Andrewes.   (c) St. Luke ix. 32.   (d) Ver. 34.   (e) St. Matth. xxvi. 38.
(f) Ver. 40.   (g) Ver. 41.   (h) Ver. 45.
(i) See St. Matth. xxvi. 41 to 46: St. Mark xiv. 38 to 42.
(k) St. Matth. xxvi. 46: St. Mark xiv. 42.   (l) St. Matth. xxvi. 48: St. Mark xiv. 44.

witness of the Resurrection should be ordained in the place of Judas,—"whi was *guide* to them that took JESUS."(*m*)

48 But JESUS said unto him, Judas, betrayest thou the Son of Mi with a kiss?

"Yea," (as it is elsewhere written,) "Mine own familiar friend, in whom I trust which did eat of My bread, hath lifted up his heel against Me."(*n*)   Concerni this act of treachery, the Reader may refer to the notes on the first Gospel.(*o*)

49, 50, 51 When they which were about Him saw what would folloj they said unto Him, LORD, shall we smite with the sword? And oi of them smote the servant of the high Priest, and cut off his right ea And JESUS answered and said, Suffer ye thus far.

"Shall we smite with the sword?"—the Apostles had inquired. "Suffer ye th far,"—was the Divine reply: whereby our SAVIOUR evidently forbade His followe to use the sword in His defence. But in the mean time, "Simon Peter having sword drew it," and performed the act of violence here recorded. "The servas name was Malchus."(*p*) See St. Matth. xxvi. 51 to 53, and the notes there; fi the first Evangelist has recorded at greatest length our LORD's discourse on th occasion. But St. Luke, (the Physician!)(*q*) alone it is who describes the mirac which follows:—

And He touched his ear and healed him.

This, by the way, is the only case recorded of the miraculous healing of a wom inflicted by external violence. Whereby our LORD set forth in example th heavenly precept of His,—"Love your enemies," "do good to them that ha you."(*r*) Consider the graciousness of such an act,—performed in favour of su an one,—and in such an hour!—"One might indeed be curious to know what effe so wonderful a cure and miracle might have had at such a time. Possibly, in th heat of the moment, the man neither noticed the wound nor the miraculous cur but still, it may have had the effect, in the end, of reclaiming him, and withdrawi him from that service."

It has also been pointed out that "in all other miracles, Faith seems to have be the essential requisite in all who required and received the benefit. But this a pears to have been performed in favour of an enemy, in whom therefore we shou not look for such faith; and as a pure act of our LORD's charity and forgivenes One cannot but suspect, however, that there might have been secretly some go in him, known to our LORD, which rendered him meet for this mercy being vouc safed to him."(*s*)

52 Then JESUS said unto the chief Priests, and the captains of th Temple, and the elders, which were come to Him,

Take notice, by the way, what a motley company had come forth from the Ci on this accursed errand: a great multitude bearing lanterns and torches, swor and staves,(*t*)—a band of soldiers with their captain, and officers of the Jews,(*u*) and among them, the chief Priests, and captains of the Temple, with the Elders I To them, said the Holy One:

53 Be ye come out, as against a thief, with swords and staves When I was daily with you in the Temple, ye stretched forth no hani against Me: but this is your Hour, and the power of Darkness.

As if He said,—"Why do ye treat Me as if I were a robber, thus coming o armed to seize Me by night? What have I done to deserve or require this? Da; have I been teaching in the Temple, and that openly. Why did ye not take I *then?*" The reason *why*, our LORD proceeds, in very remarkable language, to s sign,—or rather, He leaves His enemies to infer. They had not taken Him till no

(*m*) Acts i. 16.   (*n*) Ps. xli. 9.   (*o*) See note on St. Matth. xxvi. 47 to 56.
(*p*) St. John xviii. 10.   (*q*) Col. iv. 14.   (*r*) St. Matth. v. 44.   (*s*) Williams.
(*t*) St. John xviii. 3.   St. Matth. xxvi. 47.   (*u*) St. John xviii. 12.

because not till now had He surrendered Himself into their hands: but this was "their Hour;" and, (it is mysteriously added,) "the Power of Darkness." For a short period of time,—predetermined in the eternal counsels of God,—were they permitted to display their malice; and "the Power of Darkness" was suffered to have the ascendency,—to bruise the heel of Him who was about to bruise his head.(x) Consider what has been already offered on this subject, above, in the note on ver. 43. All this illustrates and helps to explain the marked manner in which St. John declares concerning the Traitor, that "*it was Night*" when he went out(y) from the Paschal Supper, and from the presence of his Lord.

Take notice that Christian men are declared by the Spirit yet to wrestle "against Principalities, against *Powers*, against *the Rulers of the Darkness of this World*, against spiritual wickedness in high places:"(z) but, (as it is elsewhere said,) God "hath delivered us from *the Power of Darkness*, and hath translated us into the Kingdom of His dear Son."(a)   It follows in the earlier Gospels, that at this juncture, "all the Disciples forsook Him and fled."(b)

54, 55 Then took they Him, and led *Him*, and brought Him into the High-Priest's house.

And Peter followed afar off. And when they had kindled a fire in the midst of the hall, and were set down together, Peter sat down among them.

This is related more particularly in St. John's Gospel, to which the Reader is referred.(c)   From the house of Annas, (whither our Blessed Lord was first conducted,)(d) He was led to the palace of Caiaphas, the High-Priest,—followed at a distance by St. Peter and St. John. Owing to the coldness of the weather, (for the nights in Palestine at the Passover season are intensely cold,) a charcoal-fire had been kindled in the outer part of the Hall, where the servants and officers of the High-Priest stood; and St. Peter, after standing for a while with them,(e) sat down to warm himself at the fire.(f)

It will be perceived that St. Matthew and St. Mark in this place record the proceedings of the Sanhedrin, (who find "two false witnesses;") together with the High-Priest's behaviour towards the Holy One,—who is charged with Blasphemy, and declared to be "guilty of Death."(g)   The terrible course which events were thus taking at the upper end of the Hall prepares us for the sad but instructive spectacle to which St. Luke next invites our attention. Having described St. Peter as seated among the servants at the fire, he adds:

56 But a certain maid beheld him as he sat by the fire, and earnestly looked upon him, and said, This man was also with Him.

See the note on St. Mark xiv. 67. It has been pointed out as worthy of notice, "that the women introduced on this occasion are the only women mentioned as taking part with the enemies of our Lord: and even *they* are not concerned in bringing about His condemnation, nor any further than to detect St. Peter. It is remarkable that no woman is mentioned throughout, as speaking against our Lord in His life, or having a share in His death. On the contrary,—He is anointed by a woman for His burial,—women are the last at His grave,—the first at His Resurrection: to a woman He first appeared: women ministered to His wants from Galilee: women bewailed and lamented Him: a heathen woman interceded for His Life with her husband, the Governor; and above all, of a woman He was born."(h)

57, 58, 59 And he denied Him, saying, Woman, I know Him not. And after a little while another saw him, and said, Thou art also of them. And Peter said, Man, I am not. And about the space of an hour after, another confidently affirmed, saying, Of a truth this *fellow* also was with Him: for he is a Galilæan.

(x) Gen. iii. 15.   (y) St. John xiii. 30.   (z) Eph. vi. 12.
(a) Coloss. i. 13. Compare Acts xxvi. 18.   (b) St. Matth. xxvi. 56: St. Mark xiv. 50.
(c) St. John xviii. 12 to 18,—where see the notes. See also the note on St. Mark xiv. 54.
(d) St. John xviii. 13.   (e) St. John xviii. 18.   (f) St. Mark xiv. 54.
(g) St. Matth. xxvi. 59 to 66: St. Mark xiv. 55 to 64.   (h) Williams.

See the notes on St. Mark xiv. 68, 69, 70.

60, 61 And Peter said, Man, I know not what thou sayest. A
immediately, while he yet spake, the cock crew.

And the LORD turned, and looked upon Peter. And Peter reme
bered the word of the LORD, how He had said unto him, Before t
cock crow, thou shalt deny Me thrice.

"What was expressed in that look of our Blessed SAVIOUR, thought of man ca
not conceive, and words cannot utter. That it spoke of all that had passed in a
LORD's long intimacy with St. Peter, and especially of the conversation of th
night, and that it derived a peculiar force and meaning from the indignities whi
our LORD was suffering,—that it implied something of this, we may well suppos
but what more we cannot tell. The conciseness and sublimity with which it
mentioned, resembles the account in Genesis, of His Word being spoken, at whi
the World was created. CHRIST looked,—and Light filled the soul of Peter. Th
thought of his LORD's Divinity, which he had believed, but had forgotten, no
rushed afresh on his mind. In the darkness and silence of the night, his eyes we
opened to all that had passed:"

62 And Peter went out, and wept bitterly.

The Reader is requested to read the remarks which have been already offered o
St. Peter's fall, in the Commentary on the two earlier Gospels.(i)   St. Luke pr
ceeds with the history of our SAVIOUR's Passion.

63, 64, 65 And the men that held JESUS mocked Him, and smot
Him. And when they had blindfolded Him, they struck Him on th
face, and asked Him, saying, Prophesy, who is it that smote Thee
And many other things blasphemously spake they against Him.

Concerning this portion of the Divine Narrative, the Reader is referred to t
notes on St. Matthew xxvi. 67, and on St. Mark xiv. 65. Now was CHRIST th
"poor helpless Man," of whom we read in the Book of Psalms; "persecuted," a
"vexed at the heart;" "helpless and poor," and His "heart wounded with
Him:(k) "despised and rejected of men; a Man of Sorrows, and acquainted w
Grief." "He was oppressed, and He was afflicted, yet He opened not I
mouth."(l)

How certain does it become, by the way, from a careful study of the Gospe
that the Divinity of our Blessed LORD's person cannot have been so apparen
matter as, in our devotion towards our REDEEMER and our GOD, we are sometin
apt to imagine! There must have been a very thick mantle spread over His G
head. The Glory of His Deity must have been curtained close,—so very close th
scarcely a ray, if even so much as a ray, could ever break through and meet the ey
of men. Everything in the Gospels tends to show this. He spoke in the accent
despised Galilee. He was called the "carpenter;" and deemed the son of a very p
man. No one is ever said to have been struck by His aspect. His voice did not
any means always persuade. His speech was cavilled at. Men asked Him to dep
out of their coasts. At the close of His Ministry, soldiers could strike Him with th
fists, and smite Him with their open palms,—blindfold Him,—force a thorny cro
into His pure temples,—scourge Him,—spit upon Him,—torture His parched l
with gall,—crucify Him,—thrust a spear into His lifeless side! None of th
things could have happened, had He seen fit to reveal Himself to His enemi
Once only He appeared to three of His Disciples in the nearest approach to I
proper Glory which their mortal eyes could bear to look upon; and next day, wl
He descended "the Holy Mount," the multitude came running to Him! See
Mark,—ix. 15.

It depends upon the heart of man, therefore, now as then, whether CHRIST sl
be discerned or not: discerned in the common round of daily duty,—in the lo
task,—in the unadorned pathway of common life. If we perceive Him not, it
not because He is not there, but because we have not the eyes to see Him.

(i) See the notes on St. Matth. xxvi. 75, and St. Mark xiv. 72.   (k) Ps. cix. 15, 2
(l) Isa. liii. 3, 7.

66, 67 And as soon as it was day, the elders of the people and the chief Priests and the Scribes came together, and led Him into their Council, saying, Art Thou the CHRIST? tell us.   And He said unto them, If I tell you, ye will not believe:

For our LORD had already told the High-Priest that He *was* "the CHRIST."(*m*)

68 and if I also ask *you*, ye will not answer Me, nor let *Me* go.

For, when our SAVIOUR asked questions of His enemies, they either would not, (being afraid,)(*n*)—or they could not, (being convinced and refuted,)(*o*)—return Him any answer.   Take notice that He now repeats the splendid prediction which is also found on His lips on the occasion alluded to above, in the note on ver. 67.(*p*)

69, 70 Hereafter shall the Son of Man sit on the Right Hand of the Power of GOD.
   Then said they all, Art Thou then the SON of GOD?

A most remarkable question, truly: showing how entirely His learned auditory recognized our LORD's reference to Daniel vii. 13, and how well they understood that prophecy.   He had only said, "the Son of *Man*."

71 And He said unto them, Ye say that I am.
   And they said, What need we any further witness? for we ourselves have heard of His own mouth.

This entire portion of the narrative (namely, from ver. 66 to ver. 71) will be discovered to be peculiar to the present Gospel.   It describes what took place when our LORD was brought before the high Court of Sanhedrin,—"their Council," as it is called in ver. 66.   It was now early morning, (the interval between three and six:) and the Court seems to have sat for a very brief space of time.   The words of our SAVIOUR Himself, when interrogated, rendered the calling of witnesses a superfluous form: and every instant was now precious.   His Judges therefore availed themselves of His declaration that He was indeed "the SON of GOD," to bring the solemn mockery of their judicial proceedings to a close.   And now, they are prepared to conduct Him before Pilate, and require the execution of their sinful sentence.(*q*)

(*m*) See St. Matth. xxvi. 63, 64: St. Mark xiv. 61, 62.   (*n*) As in St. Luke xx. 1 to 7.
(*o*) As in St. Matth. xxii. 41 to 46, and St. Luke xx. 23 to 26.
(*p*) See St. Matth. xxvi. 64,—and the note there.
(*q*) Compare St. Luke xxiii. 1, with St. Matth. xxvii. 1, 2, and St. Mark xvi. 1.

CHAPTER XXIII.

1 JESUS *is accused before Pilate, and sent to Herod.* 8 *Herod mocketh Him.* 11
Herod and Pilate are made friends. 13 *Barabbas is desired of the people, and is
loosed by Pilate, and JESUS is given to be crucified.* 27 *He telleth the women that
lament Him, the destruction of Jerusalem.* 34 *Prayeth for His enemies.* 39 *Two
evil-doers are crucified with Him.* 46 *His Death.* 50 *His Burial.*

1 AND the whole multitude of them arose, and led Him unto Pilate

To understand the meaning of this, the concluding note on the 22d Chapter
should be borne in mind. From this place, a new aspect of our LORD's Humiliation is presented to our notice,—namely, His sufferings at the hands of the Roman
Governor. Here begins, therefore, that train of events which ended in the memorable truth,—"He suffered under Pontius Pilate."

Having hurried the Holy One through the mock formality of a Trial before their
own Court, and so far gratified the pride of their nation, these impious men are impatient to transfer the execution of their sentence to the Roman Governor; as the
shortest, as well as the safest, method of contriving the Death of their Prisoner.
Hence, the transaction which follows. It is likely that on witnessing this result
the proceedings of the Sanhedrin, Judas set the seal upon his iniquity,—in the
manner St. Matthew describes.(a)

Our LORD was now brought before Pilate. To have taxed Him, in such a presence, with pretending to be the SON of GOD, would have been clearly ridiculous.
They must charge Him with the violation of some *Roman* Law; and according
as we learn from the present Gospel, the formal charge brought against Him, was
that of claiming to be a King. As it follows:

**2 And they began to accuse Him, saying, We found this *fellow* per-
verting the nation, and forbidding to give tribute to Cæsar, saying that
He Himself is CHRIST a King.**

He is accused of making Himself a King by the very people who would themselves by force have once made Him one.(b) Consider how Joseph, (an eminent
type of CHRIST,) submitted to punishment for the very crime which he abhorred
commit.(c) And yet, in a far different sense from what his enemies intend,
CHRIST *was* a King: so that, by successfully urging the present charge, they be-
unwilling witness to a solemn truth: and finally (albeit in mockery) procure the
true title of the SAVIOUR to be affixed to His very Cross.(d) "The fierceness of
man," (it is written in a certain place,) "shall turn to Thy praise."(e)

Take notice also that He is accused to Pilate of the very crime from the imputa-
tion of which He had in the fullest manner cleared Himself, on a recent occasion:
namely, of "forbidding to give tribute to Cæsar;"(f) and this too by the very
nation who would have rejoiced in nothing so much as in having Him for their
leader in such a cause. Consider St. Luke xx. 23, and the note thereon.

**3 And Pilate asked Him, saying, Art Thou the King of the Jews?
And He answered him and said, Thou sayest it.**

(a) See St. Matthew xxvii. 3 to 10,—where the reader is requested to see the notes.
(b) St. John vi. 15.   (c) Gen. xxxix.   (d) See below, the note on ver. 38
(e) Psalm lxxvi. 10.   (f) See St. Luke xx. 20 to 26.

A memorable question, truly; recorded by all the Four Evangelists in the self-same words:(*g*) and yet a more memorable reply. It is that "Confession" noticed by St. Paul in his first Epistle to Timothy, as the "good Confession" which CHRIST JESUS "witnessed before Pontius Pilate."(*h*) For a fuller account of His dialogue with the Roman Governor, St. John's Gospel must be consulted.(*i*) St. Luke records nothing but *the result* of that interview, in the words which follow, and which are only found besides related by St. John.

4, 5 Then said Pilate to the Chief Priests and *to* the people, I find no fault in this Man. And they were the more fierce, saying, He stirreth up the people, teaching throughout all Jewry, beginning from Galilee to this place.

To all of which, our SAVIOUR is found to have "answered nothing." "As a sheep before her shearers is dumb, so He opened not His mouth."(*k*) Pilate thereupon asked Him if He heard not the accusation of His enemies; "but JESUS yet answered nothing;"(*l*) "returned him," as St. Matthew says, "not even a single word of answer; so that the Governor wondered greatly."(*m*) There was doubtless something in our LORD's manner, so different from what is usual in a criminal, that the Judge felt something of awe and wonder before him.(*n*) In the mean while.

6, 7 When Pilate heard of Galilee, he asked whether the man were a Galilæan. And as soon as he knew that He belonged unto Herod's jurisdiction, he sent Him to Herod, who himself also was at Jerusalem at that time.

"*Also*,"—because Jerusalem was not the usual residence either of Pilate or of Herod. The Roman Governor usually lived at Cæsarea.

Pilate is the very type of a weak, irresolute statesman. Sufficiently able and inclined to recognize the right, to shrink from the commission of open and flagrant wrong; yet too fearful of consequences, to dare to be strictly just; he rejoiced in the opportunity of transferring to another the burden of a responsibility which he dared not incur in person. It must have also seemed to him a master-stroke of policy, in this manner to conciliate Herod's friendship by the self-same act which secured his own safety. And here, a new scene in our LORD's Humiliation is unfolded to our gaze. He is transferred from Pilate's judgment-seat, to that of the Idumæan Herod: whereby, the remote descendant of Jacob is confronted with the remote descendant of Esau; and experiences the same cruel treatment from him which had been experienced by all His ancestors at the hands of the same family.(*o*) Herod, who slew the Forerunner, must have a hand in the death of MESSIAH likewise.

Herod's is indeed a wonderful history. His name comes before us at the beginning of the Gospel, as the Disciple of the Baptist; next, as his destroyer: then, disturbed by a guilty conscience, it will be remembered that he supposed the murdered Saint to be the author of the miracles which were wrought by our LORD. "And Herod said, John have I beheaded; but who is this, of whom I hear such things? And he desired to see Him."(*p*) Last of all, we behold the Tetrarch face to face with the SAVIOUR of the World: and with how fearful a result!—On this entire subject, the Reader is referred to a long note on St. Luke ix. 9.

8 And when Herod saw JESUS, he was exceeding glad: for he was desirous to see Him of a long *season*, because he had heard many things of Him; and he hoped to have seen some miracle done by Him.

(*g*) St. Matth. xxvii. 11: St. Mark xv. 2: St. Luke xxiii. 3: St. John xviii. 33.
(*h*) 1 Tim. vi. 13. See also the note on St. Matth. xxvii. 11.
(*i*) See St. John xviii. 33 to 37.　　　(*k*) Isaiah liii. 7.　　　(*l*) St. Mark xv. 4, 5.
(*m*) St. Matth. xxvii. 14.　　　　　　　　　　　　　　　　　　(*n*) Williams.
(*o*) Consider the following places: Gen. xxv. 22: xxvii. 41. Exod. xvii. 8, (Compare Gen. xxvi. 12.) Numb. xx. 14 to 21. 1 Sam. xxi. 7: xxii. 18: xxx. 1, 2, &c. Obad. x. 14. Ps. xxxvii. 7. 1 Esdr. iv. 45. Lam. iv. 22. 2 Chron. xxviii. 17: xx. 1, &c. St. Matth. ii. 16: xiv. 3 to 10, &c.　　　　　　　　　　　　　　　　　　(*p*) St. Luke ix. 9.

Well may Herod have "heard many things" of our SAVIOUR,—being Tetrarch
the Province where our LORD had worked so many miracles; having moreov
Steward, whose wife was a most devoted disciple of CHRIST.(q) From those al
him, he must have become acquainted with many a divine, many a wondrous
tory; and he seems to have fallen into that fearful, but as it may be not uncom
state, where Religion becomes a mere sentiment of the heart, or matter of intel
tual curiosity; but forms no essential part of the inward life, and produces no ef
on the daily practice. He retained his vices, yet took an interest in heave
things. He listened to John, yet lived in open adultery. Just one year had elap
since the period when Herod Antipas had "desired to see" CHRIST; and now t
he saw Him, the result might have been anticipated. He was altogether surpri
and disappointed. There was no Beauty in the SAVIOUR that he should de
Him:(r) no wonders were displayed in proof of His Dominion over the powers
Nature: no reply vouchsafed to any of the curious questions with which t
Tetrarch plied Him. As it follows,

9, 10, 11 Then he questioned with Him in many words; but I
answered him nothing. And the Chief Priests and Scribes stood at
vehemently accused Him. And Herod with his men of war set Hi
at nought, and mocked *Him*, and arrayed Him in a gorgeous robe, an
sent Him again to Pilate.

Herod caused our SAVIOUR to be clad, not "in a gorgeous," but "in a wi
robe,"—such a dress as persons wore who were candidates for any high off
Here was One accused of aspiring to nothing short of the crown royal: yet He ma
His appearance unsupported by a single friend,—poor and silent,—"a worm a
no man; a very scorn of men, and the outcast of the people."(s) Claims to kin
honours, if set up by such an one, seemed to Herod a subject for ridicule, rat
than for punishment: and to mark his sense of this, he pursued the course descril
in the text,—mocking Him, *by* arraying Him in a white robe.

12 And the same day Pilate and Herod were made friends togethe
for before they were at enmity between themselves.

It has ever been thus. Men who before were at enmity will combine, and
come friends, when CHRIST Himself, or the Church of CHRIST, is to be persecuted
The occasion of the quarrel of these two is not recorded, and therefore not certai
known.(u) Far more important was it to notice this, the occasion of their rec
ciliation; whereby were fulfilled those words of ancient prophecy—"Why do
heathen rage, and the people imagine a vain thing? The Kings of the Earth
themselves, and the Rulers take counsel together, against the LORD, and agai
His Anointed"—that is, "His CHRIST." Consider the quotation of Psalm ii. 1, :
Acts iv. 25, 26; and the comment supplied by the united voice of the Apostles
verses 27 and 28, on those words of David.

It now became necessary for Pilate to act; and he is found to have summor
together not only the members of the Sanhedrin, but "the people" also, (amo
whom the Holy One certainly had many followers, many humble yet devo
friends,)(x) in order that he might have a better chance of effecting his purpo
which was, to procure our LORD's release. But no blessing ever attends crool
endeavours to do good. It follows:

13, 14, 15 And Pilate, when he had called together the Chi
Priests, and the Rulers, and the people, said unto them, Ye ba
brought this Man unto me, as one that perverteth the people: an
behold, I, having examined *Him* before you, have found no fault
this Man touching those things whereof ye accuse Him: no, nor j

(q) St. Luke viii. 3, and xxiv. 10.　　　(r) Isa. liii. 2.　　　(s) Ps. xxii. 6.
(t) See the note on St. Matth. xvi. 1.　　　　　　　　　(u) See St. Luke xiii.
(x) Consider St. John ii. 23: vii. 31: viii. 30, 31: xi. 45, 48: xii. 11. Also St. Matth.
46. St. Luke xix. 48: xxi. 38, &c. &c.

Herod: for I sent you to him: and, lo, nothing worthy of death is done unto Him.

Rather,—"nothing deserving of death has been done *by* Him." Pilate is arguing that, in Herod's judgment, our LORD can have done nothing which deserves the punishment of death,—for He has been acquitted by the Tetrarch.

Take notice by the way, in passing, how many, and what various persons bear testimony to the innocence of the Holy One. Pilate,(y) and Herod,(z) and Pilate's wife,(a) Judas himself,(b) the Thief on the Cross,(c) and the Centurion.(d)—Pilate adds:

16, 17 I will therefore chastise Him, and release *Him.* (For of necessity he must release one unto them at the Feast.)

To set a prisoner free, at the Feast of the Passover, seems to have been a privilege which the Romans granted in pursuance of a Jewish custom; and, as far as Pilate was concerned, it must have been of modern date: but it had evidently become absolute. St. Mark records that, "the multitude crying aloud began to desire him to do as he had ever done unto them."(e) Now the eager desire of the Roman Governor was, that Jesus of Nazareth might be He whom the people would desire; but the friends of the Holy One were silent, or their voices were overpowered by the rabble whom their Rulers had persuaded to procure His death.

18, 19 And they cried out all at once, saying, Away with this *Man,* and release unto us Barabbas: (who, for a certain sedition made in the city, and for murder, was cast into prison.)

Thus "denying the Holy One and the Just, and desiring a murderer to be granted unto them,"(f)—as St. Peter afterwards boldly declared.

Now, the Roman Governor knew well that it was for envy that the Chief Priests had delivered Him. Rugged, therefore, and little inclined to mercy as he is known to have been by nature,(g) he appears to have been so wrought upon by the calm majesty of his Prisoner, that he made repeated efforts to procure His release. As it follows:

20, 21, 22, 23 Pilate therefore, willing to release, JESUS spake again to them. But they cried, saying, Crucify *Him,* crucify Him. And he said unto them the third time, Why, what evil hath He done? I have found no cause of death in Him: I will therefore chastise Him, and let *Him* go. And they were instant with loud voices, requiring that He might be crucified. And the voices of them and of the Chief Priests prevailed.

24 And Pilate gave sentence that it should be as they required.

"Three times did he challenge the whole nation of the Jews, 'Why, what evil hath He done?' Three times did he make that clear profession, 'I have found no cause of death in Him.' His own wife, admonished in a dream, 'sent unto him, saying, Have thou nothing to do with that just Man:'(h) and when Pilate heard that He made Himself the SON of GOD, 'he was the more afraid.'"(i) Notwithstanding all this, he condemned and crucified the LORD of Glory.(k) It was in order to pacify the people, and retain possession of his office undisturbed and unmolested, that the Roman Governor thus acted. But his policy proved unavailing. At the end of a few years he was summoned to Rome, to meet certain charges which were brought against him; and an old Greek Chronologer, (quoted by Eusebius,) relates that he destroyed himself in desperation.—It follows:

25 And he released unto them him that for sedition and murder was

(y) St. Matth. xxvii. 24.   (z) See above, verse 11.   (a) St. Matth. xxvii. 19.
(b) St. Matth. xxvii. 4.   (c) See below, verse 41.   (d) See below, verse 47.
(e) St. Mark xv. 8.   (f) Acts iii. 14.
(g) See St. Luke xiii. 1, and the note there.   (h) St. Matth. xxvii. 19.
(i) Bp. Pearson, quoting St. John xix. 7, 8.   (k) 1 Cor. ii. 8.

cast into prison, whom they had desired; but he delivered JESUS
their will.

Then was He scourged, and stripped by the soldiers, and arrayed in the mo
ensigns of Royalty,—a crown of thorns, a purple robe, and a reed in His right ha
instead of a sceptre: while those wretched miscreants smote Him on the head, a
bowed the knee before Him in derision; and even spat in the face(l) of Him wl
is "the brightness of" the FATHER'S "Glory, and the express image of His pe
son!"(m) . . . . All this, St. Luke omits. He likewise passes over in silence th
memorable interview between our SAVIOUR and Pilate, and the many efforts whi
were made by the irresolute Roman to procure His acquittal,—"when," as &
Peter expresses it, "he was determined to let Him go;"(n) yet could not preva
with the multitude to consent to His release. On all this subject, the Gospel of St
John must be referred to, and the remarks should be read which are there offered.
It has been already pointed out,(o) and the remark deserves repetition, that the
monstrous violence of the soldiery on this terrible occasion, as well as the length of
wickedness.to which their rulers proceeded, can be referred to nothing short of the
Prince of Evil himself, who with all his forces conducted this assault against the
Son of Man. St. Paul not obscurely hints at the various ranks of those Powers of
Darkness:(p) and declares that it was, in ignorance of the marvellous scheme which
GOD had devised for Man's Redemption, that they procured the Death of the
REDEEMER: "for had they known it," remarks the great Apostle, "they would not
have crucified the LORD of Glory."(q) Of a truth they would not; for what was the
Cross but the marvellous instrument of His own victory, and their undoing? With
this, the choice weapon of the Enemy, was the Enemy himself slain. As it is
written,—"David stood upon the Philistine, and took his sword, and drew it out
of the sheath thereof; and slew him, and cut off his head therewith."(r)—But I
return.

Some hours had now elapsed. It was in fact almost nine o'clock in the morn
ing; the formal abandonment of our SAVIOUR into the hands of His bloodthirst
enemies having taken place at six.(s) On reaching the City-gate, up to which tim
He had Himself borne the Cross on which He was condemned to suffer,—

26 And as they led Him away, they laid hold upon one Simon, i
Cyrenian, coming out of the country, and on him they laid the Cross
that he might bear it after JESUS.

Concerning this incident, the Reader is requested to read what has been offere
on St. Matthew xxvii. 32, and St. Mark xv. 21.—Pleasant it is to believe that th
highly-favoured person will have become a Disciple from this hour, even if he wer
not so already; for he was one who, not in figure, but in actual truth, had fulfille
that injunction of his SAVIOUR,—"Whosoever will come after Me, let him den
himself, and take up his cross, and follow Me."(t)

27, 28 And there followed Him a great company of people, and of
women, which also bewailed and lamented Him. But JESUS turning
unto them said, Daughters of Jerusalem, weep not for Me, but weep for
yourselves, and for your children.

"Your children,"—for in their time, (namely, forty years after the Crucifixion,)
would the Siege of Jerusalem and the Fall of the City take place:(u) and "Wo
unto them that are with child, and to them that give suck in those days,"(x)—the
same Divine Speaker had already declared of that occasion. He adds a saying to
the same effect, now:

29, 30 For, behold, the days are coming, in the which they shall

(l) St. Matth. xxvii. 28 to 30: St. Mark xv. 15 to 19.   (m) Heb. i. 3.
(n) Acts iii. 13.   (o) See the note on St. Matthew xxvii. 35.
(p) Compare Eph. iii. 9 to 11, with vi. 12.   (q) 1 Cor. ii. 8.
(r) 1 Sam. xvii. 51.   (s) St. John xix. 14.
(t) St. Matth. xvi. 24: St. Mark viii. 34: St. Luke ix. 23.
(u) See the heading of the present chapter.
(x) St. Luke xxi. 23,—where see the note.

say, Blessed *are* the barren, and the wombs that never bare, and the paps which never gave suck. Then shall they begin to say to the mountains, Fall on us; and to the hills, Cover us.

Compare with this, the language of Isaiah ii. 10, 19, 21; and for a yet stricter parallel, see Rev. vi. 16. But so exact is the resemblance of the present place, in point of expression, to Hosea x. 8, that it may be regarded almost as a quotation from that ancient prophet.

31 For if they do these things in a green tree, what shall be done in the dry?

If such sufferings can befall the Innocent Man,—what shall be the fate of the ungodly Nation? If the "tree planted by the water, that bringeth forth his fruit in his season," is thus shamefully cut down,—what shall become of "trees whose fruit withereth, without fruit, twice dead?"(y)

32 And there were also two other, malefactors, led with Him to be put to death.

These men are called "thieves" in the two earlier Gospels.(z) One of them afterwards obtains such conspicuous notice, that a few words concerning the class to which they belonged, will not be out of place here. They were probably offenders of a kind which had sprung up in Palestine, in consequence of the convulsed and lawless state of the country;(a) among whom must have been found every grade of guilt,—from that of the bold insurgent and outlaw, who, with misguided patriotism, seeks to revenge his country's wrongs by violent means of his own devising, down to that of the common thief, whose trade is plunder, and who scruples not to add to his other crimes, the guilt of blood. It seems reasonable to conjecture from St. Mark xv. 7, that the two malefactors mentioned in the text were seditious men of the kind first spoken of.

33 And when they were come to the place, which is called Calvary, there they crucified Him,

It had been written full a thousand years before,—"They pierced My hands and My feet. I may tell all My bones. They stand staring and looking upon Me."(b) "The mystery here unfolded," remarks a good man, "far transcends ordinary thought. With hearts undisciplined, we shall never comprehend it; neither with the best preparation can we do more than imbibe to our soul's health some portion of that which passeth knowledge, and which angels but imperfectly apprehend."(c) Scarcely endurable, when the thoughts are engaged on a subject of such awful interest, are remarks of a purely critical character. It may, however, be thought worthy of passing notice, that "Calvary" (*Calvaria*) is merely the Latin word for "a skull;" retained (but only in this Gospel) from the Vulgate version of the Scriptures. The other three Evangelists mention that the spot to which these sinful men had now conducted our SAVIOUR, was called in the Hebrew, "Golgotha." "There they crucified Him,"—

34 and the malefactors, one on the right hand, and the other on the left. Then said JESUS, FATHER, forgive them; for they know not what they do.

This was the first of our LORD's seven sayings on the Cross. Thus did He "*make intercession for the transgressors*,"—as His ancient prophet had foretold;(d) and confirm, in His hour of bitter agony, one of His loftiest precepts,(e) by His own most holy example. And surely, a truer notion may be obtained of the stupendous nature of the transaction we are here considering, from this short Prayer of the SAVIOUR for His murderers, than could be conveyed by many words of painful ex-

(y) Ps. l. 3. St. Jude, verse 12. And compare Ezek. xx. 47 with xxi. 3, 4.
(z) St. Matth. xxvii. 38: St. Mark xv. 27.
(a) Consider St. Mark xv. 7. Acts v. 36, 37: xxi. 38.   (b) Ps. xxii. 16, 17.
(c) Dr. W. H. Mill. (d) See Isaiah liii. 12.   (e) See St. Matth. v. 44.

planation from ourselves. The occasion is one of those where (in the pious la
guage of Hooker) "our safest eloquence is our silence."

But, in proportion to our sense of the terrible sin of the actors in this black trai
action, should surely be our hatred of sin in ourselves. No less alarming than i
structive, is the warning of the great Apostle against sin in Christian men,—co
veying, as he does, an intimation that all that shocks and confounds us in the hi
tory of our SAVIOUR's Crucifixion is, after some mysterious fashion, thus repeat
and renewed,—"seeing," (he says,) "they crucify to themselves the SON of G
afresh, and put Him to an open shame."(*f*)

And they parted His raiment, and cast lots.

This will be found more particularly related by the other three Evangelists.(*
See especially the notes on St. John xix. 23 and 24.

35 And the people stood beholding. And the rulers also with them
derided *Him*, saying, He saved others; let Him save Himself, if He
be CHRIST, the chosen of GOD.

For, strange as it may appear, yet is it "next to certain, that the Death of the
MESSIAH, at the hands of His own, or any other people, was never apprehended by
the Jews as one of the events by which His Advent would be declared. This part
of His future history is foreshown indeed, as clearly as words can express, in the
xxii. Psalm, in the ix. of Daniel, and in the liii. of Isaiah; and though other
parts of these same chapters are by the Jews themselves referred to the Mes
SIAH," (the liii. of Isaiah, more expressly and more frequently than any other
single prophecy of the Old Testament;) "yet does this event appear, from the very
beginning, to have been entirely concealed from their Church." Had it not been
anciently foretold, concerning this remarkable people, that they should "grope a
noonday, as the blind gropeth in darkness?" that "the spirit of deep sleep" shoul
be "poured out upon them," and "their eyes be closed?" that they were "to hea
indeed, but understand not; and see, indeed, but perceive not?" Nay, to this day
are they not "blinded;" and "when Moses is read," is not "the veil upon the
hearts?"(*h*)

Refer besides to the notes on St. Matthew xxvii. 40, 42, and 43; and on St. Mar
xv. 31, 32.

36 And the soldiers also mocked Him, coming to Him, and offering
Him vinegar,

"They gave Him vinegar to drink, mingled with gall," St. Matthew says.(*i*
Whereby those marvellous words of ancient prophecy were fulfilled,—"They gave
Me also gall for My meat; and in My thirst, they gave Me vinegar to drink."(*k*
This they did, mocking Him:

37 and saying, If Thou be the King of the Jews, save Thyself.

In explanation of which circumstance,—("If Thou *be*,")—the Evangelist adds:

38 And a superscription also was written over Him in letters of
Greek, and Latin, and Hebrew, THIS IS THE KING OF THE
JEWS.

An inscription was set over the head of our crucified SAVIOUR, in conformity
with the Roman practice, which was, on such occasions, to specify in writing the
crime for which the offender suffered. In calling our LORD "the King of the
Jews," it may, however, well be suspected that Pilate intended indirectly to spite
the people who had forced him to violate the dictates of his own conscience. Ac
cordingly, it will be remembered that they wanted him to alter the terms of the
charge,—to which request of theirs, it was divinely overruled that the Roman
Governor did not accede.(*l*) And thus was our LORD's real character and offic
proclaimed to all men. He was *a King*.(*m*)

(*f*) Hebrews vi. 6.　　　　　(*g*) St. Matth. xxvii. 35, and St. Mark xv. 24.
(*h*) Dean Lyall,—quoting Deut. xxviii. 29.　Isa. xxix. 10: vi. 9.　2 Cor. iii. 14, 15.
(*i*) St. Matth. xxvii. 34.　　(*k*) Psalm lxix. 21.　　　(*l*) See St. John xix. 21, 22.
(*m*) See notes on St. Matth. xxvi. 65, and xxvii. 38.

The writing was in Greek,—because Greek was then the language of the world: in Latin,—because Judæa was already a Roman Province: in Hebrew,—because the Mighty Sufferer belonged by birth to the commonwealth of Israel. Grotius finely connects the diverse languages which surmounted the Cross of CHRIST, with the custom of the Roman Emperors, to carry before them the names of the "people, nations, and languages," who were subject to their sway.

Our attention is next directed to the conduct of the two malefactors; who, as we have already seen, were crucified with the Holy One. St. Luke alone, of the four Evangelists, relates the striking circumstance, "that the two men thus placed, the one on the right hand, the other on the left of our LORD, in His last agony, bore in a manner the image of those who should stand at His right and at His left in Judgment,—the elect of GOD, and the reprobate. Wonderful indeed may it appear,—if any thing after CHRIST crucified can seem wonderful,—that one of the former class should be found there, where every thing told of extreme guilt and extreme punishment: but even thus did He who came to save the lost,—and who, while we were yet sinners, in due time died for the ungodly,—even thus did He choose to manifest, even in the scene of His death, its atoning virtue to the worst of sinners repenting."(n)

39 And one of the malefactors which were hanged railed on Him, saying, If Thou be the CHRIST, save Thyself and us.

The sinful man read the inscription upon the Cross, and heard the furious railing of the disappointed rabble, as they called upon our SAVIOUR to save Himself,—if, indeed, He had any claim to the proud title written above Him.(o) "Can we wonder that he should have beheld only the contrast of his own extreme misery with the asserted power which could save, but did not,—which saved not even its professed possessor; and that, in the bitterness of anguish at the contrast, he should cast in the teeth of his fellow-sufferer the taunt of the chief priests and people,— 'If Thou be the CHRIST, save Thyself,—and us?' Can we wonder that the perception which could alone suppress these bad thoughts, was wanting to the miserable man in that hour of agony,—the perception of the majesty which sat on the bleeding brow of the CHRIST beside him, self-resigned, and praying for His murderers?

"For there is nothing in suffering, in itself considered, which has power to bring these or any other gracious feelings to minds before strangers to them: rather does it harden the heart of the carnal man, by centring his thoughts on his own woe, to the exclusion both of GOD and his fellows. Awful in this respect are all the pangs which sever soul and body. Not without reason, therefore, has the Church taught all her faithful children to say,—'Suffer us not, in our last hour, for any pains of Death, to fall from Thee!' If thus it is with those whose hearts have been disciplined and sanctified in the School of CHRIST,—how in that dismal struggle must it fare with such as have put off their repentance and piety to the last?"(p)—So asks a good man, whose observations are directed against the danger of those who defer the work of repentance to the end of life, in the vain hope that it may fare with them as it fared with the repentant malefactor. He is bent on showing that that man's blessed example is balanced by this other example of final impenitence.

40 But the other answering rebuked him,

It is impossible to say with certainty whether both of those who were crucified with our SAVIOUR were, at first, blasphemers or not: but it seems the safest plan to take the statements of the two earlier Evangelists, according to their literal force and meaning. And if both "the thieves which were crucified with Him," at first reviled Him,(q) then we have the marvellous picture of one repenting at the very latest hour, and accepted.

Be this as it may, we shall derive a sufficiently striking lesson from the wonderful history before us, if we hold fast by the revealed details of the case. Here was one who may, or may not, have been an old and hardened offender; one who may, or may not, have added the guilt of murder to robbery. What is certain, he was "a felon justly convicted, justly executed: one, whom public justice had adjudged

(n) Dr. W. H. Mill.   (o) See above, verse 37.   (p) Dr. W. H. Mill.
(q) St. Matth. xxvii. 44: St. Mark xv. 33.

to the most disgraceful as well as cruel of punishments; and to whom public mercy,—which had just saved Barabbas from a murderer's death,—had not been extended.   To such a person, therefore, was that signal mercy shown, which the brief narrative of St. Luke enables us to trace.   The repentance of the malefactor is evinced in his confession, when he rebuked his hardened comrade, (who had joined the soldiers' mockery against the Royal Messiahship of JESUS.")(r)

41 saying, Dost not thou fear GOD, seeing thou art in the same condemnation?   And we indeed justly; for we receive the due reward of our deeds:

To repentance thus hearty, at the very moment also when he was writhing beneath the bitter consequences of his crime, "he adds a Faith no less admirable; when, pointing to the Man beside him, then under that load of wrath which obscured His sacred person from all common sight, he adds to his self-condemnation and to his rebuke, the sentence,"—

but this Man hath done nothing amiss.

42 And he said unto JESUS, LORD, remember me when Thou comest into Thy Kingdom.

Rather,—"when Thou comest in Thy kingdom:" a striking prayer indeed, and worthy even of one who had companied with the Apostles "all the time that the LORD JESUS went in and out among" them.(s)   What is it but a confession that CHRIST, having taken to Himself His Kingdom, would return(t) in the Glory of that Kingdom,(u) in the latter day, to be the Judge of quick and dead?   This despised criminal could hardly have spoken more aptly had he been one of those who heard our LORD foretell His future coming in Glory.(x)

43 And JESUS said unto him, Verily I say unto thee, To-day shalt thou be with Me in Paradise.

Not, when I come in My Kingdom, will I remember thee: but, This day shalt thou be with Me.   This is the third of our LORD's seven last sayings.
"In Paradise:"—how memorable a word to be found on the lips of the Second Adam, and at such a time!   What else does it imply but that, having undone the curse,—having overcome Death by dying,—He was about to reinstate Mankind in the lost privilege of their race; to reconduct them back to that happiness from which, by the disobedience of their first Parents, they had been expelled?—So remarks the great Athanasius, and Ambrose, with many others.
Thus did our SAVIOUR convey to this man the blessed assurance of "a passage with Him through His Baptism of Blood to His rest and to His final Glory. 'To-day—in Paradise:' not in the Highest Heaven, to which our LORD Himself ascended not till afterwards: whither also, as St. Peter afterwards preached to the Jews, David himself had not yet ascended;(y) and whither to ascend at this time was surely no privilege of this penitent thief;—but in that intermediate state of faithful souls, the blessed division of that unseen region, to which on that day our LORD descended, (according to the prediction of the Psalmist,(z) and the confession in our Creed,) was the penitent Thief to be that day with CHRIST.   With the souls in that safe custody, as St. Peter writes,(a)—to whom CHRIST then declared their Redemption accomplished, and their more perfect felicity surely approaching,—was this penitent to await the full consummation of his bliss, both in body and soul.(b)
"And the conclusion from it can be none other than this,—that there is no sin so great but that the blood of CHRIST can expiate it; no sinner to whom the glad tidings of that Redemption have been borne, who may not by repentance and faith plead its benefit."(c)   Thus will the example of the dying thief ever afford unutterable consolation to the real penitent.
Let none however presume on this single recorded instance of the Divine Mercy

(r) Dr. W. H. Mill.   (s) Acts i. 21.   (t) See St. Luke xix. 12.
(u) Compare St. Matth. xvi. 28.   (x) See St. Matth. xvi. 27, 28 : xxv. 31.
(y) Acts ii. 34.   (z) Ps. xvi. 10.   (a) 1 St. Pet. iii. 19.
(b) So in effect, writes one who had been a disciple of the Apostles,—quoted by Irenæus.
                    (c) Dr. W. H. Mill.

extended to a dying Malefactor; for of a truth, very rarely in its essential features can such a case be repeated,—in its accidental features, *never*. For aught that appears to the contrary, here was a conscience only *at last* awakened; yet embracing the offer of Mercy with a free Confession, a hearty Repentance, and the prompt exercise of a most mighty Faith. When even Peter had denied his LORD, and all but St. John had forsaken Him and fled, this suffering man comes forward, an almost solitary witness to the Divinity of CHRIST: recognizing Him when "His visage was marred more than any man, and His form more than the sons of men;"(d) and confessing "a Kingdom which had the ignominious Cross as its foundation, when that mystery,—to the Jews a stumbling-block and to the Greeks foolishness,—was even to the faithful Disciples yet unknown." . . . . What possible encouragement such a history can be supposed to afford to those who delay their Repentance, reserving it for a dying bed,—it is hard to discover. Scarcely is it too much to say that the cases have no manner of resemblance. He who would be a partaker in the promise vouchsafed to the accepted malefactor, must rather imitate him in the prompt devotion of his remaining opportunities, whatever they may be, to the active service of GOD. "For while in Him we have a solitary instance of one accepted through Faith without external works, (for which he had not the opportunity,) yet by no means do we see in him a faith destitute of works, in the larger and fuller meaning of the word. For Confession and Humiliation are works; the charitable admonition of sinners is a work; and Faith itself, the direction of the mind to unseen realities against the bent of carnal feeling, is a work of no small difficulty."(e)—But enough has now been offered on this great subject

44, 45 And it was about the sixth hour, and there was a darkness over all the earth until the ninth hour. And the Sun was darkened, and the Veil of the Temple was rent in the midst.

Concerning these three hours of miraculous darkness,—at the close of which, (namely, at three in the afternoon,) our SAVIOUR expired on the Cross,—see what has been already offered in the note on St. Matth. xxvii. 45. About the rending of the Veil, see also the notes on the earlier Gospels;(f) in St. Matthew, the other prodigies which occurred on this occasion will be found recorded.(g)

46 And when JESUS had cried with a loud voice, He said, FATHER, into Thy Hands I commend My Spirit: and having said thus, He gave up the Ghost.

"With a *loud* voice,"—(a miraculous circumstance insisted upon by all three Evangelists,)(h)—did our REDEEMER resign His sinless Soul into the Hands of the Eternal FATHER: applying to Himself the language of the 31st Psalm:(i)(which is the last of His seven sayings on the Cross;) and thereby "teaching us in whose hands the souls of the departed are."(k)—St. Peter alludes to these dying words of his LORD, in his first Epistle:(l) and take notice, how the first Martyr, St. Stephen, sought to die like CHRIST in respect of his two latest sayings.(m)—"The souls of the righteous," (it is said in a certain place,) "are in the hand of GOD, and there shall no torment touch them."(n)

47 Now when the Centurion saw what was done, he glorified GOD, saying, Certainly this was a righteous Man.

The Reader is requested to read the note on St. Mark xv. 39: also that on St. Matthew xxvii. 54.

48, 49 And all the people that came together to that sight, beholding the things which were done, smote their breasts, and returned. And all His acquaintance, and the women that followed Him from Galilee, stood afar off, beholding these things.

(d) Isa. lii. 14.   (e) Dr. W. H. Mill.
(f) St. Matth. xxvii. 51, and St. Mark xv. 38.   (g) St. Matth. xxvii. 51, 52, 53.
(h) St. Matth. xxvii. 46, 50: St. Mark xv. 34, 37. See the note on St. Mark xv. 39.
(i) Ver. 5.   (k) Bp. Pearson.   (l) 1 St. Pet. iv. 19.
(m) See Acts vii. 59, 60.   (n) Wisdom of Solomon iii. 1.

Compare St. Matth. xxvii. 55, 56, and St. Mark xv. 40, 41; and see the notes the former place. See also St. Luke viii. 1 to 3.

The keen eye of Prophecy had noticed that mournful group long before. Dav speaking in the person of his great Descendant, complains,—"My lovers and friends stand aloof from my sore; and my kinsmen stand afar off."(o) It is wo observing how much is said in the Psalms of the desertion of the Disciples, (w the single exception of St. John,) throughout this dreary scene; for it would se to have constituted a special ingredient in our Lord's Cup of Sorrow. Thus, in 31st Psalm,—"I was a reproach among all Mine enemies, but especially amo My neighbours, and a fear to Mine acquaintance. They that did see Me witho fled from Me."(p) "Thou hast put away Mine acquaintance far from Me; Th hast made Me an abomination unto them. . . . . Lover and friend hast Thou p far from Me, and Mine acquaintance into darkness."(q)

50, 51 And, behold, *there was* a man named Joseph, a counsellor *and he was* a good man, and a just: (the same had not consented t the counsel and deed of them;) *he was* of Arimathæa, a city of th Jews: who also himself waited for the Kingdom of God.

In such terms is the disciple who, with Nicodemus, enjoyed the sublime privileg of providing for the Burial of his Lord, introduced to our notice. He proves t have been a member of the high Court of Sanhedrin; but, like that other memb of the same Court already named, he had had no share in the sinful proceedings the morning.(r) To "wait for the Kingdom of God," as already explained,(s) d notes the hope of every faithful Israelite for the Advent of Messiah.

52, 53 This *man* went unto Pilate, and begged the Body of Jesu And he took It down and wrapped It in linen, and laid It in a sepu chre that was hewn in stone, wherein never man before was laid.

Some remarks on these incidents will be found in the notes on St. Matthew xxv 58, 59, and St. Mark xv. 42 to 46.

54 And that day was the Preparation, and the Sabbath drew on.

The last Jewish Sabbath which the World was ever to behold! See the n which precedes St. Matth. xxvii. 57: also the note on St. Mark xv. 42.

55 And the women also, which came with Him from Galilee, follow after, and beheld the sepulchre, and how His Body was laid.

"There was Mary Magdalene, and the other Mary," (that is, "Mary the Moth of Joses,")(t) "sitting over against the Sepulchre,"—as St. Matthew relates.(u)

56 And they returned, and prepared spices and ointments; al rested the Sabbath Day according to the commandment.

Contrast the blessed calm in which these sad matrons passed their Sabbath, wi the unholy excitement of the Chief Priests and Pharisees throughout the sa solemn season.(x) These pious women, eager as they were to perform the last offi of love to their Lord, yet would not transgress the commandment. Having prepar the needful spices and unguents, they resolved to wait till the first Day of the wee should dawn, before they presumed to approach the Holy Sepulchre. How bless was the result! and how unblessed would have been the impatient yielding to the own inclination! Had they presented themselves sooner at the Grave, they woul have been grieved by the presence, perhaps molested by the rudeness, of the Roma soldiers: while their purpose could not possibly have been effected. By waitin till the Sabbath was past,—they found the guard dispersed, and their Lord alread risen! They embraced those limbs alive, which they had come to weep over, an to anoint in Death!

(o) Ps. xxxviii. 11.   (p) Ps. xxxi. 11.   (q) Ps. lxxxviii. 8, 18.
(r) See above, the note on ver. 1.
(s) See the notes on St. Mark xv. 43, and on St. Luke ii. 25.
(t) St. Mark xv. 47,—where see the note.
(u) St. Matth. xxvii. 61,—where see the note; and the verses enumerated in ver. 56.
    (x) St. Matth. xxvii. 62 to 66.

CHAPTER XXIV.

Christ's *Resurrection is declared by two Angels to the women that came to the Sepulchre.* 9 *These report it to others.* 13 CHRIST *Himself appeareth to the two Disciples that went to Emmaus.* 36 *Afterwards He appeareth to the Apostles, and reproveth their unbelief.* 47 *Giveth them a Charge.* 49 *Promiseth the* HOLY GHOST. 51 *And so ascendeth into Heaven.*

THE concluding chapter of each of the first three Gospels comprehends the history of the great Forty Days;(a) and stands in marked contrast with the chapters which immediately precede. With all the fearful events of our Blessed LORD's Passion fresh in our memory, the story of the first Easter is like the cool fragrance of morning after a night of suffering and Death. It is in fact the Birthday of the New Creation. But the History is continuous; and to understand the first verse of the present chapter, the last two verses of that which goes before must be borne in mind. "When the Sabbath was past," says St. Mark, "Mary Magdalene, and Mary the mother of James, and Salome, had brought sweet spices, that they might come and anoint Him."(b) It was therefore the first LORD's Day, and about daybreak. As it follows:

1 Now upon the first *day* of the week, very early in the morning, they came unto the Sepulchre, bringing the spices which they had prepared, and certain *others* with them.

These holy women, whose names the Evangelist will be found to specify more particularly in verse 10, desired to bestow upon the lifeless Body of their LORD the full honours of Burial; and they supposed that the rite of Anointing yet remained undischarged. The hasty ceremonial performed by the loving hands of Joseph and Nicodemus,(c) they must have deemed incomplete in this respect. How striking, however, becomes the recollection, at this stage of the sacred History,—(striking even to ourselves, but how much more striking must it have been to *them!*)—that a full week before, the sister of Lazarus was declared by CHRIST Himself to have bestowed upon His yet living Body the Anointing which was commonly reserved for the bodies of the dead!(d) And fitting it surely was. that the LORD of Life should experience so singular an anointing,—that those blessed limbs, which were destined never to "see Corruption," should exhibit in this respect a kind of prophetic intimation of the triumph which was to follow.

"Who shall roll us away the stone from the door of the Sepulchre?"(e)—the women had "said among themselves" as they came along. But they looked,

2 And they found the stone rolled away from the Sepulchre.

How this had come to pass, St. Matthew explains.(f)

3 And they entered in, and found not the Body of the LORD JESUS.

The course of the sacred narrative conducts us at once from the interment of our SAVIOUR, on the evening of Friday, to His Resurrection from Death, very early in the morning of Sunday. Concerning the whole interval, as far as the Great Captain of our Salvation is concerned, nothing whatever is revealed to us in the Gospel:

(a) Acts i. 3.   (b) St. Mark xvi. 1.   (c) See St. John xix. 39, 40.
(d) See St. Matth. xxvi. 12.   St. Mark xiv. 8.   St. John xii. 7.
(e) St. Mark xvi. 3.   (f) St. Matth. xxviii. 2.

but the momentous Truth that, during those three days, "He descended into Hell,"
hath been the constant belief of the Church, (the "Witness and Keeper of Holy
Writ,")(g) from the beginning. Not indeed that the words themselves are found
in the earliest copies of the Creed; but when Apollinaris, (who was Bishop of
Laodicea in Syria, A.D. 362,) taught that CHRIST had no human soul, but that
the Word was to Him in place of a soul, the Church put forward this well-known
doctrine, and added it to her Creed, as an eternal protest against his dangerous
heresy.

One of the purposes of our LORD's "descent into Hell," is declared in a well-
known passage of St. Peter's first Epistle. He went to "preach to the souls in safe
keeping,"(h)—according to the mysterious language of the Apostle; and the place
of their abode was "Paradise."(i) Doubtless, He proclaimed to them their Redemption accomplished, and rehearsed in their wondering ears His recent victory
over Sin and Death. A few more words on this great subject will be found in the
note prefixed to St. Mark xvi.

But the Sabbath was now passed; and the Human Soul of our LORD having returned to its fleshly Tabernacle, "perfect GOD and perfect Man," He raised Himself from Death;(k) with calm majesty, divested Himself of His fragrant garments;
and some time before the Sun had risen,—before even the Angel had descended to
hurl away the stone from the door of His Sepulchre,—after some wonderful and
unrecorded fashion, He had come forth. Hence it was, that the women, on entering the chamber of Death, "found not the Body of the LORD JESUS."

4 And it came to pass, as they were much perplexed thereabout,
behold, two men stood by them in shining garments:

More than "shining." It is implied that their garments were "*flashing*" with
light.

5 and as they were afraid, and bowed down *their* faces to the Earth,
they said unto them,

That is, the Angels said,—"Fear not ye. Ye seek JESUS of Nazareth, which was
crucified:"

Why seek ye the Living among the dead?

For they were seeking Him who proclaims concerning Himself in the Book of
Revelation,—"I am He that liveth and was dead; and behold, I am alive for evermore, Amen."(l)

6, 7 He is not here, but is risen: remember how He spake unto
you when He was yet in Galilee, saying, The Son of Man must be delivered into the hands of sinful men, and be crucified, and the third
day rise again.

8 And they remembered His words,

They remembered the memorable words recorded by St. Matthew,(m) and St.
Mark,(n) and alluded to by St. Luke,(o)—as addressed to them by their LORD
"*while they abode in Galilee*," rather more than half a year before. The Reader is
requested to refer back to the notes on St. Matthew xvii. 23, and St. Mark ix. 31,
for some remarks on this subject.—The Angels added a memorable injunction on
this occasion. They charged the women to announce to the Disciples *that* appearance on a mountain in Galilee, which our SAVIOUR was about to vouchsafe to His
followers in conformity with the promise He had made to the Apostles in His lifetime.(p) That promise, He is found to have renewed, now that He was risen:(q)
and indeed the appearance alluded to must have been one of prime importance; for,
as already shown,(r) it is almost the only event subsequent to the Resurrection, re-

(g) Article xx.   (h) 1 St. Peter iii.   (i) St. Luke xxiii. 34, where see the note.
(k) St. John ii. 19, 21: x. 18.   (l) Rev. i. 18.   (m) St. Matth. xvii. 22, 23.
(n) St. Mark ix. 31.   (o) St. Luke ix. 44.
(p) St. Matth. xxvi. 32.   (q) St. Matth. xxviii. 16.
(r) In the note on St. Matth. xxviii. 16, to which the Reader is requested to refer.

ted by St. Matthew; and may be even said to fill the concluding chapter of his
spel. St. Luke, perhaps, because he will omit all notice of the appearance in
estion, is silent also as to the Angelic announcement of it. The women, (he
ys,) remembered the words of CHRIST,

9 and they returned from the Sepulchre,

Returned,—themselves "anointed with the oil of gladness above their fellows."(s)
And as they went to tell His Disciples, behold JESUS met them, saying, All hail.
nd they came and held Him by the feet, and worshipped Him. Then said JESUS
ato them, Be not afraid: go tell My brethren that they go into Galilee, and there
all they see Me."(t) Thus charged, the company of women repaired to the City,

and told all these things unto the Eleven, and to all the rest.

10 It was Mary Magdalene, and Joanna, and Mary, *the mother* of
James, and other *women that were* with them, which told these things
unto the Apostles.

These, then, are the women alluded to in ver. 1,—to which St. Mark adds
Salome.(u) It is striking indeed to find the name of Joanna, (the wife of Herod's
Steward,) recurring at such at a time. The circumstance recalls the last place where
we met with her name, and suggests that "Susanna" may have been another of
that company of holy women, whose names, by consent, the Evangelists pass over
here in silence. Consider St. Luke viii. 2, and xxiii. 55, in connection with the
present place; and see the note on xxiii. 8.

11 And their words seemed to them as idle tales, and they believed them not.

It will perhaps occur to some, that they considered not the miracle of the raising
of Lazarus, for their heart was hardened.(x) They had also clearly forgotten the
express predictions of CHRIST Himself on this great subject: not once or twice
made, but again and again. "From that time forth,"—(from that time, namely, of
St. Peter's Confession,)—"began JESUS to show unto His Disciples, how that He
must go unto Jerusalem, and suffer many things of the Elders, and Chief Priests,
and Scribes, and be killed, and be raised again the third day."(y) One week after,
He had charged them to tell of the Transfiguration "to no man, until the Son of
Man be risen again from the dead."(z) Then followed, in Galilee, that special prediction of His Betrayal, violent Death, and Resurrection,(a) to which we have heard
the Angels refer, above, in verses 6 and 7. "Behold, we go up to Jerusalem;"
(our SAVIOUR had said to the Twelve, when He was going up to the Capital for the
last time,) "and all things that are written by the prophets concerning the Son of
Man shall be accomplished."(b) For He "shall be delivered unto the Chief Priests,
and unto the Scribes; and they shall condemn Him to Death, and shall deliver Him
to the Gentiles: and they shall mock Him, and shall scourge Him, and shall spit
upon Him, and shall kill Him, and the third day He shall rise again."(c) After such
minuteness of description, (for it is more like a narrative of the past than a prophecy of the future,) it is strange indeed to find such utter unwillingness to believe
in the fulfilment of what the lips of CHRIST had spoken: but so it was, that "*they
understood none of these things:* and this saying was hid from them, neither understood they the things which were spoken."(d) Accordingly, we shall find that
when the two Disciples returned from their walk to Emmaus, and related to the
Apostles what had befallen them on the way,—"*neither believed they them.*"(e) Well
might our risen LORD upbraid the Eleven "with unbelief and hardness of heart,
because they believed not them which had seen Him after He was risen."(f)—Take
notice of what follows.

(s) Ps. xlv. 7.   (t) St. Matth. xxviii. 10.   (u) St. Mark xvi. 1.
(x) Alluding to the language of St. Mark vi. 52.   (y) St. Matth. xvi. 21.
(z) St. Matth. xvii. 9.   (a) St. Matth. xvii. 22, 23.
(b) St. Luke xviii. 31.   (c) St. Mark x. 33, 34.
(d) St. Luke xviii. 34. And observe that the same was said before; namely, St. Luke ix.
44, which is the parallel place with St. Matth. xvii. 22, 23, above quoted.
(e) St. Mark xvi. 13.
(f) St. Mark xvi. 14,—where the Reader is requested to read the note.

12 Then arose Peter, and ran unto the Sepulchre; and stooping down, he beheld the linen clothes laid by themselves, and departed, wondering in himself

Rather,—"departed home, wondering."

at that which was come to pass.

St. John had ran with St. Peter, and outstripped him,—both in respect of speed and of Faith. The Reader will do well to compare the present verse with the parallel place in St. John's Gospel.(*f*) Both Apostles, on reaching the Sepulchre, stooped and looked into it: both, in the end, entered, and beheld the spot where their LORD had lain,—observing the tokens of One who, having "laid Him down and slept, had awakened; for the LORD sustained Him."(*g*) It had been no hurried waking, either. His grave-clothes were found deposited by themselves: "and the napkin that was about His Head, not lying with the linen clothes, but wrapped together in a place by itself."(*h*) In one of the beholders, this sight is found to have produced Belief:(*i*) in the other, only Wonder.

13 And, behold, two of them went that same day to a village called Emmaus, which was from Jerusalem *about* three-score furlongs.

The name of one of these Disciples is found to have been Cleopas; and St. Luke himself is presumed to have been the other. The conjecture, (for it is no more than a conjecture,) is a reasonable one. It is found to be the manner of the Evangelists thus to relate something concerning themselves:(*k*) and the minuteness of detail with which St. Luke describes the present interview, favours the supposition that he was a witness of the transaction he describes.

14, 15, 16 And they talked together of all these things which had happened. And it came to pass, that, while they communed *together* and reasoned, JESUS himself drew near, and went with them. But their eyes were holden that they should not know Him.

St. Mark, with reference to this appearance of our risen LORD, says that "*He appeared in another form* unto two of them, as they walked, and went into the country."(*l*) As already remarked in another place,(*m*) a wonderful change seems to have passed over the appearance of our LORD, at His Resurrection. He was the same, yet another; whence neither Mary, in the garden,(*n*)—nor Cleopas and his companion, on the road to Emmaus,—nor the seven Disciples at the Lake, at once recognized Him. The language of the Evangelist, in the last-named case, is very remarkable.(*o*) St. Luke's manner of expressing the change alluded to, is singular and suggestive.

17, 18 And He said unto them, What manner of communications *are* these that ye have one to another, as ye walk, and are sad? And the one of them, whose name was Cleopas,

(Quite a distinct person, by the way, from the "Cleophas" mentioned in St. John xix. 25, and which ought to be written "Clopas.")—Cleopas,

answering, said unto Him, Art Thou only a stranger in Jerusalem, and hast not known the things which are come to pass there in these days?

Rather,—"Thou art the only sojourner in Jerusalem who knoweth not," &c

19 And He said unto them, What things?

(*f*) See St. John xx. 2 to 10.   (*g*) Ps. iii. 5.
(*h*) St. John xx. 7.   (*i*) St. John xx. 8.
(*k*) Consider St. Matth. ix. 9, 10, &c., and the note there. St. Mark xiv. 52, and the note
there. St. John in many places.
(*l*) St. Mark xvi. 12.   (*m*) See the note on St. Mark xvi. 12.
(*n*) St. John xx. 15.   (*o*) See St. John xxi. 4, 12, &c.

As, before, He asked them the subject of their conversation, not as needing to be formed, but in order to draw them into discourse which He might turn to their struction,—so now, He is found to make inquiry concerning Himself. See the tes on St. Mark v. 9, 30: ix. 21.

20, 21 And they said unto Him, Concerning JESUS of Nazareth, hich was a Prophet mighty in deed and word before GOD and all the sople : and how the Chief Priests, and our Rulers, delivered Him to s condemned to death, and have crucified Him. But we trusted that , had been He which should have redeemed Israel : and beside all his, to-day is the third day since these things were done.

These few words declare what had been the belief,—or rather, the "hope" and "expectation,"—of the Disciples of CHRIST, concerning Him. This was the hope which had sustained them to the last:(p) and the utter destruction of this hope it ms which had paralyzed their minds, and reduced them to the strange state of perplexity, and even despair, in which, at the dawning of the first Easter, we find them every one. Even on the Day of the Ascension, we hear them timidly inquiring,—"LORD, wilt Thou at this time restore again the kingdom to Israel?"(q) Cleopas proceeds:

22, 23, 24 Yea, and certain women also of our company made us astonished, which were early at the Sepulchre ; and when they found not His body, they came, saying, that they had also seen a vision of Angels, which said that He was alive. And certain of them which were with us went to the Sepulchre, and found it even so as the women had said : but Him they saw not.

In such terms do they describe the visit of the women, and of the Apostles St. Peter and St. John, to the Sepulchre.

25, 26 Then He said unto them, O fools, and slow of heart to believe all that the Prophets have spoken : ought not CHRIST to have suffered these things, and to enter into His Glory?

First, "Suffering,"—then, "Glory." "In like manner, the two passages of all the Old Testament which speak most fully of the Humiliation of CHRIST, (the 22d Psalm and the 53d of Isaiah,) both end with the announcement of His Glory. 'Therefore will I divide Him a portion with the great, and He shall divide the spoil with the strong.' 'The Kingdom is the LORD's, and He is the Governor among the people.'"(r) Take notice, further, that St. Peter declared himself to be "a witness of the *Sufferings* of CHRIST, and also a partaker of the *Glory* that shall be revealed."(s)

It has been pointed out on St. Luke xxiii. 35, (to which the Reader is requested to refer,) that however marvellous it may seem to ourselves, the Jewish people seem never to have realized the great truth here laid down by our SAVIOUR: namely,— that it had been predicted by their ancient prophets that He should be put to death, and that through the gate of suffering He should enter into Glory. The Psalms,— the Books of Isaiah and of Daniel,—are full of this; and the Jewish Doctors freely recognized the MESSIAH in all those writings; yet, such was their blindness, they overlooked the great doctrine of what should befall Him at His first Advent.

"Slow of heart," proved the very Disciples themselves to believe "all that the Prophets had spoken" concerning CHRIST. Even *they* were slow to recognize, in the one Person of their LORD, the fulfilment of the prophetic witness to a suffering MESSIAH. Of what paramount importance this was to the fixing of their belief, and that of the early Church, on a sure basis, has been pointed out in the note on St. Luke xxii. 37: to which the Reader is invited to refer. Behold, therefore, the risen LORD Himself pours into the wondering ears of the two Disciples a Divine Commentary on "Moses and all the Prophets." As it follows:—

(p) Consider St. Luke xix. 11.　　　　　　(q) Acts i. 6.
(r) Moberly.　　　　　　　　　　　　　　(s) 1 St. Peter v. 1.

27 And beginning at Moses and all the Prophets, He expounded unto them in all the Scriptures the things concerning Himself.

Rather,—"He thoroughly interpreted."

The walk to Emmaus was not certainly the most striking incident of the first Easter; yet, *who* has not felt that if he must name the one recorded event of that glorious Day at which he would desire to have been present, it must be *this?*—The appearance vouchsafed to Mary Magdalene, in the gray of the morning,—(the first of our LORD's recorded appearances!)(*t*)—when she "supposed him to be the gardener:"—the appearance to the Ten, as they sat at meat,—when, at CHRIST's bidding, with mingled terror, joy, and wonder, the men whose names we know so well, handled Him and saw that it was He indeed; and when, with calm words of Benediction, He conveyed to them that Peace which the world can neither give nor take away;(*u*)—almost any sight of the first Easter, it were bliss beyond all telling, to have beheld. Yet, to have walked with Him, although unknown, all the way to Emmaus; and to have heard Him, "beginning at Moses,(*x*) and all the Prophets, expound in all the Scriptures the things concerning Himself,"—*this,* surely, were the *most* blessed portion of all! Surely, our hearts burn within us, even at the thought of what it must have been, to have heard *Him* so open the Scriptures. The Angels must have come down to listen, and Nature herself grown attentive to the accents of her CREATOR and her GOD!

Take notice that St. Paul, following in the footsteps of his LORD, "expounded and testified the kingdom of GOD," before his unbelieving countrymen, at Rome, "persuading them concerning JESUS, both out of the Law of Moses, and out of the prophets, from morning till evening."(*y*)

28, 29 And they drew nigh unto the village, whither they went: and He made as though He would have gone further. But they constrained Him, saying, Abide with us: for it is toward evening, and the day is far spent. And He went in to tarry with them.

Consider on how many occasions besides the present, it is intimated that constraint is necessary on the part of those who would secure the abiding presence of CHRIST. "*Pass not away,* I pray Thee, from Thy servant,"(*z*) was the respectful language of the patriarch Abraham: and, "*I will not let Thee go,* except Thou bless me,"(*a*) was the earnest exclamation of the patriarch Jacob. "Depart not hence, I pray Thee, until I come unto Thee, and bring forth my present, and set it before Thee," said Gideon to the Angel. "And He said, I will tarry till thou come again."(*b*) "I pray Thee, *let us detain Thee,*"(*c*) was the entreaty of Manoah and his wife.

St. Andrew and St. John are thus found to have followed after the SAVIOUR, till they won from His lips the word of invitation:(*d*) while the Woman of Canaan even pursued the Holy One into the House whither He had retired.(*e*) On the Sea of Galilee, about the fourth watch of the night, the Disciples saw Him coming unto them, "walking upon the Sea: and *He would have passed by them,*"(*f*) had they not cried out, and by their entreaties persuaded Him to enter the ship in which they were. The like is found to have taken place during the walk to Emmaus. By all of which we are reminded, that as, without an effort, the blessing of CHRIST's presence may not be won, so neither, without a constraining effort, may it be retained in the soul.

30, 31 And it came to pass, as He sat at meat with them, He took bread, and blessed *it,* and brake, and gave to them.

And their eyes were opened, and they knew Him; and He vanished out of their sight.

(*t*) St. Mark xvi. 9.   (*u*) See below, verses 36 to 43; and St. John xx. 19 to 23.
(*x*) "Had ye believed Moses, ye would have believed Me:" (said our LORD,) "*for he wrote of Me.*" St. John v. 46.
(*y*) Acts xxviii. 23.   (*z*) Gen. xviii. 3.   (*a*) Gen. xxxii. 26.
(*b*) Judges vi. 18.   (*c*) Judges xiii. 15.   (*d*) St. John i. 37 to 39.
(*e*) St. Mark vii. 24.   (*f*) St. Mark vi. 48.

It is impossible to read this statement without a deep conviction that a mystery lies beneath it. Here was no mere recognition; as when the unsuspected presence of a friend is discovered by his well-known gesture. It was more than that. The act described, corresponds exactly with what we read concerning the institution of the Lord's Supper;(g) and "the breaking of the bread," (which is presently alluded to, as the special act of our Saviour on this occasion,)(h) is the very expression by which the Lord's Supper itself is twice indicated in the Acts.(i) Not that it is necessary to suppose that the Holy Eucharist was partaken of at Emmaus: but it seems to be implied that the blessing of Christ served to a sacramental purpose; and that, by means of the Bread which He gave to the Disciples, "their eyes were opened." "It enlighteneth with belief," says Hooker(k) of the Holy Eucharist; "it truly conformeth us unto the image of Jesus Christ." Now, to "be like Him," and to "see Him as He is," are one.(l)

Take notice that the two Disciples, at Emmaus, had not been "forgetful to entertain strangers;" whereby, they had "entertained Angels unawares."(m)

32 And they said one to another, Did not our heart burn within us, while He talked with us by the way, and while He opened unto us the Scriptures?

"We seem to be taught by this, that in reading the Scriptures there may be an affectionate warmth and wonder as He opens them to us,—a kindling of His own Divine Love in the soul of His Disciples, however imperfect,—while He shows therein His Cross and His sufferings; and, it may be, discloses something of the Glory that is to be revealed. While we walk and are sad, from this we may yet find comfort. Discourses also which fill the hearers with a sensible warmth and fervour, and kindle a fire in their souls, may be from God; for Christ has promised that His Holy Spirit shall speak by His Ministers. But such must consist in the unfolding of the Scriptures, and in the setting forth of Christ crucified, and the Power of His Resurrection. Let the middle, and the beginning, and the end, be the setting forth of Christ crucified, that the hearts of those that hear may burn. We know not how much in these things Christ is with us, in the stirring of the heart and affections, until He vanishes from us, and it is all past.

"But if He comes to be with us when we talk of Him, and while we walk with Him, yet are we hereby taught that it is *in the Breaking of Bread* He is to be known in His Church, unto the end."(n)

33, 34 And they rose up the same hour, and returned to Jerusalem, and found the Eleven gathered together, and them that were with them, saying, The Lord is risen indeed, and hath appeared to Simon.

Take notice, that nothing is here said of the appearance to Mary Magdalene, or to the company of women. The appearance to Simon Peter is singled out in a marked way by the whole body of Disciples; and the language used concerning it, is the language of men who believe the thing they state. It perhaps had been attended by some extraordinary circumstances. St. Paul gives it the foremost place in his enumeration of our Lord's appearance after His Resurrection. "He was seen of Cephas; then, of the Twelve; after that, He was seen of above five hundred brethren at once."(o)

35 And they told what things *were done* in the way, and how He was known of them in breaking of bread.

Yet, strange to say, their report did not win belief: as St. Mark has expressly recorded.(p)

36 And as they thus spake, Jesus Himself stood in the midst of them, and saith unto them, Peace be unto you.

(g) St. Luke xxii. 19.　　(h) See below, verse 35.　　(i) Acts ii. 42 and 46.
(k) Quoting Cyprian.　　(l) St. John iii. 2.　　(m) Heb. xiii. 2.　　(n) Williams.
(o) 1 Cor. xv. 5, 6.　Consider the note on St. Matth. xxviii. 16.　　(p) St. Mark xvi. 13.

"He 'stood in the midst of them,'—suddenly, and without a sound or step being heard, or any approach or passing by noticed; noiseless as a shadow, and sightless in His coming as a dream.   He is in the midst of them, with a suddenness and silence which marks all the comings of CHRIST.   Here then was the promise visibly fulfilled, 'where two or three are gathered together in My Name, there am I in the midst of them.'"(q)   And what words may declare the joy of the Disciples at this sight of their Divine Master, thus standing among them as of old; restored to them, in a manner past all understanding, at the moment when they longed for Him most, and regarded His return as altogether impossible?

Peace,—the last word of the prophecy of Zacharias;(r) the burden of the Angelic Hymn on the night of the Nativity;(s) the Salutation which our SAVIOUR had directed His Disciples to convey with them, wheresoever they published the Gospel of Peace;(t) the precious legacy which the same SAVIOUR, on the last evening of His mortal Life, bequeathed to His Apostles:(u) Peace,—is the first word which is heard from His lips when He is again risen from the dead.

37, 38, 39, 40 But they were terrified and affrighted, and supposed that they had seen a spirit.   And He said unto them, Why are ye troubled? and why do thoughts arise in your hearts?   Behold My Hands and My feet, that it is I Myself: handle Me, and see; for a spirit hath not flesh and bones, as ye see Me have.

And when He had thus spoken, He showed them *His* hands and *His* feet.

The Reader is requested to refer to some remarks in the Commentary on St. John xx. 20.

41, 42, 43 And while they yet believed not for joy, and wondered, He said unto them, Have ye here any meat?   And they gave Him a piece of broiled fish, and of an honeycomb.   And He took *it*, and did eat before them.

Thus showing them the reality of His Body.

How is it possible here to avoid hanging upon every word with interest and wonder?   This then was the fare of the Apostles,—"broiled fish," and "honey-comb."   May there not be a meaning, also, in the food thus particularly mentioned, and partaken of on so great an occasion?

44 And He said unto them, These *are* the words which I spake unto you, while I was yet with you, that all things must be fulfilled, which were written in the Law of Moses, and *in* the Prophets, and *in* the Psalms, concerning Me.

For not only "the whole Book," but "every folding, every leaf, of this Book," is full of Him. "Thou shalt not find a Story," (says Hammond,) "a Riddle, a Prophecy, a Ceremony, a downright Legal Constitution, but hath some manner of aspect on this glass, someway drives at this mystery, 'GOD manifest in the flesh.' For example, (perhaps you have noted,) whenever you read Seth's genealogies more insisted on than Cain's, Shem's than his elder brother Ham's, Abraham's than the whole Word besides, Jacob's than Esau's, Judah's than the whole Twelve Patriarchs'; and the like passages which directly drive down the line of CHRIST, and make that the whole business of Scripture: whenever, I say, you read of any of these, then are you to note that Shiloh was to come; that He which was sent, was on His journey; that from the Creation, to the fulness of time, the Scripture was in travail with *Him*."

45 Then opened He their understanding, that they might understand the Scriptures,

(q) Williams, quoting St. Matth. xviii. 20.   (r) St. Luke i. 79.
(s) St. Luke ii. 14.   (t) St. Luke x. 5.   (u) St. John xiv. 27.

Words soon read, but involving how important a doctrine, and suggesting how many heart-stirring thoughts! "Open Thou mine eyes, that I may see the wondrous things of Thy Law,"(x) was the prayer of the devout Psalmist. The gift which he coveted, was now imparted to the Disciples of CHRIST; and by the hands of CHRIST Himself.

Consider how glorious must have been the result, when these words were spoken by Him who said, "in the beginning," "Let there be Light, and there was Light." He had already, in the case of Cleopas and his companion, "expounded in all the Scriptures," (" beginning at Moses and all the Prophets,") "the things concerning Himself."(y) But now, He caused all those dark writings to become clear to the mental eye; enabling the Disciples, by a mere act of intuition, to "*understand* the Scriptures:" not so much (be sure!) to understand the hard points in Chronology, Geography, Physical Science, Natural History, and the like, which abound in Holy Writ; as to see which portions of Sacred Story are allegorical;(z) which persons,(a) transactions,(b) and things,(c) are typical; how far typical,—and of what;—what hidden teaching lies concealed under the several enactments of the Law;(d)—what is the true reference of the several Prophecies of the Old Testament;(e)—lastly, what unsuspected mysteries and meanings lie beneath the surface of the latter, in every Work of the SPIRIT.(f)

With most convincing power must men so enlightened, so unerringly instructed in the mysteries of CHRIST's Kingdom, have proceeded to spread the knowledge of the Faith. There was once a time (we know it for certain) when certain great and curious secrets were in the keeping of the Church.(g) These, indeed, have since passed into oblivion. Yet must *the result* of such divine illumination have been permanent. The general consent of Antiquity on certain great subjects,—as the reference of our LORD's Discourse with Nicodemus to Water Baptism,—must be regarded as quite conclusive as to the mind of the SPIRIT on those subjects; and the style and method of the ancient expositors, generally, must be held to be in strict conformity with the Truth. To proceed, however. Our SAVIOUR "opened the understanding" of the Disciples:

46, 47 and said unto them, Thus it is written, and thus it behooved CHRIST to suffer, and to rise from the dead the Third Day: and that Repentance and Remission of Sins should be preached in His name among all nations, beginning at Jerusalem.

"Go ye therefore, and *teach all nations*,"—is the language of our LORD's Charge, as recorded by St. Matthew.(h) "For, from the rising of the sun to the going down of the same, My Name shall be great among the Gentiles, . . . saith the LORD."(i) The prophet Micah, in like manner, speaking of the last days, declares that "many nations shall say, Come, and let us go up to the Mountain of the LORD, and to the House of the GOD of Jacob: and He will teach us of His ways, and we will walk in His paths: for *the Law will go forth of Sion, and the Word of the LORD from Jerusalem*."(k)

48 And ye are witnesses of these things.

Take notice how distinctly the office of "witnesses" was assigned to the Apostles by their LORD; here, in St. John xv. 27, and in Acts i. 8. Accordingly, it is recognised by them on many occasions:—at the election of Matthias into the Apostolic body;(l) in St. Peter's speech, on the Day of Pentecost;(m) after the healing of the

(x) Ps. cxix. 18.　　　　　(y) See above, ver. 27.

(z) As, the History of Hagar. See Gal. iv. 21 to 31.

(a) As, Melchizedek. See Heb. vii. 1 to 17.

(b) As, the Crossing of the Red Sea. See 1 Cor. x. 1 to 6.

(c) As, the Veil of the Temple. See Heb. x. 20.

(d) As, the High-Priest's entering the Holy of Holies: see Heb. ix. 7, 8. Also, the prohibition (in Deut. xxv. 4) to muzzle the ox which treadeth out the corn: see 1 Cor. ix. 9 to 11.

(e) Consider how St. Peter expounds Ps. xvi. 8 to 11, in Acts ii. 29 to 31. Consider also St. Matth. ii. 15, 18, 23,—with the notes on each place.

(f) Consider the inference which our LORD draws from Exod. iii. 6, in St. Mark xii. 26, 27,—where see the notes: and how St. Matthew (viii. 17) explains Isa. liii. 4: and how St. Paul comments on the viii. Psalm in Heb. ii. 5 to 9. Consider also Gal. iii. 16.

(g) See 2 Thess. ii. 6.　　　　(h) St. Matth. xxviii. 19.　　　　(i) Mal. i. 11.

(k) Micah iv. 2.　　　　(l) Acts i. 22.　　　　(m) Acts ii. 32.

lame man by St. Peter and St. John;(n) before the Council ;(o) before Cornelius and his company:(p) and in St. Paul's Sermon at Antioch.(q) Consider also 1 St. Peter v. 1, and 2 St. Peter i. 16.

Hitherto we have been occupied by the History of the first Easter,—the events of a single Sunday: but the five verses which come next, give the history of our LORD's Ascension into Heaven; and therefore a long interval,—the space of Forty Days, in fact,—is interposed between what precedes and what follows.

The place from which our LORD led the Eleven Apostles "out as far as Bethany," was certainly the City of Jerusalem,—the scene of the preceding verses. He had indeed, in the mean time, manifested Himself to His Disciples on the Mountain in Galilee, and again by the Lake;(r) but they had now, once more, returned to Jerusalem. "And, being assembled together with them." (as St. Luke says in another place; where, by the way, the words should rather be translated, as in the margin, "eating together with them.") He "commanded them that they should not depart from Jerusalem; but wait for the promise of the Father, which, (saith He,) ye have heard of Me. For John truly baptized with Water; but ye shall be baptized with the HOLY GHOST, not many days hence."(s) All this is here expressed more briefly, as follows:

49 And, behold, I send the promise of My FATHER upon you: but tarry ye in the city of Jerusalem, until ye be endued with power from on High.

Which is said with obvious allusion to the great outpouring of the SPIRIT on the Day of Pentecost, which was to follow in ten days from the date of the Ascension; and for which the Apostles were to wait, (literally, to "sit" still,) in Jerusalem.

"Behold, I send." And so, in St. John's Gospel,—"The COMFORTER, whom I will send unto you from the FATHER." "If I depart, I will send Him unto you."(t) By which texts it is shown that the HOLY GHOST "proceedeth from the FATHER and the SON."(u)—The outpouring of the SPIRIT, thus alluded to, was "the promise" of the FATHER, (as it is called here, and in Acts i. 4;) for the gift had been promised in ancient days by the mouth of His holy Prophets.(x)

50 And He led them out as far as to Bethany,

From Jerusalem, then, (as explained above, in the note preceding verse 49,) He led them forth along the well-known road to Bethany; that road which, rather more than forty days before, they had seen Him daily tread, in much affliction ;(y) and thus He guided them to the summit of the Mount of Olives,—which, in common with the entire district in which it stands, was known by the name of "Bethany." "Spots consecrated by the recollection of a thousand sayings and incidents which were full of peculiar interest to them; and many of which, the events that had since occurred had now unfolded and explained ; but oh, with feelings and thoughts how different from those with which they had visited them before !"(z)

There He delivered to His Apostles His parting Charge,—as related in the concluding verses of the first two Gospels.(a) Those solemn words ended, "He lifted up His hands," bearing the marks of the wounds which He had received for them; and bestowed upon them His prevailing blessing,—as St. Luke alone records:

and He lifted up His hands, and blessed them.

The Law, therefore, began and ended with a Curse:(b) but the Gospel ends, as it began, with a Blessing.(c) And take notice that it was while our SAVIOUR was in the very act of blessing His Apostles,—His hands yet lifted up in Benediction, yet extended over them in Love unspeakable,—that He commenced His majestic ascent. As it follows:

(n) Acts iii. 15, and iv. 20, 33.   (o) Acts v. 32.   (p) Acts x. 39.   (q) Acts xiii. 21.
(r) See St. Matth. xxviii. 6, &c., and St. John xxi. 1, &c.   (s) Acts i. 4, 5.
(t) St. John xv. 26: xvi. 7.   (u) See also St. John xvi. 14, 15.
(x) See Isaiah xliv. 3, Joel ii. 28, &c.   (y) See St. Luke xxi. 37.   (z) Williams.
(a) See St. Matth. xxviii. 18 to 20, and St. Mark xvi. 15 to 19,—where the Reader is requested to see the notes.
(b) Gen. iii. 14 to 19, and Mal. iv. 6.   (c) St. Matth. v. 3 to 11, and the present place.

51 And it came to pass, while He blessed them, He was parted from them, and carried up into Heaven.

Beautiful words! denoting rather that He was *taken away* from the men He loved, than that, by an act of His own, He *left* them. For His Passion, it is said it He was impatient:(d) for His Ascension, not so. He did not *leave* His Apostles, but "*was parted* from them."

In the Commentary on St. Mark's Gospel, several remarks of a doctrinal character will be found on the subject of the Ascension,—to which the Reader is invited refer.(e)

He "sat on the Right Hand of GOD,"—as St. Mark is careful in this place to add.(f) But St. Luke's supplementary record, in the Acts, is especially worthy of remembrance here. After rehearsing a part of our LORD'S Charge and Commission, where else recorded,(g) the blessed writer adds,—"And when He had spoken these things, *while they beheld*, He was taken up; and a cloud received Him out of their sight." A chariot-cloud,—which was doubtless a host of ministering Angels: for "the chariots of GOD are twenty thousand, even thousands of Angels; and the LORD is among them, as in the holy place of Sinai."(h) "Lift up your heads, O ye gates," is their song; "and be ye lift up, ye everlasting doors, and the King of Glory shall come in."(i)

"And while they looked steadfastly towards Heaven, as He went up, behold, two Men stood by them in white apparel; which also said, Ye men of Galilee, why stand ye here gazing up into Heaven? This same JESUS, which is taken up from you into Heaven, shall so come in like manner as ye have seen Him go into Heaven." That is,—As ye have seen Him in a cloud depart, so "in clouds"(k) shall ye behold Him return. "And His feet shall stand in that Day upon the Mount of Olives, which is before Jerusalem on the East."(l)

"Then returned they unto Jerusalem from the Mount called Olivet, which is from Jerusalem a Sabbath-day's journey."(m) The record of the same Evangelist, in his Gospel, is much briefer: namely,—

52, 53 And they worshipped Him, and returned to Jerusalem with great joy: and were continually in the Temple, praising and blessing GOD. Amen.

They had been sorrowful, but their sorrow hath been turned into joy. CHRIST hath seen them again, according to His true promise: wherefore their heart rejoiceth; and now, their joy no man taketh from them.(n) They repair to the Temple; and lo, the Temple-Service becomes henceforth filled with new meanings. "The Song of Moses has become to them the Song of the LAMB." To them the Psalms speak henceforth another language, for they speak to them only of CHRIST.

Well may the Apostles have been henceforth "continually in the Temple, praising and blessing GOD!"

THE PRAYER.

ALMIGHTY GOD, who through Thine Only-begotten SON JESUS CHRIST hast overcome Death, and opened unto us the gate of everlasting Life; we humbly beseech Thee, that, as by Thy special Grace preventing us, Thou dost put into our minds good desires, so by Thy continual help we may bring the same to good effect; through JESUS CHRIST our LORD, who liveth and reigneth with Thee and the HOLY GHOST, ever one GOD, world without end. Amen.

(d) St. Mark x. 32, St. Luke xii. 50.
(e) See the note on St. Mark xvi. 19.
(g) Acts i. 6 to 8.   (h) Psalm lxviii. 17.
(k) See the note on St. Matthew xxiv. 30,—the latter part of the verse.
(l) Zech. xiv. 4.   (m) Acts i. 9 to 12.

(f) St. Mark xvi. 19.
(i) Psalm xxiv. 7.

(n) St. John xvi. 20, 22.

A PLAIN COMMENTARY

ON

HE FOUR HOLY GOSPELS.

ST. JOHN.

CHAPTER I.

h Divinity, Humanity, and office of JESUS CHRIST. 15 *The testimony of John.*
39 *The calling of Andrew, Peter, &c.*

t. JOHN wrote his Gospel long after the other three Evangelists; at a time, when
"*y deceivers*" *had "entered into the world, who confessed not that* JESUS CHRIST
come in the flesh."(a) Now, "every Spirit that confesseth not that JESUS CHRIST
was in the flesh, is not of GOD."(b) "This," (as the beloved Disciple states
badly,) "is the Spirit of Antichrist."(c) Accordingly, it was the object of the
ad writer to check the growing Heresy. "These [signs] are written," as he
was, at the end of chap. xx., (speaking of his own Gospel,) "that ye might be-
that JESUS is the CHRIST, the SON of GOD; and that, believing, ye might have
through His name."
's are prepared, after these statements, for the very express declaration con-
ing the Divinity and Humanity of CHRIST, with which the present Gospel
mences.

IN the beginning was the WORD,

In the beginning,"—to remind us of the first words of Genesis (i. 1.) See the
on St. Matthew i. 1.
.Matthew and St. Luke supply the human genealogy of CHRIST; and the for-
Evangelist begins his Gospel with it. But the Disciple whom JESUS loved, soars
r higher; and discourses at once of his LORD and ours, as "without descent,—
g neither beginning of days, nor end of life:"(d) as "*the Root*" as well as
offspring of David;"(e) the WORD, who *was* "in the Beginning;" and "*was*
" "Who shall declare *His* generation?"(f)
' this less usual name also, ("the WORD,") St. John draws away our thoughts
the Human to the Divine Nature of our Redeemer. And yet it was no new
notion, but one perfectly well recognized at the time.
e reason of the Name may be perceived by many considerations. It is designed
ich us that the SON was "with the FATHER," somewhat as a word dwells in the
L It is the utterance of the mind; and the SON is the utterance (so to speak)
e FATHER. Begotten from all Eternity, He yet abstracted nothing from the
un; whose very Image and Representation He yet was and is. And the name
is especially designed to preclude many of the thoughts which the mention of
ship is sure to awaken,—and which cannot attach to a Being "without Body,

(a) 2 St. John ver. 7.
(c) 1 St. John iv. 3; ii. 22; 2 St. John ver. 7.
(e) Revelation xxii. 16.

(b) 1 St. John iv. 3.
(d) Hebrews vii. 3.
(f) Isaiah liii. 8.

627

parts, or passions." Then, further, CHRIST was fitly called "the WORD" because He came upon Earth "to declare" the FATHER (i. 18:) whom He revealed to ever creature, somewhat as words reveal the heart and mind of man. "All things," H said, "that I have heard of MY FATHER, I have made known unto you." (xv. 15.) Accordingly, it is stated in the Epistle to the Hebrews, GOD "hath in these last days *spoken* unto us by His SON." (i. 2.) See more, in the note on ver. 18.

Lastly, it may be observed that a *word* becomes known, by clothing itself with *sound.* Expressed in writing, it becomes visible also. And somewhat thus it was that the Eternal WORD, by assuming flesh, manifested Himself to the World: and was beheld, not only by human eyes, but, as the Apostle remarks, was "*seen of Angels.*"(g)

and the WORD was with GOD, and the WORD was GOD.

The SON was "*in the Beginning:*" so that there never was a time when He was not. But lest any one should suppose from this, that the WORD was Unbegotten, the Evangelist adds immediately,—"And the WORD was with GOD." To the same effect does the Second Person in the Blessed Trinity discourse concerning Himself, in the Book of Proverbs:—"The LORD possessed Me in the beginning of His way, before His works of old. I was set up from Everlasting, from the beginning, or ever the Earth was. When there were no depths, ... before the mountains were settled, ... while as yet He had not made the Earth." (viii. 22–26.) So that there is one Person of the FATHER, and another Person of the SON. This was He whom the same St. John beheld by Revelation "clothed with a vesture dipped in blood: and His Name" was still "called the WORD of GOD."(h)

2 The same was in the beginning with GOD.

"With" Him,—yet so as to be *one* with Him: for, as it is said,—"I and My FATHER are one." (x. 30.) "He that hath seen Me, hath seen the FATHER." "I am in the FATHER, and the FATHER in Me." (xiv. 9, 10.)

The words of the text are more precise (if possible) than those which went before. They preclude the notion that the FATHER was in any way prior, in time, to the SON. WISDOM, that is, CHRIST, (compare 1 Corinthians i. 24,) says in the Book of Proverbs,—"When He prepared the Heavens, I was there: when He set a compass on the face of the depth: when He established the clouds above, ... when He gave to the Sea His decree; . . . . . then I was by Him, as one brought up with Him: and I was daily His delight, rejoicing always before Him." (viii. 27 to 30.)

3 All things were made by Him; and without Him was not any thing made that was made.

We are carried back to the very beginning of Time,—to that period which is spoken of in Genesis i. 1, and which long preceded Genesis i. 2. What, then, is here declared concerning the birthday of Creation? Even, that when GOD the FATHER, "in the beginning," "created the Heaven and the Earth,"—GOD the Son was "with" Him: "by whom also He made the worlds."(i) The Evangelist lays down this great truth first positively, and then negatively; for it is one of those mighty verities which may admit of no doubt or question. We proclaim in the Nicene Creed,—"By Whom all things were made," meaning CHRIST: and our warrant for it is the plain and repeated statement of Scripture. "There is but one GOD, the FATHER, *of* whom are all things, ... and one LORD JESUS CHRIST, *by* whom are all things."(j) But the most sublime passage of all, perhaps, is found in Colossians i. 16, 17; where it is said,—"For by Him were all things created, that are in Heaven, and that are in Earth, visible and invisible, whether they be Thrones, or Dominions, or Principalities, or Powers; all things were created by Him and for Him: and He is before all things, and by Him all things consist." . . . . . So also Ephesians iii. 9, Hebrews xi. 3, 2 St. Peter iii. 5. Also Psalm cii. 25, compared with Hebrews i. 8, 10.

It is asked in the Book of Proverbs, concerning the Author of Creation,—"What is His Name, and what is His SON's Name, if thou canst tell?" (xxx. 4.) And, i the same Book, as here, GOD's work in Creation is ascribed to the SON:—"The Lor

(g) 1 Tim. iii. 16.　(h) Revelation xix. 13.　(i) Hebrews i. 2.　(j) 1 Corinthians viii. 6.

by WISDOM hath founded the Earth." (iii. 19.) Now, Wisdom, as already explained, is one of the names of CHRIST.

4 In Him was Life; and the Life was the Light of Men.

We still linger on the threshold of Creation. "In Him was Life." "In Him,"— as in a Fountain! "For as the FATHER hath Life in Himself; so hath He given to the SON to have Life in Himself."(k) Moreover, the Life which was in Him "was the Light of Men." All the Light which our Spirits are conscious of, and whereby alone they may be said to live,—is from *Him!*.

5 And the Light shineth in Darkness; and the Darkness comprehended It not.

Our nature, since Adam's Fall, had become as it were "without form and void, and darkness was upon the face" of it. And it is said,—"the Light of men" shone athwart that darkness: but "the darkness comprehended It not." The Evangelist is hinting at the New Creation.

Compare this repeated mention of *Light* (ver. 4, 5, 7, 8, 9) with what is said in Genesis i. 3, 4, 5; and take notice how the first page of the New Testament again recalls the first page of the Old.

But observe that in ver. 9, as if with a special reference to that earlier Revelation, CHRIST is called "*the true* Light:" just as He is elsewhere called "the *true* Bread," (vi. 32,) and "the *true* Vine." (xv. 1.) All others, therefore, were but "*the figures* of the true:"(l) that is, they were but types, emblems, figures, of *Him* who created them;—who, emphatically, is *the Truth;*—and for whose sake alone, "they are, and were created."

6 There was a man sent from GOD, whose name *was* John.

The Evangelist speaks generally of the office of St. John Baptist,—concerning whom he will speak more particularly by and by. He was "sent from GOD:" whence, speaking by the mouth of His prophet, GOD says,—"Behold, *I send My Messenger!*"(m)

7 The same came for a witness, to bear witness of the Light, that all *men* through him might believe.

8 He was not that Light, but *was sent* to bear witness of that Light.

See note on verse 23.

The Baptist bore witness to the glorious Luminary which had arisen on the world, by the rays which it threw upon himself. In like manner the sunlight on the mountain informs men that the Sun has risen, though they do not yet behold the Sun's orb.

9 *That* was the true Light, which lighteth every man that cometh into the World.

In so marked and emphatic a manner is the appellation of LIGHT bestowed upon our LORD at the outset of St. John's Gospel. That Name He often took to Himself,—as in viii. 12: ix. 5: xii. 46: and it is full of high and holy teaching. The creature is evidently meant to instruct us concerning the Creator. Here, the mention of Light seems to carry our thoughts back to "the beginning." (See note on verse 5.) It suggests, moreover, that the SON came from the FATHER,—being "the Brightness of His glory, and the express Image of His Person,"(n)—somewhat as Light comes from Light ("Light of Light," as it is said in the Creed.) Now, it is the nature of Light so derived, to be co-existent, co-substantial, co-equal. Whence our LORD could say, "he that seeth Me, seeth Him that sent Me." (xii. 45.)

10 He was in the World, and the World was made by Him, and the World knew Him not.

"The World" here denotes particularly the Gentiles; and the reference is especially to the time of the Old Dispensation. St. John reminds us that CHRIST was

---

(k) St. John v. 26.   (l) Heb. ix. 24.   (m) Malachi iii. 1.   (n) Heb. i. 3.

the Author of Creation: and bids us notice the marvellous fact that, though B was ever in the World, (which was the work of His Almighty Hands,)—upholdin and sustaining it,—yet that the World did not know Him.

11 He came unto His own,

"His own,"—or "His own home," (as the same word is translated in xix. 27,) denotes the House of Israel; to which our LORD Himself declared that He was a pecially sent.(o) The World might, of course, be equally called "His own,". since, by right of Creation, all things are equally His. Yet had the Jewish peop been, from the beginning, GOD's "peculiar treasure:"(p) "a special people un Himself, above all people that are upon the face of the earth."(q) "The seed Abraham, [His] friend;"(r) "whose were the Fathers; and of whom, as concer ing the flesh, CHRIST came."(s) To them "pertained the Adoption;"—as it is sa in Exodus iv. 22,—"Israel is My Son, even My First-born." And again, "I w be a Father unto you, and ye shall be my sons and daughters, saith the LORD A mighty."(t) Well, therefore, when He was "made flesh," might the Only-Begoth of the FATHER be said to have come to "His own!"

It is written in the Song of Moses,—"When the Most High divided to the N tions their inheritance, when He separated the sons of Adam, . . . the LORD's pe tion [was] His people, Jacob [was] the lot of His inheritance."(u) Well, the fore, when He was born in Bethlehem of Judea, might our SAVIOUR be said to ha come to "His own home!"

and His own received Him not.

Observe what is here said. The World "did not know:" "His own" "did m receive Him." The "foolish heart" of the first had been "darkened," becau "they did not like to retain GOD in their knowledge."(v) They, therefore, did n know GOD. But the Jews,—"to whom pertained the Adoption, and the Glory, an the Covenants, and the giving of the Law, and the service of GOD, and the Pr mises"(x)—of them it could not be so properly said that they did not "know," s that they did not "receive," the SAVIOUR. The first had ignorance to plead for n knowing Him: for not receiving Him, the second were without excuse. Whence i came to pass that He proved a Light to lighten the Gentiles,(y) when by repentan and faith they turned to Him: whereas, of the Jewish nation, it is at last declar that, in consequence of their hard and impenitent hearts, JESUS "did hide Himsel from them."(z) "For judgment," said our Blessed LORD, "I am come into thi world, that they which see not might see; and that they which see might be mad blind." (ix. 39.)

12 But as many as received Him, to them gave He power to becom the Sons of GOD,

For though the Jews, as a nation, rejected the Messiah, yet many among th people "received Him." See, for instance, St. John ii. 23: vii. 31: viii. 30, 31 ix. 16: x. 42: xi. 45, 48: xii. 11 and 42. To these, in reward of their Faith, (a it is here said,) was given the privilege of becoming "the Sons of GOD;" concer ing which wondrous title, see 1 St. John iii. 1, 2.—CHRIST does not compel ob dience. He does but invite it.

Nor does He make men "the sons of GOD:" He does but give them "power t become" so. Implying thereby that we, being regenerate, (in Holy Baptism,) ar made GOD's children by Adoption and Grace, (by the same Blessed Ordinance,) need daily to be renewed by GOD's Holy Spirit.(a)

even to them that believe on His Name:

For, as St. John in another place declares,(b) "Whosoever believeth that JES is the CHRIST, is born of GOD."

(o) St. Matth. xv. 24.
(p) Exod. xix. 5. Psalm cxxxv. 4, and see the margin of Malachi iii. 17.
(q) Deut. vii. 6, and xiv. 2.   (r) Isaiah xli. 8.   (s) Romans ix. 5.
(t) 2 Cor. vi. 18.   (u) Deut. xxxii. 8, 9.   (v) Romans i. 28.
(x) Rom. ix. 4.   (y) Isaiah xlii. 6: xlix. 6. St. Luke ii. 32.
(s) St. John xii. 36.   (a) Collect for Christmas-Day.   (b) 1 St. John v. 1.

13 which were born, not of blood, nor of the will of the flesh, nor
of the will of Man, but of GOD.

He speaks of our Regeneration, or new Birth in CHRIST,—and contrasts it with
our natural Birth. More is said of this great mystery, in ch. iii. verses 3 to 8:
where our SAVIOUR declares that "except a man be *born of Water and of the Spirit,*
he cannot enter into the Kingdom of GOD." This explains what the Beloved Disciple only hints at in this place. See note on iii. 5.

The Only-Begotten SON of GOD, being by nature of one substance with the FA-
THER, for us men and for our Salvation, came down from Heaven and was made
Man. Baptized into Him, we become "members of His body,—of His flesh, and
of His bones."(c) We are made "partakers of the Divine Nature."(d) "The
SPIRIT itself beareth witness with our Spirit, that we are the children of GOD."(e)
Whence, in amazing condescension, GOD describes the SON as "the first-born among
many Brethren:"(f) and He Himself, (as the Apostle speaks,) "is not ashamed to
call [us] brethren."(g)

In order that Men might be born of GOD, GOD was first born of Man. Whence,
it follows—

14 And the WORD was made flesh,

That is, "*Man,*" as in Psalm cxlv. 21: Joel ii. 28: Galatians ii. 16. Now, Man
consists of Body and Soul;—so that besides human flesh, our SAVIOUR CHRIST had
a human soul also.

It is not here said that "He came to,"—or was "joined with,"—but that He was
"*made*" Man: for the WORD *came* to men often,(h) but He was *made* man only
once: and He might have been joined to man without becoming a partaker of man's
Nature. But because He was made "very man," language which can be applied
properly to man alone, is applied to Him,—as, that He wept(i)—hungered,(k)—
thirsted;(l) marvelled,(m) was grieved;(n)—wearied,(o)—and made angry.(p) It
was because He had His own body, that He was able to *bear* our sicknesses:(q)
because He had His own soul, that He was able to carry our sorrows.(r)

Lest any should be so weak, or so wicked, as to pretend that the Word, by being
"*made flesh,*" parted with the Divine Nature, or underwent any change whatsoever,
the Apostle proceeds,—

and dwelt among us.

"The fulness of the Godhead, bodily," was therefore there.(s)

"Dwelt among us" may seem only to imply that CHRIST made His dwelling with
the sons of men: but something infinitely loftier than that is meant. "Tabernacled
in us," (for so the words in strictness should be translated,) teaches that the Eternal
Son not only put on a Tabernacle of Flesh, as St. Peter and St. Paul speak,—but
that He took up His abode in that common Human Nature which belongs to all
our race: whence it is declared that He dwelt "*in us.*" As HOOKER excellently
says,—"It pleased not the WORD or WISDOM of GOD to take to Itself some one person amongst men; for then should that one have been advanced which was assumed,
and no more. But WISDOM, to the end She might save many, built Her House of
that Nature which is common unto all,—She made not *this or that man* Her habitation, but dwelt *in us.*" By thus becoming a partaker of our fallen Humanity,
CHRIST became the Restorer of it likewise: for from Him is thereby derived to every
other son of Adam those divine graces which are inherent in Himself. And this is
why He is called "the new man,"—"the second Adam,"—and "the beginning of
the Creation of GOD."(t) This supplies the reason of that contrast—"for as in Adam
all die, even so in CHRIST shall all be made alive."(u) Hence, also, it is said—"If
any man be in CHRIST, he is a new creature."(v)

(c) Eph. v. 30.   (d) 2 St. Peter i. 4.   (e) Rom. viii. 16.
(f) Romans viii. 29.   (g) Heb. ii. 11.
(h) Jeremiah i. 2, Hosea i. 2, &c.   (i) St. John xi. 35, St. Luke xix. 41, and Hebrews v. 7.
(k) St. Matth. iv. 2, and xxi. 18.   (l) St. John iv. 7, and xix. 28.
(m) St. Matth. viii. 10.   (n) St. Mark iii. 5.   (o) St. John iv. 6.
(p) St. Mark iii. 5.   (q) St. Matth. viii. 17.   (r) Isaiah liii. 4.   (s) Colossians ii. 9.
(t) Rev. iii. 14.   (u) 1 Corinthians xv. 22.   (v) 2 Corinthians v. 17.

Observe, further, that there is an allusion here to the manner in which CHRI anciently "dwelt" among His chosen people. His "Glory filled the Tabernacle;"(and *that* Glory (or "Shekinah") was the token of His special presence.(*x*) But t Tabernacle, or Temple, (by which latter name the Tabernacle is sometimes called,)(was a type of that Human Body in which our SAVIOUR's glorious Godhead was shrined.(*z*) When, therefore, the Evangelist says that the LORD "tabernacled us," by employing a Greek term which closely resembles the Hebrew word "She nah," he is evidently recalling, and reverting to, the past history of the Jew. Tabernacle and Temple ; and implying the actual fulfilment of what Haggai h predicted,—namely, that the "Desire of all nations," when He came, would so the Temple with Glory, that "the Glory of this latter House shall be greater th of the former."(*a*) And this may help to show the meaning of the exclamati which follows,—

(and we beheld His Glory, the Glory as of the Only-Begotten of t FATHER,) full of Grace and Truth.

Our LORD "manifested forth His Glory," to be sure, when He wrought His racles,—as at Cana, concerning which, see St. John ii. 11 ; and at the raising Lazarus, concerning which, see St. John xi. 4, 40. But the Evangelist, in this pla alludes to a sight which was witnessed by only two others besides himself. He fers to the Transfiguration of our LORD:—having been one of the "eye-witnesses His Majesty," and "with Him in the Holy Mount," as St. Peter speaks. See St. Peter i. 16 to 18.

15 John bare witness of Him, and cried, saying, This was He whom I spake, He that cometh after me is preferred before me; for I was before me.

The history does not begin yet. The Evangelist is but anticipating here the wi ness of the Baptist recorded in ver. 30.
He says that John "cried," because John was "the voice of one *crying* in th wilderness,"—ver. 23.

16 And of His Fulness have all we received, and Grace for Grace.

These are the words of the Evangelist; whereby he contrasts the supplies o grace under the Law and the Gospel respectively,—the one almost a type or shad of the other. "Grace for Grace,"—the New in place of the Old.

17 For the Law was given by Moses, *but* Grace and Truth came by JESUS CHRIST.

"Grace and Truth,"—as at the end of ver. 14. This contrast of the Law an the Gospel supplies the best comment on the conclusion of the former verse.

18 No man hath seen GOD at any time; the Only-Begotten Son which is in the bosom of the FATHER, He hath declared *Him*.

With one more solemn saying, the Evangelist concludes his introduction. Th none ever saw GOD, is clearly laid down in the Old Testament,(*b*) as well as in t New.(*c*) And yet, it is sometimes recorded of men in Scripture, that they "sa GOD face to face,"(*d*)—"saw the GOD of Israel,"(*e*)—"saw the LORD,"(*f*)—and t like. The meaning of those marvellous and mysterious sayings is here explained
It was the Second Person in the Blessed Trinity who thus revealed Himself. "declare the FATHER, had been the blessed office of the SON, from the beginnin It was He, who, in the person of a created Angel, so often spoke to the Fathers the Old Testament; as, to Abraham ;(*g*) to Jacob ;(*h*) to Moses ;(*i*) to the chiefs

(*v*) Exodus xl. 34; Numbers xiv. 10.
(*x*) Isaiah vi. 4, compared with 1 Kings viii. 10, 11, and Revelation xv. 8.
(*y*) 1 Sam. i. 9, and iii. 3.   (*z*) St. John ii. 19 to 21, and 1 Cor. iii. 16.   (*o*) Haggai ii. 7.
(*b*) Exodus xxxiii. 20.   (*c*) St. John v. 37: vi. 46.   1 Tim. vi. 16.   1 St. John iv. 12
(*d*) Gen. xxxii. 30.   (*e*) Exod. xxiii. 10.   (*f*) Isaiah vi. 1.   (*g*) Genesis xviii. 2–3
(*h*) xxxii. 24–30.   (*i*) Ex. iii. 2–6.

ael ;(*j*) to Gideon ;(*k*) to Manoah and his wife ;(*l*) to Isaiah, (*m*) and the rest ;—a elude, as it were, to His future Incarnation.
The Historical part of St. John's Gospel now begins.

19, 20 And this is the record of John, when the Jews sent priests d Levites from Jerusalem to ask him, Who art thou? And he con- ssed, and denied not: but confessed, I am not the CHRIST.

The attention of all the World was awakened to the probable Advent of the MES- .H about this time. It was natural, therefore, that so remarkable a person as the ptist should have called forth the inquiry,—Art thou the CHRIST? For John's ly shows that *that* was the question now put to him.

21 And they asked him, What then? Art thou Elias? And he ith, I am not. Art thou that prophet? And he answered, No.

They meant,—Art thou Elijah come back to Earth in person? For in *that* sense l the Jews interpret the two concluding verses of the prophet Malachi. To this > Baptist makes answer, "I am not." But we know that he *was* the promised ias; for our Blessed LORD expressly says so. See St. Matth. xi. 13, 14; and xvii. to 13.

"Art thou *that Prophet?*" is said with reference to that famous prediction of ises,—"The LORD thy GOD will raise up unto thee a Prophet from the midst of se, of thy brethren, like unto me; unto Him shall ye hearken;"(*n*) whereby he etold the MESSIAH, of whom he was himself, in so many respects, a type. This ond title, the Baptist of course disclaims.

22 Then said they unto him, Who art thou? that we may give an swer to them that sent us. What sayest thou of thyself?
23 He said, I *am* the Voice of one crying in the wilderness, Make aight the way of the LORD, as said the prophet Esaias.

Quoting Isaiah xl. 3.—John was but "*a Voice:*" the voice of "THE WORD." So s he but "a burning and a shining *lamp*," (for *that* is the expression in St. John 35:) going before Him who reveals Himself as "THE LIGHT of the World;"—a np kindled at the fountain of Light!
Consider how empty and vain is the mere *voice*, without the *word:* whereas, the rd needs not the voice,—except to make it known to others!(*o*) Consider also w humble is the office of the lamp; helping only to dispel the darkness, until > Day dawns!(*p*)

24, 25 And they which were sent were of the Pharisees. And they ked him, and said unto him, Why baptizest thou then, if thou be not at CHRIST, nor Elias, neither that prophet?
26, 27 John answered them, saying, I baptize with water: but there ndeth one among you, whom ye know not; He it is, who coming ter me is preferred before me, whose shoe's latchet I am not worthy unloose.

John contrasts his own Baptism, which was a mere washing with water, with the ptism of CHRIST, which was attended with the gift of the SPIRIT. He then mbly professes his own comparative littleness and unworthiness; (for to loosen > shoe or sandal, was the office of the meanest slave:) and thus ends the first orded testimony which he bore to CHRIST. The Evangelist proceeds to fix the me of this transaction.

28 These things were done in Bethabara beyond Jordan, where John is baptizing.

f) Ex. xxiv. 9–11.　　(*k*) Judges vi. 11–24.　　(*l*) Judges xiii. 3–22.　　(*m*) Isa. vi. n) Deut. xviii. 15, which is quoted both by St. Peter, Acts iii. 22, 23; and St. Stephen, Acts . 37.　　　　　(*o*) 1 Sam. i. 13, &c.　　　　　(*p*) 2 Pet. i. 19.

And why, when so many names of places are, as it seems, industriously with held, was the Evangelist guided to describe the present locality so particularly It may have been for the following reason:—

Beth-abara signifies the "House of passage,"—a name eminently allusive to th Baptist's office; for by him, the transition, passing, or *passage*, was made from th Law to the Gospel, from Moses to CHRIST. As the Israelites of old had to com through Jordan into the land of Canaan, so now were they being brought, by Ba tism in the same waters, into the true land of Promise. There was a divine fitnes therefore, that "these things" should have been "done in Bethabara *beyond Jorda* where John was baptizing."

After what we are taught concerning the name of Nazareth, in St. Matthew' Gospel, ii. 23, (where see the note,) this will not perhaps be thought a fancift Exposition of the present text.

29 The next day John seeth JESUS coming unto him, and saith, B hold the Lamb of GOD, which taketh away the sin of the World.

Surely, when the Baptist said *that*, he uttered a mighty prophecy! His word look backward, and tell of "the Lamb that was slain before the foundation of th world:"(*q*) forward also, so far as to the last Passover. They are a prophecy CHRIST's Crucifixion; ("He is brought as a lamb to the slaughter!")(*r*) and they forth the meaning of the Paschal type,—declaring therein how "Christ our Pas over is sacrificed for us."(*s*)

30 This is He of whom I said, After me cometh a Man which is pr ferred before me: for He was before me.

Alluding to what he had said the day before; ver. 27. The testimony contained in the present verse was anticipated, as already remarked, in ver. 15.

31 And I knew Him not: but that He should be made manifest to Israel, therefore am I come baptizing with water.

32, 33, 34 And John bare record, saying, I saw the SPIRIT descend ing from heaven like a dove, and It abode upon Him. And I knew Him not: but He that sent me to baptize with water, the same said unto me, Upon whom thou shalt see the SPIRIT descending, and remaining on Him, the same is He which baptizeth with the HOLY GHOST. And I saw, and bare record that this is the SON of GOD.

The Evangelist St. John describes neither the Baptism of CHRIST, nor His Temp tation. He begins his narrative (in ver. 19) at a period subsequent to both events. But in these verses he supplies some precious particulars concerning our LORD's Baptism, and explains how the Forerunner stood personally affected towards Him whom it was his office to baptize.

We learn that John had no *certain* knowledge of His mighty Kinsman, as He who should baptize with the HOLY GHOST, till the promised Heavenly sign revealed Him. When the SPIRIT descended upon our LORD from Heaven like a dove, and abode upon Him,—(with which should be compared Isaiah xi. 2,)—then, and not before, was John made conscious of the wondrous truth. Whereupon, as we learn from this place, he bore joyous testimony that "this was the SON of GOD."

35 Again the next day after John stood, and two of his disciples;

Here begins the history of the third day which St. John describes. Well may h describe it so particularly! for it was the occasion when his eyes were first blesse with the sight of the SAVIOUR of the World.—It will be perceived that th Evangelist, after his divine Introduction,(*t*) begins with the events which he pe sonally witnessed.

36 And looking upon JESUS as He walked, he saith, Behold th LAMB of GOD!

(*q*) Rev. xiii. 8.   (*r*) Isaiah liii. 7.   (*s*) 1 Cor. v. 7.   (*t*) Verses 1 to 18

As St. John *twice* uses these words of CHRIST, (in ver. 29, and in this place,) so do we, in the Litany, *twice* call upon our Blessed SAVIOUR by the same appellation.

37 And the two disciples heard him speak, and they followed JESUS.

These were St. Andrew and St. John,—men who from the very first showed themselves ready " to follow the LAMB whithersoever He goeth."(*u*)

38 Then JESUS turned, and saw them following, and saith unto them, What seek ye?

This was not perhaps a very encouraging address,—as men speak. It may warn us against expecting too much in our first approaches to CHRIST. That all His human heart was yearning towards them, all the while,—who shall doubt?

They said unto Him, Rabbi, (which is to say, being interpreted, Master,) where dwellest Thou?

Their inquiry shows that they desired to *be* with Him: to know His dwelling, in order that they might frequent it.

39 He saith unto them, Come and see. They came, and saw where He dwelt, and abode with Him that day: for it was about the tenth hour.

That is, they spent with Him *the whole day*, from ten o'clock in the morning. St. John reckons his hours in the manner of the Asiatics, among whom he wrote; and whose reckoning, strange to relate, agreed exactly with our own.

How blessed and memorable was the occasion here recorded, to the Author of the present Gospel! Well may he mark all things so accurately,—the place, and the day, and the hour of the day: the gesture of his LORD, and His gracious words. The Evangelist suppresses only the mention of himself.

If we are but in earnest in drawing near to CHRIST, He gives us ample opportunities.

40, 41 One of the two which heard John *speak*, and followed him, was Andrew, Simon Peter's brother. He first findeth his own brother Simon, and saith unto him, We have found the Messias, (which is, being interpreted, the CHRIST.)

"He *first*;"—that is, Andrew found his brother Simon, before John was able to find his brother James: but be sure the Disciple of Love was not much later in bringing his brother to CHRIST. How genuine was the zeal of these men towards GOD; which would not let either rest till he had conveyed the good tidings to his Brother!

42 And he brought him to JESUS. And when JESUS beheld him, He said, Thou art Simon the Son of Jona: thou shalt be called Cephas, (which is, by interpretation, A stone.)

Our SAVIOUR no sooner sees Simon than He bestows upon him his name of strength; foreseeing what would be hereafter. The speaker in this verse is the same who, in the Old Testament, gave new names to Abram, to Sarai, and to Jacob.

43, 44 The day following JESUS would go forth into Galilee; and findeth Philip, and saith unto him, Follow Me. Now Philip was of Bethsaida, the city of Andrew and Peter.

Thus, a fifth Apostle,—a fellow-townsman of Andrew and Peter,—is gathered into the fold!

It is impossible to think of these poor plain men without wonder and admiration. They had left their home, and forsaken their trade, in order to wait upon the stern

(*u*) Rev. xiv. 4.

Baptist, and become his disciples. Their souls were engrossed with the desire beholding the promised MESSIAH, whose advent they felt assured was at hand. I it never be thought that they received "a call," and thereupon became earne self-denying, holy. They did not become great Saints because they were called become Apostles. They were, on the contrary, called to become Apostles becas they were such great Saints.

Surely their glorious History may well teach us to look on men of the same c dition of life with interest, not to say with reverence. If Bethsaida alone contai an Andrew, a Peter, and a Philip,—there may surely be dwelling unsuspec Saints at this day among ourselves!

And can it be wrong to extend this observation to the other sex; remember that a maiden worthy to become the Mother of our Blessed REDEEMER, was for dwelling in poverty in the despised Nazareth?

45 Philip findeth Nathanael, and saith unto him, We have fou Him, of whom Moses in the Law, and the prophets, did write, JES of Nazareth, the Son of Joseph.

"JESUS of Nazareth,"—the appellation which fulfilled the prophecy noticed in Matthew ii. 23,—is here for the first time heard. Next, it is spoken by a devil see St. Luke iv. 34. It clung evermore to the Son of Man: was fastened to I cross:(x) pronounced by Angels:(y) claimed by Himself:(z) and finally became t prevailing name by which diseases were banished,(a) and in conformity with whi the first Christians were called.(b)

Take notice, that Philip speaks of Him as One who had been long known to hi self and his friends,—JESUS of the city of Nazareth, *the Son of Joseph.* "Hav been *so long time with you,* and yet hast thou not known Me, Philip?"(c)—w accordingly the question which our LORD asked him at the Last Supper.

" *We* have found;" that is, Andrew and Simon, James and John: the first nam being his own especial friend. Consider the following passages,—St. John vi. and 8: xii. 21 and 22.

46 And Nathanael said unto him, Can there any good thing com out of Nazareth? Philip saith unto him, Come and see.

Nathanael (who is called Bartholomew by the other Evangelists) was of Cana i Galilee,—as we read in chap. xxi. 2. The holy company had, therefore, by th time reached the scene of the miracle recorded in the next chapter.

Arrived at Cana, Philip straightway hastened away in search of his frien (these holy men are our examples at every step of the history!) and his announc ment, when he has found him, clearly shows how full his heart was of one gr subject. It shows, too, what studious readers of Scripture they both had be When Nathanael hesitates, Philip answers him with a saying which he had perha already learned from the lips of his Master, CHRIST. See ver. 39.

47 JESUS saw Nathanael coming to Him, and saith of him, Behol an Israelite indeed, in whom is no guile.

Our LORD (had He chosen) could have greeted His servant with a complete sol tion of the difficulty he had recently expressed concerning the supposed place CHRIST's Nativity: but we find that He took a far diviner course. He convinc Nathanael that He knew him, by declaring to him his character: thus leading t Disciple at once to the belief that he had to do with the Searcher of hearts.

By calling Nathanael "an Israelite indeed," and by the notice of his charac which follows, our LORD's words seem to have respect to the character of Isra (that is, Jacob,) as it is set down in Genesis xxv. 27. Now, to Jacob the disc ment of Angels was especially granted: consider Genesis xxviii. 12: xxxii. 1, also 24 to 30. This prepares us for the remarkable language of our LORD in ver. 5

48 Nathanael saith unto Him, Whence knowest Thou me? JES answered and said unto him, Before that Philip called thee, when th wast under the fig-tree, I saw thee.

(x) St. John xix. 19.   (y) St. Mark xvi. 6.   (z) Acts xxii. 8.
(a) Acts iii. 6, and iv. 10.   (b) Acts xxiv. 5.   (c) St. John xiv. 9

Our Saviour perceived the thought which was already springing up in His servant's heart. Nathanael suspected that surely it was Philip who had been talking to our Lord concerning him. Hence the peculiarity of our Lord's reply; by which He convinced Nathanael that He derived His knowledge from no human source.

Before the arrival of Philip, Nathanael, as if in literal fulfilment of the prophetic foreshadowings of the days of the Gospel, is found to have been "sitting under his fig-tree."(d) He had been alone. He had thought himself unobserved also. The words of our Blessed Lord just now quoted, convinced him that he had been all along in the presence of one and the same Being,—even of Him whose "eyes are in every place, beholding the evil and the good."

What might the occupation of Nathanael have been, as he sat beneath his fig-tree? Doubt not but that there is some very exquisite circumstance alluded to here; though we know it not, and cannot know it.

49 Nathanael answereth and saith unto Him, Rabbi, Thou art the Son of God; Thou art the King of Israel.

Such was his hearty confession,—produced by the discovery that he had to do with One who searcheth the heart and the reins. By the same evidence, the Woman of Samaria became a believer;(e) and the Apostles were fully convinced that Jesus of Nazareth "came forth from God."(f)

Doubt not that, evermore, Nathanael, (that is, *Bartholomew*,) felt that he was bound to Philip by a tie strong as that of blood. Not in vain, to be sure, is it recorded, that when our Lord sent forth His Apostles "by two and two,"(g) it was "*Philip and Bartholomew*" who went together. Consider the following texts,—St. Matthew x. 3: St. Mark iii. 18: St. Luke vi. 14.

50 Jesus answered and said unto him, Because I said unto thee, I saw thee under the fig-tree, believest thou? thou shalt see greater things than these.

One of the "greater things" here promised, was the miracle of the Water made Wine, which immediately follows.

51 And He saith unto Him, Verily, verily, I say unto you, Hereafter ye shall see Heaven open, and the Angels of God ascending and descending upon the Son of Man.

Our Blessed Lord directs the divine saying which follows to Nathanael, ("He saith unto *him*;") but addresses His prophecy to all who were present, ("*ye* shall see.") Most mysterious indeed are His words, and hard to explain; but they seem to mean something like this:—

Ye are about to see the actual fulfilment of that which was only shown to Jacob in a dream.(h) Henceforth, ye shall be made conscious that "Heaven" is "opened;" that a free intercourse is established between Heaven and Earth. Moreover, ye shall be witnesses how the heavenly messengers are perpetually occupied in offices of mercy towards mankind; "ascending and descending upon the Son of Man,"—that is, ministering to Him, whether in His own person(i) or in the person of His members;(k) doing His bidding in behalf of "those who shall be heirs of Salvation."(l) Whereby ye shall perceive that I am He "to whom all things in Heaven, in Earth, and under the Earth, do bow and obey;" and shall know Me to be God.

On all this, a modern Writer says beautifully,—"This introduction of the Disciples to our Lord is remarkable for its extremely quiet, and what might be called its domestic character. It is all emblematic of Him who "should not strive nor cry, neither should His Voice be heard in the Street."

"Much is of the nature of human incident, and what looks like chance occurrence. Natural ties, of Discipleship, of Kindred, and of Friendship, are the moving

(d) Compare Micah iv. 4 and Zech. iii. 10.   (e) St. John iv. 19.
(f) Compare St. John xvi. 19 and 30.   (g) St. Mark vi. 7.
(h) Gen. xxviii. 12.   (i) For example,—St. Luke xxii. 43: St. John xx. 12: Acts i. 10.
(k) For example,—Acts v. 19: x. 3: xii. 7: xxvii. 23.   (l) Heb. i. 14.

causes, as in any circumstance of daily life; and all this, in order, as with noisy
hands, (*m*) to lay the everlasting foundations of the City of GOD. The Holy Baptist
his ordinary teaching intimates to some disciples the presence of the LAMB OF G
and *that* by way of hint or incidental mention,—'as he looked on JESUS,' while
passed by. They introduce themselves to His notice, and go in silence to His ab
and are received by Him,—as a man receives his friends. The door closes on the
they are with CHRIST; but what passes is unknown. Then, the coming of the g
Apostle is through the call of Kindred; the natural tie is the apparent cause of
coming. Then, Philip also is called, as being one of the same city; and he m
rally hastens to his own friend. Friendship does now, what Kindred did before
few words are recorded; and such is the beginning of the Church whose top rea
Heaven! The grain of mustard-seed is scattered, as it were, to the mercy of
winds, till it finds fit place to take root. But it is all by Him, without whose kn
ledge not a sparrow falleth to the ground: by Him who hath the times and sea
in His own Hand, and also the hearts of men: who calleth the stars by their nan
and they answer, Here we be: or with the infant Samuel,—'Speak, LORD, for :
servant heareth!'"

THE PRAYER.

O EVERLASTING GOD, who hast ordained and constituted the servi
of Angels and men in a wonderful order; mercifully grant, that as T
holy Angels always do Thee service in Heaven, so by Thy appointme
they may succour and defend us on Earth; Through JESUS CHRIST (
LORD. AMEN.

CHAPTER II.

----

1 CHRIST *turneth water into wine; 12 departeth into·Capernaum, and to Jerusale
14 where He purgeth the Temple of Buyers and Sellers. 19 He foretelleth E
death and Resurrection. 23 Many believed because of His Miracles, but He wou
not trust Himself with them.*

1 AND the third day there was a Marriage in Cana of Galilee;

That is, the third Day after the three which the Evangelist had been describi
Thus the Gospel of St. John, like the Book of Genesis, begins with the history
a Week: the work of the sixth and the last day, (on which the second Adam "ma
fested forth His Glory,") being the chief of all, and emphatically pronounced (i
verse 10) to be very "good." On both occasions, the sixth day was signalized
the Marriage rite: on the former, by its Institution,—on the second, by "a M
riage in Cana of Galilee."
Take notice, that, as the Eternal SON had instituted Holy Matrimony "in t
Beginning,"—so now, at the very beginning of His Earthly Ministry, He d

(*m*) Consider 1 Kings vi. 7.

honour to the Marriage Rite, and blesses it anew. Surely, it was a fitting occasion
for His presence, and for the act of Almighty Power which followed: for was He
not Himself, mystically, the Bridegroom; who had come into the World to take
His Spouse, the Church?—Consider the following texts:—St. Matth. xxii. 2, &c.;
xiv. 1, &c. St. John iii. 29. Ephes. v. 22 to 32. Rev. xix. 7 to 9: xxi. 2.

The village is called by the same name ("Cana of Galilee") to this day. It is
described by a friend,(a) who has recently visited those parts, as occupying "a
gentle declivity, facing the setting sun: a sweet peaceful Village, which still arrests
the traveller with its loveliness, and makes him feel that something still lingers
there of *His* presence who makes all things blessed and lovely."

and the Mother of JESUS was there:

"Was there,"—not "was invited." It is thought that this Festivity celebrated
the Marriage of one of her relations.

2 and both JESUS was called, and His Disciples, to the Marriage.

Our SAVIOUR does not annul human relationships: He does but sanctify them
with His presence,—when He is invited to witness them. Least of all can the
Holy Estate of Matrimony be thought displeasing in His sight. He had already
blessed Virginity, by His Birth;—and Widowhood, by revealing Himself to Anna,
in the Temple. Behold Him now making a Marriage the occasion when He first
"manifested forth His glory."

Oh that He were invited to *all* our Marriage-feasts! Who shall describe the blessedness of having *Him*, at all times, for a guest?

3 And when they wanted wine, the Mother of JESUS saith unto Him, They have no wine.

The circumstance seems to have become known at once to herself,—because she
was among members of her own family. Her words to her Divine Son clearly
amounted to a request that He would supply the deficiency which began to be felt;
and they show that she knew that He had the power to do the thing she wished,—
if it were but His pleasure. It does not follow from this, that He had ever worked
a miracle before. On the contrary, we are told that this was "the Beginning
of Miracles." . . . . Observe, however, that a Mother's *request*, under ordinary
circumstances, is a *command:* for this remark will help to prepare the mind for
the words which follow.

Can the presence of so many additional guests,—perhaps the *unexpected* presence
of the six Disciples of CHRIST,—have been the occasion of this deficiency in the
supply of wine? The thing is possible; but the conjecture would not really be
worth hazarding, except for the memorable result of this day's entertainment,
which made the Bridegroom's hospitality an occasion of his enriching,—instead of
his loss. Six water-pots of wine,—(one for each guest!)—became a lasting memorial of the day, when, "not forgetful to entertain strangers," he "thereby entertained Angels unawares."(b)

4 JESUS saith unto her, Woman, what have I to do with thee? Mine hour is not yet come.

"Woman" was a respectful mode of address at the time, and consistent with the
utmost tenderness and love. See how the same Blessed Speaker addressed the
same Mother from the Cross,—St. John xix. 26.(c)

But,—"What have I to do with thee?" is the language of rebuke. This phrase
occurs in other parts of the Scripture, and always denotes that the speaker has
been unseasonably spoken to, and, as it were, interfered with.(d) In this place, it
seems to be as if our LORD had said,—What is there common to Me, thy Creator,
and thee, My creature? Thy Son I am,—after the flesh; and, as thy Son, these
thirty years have I been content to be "subject unto" thee. But I am also thy

(a) C. L. Higgins, Esq., of Turvey Abbey.
(b) Hebrews xiii. 2.						(c) Compare St. John xx. 13, 15.
(d) 2 Sam. xvi. 10: xix. 22. 1 Kings xvii. 18: 2 Kings iii. 13: 2 Chron. xxxv. 21. St.
Matth. viii. 29: St. Mark i. 24.

God; and it is only as thy God that I can do this thing. As such,—"What have to do with *thee?*"

"Mine hour is not yet come,"—probably means that the moment had not quite arrived for Him to act: but the sayings of Him who "spake as never m spake," are wondrous deep; and often, like this saying, very difficult.

5 His Mother saith unto the servants, Whatsoever He saith un you, do *it.*

Once more she gives directions to the Servants,—as one comparatively at hom It is evident that the Blessed Virgin understood, even from our Lord's disc raging reply, that He was about to grant her petition. Compare with this, wi Pharaoh said to his servants concerning Joseph, a memorable type of Christ: Genesis xii. 55.

"Whatsoever He saith unto you, do it:"—Oh, most holy and excellent couns Were it but deeply engraven in our hearts, so as to produce a life of perfect a uniform obedience,—how would Heaven begin, even on this side of Eternity! How would the issue of all our undertakings be blest!

6 And there were set there six water-pots of stone,

There is not a single word or syllable in Holy Scripture which is set down the in vain. Why, then, does St. John, who omits so many important things, infor us that the water-pots were "six" in number?

It seems likely that the number of these vessels was providentially overrule (and was therefore recorded,) with reference to the *six* Apostles of our Lord wh were present with Him on this occasion. See the note on verse 11; and conside that He was about to pour into those men, as into new vessels, the good Wine o the Gospel:(*e*) from whose ample stores the servants of Christ were to draw fort in turn; and present to every "guest" at "the Marriage-Supper of the Lamb,"(*f* severally, as much as he would. For remember,—"The Kingdom of Heaven i like unto a certain King, which made *a marriage* for His Son. . . . And the wed ding was furnished with guests."(*g*)

after the manner of the purifying of the Jews, containing two o three firkins apiece.

It was a religious custom among the Jews, to wash before meals,—as we are par ticularly informed by St. Matthew, (xv. 2,) and St. Mark, (vii. 2 to 5.) St. John mode of alluding to their practice, in this place, reminds us that he wrote his Gos pel at a distance from Judæa. He always supposes his readers unaware of th Jewish customs,(*h*) and unacquainted with the Jewish language.(*i*) Consider St John v. 2.

The "firkin" has been thought to contain about five gallons. What an over whelming supply, therefore, of wine was here! Surely, in the abundance thus un expectedly produced, we have a lively image of that Royal bounty, which is won to shower down upon us "more than either we desire or deserve!"

7 Jesus saith unto them, Fill the water-pots with water. And the filled them up to the brim.

To all appearance a very unpromising step towards remedying the want of Win but what are appearances worth, when *GOD* is the Speaker? "Hath He said and shall He not do it?" Surely, in all cases of doubt or difficulty, His Mother injunction to the servants, (in verse 5,) is the counsel which the Church addres to ourselves,—the only course which is sure to lead to Peace at last! Obedien ever inherits a Blessing.

8 And He saith unto them, Draw out now, and bear unto the Go vernor of the Feast. And they bare *it.*

It was the business of the Governor, or Ruler of the Feast, to provide for th

(*e*) St. Matth. ix. 17.   (*f*) Rev. xix. 9.   (*g*) St. Matth. xxii. 2 to 10.
(*h*) See St. John ii. 13: iv. 9: vi. 4: xi. 55. Consider also vi. 1.
(*i*) See St. John i. 38, 41, 42: ix. 7: xx. 16.

entertainment of the guests, and to taste first what was set before them. Hence our LORD's injunction.

9, 10 When the Ruler of the Feast had tasted the water that was made wine, and knew not whence it was : (but the servants which drew the water knew;) the Governor of the Feast called the Bridegroom, and saith unto him, Every man at the beginning doth set forth good wine; and when men have well drunk, then that which is worse : *but* thou hast kept the good wine until now.

"*Good* wine,"— for it came immediately from Him, whose works when they first left His Almighty hands, were pronounced *good.* The effects of the miracles of CHRIST are better than the productions of Nature.

When the Ruler of the Feast spoke these words to the Bridegroom, he stated a sad truth, — of far wider application than at first sight appears. Men seek to show their *best* at *first,*—whether of property, or sentiment, or feature. They fall away on trial. In each respect they set forth " then, that which is worse." Is it not so with Him " whose ways are not Man's ways."

CHRIST always keeps the best things till the end. They who " sow in tears, reap in joy."(i) In life " evil things,"—after death, eternal comfort.(k) " Heaviness may endure for a night, but Joy cometh in the Morning."(l)

11 This beginning of Miracles did JESUS in Cana of Galilee, and manifested forth His Glory;

Unspeakably deep and mysterious, surely, must the teaching of our LORD's first miracle be. Do we not trace therein, symbolically, the purpose with which He came into the world,—namely, to convert the weak and watery ordinances of the Law, into the " new wine" of the Gospel, which " makes glad the heart of man" for ever? Compare St. Matthew ix. 17. Not, observe, to create a new thing: but to convert the old into something better.

For our LORD did not now create something *new,*—as when, " in the beginning," He "made the Heaven and the Earth."(m) Neither did He increase and multiply a thing already existing; as when He fed the four and the five thousand. But He changed a thing which already existed, into a better thing of corresponding bulk. Just as, during the Great Six Days, He had " formed Man—*of the dust of the ground.*"(n)

"Now," (as the greatest Father of the Western Church has remarked,) " if He had ordered the Water to be poured out; and had then introduced the Wine, as a new Creation, He would seem to have rejected the Old Testament. But converting, as He did, the Water into Wine, He showed us that the Old Testament was from Himself: for it was *by His order* that the waterpots were filled." (See ver. 7.) Aye, filled to the very brim.

And so it is, that when the mind is suffered to dwell attentively on a Miracle like this, fresh points of analogy, and meanings, at first unsuspected, suggest themselves. Thus one is led to observe that, in Scripture, *Water* and *Wine,* alike are connected with the mention of spiritual gifts.(o) Moreover, it is obvious to remark that on this occasion, the use of *Water* was but *preparatory* to the Feast; whereas the Wine was an essential part of the Feast itself: and this seems to symbolize, in no obscure way, the relation in which the Law stood to the Gospel. See St. Luke v. 37 to 39.

Surely, at " the Marriage of the LAMB," the great features of *this* marriage Feast will be restored ! It will then be confessed, on all hands, that the same Almighty Benefactor hath kept " the good wine until *now ;*" for things which " eye hath not seen, nor ear heard, neither hath it entered into the heart of man to conceive," hath He prepared for those who love Him. " Thou hast kept the good wine until now." Surely *that* is the cry of Saints in bliss !

(i) Psalm cxxvi. 5.   (k) St. Luke xvi. 25.
(l) Psalm xxx. 5.   (m) Gen. i. 1.
(n) Gen. ii. 7 : compare i. 11, 20, 24, &c.
(o) Isaiah xii. 3,—compare St. John vii. 37, 38, 39. Isaiah xxxv. 6, 7 : xliv. 3. Joel ii. 28, 29, —compare Acts ii. 13, 15, 17, 18, &c. Ephes. v. 18, &c.

Verily, the Author of the Miracle which we have been considering, hath n "left Himself without witnesses,"(*p*) even to the Heathen world. For do but co sider how, year by year, the same miracle is performed, and under our very eye although, by reason of its frequency and regularity, we give no heed to it! Wh is it less than a miracle that the Rain, falling upon our vineyards, should be " ma Wine ?"

And fail not, reader, to remark, in conclusion, the severe simplicity of the pr ceding narrative. Not a word is said of the dismay which the failure of the wi occasioned,—nor of the pleasure which attended so unexpected a supply :—nothin of the surprise of the Servants,—nor of the satisfaction of the guests :—nothing, the effect which this miracle produced on the Giver of the Feast; nor of how came, at last, to his knowledge. Neither is our attention called to the largeness the miraculous supply which made him henceforth rich. We are left to study th details, and draw the inferences, and feed upon the teaching, of every part of th miracle, for ourselves. . . . . Let it be freely allowed, at least, that the number of particulars withheld, serves to impart interest and dignity, a hundredfold, to every word which is actually set down. Nothing can be in vain, where so little is re corded: nothing can be trivial, which comes from the Mouth of GOD.

and His Disciples believed on Him.

Those who delight in such inquiries, may like to pursue the hint given in these few words of the progress of the Gospel, by examining the following references: St. John ii. 23: iv. 39, 41, 42: vii. 31 and viii. 30, 31: ix. 16: x. 42: xi. 45, 48: xii. 11 and 42.

12 After this He went down to Capernaum, He, and His Mother, and His Brethren, and His Disciples: and they continued there not many days.

We have just witnessed one great Miracle. In the verses which follow we are about to be presented with another. Between the two, comes this mention of the "*Mother*" and "*Brethren*." It is the manner of the Evangelists thus to blend the Divine and Human, in describing the actions of our LORD. See the first note on St. Matthew viii. 10, and on St. Luke viii. 23. Also the note on St. Mark ii. 5, and on St. Luke iv. 30.

Concerning the "Brethren" of our LORD, see the note on St. Matthew xiii. 55 Capernaum, where this holy company now came to sojourn, and where our SAVIOUR lived so much, was a town situated at the North-Western extremity of the Sea of Galilee. No traces of it are to be seen at the present day,—according to the me morable prophecy contained in St. Matthew xi. 23. See the note on that place.

13 And the Jews' Passover was at hand, and JESUS went up to Jerusalem,

" The *Jews'* Passover,"—(as in xi. 55,) because St. John wrote at a distance from the Holy Land; and addressed his Gospel to persons who were only slightly, if at all, acquainted with Jewish customs. See the first note on the second part of ver. 6.

This, then, was the first of Four Passover seasons which are distinctly marked in the Gospels. Our LORD went up to Jerusalem on the occasion, in conformity with the requirements of the Law. See the references in the note on St. Luke ii. 41.

14 and found in the Temple those that sold oxen and sheep and doves, and the changers of money sitting:

The sheep and oxen were kept for the purpose of sacrifice. The doves were the offerings of those who came to be purified ;(*q*) especially of the poorer sort of peo ple.(*r*) The changers of money found their account in supplying those strangers and foreigners who came up, in great numbers,(*s*) to worship at Jerusalem on these occasions, and brought with them the money of other countries, in order to pur chase victims for sacrifice ; according to the express direction of the Law.(*t*) The

(*p*) Acts xiv. 17.   (*q*) Levit. xv. 14, 29.
(*r*) See Levit. xii. 6, 8 : and compare the note on Luke ii. 24.
(*s*) See Acts ii. 5 : also 8 to 11.   (*t*) Deut. xiv. 24 to 26.

payment of "tribute,"—that is, the tax of a half-shekel which all contributed towards the support of the Temple,—must have also supplied these "changers of money" with occupation.

15 And when He had made a scourge of small cords, He drove them all out of the Temple, and the sheep, and the oxen; and poured out the changers' money, and overthrew the tables;

The "scourge of small cords" was not the *instrument*, so much as the *emblem* of His wrath. It is manifest that such a Weapon must have been powerless in other hands; certainly, it would have been ineffectual to produce the mighty results here noticed. But CHRIST wrought a miracle on the present occasion; not on lifeless matter,—as at Cana; but on the hearts and minds of His rational creatures. Armed with that scourge, men beheld in Him a type of the Vengeance which will at last overtake the wicked. The traffickers in the Temple, panic-stricken, fled before the awful presence of Him, in whom they nevertheless had not eyes to discern their future Judge. And surely the spectacle is one which it will do men good to seek to realise to themselves. We love to speak of our SAVIOUR as "meek and lowly;"(u) and we do well,—for such an One He was. But, on this occasion, He revealed Himself in a very different character: terrible in His wrath,—and, as it were, consumed by His zeal for the honor of His FATHER'S House.

In truth, what we here behold is the fulfilment of that famous prophecy of Malachi:—"The LORD, whom ye seek, shall suddenly come to His Temple; even the Messenger of the Covenant, whom ye delight in. Behold, He shall come, saith the LORD of Hosts. But who may abide the Day of His coming? and who shall stand when He appeareth? For He is like a refiner's fire, and like fuller's soap: and He shall sit as a Refiner and Purifier of silver."(v) These words had a partial accomplishment, doubtless, at the Presentation in the Temple :(w) their fullest accomplishment, (as they refer to the *first* Advent of CHRIST,) when at the close of His Ministry, He purged the Temple for the second time:(x) but they were strikingly fulfilled now. See the note on the last half of St. Luke ii. 38.

Deeply emblematic, we may be sure, was this act of our blessed LORD. Besides its prophetic fulfillment, and its prophetic teaching, it set forth one great purpose of His coming ;—which was, to annul the system of carnal ordinances, and to bring to light the sublime truths which lay concealed beneath them. When He drove the victims from the Temple, He showed that a better Victim had at last appeared ; and that the Legal Sacrifices were no longer to have any place.

And will it be said that it is merely an ingenious use of the text to find in it an individual application also? "What? Know ye not that your Body is the Temple of the HOLY GHOST, which is in you ?"(y) "Know ye not that ye are the Temple of GOD, and that the SPIRIT of GOD dwelleth in you ?"(z)

16 and said unto them that sold doves, Take these things hence ; make not My FATHER'S House an house of merchandise.

"My FATHER'S House :"—the blessed Speaker had spoken of the Temple by the same name about eighteen years before ; (see the note on St. Luke ii. 49:) thereby, in express words, claiming to be the SON of GOD. See the end of the note on St. John v. 17.

On two occasions,—once at the commencement of His Ministry; next, at its close,—our SAVIOUR thus drove the buyers and sellers out of the Temple. The first incident is related by St. John only: for the second, see St. Matthew xxi. 12, 13: St. Mark xi. 15 to 18 : St. Luke xix. 45, 46.

Surely, *they* still make His FATHER'S House "a House of Merchandise," who carry thither anxieties about their secular concerns; and allow thoughts about Trade,—hopes and fears about the Market,—to find place in the Sanctuary of GOD!

17 And His Disciples remembered that it was written, The zeal of Thine House hath eaten Me up.

(u) St. Matthew xi. 29.   (v) Malachi iii. 1, 2, 3.   (w) St. Luke ii. 22 to 38.
(x) St. Matthew xxi. 12, 13.   (y) 1 Cor. vi. 19.
(z) 1 Cor. iii. 16.   Compare 2 Cor. vi. 16.   Ephes. ii. 21, 22.   Hebrews iii. 6.   1 St. Peter ii. 5.

Psalm lxix. contains many prophecies concerning CHRIST which the Apostl have noticed and applied. Verse 9 is quoted,—partly by St. John,—partly by Paul.(a) Verse 21, by St. John (xix. 29.) Verse 25, by St. Peter (Acts i. 20.)

It was *long after*, that they "remembered :" certainly not till He was risen fro the dead. See ver. 22; and compare the statement in St. John xii. 16. It may presumed, indeed, that it was not until the Ascension of CHRIST that they und stood these things; until after the out-pouring on His Disciples of *that* SPIRIT, whom it was prophesied that "He should teach them all things, and bring things to their remembrance, whatsoever CHRIST had said unto them."(b) Aft *that* great event, it may be thought that the application of Ps. lxix. 9 to this of MESSIAH, together with the real meaning of many more of our LORD's wondr sayings, presented itself to His Apostles.

It is to be observed, however, that He "opened their understanding, that the might understand the Scriptures,"(c) previous to His Ascension into Heaven.

18 Then answered the Jews and said unto Him, What sign showed Thou unto us, seeing that Thou doest these things?

It was their wont always to make such a demand. GOD had accordingly fur nished Moses with more signs than one.(d) The Prophets, in like manner, were all furnished with some visible proof of their mission. It will be remembered tha Zacharias asked for a sign; see St. Luke i. 18 to 20, and the notes there: and w find the Jewish people, on several other occasions, demanding a sign of our LORD See St. Matthew xii. 38, and the note there; also xvi. 1. St. Luke xi. 16. So also St. John vi. 30; and consider 1 Cor. i. 22.

19 JESUS answered and said unto them, Destroy this Temple, and in three days I will raise it up.

A Divine answer, truly! He gave them the most wondrous sign imaginable,— a sign which was to become the very foundation of the Christian Faith. Sublime allusive it also was, and was intended to be, to the mystical connection betwee the "House" for which He had displayed such zeal, and that "House of clay"(e in which His own Divinity was enshrined, as in a Tabernacle. Compare 2 Co v. 1, 4, and 2 Pet. i. 13, 14. Lastly, it contained a declaration of His own Go HEAD: for He professes that *He will raise Himself* from Death.

It will be remembered, that this wondrous prophecy of His own Death and R surrection supplied the enemies of the MESSIAH with a ground of accusation, and sub ject of mockery, against Him, in the end. See St. Matt. xxvi. 61,—where it wi be seen that a garbled version of it was found on the lips of the two false witness and St. Matt. xxvii. 40,—where the blasphemy of the bystanders, at the Cruc fixion, is recorded. "There seems a particular reason therefore why St. Joh should introduce the cluster of circumstances, here described : for the other Evan gelists had recorded the charge made against Him at His Death, without mention ing the occasion on which our LORD delivered it."

20 Then said the Jews, Forty and six years was this Temple i building, and wilt Thou rear it up in three days?

They spoke of that material shrine,—the second Temple, as Zorobabel's stru ture is called,—which had been restored, in a style of extreme magnificence, b King Herod the Great.

21 But He spake of the Temple of His Body.

"The Temple of His Body !" . . . How marvellously do remote, and apparent diverse places of Holy Scripture harmonize with those words,—bring out the meaning,—and, in turn, receive illustration from them ! . . . Thus we are remind that the present Evangelist, in his first chapter, (verse 14,) intimated that, in th fleshly Tabernacle of a human Body, *that* GODHEAD had come to reside, of whi the "Shekinah," or glory, in the Temple, was but a type. See the last note on th first half of St. John i. 14. The Veil of the Temple, (which "was rent in twain fro the top to the bottom,"(f) when JESUS CHRIST expired upon the Cross,) was, we ar

(a) Rom. xv. 3.   (b) St. John xiv. 26.   (c) St. Luke xxiv. 45.
(d) Exodus iv. 1 to 9.   (e) Job iv. 19.   (f) St. Matthew xxvii. 51.

expressly told, emblematic of His *flesh*,(g)—in the same hour cruelly torn: and observe, that as GOD was said to *dwell* in the Temple, so, in our SAVIOUR's Body "*dwelleth* all the fullness of the GODHEAD bodily."(h) We have just read how men, with their merchandise, defiled the Temple of GOD; and witnessed how GOD treated them: which reminds us of what is said of bodily defilement, in 1 Cor. iii. 17.

The Temple of old, and our Churches, at this day, have one extremity pointing to the East,—the other to the West. And even so point the *Temples of our Bodies*, when they are laid in the dust.

Many are the intimations in Holy Scripture that the Human Body is occupied by the Soul, as a House is occupied by its Tenant. Thus Job, as we have seen, describes Men, as "them that dwell *in houses of clay*:"(i) and GOD is said in the beginning to have "*builded*" a Woman.(k) But St. Paul calls the Body, "our Earthly Tent-House," or "Tabernacle-Residence,"—for *that* is the real meaning of 2 Corinthians v. 1: intimating thereby, (in the words of an excellent living Writer,) "that the Body is a temporary structure, easily taken down, and liable to removal at very short notice. And indeed," (he adds,) "the order of removing the Tabernacle in the Wilderness from place to place, 'when the Camp set forward,' (as prescribed in Numbers iv.) supplies a very striking emblem of the awful process of dissolution, as it takes effect upon the natural Body of Man."

As "one with CHRIST,"(l)—in whom all the Building fitly framed together groweth unto an Holy Temple in the LORD,"—we are further declared to be, spiritually, "the Temple of the Living GOD:" even "an Habitation of GOD, through the Spirit."(m)

22 When therefore He was risen from the dead, His Disciples remembered that He had said this unto them; and they believed the Scripture, and the word which JESUS had said.

See above, the note on ver. 17. The beloved Disciple here notes another of the sayings of his LORD, the meaning of which only became plain long after, to those who heard it spoken. It was, in fact, the *fulfillment* of it,—"when He was risen from the dead,"—which made it plain. "And indeed, it is evident," (says a pious Writer,) "from the subsequent mention of it by the false Witnesses, that it had been remembered in Jerusalem, and brought forth into prominent record when most needed. Thus, though it appeared no answer at the time, yet, the bread cast upon the waters was gathered after many days; and the seed sown bore a hundredfold: nor did His Word return unto Him void."

St. John tells us, besides, how the Faith of the first Believers, both in the Scripture, and in JESUS CHRIST, was confirmed thereby. And the Reader should take note that "the Scripture," (that is, the Old Testament,)—together with "the Word which JESUS had said,"—made up the sum of the Faith of the first Believers; for, as yet, the Books of the New Testament were not written.

23 Now when He was in Jerusalem at the Passover, in the Feast day, many believed in His Name, when they saw the Miracles which He did.

But what miracles were these? *One* only is recorded, in verse 15. It may be that a whole world of wonders is wrapped up in this short verse of Scripture: wonders, which are alluded to by Nicodemus, in chap. iii. 2; and which obtain further notice in chap. iv. 45.

24, 25 But JESUS did not commit Himself unto them, because He knew all *men*, and needed not that any should testify of Man: for He knew what was in Man.

To know the thoughts and intents of the heart,—to look into the mind of Man, and see what is passing there,—is in the power of GOD, and GOD only. In the words of an Eastern Father, "*He* knows what is in the heart, because it was He who fashioned it. He needs no witness to inform Him concerning the mind, be-

(g) Hebrews x. 20.   (h) Coloss. ii. 9.
(i) Job iv. 19.   (k) See the margin of Genesis ii. 22.
(l) See the Exhortation in the Communion Service.   (m) Eph. ii. 21, 22: and 2 Col. vi. 16.

cause it was His own divine contrivance." In like manner, the great Father of the West has remarked, that "the Maker knew better what was in His own work, than the work knew what was in itself:" and he quotes our LORD's prophecy to St. Peter,(n) in proof of his observation.

Consider the following texts of Scripture:—1 Samuel xvi. 7: 1 Chron. xxviii. 9: 2 Chron. vi. 30: Psalm vii. 9: cxxxix. 1, 2: Jer. xvii. 9, 10: St. Matthew ix. 4, (with which compare St. Mark ii. 8:) xii. 25: St. Luke vi. 8: St. John vi. 64: Acts i. 24: Rev. ii. 23.

THE PRAYER.

ALMIGHTY GOD, unto whom all hearts be open, all desires known, and from whom no secrets are hid; cleanse the thoughts of our hearts by the inspiration of Thy HOLY SPIRIT, that we may perfectly love Thee, and worthily magnify Thy holy Name; through CHRIST our LORD. Amen.

CHAPTER III.

1 CHRIST *teacheth Nicodemus the necessity of Regeneration.* 14 *Of Faith in His Death.* 16 *The great love of* GOD *towards the World.* 18 *Condemnation for unbelief.* 23 *The Baptism, Witness, and Doctrine of John concerning* CHRIST.

1, 2 THERE was a man of the Pharisees, named Nicodemus, a Ruler of the Jews. The same came to JESUS by night,

The name thus introduced to our notice, is one of those which are peculiar to the Gospel of St. John. Nicodemus was a member of the High Court of Sanhedrin: and, like St. Paul, belonged to "the most straitest sect" of "the Jews' religion."(a) The Evangelist elsewhere relates that, at a subsequent period, many other members of the same Court believed in our LORD; "but because of the Pharisees they did not confess Him," lest they should be put out of the synagogue.(b) Such a timid believer, as yet, seems to have been Nicodemus.

Very beautiful is the progressive history of his Faith, as it is revealed in the course of St. John's narrative; for he who now comes to JESUS under cover of the Darkness, (doubtless in order to escape notice,) is the same who, subsequently, is found openly pleading with the other Rulers in our LORD's behalf. "Nicodemus saith unto them, (*he that came to* JESUS *by night*," as St. John is careful to remind us,) "being one of them, Doth our Law judge any man, before it hear him, and know what he doeth?"(c) Whereupon the Pharisees are found to "chide with Nicodemus for taking His part."(d) Waxing bolder in the end, when Joseph of Arimathea, (another member of the same Court,) had begged the body of JESUS,— "there came also Nicodemus, (*which at first came to* JESUS *by night*,) and brought a mixture of myrrh and aloes, about an hundred pound weight;" and they two buried Him. Thus, he who was at first only a timid Disciple, soon ripened into a bold Confessor: and the same who at first believed only in secret, in the end came forward openly to assist at the Burial of the LORD of Life.

(n) Compare St. Luke xxii. 33 and 34.   (a) Acts xxvi. 5.
(b) St. John xii. 42.   (c) St. John vii. 51.
(d) See the heading of St. John vii.

Nicodemus, then, came privately to our LORD,—(being at Jerusalem, on the occasion of the first Passover; as was related in the former chapter:) (e)—

and said unto Him, Rabbi, we know that Thou art a Teacher come from GOD: for no man can do these miracles that Thou doest, except GOD be with him.

Observe how this man reasoned. He had beheld the miracles of CHRIST,—that unrecorded cluster of miracles (as it would seem,) which is alluded to in the 23rd verse of the former chapter;(f) (and concerning which it is expressly stated, that "*many believed in His Name* when they saw the miracles which He did;" and thence he had inferred, at once, the Divine Mission of Him by whose hands those works were wrought. He reasoned rightly. "I have greater Witness than that of John," said our SAVIOUR: "for *the Works* which the FATHER hath given me to finish, the same works that I do, *bear witness of Me*, that the FATHER hath sent Me."(g)

Overcome, therefore, by the force of the evidence thus presented to him, Nicodemus comes to JESUS by night; clearly, with a view to learning more of the mysteries of His Religion. But it is discovered that this learned Doctor has not discerned the MESSIAH,—the promised Redeemer of Israel,—in the meek and lowly JESUS; (which he *might* have discerned, as our LORD's words show; which so many others *did* discern, as the Gospel-narrative declares:) but only a mighty Prophet of the LORD; one come "forth from GOD as a Teacher." This seems clear from the language he employed, in addressing our SAVIOUR. Yet was it an evidence of great candor and goodness on his part, that he should have thus speedily broken through the bondage of the system in which he had been brought up, and of which he was himself an eminent professor. "He that doeth Truth, *cometh to the light*,"—as we shall presently hear our SAVIOUR Himself declare;(h) and this is what Nicodemus now did. He came to the Light, in order to have the darkness of his soul dispelled.

Our LORD, in reply, says nothing expressly to magnify Himself: but proceeds gently to correct the low views of His Disciple. Availing Himself of the readiness implied by Nicodemus to receive instruction from His lips, "He begins, in the Discourse which follows, to impart some great and fundamental truths concerning that 'Kingdom of GOD' which Nicodemus, in common with the rest of his countrymen, was expecting to see established by the MESSIAH: thus leading him to entertain juster notions of its nature and end."

3 JESUS answered and said unto him, Verily, verily, I say unto thee, Except a man be born again, he cannot see the Kingdom of GOD.

As if He had said,—"Thou art not yet born again; that is, by a spiritual begetting: and therefore thy knowledge of Me is not spiritual, but carnal and human. But I say unto thee, that neither thou, nor any one, except he be born again of GOD, shall be able to see the glory which is around Me; but shall be out of the Kingdom: for it is the begetting of Baptism which enlightens the mind."

Such seems to have been the force and bearing of the words, as they were addressed to the heart of Nicodemus, personally. As containing a great disclosure of Divine Doctrine, what do they convey but man's need of Spiritual Regeneration, or New-Birth, in order to the eternal safety of his soul? Our LORD proceeds, in verse 5, to explain His words; and it is found that He speaks of *Holy Baptism*,— "as generally necessary to Salvation." In the meantime, the answer of Nicodemus proves that he had as yet no conception of our LORD's meaning.

4 Nicodemus saith unto Him, How can a man be born when he is old? can he enter the second time into his Mother's womb, and be born?

He soars not above the carnal sense of words which *cannot* be understood carnally; and speaks like a child. "Observe," (says one of the Fathers,) "when a man trusts spiritual things to reasonings of his own, how ridiculously he talks!"—

(e) St. John ii. 13 and 23.　(f) See also St. John iv. 45; and the note on St. John ii. 23.
(g) St. John v. 36; where see the note. Consider also the following places: St. Luke vii. 20 to 22; St. John x. 25, 38: xiv. 11: xv. 24.
(h) See below, verses 20, 21.

"But do thou so understand the birth of the Spirit, as Nicodemus did the bi
of the flesh;" (remarks another:) "for as the entrance into the womb cannot
repeated, so neither can Baptism."—Our Lord proceeds to reveal more clearly
manner of our spiritual birth:

5 Jesus answered, Verily, verily, I say unto thee, Except a man
born of Water and *of* the Spirit, he cannot enter into the Kingd
of God.

As if He said,—"Thou understandest Me to speak of a carnal birth; but a m
must be born of Water and of the Spirit, if he is to enter into the Kingdom of G
If, to obtain the temporal inheritance of his human Father, a man must be born
the Womb of his Mother; to obtain the eternal inheritance of his Heavenly Fath
he must be born of the womb of the Church. And since man consists of two pa
Body and Soul, the mode even of this latter birth is two-fold: Water in the visi
part, cleansing the body; the Spirit, by His invisible co-operation, changing t
invisible soul."—Consider the truly Catholic statements on this subject contain
in our Church Catechism. It will be remembered that the Church of England,
her Baptismal Service, expressly grounds the necessity of Baptism on the press
declaration of our Lord.

"Except a man be born of Water and of the Spirit, he cannot enter into t
Kingdom of God." Famous words! which it has been the endeavor of misguid
men, in every age of the Church, to set aside or explain away. Opposing them
selves to Externals in Religion, generally, and to the two Sacraments of the Chur
in particular, sectarians have sought to fasten a strange sense on these plain wor
of Christ; contending eagerly, indeed, for the bestowal of *GOD'S* gift (the Spiri
while they have striven to make it appear that the duty required on *Man's* sid
(the Water,) can be a matter of no real importance. But,—"I hold it for a m
infallible rule in expositions of sacred Scripture," (says our wise Hooker,) "th
where a literal construction will stand, the farthest from the letter is common
the worst." And he adds, that—"Of all the ancients, *there is not one to be nam*
that ever did otherwise expound or allege this place than as implying exter
Baptism." The result of the most searching inquiry has but served to establi
the truth of this remarkable statement.

Very abundantly also is it proved by the whole tenor of Scripture, that as t
Spirit is *the necessary inward cause,* so is Water *the necessary outward means* to t
Regeneration. Thus, we are taught, that with water God doth cleanse and pur
His Church.(i) Baptism is termed by the Apostles, the bath, or laver, of Rege
ration.(k) And when the multitude, "pricked in their heart," inquired of Pe
and the rest of the Apostles, "Men and Brethren, what shall we do? . . . . Pe
said unto them, Repent, and *be baptized* every one of you in the name of Je
Christ *for the Remission of Sins,* and ye shall receive the gift of the Ho
Ghost."(l)

There have been those, however, who looking only at our Eternal Election
Christ, have been thereby led to undervalue the ordinary and immediate mea
of Life. Let such persons be reminded that Predestination does not conduct as
Life without the grace of external calling; in which our Baptism is, of necessit
implied.

Others, again, "fixing their minds wholly on the known necessity of Faith, i
agine that nothing but Faith is necessary for the attainment of all grace." I
surely, (once more to quote Hooker's words,)—"If Christ Himself which giv
Salvation do require Baptism, it is not for us that look for Salvation to sound a
examine Him whether unbaptized we may be saved; but seriously to do that wh
is required, and religiously to fear the danger which may grow by the w
thereof."

Our Saviour's weighty declaration that except a person be baptized "*he can
enter into the Kingdom of* God," has, again, deterred many from cordially accepti
His words, according to their strict literal construction: thinking themselves bou
in charity, to reject an interpretation which would press so heavily on those w
cannot obtain Baptism. The Law of Christ, however, which maketh Baptism
cessary, "must," (says the same Hooker,) "be construed and understood accordi

(i) Ephesians v. 26.   (k) Titus iii. 5.   (l) Acts ii. 37, 38.

to rules of natural equity." Thus "it is on all parts gladly confessed that there may be, in divers cases, Life *by virtue of inward Baptism*, even where outward is not found." One such case, the Church hath ever held to be *that* of unbaptized Martyrs; whose Baptism is one *of Blood*. Another such case is supplied by persons as virtuous as they, who longed indeed for Baptism, but could not obtain it, and finally died without it. *Desire of Baptism*, in both these cases, has been held to supply the place of Baptism itself.

It remains only to notice the case of infants dying unbaptized; concerning whom, Charity and Reason alike compel us to entertain a favourable hope. " We are plainly taught of GOD, that the seed of faithful parentage is holy from the very birth;"(*m*) that is, the offspring of Christian parents " bring into the world a present interest and right to those means wherewith CHRIST hath ordained that His Church shall be sanctified." It is not to be thought, therefore, that He who, as it were from Heaven, hath marked them out for Holiness by the privilege of their very birth, " will Himself deprive them of Regeneration and inward Grace, only because Necessity depriveth them of outward Sacraments." In such case, it is to be thought that the secret desire and purpose which others have in their behalf, will be imputed to *them;* and accepted as such by GOD, all-merciful to as many as are not in themselves able to desire Baptism. . . . Consider, in connection with this subject, the case of the Paralytic borne of four,—and that of the Impotent man at the pool of Bethesda; which will be found respectively discussed in the notes on on St. Mark ii. 3, and St. John v. 7.

But it is time that we notice how the Discourse proceeded. Nicodemus is wholly unable to comprehend the meaning of the Divine Speaker: our LORD therefore helps him by suggesting the analogy of our carnal birth :

6 That which is born of the flesh is flesh : and that which is born of the SPIRIT is spirit.

That is to say, The Nature which a man derives from his Parents, by virtue of his natural Birth, is corrupt, fleshly, and human : *that* which he derives from GOD, by virtue of his New Birth, is incorrupt, spiritual, and divine.

7 Marvel not that I said unto thee, Ye must be born again.

Words which reveal that CHRIST spake with one who was lost in *wonder* at the Discourse he heard.

The expression should be compared with St. John v. 28, 29, where the note may also be read. The appeal is made in both cases to something sensible, in order to assist the understanding. Here, the Author of Creation, having already dwelt on the wonder of our natural Birth, notices the mysterious rushing of the Wind :—

8 The Wind bloweth where it listeth, and thou hearest the sound thereof, but canst not tell whence it cometh, and whither it goeth : so is every one that is born of the SPIRIT.

That is,—Something similar is observed to take place in the case of every regenerate person. It becomes manifest to all that he is acting in obedience to a new principle; but *the Law* of the SPIRIT's operation,—whence it comes, or whither it goes,—how, or why, or for what length of time it will continue to affect a man,— there is none that knoweth.

The illustration may not, of course, be unduly pressed : but the Wind,—which is unseen, yet may be both heard and felt: which obeys a Law indeed, yet depends for its motions entirely upon the Counsels of GOD's Will;—the mysterious operation of *the Wind* supplies our LORD with an image, the fitness of which to express spiritual influence all can feel. In some languages, (in Greek for example,) one word stands for both *Wind* and *Spirit*. Consider also how the descent of the HOLY GHOST, on the Day of Pentecost, was manifested by a sound from Heaven as of " *a rushing mighty Wind*."(*n*) . . . Nicodemus, for all reply, confesses his utter perplexity :—

9 Nicodemus answered and said unto Him How can these things be ?

(*m*) Hooker; referring to 1 Cor. vii. 14.   (*n*) Acts ii. 2.

But his very perplexity takes the shape of a curious doubt. He claims *to understand* what he is required *to believe;* and still asks a carnal question: "*How* can these things be ?"—as before he asked "*How* can a man be born again ?"

10 JESUS answered and said unto him, Art thou a master of Israel, and knowest not these things ?

Rather,—"Art thou *The Teacher of Israel ?*" Such high and sounding titles were frequently bestowed on the Jewish Doctors. St. Paul seems to hint at several of those titles in the second chapter of his epistle to the Romans: " Behold thou art called a Jew," (he says.) . . . "and art confident that thou thyself art 'A Guide of the blind,' 'A Light of them which are in Darkness,' 'An Instructor of the foolish,' 'A Teacher of Babes.' "(*o*) On the supposition that Nicodemus enjoyed the lofty title of " The Teacher of Israel," "nothing is more probable," (remarks a learned Indian Bishop,) "than that our SAVIOUR should have taken occasion to reprove the folly of those who had conferred the appellation, and the vanity of him who had accepted it; and no occasion could have been more opportune than the present when Nicodemus betrayed his ignorance on a very important subject. Our SAVIOUR's readiness to condemn the practice here referred to, may be proved from St. Matthew xxiii. 7.

" No one," (observes the great Father of the African Church,) " is born of the SPIRIT except he is made humble; for this very humility it is, which makes us to be born of the SPIRIT. Nicodemus, however, was inflated with his eminence as a Master, and thought himself of importance, because he was a Doctor of the Jews. Our LORD casts down his pride in order that he may be ' born of the SPIRIT.' "

"Art thou then *The Teacher of Israel,*" (the words may perhaps be paraphrased,) " and rememberest thou not, that, in the days of Noah, both he and all his House were saved by water ? the like figure whereunto is the Baptism of which I speak—(*p*) Knowest thou not that all thy Fathers were baptized unto Moses in the Cloud and in the Sea ?(*q*) or hast thou not read of Naaman the Syrian, who washed in the Jordan, and was delivered from his leprosy, (the well-known type of sin,) so that ' his flesh came again like unto the flesh of a little child, and he was clean ?' " (*r*) . . . Once more does our LORD condescend to his infirmity; making use of a common argument to render what He has said credible :—

11 Verily, verily, I say unto thee, We speak that we do know, and testify that We have seen; and ye receive not our Witness.

"Sight," (says an Eastern Bishop,) " we consider the most certain of all our senses :(*s*) so that when we say we saw such a thing with our eyes, we seem to compel men to believe us. CHRIST, in like manner, speaking after the usage of men, does not indeed mean that He has seen with the *bodily* eye the mysteries which He reveals ;" (for He speaks as GOD, and ' GOD is a Spirit ;') " but it is clear that He intends to describe Himself as possessing the most certain absolute knowledge." The Reader is here requested to verify the following references,—St. John viii. 26, 28, 38, 40 : xv. 15 ; and to read the whole of the note on St. John v. 20. He will also observe the striking parallel between the present place and verse 32. lower down ; where the note may be consulted. The Baptist is there heard declaring the self-same things concerning CHRIST, as CHRIST here declares concerning Himself.

It is *ye,* (observe,) and *you :* not *thou* and *thee.* So also in the next verse, our SAVIOUR addresses not Nicodemus, but the Jewish nation at large, in the person of this their learned Doctor ; and prophesies that they will reject His testimony. Yet was He " the faithful and true witness !"(*t*) Moreover, He had the testimony, not of *one,* but of *two ;*—as we find plainly asserted in St. John viii. 16 to 18 : and *that* is perhaps the reason why the same Blessed Speaker here uses the plural number : " *we* speak," and " *our* witness."(*u*)

12 If I have told you earthly things, and ye believe not, how shall ye believe, if I tell you *of* heavenly things ?

(*o*) Romans ii. 17, 19, 20.   (*p*) 1 St. Peter iii. 20, 21.   (*q*) 1 Cor. x. 2.
(*r*) 2 Kings v. 14.   (*s*) See 1 St. John i. 1 to 3.   (*t*) Revel. i. 5 ; iii. 14.
(*u*) Compare St. Mark iv. 30.

"*Earthly* things,"—because it is here on earth that the mysteries spoken of are transacted.

"*Heavenly* things,"—seems to be said with reference to the higher mysteries of the Kingdom: eternal Truths which, to the very last, as it may be humbly thought, remained unuttered; for, on the eve of His Crucifixion, our LORD could say, "I have yet many things to say unto you; but ye cannot bear them now."(x) Observe, however, that in the case of the "earthly" and of the "heavenly things," alike, the appeal is made not to Reason, but to *Faith;* whence our LORD does not say "*understand* not," but "*believe* not."

13 And no man hath ascended up to Heaven, but He that came down from Heaven, *even* the Son of Man which is in Heaven.

A little attention will suffice to establish the connection of these words with what goes before. Our LORD is here conveying the assurance that from Himself alone could the knowledge of "heavenly things" be obtained; inasmuch as He alone had "ascended up to Heaven." His witness was worthy of all acceptation; and His only: because He spoke and testified of what He had known and seen; and, beside Himself, no man had ascended up to Heaven, to see those "heavenly things," and to know them. "What He hath seen and heard," (says the Baptist in verse 32,) "*that* He testifieth."—We have yet to set forth the meaning of this difficult place in Scripture.

The first part seems to be explained by our LORD's declaration,—"I came forth from the FATHER, and am come into the world;"(y) for *then* it was that the Eternal Son "came down from Heaven;" namely, when "He took Man's nature in the womb of the Blessed Virgin, of her substance."(z) The "*Son of Man,*" before He was conceived in the Virgin's womb, was not in Heaven; but, after His conception, *by virtue of the union of the Divine Substance,* He was in Heaven: (as He said, "the Son of Man which *is in Heaven;*" naming Himself "wholly from His humanity, as elsewhere He names Himself wholly from His divinity.") For, from the hour of His Incarnation, "two whole and perfect natures, that is to say, the Godhead and Manhood, *were joined together in One Person,* never to be divided, whereof is One CHRIST." Speaking after the manner of men, therefore, our SAVIOUR discoursed of Himself to Nicodemus, as *having ascended* into Heaven; because, whatsoever is first on Earth, and then in Heaven, must be said to have ascended into Heaven.

"Although He was made the Son of Man upon earth," writes an ancient father, "yet His Divinity,—with which, remaining in Heaven, He descended to earth,— He hath declared not to disagree with the title of Son of Man; as He hath thought His Flesh worthy the name of SON of GOD. For through the unity of Person, by which both substances are One CHRIST, He walked upon earth, being SON of GOD; and remained in Heaven, being Son of Man."—There is, in fact, an interchange of notions, when we apply the names of *GOD* and *Man* to our SAVIOUR CHRIST; so that for truth of speech, it matters not "whether we say that the SON of GOD hath created the world, and the Son of Man by His death hath saved it,—or else that the Son of Man did create, and the SON of GOD did die to save the world. Howbeit, as oft as we attribute to GOD what the Manhood of CHRIST claimeth, or to Man what His Deity hath a right unto, we understand by the name of GOD and the name of Man neither the one nor the other nature, but *the whole person of CHRIST,* in whom both natures are. When the Apostle saith of the Jews, that they crucified the LORD of Glory,(a) and when the Son of Man being on earth affirmeth that the Son of Man was in Heaven at the same instant,(b) there is in these two speeches that mutual circulation before mentioned. In the one, there is attributed to GOD, or the LORD of Glory, Death,—whereof Divine Nature is not capable; and in the other, ubiquity to man, which Human Nature admitteth not. Therefore, by "the LORD of Glory," we must needs understand *the whole person of CHRIST,* who being LORD of Glory, was indeed crucified, but not in that nature for which He is termed the LORD of Glory. "In like manner," (says Hooker, with reference to the present place,) "*the whole person of CHRIST* must necessarily be meant; who being Man upon Earth, filleth Heaven with His glorious presence, but not according to that nature for which the title of Man is given Him."

(x) St. John xvi. 12.   (y) St. John xvi. 28.   (z) Article II.
(a) 1 Cor. ii. 8.   (b) St. John iii. 13.

One of the ancients briefly sums up the matter as follows:—" So, then, He *came down* from Heaven, because He became the Son of Man; and He was *in* Heaven, because THE WORD, which was 'made flesh,' had not ceased to be THE WORD."

"Having made mention to Nicodemus, of the gift of Baptism," (remarks a third writer,) " He proceeds to the source of it, namely, *The Cross:*" "thus unexpectedly introducing this Teacher of the Mosaic Law to the spiritual sense of that Law, by a passage from the Old Testament History, which was intended to be a figure of His Passion, and of Man's Salvation:"—

14 And as Moses lifted up the serpent in the Wilderness,

—"and it came to pass that if a serpent had bitten any man, when he beheld the serpent of brass he lived:"(c)—

15 even so must the Son of Man be lifted up: that whosoever believeth in Him should not perish, but have eternal life.

For when the fiery serpents bit the Israelites, and "much people died," Moses, by the command of GOD, "made a serpent of brass, and put it upon a pole." With what result to those who beheld it, has been already stated.(d.) This, then, was a manifest type not only of *the manner*, but also of *the benefit* of CHRIST's death; as CHRIST Himself here declares to Nicodemus. Moreover, the Faith of "those who truly turn to Him," was aptly shown in the condition required of as many as were bitten of serpents, and had thus come under "the power of the Enemy."(e)

To be "lifted up" was the common phrase by which Crucifixion was expressed. Our LORD employed it on two subsequent occasions. "When ye have *lifted up* the Son of Man," (He said to the Jews,) "then shall ye know that I am He."(f) So again, at the very close of His ministry, only a day or two before He suffered— "And I, if I be *lifted up from the Earth*, will draw all men unto Me." "This He said," declares the Evangelist, "signifying *what death He should die*."(g) And indeed, it is evident that the people understood the words in that sense, from the reply they immediately made: "We have heard out of the Law that CHRIST abideth for ever; and how sayest Thou, The Son of Man must be *lifted up?*"

"Observe," says an Eastern Bishop. "He alludes to the Passion obscurely, in consideration to His hearer: but the fruits of the Passion He unfolds plainly,"—namely, "whosoever believeth in Him, shall have Eternal Life."

Hear, there, what comfortable words our SAVIOUR CHRIST saith unto all that truly turn *to Him* —

16 For GOD so loved the World, that He gave His Only-begotten Son, that whosoever believeth in Him should not perish, but have everlasting life.

It is here declared that the Only-begotten Son was given to death. As before, that which belongs to GOD was attributed to Man; so now, what belongs to Man, is assigned to GOD. Thus largely has the great mystery of Man's Redemption been already opened to Nicodemus! Our LORD moreover here enlightens him as to a great truth, unsuspected by Nicodemus and by the Jewish nation at large; namely, that MESSIAH was to be the Saviour not of that nation only, but of the whole world. "GOD so loved *the World* that He gave His Only-begotten Son." "And He is the propitiation for our sins; and not for ours only, but also *for the sins of the whole World*."(h)

"GOD commendeth His love towards us," saith St. Paul, "in that, while we were yet sinners, CHRIST died for us:"(i) in that, "He . . . . spared not His own Son, but delivered Him up for us all."(k) "In this," saith St. John again, "was manifested the love of GOD towards us, because that GOD sent His Only-Begotten Son into the World, that we might live through Him. Herein is love; not that we loved GOD, but that He loved us, and sent His Son to be the propitiation for our sins."(l) The Old Testament promised only length of days: but the Gospel promises "Everlasting Life."

(c) Numbers xxi. 9.   (d) Numbers xxi. 6 to 9.   (e) Consider St. Luke x. 19.
(f) St. John viii. 28.   (g) St. John xii. 32, 33.   (h) 1 St. John ii. 2.
(i) Romans v. 8.   (k) Romans viii. 32.   (l) 1 St. John iv. 9, 10.

17 For GOD sent not His SON into the World to condemn the World; t that the World through Him might be saved.

For GOD desireth not the death of a sinner, but rather that he should turn from ı wickedness, and live.(m)　He is called the SAVIOUR of the World, for He *wills* ı Salvation of all men.　If men perish, it is because they oppose *their* wills to a.

18 He that believeth on Him is not condemned:

On the contrary,—he "hath everlasting life, and shall not come into condemna-
m; but is passed from Death unto Life."　So it is written in St. John v. 24,—
ıere see the note.

but he that believeth not is condemned already, because he hath not
lieved in the Name of the Only-Begotten SON of GOD.

He is "*condemned*," because (as St. John Baptist declares in verse 36,) "he that
ılieveth not the SON shall not see Life: but the wrath of GOD abideth on him."
ıd he is "condemned *already;*" for although Judgment hath not appeared, yet
it already given. The LORD knoweth who are His: *who* are awaiting the crown,
ıd *who* the fire.

19 And this is the condemnation, that Light is come into the World,
ıd men loved Darkness rather than Light, because their deeds were
vil.

"The condemnation" spoken of in the preceding verse consisted in *this;* that
ıben CHRIST the true Light came into the world, men rejected Him and His Doc-
rıne: proving by their actions that they loved Darkness rather than Light. Evil
rather than Good; inasmuch as they made free choice of the one and rejected the
ıther.

The reason is added,—"Because their deeds were evil."　And this statement
exactly falls in with what we are so often elsewhere assured of; namely, that the
discernment of Truth is a moral, not an intellectual act.

20, 21 For every one that doeth evil hateth the Light, neither cometh to the Light, lest his deeds should be reproved.　But he that doeth
Truth cometh to the Light, that his deeds may be made manifest, that
they are wrought in GOD.

In the language of the SPIRIT, "Truth" is another name for *Righteousness;*
hence, "Truth" is found directly opposed to "Unrighteousness",in Psalm li. 5, 6:
John viii. 18: Rom. ii. 8:(n) 1 Cor. xiii. 6.　This is surely a most instructive circumstance; for whereas *Righteousness* is a *moral* attribute,—we are apt to regard
Truth as a purely *intellectual* matter.　And yet Holy Scripture reminds us of our
mistake in countless places; as was remarked in the preceding note. See some observations on this subject in the note on St. John vii. 17.　The frequent recurrence
ıf the words "True" and "Truth" in the present Gospel is very remarkable.

With marvellous frequency do we find our LORD discoursed of in Holy Scripture
ınder the image of *Light*.　He loved to apply to Himself this Title; and to dis-
ıourse of Himself and of His Heavenly doctrine in terms derived from this, the
lrst-born of all His creatures,—"the beginning of the Creation of GOD."(o)

Every one who is resolved to sin, (He says,) who delights in sin, hateth the
light which detects his sin.

And thus ended this memorable discourse of our SAVIOUR.　Is it not possible
ıat there was something personal, as it were, in its concluding sentences: or, at
ıast, that the season when it was spoken,—the time of *Darkness*,(p)—may have
ıggested the prevailing image with which it is brought to a close?

22 After these things came JESUS and His Disciples into the land
of Judæa;

(m) Ezekiel xxxiii. 11; xviii. 23, 31, 32.
(n) See also Romans i. 18; and consider Rev. xxi. 25; xxii. 15.
(o) Rev. iii. 14.　　　　　　　　　　(p) See above verse 2: and the note there.

That is to say, the blessed Company withdrew from the City of Jerusalem, (whither our LORD had been to keep the Passover,(q) and where the preceding Discourse with Nicodemus had taken place ;) and went to dwell somewhere on the banks of the Jordan. For, as it follows,—

and there He tarried with them, and baptized.

Not that He baptized any *Himself* Of this we are particularly assured in the beginning of the next chapter,—where it is said, " Though JESUS baptized not, but His Disciples."(r)

23 And John also was baptizing in Ænon near to Salim, because there was much water there : and they came, and were baptized.

The Evangelist describes a locality in the north of the Holy Land,—our SAVIOUR living at this time in the south of it, and therefore at a distance of many miles from the scene of the Baptist's ministration. All Samaria lay between CHRIST and His Forerunner. Salim is thought to have been the place called Shalim in 1 Sam. ix. 4. Ænon and Salim will have been in Galilee, a little to the south of Bethshan, and west of the Jordan. In this neighborhood, on account of the abundant supply of water, the Baptist had fixed himself:

24 For John was not yet cast into prison.

With this passing allusion, the beloved Disciple dismisses the imprisonment of the Forerunner, concerning which the other Evangelists have discoursed to us so largely.(s) John Baptist was not yet cast into the dungeon of Machærus,—where, at the end of two years, he was murdered,(t)—but he was on the *very eve* of that event. The discourse, therefore, which begins at verse 27, and extends to the end of the present chapter,—being the lengthiest of his recorded discourses,—may be regarded as the latest public witness which John was permitted to bear to the MESSIAH.

25, 26 Then there arose a question between *some* of John's Disciples and the Jews about purifying. And they came unto John, and said unto him, Rabbi, He that was with thee beyond Jordan, to whom thou barest witness, behold, the Same baptizeth, and all *men* come to Him.

They refer to the transaction recorded in St. John i. 19 and 32; which "took place at Bethabara, beyond Jordan, where John was baptizing."
It is clearly implied that the "question," or rather the *dispute*, arose on the part of the Disciples of John; and may very well have turned upon the efficacy of the Baptisms respectively administered by the Baptist and by our LORD. They come to their Master, as if with the language of complaint; revealing by their words how wholly unconscious they are of the surpassing majesty of CHRIST. " He who was with thee;" (and it seems to be implied, "who received Baptism at thy hands ;") "the same baptizeth." The expression "All men come to Him," is the language of Disciples jealous for their Master's Honor and Reputation. Thereby is implied, what in the first verse of the ensuing chapter is expressly stated,—namely, that "JESUS made and baptized *more Disciples than John.*"
The design of John's reply is to remove the jealousy of his ardent followers; and to conduct them to the knowledge of the Truth.

27 John answered and said, A man can receive nothing except it be given him from Heaven.

Which may either be the Baptist's vindication of our SAVIOUR's conduct; or a humble admission of his own inferiority, and dependence on GOD. It is perhaps rather, as if he had said,—I am a mere man, and cannot assume any thing more than has been freely bestowed upon me from on High.—The very argument by which his ardent followers thought to have overthrown the MESSIAH, he proceeds to turn against them :—

(q) St. John ii. 23.   (r) St. John iv. 2.
(s) See St. Matth. xiv. 3 to 12; St. Mark vi. 17 to 29 ; St. Luke iii. 19 and 20.
(t) See the notes on St. Matth. xiv. 6 to 11, and St. Mark vi. 21 to 28.

28 Ye yourselves bear me witness, that I said, I am not the CHRIST,
ut that I am sent before Him.

Alluding to the saying recorded of him in St. John i. 20, 30, 31: which doubtless
ust have contained a special reference to Malachi's prophecy, — " I will *send* My
Messenger, and he shall prepare the way *before Me.*" (u)   Now, as many as are so
ent, are servants.   The Baptist however proceeds to declare the relation in which
e stood to CHRIST by a different resemblance: as it follows:

29 He that hath the Bride is the Bridegroom:

CHRIST is that " Bridegroom ;" and His Spouse or " Bride" is the Church.   To
Him the Bride belongeth. — The language of the SPIRIT is very constant in this re-
spect.   " Thy Maker is thine Husband : the LORD of Hosts is His Name," says the
Prophet Isaiah :(x) and again, "As the Bridegroom rejoiceth over the Bride, so shall
thy GOD rejoice over thee."(y)   Again, " I was *an Husband unto them*, saith the
LORD."(z)   This thought supplies the imagery of the xlv. Psalm, and of "the Song
of Songs, which is Solomon's."   It furnishes St. Paul with illustration and argument when he discourses of the duties of the married state.(a)   Lastly, the Marriage of the LAMB, is told of in the Book of Revelation ; where the Holy City, New
Jerusalem, (that is, the Church of the Redeemed,) is seen coming down from GOD
out of Heaven, prepared as "a Bride adorned for her Husband.(b) whence it is
styled " the Bride, the LAMB's Wife."(c)— CHRIST, then, is the chief person ; for it is
"*He* that hath the Bride :"—

but the friend of the Bridegroom, which standeth and heareth Him,
rejoiceth greatly because of the Bridegroom's voice : this my joy therefore is fulfilled.

As if he said,—*That* joy, therefore, has been mine; for I have heard the voice of
CHRIST.   I, the friend of the Bridegroom, have heard the Bridegroom's voice — How
must the Disciples of John have thrilled with wonder and admiration when, a year
or two after, they heard our SAVIOUR claim to Himself the very title which the
Forerunner here bestows upon Him !   See St. Mark ii. 19, and the notes thereon.
   The expression " which *standeth*," (says an ancient Father,) "is not without
meaning ; but indicates that the part of John is now over, and that for the future
he must stand and listen.". . . . That the expression is not without meaning, either
here, or in chapter i. 35, (the place to which the Baptist's words seem to have re-
ference,) may well be suspected : but *what* its meaning precisely is, is doubtful.(d)
   Certain however it is that in this place the Baptist (calling himself " the friend
of the Bridegroom,") describes the joy which filled his heart when he first heard the
blessed sound of the SAVIOUR's Voice.   Very brief indeed appears to have been the
intercourse of MESSIAH and His Forerunner.   One only sentence is our SAVIOUR
known to have addressed to the Baptist, — or even to have uttered within his hear-
ing!   See St. Matthew iii. 15, and the last words of the note there.
   But our SAVIOUR was now about to begin His Ministry : John Baptist therefore
is ready to withdraw from the scene, — " as the Morning-Star is willingly drowned
in the brightness of the rising Sun."   It follows, —

30 He must increase, but I *must* decrease.

My reputation must grow less and less ; my followers must fall away ; the very
Disciples whom I have baptized will have to be rebaptized by Him.(e)   But *His*
Name must spread, and His Disciples increase : His Faith must extend into all
Lands, till all the World doth acknowledge Him, and Earth as well as Heaven be-
comes full of the majesty of His Glory. . . . . Such is the scope of these words of the
Forerunner: " a prophet, yea, I say unto you, and more than a prophet !"(f)

31 He that cometh from above is above all: he that is of the earth
is earthly, and speaketh of the earth : He that cometh from Heaven is
above all.

(o) Malachi iii. 1.   (x) Isaiah liv. 5.   (y) Isaiah lxii. 5.
(z) Jerem. xxxi. 32.   Compare iii. 14, 20.   Also Hos. ii. 19, 20.
(a) Ephesians v. 23 to 32.   Compare also 2 Cor. xi. 2.   And see Rom. vii. 1 to 4.
(b) Rev. xxi. 2: xix. 7.   (c) Rev. xxi. 9   (d) Compare St. John vii. 37.
(e) Acts xix. 1 to 5.   (f) St. Matthew xi. 9.

Rather, "Is above all [things] ;" which is only another way of expressing the ordinary Name of GOD,—" the MOST HIGH :" as He is called in Acts vii. 48, and as He is described in Psalm xcvii. 9.   St. John Baptist therefore in this place asserts the Divinity of CHRIST. " He that cometh from above,"— he says; or, (as our LORD expressed it in verse 13,) " He that came down from Heaven,"— is GOD.   The fore-runner is contrasting himself, earthly in his parentage, and earthly in all his thoughts, with MESSIAH, the LORD from Heaven, whose way he came to prepare.... Still speaking of Him, he continues,—

32 And what He hath seen and heard, that He testifieth; and no man receiveth His testimony.

" We speak that we do know, and testify that We have seen ; and ye receive not Our Witness ;" said our LORD in verse 11, where see the note. "As our senses are our surest channels of knowledge," observes an ancient writer, " and teachers are most depended on who have apprehended by " sight" or " hearing" what they teach, John adds this argument in favor of CHRIST, that, " what He hath *heard* and *seen, that* He testifieth ;"meaning that every thing " which He said is true."   The parallel between verses 31, 32, (the words of the Baptist,) and verses 11 and 13, (the words of CHRIST,) is very remarkable.

The Disciples of John had said, — " All men come to Him."(g)   Their Master here replies,—" And yet no man receiveth His testimony :"

33 He that hath received His testimony hath set to his seal that GOD is true.

The Baptist declares that whosoever hath received CHRIST's Testimony, hath set his seal to GOD's Truth : just as " he that believeth not GOD" is elsewhere declared to have made CHRIST " a liar ; because he believeth not the testimony that GOD gave of His SON."(h)   The words which follow are to be taken in close connection with what precedes : —

34 For he whom GOD hath sent speaketh the words of GOD.

Which supplies the reason of what goes before.   For *CHRIST*, whom GOD hath sent, speaketh the very words of *GOD*.   How remarkable are these statements of the Baptist concerning CHRIST, when compared with the similar statements made by CHRIST concerning Himself! For example,—" I have not spoken of Myself; but the FATHER which sent Me, He gave Me a Commandment, what I should say, and what I should speak .... Whatsoever I speak therefore, even as the FATHER said unto Me, so I speak."(i)   " I speak to the World those things which I have heard of Him."(k) — For the correct understanding of which sayings, and the many similar ones contained in the Gospel, the mysterious relation of the First and Second Per-son in the Blessed Trinity, as set forth in the Creeds of the Church, is to be faith-fully borne in mind.   Some remarks will be found on this subject in the notes on St. John v. 20 ; to which the reader is referred.

for GOD giveth not the Spirit by measure *unto Him.*

As unto *men* He giveth ; "dividing to every man severally as He will."(l) On the contrary : " in Him dwelleth all the fullness of the Godhead bodily."(m)

35 The FATHER loveth the SON, and hath given all things into His hands.

And so our LORD declares of Himself; saying, " all things are delivered unto Me of My FATHER."(n)   And the present Evangelist remarks concerning Him, that He knew " that the FATHER had given all things into his Hands."(o)

He speaks of the union of Deity with Manhood.   " Because ' the FATHER loveth the SON' as man, He hath, by uniting Deity with Manhood, ' given all things into His hands.' "(p)   " All things that the FATHER hath are Mine," said our SAVI-OUR :(q) because in Him is the fullness of the same Godhead ; and more than that,

---

(g) Verse 26.
(k) St. John viii. 26.
(n) St. Mark xi. 27.
(q) St. John xvi. 15.

(h) 1 St. John v. 10.
(l) 1 Cor. xii. 11.
(o) St. John xiii. 3.

(i) 1 John xii. 49, 50.
(m) Coloss. ii. 9. See also i. 19.
(p) The words are Hooker's.

ᴇ Fᴀᴛʜᴇʀ cannot have. "But since the Fᴀᴛʜᴇʀ alone is originally that Deity
ʜɪcʜ Cʜʀɪsᴛ originally is not, (for Cʜʀɪsᴛ is Gᴏᴅ by being of Gᴏᴅ, Light by issuing
ᴛ of Light,) it followeth that whatsoever Cʜʀɪsᴛ hath common unto Him with
ɪs Heavenly Fᴀᴛʜᴇʀ, the same of necessity must be *given* Him: yet naturally and
ᴇʀɴally given, not bestowed by way of benevolence and favour."(*r*)
Now, because the Fᴀᴛʜᴇʀ hath given all things into the hands of the Soɴ, He
ᴛʜ given Eternal Life into His hands also: whence, it follows immediately,—

36 He that believeth on the Soɴ hath everlasting Life: and he that
lieveth not the Soɴ shall not see Life;

Sᴛ. John says elsewhere,—"He that hath the Soɴ hath Life: and He that hath
ᴛ the Soɴ of Gᴏᴅ hath not Life."(*s*) "He that believeth on Me" (said our Sᴀ-
ᴠᴜʀ) "hath everlasting Life;"(*t*) "but he that believeth not, is condemned al-
ᴅy."(*u*) So faithfully did the Baptist (who was the Voice of the Wᴏʀᴅ) deliver
ɪ Testimony concerning Mᴇssɪᴀʜ!
The three concluding verses of the present chapter are illustrated in a remark-
ᴅᴇ manner by St. John v. 19 to 24, where Cʜʀɪsᴛ is the Speaker. The train of
ᴏᴜght will be perceived to be similar in both places.

but the wrath of Gᴏᴅ abideth on him.

"See," (exclaims an ancient Bishop) "how He refers to the Fᴀᴛʜᴇʀ when He
ᴘᴇᴀᴋs of punishment! He says not 'the wrath of the Soɴ,' though the Soɴ is
Jᴜᴅge:(*v*) but He makes the Fᴀᴛʜᴇʀ the Judge in order to alarm men more."
It is not said that on such an one *cometh* the Wrath of Gᴏᴅ; but on him the
Wrath of Gᴏᴅ (it is declared) *abideth:* "for all who are born, are under the Wrath
ᴅ Gᴏᴅ, which the first Adam incurred." We "were by nature the children of
wrath," as the Apostle speaks.(*w*) In this place therefore, the very form of the
ᴇxpression bears witness to the doctrine of Original or Birth-Sin.

———

A pious living writer, at the end of his commentary on the present chapter, ex-
ᴄlaims:—"Out of this Land of Darkness, and which lieth under the shadow of
Death, I stretch forth my hands unto Thee. O Thou who dwellest in Light which
ɴo man may approach unto, who art without variableness or shadow of turning,
from whom alone cometh every good and perfect gift,—grant unto me that Wisdom
which cometh from above, and which Thou hast promised to give unto those who
ᴀsk it of Thee. Grant me to understand Thy Words, which are from Heaven; and
ᴛo loose my hold of earthly things; and to follow Thee! Do Thou forget those
ᴛhings that are past; blot them out of Thy Book, and wash them out of my
ʜᴇart, that I may be able to see Thee who art the true Light: to see Thee and to
love Thee, in such sort that I may see and love nothing else, except what I behold
ᴀnd love in Thee!"

THE PRAYER.

O Aʟᴍɪɢʜᴛʏ Gᴏᴅ, whom truly to know is everlasting life; grant us
perfectly to know Thy Soɴ Jᴇsᴜs Cʜʀɪsᴛ to be the Way, the Truth,
ᴀnd the Life; that, following the steps of Thy holy Apostles, Saint
Philip and Saint James, we may steadfastly walk in the way that
leadeth to eternal Life; through the same Thy Soɴ Jᴇsᴜs Cʜʀɪsᴛ our
Lᴏʀᴅ. Amen.

(*r*) The quotation is again from Hooker.   (*s*) 1 St. John v. 12.
(*t*) St. John vi. 47.   (*u*) St. John iii. 18.   (*v*) St. John v. 22 and 27.   (*w*) Ephes. ii. 3.

CHAPTER IV.

1 CHRIST *talketh with a Woman of Samaria, and revealeth Himself unto her.* 27
His Disciples marvel. 31 *He declareth to them His zeal to* GOD'S *Glory.* 39
Many Samaritans believe on Him. 43 *He departeth into Galilee, and healeth the
Ruler's son that lay sick at Capernaum.*

THE former chapter ended with the record of the last public witness which the
Forerunner was permitted to bear to his LORD,—the longest of his recorded discourses. The Baptist had since been cast into prison, and the Ministry of CHRIST
was now about to begin. It had begun, in a manner, half a year before; namely,
immediately after His Baptism : but the Imprisonment of John is clearly noticed
as the event from which our SAVIOUR's public Ministry dated its more special commencement. A journey into Galilee was then undertaken,—which all the four
Evangelists concur in recording,(*a*)—and the immediate occasion of which, the
Evangelist St. John subjoins. The present chapter contains a relation of the great
incident which rendered that journey for ever memorable.

It might well have been suspected beforehand that the events of a journey undertaken at such a time must have been replete with interest and wonder : but nothing
so exquisite as the fulfillment of history, (so to speak,) which St. John here records,
could have been imagined by unassisted reason. For we shall discover that our
REDEEMER at the close of His first day's travel, arrived at that very spot of ground
where Abraham had made his first resting-place on entering the Land of Canaan.
Our SAVIOUR CHRIST, as faithful Abraham had done before Him, "passed through
the land *unto the place of Sichem ;*"(*b*) and lo, as Abraham had there been blessed
with the vision of JEHOVAH, and the promise—"*Unto thy seed* will I give this
land :" so did MESSIAH, (having taken "on Him *the seed of Abraham,*")(*c*) at once,
and at this very spot, enter on His promised spiritual inheritance ! The people of
Sichem, (here written "Sychar,") were the first to enter the Heavenly Canaan.
They became the first-fruits of the spiritual Harvest of the Land. And thus much
for the present incident, as it was a fulfillment of ancient Prophecy.

Standing in the very fore-front of the Sacred Narrative, it seems to have been
further designed to inform us that the Samaritans were included,—included, as the
remoter heathen nations were not,—in the circle to which the Gospel message in the
first instance extended ; while yet their preparation and previous character were es-
sentially different from that which belonged to the legitimate family of Abraham.(*d*)

It becomes necessary now to enter on the particular consideration of the narrative before us ; but the train of thought thus opened will be found pursued lower
down, in the notes on ver. 42.

2, 3 WHEN therefore the LORD knew how the Pharisees had heard
that JESUS made and baptized more disciples than John, (though JESUS
Himself baptized not,) but His disciples, He left Judea, and departed
again into Galilee.

The first of the four Passovers which mark the duration of our Blessed LORD'S
Ministry, was now past.(*e*) Our SAVIOUR had not returned at once into Galilee ;
but had withdrawn with His Disciples from Jerusalem to the banks of the Jordan,
where He made a brief sojourn and baptized,(*f*) and where He was now residing.
From a comparison of the Gospels, it is found that John Baptist, who in the last
chapter, "was not yet cast into prison,"(*g*) now *was* a prisoner. At this juncture,
our SAVIOUR withdraws from Judea, and returns into Galilee ;(*h*) and it is here

---

(*a*) St. Matth. iv. 12 : St. Mark i. 14 : St. Luke iv. 14: St. John iv. 3 and 43.
(*b*) Gen. xii. 6.   (*c*) Heb. ii. 15, and St. Matth. i. 1.   (*d*) Dr. W. H. Mill
(*e*) St. John ii. 23.   (*f*) See St. John iii. 22.   (*g*) St. John iii. 24.
(*h*) The references are given in the above note.(*a*).

nted that the immediate cause of His withdrawal was the jealousy of the Phari-
-es — occasioned by the number of Disciples which He made.

But why did a message, conveyed to the Pharisees at Jerusalem, to the effect that
Jesus is making and baptizing more Disciples than John,(*i*) lead to the Saviour's
ithdrawal from Judea into Galilee? Were the Pharisees inclined to become John's
isciples? or were they even jealous for the Baptist's honor? Not so. But from
:apter i. verses 19 and 24, it is found that they had long since satisfied themselves
1at *John* was not "the Christ." Fully alive to the general expectation which
1en prevailed, of Messiah's near Advent; and aroused by the tidings of one who
was baptizing," and making many disciples, "in Bethabara beyond Jordan;"
hey had sent a deputation from Jerusalem, formally to inquire whether John were
he Christ or not; and to ascertain his exact pretensions.(*k*) "When therefore the
Lord knew that the Pharisees had heard" that He was drawing to Himself *more
Disciples even than John*,—that "*all men*," in short, were "coming to Him," and
that He was baptizing them,(*l*)—(which last circumstance, however, was not strictly
true, as the Evangelist is careful to note,)—it became a measure of prudence to
withdraw from their observation into the remoter region of Galilee: whereby our
Great Pattern is found to have submitted Himself to the precept which He delivered
to His Apostles, concerning flight from persecution.(*m*)

It is obvious to remark in passing that a hint is here supplied for the probable
reason why our Saviour so frequently imposed silence on the objects of His mercy,
—forbidding them to make Him known.(*n*) Especially does that command of His,
delivered both to Apostles(*o*) and Evil Spirits, that they should not tell "that He
was the Christ,"(*p*) derive illustration from our Lord's conduct at this juncture.
To attract towards Him the notice of the chief professors of Religion among the
Jews, would probably have been the most effectual way of defeating the gracious
purpose of His Ministry. *He* knew when, and how, and to whom, to reveal Himself.(*q*) Other men, not so.

4 And He must needs go through Samaria.

Because that country occupies the centre of the Holy Land, separating Judæa
and Galilee.

5 Then cometh He to a city of Samaria, which is called Sychar, near to the parcel of ground that Jacob gave to his son Joseph.

Alluding to the act of the dying Patriarch, recorded in Genesis xlviii. 22. Sychar
is the city called (by anticipation) "Sichem,"(*r*) and "Shechem" in the Old Testament ;(*s*) after "Shechem the son of Hamor the Hivite."(*t*)　In the Acts,(*u*) the
name is written "Sychem." "The parcel of ground" here spoken of, is twice mentioned in Genesis: first, as the spot where the patriarch Jacob spread his tent, and
erected an altar to the Lord.(*x*)　Here also it was, that "the bones of Joseph, which
the children of Israel brought up out of Egypt," were buried; "and it became the
inheritance of the children of Joseph."(*y*)　Indeed, it would seem from St. Stephen's
Apology, as if *all* the patriarchs had been buried in this place.(*z*)　The spot is
clearly distinguishable at the present day,—"a field which the Lord hath
blessed."(*a*)　In the words of a recent traveller,(*b*)—"It is a most lovely spot: just
such a choice piece of ground as a Father would give to a favorite Son.　It is level
and very fertile, like a garden: just at the entrance of a pleasant valley between
hills.　I have no doubt that the very ancient tomb which stands upon it, is rightly
called Joseph's."

But *why* is it specially recorded that the incident which follows took place "near
to the parcel of ground that Jacob gave to his son Joseph?"　Chiefly, it may be

(*i*) Such is the exact translation of ver. 1.　　　　(*k*) See St. John i. 19 to 28.
(*l*) Verses 1 and 2 should be compared with verses 22 and 26 of the former chapter.
(*m*) St. Matth. x. 23.—where see the note.
(*n*) See the note on St. Mark i. 44 ; also the last note on St. Mark i.
(*o*) St. Matth. xvi. 20.　　　　(*p*) St. Mark i. 34 and iii. 12 ; St. Luke iv. 41.
(*q*) Consider St. John iv. 25, 26 : ix. 35 to 37, &c. &c.　　(*r*) Gen. xii. 6.
(*s*) See Genesis xxxiii. 18.　Joshua xxiv. 32.　　　　(*t*) See Gen. xxxiv.
(*u*) Acts vii. 16.　　　　(*x*) Genesis xxxiii. 18 to 20 : see also xlviii. 22.
(*y*) Joshua xxiv. 32.　　　　(*z*) Acts vii. 15, 16.　　　　(*a*) Gen. xxvii. 27.
(*b*) C. L. Higgins, Esq., of Turvey Abbey.

thought, in order to lead us to connect that solemn bequest of the Patriarch to his Son, with the present incident,—somewhat in the manner which will be found pointed out below, in the note on ver. 42. " To this spot of ground our LORD came, that the Samaritans, who claimed to be inheritors of the Patriarch Jacob,(c) might recognize Him; and be converted to CHRIST, the Patriarch's legal heir."(d)

Shechem, or Sychar, lay between the mountains Gerizim and Ebal; and towards this spot, ("the champaign over against Gilgal, beside the plains of Moreh,"(e) is ALMIGHTY GOD found to have directed the eyes of His chosen People, at the end of their wandering in the Wilderness. They were commanded, when they should come into the Holy Land, to repair hither and put the blessing upon Mount Geri-zim, and the curse upon Mount Ebal ;(f)—building on the latter mountain an altar, and stationing six of the tribes on Mount Gerizim to bless the people; and six upon Ebal, to curse.(g) The singular nation, known after the Captivity as " the Sama-ritans," are found to have made Shechem their chief place of residence; which lasted, as we see, down to the time of our LORD. Certain of them remain in the same locality to the present day.

Their origin has been already briefly noticed in the note on St. Matthew x. 6: the only authentic account we possess concerning them, being derived from the Bible.(h) It seems probable that along with the strange nations which the King of Assyria transplanted into the cities of Samaria, must have been mixed many of the ancient inhabitants of the Land. Such a remnant will have retained the wor-ship of the true GOD, as anciently they professed to have done,(i) notwithstanding the general idolatry of the Land ;(k) and this will account for the anxiety to be per-mitted to help the Jews, on their return from the Captivity, to rebuild the Temple. The Jews denied them the wished-for privilege; whereupon the Samaritans did all in their power to prevent the rebuilding of the City and the Temple ;(l) and out of this, grew the hatred which ever after subsisted between the two races. The Sa-maritans, in the time of Sanballat, built a rival Temple of their own upon Mount Gerizim, (the scene of ancestral worship to which the woman refers in ver. 20,) and their name, as we have seen, became henceforth a reproach, and a contemptuous by-word with the Jewish nation.(m) That the Samaritans were wholly in the wrong, in all the points of controversy between the rival races, is certain : yet may the injustice of the sentiment with which they were regarded by the Jews, be infer-red from the many favorable notices bestowed upon them by our SAVIOUR,(n)— their prompt and hearty Faith, so far surpassing that of their more favored rivals, and the astonishing use they had made of their Knowledge of the Way of Salvation, which had been wholly gleaned out of the Five Books of Moses.

6 Now Jacob's well was there.

And there it is, unmistakably, to this day : a deep well, dug as was customary in the patriarchal age, in the place of sojourn ;(o) and which Tradition has always pointed out as the well of the patriarch Jacob. It is described as "one of the most interesting objects in the Holy Land,—admitting of no doubt as to its identity with the spot St. John describes. It is exactly in the road which a traveller would take, in passing from Judæa into Galilee,—is not far from Sychar,—and above all, it is the only well in the neighborhood which fulfills the requirements of the Scripture record. This it does entirely,—being very deep, while all the other wells and springs lie near the surface, and the water of the larger portion can be reached even with the hand. The water, from its depth, is always exceedingly cool; on which account it is that persons are accustomed to visit it, in preference to other springs nearer the City."(p)

How striking a picture then is here set before us. He to whom Jacob had erected his Altar, and whom the patriarch Jacob himself foreshadowed, sits down wearied on Jacob's well: and presently we shall behold Him surrounded by the chiefs of Twelve spiritual tribes—the men who are hereafter to "judge the twelve tribes of Israel."(q)

(c) See below, ver. 12.   (d) Alcuin.   (e) Deut. xi. 30.   (f) Deut. xi. 29.
(g) Deut. xxvii. 1 to 13.   Joshua viii. 30 to 35.   (h) See chiefly 2 Kings xvii.
(i) Ezra iv. 2.   See also 2 Kings xvii. 27, 28.   (k) 2 Kings xvii. 29 to 33.
(l) Ezra iv. 11 to 16, &c.   (m) See the note on St. Luke x. 35.
(n) See St. Luke x. 33 to 35, and the note on ver. 37 : xvii. 16 to 18, &c.
(o) Gen. xxi. 25 to 30; xxvi. 15, 18 to 22, 32, 33.
(p) From the MS. already cited in the note on verse 5.
(q) St. Matth. xix. 28; St. Luke xxii. 30.

JESUS, therefore, being wearied with *His* journey, sat thus on the ell :

"Thus," in this place, means *"accordingly."* That is, our SAVIOUR was weary, id *so* He sat on the well. .

And how is it possible at this mention of a well, and the meeting which follows, avoid recalling the many occasions in the Old Testament when a well was the ene of mighty transactions in the Economy of Grace? Isaac, and Jacob, and oses, each found his future wife beside a well of water:(r) and here it is seen at one greater than these, their Divine Antitype, the Bridegroom, (as the Baptist us so lately called Him,)(s) takes to Himself His alien spouse, the Samaritan burch, at a well likewise.(t) On this head, see more in the note prefixed to the resent Chapter. Take notice then, that as His Death is our Life, so is His very eariness our refreshment. He thirsted that we might not thirst for ever.

Hunger is once recorded of the Son of Man :(u) Thirst, twice.(x) He partook f all our trials; and was made conscious, by His own mysterious experience, of ll our wants,—wants which the perfection of His nature doubtless rendered unpeakably acute and severe. It is discovered, however, from what follows, that it was not meat from the city, or drink from the well, for which He so hungered and thirsted, as for the souls of the men of Sychar,—the soul of her who came to draw water. ' Consider verses 10, 31, 32, 34, 35.

The beloved Disciple proceeds to fix with exactness the time at which the event he is describing, occurred,—which it is his manner to do, more than the other Evangelists :(y)

and it was about the sixth hour.

It was "the time of the Evening, even the time that women go out to draw water,"(z)—namely, six o'clock. It has been already pointed out that St. John does not reckon the hours after the Jewish method, (for it is clear that he wrote his Gospel at a distance from Judæa, and addressed it to persons who were familiar neither with the language nor with the customs of the Commonwealth of Israel;) (a) but, writing in Asia, he reckons time after the Asiatic method; which, singular to relate, corresponds exactly with our own. It was now *Evening*, therefore, not *Noon:* and the Son of Man, weary with the length of His day's Journey, sat Him down to rest on Jacob's Well.

7 There cometh a woman of Samaria to draw water: JESUS saith unto her, Give Me to drink.

This "woman of Samaria," or rather, "Samaritan woman," seems to have belonged to the city of Sychar. She came to draw water from the well; little suspecting that before her return to the city she should draw her first draught of living water out of the Well of Salvation !(b)

Are we to suppose that she now complied with the request of the Stranger? For she does not seem to have done so *afterwards.* Our LORD may have withdrawn from the well's mouth, while she let down her waterpot, before addressing her; and then opened the conversation in the manner recorded in the verse before us. In the meantime, the Evangelist proceeds to assign the reason why our SAVIOUR addressed His request to *her ;*—

8, 9 (For His Disciples were gone away unto the city to buy meat.) Then saith the Woman of Samaria unto Him, How is it that Thou, being a Jew, askest drink of me, which am a woman of Samaria? (for the Jews have no dealings with the Samaritans.)

(r) Gen. xxiv. 11 to 29; xxix. 2 to 10. Exodus ii. 15 to 17.
(s) St. John iii. 29.
(t) The reader is referred to the note on St. Luke xxii. 12.
(u) St. Mark xi. 12.   (x) See St. John xix. 28.
(y) Consider the following places,—St. John i. 29, 35, 39, 43; ii. 1, 13; iii. 2; iv. 52; v. 1;
vi. 4, 22; vii. 2, 14, 37; x. 22; xi. 6, 55; xii. 1, 12; xiii. 30; xix. 14, &c.
(z) Genesis xxiv. 11.
(a) See the note on St. John vi. 1. Compare with the text St. John i. 39.
(b) Isaiah xii. 3.

That is,—No familiar intercourse takes place between them. The two nations might trade together,—buy and sell, as the Disciples were even now doing: but not ask favors of one another, or even drink out of the same vessel. Take notice, however, that this rancorous feeling subsisted rather on the side of the Jews,(c) than of the singular people towards whom our LORD manifested his favor on this, and so many subsequent occasions. It was "*the Jews*" who would " have no dealings with *the Samaritans*." Hence it may be thought that our SAVIOUR's request and gracious manner,—so full of Divine Love, and gentleness unspeakable,—at once opened the heart of this Woman; even while she offered her waterpot to His parched lips, and gladly bestowed upon Him the favor which He had so far humbled Himself as to ask at her hands.

The words in the last clause, explaining the reason of the Woman's surprise at being so addressed by our LORD, are clearly not hers, but the Evangelist's.

10 JESUS answered and said unto her, If thou knewest the gift of GOD, and who it is that saith to thee, Give Me to drink; thou wouldest have asked of Him, and He would have given thee living water.

"*Living* water" is properly water from the spring,—as opposed to that which is stagnant. Our SAVIOUR speaks of the life-giving Spirit under this figure, as that which is always stirring within the heart, and refreshing the soul of him who receives it.

But, by "the gift of GOD," in this place is meant *the gift of His Only SON.* Hear our learned Hooker: " The gift whereby GOD hath made CHRIST a fountain of Life, is the conjunction of the nature of Man in the person of CHRIST; which gift, (saith He to the woman of Samaria,) if thou didst know, and *in that respect* understand *who it is* which asketh water of thee, thou wouldest ask of Him, that He might give thee living water." So that what our LORD in the last chapter said to Nicodemus, He here repeats; namely, "GOD so loved the world that He gave," (observe, the *gift*,) " His Only-begotten SON; that every one who believeth in Him should not perish, but have Everlasting Life."(d) The connection of our SAVIOUR's reply with the Woman's question thus becomes apparent. She had reminded Him of the enmity which existed between her nation and His own. His answer implies that GOD loves *the whole World*, and wills the Salvation of *every one*.

" If thou knewest," (saith our LORD,) " that GOD hath given and sent His Son; and that I who speak to thee am He; instead of rebuking Me for begging a draught of water at thy hands, thou wouldest have been the first to ask the same favor at Mine; nor would I have rebuked thee, much less would I have denied thee: but I would have given thee to drink even of the water of Life!"

He "takes occasion therefore, from the well of Jacob that was there, to discourse, according to His Divine manner, of that water of Life which conveys pardon, peace, and the purification of the soul from sin; excludes the thirst of discontent, or the feverish desire of inferior and unreal blessings; and is to every one who truly receives it a well of water springing up to Everlasting Life."(e)

And besides the illustration thus afforded of our LORD's manner in availing Himself of some accidental outward circumstance on which to base His Divine Teaching, two things here strike us. First, He is found to open His Discourse on this occasion, as on so many others, with a hard saying,—a parable as it were,—and to leave the force of what He declares to be evolved afterwards.(f) Next, we are struck with the form His Divine address to the woman takes. He wishes that she would *ask* of Him, in order that He might *give*. As a very ancient writer profoundly remarks,—" No one can receive a Divine Gift who asks not for it:"(g) and he illustrates his observation by alleging the striking language of the second Psalm; where the Eternal FATHER addressing the SON, says,—"Ask of Me, and I will give Thee the Heathen for Thine inheritance."(h) So, in another place it is enjoined,—"Ask, and it shall be given you; seek, and ye shall find; knock, and it shall be opened unto you; for every one that asketh, receiveth."(i)—" It is highly instructive to

<hr>

(c) See the note on St. Luke x. 36. Also St. John viii. 48, and St. Luke ix. 54.
(d) St. John iii. 16.
(e) Altered from Dr. W. H. Mill.
(f) Consider such places as the following,—St. John iii. 3; iv. 32; vi. 27, 33, 35; St. Matth. xvi. 6; St. Luke xvii. 37.
(g) Origen.   (h) Psalm ii. 8.   (i) St. Matthew vii. 7, 8.

see this principle in our LORD's conduct towards this woman, and indeed in all is dealings with mankind."(k)

Take notice that she has already learned to treat the unknown Stranger respectfully. She calls him " Sir ;" and instead of denying the possibility of what He has serted, asks Him to explain it.

11 The woman saith unto Him, Sir, Thou hast nothing to draw with, d the well is deep : from whence then' hast Thou that living water?

Striking indeed is the discovery that the well, concerning which we have already iefly spoken, and which Tradition has pointed out from the beginning as "Jab's well," should so remarkably retain the character here assigned to it. Travellers have found it to be of the depth of one hundred and five feet; and to this y it contains ten or fifteen feet of living water.

The woman, whose attention is now effectually aroused, seems to imply that He ust be some great One indeed, if, unaided by ordinary means, He can command eh a supply of the pure element, as shall render her future laborious journeys to is spot superfluous. She proceeds:

12 Art Thou greater than our father Jacob, which gave us the well, nd drank thereof himself, and his children, and his cattle?

Perhaps when "cattle" were supplied from a well, it was a proof that the water was abundant. Consider Gen. xxiv. 14 and 19, 20. The argument here is,—The great patriarch not only gave his children and his cattle to drink of this well, but be drank of it himself. He knew of no other resource whereby to quench his own thirst. "Art thou greater than our father Jacob?"—she therefore asks. And she already begins to suspect that she is addressing some great One indeed. That she little suspected the majesty of the Stranger, whom she had found sitting on Jacob's well, wearing the garb and using the language of a Jew, our SAVIOUR has already assured her. He proceeds to let her know that He is greater even than the Patriarch; not by vaunting Himself as such, but by contrasting the nature of the gift which it was in His power to bestow, with that of Jacob. As it follows:

13, 14 JESUS answered and said unto her, Whosoever drinketh of this water shall thirst again : but whosoever drinketh of the water that I shall give him shall never thirst; but the water that I shall give him shall be in him a well of water springing up into everlasting Life.

So spake He who proclaimed Himself of old as "the Fountain of living waters ;"(l) with whom "is the Well of Life ;"(m) and in whom whosoever believeth, "shall never thirst."(n) To the same effect on a subsequent occasion we shall hear Him cry, saying, "If any man thirst, let him come unto Me and drink. He that believeth on Me, as the Scripture hath said, out of his belly shall flow rivers of living water. But *this spake He of the Spirit*," adds the Evangelist, "which they that believe on Him should receive."(o) And of the HOLY SPIRIT our SAVIOUR speaks in this place also. It is the Water which *CHRIST* will give, because the Spirit proceedeth from the FATHER and the SON. "The fountain of Life in mortal man soon fails; but that fountain of Life which is in the SPIRIT never fails. None can fathom it, nor tell the depth nor circumference thereof. And this water of which he that drinks shall thirst again, is a type of all earthly desires, for nothing upon earth can satisfy the cravings of an immortal spirit; which, being made for GOD, can find rest in Him alone."(p)

15 The Woman saith unto Him, Sir, give me this water, that I thirst not, neither come hither to draw.

Of her history we know nothing beyond what is here recorded : but may not something be inferred even from her anxiety to be spared these daily journeys to the well?

(k) Williams.   (l) Jer. ii. 13 : xvii. 13.

(m) Ps. xxxvi. 9.   Consider Jer. xviii 14, (where see the margin,) and Rev. vii. 17 : xxi 6: xxii. 17.

(n) St. John vi. 35.   (o) St. John vii. 37 to 39,—where see the notes.   (p) Williams.

She asked in her simplicity, still supposing that it was water from the spring of which our SAVIOUR spake. What she meant, however, was, in dutiful obedience, and faith, to ask for the thing which CHRIST had bade her ask for. Seeing therefore that she came to the Fountain of all Wisdom, (who knoweth our necessities before we ask, and our ignorance in asking,) He had compassion upon our infirmities; and that thing which for her unworthiness she dared not, and for her blindness she could not ask, GOD vouchsafed to give her for the worthiness of His SON JESUS CHRIST our LORD.

Very strange and startling is the turn which the dialogue at this place takes. Observe, however, that what the woman had in effect said, was, that she desired *refreshment:* ("that I thirst not, neither come hither to draw:")—and to all such, saith not our SAVIOUR, "Come unto *Me?*" As it follows:

16 JESUS saith unto her, Go, call thy husband, and come hither.

Why did our LORD thus allude to the man with whom she appears to have been unlawfully connected? Was it only to give her an opportunity for the confession which follows?

17, 18 The woman answered and said, I have no husband. JESUS said unto her, Thou hast well said, I have no husband; for thou hast had five husbands: and he whom thou now hast is not thy husband: in that saidst thou truly.

By thus showing Himself acquainted with the past and present history of the stranger before Him, our SAVIOUR gave her the same evidence of His Godhead which He had already supplied to the guileless Nathaniel.(q) Nor can we doubt that, in either case, certain unrevealed circumstances imparted peculiar wonder to His words. He proved by a single sentence that *His* eye had been the witness of what had been transacted in strictest privacy, or with the utmost secrecy.(r)

The discovery, moreover, was attended in both cases with the same blessed results; for it follows,—

19 The woman saith unto Him, Sir, I perceive that Thou art a Prophet.

"The astonished Samaritan,—(respecting whom there is no necessity for supposing that she was now living in sin, and in whom the errors of her past life, whatever they might have been, had not obscured the perception of moral truth which our SAVIOUR ordinarily required in the hearer of His heavenly mysteries,)—confesses immediately that her informant is a prophet. None but one supernaturally enlightened could have discovered from the midst of a foreign race, what might have been probably unknown to many of her own countrymen."(s) She recognized our SAVIOUR at once as *a* prophet; and presently, as *the* "Prophet promised in the Law."(t)—Take notice that while the Jews looked chiefly for a *Kingly* (u) MESSIAH, the Samaritans seemed to have dwelt chiefly on His *Prophetic* character: while the Baptist is found specially to notice the *Priestly* office of CHRIST.(x)

Then pointing to Mount Gerizim, which stands full in sight of the spot where this conversation occurred, the woman appeals to the immemorial worship of her people there, and claims the holy patriarchs as the authors of her race; saying,

20 Our fathers worshipped in this mountain; and ye say, that in Jerusalem is the place where men ought to worship.

Does she thereby seek to give a speculative turn to the conversation, which had grown painfully personal; as we ever seek to turn to the edge of reproof, and to escape from what is private and particular, by referring to that which is general and indifferent? Surely, not so!—Or do we behold in these words the statement of a prejudice, introduced by the speaker, to outweigh a strong internal conviction? Is her conviction incomplete, from the difficulty she finds in recognizing the prophetic

(q) St. John i. 48.   (r) See the note on St. John i. 48.   (s) Dr. W. H. Mill.
(t) Deut. xviii. 15, 18. Also St. John iv. 25, 29, 39.
(u) Consider St. Matth. ii. 2. St. John i. 49: vi. 15: xii. 13: St. Luke xix. 38, &c.
(x) See St. Matth. iii. 14. St. John i. 29, &c.

character in *a Jew!*—Neither of these suggestions seems nearly so worthy of our acceptance as the following, offered by an excellent writer, who is pointing out that " her character is marked throughout with good." He says,—" The gentleness with which she first received the request of a Jewish stranger; her pious memory of the patriarch Jacob; her readiness to believe; her expressions of respect throughout, saying, ' Master;' her uncalled-for confession, that it was not her husband; and her apparent innocence on that subject, when she found herself before a Prophet: *her immediate inquiry respecting a point which was evidently nearest her heart, of the most acceptable mode of worshipping GOD;* the fullness of her faith afterwards; and the expressions that show she was evidently one of those who 'waited for the Consolation of Israel:'—all these things prove that although, like many others, she may have been chosen under circumstances apparently the most adverse, yet that her heart was in the main right towards GOD: the shadow of Gerizim, the mount of blessing, beside which she dwelt, was not in vain upon her; for she inherited the blessing of the pure of heart, in that she had eyes to discern GOD."(*y*)

And surely it is impossible to call to mind this woman's case,—that of the sinner mentioned in the vii. of St. Luke,(*z*) and again of her who is recorded in the viii. of St. John,(*a*)—as well as the case of the repentant malefactor,—without feeling that such examples are recorded not only for the consolation of great offenders, but also for the guidance of all. A great lesson of charity and forbearance is inculcated, when, from a stem to all appearance so lifeless, the fruits of the Spirit are found so abundantly to spring.

21 JESUS saith unto her, Woman, believe Me, the hour cometh, when ye shall neither in this mountain, nor yet at Jerusalem, worship the FATHER.

In neither place, (He means,) to the exclusion of all other places.—*"Believe Me,"* He begins; for that is the necessary condition of all teaching that is to profit.—It may not be out of place to remind the reader that Christian Churches do not take the place of the Jewish synagogues, but of *the temple of Jerusalem,* itself.—Our LORD's phrase, " The hour cometh," denotes how close at hand were the days of the Gospel,—when, " from the rising of the sun even unto the going down of the same," GOD's name should " be great amongst the Gentiles."(*b*)

"There was no necessity for CHRIST to show why the Fathers worshipped in that mountain, and the Jews in Jerusalem. He was therefore silent on that question; but asserted the religious superiority of the Jews on another ground,—the ground not of place, but of knowledge.(*c*) As it follows:

22 Ye worship ye know not what:

That is,—" You have lost the clear knowledge of the professed object of your worship, JEHOVAH the GOD of Israel, in forsaking that Tabernacle and Temple where He as truly fixed His habitation and His Glory in the days of David and Solomon, as He had fixed it in Shiloh of Ephraim before. You approach GOD in a way of your own invention; and have recklessly cut off all genuine record of the facts of Sacred History, subsequent to the time of Moses, with every sacred book from which the religious supremacy of Judah and Mount Sion,—the Royalty of David, and the promised descent of MESSIAH from his line,—could be learned by the people."(*d*)

we know what we worship: for Salvation is of the Jews.

"For *we,* the Jews, can trace the line of human hope from Moses, through David and all the prophets, of whom *ye* are ignorant."—" He reckons Himself among the Jews, in condescension to the woman's idea of Him: and says, as if He were a Jewish prophet, "*We* worship;" though it is certain that He is the Being who is worshipped by all. The phrase " for Salvation is of the Jews," means that every thing calculated to amend and save the world,—the knowledge of GOD, the abhorrence of idols, and all the doctrines of that nature; even the very origin of our

(*y*) Williams.   (*z*) St. Luke vii. 37, &c.   (*a*) St. John viii. 3, &c.
(*b*) Malachi i. 11.   (*c*) Chrysostom.   (*d*) Abridged from Dr. W. H. Mill.

religion,—comes originally from the Jews,"(e) "to whom pertaineth the Adoption," as the Apostle speaks, "and the Glory, and the Covenants, and the giving of the Law, and the service of GOD, and the promises : whose are the Fathers; and *of whom as concerning the flesh* CHRIST *came."*(f) — Our LORD proceeds:

23 But the hour cometh, and now is, when the true worshippers shall worship the FATHER in spirit and in truth : for the FATHER seeketh such to worship Him.

"The Jewish worship then was far higher than the Samaritan ; but even *it was* to be abolished."(g) And the accepted ones would no longer be those of a particular nation ; but the distinction would be into false worshippers and true. Our LORD had already said, "The hour is coming,"(h) but here He adds, "*and now is,*" —to imply that the event foretold was not remote, like the predictions of the ancient Prophets ; but close at hand, even at the doors.

Having said thus much concerning the place and the manner of acceptable worship, the Divine Speaker thus concludes :

24 GOD *is* a Spirit ; and they that worship Him, must worship *Him* in Spirit and in Truth.

Of these words, and of those which go before in verse 21, it would clearly be a wanton abuse to suppose that they convey a condemnation of externals in Religion ; or imply that the place of Divine Worship is a matter of indifference to Almighty GOD.—Not so. But in an age when it was believed that *in Jerusalem only,* might GOD be acceptably worshipped ; and among a people whose Law of ceremonial and outward observances had become so burdened by carnal traditions, that spiritual worship had well nigh disappeared altogether, it was of the last importance to vindicate the Mind and Will of Him who said " I will have Mercy and not Sacrifice ;"(i) and, by His Prophets, had so often claimed the spirit and the truth of those ordinances which, in respect of the letter and the type, had been punctually enough fulfilled.(k)

25 The woman saith unto Him, I know that MESSIAH cometh, (which is called CHRIST :) when He is come, He will tell us all things.

Her words seem to have respect to what had gone before. She had asked concerning *the place* of Divine Worship : the stranger had spoken concerning *the manner* of it also. In reply, she declares her belief in the near Advent of the MESSIAH,—(a Hebrew word, which St. John, for the second time,(l) explains to mean the "CHRIST," that is, "the Anointed One ;")—and implies that all doubts of this nature will be effectually solved by *Him,* at His coming: " a confession truly extraordinary, whether we consider the previous materials of this conviction, or the occasion that now drew it forth. The occasion which now drew forth this recognition of the great hope of mankind was simply what had just been spoken concerning the approaching establishment of a spiritual religion and worship. Her introduction therefore of the MESSIAH upon this, proves that it was a spiritual Leader,—a teacher of the true worship of GOD,—that she expected under that name and character. How different from the Jewish expectation of a conquering hero, and temporal deliverer? And how much more remarkable does this difference appear when we compare the materials for their respective convictions!(m) The truth has been discovered by the Samaritans, possessing only the Pentateuch ; and missed by the Jews, though David and all the Prophets were theirs.—Little prepared, however, was the woman for the disclosure which was to follow :—

26 JESUS saith unto her, I that speak unto thee am *He.*

"And the result of this announcement was the conversion, not only of this woman, but of many of her countrymen." It is the first open declaration of the same nature which our SAVIOUR is recorded to have made. The next is to the man born blind. See St. John ix. 37.

(e) Chrysostom. (f) Romans ix. 4, 5. (g) Chrysostom. (h) See above, verse 21.
(i) St. Matthew ix. 13, quoting Hosea vi. 6. (k) Consider Isaiah i. 11 to 17, &c.
(l) See St. John i. 42. (m) Dr. W. H. Mill.

27 And upon this came His Disciples, and marvelled that He talked ..th the woman: yet no man said, What seekest Thou? or, Why talk-t Thou with her?

Many are the recorded tokens of the deferential respect with which our LORD as regarded by His faithful followers. The reader may be pleased at having such aces as the following recalled to his remembrance:—ver. 33, below: St. John xii.) to 22: xiii. 22 to 24: xvi. 17 to 19: xxi. 12. St. Mark ix. 32.

But what was the precise ground of wonder to the Disciples on this occasion? ..ot, probably, so much at beholding their Divine Master discoursing with a female; .r many followed His footsteps, and ministered to His needs; moreover, He is re-..rded on many occasions to have spoken to women. The Disciples seem rather to ave been astonished at finding Him engaged in converse with *such* a woman, and .t *such* a place. They were at a loss, (as the Evangelist himself, who was one of their number, expressly intimates,) to know what He could want? or what could possibly ..e the subject of His conversation with her? Moreover, if the juncture at which they came up is considered, it will perhaps be thought that the woman's astonish-..ent, so far exceeding their own, must have added not a little to their perplexity and surprise.

They knew not that they beheld the Good Shepherd rejoicing over the recovery of the sheep which He had lost.

28 The woman then left her waterpot, and went her way into the city;

An ancient writer remarks,—" The woman is almost turned into an Apostle. So forcible are His words, that she leaves her water-pot to go to the city, and tell her townsmen of them."(n) Another points out that "as the Apostles on being called, left their nets, so does she leave her water-pot, to do the work of an Evangelist. She calls not one person, but a whole city."(o) As it follows:—

29 and saith to the men, Come, see a Man, which told me all things that ever I did: is not this the CHRIST?

"Come, see" Him!—Like Philip, when he invited Nathanael, (p) she knew that to see Him would be enough; and that belief must surely follow. How eager are the Saints of GOD ever found to be for the salvation of others! how impatient to communicate to their brethren the knowledge of the way of Life! Consider the conduct of those whom our SAVIOUR first called,—St. Andrew, and St. Peter, and St. Philip.(q) "Come and hear," (they seem to say,) and I will declare what GOD hath done for my soul."(r)

30 Then they went out of the city, and came unto Him.

We shall be told, in ver. 39, that "many of the Samaritans of that city believed on Him for the saying of the woman" here recorded. How they acted when they came to CHRIST, we learn in verse 40.

In the meantime, it seems incumbent on us to notice how much of ministerial guidance, how many precious lessons, are obtainable from the portion of sacred narrative before us. First, the case of none is to be regarded as hopeless, or be-yond the reach of ministerial zeal. Next, in so sacred a cause, we may converse with such as this fallen woman was: for "not of Apostles only, but of Believers generally, it was said 'Ye are the salt of the earth;' and *salt must mix with that which is to be salted*. It is to be remembered that our LORD ate and drank with Publicans and Sinners, neither refused He the invitation of the Pharisee. Such is our duty; such is the great exemplar of our lives."(s) Nay more, from such in-stances of conversion to GOD, it is not obscurely hinted that the most blessed results of all may be hoped for. It seems to be implied, in addition, that discourse of this nature may most fitly take its rise from some accidental circumstance, and be sug-gested by the events of the moment. From what follows, it is further found that

(a) Origen.   (o) Chrysostom.   (p) St. John i. 46.
(q) See John i. 40, 41, 45, and the note on 46.   (r) Ps. lxvi. 16.
(s) From a MS. Sermon by the Rev. W. J. Palmer.

the pursuit of a lost soul should be meat and drink to him who is called to be a Shepherd of souls: and lastly, it may not be overlooked, that by conversing with this sinful woman openly, and in a public place. He teaches us to join the wisdom of the serpent to the harmlessness of the dove,—to give the enemy no opportunity for injurious insinuation.

And now the Evangelist proceeds to detail what took place when the Disciples returned from Sychar, with the supply of food for the evening meal which they had been sent thither to provide.

31 In the meanwhile His Disciples prayed Him, saying, Master, eat.

"All ask Him at once. This is not impatience in them, but simply tenderness for their Master."(t)

32 But He said unto them, I have meat to eat that ye know not of.

Thus, in conformity with His Divine practice on other occasions, already noticed,(u) our SAVIOUR is found to have opened with a hard saying the subject on which He was no less desirous of enlightening His Disciples than they were of asking Him. He is willing that they should rejoice with Him over the recovery of His lost treasure,(x) but He leads them to the subject by degrees; first arresting their attention by a few dark words, from which He may afterwards lead them up to something higher and spiritual.—Very Man, He truly hungered, truly thirsted. Yet were His bodily needs as nothing compared to the longings of His Human soul towards the Race which He had come to save; and these longings had been largely satisfied, while those needs continued urgent as ever. But all this the Disciples had yet to learn. They "knew not" as yet the depth of the REDEEMER'S Love: they knew nothing as yet, experimentally, of a heart finding in Obedience the full supply of every earthly want: they "knew not" that the woman whom they saw retiring from the well, was about to bring a whole city to the knowledge of the Truth.

33 Therefore said the Disciples one to another, Hath any man brought Him *ought* to eat?

"What wonder," (exclaims Augustine,) "that the woman did not understand about the water? Lo, the Disciples do not understand about the meat!"

Observe that they said this "one to another."(y)—with that respectful reverence of which we find so many traces in the Gospels. And it is done in Heaven as it was done on Earth; for "Isaiah in a vision of the LORD in His Glory," when he heard the Seraphim crying, "Holy, Holy, Holy," noticed that besides covering their faces with their wings, one so "*cried unto another*."(z)—Our LORD hastens to release them from their perplexity.

34 JESUS saith unto them, My meat is to do the will of Him that sent Me, and to finish His work.

Our SAVIOUR here speaks of Himself not as GOD, but as Man. As Man, it was His meat and drink to do the FATHER'S Will. The Human Will in the One Person of our SAVIOUR CHRIST, we know was in all things conformed to His Divine Will, although it existed independently of it.(a) His Divine Will was altogether one with the FATHER'S.

"My *meat* is to do *the Will* of Him that *sent* Me:" for, Behold, I am come *to do Thy Will*, O GOD,(b)—was the prophetic language in which our SAVIOUR long before had spoken of His own future Advent in the flesh; adding that he found His "*delight*" therein. That CHRIST was the "*sent*" of GOD, is the constant declaration of Holy Scripture. It shall suffice, once for all, to enumerate the chief statements to this effect which are supplied by the writings of St. John alone.(c)

(t) Chrysostom.
(u) See above, the note on ver. 10.   (x) Alluding to St. Luke xv. 6, 7, and 9, 10.
(y) Compare Mal. iii. 16.   See above the note on ver. 27.   (z) Isaiah vi. 3.
(a) See St. John v. 30 and vi. 38, where see two notes.
(b) Psalm xl. 7, 8: as quoted in Heb. x. 9.
(c) See,—St. John iii. 17, 34: v. 23, 24, 30, 36, 37, 38: vi. 29, 38, 39, 40, 44, 57: vii. 16, 18, 28, 29: viii. 16, 18, 26, 29, 42: ix. 4: x. 36: xi. 42: xii. 45, 49: xiv. 24: xv. 21: xvi. 5: xvii. 3, 8, 18, 21, 23, 25: xx. 21.—1 St. John iv. 9 10, 14.

But the Salvation of Mankind is the special "*Will* of GOD" here intended; for
D "willeth that all men should be saved."(*d*)   This is also "His *Work ;*" for He
the sole cause of Salvation in Man: GOD not only "*willing*" our Salvation, but
o "*working* in us both to will and to do."(*e*)
Not only so; but the entire scheme of man's Redemption was GOD's great work,
the Apostle so often declares :(*f*) a work which addresses itself throughout to
un's Faith.   Whence our SAVIOUR's declaration : "This is the work of GOD, that
believe on Him whom He hath sent."(*g*)   And " to *finish*" this work is found to
re been the great object of all He said and did on earth : from the Day of His
ptism until the day of His Crucifixion ; when He said "*It is finished ;*" and bowed
s head : and gave up the Ghost."(*h*)
With obvious reference therefore to the " door of Hope"(*i*) which was even now
ing opened to the men of Sychar, our LORD intimates that He has been re-
shed and supported during the Disciples' absence by having effectually done the
ork of Him that sent Him.

85 Say not ye, There are yet four months, and *then* cometh harvest?
:hold, I say unto you, Lift up your eyes, and look on the fields ; for
ley are white already to Harvest.

The interval between the season of sowing and the season of reaping in Judæa,
as four months.   Our LORD's words are allusive to this circumstance, and perhaps
) some proverbial saying which may have grown out of it.   But the entire passage
efore us has been thought difficult, and given rise to so much conjectural criticism,
bat it may be as well in explaining it to show its connection with what goes before
and what follows.
The Disciples had been pressing our Divine LORD to partake of food.   He told
them in reply that it was food to Him to do His FATHER's will, and to finish
His work.   Then, addressing them as the men who were destined to become
His blessed instruments therein : — "At seed-time," saith He, " say ye not: Pass
four months and it will be Harvest?   But look abroad on yonder fields, and take
notice that the wheat is ripe already, and the time of Harvest *hath come.*"   It was
in fact shortly after the Passover season that He thus spake.   The wheat was therefore fully ripe ; presenting that *whitish* appearance, which many ancient writers have
described, and a few modern travellers have noticed.
We are of course left to infer that to the Divine Speaker's inner vision, a corresponding spectacle discovered itself in respect of that part of the region where that part of
spiritual " Harvest of the Earth" was also " ripe" already ;(*k*) and that He beheld
the season for thrusting in the sickle, close at hand.   Moreover, He seems to imply
that as the fields of Samaria were now teeming with ripe grain, in the sowing of
which His Disciples had had no share,—just so was it in respect of the fruits of the
spiritual Kingdom.   The Patriarchs and Prophets of old had *sown ;* the seed had
fallen into honest and good hearts; and there had been an abundant increase.   The
Apostles of CHRIST would therefore now have but to *reap ;* that is, to bring to the
full knowledge of the Gospel, hearts already well prepared and fully disposed to receive the Heavenly message.   The privilege of such reaping is stated in the words
which follow :

86 And he that reapeth receiveth wages, and gathereth fruit unto
ife eternal :

That is, — Between an ordinary reaper and yourselves, there will be this mighty
difference ; that whereas *he* receiveth wages, and garnereth for another in an earthly
ara, the fruit which wasteth away and perisheth,—*ye*, besides your great hire, shall
gather immortal souls into the Heavenly Garner, unto Life Eternal, to be your
own of rejoicing in the Great Day of the LORD.(*l*) — With such language does the
Blessed Speaker sustain the spirits, and kindle the desires of His lowly followers :
adding,

(*d*) 1 Tim. ii. 4.   (*e*) Phil. ii. 13.   (*f*) See Ephes. i. 5, &c.
(*g*) St. John vi. 29.   (*h*) St. John xix. 30.
(*i*) Hos. ii. 15.   May not that prophecy have had reference to this very occasion?   Observe
that the situation of the valley of Achor is unknown ; but it seems to have been not far from
Gerizim.
(*k*) Rev. xiv. 15.   (*l*) Consider 1 Thess. ii. 19.

that both he that soweth and he that reapeth **may rejoice together.**

Our LORD is declaring another point of contrast between earthly and heavenly reaping. It is as if He had said. — Now, here on earth, he that sows hath all the labor, and he that reaps hath all the joy ; but the consequences of what I have been describing will be that the Sower shall partake in the Reaper's bliss : My ancient Saints,—the Patriarchs and the Prophets of Israel,—shall rejoice together with you, My Apostles. — "*Rejoice* together :" for if the Repentance of one sinner sufficeth to fill beholding Angels with Joy,(m) what rapture at the eternal bliss of many Saints, must fill the hearts of such as have been GOD's instruments in turning these to righteousness !(n)

And surely, thrice glorious is the anticipation thus held out, — the hint, namely, of the bliss in store for all those who have already gone to their rest, and who hereafter shall go, with nothing but the experience of labor, for which they beheld no fruit ? Doubtless, they who thus went on their way weeping, and bearing forth good seed, shall come again with joy, and even bring their sheaves with them !(o)

37 And herein is that saying true, One soweth, and another reapeth.

The meaning is, — That common proverb, "One soweth and another reapeth," is nevertheless true ; and its truth consists in the fact, that here also, he who reaps is a different person from him who sowed. As it follows :

38 I sent you to reap that whereon ye bestowed no labor : other men labored, and ye are entered into their labors.

The sower and the reaper are therefore different persons ; and so far the saying is true : but as the saying is commonly employed to denote that one has all the labor, the other all the rejoicing, it is no longer applicable ; for *the rejoicing* to the sower and to the reaper is the same.

"I *sent* you to reap :" not that their LORD had sent them yet ; but since they were named "Apostles," that is " [men] sent," from the first,(p) the expression was correct at all times after they had once been called. The rest of the verse has been explained already, by anticipation. But the repeated mention of ministerial labor in this place, suggests a reference to such passages of St. Paul as are noticed at foot :(q) while the allusion in ver. 36, to the "joy in harvest," recalls Isaiah ix. 3.

The Evangelist now proceeds with the history of the Samaritans.

39 And many of the Samaritans of that city believed on Him, for the saying of the woman, which testified, He told me all that ever I did.

In illustration of this and the next verse, what the Evangelist has already stated in verses 29 and 30 should be recalled. Take notice of the largeness of the faith here described ; surpassing even that of the Woman herself. "Is not this the CHRIST?" she had timidly asked : but many of these men are found to have "believed on Him,"— that is, to have believed that it *was* He,—from her report alone. Whatever her own faith may have been, she had at least seen our SAVIOUR: but the men of Sychar were more blessed, in that though they had not hitherto seen Him, they had yet believed.(r) All this was, however, *His* gift ; no less than the request which follows.

40 So when the Samaritans were come unto Him, they besought Him that He would tarry with them : and He abode there two days.

Bequeathing to the City which so honorably entertained Him, as it would seem, an abiding blessing. Unlike Capernaum, Chorazin, and Bethsaida, where our LORD was rejected and despised, and which have since utterly disappeared, Sychar, (or as it is now called, "Nablous,") is in a flourishing condition to the present day. "Its prosperity is far too striking to be overlooked by the traveller ; having nothing of the lifeless, indolent, poverty-stricken appearance of almost all the other towns

(m) St. Luke xv. 7, 10.   (n) Dan. xii. 3.
(o) Ps. cxxvi. 6.   (p) St. Luke vi. 13.
(q) 1 Cor. xv. 10.   2 Cor. xi. 23.   Gal. iv. 11.   Col. i. 29.   Phil. ii. 16.   1 Thess. ii. 9; iii. 4.
2 Thess. iii. 8.   1 Tim. iv. 10: v. 17, &c.
(r) St. John xx. 29.

the country. On the contrary, its neighborhood is fertile ; refreshing springs
n through its streets: a great amount of activity and bustle is found among the
habitants, who seem a thriving prosperous people: the bazaars are crowded ; and
together its appearance is so different from other places, that you are induced to
ink that there must be some especial circumstances connected with its locality,
ore favorable than ordinary. This however does not appear to be the case."(s)
Josephus remarks that it is a three days' journey out of Judœa into Galilee. The
ro days therefore which would have sufficed to conduct our SAVIOUR back to Ca-
rnaum, He passed among the men of Sychar: and thus the faith of the "noble-
an," of whom we shall read in ver. 46, and whose son was even now a-dying, was
xed to the uttermost. See more in the note on ver. 47 ; and consider, in connecon with the constraint exercised by the men of Sychar, the remarks which were
ffered on St. Luke xxiv. 29.—It follows:

41 And many more believed because of His own word: and said
unto the Woman, Now we believe, not because of thy saying : for we
have heard *Him* ourselves, and know that this is indeed the CHRIST,
the SAVIOUR of the world.

"Because of His own *Word*," the men of Sychar became believers : not because
of any *Miracles* which He wrought among them. "Their grounds were therefore
not those overpowering proofs of His Divinity which were yet insufficient to convince the stubborn Jews. All that these good Samaritans appear to have possessed, or sought, was the sober conviction with which our LORD's prophetic character inspired them ; and on the strength of which they proclaim Him, in the true
spirit of knowledge and charity united, the SAVIOUR of the whole World !"(t)
And truly, if their faith was so readily kindled, even from the Woman's report
of Him, what must have been the effect of His prolonged converse on their hearts !
If the rising of the Day-Star filled them with light and heat, what must have been
wrought in them by the noontide glow of CHRIST's actual presence ! "We have
heard Him ourselves," they say, "and *know:*" for "Faith cometh by hearing."(u)
Accordingly, their Faith is ample, and their Confession complete:—"This is indeed
the CHRIST, the SAVIOUR of the World !"
It has been admirably pointed out, that "this was not however their final state ;
nor designed to be represented by the inspired historian as such. When the mysteries of human Redemption were accomplished, and CHRIST was glorified, then we
are told by St. Luke, in the book of Acts, how Samaria received the Word of GOD ;
first, by the preaching and *Baptism* of Philip the Evangelist, and afterwards by
Apostolic *Confirmation,* and the imposition of hands. Thus, doubtless, were these
men of Sychar in particular actually admitted into that Kingdom for which their
previous reception of its LORD had prepared them, and which He described as on
the point of manifestation to the World."(x)
It is impossible to dismiss this great incident,—which is none other than the
beginning of the fulfillment of the prophecies made to Abraham, confirmed to
Isaac, and renewed to Jacob, without dwelling a little further upon its precious
details. We have read of the first great gathering in of the aliens, (for the Samaritans were reckoned almost with the very heathen,)(y) into the fold of CHRIST.
Here it is that the Heavenly Canaan first opens to our sight. Viewed from this
spot of holy ground, what new and unexpected light is found to fall on many a
familiar incident of Old Testament history ; and how beautifully does the design
of the inspired narrative straightway become !
We are reminded, before all things, of that original mention of Sichem as the
first place of the Patriarch Abraham's rest, to which attention was called above.(z)
There he received the promise ; there JEHOVAH (and it was none other than CHRIST
Jesus Himself !) appeared to him ; and there, he builded his first altar. The spot
thus singularly hallowed as the first place at which GOD had appeared to man, remained for ever holy in the eyes of Abraham's descendants. Here Jacob, when
he returned with his family into Canaan, hid all the strange gods which were in
their hand.(a) Here arose "the Sanctuary of the LORD,"(b) and here was one of

(s) From the MS. quoted above, on verses 5 and 6.
(t) Dr. W. H. Mill.   (u) Rom. x. 17.   (x) Dr. W. H. Mill.
(y) St. Matt. x. 5.   (z) See the first note on the present chapter.
(a) Gen. xxxv. 4.   (b) Josh. xxiv. 26.

the cities of refuge.(c) To this place, Joshua solemnly summoned the Twelve
Tribes before his death, and renewed the covenant with them after the conquest
and partition of the Land.(d) Here Abimelech, (Joseph's descendant,)(e) was
made king;(f) and here Rehoboam was crowned,(g) Jeroboam likewise "built
Shechem in Mount Ephraim,(h) and dwelt therein."(i) Here, therefore, where the
Ten Tribes rebelled against the house of David,(k) was David's Son about to
"gather together in one the children of God that were scattered abroad."(l)

Very striking is the consideration, suggested by the actual record of the Evangelist,(m) that the spot of ground where our Saviour now rested, and where He
was destined to receive the first earnest of His spiritual inheritance,(n) was the
same which had become the first possession of any of His Ancestors after the flesh.
Machpelah seems to have been a place of burial, and no more; not so the "parcel
of a field" where Jacob spread his tent on returning to Canaan after his absence
of twenty years at Haran. This piece of ground had already been the property of
his grandfather Abraham,(o) and now became his own by renewed purchase of
the same family from whom Abraham had originally obtained it.(p) Subsequently,
by right of conquest also,(q) had the Patriarch secured this precious spot of ground
to himself and his family; bequeathing it to Joseph, "a portion," (or "Shechem,"
as the Hebrew expresses it,) "above his brethren,"—in token that the right of
primogeniture should be his.(r) To Joseph's descendants (the tribe of Ephraim)
this piece of territory is accordingly found to have afterwards belonged: among
the rest to Joshua, the temporal Jesus, Joseph's immediate descendant, who conquered the entire Land,—beginning his conquest almost at this very place.(s) The
spot is found to have been very fertile and well adapted from the beginning for
pasturing of sheep;(t)—a character which it preserves in a remarkable manner to
the present day.

An ancient writer says strikingly,—"This parcel of ground I conceive to have
been left not so much to Joseph as to Christ, of whom Joseph was a type; and
whom the Sun, the Moon, and all the Stars, truly adore."(u) It was in fact the
scene of the youthful patriarch's dreams;(x) and, (what is remarkable,) after an
interval of just 1700 years, this "parcel of ground" is found to have retained its
ancient distinction of fruitfulness in corn; for, as we have seen, the abundant harvest which grew on the spot suggested the form of discourse which our Saviour
adopted in addressing His Disciples on the present occasion.(y) At Jacob's well,
therefore, and in "the parcel of ground that Jacob gave to his son Joseph," did
the discourse above recorded, and which led to such memorable results, occur;
whereby Joseph became that "fruitful bough, even a fruitful bough by a well,"(z)
of which the dying Patriarch spake; "whose branches run over the wall."

43 Now, after two days He departed thence, and went into Galilee.

Our Lord was on His way from Judæa into Galilee, when the incident occurred
which led to His sojourn of two days at Sychar.(a) Those two days ended, He
proceeded on His journey; but He did not return to Nazareth, which for thirty
years He had made His home, (and which is hence called in the Gospels,(b) "His
own country;")—and that, for the reason which the Evangelist proceeds to give:

44 For Jesus Himself testified, that a Prophet hath no honor in his
own country.

The Evangelist alludes to the proverbial saying which our Lord is recorded to
have addressed to His fellow-townsmen in the Synagogue of Nazareth, on two
subsequent occasions. See St. Matthew xiii. 57, and St. Mark vi. 4.

(c) Josh. xx. 7 : xxi. 21, and 1 Chron. vi. 67.
(e) Compare Joshua xvii. 2, with Judges vi. 11, vii. 1, and ix. 1.
(f) Judges ix. 1 to 6.
(h) For Abimelech "had beaten down the city, and sowed it with salt."—Judges ix. 45.
(i) 1 Kings xii. 25.   (k) 1 Kings xii. 1 to 20.
(m) In ver. 5.   (n) Consider Ps. ii. 7, 8.
(p) Gen. xxxiii. 19. Joshua xxiv. 32.
(r) Deut. xxi. 17. 1 Chron. v. 2. Ezek. xlvii. 13.
(t) Gen. xxxvii. 12, 13.
(u) Alcuin.   (x) See Genesis xxxvii. 5 to 9.
(z) Consider also Deut. xxxiii. 28.
(b) See St. Matth. xiii. 54, and St. Luke iv. 23.

(d) Joshua xxiv. 1 to 28.

(g) 1 Kings xii. 1.

(l) St. John xi. 52.
(o) Acts vii. 16.
(q) Gen. xlviii. 22.
(s) See Joshua vii.

(y) See above, ver. 35 to 38.
(a) See above, ver. 3.

45 Then when He was come into Galilee, the Galileans received
Him, having seen all the things that He did at Jerusalem at the Feast :
for they also went unto the Feast.

"Received Him," denotes that they welcomed Him back, and gave Him a *kind*
ception.(c) In assigning the reason of this, the Evangelist alludes for the third
me to the Miracles (doubtless very surprising ones!) which our SAVIOUR had
tely wrought at Jerusalem, and which the Evangelist has nowhere described par-
:ularly.(d) It was the sight of those wonders which wrought conviction in Ni-
demus:(e) and from the present verse it is discovered that they prevailed with
e Galileans likewise. How far more noble was the faith of the men of Sychar,
ho "believed—*because of His Word!*"(f) "Except ye see signs and wonders,
e will not believe," was our LORD's reproachful address to the nobleman of Ca-
ernaum.(g)

46 So JESUS came again into Cana of Galilee, where He made the
rater wine.

Instead of returning to Nazareth, our LORD revisits Cana,—which was probably
he abode (as before suggested)(h) of some of the relations of the Blessed Virgin
Mary. . . . "Cana of Galilee, *where He made the Water Wine:*"—how much is this
in St. John's manner! It is his wont thus to identify places and persons, by some
single circumstance which rendered them forever memorable. Nicodemus, as often
as his name recurs, is mentioned as he "*which at the first came to JESUS by night:*"
(i)—the miraculous feeding of the five thousand, was performed "*after that the* LORD
had *given thanks:*"(k)—Philip. we are reminded, was "*of Bethsaida of Galilee :*"
(l)—and the Evangelist himself desired to be remembered by the Church, as "*the
Disciple which* JESUS *loved ; . . . which also leaned on His breast at Supper, and said,
LORD, which is he that betrayeth Thee?*"(m)

And there was a certain Nobleman, whose son was sick at Capernaum.

It is uncertain who and what this person was ; but probably he belonged to the
Court and Palace of King Herod. Hence the marginal suggestion that we should
translate "Courtier." If Chuza, (Herod's steward,) was a believer as well as his
wife,(n) the "Nobleman" may have been Chuza himself. But he was doubtless a
Jew; one of those Galileans, it may be thought, who are spoken of above as having "seen all the things which JESUS did at Jerusalem at the Feast."

47 When he heard that JESUS was come out of Judæa into Galilee,
he went unto Him, and besought Him that He would come down, and
heal his son : for he was at the point of death.

Let us notice what is here revealed, (doubtless for *our* profit,) and not miss the
precious teaching which it seems intended to convey.—Here was a child sick of a
fever at Capernaum. His father had been anxiously expecting our SAVIOUR's return to that city ; but in vain. He knew that CHRIST could save his child, and
despaired of help from any other source. Every hour at last became of importance. Presently, he is told that the Great Physician has arrived at Cana. We
may judge of the father's distress and anxiety, by finding that he trusts no messenger, (though a man of such rank as to have many servants at his command,)(o)
but leaving the object of his love *at the point of Death* at Capernaum, repairs in
person to Cana,—a distance of some six or eight hours. How untoward must he
have thought our LORD's prolonged absence! How "unlucky" must that two
day's sojourn at Sychar, and now this halt at Cana, have seemed! Yet, perceive
we not that the Great Physician had been thereby dealing no less lovingly with
the father, than He was prepared now to deal with the son? Was it not to try
the man's faith, and because He designed his great blessedness, that CHRIST had

(c) So in St. Luke ix. 11.   (d) St. John ii. 23.   (e) St. John iii. 2.
(f) See above, ver. 41, 42.   (g) See below, ver. 48.   (h) See the last note on St. John ii. 2.
(i) See St. John iii. 2; vii. 50; xix. 39.   (k) St. John vi. 11 and 23.
(l) St. John i. 44; xii. 21.   (m) St. John xiii. 23, 25; xxi. 20.
(n) St. Luke viii. 3.   (o) See below, verse 51.

44

first lingered on the road, and now directed His steps not to Capernaum, but to Cana:—"knowing that tribulation," as St. Paul testifies, and "the trying of faith," as St. James declares,(p) "worketh patience; and patience, experience; and experience, hope; and hope maketh not ashamed?"(q)—For more on this subject, see the note on St. Luke v. 17; and especially the notes on St. Mark v. 24, and 35.

It was doubtless Faith which brought this man from Capernaum to Cana, in search of our SAVIOUR: yet it is found to have been a most imperfect Faith. Thus, he does not believe that CHRIST can cure his son at a distance.(r) He thinks (like the Ruler of the Synagogue) that He must perforce "come down," and perhaps that He must lay His hand upon the sufferer, in order to his recovery.(s) He reminds us of the father of the lunatic boy,(t) rather than of the Gentile Centurion,(u) or the woman of Cannan,(x) or even the Ten Lepers.(y) To this slowness of heart, therefore, our SAVIOUR replies in the first instance.

48 Then said JESUS unto him, Except ye see signs and wonders, ye will not believe.

"Ye,"—that is, ye Jews, My countrymen: so unlike those Samaritan aliens whom I have lately left, and among whom I wrought no signs. Take notice that these words fully disclose to us the reason of the discipline to which the Holy One was subjecting the man who addressed Him; and who, while he came to obtain help for his son, little suspected that he was even in greater want of the Divine Physician himself. Nothing but *the sight* of miracles and wonders would produce conviction:(z) whereas Faith and Sight are in a manner opposites. What a contrast, by the way, was all this to the scene we have been so lately witnessing beside Samaria's Well,—where He who spoke was a stranger, and they who listened were members of a despised race!

49 The Nobleman saith unto Him, Sir, come down ere my child die.

For he had left him "at the point of death;"(a) and his agony will brook no delay. From his reply, we perceive yet more clearly the limits of the nobleman's faith. He supposes CHRIST's power will be ineffectual if his child dies.(b) How far was he, in the meantime, from realizing the object of those miraculous cures which he seems to have been already acquainted with, and of which he was even now imploring the repetition! He knew not that the purpose of CHRIST's coming was to build up the feeble in Faith; and that the chief object with which He healed bodily sickness, was to remedy spiritual infirmity.

50 JESUS saith unto him, Go thy way, thy son liveth.

The Physician of souls, seeing that His first medicine avails not, mercifully tries another treatment: and wins by benefits the man whom he could not move by reproaches. Thereby teaching those in the Ministry that by various methods are men to be gained over; and reminding us that resources may yet be discovered, even after our best-devised plans have failed.

Take notice of the Wisdom of the course our SAVIOUR pursued with this man. Had He complied with his request,—gone down with him to Capernaum, and there healed his son,—the nobleman's faith must forever have remained weak; for he would have ascribed to CHRIST's *presence* what was the result only of His *power*. Had He, on the contrary, sent the nobleman away disappointed, the small spark of faith in him would have been entirely quenched. By granting one half of the man's petition, and denying the other, He fanned that spark at once into a flame.(c)

When the Centurion told our SAVIOUR of *his servant* "lying at home sick of the palsy, grievously tormented," he received for answer, "I will come and heal him" (d)—a favour which he had not asked. Here our LORD is entreated by a Nobleman to come down and heal *his son*, and He refuses. The reason of this diversity of treatment is to be found in the spiritual condition of these two individuals, respectively. The nobleman's imperfect faith was perfected by our LORD's *refusal* to come down;

(p) St. James i. 3.   (q) Romans v. 3 to 5.   (r) And see below, the note on ver. 48.
(s) See St. Matth. ix. 18.   (t) See St. Mark ix. 22.   (u) See St. Matth. viii. 8, 9.
(x) See St. Matth. xv. 27.   (y) See St. Matth. viii. 2.   (z) Consider 1 Cor. i. 22.
(a) See verse 47.   (b) See above, the latter part of the note on verse 47.
(c) From Toletus.   (d) St. Matth. viii. 6, 7.

e perfection of the Centurion's faith was displayed by our LORD's *proposal* to come
wn. Both men become the Church's instructors: the first, in the way of warn-
g; the second, in the way of example.

It seems worth pointing out that as our SAVIOUR abode for "two days" at Sychar,
id then restored the young man, so also when He heard that Lazarus was sick,
He abode two days in the same place where He was," and then announced His
tention of going to "awake him out of sleep."(e) Were not these acts typical of
is own Resurrection "on the third day?" according to that of the prophet,—
After two days will He revive us: in the third day He will raise us up, and we
iall live in His sight."(f)

And the man believed the word that JESUS had spoken unto him, nd he went his way.

Retracing his steps as we may suppose to Capernaum, with joy not unmingled
with anxiety: and travelling, as we shall presently discover, by night.(g) Take
notice that it is not here said of the nobleman that he believed in CHRIST. This
effect was to follow, and is declared to have followed in ver. 53; but the first necessary step had been taken, inasmuch as *he believed His word*: that is, he believed
it would be as CHRIST had said; and departed convinced that his son was already
in the way of recovery. He will have afterwards attained the conviction that the
Holy One, besides announcing his child's recovery, had been the Author of it likewise.

51 And as he was now going down, his servants met him, and told him, saying, Thy son liveth.

As soon as the wonderful change in the young man's state was witnessed, the
servants had been dispatched in quest of their master; and now they greet him with
the very words which he had already heard from the lips of CHRIST.

52 Then inquired he of them the hour when he began to amend.

How natural is this! "He wished to find out," (observes Chrysostom,) "whether
the recovery was accidental, or owing to our LORD's Word."

And they said unto him, Yesterday at the seventh hour the fever left him.

He asked his servants when the child *began to amend*. They tell him in reply,
that this has been no progressive recovery: but that, yesterday evening, his son
suddenly—*got well*. "At the seventh hour, *the fever left him*." . . . The reader is
referred to what has been already offered on this striking subject in the Commentary on the latter part of St. Mark i. 31.

"The seventh hour" in the present Gospel denotes either seven o'clock in the morning, or seven o'clock in the evening: not *one* o'clock,—according to the Jewish mode of
reckoning Time. This has been already explained on ver. 6. In this place, therefore, it will have been seven o'clock in the *evening*; for Capernaum is certainly not
more than 8 hours distant from Cana, and the servants met the nobleman on his
way back,—probably when he had got about half way. It was, however, *the morrow* when they met, as we discover from the servants' language: which could not
have been the case had the ·miracle been wrought, and the journey commenced, in
the morning.

We have heard the nobleman's inquiry, and his servants' reply. The result will
remind us of the truth of the remark, that the more attentively we scrutinize the
Works and the ways of GOD, will our faith be nourished and increased.

53 So the father knew that *it was* at the same hour,

Rather; — "that [the fever left him] at the same hour,"—

in the which JESUS said unto him, Thy son liveth: and he himself believed, and his whole house.

(e) St. John xi. 6. 11.   (f) Hosea vi. 2.
(g) See below, the note on ver 52.

Words which evidently imply at least thus much ; — that when the father heard that his child had been restored to perfect health at seven o'clock on the previous evening.—and connected with this, the circumstance that in the self-same hour our LORD had conveyed to him the comfortable assurance, " Thy son liveth,"—the mist cleared up from his soul at once, and he became a true believer in JESUS CHRIST. He had arrived, although by slow and painful steps, at that point of Faith with which the Centurion originally came to CHRIST. He perceived that he had been discoursing with One who could say to a fever, as to a servant, " Go, and he goeth."(h)   Thus a single sentence from the lips of the LORD of Life, (as Cyril of Alexandria remarks,) brought healing at once to two souls ! The nobleman " himself believed ;" nor only so, but he became the head of a believing h̄ousehold. Such then was the gracious design with which illness had been sent into this man's family ! It was the Hand of Love which had brought his child to the brink of the grave, and rendered the skill of the physicians ineffectual. Now all these things " were written for our learning, that we through patience and comfort of the Scriptures might have hope."(i)

Venerable Bede points out that " Faith, like the other virtues, is formed gradually ; and has its beginning, growth, and maturity. The nobleman's faith had its beginning when he asked for his son's recovery ; its growth when he believed our LORD's words, ' Thy son liveth ;' but it did not reach maturity, until the announcement of the fact by his servants."

54 This *is* again the second miracle *that* JESUS did, when He was come out of Judæa into Galilee.

Rather,—" This second miracle again JESUS did." The Evangelist has described one other famous miracle, (the Water made Wine,) and this is the second. Both were wrought at Cana of Galilee ; and they are brought into mysterious prominence by the very manner in which St. John records them : the one, as the " *beginning* of miracles ;"(k) the other, as the " *second* miracle."

CHAPTER V.

---

1 JESUS *on the Sabbath day cureth him that was diseased eight and thirty years.* 10 *The Jews therefore cavil, and persecute Him for it.* 17 *He answereth for Himself, and reproveth them, showing by the testimony of His* FATHER, 32 *of John,* 36, *of His Works,* 39 *and of the Scriptures, who He is.*

1 AFTER this there was a Feast of the Jews ; and JESUS went up to Jerusalem.

The Feast of the Passover is probably intended,—the second of the four Passover Seasons indicated in the Gospels.

2 Now there is at Jerusalem by the sheep *market* a Pool, which is called in the Hebrew tongue Bethesda, having five porches.

Rather,—" by the Sheep-*gate*,"—as in the margin.(a) " Bethesda" means either " House of *Mercy*," or, " House of *Washing*." See the note on St. John vi. 1. It may be also worth observing that the Greek word which here (and in St. John ix. 7,) is translated " Pool," (literally " a Bath for *swimming* in,") was the name which the early Christians gave to their Baptisteries, and to their Baptismal Fonts. Com-

(h) See the note on St. Matth. viii. 9.   (i) Rom. xv. 4.
(k) St. John ii. 11.   (a) Compare Nehemiah iii. 1 : xii. 39.

der the foot-note on St. Luke v. 10: and the first note on St. Matthew xiii. 47. Bethesda itself, with its five porticos, was evidently a considerable edifice; for it llows:—

3 In these lay a great multitude of impotent folk, of blind, halt, ithered, waiting for the moving of the water.

The water of this Bath, which availed to heal every form of disorder, (as we read the next verse,) was clearly typical of the Water of Baptism: which heals the ul by virtue of a Divine Efficacy imparted to it. Mark the contrast, however, be-ween the Laver of Regeneration,(b) unexhausted and inexhaustible,—the "Foun-in opened to the House of David and to the inhabitants of Jerusalem for Sin and r Uncleanness,"(c)—and the Pool of Bethesda, available only for a single cure! . . . It was because a created Angel imparted healing virtue in the one case; whereas the CREATOR Himself, by going down into Jordan, sanctified all Waters 'to the mystical washing away of Sin."(d) See more in the note on verse 7.
The analogies of Holy Scripture are endless. As in Nature, so in Grace, the more attentively we gaze, the more we seem to discover. Pursuing the contrast already hazarded, how obvious is it to remark that the Law, (having five Books, like the Building here described, "having five Porches,") did but display,—revealed without being able to remove,—the different aspects of Human Infirmity!

4 For an Angel went down at a certain season into the pool, and troubled the water; whosoever then first after the troubling of the water stepped in, was made whole of whatsoever disease he had.

Perhaps, all that met the eye, in the Pool of Bethesda, was "the moving of the water,"—that is, the agitation of its surface. And this may possibly have been re-ferable to some natural cause,—as, to a spring which bubbled up from below; or to a gust of wind which came down upon it: either of which causes would suffice to produce a ripple on the water. But the Bible lifts the veil from the unseen world, and tells us of things which unassisted Reason could never have suspected. It discovers to us the Ministry of Angels. Reason may have known that the Wind was moving the Water; but Faith here informs Reason that an Angel was moving the Wind. See the note on St. Luke xxii. 3.

5 And a certain man was there, which had an infirmity thirty and eight years.

While so many things which we earnestly desire to know, are carefully kept from us in the Gospels, why are we informed of such a thing as this, which does not seem to concern us much? The same reverent inquiry is also suggested by St. Luke viii. 42 and 43: xiii. 11, 16. Are we, in this case, to see an emblem of Israel's punishment, in the sufferings of one of Israel's descendants; and to connect his thirty and eight years of affliction, with theirs?(e) This suggestion, which is an old one, and is humbly repeated, shall not be pressed. Neither shall the analogy suggested, be pursued. It shall but be observed concerning it, that such remarks are not foreign to the spirit of Inspired Scriptural Exposition: and that as the dig-nity, depth, and importance of every word and deed of the Incarnate JEHOVAH can-not possibly be over-rated; so neither can the written record of His actions be sup-posed to be in any respect trivial, unmeaning, or superfluous, either.

6 When JESUS saw him lie, and knew that he had been now a long time in that case, He saith unto him, Wilt thou be made whole?

Into the House with the five porches, our SAVIOUR enters; and moving past the crowd of sufferers described in verse 3, He singles out to be the special object of his Mercy one infirm person, who seems to have been in greater need than any of the rest:—a man without a single friend; and in whose case Hope deferred for eight and thirty years must have made the heart very sick. Let the infirm, and the friendless, and the despairing, take comfort from this wondrous narrative.

(b) See Tit. iii. 4,—where the word "Laver" is rendered "Washing."
(c) Zechariah xiii. 1.   (d) See the Baptismal Service.
(e) Deuteronomy ii. 14.

7 The impotent man answered Him, Sir, I have no man, when the
water is troubled, to put me into the pool: but while I am coming, another steppeth down before me.

He makes no churlish answer, observe. He simply states his great misery and
his extreme need. He perhaps secretly wished, that the "Man" he spoke to would
befriend him when next the troubled water betokened the Angel's presence. Little
did he suspect that it was the Creator of Angels with whom he was conversing!
His utter helplessless reminds us of another case of suffering.—*that* of the Paralytic,
who depended entirely on the active piety of four friends to bring him to Christ.
The reader is referred to the latter part of the note on St. Mark ii. 3: also to the
note on St. Luke v. 20: after calling attention to which, it is only fair to remark
that the present miracle seems further to teach that God does not so *tie Himself* to
Sacraments,—has not so annexed the bestowal of his favors to outward and appoint-
ed means,—as that He will never, under *any* circumstances, be induced to bestow
Sacramental grace without the Sacramental sign. The same lesson is taught by
Numbers xi. 16, 17, and 24 to 26. · See the notes on St. John iii. 5: also on St.
John vi. 23.

Not only in his peculiar *helplessness* does this man remind us of the Paralytic;
but in the mention made, in the case of either, *of his sins*. Compare St. Mark ii.
5, and the notes on the latter part of that verse.

See also the notes on the next verse, (verse 8,) of the present chapter.

8 Jesus saith unto him, Rise, take up thy bed, and walk.

The same three acts of Faith which our Lord required of the man sick of the
Palsy. See St. Mark ii. 9. and the notes on St. Mark ii. 11 and 12.

Observe that the man, (in the third chapter of the Acts,) not *walked*, but *leaped*,
when healed by St. Peter and St. John; neither is he said to have carried his bed:
perhaps, because in *his* case, there had been no punishment overtaking; but he had
been "*lame from his mother's womb*."(*f*)

9 And immediately the man was made whole, and took up his bed,
and walked: and on the same day was the Sabbath.

On which day our Blessed Lord is repeatedly declared to have performed his acts
of Mercy. See the note on St. Luke iv. 36; and consider the following places:—
St. Mark iii. 1 to 5. St. Luke iv. 31 to 35: also 38 to 39: xiv. 1 to 4. St. John
ix. 14. Thereby, He declared plainly that the Jewish Sabbath was only a temporary institution, which had attained its fulfillment in Him; since *in Him* is our
Eternal Rest,—which the Sabbath foreshadowed. See Colossians ii. 16, 17.

10 The Jews therefore said unto him that was cured, It is the Sabbath day: it is not lawful for thee to carry *thy* bed.

Consider the following texts:—Exodus xxxi. 14, 15; Numbers xv. 33 to 36: Nehemiah xiii. 19, (where burdens *of merchandise* alone are forbidden;) Jeremiah
xvii. 21, 22: St. Mark ix. 16.—Concerning "the Jews," see the note on ver. 15.

11 He answered them, He that made me whole, the same said unto
me, Take up thy bed, and walk.

The character of the man whom our Saviour had restored, begins immediately
to display itself. He says,—I have a mighty warrant for carrying my bed. It
was the command of One, who by a single word cured me of an infirmity of which I
have suffered for thirty-eight years. He must needs be a Teacher come from God;
for no man can do such miracles except God be with him !(*g*)

12 Then asked they him, What man is that which said unto thee,
Take up thy bed, and walk?

These hypocrites do not ask, *What man is that which made thee whole?* but name,
instead, the pretended *offence* of the Holy One.

(*f*) See Acts iii. 2 to 8.   (*g*) St. John iii. 2.

13 And he that was healed wist not who it was: for JESUS had con-
,yed Himself away, a multitude being in *that* place.

The expression in the original is remarkable. It denotes a swift and silent glid-
g (literally *swimming*) out of, and away from the crowd.

14 Afterward JESUS findeth him in the Temple,

The Impotent man is found next *in the Temple.* Doubt not but what he hastened
ither to pour out his heart in gratitude to the Author and Giver of all good
ings !(*h*) The character of those whom our SAVIOUR selected to be the objects of
is Mercy, should always be carefully noticed.

and said unto him, Behold, thou art made whole: sin no more, lest a
orse thing come unto thee.

"A worse thing," (observes a thoughtful living writer,) "than 38 years of Pain
d Infirmity ! — words which give us an awful glimpse of the severity of GOD's
judgments. This infirmity had found the man young, and left him old: it had
thered up his manhood, and yet 'a worse thing' even than this is threatened him,
hould he sin again...... What the past Sin of this sufferer had been, to which
ur LORD alludes, we know not; but the man himself knew very well. His consci-
nce was the interpreter of the warning."

Sometimes, therefore, bodily sickness and suffering are to be regarded as correc-
tive of past Sin, — the direct consequence to the sinner of Sin in himself: but by no
means always. It was indeed so in Gehazi's case,(*i*) — in the case of Ananias and
Sapphira,(*k*)—of Elymas.(*l*)—and of Herod.(*m*) Consider further 1 Corinthans xi.
30. David, however, was punished for his adulterous connection with Bathsheba,
by *the death of his child*:(*n*) and many are the cases where Sickness, Suffering, and
Death itself, have been brought on the individuals of a nation by the sin of their
rulers. Consider Genesis xii. 17; xx. 18. 1 Samuel v. 6 to 12. 2 Samuel xxi. 1:
xxiv. 10 to 17. Then further.— Bodily Ailment may be sent, not for the correction
of past sins, but for the prevention of future,— as in the case of St. Paul.(*o*) Lastly,
its purpose may be to try and prove the patience of the Saints,—as in Job's case:(*p*)
or "that the works of GOD may be made manifest," — as in the case of the Man
born blind.(*q*)

"We learn besides from our LORD's words," remarks an ancient Bishop, "that if,
after undergoing a heavy punishment for our sins, we fall into them again, we shall
incur another and a heavier punishment." See the notes on St. Matthew xii. 43
to 45.

15 The man departeth, and told the Jews that it was JESUS, which
had made him whole.

Not—" which had said, *Take up thy bed* and walk ;" (for *that* was an offence to
the Jews, and was not the ground of the speaker's joy:) but—" which had *made him
whole.*" Compare verse 12, and the note there. And here we lose sight of the
man; who goes forth, preaching CHRIST !

But it is time to point out concerning the personages whom St. John in ver. 10,
in this place, and in ver. 15, calls "*the Jews,*" that the Rulers of the People (as in
chap. vii. 48,) are clearly spoken of: members of the Sanhedrin, or Great Council
of the Nation, who were chiefly of the sect of the Pharisees. Compare ver. 33,
below. with chap. i. 19, 24. Consider also the following places : — St. John vii. 1,
13: ix. 18 to 22, (and 13, 15 :) xviii. 12, 14. The actual power in the hands of
these persons(*r*) was what rendered their enmity so formidable: as it follows,—

16 And therefore did the Jews persecute JESUS, and sought to slay
Him, because He had done these things on the Sabbath day.

17 But JESUS answered them, My FATHER worketh hitherto, and I
work.

(*h*) See 2 Kings xx. 8.　　　　　　　　　(*i*) 2 Kings v. 20 to 27.
(*k*) Acts v. 1 to 10.　　　　(*l*) Acts xiii. 8 to 11.　　　(*m*) Acts xii. 23.
(*n*) 2 Sam. xii. 14.　　　　(*o*) 2 Cor. xii. 7.　　　　(*p*) Job ii. 3, &c.
(*q*) See St. John ix. 1 to 3.　　　(*r*) St. Matthew xxvii. 65. St. John vii. 32, 45. &c.

That seems to mean,—Ye seek to slay Me for having, as ye say, broken the Sabbath : whereon, according to the Commandment, men must rest,—after the pattern of GOD, who "*rested* on the seventh day." But if upon acts of Mercy, Providence, and Goodness, ye bestow the name of "works," learn ye that " My FATHER worketh hitherto,"—hath been "working" up to this very hour, — with sleepless watchfulness, unremitting energy, untiring love. Learn that, by "rested" (in Genesis ii. 2, 3.)(*s*) it is implied only that GOD, at the end of six days, ceased *from the Work of Creation,*—made no more new creatures. *Those* were "the works" which "were *finished* from the foundation of the world."(*t*) But from that time until now, GOD has been carrying on the *government* of those creatures,—upholding and sustaining them. Were He to cease from *such* working, the World itself would cease to exist. Why then do ye desire to kill *Me* for displaying a similar care and concern for the Lives of men ?

But by saying "*MY FATHER* worketh hitherto, *and I* work," — the Divine Speaker was declaring a glorious Doctrine. First, His own Divinity : for He calls GOD His " FATHER,"—evidently in a different sense from that in which men, addressing the same Almighty Being, are taught to say " *Our* Father." Consider St. Matthew vi. 9, in connection with Isaiah lxiii. 16. "*My,*" implies *equality.* Consider St. John x. 30, 33, 36. — Next, our LORD conveys the Doctrine that He is Himself " of one substance with the FATHER,"—" in the FATHER," as the FATHER is in Him : so that as the " FATHER worketh hitherto," *He* also " worketh." Consider Hebrews i. 3. And thus it was that the Jews understood His words, — nor did He deny the correctness of their inference : —

18 Therefore the Jews sought the more to kill Him, because He not only had broken the Sabbath, but said also that GOD was His FATHER, making Himself equal with GOD.

Strange that these impious men should have seen so clearly in our LORD's Words, — (namely, in the statement "that GOD was *His own FATHER,*")(*u*) — the great Truth which many an Unbeliever of the present day declares that he cannot find there !

If the reader will call to mind what was said in the second note on verse 15, above, and then observe the exceeding solemnity of the words which follow—(than which anything graver, grander, and more momentous is not to be found in the whole of the Gospel.) — he will probably be of opinion that from verse 17 to the end of the present chapter is to be regarded as the Defence of the SAVIOUR of the World when cited before the Bar of His Enemies : a formal Address which He delivered before the Court of Sanhedrin.

19, 20 Then answered JESUS and said unto them, Verily, verily, I say unto you, The SON can do nothing of Himself, but what he seeth the FATHER do : for what things soever He doeth, these also doeth the SON likewise. For the FATHER loveth the SON, and showeth Him all things that Himself doeth :

Compare this, with what is said in ver. 30 : — " I can of Mine own self do nothing : as I hear, I judge." The terms " hearing" and " seeing," when applied to GOD,(*x*) as in chap. iii. 11 and 32, — should create no surprise. In no better way can Heavenly mysteries be revealed to human hearts and minds than by using such ordinary forms of human speech. GOD speaks to us in the Bible, as we speak to little children. We tell them *the Truth ;* but we put the Truth into language which they can understand. When full-grown, they do not reproach us with having deceived them. Far from it. They in turn, use the self-same language to the children of the next generation.

Now, it may be convenient, before we pass on from verses 19 and 20, to bring under one point of view some other similar places of St. John's Gospel ; and to offer a few remarks upon them all together, instead of dividing our remarks, or repeating them. Thus, then, in St. John viii. 26 to 28, it is said, — " He that sent

(*s*) Compare Exodus xxxii. 17.   (*t*) Hebrews iv. 3.
(*u*) Compare Romans viii. 32, — where JESUS CHRIST is called God's "*own* SON."
(*x*) Consider the following places : — Genesis i. 4, 10, 12, &c. : xi. 5 : xviii. 21 : xxi. 17. Exodus iii. 7.

e is true; and I speak to the World those things which I have heard of Him. They understood not that He spake unto them of the FATHER.) Then said JESUS . . . I do nothing of Myself; but as My FATHER hath taught Me, I speak these ings." Again, in St. John xii. 49, 50,—" I have not spoken of Myself; but the ATHER which sent Me, He gave Me a Commandment, what I should say, and what should speak . . . . Whatsoever I speak, therefore, even as the FATHER said unto a, so I speak." Again, in St. John xiv. 10:—'' Believest thou not that I am in e FATHER, and the FATHER in Me? The words that I speak unto you, I speak st of Myself: but the FATHER that dwelleth in Me, He doeth the work.(y)—In l these places a high and heavenly Doctrine is set before us: concerning which if words should be wary and few.

There are certain great Truths—held by all men, held at all times, held in all laces,—fundamental Truths concerning the Three PERSONS in the GODHEAD,—(the mystery of the Blessed Trinity, as it is called,—Truths *above* Reason, yet not *against* Reason, which have been certainly gathered by the Church out of GOD's Word; and which enable it to explain other places in Holy Writ which would else have been hopelessly dark and difficult. Thus, the Doctrine of the Eternal Generation of the SON, rightly stated, will be found to bring all the texts above quoted within the limits of Man's understanding.

For the Church teaches, and hath ever taught, that the Divine Essence of GOD THE SON, He hath not of Himself, but by communication from GOD THE FATHER: yet is this statement, and others like it, made without reference to *Time*. We cannot talk of "One Person of Himself originally subsisting,(z) without straightway inquiring,—Was there ever a time when the other two Persons in the Godhead did not exist? To which the Church answers, "In this Trinity, *none is afore or after other ;*" "The FATHER, eternal: the SON, eternal: and the HOLY GHOST, eternal.(a) There never was *a time*, therefore, when any One of the Three Persons was not; and yet the SON was "begotten" of the FATHER: the HOLY GHOST "proceeded" from the FATHER and the SON.

"All things that the FATHER hath are Mine," saith CHRIST ;(b) because in Him is the fullness of the same GODHEAD; and more than that, the FATHER cannot have. But yet, in that perfect and absolute equality, there is notwithstanding this disparity,—that the FATHER hath the Godhead not from the SON, nor any other; whereas the SON hath it from the FATHER. CHRIST is the True GOD, and Eternal Life; but that He is so, is from the FATHER: "for as the FATHER hath Life in Himself, so hath He *given* to the SON to have Life in Himself;"(c) not by participation, but by communication. It is true, our SAVIOUR was so "in the form of GOD," that He "thought it not robbery to be equal with GOD:" but when the Jews sought to kill Him, because He made Himself equal with GOD, He answered them,— "Verily, verily, I say unto you, the SON can do nothing of Himself but what He seeth the FATHER do :" by that connection of His operations, showing the reception of His Essence; and by the acknowledgment of His Power, professing His Substance from the FATHER.

When, therefore, our LORD says, (in verse 30,) "I can of Mine own self do nothing,"—it is because He is not of Himself; and whosoever receives his Being, must receive his Power from another; especially where the Essence and the Power are undeniably the same, as in GOD they are. "The SON," then, "can do nothing of Himself, but what He seeth the FATHER do,"—because He hath no Power of Himself but what the FATHER gave: and since the FATHER gave him all the Power, so communicating His entire and undivided Essence, therefore, "what things soever He doeth, these also doeth the SON likewise," by the same Power by which the SON worketh; because He had received the same Godhead in which the FATHER subsisteth.

The reader is also referred to the note on St. John xiv. 28, for some remarks on this great subject. Speaking of what things the FATHER showeth the SON, our LORD proceeds :

21 and He will show Him greater works than these, that ye may

(y) St. John iii. 34 may be also referred to ; where a similar statement concerning our SAVIOUR made by His Forerunner.

(s) These words, and many others in the present note, are borrowed from the great Work f the learned and wise Bishop Pearson.

(a) See the Athanasian Creed,—the great Treasury of Catholic Truth.

(b) St. John xvi. 15.   (c) St. John v. 26.

marvel. For as the FATHER raiseth up the Dead, and quickeneth *them;* even so the SON quickeneth whom He will.

To raise the dead would be a more marvellous work than that performed upon the Impotent Man. But our LORD's language seems to be intentionally made capable of a double interpretation; being applicable either to the quickening of those who are "dead in trespasses and sins,"(d) or to the raising of the dead at the last day: to which allusion is made in chap. vi. 39, 40, 44, 54. And this may have been done, because while the relief of bodily suffering was the actual subject of our LORD's discourse,—Sin and Eternal Death, (of which Sickness(e) and Dissolution are but the emblems,) were in reality the objects at which His gracious words pointed.

All this is made plainer in the sequel: for, while verses 24, 25 and 26, declare the spiritual Resurrection which takes place in Time,—verses 28 and 29 will be found to set forth bodily Resurrection which is for Eternity. Verse 27 may be compared with ver. 22.

"*Whom He Will:*"—*that* is the Prerogative of GOD alone. Of GOD the FATHER, —as in St. James i. 18: of GOD the SON,—as in St. Matthew viii. 3, and in this place: of GOD the HOLY GHOST,—as in 1 Corinthians xii. 11.—GOD, and GOD *only*, may do *as He will*. Yet is it certain that the Will of GOD is not arbitrary: for, (as the Apostle declares,) He worketh all things "after *the counsel* of His own Will;(*f*) "and whatsoever is done with counsel or wise resolution, hath of necessity some reason why it should be done."

22 For the Father

—who never took upon Him the nature of men or of angels,—

judgeth no man, but hath committed all Judgment unto the SON:

As stated in Acts xvii. 31 and x. 42. And the reason why He hath committed it to Him, is because He is not only the SON of GOD, (as verses 22 and 23 imply, and verse 25 clearly states,) and so, truly GOD:—but also "the SON of Man," (as stated in verse 27,) and so truly Man: *that* Son of Man who suffered so much for the sons of men.

There is therefore an original, supreme, judicial power: and there is a judicial power derived, given by commission. CHRIST, as GOD, hath the first, together with the FATHER: CHRIST, as Man, hath the second from the FATHER. And the reason of this delegated authority is set forth in the next verse:—

23 that all *men* should honor the SON, even as they honor the FATHER. He that honoreth not the SON, honoreth not the FATHER, which hath sent Him.

For the SON could not be the SON, but for the FATHER: nor could He be the FATHER if He had not the SON.

24 Verily, verily, I say unto you, He that heareth My Word, and believeth on Him that sent Me,

Our LORD says not "on *Me:*" but "on *Him that sent* Me:" and the reason is plain He is "*declaring the* FATHER:"(*g*) is engaged in revealing to the Jews the mysterious relation in which Himself, (the SON,) stood to the FATHER. It will suffice, therefore, if He can persuade them to "believe on *Him that sent:*" for if "every one that *loveth* Him that begat, loveth Him also that is Begotten of Him,"(*h*) certainly *Belief* on Him that *sent* will produce Belief also in Him that *is* sent. See above (ver. 23.) how the honor of the FATHER and of the SON are declared, mutually, one to imply the other. Consider St. John xii. 44: xv. 23.—He then, so hearing and believing,

hath everlasting Life, and shall not come into Condemnation; but is passed from Death unto Life.

"To hear," in the language of the SPIRIT, is "*to obey*." "He that heareth My

(d) Ephesians ii. 1.   (e) See above, verse 14.   (f) Ephes. i. 11.
(g) St John i. 18.   (h) 1 St. John v. 1.

Word," is therefore "He that keepeth My commandments." See the note on ver.
21. Of such an one it is said.—he "*hath* Everlasting Life:" he "*is passed* from
Death unto Life." That is, he has begun *already* to be a partaker of it. The Eternal Life which he obtains here, is as it were, an earnest of that which is to follow.
Remember what is said in St. John xi. 25, 26: and take notice how exactly it corresponds with what is here declared of a passage, in *this* World, "from Death unto
Life." Consider St. John vi. 47, and the note.

25 Verily, verily, I say unto you, The hour is coming, and now is,
when the Dead shall hear the Voice of the SON of GOD: and they that
hear shall live.

"Hear," so as *to obey:* as explained in the preceding note. Spiritual deadness,
obviously, is here spoken of. A state of *Sin* is set forth under the image of *Death*,
as in so many other places ;(*i*) while *Repentance* is spoken of as *Life* itself. Compare St. Luke xv. 24, 32. Also Ephes. ii. 1, 5; v. 14. Coloss. ii. 13. 1 St. John
iii. 14. And see the note on St. Matthew ix. 25.

26 For as the FATHER hath Life in Himself; so hath He given to
the SON to have Life in Himself.

The *likeness of Nature* between the First and Second Persons of the Blessed Trinity is here declared. Both the FATHER and the SON have the same life: both have
it in themselves; both in the same degree; *as* the One, *so* the Other: but only with
this difference,—the FATHER (from all Eternity) giveth it; the SON (from all Eternity) receiveth it. And this has been already explained in the note on verse 20.
From whence, in a certain place, CHRIST professeth that "the living FATHER sent
Him, and that *He liveth by the FATHER;*"(*k*) and here, that the FATHER "*gave
Him to have Life* in Himself:" which is tantamount to saying that the FATHER
"begat" Him.
In Him dwelt all the fullness of the GODHEAD bodily ;(*l*) and this, He sufficiently
showed by His acts of Divine power: not only healing diseases, and casting out
devils; stilling the winds and waves, and even raising the dead; but from Him as
from a fountain, without word or sign, Healing Virtue went into as many as
touched His garments in Faith.(*m*) More than this, He was able, at will, to impart to others a measure—as much as He would—of His own Divine power.(*n*)
So that, most truly, "*in Him was Life.*"(*o*)—It follows:

27 And hath given Him authority to execute Judgment also, because He is the Son of Man.

That is, because, of the three Persons which are GOD, He only is also the Son of
Man. And therefore, because of His alliance with man's nature,—because of His
sense of man's infirmities,—because of all He did and suffered for man's sake, as
the Son of Man,—He is most fit, as well as most worthy, to be Man's Judge. See
above, on verse 22.
Yet further,—since "Son of Man" is a title of our LORD which often stands for
"The Messiah," (as was explained in the second note on St. Matthew viii. 20,) it
seems to be here implied that the Divine Speaker must needs duly perform that
part of the Mediatorial office which made Him Judge both of quick and dead.

28 Marvel not at this:

Referring, probably, less to what He had just before said of Judgment to come,
than to the statements in verses 24 and 25 concerning spiritual Resurrection:

29 for the hour is coming, in which all that are in the graves shall
hear His Voice, and shall come forth; they that have done Good, unto
the Resurrection of Life; and they that have done Evil, unto the Resurrection of Damnation.

(*i*) See St. Matthew viii. 22, and the note there.   (*k*) St. John vi. 57.
(*l*) Colossians ii. 9.   (*m*) St. Mark v. 28, 29; St. Luke vi. 19.
(*n*) St. Luke x. 19; St. Matthew x. 8; St. Mark xvi. 17; St. John xiv. 12.
(*o*) St. John i. 4.

In this way our LORD repeatedly reasons. Consider the following places:—St. John i. 50, 51: iii. 7, 8: vi. 61, 62. St. Mark ii. 9 to 11. &c.

These two verses, then, stand in marked contrast with verses 24 and 25, and should be compared with them, throughout. *There* the Resurrection which takes place in *this* World,—the Resurrection of the Soul from the Death of Sin to the Life of Righteousness was spoken of: *here*, the Resurrection of Soul and Body at the Last Day is declared. Hence, in the former place, the phrases,—"now *is*," "the *dead*," (whether *all* or *some* is not stated,) "shall *live;*" in the latter,—"*is coming*," (for the Judgment is yet future:) "*all*," (for we must *all* stand before the Judgment Seat of Christ;) "in the *Grave*," and "shall *come forth*," (for the Resurrection of *the Body* is intended.)

It might be thought by one who should contend for the mere letter of verse 24, that the phrase "he that heareth My Word" should not be interpreted of *works of Obedience*. The language in that place may seem to some, little else than a declaration that "Faith cometh by hearing, and hearing by the Word of GOD."(*p*) Let such "hearers," however, attend to the description (in ver. 29) of those who "shall come forth . . . unto the Resurrection of Life" Eternal. It is "*they that have done good*,"—and none other.

30 I can of Mine Own Self do nothing: as I hear, I judge:

This is said because the SON is not of Himself, but was from all Eternity begotten of the FATHER; and whosoever receives his Being, must receive his Power, from another; especially where the Essence and the Power are the same, as in GOD they are.—The reader is referred to verse 19, and the note there. See also the note on the last words of St. John xiv. 28, for a few more words on this great mystery.—"As I hear, I judge."

and My Judgment is just; because I seek not Mine own Will, but the Will of the FATHER which hath sent Me.

The reader is referred below, to the notes on ver. 44; and will observe that our LORD pronounces here, "in reference to His own conduct and example, that Humility, Submission, and entire Singleness of purpose,—founded upon implicit Obedience to GOD,—are the true rudder to guide us to Truth in reasoning."

Not that the Will of GOD the SON is here spoken of as something distinct from the Will of GOD the FATHER; for *that* were absurd: but, *as the Son of Man*, our Blessed SAVIOUR had a Human Will,—distinct from the Divine; though never at variance with it. Consider by all means the memorable words in St. Luke xxii. 42. In this place, then, our LORD declares, that His Will is not His own in such a sense, as to be different from the FATHER's: that, as Man, He seeks not His own Will in opposition to that of GOD. "For" (says a great African Bishop) "men do their own Will, not GOD's, when, to please themselves, they violate GOD's commands. But when they do what they wish, so as at the same time to follow the Will of GOD, they do not their own Will, but GOD's."—Compare St. John vi. 38.

See some remarks in the notes on St. Matthew ix. 13, on the expression "and Mine own . . . *but;*" and compare in the present Gospel, iii. 17: vi. 27: vii. 16: ix. 3: xii. 44, 47: xiv. 24.

31, 32 If I bear witness of Myself, My witness is not true. There is Another that beareth witness of Me; and I know that the witness which He witnesseth of Me is true.

Our LORD means, that they would not allow Him to bear witness of Himself; that they would pronounce such witness untrue,—as they actually did, in chapter viii. 13. And further, that His witness as Man, without the witness of another.(*q*) —without the witness of GOD,—was inconclusive. (Consider Acts ii. 22, and Hebrews ii. 4. See also verse 36, below; and the note there.) He proceeds therefore to remind them that He had, besides, a fourfold witness:—(I.) the witness of St. John Baptist,—(II.) the witness of His own miraculous works, (verse 36,)—(III.) the witness of the FATHER, (verse 37,)—and (IV.) the witness of the Holy Scripture,(*r*) (verse 39, &c.) . . , First, He reminds them of the Baptist's Testi-

(*p*) Romans x. 17.   (*q*) St. Matthew xviii. 16.
(*r*) See the heading of the present chapter.

*ony, which was the least of all; and, as if to anticipate their objection that it *ight not be *true*, He adds:

33, 34 Ye sent unto John, and he bare witness unto the Truth. But [receive not testimony from man: but these things I say, that ye might be saved.

That is, — Ye sought him yourselves, to inquire of him; (alluding to chap. i. 19 o 27:) *that* is why I use his testimony, — that ye might be saved. For I, being God, need not the Testimony of Man.

35 He was a burning and a shining light: and ye were willing for a season to rejoice in his light.

Rather, — "He was the burning and shining Lamp." The reader is referred to the notes on St. John i. 23.

36 But I have greater witness than *that* of John: for the works which the FATHER hath given Me to finish, the same works that I do, bear witness of Me, that the FATHER hath sent Me.

Our LORD says that His miracles not only proved Him to be *GOD*, but proved Him to be *the MESSIAH* likewise, — by corresponding with the predictions of Prophecy: Isaiah xxix. 18: xxxii. 3, 4: xxxv. 5, 6: xlii. 6, 7, &c. He often thus appealed to the witness of His miracles, — as in St. Luke vii. 20 to 22. St. John x. 25, 38: xiv. 10, 11: xv. 24, &c.

37, 38 And the FATHER Himself, which hath sent Me, hath borne witness of Me. Ye have neither heard His voice at any time, nor seen His shape. And ye have not His Word abiding in you: for whom He hath sent, Him ye believe not.

"GOD is *a Spirit* ;"(s) "without body, parts, or passions."(t) He hath no voice, therefore, — neither hath He a shape. And this is what our LORD here declares. Consider Exodus xxxiii. 20: Deut. iv. 12: 1 Tim. vi. 16: 1 St. John iv. 12. But the Voice from Heaven, which attended the Baptism of our SAVIOUR, and proclaimed Him as the "Beloved SON," was doubtless *part* of the "witness" borne to Him by the FATHER.(u)

In this place, however, our LORD certainly does not refer in any *special* manner to that remarkable Testimony. Rather may it be thought that He even draws away the attention *from* it. The FATHER, by giving to the Jews His Words, (that is, *the Gospel*,(x) through the SON, and thereby "borne witness" to Him. But their actions proved that they had not *that* Word abiding in themselves;(y) — namely, the Commandments of GOD, in the true spirit of them: for (He adds,) "Whom He hath sent, Him ye believe not." Now, as our LORD declared on another occasion, — "If any man will *do His Will*, He shall know of the Doctrine, whether it be of GOD, or whether I speak of Myself."(z)

39 Search the Scriptures; for in them ye think ye have Eternal Life: and they are they which testify of Me.

"Of Me, — through whom alone that Life may be obtained."

40 And ye will not come to Me, that ye might have Life.

Perhaps this ought to be read, — "Ye search the Scriptures." The meaning is, that though the Scriptures bore such clear testimony to CHRIST, *yet* the Jewish nation, to whom those Books belonged,(a) would not come to CHRIST.

(s) St. John iv. 24.   (t) Article I.
(u) See St. Matth. iii. 17, and St. Luke iii. 12, — where (in the words of the heading of the chapter,) "CHRIST receiveth testimony from Heaven." See also St. Matthew xvii. 5: but observe, the Transfiguration was an event yet future.
(x) Compare St. John vii. 16: viii. 28: xii. 49: xiv. 10, 24.
(y) Compare 2 St. John ii. 14.   (s) St. John vii. 17.   (a) Romans iii. 2.

It was said, above, (in the note on verse 32,) that our LORD appealed to a four-fold testimony. It should be observed that a gradation, as well as a connection, is discernable between every link in the chain. — Ye chose the witness of John (I.): but the witness of My miracle is far greater; for those works are the confirmation of his words (II.). Still weightier witness do My doctrines supply, that I came forth from GOD, and am the MESSIAH (III.). But the most mighty testimony of any is supplied by the writings of Moses, — by the whole volume of Scripture; which, in Types and Shadows, — Histories and Laws, — Civil and Religious Enactment, — Feasts and Sacrifices, — Prophecies and Psalms, — is *full*, from end to end, *of Me* (IV.).

It seems as if it were further implied. — I do not bring forward this fourfold testimony because I seek My own glory.(*b*) "I complain not of your being unwilling to come to Me, as though I should gain honour from your coming; for,"—

41 I receive not honour from men. But

" I speak thus of you, because"

42 I know you, that ye have not the love of GOD in you.

To convince you that it is not from your love of GOD that you persecute Me: for He bears witness to Me, as I have shown, by My Doctrine, by My works, and by the Scriptures.

43 I am come in My FATHER'S Name, and ye receive Me not: if another shall come in his own name, him ye will receive.

Alluding to the "false Christs and false Prophets," which our LORD foretold St. Matthew xxiv. 24. "Here, then." observes an old Eastern Bishop, "is the crowning proof of their impiety." He says, — "If it was the Love of GOD which made you persecute Me, you would persecute Antichrist, (who will come in his own name.) much more: for he will not profess to be sent by the FATHER, or to come according to His will; but, on the contrary, usurping what does not belong to him, will proclaim himself to be GOD over all." Whereas, Antichrist ye *will* receive.

" The true disciples of our LORD were few; though in one instance four, and in another five, thousand were miraculously fed by Him. But a Jew, who afterwards came from Egypt, with no other credentials but self-confident boasting, led away to Olivet, as Josephus informs us, no less a number than 30,000 deluded followers. And though, as far as appears, neither he nor any of his brethren in imposture actually assumed the title of MESSIAH; yet their general conduct showed to what their ambitious views aspired."

44 How can ye believe, which receive honor one of another, and seek not the honor that *cometh* from GOD only ?

Mark the contrast between the disposition implied by these words, and what our LORD states concerning Himself, in verse 41.

This is one of those marvellous places, (places in which are scattered with no sparing hand throughout the Book of Life,) in which a secret is revealed to us concerning ourselves. It is found that the disposition which courts honor at the hands of man, and is content to rest in such honor, is at enmity with the spirit of Faith. Compare chapter xii. 42, 43. St. Matthew xxiii. 5. Rom. ii. 29. — There is, indeed, "scarcely any doctrine or precept of our SAVIOUR more distinctly and strongly stated, than that the capacity for judging of, and for believing the Truths of Christianity, depends upon moral Goodness, and the practice of Virtue." The reader will do well to consider the texts indicated at foot.(*c*)

45 Do not think that I will accuse you to the FATHER : there is one that accuseth you, *even* Moses, in whom ye trust.

He answers them out of their own authorities: John, — to whom *they sent; the*

(*b*) Compare St. John vii. 18: viii. 50, 54.
(*c*) St. John vii. 17: viii. 12. Eccles. i. 26: xxi. 11. St. Matth. v. 8. Psalm xix. 8: cxix. 100. And see above, the first note on the latter half of verse 30; and the note on St. Luke xi. 33 and 43.

kriptures, wherein *they thought they had eternal Life;* Moses, — in whom *they trusted.* And he warns them that their trust in Moses is based on a foundation of sand : that the great Lawgiver himself will prove the accuser of the nation,—nay, i their accuser already. And the memorable reason follows :

46 For had ye believed Moses, ye would have believed Me; for he rrote of Me.

A wondrous declaration, truly, if we consider who is the Speaker.(*d*) O to have nown what he said on this subject to Cleopas and his companion as they went to Emmaus ! But the Books of Moses are in our hands. *Where* then does he write of Christ ? Shall it suffice to appeal to ten or twenty places in the Pentateuch,— uch as the reader will find enumerated at foot of the page ?(*e*) Surely, those places do not come up to the largeness of our Lord's statement !(*f*) Where does Moses say "that Christ should suffer ?"—or "that He should be the first that should rise from the dead ?"—or that He "should show Light unto the people, and to the Gentiles ?" And yet, St. Paul found some, if not all, of these things in "Moses !"(*g*) The plain truth is, that *we do not thoroughly understand the Bible;* and the next best thing to understanding it, is to know that we understand it not.

47 But if ye believe not his Writings, how shall ye believe my Words ?

That is,—If ye practically disbelieve the ancient Writings of one whom ye profess to hold in such honour, how should ye believe the mere Sayings of One for whom ye entertain no respect ?

With such words does our Saviour conclude a discourse which yields to none in Holy Scripture, in dignity, difficulty, and mysterious importance. In declaring the eternal relations of the Father and of the Son, this chapter may be regarded as a very "pillar and ground of the Truth."

CHAPTER VI.

1 Christ *feedeth five thousand men with five loaves and two fishes.* 15 *Thereupon the people would have made Him King.* 16 *But withdrawing Himself, He walked on the sea to His Disciples:* 26 *reproveth the people flocking after Him, and all the fleshly hearers of His Word:* 32 *declareth Himself to be the Bread of Life to believers.* 66 *Many Disciples depart from Him.* 68 *Peter confesseth him.* 70 *Judas is a devil.*

The Evangelist St. John does not record the Institution of either of the two Sacraments. But what the other evangelists have set down in the way of historical narrative, St. John is found to deliver in the way of doctrinal statement. Accordingly, our Lord's discourse with Nicodemus, in the third chapter of St. John's Gospel, is allowed by the Universal Church to relate to Holy Baptism : while the Discourse in the Synagogue of Capernaum, in the present chapter, as plainly relates to the great mystery of the Holy Eucharist.(*a*) A singular coincidence is moreover observable in the manner and arrangement which runs through the chapters in which these two Sacraments are predicted ; as will be found pointed out below in the notes on verses 52 and 62.

In the Miraculous feeding of the Five Thousand, which precedes the Discourse

---

(*d*) Compare St. John i. 45. St. Luke xxviii. 27. Acts xxviii. 23.
(*e*) Gen. iii. 15 : xii. 3 : xviii. 18 : xxvi. 4 : xlix. 10. Numb. xxi. 9. Deut. xviii. 15, 18.
(*f*) See above, the note on ver. 40. (*g*) See Acts xxvi. 22, 23.
(*e*) See below, the note on ver. 35.

in the Synagogue of Capernaum, our LORD mystically showed the virtue of His own Incarnation and Sacrifice. No fitter preparation for that Discourse can therefore be imagined, than is here supplied: and thus it may be declared briefly that the Incarnation, and the Eucharist as connected with it, is the one pervading topic of the whole chapter.

AFTER these things JESUS went over the sea of Galilee, which is *the sea* of Tiberias.

Between chapter v. and chapter vi., a whole year elapses, — the second year of our LORD's Ministry. St. John, because he wrote his Gospel at a distance from the Holy Land, and addressed it to a people unacquainted with the language or religion, the customs or geography of Judæa, is found frequently to explain his own statements, and the terms which he himself employs. Thus, in the first chapter of his Gospel, we meet with an explanation of the words, "Rabbi," "Messias," and "Cephas."(*b*) Below, in ver. 4, he informs his reader that "the Passover" is "*a Feast of the Jews;*" and towards the close of his Gospel, he explains what is "the manner of the Jews to bury."(*c*) In the fourth chapter, he explains that one journeying out of Judæa into Galilee, "must needs go through Samaria ;"(*d*) and, in the verse before us, he identifies the mountain Lake, known in Palestine as "the Sea of Galilee," by mentioning the most considerable city which stood upon its shore. Tiberias, situated on the western side of the Lake, was built by Herod Antipas, and named after the Roman Emperor Tiberius.

2, 3 And a great multitude followed Him, because they saw His miracles which He did on them that were diseased. And JESUS went up into a mountain, and there he sat with His Disciples.

At all to understand the history of the transaction thus alluded to, rather than described, — (the reason, namely, why our LORD "went over the Sea of Galilee," and the manner of the pursuit adopted by the "great multitude,") — the reader should consult the narratives of the three earlier evangelists.(*e*) He will be disposed to remark, when he has done so, that this part of St. John's Gospel does not by any means produce a corresponding impression on the mind. To which it may be answered, that *neither was it intended* that it should. St. John passes very briefly over the previous history, (which had been so fully treated by the Evangelists who wrote before him ;) being chiefly anxious to describe the miraculous feeding of the Five Thousand which followed, and above all to record the Divine Discourse of our SAVIOUR, to which none of the other Evangelists had been guided even to make allusion. Take notice of his remarkable method, as exemplified in the very next verse :—

4 And the Passover, a feast of the Jews, was nigh.

The reader may be invited, in passing, to compare this explanation of the term "Passover" with what is found in St. John ii. 13, and xi. 55. See above, the note on verse 1; and the note on the latter part of chap. ii. 6.

But it is far more important that he should consider what may have been the object of the blessed writer in introducing here the statement that the Passover was nigh. Was it done *merely* to mark the close of the second year of our SAVIOUR's Ministry? We cannot believe it. Much worthier seems the supposition that the HOLY SPIRIT thereby guides Believers to connect the miracle which follows, with the Paschal season: to view therein a lively symbol of the Efficacy of the Sacrifice of "CHRIST, our Passover ;"(*f*) and thus to regard the entire transaction as having mysterious reference to the great event which took place at Jerusalem exactly one year after the date of the present transaction. For, as the HOLY ONE Himself declared on this occasion,—"*I* am the Bread of Life,"—"the living Bread, which came down from heaven ;" "and the Bread which I will give is *My flesh*, which *I will give for the life of the World.*" "Verily, verily, I say unto you, Except ye eat *the flesh of the Son of Man,* and drink *His blood,* ye have no life in you."(*g*) That these words have reference to the blessed Sacrament of CHRIST's Body and

(*b*) St. John i. 38, 41, 42.   (*c*) St. John xix. 40.   (*d*) St. John iv. 4.
(*e*) St. Matthew xiv. 3 to 14: St. Mark vi. 32 to 34: St. Luke ix. 10 and 11.
(*f*) 1 Cor. v. 7.   (*g*) See below, verses 35, 41, 51, 53.

d, the Church allows:(h) and indeed can we doubt that *both* miracles of feed —*this*, performed for the relief of the Five Thousand, and *that* for the relief of Four,(i)—were emblematic of the same Heavenly Feast, which was expressly ined for the support of souls fainting in this World's wilderness?

ut our attention is invited to the mountain's side, on the north-eastern extremity ie Lake, where our SAVIOUR has withdrawn with His Twelve Apostles.

, 6, When JESUS then lifted up *His* eyes, and saw a great company ie unto Him, He saith unto Philip, Whence shall we buy bread, that se may eat? And this He said to prove him:

ut *why* did He address this inquiry to Philip? The Evangelist himself supplies reason: "this He said to prove him," that is, to make trial of the Apostle's h. Was then CHRIST ignorant of what would be St. Philip's reply? GOD for- that such a thought concerning the Searcher of hearts should be seriously en- ained! Effectually to preclude it, the Evangelist adds —

or He Himself knew what He would do.

He only intended to draw forth by His question the mind of that Apostle and rest, who had besought Him to send away the multitude to buy food for them- ies in the nearest villages.(k) All were to be made fully aware of the insuffi- ncy of their own resources for such a multitude; and to feel that a power no less in Divine was concerned in supplying the deficiency.(l)

But the question recurs, Why was *Philip* singled out for the inquiry recorded in i text? The clue is probably to be found in our SAVIOUR's dialogue with him re- rded in the xiv. chapter of the present Gospel.(m) A certain slowness of heart recognize the Godhead of the Incarnate SON, may be presumed thus on *two* re- rded occasions to have suggested words, the tendency of which was to reveal . Philip to himself.—His reply sufficiently shows that he dreamed of nothing less in a display of miraculous power.

7 Philip answered Him, Two hundred pennyworth of bread is not fficient for them, that every one of them may take a little.

And yet, this was the same Philip who, in the beginning of the Gospel, "findeth athanael, and saith unto him, We have found Him of whom Moses in the Law, id the Prophets, did write."(n) Strange that one who was prepared to make such confession, should have been unprepared for the inferences which, to *us*, seem so iavoidable! Instead of replying,—"The eyes of all wait upon Thee, O LORD; id Thou givest them their meat in due season. Thou openest Thy hand, and llest all things living with plenteousness?"(o)—we find him adverting only to the ender store of money contained in their common purse,—which may have amount- l in value to about 7l. or 8l. sterling.

8, 9 One of His disciples, Andrew, Simon Peter's brother, saith nto Him, There is a lad here, which hath five barley loaves, and two nall fishes:

On which one of the ancients suggests beautifully,—"Probably he had some rea- s in his mind for this speech. He would know of Elijah's miracle, by which *a* adred men were fed with *twenty* barley loaves.(p) This was a great step, but re be stopped. He did not rise any higher: for his next words are,—

but what are they among so many?

"He thought that less could produce less in a miracle, and more, more: a great intake; inasmuch as it was as easy for CHRIST to feed the multitude from a few he, as from many. He did not really want any material to work from; but only

(h) "For then we spiritually eat the Flesh of CHRIST, and drink His Blood." (From the zhortation in the Communion Service.)
(i) See St. Matthew xv. 32, and the note there.
(k) See St. Matth. xiv. 15: St. Mark vi. 36: St. Luke ix. 12.
(l) Dr. W. H. Mill.　　　(m) St. John xiv. 7 to 11.　　　(n) St. John i. 45.
(o) Psalm cxlv. 15, 16.　　　(p) 2 Kings iv. 42 to 44.

made use of created things for this purpose, in order to show that no part of the Creation was severed from His wisdom." See the note on St. Matthew xiv. 17.

"*A lad*" carried these loaves; thus the young obtain an interest in the Gospel,—becoming the objects, or the instruments, of God's Mercies in CHRIST. There are some beautiful verses on this subject in the "*Lyra Innocentium*," beginning;—

> What time the SAVIOUR spread His feast
> For thousands on the mountain's side,
> One of the last and least
> The abundant store supplied.

10 And JESUS said, Make the men sit down. Now there was much grass in the place. So the men sat down, in number about five thousand.

This was the number of "*the men*." Including the women and the children,(r) there must have been far more than twice five thousand. Each Apostle will therefore have had about as many to minister unto, as experience shows may not unreasonably be left to the pastoral care of a single individual. St. Mark relates that the vast assembly was further subdivided into companies of fifty and a hundred.

"There was much grass in the place,"—and the grass was "green;"(s) for it was in the month of March or April, as we learn from what was stated in the 4th verse. As, in all the accounts of the Institution of the Holy Eucharist, it is expressly mentioned that, in the first instance, our SAVIOUR "*took* bread,"(t)—so, in all the four accounts of the present miracle, does the same act find special record likewise.(u) As it follows:

11 And JESUS took the loaves; and when He had given thanks, He distributed to the Disciples, and the Disciples to them that were set down; and likewise of the fishes as much as they would.

"The distribution is preceded by a solemn giving of thanks; which, emphatically repeated both in the narrative itself, and the subsequent allusion in the 23d verse, shows that the eucharistic act was an essential part of the mystery."(v)

By thus giving thanks, CHRIST further teaches us what should be *our* habit whenever we sit down to meat.—By His distribution "*to the Disciples*,"—He shows that the Bishops and Pastors of His flock are the appointed channels for the conveyance of His gifts. Both which circumstances will be found already remarked upon in the notes on St. Mark's Gospel,—chap. vi. 41.—The marvellous increase of food which followed, has been the subject of some observations in the notes on St. Matthew xiv. 19, 20; and St. Luke ix. 16. It was achieved by the same creative power which produces a harvest out of a few grains: for those five loaves were as seeds in CHRIST'S Hands,—seeds which yielded to the Great Husbandman a *thousandfold*.

How marvellous must have been that growth,—so rapid and so abundant, yet eluding observation and defying understanding! The bread is broken, yet not diminished: each loaf is divided into parts, yet the sum of the parts is found to be greater than the whole: half is given away, yet all remains! . . . . . Above all, there remained at last a far larger supply than existed at the beginning. And thus the saying of the wise man came literally true,—"There is that scattereth, and yet *increaseth*."(x)

12 When they were filled, He said unto His Disciples, Gather up the fragments that remain, that nothing be lost.

These memorable words are peculiar to the present Gospel. A most precious injunction this will be felt evermore to be; and a might warrant, even amid the greatest abundance, that no *Waste* should be allowed. The reason of this, in such as we are, is indeed plain enough; for every thing we call our own, is in reality "another man's."(y) We are not Lords and Masters of anything. We are but

(r) St. Matthew xiv. 21.
(s) St. Mark vi. 39.   (t) St. Matth. xxvi. 26.   St. Mark xiv. 22.   St. Luke xxii. 19.
(u) See the end of the note on St. Luke ix. 16.   (v) Dr. W. H. Mill.
(x) Proverbs xi. 24.   (y) St. Luke xvi. 12.

wards and Servants; and of this, the Gospel often reminds us. But even the up of the whole earth,—at whose will a table was furnished in the wilderness, bread provided for His people.(a)—even *He*, the LORD and Master of all, bade us gather up the fragments, and was solicitous that *nothing* should be *lost!* Other inferences besides this, have been drawn from our LORD's injunction; some which are indeed sufficiently obvious. Who does not feel, however, that there at be a yet deeper meaning here than meets the eye? The Evangelist proceeds to record the necessary result of the injunction before —which was delivered to *Twelve* Men :—

13 Therefore they gathered *them* together, and filled twelve baskets th the fragments of the five barley loaves, which remained over and ove unto them that had eaten.

It cannot be without an object that St. John has twice reminded us that these are "*barley* loaves." What may that object, therefore, be presumed to be? And ay do all the Evangelists so often state that the loaves were *five* in number? re we simply to see in the material of the loaves an indication of *the season* of e year :(b) in their number, a careful distinction of the present miracle from at other occasion when *seven* loaves furnished forth a banquet for four thousand ?(c)

The perfect safety of such criticism forcibly recommends it to writers and readers of every description: and very far are we from disparaging a style of remark which we believe to be in itself perfectly true, and which is doubtless highly valuable also. But the question arises,—Is it *the whole* truth? May there not have been yet another object in the writer's mind for dwelling on the fact that the present miracle was wrought with *five* loaves of *barley* bread? But we forbear to speculate. It shall suffice to have invited the reader's attention to the subject; and to have avowed our own suspicions. The reference of the present miracle to the coming Sacrifice of CHRIST, and to the benefits consequent thereon, is however, something more than a mere matter of opinion. "Certainly," as one of the greatest of our Divines(d) has remarked, "no more significant act,—none more pregnant with meaning and mystery,—appears in the whole course of CHRIST's humiliation, than this feeding of the Five Thousand." "It is the only event before the Passion and the Resurrection, which is found related by *all the four* Evangelists. . Not without reason is it that the Church repeats this, as no other is found repeated, in her cycle of Gospels; giving this narrative from St. John, not only on Mid-Lent Sunday, as preparatory to the approaching Paschal Eucharist,—but again, divested of its significant preface, in the concluding Gospel of her year.(e) On one of the intermediate Sundays, (the Seventh Sunday after Trinity,) we are also presented with the other miraculous feeding from St. Mark,—chap. viii. 1 to 9.

"It is not mere stupid astonishment, then, which seizes on this great multitude, such as we sometimes see to be the sole effect of our LORD's miracles; their thoughts ascend from the gift to the giver." As it follows:

14 Then those men when they had seen the miracle that JESUS did, said, This is of a truth that Prophet that should come into the world.

The prophet, namely, *like unto Moses*, whom the same Moses had foretold that the LORD GOD would raise up unto the Israelites, of their brethren :(f) for CHRIST had now fed them, (as Moses did,) with manna in the wilderness. Consider the questions which were put to the Baptist in the early part of his Ministry ;(g) and take notice that the multitude here spoken of, seem, from what follows, to have identified "the Prophet," with CHRIST, the promised *King*. Accordingly, it is added,—

15 When JESUS therefore perceived that they would came and take Him by force, to make Him a King, He departed again into a mountain Himself alone.

(a) Psalm lxxviii. 19, 20. (b) Compare Exodus ix. 31, and 2 Kings iv. 42.
(c) St. Matth. xv. 32, &c. St. Mark viii. 1. (d) Dr. W H. Mill.
(e) See the Gospel for the fourth Sunday in Lent, (which is St. John vi. 1 to 14,) and for the Twenty-fifth Sunday after Trinity; which last begins at verse 5.
(f) Deuteronomy xviii. 15, 18. (g) St. John i. 20, 21.

Rather,—"IIe withdrew again to the mountain," already mentioned in verse 3; and that, as St. Matthew(*h*) and St. Mark(*i*) relate, for the purpose of *prayer*: thereby teaching us, (as a great man remarks,) that whenever escape is necessary, there is necessity for prayer also. "Dismissing His Disciples to the Lake by themselves, and eluding the carnal-minded multitudes, He retires for private prayer to the mountain; to add one vigil more of fasting and devotion to a life perpetually offered up in sacrifice to IIis FATHER for the sin and madness of mankind."

One of the charges which the enemies of our LORD brought against Him, at the time of His Passion, was, that He claimed to be "CHRIST *a King* ;"(*k*) so that He is found, like Joseph, to have suffered for the very offence which He had shown Himself most careful to avoid (*l*) Not but what He *was* and *is* a King :(*m*) nay, more.—KING of Kings, and LORD of Lords."(*n*) Yet was His Kingdom "not of this World :"(*o*) neither was He a King by the will of man; but because He reigned from all Eternity with the FATHER.

16, 17 And when even was *now* come, His Disciples went down unto the sea, and entered into a ship, and went over the sea toward Capernaum.

Rather,—"And when the Evening was come, His Disciples had gone down to the sea, and having entered the ship, were going over the sea to Capernaum." "It is easy," says the great Father of the West, "to perceive that John relates *that as done afterwards* by the Disciples, which our LORD had ordered them to do before His departure to the mountain."

And it was now dark, and JESUS was not come to them.

Darkness,—Desertion,—a Storm raging around: from such causes spring terror; whether assailing the Church of CHRIST, or any of its individual members. When, in the Baptismal Service, we speak of "so passing the waves of this troublesome World, that finally we may come to the Land of Everlasting Life,"—what do we but supply a key to the mystical interpretation of the present incident? If, in the miraculous feeding of the Five Thousand, our SAVIOUR set forth in emblem the virtue of His Incarnation and Sacrifice,—what but a type of "the Ark of CHRIST's Church," when deprived of its Head, did the Disciples' storm-tossed bark supply?

18 And the sea arose, by reason of a great wind that blew.

This circumstance of the Wind, (which, as St. Matthew and St. Mark relate, "was contrary,"(*p*) explains why, at the end of many hours, the Disciples had not got much more than half-way across the Lake,—which is nowhere more than eight miles in breadth. As it follows:

19, 20 So when they had rowed about five-and-twenty or thirty furlongs, they see JESUS walking on the sea, and drawing nigh unto the ship: and they were afraid. But He saith unto them, It is I : be not afraid.

Literally,—"I AM: fear not!" Thus the Greek idiom in more than one place, (*q*) recalls the Divine Name itself.(*r*)

21 Then they willingly received Him into the ship.

Rather,—"Then they wished," or "were eager to receive Him." St. John says nothing of St. Peter's miraculous walking on the water, which occurred at this juncture :(*s*) "all, events full of mystery,"—remarks a truly great writer.(*t*) Indeed, the entire transaction clearly bears a symbolical character,—as we have

(*h*) St. Matthew xiv. 23.
(*k*) St. Luke xxiii. 2.
(*m*) Jeremiah xxiii. 5. Zechariah ix. 9, (quoted St. Matthew xxi. 5; St. John xii. 15;) St. John i. 49: St. Luke xix. 38: St. Matthew xxvii. 11: St. John xviii. 37, &c.
(*n*) 1 Tim. vi. 15: Rev. xvii. 14: xix. 16.
(*p*) St. Matthew xiv. 24: St. Mark vi. 48.
(*r*) Exodus iii. 14.
(*t*) Dr. W. H. Mill.
(*i*) St. Mark vi. 46.
(*l*) Consider Genesis xxxix. 8, 9, 12 and 14.
(*o*) St. John xviii. 36.
(*q*) So in St. John viii. 58 : xviii. 5, 6, 8,
(*s*) See St. Matthew xiv. 28 to 31.

ady suggested; and as was more fully pointed out in the note on St. Mark vi.
How lively an image of the Church, "tossed with waves," did that Ship with
little company present; when "the sea arose by reason of a mighty wind that
r !" The small progress effected, in spite of the incessant labor; and the oppo-
on continually experienced, as well as the storm patiently sustained; are all cir-
aistances which suggest their own obvious interpretation. CHRIST walking upon
Sea, — drawing near to the Ship, — and only then remedying the distress of its
w, when at last He blesses them with His actual presence,—completes the sacred
gory. For verily there is found to be much toil here below. without Him, and
little advance. Meantime, we know that He keepeth His Eye lovingly on his
arch ;(*u*) and maketh intercession for it from afar. "The LORD hath gone up on
;h," and "is mightier than the noise of many waters, yea, than the mighty waves
the sea."(*x*) He delays His coming, indeed ; and will delay it till "the night is
spent, and the Day is at hand:" but then, He will come with power; and Rest
d Joy will come with Him.

and immediately the Ship was at the land whither they went.

Many have thought that a quick miraculous gliding of the Vessel to its destina-
on is here spoken of. But the words in themselves, do not, by any means, imply
is. "Immediately" merely signifies that "forthwith," "straightway," the Dis-
iples reached "the haven where they would be."(*y*)
The Evangelist proceeds to explain what took place on the morrow. with respect
o the multitude which our SAVIOUR had left on the Eastern side of the Lake.

**22 The day following, when the people which stood on the other side
of the sea saw that there was none other boat there, save that one
whereinto His Disciples were entered, and that JESUS went not with
His Disciples into the boat, but *that* His Disciples were gone away
alone ;**

St. John was about to add, that the multitude, when they saw this, (or rather,
having noticed this over-night,) took ship and crossed over to Capernaum in pursuit of our SAVIOUR. He checks himself, however; for he has not yet explained
how this was possible. If "there was none other boat there, save that one whereinto His Disciples where entered,"—how could hundreds of persons cross the Lake
in boats? He explains as follows:

**23 (howbeit there came other boats from Tiberias nigh unto the
place where they did eat bread, after that the LORD had given thanks:)**

That is to say,— Although, at the time when the Disciples set out for Capernaum,
there was only one boat to be seen on the shore, yet did the wind of the preceding
night, (which to the Disciples rowing in a westerly direction, had been contrary,)(z) compel many boats from Tiberias, (on the western side of the Lake,) to put
in, for security, to the eastern shore, — "nigh unto the place where they did eat
bread, *after that the* LORD *had given thanks.*" Take notice, by the way, of the significant manner in which St. John speaks of the great miracle we have been considering above ;(*a*) and connect his present reference to the Eucharistic act by which
it had been prefaced, with his former allusion to the Paschal Season at which it had
been performed.(*b*) Having thus explained that, on the morrow, owing to the recent stress of weather, there was no lack of shipping on the north-eastern side of
the Lake, where the multitude yet lingered, earnestly but vainly expecting to see
our SAVIOUR re-appear among them, — St. John adds:

**24 when the people therefore saw that JESUS was not there, neither
His Disciples, they also took shipping, and came to Capernaum, seeking for JESUS.**

Rather, — "they also went on board the boats." That is, they persuaded their

(*u*) St Mark vi. 48.   (*x*) Ps. xciii. 4.
(*y*) Ps. cvii. 30.   (*z*) See the note and references above, on ver. 18.
(*a*) See the first note on·verse 11, above; also the note on St. John iv. 46.
(*b*) See above, the note on ver. 4.

owners, on setting sail, to take them on board with them, and give them a passage to Capernaum, — the city of our LORD's habitual residence.

25 And when they had found Him on the other side of the sea, they said unto Him, Rabbi, when camest Thou hither?

They do not ask Him "*how*," but "*when*" He came.   There was but one boat; and the multitude had seen the Disciples depart in that boat alone.(c)   The Holy One therefore, as they supposed, must have eluded their vigilance; and in the course of the night, walked to Capernaum.   Accordingly they inquire, "*When* camest Thou hither?"   All their thoughts about our LORD are low and groveling.   They little thought that they had to do with Him of whom it had been written, — "Thy way is in the Sea, and Thy path in the great waters, and Thy footsteps are not known!"(d)

Very instructive is it to observe how our LORD dealt with the inquiry, — "Rabbi, when camest Thou hither?"

26 JESUS answered them and said, Verily, verily, I say unto you, Ye seek Me, not because ye saw the miracles, but because ye did eat of the loaves, and were filled.

The Searcher of hearts exposes these men to themselves.   "Verily, verily," He begins, — speaking from the depths of His own certain knowledge.   "Not for My sake, but for *your own*, have ye followed Me.   My miracle hath wrought in you no conviction, — but only a desire that the abundance of yesterday might be re-produced to-day."

"In the banquet of which they had been the astonished partakers," says a great writer, "these men saw only a foretaste of the abundance with which the anointed Son of David would enrich His followers.   With no higher or purer affection than this, they looked for the expected Kingdom."

Having therefore replied in this manner to their inquiry in verse 25, by reproving the low and sensual motive which had led them to follow Him to Capernaum, He indicates what had been the true import of His gracious work, — "by exhorting them to labor for the meat which the Son of Man was able and ready to impart to the soul that hungered after Righteousness."(e)

27 Labor not for the meat which perisheth, but for that meat which endureth unto everlasting Life, which the Son of Man shall give unto you:

As if He had said, — Labor, if you will, for bodily food; such perishable bread as ye partook of yesterday : but labor rather(f) for that Heavenly Bread which perisheth not, — "the Bread which availeth for the eternal Life of Soul as well as Body."(g)   In which words of our LORD, the same Divine Wisdom is discoverable which we noticed in His address to the Woman of Samaria ; when he had sought, (not vainly as now !) to awaken a desire for something loftier than human food.(h)

Then, lest His hearers should suppose that He spoke of that which their own un-assisted labor might procure, He adds that this must be *His* gift, — a gift which "the Son of Man" is not only able, but also willing to impart.   By which words, He openly proclaims his own Godhead ; yet does He not call himself the Son of GOD, in respect of this gift, but the Son of Man, — because it was not as *GOD*, but as *Man*, that He would give His Flesh for the Life of the World.(i)   The explanation follows:

for Him hath GOD the FATHER sealed.

That is, — for GOD the FATHER hath set His seal upon Him, by joining the God-head to the Manhood in His Person.   The order of the words in the original suggests that it is further implied, — That the FATHER had thus sealed Him, in that the FATHER is GOD.   And thereby it is explained how the Son of Man, (being Himself Very GOD,) can impart to others the Bread of Eternal Life ; as well as how it comes

---

(c) See above, ver. 22.   (d) Ps. lxxvii. 19.   (e) Dr. W. H. Mill.
(f) See the note on St. Matth. ix. 13, and the end of the note on St. John v. 30, &c.
(g) Consider Isaiah lv. 2.   (h) See the note on St. John iv.   (i) See below, verse 51.

pass that His flesh,) so conjoined with Godhead,) should actually *be* to others
it Bread of Life.

Besides the notion of *attestation* implied by this remarkable saying, consider what
"the nature of an impression from a signet. It exhibits accurately, as well as
tirely, the character of that which impresses: and while it is altogether a reci-
ent, in respect of the signet which produces the impression, it supplies every whit
the substance which sustains that impression."(*j*)

28 Then said they unto Him, What shall we do, that we might work
e works of GOD?

"Our LORD having exhorted the people to work for that meat which endureth
to Everlasting Life," they here (as again at the end of ver. 30) in allusion to His
iguage, ask how they "may work the works of GOD,"—that is, do the works
iich GOD requires and will accept, so as to obtain that meat. Thus in Ps. li. 17,
he sacrifices of GOD," are "the sacrifices acceptable to GOD;" and in St. James i.
, the "Righteousness of GOD," is the "righteousness which GOD requires."(*k*)—
ike notice that the word translated "labour," in ver. 27, is translated "work,"
the present verse.

29 JESUS answered and said unto them, This is the work of GOD,
iat ye believe on Him whom He hath sent.

The Blessed Speaker so far condescends to their weakness, as to reply to them
y using their own expression. The "work" required of them was "*Faith* in Him
hom GOD had sent:"(*l*) that is, they were required to believe in CHRIST as the
or of GOD sent for the Salvation of Mankind.

"But when these men do indeed understand that it is as One sent from Heaven,
id not as an Earthly King, that He requires their submission and obedience, the
we of their discourse is immediately altered from that of deference and veneration,
i that of questioning and unbelief."(*m*)   As it follows:

30 They said therefore unto Him, What sign showest Thou, then,
iat we may see, and believe Thee?

That is,—"Thou declarest Thyself to be the MESSIAH, and claimest to be be-
eved in as such. Now, all who have ever put forth any lofty pretensions, have
en able to appeal to some *sign*. 'What sign therefore showest *Thou?*' Thou
iust display some transcendant miracle which may suffice to prove the justice of
by claim." By which demand, it is implied that the miraculous feeding of the
ive thousand which had taken place on the previous day, was in their estimation
iafficient for the purpose. But our LORD, having therein given them an abun-
antly sufficient sign, "instead of complying with their demand, proceeds to lay
efore them some deep truths which it required an earnest personal affection, and a
rm conviction of the authority of His teaching, to accept. Very different was the
imper of the men, who continue as follows:

31 What dost Thou work? Our fathers did eat manna in the de-
ert; as it is written, He gave them bread from Heaven to eat.

They refer to the miracle recorded in Exodus xvi. 4, 15. Their argument seems
i be: "Moses fed 600,000 Israelites with manna, during their wanderings in the
ilderness: a sign from Heaven! for as it is said in the seventy-seventh Psalm, He
ive them bread *from Heaven* to eat. Now, this lasted for a long series of years.
loreover, this miracle was repeated daily: and yet Moses raised no such preten-
ons as Thou raiseth; nor was he ever so believed in, as Thou requirest us to be-
eve in Thee." . . . *A sign from Heaven*(*n*) seems, in fact, to have been the thing
iich these unbelievers thought requisite for their conviction.

Here then was a two-fold requirement. First, "We must *see*," (say they,) "in
der that we may believe:" next, "We must have a sign *from Heaven*, such as
ir Fathers had." . . . To their first requirement, our LORD's reply is found to

(*J*) Hilary.   (*k*) Lonsdale and Hale.   (*l*) See the foot-note (*e*) on St. John iv. 34.
(*m*) Dr. W. H. Mill.
(*n*) Consider Isaiah vii. 11. Also St. Matth. xii. 38, compared with St. Luke xi. 16.

have been,—"Ye have *seen* already; yet have ye not believed." This, we shall discover by and by, from his language in ver. 36.—To their second demand His reply is as follows :

32 Then Jesus said unto them, Verily, verily, I say unto you, Moses gave you not that bread from Heaven.

There is a double emphasis here. "The bread you speak of did not come down *from Heaven;* but only from that upper region of the air, to which the name of Heaven is sometimes popularly given.(o) Moreover, it was not *Moses* who gave you that bread."

but My Father giveth unto you the true Bread from Heaven.

Here, also, there is a double emphasis. Besides implying that the Bread spoken of was given them by *GOD,* not by *Moses,* our Saviour proceeds,—"But the gift of My Father is the *true* Bread : that spiritual Bread, namely, of which Manna was but the type or shadow.(p) And this Bread truly cometh down *from Heaven itself,*—even from that Heaven of Heavens where God dwelleth."

By saying, "*My FATHER* giveth,"—the Divine Speaker implies that He is Himself the Son of God; and yet of equal power with God. Consider St. John v. 17, 18; and the notes there. The Jews understood Him in this sense,—and not as contradicting what He had said before :(q) for we shall find them presently saying, —"Lord, evermore give us this bread !"(r) . . . . "*Giveth*" obviously implies "is willing," "is prepared to give."

33 For the Bread of God is He which cometh down from Heaven, and giveth life unto the world.

Rather, "For the Bread of God is *that* which cometh down from Heaven." Our Lord does not, apparently, explain that He is speaking of *a person,* until ver. 35.

In three other respects then is the Bread of which our Lord discourses, declared to be superior to the Manna which fed the Israelites : first, because it "*came*" (not "was poured,") "down" from Heaven ; next, because it conveyed the gift of eternal life ; lastly, because it was to be a portion, not to the Jews alone, but "unto the World."

In these three verses and the seventeen which follow, our Lord asserts the great truth of His Incarnation ; and tells the Jews that this was the reality, of which the gift of Manna was but a sign. "He states to them that the relation between Man and God, on which depended Man's happiness, was only to be maintained through Himself, as a Mediator ; that into His Man's nature the Godhead had poured its gifts, and thus had constituted Him the real food and sustenance of men's souls. This was the fact which it had pleased God to exhibit by way of type, when He fed His people with manna in the wilderness ; and He Himself, by coming into the World, had brought down among the true principle of spiritual existence."

34 Then said they unto Him, Lord, evermore give us this bread.

Their answer, which recalls that of the Samaritan woman,(s) is expressive of some degree of Faith. "Lord !"—it begins. They still suppose, however, that Christ speaks of bodily food,—of a more nutritious kind, indeed, than their boasted manna ; yet, like it, requiring to be periodically renewed. Wherefore they exclaim, —"*Evermore* give us this bread !" That is, "Give us *day by day.*"

35 And Jesus said unto them, I am the Bread of Life : he that cometh to Me shall never hunger ; and he that believeth on Me shall never thirst.

The Divine Speaker Himself was the "Bread" of which He had spoken. To be made partakers thereof, men must "come to Him ;" that is, must *believe* in Him.(t)

(o) As in Gen. i. 20 : vii. 11 : viii. 2, &c.
(p) Compare St. John xv. 1. Also Heb. viii. 2 : ix. 24.
(q) In ver. 27.　　(r) See below, ver. 24.　　　　(s) See St. John iv. 15.
(t) Consider verses 37, 44, 35 : also v. 40 : vi. 37 : and St. Matth. xi. 28,—with the note. Rev. xxii. 17.

As many as do this will not require that He should "evermore" supply their seeds: but will never hunger, never thirst again. This last saying further recalls our SAVIOUR's discourse to the Woman of Samaria ;(u) and the meaning of His words is in both places the same. He teaches that even here below, in the case of believers in His Divine Doctrines, *that* longing for unreal joys,—which may be fitly called thirst and hunger,—will altogether cease; while those lofty desires of the soul, which in eternity will assuredly be fully appeased, will even here have their partial gratification. The analogy of other parts of Scripture(v) abundantly prepares us for such metaphorical language. But it is time to remind ourselves of the very holy ground which we are approaching; and to ascertain the general structure of the entire Discourse.

The great subject of the present Chapter has been already declared to be the octrine of the Holy Eucharist; but it cannot for a moment be thought that this lengthy specimen of our SAVIOUR's teaching refers directly, throughout, to that grand mystery. Indeed, the verses which have *exclusive* reference to the Sacrament of CHRIST's Body and Blood,(x) will perhaps be found to be very few in number. Let the plain meaning of the words before us be attentively considered; and we shall be disposed to admit that although, in subsequent parts of the present chapter, (y) a Eucharistic meaning is so unequivocally fastened upon the expression "The Bread of Life," that the covert reference of the phrase in the present verse the Holy Eucharist may reasonably be suspected,—yet would it be to deal unfairly with language to doubt that our LORD is here rather declaring His own Divinity; and inviting men to Faith and Obedience. While a general promise is added, that spiritual sustenance, even unto Life Eternal, will be the corresponding gift on the part of GOD."(z)

On a review of the contents of the entire chapter, it will perhaps be thought that from ver. 26 to ver. 33, inclusive, is, as it were, introductory of the subject: that ver. 35 to ver. 50 treats of the Incarnation of CHRIST, and of Faith therein as the means of Life: while ver. 51 to ver. 58 is a building of the Doctrine of the Holy Eucharist on the Doctrine of the incarnation: the Divine Speaker in that place advancing a step in His solemn discourse, by the mention for the first time of His '*flesh.*" From the lesser acts of Faith, He thus goes on to speak of the highest of all; and because His whole discourse points in the direction of the Holy Eucharist, even that part of it which relates to ordinary Belief, is conceived in language which has covert reference to Sacramental communion.

The *progressive* character of our LORD's teaching is in fact nowhere more clearly distinguishable than here. From the mention of "Bread," (in verse 31,) He takes occasion, first, (in verse 32,) to speak of the "*true* Bread;" next, (in verse 35,) He proclaims that He is *Himself* that Bread: then, (in verse 39,) He hints at *Resurrection* as the consequence of union with Himself: presently, (in verse 51,) He explains that His *Flesh* must be eaten: lastly, (in verse 53,) He makes open and repeated mention of His Flesh *and His Blood.*

He proceeds:

36 But I said unto you, that ye also have both seen Me, and believe not.

"*I said* unto you:" from which it appears likely that He had used these words already; as will be found pointed out at the end of the note on ver. 31.(a) What follows should be translated "Ye have *both* seen Me," &c. It has reference to the demand of the Jews, in ver. 30; and is a refutation of the pretended need of some sign "which they might *see*," and on which they might base a rational belief in Him as CHRIST. The Jews had already beheld Him perform many miracles, (He tells them,) whereby they might have known Him to be the MESSIAH; and yet they believed not.—How this came to pass, His next words explain; and it was in order that He might supply those words of explanation that He repeats the saying before us for the second time.

37 All that the FATHER giveth Me shall come to me;

(s) See St. John iv. 13, 14.
(v) Such as Deut. viii. 3. Is. lv. 1, 2. Jer. xv. 16. Amos viii. 11. St. Matth. v. 6. St. John iv. 13, 14: vii. 37. Heb. v. 12, &c.
(x) As verses 53 to 56.   (y) As verses 51 to 58.   (z) Bp. Turton.
(a) Consider St. John xi. 28 and 40, which are also instances of the same method.

That is, — No sign in and by itself can produce real conviction in the heart of man. Faith is GOD's own Gift. There must be an inward calling from the FATHER to enable any one to obey such an invitation as is contained in ver. 35, and come to CHRIST. " A man must be given to Me, in order for him to become Mine." This our LORD will be found to state more plainly lower down, in ver. 45, — where see the note. In illustration of this expression, see the references at foot.(b)

" All," or rather, " everything" " that the FATHER giveth Me, shall come to Me." " Everything," — whether male or female, learned or young, rich or poor, learned or simple, Jew or Gentile. — These words are prophetic of the Call of the Gentiles, while they imply the unbelief and consequent rejection of many of the Jews.

and he that cometh to Me I will in no wise cast out.

By which words, our LORD declares that His Will is one and the same with that of the FATHER; and that every individual believer whom the FATHER has willed should come to Him, He will graciously receive, and sanctify, and save. — To be " cast out" is a well-known expression in the Gospel, descriptive of the fate of lost souls.(c)

38 For I came down from Heaven, not to do Mine own will, but the Will of Him that sent Me.

That is,—" For I came down from Heaven for this very purpose; namely, to perform the merciful Will of GOD towards mankind."(d) — He speaks as the Son of Man. Now, as such, the FATHER's Will was prior, in point of time, to His: as well as, in its nature, independent of it. But in the next two verses, He will speak as GOD—that raiseth the dead.—Compare the form of the expression in ver. 38, with what is met with in St. John v. 30.

In the meantime, consider " the Will" of GOD with respect to the World, as it is declared in a former chapter. " GOD so loved the World that He gave His Only Begotten SON, that whosoever believeth in Him should not perish, but have everlasting life."(e) The process of Salvation is here declared more plainly:—

39 And this is the FATHER'S Will which hath sent Me, that of all which He hath given Me I should lose nothing, but should raise it up again at the Last Day.

Literally,—" And this is the will of Him that sent Me, [even] the FATHER; that of nothing which He hath given Me, should I lose [any part."] See above, the latter part of the note on first clause of ver. 37. — Compare St. John xvii. 12.

The connection of these words with those which precede will be perceived to be of the closest kind. The entire verse is more than an expansion of ver. 37, above. It explains that entire statement likewise: showing that "casting out" implies " loss;" showing also, that the momentous consequence of becoming CHRIST's, is to be raised up by Him on the last day, and to be made a partaker in the Resurrection of the Just.

40 And this is the Will of Him that sent me, that every one which seeth the SON, and believeth on Him, may have Everlasting Life; and I will raise him up at the Last Day.

An important verse; for it contains an explanation of two of the sayings which have gone before. Who, (it might be asked,) are they whom " the FATHER giveth the SON?" They are as many as " behold the Son, and believe in Him."(f) And next,—What is meant by not being " lost?" The enjoyment of " Everlasting Life" is meant thereby; which will be the consequence of being by Him raised up in the Last Day.

The several statements contained in this Discourse of our LORD, will be perceived on consideration to be, one and all, of the highest importance; and even for what He omits, a reason is discoverable. Thus, if He says nothing of the Resurrection of unbelievers, it is because He is revealing Himself throughout as the Bread of Life. — But why does He say so much about Resurrection at all? It is, lest His

(b) See ver. 39: also x. 29: xvii. 2, 6, 9, 11, 12, 24: xviii. 9.   (c) See St. Matth. xxv. 30.
(d) See the note on St. John iv. 34.   (e) St. John iii. 16.   (f) Consider ver. 36.

ere should suppose, either that in consequence of participation of the Bread of
, men would never die; or dying, would experience no further benefit from the
enly food of which they had been partakers. He explains therefore, that
stian men, after being so nourished, must indeed taste of Death; but, by virtue
ich participation, will be restored to Life Eternal. "For doth any man doubt,"
a Hooker,) "but that even from the flesh of CHRIST our very bodies do receive
life which shall make them glorious at the latter day; and from which they
already accounted parts of His Blessed Body?"

**:1 The Jews then murmured at Him, because He said, I am the
:ad which came down from Heaven.**

ake notice that our LORD is nowhere recorded to have said these words; but
Jews rightly connect a clause in ver. 35 with a clause in ver. 33, and make a
plete sentence out of them: rightly,—for our LORD Himself so speaks in ver. 51.
content with disbelieving His statements, however, they are found to murmur
bem likewise,—in the verses which follow:

**42 And they said, Is not this JESUS, the son of Joseph, whose Father
d Mother we know? how is it then that He saith, I came down from
eaven?**

They are offended by the Humanity of CHRIST, who was *legally*, (and as they
ppo-ed, *naturally*,) the Son of Joseph,—whose father Jacob,(g) (or, Heli,)(h) as
ell as his mother, they also knew. Their blame lay not in this supposition; but
failing to recognize in His miracles, (if not in His discourse,) the evidence of
ne who was not mere Man. See St. John v. 36, and the note there.—Compare
ith the language of these unbelievers, what is found in St. Matthew xiii. 55, and
t. Mark vi. 3: where see the notes.—Observe also, in passing, that our SAVIOUR
oes not undeceive these men with reference to the mystery of His birth. That
reat secret must as yet be kept hid from men and devils.

**43, 44 JESUS therefore answered and said unto them, Murmur not
nong yourselves. No man can come to Me, except the FATHER
rhich hath sent Me, draw him:**

Murmur not at My sayings, as if they were contrary to reason. The fault is not
n My side, but on yours; who are without that preventing grace, which is re-
uisite. before ye can come to Me and believe My words. A man needs to be drawn
y My FATHER before he can come to Me.(i) Or, as the present text is re-worded
elow, in ver. 65,—"No man can come unto Me, except it were given unto him of
ty FATHER:"

and I will raise him up at the last day.

Compare that solemn address to the FATHER, where the SON says of Himself,—
'Thou hast given Him power over all flesh, that *He should give Eternal Life* to as
any as *Thou hast given Him*."(k)
"*I* will raise:"—which, unless He were the Bread of Life, He could not do. By
hus reminding them of His Divine Power, He exposes to them the danger of mur-
uring at His words in a spirit of Unbelief. At the same time, He asserts His
quality to the FATHER:(l) which was necessary; lest, from his repeated assertion
hat no one could come to Him unless the FATHER draw him, His hearers should
uppose that, as touching His Godhead, He was inferior to the FATHER.

**45 It is written in the prophets, And they shall be all taught of
GOD.**

In other words,—What I have said of the impossibility of a man's coming to me

(g) St. Matth. i. 16.   (h) St. Luke iii. 23.
(i) Take notice how many of our Collects embody this doctrine: e. g. Second Collect at Even-
: Prayer; 5th after Easter; 1st, 9th, 17th, 19th, after Trinity; the Fourth Collect after the
mmunion Service, &c.
k) St. John xvii. 2.
l) See the notes on St. John v. 17, 18: also above the note on the latter part of ver. 32.

with Faith, "except the FATHER draw him," is the fulfillment of what "the prophets," and Isaiah in particular, foretold; when they described the Covenant of the Gospel, as one under which all should be "taught of GOD."(*m*)

Every man therefore that hath heard, and hath learned of the FATHER, cometh to Me.

That is, — "Every one, therefore, who," — like Simon Peter on a previous occasion.(*n*) — "hears the FATHER's teaching, and is willing to learn of it, is drawn by My FATHER, and so cometh, as a believer, unto Me."(*o*) Consider what is said of Lydia, in Acts xvi. 14.

These words of course are not intended to depreciate the human preaching of the Gospel: for consider Romans x. 14, 15. They do but declare that no external helps can avail without an inward drawing of the heart, and illumination of the soul, by GOD. As it is written, "Neither is he that planteth, any thing; neither he that watereth; but GOD that giveth the increase."(*p*)

Then, to guard against any gross misconception of His Divine meaning, He adds:

46 Not that any man hath seen the FATHER, save He which is of GOD, He hath seen the FATHER.

In other words,—Not that the hearing and learning of the FATHER which I speak of, is effected with the bodily organs,—as when pupils *see* the Teacher who instructs them. He which is Begotten of the FATHER, and He which Proceedeth from the FATHER, alone hath so seen the FATHER.

In ver. 44, our LORD asserted (1) the need of a Heavenly drawing, to enable a man in the first instance to come to Him ; — and (2) He promised Resurrection to Eternal Life, as the final result of such coming. Verses 45 and 46 contain some explanation of the former of those two sayings. The latter saying, in an expanded form seems to be repeated in ver. 47, which follows ; and the Blessed Speaker, because He is about to resume and enforce a Doctrine already laid down, begins, (as His Divine manner is,)(*q*) with the well-known phrase of solemn asseveration,—a phrase peculiar to St. John's Gospel.

47 Verily, verily, I say unto you, He that believeth on Me hath everlasting Life.

This should be compared with St. John v. 24,—"Verily, verily, I say unto you, He that heareth My Word, and believeth on Him that sent Me, hath Everlasting Life, and shall not come into Condemnation ; but is passed from Death unto Life." See the notes on that passage.

Take notice therefore that the very foundation of all that follows, is Faith.

"*Hath* everlasting Life," — because he hath the present right to it. "*Hath*" it, also, — because he hath already entered upon the present enjoyment of that which will become Everlasting Life hereafter. "This is Life Eternal," (said our SAVIOUR on another occasion,) "to know Thee the only true GOD, and JESUS CHRIST whom Thou hast sent."(*r*)

First, then, the reason is briefly assigned why those who believe in CHRIST have everlasting Life:

48 I am that Bread of Life.

"And," (it is implied,) "I nourish those that come to Me."

When our LORD is called "the living Bread," (as in ver. 51,) it seems to be taught that he hath the principle of Life in Himself: when, "the Bread of Life," as here, — that in Him is vested the lofty privilege of conveying the gift of Life to others.

49, 50 Your fathers did eat manna in the wilderness, and are dead. This is the Bread which cometh down from Heaven, that a man may eat thereof, and not die.

(*m*) Is. liv. 13. See also the other places referred to in the margin.
(*n*) See St. Matth. xvi. 17.   (*o*) Lonsdale and Hale.
(*p*) 1 Cor. iii. 7. And consider Ephes. 17. 18.
(*q*) As in St. John iii. 2, 5, 11 : v. 19 : vi. 26, 32 : x. 1, 7 : xiv. 12, &c.
(*r*) St. John xvii. 3.

ecause He speaks of Himself in this place as GOD: He says "*Your* fathers," "Our,"—as in chap. iv. He then contrasts the manna, given by Moses, with gift of this Bread which came down from Heaven. Those who partook of the ner bread, were thereby sustained in temporal life, yet not preserved from death. y all died: and the manna will not avail to raise them up at the last day. But Bread which CHRIST giveth—though the recipient thereof, in due course of na- ·, must perforce die,—availeth to raise up to a blessed Immortality that Body me mere temporal life it was never intended to sustain. He continues:

51 I am the living Bread which came down from Heaven: if any n eat of this Bread, He shall live for ever:

lee above, the note on verse 41.—In that CHRIST is "*Bread*," He is the support those who feed upon Him. In that He is "the *living* Bread," and hath the nciple of Life in Himself, He is able to impart the gift of Life to others. In s He came down "*from Heaven*," this Life of His is Heavenly, not Earthly,— rnal, not transitory. Hence, the Blessed Speaker adds,—"If any man eat of s Bread, he shall live forever."
The next words introduce a fresh statement. It should not perhaps be said that re is here a transition to another subject. The Divine Speaker seems rather to rance one step in His solemn Discourse,—distinctly alluding, in all that follows, the Sacrament of the LORD's Supper.

and the Bread that I will give is My Flesh, which I will give for the e of the world.

That the "Bread" of which He had been hitherto speaking was His own Flesh," our LORD here explains for the first time. He adds that this was to be a opitiatory sacrifice *on behalf of* mankind; and declares that it would be His own e gift. So singular an announcement is found to produce strife and debate ong His auditory.

52 The Jews therefore strove among themselves, saying, How can is Man give us *His* flesh to eat?

Compare the inquiry of Nicodemus, in chapter iii. 4. When our LORD had said, Except a man be born again, he cannot see the Kingdom of God,"—the other ade answer, "How can a man be born when he is old?" Our SAVIOUR, in reply, ith peculiar solemnity and claim to attention, pointed out the possibility and the eans of being born again; as well as the necessity of such Regeneration: "Ve- y, verily, I say unto thee, Except a man be born of Water and of the Spirit, he unnot enter into the Kingdom of God."—On the present occasion, His answer rresponds to that given to Nicodemus, even to the very turn of the sentence.(s)

53 Then JESUS said unto them, Verily, verily, I say unto you, Ex- ept ye eat the Flesh of the Son of Man, and drink His Blood, ye have o Life in you.

It will be perceived that He does not seek to abate the wonder which His words ave occasioned, by simplifying, much less by withdrawing any part of His former sertion. On the contrary, He repeats the statement with solemn asseveration,— entions His Blood, in addition to His Flesh,—and concludes with the startling surance that without participation in these, men have "no life" in them.—Take otice, in passing, that our Church, as a faithful witness and keeper of Holy Writ, ath not failed to remind her children, in the Exhortation "at the time of the cele- ration of the Communion," of the solemn statement contained in this verse and verse 56.
Notwithstanding this plain declaration, however, and the express command, Drink ye *all* of it,"—one mighty section of the Church of CHRIST, perseveres in e sinful novelty of denying the Sacrament of His Blood to the laity."(t)
It would be almost an omission to pass on, without calling attention to the noble xposition of Catholic Truth contained in the following passage of our own Hooker,

(s) **Bishop Cleaver.**   (t) Consider St. Matthew xxvi. 27, and the note there.

" The grace which we have by the Holy Eucharist doth not begin but continue
Life.   No man, therefore, receiveth this Sacrament before Baptism, because no
dead thing is capable of nourishment.   That which groweth must of necessity first
live.   If our bodies did not daily waste, food to restore them were a thing superfluous.   And it may be that the grace of Baptism would serve to Eternal Life, were
it not that the state of our spiritual being is daily so much hindered and impaired
after Baptism.   In that life, therefore, where neither body nor soul can decay, our
souls shall as little require this Sacrament as our bodies corporeal nourishment;
but as long as the days of our warfare last, during the time that we are both subject to diminution and capable of augmentation in grace, the words of our LORD
and SAVIOUR CHRIST will remain forcible,—' Except ye eat the Flesh of the Son of
Man, and drink His Blood, ye have no life in you.'

" Life," he continues, " being therefore proposed unto all men as their end, they
which by Baptism have laid the foundation and attained the first beginning of a
new life, have here their nourishment and food prescribed for *continuance of life*
in them.   Such as will live the life of GOD must eat the Flesh and drink the Blood
of the Son of Man; because this is a part of that diet which, if we want, we cannot live."

The Rubric at the end of " the Communion of the Sick," will here occur to some
readers:—" But if a man, either by reason of extremity of sickness, or for want
of warning in due time to the Curate, or for lack of company to receive with him,
or by any other just impediment, do not receive the Sacrament of CHRIST'S Body
and Blood, the Curate shall instruct him, that if he do truly repent him of his sins,
and steadfastly believe that JESUS CHRIST hath suffered death upon the Cross for
him, and shed His Blood for his Redemption,—earnestly remembering the benefits
he hath thereby, and giving Him hearty thanks therefor,—he doth eat and drink
the Body and Blood of our SAVIOUR CHRIST profitably to his Soul's health, although
he do not receive the Sacrament with his mouth."   It might appear undutiful, were
we to omit so remarkable a statement of Doctrine, while on this subject; especially
after the extracts from Hooker which precede.

Let no one, however, be so perverse as to suppose that the Church is here sanc-
tioning the monstrous opinion that " every holy prayer and devout meditation render the faithful soul a partaker of CHRIST *in the same sense* that His own Divine
Sacrament does."(*u*)   And yet, by parity of reasoning, what we hold concerning
certain persons who die unbaptized, we may well hold concerning some who die
uncommunicate.   As " it has been constantly held, as well touching other believers
as martyrs, that Baptism *taken away by necessity* is supplied by desire of Baptism,"
(*v*)—the same may reasonably be thought touching cases as strong in regard to the
Eucharist.   Far safer, however, is it, not to speculate, but by all means to endeavor
to obey.   " With GOD," remarks an old writer, " inasmuch as He is their Author,
the Sacraments may be dispensed withal: with Man, inasmuch as his duty is to
obey, they may not possibly be dispensed with.   For it is in the power of GOD, independently of them, to save: but it is not in the power of any, without them, to
attain to Salvation."(*x*)—On all this subject, the reader is referred to the note on
St. John iii. 5.   And now to proceed,—

54 Whoso eateth My Flesh, and drinketh My Blood, hath eternal
Life; and I will raise him up at the last day.

"And," in this place, denotes *consequence*,—as in verse 44.   The promise is thus
repeated for the fourth time.(*y*)

The *progressive* character of our LORD's teaching, observable throughout all His
Discourses, and in none more clearly than in this, (as was pointed out above, in
the note on verse 35.) may be recognized even here; where, to an inattentive reader, He may seem to be merely repeating what He had said in the previous verse.
For (1st,) By the new word which He employs to denote " eating," (and which He
repeats in verses 56, 57 and 58,) He puts it out of all doubt that what He refers
to is a " pressing with the teeth" of " the Sacrament of the Body and Blood of
CHRIST.(*z*)   And (2dly,) What our SAVIOUR delivered negatively in the former
verse, He here delivers with affirmation,—using the language of encouragement, not

(*u*) Keble.   (*v*) Hooker.   (*x*) Hugo, referred to in a note by Hooker.
(*y*) See above, verses 39, 40, 44.
(*z*) The word recurs in St. John xiii. 18,—a memorable place.

threatening. Consider in connection with the declaration of our LORD, at the end
the verse, the language used in delivering the consecrated elements. "The
dy of our LORD JESUS CHRIST, which was given for thee,"—"The Blood of our
RD JESUS CHRIST, which was shed for thee,—preserve thy *body and soul to ever-
sting Life.*"

55 For My Flesh is meat indeed, and My Blood is drink indeed.

That is why CHRIST, in the two verses which precede, has been insisting on the
cessity of participation. He proceeds to explain how it happens that they are
strumental for the transmission of Eternal Life.

56 He that eateth My Flesh, and drinketh My Blood, dwelleth in
[e, and I in him.

Rather "*Abideth* in Me." That is,—"Becometh mystically united to Me:" "Is
ade one with Me, and I with him, by a secret and spiritual union.(*a*)—And thus,
r the fourth time, in four successive verses, our SAVIOUR makes mention of His
rn Flesh to be eaten, His own Blood to be drunk,—thereby forcibly calling atten-
on to that very remarkable expression, and putting it out of doubt that He is al-
ding to that Blessed Sacrament; whereof "the inward part, or thing signified,"
declared in our Catechism to be "the Body and Blood of CHRIST, which are
rily and indeed taken and received by the faithful in the LORD's Supper."
Of *the manner* of our LORD's presence in this great Sacrament, we are not dis-
sed to dispute. "Where GOD Himself doth speak those things which either for
ight and sublimity of matter, or else for accuracy of purpose we are not able to
ach unto, as we may be ignorant without danger, so it can be no disgrace to con-
s we are ignorant."(*b*) Enough for us to know that "the Cup of Blessing which
bless" *is* "*the Communication of the Blood of* CHRIST,"—"the Bread which we
eak, "*the Communication of His Body;*"(c) and that, "by the faithful in the
RD's Supper," His "Body and Blood are verily and indeed taken and received."
rmly embracing this blessed Truth, let us be content to "feed on Him in our
arts by Faith, with Thanksgiving;" and, (in the words of an ancient Father,)
dore, while others dispute."(*d*)
Our LORD proceeds:

57 As the living FATHER hath sent Me, and I live by the FATHER,
he that eateth Me, even he shall live by Me.

It is not quite certain whether our SAVIOUR here speaks of Himself as GOD, or as
an. But it is true, even as GOD, that He "lives by the FATHER."(*e*) This is but
nother way of expressing His eternal Generation.
The words before us may perhaps be thus paraphrased,—As the living FATHER
ent Me in the flesh; and by virtue of the consequent Union of the Godhead,
[which I have by Communication from Him,) with the Manhood, Eternal Life is conveyed to this else perishable Human Body;—even so shall he, who by sacramental
participation unites himself with Me,—even he shall live by Me.—The entire passage recalls St. Paul's argument in Romans viii. 11.—"Sacraments," (says Hooker,)
"are the powerful instruments of GOD to Eternal Life. For as our natural Life
consisteth in the union of the Body with the Soul; so our life supernatural in the
union of the Soul with GOD."

58 This is that Bread which came down from Heaven: not as your
fathers did eat manna, and are dead: he that eateth of this Bread shall
live for ever.

And thus does our LORD conclude the entire Discourse, and dismiss His mighty
theme,—repeating some of the sayings which He will be found to have delivered
in verses 32, 33, and 49, 50, 51.—As if He said,—"This then is the Bread I spake
of, as coming down from Heaven, and giving Life unto the World: and herein is it
superior to that Manna which your Fathers partook of, and which had no power to
bestow eternal Life."

(*a*) See the note on St. John xiv. 20.   (*b*) Hooker.
(*c*) 1 Cor. x. 16.   (*d*) Augustine.
(*e*) See more in the notes on St. John v. 20, and 26: also xiv. 28.

Hooker, in his majestic way, observes,—"CHRIST having Adam's nature as we have, but incorrupt, deriveth not Nature but Incorruption, and that immediately, from His own person into all that belong to Him. As therefore we are really partakers of the Body of Sin and Death received from Adam, so except we be truly partakers of CHRIST, and as really possessed of His Spirit, all we speak of Eternal Life is but a dream."—Ignatius, the earliest of the Fathers, has a brief but pregnant allusion to the present Discourse of our LORD, when he declares the Sacramental Bread to be "an antidote against Death,—the Medicine of Immortality."

59 These things said He in the Synagogue, as He taught in Capernaum.

St. John, as his manner is,(*f*) fixes the locality in which this momentous discourse was delivered;—the same Synagogue, doubtless, which the faithful Centurion built in order to show his love toward the Jewish nation !(*g*)—"Other discourses in St. John, as that in the former Chapter,(*h*) seem as if they were delivered before some formal assembly or Council, though it is not mentioned; and here it only seems to be introduced incidentally, though doubtless not so; and it is an interesting and remarkable addition to the discourse.(*i*)

60 Many therefore of His Disciples, when they had heard *this*, said, This is an hard saying; who can hear it?

"A hard Doctrine," truly: yet was the hardness which called for complaint, wholly their own. Judging from our SAVIOUR's discourse which follows, and the expressions in ver. 58. above,—two things seem chiefly to have perplexed His Disciples: (1) His assertion that He had come down from Heaven,—(2) His requirement that His flesh must be eaten. Accordingly, it follows:

61 When JESUS knew in Himself that His disciples murmured at it, He said unto them, Does this offend you?

Is it a stumbling-block in the way of your belief that I should say,—"I am the living Bread which came down from Heaven?"(*k*)

62 *What* and if ye shall see the Son of Man ascend up where He was before?

By this prophecy of His future Ascension,—(an event which in St. John's Gospel is twice alluded to,(*l*) but nowhere described,)—our LORD may be thought to have supplied a seasonable check to the unbelief, which His hearers had conceived on hearing Him say that He had come down from Heaven; while His words will have suggested that, not as Man, but GOD, His flesh was to prove the channel of life to mankind.(*m*)

But the true purpose of this saying was doubtless of a yet loftier nature. He intended thus to cure His auditory of low carnal notions concerning what He had been delivering; and lift them up to the spiritual appreciation of His heavenly discourse. He asks,—"If therefore ye behold the Son of Man ascending up where He was before;" (evidently implying.)—"What will ye say *then*? Ye will no longer ask, How can this Man give us His flesh to eat? Ye will be constrained to give up all such carnal imaginations, and to believe that only as GOD, and after some lofty spiritual fashion, I propose to do this thing."(*n*) Consider His marvellous words to Mary in the garden, when (doubtless) she stretched out her arms, as if to embrace His knees:—"Touch me not; *for I am not yet ascended.*"(*o*)

We are once more forcibly reminded of the discourse with Nicodemus. "How can these things be?" exclaimed the master of Israel: to which our LORD replied, —"Knowest thou not these things? . . . . If I have told you earthly things, and ye believe not, how shall ye believe, if I tell you of heavenly things?"(*p*)—words which seem very well to introduce the saying which follows:

(*f*) See the note on St. John iv. 6, foot-note (y) p. 107.
(*g*) See St. Luke vii. 5,—which ought to be translated "*the* Synagogue." There doubtless was but one, at Capernaum.   (*h*) See the note on St. John v. 18.
(*i*) Williams.   (*k*) See above, ver. 51.   (*l*) See St. John xx. 17.
(*m*) Cyril.   (*n*) Amplified from a hint of Athanasius.
(*o*) St. John xx. 17, where see the note.   (*p*) St. John iii. 9 to 12.

63 It is the Spirit that quickeneth ; the Flesh profiteth nothing.

Literally — " the Spirit is that which giveth life ;" or " maketh alive." By which
same, (of Spirit,) in this place, our SAVIOUR speaks of " His Divine, as opposed to
His Human Nature. He explains to His wondering Disciples that those miracu-
ous effects which were to attend the reception of His Flesh, would not arise from
its natural influence, (as the flesh of Man,) but from that supernatural efficacy with
which it was endowed," in consequence of the entire Union of the Godhead with
the Manhood in His Person. " The word *Spirit* in our LORD," (says Bishop Bull,)
is commonly employed in Holy Scripture and in the writers of the first age, to
express that Divine Nature in Himself to which it properly pertaineth to quicken,
r give life to mortals; in respect whereof, CHRIST is called the ' Prince of Life,'
1 Acts iii. 15 ; and ' Life' itself, in St. John i. 4." The truth here revealed there-
ore, is, that our LORD'S Manhood was to be the principle of Life, by reason of the
Godhead with which it was united. Hence, in his chapter on the Resurrection of
he Body, St. Paul is found to use these same words concerning CHRIST. " The
rst man Adam," (he says,) " was made a living soul : the last Adam was made *a
quickening Spirit.*"(q)

The words that I speak unto you, *they* are spirit, and *they* are life.

Some explain it thus,—Let what I have spoken to you be understood spiritually.
e may not eat of this flesh which ye behold with your eyes, nor drink the crimson
urrent which flows in these veins ; yet, under sacramental emblems, shall faithful
en verily and indeed become partakers of both in My Supper.
But the following seems better :—" I perceive from the reasonings of your hearts,
iat ye foolishly suppose Me to have said that this Earthly Body can naturally
apart Life. Far different was the purport of My discourse. I spoke altogether
oncerning the Divine Spirit, and concerning Life Eternal . . . Wherefore, the
ords which I have spoken unto you, ' are Spirit,'— that is, they are spiritual, and
bout the Spirit : ' and are Life ;' that is, are life-giving, and concerning that which
in its essential nature, Life."— So, Cyril of Alexandria in his noble Commentary
1 the Gospel of St. John.

64 But there are some of you that believe not.

He foresaw that some were about to forsake Him. He therefore assigned before-
ind the true occasion of their departure : which lay not in anything which *He* had
oken, but in *their unbelief.*—The present sentence will be found continued below,
. ver. 65 : " Therefore said I unto you, that no man can come unto Me," &c.

(For JESUS knew from the beginning who they were that believed not,
ad who should betray Him.)

Which parenthetical words of the Evangelist have reference partly to what fol-
ws in ver. 66, and partly to what follows in ver. 70, 71.—" The Evangelist wishes
show us, that CHRIST knew all things before the foundation of the World ; which
as a proof of His Divinity."(r) He continues to relate the saying of CHRIST,
hich he had interrupted half-way :

65 And he said, Therefore said I unto you, that no man can come
ato Me, except it were given unto him of My FATHER.

That is, — because I was made aware by the Spirit within Me, that some among
ou are unbelievers, I made the remark some time since, — " No man can come to
e, except the FATHER which hath sent Me draw him."(s)   " As if He said, —
en's unbelief does not disturb or astonish Me. I know to whom the FATHER
ath given to come to Me"(t) . . . And this is the end of the subject.

66 From that *time* many of His Disciples went back, and walked no
ore with him.

It is not *certain* that St. John meant to say that "from that time" many

(q) 1 Cor. xv. 45.   (r) Theophylact.   (s) Ver. 44.
(t) Chrysostom.

fell away from CHRIST. He may have meant, that it was "from this [circumstance,"] — "in consequence of this [discourse,"] — or the like . . . . . . "When you hear, however, of His Disciples "murmuring" and "going back" understand not those really such; but rather some who, as far as their behaviour went, seemed to be receiving instruction from Him. For, among His followers were some of the people, who were called Disciples, because they companied with His Disciples."(u)

67 Then said JESUS unto the Twelve, Will ye also go away?

Take notice that although he had all along foreseen this defection of certain of His followers, (miserable men!) yet had he continued lovingly to plead with them till now. Seeing many thus fall away from Him, He sadly asks the Twelve whether they intend to go away likewise? Words which at once implied the freedom of the will in those whom He addressed, and provoked them to a noble confession by the largeness of the good at stake, which His recent discourse had brought before them. — Simon Peter returns answer in the name of all the rest:(v)

68, 69 Then Simon Peter answered Him, LORD, to whom shall we go? Thou hast the words of Eternal Life. And we believe and are sure that Thou art that CHRIST, the SON of the living GOD.

"This is an hard saying," — the others had declared. Better taught, the Apostle, (with allusion to what his LORD had said in ver. 63,) confesses that His Master's sayings have the savor of "Eternal Life." — Some again there were "that believed not:"(x) but "We," (says St. Peter, in behalf of His fellow-Apostles,) "We believe and know that Thou art the CHRIST, the SON of the living GOD!"

70 JESUS answered them, Have I not chosen you Twelve, and one of you is a devil?

"Chosen" by CHRIST: yet able to become "a devil!" Therefore hath GOD left the will of Man perfectly free! "His election does not impose any necessity upon the person with respect to the future; but leaves it in the power of his will, to be saved or perish."(y)

Notice the rebuke implied in these words of our LORD. "We believe and know," St. Peter had said; and the whole body of his fellow-Apostles will have largely sympathized in the loving forwardness of that prompt Confession. They will have beheld some of the other Disciples wavering: perhaps they will have heard some openly professing their resolve to walk with CHRIST no longer. Meantime, a hedge seemed to have been set about themselves; and standing, as they probably did, apart from the multitude, and keeping together, (which appears to have been their wont on other occasions besides the present,)(z) they may have felt as if entire faithfulness and perfect security were at least their portion. "Have not I made choice of you, — the Twelve?" (exclaims our LORD,) "and yet one of you is a devil!" — showing that his language in ver. 64 was applicable, and had doubtless been addressed, to one of themselves also. He calls Judas "a devil, not only because, by his means, Satan was to assail CHRIST; but also because he was to fall, (if be had not already fallen,) from a state of uprightness, as Satan himself had done, to a state of utter and hopeless wickedness.

By this solemn word of warning, doubtless, the entire company of the Disciples will have been rendered more humble, more watchful, more apprehensive. The name of the traitor was mercifully withheld, — whereby all were profited; for each one trembled lest he might prove the guilty man. "Mark the wisdom of CHRIST," (says Chrysostom:) "He neither, by exposing Judas, makes him shameless and contentious; nor again emboldens him, by allowing him to think himself concealed."

The checks, hints, warnings which from first to last, are addressed to Judas Iscariot, exceed in number what any one would suppose who had never attended to the circumstance. Some remarks have been already offered on the subject in the note on St. Mark xiv. 25. Take notice that Judas must have been a good man when CHRIST chose him, — namely, about a year before; and it is not certain from the present words that Judas had even yet fallen. The words of CHRIST are therefore words of warning addressed to Judas, — whom he nevertheless "knew should betray Him."

(u) Theophylact.   (v) So Cyril and Chrysostom.   (x) Ver. 64.
(y) Chrysostom.   (z) Consider St. Matthew xii. 49.

e are unexpectedly brought upon the contemplation of one of the most perplexing questions in speculative Divinity, concerning which it editate than to argue; and safest of all *to obey*. " The secret things the LORD our GOD: but those things which are revealed, belong unto r children forever, that we may *do* all the words of this Law."(*a*)

pake of Judas Iscariot *the son* of Simon: for he it was that :ay Him, being one of the Twelve.

the seventh or eighth time in the course of one brief chapter, did our w that the future as well as the unseen present, is all exposed to His :n.(*b*) Take notice that, on the first four occasions on which St. of Judas Iscariot, he always adds "the son of Simon,"(*c*)—to distin- om St. Jude, his namesake, our LORD's cousin. That short clause — of the Twelve,"—is added with special reference to the four preceding is the only comment, if comment it can be called, which the four Evan- rhere make on the traitor's crime.(*d*) y remarkable," says a pious writer at the close of his Commentary on " that as so much is said of the Holy Eucharist being a savor of Life · of Death unto death, — even *Discourse* respecting it is found to work same effects. Thus, on the present occasion, not only many Disciples)ut even among the Twelve, it brings forth fearfully, for the first time, d the shade: — in St. Peter, the blessed Confession unto Life; and in ndas, the first disclosure as to his having a devil. . . . Great reason : for caution when this awful doctrine is discussed !"(*e*)

CHAPTER VII.

·oveth the ambition and boldness of His kinsmen: 10 *goeth up from the Feast of Tabernacles:* 14 *teacheth in the Temple.* 40 *Divers opinions* ·*ong the people.* 45 *The Pharisees are angry that their officers took Him* ·*hide with Nicodemus for taking His part.*

:hese things, JESUS walked in Galilee: for He would not walk because the Jews sought to kill Him.

gelist St. John thus assigns the reason why our SAVIOUR did not go up ı to keep the Third Passover. To speak more accurately, — he is here for our SAVIOUR's absence from the Capital for the entire space of ınths. He abode in Galilee, instead: or rather, He "*walked*" there; eriod comprised in the present verse is to þe referred the journey into f Tyre and Sidon, which comprised a circuit East of the Sea of Gali- be same period belongs the miraculous feeding of the Four Thousand:(*g*) through the towns of Cæsarea Philippi; and the transfiguration.(*h*) of our SAVIOUR's Ministry had in fact elapsed, since the miracle re-

xix. 29. (*b*) Consider verses 6, 15, 26, 43, 51, 61, 64, 71.
ı vi. 71: xii. 4: xiii. 2: xiii. 26. There was no fear or mistake in verse 29, or

note on St. Matth. xxvi. 47. (*e*) Williams.
:th. xv. 21 to 29. St. Matth vii. 24 to 31
th. xv. 32 to 39. St Mark viii. 1 to 9.
th. xvii. 1 to 8. St. Mark ix. 2 to 8. St. Luke ix. 28 to 36.

corded in the former chapter: concerning which interval the beloved Disciple was divinely guided to preserve no single word of record; but to pass on at once from the Passover season to the Feast of Tabernacles.

The occasion of this prolonged retirement in Galilee proves therefore to have been the murderous intentions of "the Jews;" of which we had the first intimation in chap. v. 16, 18; and which seem to have dated from the time of the cure of the impotent man at the Pool of Bethesda, recorded in chap. v. Those intentions are found to have been rife in the Capital, at this very season; as our Saviour's language on confronting His enemies shows;(*d*) and as their subsequent conduct abundantly attests.(*e*) The pretended ground for these wicked designs is zeal for God's honor, — occasioned by our Lord's supposed breach of the Fourth and First Commandments.(*f*) Amazing blindness! which nothing but a long course of Sin can be supposed to have produced. And take notice, that it was the publicity which the Miracle had acquired by the formal defence of the Holy One before the Court of Sanhedrin,(*g*) which must be presumed to have rendered its author so obnoxious in the eyes of the Jewish Rulers. Their enmity was not one whit abated, though a full year and a half had elapsed since the transaction alluded to took place.

2 Now the Jews' Feast of Tabernacles was at hand.

It was therefore now the Autumn of the year; for the Feast of Tabernacles, or of Ingathering, as it was sometimes called, was "in the end of the year, when thou hast gathered in thy labors out of the field,"(*h*) — "thy corn and thy wine."(*i*) It began on the fifteenth day of the seventh month, Tisri, which corresponds with part of our September and October; and lasted for eight days, — the first and last being "a solemn assembly," and "a sabbath."(*j*) The Festival itself was intended as a memorial of the time when the Israelites dwelt in tents in the wilderness;(*k*) and it beautifully shadowed forth that season, yet future, when Christ should tabernacle in the flesh, and "dwell among us."(*l*) It was, in fact, one of those three great annual Feasts, when as many of the Commonwealth of Israel as were able, being males, presented themselves before the Lord in His Temple:(*m*) and our Saviour, (like a Son in His own house,)(*n*) is found to have appeared with them.

Many were the august ceremonies with which this Festival was kept; one of which will be found alluded to in the note on ver. 37. But the Jewish people do not seem to have obeyed the letter of their Law, which required that they should "take boughs of goodly trees, branches of palm-trees, and the boughs of thick trees, and willows of the brook;" and rejoice before the Lord their God, "dwelling in booths seven days."(*o*) One such observance of this solemn festival, indeed, took place in the time of Nehemiah; when the Children of the Captivity are said to have "found written in the Law" "that they should proclaim in all their cities and in Jerusalem, saying, Go forth unto the Mount, and fetch olive branches, and pine branches, and myrtle branches, and palm branches, and branches of thick trees, to make booths:" (which may perhaps be regarded as an ancient Jewish exposition of Levit. xxiii. 40, 42, already quoted.) Thereupon it is recorded that "the people went forth, and made themselves booths, every one upon the roof of his house, and in their courts, and in the courts of the House of God, and in the street of the water gate, and in the street of the gate of Ephraim:" but it is expressly added that "*since the days of Joshua the son of Nun* unto that day, had not the children of Israel done so."(*p*) That is, they had failed to obey this part of the Law for a thousand years.

How this Festival was observed in the time of our Lord, is not known precisely: but inasmuch as it was the practice of every pious Israelite who was able to comply with the requirement of the Law, to repair to Jerusalem, "in the Feast of unleavened Bread, and in the Feast of Weeks, and in the Feast of Tabernacles,"(*q*) — it follows:

(*d*) See below, ver. 20 and 25.
(*f*) See St. John v. 16, 18.
(*h*) Exod. xxiii. 16.
(*j*) Numb. xxix. 12 to 38. Compare Levit. xxiii. 36, 39: Numb. xxix. 35.
(*k*) See Levit. xxiii. 43.
(*m*) Exod. xxiii. 14 to 17. Deut. xvi. 1 to 17. See St. Luke ii. 41.
(*n*) Hebrews iii. 6.
(*p*) Nehemiah viii. 13 to 17

(*e*) See below, verses 30, 32, 44, 45.
(*g*) See the note on St. John v. 18.
(*i*) Deut. xvi. 13.

(*l*) See St. John i. 14 and the note there.

(*o*) Levit. xxiii. 40, 42.
(*q*) Deuteronomy xvi. 16.

3, 4 His Brethren therefore said unto Him, Depart hence, and go into Judæa, that Thy Disciples also may see the works that Thou doest: for *there is* no man *that* doeth any thing in secret, and he himself seeketh to be known openly. If Thou do these things, show Thyself to the World.

The scene where these words were spoken is not recorded. It seems likely, however, that Nazareth was the place,—*that* being the home of CHRIST's "Brethren" after the flesh. Concerning the persons alluded to, see what has been offered on the places indicated at foot.(r) They were probably the sons of another Mary, who was wife of Clopas, and sister of the Blessed Virgin; and their names,—James, and Joses, and Simon, and Judas."(s) Of these brothers, one at least (Jude) was a member of the Apostolic body.(t) It was not therefore *all* "the Brethren of CHRIST who addressed Him in the manner here recorded. Indeed, the suggestion in the heading of the chapter, may very well be correct; namely, that the speakers were certain of His "Kinsmen," generally.

These men therefore urge our LORD to proceed to the Capital, and there to show Himself openly; not to continue his residence in the remote region of Galilee,—travelling about secretly,(u) and seeking (however vainly) to be hid.(v) Marvellous works our SAVIOUR did indeed perform in that despised district: and "the Brethren" are observed here to make two distinct allusions to them: but these did not attract the same measure of attention, nor procure for their Divine Author the same renown, which was achieved by His few miracles wrought at Jerusalem. Thus, the cure of the impotent man, recorded in St. John v., had evidently obtained such notoriety, that at this very time our LORD's personal safety in the Capital was endangered. Consider verse 21, lower down, and see the note there.

But while malignity was devising the destruction of the Holy One in the very spot where He had wrought such stupendous acts of Mercy, not a few faithful hearts are found to have entertained towards Him a humble measure of faith and love.(x) Our SAVIOUR had already many "Disciples" in Jerusalem; and His cousins at Nazareth are found to have grown impatient that their great Kinsman should gather these about Himself,—openly declare His pretensions, and proclaim His Mission. Such is apparently the purport of the sayings in verses 3 and 4.

The worldly spirit which that address of "the Brethren" reveals, is much to be noticed. The speakers knew nothing of that goodness which seeks "the honor that cometh from GOD only."(y) As little did they know of that heavenly method which our SAVIOUR CHRIST was at this very time pursuing,—in gathering together the outcasts, and fetching home the wanderers from the fold; extending His kingdom upon Earth by methods which to men seemed foolishness; building up His Church out of the "base things of the world, and things which are despised, yea, and things which are not."(z) They were ambitious of human honor; and thought all lost which was done in secret. Thus, they were led to reject their Mighty Kinsman, (as the people of Nazareth had twice done before,)(a) and to regard Him with secret unbelief. Of this, the Evangelist himself assures us in the very next verse. "How can ye believe," (our SAVIOUR had already asked the Jews at Jerusalem,) "*which receive honor one of another?*"(b)

5 For neither did His Brethren believe in Him.

This truly marvellous statement suggests many important inferences as to what must have been our SAVIOUR's method with His immediate followers. There had been no special works wrought for their personal conviction. Much less had any constraint been put upon their wills and affections. And perhaps it was to guide us to some such reflections, that the Evangelist here records the unbelief of "the Brethren" of CHRIST.

(r) St. Matth. xii. 47: xiii. 55. St. Mark iii. 31: vi. 3.
(s) See St. Matth. xiii. 55, and St. Mark vi. 3.
(t) See the note on "Thaddæus," in St. Mark iii. 18,—vol. ii. p. 74.
(u) St. Mark ix. 30.　　　　　　　(v) See St. Mark vii. 24.
(x) See St. John ii. 23; vii. 31.
(y) St. John v. 44.　　　　　　　　　　　(z) 1 Cor. i. 28.
(a) See St. Luke iv. 16 to 30, and St. Matth. xiii. 54 to 58.
(b) St. John v. 44.

6 Then JESUS said unto them, My time is not yet come:

Rather, " My season."   A certain moment is spoken of, well known in the deep counsels of GOD: the hour, namely, " that He should depart out of this World unto the FATHER."(c)   Until that " hour" had " come," CHRIST would not show himself openly; nor indeed could any " lay hands on Him."(d) It came at last; and then He distinctly proclaimed its arrival,(e) and " steadfastly set His face to go to Jerusalem."(f) In the meantime, the Blessed Speaker contrasts the position of His kinsmen after the flesh with His own position; and explains what prevented His going up to Jerusalem with them, openly, now. It follows:—

but your time is alway ready.

Our SAVIOUR tells His " Brethren" that they may visit Jerusalem at any time with perfect safety. They were not objects of public hatred, and secret conspiracy, like Himself.

7 The World cannot hate you;

" For you urge the principles of the World, and ' the World will love its own.' "(g)

but Me it hateth, because I testify of it, that the works thereof are evil.

" This is the secret of the World's hatred. The words, the deeds, the presence, the very thoughts of the good, are a witness which it will not endure,—as Cain could not endure Abel. ' He is grievous unto us, even to behold.' ' He abstaineth from our ways, as from filthiness.' "(h)

The beloved Disciple in a certain place inquires, Wherefore Cain slew Abel? And the answer which he subjoins, forcibly recalls the present place of his Gospel. " Because his own works were evil, and his brother's righteous. Marvel not, my brethren, *if the World hate you*."(i)

8 Go ye up unto this Feast: I go not up yet unto this Feast; for My time is not yet full come.

The meaning of these words was of course hid from the men to whom He spake. They supposed that our LORD was alluding only to the period at which it would please Him to go up to the Feast of Tabernacles; whereas all His words may have had a deeper meaning; and His concluding saying certainly had. They little knew the nature of the manifestation for which they expressed impatience, or suspected what was to follow at " the fullness of Time."

In the meanwhile, it is to be observed that our LORD here announces His actual intention of being present at the approaching solemnity. He does but declare that He proposes not to go up *yet*. Accordingly, it follows:

9, 10 When He had said these words unto them, He abode *still* in Galilee. But when His Brethren were gone up, then went He also up unto the Feast, not openly, but as it were in secret.

How long He staid in Galilee does not appear: for the space of a few days, it may be thought. " The Brethren" having departed, our SAVIOUR followed, journeying privately; and when He reached the Capital, (which may well have been on the first day of the Feast of Tabernacles,) He probably lived there for three days in perfect seclusion. See below, verse 14.

11 Then the Jews sought Him at the Feast, and said, Where is He?

Showing that the memorable events which had attended our SAVIOUR's last visit to the Capital, (recorded in chapter v.) had obtained such notoriety, that His presence was eagerly looked forward to at Jerusalem, and His arrival diligently inquired after, as often as the greater Festivals of the Church came round. " The

---

(c) St. John xiii. 1.   (d) See below verse 30.   Also chap. viii. 20.
(e) St. John xii. 23: xvii. 1. St. Mark xiv. 41.   (f) See St. Luke ix. 51.
(g) St. John xv. 19.   (h) Williams, quoting Wisdom ii. 15, 16.
(i) 1 St. John iii. 13.   Consider also St. John xv. 18 and xvii. 14.

Jews"(k) are the most diligent seekers after Him; who nevertheless cannot bring themselves to mention His hated Name; but,—"Where is He?" they ask. The word is emphatic.

12 And there was much murmuring among the people concerning Him: for some said, He is a good Man: others said, Nay; but He deceiveth the people.

In verse 43, below, it is also said that the populace were divided "because of Him." "Some" there were, in fact, of "the common people," who "hung upon" His words,(l)—"heard Him gladly,"(m)—and came to Him "early in the morning,"(n) in the Temple. "Others," were the partizans of those hypocritical Chief Priests, who finally compassed His death. These were taught to call Him a "Deceiver," to the very last.(o)

13 Howbeit no man spake openly of Him for fear of the Jews.

Rather,—"spake *freely* of Him:" by which it is implied that some would have spoken in His favor, had they dared. "The Jews," in this place, as in so many others, is a phrase which indicates a certain section of the people,—that large and powerful body of Pharisees, whose enmity kept in awe Joseph of Arimathæa,(p) and many other of the Rulers.(q) See the note on St. John v. 15.

14 Now about the midst of the Feast JESUS went up into the Temple, and taught.

It was now the fourth day of the Festival; and our SAVIOUR, who was already in Jerusalem,(r) made His appearance in the Temple,—no longer remaining hid, but revealing Himself openly, and assuming the office of a public Teacher. Very astonishing must His remarks on their Sacred Books have appeared to the Jewish Rulers,—blinded though they were by prejudice, and hardened against conviction, by Sin: for *He* knew, as no one else could know, not only the recondite meanings of the Law and the Prophets, but also what observations upon them would affect His auditory most. Accordingly, it follows:—

15 And the Jews marvelled, saying, How knoweth this Man letters, having never learned?

Rather,—"How does this [person,]" (or "fellow,") "know *the Scriptures?*" The expression recurs in St. John v. 47, and 2 Tim. iii. 15.—These blind Teachers give little heed to His Divine Doctrine. Too proud to acknowledge their admiration of its sublimity, their very surprise at *what He says* is swallowed up in wonder as to *how He knows it*. They marvel "how" such treasures of wisdom can dwell with One who has never studied in their schools,—(for it is not here implied that our SAVIOUR had never been a learner; but only that He had attained His marvellous acquaintance with the Scriptures without having sat at the feet of any of their famous Rabbis.) The inference was indeed sufficiently obvious,—namely, that He must have been divinely assisted: but this they were not in a condition to perceive.

Our SAVIOUR; knowing the thoughts of their hearts, makes answer to their doubts; accounting for the admiration which His Teaching had occasioned them, and explaining the source of His Knowledge,—which was neither human, nor yet demoniacal, as some of them may have suspected.

16 JESUS answered them, and said, My Doctrine is not Mine, but His that sent Me.

This form of expression we have met with so repeatedly before, that it is almost needless to explain it further.(s) "*Not* Mine, *but* His that sent Me,"—obviously conveys no denial that the Doctrine which our SAVIOUR delivered was His own, as GOD; but only the assertion, that whatever He, the Eternal SON, had,—whether

(k) See below, the note on verse 13.
(m) St. Mark xii. 37.
(o) See below, verse 47. Also St. Matthew xxvii. 63.
(q) St. John xii.
(s) See the notes on St. Matthew ix. 13, and St. John v. 30.

(l) St. Luke xix. 48.
(n) St. John viii. 2.
(p) St. John xix. 38.
(r) See above, on ver. 10.

Doctrine, or any other thing,—He derived from the FATHER; inasmuch as He derived from *Him* His Essence, by virtue of that Eternal Generation of which we have already spoken particularly, elsewhere.(*t*) It matters nothing, therefore, whether our SAVIOUR here speaks of Himself as GOD, or as Man. In either case He would have referred His wisdom to the Eternal FATHER. As GOD,—because that relation whereby the SON receives all things of the FATHER, (whereas the FATHER receives nothing of any,) is the fundamental truth of the Gospel.(*u*) As Man,—because although His own Divinity was doubtless the source of that Divine Wisdom whereby He spake, yet if He had failed to ascribe that Wisdom to the FATHER, a door would have been opened to misconception and error. Men might have doubted whether He was *Begotten* of the FATHER, and of *One Substance* with Him.

Concerning the superiority implied by the Mission here spoken of, (" His that sent Me,") hear what Cyril says;—" Our SAVIOUR does not hereby represent Himself as inferior to the FATHER in honour: nor may His being " sent" be thought of as if it were something servile,—true though it be that He took upon Himself the form of a Servant.(*v*) He was " sent" as a word from the mind, or a sunbeam(*x*) from the sun;—things which are disposed to project themselves, so to speak, from that wherein they abide, by reason of their innate tendency to external manifestation: while yet they are naturally inherent in their respective sources, and inseparable from them. For when a word hath been uttered from the mind, or brightness from the sun, it is not supposed that the source which begat hath experienced loss or privation in respect of that which is begotten: but on the contrary, either is supposed still to remain in the other."

In the verse before us then, our LORD by a few mysterious words explains the source of that Divine Knowledge in Himself which so perplexed His enemies. He straightway adds,—

17 If any man will do His Will, he shall know of the Doctrine,— whether it be of GOD, or *whether* I speak of Myself.

Whereby it will be perceived that He further explains to His enemies the reason of their perplexity and unbelief. As though He had said,—" If ye were faithful doers of the Will of Him that sent Me, ye would recognize My Doctrine to be His, likewise." . . . "*Of Myself*," in this place, is evidently put in opposition to that which is " of GOD." This is made plainer in the next verse.

These famous words may be looked upon not only as conveying a most gracious promise; but also as embodying a great and most important precept,—namely, that the perception of Truth depends upon the practice of Virtue. It is a favorite maxim of the present day, that increased Knowledge will bring with it growth in Godliness. Holy Scripture, at all events, exactly reverses the process. The way to " know of the Doctrine, whether it be of GOD," is—*to do* "*His Will*." And to this agree many other declarations of Holy Scripture.(*y*)

Literally,—" If any man wills," that is, wishes, sincerely desires, to do GOD's Will, " he shall know." Thus, the love of GOD has the promise of conducting to the Knowledge of GOD. The words are full of consolation; yet full of terror likewise; for they remind us that the " rejection of true doctrine is a proof of an evil heart." " Understanding," (says Augustine,) " is the reward of Faith. Seek not to know, in order that thou mayest believe; but seek to believe in order that thou mayest know." GOD hath indissolubly linked together our intellectual and our moral nature; and will call us to account for our views and opinions, no less than for the actions of our lives. This is an unfashionable Doctrine, but it is *true.*

18 He that speaketh of himself seeketh his own glory.

And he that seeketh his own glory, the same " is a deceiver and an antichrist." (*z*) " My Doctrine," (saith our SAVIOUR,) " is not Mine, but His that sent Me:"(*a*) and the character of Him that seeketh the Glory of Him that sent Him, follows:

but He that seeketh His Glory that sent Him, the same is true, and no unrighteousness is in Him.

(*t*) See the notes on St. John v. 20, &c.   (*u*) See St. John xx. 31.
(*v*) Philippians ii. 7.   (*x*) Cyril says " brightness,"—recalling Hebrews i. 3.
(*y*) See the places referred to in note (c) at page 686,—in the Commentary on St. John v. 44.
(*z*) 2 St. John verse 7.   (*a*) See above, verse 16.

" True,"—and therefore no deceiver of the people,(b) as some of them had said.(c)
"Unrighteousness" here stands for *Falsehood*, as in so many other places of Scripture.(d) It is further implied that the Pharisees, who sought " honor one of another,
and not the honor that cometh from God only,"(e) were both liars and unrighteous:
liars, — because they taught for doctrines the commandments of men ;(f) unrighteous, — because they were themselves trangressors.   As it follows:

19 Did not Moses give you the Law, and *yet* none of you keepeth
the Law?   Why go ye about to kill me?

This is said with allusion to their alleged ground of offence against our .Lord;
namely, His supposed violation of the Mosaic Law.(g)   The argument is, — " Ye
profess honour for the Law of Moses.   Why go ye about to kill Me, in whom is no
unrighteousness; and thus prove by your actions that ye despise that Law which
so strictly forbids murder?"
This was the question of Him "unto whom all hearts be open, all desires known,
and from whom no secrets are hid."   Our Lord knew the murderous intentions
which already filled the hearts of His enemies: He knew also the occasion of their
hate.   But this has been explained already in the note on verse 1.
Take notice that on a former occasion, also, the same Divine Speaker had asked
His enemies a question very like the present.   It was the Sabbath-day: He was
about to restore a man which had a withered hand: the Scribes and Pharisees murmured at Him for doing what was unlawful on the Sabbath, and evidently designed
nothing less than His destruction.   Accordingly, He addressed to them the wither-
ng inquiry, — " Is it lawful to do good on the Sabbath-days, or to do evil? to save
life, or to kill?"(h)
His enemies in the meantime ascribe to demonical possession His knowledge,
the *reality* of which they are unable to deny: —

20 The people answered and said, Thou hast a devil: who goeth
about to kill thee?

Without condescending to notice their calumnious charge, or their question,—our
Saviour at once exposes the source of their malignity ; —

21 Jesus answered and said unto them, I have done one work, and
ye all marvel.

"Marvel" is here thought to signify "are inflamed." "enrage yourselves." —
Take notice that He says not,—" I restored to health on the Sabbath-day one hopelessly diseased."   He simply describes the miraculous cure described in the v. chapter, as "a work" which He had done, — thereby soothing the feelings of his excited
auditory.   It seems to be implied, — "For this one work, although wrought for a
sick man's perfect restoration, ye persecute Me as if I were a malefactor, guilty of
some monstrous crime.   Ye pretend to be actuated only by jealousy for the honor
of the Sabbath : yet might your regard even for *that* Institution well give way at the
sight of One standing among you so manifestly invested with Divine Power as Myself.   Ye marvel at *My* disregard of *Moses'* Law, inasmuch as I have done this *one*
work: what then, think ye, must be the wrath of Almighty God against *yourselves*,
for your *numberless* offences against *Him!*"(i)

22, 23 Moses therefore gave unto you Circumcision: not because it
is of Moses, but of the Fathers;'and ye on the Sabbath-day circumcise a man.   If a man on the Sabbath-day receive Circumcision, that
the Law of Moses should not be broken ;

Not that the Law of Moses any where commands Circumcision on the Sabbath-
day.   In only one place does the ancient Lawgiver prescribe the observance of this

(b) Consider 2 Cor. vi. 8: "as *deceivers* and yet *true*."   (c) See above, ver. 12.
(d) Consider St. John iii. 21, (where see the note.)   Rom. i. 18: ii. 8.   1 Cor. xiii. 6.   2
Thess. ii. 12.
(e) St. John v. 44.   (f) St. Matth. xv. 3, 6, 9.   (g) See St. John v. 16 and 18.
(h) See St. Mark iii. 4, and the note there.
(i) From Cyril.

sacred rite at all; and there, he merely says of the "man child," — "In the eighth day, the flesh of his foreskin shall be circumcised."(k) Our LORD, in verse 22, says "Moses *gave you* Circumcision," because the Jewish nation rested their continued observance of that sign of GOD's covenant with Abraham(l) on the passage already quoted from the Law of Moses.

But the remarks thus offered, instead of removing, seem rather to increase the difficulty of the place; the meaning of which will perhaps best appear from some such a paraphrase as this: —

"On the following account(m) Moses gave you Circumcision:—not, because it was any part of the Law which he received new from GOD; but, on account of its being a Patriarchal Rite. His command to circumcise, amounts therefore only to his sanction of a Patriarchal Precept. And yet, though Circumcision is nothing more than this, you hesitate not to circumcise on the Sabbath-day, — thus transgressing the letter of the Fourth Commandment; and violating (according to your own standard of strictness,) the oldest and most solemn of the Divine Institutions. If, then, ye yourselves practice a wounding of the flesh on the Sabbath-day, are ye angry at *Me*,"—

are ye angry at Me, because I have made a man every whit whole on the Sabbath-day?

That is,—"Now, if Circumcision, which is a *wounding* and *partial mutilation* of the Body, must needs be performed even on the Sabbath, in order that the Law of *Moses* may be preserved inviolate, — are ye angry at *Me* because I made the *whole frame* of a man *healthy* on the same day?"(n) In which words, a contrast seems to be implied between Moses, who, "verily was faithful in all his house, *as a servant*;" and "CHRIST *as a Son* over his own House."(o)

24 Judge not according to the appearance, but judge righteous judgment.

This does not mean, "judge not *according to what appears*;" as if the Divine Speaker implied that appearances are often deceptive. It means, — *Be not partial* judges; but learn to give an *impartial* judgment. Do not assent to what Moses requires, and yet charge Me with Sin: but regard your own act, and Mine, with fair and impartial eyes; for the Law of the Sabbath is equally binding on us all. Ye consider that ye circumcise on the Sabbath-day by Moses' requirement. Be it so. Contrast therefore the bloody rite of Circumcision, practised on a Babe, with the glorious recovery of entire soundness in the case of one who had been diseased for 38 years. Look at the *work*, and judge fairly. Be "not acceptors of persons."

25 Then said some of them of Jerusalem, Is not this He, whom they seek to kill?

Showing that the intention of the Jewish Rulers was no secret to the people.

26 But, lo, He speaketh boldly, and they say nothing unto Him. Do the Rulers know indeed that this is the very CHRIST?

Rather,—"Have the Rulers," (that is, the members of the High Court of Sanhedrin,) "perhaps really ascertained that this is indeed the MESSIAH?" . . . . These words of the people convey a lively picture of the majesty and power with which our SAVIOUR must have spoken the preceding words; for His enemies are seen silent and confounded in His presence, — the presence of One whom, it was notorious, they only wanted to get into their power in order to destroy. Here He is, and they are powerless! Nay, so awe-struck do they appear, that a looker-on would suppose them *conscious* that MESSIAH stood before them. . . . . Unbelief however soon interferes to prevent the person who threw out this suggestion, from accepting it for their own souls' health. It follows:

(k) Levit. xii. 3.   (l) Gen. xvii. 9 to 14.
(m) The learned reader should compare, for the construction, St. John v. 16, 18: viii. 47: 1: 17: xii. 18, 39. St. Matth. xiii. 13. 1 St. John iii. 1. The word "therefore" must not be connected with the preceding verse.
(n) See above the note on ver. 1.   (o) Heb. iii. 5, 6.

27 Howbeit we know this Man whence He is:

The reasoners knew that JESUS of Nazareth was the reputed son of Joseph, "the carpenter," and Mary his wedded wife. They might have found out, however, had they pursued the investigation with real care, that Bethlehem had been the place of His actual Birth; and it was within the limits of inquiry to ascertain that His Parents claimed to be of the House and lineage of David.(*p*) All this however the inhabitants of Jerusalem were little likely to suspect. Their boast on every occasion was, that they "knew" whence CHRIST was; that is, they knew His Parentage and connections.(*q*) A veil had been drawn over the early history of the Holy One,—a thicker veil than men, or even the Prince of Evil himself, could penetrate. The flight into Egypt and subsequent return to Nazareth,—the home (and probably the birth-place) of the Blessed Virgin Mary,(*r*) as well as of her saintly Husband,— must have effectually obliterated the memory of the Nativity at Bethlehem. Wonders had attended that event indeed; but, on reflection, it will be felt that every part of this "crying mystery," as Ignatius speaks concerning the Incarnation, had been "wrought in the silence of GOD."(*s*) The portentous Star and the arrival of the Magi at Jerusalem must have been the events of a single day; while the visit and the offerings of those royal persons to the Infant "King of the Jews," must have been scarcely less secret a matter than the homage of the shepherd-swains which had preceded it. The Presentation in the Temple was altogether a private transaction. The very Murder of the Babes of Bethlehem must have been looked upon as little more than one of the many acts of cruelty which disgraced the latter days of Herod,—a thing to be condemned, deplored, and forgotten. In the meantime, the Holy Family disappeared from the Holy Land for a period: and when Joseph and Mary returned, it was not to the scene of their late singular distinction. They had come back to dwell in extreme poverty among the despised race to which they belonged; and in a city where no persons knew what had befallen them since their departure. Thirty troublous years had elapsed since then; and a fresh generation had sprung up. The title "*Jesus of Nazareth*" had now become the established appellation of our SAVIOUR.(*t*) Men were able, therefore, with confidence, to say, "We know this Man whence He is!" Consider below, verses 41, 42. It follows:

but when CHRIST cometh, no man knoweth whence He is.

They allude to the declaration of the prophet Micah, that the "goings forth" of Him "that is to be Ruler in Israel," "have been from of old, from everlasting:"(*u*) and again to those words of Isaiah respecting him: "Who shall declare His generation?"(*v*) Hence, they reason thus: Concerning CHRIST, it will not not be known whence He cometh (alluding to His Parentage;) but we know whence this Man cometh. Therefore He is not CHRIST. . . . A melancholy specimen of perverse reasoning, truly! They had nothing to advance against the Holy One; nothing whereon to rest their unbelief; except the inconvenient fact that they knew (or thought they knew) His origin.(*x*) He proceeds to deprive them even of this excuse:—

28 Then cried JESUS in the Temple as He taught, saying, Ye both know Me, and ye know whence I am: and I am not come of Myself, but He that sent Me is true, whom ye know not.

He spake this with a loud Voice, as if proclaiming the Truth in triumph. The sense is: "Ye both know Me, and ye know whence I am." So ye say: and in a certain sense, ye say truly. "And yet, I came not of Myself: but He is faithful and true that sent Me,—fulfilling His promises made to the Fathers. And *Him*, ye know not." . . . Hence, it is implied that the enemies of CHRIST, in reality, *knew not whence He was*. And so our LORD says in another place :(*y*) adding, in express words, "Ye neither know Me nor My FATHER."(*z*) It follows:

(*p*) See St. Luke ii. 4, and the note.
(*q*) St. Matth. xiii. 55 to 57. St. Mark vi. 2, 3. St. Luke iv. 22. St. John vi. 42.
(*r*) St. Luke ii. 39. (*s*) See the note on St. Luke ii. 35.
(*t*) Consider St. John i. 45, (where see the note,) xix. 19, St. Matth. xxi. 11, and especially Acts xxii. 8.
(*u*) Micah v. 2. (*v*) Isaiah liii. 8.
(*x*) Compare the place with St. John ix. 29, where see the note.
(*y*) See St. John viii. 14. (*z*) St. John viii. 19. See also St. John xvi. 3.

29 But I know Him:

" The Son alone knoweth the Father, as being of one substance with Him; and He only can reveal Him. The peculiar knowledge here spoken of implies a peculiar Generation from which it springs. For since the knowledge of the Father is peculiar to him, as being from Him, then the being from Him is peculiar to Him also; that is, the being the true Son of God, by nature."—(a)

for I am from Him, and He hath sent Me.

" ' From whom I received My Essence by communication, from Him also received I this commission.' Thus He which begotteth sendeth, and He which is begotten is sent."

" 'I know Him' (saith Christ), 'for I am from [or of] Him.' And because He is from [or of] the Father, therefore He is called by those of the Nicene Council, in their Creed, 'God of God, Light of Light, very God of very God.' " In fact, they gathered those words of their Creed from this place; but not immediately, for (as Bp. Pearson remarks) they were in some of the Oriental Creeds before. He goes on to explain: " The Father is God, but not of God: Light, but not of Light. Christ is God, but of God: Light, but of Light. There is no difference or inequality in the Nature or Essences, because the same in both; but the Father of our Lord Jesus Christ hath that Essence of Himself, from none; Christ hath the same, not of Himself but from Him."(b)

By these words, then, the Eternal Son declares Himself to be the Only-Begotten of the Father, and asserts His Eternal Generation; as well as proclaims His Incarnation and divine Apostleship.(c) He had, in fact, now repeated the solemn Doctrine which we met with in chap. v.; and accordingly, in the estimation of His hardened auditory, He was guilty of the same offence which is recorded of Him on that earlier occasion;(d) and it is attended by the same consequence. Namely:

30 Then they sought to take Him: but no man laid hands on Him, because His hour was not yet come.

That is,—It was divinely overruled that none should lay hands upon Him: because, "His Hour" was yet future. Concerning that phrase, see above, the note on ver. 6. "He laid invisible hands on their power" (remarks Williams); "for it is He who hath said to the Sea,—Hitherto shalt thou come and no farther."

31 And many of the people believed on Him, and said, When Christ cometh, will He do more miracles than these which this _Man_ hath done?

Showing the nature of the expectations which were popularly entertained concerning Messiah. These men were wrought upon by the same considerations which prevailed with Nicodemus;(e) the witness, namely, of "the works" of Christ. See St. John v. 36.

They believed therefore with their heart, and confessed Him with their lips. In this manner were the Israel of God by slow degrees gathered into the Fold. A similar statement will be found in the ensuing chapter;(f) and the reader is referred to the note on the last words of St. John ii. 11. In the meantime, the words which wrought so blessed an effect on "many out of the crowd," or "common people," did but harden the hearts of their Rulers. As it follows:

32 The Pharisees heard that the people murmured such things concerning Him; and the Pharisees and the Chief Priests sent officers to take Him.

It will be perceived by a comparison with other parts of Scripture that the persons spoken of were the Court of Sanhedrin.(g) These men were those "blind guides" whom our Lord rebuked so severely;(h) for such acts as the present, denouncing

(a) Williams, from Hilary.   (b) Bp. Pearson. See the note on St. John xiv. 23.
(c) See above, the note on ver. 16.   (d) St. John v. 16, 18.
(e) St. John iii. 2.   (f) See St. John viii. 30.
(g) See St. John xi. 47, and Acts v. 21. (h) See Matth. xxiii. 16 and 24.

ght woes upon them. "Woe unto you Scribes and Pharisees, hypocrites! for ye
ut up the Kingdom of Heaven against men; for ye neither go in yourselves, nei-
er *suffer ye them that are entering to go in.*"(i)

33 Then said JESUS unto them, Yet a little while am I with you,
nd *then* I go unto Him that sent Me.

He says, "Yet *a little while*,"—because at the ensuing Passover He will suffer
ath. "*I go*,"—for CHRIST laid down His life by His own free will.(k) "Unto
im *that sent* Me,"—implying that He is "Very GOD of very GOD;" "the Only-
egotten SON of the FATHER." . . . These words were possibly addressed to the Of-
cers who were sent to apprehend the Holy One. The effect which our LORD's Dis-
ourse produced upon those men, we shall discover lower down, in verses 45, 46.
"Yet a little while am I with you." Notice the tenderness of that plea, which
ur SAVIOUR so often urges: "words" (says Williams) "which make the strong
an of wrath as a little child; the subject which, of all others, lies the nearest to
uman tears! And not only such as to soften enemies, but, as Chrysostom ob-
erves, such as to make those who were in earnest more eager to hear Him, as having but a little while to do so." Consider the places at foot.(l) In the meantime,
He proceeds:

34 Ye shall seek Me, and shall not find *Me*:

This is at once a prophecy and a threat,—that after the close of our LORD's Ministry, when He had returned to the FATHER, they who now despise Him will too
late discover their mistake, and be made conscious of their sin. According to that
of Hosea,—"They shall go with their flocks and with their herds to seek the LORD;
but they shall not find Him; He hath withdrawn Himself from them.(m) Then,
(as it had also been prophesied of old,) 'though they shall cry unto Me, I will not
harken unto them.'"(n) And again,—"When ye spread forth your hands, I will
hide Mine eyes from you; yea, when ye make many prayers, I will not hear."(o)
"Because I have called, and ye refused; I have stretched out my hand, and no
man regarded; . . . I also will laugh at your calamity; I will mock when your fear
cometh."(p) The allusion may be specially to the time of the Siege, as Chrysos-
om suggests. Our SAVIOUR adds:

and where I am, *thither* ye cannot come.

He speaks of course of Heaven; and the same saying will be found repeated in
hap. viii. 21, and is alluded to by CHRIST Himself in chap. xiii. 33. A slight difference, however, is discoverable between the two places. For it is not here said
whither I go, ye cannot come;" but "*where I am;*"—a saying which recalls the
ublime assertion already considered in the note on chap. iii. 13.
Moreover, it is observable that this is one of those sayings of our LORD, (of which
ere are indeed so many,)(q) which evidently obtains a different meaning in dif-
rent places. The expression does not seem to signify the same thing here, and
chap. xiii. 33. Here, it implies that our SAVIOUR was about to withdraw to that
lessed Region, whither His saints should follow Him; (for indeed He went to
repare a place for their reception:) but whither the unbelieving and impenitent
ews, His enemies, would never arrive. The Marriage Feast, the Great Supper,
e Everlasting Habitations, the Many Mansions, the Heavenly Jerusalem,—all
is was not for them. Yea, to this day, their descendants seek Him, yet do not
d Him; and (strange to think!) it is precisely for the reason which their fore-
hers, in the very next verse, suggest:—

85 Then said the Jews among themselves, Whither will He go, that
e shall not find Him? will He go unto the dispersed among the Gen-
iles, and teach the Gentiles?

The meaning of the original seems to be rightly given here. They ask,—Will
HRIST then go "to the Twelve Tribes in the dispersion," (or "scattered abroad,"

(i) St. Matthew xxiii. 13.
(l) See St. John xiii. 33: xiv. 19: xvi. 16.
(n) Jeremiah xi. 11.   (o) Isaiah i. 15.
(q) See the note on St. Matthew xix. 30.

(k) Consider St. John x. 18.
(m) Hosea v. 6.
(p) Proverbs i. 24, 26.

as we render the place ;)(r) "and teach the Gentiles,"—literally, "the Greeks?" In which words there seems to be a tacit allusion to the prophecy in Isaiah xlix. 6. They add:

36 What *manner* of saying is this that He said, Ye shall seek Me, and shall not find *Me:* and where I am, *thither* ye cannot come?

And thus ended the dialogue. Our attention is next invited to a memorable scene which took place in the Temple, four days later,—namely, on the eighth day of the Feast of Tabernacles.

37 In the last day, that great *day* of the Feast, JESUS stood and cried, saying, If any man thirst, let him come unto Me, and drink.

It was on the eighth,(s) which had come to be regarded as the principal day of that Feast which the Jews observed with most veneration, and attended in largest numbers; a day observed with peculiar solemnity, as that which closed not only the Feast of Tabernacles, but also all their yearly festivals;—in the presence of a mighty concourse, therefore, it was, that the SAVIOUR of the World took His stand, and spake these words. It cannot in vain be recorded of Him that He "*stood and cried*." There must have been something exceedingly solemn in that attitude, and that voice. He "stood,"—where all might see:(t) He "cried,"—that all might hear. "If any man thirst," was His cry,—"let Him come unto Me and drink!" And how must those words have recalled the exclamation of the Prophet,—"Ho, every one that thirsteth, come ye to the Waters, and he that hath no money; come ye, buy and eat!"(u)

Consider that this was *the last time* that our LORD was ever to keep one of the three great Festivals at Jerusalem; and it was *the last day* of that Festival. He "cried," therefore, that the deaf ears might hear; and the careless ones be made attentive. It was a strong cry of reproof, of warning, of invitation. "Wisdom," (as it is written concerning CHRIST Himself,) "crieth in the chief place of concourse, in the openings of the gates: in the city she uttereth her words, saying, How long ye simple ones will ye love simplicity? and the scorners delight in their scorning, and fools hate knowledge? Turn you at My reproof: behold, *I will pour out My Spirit unto you.*"(x) . . . The words are almost a prophecy!

It is of *the Soul's Thirst* that our LORD here speaks. He might have said "Hunger," had He willed,—as in St. John vi. 35; and the meaning would have been the same. Why then is it Thirst, in this place, and not Hunger? Plainly because Thirst is the keener want: because, also, it is the manner of Scripture to discourse of *the Spirit* under the figure of *Water;* and our SAVIOUR was revealing Himself to His countrymen,—fetching water, as on this day they did, from "Siloa's brook, (z) that flowed fast by the Oracle of GOD," and bringing it with pomp and ceremony into the Temple,—as *Himself* the Living Fountain,—the true source of spiritual refreshment to Israel.

Here then is a most gracious invitation, and most loving promise. "Let him come unto *Me:*" there is the invitation. "Let him *drink:*" there is the promise. To appreciate the blessedness of these words, we have but to call to mind the things which the soul most ardently longs for; as Happiness,—Love,—Knowledge,—Holiness: and further, to remember how the thirst for these becomes aggravated by Misfortune,—Bereavement,—Perplexity,—Falls. We know too that the things of Time cannot, were not meant, to satisfy those immense desires which will find their full gratification only in Eternity. Their office is to lead on to something higher, and purer, and better. The thirst of Happiness was meant to guide us to GOD's Right Hand:(a) and of Love, to Him who is ever with us:(b) and of Knowledge, to the presence of Him who dwelleth in Light:(c) and of Holiness, to Him who alone maketh holy.(d) "Come unto Me," (it is therefore written,) "all ye that labour and are heavy laden, and *I* will give you rest."(e) "I am Alpha and Omega, the Beginning and the End. I will give unto Him that is athirst, of the

(r) St. James i. 1. Compare 1 St. Peter i. 1.
(s) See Leviticus xxiii. 36, 39, and Numbers xxix. 35.
(t) Compare St. John i. 35.　　　　(u) Isaiah lv. 1.　　　　　　(x) Proverbs i. 20 to 23.
(z) See St. John ix. 7.　　　　　　(a) Psalm xvi. 11.
(b) Hebrews xiii. 6,—see the margin.
(c) 1 Timothy vi. 16.　　　　(d) 1 St. Peter i. 16.　　　　(e) St. Matthew xi. 28.

Fountain of the Water of Life freely."(*f*)   "If any man thirst, let him come unto *Me*, and drink !"

A partial fulfillment, then, these words would have had at the time when they were spoken.   A yet larger fulfillment they will have obtained at the feast of Pentecost.   But their entire scope belongs to that period, yet future, when the "Spirit and the Bride will say, "Come :"(*g*) when "a pure river of Water of Life, clear as crystal," will be seen "proceeding out of the Throne of GOD and of the LAMB."(*h*) There, (in "that great City, the Holy Jerusalem,") the Saints of GOD shall "hunger no more, *neither thirst any more;* neither shall the Sun light on them, nor any heat. For the LAMB which is in the midst of the Throne shall *lead them unto living fountains of Waters;* and GOD shall wipe away all tears from their eyes !"(*i*)

38 He that believeth on Me, as the Scripture hath said, out of the belly shall flow rivers of living Water.

It is well known that nowhere in the Bible are these words to be found ; and it is not by any means likely that we ought to explain the passage with Chrysostom and others, — "He that believeth on Me as," (that is, "in conformity with what,") "the Scripture hath said ;" making the words which follow, a promise which had been reserved for the New Covenant.   The true meaning of our LORD's words is, that as many of the goodly fellowship of the Prophets as have discoursed in dark, deep phrase, of the largeness of spiritual endowments, — that free outpouring and indwelling, even to overflowing, of the SPIRIT, which was to mark the reign of MESSIAH ;(*k*) — all these, more or less implicitly, have said the thing which He by whose Spirit they spake(*l*) here attributes to them.   The language used by our LORD on this occasion, seems, therefore, to be as nearly as possible tantamount to that which He used in addressing the Woman of Samaria ;—"Whosoever drinketh of this water shall thirst again ; but whosoever drinketh of the water that I shall give him shall never thirst; but the water that I shall give him shall be in him *a well of water springing up into Everlasting Life.*"(*m*)   In both places it is distinctly marked not only that he that drinketh shall have no lack for evermore ; but that he shall have in himself a well-spring of blessedness, — derived indeed from Him with whom all fullness dwells ; yet flowing away in rivers even from the earthen vessel to which it had been imparted.   "The manner of our SAVIOUR's expression implieth that the SPIRIT should be poured out in such a plentiful measure as would be not only sufficient to satiate the souls of them that thirsted after it, but in a manner overflow to the Salvation of others."(*n*)   Hence, that word of the Apostle,—"As every one hath received the gift, so let him minister."(*o*) . . . The "belly," in this place, of course denotes the whole "*inner man.*"

And take notice that this is one of the occasions, (so much more numerous than is supposed,) when the Evangelist himself comes forward to prevent mistake, or misconception : adding,

39 (But this spake He of the Spirit, which they that believe on Him should receive :

St. John says, — Seek not for this saying of our LORD, (thine and mine,) in any special place of the Old Testament.   Thou wilt strive to discover this particular passage, all in vain : for "this spake He of the Spirit, which they that believe on Him should receive ;" "the streams whereof shall make glad the City of GOD."(*p*) Take notice however that "each is filled according to the size of that vessel of faith which each brings to the Fountain.   If the love of the World dwelleth in thee, there is no room in thee for the love of GOD.   Thou art a vessel, but thou art full.   Pour forth what thou hast, that thou mayest receive that which thou hast not.   Pour forth the love of the World that thou mayest be filled with the love of God.   Each according to his thirst, shall find drink in GOD."(*q*) — St. John adds,

(*f*) Rev. xxi. 6.   (*g*) Consider Rev. xxii. 17.
(*h*) Rev. xxii. 1.   (*i*) Rev. vii. 16, 17.
(*k*) As Is. xii. 3 : xxxv. 6, 7 : xli. 18 : xliii. 19 : xliv. 3 : lv. 1 : lviii. 11.   Ezek. xxxix. 29. Joel ii. 28, 29.   Zech. xii. 10 : xiv. 8, 16, &c.
(*l*) 1 St. Peter i. 11.   (*m*) St. John iv. 13, 14.
(*n*) Dr. Jackson.   (*o*) 1 St. Peter iv. 10.   (*p*) Ps. lxvi. 4.
(*q*) Williams, quoting Augustine and Ludolph.

for the HOLY GHOST was not yet *given ;* because that JESUS was not yet glorified.)

The allusion here to the great Pentecostal effusion(r) is unmistakable. "The Spirit" was a gift yet future,—something which believers "*should* receive." Hence it is said "*for* the HOLY GHOST was not yet given." The waters of Life would not flow till the Rock was smitten. It is the manner of St. John in this way *to allude* to events which he yet does not describe.(s)

Take notice also of that expression —"JESUS was not yet glorified." It is thus that not only St. John, but our SAVIOUR Himself, elsewhere speaks of His Triumph over Death, and His subsequent exaltation to the Right Hand of GOD.(t) Moreover, *that* out-pouring of the Spirit, which was to take place ten days after our LORD's Ascension into Heaven, He expressly makes *dependent* on His Ascension. "It is expedient for you that I go away," (He said to His sorrowing Disciples ;) "for if I go not away, the COMFORTER *will not come* unto you; but *if I depart, I* will send Him unto you."(u) This sequence and order is marked also in the sixty-seventh Psalm: "Thou hast ascended on high, Thou hast led captivity captive: *Thou hast received gifts for men.*"(v) — Hence the word "Because," in the text.

But verse 39 is parenthetical and explanatory. In the next verse we are informed what was the effect produced on our LORD's auditory by the very remarkable sayings in verses 37 and 38.

40 Many of the people therefore, when they heard this saying, said, Of a truth this is a Prophet.

Referring to the famous prediction in Deuteronomy xviii. 15, 18, — of a Prophet like unto Moses which GOD should raise up, in the latter days. Compare St. John i. 21, and the note there.

41 Others said, This is the CHRIST.

Hazarding a yet bolder confession : for it is found to have been a different one from the other.(x)

But some said, Shall CHRIST come out of Galilee ?

"Ever stifling, by the Scripture itself, the yearnings of Faith." A true sample this, of the World's wisdom in things spiritual,—knowing so much, yet knowing so little! Sufficiently clever in suggesting technical difficulties; not skillful enough to suggest their solution. Surely the dawn of the truth was discoverable even from Isaiah ix. 1, 2.

42 Hath not the Scripture said, That CHRIST cometh of the seed of David, and out of the town of Bethlehem, where David was ?

The objection thus raised against our LORD is a striking confirmation of the truth of what was offered above in a note on verse 27 ; for it is quite evident that a belief had firmly obtained that "JESUS of Nazareth" was *a native* of Galilee. Neither does it seem to have been generally known that the Husband of the Blessed Virgin claimed to be of "the House and Lineage of David." — The prophecies which had gone before respecting the Royal descent(y) and Birth-place of MESSIAH,(z) were in the meantime, a matter of notoriety.(a)—"Bethlehem, *where David was,*" seems to be said to distingush this Bethlehem from another in the Tribe of Zabulon. See the note on St. Matthew ii. 5.

43 So there was a division among the people because of Him.

(r) Acts ii. 1 to 4.
(s) As, to the institution of Baptism in chap. iii., and of the LORD's Supper in chap. vi.: to the Ascension, in chap. vi. 62 and xx. 17. In this place, to the Day of Pentecost.
(t) St. John xii. 16, (with which compare xiv. 26,) and xii. 23, (with which compare xvii. 1 and 5.) Also St. John xiii. 32. And consider such places as the following : St. Luke xxiv. 26. Rom. viii. 17. 1 St. Peter i. 11 : iv. 13 : v. 1, &c.   (u) St. John xvi. 7.
(v) Ps. lxviii. 18, quoted in Eph. iv. 7 to 12. See Acts ii. 33.   (x) St. John i. 20.
(y) 2 Sam. vii. 12 ; Jer. xxiii. 5, 6 : xxxiii. 15, 16 ; Ps. cxxxii. 11, &c. (z) Micah. v. 2.
(a) Acts ii. 30. Rom. i. 3, &c. Also St. Matth. ii. 6.

"His own prophecy began already to be fulfilled, that He came to send Division upon Earth: though God is not the Author of Confusion, but of Peace."(b)   See also St. John ix. 16, x. 19, and xii. 42.

44 And some of them would have taken Him; but no man laid hands on Him.

The allusion does not seem to be to those officers who were despatched in verse 32: for compare verse 30.   There doubtless was a large party of miscreants in Jerusalem, completely at the disposal of the Chief Priests and Pharisees; and who, at this very time, were ripe for those atrocities which six months after they perpetrated with greediness.(c)   But their purpose was overruled for the present by an unseen Arm; because the Hour appointed in the Divine Counsels for CHRIST's Death was not yet come.   See above, on verse 30.

In the meantime, the officers who (as we read in verse 32) were despatched to apprehend the Holy One return; and from the general tenor of all that follows, it would seem as if the Sanhedrin, (consisting of the Chief Priests and Pharisees,) were now assembled in Council.

45, 46 Then came the officers to the chief Priests and Pharisees; and they said unto them, Why have ye not brought Him?   The officers answered, Never man spake like this Man.

Take notice that they complain neither of want of opportunity, nor fear of the populace, as on a subsequent occasion they might have done.(d)   His innocence has disarmed them, and the majesty of His Discourse has made them afraid. "Never at any time so spake man as this Man speaketh." — The Doctrine, so unearthly: the eloquence, so convincing: the aspect, so awful: the manner, so divine. It is as if they said.—He is not Man, but God!   In short, they prefer braving the anger of their employers to incurring the danger of laying violent hands on such a Being.   Nay, they are converted into Apostles; and come back to the Sanhedrin, —preaching CHRIST!

47 Then answered them the Pharisees, Are ye also deceived?

For they wickedly called CHRIST a "Deceiver,"—that is "an Impostor."(e)   They seek to convince their servants of the error of believing in CHRIST, by appealing to the estimation in which He was held by their own learned body, (who perforce, it is implied, must be the best judges of such a matter;) asking with scorn,—

48, 49 Have any of the Rulers or of the Pharisees believed on Him?   But this people who knoweth not the Law are cursed.

This was their customary way of denouncing their unlearned brethren.   Take notice however that even "among the chief Rulers, many believed" in JESUS CHRIST already; "but because of the Pharisees, they did not confess Him, lest they should be put out of the Synagogue."(f)   The faith of Jaïrus,(g) of Joseph of Arimathæa, and perhaps of more(h) who are mentioned in the Gospel, remained therefore yet a secret.   The well-known name of a third member of the Sanhedrin follows.   He was present; and felt constrained to speak.

50, 51 Nicodemus saith unto them, (he that came to JESUS by night, being one of them,) Doth our Law judge *any* man, before it hear him, and know what he doeth?

Concerning Nicodemus, who was mentioned at first as a secret Disciple of CHRIST, and who now comes forward as His open Apologist,—(hereafter to show himself a bold Confessor likewise,) the reader is referred to the note on St. John iii. 2: and he is also requested to peruse the note on St. John iv. 46.—"Wisely appealing to

(b) Williams, quoting St. Luke xii. 51.   1 Cor. xiv. 33.
(c) Consider St. Matth. xxvii. 20.   St. Mark xv. 11.   (d) St. Luke xix. 47, 48.
(e) See above, on ver. 12.   (f) St. John xii. 42: see xix. 38.
          (g) Compare St. Mark v. 22 with St. Matth. ix. 18.
          (h) Consider St. Luke xvi. 1, and xviii. 18.

their own law,(*i*) and secretly pleased to find the officers so affected with awe, Nico-demus hoped that the Rulers themselves might, in like manner, be overcome by the presence of CHRIST."(*k*) Take notice that, instead of argument, certain members of their assembly assail their brother counseller with insult: asking, in derision, if they may attribute his taking of our LORD'S part, to the bond of a common Country.

52 They answered and said unto him, Art thou also of Galilee? Search and look: for out of Galilee ariseth no prophet.

Their taunt, in the original, runs thus,—"Surely, *thou* too art not of Galilee, [art thou?"] "Search and see," they add: that is,—"Search the Scriptures,"(*l*) and notice what is there written: for it is nowhere foretold "that the Prophet is to arise(*m*) out of Galilee;" in other words, "is to be born" there.

This is certainly what the speakers meant. They were far too learned not to know that many of "the goodly fellowship of the prophets" had been Galilæans,—as Elijah and Elisha, Jonah, Amos, Hosea, and Nahum.—In the meantime, the remonstrance of Nicodemus is found to have been attended with the result which he must have mainly intended; for the Council evidently broke up,—as usual with them, after the evening daily sacrifice. Accordingly, we read:

53 And every man went unto his own house.

But "JESUS" (it is added,) "went unto the Mount of Olives." Why then are those words severed from their context, and made the commencement of a new chapter?(*n*) The balance of the sentence is thereby destroyed; the affecting contrast between its two members, lost; and only half the Evangelist's meaning conveyed. What GOD had so joined together should not have been put asunder.

CHAPTER VIII.

1 CHRIST *delivereth the woman taken in adultery.* 12 He preacheth Himself the Light of the World, and justifieth His doctrine: 33 answereth the Jews that boasted of Abraham, 59 and conveyeth Himself from their cruelty.

1 JESUS went unto the mount of Olives.

Concerning the import of these few words, enough has been said at the close of the preceding chapter,—to which, in fact, they properly belong. It will be remembered that the time spoken of is "the last day, that great day of the Feast" of Tabernacles, — a Festival which marked the close of the Sacred year; and which, in this place, indicates the commencement of the last half-year of our LORD'S Ministry.

2, 3, 4 And early in the morning He came again into the Temple, and all the people came unto Him; and He sat down, and taught them. And the Scribes and Pharisees brought unto Him a woman taken in adultery; and when they had set her in the midst, they say unto Him, Master, this woman was taken in adultery, in the very act.

Concerning the position given to the accused person, compare Acts iv. 7. It

(*i*) To such places as Exod. xxiii. 1. Levit. xix. 15. Deut. i. 17: xix. 15.
(*k*) Williams.   (*l*) Compare St. John v. 39.
(*m*) The learned reader will perceive that this is one of the cases where the Vulgate discharges the office of a Commentary.
(*n*) See foot-note (*b*) on St. Mark ix. 1.

should be observed that her accusers belonged to the class which occupies such prominent notice in St. Matthew xxiii.

5 Now Moses in the law commanded us, that such should be stoned: but what sayest Thou?

"Thou,—who pretendest to have an authority greater than that of Moses?"(a) It is remarkable that this command is not found in the Pentateuch; which however mentions, that stoning should be the punishment for a *betrothed* person.(b) It must therefore have been the ancient gloss of the Scribes on Leviticus xx. 10,—which only declares that the guilty parties shall "be put to death;" without specifying how. This mode of punishing adultery appears however to be alluded to in Ezekiel xvi. 38, 40.

6 This they said, tempting Him, that they might have to accuse Him.

By which last words, the beloved Disciple explains the design of these sinful men in bringing the case of the woman taken in adultery before the Holy One. Remarkable indeed is the necessary inference from what is here revealed of their conduct and intentions: for it shows how just an opinion they had conceived of our SAVIOUR's clemency. What else was the difficulty to which they exposed Him? Why should He not have simply confirmed Moses' sentence, and so dismissed the case? But they had learned, by the experience of His past acts and saying, that it was improbable He would do so. "It was unlike His mercies to condemn; yet, if He did not, they would charge Him as a transgressor of the law. 'In the same net which they hid privily, is their foot taken,'"(c)—as we shall presently discover.

But JESUS stooped down, and with *His* finger wrote on the ground, *as though He heard them not.*

Take notice that the words in italics ("*as though He heard them not*") form no part of the sacred record. They are not the words of Inspiration; but the pious suggestion of some very ancient reader, who inscribed them in the margin of his copy of St. John's Gospel: and the Church has so far respected them, as to retain them to this day,—distinguished from the words of the Evangelist by the difference of type. The commentary thus supplied is indeed too valuable to be lost sight of. We read that our SAVIOUR was sitting at early morning in the Temple, and that He was teaching a multitude of persons. While thus engaged,—the hour and the place, the solemn Season and His Divine occupation, all suggesting thoughts of holiness and acts of forbearance, and words of love,—the Scribes and Pharisees suddenly enter; and disturb the flow of His heavenly teaching by a filthy accusation, and that confusion and excitement which are inseparable from public transactions of a semi-judicial nature like the present. Here was the accused and her many accusers,—powerful men attended by their servants and followers, as well as by a noisy rabble,—all crowding into the SAVIOUR's presence, and challenging His notice. Very striking therefore must have appeared the gesture of One who, at such a moment, could stoop down, and with His finger trace words on the dusty floor, as if heedless of what they were saying. His action must truly have been 'as though He heard them not." Viewed as conveying a lesson to ourselves, it seems to say—"Turn away mine eyes, lest they behold vanity."(d) What, however, may have been our Blessed SAVIOUR's purpose and meaning in thus "stooping down?" and what may He be supposed to have "written on the ground?" The matter is certainly obscure and difficult; but a clue to the entire mystery seems discoverable from a careful study of the ancient law concerning the punishment of an adulteress,—that law which was delivered to Moses by CHRIST Himself. A few suggestions on the subject will, however, be most conveniently submitted to the reader in a collected form, when we have reached the end of the present narrative. See below, the long note on the concluding words of verse 9. The accusers of the woman, in the meantime, are not to be so put off. They persevere in their inquiry, and will have an answer.

(a) Lonsdale and Hale: referring to St. Matth. v. 21, 22: 27, 28: 31, 32, &c.: xii. 8: xix. 9. (b) See Deut. xxii. 24. (c) Williams, quoting Ps. ix. 15. (d) Ps. cxix. 37.

7 So when they continued asking Him, He lifted up Himself, and said unto them, He that is without sin among you, let him first cast a stone at her.

Rather, "Let him that is without sin among you *be the first to cast his stone at her:*" for the Law which prescribed death by stoning, commanded likewise that "the hands of the witnesses should be first upon" the guilty one to put him to death, "and afterwards the hand of all the people."(*e*) It would seem as if these accusers had presented themselves before the great Judge, prepared to execute the sentence of the Law, and armed with the instruments of destruction.

8, 9 And again He stooped down, and wrote on the ground. And they which heard *it*, being convicted by *their own* conscience, went out one by one, beginning at the eldest, *even* unto the last:

How terrible a picture, by the way, of moral degradation! Can we read such things, and then wonder at the severity of our LORD's denunciations pronounced against these very men?(*f*) St. Matthew xii. 39 may therefore be taken literally! Consider also St. James iv. 4.

Take notice that He has neither condemned the Woman, nor yet absolved her. He has, in fact not answered the question of His hypocritical assailants at all; and yet He has defeated their malice, and ridded Himself of their molestation. Nay, He sends them away covered with shame; and yet it is not He that has condemned them, but they have been made to condemn themselves.

and JESUS was left alone, and the woman standing in the midst.

In the midst, probably, of that circle of attentive listeners whom our LORD was addressing when these hypocrites entered. And thus they stood,—" Misery and Mercy,—the pitiable one, and He that is Pity itself,—confronting each other."(*g*) "It was a fearful sentence, to stand before Him and to be forgiven!"(*h*) "There is mercy with Thee: therefore shalt Thou be feared."(*i*)

What, in the meantime, is to be said in the way of *interpretation* of the striking narrative which precedes? Observe that the matter in hand was the trial of a woman taken in adultery: but our LORD sees fit to treat the case as if it were what is called in the Law, "the trial of Jealousy." This trial by the bitter water (or water of conviction),(*k*) was a species of ordeal, intended by the ALMIGHTY for the vindication of innocence, and the conviction of guilt. There is reason for believing that, in common with many other enactments of the Divine Law, it had fallen into practical disuse at this time,—in consequence of the great prevalence of the special sin against which it was directed: but He who gave the Law is here found to enforce it; and *that*, after a divine and unexampled, as well as a wholly unexpected manner.

It is worth observing that, according to the Jewish tradition and belief, this test proved effectual only in the case of the woman whose husband was himself innocent of the crime with which he charged his wife. If *he* were just as guilty as herself, no conviction followed. This circumstance helps to explain the merciful treatment which the "woman taken in adultery" meets with at our LORD's hands. For it will be found that He exactly reverses the process which her accusers intended; and treats *them* as the accused party. Let the language of Numbers v. 16 to 24 be carefully considered; and then, the truth of what has been asserted will at once appear. We read:—"The priest shall bring her near," (that is, the accused woman,) "and set her before the LORD: and . . . take holy-water in an earthen vessel; and of the dust that is in the floor of the tabernacle the priest shall take, and put it into the water." "And the priest shall have in his hand the bitter water that causeth the curse; and . . . shall charge her by an oath, and say unto the woman, If no man have lain with thee, . . be thou free from this bitter water that causeth the curse: but if thou hast gone aside to another instead of thine husband, and if thou be defiled, . . . then the priest shall charge the woman with her oath of cursing" (which follows), "and the woman shall say, Amen, amen. And the priest shall write these

(*e*) Deut. xiii. 9 : xvii. 5 to 7.   (*f*) See all St. Matth. xxiii., especially ver. 27, 28.
(*g*) Augustine.   (*h*) Williams.   (*i*) Ps. cxxx. 4.
(*k*) So interpreted by the Septuagint in Numb. v. 18, 19, 23, 24.

curses in a book, and he shall blot them out with the bitter water ;(*l*) and he shall cause the woman to drink the bitter water that causeth the curse. And the water that causeth the curse shall enter into her, and become bitter." Thereupon, if the woman were guilty, she immediately fell under a visible penalty ; her body testifying terribly to her sin. If innocent, nothing followed. Such were the provisions of the Law.

And now, with all this before us, who sees not that our Blessed SAVIOUR has been dealing with these adulterous hypocrites exactly as if *they* had been the culprits, instead of the wretched woman whom they had dragged into His presence?

Terribly "near" to the incarnate JEHOVAH had they themselves been brought. Before Him they had been "set ;" and doubtless, when He stooped down and wrote upon the ground, it was a bitter sentence against the adulterer and adulteress which He wrote in "the dust of the floor of the tabernacle." We have but to assume that the words which he had thus traced on the ground, had some connection with the words which he uttered with His lips, and He will indeed have "taken of the lust and put it on the water," and "caused them to drink of the bitter water which causeth the curse!"

For, when by His Divine Spirit our Great High Priest addressed Himself to these adulterers,—what did He, but, (in the very phrase of the Apostle,) present them with living water,(*m*) "*in an earthen vessel ;*"— an expression which St. Paul explains to denote the "earthly tabernacle" of the body ?(*n*) Did not the Great Priest of the Temple further charge these men with an oath of cursing ; saying, "*If ye have not gone aside to uncleanness,* be ye free from this bitter water : but if ye have gone aside to others instead of your wives, and if ye be defiled,"—On which alternative being presented to them, did they not, self-convicted, go out one by one ? And what was this, but themselves pronouncing the acquittal of the sinful woman or whose condemnation they were, or seemed to be, so impatient ? for, according to their traditional belief of what happened in such cases, (as already explained,) she must perforce have submitted to the ordeal with impunity.

Meanwhile, our LORD is found to have resumed His former attitude and occupation. Did He continue writing on the ground the curses of the adulteress ; making the "floor of the Tabernacle" His "book ?" It seems likely that He did so ; and if He did, it would be no more than a mere matter of fact that in the case of the sinful woman before Him, He also *blotted out* those curses by her acquittal ; and, as one may say, with that very bitter water too which He had compelled her accusers to drink. For it follows :

10 When JESUS had lifted up Himself, and saw none but the woman, He said unto her, Woman, where are those thine accusers ? hath no man condemned thee ?

"Hath no one remained to demand the enforcement of the Law against thee ?"

11 She said, No man, LORD. And JESUS said unto her, Neither do I condemn thee : go, and sin no more.

Our LORD says not, "Neither do I condemn *thy sin ;*" but "Neither do I condemn *thee.*" Take notice also that He speaks of a judicial sentence,—*that* judicial sentence which He first inquired if no one else had enforced against the woman ? On being told that no man had done this, He declines, on this occasion, to assume the judicial office.(*o*) In the words of the heading of the chapter, He simply "*delivereth the Woman.*" The sin of Adultery He heavily condemns,(*p*) but this individual offender He is mercifully pleased to acquit,—an instance of His clemency, which, like His forgiveness of the repentant malefactor, cannot but prove a source of unspeakable consolation to us all.

Strange, that this entire history, (from chap. vii. ver. 53 to ver. 11 of the present chapter inclusive,) should be found wanting in so many ancient manuscripts of the Gospels! The inference is obvious,—namely, either that men must have suspected the authenticity of the passage, or that they must have dreaded lest so merciful a

---

(*l*) That is, he was to write the curse so superficially, that by pouring water over it the writing was to disappear.
(*m*) So the ancient Greek version renders "holy water" in Numb. 17.
(*n*) 2 Cor. iv. 7, and v. 1.　　　　　　　　　(*o*) So also in St. Luke xii. 13, 14.
(*p*) As in St. Matth. v. 27 to 32.

sentence should prove productive of evil in the Church of CHRIST. But who and what are *we* that we should presume thus to judge of the Work of the SPIRIT? "It is GOD that justifieth. Who is he that condemneth?"(q) What know we of this woman's age, history, character, mind, heart? The reader is invited to refer to some remarks on this subject which have been already offered in the note on St. John iv. 20.

The chief lessons derivable from the present narrative seem to be (1st,) one of solemn warning to ourselves against the condemnation of others ;—(2d,) one of encouragement to the greatest of offenders, never to despair of forgiveness :—(3d,) one of exhortation to all ; for we are hereby reminded that the very condition of mercy, is to "*sin no more.*" Compare St. John v. 14.—" By occasion of " this woman, the Holy One showeth, (as is said in the heading of St. Luke vii.) "how He is a friend to sinners, not to maintain them in sins, but to forgive them their sins, upon their Faith and Repentance."

Whether what follows took place at the same time as what precedes, does not appear. The locality was the same,—as we learn from ver. 20 ; and there are some allusions in our LORD's discourse which recall the scene of the preceding incident; but on the whole, it seems to belong to another occasion ; for observe, it begins: "Then spake JESUS *again* unto them." It may have occurred somewhat later in the same day.

12 Then spake JESUS again unto them, saying, I am the Light of the World : he that followeth Me shall not walk in darkness, but shall have the Light of Life.

"The Light of the World!" This title our LORD assumes in the manner of the Doctors of His nation ;(r) with a propriety of which they could have no conception, and with a sublimity surpassing even our own assisted powers of thought. But the chief thing to be noticed is, that He hereby claims to Himself one of the well-known appellations of the MESSIAH. Consider Isaiah xlii. 6, xlix. 6, and lx. 3; and see the end of note on St. John x. 24.

Some remarks will be found upon this highly significant title, which our SAVIOUR claims on many occasions, in the Commentary on St. John ix. 5, to which the reader is accordingly referred ; but he is requested to take notice that the aspect of this appellation there enlarged upon, is not precisely the aspect which gives it such peculiar propriety *here.* In *this* place it seems to have reference to what has immediately gone before. Our SAVIOUR had been making manifest the filthy wickedness of the Scribes and Pharisees: now, "*whatsoever doth make manifest is Light.*"(s) See what has been said on the subject of "Darkness" in the note on St. John xii. 35 ; and compare the entire place with St. John xii. 46, 35, and 36.

13 The Pharisees therefore said unto Him, Thou bearest record of Thyself ; Thy record is not true.

These sinful men, (members of the sect already mentioned in ver. 3, but probably not the same individuals,) allude to a well-known precept of the Law, which allowed not that any should bear testimony for himself. In His Discourse on a former occasion, our SAVIOUR had anticipated them in their present sentence: "If I bear witness of Myself," (He said,) " My witness is not true."(t) He proceeded however on that occasion, as he proceeds on this, to show that His record is true, —even though he bears it of Himself: for that, in effect, it was the Eternal FATHER who bare Him record.

14 JESUS answered and said unto them, Though I bear record of Myself, *yet* My record is true : for I know whence I came, and whither I go ; but ye cannot tell whence I come, and whither I go.

That is,—Even though I, the SON of GOD, bear record of Myself, My record is true : for I have a true and perfect knowledge concerning My own mysterious nature and origin, My present mission, and My everlasting purposes,—a knowledge not liable to error, as all human evidence is. " But ye know not" (for so the words

(q) Rom. viii. 33, 34.   (r) See the notes on St. John iii. 19.
(s) Eph. v. 13. Consider verses 8 to 14.   (t) St. John v. 31.

should be translated) "whence I come and whither I go." "Take notice that Christ says He must *go back* to the place from whence He declares that He first *came; that is, back to Heaven, from whence He had been 'sent.' By 'coming,' therefore, from that region whence Man cannot come, He shows that He is God."(*u*)

15 Ye judge after the flesh; I judge no man.

He spoke in ver. 14 of His Testimony. Here, He speaks of His Judgment; and He contrasts it with theirs,—which, He says, is "after the flesh;" that is, founded in external evidence, and the mere appearance of things. With this fallible judgment they presumed to judge even Him: and their judgment was false; for in consequence of their own carnal mind, they looked upon Him as mere Man.—"I judge no one," our LORD proceeds: by which He seems to imply that His season of Judgment is yet future.(*v*) This will be found more fully noticed below, in the note on ver. 26. Is there, perhaps, a passing allusion in that saying to the case of the Woman taken in adultery, whom He had neither judged nor condemned?

16 And yet if I judge, My judgment is true: for I am not alone, but I and the FATHER that sent Me.

Thus He gives His hearers a nearer insight into His own mysterious Nature, whereby He was one with the FATHER. The present statement recurs below, in ver. 29.(*x*) Compare the entire verse with St. John ver. 30.

Our SAVIOUR proceeds to apply this great Doctrine to the matter in hand; and very surprising is the use which He makes of it.

17 It is also written in your Law, that the testimony of two men is true.

Referring to Deuteronomy xvii. 6, and xix. 15.

18 I am One that bear witness of Myself, and the FATHER that sent Me beareth witness of Me.

When our LORD says that the FATHER bears witness of Him, He means chiefly by the miraculous Works which the FATHER gave the SON to do: as it is elsewhere said,—"The Works which the FATHER hath given Me to finish, the same Works that I do, *bear witness of Me, that the FATHER hath sent Me*."(*y*) And again, "the FATHER that dwelleth in ME, He doeth the Works."(*z*) The twofold testimony therefore to which our SAVIOUR here appeals is, (1st,) His own declarations concerning Himself: (2ndly,) His Miracles, which were a proof that the FATHER was with Him. And herein we have the witness of *two* Persons; because "there one Person of the FATHER, another of the SON."

This will be at once felt to be a surprising method of reasoning. The enemies of CHRIST would of course deny the validity of the argument. His works (they would say) were inseparable from Himself: and His own witness in such a case, (as they had already declared,)(*a*) was inadmissible.—We are reminded of a remark already elsewhere offered, that the Divine Logic is always perplexing. It has a lofty marvellousness of its own; and reminds Faith herself that she has many lessons yet to learn. Above all, it convinces her, how little she understands that Scripture for which she professes so great a reverence. CHRIST unfolds the Book,—nay, His very Apostles unfold it,—and straightway their remarks are unlooked for,(*b*) their reasoning improbable,(*c*) their comment unearthly.(*d*) Things little suspected are found to be lying on the surface of that familiar page; and we are driven to theories of Allusion and Accommodation in excuse and apology for the blessed speaker, but in reality to cover our own ignorance of the Book of Life. See what has been already offered on this subject in the notes on St. Mark xii. 27, and St. Luke iv. 6.

(*u*) Novatian, A.D. 250.　　　　　　　　　　　(*v*) So Augustine and Chrysostom.
(*x*) See also St. John x. 38: xiv. 10, 11, 20: xvi. 32: xvii. 21 to 23.
(*y*) St. John v. 36. Compare also x. 37, 38, and xiv. 10, 11.
(*z*) St. John xiv. 10.　　　　　　　　　　　　　(*a*) See above, verse 13.
(*b*) As in St. Luke xvii. 32: St. Matthew ii. 23, and in 2 Cor. viii. 15: Hebrews iv. 4.
(*c*) As in St. Mark xii. 27, (where see the note,) and 1 Cor. x. 1 to 6.
(*d*) As in this place: St. Matthew viii. 17, and in Romans x. 4 to 10: Gal. iv. 21 to 31: 1 Cor. i. 9 to 11: Hebrews ii. 5 to 9.

Concerning the place in Deuteronomy referred to, in ver. 17, we will but suggest (in the words of a pious writer) "that those words of the Law respecting the two witnesses, do refer to the Doctrine of the Trinity, and the twofold Witness of the FATHER and the SON, before the HOLY GHOST was yet given, who was the Third Witness. For, on referring to the passage in Deuteronomy, we find that it is said 'two *or three* witnesses:'(e) and may not the words 'or three' be here dropped in our LORD's statement for the reason assigned; namely, that the Third Witness had not yet been brought forward?"(f)   Certain it is that on the other occasion when our SAVIOUR referred to the same enactment, (namely, in St. Matthew xviii. 16,) He failed not to notice the exact terms in which it was originally delivered.— "How" (asks the greatest of the Fathers) "must we understand the precept— 'By the mouth of two or three witnesses, shall every word be established,' except as an intimation of the mystery of the Trinity, in which is perpetual stability of Truth ?(g)

Whatever may be thought of this suggestion, it is a plain matter of fact that our LORD's reasoning is such as we have described it to have been. Moreover, whether satisfactory to His audience or not, it was evidently meant to be conclusive. Nothing remains, therefore, but that we should meditate upon it humbly and reverently. The only rejoinder which His enemies ventured to make in reply, cannot find place on *our* lips.

19 Then said they unto Him, Where is Thy FATHER ?

Thus do they immediately afford evidence of that carnal judgment with which our SAVIOUR had charged them in ver. 15.(h) They suppose He speaks of a human Parent; just as, in ver. 32, they suppose that He speaks of deliverance from bodily servitude; and, in ver. 53, of deliverance from temporal Death. The present is, in fact, rather a scoff than a question ; and our LORD treats it accordingly.

JESUS answered, Ye neither know Me, nor My FATHER.

"As if He said,—Ye ask, Where is My FATHER? as if ye knew *Me* already, and I were nothing else but what ye see. But ye know Me not; and therefore I tell you nothing of My FATHER. Ye think Me indeed a mere Man, and therefore among men look for My FATHER. But inasmuch as I am different altogether, according to My seen and unseen natures, and speak of My FATHER in the hidden sense according to My hidden nature; it is plain that ye must first know Me, and then ye will know My FATHER."(i)

if ye had known Me, ye would have known My FATHER also.

"Which expression, of course, implies Unity of Substance : for it cannot properly be said of any one, that in knowing him, you know another, unless they both are one. Much less can it be said that in knowing the creature, ye know the Creator. How striking and beautiful the change in the tone and language, when the same occurs with one of the Disciples in humble inquiry!—' If ye had known Me, ye should have known My FATHER also. . . . Philip saith unto Him, LORD, show us the FATHER, and it sufficeth us. JESUS saith unto him, Have I been so long time with you, and yet hast thou not known Me, Philip? He that hath seen Me, hath seen the FATHER.' "(k)

20 These words spake JESUS in the Treasury, as He taught in the Temple : and no man laid hands on Him; for His hour was not yet come.

CHRIST spake thus, openly, in that part of the Temple which was called the "Treasury ;" "and yet no one laid hands on Him ;" and the mysterious reason is added, which will be found already discussed in the note on St. John vii. 6.—The Court of the Women was called by this name, because the gold and silver vessels of the Temple were kept there. This had been the scene of the interview with the woman taken in adultery.

And thus ends this portion of our LORD's Divine Teaching. "That Discourse of

(e) Deuteronomy xix. 15.   (f) Williams.   Consider 1 St. John v. 6 to 9.
(g) Augustine.   (h) Augustine.   (i) Augustine.
(k) Williams, quoting St. John xiv. 7 to 9.

Light of the World," (says Bp. Pierson,) "was in the Treasury. That which weth, was not: at least, appeareth not to be so."

1 Then said JESUS again unto them, I go My way, and ye shall t Me, and shall die in your sins: whither I go, ye cannot come.

nder the name of "departing," (or as the word is here rendered "going His ,") our SAVIOUR speaks of His approaching Death and Resurrection: thereby nating that submission to Death was the act of His own free-will. This he "again;" having already said it in chap. vii. 33, 34, — where the notes may be ulted. Or the word "again" may have reference to the occasion on which the ls before us were spoken; which was perhaps subsequent to that specified in 20.—"Ye shall die in your sins" will be found repeated below, in ver. 24, and ained by our LORD himself.

2 Then said the Jews, Will He kill Himself? because He saith, ither I go, ye cannot come.

ir SAVIOUR's announcement to His enemies that, Whither He went, they would it impossible to follow Him, perplexes them now as it perplexed them before: the solution which they now propose of the difficulty, is not the same which before proposed. Compare this place with St. John vii. 35.

8 And He said unto them, Ye are from beneath; I am from above: are of this World; I am not of this World.

iese words seem to be a continuation of the discourse which the Jews inter-ed when they asked the question contained in ver. 22. Without alluding to so ous a matter as His Humanity, (in respect of which, He *was* "from beneath,") SAVIOUR declares concerning Himself, as GOD, that He is "from above," and t of this World:" contrasting thereby His Divine Nature with that of His al persecutors; and implying that He would deliver Himself out of the hands lis enemies by at last transferring Himself to that region of Light and Glory which He originally came, and which was in fact His proper home. Consider , in chap. iii. 13, He is found to have declared, even in the days of His Humi-on, that "the Son of Man *is in Heaven;*" on which place, see the note. Of this World" and "not of this World" are not merely words explanatory of g "from beneath" and "from above;" but they describe and contrast *the* acter of CHRIST and of His assailants. They should be compared with what is d in St. John xv. 19, xvii. 14, and 1 St. John iv. 5; and will be perceived to ly a connecting link with what immediately follows:

4 I said therefore unto you, that ye shall die in your sins: for if believe not that I am *He*, ye shall die in your sins.

ius then our SAVIOUR explains what He had said in ver. 21. It is found that any as are "of the World," inasmuch as "therefore speak they of the World,"(*l*) ither words, inasmuch as they are "earthly and speak of the Earth;"(*m*) and that wisdom which is not from above, are "earthly, sensual, devilish;"(*n*) — men believe not in CHRIST, and by consequence "die in their sins." it our LORD's saying, in strictness, runs thus,—"If ye believe not that I AM:" h recalls the observation already offered on St. John vi. 20.(*o*)

5 Then said they unto Him, Who art Thou?

ith that blindness which is ever the mark of the carnal mind, these sinners do recognize the Divine Name, even when they hear it pronounced by CHRIST elf. And yet they have heard all that Moses heard, when he inquired of the : Second Person in the Blessed Trinity concerning His Name!(*p*)

nd JESUS saith unto them, Even *the same* that I said unto you from beginning.

1 St. John iv. 5.   (*m*) St. John iii. 31.   (*n*) St. James iii. 15.
See below, the note on ver. 58.   (*p*) See Exodus iii. 14.

The Greek properly implies "What I am saying unto you all along from the beginning;" — in less classical English, "what I said at first, and what I keep on ever since saying unto you."

Take notice that our Saviour had again and again declared to the Jews His Divine Origin, the union of the Divine and Human Natures in His One Person, His Mission from the Father, and the purpose of His Coming into the World : together with whatever else it can profit a man to know for his soul's health. A glance over the fifth, sixth, and eighth chapters of the present Gospel will abundantly establish this. — He proceeds:

26 I have many things to say and to judge of you: but He that sent Me is true ; and I speak to the World those things which I have heard of Him.

This seems to mean that though the Divine Speaker had a heavy witness to bear against the men of that generation ; and a terrible judgment hereafter to pronounce upon them, yet, the season for Judgment had not arrived. "I judge no man," as our Saviour said in ver. 15. Or, as He here proceeds — "But He that sent Me is true;" implying thereby that God would be faithful to fulfill his promises, and execute His purposes of Mercy. Now, 'God sent not His Son into the World to condemn the World ; but that the World through Him might be saved."(q) "The Father sent the Son to be the Saviour of the World."(r) "If any man hear My words," (saith Christ,) "and believe not, I judge him not: for I came not to judge the World, but to save the World."(s) The Holy One speaks of His first Advent. At His second Coming, He will appear as the Judge of quick and dead :(t) "for the Father judgeth no man, but hath committed all judgment unto the Son."(u)

Concerning the concluding words of this verse, ("I spake to the World those things which I have heard of Him,") the reader is referred to a long note on St. John v. 20. It is obvious to compare the place with St. John iii. 11, 32, and xv. 15.

27 They understood not that He spake to them of the Father.

28 Then said Jesus unto them, When ye have lifted up the Son of Man, then shall ye know that I am He, and that I do nothing of Myself; but as My Father has taught Me, I speak these things.

Our Lord here prophecies that from the period of His Crucifixion, the Jewish people should begin to recognize His Divinity ; and so we find they did.(x) To be "lifted up," was a well-known phrase for being "crucified," — as we have already explained elsewhere.(y) The rest of the verse has been sufficiently commented upon in the note on St. John v. 20, which has been more than once referred to.

29 And He that sent Me is with Me: the Father hath not left Me alone ; for I do always those things that please Him.

By such statements it seems ever to have been the intention of the Divine Speaker to correct any erroneous opinions which the imperfection of language might have caused His hearers to entertain concerning Himself. Thus, in verses 26 and 29, our Saviour had said that He was "sent:" and in ver. 28, that He "did nothing of Himself," but "spake as He was taught of the Father." It became necessary to add that the Father, who sent, had not thereby separated Himself from the Son, who was sent; but was "with" Him. This doctrine has been already opened in ver. 16, where see the note.

And the words, "for I do always those things that please Him," express not the cause why the Father leaveth not the Son alone, the consequence, or rather the evidence of that inseparable union of Natures. The same thing is here said, in effect, which is said in St. John v. 19, — namely, that "what things soever [the

---

(q) St. John iii. 17.   (r) 1 St. John iv. 14.   (s) St. John xii. 47.
(t) Acts x. 42: xvii. 31. 2 Cor. v. 10. 2 Tim. iv. 1. 1 St. Pet. iv. 5.
(u) St. John v. 22: and see ver. 27.
(x) Consider such places as the following: St. Matth. xxvii. 54. St. Luke xxiii. 48. Acts ii. 41: vi. 7: xii. 24: xix. 20, &c.
(y) See the note on St. John iii. 15. The attentive reader will perceive that our Saviour's words on this occasion are alluded to by the people, in St. John xii. 34.

'ATHER] doeth, these also doeth the SON likewise." The note on that famous
scripture passage must be again referred to.

30 As He spake these words, many believed on Him.

This becomes a very striking statement when it is considered that the meaning
f our LORD's prophecy in ver. 28 was perfectly well understood by His auditory.
ee the note on St. John vii. 31 : and for an enumeration of the places in this
Gospel, where the Church's growth and increase is recorded, the reader is referred
) the note on the last words of St. John ii. 11. He may also be invited to read the
ote on the last verse of chap. x.
Bp. Pearson considered it " very probable that a new Discourse is again begun"
t this place.

**31 Then said JESUS to those Jews which believed on Him, If ye
ontinue in my Word, *then* are ye My Disciples indeed :**

Observe how prompt He is to sustain the first beginnings of Faith ! There had
een many Disciples before now, who "went back, and walked no more with
lim,"(z)—men whose Faith had suddenly declined and perished under the trial of
ard doctrine. Our LORD therefore reminds "those Jews which believed on Him,"
rat truly to be His Disciples, they must "*abide* in His Word." Consider, in con-
ection with this, St. John xv. 4 to 7, and see the notes there.
It may be worth the while of any Christian man to notice, as he reads the Bible,
'hat amazing stress is laid throughout on Perseverance *to the end*.(a) Patience
rust " have her *perfect* work."(b) But this circumstance has been already pointed
ut in the Commentary on St. Matthew x. 22 and xxiv. 13. — The privilege which
rould result from being " Disciples indeed," follows.

**32 And ye shall know the Truth, and the Truth shall make you
ree.**

"This is Life Eternal," (saith our LORD,) " that they may know Thee the only
rue GOD, and JESUS CHRIST whom Thou hast sent :"(c) to know Him, namely, who
mphatically styles Himself "the Way, *the Truth*, and the Life."(d)
And why is CHRIST called " the Truth ?" Not only because His Doctrine is true ;
rat because all the types and shadows of the Law point to Him as their object ;
rhile in Him all the promises of GOD, made to the ancient Fathers, find their com-
letion and fulfillment.
The nature of the "freedom" which was to follow from the knowledge of the
fruth is deserving of our best attention. The very term implies a state of slavery
rom which men are to be liberated. It is from the bondage of Sin that our
laVIOUR here promises His Disciples that they shall be released. See ver. 34.

**33 They answered Him, We be Abraham's seed, and were never in
iondage to any man : how sayest Thou, Ye shall be made free ?**

These men cannot rise above the letter of our LORD's Discourse, but put a carnal
ense on every sublime truth which He delivers. Even so, however, they boast
alsely : for had not their Fathers been in bondage,—first, in Egypt ; then " by the
raters of Babylon ?" Were they not themselves, even now, tributary to the Ro-
aans ?—The echo of that boast of theirs, " We be Abraham's seed," will be found
iot to die away until the end of the present chapter.

**34 JESUS answered them, Verily, verily, I say unto you, Whosoever
iommitteth sin is the servant of Sin.**

"For by whom a man is overcome," writes the Apostle Peter, (discoursing of the
'servants of corruption,") "unto the same is he also brought in bondage."(e)
This is the only slavery of which CHRIST would have men ashamed ; and truly, it

(z) St. John vi. 66.
(a) It will be found worth while to refer to Ps. cxix. 33, 112. St. Luke xi. 28. 1 Cor. xv.
, 2. Col. i. 23. Heb. iii. 6, 14 : vi. 11. Rev. ii. 26, &c.
(b) St. James i. 4.   (c) St. John xvii. 3.   (d) St. John xiv. 6.
(e) 2 St. Pet. ii. 19.

is the most terrible bondage of any. The reader will readily call to mind a multitude of passages, from either Testament, where, under the metaphor of enslavement, the subjection of the soul to the Law of Sin is described.(*f*)

35 And the servant abideth not in the House forever : *but* the Son abideth ever.

Thus Moses, however "faithful in all his House as a servant," makes way for CHRIST "as a Son over His own House."(*g*)   And we know that the Hebrew slave was dismissed at the end of seven years of servitude.(*h*)   By this casual allusion therefore to the practice of His people under the Law, our SAVIOUR glances prophetically at the destiny of the Jewish nation.   "Cast out the bondwoman and her son," (was the language of one who lived under the ancient Covenant:) "for the son of the bondwoman shall not be heir with the son of the freewoman."(*i*)   Ishmael must accordingly make way for Isaac,—the Jews for ourselves ; inasmuch as "we, as Isaac was . . . . are not children of the bondwoman, but of the free."(*j*)   The Holy One here seems to make a tacit allusion to the history of Isaac and Ishmael.

"Yet it is not the Bondage of the Law which is here being discoursed of, but the Bondage of Sin. 'The Truth' is not opposed to legal shadows, but to worldly deceits."   CHRIST is therefore emphatically "*the SON*" here spoken of, who alone can give us "sonship and freedom, as being Himself sinless among sinners: made a slave, in order that we might become sons: 'made sin for us'(*k*) to redeem us from the power of sin: dying that we might live for ever."(*l*)   Consider Galatians iv. 4 to 7. It follows,—

36 If the Son therefore shall make you free, ye shall be free indeed.

"Our LORD having compared the habitual sinner to a slave,(*m*) here continues the comparison ; and intimates to His hearers that as the slave had not that right which the son and heir of the family had, of remaining for ever in the house where he dwelt, and of enjoying all its privileges, so the Jews could not have a right to remain in the Family of His FATHER, unless He, the SON, should *make them free* from Bondage, and admit them to be partakers with Him of the privileges of sons."(*n*)   Consider St. John i. 12.

37 I know that ye are Abraham's seed; but ye seek to kill Me, because My Word hath no place in you.

Our LORD thus reverts to their boast in verse 33; and He is about to convict them of that sinfulness which He laid to their charge in verse 34. This He will do distinctly below, in verse 40. — In the meantime, take notice that the reason why these murderers were bent on destroying CHRIST, was because His Heavenly Doctrine found no place in their hearts. He proceeds:

38 I speak that which I have seen with My FATHER : and ye do that which ye have seen with your Father.

Namely, the Devil, — as He will be found to explain in verse 44. All this, our LORD seems to have added lest they should impute to His Doctrine the blame which was wholly due to themselves. Accordingly, in language which has already been sufficiently explained,(*o*) He vindicates the Divine origin of the one, and denounces the infernal authorship of the other.

39 They answered and said unto Him, Abraham is our Father.

"Not fully understanding, it appears, but suspecting that He spake of some one beside Abraham." Take notice that we have here the ancient boast of the degenerate sons of Abraham,—referred to by the forerunner,(*p*) and in what follows, solemnly refuted by MESSIAH Himself.

(*f*) See Ps. xi. 12.   Prov. v. 22.   Rom. vi. 12 to the end of the chapter: viii. 21, &c.
(*g*) Heb. iii. 5, 6.   (*h*) Deut. xv. 12.
(*i*) Gal. iv. 30, quoting Gen. xxi. 10.   (*j*) Gal. iv. 28 and 31.
(*k*) 2 Cor. v. 21.   (*l*) Altered from Williams.
(*m*) See above, ver. 34.   (*n*) Lonsdale and Hale.
(*o*) See above, the notes on ver. 26, 27.   (*p*) See St. Matth. iii. 9, and St. Luke iii. 8.

JESUS saith unto them, If ye were Abraham's children, ye would do ₃ works of Abraham.

"If ye were Abraham's children, so as to inherit the promise made unto Abram:" thus, interpreting the promise which He had Himself made to that Patriɪh, and to his seed, almost two thousand years before! And to the same purpose, ₃ Apostle Paul: "Not as though the Word of GOD hath taken none effect. For ₃y are not all Israel, which are of Israel: *neither, because they are the seed of ₃aham, are they all children:* but, '*In Isaac* shall thy seed be called.' That is, ₃y which are the children of the flesh, these are not the children of GOD: but the ɪldren of the promise are counted for the seed."(q) As the same Apostle else₃ere writes,—"they which are of Faith, the same are the children of Abraham."(r)

ɪn the controversy so often senselessly waged concerning *Faith* and *Works*, are ₃n careful to remember that our SAVIOUR Himself appeals to "*the Works* of Abra₃m?"—that is, to his obedience,(s) his piety,(t) his patience,(u) his resignation; ₃ve all, to his daily walk of Faith?

40 But now ye seek to kill Me, a Man that hath told you the truth ɪɪch I have heard of GOD: this did not Abraham.

ɔur LORD assigns the reason of their enmity. It was because He had delivered ₃hem *Divine Doctrine:* "the truth which I have heard *of GOD*." And these ₃ words declare more than is found in verses 26 and 28. Coupled with those ₃lier statements, here is our SAVIOUR's express declaration that 'GOD is His ₃HER.—" The condemnation of the Jews was, that they saw a Holy Man, with ₃dence that He came from GOD, and that GOD was with Him;" but received Him ₃ If they had but received Him then, as such, the higher doctrines of the Incarna₃n, and Atonement, of His Godhead, and of the SPIRIT, would have followed."(v) ɔrigen has a striking remark on this verse. " To some it might seem superflu₃ to say that Abraham did not seek to kill CHRIST; for it was impossible, since ₃IST was not born at that time. But the Saints were never without the spiritual ₃vent of CHRIST. I understand then from this passage that every one who, after ₃generation, and other divine graces bestowed upon him, commits sin, does by his re₃n to evil, incur the guilt of crucifying the SON of GOD; which Abraham did not do." '*Abraham sought not to kill Me*; *but ye do seek*." Presently(x) we shall read, ₃braham rejoiced to see My Day;" *but* (it is implied) *ye rejoice not.* " Ye do that ₃ did not: ye do not that he did. How can these be Abraham's sons? Those are ₃ons that do as he did !"(y)

Now, since men are said to be the children of him whom they resemble in their ₃ions, (as our LORD explained in His Sermon on the Mount,)(z) He proceeds at ₃e to assign the terrible parentage of the men who sought His life.

41 Ye do the deeds of your Father.

' Our LORD says this with a view to put down their vain boasting of their de₃nt; and persuade them to rest their hopes of Salvation no longer on the natural ₃ationship, but on the Adoption. For this it was which prevented them from ₃ning to CHRIST,—namely, their thinking that their relationship to Abraham was ₃cient for their Salvation."(a)

Then said they to Him, We be not born of fornication we have one ₃ther, *even* GOD.

ɾhey reply that they are not a race of idolaters, who worship many gods, and ₃rd them as fathers: but that they had one Father, even GOD.(b) ₃o long as they understand our LORD to speak of natural descent, these men claim ₃e the seed of Abraham. But when they discover that His words are to be taken ₃ spiritual sense, they straightway claim to be sons of the true GOD. " Not born ₃rnication," is a phrase plain enough to those who remember the constant sense ₃e same metaphor in the writings of the Prophets:(c) but the boast of the Jews

q) Rom. ix. 6 to 8. (r) Gal. iii. 7. (s) Heb. xi. 8. Gen. xxii. 2, 3.
t) Gen. xviii. 17 to 23: xxiv. 2, &c. &c. (u) Gen. xii. 4 and xvii. 1.
v) Williams. (x) In verse 56. (y) Bp. Andrewes.
z) St. Matth. v. 44, 45. (a) Chrysostom. (b) Lonsdale and Hale.
(c) As Isaiah i. 21. Jer. iii. 8, 9, 14: xxxi. 32. Hos. ii. 4. See Judges ii. 17, &c. &c.

in respect of their *spiritual* sonship, was as vain as their reliance on their descent from Abraham. The evangelical Prophet had called their Fathers, "the seed of the adulterer and the whore ;"(d) and our LORD Himself repeatedly denounced them as "an adulterous generation."(e)

"In this, (says the beloved Disciple,) "the children of GOD are manifest, and the children of the Devil ; whosoever doeth not Righteousness is not of GOD:"(f) whereas "every one that doeth Righteousness is born of Him."(g)   "He that committeth sin is of the Devil."(h)

42 JESUS said unto them, If GOD were your FATHER, ye would love me : for I proceeded forth and came from GOD ;

Rather, "and am come."   By *proceeding forth* from GOD," our LORD, "whose goings forth have been from of old, from Everlasting,"(i) declares his Eternal Generation: by "being *come*," He declares his Incarnation.   Compare and consider that place in Hebrews, quoted from Psalm xl. 7,—" Lo, *I am come* to do Thy will, O GOD ;"(j) which, as the Apostle remarks, is what "*when He cometh into the World, He saith.*"(k)   The reader is also requested to refer to the two following places in the present Gospel,—chap. xvi. 28 and xvii. 8.

neither came I of Myself, but He sent Me.

The Hebrew idiom of these words need not be further remarked upon.(l)   But observe our LORD's ever-recurring declaration that He was "sent" by the Eternal FATHER ;(m) and consider whether the absolute need of ecclesiastical mission, by one duly authorized to send, is not thereby indirectly implied and enforced.   As says the Apostle,—" How shall they preach, *except they be sent ?*"(n)

43 Why do ye not understand My speech, *even* because ye cannot hear My Word.

That is—" What is the reason that ye find My Discourse unintelligible?   It is because ye have so hardened your hearts that ye are no longer able to receive My Doctrine."

44 Ye are of *your* Father the Devil, and the lusts of your Father ye will do.

Rather,—" ye desire to do :" "ye are bent on doing."   For example, they desired to slay CHRIST, "as Cain, *who was of that wicked one,* slew his brother.   And wherefore slew he him ?   Because his own works were evil, and his brother's righteous."(o)   These murderers were therefore actuated by the self-same motive as Cain.(p)   Here then our SAVIOUR explains what He had only hinted at before, in verses 38 and 41 ; namely, that the Devil was the Father of this "generation of Vipers."(q)   The reader should connect with the present passage such places as St. Matthew xiii. 38.   Acts xiii. 10.   1 St. John iii. 8.—Our LORD adds a few solemn words concerning Satan, the chief of the fallen Angels, and the author of the ruin of our race,—to destroy whose works, is declared to have been the great purpose of our LORD's manifestation in the Flesh ;(r) and concerning whom, every syllable which CHRIST Himself hath spoken cannot but be of most awful interest to ourselves.

He was a murderer from the beginning, and abode not in the Truth, because there is no Truth in him.

"A murderer," because he brought death into the World by Adam's transgression : and to this he seduced our first parents by a lie.(s)

But those words, "he abode not in the Truth," imply far more than this. They

---

(d) Isa. lvii. 3.
(e) St. Matth. xii. 39 : xvi. 4.   St. Mark viii. 38.   See the note on St. John viii. 9.
(f) 1 St. John iii. 10.   (g) 1 St. John ii. 29.   (h) 1 St. John iii. 8.
(i) Micah v. 2.   (j) Heb. x. 7, 9.   (k) Heb. x. 5.
(l) See the notes on St. Matth. ix. 13, and the end of the note on St. John v. 30, &c.
(m) See the note (c) at foot of p. 668.   (n) Rom. x. 15.
(o) 1 St. John iii. 12.   (p) See above the note on ver. 40.
(q) See the note on St. Matth. xii. 34.   (r) 1 St. John iii. 8.
(s) Gen. iii. 4.

s, in fact, a glorious vindication of God's Justice, and a formal assertion of the rightness in which Satan (like the rest of his peers,) was originally created by in. And hereby the intricate and insoluble question of the Origin of Evil is ened; "on which deep subject all that we are given to know is that while to oral and intellectual agents freedom of choice is an inseparable attribute, *that* iedom implies the possibility of an evil choice; while an evil choice once admitted d uncured, leads to interminable disorder, confusion, and wrong in the spiritual ation; and intercepts those communications of Goodness from the original Source, which alone the moral constitution is preserved in virtue and in happiness. iat such was the case with Satan, Christ has Himself told us in one word; in ying that he was a murderer and liar from the beginning, simply because he *ode not* in the Truth; that is, *in the Truth and rectitude of his original Crea-n.*"(*t*) He was the Leader of those "Angels which *kept not their first estate.*"(*u*)

When he speaketh a lie he speaketh of his own: for he is a liar and e father of it.

This either means, "When he gives utterance to falsehood, he speaks from the states of his own nature; for he is a liar and the father of lying:" or it may an, "When any of you speaks falsehood, he speaks after the manner of his kin-ed; for his father also is a liar." But the former interpretation, which is the ore obvious, probably represents the true meaning of the Evangelist.(*v*)

45 And because I tell *you* the Truth, ye believe Me not.

A striking argument that they were the children of the Devil,—the Father of lies.

46 Which of you convinceth Me of sin? And if I say the Truth, iy do ye not believe Me?

" Which of you convicteth Me of such sin as would make it probable that I should ak falsehood?"(*x*) — As our Lord said on a subsequent occasion, — " If I have oken evil, bear witness of the evil: but if well, why smitest thou Me?"(*y*)

47 He that is of God heareth God's Words: ye therefore hear *them* it, because ye are not of God.

Our Lord's argument, put into human form, would be expressed thus: " They it are not of God hear not God's words:(*a*) ye are not of God: therefore ye hear t God's words." But He graciously begins with the more comfortable statement, it "*He that is of GOD* heareth God's words." . . . "And on this is founded the iole system of Man's Redemption through Faith in Christ: that hearing of trist's Word is the proof of being of God; not being able to hear it, is Reproba-n, the proof of being not of God."(*b*)

48 Then answered the Jews, and said unto Him, Say we not well at Thou art a Samaritan, and hast a devil?

These men are nowhere recorded to have applied the former taunt to our Divine ard; but they had evidently many a time reviled Him in this manner among emselves. In chap. vii. 20, they are found however to say " Thou hast a devil." ike notice of the evidence their words afford of the enmity with which the Jews garded the people of Samaria.(*c*) It has been pointed out that the "Good Samari-n," in His reply, denies only the latter half of their accusation.

49 Jesus answered, I have not a devil; but I honour My Father, ad ye do dishonour Me.

Whereby, they dishonoured God Himself.

(*t*) Dr. W. H. Mill. (*u*) St. Jude ver. 6. (*v*) Rev. T. S. Green.
(*x*) Lonsdale and Hale. (*y*) St. John xviii. 23.
(*a*) This follows from the proposition, " They that are of God, hear God's words." Comp. St. John iv. 6. Consider also St. John i. 3 : x. 26, 27.
(*b*) Williams.
(*c*) See the note on St. Luke x. 35. See also above, p. 659–60.

50 And I seek not Mine own Glory: there is One that seeketh and judgeth.

Rather,—"*But* I seek not Mine own Glory." He who sought the Son's Glory,(*d*) and judged between Him and the Jews, was the Eternal FATHER,—who raised CHRIST from the dead and set Him at His own Right Hand, until He made His enemies His footstool.(*e*) This, our LORD declares below, in ver. 54.

51 Verily, verily, I say unto you, If a man keep My saying, he shall never see death.

Rather, "If any one keep My Word;" that is, "believe My doctrines, and obey my commands." "He says *keep:* that is," (observes Chrysostom,) "not by Faith, but by purity of Life." . . . . These words seem to have no connection with what immediately goes before, but they cohere closely with what was commenced in verse 47,—at which part of his divine discourse, the Jews had interrupted our SAVIOUR. And because He is now about to resume and enlarge upon a Doctrine already partly delivered. He begins with His well-known phrase of solemn assertion.(*f*) . . . . The declaration contained in the present verse should be compared with what is found in St. John v. 24, vi. 47, and xi. 26. But take notice that our LORD's Divine meaning is mistaken by His carnal hearers, who assume that He is speaking of temporal death; whereas He speaks of "the second death,"(*g*) which is *eternal*.

52 Then said the Jews unto Him, Now we know that Thou hast a devil. Abraham is dead, and the Prophets; and Thou sayest, If a man keep My saying, he shall never taste of death.

"Were the Jews right," (asks Origen,) "in saying that Abraham was dead? For he heard the Word of CHRIST, and kept it; as did also the Prophets." Consider St. Matthew xxii. 32. They proceed:

53 Art Thou greater than our Father Abraham, which is dead? and the Prophets are dead: whom makest Thou Thyself?

"They might have said, Art Thou greater than GOD, whose words *they* are dead who heard? But they do not say this; because they thought Him inferior even to Abraham."(*h*) To their concluding question, ("Whom makest Thou Thyself?") our SAVIOUR proceeds to direct His reply.

54 JESUS answered, If I honour Myself, My honour is nothing: it is my FATHER that honoureth Me;

Rather, "If I glorify Myself, My Glory is nothing." By which words our LORD meets the insinuation of His enemies that He had been guilty of vainglorious human boasting. By the words, "It is My FATHER who glorifieth Me,"—He further refers to the Eternal FATHER all those signs of his own Godhead which He so freely manifested in the sight of the nation to which He had been sent. Adding,

55 of whom ye say, that He is your GOD. Yet ye have not known Him; but I know Him: and if I should say, I know Him not, I shall be a liar like unto you: but I know Him, and keep His saying.

Rather, "keep His Word,"—that is, "His Commandments:" as in verse 51. Compare St. John xv. 10.

56 Your Father Abraham rejoiced to see My Day: and he saw it, and was glad.

It is not necessary to limit the "Day" thus spoken of, to the day of the Nativity or the Passion of CHRIST, as some of our Fathers in the Faith have done. "There be but two such eminent days," (writes good Bp. Andrews,) "the first and the

(*d*) See St. John xiii. 32.　　　　　　　　　　　(*e*) Psalm cx. 1.
(*f*) See the latter part of the note on St. John vi. 46.
(*g*) Rev. ii. 11: xx. 6, 14: xxi. 8.　　　　　　　(*h*) Chrysostom.

st. The first,—of His Genesis, or coming into the world; the last,—of His Exdus, or going out: His Nativity and His Passion." We are unwilling however to rplain the Day of CHRIST as having exclusive reference to either of these great rents. "The acceptable Year of the LORD,"(i) in like manner, we do not restrict any particular year of our SAVIOUR's Ministry; but we consider either phrase denote *the times of the Gospel* generally,—and emphatically, the period of the irst Advent, the season when our SAVIOUR came to dwell with men.

The original *seems* rather to mean, "Abraham rejoiced with desire to see My ay:" unlike yourselves, (it is implied,) who are grieved at beholding it, and ould slay Me if you could. And so Bishop Andrewes understood the place. He oints out that joy may naturally enough be felt in actual *fruition;* but, that it ould be felt "in *desire*, is altogether unusual. That Abraham should have re-iced *to see,* may well be understood: that he should have *rejoiced with desire to* , not so well. . . . Judge then how great a good is the good of this Day; that not the enjoying, but even in the desiring," did so affect our father Abraham; "and rought from him this act, the act of exultation, and made him even young again. ut" (adds the same holy man,) "I will tell you yet of another as strange: for the me word, you shall observe, is used of the Baptist while he was yet in his moth-'s womb, and 'leaped for joy' at the voice of the Blessed Virgin Mary. So that e see both old and young, Abraham and John Baptist, from the eldest in years the child unborn,—it concerns all! All need it; all are bound to be glad of it; l is for the joy and honour of this Day."

But whatever may be the meaning of the former part of the sentence, take no-e that Abraham "*saw*" the Day of CHRIST,—as "seeing Him who is invisible:" not having received the promises, but having seen them afar off, and been per-aded of them, and embraced them."(j) For "Faith is the substance of things ped for; the evidence of things not seen."(k)

Is there perhaps an allusion in the rejoicing and gladness of Abraham, here no-ed, to the occasion when Abraham, on receiving the promise of Isaac, "fell upon s face and *laughed?*"(l) However this may be, such a statement as the present, om the lips of CHRIST Himself, (the same who talked with faithful Abraham!) ust be felt to be most precious. It conveys a marvellous notion of the vigour of e Patriarch's Faith: not feeding, (like our own,) on definite mercies fulfilled in ime past; but exulting in the contemplation of designs yet future, of boundless ttent, and only partially revealed. What else signified the mysterious oath which e Patriarch took of his servant, causing him to put his hand under his thigh,(m) at that he certainly foresaw that the SON of GOD was thence to take flesh?"(n)

57 Then said the Jews unto Him, Thou art not yet fifty years old, nd hast Thou seen Abraham?

The natural rejoinder would have been,—"And hath Abraham seen *Thee?*" But is obvious that our LORD had said neither the one thing, nor the other. He had mply declared that Abraham had seen *His Day.* The carnal temper which at ice invents a difficulty of its own, and assumes that our LORD has said that He ad Abraham, like two ordinary mortals, were living upon earth at the same time, -is very striking.

As concerning our LORD's age, it is evident that they spoke only in a general ay. CHRIST was *certainly* "not yet fifty years old;" and that is all His enemies eant to express. He was, in fact, but thirty-three. It is scarcely in point, there-re, to lay any stress on those affecting words of the Evangelical Prophet, "His sage was so marred more than any man,"(o) as if they were specially illustrative the present place of Scripture.

Our LORD's reply shows that He was chiefly bent on removing from the minds His hearers their fundamental error in regarding Him as mere man.

58 JESUS said unto them, Verily, verily, I say unto you, Before braham was, I am.

(i) St. Luke iv. 19.   (j) Hebrews xi. 27, 13.   (k) Hebrews xi. 1.
(l) Genesis xvii. 17. Take notice that the name "Isaac" signifies *Laughter.*
(m) Genesis xxiv. 2: a sign repeated by his grandson Jacob, in Gen. xlvii. 29. See also the margin of 1 Chron xxix. 24.
(n) Notice the margin of Judges viii. 30.   (o) Isaiah liii. 14.

Rather, "Before Abraham was born, I AM." So stupendous a declaration is introduced with the formula of solemn assertion.

The idiom of the language, which is thus forever presenting us with the mysterious Name of the Second Person in the Trinity, in the Discourses of our SAVIOUR, has been already made the subject of remark.(p)

Our LORD'S words, (says Bishop Pearson,) "plainly signify thus much: 'Do you question how I could see Abraham, who am not yet fifty years old? Verily, verily, I say unto you, Before ever Abraham, the person whom you speak of, was born, I had a real being and existence, (by which I was capable of the sight of him,) in which I have continued until now.' In this sense certainly the Jews understood our SAVIOUR'S answer, as pertinent to their question, but in their opinion blasphemous; and therefore they took up stones to cast at Him." As it follows:

59 Then took they up stones to cast at Him: but JESUS hid Himself, and went out of the Temple, going through the midst of them, and so passed by.

Many are the recorded occasions when the Holy One was thus obliged to save Himself by flight from the murderous designs of the very people whom He came to save.(q) Wickedly charging Him with blasphemy, and burning with impatience to execute against Him the sentence of their Law,(r) these sinners have armed themselves with such stones as the locality sets within their reach, (for the work of building is related to have been going on about this time in the Temple;) but CHRIST hides Himself, and escapes out of their hands. Yet not, (as it has been truly pointed out,) by taking refuge in a corner. On the contrary, He passed *through the midst* of His enemies: by an effort of Divine power, (as it may reasonably be thought,) rendering Himself invisible to them; for His hour " was not yet come." It was the Divine act of Him who is the "hiding-place of His Saints;(s) yea, who hideth them privily *by His own presence* from the provoking of all men."(t)

CHAPTER IX.

---

1 *The Man that was born blind restored to sight.* 8 *He is brought to the Pharisees.* 13 *They are offended at it, and excommunicate him: 35 but he is received of JESUS, and confesseth Him.* 39 *Who they are whom* CHRIST *enlighteneth.*

THE ninth chapter of St. John's Gospel is occupied with the history of a single incident in the Ministry of our Blessed LORD,—the giving of sight (not its *restoration*, as in the heading of the chapter,) to a man who was born blind. Blind must he be who perceives not that the wondrous prominence thus given to a few transactions in our LORD'S Life by the beloved Disciple, vindicates for those transactions a high degree of significancy, and entitles them to more than ordinary attention at our hands. What more fitting emblem can be imagined of the declared purpose of our SAVIOUR'S Coming, which was to be " a Light of the Gentiles,"(a)—a Great Light springing up " to as many as sat in the region and shadow of Death,"(b)—

(p) See above, the notes on verse 24.
(q) See St. Luke iv. 30. St. John x. 39: xii. 36. Consider the teaching of St. Mark xii. 7.
(r) Leviticus xxiv. 16.—The reader may also refer to the following passages: 1 Kings xxi. 10 and 13. Acts vii. 58, 59 connected with vi. 11; and see St. John x. 30 to 36.
(s) Ps. xxviii. 5. See also Ps. xvii. 8.　　　　(t) Ps. xxxi. 22.—Prayer-Book version.
(a) Is. xlix. 6, (quoted in Acts xiii. 47,) and xlii. 6, (referred to in St. Luke ii. 32.) See also Isaiah lx. 3.
(b) St. Matth. iv. 16, quoting Is. ix. 2.

than this opening of the blind eyes? How could He have more aptly shown that He had come to enlighten the spiritual Darkness of mankind, "to bring out the prisoners from the prison, and them that sit in darkness out of the prison-house,"(c) than by thus bestowing the gift of Sight on a beggar, who had been blind from his birth? The Evangelical Prophet had foretold that "in that day shall . . . . the eyes of the blind see out of obscurity and out of darkness. The meek also shall increase their joy in the LORD, and *the poor among men* shall rejoice in the Holy One of Israel:"(d) and so it came, even literally, to pass.

It is worth observing that more of our SAVIOUR's miracles are recorded as having been wrought on blindness than on any other form of human infirmity. One deaf-and-dumb man(e) is related to have had the gifts of speech and hearing restored to him: one case of Palsy,(f) and one of Dropsy,(g) find special record: twice was Leprosy,(h) and twice was Fever,(i) expelled by the SAVIOUR's Word. Three times were dead persons(j) raised to life. But the minute and particular records of His cures wrought on blindness are *four* in number:(k) and the circumstance cannot be without a meaning. Indeed the record may be said to extend to *six* cases in all.(l) In like manner, the prophet Isaiah will be found to hint at the recovery of sight to the Blind more frequently than to any other act of Mercy symbolical of the Day of CHRIST.(m)

The language of the original seems to connect the stupendous Miracle which follows, in the closest manner, with the narrative which immediately precedes it. It will belong therefore to that Sabbath day with which the Feast of Tabernacles concluded.(n) Our SAVIOUR was flying from His enemies, and effecting His miraculous escape from their violence. He went "through the midst of them, and so *passed by*."(o) "And *as He passed by*," (it follows,) He encountered the man on whom He wrought the miracle. All this however does but amount to a probability,—as every attentive student of these blessed Narratives will at once admit. It is not impossible that all that follows, down to the 21st verse of the next chapter, took place at the Feast of Dedication,—namely, about two months later than the Feast of Tabernacles.

And as JESUS passed by, He saw a man which was blind from *his* birth.

In which last circumstance the present case of blindness differs from every other one recorded in the Gospels. The act of Divine power displayed on the ensuing occasion was not greater indeed, in any respect, than when our LORD wrought other miracles on the blind: but it strikes *us* as more stupendous; and for the very reason which the sufferer himself points out in ver. 32, — namely, because it was never "heard of that any one opened the eyes of a man blind *born*."

He who reads the Gospel with care, learns at last that not even the commonest statements are made without a meaning. Thus, since the Disciples are found in the very next verse to ask our SAVIOUR a question concerning this blind man, the suspicion arises that by saying, "*He saw* a man which was blind from his birth," St. John implies that our SAVIOUR fastened His eyes upon the sufferer in a manner which arrested their attention. The man probably sat and begged,"(p) as our LORD passed by: and his misfortune seems to have been a well-known circumstance at Jerusalem; both from the allusion made to it by the Disciples, in the next verse, and from the manner in which his case is noticed by the neighbours and others, in verses 8 and 9.

(c) Is. xlii. 7.   (d) Is. xxix. 18, 19. See also Is. xxxii. 3: xxxv. 5.
(e) St. Mark vii. 31 to 37.
(f) St. Matth. ix. 1 to 8, [St. Mark ii. 1 to 12, St. Luke v. 17 to 26.]
(g) St. Luke xiv. 1 to 6.
(h) St. Matth. viii. 1 to 4, [St. Mark i. 40 to 45, St. Luke v. 12 to 16:] and St. Luke xvii. 11 to 19.
(i) St. John iv. 46 to 54: and St. Matth. viii. 14 to 17, [St. Mark i. 29 to 31, St. Luke iv. 38 to 39.]
(j) St. Matth. ix. 18 to 26, [St. Mark v. 22 to 43, St. Luke viii. 41 to 56:] and St. Luke vii. 11 to 16: and St. John xi. 1 to 54.
(k) St. Matth. ix. 27 to 31: and St. Mark viii. 22 to 26: and St. Matth. xx. 29 to 34, [St. Mark x. 46 to 52, St. Luke xviii. 35 to 43:] and the present place.
(l) See St. Matth. xii. 22, and xxi. 14.
(m) See Isaiah xxix. 18: xxxii. 3: xxxv. 5: xlii. 7.
(n) Lev. xxiii. 39.   (o) See the last words of St. John viii.
(p) See below, ver. 8: and consider St. Matth. xx. 30.

That the sufferer knew *something* about our Blessed LORD, is quite certain. (How many things the Evangelist must pass over in silence!) The amount of this man's knowledge, it is of course impossible to define: but it may perhaps be safely assumed that he had lent a faithful ear to the reports of others concerning the Holy One, as well as that he had been careful to ascertain that His Name was JESUS.(q) How accurate were his notions on the subject of Natural Religion, his subsequent discourse proves in a most remarkable manner:(r) while his intrepid spirit and generous nature shine out to great advantage in contrast with the crooked villany of his persecutors. But of this, hereafter. "As JESUS passed by," He saw this man:

2 And His Disciples asked Him, saying, Master, who did sin, this man, or his Parents, that he was born blind?

What first here strikes us with surprise, is, to find our LORD, — who is supposed just before to have been flying from His enemies, — in what seems to be calm converse with His Disciples. But this ought perhaps to remind us of the very little we know of the transactions recorded in the Gospels, of which particulars have been withheld by the Evangelists. Thus, the dialogue related in St. John viii. 31 to 59, may possibly have taken place in a corner, — where the attempted violence would have been perpetrated without risk of raising a tumult, or encountering molestation. Once abroad, our SAVIOUR was perhaps secure. He may have transferred Himself to a remote quarter of the crowded City, and there regained the society of His Disciples. Moreover, if the character of the present miracle is attentively considered, it will be found to have been one in which the Divine person of our LORD absolutely disappears. He addresses a blind man, and at once withdraws Himself from His observation, — leaving the other to bear his witness before the Sanhedrin alone; and not re-appearing, except for a few moments at the close of the history, (and *then*, perhaps, after an interval of two months,) to bring the object of His former mercy into the better light of the Gospel, and to the knowledge of Himself. As already admitted, however, there is no *proof* that the events recorded in this chapter and the last are not severed by a wide interval of time.

Even more surprising and singular is the question which the Disciples ask. To submit their words to a process of rigid philosophical investigation, is however unreasonable. We should perhaps regard those words as embodying the general belief of the Jewish people in the immediate connection of calamity with crime; of which we have other instances in the Gospel besides the present.(s) It is obvious also that such a belief derived no small sanction from the words which our LORD Himself addressed to the impotent man whom He healed at the Pool of Bethesda, "Sin no more, lest a worse thing come unto thee."(t) The Disciples, in their question, simply assume that Human suffering is always judicial. But this man was *born* blind. With whom then rested the sin, they ask: with him, or with his parents? Some of the nation taught the transmigration of souls which had sinned; and the Disciples may have wished to obtain from our LORD some information on the general subject.

3 JESUS answered, Neither hath this man sinned, nor his Parents; but that the works of GOD should be made manifest in him.

Rather,—"Neither *did* this man sin."— It is of course obvious that our LORD is not here asserting the sinlessness of any persons; but only that neither this man's Sin, nor the Sin of the authors of his being, was the cause of his having been born blind.

Not to repeat what has already been offered in the Commentary on St. John v. 14, on the various causes for which bodily sickness and suffering are found to have been inflicted on mankind, it shall be only observed that our LORD's reply seems to intimate that GOD's design in causing this man to be born with sightless eyes, was to make him a monument of His mercy, by causing a transcendent miracle of Love to be performed upon him; whereby not only his own highest good in Time and in Eternity would be secured, but MESSIAH Himself would be manifested to the World. A glorious mission truly! and a no less wonderful revelation of the

(q) See below, ver. 11.   (r) See below, ver. 30 to 33.
(s) See St. Luke xiii. 1 to 5, and the notes there.
(t) St. John v. 14; where the note may be consulted.

fruitfulness of wisdom displayed in GOD's puposes,—where seeming severity proves to be but the condition of exceeding Love. Thus the Sickness of Lazarus was not unto Death, but for GOD's Glory, that the SON of GOD might be glorified thereby.(u) Here, the blind eyes were but preparatory to spiritual as well as to bodily illumination: and a suffering, sightless wretch becomes transformed in a few hours into an Apostle and Confessor of CHRIST! . . . . All this is not offered as a complete account of the matter; but only as some explanation of our SAVIOUR's words. Sin and suffering do indeed go together, as cause and effect,—Crime and the penalty of Crime;(v) but we may not presume to interpret GOD's judgments in particular; nor discourse about such an intricate moral problem as if we understood it.

4 I must work the Works of Him that sent Me, while it is Day:

Rather,—"I must *needs* work," &c. Consider St. John vi. 38, and the last words of x. 18.

This then which was to follow, was one of the Works, like those of the FATHER, which the SON wrought continually,(x) in token of His Divine Mission: one of the Works which his FATHER had given Him to finish,(y) and which he had been sent into the world to perform.(z) Chrysostom says that the words mean,—"I must manifest Myself, and show that I do the same that my FATHER doeth."

the Night cometh, when no man can work.

"Not that any night can overtake CHRIST; but as Night is given to mankind to be an emblem of Death; and the life of each is to the appointed day of his work; our LORD adopts the same figure for His own course in the flesh. As "Man goeth forth unto his work, and to his labor until the evening."(a) In like manner this His Day was on the wane, and verging to its close."(b) . . . But our LORD straightway adds,

5 As long as I am in the World, I am the Light of the World.

By which words, we are reminded of the singular manner in which our SAVIOUR's sayings ever assume an unexpected meaning, and demand a breath of application for which we were at first unprepared. "The Day," then, of which He spake before, (*that* Day which Abraham "saw and was glad,")(c) however protracted its future glories, yet in the strictest sense of the term, had the same duration as His own Ministry; lasted as long as He Himself continued in the World. The Sun of Righteousness was now about to be withdrawn from the eyes of men; and accordingly the Day of which He spake was itself now rapidly drawing to a close. "The Night cometh," (saith He,) "when no man can work:" words which, as we now perceive, must have a broader meaning than was assigned to them above. They must imply, that "the hour was at hand when men could no longer have the opportunity of beholding and believing in CHRIST, but would be overtaken by spiritual darkness. Compare ver. 4 and 5 with chap. xi. 9, 10, and xii. 35, 36.

"I am the Light of the World,"—saith our LORD. How precious a saying for Faith and Love to feed upon! Yea, He "is the true Light, which lighteth every man that cometh into the World."(d) The Sun which glorifies Creation,—filling the air with brightness and the heart with joy,—is therefore but a faint type or shadow of Him, who is "the *true* Light." CHRIST alone is the "Light of the World!"

And if He *be* the Light of the World, (as He repeatedly declares of Himself,)(e) then should men learn to rejoice in His shining, and to regard all things as dark and gloomy where He is not. They should try to behold everything as it must appear in *His* presence; and let every thing depend for its due place, and form, and colour upon *Him*. What safety in a path which *He* has not revealed? What joy in a prospect which *His* smile does not adorn? "In Thy Light," (exclaims the Psalmist,) "shall we see Light!"(f)

(u) St. John xi. 4.
(v) See Gen. iii. 16 to 19. Also the note on St. Luke xiii. 3.
(x) St. John v. 17: and see ver. 19.   (y) St. John v. 36: xvii. 4.
(z) St. John iv. 34.   (a) Ps. civ. 23.   (b) Williams.
(c) St. John viii. 56.   (d) St. John i. 9.
(e) See St. John viii. 12. Compare also iii. 19: xii. 35, 36, and especially 46.
(f) Ps. xxxvi. 9.

The saying thus remarked upon prepares us for the miracle which follows, in the manner explained in the note prefixed to the present chapter.

6 When He had thus spoken, He spat on the ground, and made clay of the spittle, and He anointed the eyes of the blind man with the clay.

Three times is our SAVIOUR related to have employed the moisture of His Divine Mouth in working miraculous cures : once, in relief of a stammering tongue,(g)— twice, for the cure of blindness.(h) But only on this occasion do we read of "clay" made with spittle being employed as an instrument of cure. The washing in the Pool of Siloam as a superadded condition, is without a parallel in the recorded miracles of our Blessed LORD. The thing to be observed however, is, that neither in the thick clay, nor in the sacred moisture, nor in Siloa's brook, — in no sacramental sign, did the power of vision lie ; but in the Faith of him who obediently availed himself of the covenanted means of Grace. CHRIST prescribed the means of illumination : the sufferer, blind from his birth, complied with those conditions; and the gift followed, as a matter of course. . . . . . Concerning the symbolical nature of the transaction, see below, the note on verse 7.

It is a highly interesting circumstance, that the ancients believed in the healing virtue of saliva, in the case of disorders of the eyes. Even the anointing *with clay* was a recognized method of cure. What then is to be thought of our SAVIOUR'S employment of such media,—utterly unavailing as they must have been in directly furthering His Divine purpose? They were perhaps intended to help the Faith of the sufferers themselves. Neither spittle nor clay will have been needed by the noble pair at Jericho, whose Faith made them even clamorous for Mercy. Saliva alone may have sufficed (though it barely sufficed)(i) for the blind man of Bethsaida, who seems to have merely lost a faculty which he once possessed. But the man *blind from his birth* may have required the most help of all. He will have *understood*, as well as *felt*, the anointing with clay : a less palpable outward sign in his case, would have been, perhaps, ineffectual.

If it be asked why then the man who had only an impediment in his speech was so assisted, let it be suggested that his was precisely a case where we seem to recognize some defect in the moral condition of the object of our SAVIOUR's mercy. On the occasion of no other miracle is He said to have *sighed*.(k) — But, to return Our LORD " spread the clay [like ointment] over the eyes of the blind man,"—

7 and said unto him, Go, wash in the pool of Siloam, (which is by interpretation, Sent.) He went his way therefore, and washed, and came seeing.

Take notice then that this was a *double* miracle. Our LORD had not only bestowed upon the man the faculty of Sight, but He had given him the astounding power to use that newly acquired faculty as completely as if he had never known the lack of it. This has been already remarked upon in the Commentary on the latter part of St. Mark i. 31.—The implicit faith in CHRIST, shown by the Beggar's immediate obedience to directions apparently so little calculated to afford him any benefit, becomes even more striking when contrasted with the reluctance of Naaman on a similar occasion.(l)

Thus did *He* give light to the blind eyes on the first Day of the week,(m) who in the beginning had called forth the Light itself on that Day. His making clay while engaged in this act, so highly symbolical of the New Creation, reminds us of the history of the Creation of Man.(n)

That the entire transaction was symbolical, may be fairly assumed ; and the analogy of other places of Scripture, (as the History of Naaman's Leprosy,)(o) added to the concurrent testimony of the Fathers, leads us to refer the concluding act of the miracle to that Baptismal washing, so clearly revealed in Scripture as " generally necessary to Salvation ;" and declared to be a rite indispensable, even in the case of those who, by Faith, have been already brought as Catechumens or Con-

(g) St. Mark vii. 33.
(i) See the note on St. Mark viii. 25.
(l) 2 Kings v. 10 to 14.
(n) See Gen. ii. 7.

(h) See St. Mark viii. 23.
(k) See the notes on St. Mark vii. 34.
(m) See below, ver. 14.
(o) See 2 Kings v. 10 to 14.

fessors into the marvellous Light of the Gospel of CHRIST. The reader should examine the places referred to at foot ;(*p*) and he is requested to observe that, in the Apostolic Age, "Illumination" or "Enlightenment" was actually a name for Baptism itself.(*q*) What has been already offered on the word "Pool," in connection with Holy Baptism, shall not be here repeated.(*r*)

But the chief difficulty of the passage yet remains untouched: for it requires no great familiarity with Scripture to feel convinced that our LORD's injunction to "go, wash in the pool of *Siloam*," was not delivered without a deep meaning. If this could be for an instant doubted, the interpretation of the word, so significantly introduced, would be enough to establish the fact.

It shall suffice to point out, very briefly, the probable meaning of this interesting passage.—"Siloam," (says the beloved Disciple,) signifies "[a man who hath been] sent." That this was our LORD's own special designation, has been already sufficiently shown.(*s*) In requiring, therefore, as the condition of the blind man's obtaining the gift of sight, that he should "go *wash in Siloam*," it seems to be plainly declared that the blindness of the Jewish Church, (aptly prefigured by the weak-eyed Leah,) could not be healed until she betook herself to the "*Sent*" of GOD,(*t*)—even to Him who "*washed us from our sins in His own blood.*"(*u*)

It is further evident that the clay with which our SAVIOUR had overspread the man's eyes, was in itself calculated only to obstruct the Light. It could only act as a hinderance, not as a help, to the approach of vision. In the waters of Siloam, however, this obstacle would disappear entirely. And what does all this seem to signify but that our LORD's Humanity was a hinderance to the Jews, and in itself only helped to blind them to "the true Light?" *That* form of clay, wherein Deity had been pleased to unite itself to the dust, and which was all that met the eyes of men, was a mere obstacle, until they freely betook themselves to Him that had been "Sent;" when the difficulty at once vanished, and their eyes were opened.

Here then was displayed, in a most lively and instructive parable, the consequences to the Jewish Nation of our LORD's Advent. Blind like this Beggar, though little suspecting that like him they were wretched, and miserable, and poor, and blind, and naked,(*v*)—as many as received not the "Sent" One, henceforward became even more hopelessly dark. This is what our LORD will be found presently to declare, in those words—"For judgment am I come into this World, ... *that they which see*," (that is, who think they see, yet reject Me their SAVIOUR,) "*might be made blind:*"(*x*) and to this agree the writings of the Prophets(*y*) and Apostles.(*z*)

Lastly, by this mention of Siloam, our SAVIOUR may have intended to direct attention to a well-known place in the writings of His Evangelical Prophet, and even to guide the Church to its true spiritual application. The threat anciently denounced against Israel that they should be subdued by the King of Assyria, "*forasmuch as this people refuseth the waters of Shiloah* that go softly,(*a*) was doubtless not without reference to the days of MESSIAH: and may well have implied that on the Jews' rejection of Him whom GOD had "sent," He would "send forth His armies, and destroy those murderers, and burn up their City."(*b*)

It may be added that "the pool of Siloam" is recognized at the present day "as a small deep reservoir in the form of a parallelogram, into which the water flows from under the rocks through a long subterraneous channel." It stands at the foot of Mount Sion, towards the southeast of the ancient City: and has ever been remarkable for the irregular flow of its water,—the cause of which phenomenon does not

---

(*p*) See Acts ii. 37 to 41: viii. 12, 36, 38: ix. 8 to 18: x. 44 to 48: xvi. 30 to 33: xix. 1 to 5, &c. See also the note on St. John iv. 42, p. 137-8.

(*q*) See Heb. vi. 4: x. 32.　　　　　　　　　(*r*) See the note on St. John v. 2.

(*s*) See the note (*c*) on St. John iv. 34, at p. 668.

(*t*) Is it possible that Gen. xlix. 10, is to be connected with this name? We humbly suspect not. "Shiloh" probably means "He whose it is,"—"He for whom it is reserved,"—or (as the prophet Ezekiel (xxi. 27,) explains the place,) "*He whose right it is.*" Moses perhaps refers to this name in Exod. iv. 13.

(*u*) Rev. i. 5. See also Eph. v. 26.

(*v*) Rev. iii. 17.　　　　　　　　　　　　　(*x*) See below, ver. 39.

(*y*) Is. vi. 10.　　　　　　　　　　　　　　(*z*) Rom. xi. 7 to 10, also 25.

(*a*) Is. viii. 6. The final letter of Siloam was added by the Jews of our SAVIOUR's time to the ancient form of the word—Siloa.

(*b*) St. Matth. xxii. 7.

seem to be understood.   The "Tower in Siloam," mentioned in St. Luke xiii. 4, is thought to have been close by this Pool ; which is only noticed besides in Nehemiah iii. 15.   It was always famous for the salubrity of its waters.

8 The neighbors therefore, and they which before had seen him that he was blind, said, Is not this he that sat and begged ?

He was therefore poor as well as blind.   A blind beggar !   Such are the Gospel Heroes.(c)   The man had now returned to the dwelling of his parents; and the neighbours as was natural crowded to see him.

9 Some said, This is he: others *said*, He is like him : *but* he said, I am *he*.

The thing seemed impossible ; and therefore opinion was divided as to the man's identity.   But the Beggar's testimony settled the question.

Nothing more alters the general expression of the face, which before presented an utter blank, than the addition of the organs of sight.   The neighbours scarcely recognized the blind beggar after he had been the object of our SAVIOUR's mercy. They saw merely a resemblance in the man to his former self.   "But he said, I am he."   This, it has been well observed, is the emblem of a sinner whose eyes God hath touched and enlightened by His Grace; who hath, in consequence, become a man so altered in his views and opinions of all things, that he appears to others scarcely the same person : but he knows himself to have been he that was " miserable, and poor, and blind, and naked ;" and that through the Grace of GOD he is other than he was.(d)

10, 11 Therefore said they unto him, How were thine eyes opened? He answered and said, A Man that is called JESUS made clay, and anointed mine eyes, and said unto me, Go to the pool of Siloam, and wash : and I went and washed, and I received sight.

He had therefore ascertained that his great Benefactor bore the name, as well as exercised the office, of a SAVIOUR ; and his language shows that he had, in the strictest manner, fulfilled the instructions which our LORD had given him.   The result, he describes with the same sublime simplicity as if he were describing the work of the first day of Creation,—when "GOD said, Let there be Light: and there was Light."(e)

"Mark his exactness.   He does not say how the clay was made ; for he could not see that our LORD spat on the ground.   He does not say what he does not know: but that our LORD had anointed his eyes, he could *feel*.   Our LORD's words, too, he could declare from having *heard* them."(f)

12 Then said they unto him, Where is He ?   He said, I know not.

Obviously.   He had hitherto only heard, not seen, his Benefactor ; and can have known nothing of the movements of One who in fact " had not where to lay His Head."   Compare the case of the impotent man, in St. John v. 12, 13.

13 They brought to the Pharisees him that aforetime was blind.

" These men, when they asked, Where is He? were desirous of bringing our LORD before the Pharisees : but as they could not find Him, they bring the blind man instead,(g) in order that the Pharisees might examine him the more closely." The pretence for this proceeding on their part, follows in the next verse.

14 And it was the Sabbath day when JESUS made the clay, and opened his eyes.

So, after recording the cure of the impotent man, St. John adds,—"And on the same day was the Sabbath."(h)

One of the Evangelist's reasons for adding this circumstance (though by no means the only reason) was doubtless that assigned by Chrysostom ; namely, to ex-

---

(c) See St. James ii. 5.
(e) Gen. i. 3.
(g) Chrysostom.

(d) Williams.
(f) Chrysostom.
(h) St. John v. 9.

the real design of these men in their present proceeding. This was, to accuse SAVIOUR of a breach of the Commandment, and thus to detract from the miracle. ording to these hypocrites, the "making the clay" was a violation of the Fourth mandment.

.5 Then again the Pharisees also asked him how he had received sight.

hey asked him the same question as "the neighbours" had asked already. y perhaps wished to intimidate the Beggar, and to give him an opportunity of ying that any cure had been wrought upon him by CHRIST at all.

Ie said unto them, He put clay upon mine eyes, and I washed, and see.

Iark his firmness. He had already borne his testimony before "the neighrs;" but he had nothing then to fear. Here, he beholds a formidable Court yed before him, and he repeats his story fearlessly,—omitting only such parlars as he knows to be superfluous.

16 Therefore said some of the Pharisees, This Man is not of GOD, ause He keepeth not the Sabbath day.

Some," not *all:* for others (like Nicodemus) were believers already; "had their eyes anointed," as Augustine speaks. "Some," however, "passing over miracle in silence, give all the prominence they can to the supposed transgresi; not charging our SAVIOUR with *healing* on the Sabbath, but with *not keeping* Sabbath."(*i*) They were guilty of the same malicious suppression on a former sion.(*j*)

Others said, How can a man that is a sinner do such miracles?

Jo we not here recognize the voice of him who at first "came to JESUS by night, I said unto Him, Rabbi, we know that Thou art a Teacher come from GOD: *for men can do these miracles that Thou doest except GOD be with Him?*"(*k*)—Come chap. x. 19, 20, 21,—in which last verse, the voice of Nicodemus seems to be in plainly discernible.

And there was a division among them.

For this was He," (says Augustine finely,) "who in the beginning divided the ht from the Darkness."— See the note on St. John vii. 43.

17 They say unto the blind man again, What sayest thou of Him t He hath opened thine eyes?

This is a single question: "What doest *thou* say about Him for having opened," "in that He hath opened thine eyes?"—Observe how artfully these wicked men ceed. They attempted at first to obtain from the beggar a denial of his cure. led in this endeavour, they seek to draw from his ignorant lips some opinion cerning our LORD which they may turn to His prejudice. The beggar's reply eals the amount of his belief concerning our LORD,—namely, that He was a man h a Divine Commission; a man sent from GOD.(*l*)

He said, He is a Prophet.

18 But the Jews did not believe concerning him, that he had been nd, and received his sight, until they called the parents of him that I received his sight.

For then either,—according to the well-known use of the present idiom, so often lained already. See the places at foot.(*m*)

---

l) Chrysostom.
k) St. John iii. 2.
m) See the notes on St. Matthew L 25: xviii. 34: xxviii. 20.

(j) See St. John v. 12, and the note there.
(l) See below, ver. 33.

19 And they asked them, saying, Is this your Son, who ye say was born blind? how then doth he now see?

The Beggar was removed from the Court,(n) while this iniquitous attempt was made to extort from the lips of a humble pair something which might be wrested to our LORD's disadvantage. "*Ye say*" that your Son was born blind. Is it really the case? His look is so altered, that the very neighbours are in doubt whether this is the man who "sat and begged." Are ye *sure* that this is your son? . . . . Overawed as the poor creatures evidently were by the interrogations of such men, they are yet found to bear most pertinent witness to the Truth on both these points.

20, 21 His Parents answered them and said, We know that this is our Son, and that he was born blind : but by what means he now seeth, we know not ; or who hath opened his eyes, we know not. He is of age ; ask him. He shall speak for himself.

They answer in fear, as St. John mentions in the next verse: but they bear witness to the only points of any importance,—namely, that *this was their Son; and that he was born blind.* That he now possessed the faculty of sight, was a plain fact,—to be accounted for, they cared not how. And thus, as Chrysostom truly observes, "the Truth becomes strengthened by the very snares which are laid against it. A lie is its own antagonist, and by its attempts to injure the Truth, sets it off to greater advantage. So was it now: for the argument which might otherwise have been urged that the neighbours knew nothing for certain, but spoke from a mere resemblance, is cut off by the introduction of the Parents,—who could of course testify to their own Son."

22 These *words* spake his Parents, because they feared the Jews: for the Jews had agreed already that if any man did confess that He was CHRIST, he should be put out of the Synagogue.

So sinfully had these Pharisees prejudged the case into which they pretended to inquire! "Nor shall any such sentence of excommunication be void; for if pronounced with injustice, it falls back on the authors of it: never more signally than now, for while CHRIST received this man into His Church, those Jews are cut off from the Church unto this day. An awful instance of the serious consequence of using wrongly and unjustly such sacred powers."(o) Concerning "the Jews," the reader is referred to the second note on St. John v. 15 ; and he should compare ver. 22, above, with chap. xii. 42.

23 Therefore said His Parents, He is of age ; ask him.

"By which words" (remarks an old writer,) "the Evangelist shows that it was not from ignorance, but fear, that they gave this answer."(p) The Man who had received his sight was now again brought in.

24 Then again called they the Man that was blind, and said unto him, Give GOD the praise : we know that this Man is a sinner.

Rather, "Give glory to GOD,"—which does not mean "Give it to GOD, and not to this man :" it is simply a solemn abjuration to the Beggar to speak the truth,— as when Joshua in the self-same words addressed Achan."(q) "We, the learned Doctors of the Law," (say they,) "have fully satisfied ourselves that this man is a Sinner,"—that is, a notorious offender: "do not thou persevere in thy lie!" (a method of argument, or rather of intimidation, which we have heard the same speakers employ before:)(r) and they seem to wish by this saying to confound and overbear the humble individual who has just been brought into their presence for the second time ; whom they would fain impress with the belief that they have been making discoveries during his absence, which prove that the whole of this miraculous transaction has been a fraud.

(n) Consider below, ver. 24. (o) Williams. (p) Alcuin.
(q) See the Greek version of Josh. vii. 19. The formula is found in other places,—as 1 Sam. vi. 5. Jer. xiii. 16. Mal. ii. 2. Rev. xi. 13: xiv. 7: xvi. 9.
(r) See St. John vii. 48, 49, and the note on ver. 47.

25 He answered and said, Whether He be a sinner *or no*, I know not: one thing I know, that, whereas I was blind, now I see.

He refuses to go into any irrelevant question with them. That the "man called Jesus" was a sinner, the Pharisees said "*we know*." Whether this be the fact, or the contrary, exclaims the Beggar, "*I know not*." . . . One thing only he chooses to know; but *that* one thing it is which creates all the present difficulty.

26 Then said they to him again, What did He to thee? how opened He thine eyes?

Was this the language of utter perplexity? or of real curiosity? or did these sinners seek thus to entrap the man into some contradiction of himself? Chrysostom compares them to dogs which, when the scent fails, go back to some old scent.

27 He answered them, I have told you already, and ye did not hear; wherefore would ye hear *it* again? will ye also be His Disciples?

Observe that he here makes a glorious confession of his Faith in Christ. The bold irony of his reply is admirable: "what is the object," (he asks,) "of all this tedious questioning, and rigorous investigation of so plain a matter? Do you wish to discover that the miracle is true, in order that *you* also,—you as well as myself, —may become the Disciples of Jesus?" . . . So that his generous spirit has waxed bolder under the fire of persecution: every instinct of his "honest and good heart" being at last outraged by what he has witnessed in the World to which his eyes have been only newly opened. Cited at first before the Pharisees, in order to make him give information prejudicial to his Benefactor: a witness, next, of the shallow reasoning which would set aside so astounding a miracle on the frivolous pretext that it was wrought on the Sabbath-day: then, plied with an insidious question, whereby he might be brought to inculpate either our Saviour or himself: made to withdraw, while a mean endeavor is made to confound and intimidate his poor and probably aged parents; and only recalled before the sinful Pharisees in order to be overawed and insulted by them;—the Blind man evidently became warmed by a noble courage, which made him at last spurn and defy the malice which he saw arrayed against him: and his taunt is found to have cut his adversaries to the quick.

28, 29 Then they reviled him, and said, Thou art His Disciple; but we are Moses' Disciples. We know that God spake unto Moses: *as for this fellow*, we know not from whence He is.

Thus to set up Moses against Christ, and to contrast their respective claims, is found to have been the favourite practice of these speakers. See St. John vi. 31, 32, and the notes there: also viii. 5: and consider St. John v. 45 to the end.

"*Thou* art a Disciple of *Him*," (say the Pharisees;) "but *we* are Disciples of *Moses*." The words are all emphatic. "May such a malediction as the former saying was meant to imply, be upon us and upon our children!" piously exclaims Augustine. On a former occasion, we heard these men urge their knowledge of Christ's origin as a reason for rejecting Him. "We know this Man whence He is: but when Christ cometh, no man knoweth whence He is."(*s*) Here, they seem to profess no knowledge on the same object: but what they mean is, that they know not the source whence He obtained His Commission, nor the ground of His pretensions to be sent of God.

30, 31, 32, 33 The man answered and said unto them, Why herein is a marvellous thing, that ye know not from whence He is, and *yet* He hath opened mine eyes. Now we know that God heareth not sinners: but if any man be a worshipper of God, and doeth His will, him He heareth. Since the world began was it not heard that any man opened the eyes of one that was born blind. If this Man were not of God, He could do nothing.

(*s*) St. John vii. 27,—where see the notes.

The exceeding wit of this prompt rejoinder is scarcely less remarkable than its bitter irony; while the instincts of natural Piety which it discovers are truly admirable. "Why!" (exclaims the man,) "this is a wonderful feature of the case indeed. Ye,—the wise Doctors of the Law, whose office it is to try the spirits whether they be of God, to distinguish between false Prophets and true,—ye profess yourselves unable to say whether this Man be from Heaven, or not: and ye He hath wrought a miracle on me, without a parallel in the World's history!(t) Listen then while I solve the problem for you. You have yourselves declared that God heareth not sinners:(u) and I quite agree. It is even proverbial that God heareth not the hardened and the impious,(v) but only those who do His will.(x) Now God *hath* heard this Man. He is therefore *not* 'a sinner,' in your sense of the word, but must be from God. If He were not, He could do nothing at all in this way; much less could He have wrought such a stupendous act of power as this!" . . The rage of such a body of persons at being so addressed, might be foreseen.(y) The relation between the speakers had become reversed. The Beggar was the teacher: the Pharisees, the taught. They stood convicted at once of folly and of malice; and are found to be no longer at any pains to conceal their anger and their scorn.

34 They answered and said unto him, Thou wast altogether born in sins, and dost thou teach us?

They allude to the man's natural defect, and taunt him with having come into the world with the penalty of Sin branded on his entire person, in that he was born blind. This seems to be the meaning of "altogether;" for "the lamp of the body is the eye,"(z) as our Saviour said on another occasion; and its office is to fill the whole body with light. But the wretched speakers forget that they are already asserting the very thing which they were lately so bent on disproving! They forget also, that "if Blindness were indeed the sign of Sin, then, to remove Blindness proved a power to remove the penalty of Sin."(a) Lastly, they seem regardless of the fearful truth that by such words they are reproaching their Maker:(b) for "who maketh the dumb, or deaf, or the seeing, *or the blind?* have not I the Lord?" (c)—said God to His servant Moses. All is forgotten in the unbearable thought that they, "the Guides of the Blind," as they vainly styled themselves,(d) were receiving instruction at the hands of this blind Beggar. "It was they themselves," (as Augustine observes,) "who had made him the teacher; themselves, who had asked him so many questions." But that "Lights of them which are in Darkness," "Instructors of the Foolish," "Teachers of Babes,"(e) should be thus schooled by an illiterate person who but yesterday had "sat and begged,"—all this was not to be endured. Accordingly, "his clear and forcible eloquence is met by one argument alone; namely, thou art a sinner, but we are righteous: thou art ignorant, and we learned in the Law: we sit in Moses' seat,(f) thou art the blind follower of this Galilean deceiver."—So much then for *Evidence*, as a means of convincing men of the truth of Christianity! Here had been a judicial inquiry; and it was attended with this result!(g) A change of heart, not more Light, in such matters is the thing needed. The perception of Truth is a moral, rather than an intellectual act. But this has been often pointed out already.(h) It follows:

And they cast him out.

That is, they pass a formal sentence of Excommunication upon him,—and doubtless cause him to be ejected from their presence likewise; thereby making him the foremost of that glorious Army of Confessors who praise God for evermore. Take notice therefore how literally in him was fulfilled the blessing pronounced by our

(t) See the note on verse 1.   (u) See above, verses 16 and 24.
(v) *That* is what is meant by "sinners" in verses 16, 24 and 31. Consider Job xxvii. 8, 9.
Psalm lxvi. 18.   Prov. i. 24 to 30: xxviii. 9.   Isaiah i. 15: lix. 2.   Jer. xiv. 10, 13. Micah iii. 4, &c.
(x) See Psalm xxxiii. 18: xxxiv. 15.   1 St. Peter iii. 12.
(y) Consider the character which our Lord Himself gave of them in St. Matthew xxiii.
(z) St. Matthew vi. 22.   (a) Williams.
(b) Consider Proverbs xvii. 5: xiv. 31.   (c) Exodus iv. 11.
(d) See Romans ii. 19: and the note on St. Matthew xxiii. 16, 17.
(e) See the note on St. John iii. 10.   (f) Williams.
(g) See on St. Mark iii. 22.   (h) See on St. John v. 11.

ᴏʀᴅ Himself on those whom men should "hate," and "separate from their com-ᴀɴy," and "reproach," and cast out their name as evil, for the Son of Man's ᴀke.(i)

It will be seen that in the next verse, our Sᴀᴠɪᴏᴜʀ reappears. We heard of Him ᴛᴇᴛ in verse 7. Henceforward we do not lose sight of Him till the Feast of the ᴅedication :(k) and He seems to have been all the while at Jerusalem. Between ᴇʀᴇᴇs 34 and 35, therefore, some weeks may *possibly* have elapsed ; namely, from ᴛᴇ latter part of October to the beginning of December, in the last half year of our ᴏʀᴅ's Ministry.

35 Jᴇsᴜs heard that they had cast him out; and when He had found ᴛim, He said unto him, Dost thou believe on the Sᴏɴ of Gᴏᴅ ?

An interval has occurred. Our compassionate Lᴏʀᴅ, who never forsakes His ᴇᴏᴘle, then proceeds, (as on a former occasion He had done,)(l) in search of (m) ᴛe late object of His Mercy ; whose Faith, the experience of the interval has suf-ᴄed to ripen fully, and who is now in a condition to receive the knowledge of His ᴅivinity. He who knoweth all things, knows where to find the man; and when ᴛe has found Him,—and, as we may suppose, further revealed Himself as the Great ᴛʜysician who had brought him out of thick darkness into the dazzling light of an ᴛastern Day,—He asks, "Dost thou believe in the Sᴏɴ of Gᴏᴅ ?" Nothing short of ᴛɪs is a saving Belief. The Beggar must confess with the Confession of St. Peter, ᴛough he cannot yet speak with the largeness of the Apostle's Faith.

36 He answered and said, Who is He, Lord, that I might believe on ᴛim ?

Rather, "Who is He, *Sir ?*" And so in verse 38.—"The language of a longing ᴛd earnestly desirous soul."(n) Only tell me who He is, (he seems to say,) and, ᴛ Thy Word, I will believe on Him.

37 And Jᴇsᴜs said unto him, Thou hast both seen Him, and it is He ᴛat talketh with thee.

"Thou hast not only *seen* Him, — (by which our Sᴀᴠɪᴏᴜʀ reminds him of his ᴇᴄent cure,)(o)—but He that is talking to thee is He." By sight and by hearing ᴛth, thou art making thyself acquainted with Him. So gracious a revelation, our ᴏʀᴅ is only once before recorded to have made.(p) "Those who suffer for the Truth's sake," observes Chrysostom, "come to ᴛeatest honour; as we see in the instance of this Blind man. The Jews cast him ᴛt of the Temple, but the Lᴏʀᴅ of the Temple found him; and received him as ᴛe Judge doth the wrestler after his labours, and crowned him."

38 And he said, Lᴏʀᴅ, I believe. And he worshipped Him.

Thus adding the deed to the word,—the act of bodily adoration to the confession ᴛ the heart.—In one deep sentence our Sᴀᴠɪᴏᴜʀ seems to sum up the entire ᴛatter; delivering a solemn comment on all the events which we have been ᴇᴄently considering. The miracle itself does not so much as *suggest* the image ᴛhich He employs, as receive its interpretation from His lips:

39 And Jᴇsᴜs said, For judgment I am come into this World, that ᴛey which see not might see; and that they which see might be made ᴛlind.

"Judgment" is not here used in an active sense. The "Judgment" spoken of ᴛ the condemnation implied by the severing of men into good and bad, which was ᴛe consequence, (not the purpose,) of Cʜʀɪsᴛ's coming into this World. He was 'ᴇet for the *fall* and the *rising* of many," as holy Simeon declared; for this was ᴛe Stone on which some were to build and be saved, — others, to stumble and be

(i) St. Luke vi. 22.   (k) St. John x. 22.   (l) St. John v. 14.

(m) St. John xii. 14, compared with St. Matth. xxi. 1 to 7.

(n) Chrysostom.   (o) Theophylact.   (p) See St. John iv. 26.

broken.(q) He was to be "a sign which should be spoken against, *that the thoughts of many hearts might be revealed*.(r) There was no formal judgment indeed to be pronounced as yet. This was reserved for the end of all things.(s) But in the meantime he that believed not, was just as effectually condemned already ; because he believed not in the Name of the Only Begotten SON of GOD. "And this is the condemnation," (said our SAVIOUR to Nicodemus,) "that Light is come into the World, and men loved Darkness rather than Light, because their works were evil."(t)

It is therefore in the sense which the words last quoted suggest, that our SAVIOUR here says, "For judgment came I into this World." Had it not been prophesied, concerning His appearing, that He should be "like a refiner's fire," "purifying the Sons of Levi, and purging them as gold and silver?"(u) Was not this He, "whose fan is in His Hand, and He shall thoroughly purge His floor;" making a separation between the chaff and the wheat?"(v) But neither of these images is here employed. CHRIST is here "*dividing the Light from the Darkness*," — which had also been His work on the Birthday of Creation. Men promptly showed themselves to belong to the one or to the other state, (for "Darkness" is *a moral state* in the language of Scripture;) and by thus arranging themselves in two great classes, they anticipated, as it were, their own final sentence ; and the Work of the Great and terrible Day became exhibited in emblem, even at the *first* Advent of CHRIST.

The consequence was, that the blind, (that is, simple and ignorant, yet meek and faithful men,) saw ; while the seeing, (that is, the vain pretenders to discernment, proud and presumptuous persons,) were made blind. And this had been the well known prediction of prophecy from the first.(w)

40 And *some* of the Pharisees which were with Him heard these words, and said unto Him, are we blind also ?

Some "*which were with Him*," — to show that they heard Him utter this saying, themselves. The expression seems also to imply that certain of the Pharisees maliciously followed our SAVIOUR about. Their question seems to be asked in anger. They fully apprehended the sense of His words ; perceived that He spoke of spiritual blindness, (although with an allusion to His recent miracle ;) and indignantly inquire whether He means to insinuate that *they* labour under the infirmity of which He speaks?

41 JESUS said unto them, If ye were blind, ye should have no sin: but now ye say, We see; therefore your sin remaineth.

A terrible sentence truly! Our SAVIOUR says, — "If ye were indeed in a benighted condition, there would be excuse for you: or if, being blind, ye were eager to "anoint your eyes with eye-salve, that ye might see(x) — if ye were ready to confess your blindness, and to pray for its removal,—it should be removed. But whereas ye make a boast of living in the full blaze of Light, — behold, your sin remaineth."

CHAPTER X.

1 CHRIST *is the Door, and the Good Shepherd.* 19 *Divers opinions of Him.* 24 *He proveth by His Works that He is* CHRIST *the* SON *of* GOD: 39 *escapeth the Jews:* 40 *and went again beyond Jordan, where many believed on Him.*

It is reasonable to presume that the present Discourse should be regarded as

(q) See 1 St. Pet. ii. 6 to 8, and 2 Cor. ii. 16.   Is. viii. 14, and also Rom. ix. 33.
(r) St. Luke ii. 34, 35.   (s) See the note on St. John viii. 26
(t) St. John iii. 18, 19, — where see the note.
(u) Mal. iii. 2, 3.   (v) St. Matth. iii. 12.
(w) See Is. vi. 10: also Rom. xi. 7 to 10.   (x) Rev. iii. 18.

,ving immediate connection with the short dialogue with which chapter ix. con-
.des. Indeed, were it not for the division into chapters, no break would probably
.ve ever been suspected. If there was any truth, therefore, in the suggestion
.arded at the end of the note on chap. ix. 34, our SAVIOUR will have already
rived at Jerusalem in order to keep the Feast of Dedication, which obtains
ecial notice below, in verse 22. But it is impossible to pronounce with any
.gree of certainty on this subject; and a very careful reader is able to form as
.astworthy an opinion as his guide. Learned men are not agreed whether the
.aling of the Blind Man, recorded in chapter ix., took place at the Feast of
.bernacles, or afterwards :(a) and till this is decided, the arrangement of the rest
.the narrative must perforce be uncertain. It is a satisfaction to reflect, on all
.ch occasions, that if it were at all needful that we should enjoy the sense of
rtainty, the witness of the SPIRIT would have been express. An instructive
.ference may surely be drawn from the very silence and seeming indifference of
.e Evangelists in such matters. The subject, (they seem to say,) is of no real
.aportance. Give heed to *what* thy LORD tells thee, rather than trouble thyself
.out discovering *when* He said it. . . . . It would be easy to expand these remarks;
.t the subject shall be left for the thoughtful reader to pursue for himself.
The formula by which the parable of the Door of the Sheep is prefaced in verse
.and proceeded with in verse 7, sufficiently proclaims its solemnity and impor-
.nce : (see the last words of the note on St. John vi. 46 :) while a little attention
.the Discourse itself is enough to convince any one of its extreme difficulty like-
.ise. In its *progressive* character, it reminds us of our LORD's discourses recorded
.the fifth and sixth chapters of the present Gospel. See the latter part of the
.mmentary on St. John vi. 35.

1 Verily, verily, I say unto you, He that entereth not by the
.oor into the sheepfold, but climbeth up some other way, the same is a
.ief and a robber. But He that entereth in by the door is the Shep-
.erd of the sheep.

Rather "*a* Shepherd of the sheep." CHRIST alone is "*the* Shepherd :" and He
.ill be found presently, (namely, in verse 11,) to reveal Himself by that name.
.t first, (namely, from verses 1 to 10 of the present chapter,) He discourses of
.imself as "*the Door*" of the sheep: and the shepherds spoken of are all those
.whom He gives a commission to "feed His sheep."(b) That the attributes of a
.ood Shepherd which our LORD proceeds to indicate, (and this one among the rest,)
.re fully exhibited in His own person alone, is true; but this does not affect our
.terpretation of the Parable. Every expression in it has a marked reference to
.HRIST. His language, in order to be fully understood, must be interpreted of
.imself. But still, it is plain that it is not of Himself that He is *primarily*
.eaking.
What then may be the connection between the present Discourse and that which
.ent before ? Our LORD's intention seems to have been to pass a sentence of
.tter condemnation on the sinful individuals who had recently excommunicated(c)
.e Man born blind, and denounced Himself as a sinner.(d) So far from allow-
.g *them* to be faithful Pastors who had thus ejected from Church-membership one
.hose offence had been that he believed in *Him*, our SAVIOUR informs them, first,
.at admission to the Ministry can only be procured through Himself: and that as
.any as obtain the pastoral commission in any other way except by Faith in Him,
.re but "thieves and robbers."— Next, whereas the Pharisees had excluded the
.an born blind from the Fold of the Church, our LORD gives them to understand
.hat a terrible mistake they labour under. In the exercise of the power of the
.ys with which they were entrusted, they had thought themselves at liberty to
.ose the door against this man.(e) But, — "*I am the Door*," saith our SAVIOUR
.HRIST ! "By Me if *any man* enter in, he shall be saved." Thus, the first part
.f the parable, (down to verse 6,) refers chiefly to the Pharisees: the latter part,
.erses 7 to 10,) chiefly to the object of their recent cruelty.
What is it then for a Shepherd to enter the sheepfold "by the Door," that is,

(a) See the conclusion of the note prefixed to St. John ix.
(b) Alluding to St. John xxi. 16, &c.
(c) See St. John ix. 34.
(e) Consider St. John xvi. 2.   (d) S. John ix. 24, 25, 29, 30.

CHRIST? Doubtless, it is above all things to be called lawfully, — that is, *according to CHRIST'S Institution.* "And when our LORD, as Man, took upon Himself the care of the flock, He set a perfect example of conformity to the laws of entering upon and bearing that office." He "glorified not Himself to be made an High Priest; but He that said unto Him, Thou art My SON, to-day have I begotten Thee."(*f*) "Accordingly, in setting forth those laws which regulate man's life in the Fold of GOD, and the order and government of it, He does not omit to speak of His own lawful entrance, and faithful endurance; and to make these the living and visible rule for all Pastors to follow."(*g*)

But, (it will be asked,) had not the men then whom CHRIST addressed, been lawfully called? As far as external vocation goes, they had, doubtless. They sat in Moses' seat,(*h*) and were armed with GOD's authority to dispense His Word and Sacraments. But something more than external vocation is necessary in GOD'S sight, without which the highest privileges may be forfeited. Thus, when these pastors were for thrusting CHRIST aside,—CHRIST, "the end of the Law,"(*i*) by and through whom they held their very commission,—*who* sees not that they were virtually undoing the work of their Ordination, and rejecting the Rock on which they were themselves built? CHRIST therefore denounces them by the appellation which belongs to as many as, neglecting the door, climb up into the sheepfold "some other way." He calls them "thieves and robbers;" that is, men who to acts of secret fraud are prepared to add deeds of open violence. As a proof how richly they deserved the former appellation, the reader has but to consider the villany hinted at in St. Matthew xxiii. 14 and 17; also in St. Mark vii. 13; on all of which three places he is requested to read the notes.(*k*) In illustration of the latter term of reproach, it may be enough to refer to the conduct of the Pharisees described in the former chapter, and lower down in verses 31 and 39; as well as elsewhere in the Gospel.(*l*) And take notice how both classes of offenders receive their sentence in those words of GOD's ancient prophet,—"Woe be to the shepherds of Israel that do feed themselves! should not the shepherds feed the flocks? Ye eat the fat, and ye clothe you with the wool, ye kill them that are fed: but ye feed not the flock. . . . With force and with cruelty have ye ruled them."(*m*) What a contrast is afforded by the conduct of Jacob,—an eminent type of CHRIST! "The rams of thy flock have I not eaten. That which was torn of beasts, I brought not unto thee; I bare the loss of it. Of my hand didst thou require it, whether stolen by day, or stolen by night. Thus I was: in the day the drought consumed me, and the frost by night; and my sleep departed from mine eyes."(*n*) "Which things are an allegory."

We may not doubt too that in the case of many who boast of Apostolic Ordination, there may have been no effectual entering "by the Door" into the sheepfold. The line of succession may be unbroken: every condition of a lawful Call to the Ministry may have been observed;(*o*) but if Faith and Humility, Love and Self-denial, be wholly wanting, there has been no effectual entering by CHRIST. In the words of a pious living writer:(*p*) "No self-confident Deacon; no ambitious, or covetous, or ease-loving Priest; no proud Prelate; none of these, though in right lineal descent from the Twelve or the Seventy, enter the sheepfold by CHRIST the Door."

Another excellent Divine has said, — "CHRIST may well be understood to mean that all who should be pastors under Him must enter by the door of His Commission, and perchance of imitation too. O awful thought for one who is entering into the sacred ministry of CHRIST's Church, and into the charge of His flock! The outward transactions, and the ceremonies of Ordination, solemn though they be in themselves, do but veil CHRIST. Under the lintel of His Cross and His extended Hands, do they pass to the sheep which He has purchased with His Blood.

"Surely it is one part of a right entrance into the fold to comply with the example of our LORD; and again, earnestly to seek the personal inward grace, as well as duly to receive the external commission and grace of authority. Whatsoever conformity to CHRIST can be obtained by humility and zeal, whatsoever can

---

(*f*) Heb. v. 5.   (*g*) Rev. C. Marriott.   (*h*) St. Matth. xxiii. 2.
(*i*) Rom. x. 4.   (*k*) See also St. Luke xvi. 14.
(*l*) St. John vii. 1, 30, 45: viii. 59: ix. 22 to 34. See below, ver. 31, 39, &c., &c. And take notice that St. Matth. xxi. 13 should be translated "a den of *robbers.*"
(*m*) Ezek. xxxiv. 2, 3, 4.   (*n*) Gen. xxxi. 38 to 40.
(*o*) Heb. v. 4.   (*p*) Williams.

be won by prayer and fasting, whatsoever by patient endurance, all will go towards the blessed result of being known by His sheep for His, and feeding them
safely in His Name."(q) . . . . . Accordingly, it follows :

3 To Him the Porter openeth ;

This mention of "the Porter" shows that a very different kind of "sheepfold" is
intended from those with which we are best acquainted. Consider Numbers xxxii.
16, 24 and 36.

By "the Porter" is intended the HOLY SPIRIT,—who, at Ordination, conveys
spiritual powers to the candidate for the Pastoral Office, and is ready to confer
spiritual gifts upon him likewise. But he must strive to show himself a "shepherd *of the sheep ;*"(r) that is, one who "takes the oversight of the flock" *for the
sake of the flock,* and not "for filthy lucre's sake."(s)—To such, (our LORD says,)
the Porter openeth :

and the sheep hear His voice : and He calleth His own sheep by name, and leadeth them out.

Consider what intimate knowledge, as well as what particular care of every
member of the flock, is implied in this characteristic of a faithful shepherd. To
understand the full import of the language of the text, refer to Exodus xxxiii. 12
and 17 : also to Isaiah xliii. 1, and xlv. 4. The "Great Shepherd of the sheep,"(t)
in like manner, "calleth them all by their names,(u) having first bestowed on every
member of His flock a name at his Baptism.

He "leadeth them out" beside the still waters, and into green pastures :(x) that
is, He procures for them spiritual refreshment, and guides them into the paths of
Peace. But "the Great Shepherd of the sheep" doeth even more for "the people
of His pasture and the sheep of His Hand."(y) That the sheep "hear His voice,"
is more fully dwelt upon below, in verses 4 and 5. For the present, it shall suffice
to draw therefrom the obvious inference that the shepherd must not be *silent* while
he is among his sheep. The language of verse 27 will be found to supply a clue to
our SAVIOUR's sacred meaning in dwelling thus remarkably on the knowledge enjoyed by the sheep of their Shepherd's voice.

4 And when He putteth forth His own sheep, He goeth before them, and the sheep follow Him ; for they know His voice.

Not only in the East, and in the south of Europe, but in many parts of England,
(on the Berkshire Downs for instance,) shepherds walk *before* their sheep ;—an exquisite type of the duty which attaches to the Pastoral Office, of being not only
guides, but also "ensamples to the flock :"(z) making "ourselves an ensample unto
you to follow us,"—as St. Paul writes to the Thessalonians.(a) Our SAVIOUR is
related more than once *literally* to have walked in advance of His Disciples ;(b) and
it is worth observing that on one occasion He is found to have gone first expressly
in order to encounter danger, and to protect His Disciples from it.(c)
The sheep follow their Shepherd, therefore, because "they know his voice."
They are familiar with its loving accents, and they recognize it instantly. The
experience of past years has convinced them that he desires nothing so much as
their own greatest good ; they are ready therefore to follow his footsteps whithersoever he may lead the way.

5 And a stranger will they not follow, but will flee from him : for they know not the voice of strangers.

By the same instinct which enables them to recognize the voice of their own

---

(q) Rev. C. Marriott.   (r) Consider Heb. xiii. 20.
(s) 1 St. Pet. v. 2.   (t) Heb. xiii. 20.
(u) Ps. cxlvii. 4.   Compare 1 Cor. xv. 41: and consider St. Luke xix. 5, St. John i. 48 : xi.
43, &c.
(x) Ps. xxiii. 2.   (y) See below, the note on ver. 28.
(z) 1 St. Pet. v. 3.
(a) 2 Thess. iii. 9. See also Phil. iii. 17. 1 Tim. iv. 12. Tit. ii. 7.
(b) See St. Mark x. 32. Also St. Matth. xxvi. 32.
(c) St. John xviii. 4, 8.

Shepherd, they at once discern the voice of a stranger. They flee from his guidance, and are regardless of his call. And hereby, that spiritual discernment seems alluded to, which causes "the people of God's pasture and sheep of His care" to shrink away from and refuse to follow false teachers.

6 This parable spake JESUS unto them: but they understood not what things they were which He spake unto them.

The parable, or figurative language, here employed is indeed dark, even to us; but it must have been hopelessly obscure to *them*. Our LORD proceeds, in the next four verses, partially to explain Himself.

7 Then said JESUS unto them again, Verily, verily, I say unto you, I am the Door of the sheep.

We have been compelled, in a manner, to anticipate the great announcement which is here made for the first time; namely, that CHRIST is Himself "*the Door.*" It is introduced by the formula of solemn assertion, "Verily, verily,"—which, by the way, our SAVIOUR's auditory much needed; for, in their estimation, to be of the seed of Israel "was the fold, and the door, and all things."(d) Here then begins *the interpretation* of the Parable. The Divine Speaker's meaning is felt to be difficult: wherefore by the Door Himself is the door unfolded.

Take notice that He says not "the Door *of the Sheepfold,*" but "the Door—*of the sheep.*" That is, He is *our* "Door;" for through Him we offer up our prayers, and by Him have access to the FATHER.(e) By Him alone we enter the Church, and through Him we look for Salvation. Thus, the largeness of our SAVIOUR's meaning begins to appear. He has already begun to divert our attention from the shepherd to *the sheep*: but He will be found to do so more fully below, in verse 9.

8 All that ever came before Me are thieves and robbers : but the sheep did not hear them.

The first words are said with manifest reference to verse 1 of the present chapter: and, "Woe be unto the pastors that destroy and scatter the sheep of My pasture! saith the LORD."(f) Literally, "All, as many as came." But the expression "all" requires interpretation; for of course "the goodly fellowship of the Prophets," who came before CHRIST, are not here intended. Nay, all these *had* duly entered the sheepfold by CHRIST, the Door, and were the authorized heralds of His approach. But allusion is made to those *false Christs*, those pretenders to be themselves "the Door," (such as Judas of Galilee, Theudas,(g) and the rest,) whom "the sheep did not hear; and yet more, as it seems, to those shepherds alluded to, whose shameful spoiling of the flock of CHRIST had been sternly denounced by His prophets Ezekiel and Zechariah ;(h) a race which it is evident were not yet without living representatives. For what else but "thieves" were the men who "devoured widows' houses,"(i) and had transformed the Temple of GOD not only into "a house of merchandise,"(j) but even into a very "den of thieves,"(k) Their violence made them as robbers; and when they drew away disciples, what did they else but rob GOD? Nay, "in tithes and offerings," like their fathers, had they robbed Him ;(l) and that, shamelessly. See above, the note on ver. 1.

9 I am the Door: by Me if any man enter in, he shall be saved, and shall go in and out, and find pasture.

And thus, the interest which all men have in CHRIST, is plainly proclaimed: for He is declared to be the entrance not for shepherds only, (that is, for those in the Ministry:) but for the sheep likewise, that is, "any man,"—as our LORD Himself explains. By this door, (says the holy martyr Ignatius,) "Abraham and Isaac and Jacob enter: the Prophets also, and the Apostles, and the Church." The preventing Grace of the HOLY SPIRIT, (the Porter,) opens this Door to those who knock in Faith; and Salvation is freely promised to as many as shall enter the sheepfold,

---

(d) Lightfoot.   (e) St. John xiv. 6. Eph. ii. 16.   (f) Jer. xxiii. 1.
(g) Acts v. 36, 37.   (h) See Esek. xxxiv. and Zech. xi.
(i) St. Matth. xxiii. 14.   St. Mark xii. 40.   St. Luke xx. 47.
(j) St. John ii. 16.   (k) St. Matth. xxi. 13.
(i) Malachi iii. 8, 9, &c.

(that is, the Church,) by Him.(m) "For through Him," (as it is written,) "we both," (that is, Gentiles as well as Jews,) "have access by one SPIRIT unto the FATHER."(n)

The concluding words describe the security and enjoyment which thereupon ensue, and which are the privileges of God's people. To "go in and out," is to transact the business of each day's life, its rest and its labor, the beginning and the end of every work. The Hebrew phrase denotes a man's whole life and conversation, as in Acts i. 21, and elsewhere :(o) while the promise closely connected therewith, of "finding pasture," seems to imply that in that daily walk, (it may be in the World's "dusky lane and crowded mart,"(p) the people of GOD will find spiritual support and consolation; even meat for their souls which the World knows not of.(q) Elsewhere, indeed, the phrase will be found almost invariably to be, — "go out and come in." Here, (not without meaning doubtless,) the expressions are transposed. The former is, in fact, the order of Nature: the latter the order of Grace.

"In considering CHRIST as 'the door of the sheep,' much will appear that is important to all shepherds of His flock. For by him must be their going out and coming in, if they are to go in and out before His sheep, and to find the pasture that is provided for them."(r)

10 The thief cometh not, but for to steal, and to kill, and to destroy: I am come that they might have life, and that they might have it more abundantly.

Rather, "in abundance." — Our LORD says, "The false teacher comes only to gratify his evil desires, by the plunder and destruction of the flock. I am come, on the contrary, that they who follow Me may have life; and that they may have it in the fullest measure, even Life Eternal."(s)

This verse, in which the Blessed Speaker contrasts the purpose of His own coming with that of the pretenders who had assumed His Name and laid claim to His office, forms an easy transition to the parable of the Good Shepherd, which follows; wherein our LORD not only comes before us under a most engaging image, but explains His right to a title which, from the very beginning, by type,(t) and parable,(u) by psalms,(x) and prophecies,(y) He had made particularly His own.(z) "What is all History," (asks a thoughtful writer,) "but the traces of His iron rod, or His shepherd's staff ?"(a)

Still better worthy of our notice is the fact, that by claiming this character of "Shepherd," He was claiming a well-known title of MESSIAH. Whence the question recorded below, in verse 24,—where see the note.

11 I am the Good Shepherd: the Good Shepherd giveth His life for the sheep.

Rather, "layeth down His life;" as in verses 15, 17, 18.—Observe the expression, "The Good Shepherd;" as elsewhere, "the True Light,"(b) and "the True Bread,"(c) and "the True Vine."(d) All others, it is implied, are but vague shadows, and imperfect resemblances of Him. . . . And thus, in a single sentence, our SAVIOUR distinctly claims the title which we have hitherto only inferred to be rightfully His. He called Himself, in the first instance, "the Door," but He was also the Shepherd. Here, He calls Himself "the Shepherd;" but He is still the Door. Nor let any one presume to say that there is any confusion in this; or that any perplexity is

(m) Compare Acts xvi. 31. St. John iii. 16, 36: vi. 47.
(n) Eph. ii. 18.
(o) See Deut. xxviii. 6. Ps. cxxi. 8. 1 Sam. xxix. 6. 2 Sam. iii. 25. 2 Chron. i. 10.
(p) Keble. (q) Consider St. John iv. 32.
(r) Rev. C. Marriott. (s) Lonsdale and Hale.
(t) Gen. iv. 2: xxxi. 38 to 40: xxxvii. 2. Exod. iii. 1. 1 Sam. xvii. 15, 34 to 36, &c.
(u) St. Luke xv. 3 to 7, with the notes.
(x) Ps. lxxvii. 20: lxxviii. 52: lxxix. 13: lxxx. 1, &c. Consider Ps. xxiii.
(y) Isaiah xl. 11: lxiii. 11. Ezek. xxxiv. 23: xxxvii. 24. Jerem. xxxi. 10. St. Matth. xxv. 32, 33, &c.
(z) See the note on the latter part of St. Luke v. 10.
(a) Rev. C. Marriott; alluding to Ps. xxiii. 4. See Ps. ii. 9. Micah vii. 14. Rev. ii. 27, &c.
(b) St. John i. 9. (c) St. John vi. 32. (d) St. John xv. 1.

hereby occasioned. CHRIST is all things at once to all men. Every duty, every office, every relation, has its true exhibition and entire fulfillment in *His* sacred person. Thus, besides being our Door, and our Shepherd, in Him are we as in a Fold: To us He opens, as the Porter: yea, and in Him, (in His Word and in His sacraments,) we find the food of our souls likewise. Lastly, is not this THE LAMB *that* was "slain from the foundation of the world?"(*e*)

To this announcement concerning Himself, He adds a solemn prophecy, (the first of four successive prophecies,) of His own Death; as well as explains the purpose of it: namely, that He might prove a ransom for all.(*f*) "Hereby perceive we the Love of GOD," (says the Beloved Disciple,) "because He laid down His life for us: and we ought to lay down our lives for the brethren."(*g*) In solemn contrast with this, our SAVIOUR CHRIST declares the conduct of one who "takes the oversight" of the flock "for filthy lucre:"(*h*) seeking not *them*, but *theirs*.(*i*) The proneness of man's unassisted nature to render such a mercenary service, appears sufficiently from the many warnings against it contained in the Apostolical Epistles.

12 But he that is an hireling, and not the shepherd, whose own the sheep are not, seeth the wolf coming, and leaveth the sheep and fleeth: and the wolf catcheth them, and scattereth the sheep.

"When the wolf cometh is the trial;" for, (as Gregory the Great says,) "Whether a man be a shepherd or a hireling, cannot be told for certain, except then. In tranquil times, the hireling generally stands on watch like the shepherd."—He flees, (as the same writer and Augustine explain the saying,) "not by change of place, but by shrinking from duty."(*k*)

Take notice that CHRIST Himself, "the Good Shepherd," acted not thus in the hour of the greatest danger:(*l*) but suffered himself to be smitten, in order that the sheep might go their way.(*m*) Jacob also, and Moses and David, those three eminent types of CHRIST, are found to have typically exhibited the same devotion of themselves on behalf of their respective flocks.(*n*) — Consider the language of St. Paul, (himself a faithful shepherd,)(*o*) to the Elders of Ephesus, concerning the heretics and others who should hereafter ravage "the flock over the which the HOLY GHOST had made them overseers;"(*p*) taking notice however that *all* the agents of Satan are "wolves" in GOD's sight,—whether open persecutors, as Pharaoh, or secret instigators, to sin, as Balaam.

13 The hireling fleeth, because he is an hireling, and careth not for the sheep.

What is here meant by "an hireling," has been already sufficiently explained at the end of the comment on verse 11. As many as look chiefly to their earthly recompense, are "hirelings:" and they flee from danger, simply because the sheep over whom they are set, are nothing to them.

14 I am the Good Shepherd, and know My *sheep*, and I am known of Mine.

He claims for the second time "the appellation of the Good Shepherd,"(*q*) as He had twice claimed to be "the Door."(*r*)—And because "the foundation of GOD standeth sure, having this seal, The LORD knoweth them that are His."(*s*) He further declares His particular knowledge of every member of His flock.—While noticing the mysterious intimacy which thus subsists between Himself, and "the sheep of His pasture," He traces the origin and progress of that mutual sentiment. "*I know* My sheep, — and am *known* of Mine." "We love Him," (as it is elsewhere written,) "because He first loved us.(*t*) See below, on ver. 27. — But the words which follow are wrongly translated.

(*e*) Rev. xiii. 8.   (*f*) 1 Tim. ii. 6.   (*g*) 1 St. John iii. 16.
(*h*) 1 St. Pet. v. 2.   (*i*) 2 Cor. xii. 14.
(*k*) Williams.   (*l*) St. John xviii. 4, 8, 9.
(*m*) Consider Zech. xiii. 7, quoted by St. Matth. xxvi. 31.
(*n*) Gen. xxxi. 38 to 40.   Exodus xxxii. 32.   1 Sam. xvii. 34 to 36.
(*o*) See 2 Cor. xii. 15.   (*p*) Acts xx. 28, 29.
(*q*) See verse 11.   (*r*) See verses 7 and 9.   (*s*) 2 Tim. ii. 19.
(*i*) 1 St. John iv. 19.

15 As the FATHER knoweth Me, even so know I the FATHER:

This should be,—"even as the FATHER knoweth Me, and I know the FATHER;" the sentence being a continuation of that which precedes, and as it were an explanation of it. The mutual knowledge which subsists between the FATHER and the SON, (it is hinted,) is the source and cause of the corresponding knowledge between CHRIST and His people.(*u*)

A profoundly intimate knowledge does indeed here seem to be hinted at, as well on the side of Man towards GOD,(*x*) as of GOD towards Man. Holy persons are accordingly found to discourse with amazing fervour of their blessed experiences in this behalf; so that, to such as we are, their words may sometimes even seem extravagant and unreal.(*y*) ... But who shall pretend to prescribe the depth of *His* knowledge, (or rather the measure of His *Love*,) who said, "*I know My sheep?*" Adding,

and I lay down My life for the sheep.

Now, what is "laid down" may be "taken up again;" so that these words are a prophecy of our LORD'S Resurrection. Obvious is it to remark that He thus, for the second time foretells His Death, together with the purpose of it, as well as explains that it was a voluntary act. But this last circumstance is declared more fully in verse 18.—Take notice, by the way, that these words ("and I lay down My life for the sheep") are to be read in connection with verse 14; the clause which has come between being only explanatory. So that the whole is equivalent to saying that CHRIST so entirely loves His sheep, that He is ready to die for their sake. This momentous matter is repeated in verses 11, 17, and 18.

"And after laying down my life for them, (it is implied,) when GOD shall 'bring again from the dead ... that Great Shepherd of the sheep,' "(*z*)—then will it be found that other sheep I have: (as it follows:)

16 And other sheep I have, which are not of this fold: them also I must bring, and they shall hear My voice; and there shall be one Fold, *and* one Shepherd.

Rather, "And it shall become one *Flock*, one Shepherd:" as if in allusion to those words of Ezekiel,—"I will set up *one Shepherd* over them, and he shall feed them, even My servant David; he shall feed them, and he shall be their shepherd." (*a*) The "other sheep," which our blessed LORD speaks of, were not "the lost sheep of the House of Israel," but those heathen nations which were about to be evangelised by His Apostles. For "the LORD GOD which gathereth the outcasts of Israel, saith, Yet will I gather others to him, besides those that are gathered unto him."(*b*) And to this St. Peter bears witness in writing to the Gentiles,—"Ye were as sheep going astray; but are now returned unto the Shepherd and Bishop of your souls." (*c*)—They were as yet enclosed within an inanimate *Fold*; but henceforth, they were to become members of a living *Flock*.—"All these sheep," He says, "*I have*;" because with Him is neither Past nor Future.(*d*)—And "they shall hear My Voice," because the success which was to attend the preaching of the Word was to Him fully known before.—"Them also I must needs *bring*," He declares; because the Apostles of CHRIST "*went forth* and preached everywhere, *the LORD working with them:*"(*e*) as how should the Heathen "believe in Him of whom they had not heard? and how shall they hear without a preacher?"(*f*) Nay, St. Paul in a certain place hesitates not to assert that this was the act of CHRIST Himself.

(*u*) Consider further such places as the following: St. John vi. 57: xvii. 11: xx. 21.
(*x*) See Philippians iii. 8.   2 St. Peter i. 8: iii. 18.
(*y*) For instance, pious Hooker, when speaking of the comforts of Holy Communion: "They are things wonderful which he feeleth, great which he seeth, and unheard of which he uttereth, whose soul is possessed of this Paschal Lamb, and made joyful in the strength of this new wine." —"There is an intimate communion with GOD," (says a living writer,) "the joy of which is unutterable; and which those who have it can suppose to be in others, but cannot see in them, or know in them by description. They have it to themselves."—Marriott.

(*z*) Williams, quoting Hebrews xiii. 20.   (*a*) Ezekiel xxxiv. 23.
(*b*) Isaiah lvi. 8, quoted by Williams.   (*c*) 1 St. Peter ii. 25.
(*d*) Consider Acts xviii. 10, and St. John iv. 35.
(*e*) St. Mark xvi. 20.   (*f*) Romans x. 14.

(g)—He "*must needs* bring;" because to gather together in one the children of
GOD that were scattered abroad,"(h) was a part of the "commandment" which He
had "received of the FATHER;"(i) and was "necessary, in order to the fulfillment
of those Divine purposes respecting the Gentiles, which were declared in the prophecies of the Old Testament."(j) Consider Hebrews xi. 40.—"It shall become
one Flock," our LORD finally foretells; because, (in the words of His Apostle,) "He
hath made both [Jews and Gentiles] one, and hath broken down the middle wall
of partition" between them.(k) There was therefore henceforth to be but one
Church, collected out of Jews and Gentiles alike;—"One Body and one Spirit,"
(as St. Paul says;) "one LORD, one Faith, one Baptism."(l)

In the Old Testament, consider what an interesting commentary on this verse is
supplied by the xxxvii. chapter of Ezekiel, verses 21 to 28: also by xxxiv. 13: and
Jeremiah xxiii. 3 and xxxii. 37. In the New Testament, Ephesians ii., iii., and
the first six verses of chapter iv. will be also studied with advantage in connection
with this subject.

The Blessed Speaker before concluding His Discourse, recurs prophetically to
the subject of His own Death.

**17 Therefore doth My FATHER love Me, because I lay down My
Life, that I might take it again.**

Literally, "On this account doth the FATHER love Me, [namely,] because,"(m)
&c.—Lest His hearers should overlook the Divinity of Him who spake, this He
adds concerning His own Death,—which was to be His own free choice, and a glorious portion, though, (as far as the authors of the crime were concerned,) an unspeakable indignity offered to "the LORD of Glory."(n) Because He thus submitted Himself to the will of the Eternal FATHER, and became "obedient unto Death,
even the Death of the Cross, GOD also hath highly exalted Him, and given Him the
Name which is above every Name."(o)

The last clause, ("that I might again resume it,") whereby our LORD alludes to
His Resurrection from the grave, is not vainly added. If He was "delivered *for
our offences,*" He was "raised again *for our Justification.*"(p) "If CHRIST be not
raised, your faith is vain," (writes St. Paul;) "ye are yet in your sins."(q)—Take
notice also that this short sentence, ("I lay down My life that I may take it
again,") "is the essential principle of all martyrdom."(r)

18 No man taketh it from Me, but I lay it down of Myself.

Rather, "No [one] taketh it."—Our SAVIOUR says this, not, of course, as denying the bitterness of the portion which awaited Him, and from which all the blameless instincts of His humanity recoiled,—(as witness His Agony in the Garden, His
Prayer to the FATHER,(s) His sufferings on the bitter Cross;) still less as acquit-
ting His murderers of the horrible sin of compassing His Death.(t) But He asserts
His own Almighty power and Godhead. His enemies could have done nothing
against Him, except He had suffered them. Until His "Hour had come," their
murderous attempts proved fruitless;(u) and when they were in the very act of
apprehending Him, "Thinkest thou that I cannot now pray to My FATHER," (He
asked,) "and He shall presently give Me more than twelve legions of Angels?"(v)
"For it was in His power whether He would come into the hands of His enemies:
it was in His power to suffer or not to suffer the sentence of Pilate, and the nailing
to the Cross: it was in His power to have come down from the Cross, when He was
nailed to it."(x) . . . Take notice that "the *loud* cry" with which our Blessed Sa-
VIOUR expired, was a plain witness that by His own free will He so "gave up the
Ghost:" that He "had power" to resign, or to retain it. All this has been already
explained in the note on St. Mark xv. 39.—He adds:

(g) Ephesians ii. 17.
(i) See below, the end of verse 18; where see the note.
(j) Lonsdale and Hale.
(l) Eph. iv. 4, 5.
(n) 1 Cor. ii. 8.
(p) Romans iv. 25.
(r) Williams.
(t) Consider St. Luke xxiii. 34, and St. Matthew xxvi. 24.
(u) See the notes on St. John vii. 30, 44, and viii. 59.
(v) St. Matth. xxvi. 53.

(h) St. John xi. 52.

(k) Eph. ii. 14.
(m) See the note (m) on St. John vii. 22, p. 714.
(o) Phil. ii. 8, 9.
(q) 1 Cor. xv. 17.
(s) St. Matthew xxvi. 39, 42, 44.

(x) Bishop Pearson.

I have power to lay it down, and I have power to take it again.

Very Man, "to lay it down" by Death; very GOD, "to take it again by Resurrection: whereby our SAVIOUR declares the union of the two natures in His One Person. For, "by that power which He had within Himself, He did take His life again which He had laid down; did reunite His Soul unto his Body, from which He separated it when He gave up the Ghost; and so did quicken and revive Himself. Therefore it is a certain truth, not only that GOD the FATHER raised the SON,(y) but also that GOD the SON raised Himself.(z)

This commandment have I received of My FATHER.

By these few words, repelling the possible insinuation that He was unduly assuming to Himself the Mediatorial character. His Death and Passion, His Descent into Hell and subsequent Resurrection from the dead, — the whole of the sufferings which he was about to undergo, He encountered in submission to the FATHER's Will.(a) He "proved obedient," (as the Apostle says,) "unto Death;"(b) that is, "submissive to the FATHER's will unto the extremity of suffering Death," For in the very notion of Obedience is implied on external Will.(c) — And thus, for the hundreth time, "Humiliation and Greatness unspeakable are found expressed at the same time. Union with the FATHER, combined with the laying down of life;" the power of Resurrection, with the receiving of commandment. As Godhead and Manhood are inseparably united, so is every attribute of both."(d)—And this is the end of our LORD's Discourse.

19 There was a division therefore again among the Jews for these sayings.

"Again," as there had been before, among the Pharisees; namely in St. John ix. 16. The present seems to have been *another visit* to Jerusalem; and the beloved Disciple remarks that it was the occasion of *another "division* among the Jews."

20 And many of them said, He hath a devil, and is mad; why hear ye Him?

Take notice that when our LORD either gave evidence of supernatural knowledge,(e) or delivered Doctrines of extraordinary sublimity,(f) the resource of His sinful hearers was to ascribe His words to demoniacal possession. On this occasion they call Him "mad." It was the charge which Festus brought against St. Paul;(g) the charge which the World is ever bringing against those who act on unearthly motives.(h) — No reply is vouchsafed to His present calumniators by CHRIST Himself. He leaves to others the privilege of repelling so blasphemous an insinuation.

21 Others said, These are not the words of him that hath a devil. Can a devil open the eyes of the blind?

Alluding to the miracle described in the last chapter,(i) and which again obtains notice in chapter xi. 37. — See the note on St. John xi. 36.
Surely it was Nicodemus in particular who said this! as well as what we met with in chap. ix. 16, where see the note. Take notice that he has already taken our SAVIOUR's part, — "being one of them;(j) and that the argument used both here, and in chap. ix. 16, is the very same which, in his first interview with our LORD, Nicodemus urged in explanation of his own belief. This was the consideration which had wrought conviction in himself.(k) *Then,* he was overcome by the sight of our SAVIOUR's Works; to which is *now* added the evidence of His spoken Words.

(y) Gal. i. 1. Acts v. 30. Eph. i. 20.
(z) Bp. Pearson. Consider St. John ii. 19.
(a) Heb. x. 7.   (b) Phil. ii. 8.
(c) See above. in the note on ver. 16. See also in St. John vi. 38, xiv. 31, and xv. 10. Also Isaiah liii. 10, 12.
(d) Williams.   (e) St. John vii. 20.
(f) St. John viii. 48, 52, and here.   (g) Acts xxvi. 24.
(h) Consider St. John vii. 7 and xv. 19.   (i) St. John ix. 7, &c.
(j) St. John vii. 50 to 53.   (k) See St. John iii. 2.

22 And it was at Jerusalem the Feast of the Dedication, and it was winter.

St. John, as his manner is beyond the other Evangelists, thus fixes a definite period in the Sacred Year; but whether only in order to mark the occasion of the Discourse, which follows, or for the further purpose of indicating when much that goes before was spoken, it is impossible to pronounce with certainty. The allusions in verse 26 to 29, certainly favour the latter view. A short interval is perhaps all that intervened between what immediately goes before and what follows.

The Feast of Dedication began in the middle of December, and lasted for eight days. It had been instituted about 165 years before the Birth of CHRIST, and was intended to commemorate the Purification of the Temple after its profanation by Antiochus Epiphanes. Take notice that here was a religious Festival not of Divine institution, and yet our SAVIOUR is found to keep it, like the rest of His nation. Judas Maccabæus was its author.(*l*)

This Feast was kept with a general Lighting of Candles ; and, (unlike the three great Festivals which could be celebrated only in Jerusalem,) it was observed everywhere throughout the whole Land, — whence it was not superfluous, in the present instance, for the Evangelist to say, "*It was at Jerusalem.*"

But why does St. John inform us that "it was Winter." Was it simply to prepare us for the statement which follows,—namely, that our SAVIOUR "was walking" in a *covered* part of the Temple? Nothing of the kind, we suspect: and the reader is warned against this kind of plausible, yet very shallow criticism. . . . . . The question is asked in the profound conviction that many of these trivial, and seemingly unimportant particulars of time and season, age and place, are the strong hinges on which the gates of eternal Truth will often be found to turn.

23, 24 And JESUS walked in the Temple in Solomon's porch. Then came the Jews round about Him, and said unto Him, How long dost Thou make us to doubt? If Thou be the CHRIST, tell us plainly.

That the scene of the ensuing dialogue was an ordinary place of resort and concourse, appears from Acts iii. 11 and v. 12. If it be the same structure which is described in 1 Kings vi. 3, (a kind of cloister, or covered colonnade,) it will have been a portion of the edifice which escaped destruction when Solomon's Temple was burned by Nebuchadnezzar.

"The Jews" hem our Blessed SAVIOUR round,(*m*) as He "is walking" in the Porch of the Temple, and under pretence of being actuated by nothing but an earnest desire to behold the MESSIAH in His Person, request Him to keep their souls no longer in suspense and anxiety ; but to tell them plainly if He be the CHRIST? In reality, they seek nothing else but a ground of accusation against Him.—By "plainly," is meant without dark speech or parable,—as when, dropping the metaphor of Sleep, He "said unto them *plainly*, Lazarus is dead."(*n*)

And here it is necessary to point out what was the occasion of this inquiry. By styling Himself "the Good Shepherd," our LORD was claiming a well-known title of MESSIAH. The reader should refer to Ezekiel xxxiv. 7 to 16; especially verse 23 ; also to Isaiah xl. 11: and he is invited to read the note above, which precedes verse 11. A similar remark was offered on our LORD's Declaration that He is "the LIGHT of the World."(*o*) His learned auditory perceived clearly enough the import of these titles; and were impatient to hear Him speak of Himself "plainly," without a figure.

25 JESUS answered them, I told you, and ye believed not:

Rather, "and ye believe not."

the works that I do in My FATHER'S Name, they bear witness of Me.

"In the name of My FATHER,"—He says: "ever expressing with infinite care that He, in all His works and words, is in no way different from the FATHER."(*p*)

(*l*) See 1 Macc. iv. 36 to 59. Compare 2 Macc. x. 5 to 8.
(*m*) Consider Ps. xxii. 16: cxviii. 12.
(*n*) St. John xi. 14. Compare xvi. 25, 29.
(*o*) See the note on St. John viii. 12.   (*p*) Williams.

Our SAVIOUR's *Works*, then, were a sufficient evidence of His Divine Mission; proving Him to be "He that should come;"—as His reply to the Disciples of John Baptist fully shows.(q)   More will be found on this subject below, on verses 37 and 38.   See also St. John v. 36, and the note there.

He had told them in St. John v. 36, and again in viii. 42, that He was "the Sent" of GOD,—and that His Works bore witness to His Heavenly Mission.   Again, in chapter viii., it is evident that His enemies understood that He claimed to be the CHRIST, for they objected to His testimony as invalid: and He in reply referred them once more to the evidence of His Works.(r)   Of what conviction were men capable who ascribed His miracles to fraud, and His Divine Wisdom to Satanic possession?   Our SAVIOUR has already told them that their unbelief does not result from insufficient evidence.   He proceeds, in the next verse, to tell them what is its true cause.

26 But ye believe not, because ye are not of My sheep, as I said unto you.

That is,— not because I am not your Shepherd, but because ye are not My sheep.(s)—The nearest approach to this which our LORD is related to have said to them was, "He that is of GOD heareth GOD's words: ye therefore hear them not, because ye are not of GOD."(t)   "Not of My sheep," clearly denotes the *unwilling-ness* of the men He addressed to follow Him as their Shepherd, and acknowledge Him as their Guide.   Hence, our SAVIOUR adds:

27 My sheep hear My voice, and I know them, and they follow Me:

It is implied,—"But ye hear not my Voice; therefore are ye not My sheep." Compare this with what was said above of the sheep and their Shepherd, in verses 4, 5 and 6. . . . . Surely, every word here is full of momentous import! For what is this but a revelation of the Divine method,—a history of the way of Salvation,— declared in a parable by CHRIST Himself? "My sheep hear My voice,—and I know them,— and they follow Me."— The reader is referred to verse 14, and the note upon it.

28 and I give unto them Eternal Life; and they shall never perish, neither shall any *man* pluck them out of My Hand.

"Eternal Life," therefore, is that green pasture to which the Good Shepherd "leadeth out" His flock.(u)—He says "My *Hand*," because it is with this mem-ber that we retain, cherish, and protect, whatever is committed to our care. Hence, "I have graven thee" (saith He,) "*upon the palms of My Hands*."(x) And His departing saints, because they know that "the souls of the righteous are in the Hand of GOD, and there shall no torment touch them,"(y) commend to Him their spirits, even with their dying breath;(z) saying, after the example of their LORD, "*Into Thy Hands I commend my spirit.*"

The sayings in verse 28 do not apply to *the elect* only, but to *all*. Our SAVIOUR CHRIST, when He had "overcome the sharpness of Death," opened "the Kingdom of Heaven to all Believers."   The gift of Eternal Life He offers freely to as many as believe in Him, and persevere steadfastly to the end; nor can any forcibly snatch them out of His Hand: no, "neither Death," (nor Satan, who "had the power of Death,"(a) and who is emphatically "the wolf" alluded to in verse 12; who, more-over, seems to be the "being" specially alluded to in this and the next verse ;)(b) "neither Death, nor Life, ... nor things present, nor things to come, nor Height, nor Depth, nor any other creature."(c)   Yet are men left free to withdraw them-selves from the inner circle of GOD's providential care; and even hopelessly to fall away from Him.   All this, St. Paul has clearly pointed out from the writings of

(q) See St. Matth. xi. 2, 3, and the note on verses 4, 5.
(r) St. John viii. 13 and 18.   (s) Chrysostom.
(t) St. John viii. 47.   (u) See above ver. 3, and the note.
(x) Is. xlix. 16.   (y) Wisdom iii. 1.
(z) Acts vii. 59 : compare St. Luke xxiii. 46.
(a) Hebrews ii. 14.
(b) There is no word answering to "*man*" in the original ; either here, or in ver. 18.
(c) Rom. viii. 38.

the prophet Habakkuk;(d) though pains have been sometimes taken to obscure the important truth.

29 My FATHER which gave *them* Me, is greater than all; and no *man* is able to pluck *them* out of My FATHER's Hand.

Here, as elsewhere, the Eternal SON speaks of the Eternal FATHER as supreme. In what sense He is greater than the SON,(e) "greater than all," has been already partly treated of in the commentary on St. John v. 20, and will be found more fully explained on St. John xiv. 28.—Having thus plainly declared the distinction *of the Persons* of the FATHER and the SON, our SAVIOUR proceeds to assert their *Oneness of Nature:* adding a sentence which does in fact explain how it comes to pass that no man can pluck the sheep of CHRIST out of CHRIST's Hand.   Namely,

30 I and *My* FATHER are One.

Rather, "I and *the* FATHER are One."   One, that is, *in Essence.*   The "Hand" of CHRIST is therefore the "Hand" of the FATHER: for "our GOD is One, or rather very Oneness, and mere Unity, having nothing but Itself in Itself, and not consisting, (as all things do besides GOD,) of many things.   In which essential Unity of GOD, a Trinity personal nevertheless subsisteth, after a manner far exceeding the possibility of man's conceit."(f)   And that it was in this lofty sense that our Blessed LORD spake of Himself as One with the Eternal FATHER, and not after any lower method of Unity, the Jews saw clearly enough, as their conduct described in the next verse plainly shows.

31 Then the Jews took up stones again to stone Him.

"Again," in allusion to the last occasion when they had attempted the same act of violence; namely, at the Feast of Tabernacles.(g)   See above, the note on ver. 19.

32 JESUS answered them, Many good works have I showed you from My FATHER; for which of those works do ye stone Me?
33 The Jews answered Him, saying, For a good work we stone Thee not; but for blasphemy; and because that Thou, being a man, makest Thyself GOD.

Rather,—"even because Thou."—Take notice how exactly our Blessed LORD's true meaning was apprehended by these sinful men; namely, that He is *of one Substance with the FATHER.* Clear-sighted enough were they to see in His words the assertion of that sublime truth which modern unbelievers have professed themselves unable to discover there. . . . . Against those unbelievers, surely "the very stones" in these men's hands "cry out!"(h)
We shall be told (in verse 36) that our SAVIOUR had said concerning Himself, "I am the SON of GOD:" and that He had done so, in effect, is plain from His repeated mention of GOD as His FATHER, joined to His recent assertion that He and the *FATHER* are *One.*   This then was the explicit answer to the request of His enemies that "if He were the CHRIST, He would tell them plainly;"(i) for it is Matthew xxvi. 63,(k) as from many other places in the Gospel,(l) that it was the established belief of the nation that "the CHRIST" might be also called "the Son of GOD."   What then must be thought of the wickedness of persons who no sooner obtain a plain answer to their inquiry, than they take up stones in order to effect the destruction of "the poor helpless Man,"(m) whom, a moment before, they had so insidiously approached with a seemingly friendly question!   They accuse Him of blasphemy; but (on their own showing) there had been no blasphemy at all, if our SAVIOUR were indeed the CHRIST.

(d) See Hab. ii. 4, quoted in Hebr. x. 38; where be careful to observe that instead of "*any man,*" in italics, it should be, "*he,*" in Roman letters.
(e) St. John xiv. 28.
(f) Hooker.
(g) See chap. viii. 59, and the note.
(h) Maldonatus.
(i) See above, ver. 24.
(k) As well as in St. Mark xiv. 61.
(l) Consider the terms of St. Peter's confession, in St. Matth. xvi. 16: also in St. John vi. 69. See also St. John xi. 27.   Acts viii. 37, and in ix. 20.
(m) Ps. cix. 15.

Our attention is now invited to a circumstance of unusual interest. The Holy One proceeds to repel the charge of blasphemy which His enemies have brought against Him: and He does so by a citation of Scripture, on which He makes an important remark, and from the terms of which He proceeds to draw a striking inference. Need it be observed that every passage by Him cited from the Book which is inspired by His SPIRIT, and emphatically styled His own, is entitled to special reverence and attention at our hands?

34 JESUS answered them, Is it not written in your Law, "I said, Ye are gods?"

"Law," here denotes the whole body of the Jewish Scriptures.(n) — Our LORD quotes from Psalm lxxxii. — which begins with the awful announcement, that GOD standeth in the assembly of the Magistrates, and that He judges among the Judges, (or "the gods" as they are called in the Law;)(o) the entire psalm being an exhortation to the Judges of Israel, and a reproof of their negligence. Our LORD, having thus referred to the 6th verse of this psalm, where it is written, "I have said, Ye are gods; and all of you are children of the Most High,"—proceeds to make the following striking comment upon it:

35 If he called them gods, unto whom the Word of GOD came, (and the Scripture cannot be broken;)

Literally, "be loosened," or "undone:" implying that Holy Scripture is *binding*. —Before passing on, it is well worthy of observation that our SAVIOUR here assigns the reason *why* Magistrates and Judges are called "gods." It is because *to them the Word of GOD came:* that is, because, besides being endowed with the godlike gift of Reason, and being blessed with the knowledge of His Law, (so that they might, if they would, conform their will to GOD's Will, and work with Him;) *they had received authority from* GOD; and were by Him commissioned to exercise portions of His Power in the World: ("for there is no Power but of GOD; the powers that be are ordained of GOD:"(p) and were therefore, in a manner, "gods," each in the place which GOD had assigned them. "Take heed what ye do," (it was said to them anciently,) "for ye judge not for man, but for the LORD, who is with you in the judgment."(q)

So dignified and important a statement from the lips of Him who is the source of all authority and power will be felt to supply matter for solemn and profitable meditation. Let the whole psalm be studied, and it will be felt that "when GOD had spoken to men, and called their spirit (which was made in His image) to awake and work with Him, then He said "Ye are gods," that He might put strongly before them the truth that they were made in His image, and must not think to live a mere carnal life without being judged for it. That life they were choosing indeed, and living according to it, and not according to GOD; and so they are warned that they are forfeiting their best portion and true honour: "Ye shall die like men, ye shall fall like one of the princes." Truly, a sad end for those who had a calling from GOD, and a spiritual life which they might live in His glory for ever, if they would but use the powers He gave them according to His will!"(r)

To return, however, to the Divine argument. — If (says our SAVIOUR) Holy Scripture calleth certain men "gods," for no other reason than because unto them GOD's commission came, — (and the authority of every statement contained in the Law is undeniable, nor may it on any account be made light of and disregarded,) —

36 say ye of Him, whom the FATHER hath sanctified, and sent into the World, Thou blasphemest; because I said, I am the SON of GOD?

"Him" should be in italics. It is rather, "Say ye of *Me*."(s) That is, Do ye presume to charge *Me* with blasphemy, whom the FATHER hath consecrated, and commissioned to the most eminent and extraordinary office, because I said I am the

(n) So in St. John xii. 34: xv. 25; and Rom. iii. 19.
(o) Exod. xxii. 8, 9, 28, though the word is translated "gods" only in the 28th verse.
(p) Rom. xiii. 1.   (q) 2 Chron. xix. 6.   (r) Rev. C. Marriott.
(s) The same mistake occurs in the translation of St. John xix. 37, — where see the note.

SON of GOD? — See above, the note on verse 33. — And take notice that although it be true that the HOLY GHOST " was bestowed without measure on the Incarnate SON, whose Humanity He sanctified from the beginning, and continued progressively to sanctify to the end,"(t)—yet, by the phrase "whom the FATHER *hath sanctified*," is meant not this; but rather, that act of special Sanctification of the Manhood of CHRIST which consisted in the union of Godhead therewith. The expression is therefore equivalent to what we met with in St. John vi. 27, — namely, "for Him," (that is, the Son of Man,) "hath GOD the FATHER *sealed*."

The argument will therefore be of the following kind: — If *mere men*, because they enjoy God's delegated power and authority, may without blame be styled "gods," with how much better right may *I*, — declared as I am to be God's own SON, by the evidence which My works afford that the Godhead is united to the Manhood in My person, — lay claim to the same title! . . . . . In which words, Bishop Bull directs attention to a peculiar nicety of expression. Our SAVIOUR speaks not of Himself as One "whom *GOD* hath sanctified; but, "whom the *FATHER* hath sanctified:" thereby giving His hearers to understand that God began not *then* to be His FATHER when He sanctified Him, and sent Him into the World; but on the contrary, that being already His FATHER, GOD sanctified and sent Him. And this great truth is further marked by the expression "*sent into the World*;" which implies that CHRIST had first been the SON of GOD *in Heaven*.(u)

Lastly, — it will be perceived that our LORD's words do not by any means imply (as at first sight might appear) that He claimed to be "God," in no other sense than that in which the Judges of Israel are styled "gods" in the Law. His words, on the contrary, altogether exclude such a supposition; for He speaks of Himself expressly as One "*whom the FATHER hath sanctified and sent into the World*." The purport of His remonstrance is therefore simply this: "How can GOD's own SON, being very GOD, be guilty of blasphemy for saying, I am the Son of GOD, if there be no blasphemy in calling those persons "gods," and "sons of GOD,"(x) to whom merely the Word of GOD came?" . . . . In the words of an excellent writer, — "He who had such a witness as St. John, and who could do such works Himself, in proof of His being from GOD, had a right to call upon them to hear Him, as being the person "whom GOD the FATHER had sanctified, and sent into the world." The words of such a person they were not lightly to charge with blasphemy. They ought rather to have heard them with reverence; and if any thing struck them as strange and different from what they had expected, they ought to have supposed they did not quite rightly understand it, and asked the meaning of it humbly, instead of setting themselves up for His judges."(y)

It is not of course denied that, in point of fact, our SAVIOUR was really making Himself equal with GOD, whereas the Psalmist never meant to say that those he spoke of were really gods. Purposely however did He use words which might not at once show the whole truth, in order to lead His hearers on by degrees, (if they would hear,) to the fuller knowledge of Himself.

But in the meantime, the obvious answer to His entire remonstrance would have been a denial that the FATHER had so sanctified Him, and sent Him into the World. Accordingly, in the very next verse, He proceeds to establish this, — to assert the Godhead which He had in common with the FATHER, — by an argument derived from His own miracles. As it follows:

37, 38 If I do not the works of My FATHER, believe Me not. But if I do, though ye believe not Me, believe the works: that ye may know, and believe, that the FATHER *is* in Me, and I in Him.

That is,—Because I styled Myself emphatically the SON of GOD, and said that "I and the FATHER are One," ye charged Me with blasphemy. In which proceeding of yours, there would perhaps have been some reason if I had sought to establish My Divinity by My words only, and not by My acts as well. Inasmuch however as ye see Me perform the self-same almighty works with My FATHER, wherefore do ye not believe Me to be of the self-same Nature with him? I require not of you

(t) Dr. W. H. Mill.
(u) Consider St. John xvi. 28, — where see the note.
(x) "Children of the Most High." Ps. lxxxii. 6.
(y) Rev. C. Marriott.

hat ye should believe My testimony concerning Myself, but only that ye would be ersuaded by My works that the FATHER is in Me, and I in Him: in other words, 1at, (as I said,) "I and the FATHER are One."(z)

In all this, the attention which our SAVIOUR emphatically calls to His Works, and he great stress which He lays upon these as the special evidence of His Divine iature and Commission, is much to be noticed; and should be studied in connecon with the other places referred to at foot.(a) For "in almost every expression hroughout this Gospel," (as a pious writer remarks,) "there is the building up of higher doctrine, like a solemn Creed, set to the music which is in Heaven; with 1e same cadences ever and again returning."(b)

39 Therefore they sought again to take Him: but He escaped out f their hand,

"Again,"—as they had doubtless done before, in verse 31; when, having armed 1emselves with stones, they must have intended to drag our LORD out of the 'emple,(c) in order to put Him to death. "But He escaped out of their hand,"— iiraculously preserving His life, as on a former occasion. See chapter viii. 59, and 1e note there. "They apprehended Him not," (says Augustine,) "because they ad not the hands of Faith: (by which, GOD grant that we may apprehend Him, nd not let Him go!") To be near to GOD, without Faith, is to be of all the furthest rom Him. For Him to come near unto us in Love, and not to be loved in return y us, by some inscrutable mystery of our nature, engenders deepest hate of Goodess. No death is so hopeless as his who dies near the very source of life!(d)

Our SAVIOUR therefore, fleeing from the murderous designs of His enemies, now ift Jerusalem; agreeably to the precept which He had delivered to His Disciples n a former occasion:(e)

40 and went away again beyond Jordan into the place where John t first baptized; and there He abode.

"Again,"—as He may have done after the Feast of Tabernacles.(f) He abode t the place where the Forerunner "at first baptized," namely, "Bethabara beyond ordan." See St. John i. 28, 29.

It is interesting to reflect on what must have been the joy and wonder of many a umble believer, on beholding our SAVIOUR's return to the scene of His Baptism; 1e locality where the miraculous manifestation which had attended that great vent(g) must still have been well remembered; and where the witness of John 1ust have at once recurred to the memory of all. Full three years had elapsed ince then. The statements which follow, do not in the least surprise us: namely,—

41 And many resorted unto Him, and said, John did no miracle: but ll things that John spake of this man were true.

This is one of those highly suggestive places, which, in addition to all they tell s, leave us to infer so many things besides. Thus we learn, first, that many of the eople of the place "came" to our LORD, when He went to live among them. Next, 'hile we obtain the striking information that John Baptist "did no miracle;" and re left to infer how mightily the Grace of GOD must have wrought with him, that, naided by that particular species of evidence which the Jews were so prone to squire,(h) (but which it was nevertheless reserved for MESSIAH to exhibit,) he hould have succeeded in drawing multitudes to his Baptism;(i) the present place irther suggests that our SAVIOUR, during His residence at Bethabara, wrought

(z) From Bp. Bull.
(a) See above, ver. 25, and the note there. Also, St. John v. 36: xiv. 10, 11: xv. 24. Conder also St. Matth. xi. 2 to 6. St. Luke vii. 19 to 23.
(b) Williams. (c) See above, ver. 23.
(d) Williams.
(e) See St. Matthew x. 23, and the places referred to in the margin.
(f) St. John ix. 7.
(g) See St. Matthew iii. 16, 17, and St. John i. 32, 33.
(h) See St. Matthew xii. 38: xvi. 1. St. John ii. 18: vi. 30:—on any of which places, see he commentary.
(i) St. Matthew iii. 5: St. Mark i. 5: St. Luke iii. 7.

many miracles; the sight of which produced the testimony of contrast, here recorded by the Evangelist.

Then further, if the known sayings of the Baptist are attentively examined, it will perhaps be felt that to none of them can these words of the men of Bethabara be thought to apply. Those sayings do but amount to a declaration that CHRIST was to be a greater One than the Baptist himself,(*k*) even the SON of GOD,(*l*) but there will have been several more minute predictions concerning MESSIAH, certain infallible notes which John will have taught them to look for; all of which our SAVIOUR will have displayed during His present residence among them.

The saying recorded in the text amounts therefore to this :— How safely and wisely shall we yield to *Him* our hearty and entire belief; who by so many miraculous signs supports His claim to be the MESSIAH! If all things which John spake concerning Him be true, why should we except the Baptist's plain declaration that this is indeed the CHRIST? . . . Accordingly it follows:

42 And many believed on Him there.

A brief, but emphatic notice; reminding us of the many places where the Church's progressive increase is incidentally alluded to; and which will be found enumerated in the note on the last words of St. John ii. 11.

Delightful and refreshing is it, amid the many examples of the "contradiction of sinners"(*m*) which distress us in the Gospel, to meet with these brief notices of the Church's early increase. Silently and calmly in the despised Galilee, in the hated Samaria, in the parts beyond Jordan, at Bethany, in the hostile capital itself,— silently and secretly are the living stones found to have been wrought into beauty by the Hand of the Divine Artist; whereby *that* came to pass in respect of GOD's spiritual Temple which had been exhibited in type in the construction of His material Shrine;—"the House, when it was in building, was built of stone made ready before it was brought thither: so that there was neither hammer nor axe, nor any tool of iron heard in the House while it was in building."(*n*)

CHAPTER XI.

1 CHRIST *raiseth Lazarus, four days buried.* 45 *Many Jews believe.* 47 *The High-priest and Pharisees gather a council against* CHRIST. 49 *Caiaphas prophesieth.* 54 JESUS *hid Himself.* 55 *At the Passover they inquire after Him, and lay wait for Him.*

IT is a remarkable feature in the present Gospel that each chapter seems to contain some one great subject,—the narrative chiefly of a single incident: so that we are able by a short phrase to bring the whole of each chapter before the memory. Thus, THE WORD, Cana, Nicodemus, the Woman of Samaria, the Pool of Bethesda, the Miracle of the Loaves, the Woman taken in Adultery, the Man born blind, the Good Shepherd, — these few words seem to set before us, with sufficient exactness, the ten chapters of St. John which have gone before. The present chapter, in like manner, is entirely devoted to *the Raising of Lazarus;* which, as Augustine truly remarks, is more spoken of than any of our LORD's miracles.

The circumstance is certainly worthy of attention that so stupendous an event should be not only unrecorded, but not even alluded to, either by St. Matthew,

---

(*k*) St. John i. 26, 27. Take notice that the longest recorded discourse of the Baptist, (St. John iii. 27 to 36,) was pronounced at "Ænon near to Salim,"—St. John iii. 23.
(*l*) St. John i. 34.   (*m*) Hebrews xii. 3.   (*n*) 1 Kings vi. 7.

St. Mark, or St. Luke. The same thing may be said, however, with almost equal truth, of the whole contents of St. John's Gospel. And the *reason* of it seems hardly a legitimate subject of inquiry. The silence of St. Matthew concerning our LORD's Ascension into Heaven might perhaps surprise us; for it is an Article of the Creed. Not so the last of the three miracles of Raising the Dead; however surpassing the other two in wonder, as things seem wonderful to us.

What may be the correct *inference*, however, to be derived from the silence of the other Evangelists on this great subject, seems to be highly deserving our attention: nor is it hard to discover it. How sublime a comment does it afford on that statement of the beloved Disciple, — that "there are also *many other things* which JESUS did; the which, if they should be written every one, I suppose that even the World itself could not contain the books that should be written!"(a)

Now a certain *man* was sick, *named* Lazarus of Bethany, the town of Mary and her sister Martha.

We are indebted to St. John's Gospel for our knowledge of the family of Bethany, — that brother, and that pair of holy sisters, whom the Son of Man "loved;"(b) and who seems to have enjoyed the amazing privilege of furnishing Him with a shelter during His residences at Jerusalem. Those departures from the capital during the last days of His Ministry, when He is said to have gone out to Bethany,(c) may well indicate His withdrawal for the night to the house of Martha, — for we find it spoken of in a certain place,(d) as if *she* were actually the mistress of the house. — St. Luke indeed just mentions the two sisters, as well as St. John: but the present Evangelist alone mentions Lazarus; whose name occurs for the first time in the passage before us. A name divinely significant, truly! for Lazarus, or rather *Eleazar*,(e) which is the same word, denotes one "*whom GOD aids*." . . . . When our LORD heard that this man "was sick," He was Himself residing with His Disciples at Bethabara, on the eastern side of the Jordan, as recorded at the close of chapter x.(f)

2 (It was *that* Mary which anointed the LORD with ointment, and wiped His feet with her hair, whose brother Lazarus was sick.)

This incidental remark, whereby the blessed writer identifies the Mary of whom he is about to speak, and distinguishes her from all the other Marys who are named in the Gospel, suggests two observations: the first, critical, — namely, that St. John is here alluding to a transaction which took place *after* the raising of Lazarus. The entire history having long since elapsed, at the time when the Evangelist wrote his Gospel, he very naturally speaks of the anointing in the past tense, though it was yet future when our SAVIOUR heard of the sickness of Lazarus.

The other observation has been already offered in connection with the first words of St. John iv. 46: namely, that it is altogether in the manner of the beloved Disciple to identify persons and places by some one incident which rendered them for ever famous. His allusion to Cana of Galilee, and Bethabara beyond Jordan, will occur to the reader at once.(g) His method of identifying Nicodemus,(h) Lazarus,(i) the sister of Lazarus,(j) Caiaphas,(k) and himself,(l) are even more striking.

The act of Mary which unassisted human judgment would probably have rather pitched upon as characteristic, would have been her sitting at the feet of JESUS, recorded in St. Luke x. 38 to 42, — where the notes may be referred to.

3 Therefore his sisters sent unto Him, saying, LORD, behold, he whom Thou lovest is sick.

From which it appears that they knew, at Bethany, the place of our SAVIOUR's

---

(a) St. John xxi. 25.   (b) See below, ver. 5.
(c) St. Mark xi. 12, [St. Matth. xxi. 18.] 19. St. Luke xx. 37.
(d) St. Luke x. 38.
(e) The name occurs twenty or thirty times in the Old Testament; first, in Exod. vi. 25.
(f) St. John x. 40, — where see the note.
(g) St. John iv. 46 and x. 40.   (h) St. John vii. 50: xix. 39.
(i) St. John xii. 1.   (j) Alluding to the present place.
(k) See St. John xviii. 14, alluding to xi. 50.   (l) St. John xxi. 20.

sojourn; which is somewhat remarkable. It is evident however from St. John x. 41, 42, that He was not living in any privacy at Bethabara.—Unlearned readers may like to be told that what St John actually says is,—"*The* sisters then sent unto Him:" but all may be invited to take notice that these holy women send no direct *petition* to our Saviour. They neither say "Come down ere he die :(m) nor "Come and lay Thy hand on him, and he shall live :(n) nor even "Speak the word only, and he shall be healed."(o) They do but remind Him of *His love* for their dying brother, and are content with having urged that tender plea. After thus, without request, "making their requests known unto God," it seems as if they sought to be "careful for nothing."(p) Consider St. John ii. 3.

4 When Jesus heard *that*, He said, This sickness is not unto death, but for the Glory of God, that the Son of God might be glorified thereby.

The saying of One who seeth the end from the beginning! These words may be supposed to have been addressed to the messengers of Martha and Mary. The meaning is sufficiently obvious ; namely, that the design of God in sending this sickness, (of which our Lord shows Himself to be perfectly well aware,) was not with a view to the present dissolution of Lazarus, but to convert his Death into an occasion of His own Glory. In this respect, the present place deserves to be compared with St. John ix. 3,—on which passage the reader is invited to read what has been already offered. Both the present miracle and that just now alluded to promoted God's Glory in a singular manner by affording such transcendent evidence of His Divinity; and as a necessary consequence, by convincing so many of the Divinity of Christ.(q)

"Inseparable," (says Hilary;) "is God's honour from the honour of Christ. How altogether one and the same they are, may be shown from this very passage. Lazarus dies for the Glory of God, that *the SON of GOD may be glorified*. What doubt can there be that the Glory of God consists in the Glory of God's Son, since the death of Lazarus, which was conducive to God's Glory, was designed to bring Glory also to the Son of God?"

Take notice that by such words, our Lord prepared the minds of His hearers "beforehand, as He often did, for some miraculous interposition."(r)

Truly has it been remarked that "the Son of God, who was glorified through the death of Lazarus, will have His Glory, somehow or other, in the death of each of ourselves."(s) .... *We*, in the meantime, be it observed, have learnt the meaning of language to which even such saints as Martha and her sister were as yet strangers. When their messengers returned to Bethany, as doubtless they did at once, with these words on their lips,—how enigmatical must the message have sounded in the ears of the sisters! "This sickness not unto death :" nay, but Lazarus has been already dead for one whole day! And what can their mighty Friend mean by the event being intended "for the Glory of God: that the Son of God might be glorified thereby?" .... It will be found suggested below, (in the note on verse 40,) that Martha asked concerning this matter, as soon as she came into our Saviour's presence.

5 Now Jesus loved Martha, and her sister, and Lazarus.

"I love those that love Me," (saith the Spirit;) "and those that seek Me early shall find Me."(t)

Well may such a statement be exhibited by itself, and occupy a separate verse! What a world of blessedness is implied in those few words! How many acts of unutterable condescension on the part of Him whose ways, at the birthday of Creation, caused the very morning-stars to sing together, and the sons of God to shout for joy!(u) On the part of the little family of Bethany, how much of reverence and gratitude, as well as singleness and purity of heart! . . . . . Let those who have

(m) St. John iv. 49.　　　　　　　　　　(n) St. Matth. ix. 18.
(o) St. Matth. viii. 8.　　　　　　　　　(p) Phil. iv. 6.
(q) See St. John ix. 16 : x. 21 : xi. 37.—See also below, ver. 45, 48 : xii. 11, 17 to 19 and 42.
(r) Williams.
(s) From a MS. Sermon by the Rev. E. Hobhouse.
(t) Prov. viii. 17.　　　　　　　　　　　(u) Job xxxviii. 7.
(v) See the note on St. Mark vii. 44.

presumed to think of Martha as of one engrossed with domestic cares, to the neglect of her spiritual condition, consider what is implied by the statement, " JESUS *loved Martha.*" We make wondrous free with GOD's saints. It is "unbelieving Thomas," (!) and "busy Martha," (!) More complaisant to ourselves, we do not hesitate to assert that we have given our "mite," when we have cast into the offerings of GOD so paltry a sum that we are literally ashamed to say how small it was.(v)

Take notice, by the way, that though our SAVIOUR loved these two sisters and their brother Lazarus, yet the first were at this time drowned in sorrow ; the last, sick nigh unto death. " Whom the LORD *loveth,*" therefore, " He *chasteneth :*"(x) and of this we are careful to remind our sick, when we visit them with the consolations of our Holy Religion.(y) To remind *us* of it, may have been one of the Evangelist's reasons for mentioning the SAVIOUR's *love* for the little family of Bethany.

6 When He had heard therefore that he was sick, He abode two days still in the same place where He was.

As already explained, at Bethabara, on the eastern side of the Jordan. We can but entreat attention to the progress of the sacred narrative. Here was no want of love towards the sick man, or his relations : on the contrary, " JESUS *loved Martha, and her sister, and Lazarus.*" We are not left to draw inferences : the fact is expressly stated. Neither was Prayer wanting : for the messengers of Martha and Mary, though they asked nothing, showed clearly enough what was the longing desire of their souls. Notwithstanding all this, our SAVIOUR is found to remain " two days still in the same place where He was." In the meantime, Lazarus, from being ill, actually dies, and is buried ! . . . . Now all these things " were written for *our* learning, that we through patience and comfort of the Scriptures might have Hope."(z)

A pious writer remarks : " To faithful suppliants, there is no better sign than for their prayers not to be soon answered, for it is a pledge of greater good in store. The conduct of our LORD is the sensible embodying to our sight of what we experience in the ways of His Providence. In the family which JESUS loved, one is dying, the other two in distress. They omit no means of obtaining the Divine aid. They are heard by Him who is as if He heard not : He waits, and for two days moves not, nor deigns them any consoling reply. And this, not for want of Love, but from the greatness of His Love towards them. This, as it is a matter of familiar occurrence, so is it often alluded to throughout the Scriptures. " Shall not GOD avenge His own elect, which cry day and night unto Him, though He bear long with them? I tell you that He will avenge them speedily."(a) And yet from beneath the Altar, they cry " How long ?"(b)

The reader is invited to refer to what has been already offered on the subject of Divine delays, in the notes on St. John iv. 47, St. Mark v. 24 and 35, and St. Luke v. 17. Those remarks here suggest themselves again, but may not be repeated.

Our SAVIOUR "abode *two days* still in the same place where He was," and then set out for Bethany. On arriving, He found that Lazarus had been *four days* dead and buried.(c) Now, from Bethany to Bethabara is found to have been about a single day's journey. Lazarus must therefore have been at his last extremity when the Sisters sent to CHRIST. The very same thing was observed in the case of the Nobleman's son,(d) and the daughter of Jairus.(e) Is it not a type of what we see happening around us, of what happens to ourselves, every day? When all beside is hopeless, when help from every other quarter is excluded, we bethink ourselves of Him! . . Does not He also often reserve His aid until all earthly means have failed ; as if to remind us that man's extremity is GOD's opportunity?

7 Then after that saith He to *His* Disciples, Let us go into Judæa again.

(v) See the note on St. Mark xii. 44.
(x) Heb. xii. 6.
(z) Rom. xv. 4.
(b) Williams, quoting Rev. vi. 10.
(c) See verses 17 and 39.
(e) St. Mark v. 24 and 25, where see the notes.

(y) See the Communion of the Sick.
(a) St. Luke xviii. 7, 8.

(d) St. John iv. 47 and 49.

So spake *He* concerning whom it is said,—"After two days will He revive us; in the third day He will raise us up, and we shall live in His sight."(*f*)

8 *His* Disciples say unto Him, Master, the Jews of late sought to stone Thee; and goest Thou thither again?

They allude evidently to the transaction recorded in chapter x. 31 to 39. Take notice that the word translated " of late," (literally " [but] now," " [just] now,")(*g*) indicates that the attempt to stone our LORD had been of very recent occurrence. But we know that the Feast of Dedication, about which time it happened, was in December. It will have been at our *Epiphany* Season therefore that our LORD will have *manifested forth His Glory* by the raising of Lazarus.(*h*)

9 JESUS answered, Are there not twelve hours in the day? If any man walk in the day, he stumbleth not, because he seeth the light of this world.

Mysterious words! which recall His sayings immediately before He bestowed sight on the man born blind ;(*i*) and which require to be interpreted in somewhat the same manner as those sayings. Indeed the two places singularly resemble and illustrate one another. When He mentions " The Light of this World," the Sun of Righteousness is speaking of His visible emblem in the Heavens.

The words before us may perhaps be paraphrased somewhat as follows:—"Are there not in the Day twelve hours of Light?"(*k*) (for the Jews divided the period between sunrise and sunset into twelve equal parts,—whatever the season of the year:) " and until the last of those twelve hours has run out, is it not certain that Darkness cannot overtake a man? None can stumble for want of Light, so long as any part of the appointed period of sunshine remains.—Just so is it with respect to Myself. The period fixed in the counsels of GOD, for the duration of the Ministry of the SON of Man, hath not yet expired. "Mine hour is not yet come." It is " the eleventh hour" with Me, indeed, but there yet remains to Me one full hour more. Learn therefore that your present fears for My personal safety are groundless." . . . . The place may be usefully compared with St. Luke xiii. 32, 33,—where the fixed period of our SAVIOUR's Ministry is in like manner indicated by the mention of " to-day, and to-morrow, and the day following."

Such seems the literal sense of what was spoken: but it is obvious that a spiritual meaning lies beneath the surface of the letter. Hence, the parabolical character of the language employed:—" the Day," " twelve hours," " walking," " stumbling," " the light of this World." Could any one indeed desire a better commentary on our LORD's hidden meaning than what He Himself supplies by His words on a subsequent occasion, in reply to the inquiry of the people, " Who is this Son of Man?" Hear His answer:—" Then JESUS said unto them, Yet a little while is THE LIGHT with you. *Walk while ye have THE LIGHT, lest Darkness come upon you:* for he that walketh in Darkness knoweth not whither he goeth. While ye have THE LIGHT, believe in THE LIGHT, that ye may be the children of Light"(*l*) " I, LIGHT, came into the World, *that every one who believeth in Me, should not abide in Darkness.*"(*m*) "As long as I am in the World, *I am the Light of the World.*"(*n*) These sayings are enough to vindicate for our LORD's present Discourse the same breadth of meaning which was claimed for St. John ix. 4, 5, in the note on the latter of those two verses. They prepare us in fact for the turn which the thought immediately takes.

10 But if a man walk in the night, he stumbleth, because there is no light in him.

By which words, attention is directed from the Speaker to His Disciples, and to

(*f*) Hosea vi. 2. See the last paragraph of the notes on the first half of St. John iv. 54. Consider also the following places,—Gen. xxii. 4: xl. 20: xli. 1: xlii. 17, 18. St. Luke ii. 44. Acts ix. 9.

(*g*) As in St. John xxi. 10.   (*h*) Consider St. John ii. 11: xi. 4, 40
(*i*) See St. John ix. 4, 5, and the notes there.
(*k*) Our Version gives the exact meaning of the original here, though it does not appear to do so. The same, of verses 25, 26.
(*l*) Compare St. Luke xvi. 8.   (*m*) St. John xii. 35, 36, 46.
(*n*) St. John ix. 5.

the Jewish nation generally. It is not so much a new thought which is here brought forward, as the practical application to our LORD's hearers of the Divine saying which went before; which is here brought out and applied. The beloved Disciple will be found to refer to these words of his LORD in 1 St. John ii. 10, 11: while many a passage in the writings of the Apostles of CHRIST explain the spiritual force of the expression "to stumble."(o) Concerning the phrase "there is no Light in him," it may suffice to refer the reader to St. Matthew vi. 22, 23.

Before passing on to another subject, the reader is invited to consider the fearful significance which the present sayings of our LORD give to that well-known expression of His,—"This is your hour and *the Power of Darkness*,"(p) spoken at the time of His apprehension in the garden: also, to the Evangelist's remark, on occasion of the departure of Judas,—"Now, *it was night:*"(q) and, not least of all, to the *darkness* which covered "all the Land"(r) at the eclipse of "the *True* Light" upon the Cross.

11 These things said He: and after that He saith unto them, Our friend Lazarus sleepeth; but I go, that I may awake him out of sleep.

Take notice how He includes them all with Himself, as friends of Lazarus: "*Our friend Lazarus*." Yet more, take notice that death is, in GOD's sight, but a *sleep*. Now, from all sleeping there must be a waking; so that in this very term is contained the doctrine of the Resurrection. The same remarks were suggested by our SAVIOUR's declaration concerning the daughter of Jairus, "The maiden is not dead, *but sleepeth*."(s)

This way of regarding death is not peculiar to the Gospel, as some have thought. See the references at the end of the note on St. Mark v. 39. It is true, however, that what was only the language of exalted Faith under the Old Covenant, is the ordinary speech of believers under the New.(t)

12 Then said His Disciples, LORD, if he sleep, he shall do well.

As much as to say, "If it be indeed merely a state of lethargy into which our friend has fallen, he is safe, and will get well; nor can it be needful that Thou shouldst go down to the scene of danger, in person." Or they may have meant that the sleep of Lazarus was a sign that he was on the road to recovery. Either way, their speech is dissuasive: and recalls what we meet with in St. Matthew xvi. 22. It reveals also a thing which the Evangelist has not yet mentioned,—namely, that our LORD's Disciples knew that Lazarus was *ill*.

13 Howbeit JESUS spake of his death: but they thought that He had spoken of taking of rest in sleep.

On this, (as on so many other occasions,) we are struck by the childlike manner in which these holy men are found to receive the sayings of their LORD. They evidently interpreted them in the *most literal* manner possible. Consider their remarks on His injunction to "beware of the leaven of the Pharisees and of the Sadducees,"(x)—on His declaration, "I have meat to eat, that ye know not of,"(y) —on His admonition that "he that had no sword, should sell his garment and buy one."(z)

14 Then said JESUS unto them plainly, Lazarus is dead.

Compare St. John x. 24: xvi. 29. He does not add,—"But I go that I may raise Him from death!"

15 And I am glad for your sakes that I was not there, to the intent ye may believe;

(o) See St. Matthew xviii. 7, 8 (compare v. 29, &c.). Romans ix. 32: xiv. 21. 1 St. Pet. ii. 8. Consider likewise St. Luke ii. 34, and 1 Cor. i. 23.
(p) St. Luke xxii. 53.   (q) St. John xiii. 30.
(r) St. Matthew xxvii. 45.
(s) See the notes on St. Matthew ix. 24, and St. Mark v. 39.
(t) See St. Matthew xxvii. 52. Acts vii. 60: xiii. 36. 1 Cor. xi. 30: xv. 6, 18, 20, 51. 1 Thess. iv. 13, 14, 15. 2 St. Peter iii. 4.
(x) St. Matthew xvi. 6 to 12, &c.   (y) St. John iv. 32 to 34.
(z) St. Luke xxii. 36, 38.

Clearly implying, (as will be found explained in the note on ver. 32,) that Lazarus would not,—*could* not have died,—had the LORD of Life been present.

"Instead of raising up Lazarus from sickness, as they whom He loved had desired, they are all by this miracle to be raised up together with Lazarus unto the life of Faith, which will never die."(a)   And here the progressive nature of Faith,—its several degrees, and the accessions of which it is capable,—is much to be noticed.   After the water made wine, at Cana of Galilee, "His Disciples believed on Him;"(b) and after the stilling of the storm on the Lake, all worshipped Him, with the confession, "Thou art the SON of GOD."(c)   Simon Peter twice confessed Him as the "CHRIST, *the SON of the living GOD:*"(d) and we have already heard Martha say, "I believe that Thou art the CHRIST, the SON of GOD, which should come into the world."(e)   Yet, *because of their unbelief*, it was that nine of the Apostles were unable to heal the lunatic boy: they had not "faith as a grain of mustard-seed."(f)   "O thou of little faith!" exclaimed our SAVIOUR to Simon Peter.(g)   "*Have faith in GOD,*"(h) was His word to the Twelve after cursing the Fig-tree: and Lazarus is now to be raised from the dead to the intent *they* "*may believe.*" . . . Our SAVIOUR adds,—

nevertheless let us go unto him.

16 Then said Thomas, which is called Didymus, unto his fellow-disciples, Let us also go, that we may die with Him.

We know very little about the Apostle Thomas,(i) (who as St. John thrice remarks,) was called "Didymus" by the Greeks as he was called "Thomas" by the Hebrews.(j)   He comes prominently before us on only three occasions, of which this is the first:(k) but from the very expressive indications which the Gospels supply, we have sufficient materials to enable us to conceive his character.   He appears to have been a man of earnest mind, capable of strong and disinterested attachments; but of that temperament which looks habitually to the darker side of things; which, out of several future events equally possible, is ever disposed to consider the least welcome as the most probable, and to distrust extraordinary good news all the more from the circumstance of its being good.   This habit of mind we find strongly exemplified on the present occasion.   The Twelve, with one accord, deprecate our LORD's self-exposure to the powerful enemies in the capital who had so lately threatened Him with stoning: and doubtless those of the number who shared in any degree the sanguine temper of their chief member,—his willing disbelief of the possibility of the LORD's subjection to shame and death,—must have remonstrated in the hope either that their dissuasions would be effectual; or that their LORD, if He choose to brave the danger, would by His experienced power surmount it.   But not so thinks Thomas.   He is the first to recognize the adverse determination of his Master, and while perceiving, despairingly to acquiesce in it; and he says immediately to his fellow-disciples,—"Let us also go, that we may die with Him;" thus uniting, with a feeling of entire self-devotion, the anticipation that the worst must follow; that in the death of their beloved Master, all hope was gone; and that it was well for them who had contentedly shared His fortunes hitherto, to perish also contentedly with Him by the hands of His triumphant enemies.(l)

Chrysostom points out that he who now scarcely dared to go to Bethany in company with his LORD, afterwards fearlessly traversed the whole East, without Him, in the midst of those who sought his death.   St. Thomas is the Apostle of India.

17 Then when JESUS came, He found that he had *lain* in the grave four days already.

Of this, we are twice reminded.(m)   Four days! a hopeless period: one day more than the third day, which is the third day of Resurrection!   The appointed

(a) Williams.   (b) St. John ii. 11.
(c) St. Matthew xiv. 33   (d) St. Matthew xvi. 16.
(e) See below, verse 27.   (f) St. Matthew xvii. 19, 20.
(g) St. Matthew xiv. 31.   (h) St. Mark xi. 22.
(i) See a short notice of him in the Commentary on St. Mark iii. 18.
(j) Namely, in St. John xi. 16: xx. 24: xxi. 2: for the Evangelist is not here *translating* the Hebrew word, and explaining that it means "Twin."
(k) The other two being St. John xiv. 5, and xx. 24 to 29.
(l) Dr. W. H. Mill.   (m) See verse 39.

days of "weeping" were ended: those of lamentation had begun.] Dying on the very day when the sisters had sent to our SAVIOUR, (who was distant about one day's journey from Bethany,) in consequence of the two days still spent at Betha-bara, Lazarus will now have been dead four days; and since it was usual with the Jews to inter their dead on the day of death.(n) he will have "been four days in the grave" also. From this verse would it not seem as if our SAVIOUR on reaching the outskirts of the village, had been *told* by some one of what had befallen His friend?

18, 19 Now Bethany was nigh unto Jerusalem, about fifteen furlongs off: and many of the Jews came to Martha and Mary, to comfort them concerning their brother.

Rather, "*had come* to Martha and Mary:" yet chiefly to comfort *Mary*. Con-sider verses 31 and 45.—The nature of the errand thus alluded to, will be found noticed below, in the latter part of the note on verse 46. The office of the com-forters, (like that of the mourners)(o) on such occasions, had grown a miserable piece of lifeless formalism. The days of grief were fixed at thirty; of which it was prescribed that the three first should be for weeping, the next seven for lamen-tation, and so forth. More than one Jewish treatise is extant on this subject. Happily for the sisters, a better Comforter was already on the way to their dwelling!

By stating that the village of Bethany was scarcely two miles distant from the capital, St. John (who writes for strangers, as already often pointed out,)(p) seems to explain how it happened that "many of the Jews" were enabled to come on the pious errand here described. . . . "So entirely was it a scene of mourning! as in a family where death and the funeral are passed."(q)

20 Then Martha, as soon as she heard that JESUS was coming, went and met Him: but Mary sat *still* in the house.

Some one seems to have come in advance, in order to warn the sisters of the approach of their Divine Friend. Martha, (probably because the tidings were first conveyed to herself,) hastens to receive Him; and meets Him, (as we learn from ver. 30,) outside the village. There the ensuing dialogue takes place. Mary in the meantime, with characteristic calmness, is sitting still in the house. Surely the act of either sister is equally lovely! If the repose and sanctity of Mary's course affects the heart most, who does not feel the blessedness of Martha in thus going forth to meet her LORD and ours! "To meet a friend coming to us in our affliction, is something," (says the pious writer last quoted:) "but this meeting was with such feeling as none can know but they who beheld in the flesh Him who raised the dead."

21 Then said Martha unto JESUS, LORD, if Thou hadst been here, my brother had not died.

And so presently said Mary,—as will be found in ver. 32, where see the note. It is striking to observe that our SAVIOUR also, in effect, had said the same thing, when His friend's sickness was first reported to Him: for *what* was implied by the words, "I am glad for your sakes that I was not there,"—if not the admission that in that case, "Lazarus had not died?" . . . Martha proceeds:

22 But I know that even now, whatsoever Thou wilt ask of GOD, GOD will give *it* Thee.

What may the pious woman have meant? That CHRIST could give her back her brother even now? It does not indeed seem that she meant nothing less. But faith itself breaks down when the trial of faith comes on; for consider her words in verse 39. . . . Observe however that even yet she perseveres in the lowly course which we recognized both the sisters at first as pursuing: namely, she makes no *request*.

(n) Acts v. 6 to 10. (o) See the note on St. Mark v. 38.
(p) See the notes on St. John ii. 6 and vi. 1.
(q) Williams.

Meantime, the weak point in her confession clearly is that she does not recognise CHRIST *as GOD*. Whatever He might ask of GOD, she was sure that GOD *would give Him* : but this is no more than is promised to every one of ourselves.(r) She does not know that He and the FATHER "are *One:*" that whosoever seeth *Him*, hath seen the FATHER. And yet, had He not declared as much by His message to the sisters in verse 4?

Even that faithful saying,—"LORD, if Thou hadst been here,"—discovers a want of Faith. Is CHRIST therefore "mighty to save" only when *present ?*

23 JESUS saith unto her, Thy brother shall rise again.

By which words, He begins to prepare her, (as His Divine manner ever was,) for the miracle which was to follow. The afflicted woman, however, regards His Divine words as merely conveying the usual language of consolation,—like that which St. Paul addressed to the Thessalonians.(s)

24 Martha saith unto Him, I know that he shall rise again in the Resurrection at the Last Day.

Whereby she seems to imply that she had dared to hope for something more. "In the Resurrection, at the Last Day, *all* must rise. I *know* that he will rise *then !*" ... Are we perhaps at liberty to suspect that our LORD Himself had been her Teacher here? or may we presume, (on the strength of Job xix. 25,) that the same hope was confidently entertained by the best informed of the Jewish nation in general?

25 JESUS said unto her, I am the Resurrection and the Life:

Blessed words! and rightly chosen to be the first which shall greet the mourner's ear when he enters the place of graves! Shall we ever listen to them, without considering the occasion on which they were first spoken, and calling to mind the largeness of the bliss of which they were the solemn, aye, the *immediate* precursors?

"I am the Resurrection and the Life," saith our LORD: and by taking again the life which He had already laid down, He *proved His right* to that title.(t) He is "*the Resurrection,*" because He is the sole cause of Resurrection to us. "As in Adam all die, even so in CHRIST shall all be made alive.(u) "For since by man came Death, by man came also the Resurrection of the dead."(v) ."Doth any man doubt," (asks Hooker,) "but that even from the flesh of CHRIST our very bodies do receive that life which shall make them glorious at the latter day?" ... He also is "*the Life,*" because our only true life is derived from Him,—of whom it is said, "in Him was *Life:*"(w) and "as the FATHER hath Life in Himself, so hath He given to the SON to have *Life in Himself.*"(x) Hence, in another place, our LORD says, — "I am the Way, the Truth, and *the Life;*"(y) St. Peter calls Him "the Prince," (or "Author,") "of Life;"(z) and the Apostle Paul declares, "When CHRIST, *who is the Life,* shall appear, then shall ye also appear with Him in glory."(a) ... It was implied, therefore, on the present occasion,—What need to wait for "the Last Day," when *He* stands before thee who is more than the cause of Resurrection to others: yea, who is the very Resurrection and the Life itself!

Martha had said, "I know that whatsoever Thou wilt ask of GOD, GOD will give it Thee." Our LORD makes answer:

26 He that believeth in Me, though he were dead, yet shall he live: and whosoever liveth and believeth in Me shall never die.

The first clause was evidently designed to bear a twofold meaning. The believer in CHRIST, though he suffer dissolution, yet shall surely rise again from Death, and live with CHRIST for ever. Even so, "GOD, who is rich in mercy, for His great love wherewith He loved us, even when we were *dead in sins,* hath quickened us together with CHRIST."(b) Of the Prodigal son it is declared in like manner that "he *was dead,* and *is alive again.*"(c).

(r) St. Matth. xxi. 22. St. John xiv. 13, 14: xv. 7, 16: xvi. 23, 24.
(s) 1 Thess. iv. 13 to 18. (t) So Bp. Pearson.
(u) 1 Cor. xv. 22. (v) 1 Cor. xv. 21.
(w) St. John i. 4. (x) St. John v. 26. (y) St. John xiv. 6.
(z) Acts iii. 15. (a) Coloss. iii. 4. (b) Eph. ii. 45.
(c) St. Luke xv. 24, — where see note.

The second clause of the sentence, however, claims for itself nothing but a spiritual interpretation. Whosoever lives that Life which alone in God's sight deserves the name of living, — (the Life of Faith in the Incarnate Son,) — this man shall never die: that is, he shall know nothing of that "second Death,"(d) which alone deserves the name of dying. These two sayings are therefore an expansion of the declaration which went before,—" I am *the Resurrection* and *the Life.*"

And here, we may not fail to remind the reader how "exceedingly little is said in the New Testament about *Death.* Christ is declared to have "*abolished*" it ;(e) and accordingly, it almost disappears from the Christian scheme: *the Coming of CHRIST* being the topic which takes its place. "The two *natural* eras of our being, — our Birth and our Death, — are not the *Christian* eras. All things are become new to us. Our span is different; our points are different. We begin with the Sacrament of our New Birth, when Christ gives us His grace: we end with that hour, when He shall come" to take unto Him His elect, and to reign.(f) . . . "Verily, verily, I say unto you, He that heareth My word, and believeth on Him that sent Me, *hath everlasting Life,* and shall not come into condemnation; but *is passed from Death unto Life.*"(g)   How glorious an intimation from the very "Prince of Life!"(h)   See the beginning of the note on St. Luke xvi. 9 . . . . . To each one of us, as well as to Martha, He addresses the solemn question which follows:—

Believest thou this?

For this sublime doctrine was more than Martha had yet professed her belief in.

Take notice that our Saviour, who can do nothing where there is not Faith,(k) requires a confession from Martha before He raises Lazarus from the grave ; as He required a confession from the Twelve before He suffered three of their number to behold His Transfiguration.(l) . . . "Believe ye that I am able to do this?" — He asked of the two blind men who followed Him crying for mercy.(m)   "If thou canst believe," — was his saying to the father of the lunatic child,(n) before He proceeded to cast out the dumb and deaf spirit.

27 She saith unto Him, Yea, Lord: I believe that Thou art the CHRIST, the Son of God, which should come into the World.

A marvellous confession, truly ; and, *implicitly,* all that could be wished for ; yet does it not appear to have been the *explicit* confession which our Saviour had required of her.   So thought Chrysostom: who remarks, — "She seems not to have understood His words.   She saw that He meant something great, but did not see what it was.   She is asked one thing and answers another."   Yet observe her language, "Yea, Lord," she begins, "*I have believed:*" thereby, as it would seem, expressing what had long been the abiding conviction of her soul; and she proceeds to declare her full belief in our Lord's Divinity.   Augustine, accordingly, understands her to imply, — "When I believed that thou wert the Son of God, I believed also that Thou wert the Resurrection, and that Thou wert the Life:" and that "he that believeth in Thee, though he die, yet shall he live." . . . "The Anointed,"—"the Son of God,"—"He that should come,"(o)—she names Him by three of His great Names.   Yet have we heard her, in ver. 22, ascribe to Him the conduct of a created being!

It will, in fact, have struck every intelligent reader of the Gospel with some surprise that persons capable of such magnificent confessions as we sometimes meet with, should *practically* have shown that they entertained very erroneous, or very unworthy notions of our Lord.   This circumstance, however, need not cause perplexity.   Assisted by the Creeds and Confessions of the Church Catholic, the meanest among us (blessed be God for it!) are now enabled to reason aright concerning our Saviour: but in the days of Messiah, it was not so.   The Incarnation,

(d) Rev. ii. 11: xx. 6, 14: xxi. 8; and consider xxi. 4.
(e) 2 Tim. i. 10.
(f) From a MS. sermon by the Rev. C. P. Eden (17th Dec. 1854).
(g) St. John v. 24.   (h) Acts iii. 15.   (k) St. Matth. xiii. 58.
(l) Consider St. Matth. xvi. 15, 16, and xvii. 1, 2.
(m) St. Matth. ix. 28.   (n) St. Mark ix. 23.
(o) The reader is referred to the note on St. Matth. xi. 3.

— that great "mystery of godliness,"(*p*)—as it was the fruitful parent of most of the early heresy, so might it well prove a difficulty in the way of every indiviual believer; leaving Reason far behind, and tasking Faith itself beyond its utmost unassisted powers.

28 And when she had so said, she went her way, and called Mary her sister secretly, saying, The Master is come, and calleth for thee.

Is it not perhaps rather,—"secretly saying?" Martha seems to have retraced her steps; called her sister Mary aside; and privately to have poured the blissful message into her ear. Martha found her sitting among those members of her own nation who had come to comfort the sisters, — as may be gathered from verses 19, 29 and 31, where see the note. The prescribed rule on such occasions was, that the "comforters" sat in silence upon the floor, till the mourner spoke.

The word here, and generally elsewhere, translated "Master," rather implies a "Teacher." But it is in fact the nearest Greek equivalent to the Hebrew "Rabbi," as St. John informs us in chapter i. 38. By this name the little family at Bethany are found to have designated our LORD in conversation with one another.

Take notice that it is not actually *recorded* that our SAVIOUR asked for Mary. That He "called her," we learn from these words of her sister. In this way, many little circumstances, perhaps unsuspected by careless readers, are revealed both in the Old and New Testaments. A few examples of this are set down at foot of the page; which it may be found worth while to refer to.(*q*) Indeed, one other saying of our blessed LORD, on this same occasion, though not recorded in its historical place, is discoverable from a subsequent part of the present chapter; and is so related there, as even to suggest a further portion of Martha's dialogue with our SAVIOUR. See below, the note on ver. 40.

But to return to the narrative. Mary is told that the LORD has asked for her :—

29 As soon as she heard *that*, she arose quickly, and came unto Him.

The Evangelist will be found *twice* to notice the promptness with which Mary obeyed our LORD's summons. Such a circumstance may be thought to make the supposition the more probable, that she had not before been aware of His approach. It has been thought that Martha's more active habits had put her in the way of hearing the rumor of that event before her sister. The objection to this supposition is, that it seems unlikely that Martha would have kept our LORD's arrival a secret from her sister: while His *summons* would fully explain the alacrity with which Mary at last went forth to meet Him.

30 Now JESUS was not yet come into the town, but was in that place where Martha met Him.

This is divinely contrived. (What is not divinely contrived which CHRIST contrives?) By remaining without, somewhere near the burial-ground we may suppose, (which was always outside the town,)(*r*) the whole company of Mary's comforters, in following *her*, are brought to *Him*. As it follows:

31 The Jews then which were with her in the house, and comforted

---

(*p*) 1 Tim. iii. 16.

(*q*) e. g. in the Old Testament:—Gen. xxxi. 30, (of which "sore longing" we have no hint given us between xxix. 20 and xxx. 43) Gen. xliii. 21, (which "anguish and "beseeching" was not even alluded to in xxxvii. 21 to 28.) Gen. xliii. 7, (which earnest inquiries on the part of Joseph, concerning his father and brother, were passed over in perfect silence between xlii. 7 and 26.) Gen. xliv. 19 to 23, (where a few more particulars of the same interview are revealed.) Gen. xliv. 27 to 29, (were more of Jacob's words are related than in Gen. xliii. 7.) Hosea xii. 4, (which "weeping" and "supplication" is not mentioned in Gen. xxxii. 24 to 26.) Deut. iii. 25, 26, (which prayer, together with its rejection, is nowhere else even alluded to.)— In the New Testament:—St. John i. 20 reveals that the unrecorded inquiry of the "Priests and Levites from Jerusalem" was "Art Thou the CHRIST?" St. John vi. 36 mentions a thing as said before, yet not recorded. Hebrews v. 7 relates a circumstance of our LORD's Passion which none of the Evangelists had particularly mentioned.

(*r*) Compare St. Luke vii. 12.

her, when they saw Mary, that she rose up hastily and went out, followed her, saying, She goeth unto the grave to weep there.

They attribute to a sudden pang of grief, Mary's sudden rising ; and, as might be expected, rise and follow her, weeping like herself.(*s*) . . . . Such was the mournful company which the Apostles must have beheld approaching them, as they stood with our SAVIOUR at the entrance of Bethany, outside the village. And thus had the providence of GOD overruled it, that a multitude *from the capital* should witness the great wonder which was to follow: while yet the publicity which would have attended the miracle, if wrought within the capital itself, was avoided. . . . . For the inhabitants of Jerusalem, a yet greater miracle was in store. CHRIST *will raise Himself* from death, at the end of two or three months from this time.

32 Then when Mary was come where JESUS was, and saw Him, she fell down at His feet, saying unto Him, LORD, if Thou hadst been here, my brother had not died.

"And *saw* Him." How numerous and delicate are the touches in these divine Narratives!
Martha, it may be, had fallen at His feet likewise : but it is not so stated. Whatever the *actions* of the two sisters may have been, their *words* on coming into our SAVIOUR's presence are found to be *identical*,—clearly revealing what had been a constant saying between them ever since their brother's death : " If the Master had but been here, Lazarus had not died !" . . . . Is it not promised, " If two of you shall agree on earth as touching anything that they shall ask, it shall be done for them of My FATHER which is in Heaven ?"(*t*)
As already hinted, our LORD's saying before He set out for Bethany, ("I am glad for your sakes that I was not there,")(*u*) is a proof that Mary and her sister were right when they expressed their belief that Lazarus would not have died had *He* been with them : and what a striking revelation does this afford as to what was usual where our LORD was! What a blissful experience do the sisters seem to have enjoyed of the consequence of CHRIST's presence ! They say,—" LORD, while Thou wast with us, no sickness dared show itself in a family with which the Life deigned to take up His abode."(*v*) . . . . None can have ever applied to Him in faith for the relief of disease, and have been refused. He had come into the world " that through Death He might destroy him that had the power of death, that is, the Devil."(*x*) "In Him was Life :"(*y*) and, by consequence, where He was, there Death could not enter !

33 When JESUS therefore saw her weeping, and the Jews also weeping which came with her, He groaned in the spirit, and was troubled,

Literally, " and troubled Himself." This was when He " *saw*" their tears. See above, on verse 32.—The word in the original for " groaning," (here and in verse 38,) is a term of large and portentous meaning, and of rather rare occurrence. It conveys the notion of exceeding wrath, which breaks forth into threatening : but it is difficult at first sight to find scope for such notions here,—unless we suppose the Holy One to be thus deeply stirred at the sight of the usurped empire of His great enemy, the Devil. Truly, the thoughts of the CREATOR while He dwelt in the flesh among His creatures must have been of a nature which we may not hope to fathom. We can but avail ourselves of every hint; and with dutifulness and gratitude follow it out into its lawful consequences. Thus, when we read that, at the sight of bereavement and sorrow,— tears and groans,— the Incarnate SON was agitated with a mighty *anger*,—an indignation which threatened to break out into some external manifestation of its intensity,— it seems impossible to resist the suspicion that it was the sight of the fair work of Creation so shamefully marred and disfigured, which stirred up the awful wrath of the Most High. "An enemy hath done this !"(*z*)—He seems to say. And indeed, what is every scene of suffering but the work of Sin,—the remote consequences of the Fall,—signs of an usurped

(*s*) This appears from ver. 33.   (*t*) St. Matthew xviii. 19.
(*u*) See above, ver. 15.   (*v*) Alcuin.   (*x*) Heb. ii. 14.
(*y*) St. John i. 4.   (*z*) St. Matth. xiii. 28.

dominion over beings destined for happiness, and innocence, and immortality?...
The Evangelist further declares that our LORD "was troubled,"—

34 and said, Where have ye laid him?

Do we not seem to feel that these words are spoken in all the consciousness of superhuman power,—spoken by One who is about to snatch the prey from the jaws of the spoiler, and vindicate His own empire over Death itself; a solemn earnest of His intended destruction, in the end, of *that* enemy also?(a)

He asked, therefore, (as on so many other occasions,)(b) not as *needing* to be informed; but as desiring to arrest the attention of the by-standers, and to direct special notice to what He was about to do. Thus, before converting Moses' wand into a serpent, He is found to have inquired,—"What is that in thy hand?"(c)

Athanasius has some good remarks on this subject. "Ignorance," (he says,) "is proper to Humanity: in Godhead, it can have no place. Take notice that our LORD, though He asked 'where they had laid Lazarus?' had already declared, while a long way off, the *death* of Lazarus. Nay, this is He who knew beforehand the thoughts of His disciples, and who read what was in the heart of each, and knew what was in Man.(d) Above all, He alone knoweth the FATHER;(e) and saith of Himself, 'I am in the FATHER, and the FATHER in Me.'"(f)

They said unto Him, LORD, come and see.

They who are able to repress the outward display of their grief, while suffered to be silent, are often observed to break forth passionately when spoken to, and constrained to make answer. So may it have been the case now: for it is observable that it was after He had drawn from the sorrowful company the invitation to "come and see" the place where they had laid Lazarus, that something occurred which moved the Son of Man to tears.

35 JESUS wept.

"Himself borne along with, and not seeking to resist, this great tide of sorrow."(g) He weeps with those that weep,(h)— our pattern in all things! weeps, "because He is the Fountain of Pity."(i) Thus hath He sanctified our sorrows, and sanctioned on such occasions our very tears! For the word here is "JESUS *shed tears*,"— an expression confined to this single place in the Gospel.

Amazing proof of the perfection of either nature, the Divine and human, in the One Person of our LORD, that He should have shed tears of human sympathy even when He was about to assert His empire over Death and Hell!(j) His "suffering humanity is as marked throughout this occasion as the power of his Godhead." Indeed, Chrysostom observes that "St. John, who enters into higher statements respecting our LORD's Nature than the other Evangelists, descends also lower than any other in describing His bodily affections."(k) But this may be doubted.(l)

Thrice is our SAVIOUR related to have "wept."(m) It is not once said of Him that He smiled. And take notice that His tears, recorded in the Gospels, were called forth by the contemplation of human grief. This sign of the compassion of Him who in His unspeakable condescension calls Himself our *Brother*, (at the same time that He is our GOD!) cannot but prove a source of deepest solace to every afflicted member of the great human family. Our LORD may seem to deal harshly with us, at times: but Love is ever present in all His dispensations. When Joseph, (that most eminent type of CHRIST,) "took from them Simeon, and bound him before their eyes," is it not expressly declared that he first "turned himself about from them, *and wept?*"(n)

(a) See 1 Cor. xv. 26.
(b) e. g., St. Matth. xvi. 13. St. Mark ix. 21: vi. 38. St. Luke viii. 30, 45. St. John vi. 6, &c.
(c) Exod. iv. 2.   (d) St. John ii. 25.
(e) St. Matth. xi. 27.   (f) St. John xiv. 11.
(g) Trench.   (h) Rom. xii. 15.   (i) Alcuin.
(j) See the first note on St. Matth. viii. 10: St. Luke viii. 13. Also the notes on St. Luke vii. 13: St. Mark iii. 5: viii. 3, &c.
(k) Williams.   (l) Consider St. Luke xxii. 44.
(m) Besides the present place, St. Luke xix. 41, and Heb. v. 7.
(n) Gen. xlii. 24.

The name of Joseph indeed suggests the further remark that the saints of GOD are all described, (and Joseph in particular,) as men of tears. It is believed that the passages specified at foot will be found worth referring to, in connection with this mention of the tears of the Son of Man.(o)

36 Then said the Jews, Behold how He loved him.

So said certain of them. "*But* some," it follows, (not "*And* some:") as if marking the different dispositions of those present; and intimating, (as is very plainly done a little further on),(p) that the present miracle was beheld by two distinct classes of persons, whose respective characters were thereby prominently brought out. And this, be it observed, is one of the effects constantly found to attend every greater manifestation of the Son of Man. He had come into the World that the thoughts of many hearts might be revealed :(q) instances of which, well worthy of thoughtful attention, will be found in the following places of the present Gospel,—chap. vii. 12, also 40 to 43; ix. 16; and x. 19 to 21. See also the note on chapter ix. 39, and the concluding note on chapter vi. He was for ever separating the Light from the Darkness. Accordingly, what next follows sounds like a murmur on the part of some.

37 And some of them said, Could not this Man, which opened the eyes of the blind, have caused that even this man should not have died?

"There is a depth of truth in these words which they who asked the question little knew of. True it was that JESUS *could* have stayed the hand of Death as easily as He made the blind to see. But He heeded not to answer in words: He was about to answer in *deeds*, by undoing the work of Death, and calling forth the dead from the grave. None will have doubted that He *could* have caused that that man should not die, if He could bring him back again from the dead. And all this was done that He might appear to be *the* LORD *of the issues of Life and Death.*"(r) Take notice, by the way, how deep an impression had been made by the miracle performed on the man born blind, as well as how general the knowledge of it had become, that thus, for the second time,(s) it should be put prominently forward by the Jews on a public occasion. Compare our LORD's allusion (in St. John vii. 21,) to His healing of the man at the Pool of Bethesda.

38 JESUS therefore again groaning in Himself cometh to the grave.

Thus our SAVIOUR's human sorrow is for the third time noticed.(t) The occasion was indeed stupendous, and the scene must have been awfully impressive beyond all words. Are we not to look a little onwards, however, and to discover in verses 46 to 53 the main cause of that portentous anguish which now oppressed the Son of Man? . . Concerning the sepulchre of Lazarus, St. John adds:

It was a cave, and a stone lay upon it.

Take notice, reader, that this little graphic touch, (like so many in the Gospels!) is clearly from the pencil of an eye-witness. The "cave" may have been a natural formation ;(u) but it was more probably a sepulchral chamber hewn out of the rock.(v) The "stone," (as in the case of our SAVIOUR's Sepulchre,) served the purpose of a door. Still blending the human with the Divine, He who inquired where they had laid Lazarus, and wept on His way to the place, now requires the bystanders to take away the stone which closed the entrance of the sepulchre. As it follows:

39 JESUS said, Take ye away the stone.

One design of this injunction, (as of that in verse 44,) may have been to exclude

(o) Thus Jacob, Gen. xxix. 11 : xxxiii. 4: xxxvii. 35.—Joseph, Gen. xlii. 24: xliii. 30: xlv. 2, 14, 15: xlvi. 29 : l. 1, 17.—David, 1 Sam. xx. 41 : 2 Sam. iii. 32: xii. 21, 22: xv. 30: xviii. 33: xix. 1.—St. Paul, Acts xx. 19 and 31. 2 Cor. ii. 4.—St. John. Rev. v. 4, 5.
(p) See below, ver. 45 and 46. Take notice that ver. 46 begins in the same way as ver. 37.
(q) St. Luke ii. 35.
(r) From a MS. sermon by the Rev. Edw. Hobhouse.
(s) See St. John x. 21; the reference in both places being to St. John ix. 7.
(t) Verses 33, 35, 38.   (u) As Gen. xxiii. 9.
(v) Compare Is. xxii. 16, or St. Matth. xxvii. 60.

doubt and unbelief, at every avenue. The Jews are commanded to remove the stone and convince themselves that the body of Lazarus is yet lying within the sepulchre. Presently, they will see him come forth; and then they will be required, with their own hands, to divest him of his grave-clothes, and to *let him go.* They shall not be able to pretend, as they would fain have done in the case of the man born blind,(w) that there is no doubt as to the identity of the person raised from death with him who died and was buried. The Jews from Jerusalem, the mourners, the comforters, *all* shall see this miracle; all shall be convinced of its reality in all its parts. The tender sister herself shall remonstrate, and give her terrible reason. As it follows:

Martha, the sister of him that was dead, saith unto Him, LORD, by this time he stinketh: for he hath been *dead* four days.

Rather "[*buried*] four days." The circumstance is thus mentioned for the second time.(x) She speaks, as knowing what must of necessity have been the case. Her notion of the Divine powers of CHRIST did not extend so far as to suppose that His mighty word could undo at once the work of the Grave, and the work of Death: annihilate Corruption, as well as repair Dissolution.

It may perhaps strike an attentive reader as a strange addition to the name of Martha, that she should be described as "the sister of him that was dead;" a thing already made so plain by all that has gone before. The truth is, St. John expresses himself somewhat differently. At the command to remove the stone, his words are;—"Saith to Him the sister of the dead." Then, as if to make it clear which of the two sisters he is speaking of, he adds,—"Martha."

40 JESUS saith unto her, Said I not unto thee, that, if thou wouldest believe, thou shouldest see the Glory of GOD?

An unrecorded saying,—as already pointed out in the note on ver. 28: but it sends the reader's eye back to the earlier part of the chapter, to ascertain if any trace of it be discoverable there. Nor is the search altogether fruitless. It will be remembered that our LORD's words to the messengers who brought tidings of His friend's sickness, were, — "This sickness is not unto death, *but for the Glory of GOD.*"(y) This became, in fact, the message which those envoys will have carried back to Bethany. Is it not natural then to suppose that, on our LORD's arrival Martha will have timidly inquired the meaning of that comfortable, yet most enigmatical saying; and drawn from Him the assurance that if she had Faith, her eyes should *behold* that "Glory of GOD" of which He had spoken? . . . . The reader must forgive such speculations, if they offend him. They are but submitted to his judgment.

It is to be noticed that Martha's very remonstrance was a mark of failing Faith; showing that she required the timely succour thus mercifully supplied her by our LORD: and which is as when He stretched forth His hand to save His sinking Apostle on the troubled sea.(z) . . . . In the meantime CHRIST's order has been obeyed:—

41 Then they took away the stone *from the place*, where the dead was laid. And JESUS lifted up *His* eyes, and said, FATHER,

The same gesture of our Divine LORD will be found noticed on other occasions,—as St. Mark vii. 34, and St. John xvii. 1. By directing His eyes to Heaven, He indicated that His FATHER, to whom He addressed His mysterious thanksgiving, was in Heaven. He said, "FATHER,"

I thank Thee that Thou hast heard Me.

Words which marvellously indicate the union of the Divine and human nature in the One Person of CHRIST. "He was heard before He prayed," (remarks Origen;) "and therefore He begins with giving thanks: 'FATHER, I thank Thee that Thou hast heard Me.'" "*Before they call, I will answer,*" saith the LORD concerning His

(w) St. John ix. 9, 19, 20.　　　　　　　　　　　　　　(x) See above, ver. 17.
(y) See above, ver. 4.
(z) St. Matth. xiv. 31.　See also the note on St. Mark v. 36.

saints.(a) "That is," (proceeds Chrysostom,) "there is no difference of will between Me and Thee." "Thou hast heard Me," does not show any lack of power in Him, or that He is inferior to the FATHER. That the prayer is not really necessary, appears from the words that follow,—

42 And I knew that Thou hearest Me always : but because of the people which stand by I said it, that they may believe that Thou hast sent Me.

Rather, "on account of the multitude which stand around." See above, the note on ver. 31.—As if He said, "I need not prayer to persuade Thee; for Ours is one Will." He hides His meaning on account of the weak faith of His hearers: for God regards not so much His own dignity as our Salvation: and therefore seldom speaks loftily of Himself. Even when He does, He speaks in an obscure way; whereas humble expressions abound in His discourses."(b) Hilary adds,—"He did not therefore need to pray. He prayed for our sakes, that we might know Him to be the SON. His prayer did not benefit Himself, but it benefitted our faith. He did not want help, but we want instruction."

"I *know* that Thou hearest Me *always.*" Thus the Divine Speaker precludes the derogatory suspicion which the bystanders might have else conceived that He knew not till now that He had been "heard;" or again, that sometimes He was "heard;" sometimes not. The intent of all was that "the people which stood by" might be convinced that "the FATHER had *sent* Him;" that is, that they "might see that He was from God, and that the miracle which He was about to perform was in accordance with GOD's Will.(c) "The sense is," (remarks a living commentator,) "I say not this as though I had doubted whether Thou wouldst hear Me, or not; for "I know that Thou hearest Me always:" for I have thus thanked Thee openly for the sake of the many witnesses who are present: that they, hearing Me, thus address Thee, and seeing the work which I am about to do, "may believe that Thou hast sent Me," and that all My works are done according to Thy will."(d)

On this great subject, Bp. Pearson writes as follows: — "Whatsoever miracle Moses wrought, he either obtained it by his prayers, or else consulting with God, received it by commandment from Him; so that the power of miracles cannot be conceived as inhering in him. Whereas this power must of necessity be in JESUS, 'in whom dwelt all the fullness of the Godhead bodily,'(e) and to whom the FATHER had given 'to have life in Himself.'(f) This He sufficiently showed by working with a word, commanding the winds to be still, the devils to fly, and the dead to rise. . . . Once indeed CHRIST seemeth to have prayed, before He raised Lazarus from the Grave ; but even that was done 'because of the people which stood by.' Not that He had not power within Himself to raise up Lazarus, who was afterwards to raise Himself; but 'that they might believe the FATHER had sent Him.' Chrysostom, in the same spirit, bids us remark that He does not say 'In my FATHER's Name, come forth;' or 'FATHER, raise him;' but, throwing off the whole appearance of one praying, He proceeds to show His power by acts. This is His general way. His words show humility ; His acts power."

A living writer, whose piety is always edifying, remarks,—"God created Man by a word, without effort: but recalls him to life not without many groans, and tears, and intercessions ; amid all around weeping,—samples as it were of the whole Creation groaning and travailing together with pain, waiting for the Redemption."(g)

43 And when He thus had spoken, He cried with a loud voice, Lazarus, come forth.

He "cried," that all might notice *Him* as the Author of this mighty miracle.— His "loud Voice" was like the Voice of the Archangel, and the trump of God, whereat "the dead in CHRIST shall rise,"(h) at the last Day.—It is *by name* that He calls Lazarus, (says Augustine strikingly,) lest He should bring out *all* the dead. And indeed, He who called, hath a personal knowledge of each. As in life, so in death, "*He calleth them all by their names.*"(i)

(a) Is. lxv. 24. See Ps. x. 17.   (b) Chrysostom.
(c) Chrysostom.   (d) Lonsdale and Hale.   (e) Col. ii. 9.
(f) St. John v. 26.   (g) Williams.   (h) 1 Thess. iv. 16.
(i) See the note on the latter part of St. John x. 3.

Chrysostom points out that our LORD does not say "Arise," (as He said to the daughter of Jairus,(*j*) and to the Widow of Nain's son;(*k*) but "Come forth;" "speaking to the dead as if he were a living person."—Consider Romans iv. 17.

44 And he that was dead came forth, bound hand and foot with grave-clothes; and his face was bound about with a napkin.

The summons to Lazarus was literally, "*Come out.*" It was a cave; and from its dark recess, at the command of Him who, in the beginning, "said, Let there be light and there was light,"—"he that was dead *came out.*" How fitting an emblem of the hour which "is coming, ... when the Dead shall hear the Voice of the Son of GOD; and they that hear shall live;" yea, "the hour . . . . in the which all that are in the graves shall hear His voice, and shall come forth?"(*l*) . . . . "CHRIST raised the dead in the chamber and in the street, from the bed and from the bier," (remarks Bp. Pearson;) "and not content with these smaller demonstrations, proceedeth to the grave. These three evangelical resuscitations are so many preambulary proofs of the last and general Resurrection."

O miracle of miracles! How is it possible to dwell in thought upon the incident thus simply yet strikingly narrated, without a growing sense of the unspeakable majesty of the entire transaction? . . . On the one side our SAVIOUR is standing, attended by His Apostles, and doubtless a multitude which has followed the blessed company from beyond the Jordan: on the other are the sisters, the Jews, and the people of Bethany. The entire assembly have met in the place of graves, outside the town, and form a mighty circle round the tomb of Lazarus.(*m*) The vault in which his dead body had been deposited, is uncovered at the command of Him who, as it is well remembered, has lately "opened the eyes of the blind." Expectation is raised to the highest pitch; and the gaze of all is directed towards our SAVIOUR; whom, with uplifted eyes, still exhibiting traces of His human sorrow, they behold engaged in mysterious intercourse with His FATHER. Then, *with a loud voice* which rings awfully through the silent air, and rivets the attention of every bystander, He cries, "Lazarus, come out!" Attention is drawn straightway to the darksome chamber of death, to observe what will follow: and lo, to the amazement and consternation of all present, the figure of the dead man comes to view! Lazarus comes forth,—moving as a shrouded corpse may be imagined (but as it was never, except on this one occasion, *seen*) to move,—not only blinded by the napkin which veiled the face,(*n*) but completely swathed about with linen bandages also;(*o*) or, as it is here expressed, "*bound hand and foot with grave-clothes;*" obedient to the summons of Him whose powerful Voice had penetrated into the very abode of departed spirits, had shaken the powers of the unseen world, and already for the third time burst the bars and broken the gates of the Grave!

The reader will notice that every word here affords evidence of a most attentive eye-witness.

JESUS saith unto them, Loose him, and let him go.

He who rose before the stone was rolled away from the door of His own Sepulchre, could have dispensed with the removal of the stone from the Sepulchre of Lazarus. He who could first break the cords of Death which bound him, could have also undone the grave-clothes which confined his body. But the Holy One thus provided that as many as chose, should handle Lazarus *at once*, and see that it was he indeed.(*p*) By commanding the bystanders not only to "loose him" from the bandages of the grave, but also to "let him go," (literally, to "let him *depart*,")it was further provided that all should behold Lazarus moving before them,—alive, and at liberty to withdraw whithersoever he pleased.

The description of the raising of Lazarus, strictly speaking, ends here. Over how much of wonder, how much of interest which must inevitably have followed, does the sacred writer draw a veil!

Can it be necessary in taking leave of this great transaction, to point out that it was clearly symbolical throughout,—emblematic, that is, of the restoration of a soul, "tied and bound with the chain of sins," and to all human appearance irrecoverably

(*j*) St. Mark v. 41.   (*k*) St. Luke vii. 14.   (*l*) St John v. 28, 29.
(*m*) See the first words of the note on verse 42.
(*n*) Compare St. John xx. 7.   (*o*) See St. John xix. 40, and Acts v. 6.
(*p*) Alluding to the language of St. Luke xxiv. 39. See above, the note on ver. 39.

lost? CHRIST must speak powerfully to the heart of such an one; who thereupon comes forth from the darkness of his former corrupt life, is endued with new powers, and asks but external loosing by the hands of CHRIST'S servants, in order that he may go perfectly free. — The reader is invited to refer to what has been already offered on the subject of the three cases of raising the dead, recorded in the Gospels, in the notes on St. Matthew ix. 25. — Gregory the Great observes: "The maiden is restored to life in the house; the young man outside the gate; Lazarus, in his grave. She that lies dead in the house, is the sinner lying in sin: he that is carried out by the gate, is the openly and notoriously wicked: and one there is who lies dead in his grave, weighed down by habits of Sin. But the Divine Grace has regard even unto such, and enlightens them." . . . . "We do not," says Agustine, (after insisting, as all the ancient writers do on the allegorical character of the fore-going miracle,)—"We do not, because we trace an allegorical or mystical meaning in facts, forfeit our belief in them as literal occurrences." GOD forbid!

Of Lazarus himself it is impossible to think without feelings of the deepest awe, wonder, and curiosity. Here was one who *for four days* had been gathered to the world of Spirits; and was afterwards recalled to the world of sense. Was he perhaps engaged in converse with some departed soul, when the "loud Voice" of the Incarnate JEHOVAH summoned him back to earth, — leaving the other amazed and confounded at the all but unparalleled strangeness of his withdrawal? There had been three such cases in three years; but not one so strange as this! The tradi-tional account of the subsequent duration of his earthly life, (thirty years,) and of his demeanour, (how that he never smiled again,) cannot be entitled to serious attention. In the words of the poet, —

> "The rest remaineth unreveal'd.
> He told it not; or something seal'd
> The lips of the Evangelist."

45 Then many of the Jews which came to Mary, and had seen the things which JESUS did, believed on Him.

Whereby that came to pass which our SAVIOUR had foretold, namely, that this sickness was "not unto death, but for the Glory of GOD."(q) The reader is requested to read the last note on chapter x.

46 But some of them went their ways to the Pharisees, and told them what things JESUS had done.

Doubtless with an evil intent: and thus, (as was pointed out at some length above, in the note on ver. 36,) our LORD'S words and actions were for ever revealing what was in the hearts of men; and throwing them into two opposite classes. So truly, of some, had it been foreseen and foretold by our SAVIOUR that if "they heard not Moses and the Prophets, neither would they be persuaded *though one rose from the dead!*"(r) The grand exhibition of the truth of that saying was indeed future; being reserved for our LORD'S Resurrection on the third day: yet was the present even a more palpable sign of the Godhead of Him who wrought. What is strange, here was one raised from Death, bearing the very name of the individual mentioned in the parable,—as if purposely to remind them of our SAVIOUR'S former teaching, and to render their unbelief without excuse.

If it should appear strange to any, (as indeed at first sight it may well appear somewhat strange,) that persons who were capable of coming on so pious an errand as the consolation of the bereaved sisters, should have been also capable of the malignity here ascribed to certain of their body, — the real character of the act described in verses 19 and 31,(s) requires to be further explained. The same wretched formalism which had corrupted the sacred Oracles, and reduced the spirit of the Divine law to the lifelessness of its letter,—is found to have obtruded itself also into the house of mourning; reducing sorrow to a ceremony of thirty days' duration, during which, every observance was a matter of routine, to be performed by rule and number. It is obvious that, dwelling among a people where the very chamber of Death was not exempt from intrusions of this sort, it may easily have come to pass

(q) See above, ver. 4.　　　　(r) St. Luke xvi. 31.
(s) And alluded to in ver. 45.

that the sisters of Bethany were followed to the grave of their brother by some "mourners" little disposed to rejoice in the presence of their great Benefactor.·

47 Then gathered the chief priests and the Pharisees a council, and said, What do we? for this Man doeth many miracles.

Rather, "What must we do?" or "What are we to do?" (as in chap. vi. 28:) the meaning of which words will be found more fully explained below, in the note on verse 49. Thus the Court of Sanhedrin,—(for take notice that the word here translated "Council" is the Greek word which the Jews pronounced *Sanhedrin*,)—this Court admit the truth of the Miracles; but for political reasons, are apprehensive of their results. As it follows:

48 If we let Him thus alone, all *men* will believe in Him: and the Romans shall come and take away both our place and nation.

They apprehended the jealousy of the Roman Emperor, whom they knew would be incensed if tidings should reach the imperial City that One claiming to be the MESSIAH, (and therefore *a King*, was drawing away large bodies of the people after Him. A true specimen, this, of the worthless reasoning of the wicked! We know that the very reverse of what they anticipated would have taken place. Jerusalem would, on the contrary, have been standing to this day!

In the meantime, the very thing they desired to guard against, actually occurred. This miracle procured for our SAVIOUR many Disciples;(*t*) while the catastrophe which they apprehended, they brought about, though in a different manner from what they anticipated, by the sinful measures they were adopting in order to prevent it. . . . Those who "seek first the Kingdom of GOD and His Righteousness" have all other things added unto them.(*u*) Those on the contrary who seek not GOD, not only lose Him, but they lose the World besides.

49 And one of *them* named Caiaphas, being the High-priest that same year, said unto them, Ye know nothing at all:

An expression as it seems, of displeasure and impatience with the Council. He had heard the rest deliver their sentiments, and now comes forward to offer his own. — "What are we to do?" the others had said: implying thereby, plainly enough, that they were at a loss how to act, in consequence of their conviction of our Blessed LORD'S innocence. If the barest pretext for charging Him with any crime had occurred to them, they would have known full well what to do. His innocence it was which created all their difficulty. Caiaphas therefore puts down their scruples, and delivers his own opinion, which he declares roundly is based altogether on his view of political expediency. "Ye know nothing at all," (he begins,)—

50 nor consider that it is expedient for us, that one man should die for the people, and that the whole nation perish not.

"One MAN." The expression which is marked in the original, did not escape the ancients. "It was as *Man* that CHRIST died for the people," observes Origen; "in so far as He is the image of the invisible GOD, He is incapable of Death." The word seems used as it were contemptuously, as in ver. 47; also in chap. v. 12.

Little can the speaker have suspected the Divine fullness of meaning which his angry and murderous words contained! On this subject, see below, the note on ver. 52. Very well worthy of our attention is the Evangelist's comment, which follows: and the reason which he *twice* assigns for the prophetic character which belonged to the words of Caiaphas, — namely, that he was the High Priest of GOD's chosen people. An important inference from this statement will be offered presently.(*x*) For the moment, it shall suffice to call attention to the peculiar phrase employed by the Evangelist; the precise force of which has never been explained. He says that Caiaphas was "High-priest *that year*." The office was indeed no longer held for life, according to the Divine appointment; but had been lately conferred on many individuals in succession; and it had been held for only one *year*, by some.

(*t*) See St. John xii. 10, 11, 17 to 19.　　　(*u*) St. Matth. vi. 33.
(*x*) See the end of the note on ver. 52.

Caiaphas, on the other hand, *seems* to have been High-priest for several years. The Evangelist's allusion is perhaps to some circumstance in the history of the priestly office about this period which is nowhere expressly recorded.

This prophecy, which the Evangelist proceeds to explain, is so far characteristic of the man, as to be referred to in a subsequent chapter, as the most fitting circumstance whereby to identify him. Consider St. John xviii. 14.

51, 52 And this spake he not of himself: but being High-priest that year, he prophesied that JESUS should die for that nation ; and not for that nation only, but that also He should gather together in one the children of GOD that were scattered abroad.

A divine interpretation truly of that evil man's unsuspected prophecy ! "The meaning of Caiaphas was insincere, mean, and timid: the meaning of the HOLY GHOST in his words was awful, mysterious, and divine."(y) All that Caiaphas *intended* to say clearly amounted to this,—that our SAVIOUR's destruction must any how be effected, and *that* speedily. His argument was, that the Death of One would thus be productive of general good,—by diverting from the nation the wrath of their Roman masters.

But his speech was overruled by a higher power, and the words which fell from his lips proved susceptible of a double meaning: the HOLY GHOST deigning to employ even this sinful organ, (as He had already spoken by the mouth of Balaam,) to convey nothing less than a wondrous prophecy concerning the propitiatory nature of the approaching sacrifice of CHRIST's Death, and its marvellous result to "the Israel of GOD"(z) scattered throughout the world; not only, (that is,) to the Jewish nation, but to the Gentiles as well.(a) A far-sighted prophecy truly ! extending infinitely beyond the anticipations, as yet, of any even of the Apostles themselves. Our SAVIOUR alone has hitherto mentioned "other sheep" "not of this fold" which must yet be brought, and made "one flock under one Shepherd." (b) The blessed result of His Cross and Passion, thus darkly hinted at, St. John describes in language formed upon Deut. xxx. 3. It will be found also to resemble Isaiah lvi. 8.(c)

Irenæus, (the disciple of Polycarp, who was the disciple of St. John,) records it as a saying of "one of the elders," that "by the extension of His Divine Hands," our Crucified LORD "gathered to One GOD the two people scattered to the ends of the earth." This thought, which is full of pious beauty, found great favour with the ancient Church. It recurs perpetually in the primitive fathers.

The reason why the HOLY GHOST saw fit to prophesy by the mouth of Caiaphas deserves to be noticed. It was because that individual happened to fill the place of High-priest. But he was an unauthorized intruder into the sacred office; having no other title to it than the will of the Roman Procurator, and the power of the Roman legions. Let us not therefore overlook the intimation thus conveyed, that the unworthiness of *the individual* does not affect the sanctity of *his office.* This remains unimpaired. A solemn thought both for clergy and people; rulers and subjects ! Chrysostom draws a double inference : "See the great virtue of the HOLY SPIRIT," (he says,) "in drawing forth a prophecy from a wicked man. And see, too, the virtue of the pontifical office; which made him, though an unworthy High-priest, unconsciously prophesy. Divine grace used only his mouth: it touched not his corrupt heart."

53 Then from that day forth they took counsel together for to put Him to death.

"Many, indeed, had been the designs against His life: but from this time the purpose was formal, deliberate, and determined; under the usual plea by which Martyrs and Kings are slain,—that of public expediency."(d)

54 JESUS therefore walked no more openly among the Jews : but

(y) Williams.　　　　　　　　　　　　　　　　　　　(z) Gal. vi. 16.
(a) Compare 1 St. John ii. 2. Consider also the Divine comment on the place, supplied by Ephes. ii. 13 to 22.
(b) St. John x. 16.
(c) See also Psalm cxlvii. 2: Jer. xxxii. 37: Ezek. xxxiv. 13.
(d) Williams.

went thence unto a country near to the wilderness, into a city called
Ephraim, and there continued with His Disciples.

The city thus mentioned is thought to have been situate between Jericho and
Bethel. Thither our Saviour now retires, and passes the season preparatory to
His Crucifixion, in mysterious privacy with His Disciples. But first, "He puts
forth this most astonishing of all miracles to speak aloud of itself to Jerusalem.
His goodness had contended with their malice. They would have stoned Him for
declaring Himself God: He retires from them, and in retiring leaves this miracle
to tell them who He is; and leaves them to consider it awhile,—then coming Himself to die for them. . . . Lazarus had thus come from the grave to warn his brethren. Living at Bethany, in the very neighbourhood of Jerusalem, he continued
after he had been raised from the dead to be a living witness for a time unto those
who would not 'hear Moses and the Prophets.' So much was this the case, that
at the concourse of the festival, (described in the next chapter,) many went from
Jerusalem to Bethany, 'not for Jesus' sake only, but that they might see Lazarus
also, whom He had raised from the dead.' "(e)

Why does St. John mention the name of the present place of our Lord's retreat?
. . . It follows:

55 And the Jews' Passover was nigh at hand:

The last year of our Blessed Lord's Ministry had now very nearly come to a
close. In the seventh chapter of the present Gospel, we were reminded of the
events of October; in the tenth chapter, a Festival kept in December obtained notice.(f) The Passover season, (belonging to March or April,) is now approaching.
To the month of January or of February therefore, the raising of Lazarus, which
has hitherto occupied our attention, may be loosely referred; and the intervening
weeks, according to the statement in verse 54, will have been spent at Ephraim.
If the suggestion hazarded in the note on verse 8 be correct, the period of sojourn
at Ephraim will have commenced some weeks earlier.

and many went out of the country up to Jerusalem before the Passover, to purify themselves.

For cleanness, according to the Law of Moses, was required of all persons(g)
who would keep the Feast of the Passover at the time appointed.(h) The "many"
therefore, who are here spoken of, were such as had contracted some legal defilement, from which they could not be purified without the performance of certain
rites in the Temple.(i)

A thoughtful writer observes,—"They who went up to purify themselves in order
to keep the Feast, were nevertheless desirous to embrue their hands in innocent
blood! It was to this, therefore, that the Holy Spirit had particularly called their
attention throughout the Prophets: pointing out this 'spot in their Feasts' by the
finger of reproof, and one also of prophetic warning. It was to this circumstance
also that our Lord had always directed His teaching of the Pharisees, as knowing
what was in the heart of man; and foreseeing this consummation of hypocrisy to
which they were tending. And even now, had they been at all desirous to 'purify
themselves' in reality, by that cleansing of the heart by repentance which the Law
signified, as well as by the external rites which it ordained, they would have been
preserved from that great wickedness; they would have received the Christ; they
would have laid aside their own corrupt leaven, and kept the Feast "in sincerity
and truth."(k)

"This purification required by the Law," (continues the same pious writer,)
"was like that call to Repentance which preceded the coming in of the Kingdom;
for without Repentance the eyes of flesh could not 'see the salvation of God.'(l)
It is like the Lent which precedes Easter, in order to give us eyes to discern
Christ crucified. Nay, it is so with the Gospel itself; for we must purify ourselves lest we should not behold Christ therein, even though He sitteth in His own
Temple."

(e) Williams, quoting St. John xii. 9.
(g) Numb. ix. 6 to 13: 2 Chron. xxx. 17 to 19.
(h) Exodus xii. 3 to 6.
(k) Williams, quoting 1 Cor. v. 8.

(f) St. John x. 22.

(i) Lonsdale and Hale.
(l) Isaiah iii. 10.

56 Then sought they for JESUS, and spake among themselves, as they stood in the Temple, What think ye, that He will not come to the Feast?

57 Now both the chief Priests and the Pharisees had given a commandment, that, if any man knew where He were, he should show *it*, that they might take Him.

"Well therefore did our LORD say unto them by His own Evangelical Prophet, when He began more distinctly to prefigure to them the coming in of this dispensation,--' Your new moons and your appointed feasts My soul hateth : they are a trouble unto Me ; I am weary to bear them.' 'Wash you, make you clean.' '*Your hands are full of blood.*'(*m*)   More, indeed, than they meant did they say in the Temple when they spoke of His coming to the Feast, and apprehended that they should not find Him there !"(*n*)

It is somewhat affecting to read such an account as the following, of the aspect which Bethany now presents. Let us remember that we are bearing about the frequent and favourite resort of our adorable REDEEMER: let us call to mind how often He withdrew from the murderous capital to sanctify that quiet abode of loving hearts,—treading with "beautiful feet"(*o*) the eastern slope of the Mount of Olives, in quest of a friendly roof beneath which He might lay His weary head.(*p*) This, and His miracles of Love, and His words of Eternal Truth, — all the unspeakable blessedness and beauty which must have attended His " going out and coming in,"(*q*) must be considered ; after which, it seems impossible to read the following words of an American traveller(*r*) without painful emotion :—" Bethany is a poor village of some twenty families ; its inhabitants are apparently without thrift or industry. In the walls of a few of the houses there are marks of antiquity,—large hewn stones, some of them beveled ; but they have all obviously belonged to more ancient edifices, and been employed again and again in the construction of successive dwellings, or other buildings. The monks, as a matter of course, show the house of Mary and Martha, that of Simon the Leper, and the sepulchre of Lazarus. The latter is a deep vault, like a cellar, excavated in the limestone rock in the middle of the village ; to which there is a descent by twenty-six steps. It is hardly necessary to remark, that there is not the slightest probability of its ever having been the tomb of Lazarus. The form is not that of the ancient sepulchres ; nor does its position accord with the narrative of the New Testament, which implies that the tomb was not in the town."

But this writer's concluding statement is of real value. "The Arab name of the village," (he says,) " is *el-Aziriyeh*, from el-Azir, the Arabic form of ' Lazarus.' The name Bethany is unknown among the native inhabitants." Thus the celebrity of the miracle we have been considering proves to have been so great, that, at the end of eighteen hundred years, the very stones have learnt to cry out; and the name of " Lazarus" will cleave to the locality to the end of Time !

CHAPTER XII.

THEN JESUS six days before the Passover came to Bethany, where Lazarus was which had been dead, whom he raised from the dead.

(*m*) Isaiah i. 14, 15, 16.
(*o*) Isaiah lii. 7.
(*q*) See the note on St. John x. 9.
(*n*) Williams.
(*p*) St. Matth. viii. 20.
(*r*) Dr. Robinson.

"As the time approached at which our LORD had resolved to suffer, He approached the place which He had chosen for the scene of his suffering."(a)

St. John proceeds to describe the Supper at Bethany ; restoring that incident to its actual historical place, namely, the Sabbath before the Passover ; from which St. Matthew,(b) (and St. Mark(c) after him,) had displaced it. They did so for an excellent reason, which has been pointed out in the note immediately preceding St. Matth. xxvi. 6 ; but which, as the attentive reader will perceive, would not have been discoverable, but for the statement of the present Evangelist below, in ver. 4. From this period, the sacred Writers do not suffer us to lose sight of our LORD, until the dawning of the first Easter-Day. — He had now come to Bethany ; and it follows,—

2 There they made Him a supper ; and Martha served ; but Lazarus was one of them that sat at the table with Him.

Take notice, that to eat and drink proves the reality of a corporeal, as distinguished from a merely spiritual presence. Thus St. Peter, to demonstrate the truth of our LORD'S Resurrection from the dead, appeals to having, (with the Twelve,) "ate and drank with Him"(d) after that event. Our SAVIOUR, in like manner, on the evening of the first Easter-Day, to convince the Apostles that they beheld no spectral appearance, partook of food in their presence. "While they yet believed not for joy, and wondered, He said unto them, Have ye here anything which may be eaten? And they gave Him a piece of broiled fish, and some honey-comb. And He took it, and did eat before them."(e)

The incident here recorded took place "in the house of Simon the leper,' (f)—who is mentioned only on this occasion, and about whom nothing else whatever is known. . . . Both sisters served the LORD faithfully and well. Martha, (like Simon Peter's mother-in-law, at the beginning of our LORD's Ministry,)(g) waits upon Him, as He reclines at the table ; which had also been her chosen office on a former occasion.(h) Mary does Him honour in the way next described.

3 Then took Mary a pound of ointment of spikenard, very costly, and anointed the feet of JESUS, and wiped His feet with her hair:

The two first Evangelists omit the name of the author of this famous, and, (as our SAVIOUR Himself testified,) mysterious action: famous, — for it enjoyed the immediate prophecy that it should be spoken of throughout the World ; mysterious, —for Mary was declared to have, unconsciously, "came beforehand to anoint" the LORD's "Body to the burying."(i) They relate, however, that she poured the ointment on His Head; and St. Mark relates that, in the impatience of her love, Mary "brake the box:"(j) brake it,—" so that nothing should be spared, and that nothing should remain behind for any other purpose.(k) . . . . Can we wonder at her Love? Lazarus was at the table!

Refer back to chapter xi. 2, and see the note there. — It need not, surely, be remarked that this transaction is not to be confounded with that recorded in St. Luke vii. 36 to 38, — however strikingly like it. . . . St. John adds,

and the house was filled with the odour of the ointment.

Not that "house only, but the universal Church of CHRIST, has been filled with the fragrance of her action. See the beautiful allusion of Ignatius to it, quoted in the note on St. Matthew xxvi. 7. The Fathers often point out that the House at Bethany was a type of the Church,—wherein the name of CHRIST " is as ointment poured forth."(l)

A modern writer remarks, in an ancient spirit,—"Here then was CHRIST sitting at supper with the Leper who was cleansed, and with the dead man whom He had raised to life : and what is this but a figure of His Church, where he who is cleansed, and he who is raised from the death of sin, sit with CHRIST, and eat and drink in His Kingdom, which is filled with the odour of His Death ?"(m).

(a) Alcuin.
(c) St. Mark xiv. 3 to 9.
(e) St. Luke xxiv. 41 to 43.
(g) St. Matth. viii. 15.
(i) St. Mark xiv. 8.
(k) Williams.
(m) Altered from Williams.

(b) St. Matth. xxvi. 6 to 13.
(d) Acts x. 41.
(f) St. Matth. xxvi. 6: St. Mark xiv. 3.
(h) See St. Luke x. 38 to 42.
(j) See the note on St. Mark xiv. 3.
(l) Song of Solomon i. 3.

The fragrance of the precious ointment proved an offence to Judas. As it follows:—

4, 5 Then saith one of His Disciples, Judas Iscariot, Simon's *son*, which should betray Him, Why was not this ointment sold for three hundred pence, and given to the poor?

Take notice that St. John, by that short clause,—"*which should betray Him*,"—guides us to connect the crime of Judas with the present transaction. St. Matthew and St. Mark, as we have seen, even place the Supper at Bethany, and the Betrayal of our Saviour, side by side, in their Gospels.(*n*) What now took place seems to have provoked the traitor to his accursed crime.

Pliny has a remark which is very much in point here, on the extravagant price which used to be paid for certain ointments. He informs us with indignation that "there were some ointments in the shops, made of such costly ingredients, that every *pound* weight was sold at *four hundred Roman pence;* which, by computation," (remarks Bishop Sanderson,) "allowing to the Roman penny sevenpence-halfpenny of our coin, cometh to above twenty-two pounds English." This Roman writer thus, without intending it, bears witness to a fact which we might have suspected indeed, but which we could not else have certainly known; namely, that the sister of Lazarus, when she was intent on showing honour to her Lord and ours, purchased *the most expensive offering she could procure*. Let it be remarked without offence, that our Saviour's emphatic commendation of her action becomes the abiding warrant for munificence on every similar occasion; and the perpetual rebuke of those who seem to think that anything is good enough for the House of God, while they yet deny themselves in no single luxury at home. The same lesson is unmistakably conveyed by the words which fell from the same gracious lips in commendation of the Widow's mite. See the note on St. Luke xxi. 4. Surely, the faithful service of God must have a wonderful tendency thus to unlock the heart, and make it liberal. Consider the language of David,(*o*) and of Zacchæus.(*p*) In the meanwhile, take notice that "the evil eye of the wicked serves only to do honour to God's servants; for had it not been for the reproof of Judas, the costliness of Mary's offering had not been thus known and honoured."(*q*) It is ever thus. The malice of Man is always overruled to the glory of God.

Judas Iscariot it was, who presumed to assail this pious woman with the reproach of wasteful extravagance; in which, it seems certain from St. Matthew's language, that others of the Disciples inadvertently joined.(*r*) It has been suggested, indeed, that the plural is here used by St. Matthew for the singular, according to a known idiom of the language; but observe that he records the Divine *reply* as addressed to *many* also.(*s*)—Judas affects to lament the loss of such an opportunity of showing kindness to the poor: but, (as St. John proceeds to declare,)—

6 This he said, not that he cared for the poor; but because he was a thief, and had the bag, and bare what was put therein.

Judas thus becomes the type of those who make Religion a cloak for Covetousness. Christ yet suffered this man to retain his place among the Apostles; thereby teaching us not to look for a Church where *all* shall be Saints.(*t*)

Awful discovery of motives the vilest, for words which must have seemed to all who heard, brimful of sweetest Charity! . . . "Not that *he* cared for the poor!"—though all the Disciples, to the very last, thought that the poor were uppermost in his regard:(*u*) "but because he was *a thief; and had in his keeping the money-box ;*(*x*) and *was in the habit of pilfering* from the moneys which from time to time were cast into it." . . . And thus we are, as it seems, let into the secret of what led to this man's final downfall. O mystery of iniquity, too little attended to! Ought not the terrible history of Judas Iscariot to be more in our thoughts, and

(*n*) See the note on St. Matth. xxvi. 5.
(*o*) 2 Sam. xxiv. 24. See also 1 Chron. xxix. 14.
(*p*) See St. Luke xix. 8, and the note there.
(*q*) Williams.　　　　　　　　　　　　　(*r*) See St. Matth. xxvi. 8.
(*s*) St. Matth. xxvi. 10, and St. Mark xiv. 6.
(*t*) Grotius.　　　　　　　　　　　　　(*u*) Consider St. John xiii. 29.
(*x*) The word is uncommon. It is the translation of "a chest," in the Septuagint version of 2 Chron. xxiv. 8, 11.

on our lips, than it is to be feared is the case? If he had fallen by the commission of some splendid crime, men would have put his history away, as something which was altogether above and beyond them. Is he then beneath us also, because he sinned on so petty a scale, and lost his soul for a bribe so exceedingly paltry?

Take notice that there is reason for supposing that the "bag," or "money-box," which held the common fund of the Twelve and their LORD, (and which we are *twice* told was entrusted to the keeping of Judas,)(y) did not generally contain so large a sum of money as this single offering was supposed to be worth. Consider St. Mark vi. 37, and the note there.—Observe also, how large a sum this must have seemed to the Traitor, who could perhaps betray his Master for perhaps one-eighth of the amount! Since, at the time when the Gospel was written, "a penny a day" was the hire of a labouring man,(z) we cannot be far wrong in regarding three hundred pence as equivalent to about 25*l.* of our money.

> 7 Then said JESUS, Let her alone: against the day of My Burying hath she kept this.

Not that Mary need have *known* what she did. It cannot be supposed that she had been preserving this precious offering against the day of our SAVIOUR's Burying; or that she suspected that she was now "anticipating," (to use St. Mark's expression,(a) an act which it was usual to perform immediately after death. But "the humble actions of good Christians, done for GOD, and with a kind of instinctive sense of what may be pleasing to Him, bear onward to the future with some significancy; and because they are reproved by the World, are magnified and honoured by CHRIST."(b) It was not fitting that our SAVIOUR's "precious Death and Burial" should have wanted this mark of reverence and honour: and pious Mary was allowed the life-long satisfaction of reflecting that *her* hands had bestowed in this marvellous and unexpected manner, what others, seven days later, sought to bestow upon the sacred Body of our LORD, in vain.(c)—He adds,

> 8 For the poor always ye have with you; but Me ye have not always.

"The poor shall never cease out of the land,"(d) saith Almighty GOD in either Testament. They will be with the Church of CHRIST to the end,— in order that His people may show them kindness for His sake.(e)—"The Day of *My Burying*," —"Me ye have *not always:*"—by such allusions, prophetic of His near departure, did the Holy One seek to move and soften Judas; even while His words must have melted every other person whom He addressed. For who ever entertained a grudging thought under such a prospect? Nay, what mourner's heart has not ached through sorrow that he had not himself a timely warning given him, in order that he might have done more!

St. John will be found to exhibit our LORD's rebuke, and very memorable reply to the assailants of this holy woman, more briefly than the two first Evangelists. He also omits the striking prophecy which followed, and which has already found, (as we ourselves are witnesses,) such ample fulfillment in the Church of CHRIST; namely, that the fame of this act should become as widely spread as the very Gospel itself.(f) That it was published among "those who inhabit the British Isles," was remarked even in the days of Chrysostom. In this prophetic announcement, then, on the part of our LORD, was there not abundant comfort provided for Mary, under the rebuke of Judas, and a consideration suggested which might well have roused the Traitor's fears?

A transaction of this very remarkable nature should not be lightly dismissed. "Let us observe what the nature of the action is which our LORD selects as the one of all others that shall receive an earthly memorial. It is one done as it were in secret, in a private room: an expression, not of want, nor of personal need; but a free and spontaneous act of thanksgiving. It has no purpose but that of doing honour to our LORD; being not only not done to please men, but even done in

---

(y) Also at St. John xiii. 29.   (z) St. Matth. xx. 2.
(a) St. Mark xiv. 8. See St. Matth. xxvi. 12.
(b) Williams.
(c) St. Mark xvi. 1, 2: St. Luke xxiv. 1.
(d) Deut. xv. 11.
(e) St. Matth. xxv. 40, 45.
(f) Compare verses 7 and 8 with St. Matth. xxvi. 10 to 13, and St. Mark xiv. 6 to 9.

spite of their reproof,—the free-will offering of deep reverential love. It seeks not human fame, and therefore shall receive it."(g)

In the meantime, the news that our SAVIOUR had returned from Ephraim, the scene of His retirement,(h) and had reappeared at Bethany, quickly spread to the Capital; and the consequence might have been foreseen. As it follows:—

9 Much people of the Jews therefore knew that He was there: and they came not for JESUS' sake only, but that they might see Lazarus also, whom He had raised from the dead.

These were *from Jerusalem*.(i) "Curiosity brought them, not Love:" curiosity to see the Physician and His Patient together. "The news of this great miracle had therefore spread everywhere; and was supported by such clear evidence, that the Rulers could neither suppress nor deny the fact."(j) The reader is invited to refer to the latter part of the Commentary on verses 17, 18.

10 But the chief priests consulted that they might put Lazarus also to death;

Rather,—"But the chief priests *determined to put*," &c.—"Lazarus also," as well as CHRIST; against whom the Sanhedrin had conspired ever since the day when he raised Lazarus from the dead.(k) Notice the rapid *growth* of Sin. Apt disciples these in the school of Caiaphas !(l)—"O blind rage!" (exclaims Augustine;) "as if the LORD who raised the dead, could not raise the slain. Lo, He did both. He raised Lazarus, and He raised Himself." . . . . They conspired against Lazarus then,

11 Because that by reason of him many of the Jews went away, and believed on JESUS.

"Went away from their former teachers, the Scribes and Pharisees. The word is the same as that used in chap. vi. 67, where our LORD asks His Disciples if they were inclined to 'go away' from Him." . . . The reader is requested to refer to the note on St. John xi. 54.—"No other miracle," (says Chrysostom,) "excited such rage as this. It was so public, and so wonderful, to see a man walking and talking after he had been dead four days. And the fact was so undeniable. In the case of other miracles, they had charged Him with breaking the Sabbath; but here there was nothing to find fault with, and therefore they vent their anger upon Lazarus."

The event which follows belongs to "Palm Sunday,"—as the Sunday next before Easter was anciently, and is sometimes still, called. "It was a precept of the Law that on the tenth day of the first month, the lamb or kid was shut up in the house until the fourteenth day of the same month, when it was slain in the evening.(m) Wherefore also the True Lamb, chosen without spot out of all the flock to be slain for the sanctification of the people, five days before, that is on the tenth day, goeth up to Jerusalem."(n)

12, 13 On the next day much people that were come to the Feast, when they heard that JESUS was coming to Jerusalem, took branches of palm-trees, and went forth to meet him, and cried, Hosanna: Blessed is the King of Israel that cometh in the name of the LORD.

Thus was prefigured the time, of which St. John speaks in the Book of Revelation, when lo, a great multitude, which no man can number, will stand "before the Throne, and before THE LAMB, clothed with white robes, and *palms in their hands;*" and will cry "with a loud voice, saying, Salvation to our GOD which sitteth upon the Throne, and unto THE LAMB."(o)

All this is related in a manner somewhat explanatory of the same incident as de-

(g) Williams.   (h) See St. John xi. 54.
(i) See St. John xi. 18, 19, and the notes there.
(j) Augustine.   (k) See St. John xi. 53.
(l) See St. John xi. 49, 50.   (m) Exodus xii. 3.
(n) Chrysostom.   (o) Rev. vii. 9, 10.

scribed by St. Matthew xxi. 8, 9, and St. Mark xi. 8, 9, — to both of which places
the reader is requested to refer, as well as to the Commentary thereon.

It is observable that our SAVIOUR now approached Jerusalem in a manner different from any former occasion. Hitherto, His coming had been "as it were in secret:" but His hour had at length come ;. and He does all things openly, and without reserve. See the note on St. Mark x. 32. The news of the SAVIOUR's intended
approach to the Capital seems to have spread rapidly ; and it brings forth a multitude, at once, to meet Him. Very royal, surely, even in its lowliness, is the mysterious pageant thus set before us !

14 And JESUS, when He had found a young ass, sat thereon ;

This is very concisely related by St. John. The curious and careful search which
our LORD ordered two of His Disciples to make for the colt on which he was to enter Jerusalem in triumph, is recorded by the three first Evangelists in the places
mentioned at foot,(p) where the notes on St. Matthew and St. Mark may be consulted. "When He had found" this creature, "He sat thereon :"

15 As it is written, Fear not, daughter of Sion : behold, thy King
cometh, sitting on an ass's colt.

These are not precisely the words of Zechariah ix. 9 ; but they exhibit the meaning of the prophecy referred to, and preserve *its substance.* Let us be on our guard
against the flagrant absurdity which, on occasions like the present, can suggest
that St. John "quoted *from memory !*" Such a suggestion, if it proceeds from a
Teacher of Divinity, must make the Angels weep. Let us be well assured that St.
John's memory was perfectly trustworthy as often as he saw fit to trust it. But,
in truth, these blessed writers "neither spake nor wrote any word of their own, but
uttered syllable by syllable as the SPIRIT put it into their mouths."(q) The suppression, in two of the Gospels, of the language of exultation with which the ancient
prophecy commences, is probably a circumstance full of mysterious meaning. See
St. Matthew xxi. 5, and the note there. The present Evangelist, — because he is
silent about the "ass," which we know that our SAVIOUR commanded the Disciples
to bring Him, as well as the foal on which He was to ride, — omits that clause of
Zechariah's prophecy which notices the elder animal, whereby the Jewish nation
was typified.(r)

16 These things understood not His Disciples at first : but when JESUS
was glorified, then remembered they that these things were written of
Him, and *that* they had done these things unto Him.

Take notice, therefore, that there is something *to be "understood"* in all this ;(s)
something which the Disciples themselves did not understand until the day of Pentecost. Then, according to their LORD's true prediction, "the HOLY GHOST taught
them all things, and brought everything which CHRIST had spoken to their remembrance."(t) Consider in illustration of the statement, St. John ii. 17 and 22 : viii.
28 : xiii. 7 : xvi. 12, 13 ; and St. Luke xxiv. 8 and 45 ; on each of which places the
notes should be read. "The HOLY GHOST was not yet given, because JESUS was
not yet *glorified :*" on, which expression, as well as on the doctrine involved by what
precedes, the reader is referred to the Commentary on the latter part of St. John
vii. 39 : also, on xiii. 7.

Besides that, hereby, the words of Zechariah found their accomplishment, may
not the Disciples have perhaps afterwards "understood" that, when our LORD thus
entered Jerusalem, *that* "binding" of "his foal unto the Vine, and his ass's colt
unto the choice Vine,"(u) took place, of which dying Jacob spoke, when he foretold
what should befall Judah "in the last days ?" Now, of a truth, was CHRIST binding the Gentiles, (the colt,) unto Himself, "*the True Vine ;*"(v) and, (singular to
relate,) an ancient Jewish Commentary on the words of the Patriarch last referred
to, declares that Jacob thereby "showeth us that when the CHRIST shall come to

(p) St. Matth. xxi. 1 to 7 : St. Mark xi. 1 to 7 : St. Luke xix. 29 to 35.
(q) Hooker.   (r) See St. Matth. xxi. 2, and the note there.
(s) Consider St. Matth. xvi. 9 : St. Mark viii. 17.
(t) St. John xiv. 26.   (u) Gen. xlix. 11.
(v) St. John xv. 1.

save Israel, He shall make ready His ass, and ride upon him, and come unto Israel with poverty."(x)

"But we may well ask," (observes Williams,) "how could a sensation so great as this be at this time occasioned? And St. John himself proceeds to explain it. It was from that great type of the Resurrection which had occurred among them so lately: the great miracle which our LORD had reserved for the last of all, as so divinely suited to the dispensation which was now to follow."

17, 18 The people therefore that was with Him when He called Lazarus out of his grave, and raised him from the dead, bare record. For this cause the people also met Him, for that they heard that He had done this miracle.

Two distinct multitudes are here spoken of. "The people that was with Him when He called Lazarus out of his grave," is the multitude whose presence is noticed in St. John xi. 31, (where see the note,) 42, and 45. The people who "met Him," (and who are the multitude also mentioned above, in verses 12, 13,) knew of the miracle only by hearsay from the others. The former are said to have "borne record;" that is, they bare renewed witness to the truth of the miracle which they had witnessed with their own eyes. (The reader is invited to refer back to the remarks which were offered in the Commentary on St. John xi. 31, 42.) It is evident that the raising of Lazarus was *felt* to be one of those stupendous acts of Divine Power which admitted not of suspicion, much less of denial. The miracle had been wrought in broad daylight,—before a crowd,—with evident care to preclude all doubt as to its reality.(y) Moreover, Lazarus was before them, alive, —whom they *knew* to have been four days dead! Their amazement may be inferred from a well-known assertion of the elder Pliny: "It is some consolation to poor human nature," (he remarks,) "that GOD cannot do all things. He cannot bestow upon mortals the gift of Immortality, *nor recall the dead to life.*"

19 The Pharisees therefore said among themselves, Perceive ye how ye prevail nothing? behold, the world is gone after Him.

The endeavors of the Pharisees, already noticed,(z) to prevent the people from following CHRIST, had proved an utter failure, and they were compelled to confess it. More than is here set down, these hypocrites said,—as may be seen in St. Luke xix. 39, 40; where the memorable rebuke which our LORD addressed to them on this same occasion, is also recorded.

And thus St. John takes leave of our LORD's triumphal entry into Jerusalem; concerning which, it is necessary to refer to the three earlier Gospels, if we would know more.(a) At this place, indeed, the present Evangelist suspends his History of Holy Writ altogether, with the memorable exception of the incident which immediately follows, (the Greeks brought to CHRIST;) not resuming that History, until he describes the washing of the Disciples' feet, which took place at the Last Supper. This will be found more fully pointed out in the note at the end of the present chapter.

An incident of the highest interest follows: as it were the first streak of dawn: announcing the coming Day of the Gentiles. Certain Greeks are brought to CHRIST, proselytes, as it seems, who had come up to Jerusalem to worship:(b)—

20, 21 And there were certain Greeks among them that came up to worship at the Feast: the same came therefore to Philip, which was of Bethsaida of Galilee, and desired him, saying, Sir, we would see JESUS.

Rather, "*We wish* to see."—What may have been the object of these men in thus desiring to be brought to CHRIST? for it is certain that they desired to do *more* than "see" Him. Had they, perhaps, heard of the acclamations with which He

---

(x) Bereshith Rabba.
(y) See the notes on St. John xi. 39, and on verse 44.
(z) See St. John ix. 22: xi. 47, 48: xii. 42.
(a) St. Luke xix. 41 to 44: St. Matth. xxi. 10, 11: and St. Mark ix. 11.
(b) Consider Acts xvi. 4. Also Acts viii. 27. The case was contemplated at the Dedication of the Temple: see 1 Kings viii. 41 to 43.

had been lately greeted on entering the Capital; and of the waving branches of palm which, as Greeks, they well understood to be emblematic of royal rank?... They were destined to be strangely disappointed when they were brought into the presence of JESUS of Nazareth, and heard, (as it is reasonable to suppose they did,) the tenor of His wondrous Discourse, which follows.

The name "Philip," is of Greek origin. Does this, perhaps, explain why these Greeks addressed themselves to *him?* Or were they perhaps Syro-Phœnicians,(c) and therefore not unlikely to know an inhabitant of Bethsaida of Galilee?

22 Philip cometh and telleth Andrew: and again Andrew and Philip tell JESUS.

Take notice, here, of the respectful conduct of these lowly men, in their approaches to CHRIST: the deference, and form, with which they proceeded on an occasion like the present. This circumstance has been already pointed out, in the note on St. John iv. 27. It is obvious however to suspect, as well from the formal request of the strangers, as from the hesitation of the two Apostles, that the desired interview was of no ordinary kind. Our LORD's prohibition, in St. Matthew x. 5, affords no sufficient clue to the conduct of His servants here recorded.

Philip singles out *Andrew,*—perhaps because Andrew was his fellow-towns-man; (d) and it may have been in order to suggest this inference, that St. John states, in verse 21, that Philip *"was of Bethsaida of Galilee."* The names of these two Disciples are found connected also in St. John vi. 5 and 8: and they are doubtless the "two" which are omitted in chap. xxi. 2.

It has been pointed out that "as there were two Apostles sent for the colt which represented the Gentiles, so there are two who now tell JESUS of the approach of the first-fruits of the Gentiles. . . . Our Blessed LORD sees therein the sign of His own approaching Death; for the calling of the Gentiles could not take place until the Jews had rejected and crucified Him."—"Listen to the voice of the Cornerstone:(e)—

23 And JESUS answered them, saying, The hour is come, that the Son of Man should be glorified.

"Glorified,"—as above, in verse 16: where the reader is requested to read the note.—"Did He think Himself glorified, because the Gentiles wished to see Him? No. But He saw that after His Passion and Resurrection the Gentiles in all lands would believe on Him; and He took occasion from this request of some Gentiles to see Him, to announce the approaching fullness of the Gentiles: for that the hour of His being glorified was now at hand, and that after He was glorified in the Heavens, the Gentiles would believe.(f) It was certain that this reply was made in the presence of a large assemblage of persons;"(g) and it is reasonable to suppose that the "Greeks" themselves heard it. The object of the Divine Speaker "appears to have been to correct the wrong notions as to the glories of His Kingdom, which His triumphant entry into Jerusalem had led these Greeks, in common with many others, to entertain."(h)

That "hour," therefore, so often mysteriously spoken of as "not yet come,"(i) had at length arrived. Consider the following places, where the same announcement is repeated:—St. John xiii. 1: xvii. 1: St. Mark xiv. 41: St. Luke xxii. 53.

"But it was necessary that His Exaltation and Glory should be preceded by His Humiliation and Passion: wherefore He says,"—

24 Verily, verily, I say unto you, Except a corn of wheat fall into the ground and die, it abideth alone: but if it die, it bringeth forth much fruit.

"CHRIST Himself, of the seed of the Patriarchs, was sown in the field of the World; that, by dying, He might rise again with increase. He died alone: He

---

(c) Consider St. Mark vii. 26. So Grotius.
(d) See St. John i. 4.
(f) Augustine.
(h) Lonsdale and Hale.
(i) For instance, in St. John ii. 4: vii. 30, and viii. 20.

(e) Augustine.
(g) See below, verses 29 and 34.

se again with many."(j) "In the ears of those who heard Him, however, His ords contained a simple intimation that although the time had arrived when He vould "be glorified," yet must He first die before He could "enter into His ory."(k) And He proceeds, in the two next verses, to declare that they who ould share that glory with Him,(l) must show themselves His servants by follow-g Him in His sufferings, and giving up "life in this world" for "Life Eter-l."(m)

"Except a corn of wheat fall into the ground and die." How do such words on the ps of the CREATOR serve to remind us that the whole World is but one mighty Para le, to which the Gospel supplies the clue! Compare with the present place, the rocess described in St. Luke xiii. 19; and take notice that St. Paul, when dis-ursing of the mystery of Death and Resurrection, derives his language from the scay, and subsequent growth of seeds; as "bare grain,—*it may chance of wheat.*" he body, "raised in power," is "*sown,*" (he says) "in weakness."(n) The lesson derived from seeds in the present place, however, is not the change osn dishonour to glory, which takes place when they are sown into the earth; nor le change of body with which the plant at last appears. The *prodigious increase* hich follows upon their decay, is the one circumstance to which attention is irected. A seed, unless it dies, "abideth *alone,*" our LORD says: it continues *bare* grain;"(o) "but if it die, it bringeth forth much fruit." The figure may have ven suggested by the circumstance that these Greeks were the "first-fruits." CHRIST Himself, on His rising on Easter-Day, was the offering of the first sheaf a the morrow after the Sabbath;(p) and the coming in of the Gentiles, on the ay of Pentecost, was the gathering in of the harvest."(q) — It follows:

25 He that loveth his life shall lose it; and he that hateth his life i this World shall keep it unto Eternal Life.

"*He* loves his life in this world, who indulges its inordinate desires: *he* hates it, ho resists them."(r) "It were harsh to say that a man should hate his life; so ir LORD adds "*in this World;*" that is, for a particular time, not for ever. And e shall gain in the end by so doing; for we shall thereby enter into Life Eter-l."(s) This is one of those almost proverbial sayings which are of most frequent recur-nce on our LORD's lips. It is repeated, with small varieties, no less than four istinct times:(t) and, on the two first, it is found connected, (as here,) with the following of CHRIST."

26 If any man serve Me, let him follow Me; and where I am, there iall also My servant be: if any man serve Me, him will *My* FATHER onour.

This, then, is the Christian's great reward: to be, throughout the Ages of Eter-ity, in that blissful region where his Master is! After Death, will come the lorious Resurrection to Eternal Life, of as many as have been faithful followers CHRIST in this World. By making them partakers thereof, the FATHER will honour" them: "for what greater honour can GOD's adopted sons receive than to i where the Only SON is?"(u)

27 Now is My Soul troubled; and what shall I say? FATHER, ive Me from this hour: but for this cause came I unto this hour.

"Thus did our LORD draw us near to Himself by showing how deeply He partook our human fears and sorrows; as if thereby to lead us on to something better."(y) ake notice, that in these sayings, (which are a kind of foretaste of the scene in the

(f) Bede. — Consider St. Matth. xxxii. 52, 53.
(k) St. Luke xxiv. 26.
(m) Lonsdale and Hale.
(o) 1 Cor. xv. 37.
(q) Williams.
(s) Theophylact.
(t) St. Matth. x. 39: St. Matth. xvi. 25, (which is St. Mark viii. 35, and St. Luke ix. 24:) St. ake xvii. 33; and the present place.
(u) Chrysostom.

(l) St. John xvii. 24.
(n) 1 Cor. xv. 36, 37, 42, 43.
(p) Levit. xxiii. 11.
(r) Chrysostom.

(y) Williams.

Garden of Gethsemane,(z) we have a striking evidence of the reality of His Human Nature ; which shrank, (as our Nature ever must shrink,) from Pain and Death. The Humanity of our LORD,—*Soul* as well as Body,(a)—becomes more and more apparent, as His Cross draws nearer in sight. But, besides partaking all our natural instincts and infirmities, (not one of which is in itself sinful,) the present trouble of our SAVIOUR'S Soul may well be thought to have mainly arisen from the prospect of the terrible conflict with the Power of Darkness which was now close at hand. Consider all that follows, down to verse 32,(b) inclusive : and interpret the last words of ver. 27, by comparing them with 1 St. John iii. 8.

Having exhorted His Disciples to endurance, and the patient treading in His own footsteps, He straightway reveals Himself as "a Man of Sorrows, and acquainted with grief."(c) His soul is full of agony at the prospect of all that awaited Him; and His affecting language in the text is that reasoning whereby He calms His troubled soul, setting us thereby an example. . . . On this, Augustine exclaims :— "Thou biddest my soul follow Thee ; but I see Thy soul troubled. What foundation shall I seek, if the Rock gives way ? LORD, I acknowledge Thy mercy. Thou, of Thy love, wast troubled, to console those who are troubled through the infirmity of nature ; that the members of Thy Body perish not in despair. The Head took upon Himself the affections of His members."

"It is as if our LORD had said,—I cannot say why I should ask to be saved from this hour ; for, for this cause came I unto this hour. . . . I am troubled, yet I ask not to be spared. I do not say, "Save Me from this hour ;" but,—

28 FATHER, glorify thy Name.

"To die for the Truth was to glorify GOD, as the event showed : for, after His Crucifixion, the World was to be converted to the knowledge of GOD."(d)

Then came there a Voice from Heaven, *saying*, I have both glorified *It*, and will glorify *It* again.

"'I have glorified it,'—that is, when Thou wast born of a Virgin ; didst work miracles ; wast made manifest by the HOLY GHOST descending in the shape of a dove : 'and I will glorify it again,'—that is, when Thou shalt rise from the Dead; and, as GOD, be exalted above the Heavens, and thy Glory above all the Earth."(e) Supremely was the FATHER "glorified" by the proofs which the SON gave of His Divinity, as he hung upon the Cross ; as well as by the stupendous miracles which followed upon His Ascension. See the notes on St. John xiii. 31. . . Chrysostom points out that our LORD'S announcement in verse 31, "fits on to the preceding words ; as showing *the mode* in which GOD was glorified." The remark seems just; and reminds us that as GOD had been already glorified by the issue of the Temptation in the Wilderness, so was He now about to be glorified again by the entire and final conquest over the same Enemy, which our LORD obtained on the Cross.(f) For "through Death," (as we know,) He destroyed "him that had the power of Death, that is, the Devil."(g)

Thrice was the Divine Voice heard from Heaven : first, at our LORD'S Baptism,(h) when He seems to have been specially designated to His *Priestly* Office : next, at His Transfiguration,(i) when, by the departure of Moses and Elijah, He was discovered as the great *Prophet* of His People ; lastly, on the present occasion, when He is not only revealed to Sion, as her *King ;* and beholds the first fruits of those Gentiles who should hereafter press so largely into His Kingdom : but is invested, although in mockery, with all the insignia of Royalty ; and wears His title ("the King of the Jews,") upon the very Cross.

29 The people therefore, that stood by, and heard *it*, said that it thundered : others said, An Angel spake to Him.

Take notice that when GOD speaks, His voice is now, loud as the sound of many

(z) Consider St. Luke xxii. 42, &c.
(b) See especially the note on verse 31.
(d) Chrysostom.
(f) See below, the note on ver. 31.
(h) St. Mark i. 11.

(a) See the note on St. John xiii. 31.
(c) Is. liii. 3.
(e) Augustine.
(g) Heb. ii. 14.
(i) St. Matth. xvii. 5.

waters ;(*j*) and terrible, as the thunder :(*k*) now, it is "a still small voice,"(*l*) like that of Infancy, or Age.(*m*) And to some, it is but a confused sound ;(*n*) while, to others, it is distinctly audible, and articulate.

30 JESUS answered and said, This Voice came not because of Me, but for your sakes.

"As He had said, at the Grave of Lazarus, that for the sake of others He spake aloud unto the FATHER,(*o*) so now also, for their sakes," (not for His own, who needed no such testimony,) "did the FATHER speak aloud to Him."(*p*) And Augustine points out that "as that Voice did not come for His sake, but for theirs, so was His Soul troubled for their sake, not for His own." . . . We look narrowly at the next words which our SAVIOUR is recorded to have spoken, in order to discover whether they supply any clue to this supernatural manifestation ; nor are we disappointed.

31 Now is the judgment of this World : now shall the Prince of this World be cast out.

Is it possible to read such an announcement,—(duly considering *by* whom, and *of* whom, and *when* it was spoken,)—without the deepest awe, curiosity, and wonder ? The miraculous Voice which had been just heard, is declared to have marked the juncture at which "*the Prince of this World*" *was about to be* "*cast out*." The expression "Prince of this World,"—(which derives singular illustration from the boastful, and certainly not altogether vain, language of St. Luke iv. 6,)— is found in two other places, and denotes unmistakably the arch-fiend Satan ; who is elsewhere called "the god of this World,"(*q*) and "the Prince of the Power of the air."(*r*) Thus, in St. John xiv. 30, our SAVIOUR speaks of "the Prince of this World" as coming, and finding nothing in Him. But the most remarkable place, in connection with the present, is chap. xvi. 11,—to which the reader is requested to refer. By that expulsion of the Prince of Evil, therefore, GOD was about to "glorify His Name." Was not this, in fact, the fulfillment of the first great prophecy, that the promised Seed should "*bruise*" the Serpent's "*head ?*" (*s*)

The Cross of CHRIST, now full in view, was doubtless the scene of the mighty Triumph here proclaimed beforehand. The Enemy repulsed in his threefold assault in the Wilderness, had departed from the Holy One, (as we there read,) "until a [future] season,"(*t*)—which season had now at length arrived. The attack was therefore about to be renewed, with all the violence which the desperation of Devils can suggest, and which infernal malice can call to its aid. As *then*, through every avenue of Pleasure, so *now*, through every avenue of Pain, the Devil will seek to shake the Almighty One from His steadfastness, and gain some advantage over Him. With what chance of success,—he may have heard our LORD declare beforehand. Yet will he persevere, and at least do his worst. By the contradiction of sinners ; by the blasphemy of the multitude ; by the blindness of the Jewish Rulers, wilfully persevered in to the very last ; by the treachery of Judas ;(*u*) by the Agony in the Garden, resulting it may be in part from a conflict with the Power of Darkness ; by the desertion of the Apostles ; by the multiplied cruelties, and prolonged tortures of His Passion ; finally, by His sufferings on the bitter Cross ;—by all these means, the enemy will seek to avert his own threatened doom, and to defeat GOD. But he is destined to be hopelessly foiled in every endeavour. He falls, as Lightning falls from Heaven :(*v*) and the Cross, which was to have been the instrument of his victory, proves, (as we have elsewhere shown,) the very means of his own discomfiture and downfall. "All the Fathers, from Ignatius to Bernard, represent Satan as snared by his own success ; and by taking away the life of the One Immaculate human subject, losing for ever that proprietary right over the lives of all the rest, which had been his through the penal consequence of the first sin."(*x*)

(*j*) Rev. i. 15.
(*l*) 1 Kings xix. 12.
(*n*) As here, and in Acts ix. 7 : xxii. 9.
(*p*) Williams.
(*r*) Ephes. ii. 2.
(*t*) See the note on St. Luke iv. 13.
(*u*) See the note on St. John xiii. 20.
(*v*) See St. Luke x. 18, and the note there.
(*x*) Dr. W. H. Mill.

(*k*) Ps. xxix. 2 to 9.
(*m*) 1 Sam. iii. 5.
(*o*) St. John xi. 42.
(*q*) 2 Cor. iv. 4.
(*s*) Gen. iii. 15.

He will henceforth cease to be "the Prince of this World," except in an inferior
sense. He is about to be dethroned, and "cast out." Our Race had indeed sold
themselves to him : (and although we had no right to do so, seeing that we are
not our own, yet was the contract binding, as far as men were concerned :) "our
act then barreth us. And yet it cannot bar the right Owner from challenging His
own wheresoever He finds it. And therefore we may be well assured that God will
not suffer the Devil, who is but an intruder and cheater, quietly to enjoy what is
God's, and not his ; but He will eject him, and recover out of his possession that
which he hath no right at all to hold."(y)—On this great subject, the reader is requested to read the notes on St. Matthew xxvii. 35, 38, and 40 : St. Luke xxii. 43,
44; xxiii. 25. He is also invited to refer to the observations prefixed to St. Matthew iv. It must be almost superfluous to point out that the Parable of "the strong
man armed keeping his goods" should be considered in connection with all that
goes before. See the note on St. Luke xi. 22.

This mighty transaction, then, is called by our Lord, "the Judgment of this
World ;" words which seem to imply that a sentence of condemnation was now
virtually passed on Sin and Satan : the evidence whereof was that the Evil One and
his wicked Angels, the "Rulers of the Darkness of this World," as they are termed
by St. Paul,(z)—(and these "Devils, or Princes of the Air," are all one with the
"Princes of this World,"(a)—no longer reigned over the bodies of men as they had
done in times past. For "we learn from repeated divine testimonies, that before
the price of our Redemption was paid, the World and its Kingdom were suffered by
God to remain under diabolical control to a degree which we cannot now readily
conceive."(b) The Disciples had power given them to tread under foot "all the
Power of the Enemy ;"(d) and this casting out of the Devils became a part of their
abiding Commission."(e) The reader is requested to read the note on St. Luke x.
18. . . . . Enough has been said, in the course of the present note, to show the
close, yet secret connection of the words which immediately follow with those which
precede. Not only is there an allusion *to the Cross*, as the instrument whereby
Messiah was to do such wonders for His people, but it seems to be also implied that
men,—from his empire over whom Satan was about to be expelled,— would be the
more easily drawn to Himself, when released from the tyranny of such an usurper.

32 And I, if I be lifted up from the Earth, will draw all *men* unto
Me.

Rather,—"*when* I am lifted up :" for the meaning of which phrase, see the note
on the next verse.—It will be perceived that our Saviour blends some intimation
of His Greatness and Godhead with almost every allusion to His coming Humiliation. Thus even while He indicates the ignominious death by which He will soon
see fit to die, He delivers a glorious hint concerning the consequences to mankind
of that act of self-abasement: namely, that He will thereby "*draw all men*" *unto
Himself;* cause men of all nations to become subjects of His Kingdom.(f) And
what is this but looking beyond His own Resurrection from Death, and Ascension
into Heaven to the gift of the Holy Ghost which was to follow? What is it but
to claim to Himself, as God, that marvellous operation of Divine Power whereby
the hearts of men must first be effectually *drawn*, before they can come to God?
Consider St. John vi. 44,—where this "drawing" is ascribed solely to the Father.
. . . . The reader is requested to refer to the third paragraph of the note on St.
John xi. 52. He will be reminded by the place of Scripture thus referred to, that
the great purpose of our Saviour's Advent upon Earth, was to die, not for His own
nation only, but to "gather together in one the Children of God that were scattered
abroad."

"When I am lifted up from the Earth, I will draw all men unto Me," saith our
Saviour: and if those words were true of His Crucifixion, how powerful ought they
to be in reference to His Ascension! "When the Lord would take up Elijah into
Heaven, Elisha said unto him, 'As the Lord liveth, and as thy soul liveth, I will not
leave thee :'(g) when Christ is ascended up on high, we must follow Him with the

(y) Bp. Sanderson.   (z) Eph. vi. 12.   (a) Bp. Pearson. Consider 1 Cor. ii. 6, 8.
(b) Dr. W. H. Mill. — Not that Satan ever claims more than a delegated power: See St.
Luke iv. 6. ·
(d) St. Luke x. 19.   (e) St. Mark xvi. 17.
(f) Consider Colossians i. 13.   (g) 2 Kings ii. 1, 2.

wings of our meditations, and with the chariots of our affections." So far, Bishop
Pearson.—The Evangelist remarks on the words of his LORD,—

. 33 This He said, signifying what death He should die.

And those who heard, understood this signification of His words perfectly well;
as appears from what follows. The reader is requested to refer to the note on
St. John viii. 28.

34 The people answered Him, We have heard out of the Law that
CHRIST abideth for ever:

Observe the perversity and malice of this rejoinder. Our LORD had not denied
that "the CHRIST abideth for ever." The ancient Scriptures are full of it. His
throne was to be "as the Sun," and "established *for ever* as the Moon."(h) He was
to be "a Priest" and a "Prince *for ever*."(i) "Of the increase of His Government"
there was to be no end."(k) His Dominion was to be "an everlasting Dominion
which shall not pass away, and His Kingdom that which shall not be destroyed."(l)
He was Himself to "reign over them in Mount Sion from henceforth, even *for
ever*."(m) What therefore they had "heard out of the Law," CHRIST had not
denied. He had merely declared the chief previous article of *His passion*,—
namely, the bitter Cross. Could they say that they had heard out of the Law that
CHRIST *doth not suffer?* The very reverse was notoriously the case. It is worth
referring to such places as St. Luke xxiv. 26, and 44 to 46: 1 St. Peter i. 11.—
They proceed:

and how sayest Thou, The Son of Man must be lifted up? who is
this Son of Man?

"What kind of a MESSIAH is this, who, Thou sayest, must be 'lifted up?' How
can He be the MESSIAH of whom the Prophets speak?"(n) But it is worth remark
that our SAVIOUR had not said "The Son of Man must be lifted up," on *the present
occasion*. Unless indeed this be another example of what was pointed out above,
in the note on St. John xi. 28. He will be found to have so prophesied of His
Crucifixion, at the Feast of Tabernacles, about six months before.(o) The actual
words, (strange to relate,) are found only in His Discourse to Nicodemus,—
recorded in St. John iii. 14.

The title "Son of Man" occurs in Daniel vii. 13,—and is thence quoted by our
LORD in St. Matthew xxiv. 30, and xxxvi. 64.—To the inquiry proposed to Him by
the people concerning His language, the meaning of which must have been abundantly plain, our SAVIOUR vouchsafes no direct reply. The Discourse which follows,
and which, (broken only by some precious remarks of the Evangelist himself,) extends to the end of the present Chapter, appears to have been the last of our LORD's
public Discourses; and it has all the solemnity which might have been expected in
such a leave taking of His hard-hearted Countrymen. His very language is of
Twilight, and turns on the approach of Night,—as implying that the Day of Grace
was now rapidly on the wane, if it had not indeed already expired. Truly has it
been remarked, however, that, in what follows, our LORD speaks "as if His Death
were but the going away for a time; as the Sun's light only sets to rise again."(p)

35 Then JESUS said unto them, Yet a little while is the Light with
you. Walk while ye have the Light, lest Darkness come upon you:
for he that walketh in Darkness knoweth not whither he goeth.

Thus,—and for the last time!—does "the Light of the World" discourse of Himself under this favorite and most instructive image; concerning which it must suffice to refer the reader to what has been already offered on the notes on St. John
i. 9: viii. 12, and ix. 5. But the passage most in point is St. John xi. 9 and 10,
which should be attentively considered. See also below, on verse 46. . . . . The
attentive student of St. John's writings will recognize a reference to these sayings

(h) Ps. lxxxix. 36, 37.   (i) Ps. cx. 4: Ezek. xxxvii. 25.
(k) Is. ix. 7.   (l) Dan. vii. 14.
(m) Mic. iv. 7.   (n) Lonsdale and Hale.
(o) See St. John viii. 28.   (p) Chrysostom.

of our SAVIOUR, (or to St. John viii. 12,) in St. John's first Epistle,—i. 5 to 7, and ii. 11. May it be thought that His words were intended to recall the exhortation of His ancient prophet Jeremiah ? — "Give glory to the LORD your GOD before He cause darkness, and before your feet stumble upon the dark mountains, and while ye look for Light, He turn it into the shadow of Death, and make it gross darkness ?"(q) In language not dissimilar, at least, does our LORD warn the Jews, for the last time, of the spiritual Darkness which had already all but entirely overtaken them; and which, if they refused to walk in His Light, would effectually blind their eyes, and cause them terribly to err from the right way. And so it came to pass(r) when they had "crucified the LORD of Glory. *Quite* benighted were they at the time of the siege of their city.

Such solemn words, from Him who is our light, on the subject of "Darkness," seem to call for special comment. "What then is *Darkness?* In GOD there is none, that is, none *to* Him, for the Darkness is no Darkness with Him.(t) All Darkness, then, is in the creature; in Satan, and in his evil Angels, and in Man. Men walk in Darkness "because the god of this World hath blinded their minds."(u) The Light is around them, and the Eye of GOD pierces through them: the Darkness is *to* them, and *within* them. The Light that is in them is Darkness, and how great is that Darkness !(o) They shut their eyes to the Light of GOD, and make to themselves a false Light; referring everything to self instead of to Him: so that all things take false proportions and false relations.

"Nor is there anything in Nature that can fully represent the perversion which takes place in the mind when it chooses to regard everything in relation to itself, and its own will. Nothing short of Blindness can express it; but in the case of Blindness, we have no *false* Light to put in the place of the *true*. Dreaming comes nearer to the image required; yet, even in Dreaming, we are usually protected by the half-conscious recollection of objects, or the unseen care of Angels, from the wreck we should work if we really acted upon the view that is in our eye. Madness does not commonly go the length of the folly and contradiction of a wicked man's Life. It is not often that madmen so grossly mistake the nature and appearances of sensible objects, as ordinary men do daily mistake the real nature and relations of things that concern them far more nearly. Madness, Dreaming, Darkness, all combined, make but a shadow of that "darkness which may be felt,"(x) — *an ungodly Will.*"(y) . . . . Our LORD concludes:

36 While ye have Light, believe in the Light, that ye may be the children of Light.

Rather, — "While ye have *the* Light." No better Commentary can be desired on the rest of the verse, than is supplied by ver. 46. The phrase "children of Light" recalls the language of St. Luke xvi. 8.

These things spake JESUS, and departed, and did hide Himself from them.

He "hid Himself from them," as He had done on so many former occasions; some of which will be found specified at foot.(z) The phrase here employed is met with also in Psalm lv. 12. — It may well have been the Evening of the Day, when our LORD addressed these solemn words to His enemies; hiding Himself at last from their gaze, as His visible emblem in the Heavens(a) sunk behind the western hills. . . . . The Evangelist proceeds to make some weighty remarks on the unbelief of the Jews with respect to the transactions he has been describing.—And first, he shows that however strange, and even inexplicable to Human Reason, may have been the reception which our LORD's miracles met with at the hands of His own chosen people, that result had been clearly foreseen in the Divine Counsels, from the very beginning

(q) Jer. xiii. 16.
(t) Ps. cxxxix. 12.
(v) St. Matth. vi. 23.
(y) Rev. C. Marriott.

(r) Rom. xi. 7 to 10, and 25.   2 Cor. iii. 14, 15.
(u) 2 Cor. iv. 4.
(x) Ex. x. 21.

(z) See St. Luke iv. 30. St. John viii. 59, (where the same expression occurs:) and x. 39.
(a) It would be interesting to collect the occasions when our LORD's discourse may be thought to have been suggested by external phenomena. Consider St. John iv. 35: vii. 37: xv. 1. St. Luke xiv. 1, 7, 12, 15, 16: xxi. 29, 30, &c., &c.

37, 38 But though He had done so many miracles before them, yet they believed not on Him : that the saying of Esaias the prophet might be fulfilled, which he spake, LORD, who hath believed our report? and to whom hath the Arm of the LORD been revealed?

By the first clause in this prophetic saying, the SPIRIT intended to imply the rejection of the Gospel. Hence, St. Paul says, — "They have not all obeyed the Gospel. For Esaias saith, LORD, who hath believed our report?"(b) . . . . In the latter part of the sentence, Augustine saw a plain reference to the SAVIOUR. "It is evident," (he says,) that "the Arm of the LORD" is here the SON OF GOD Himself :(c) who is so called, because all things were made by Him."(d) The reader is invited to read what has been offered in another place on the kindred expression, — "The finger of GOD."(e) Isaiah's words have thus been paraphrased :— "LORD, who will believe the testimony of us Thy prophets respecting CHRIST? and to whom will Thy power, put forth in Him, be so revealed that they will see and acknowledge it to be Thine?"(f)

A few words will perhaps be expected on the very difficult subject which is opened by the form of speech employed by the Evangelist, in this and so many other places.(g) It must suffice to point out that, as far as the usage of the original language goes, the expression in verse 38, ("that the saying of the prophet might be fulfilled,") *need not* mean anything more than, "*So that* the saying of the prophet *was fulfilled.*" Utterly absurd, of course, would be the supposition that an inspired writer could wish to imply that a spirit of unbelief had been forced upon the nation of the Jews in order to save the credit of one of GOD's ancient Prophets. The ambiguity of the original expression, when received into "an honest and good heart," will perhaps occasion no real difficulty. Doubtless, (it will be felt,) when GOD hath spoken, the thing *must* come to pass. On the other hand, unless the thing had been *certainly* destined to come to pass, GOD would never have spoken. The prophecy *depended* on the event: it did not *make* it. Where this truth is borne in mind, and GOD's perfect Justice together with Man's Free-will is fully admitted, more words on this confessedly difficult subject, will not perhaps be wished for.

Having thus brought forward the well-known beginning of the fifty-third of Isaiah, the Evangelist proceeds to quote from the sixth chapter of the same prophet; not setting down the words exactly, but rather giving their sense and substance.

39, 40 Therefore they could not believe, because that Esaias said again, He hath blinded their eyes, and hardened their heart ; that they should not see with *their* eyes, nor understand with *their* heart, and be converted, and I should heal them.

"The Evangelist says "*could not,*" to show that it was impossible that the Prophet should lie; not that it was impossible that they should believe."(h) "If any ask *why* "they could not believe," I answer, *Because they would not.*"(i) See on St. Matt. xiii. 15.

Verse 40 should not begin "He hath blinded their eyes," &c., — but "*They have* blinded:" as when our SAVIOUR,(k) and St. Paul,(l) quote the same place. An aspirate makes all the difference!(m) . . . . . The few words of explanation thus offered will be felt to remove the apparent harshness of the expression. At the same time, it is not meant that *never* does GOD blind the eyes, and harden the hearts of men. If men resist the motions of His Good Spirit, He will certainly withdraw that blessed influence; and, (as in the case of Pharaoh,) will *harden* the heart at last.(n) "For He does not leave us, except we wish Him to do so. . . . It is plain that we begin to forsake first, and are the cause of our own perdition."(o)

(b) Rom. x. 16.   (c) Compare Is. li. 9 : also Acts xiii. 17.
(d) Consider St. John i. 3, and the note there.
(e) See the note on St. Luke xi. 20.   (f) Lonsdale and Hale.
(g) For instance, — St. Matth. ii. 15 : iv. 14 : xxi. 4, 5 : xxvii. 35, &c.
(h) Chrysostom.   (i) Augustine.
(k) St. Matth. xiii. 15.   (l) Acts xxviii. 27.
(m) The learned reader will perceive that "This people," (not "GOD,") is the nominative to the verb.
(n) Exodus ix. 12 : x. 20, 27 : xi. 10.   (o) Chrysostom, — quoting Hos. iv. 6.

St. Mark, instead of, "And I should heal them,"—gives (from the Chaldee Paraphrase) "And their sins should be forgiven them."(*p*)

41 These things said Esaias, when he saw His Glory, and spake of Him.

" He saw *His Glory,*" not *Him.* The Eternal Son is " equal to the FATHER, as touching His Godhead," and therefore invisible. Not until He took our nature upon Him, was it possible that He should be " seen of Angels,"(*q*) or of Men. When He appeared to the Patriarchs of old, it was in the person of a created Angel.(*r*)

Take notice, in the meantime, that Isaiah declares that his eyes had " seen the King, JEHOVAH Sabaoth,"—that is, " the LORD of Hosts."(*s*) But St. John declares that it was the Glory of *CHRIST* which the prophet Isaiah saw, and that he "spake *of Him.*" CHRIST is therefore JEHOVAH.(*t*) . . . . The entire chapter of Isaiah should be here referred to; exhibiting, as it does, a magnificent picture of that Glory which He, of whose humiliation we are reading, had with the FATHER before the World was.(*u*) To CHRIST, therefore, do the Seraphim cry " Holy, Holy, Holy !" . . . . The Evangelist proceeds:

42 Nevertheless among the chief Rulers also many believed on Him;

The warning conveyed in so many other parts of Scripture is not wanting on the present occasion,—when, from the sweeping condemnation which went before, it might be supposed that there was no exception to the general rule of Unbelief which the Evangelist has been noticing. Even " among the Rulers,"(*x*) that is, in the very Sanhedrin itself, there were " many" who believed in CHRIST. Nicodemus and Joseph of Arimathæa are not here specially intended ; for these men boldly confessed CHRIST. St. John speaks of others ; who believed indeed,—

43 But because of the Pharisees they did not confess *Him,* lest they should be put out of the synagogue: for they loved the praise of men more than the praise of GOD.

Concerning the love of human Praise, as a hindrance to Faith, consider our LORD's saying recorded in St. John v. 41 and 44. On the form of enmity here alluded to, see chap. ix. 22 and 34.

The Evangelist proceeds with what we suspect to have been part of *the same* Discourse which was interrupted above, at ver. 36.—Take notice that JESUS is said to have " cried," when He spake the words which follow. This was probably for the reason assigned in the commentary on St. John vii. 37 ; namely, because it was " the last time ;"(*z*) and because " the time was short."(*a*) See the second paragraph of the note referred to.

44, 45 JESUS cried and said, He that believeth on Me, believeth not on Me, but on Him that sent Me. And He that seeth Me, seeth Him that sent Me.

" So little difference is there between Me, and Him that sent Me, that he that beholdeth Me, beholdeth Him. . . . . He does not hereby withdraw the believer's faith from Himself, but gives him a higher object for that faith, than the form of a servant."(*b*) This is one of the places of Scripture from which the ancients proved the Son's Divinity ; since to believe in Him, is to believe in the FATHER. Notice here the difference between " *believing*" a person, and " *believing in*" a person. The former is said *of men:* the latter *of GOD.* . . . . Chrysostom remarks that, " It is

(*p*) St. Mark iv. 12.   Consider St. Luke v. 17: and compare the 20th verse of the same chapter with the 23rd and 24th.
(*q*) 1 Tim. iii. 16.
(*r*) See the note (*k*) on St. Matth. xv. 27.
(*s*) Is. v. 5.
(*t*) So Pearson, following Athanasius, and the ancients generally.
(*u*) St. John xvii. 5.   (*x*) Not " the chief rulers," in the original.
(*z*) 1 St. John ii. 18.   (*a*) 1 Cor. vii. 29.
(*b*) Augustine.

as if our SAVIOUR had said, He that taketh water from a stream, taketh the water not of the stream, but of the Fountain." Then, to place the matter out of all doubt, and to show that the Nature of the FATHER and the SON is strictly one and the same, our SAVIOUR adds that to behold the SON is to behold the FATHER. Compare this with St. John xiv. 9. . . . "I and My FATHER are *One*,"— said our LORD on a former occasion.(c)

It can scarcely be necessary, with reference to the mode of expression in ver. 44, to do more than request attention to the note on St. John vii. 16.

46 I am come a Light into the World, that whosoever believeth on Me should not abide in Darkness.

"Whereby it is evidently implied that He found all the World in Darkness." Consider Genesis i. 2. "In which Darkness, if men wish not to remain, they must believe in the Light which was come into the World," and was now so near its setting. "He once said to His Disciples, 'Ye are the Light of the World :'(d) but He did not say, 'Ye are come a Light into the World, that whosoever believeth on you should not abide in Darkness.' All Saints are lights; but they are so by Faith, —because they are enlightened by Him, from whom to withdraw is Darkness."(e) . . . On this great subject, the reader is referred to the note on verse 35. He will also profitably call to mind St. Paul's striking declaration, that GOD " hath delivered us from the Power of Darkness, and hath translated us into the Kingdom of His dear SON :"(f) called us out of Darkness into His marvellous Light."(g)

Take notice that the very form of the expression, ("I am come a LIGHT into the World,") shows, 1st, that CHRIST existed before His Incarnation ;(h) even as the Sun exists before it appears above the Eastern hills. 2ndly, It is implied that He was the one SAVIOUR of the World, as there is but one Sun. Lastly, that He came not to one nation only, but to *all* ;(i) even as the Sun's "going forth is from the end of the Heaven, and his circuit unto the end of it: and there is nothing hid from the heat thereof."(k)

47 And if any man hear My Words, and believe not, I judge him not :

"That is, I judge him not now. He does not say, I judge him not at the Last Day, for that would be contrary to what is elsewhere written.(m) The reason follows, why He does not judge *now :*"

For I came not to judge the World, but to save the World.

"Now is the time of Mercy : afterward will be the time of Judgment."(n) Compare St. John iii. 17.

48 He that rejecteth Me, and receiveth not My Words, hath one that judgeth him : the Word that I have spoken, the same shall judge him in the Last Day.

That is,—A Judge will nevertheless not be wanting, at the Last Day, who shall condemn those unbelieving ones whom yet CHRIST did not condemn. The Word, namely, which the Jews had heard spoken by His own Divine Lips, and which they had refused to believe, will rise up in judgment against them, (our LORD says,) and declare them to be deserving of everlasting punishment. For, (as it is elsewhere written,)—" If I had not come and spoken unto them, they had not had sin: but now they have no cloak for their sin."(o) . . . " They could not but know that that Word was true, confirmed as it was by the evidence of so many mighty Works: wherefore that Word shall judge them, and accuse them, and condemn them. Where then will be the tribunal of such a Judge? From what judgment-seat will he pass his awful sentence? He will be very nigh the culprits. His throne will be within each guilty breast. He will speak fearfully to the conscience

(c) St. John x. 30.   (d) St. Matth. v. 14.   (e) Augustine.
(f) Coloss. i. 13.   (g) 1 St. Pet. ii. 9.   Consider 1 Thess. v. 4, 5.
(h) See the second paragraph of the note on St. John x. 36.
(i) Consider St. John i. 9.   (k) Ps. xix. 6.
(m) St. John v. 22, and 27 to 29.   (n) Augustine.
(o) St. John xv. 22.

of each terror-stricken unbeliever."(*p*) .... This prophecy is therefore more alarming than that in chap. v. 45; where *Moses* is declared to be the great accuser of the nation.

It is striking to notice in how many respects the attributes of CHRIST Himself are ascribed to His word also. It is declared to be "a discerner of the thoughts and intents of the heart:"(*q*) it is eternal, and "will never pass away:"(*r*) it is "the Power of GOD unto Salvation:"(*s*) it shall "judge" mankind.(*t*)—Pursuing the train of thought thus opened, it is well worthy of observation how strictly the Gospel of CHRIST resembles its Author,—in its nature, (at once Human and Divine;) in its unattractive aspect:(*u*) in its hidden sweetness;(*v*) and in the reception which it daily meets with at the hands of men. It bears the very name of its Object and Author,—"The Word."(*w*) No fanciful statement therefore, is it, but a simple *fact*, that, in *that* Word, CHRIST is forever truly present with Mankind. St. Paul surely implied no less, when he reproached the Galatians with inconstancy,—"*before whose eyes* JESUS CHRIST hath been evidently set forth, crucified among you." (Gal. iii. 1.) ... If this be a digression, the reader will forgive it.— Our LORD proceeds:

49 For I have not spoken of Myself; but the FATHER which sent Me, He gave Me a commandment, what I should say, and what I should speak.

Thus, then, the reason is assigned why CHRIST's Word should judge those who did not believe;—namely, because He spoke not from Himself, but from the FATHER. By which saying, our LORD adapts His argument to the powers of His hearers. It is as if He had said,—"Supposing even that I were a mere man, as ye suppose; yet, even thus, ye ought to believe My Word; since it is not Mine, but the FATHER's who sent Me." ... By which words, however, take notice that it is by no means to be assumed that our SAVIOUR speaks of Himself *as He was the Son of Man*. Whether as GOD, or as Man, the eternal SON would refer all His Wisdom to the Eternal FATHER. This has been already explained in the commentary on St. John vii. 16, to which the reader is requested to refer. Compare also, and consider the following places:—St. John iii. 32: v. 19, 30: vii. 16: viii. 38: xii. 50: xiv. 10, 24: xvii. 8.

"What I should *say*, or what I should *speak*," seems intended to comprehend every class of Discourse,—as well the words of familiar intercourse, as the grave and solemn addresses of the SAVIOUR. The entire sayings in the two last verses seem clearly intended to recall the famous prophecy concerning MESSIAH in Deuteronomy xviii. 18, 19.

50 And I know that His Commandment is Life Everlasting: whatsoever I speak therefore, even as the FATHER said unto Me, so I speak.

"This is Life Eternal," (saith our LORD in another place:) "that they might know Thee, the only True GOD, and JESUS CHRIST whom Thou hast sent."(*x*) The sense, in both cases, is evidently the same: namely, that the keeping of GOD's Commandment, is the path which leads to Life. This, our SAVIOUR declared that He "knew," with all the fullness of Divine knowledge: and He probably said it, in order yet further to arouse, and attract the sluggish hearts of His auditory.... "I know," (He says,) "that the end for which I received this authority from My FATHER is, that Life Everlasting may be given to as many as believe My words."(*y*)

It will be perceived by those who read the Gospel with any degree of attention, that with the exception of a single incident of uncertain date, viz., *that* recorded above, (ver. 20 to the end,) St. John proceeds at once from Palm-Sunday, to the evening of Thursday in Holy Week; beginning his next chapter (the thirteenth,) with the washing of the Disciples' feet, which took place at the Last Supper. The pre-

(*p*) Rupertus.   (*q*) Heb. iv. 12.
(*r*) St. Matth. xxiv. 35.
(*s*) Rom. i. 16. See also 1 Cor. i. 18, compared with 24.
(*t*) St. John xii. 48.   (*u*) Is. liii. 2, and 1 Cor. i. 18, 21, 23.
(*v*) St. John vi. 68, and Ps. cxix. 103.   (*w*) Rev. xix. 13.
(*x*) St. John xvii. 3.   (*y*) Lonsdale and Hale.

sent Evangelist, therefore, is silent with respect to a period of the Ministry concerning which the three first Evangelists are singularly full and particular. Especially may it be thought deserving of notice, that the prophetic discourse delivered on the Mount of Olives, so elaborately recorded by St. Matthew, St. Mark, and St. Luke, is not even alluded to by St. John. " It has been said that these prophecies are recorded by the three first Evangelists, because they concerned an event which had not taken place when they wrote; viz. the taking of Jerusalem: but that St. John abstains from recording those prophecies because he composed his Gospel after the destruction of the City." This however is shallow criticism indeed; for it would imply that the scope of our LORD's Discourse on the Mount of Olives was limited by the events of the Siege of Jerusalem; whereas, His far-sighted words are found to reach on even to the end of the World.

" May it not be suggested that the true reasons why St. John abstained from recording these prophecies, were, (1st) because they were sufficiently recorded by the other three Evangelists; and, (2dly) because he himself, in another Canonical Book, had very fully declared all that it was needful for the Church to know of her own future condition, even to the Second Advent, viz. in the Apocalypse? . . . If any thing more had been necessary to be known on this matter, St. John (we may reverently suppose) would have added it in his Gospel, as supplementary to the prophecies in the other three Gospels, and in the Apocalypse. His silence proclaims, I conceive, the *completeness* of what his three predecessors, and he himself, had written: it consummates and canonizes it."(z)

CHAPTER XIII.

1 JESUS *washeth the Disciples' feet: exhorteth them to Humility and Charity.* 18 *He foretelleth and discovereth to John by a token, that Judas should betray Him:* 31 *commandeth them to love one another,* 36 *and forewarneth Peter of his denial.*

THE reader should not enter upon the present chapter of St. John's Gospel, without taking notice of the remarks which were offered at the conclusion of the Commentary on the preceding chapter. Not a word is here found about any of those august events, so numerous and so significant,—those discourses, so prolonged and so portentous,—which mark the days of Holy Week, and which the three earlier Evangelists have described with such unusual minuteness of detail. St. John passes on at once to the Last Supper; which, however, he does not describe; but contents himself with narrating an occurrence which the other three Evangelists had omitted to narrate. He alone further subjoins the heavenly Discourses of our SAVIOUR when the solemnity of the Last Supper was ended.

Let us beware, however, how we speak of these Divine Writings. Let not reference be made to the structure of the Gospels as if they were ordinary narratives. We may not say that one supplies what the other omits, as if we thought that there had been *incompleteness* in that other. Still less may it be supposed that the supplementary parts of St. John's Gospel impart to his entire narrative a fragmentary character,—as if the study of another Evangelist were required for the completeness of St. John. It is not so. Each of the Gospels is complete in itself. St. John was divinely guided to begin, at this place, *his* history of our SAVIOUR's Cross and Passion; and he enters upon it, by describing one highly symbolical transaction,—of which, hereafter: and the date of it, he solemnly fixes to the eve of the Feast of the Passover.

It may be pointed out, however, in passing, that " the Disciple whom JESUS loved," by his silence concerning the Institution of the LORD's Supper, sets his

(z) For these valuable remarks the writer is indebted to a MS. communication from the Rev. Christopher Wordsworth, D.D.

seal in the most emphatic manner to the accounts thereof, given by St. Matthew, St. Mark, and St. Luke. And it may further be suggested, concerning his silence, that just as he has supplied in the Book of Revelation what may very well be regarded as an equivalent to the prophecy delivered by our LORD on the Mount of Olives,(a) so did he furnish in his sixth chapter, a full equivalent to his silence concerning the Holy Eucharist, now.

Now before the Feast of the Passover, when JESUS knew that His hour was come that He should depart out of this World unto the FATHER,

The last of the four Passovers within which the Ministry of our Blessed LORD was contained, had at last arrived; a Feast which derived its name from GOD's promise, that when He saw the blood of the Paschal Lamb "on the two side-posts and on the upper door-post of the houses" of the Israelites, He would *pass over* them and spare them.(b) "All was now to take place in reality, of which the Jewish Passover was the type. CHRIST was led as a Lamb to the slaughter; whose blood, sprinkled upon our door-posts, (that is, the sign of whose Cross marked upon our foreheads,) redeems us from the dominion of this World, as from Egyptian bondage;"(c) at once cleansing us from all sin, and delivering us from the Divine wrath.(d) St. John says "*before* the Feast of the Passover," because he relates what happened on the evening of the fourteenth day of the month; at which time the Passover was eaten: but, (as it is expressly mentioned in the Law,) "*the Feast*" was "*on the fifteenth day*."(e)

Here, then, every word is full of great and awful interest. We seem at first to be reading of an ordinary transaction, in that Washing of the Disciples' feet which follows; but, on closer inspection, it is found that it cannot have been such. Neither, in fact, may any of our LORD's sayings be passed by as if they were ordinary. *He* probably explains those words and actions best, who sees in either the greatest depth of meaning.

The "hour," so often mysteriously alluded to by our SAVIOUR,(f) and described by Himself in the former chapter as the hour when "the Son of Man should be glorified,"(g) had now at length arrived. The holy Evangelist speaks of it in terms different indeed, but in terms of quite the same import; namely, as the hour when JESUS "should depart out of this World unto the FATHER." Take notice therefore that, in the view of the SPIRIT, *Death* is but a "departure;" and remember what has been already offered on this head in the note on St. John xi. 26, and St. Luke xvi. 9. The Evangelist may have used this particular expression, in order to recall the signification of the Chaldee word "Pascha" (*Passover*) which precedes. We noticed a specimen of the same method in St. John's first chapter;(h) and a yet more apposite example is supplied by St. Luke ix. 31,—where our SAVIOUR's Death is called His "Exodus." . . . St. John here declares that our LORD "knew" that His hour was come, to remind us of His Divinity. From all Eternity, He knew that the present hour awaited Him: by His Divine Knowledge, He knew that His hour was at last come. Hence, it is added,—

having loved His own which were in the world, He loved them unto the end.

"*His own,—which were in the World*." The Apostles of CHRIST are here called "His own," partly on account of the love He bare them, whereby they became His "brethren:"(i) partly because of the intimate(k) relation in which the true Disciple stands to his LORD,—which was noticed at some length in the commentary on St. John x. 3, 14, 15. And the clause "which were in the World," is added in order to explain and account for the unbounded condescension and love which our SAVIOUR displayed towards His Disciples on the present occasion. He Himself, indeed, was about to exchange "this troublesome World" for the immediate pre-

(a) See the note on the last verse of St. John xii.
(b) Exodus xii. 7, 13.
(d) 1 St. John i. 7, and 1 Thess. i. 10.
(f) St. John ii. 4: vii. 30: viii. 20: xii. 23, &c.
(g) St. John xii. 23.
(h) See the note on St. John i. 14.
(i) See the note on St. Matthew xxviii. 10.

(c) Augustine.
(e) Lev. xxiii. 6: Numb. xxviii. 17, &c.

(k) So far, Chrysostom.

sence of the FATHER. All Peace and Joy, therefore, awaited Himself. But they,—the men whom He had chosen out of the World, yet now was about to leave behind Him "in the World,"—could He fail at such a moment to pity *them?* They, on the eve of orphanhood, were objects for His compassion indeed !

The Evangelist says therefore, that JESUS, who had all along so fondly loved "His own," now that the hour of His departure was at hand, still loved them on, to the very last; leaving nothing undone which might witness to them the boundless extent of His Love. One great example follows,—namely the unspeakable act of condescension which the Evangelist proceeds to describe; and which was only preliminary to another crowning act of Love, — namely, the Communion of His Body and Blood.

2 And supper being ended,

Rather, "And at Supper-time;" or, "And during supper,"—

3, 4 the Devil having now put into the heart of Judas Iscariot, Simon's *son*, to betray Him; JESUS knowing that the FATHER had given all things into His hands, and that He was come from GOD, and went to GOD; He riseth from Supper,

The "Supper," here spoken of, from which our LORD now arose, was not that sacred thing which we have learned (after St. Paul's example,)(*l*) to call "the LORD's Supper;" but that part of the Paschal Feast which consisted in the eating of the Lamb. . . . The Solemn Washing which follows was doubtless symbolical of that cleansing of the heart which is required by all men before they present themselves at the Table of the LORD, — as the prayer for Purity, at the beginning of our Communion service sufficiently bears witness.

The lofty meaning of the entire passage under consideration will perhaps be best shown by a somewhat lengthy paraphrase. St. John seems to say, that,—At a certain period of the Paschal Supper, when the Hour of our SAVIOUR's Passion was so near at hand that Satan had already filled the soul of Judas with the intention of betraying his LORD: at that period, notwithstanding, that the familiar friend, whom He trusted, was even now sitting at the table with Him, entertaining the infernal design of compassing His Death : — even *then* it was that the Holy JESUS, fully conscious, ("*knowing*," as it is said for the second time,) that the hour was at last arrived when "all things," were to be freely given into His Hands by the FATHER; all things, that is, appertaining to the Redemption and Salvation of Mankind ; for *that* is what seems here to be especially meant:(*m*)—that inasmuch as He is now about to "go to GOD;" and therefore, about to receive the fullness of that Power and authority over "all things"(*n*) which He had begun to receive when first He "came from GOD:"—the last evening, therefore, of His earthly Life having now arrived ; the last occasion on which the SAVIOUR would be able to display the largeness of His Divine Love towards "His own ;" the season, moreover, when He was about to return to the FATHER who loved Him, — the FATHER whom He loved,—with a perfect Love; and when He must be able to say "It is finished;" "I have finished the work which Thou Gavest Me to do :" He, therefore *knowing that this period had arrived,*—"riseth from supper."

Hear Bishop Pearson on the latter part of this very mysterious place. "The dominion given unto CHRIST, in His Human Nature, was a direct and plenary Power over all things, but was not actually given Him at once : but part, while He lived on Earth; part, after His Death and Resurrection. For though it be true that JESUS knew before His Death, 'that the FATHER had given all things into His hands ;' yet it is observable that in the same place it is written that He likewise knew ' that He was come from GOD, and went to GOD :' and part of that Power He received when He came from GOD ; with part He was invested when He went to GOD : the first, to enable Him; the second not only so, but also to reward Him."

The Evangelist is therefore here declaring, partly, the circumstances under which the Holy One performed the two great acts of Love which followed ; partly,

(*l*) See 1 Cor. xi. 20.
(*m*) Consider St. John xvii. 2: iii. 35: v. 21, 22. Also St. Matth. xi. 27 or St. Luke x. 22,
(*n*) Consider St. Matth. xxviii. 18.

he is setting forth the considerations which moved Him to perform them.—CHRIST, then, "riseth from Supper,"—

and laid aside His garments ; and took a towel and girded Himself.

Concerning all that follows, it is surely needless to dwell at any length on the fact, (adverted to by our LORD Himself in verses 14, 15,) that He here sets before us a wondrous *lesson of Humility*. This, (which would seem to be sufficiently obvious,) is much dwelt upon by the commentators. "The FATHER," (says Theophylact,) "having given up all things into His hands, (that is, having given up to Him the Salvation of the faithful,) He deemed it right to show them all things that pertained to their Salvation ; and gave them a lesson of Humility by washing the Disciples' feet." . . . . Let us beware how we *rest* in this view; as if it really embodied all that is to be said about one of the most clearly symbolical transactions in the Bible. See below, on verses 5, 7, 8, and 15.

The first thing which here strikes us, is the Evangelist's minuteness ; and he is so minute, doubtless, only because everything here is big with mysterious meaning. He has already dwelt upon the circumstances under which the washing of the Disciples' feet took place : he now dwells upon each particular of that memorable transaction : and every feature of his description helps to impress us more and more deeply with the immense condescension of Him who could so act. Take notice that He rose "*from Supper*" to do this lowly thing;—the most uncongenial moment, perhaps, which could be imagined for such a service. Was it not a true representation of the Love of Him, who, "being in the form of GOD," was content to come down from the highest Heaven, in order to become like one of ourselves? He next "laid aside His outer garment,"—even as already, in order to be "made Man," He Had emptied Himself of His Glory.(o) He "took a towel, and girded Himself ;" and had He not already, as in the first step towards the work of Redemption, "made Himself of no reputation, and taken upon Himself the form of a Servant?" Doubtless it was our SAVIOUR's express intention, by His gesture on the present occasion, — not only, observe, by performing a servile act, but by even assuming a Servant's attire (p) as a preparation thereto,—to exhibit in emblem the character which He had seen fit, in the fullness of His Divine condescension, to assume.(q) "I am with you," (He declared openly,) "as He that *serveth*."(r) He seems to have wished to show them that "the Son of Man came not to be ministered unto, but *to minister*." Did He not also, by the act which follows, set forth in a figure that He came "to give His Life a ransom for many?"(s) For we read :

5 After that He poureth water into a bason, and he began to wash the Disciples' feet, and to wipe *them* with a towel wherewith He was girded.

And what was this but the act of "Him that loved us, and washed us from our sins in His own Blood?"(t) of Him who by His own precious blood-shedding was even now about to wash away the defilement of His Disciples ; and with the flesh wherewith He was clothed, to make them clean? Thus, in our "prayer of humble access," we are taught to pray "that our sinful bodies may be made clean by His Body, and our souls washed through His most precious Blood." . . . If such a commentary on the text strikes any one as fanciful, and far-fetched, let him ponder well the meaning of verses 6 to 11 : and he will probably see the reason to reverse his judgment.

Many of the ancient writers point out that our attention is here evidently called to the fact that our SAVIOUR performed the present servile office *alone ;* suffering no one to help Him, even so far as to pour the water for Him into the bason. Hence, they bid us derive a lesson of strenuous personal exertion in whatsoever labor we undertake ; the lesson, in fact, which is conveyed by that precept of the Preacher, — "Whatsoever thy hand findeth to do, do it with thy might."(u) But surely, far loftier teaching than this, awaits us here ! "Wherefore art Thou red in Thine apparel," (asks the Prophet,) "and Thy garments like him that treadeth

(o) Philippians ii. 7.
(q) Consider Isaiah xlii. 1, &c.
(s) St. Matth. xx. 28.
(u) Eccles. ix. 10.

(p) See St. Luke xii. 35, 37.
(r) St. Luke xxii. 27.
(t) Rev. i. 5.

in the wine-fat?" Our SAVIOUR makes answer:— *"I have trodden the wine-press alone: and of the people there was none with Me."*(x)

6 Then cometh He to Simon Peter: and Peter saith unto Him, LORD, dost Thou wash my feet?

Many have thought from this that our LORD began first with Judas, or some other, and came *last* to Simon Peter. Would it not rather seem, on the contrary, that Simon was *the first* whom the Son of Man approached on the present mysterious occasion? (Take notice that *"began* to wash," in ver. 5, merely signifies *"washed."*) Amazed at the intended act of condescension, the Disciple exclaims, " LORD, art *Thou* about to wash *my* feet?" . . . . But the language of the original is far more striking; for, first, there is a marked contrast between " Thou" and " my ;" (the words come close together, and we are left to infer the emphasis with which the Apostle will have pronounced them :) next, all by itself, comes the question about the washing of the feet. Was such an act possible, on the part of " the CHRIST, the SON of the living *GOD*,"(y) towards one who knew himself to be " a sinful *man?*"(z)

7 JESUS answered and said unto him, What I do thou knowest not now; but thou shalt know hereafter.

There was therefore more than met the eye in the lowly act which we have been hitherto considering. *What* is signified, our SAVIOUR will be found Himself partly to explain in verse 8 : but the full understanding of it, we learn, was reserved until " hereafter:" a saying which reminds us of the many intimations in the Gospel that after our LORD's Ascension, it would be the office of the HOLY SPIRIT to bring " all things" to the remembrance of the Apostles,—both the sayings and the actions of their Divine Master: as well as to discover the wondrous, and wholly unsuspected, meaning of either. See the note on St. John xii. 16, and the places there referred to.

St. Peter seems to have been too much confounded by the largeness of the intended condescension to attend to our LORD's hint that this was no common service. Accordingly,—

8 Peter saith unto Him, Thou shalt never wash my feet. JESUS answered him, If I wash thee not, thou hast no part with Me.

Far more therefore, than a pattern of *Humility*, did our SAVIOUR set forth when He performed this lowly office for the Twelve. Far more also was thereby intended than the display of His *Love* for " His own," when he was about to depart out of the World, and to leave them behind Him. Simon Peter hath " *no part with*" CHRIST, if CHRIST doth not wash him! Further on,(a) we shall find the present washing connected with the cleanness which *all but one* possessed. " There is therefore a deeper meaning here than the mere relief of suffering Humanity." " Let those who refuse to allegorize(b) these, and the like passages," (says Origen,) " explain how it is probable that he who out of reverence for JESUS said, " Thou shalt never wash my feet," would have had no part with the SON of GOD ; as if not having his feet washed were a deadly wickedness." By this symbolic action, it was doubtless intended, (as we have already hinted above on ver. 5,) to set forth the cleansing power of CHRIST's Blood; which, sacramentally conveyed to the souls of CHRIST's people, washes away the guilt of their souls, and renews to purest life. In the person of Simon, our SAVIOUR therefore addresses the whole Human Race, and teaches that no one can have any part with Him who is not first washed by Him.

9, 10 Simon Peter saith unto Him, LORD, not my feet only, but also *my* hands and *my* head. JESUS saith to him, He that is washed needeth not save to wash *his* feet, but is clean every whit :

Terrified at the prospect of having no part with CHRIST, but still at a loss to

---

(x) Is. lxiii. 2, 3.　　　　　　　　　　　(y) St. Matth. xvi. 16.
(z) St. Luke v. 8.　See St. Matth. iii. 14.　　(a) In verses 10, 11.
(b) The reader, it is hoped, will not require to be reminded that the word is used in St. Paul's sense,— Gal. iv. 24.

understand his Master's meaning, — Simon, with characteristic eagerness, professes his desire for the completest possible washing, if only thereby he may obtain the largest possible interest in CHRIST. Our LORD's answer is full of sacramental import. He that hath once been *washed all over*, — (for so it is implied by our LORD's words, in the original; whereby, doubtless, He alluded to that "one Baptism for the remission of sins," which may never be repeated,)—" needeth not save to wash his feet." "From which, (as Augustine observes,) we understand that Peter was already baptized." The meaning of the words has been thus given by the same commentator :—" The whole of a man is washed in Baptism; not excepting his feet. Inasmuch however as we have to live in the World afterwards, we are compelled to tread upon the ground. Those human affections therefore, without which we cannot live in this world, are, as it were our feet, which connect us with human things; and so connect us, that "if we say we have no sin we deceive ourselves; and the Truth is not in us." Daily therefore does *He* wash our feet who " maketh intercession for us :"(c) and that we need this daily washing of our feet, (that is the cleansing of our ways,) we confess in the LORD's Prayer, when we say "Forgive us our debts, as we forgive our debtors:"(d) for "if we confess our sins," (as it is written,) then most assuredly will He, who washed His Disciples' feet, prove faithful and just to forgive us our sins, and *to cleanse us* from all unrighteousness:"(e) that is to say, He will cleanse us down to the very feet wherewith we hold our converse with Earth:"(f) the defilement which we contract in our daily intercourse with the World will be daily done away.

"He that is washed needeth not save to wash his feet, but is clean every whit." "Does not this warn us," (asks a zealous parish priest,) "that in every soul to whom we minister within the Kingdom of GOD, we should remember the Baptism of earlier years? We should never forget that they may have been, even as we, recipients of His grace: nay, we may believe, (what we shall seldom fail to find,) that in every man, beneath the most rugged manner and coarsest spirit, there is some, if it be but one, remaining element of good."(g) — The Blessed Speaker adds.

and ye are clean, but not all.

May these last words have been added by our SAVIOUR after He had completed His lowly task? It seems very probable. "And now, ye are clean," (He says,) "but not all of you." The Traitor, though washed by the Hands of CHRIST Himself, was "filthy still."(h) Compare chap. xv. 3.

Note here the *progressive* character of our LORD's Discourse.(i) At first, it might have been thought that an external washing with water, and the removal of bodily defilement, was all that He wished to display on this occasion; and that He intended thereby to set before His followers an example of Humility. He gives a hint that His act contained a higher meaning in verse 7: He declares plainly that it *had* a higher meaning, in verse 8. — So, in the former part of the present verse, He darkly intimates that it is not mere bodily impurity to which He seeks to direct the attention of His Disciples: and here, at the close of the verse, He declares that His words actually point to *spiritual* defilement. These few last words are therefore the key to all that went before. They declare our SAVIOUR's act to have been symbolical throughout: the washing,—a symbolical cleansing; the uncleanness,— a symbolical impurity.

11 For He knew who should betray Him; therefore said He, Ye are not all clean.

"Rather '*him that was betraying Him ;*' that is, the Disciple who was meditating to do so."(j)

12 So after He had washed their feet, and had taken His garments and was set down again, He said unto them, Know ye what I have done to you?

(c) Rom. viii. 34.
(e) 1 St. John i. 9
(g) From an Ordination Sermon, by the Rev. T. T. Carter, of Clewer; preached at Christ-Church, Oxford, Dec. 23, 1849.
(h) Rev. xxii. 11.
(j) Burton.
(d) St. Matth. vi. 12.
(f) Augustine.
(i) See the end of note on St. John vi. 34.

He had now gone the circuit of that upper chamber: He had bowed Himself down before each one of His Disciples, — had washed the feet of each, — had dried them with the towel wherewith He was girded. Even Judas had been washed. Hereafter, of each of the Eleven it will be said, "How beautiful are the feet of him that bringeth good tidings!"(k) CHRIST then resumed His place at the Paschal Supper; and while the rest of the Disciples proceeded with their meal,(l)—"Know ye what I have done unto you?" He asks:

13, 14 Ye call me Master and Lord: and ye say well, for *so* I am. If I then, *your* LORD and Master, have washed your feet; ye also ought to wash one another's feet.

This is one of the Blessed Speaker's most usual methods of reasoning.(m) "If *I*, who am your LORD and Master, have not disdained to perform this servile office towards *yourselves*, who are My creatures and My servants,—how much more should ye, who are all brethren,(n) do the like towards one another!"

Take notice, here, with how much delicacy and gentleness our LORD introduces the Divine precept which follows. He does not begin "I am your LORD and Master;" but from the confession of their own lips, He instructs them: so that His manner on this occasion becomes a sublime kind of illustration of the precept found in Prov. xxvii. 2. The place of Scripture, however, to which the reader's thoughtful attention should be especially directed, in connection with verse 13, is St. Matthew xxiii. 8 and 10.—Let it further be observed, that when our SAVIOUR might have drawn a very different inference as to the duty of the Disciples, as servants He is content to exact nothing more than conformity to His own example, though He is their LORD. As it follows:

15 For I have given you an example, that ye should do as I have done to you.

An example of *Humility* and *Love;* the special act which had been singled out as a pattern of those graces, being the servile act(o) of Washing of the feet: just as, in the Decalogue, when the graces of Purity and Temperance, Honesty and Liberality, are enjoined, special mention is made of *Adultery* and *Theft*. "But it is not necessary for any one who wishes to obey all the commandments of JESUS, literally to perform the act of washing feet. This is merely a matter of custom; and the custom is now generally dropped,"—says one who wrote in the beginning of the third century.(p) "The washing of the feet is rather a symbol of the relief that should be given amidst the evils which settle upon man in his continual struggle with the World. All mercies centre in the Apostolic Commission."(q) And "learn of Me;" (saith our Blessed LORD;) "for I am meek and lowly of heart: and ye shall find rest unto your souls."(r)—How much these lowly followers of THE LAMB needed such a precept, the events of this very Paschal Supper very quickly showed. St. Luke relates that, soon after the Institution of the LORD's Supper, "*there was a strife among them*, which of them should be accounted the greatest."(s)

There was a deeper purpose, however, as we have seen,(t) in this act of our REDEEMER, than the example of lowly Love which He thereby set to His Disciples. He designed, symbolically to prepare them for the blessed rite which was to follow; and bodily ablution had been the well-known typical means, under the Law, of attaining the purity which is requisite on similar occasions.(u) By such remarks we are naturally guided to the loftier intention of the present precept. "What else can be our LORD's meaning therein," (asks Augustine,) "than what St. Paul plainly rejoins?—'Forgiving one another, if any man have a quarrel against any: even as CHRIST forgave you, so also do ye.'(w) Let us then forgive one another,

(k) Is. lii. 7.   (l) Consider St. Matth. xxvi. 26.
(m) Consider St. Luke xiii. 16: xiv. 5.   (n) St. Matth. xxiii. 8.
(o) To know what this act implies, consider 1 Sam. xxv. 41, and St. Luke vii. 36. Observe also our LORD's comment upon it, — St. Luke xxii. 27.
(p) Origen. This ceremony, however, was observed by the Church of Milan, until the time of Ambrose. — Consider 1 Tim. v. 10.
(q) Rev. T. T. Carter.   (r) St. Matth. xi. 29.
(s) St. Luke xxii. 24. Consider the place, and all that follows.
(t) See above, the notes on verses 5, 7, 8.
(u) Consider Exodus xxx. 19, 20. Ps. xxvi. 6: lxxiii. 13. Also Ps. li. 2.
(w) Col. iii. 13.

and pray for one another; and thus, in a certain sense, let us wash one another's feet. GOD hath Himself committed to us a Ministry of Humility and Love: promising that He will Himself hear us; that through CHRIST, and in CHRIST, He will cleanse us from all our sins; and that whatsoever, by acts of forgiveness, we loosen here on Earth, shall by Him be loosened also in Heaven."

16 Verily, verily, I say unto you, the Servant is not greater than his Lord; neither he that is sent greater than he that sent him.

A proverbial saying very like the present, (namely, "The Disciple is not above his Master,") is found on our SAVIOUR's lips on two occasions:(x) being conjoined, on the second time of its occurrence, with the present saying, — "The Servant is not greater than his Lord." Words full of solemn meaning, doubtless; for our SAVIOUR recurs to them in St. John xv. 20. Their purpose in this place seems to be, to convey to the Apostles a general lesson of warning and guidance; "as if to say, if I do it, much more ought you."(y) "This was a necessary admonition to the Apostles, some of whom were about to rise to higher, others to lower, degrees of eminence. That none might exult over another, He changes the hearts of all."(z) — Take notice that these words are introduced with the formula of solemn assertion:(a) and see below, on ver. 19.

The latter clause of this sentence inevitably loses half its point in our language, which has not a word, (like "Apostle,") formed from the verb "to send," to indicate "one that is sent."

17 If ye know these things, happy are ye if ye do them.

"These words immediately refer to the lesson which our Blessed SAVIOUR had given to His Disciples, that they should do to one another as He had done unto them, in washing their feet. But they are the words of Him who spake as never man spake; and we must not confine their meaning to the single case which called them forth. They declare a principle applicable to every part of a Christian's life;"(b) even this, that the *knowledge* of Religion is worthless apart from the *practice* of it.

The mere mention of the "happy," (or, as the word is rendered in the Sermon on the Mount, the "blessed,") seems to have suggested thoughts so wholly foreign to the case of *Judas*, that our SAVIOUR at once adds:

18 I speak not of you all: I know whom I have chosen:

"Chosen," that is, to *worthy* Apostleship. Our LORD does not seem to be here speaking of those whom GOD "hath chosen in CHRIST out of mankind," and hath decreed "to bring by CHRIST to everlasting Salvation."(c) He speaks rather of those whom He had chosen to be of the number of the twelve, — as in chap. vi. 70 ;(d) chosen, doubtless, with a view to their Eternal Blessedness. Yet, forasmuch as one of them "was a Devil," our LORD, (who saw the end from the beginning, and "from whom no secrets are hid,") — speaks of *that* one as never having been the object of His choice. Hence, "I speak not of you all," He says: "I speak not as if ye were *all* about to be thus happy in practising the lesson which I have taught you;"(e)

but that the Scripture may be fulfilled, He that eateth bread with Me hath lifted up his heel against Me.

As if He said, — "But it was foreseen from the beginning that all things would thus fall out. Words darkly descriptive of the event were divinely suggested to the author of the forty-first Psalm; and *Judas* is the individual man, concerning whom, that sure word of prophecy was written." . . . How precious a circumstance is it that we should be thus informed, by the very lips of CHRIST, that the forty-first Psalm has direct reference to *Himself!*

(x) St. Luke vi. 40: and St. Matthew, x. 24.
(y) Chrysostom.   (z) Theophylact.
(a) See latter part of note on St. John vi. 46.
(b) From a sermon by Rev. Rob. Scott, D.D., Master of Balliol.
(c) Article of Predestination and Election.
(d) Compare St. Luke vi. 13.   (e) Lonsdale and Hale.

The phrase, "lifting up the heel," seems most probably to imply the attempt of a wrestler, or racer, *to trip up* his antagonist; (in which sense Jacob was called a "supplanter;")(*f*) whence it comes to signify *behaving treacherously;* plotting against another *so as to procure his fall.*—The circumstance that Judas "did eat of CHRIST's bread," is noticed as a peculiar aggravation at once of the Traitor's cruelty, and of his guilt. Cruelty,—for if he had been an open enemy, his conduct would have been bearable: if his hatred had been a known thing, then might it have been avoided; "but it was even thou; My companion, My guide, and Mine own familiar friend,"(*g*) Guilt,—for it was the consecrated Bread of the Holy Eucharist of which he was now about to be made a partaker.(*h*) . . . The reader is referred below to the note on ver. 30, for some remarks on the character of Judas, and the loving treatment which he was at this time obtaining at the hands of his Divine Master. Chrysostom points out that, "if injured ever by our servants or inferiors, we should not be offended. Judas had received infinite benefits, and yet thus requited his Benefactor."

It has been already elsewhere admitted,(*i*) that the expression—"that the Scripture might be fulfilled," occasions a difficulty: but the most simple-hearted and honest-minded man will probably be the least conscious of it. None can doubt that Judas, when he was called to the Apostleship, was, (like Saul,) full of fairest promise: but freedom of action was not *taken from him* because he was chosen to follow CHRIST. GOD constrains the will of none. Adam was even *created upright:* yet he fell; and it was by *his own choice* that he fell.

But if Judas was not constrained to continue holy, still less was he constrained to become wicked. The very thought would be blasphemous, if it were not so absurd. In the meantime, the all-seeing GOD clearly *foresaw* his fall; and David, moved by the HOLY GHOST, predicted it plainly:(*j*) the intention of the HOLY GHOST, thereby, being the same which now induced our LORD to allude to the circumstance,—an intention which He will be found to declare in the very next verse.

19 Now I tell you before it come, that, when it is come to pass, ye may believe that I am *He*.

The treachery of Judas, thus foretold by our LORD, and therefore clearly foreseen by Him: foreshadowed, a thousand years before, in the Psalms of David, and now shown by the same LORD to be there foreshadowed,—His finger indicating the very place of the Prophet where His own inspiring Spirit(*k*) had caused him to describe the Traitor's great wickedness:—*this* would be a convincing proof to the Disciples, hereafter, that He who now spake to them was none other than the Eternal GOD. Compare, for the expression, St. John viii. 28. Accordingly, St. Peter's *very first words*, after the Ascension, are found to be an appeal to the fulfilment of prophecy, as exhibited in the person of Judas. Consider Acts i. 15 to 20.—The saying which follows, is introduced by the formula of solemn assertion:—

20 Verily, verily, I say unto you, He that receiveth whomsoever I send receiveth Me; and he that receiveth Me receiveth Him that sent Me.

At first, the connection of this verse with what goes before, is not obvious. The truth is, verses 18 and 19 are of the nature of a digression, occasioned by the language of verse 17. "Verily, verily," here, (as in verse 16,) indicates that the Divine Speaker is about to resume the subject which He had already treated of from ver. 13 to ver. 17; namely, the relation in which His Disciples stood towards Himself,—the duties which they should be prepared to discharge towards one another,—and the consideration in which they were to be held by the World. To the Clergy, then, belongs a Ministry of unfeigned Humility, Charity, Forgiveness: but, lest the World should presume on this to set at nought GOD's ambassadors, and to refuse their message, our LORD spreads over their ministrations the awful sanction of His own special presence; declaring that the favour which they experience He will graciously accept as offered to Himself. Woe to those who forget

(*f*) Gen. xxvii. 36.   (*g*) Ps. lv. 12 to 14.
(*h*) See 1 Cor. xi. 27 to 31.   (*i*) See the note on St. John xii. 38.
(*j*) Consider Acts i. 16.   (*k*) Consider 1 St. Pet. i. 11.

that the reverence thus shown them by the World is in reality shown *to their Master!*

Judas, in the meantime, was reclining beside the Holy One, unmoved. With a heart full of murderous thoughts against His Benefactor,(*l*) he had beheld that Benefactor, like some " poor helpless Man,"(*m*) kneel before him,—as if to abandon his wicked purpose; and, while yet it was in his power, to repent of his sin. He had felt those loving Hands wash his feet, "swift to shed blood;"(*n*) had heard Simon Peter's conscience-stricken cry, "*Thou*, my King and GOD, shalt *never* wash the feet of such a wretch as I! Depart from me, for I am a sinful man, O LORD!" He had been made aware, next, that the act was symbolical; and he *must* have known that it was symbolical of that very inward cleansing which he needed so much more than all the rest. He had heard our LORD, while yet engaged in His lowly task, say—" Ye are clean, but *not all*."(*o*) On resuming His place at the table, the same Divine lips had said,—" I speak not of you all. I know whom I have chosen;"(*p*) and the rest. Our SAVIOUR, therefore, had now brought His Discourse to a close; and can we wonder at what we read in the next verse concerning His demeanor on this most affecting occasion?

21 When JESUS had thus said, He was troubled in Spirit, and testified, and said, Verily, verily, I say unto you, that one of you shall betray Me.

Thus bringing home to each breast the warning which had hitherto been only general. It follows:

22 Then the Disciples looked one on another, doubting of whom He spake.

Notice their sweet charity! We do not read that all eyes were turned towards Judas. They suspected no one in particular. They "looked *one on another;*" each one of the Eleven dreading, lest it might prove to be *himself!* "And they were exceeding sorrowful," (we read;) " and began every one of them to say unto Him, LORD, is it I?"(*q*) "'And another said, Is it I?"(*r*) . . . If the reader desires for more information concerning this solemn scene, he will find it in the notes on St. Matthew xxvi. 21 to 25 : indeed, he is invited to refer thither.

The Christian Passover was next instituted. Our LORD proceeded at this juncture, to deliver to His Disciples,—(and to Judas among the rest,)—" the most comfortable Sacrament of His Body and Blood." Several remarks on that stupendous transaction will be found in the notes on St. Matth. xxvi. 26 to 29 : St. Mark xiv. 21 to 25 : St. Luke xxii. 15 to 20 : to which it is hoped that the reader will find it worth his while, in this place, to refer.

" But behold," (said our SAVIOUR, at the end of this, the last Paschal Supper,) " the hand of him that betrayeth Me is with Me on the table. And truly the Son of Man goeth, as it was determined: but woe unto that man by whom He is betrayed! And they began to inquire among themselves, which of them it was that should do this thing."(*s*)

23 Now there was leaning on JESUS' Bosom one of His Disciples, whom JESUS loved.

What a head must *his* have been, to have found such a pillow! . . . St. John here describes himself for the first time, as " the Disciple whom JESUS loved." Our SAVIOUR CHRIST did indeed "love" *all* His Disciples:(*t*) but it was the unspeakable joy of St. John, to deserve this mode of designation beyond all the rest; to be able truly to describe himself as " the Disciple whom JESUS loved"(*u*) with strong human Love, as *His friend*. . . . The only other persons, by the way, whom our SAVIOUR is expressly *stated* to have loved, are Lazarus and his sisters.(*v*)

(*l*) St. John xiii. 2.   (*m*) Ps. cix. 26.
(*n*) Rom. iii. 15, quoting Prov. i. 16.   (*o*) Ver. 10.
(*p*) Ver. 18.   (*q*) St. Matth. xxvi. 22.
(*r*) St. Mark xiv. 19.   (*s*) St. Luke xxii. 21 to 23.
(*t*) St. John xiii. 34: xv. 9, 12, &c.
(*u*) The expression recurs in St. John xix. 26: xx. 2: xxi. 7 and 20.
(*v*) St. John xi. 5. St. Mark x. 21 is not, of course, in point.

It is found from this verse, and what follows, that St. John reclined at the table next to our SAVIOUR; while St. Peter was so far off as to be obliged to explain *by signs* the question which he wished "the other Disciple" to put to their Divine Master. One can easily picture the gesture, slight but expressive, which would have conveyed the inquiry which follows:—

24 Simon Peter therefore beckoned to him, that he should ask who it should be of whom He spake.

Rather, "who *it was.*"—Take notice of the respect of the Twelve, (of which we have already noticed so many examples,) in their approaches to our LORD.(*x*)

25 He then lying on JESUS' breast saith unto Him, LORD, who is it?

Or, perhaps he said,—"LORD, which is he that betrayeth Thee?" ... This passage in the life of the beloved Disciple appeared to himself important enough to become the act by which, in his old age, he wished the Church of CHRIST evermore to identify him. Consider St. John xxi. 20.

He seems to have leaned forward, and sunk upon his Master's breast; and so whispered this question. In a very soft whisper also, it is quite certain, (*for no one present heard the words, except St. John,*) did our LORD return answer.

26 JESUS answered, He it is to whom I shall give a sop when I have dipped *it*. And when He had dipped the sop, He gave *it* to Judas Iscariot, *the son* of Simon.

These words were whispered, then, into the ear of St. John *alone;* and it is plain from what we read in verses 28 and 29, that St. Peter himself was not permitted to know what answer the LORD had returned to his inquiry.

Does it not almost follow, from the portion of narrative before us, that while St. John was reclining on one side of our LORD, *Judas Iscariot must have been reclining on the other?* Take notice, that no one present either heard what our LORD had said, or seems to have noticed what He had done. If He had had to reach across the Table, or beyond any one sitting next to Him, the act would have infallibly attracted attention. But if St. John and Judas,—(the first in purity, and the last in defilement!)—occupied the two extremities of the line of Disciples which met and centered in their LORD, so that *one was on His Right Hand, and the other on His Left,* all becomes quite plain. And thus will have been exhibited at the Paschal Supper, what was exhibited afterwards on the Cross; namely, the SAVIOUR immediately between two men, who "bore in a manner the image of those who should stand at His Right, and His Left,—the elect of GOD, and the reprobate."(*a*) St. John, at all events, was now *at our LORD'S Right Hand;* for it was customary, at meals, to lean on the left elbow; and he "was reclining on JESUS' bosom."

CHRIST, therefore, "when He had dipped the sop," (or, rather, "the morsel of bread,") "gave it to Judas Iscariot."

27 And after the sop Satan entered into him.

Which becomes evermore the warning of the unworthy Communicant,—as the Church faithfully reminds us, in her first Exhortation.

The attentive student of the Gospel will remember, that St. Luke mentions in connection with the history of the previous day, (namely, Wednesday,) that " Satan entered into Judas Iscariot:"(*b*) and in our note on that passage it was suggested that the Enemy had obtained a footing in this sinful man's soul at a yet earlier period; namely, immediately after the supper at Bethany. Doubtless, Satan gets possession of a man *by degrees;* and yet, (as in taking a town,) the final *assault* must come at last. Now *this* is just what seems to be here indicated by the blessed Evangelist, in the case of the Traitor. *Two years before* our SAVIOUR spoke of him as being "a devil."(*c*) Above, in verse 2, it was said that the Enemy had "now put it into the heart of Judas" to betray his LORD. Here, finally, Satan "*enters*

(*x*) See the notes on St. John iv. 27, and xii. 22.
(*a*) See the notes on St. Luke xxiii. 38. (*b*) St. Luke xxii. 3.
(*c*) St. John vi. 70, where see the note.

into" Judas. Compare the language of Acts v. 3. He finds the "house" swept and garnished; "enters in, and dwells there." "And the last state of that man is worse than the first !"(*d*)

The following remarks on the terrible statement before us, seem deserving of attention,—" When it is said that ' Satan entered into' Judas, we are not to understand that the man became transformed into a demoniac; or that he was now for the first time inflamed with wicked designs. He had in fact already yielded himself to the suggestions to the Tempter. But, roused and exasperated by the suspicion that he was being marked out as the intended betrayer of CHRIST, he opened all his soul to the instigations of the Evil One: and, while he resolved on the act of wickedness, determined in his own heart to carry it into immediate execution, likewise. Satan therefore is said to enter into him, because he obtains a firm footing within him, and gets him quite into his power; for Judas, in renouncing Discipleship, separated himself from CHRIST. And the receiving of the sop at our SAVIOUR'S Hands, marked the instant at which this separation took place. Hitherto, while Judas remained of the number of the Twelve, Satan had not dared to enter into him; but had been merely assailing him from without. From this instant, however, he boldly made him his own. Accordingly, Judas may no longer even remain in the society of the Apostles, but goes out."(*e*)

Need it be added that "the sop" was not the efficient cause of Satan's victory over Judas? It was a good gift: a sign of tender Love: a pledge, (it may be,) that forgiveness was yet in store, if Judas would repent. But despised blessings become the occasion of our severest downfalls.

And it is not at all unlikely, that because Judas supposed himself on the very eve of detection,—when, with the quick eye of conscious guilt, he noticed St. Peter making signs to St. John, and St. John whispering to our LORD, and lastly our LORD guiding His hand to *him*,—he became hardened and reckless. The mask, (as he thought,) was all but torn from his face. It was useless therefore to maintain appearances any longer.

Then said JESUS unto him, That thou doest, do quickly.

Proving to the Traitor, by those few words, that the foul intentions of one whom, by so many fruitless endeavors, He had sought to reveal to himself, were at least all fully known to *Him*. CHRIST does not *bid* Judas go on his accursed errand. He does but *permit* his departure: as indeed nothing can take place without GOD'S permission. The words also contain a reproof: "convey an intimation that the Blessed Speaker would offer no hindrance to the intended wickedness;"(*f*) and, lastly, they are words of sad dismissal.

28 Now no man at the table knew for what intent He spake this unto him.

St. John proceeds to show how very wide of the Truth were their conjectures. "*For*," (he says,)—

29 For some *of them* thought, because Judas had the bag, that JESUS had said unto him, Buy *those things* that we have need of against the Feast: or, that he should give something to the poor.

By this time, then, it is found that the eyes of the Apostles began to be attracted towards Judas. They all perceived that our SAVIOUR had whispered *something* into his ear; for it is expressly said that "*no man at the table* knew *for what intent*" CHRIST had spoken. Some, again, are declared to have speculated as to what might have been the nature of our LORD'S communication; and since their thoughts are here set down, it is to be supposed that they mentioned them afterwards to St. John. But it does not seem clear that a single person present heard the actual words which our SAVIOUR uttered. What is *quite* certain, even St. John himself, if he heard them, did not understand their import.

Everything here is suggestive. Every word, almost, is a homily. And well may it be so: for we have reached a part of the narrative, from which, wherever we turn, we are met by new combinations of past incidents, and obtain a fresh view of the entire subject. The custody of " the bag," or money-chest, which rested with Judas,

---

(*d*) St. Luke xi. 25, 26.   (*e*) Toletus.   (*f*) Chrysostom.

here noticed for the second time,(*g*) is a circumstance full of tremendous warning. The two supposed errands of the Traitor have both to do with money: and by coupling them with the statement that "Judas had the bag," St. John seems to imply that the Traitor, impatient for his bribe, on rising to leave the table, was observed to grasp the intended receptacle of the silver pieces. What things a pious Israelite was likely to procure overnight, on the 14th of Nisan, "against the Feast," we will not here conjecture. But *who* can read without emotion the hint as to our REDEEMER's practice with respect to "the poor?" Judas was therefore the *Almoner* of CHRIST: and surely, if his office of *Treasurer* exposed him to fiery temptation, the insight which he must have obtained, in his other capacity, into the depth of Human Misery, and the height of Divine Love, should have sufficed to quench the flame! Here was the antidote side by side with the poison.

From this point, we seem to have the clue supplied us to our SAVIOUR's many warnings against Covetousness:(*h*) His repeated exhortations to His Disciples to "*watch :*"(*i*) His many hints that "the first should be last :"(*k*) that of the many "called" few would be "chosen :"(*l*) that there was danger lest, out of many, *one* should prove a castaway,(*m*)—a subject which has been already alluded to, in the notes on St. Mark xiv. 25. Here, also, we are reminded of the many direct hints and warnings which Judas is related to have received, from first to last, at our LORD's hands; concerning which, see the note on St. John vi. 70; and above, on verses 20, 21. Indeed, the present chapter is full of them. It is alike awful and instructive to discover, that, as if to give the Traitor no excuse, — in order to leave nothing, either in the way of warning or of kindness, untried, — our SAVIOUR *twice* before Judas rose and left that upper-chamber, said openly—"The Son of Man goeth, as it is written of Him: but woe unto that man by whom the Son of Man is betrayed! *It had been good for that man if he had not been born.*"(*n*)

Finally, the reader is requested to refer to what has been offered on the character of Judas, and the temper of the Twelve, in the commentary on St. Matthew xxvi. 22: St. Mark xiv. 25: St. Luke xxii. 23. The amazing contrast between the Traitor's outer and inner life; as well as the success with which he kept his wickedness a secret from the rest of the Apostles to the very last; are perhaps among the most astonishing and instructive warnings in the Gospel. Equally does the largeness of the charity displayed by all the rest, on this occasion, become our bright example.

It shall only further be pointed out, (and to fail to do so, would be an omission indeed,) that the Ministers of CHRIST, "following their Divine Master in their earnest search for souls, are to leave none, no, not even the most abandoned, untried by their hand. Even Judas was washed. The LORD was seeking even then to awaken his darkened soul, before Satan finally "entered in," and possessed him. So surely would a Pastor fail to fulfill the Commission of his Master, if he passed one house as too degraded for his foot, or left one soul as beyond hope."(*o*) The Traitor received *so many* warnings, in the course of the Last Supper, only that he might profit by *one*.

The transaction however which has called forth these remarks, was but the work of a few silent moments. Simon Peter motioned, — St. John whispered, — our Divine LORD breathed His inaudible reply. A morsel of bread was in His hand. He dipped it; and, turning to the most guilty as well as the most miserable of mankind, presented it to him. In the dark recesses of the Traitor's soul a horrible thing was wrought; and the SAVIOUR let fall a few words which sealed his fate. We read that the result was *immediate ;—*

30 He then having received the sop went immediately out: and it was Night.

Judas went "immediately" on his accursed errand. Satan hurried him on, lest he should consider,—and repent. Such violence and promptness are observed ever to characterize the acts of the Evil One. Consider Job i. 16, 17, 18; St. Matthew

(*g*) See St. John xii. 6, and the note there.
(*h*) As St. Matth. vi. 19 to 24: St. Luke xii. 15, &c.
(*i*) St. Matth. xxiv. 42 : xxv. 13, &c.
(*k*) See St. Matth. xix. 30; St. Mark x. 31, and the notes there.
(*l*) See St. Matth. xx. 16 : xxii. 14.
(*m*) See the note on St. Matth. xxii. 11, 12 : xxv. 28 : and on St. Luke xix. 13.
(*n*) St. Matth. xxvii. 24, and St. Mark xiv. 21, are distinct from St. Luke xxii. 22.
(*o*) Rev. T. T. Carter.

viii. 31, 32. "The sop," or rather "the morsel of bread," is thus mentioned for the fourth time :(*p*) perhaps to remind us of the *literal* fulfillment of the Prophecy quoted in ver. 18.

"It was Night" when this happened. There is doubtless the deepest significance in the announcement. Dark Night was it, when Judas was led captive by the Power of Darkness(*q*)—made subject to the "Ruler of the Darkness of this World."(*r*) The reader is invited to refer to what was offered on St. John xii. 35.(*s*) So also is the statement, (twice repeated,) that Judas "*went out*," full of awful meaning. In departing from that upper-chamber, Judas, like Cain, "went out from the presence of the LORD :"(*t*) cast himself forth from what was a type of "the Marriage Supper of THE LAMB,"—a scene of Light and Joy,—into the image of that "outer Darkness" which is spoken of in the Gospel as the portion of the damned. Consider St. Matthew viii. 11 and 12, and the notes there.(*u*) "He *went out* indeed," (remarks Origen,) "not only from the house in which he was, but from JESUS altogether."

31 Therefore, when he was gone out, JESUS said, Now is the Son of Man glorified, and GOD is glorified in Him.

Up to this period, the Discourse of our LORD had the Traitor for its especial object. It seems to have been altogether intended to reclaim *Judas* from his intended crime. The Good Shepherd had left His eleven sheep in the Wilderness, and gone in search of that which was lost.(*x*) (Take notice, by the way, that if even HE did not succeed in bringing back the object of His Love and Pity, "on His shoulders, rejoicing,"—the minister of CHRIST may be permitted to find comfort under failures, also.) But, "when Judas *was gone out*," the REDEEMER's words of counsel and consolation could flow forth freely ; and His address to the Eleven is found to fill three entire chapters, — besides the conclusion of the present chapter; being followed by His Prayer to the Eternal FATHER, which occupies the seventeenth of St. John.

"Now is the Son of Man glorified," saith our LORD. Instead of speaking of His *Death*, He speaks of His "glorification ;" in order thereby to raise the spirits, and comfort the failing hearts of His Disciples ; describing His Crucifixion by this name, because of the glory which was to follow ;(*y*) and because of the evidence which would then be afforded to the World that "*the Son of Man*" was also "the Son of GOD."(*z*) "*Is* glorified," as if the transaction was already over: because it was so very close at hand ; so very certain ; and because, when Judas "went out" to betray Him into the hands of His murderers, surely, some of the bitterness of Death itself was already past.(*a*) This first terrible earnest of what was coming did indeed bring our SAVIOUR's Cross and Passion so clearly to view, that He is able to say, "*Now* is the Son of Man glorified." True it is that He had been frequently glorified already, (that is, the Godhead had been frequently revealed by His miracles:(*b*) but those manifestations had been as nothing, compared to the evidence which was in store, and which was to come abroad only after our SAVIOUR had trod the avenue of Pain and Death.(*c*) It may also be thought that the triumph over the Powers of Hell, which was achieved by the Son of Man while He hung upon the Cross,(*d*)— a triumph not witnessed by human eyes indeed, but gazed on doubtless with awe and admiration by every member of GOD's spiritual Creation ; and which is hinted at, in no obscure language by our SAVIOUR CHRIST Himself;(*e*) *that* triumphant display of Incarnate Deity, (may we not presume?) will have formed no inconsiderable part of the "glorification" here alluded to.(*f*)

The entire passage, ("Now is the Son of Man glorified, and *GOD is glorified in Him*,") appears to have reference to the incident recorded in chap. xii. 28.(*g*) "FATHER, glorify Thy Name," our LORD had there said. "I have both glorified

---

(*p*) Verses 26, 27.   (*q* St. Luke xxii. 53.   (*r*) Ephes. vi. 12.
(*s*) Origen further reminds us of 1 Thess. v. 5 to 7.
(*t*) Gen. iv. 16.   Consider St. Matthew xviii. 28 ; and the note on St. Matthew xviii. 30.
(*u*) See also St. Matth. xxii. 13, and xxv. 30.
(*x*) St. Luke xv. 4.   (*y*) 1 St. Pet. i. 11.
(*s*) St. Matth. xxvii. 54.   (*a*) Alluding to 1 Sam. xv. 32.
(*b*) Consider St. John ii. 11.   (*c*) Consider Phil. ii. 9, 10.
(*d*) Consider by all means Coloss. ii. 15, and Ephes. iv. 8.
(*e*) See St. John xii. 31.   (*f*) See the notes on St. John xii. 28.
(*g*) Where see the notes.

it, and will glorify it again," was answered by "a Voice from Heaven." Accordingly, the moment *has arrived*, when, by the Son of Man's glorification, GOD is to be "glorified in Him." In other words, GOD is about again to glorify that Name which He had already glorified so abundantly: for the honour of the SON, is the honour of the FATHER; and the glorification of the One implies the glorification of the Other in Him, also. Some light is thrown on the FATHER's being "*glorified*" by the Death of the Son of Man," by what we read in St. John xxi. 19, concerning the death of St. Peter; and in xi. 29, 30, concerning the death of Lazarus. See the note on St. John xi. 4; and consider St. John vii. 18. Our LORD proceeds:

32 If GOD be glorified in Him, GOD shall also glorify Him in Himself, and shall straightway glorify Him.

"If," does not imply *uncertainty* in this place.(*h*) The meaning appears to be, that the FATHER, being thus glorified in the SON, will Himself glorify the SON; (for "*in* Himself" would seem here to mean "*by* Himself;") and will do so forthwith. That is,—"not at any distant time, but immediately, while He is yet on the very Cross," the FATHER will cause "His glory to appear. For the Sun was darkened, the rocks were rent, and many bodies of those that slept arose,"(*i*) at the moment when CHRIST expired. Lastly, His dying cry was a miracle;(*k*) and miraculous was the fountain which flowed from His wounded side:(*l*) all which things, we read, led to the conversion of many.(*m*) It may further, even chiefly, be meant that the FATHER would speedily raise the Son of Man from Death;(*n*) would highly exalt Him;(*o*) and "set Him at His own Right Hand in the heavenly places, far above all principality, and power, and might, and dominion, and every name that is named, not only in this World, but also in that which is to come."(*p*)

33 Little children, yet a little while I am with you. Ye shall seek Me : and as I said unto the Jews, Whither I go, ye cannot come ; so now I say to you.

He calls His Disciples on this one occasion His "*little* children," to indicate the exceeding tenderness of His fatherly love towards them. Moreover, they were as yet but "babes in CHRIST;"(*g*) and He was now to be withdrawn from the World, and from them. . . . . So sweet did this appellation sound in the ears of one of those who heard it, that, in his old age, he often addressed his own disciples, in turn, by this very name.(*r*)—"Yet a little while," (or, "Only a little longer,") our Blessed SAVIOUR says; (alluding to His Death rather than to His Ascension;)(*s*) because in less than twenty-four hours from the time when He spake, they will become orphans.(*t*) How must it have melted the hearts of the Disciples to hear their Divine Master thus speak! Consider, however, St. John viii. 33, and read the note on the place.

The rest of the verse presents no difficulty. Our LORD foretells that, in their adversity, the Disciples will "seek" Him; that is, long for Him back; "desire to see one of the days of the Son of Man."(*u*) But in vain! Pass forty days, and He will have withdrawn from their eyes entirely, and for ever. . . . . He reminds the Disciples, therefore, of what He had said to the Jews six months ago, at the Feast of Tabernacles; words which, in a certain sense, (He says,) are as applicable to themselves, as to their unbelieving countrymen. A striking difference, however, is discoverable between what was spoken on the two occasions. Our LORD begins by calling the Disciples, His "little children." Next, He does not *now* declare as He did *then*, "Ye shall seek Me, *and shall not find Me;*" still less does He say that they shall *die in their sins.*"(*v*) To the Jews, He had predicted that their repent-

(*h*) Compare St. Matth. xxii. 45.
(*i*) Chrysostom,—quoting St. Matth. xxvii. 51 to 53.
(*k*) See the note on St. Mark xv. 39.　　　　　(*l*) See the note on St. John xix. 34.
(*m*) St. Matth. xxvii. 54.
(*n*) Phil. ii. 9. Acts ii. 24, 42: iii. 15: iv. 10: x. 40: xiii. 30: xvii. 31. See the place enumerated in the margin of Acts ii. 24.
　　(*o*) Acts ii. 33: v. 31. Heb. ii. 9, &c.　　　　　(*p*) Eph. i. 20, 21.
　　(*g*) 1 Cor. iii. 1.
　　(*r*) See 1 St. John ii. 1, 12, 28: iii. 7, 18: iv. 4: v. 21.
　　(*s*) Consider St. Luke xxiv. 44.　　　　　(*t*) St. John xiv. 18.
　　(*u*) St. Luke xvii. 22.
　　(*v*) St. John vii. 34, where the note should be read; also, viii. 21.

ance would be fruitless; so that they would never attain to the knowledge of Him whom they had once deliberately rejected. To the Disciples, He merely announces that until the laborious years of their earthly pilgrimage have fully expired, they will not be permitted to follow Him; and He adds the prophetic warning that they will ere long find themselves severed from His presence entirely. . . The intention of all this seems to have been, partly, to show them that this hour had been all along very present to His mind; and partly, to prepare their hearts for the trials which must soon befall them.—He adds a few words of precious counsel; gathering up the substance of many commands into a single precept,—which must henceforth be the Disciples' great Rule of life; and which, (because men are observed ever to heed most what is spoken with dying lips,) He is found to have put off until now. This legacy of Love follows:

34 A new commandment I give unto you, That ye love one another; as I have loved you, that ye also love one another.

Being now on the point of departure, our SAVIOUR gives His Disciples a parting charge. Countless precepts He had already given them: but this, of *mutual Love*, He had reserved till the last; and the chord thus clearly struck by the Master's Hand, never ceases to vibrate, until the close of the inspired Canon. Our LORD repeats His "new Commandment" in chap. xv. 12. St. John alludes to it very distinctly, in the many places of his first and second Epistles, indicated at foot of the page.(w) St. Peter possibly,(x) St. Paul, without a doubt,(y) allude to this place of Scripture. Long after the last page of the New Testament was written, St. John, surviving the Eleven, is related to have had the words, "Little children, love one another!" for ever on his lips.

But, in what sense was this "a *new* Commandment?" and, wherein did it differ from that ancient precept of the Law, "Thou shalt love thy neighbour as thyself?"(z)—It differed from the requirement of *universal* Charity, because the love which it inculcates is that which Christian men ought to show towards one another, *because they are Christians*. As members of CHRIST's mystical Body, we are commanded to love one another with a peculiar love. "Whether one member suffer," (it is written,) "all the members suffer with it; or one member be honoured, all the members are honoured with it."(a) "Let us do good unto all men," (says the same Apostle;) "especially unto them who are of the Household of Faith."(b) Consider, again, St. Paul's reference to these words of our LORD, in 1 Thess. iv. 9;(c) noticing how clearly it is implied by all that follows, down to ver. 12, inclusive, that he is speaking of the love which Christians ought to bear towards one another *as such*.(d) This appears even more plainly by what is added below, in ver. 35; namely, that this mutual Love of Christians was to be the very token of their Discipleship.

It will be perceived that our SAVIOUR sets before His Disciples, for their imitation, His own Divine example, in those words,—"As I have loved you, that ye also love one another." This recalls the many places of Holy Scripture in which the same lofty pattern is held up to view. "Be ye therefore merciful, as your FATHER also is merciful."(e) "As He which hath called you is holy, so be ye holy in all manner of conversation."(f) "Be ye therefore perfect, even as your FATHER which is in Heaven is perfect."(g) These are *true* "counsels of Perfection." It is not meant that the Love, the Mercy, the Holiness, the purity,(h) of the Eternal GOD can be exhibited by us, His fallen creatures. All that is required of us, is, that we should act up to *the perfection of our nature*. We may show Love towards one another, *as truly as* CHRIST showed Love towards us. But the affection will differ infinitely in degree, and almost in kind.

Ancient commentators on the present passage, with general consent, find the

(w) Especially 1 St. John ii. 7 taken along with iii. 11 and 16: also 2 St. John, ver. 5. Next, 1 St. John iii. 23: iv. 21. Next 1 St. John iii. 14: iv. 7, 10, 11.
(x) 1 St. Pet. i. 22: ii. 17.   (y) 1 Thess. iv. 9.
(z) Levit. xix. 18, quoted St. Matth. xxii. 39: also, in xix. 19.
(a) 1 Cor. xii. 26: consider ver. 12 to ver. 27.
(b) Gal. vi. 10.   (c) He seems to allude hither again in Ephes. v. 2.
(d) Consider, in like manner, what is implied by the verse which follows 1 St. Pet. i. 22.
(e) St. Luke vi. 36.   (f) 1 St. Peter i. 15.
(g) St. Matth. v. 48.   (h) See 1 St. John iii. 3.

reason why our SAVIOUR called this "a *new* Commandment," in the concluding clause of it,—"*as I have loved you* that ye also love one another." This is more than to love one's neighbour *as one's self*, (they say:) it is to prefer another's good to one's own. . . But it will be felt that although this is a true picture of CHRIST's love towards Man ; and although His love towards Man is, in this very respect, again and again set before us as a pattern ;(*i*) yet this does not seem to supply a sufficient reason why CHRIST should have called His Commandment a "*new*" one. Indeed, its concluding clause is sometimes not alluded to by St. John when he afterwards quotes the precept in question.(*k*)

If therefore we were called upon to assign a reason, besides *that* already offered, (in the second paragraph of the present note,) why this is called "a *new* Commandment," we would humbly suggest that it was put forth at the moment when He, by whom, "in the beginning," "all things were made,"(*l*)—was about to renovate the World.(*m*) He was Himself the beginning of "*a new Creation.*"(*n*) By becoming a partaker of His Nature, Man was henceforth to become "*a new Creature.*"(*o*) "*A new Covenant*" was now on the point of being ratified :(*p*) and the Law was to be written anew, after a more heavenly manner.(*q*) There was to be a "new Heaven and a new Earth."(*r*) Old things were passing fast away; and behold, even in that upper chamber where the Eleven Disciples were assembled with their LORD, all things were already becoming *new*.(*s*) It was declared that the very "fruit of the Vine," when next partaken of by that Blessed Company, would be drank "*new*" in the Kingdom of GOD."(*t*)—The Commandment under discussion is therefore called "new," because it was destined to become *the great Law of the New Creation ;* and because the Love which it enjoined was a higher and a purer sentiment than anything with which the World had, as yet, been acquainted : a Love growing out of a lofty, and hitherto unheard-of relationship; namely, our common Brotherhood in CHRIST, — "the *second* Man," "the *last* Adam."(*u*)   For, "as in Adam and CHRIST are the two roots of Mankind, so there is a twofold Brotherhood amongst men, correspondent thereunto : first, a brotherhood of Nature; secondly, a brotherhood of Grace. As men, we are members of that great body, the World. As Christians, we are members of that mystical Body, the Church. And, as the Moral Law bindeth us to love *all men* as our brethren, and partakers with us of the same common nature in Adam ; so, the Evangelical Law bindeth us to love *all Christians* as our brethren, and partakers with us of the same common Faith in CHRIST.(*x*)   Accordingly, St. Peter after bidding us "Honour all men," requires us to "*Love the Brotherhood.*"(*y*) . . . If these should seem to be many words about a small matter, let it be asked, What then is great, if the Dying command of our SAVIOUR CHRIST is not great ? — He continues :

85 By this shall all *men* know that ye are My Disciples, if ye have love one to another.

This has been already in part explained above, at page 820. Take notice that it is not said that the Disciples of CHRIST should be known by *their power of working Miracles.* The greatest miracle of all would be their oneness of heart and soul :(*z*) and thereby, they would be fitly recognized as the Disciples of "Him that loved us, and washed us from our sins in His own blood,"(*a*) "and gave Himself for" us :(*b*) of Him, in short, who "*is Love*" itself.(*c*) . . . Our LORD's precept was faithfully obeyed by the early Christians ; and the result was exactly that which

---

(*i*) Rom. xv. 2, 3. 2 Cor. viii. 9. Eph. v. 2. Phil. ii. 3 to 8, &c.
(*k*) e. g. in 1 St John iii. 23: iv. 21. Also, 2 St. John ver. 5. — On the other hand, it will perhaps be thought that, in the following places, St. John alludes to the whole of the precept : 1 St. John ii. 7, taken along with iii. 11, and especially 16: also iv. 7, taken along with 10, 11. — St. Paul's reference to the whole of St. John xiii. 34, or xv. 12, (in Ephes. v. 2,) is very striking.
(*l*) St. John i. 3.   Read the noble passage Coloss. i. 15 to 18.

(*m*) Rev. xxi. 5.	(*n*) Rev. iii. 14.
(*o*) 2 Cor. v. 17.	(*p*) Heb. vii. 22: viii. 6: ix. 15: xii. 24.
(*q*) Heb. viii. 10 : x. 16 : — quoting Jer. xxxi. 31 to 33.	
(*r*) 2 St. Pet. iii. 13. Rev. xxi. 1.	(*s*) See 2 Cor. v. 17.
(*t*) See St. Mark xiv. 25 : also St. Matth. xxvi. 29, — where the note should be referred to.	
(*u*) 1 Cor. xv. 45, 47.	(*x*) Abridged from Bp. Sanderson.
(*y*) 1 St. Pet. ii. 17.	(*z*) Acts iv. 32.
(*a*) Rev. i. 5.	(*b*) Gal. ii. 20.
(*c*) 1 St. John iv. 8, 16.	

the Blessed Speaker here, in a manner, predicts. The sight was deemed extraordinary, and attracted attention. "See," (it was said,) "how these Christians love one another !"(d)

36 Simon Peter said unto Him, LORD, whither goest Thou? JESUS answered him, Whither I go thou canst not follow Me now; but thou shalt follow me afterwards.

Simon Peter, passing over what our LORD had said in the last two verses concerning the Christian duty of mutual Love, inquires, (with reference to our LORD's sayings in ver. 33,) "Whither goest Thou?" Bent on nothing so much as following the Master whom he loved, he asks this question in the fullness of his earnest zeal; supposing perhaps that when CHRIST said, "Whither I go, *ye cannot come,*" He alluded only to difficulties which must be surmounted, or to dangers which must be faced, by those who would follow Him. As yet, St. Peter understood nothing of that mystery of the Cross, which was now so very near at hand.

Our SAVIOUR, in reply, does not refuse to Simon the privilege of following Him. He only warns him that he cannot follow Him *now.* In a very different sense from that which the Apostle intended were these words spoken; as well as the promise given that he should follow CHRIST afterwards. Our LORD meant that a life of hardship first awaited St. Peter; that he had not yet the spiritual courage which he would require in order to face death boldly; but that, finally, he should follow his Divine Master, even in the very manner of his suffering; namely, by being crucified.(e)

37 Peter said unto Him, LORD, why cannot I follow Thee now? I will lay down my life for Thy sake.

He suspects that our SAVIOUR doubts either his courage, or his zeal: he therefore professes himself ready to *die* for CHRIST's sake. As in the case of St. Thomas, the risk of perishing is the worst alternative which presents itself to his imagination. See St. John xi. 16.

38 JESUS answered him, Wilt thou lay down thy life for My sake? Verily, verily, I say unto thee, The cock shall not crow, till thou hast denied Me thrice.

This was a humiliating assurance indeed! The Disciple, thinking of nothing but temporal danger, had professed his readiness to forfeit his life for CHRIST's sake; but even this poor sacrifice, his LORD informs him, will be found to surpass his powers. Nay; so far from "*laying down his life*" for CHRIST's sake, he will even deny that *he knows* CHRIST at all: not *once* will he disclaim all knowledge of the SAVIOUR, but *three times* in succession: not *hereafter,* when his faith has begun to wax cool, will he do this; but now, even *before the cock crow!* — The reader is referred on this subject to the notes on St. Matthew xxvi. 34; but it is St. Luke, (not St. Matthew,) who relates the present mournful prediction. See St. Luke xxii. 34.

CHAPTER XIV.

1 CHRIST *comforteth His Disciples with the hope of Heaven:* 6 *professeth Himself the Way, the Truth, and the Life, and One with the* FATHER: 13 *assureth their prayers in His name to be effectual:* 15 *requesteth love and obedience:* 16 *promiseth the* HOLY GHOST *the Comforter:* 27 *and leaveth His peace with them.*

THE connection of the present chapter with that which precedes, is of the closest

---

(d) Tertullian.   (e) Consider St. John xxi. 18, 19, and compare 2 St. Pet. i. 14.

kind. The Discourse which was begun in the thirty-first verse of the former chapter would have flowed on unbroken, until the end of chap. xvii.,—but for the interruptions, first, of St. Peter ;(*a*) next, of St. Thomas ;(*b*) lastly, of St. Philip.(*c*) Our SAVIOUR graciously replied to each of His distressed Disciples, in turn ; and straightway proceeded with His Discourse,—which is "like an Eucharistic sermon ; more than human in sympathy, more than angelic in sweetness, most Divine in Doctrine." (*d*) Thus, His first words in chap. xiv. will be found to be a continuation of what He was saying in chapter xiii. 35, or rather 33 ; and in order to understand these opening words, reference should be made to what immediately went before St. Peter's inquiry,—namely, to St. John xiii. 36.

LET not your heart be troubled : ye believe in GOD, believe also in Me.

That is,—"Let not your heart be troubled at hearing that whither I go ye cannot come.(*e*) As ye believe in GOD, a very present help in trouble, so believe also in Me !" . . . Thereby implying that He was GOD ; and inviting His Disciples to repose the same absolute confidence in Himself, which they were accustomed to repose in GOD, "the FATHER Almighty."

But, besides the general trouble which had overtaken the Eleven Apostles ever since the announcement that their Divine Master was about to leave them, *ten* of their body were as yet without the comfortable assurance that they should follow CHRIST at some future time. He therefore proceeds to inform them, in the next place, that He had been making no special exception in favour of Simon Peter : but that,

2 In my FATHER'S House are many mansions :

Rather, "abodes,"—as in verse 23, where the word is the same : a word happily expressive, in this place, of that *perpetuity* which distinguishes the heavenly from the earthly home of GOD's people. There is, therefore, "a place" for *all*, where the "mansions" are "many."

This is one of the texts from which it was anciently(*f*) (and is still) argued that there will be different degrees of bliss in Heaven. "The multitude of mansions in Heaven seems hardly intelligible, without admitting a difference of degrees in the Heavenly Glory. For if all the Saints should be placed in one and the same degree or station of bliss, they would have one and the same mansion in Heaven ; but in our Heavenly FATHER'S House there are 'many mansions ;' some higher, some lower, according to the measure of proficiency in virtue which men have attained to in this life."(*g*) Not that it will result from this that any will feel lack. All will have received "a penny ;" that is, one and the same joy, arising from the vision of their Maker.(*h*)—Our LORD continues :

if *it were* not *so*, I would have told you. I go to prepare a place for you.

That is,—I would have told you at once, and not suffered you to cherish a false hope, were it otherwise. . . . It might be asked,—Since there were those "many mansions," why did CHRIST "go to *prepare* a place for His Disciples ?—It was because the Kingdom of Heaven could not be "opened to all believers," until He had first "overcome the sharpness of Death." By His precious blood-shedding.(*i*) He led the way into the Land of Everlasting Rest ;(*j*) and "*prepared a place*" for those who before could not come thither :(*k*) whence He is called "the Forerunner ;" and is declared to have "entered in on our behalf."(*l*) CHRIST *then* entered into the Heavenly Sanctuary, (the true Holy of Holies ;) as St. Paul in his Epistle

(*a*) St. John xiii. 36.
(*c*) See below, verse 8.
(*e*) St. John xiii. 33.   Consider xvi. 6, 22.
(*f*) By Clement of Alexandria, Tertullian, Origen, Cyprian, &c.—The same doctrine is gathered from 1 Cor. xv. 41, 42.
(*g*) Bishop Bull.
(*h*) Gregory the Great.   See the note on St. Matthew xx. 16.
(*i*) Hebrews ix. 12, 24.
(*k*) Consider Hebrews xi. 39, 40.

(*b*) See below, verse 5.
(*d*) Williams.

(*j*) Hebrews iv. 14.
(*l*) Hebrews vi. 20.

to the Hebrews explains: "the HOLY GHOST, [by those two Tabernacles, and the High-priest's necessary entrance into the first, before he entered the second,] this signifying,—that the way into the Holiest of all was not yet made manifest, while as the first Tabernacle was yet standing."(*m*)   But at CHRIST's Passion, the Veil was rent, (both the Veil of the Temple,(*n*) and that which it typified, "that is to say, His Flesh ;")(*o*) and our Great High-priest straightway entered into "the Holiest of all:"(*p*) the gracious purpose thereof, as He here assures us, being "to prepare a place" for those who love Him! . . . It may yet be true that in the text, He employs the language of those who, when they travel, are preceded by one of their party, who prepares a place for the reception of all the rest when they shall come to the end of their day's pilgrimage :(*q*) but we much prefer the analogy suggested by what we read of the Ark of the Covenant: namely, that it went before the Israelites "in the three days' journey, to search out a resting-place for them." (*r*)—CHRIST continues,—

3 And if I go and prepare a place for you, I will come again, and receive you unto Myself; that where I am, *there* ye may be also.

Literally,—"Take you with Me to Myself;" that is, "to where I dwell."(*s*) He foretells His Second Advent; and promises that He will then "receive" those who might not follow Him now.   There was therefore no room for trouble or grief at this delay.   The place was not yet prepared for them; the path which they must tread was not yet made smooth; the gate was yet unopened by which they must hereafter be admitted.

Full well did the Blessed Speaker know how much the Disciples desired to be told whither their LORD was going.   To lead them, therefore, to ask Him this question, as well as to afford Himself an opportunity of affording them Heavenly instruction, our SAVIOUR adds:

4 And whither I go ye know, and the way ye know.

He thus administers strong consolation : for, at the departure of one deeply beloved, what greater joy is there than to know whither he goes, and the way by which we may come where he is ?(*t*)

Because the Disciples knew the FATHER, whom CHRIST had so often declared unto them, they are said to know "whither" CHRIST went; for it was to the FATHER that He went.   Again: because they knew *CHRIST*, they are said to "know *the Way*" to the FATHER ; for CHRIST is Himself "the Way."(*u*)   *This*, however, they did *not* as yet know.(*w*)   Accordingly, it follows:

5 Thomas saith unto Him, LORD, we know not whither Thou goest; and how can we know the way ?

Since we know not so much as the place to which Thou goest, how can we possibly know the way thither? . . . . This is the mournful language of complaining love ; corresponding entirely with the view we have already taken of the character of St. Thomas.   See the note on St. John xi. 16.   Take notice of what is implied by our LORD's answer ; which follows.

6 JESUS saith unto him, I am the Way, the Truth, and the Life: no man cometh unto the FATHER, but by Me.

The teaching implied by the form which our LORD's reply assumes is remarkable.   "*Thou* sayest that ye know not 'the Way,' because ye know not 'whither' I go: but *I* tell thee that ye know not 'whither' I go, *because ye know not 'the Way.'*"   "The Way" is not to be discovered by knowing the "whither :" but, on the contrary, the "whither" is to be discovered by knowing "the Way."   That is, Only by knowing Me, can ye know the FATHER,—to whom I go. . . . . . CHRIST intimates, therefore, His approaching departure to the FATHER ; and explains that

(*m*) Hebrews ix. 8.
(*o*) Hebrews x. 20.
(*q*) Grotius.   Consider St. Mark xiv. 12 to 16, and Philemon 22.
(*r*) Numbers x. 33.
(*t*) Toletus.
(*w*) Consider the method in St. John ix. 35 to 37.

(*n*) St. Matthew xxvii. 51.
(*p*) Hebrews ix. 3.

(*s*) Lonsdale and Hale.
(*u*) See below, verse 6.

He calls Himself "the WAY," because "no man cometh to the FATHER" but by Him. . . . . The title further reminds every follower of CHRIST that he must, with hearty Faith, steadily fasten his eyes on his Divine Master; must, with dutiful obedience, tread in His footsteps; taking up the Cross daily, (if need be,) and following Him. Such an "Imitation of CHRIST" is a true walking in "the Way" whereby a man "cometh unto the FATHER."

But doubtless it is because our "Faith in His Name" is the foundation of all our Christian Hope, that our SAVIOUR here calls Himself "the Way." All our prayers to the Throne of Grace are offered up "through JESUS CHRIST our LORD." Thus, we draw near to GOD "by a new and living Way:"(x) "for *through Him*, we . . . have access . . . unto the FATHER,"(y) as St. Paul speaks. He is "the Door of the sheep:"(z) "neither is there Salvation in any other," (as St. Peter testifies;) "for there is none other Name under Heaven given among men, whereby we must be saved."(a) "Man's way to GOD," (says Augustine,) "is through Him who is at once GOD and Man; that is, JESUS CHRIST." . . . Is there not an allusion here to Isaiah xxxv. 8?

But the very largeness of our SAVIOUR's reply occasions a little embarrassment. He not only explains that He is Himself "the Way;" but declares that He is "*the Truth, and the Life*," as well. The words have been thus paraphrased:(b) — "'I am THE TRUTH,' who not only cannot lie, nor deceive, but who will faithfully perform whatsoever I promise. Doubt not, therefore, that I will come to you, and take you to Myself. Believe Me, and believe *in* Me, for I am 'the Way;' and look confidently for the due fulfillment of that which I promise, for I am 'the Truth.' Further, lest at any time your hearts should be troubled at the prospect of Death for My sake, learn too that 'I am THE LIFE;' who will raise you from Death, and will take you to Myself. Death itself will not separate you from Me, for I am none other than the 'Prince of Life.'"(c) Concerning this last title, see also the note on St. John xi. 25.

7 If ye had known Me, ye should have known My FATHER also: and from henceforth ye know Him, and have seen Him.

The first words are almost a repetition of the latter part of St. John viii. 19, where see the note.(d) Thus then, the Blessed Speaker explains how it happened that St. Thomas, in the name of the rest, was able to declare with truth that he knew not whither our LORD was going. It arose out of *their imperfect knowledge of Himself*. For, as the Godhead of the FATHER and of the SON is one and *indivisible*, so does the knowledge which has the Second for its Object, involve the knowledge of the Former also. This is made clearer in verse 9.

8 Philip saith unto Him, LORD, show us the FATHER, and it sufficeth us.

A saying which reveals the limited knowledge of Divine things to which the Apostles themselves had as yet attained. St. Philip thinks that he may with his bodily eyes behold the FATHER, as he already beholds CHRIST; forgetting that no man may "see Him and live!"(e) So to know the FATHER, as he thinks he already knows the SON, is all that he requires. "It sufficeth us," he says. Our SAVIOUR proceeds at once to show him the largeness of his error.

9 JESUS saith unto him, Have I been so long time with you, and yet hast thou not known Me, Philip?

Take notice that instead of saying,—"and yet hast thou not *seen the FATHER*, Philip?" our LORD says, — "and yet hast thou not *known Me?*" implying (1st,) that, hitherto, Philip and the other Apostles not only did not know the FATHER, but knew not *Himself;* whom they beheld with their eyes, and fancied they knew full well. . . . . His words (2ndly,) guided those who heard Him to this higher truth, that the Divine Nature is to be "known," not "seen:" or, if "seen," — (and our SAVIOUR Himself employs the metaphor of Sight in what immediately follows, in

---

(x) Heb. x. 20.   (y) Eph. ii. 18.
(z) St. John x. 7.   (a) Acts iv. 12.
(b) By Toletus.   (c) Acts iii. 15.
(d) Consider Heb. i. 3.   (e) Exod. xxxiii. 20.

order to adapt His answer to Philip's request,)—it is *the eye of the heart and mind*, not the bodily organ which must be employed. It follows:

he that hath seen Me hath seen the FATHER; and how sayest thou *then*, Show us the FATHER?

Philip therefore, though he had been for three years living with CHRIST, had not hitherto "seen" Him! The Apostles had seen His Manhood, indeed. His Godhead, as yet they had not seen!

Take notice here, how plainly the great fundamental Doctrines of our most Holy Faith are laid down. So indivisible is the Godhead of the Persons in the ever-Blessed and Glorious Trinity, — so inseparable is the FATHER from the SON in Essence, though distinct from Him in Person. — that when the Eternal WORD was "made Man,"(*f*) whosoever beheld *Him, beheld the FATHER also!* . . The same great Doctrine is further declared in what next follows: concerning which, our words are not more numerous, only because the statements themselves are so emphatic and plain.

The *statements* are plain, and their meaning is not to be mistaken; but the *Doctrine* which they embody, is confessedly above us. Such a mighty Mystery is it, that, (in the words of Bishop Bull,) "instead of curiously scrutinizing, our part must rather be devoutly to adore. No comparison which can possibly be devised for the illustration of it is altogether adequate: no method of speech can set it forth with sufficient dignity. The union spoken of towers over every other union that is known. In the darkness of our present being, we think and talk of this, and other Divine mysteries, like very children: yea rather, we talk with stammering tongues. So long as we are here below, we behold our GOD "as in a glass darkly."(*g*) The time will come, however, when we shall behold Him face to face. The beatific Vision of GOD will then chase away all shadows from our minds. May *He*, of His infinite Mercy, make us capable thereof! Day and Night let this be our earnest prayer."(*h*) . . . . See a few words more on this subject, in the note on verse 11.— Our SAVIOUR asks:

10 Believest thou not that I am in the FATHER, and the FATHER in Me?

Let us beware how we pass these glorious passages by. Most fruitful are they; and each, a very "sword of the SPIRIT," wherewith to repel heresy and sever Truth from Falsehood. We would rather feed upon them, however, than discuss them polemically. . . The FATHER, we discover, "is in the SON, and the SON in Him; they both in the SPIRIT, and the SPIRIT in both them. So that the FATHER'S Offspring, which is the SON, remaineth eternally in the FATHER; the FATHER eternally also in the SON, no way severed or divided, by reason of the sole and single Unity of their Substance. The SON in the FATHER, as Light in that Light out of which it floweth without separation: the FATHER in the SON, as Light in that Light which it causeth and leaveth not."(*i*) — The statement before us is repeated in the next verse, (where see the note,) and is also found in St. John x. 38, and xvii. 21. Consider further St. John x. 14, 15. See also below, on verse 20.

the words that I speak unto you I speak not of Myself: but the FATHER that dwelleth in Me, He doeth the works.

This, according to the idiom of our own language, would perhaps have been expressed thus:—"The words which I speak unto you, I speak not of Myself; and the works which I do, I do not of Myself: but the FATHER that dwelleth in Me, He speaketh the words, and He doeth the works.". . . As one common Nature belongs to the FATHER and the SON, so are the words and the works of the One, declared to be the words and works of the Other also.

It must suffice to refer the reader to the note on St. John v. 19, 20, where these mysterious sayings will be found commented on.—Our SAVIOUR implies that His Discourses were in themselves sufficient to show that He was not mere man;(*l*)

(*f*) St. John i. 14,—literally "made flesh."
(*h*) End of Bp. Bull's Defence of the Nicene Creed.
(*i*) Hooker.
(*g*) 1 Cor. xiii. 12.
(*l*) Compare St. John vii. 17.

as indeed His very enemies had confessed already.(m) His Discourses declared Him to be none other than the Son of God.(n) His Works, in like manner, proclaimed the indwelling of the Father,(o) as our Lord further states. This latter evidence, indeed, might not be overlooked or denied :(p) and accordingly, the Blessed Speaker proceeds to lay great stress upon it, as He had already done on a former occasion.(q)

In what follows, the Discourse is turned to the other Ten Apostles. It has been hitherto specially addressed to St. Philip,—on whose Festival, this portion of the Gospel is duly read. The reader will call to mind with advantage what was offered in the notes on St. John vi. 6, in explanation of the probable reason why our Saviour directed an inquiry to Philip before the miraculous Feeding of the Five thousand. It may perhaps be regarded as indicative of a peculiar slowness of heart in this Disciple to recognize the Godhead of the Incarnate Son, that the request to be shown the Father should have proceeded from his lips on the present occasion.

11 Believe Me that I *am* in the Father, and the Father in Me: or else believe Me for the very works' sake.

After what has been offered above on verse 10, it must suffice to refer the reader, concerning these words, to St. John x. 38. "We worship one God in Trinity, and Trinity in Unity; neither confounding the Persons, nor dividing the Substance:" and these passages are our instructors, and our warrant for so doing. This intimate and mutual inhabitation of the three Divine Persons, the ancients described by a peculiar term; *expressive* of the inscrutable mystery, indeed, yet no ways *explanatory* of it. Rather is it a thing to be reverently adored, than curiously scanned, says Bishop Bull, (whose words will be found quoted above, in the note on the latter part of verse 9:) for, "what the Oneness of the Son with the Father, is; what the Fellowship of the Father with the Son; what the Spirit; what the union of these Three Divine Persons, and what the distinction of them, so united, — the Spirit, the Son, and the Father :"(t)—this, during the days of our pilgrimage, we desire, rather than are able, to attain to the knowledge of."(u)

The present verse, then, though addressed to all the Eleven, terminates the reply to St. Philip's inquiry in verse 8. Our Lord continues:

12 Verily, verily, I say unto you, He that believeth on Me, the works that I do shall he do also : and greater *works* than these shall he do : because I go unto My Father.

Take notice that *Faith in CHRIST* is the strong root out of which all these wonders were to spring. When our Divine Lord says—" he that *believeth on Me*," He refers the wonder-working power of which he speaks, to its true and only Source,—namely, to *Himself*.(v) Without such an explanation, the words before us would be unintelligible indeed. Accordingly,—"I can do all things," (saith the great Apostle,) "*through CHRIST which strengtheneth me*:"(w) and, on another occasion,—"I laboured more abundantly than they all; yet not I, but *the Grace of GOD which was with me*."(x)

But what " greater works" were to be wrought by the Apostles, than those which as yet Christ Himself had wrought? (For take notice, it is not said that believers should do greater works *than CHRIST Himself would do*. The works to be done by them were *His*, not *theirs*. He was still to work by *them*, His instruments.) What then are the works alluded to? They are probably such as that recorded in Acts ii. 41; when *three thousand souls* were gathered into the Church's fold, after a single sermon. And, when the rapid progress of the Gospel in the World during the first ages is considered, how many unrecorded marvels of the same nature must have occurred ! . . . Our Fathers in the faith pointed besides confidently to Acts

(m) St. John vii. 46.
(n) Consider the following places : St. John iii. 11 : vii. 16 : viii. 28 : xii. 49.
(o) See St. John v. 19 and viii. 28.　　　　　(p) See St. John iii. 2.
(q) See St. John v. 36, and x. 25, 38. Consider also xv. 24.
(t) Athenagoras, who flourished A.D. 177.　　(u) Bp. Bull.
(v) Observe how to *His* Name, and to *Faith* in His Name, the Apostles ascribed all their powers : — Acts iii. 6, 16 : iv. 10, 30 : ix. 34, &c.
(w) Phil. iv. 13.　　　　　　　　(x) 1 Cor. xv. 10.

v. 12 to 16. (laying special stress on ver. 15,) as the fulfillment of our LORD's prediction. But we feel disposed to question their wisdom in this particular. No
miracles of healing recorded in the Acts of the Apostles, are so surprising as what
we meet with in St. Mark vi. 56 :(y) the *effect* however, of the healing of Æneas,(z)
is perhaps without a parallel in the Gospels. Can we be wrong, at all events, in
asserting, that the marvellous result described in Acts ii. 43 to 45, and iv. 32 to 35,
was something wholly unknown, at least on so large a scale, during the days of the
Son of Man? Contrast with it, what we meet with in St. Matthew xix. 21, 22...
Thus then will our SAVIOUR's prophecy in the text, have found fulfillment! CHRIST's
greatest miracles, ("wrought by the hands of the Apostles,"(a) indeed, yet still
CHRIST'S miracles, not *theirs;*) were reserved until after His ascension into
Heaven; as indeed they were the direct *consequence* of that event. Hence, it is here
added,—"*Because* I go to My FATHER." The HOLY GHOST was then poured out in
full measure on the Church :(b) and it was by the Divine aid thus liberally vouchsafed, that the Apostles were enabled to "do" so "wondrously."(c)

It seems likely, then, that in this last clause the reason is assigned not so much
why believers in CHRIST should do "greater works than these" which CHRIST had
done, but why they should "do also" the works which CHRIST did. If *He* reserved
His greatest works until after His Ascension, it was because those works would not
have furthered the purpose of His Ministry, nor have been suited to the period of
His humiliation. He had been constrained, till now, to keep the rays of His Godhead from shining forth too brightly.(d) He had found it needful to curtain His
Divinity very closely round with the Veil of His human Flesh.(e) Not until He
was lifted up from the Earth, would He draw all men unto Himself.(f) Not until
He was "by the Right Hand of GOD exalted," and had "received of the FATHER
the promise of the HOLY GHOST," would He shed forth that which, on the first
Christian Pentecost, was seen and heard.(g)

Our LORD's entire argument will therefore have been of the following nature :—
By the works He had Himself wrought, the Apostles might have known that He
was in the FATHER, and the FATHER in Him. Much more, however, would they
be convinced of this by those greater works which they were about themselves to
perform by His Power and authority; and which would therefore come home to
them so much more nearly. These assurances, it will be felt, were consolation of
a very high order.—Take notice that the last words of verse 12, ("Because I go to
My FATHER,") cohere closely with the words which follow.

**13 And whatsoever ye shall ask in My Name, that will I do, that
the FATHER may be glorified in the SON.**

"*In My Name.*" Not, as hitherto, were the names of Abraham, Isaac, and Jacob
to be pleaded at the Throne of Grace. From henceforward, all petitions were to
be offered up "through JESUS CHRIST." The command is repeated in verse 14, and
in xv. 16: xvi. 23, 24, 26; and must have been at once obeyed. See Romans i. 8.

Our LORD says not, — "that will the FATHER do;" nor, "that will I pray the
FATHER to do;" but, — "that will *I* do:" showing thereby that He is very GOD:
the GOD who, by His own authority, answers prayer. The FATHER would thereby
"be glorified in the SON," because the Godhead of the FATHER would be shown to
be in Him. The SON would be shown to be of one Substance with the FATHER.

Moreover, by thus coming forward as the Agent, ("that will *I do*,") our SAVIOUR
explains that the "greater works" promised to believers, will be still His own,—
wrought, as much as ever, by Himself; but graciously reserved until now, to be
put forth from time to time in answer to the prayer of Faith.—Consider, in illus-
tion of all this, our Blessed LORD's words to the Twelve, recorded in St. Matthew
xvii. 19, 20, and xxi. 20 to 22. — It follows:

14 If ye shall ask anything in My Name, I will do *it*.

Why did our SAVIOUR repeat this a second time? Is the saying "doubled,"

(y) See the note on St. John xv. 24.   (z) Acts ix. 33, 34. Consider ver. 35.
(a) Acts v. 12.
(b) Consider St. John vii. 39, and the note.
(c) Judges xiii. 19.   (d) St. John vi. 15. St. Mark vii. 24, &c.
(e) St. Matth. ix. 30: xvii. 9 St. Mark i. 43 to 44. St. Luke v. 14 to 16, &c.
(f) St. John xii. 32.   (g) Acts ii. 33.

"because the thing is established by GOD?"(h) and was it repeated, simply in order to impress it more deeply upon His hearers? Or, may it be supposed that the words which, in verse 13, are to be taken in connection with the promise of "greater works" than CHRIST's to be done in CHRIST's Name, are here, designed for the consolation of believers in general; and, quite apart from the context, are simply intended to convey an abiding encouragement to Prayer? They do indeed contain a most large, as well as a most blessed promise; and it is a comfort to the distressed soul to find that the words were spoken not once, or twice; but again and again by our Divine LORD. See St. John xv. 16, and especially xvi. 23, 24,—where the notes may be referred to.

But besides Faith, in order that Prayer may be availing, there must be *Obedience;* wherefore our LORD continues:—

15 If ye love Me, keep My commandments.

On which word ("If") pious Bp. Andrewes discourses with beautiful indignation. . . . Our LORD thus reminds us that *Obedience* is ever the Divine test of *Love.* Compare below, verse 23, where the doctrine is repeated; verse 21, where its converse is stated; and verse 24, where the negative statement is found, of what is here stated affirmatively.—See also 1 St. John v. 3; where "the Apostle of His bosom,"(i) evidently alluding to the present place, says,—"This is the Love of GOD, that we keep His Commandments."(j) It is obvious to suspect that the "new Commandment," already so largely commented on,(k) is that to which our LORD here chiefly refers.

16 And I will pray the FATHER, and He shall give you another Comforter, that He may abide with you forever;

Accordingly, it was while the Apostles "were *all with one accord in one place,*"(l) that the HOLY GHOST was bestowed.—"His promise is in the manner of a Deed; not absolute, but as it were with articles on both parts. A Covenant on His part: a condition on theirs. He covenants two things: the one supposed,—Love; 'If ye love Me:' the other imposed,—then 'Keep My Commandments.' These two on their part well and truly performed and kept, He stands bound to 'pray,' and praying to procure them a 'Comforter;' another in His stead. . . . Those articles were here drawn from them; but he that liketh the same conditions may have title to the same Covenant to the World's end."(m) "If we love Him and keep His Commandments, we have a right to expect a secret and inward working of His HOLY SPIRIT, such as may be in some measure known to ourselves, though hidden from the ungodly World. Not that we first love Him; but that He, in exceeding love to us, hath begun the work; and that, if our will is with Him, we are promised the continuance of it."(n)

"I will pray,"—(or rather, "I will *ask;*")—to imply that "the Comforter, which is the HOLY GHOST,"(o) was sent in consequence of CHRIST's all-sufficient merits, and at *His* prevailing intercession, as the SON of Man: sent, however, by Himself,(p) no less than by the FATHER.(q) . . . "A special high benefit it is, we may be sure," (observes Bp. Andrewes.) "An Angel served to annunciate CHRIST's Coming: no Angel would serve for *this* Coming. CHRIST Himself did it."

"*Another* Comforter,"—besides CHRIST: whereby the difference of persons is established. Indeed, the mystery of the Blessed Trinity is revealed to us here: "the SON praying: the FATHER granting: the HOLY GHOST comforting. A plain distinction."(r)

It should be pointed out, however, that the term which our SAVIOUR actually employed on this occasion,(s) was "Paraclete,"—a Greek word which had passed into the Syriac language, and signifies an "Advocate;" or rather an *Intercessor;*

(h) Gen. xli. 32.
(j) See also 2 St. John 6.
(l) Acts ii. 2.
(n) Rev. C. Marriott.
(i) Pearson.
(k) See St. John xiii. 34, and the note there.
(m) Bp. Andrewes.
(o) See below, ver. 26.
(p) See St. John xv. 26: (where the note should be consulted:) xvi. 7. Also Acts ii. 33, and Eph. iv. 8, (quoting Ps. lxviii. 18).
(q) See below, ver. 26.
(r) Bp. Andrewes. So in St. Matth. iii. 17, &c.
(s) Also below, in ver. 26, and in chap. xv. 26: xvi. 7.

one whose function it is to *intercede* for the accused by prayer and entreaty. His work is therefore the direct opposite of Satan's,—" the *Accuser* of our brethren ... before our GOD day and night."(*t*) On this office, as discharged by CHRIST Himself, " who also maketh intercession for us,"(*u*) consider 1 St. John ii. 1 : and, as discharged by "*another* Intercessor," even the HOLY GHOST, " who maketh intercession for us with groanings which cannot be uttered,"— consider Romans viii. 26, 27.—Unlike our SAVIOUR, then, who had interceded for the Disciples till now,(*v*) but who now was about to be withdrawn from their eyes, that "*other* Intercessor" whom He promised them, would abide with them "*forever*." This then was a topic of lofty consolation indeed. Nor can we forbear suspecting that in the very name of " Paraclete," (notwithstanding all that has been written on this subject,) was suggested to the Disciples a sense of coming *consolation* akin to what the title of " *Comforter*" conveys to an English ear. An attentive perusal of 2 Cor. i. 2 to 7, will confirm the learned reader in this opinion :(*x*) and will perhaps incline him to the belief that by our translation of "*Paraclete*," we do in truth retain a precious and most ancient *commentary* on our LORD's language, which is embodied in the ancient Latin version. Truly has it also been remarked, that,—" If they had been perplexed, He would have prayed for the Spirit of *Truth*: if in any pollution of Sin, for the *sanctifying* Spirit. But they were, (as orphans,) cast down and comfortless.(*y*) The Spirit of Truth, or of Holiness, would have done them small pleasure. It was *Comfort* they wanted. A *Comforter* to them was worth all !"(*z*) See a few words more, below, on verse 26: and, take notice, that in St. John iv. 26, the meaning of " Paraclete" seems somewhat different.

On the perpetual abiding of the HOLY GHOST, as contrasted with the short duration of our LORD's earthly life, Bp. Andrewes remarks beautifully: " Therefore CHRIST's abode is expressed by the *setting up of a Tent, or Tabernacle.*(*a*)— to be taken down again, and removed within a short time. But the HOLY GHOST shall continue with us still ; and therefore He is allowed *a Temple*,—which is permanent, and never to be taken down."(*b*)

17 *Even* **the Spirit of Truth: whom the World cannot receive, because it seeth Him not, neither knoweth Him: but ye know Him; for He dwelleth with you, and shall be in you.**

Many unsatisfactory reasons have been offered why the HOLY GHOST is called " the Spirit of Truth ;"(*c*) which we will not enumerate. We shall perhaps feel the force of the expression best, if we keep steadily in mind what is the Gospel-view of " Truth." Now, "*Truth*" consists in *conformity to the Mind and Will of GOD*: and whatever is opposed to this, is emphatically termed "*a Lie.*"(*d*) GOD's Holy Word, then, because it declares His mind and will, is called " Truth" itself.(*e*) Accordingly, we often find the word " Truth" opposed to Unrighteousness ; as in 1 Cor. xiii. 6 ; Rom. ii. 8 : 2 Thess. ii. 12. Again, we read of " *doing* Truth," in St. John iii. 21, and 1 St. John i. 6 :—of " *walking* in Truth," in 2 St. John ver. 4, and 3 St. John ver. 4. In like manner, actions, as well as persons, are called " true," which in other writings would probably have been called " holy," " just," or " righteous ;" as in St. John vii. 18: Phil. iv. 8 ; and throughout the Book of Revelation, where " true" is a frequent epithet of Him who declared Himself to be " the Way, *the Truth*, and the Life ;"(*f*) and who, in the days of His humiliation, was seen to be "*full of* Grace and *Truth*."(*g*) In the writings of St. John, (who is called " the Divine" because He discourses so largely of the Divine Nature of CHRIST,) it is found that the words " True" and " Truth" occur more frequently than in all the other Books of the New Testament put together.

(*t*) Rev. xii. 10.　　　　　　　　　　(*u*) Rom. viii. 34.

(*v*) Consider St. John xvii. 9, 11, 15, 17, 20, 24. Also St. Luke xxii. 32.

(*x*) See also Acts ix. 31.　　　　　　　(*y*) St. John xvi. 6.

(*z*) Bp. Andrewes.

(*a*) See the note on St. John i. 14.

(*b*) Alluding, doubtless, to 1 Cor. vi. 19 : iii. 16, 17, and 2 Cor. vi. 16.

(*c*) Here, and in chap. xv. 26 : xvi. 13.

(*d*) Rev. xxi. 27 : xxii. 15. Consider St. John viii. 44.

(*e*) St. John xvii. 17. Compare 2 Cor. vi. 7: Eph. i. 13: Col. i. 5: 2 Tim. ii. 15: St. James i. 18.

(*f*) See above, ver. 6. See Rev. iii. 7 and 14 : vi. 10: xix. 11, &c.

(*g*) St. John i. 14 and 17.

The HOLY GHOST is therefore here called "the Spirit of Truth," because it was to be His blessed office, hereafter, to "testify of CHRIST,"(*h*) who is Truth itself: to teach the Apostles all things, (*i*) "that pertain to Life and Godliness ;"(*j*) in other words, to "guide them into all Truth ;"(*k*) and to bring their lives and doctrines *into entire conformity with the mind of GOD*. . . . Consider the places referred to at foot of the page.(*l*)

This "Spirit of Truth," our LORD declares that "*the World* cannot receive, because it seeth Him not, neither knoweth Him: but" (He adds) "*ye* know Him ;" thus opposing "the Spirit of the World" to "the Spirit which is of GOD ;" and intimating that "the natural Man receiveth not the things of the Spirit of GOD, for they are foolishness unto him: neither can he know them, because they are spiritually discerned."(*m*) . . . . The terms "seeing" and "knowing" are probably here used, as above in verse 17, with reference to that inner vision which is the truest Sight, and yields the most perfect knowledge.

18 I will not leave you comfortless : I will come to you.

Rather, "I will not leave you *orphans:*" thereby declaring Himself their Father, —as He had lately addressed them as His "little children ;"(*n*) and adding words of larger and yet larger consolation. *Him* it was that the Apostles desired, and longed for ; and full well He knew it. He promises therefore that He will *Himself* come back to them ; not leave them in their orphanhood.

But *when* did He mean that He would "come ?" We may not presume to speak positively on this subject, as if we knew for certain the meaning of words which the Fathers explain diversely. The most trustworthy opinion, however, seems to be that the reference is to that real but mysterious presence with His Church which was to date from the descent of the HOLY SPIRIT.

With equal truth and beauty has it been remarked as "wonderful" how the highest points of doctrine respecting the FATHER, and the SON, and the HOLY GHOST, are interwoven throughout; so as to render them, humanely speaking, replete with difficulties and contradictions, for which no key is furnished but by the Catholic FAITH : discords moulded into a Divine harmony, which nothing less than Eternity can unravel. Our LORD will ask the FATHER, and He will give the Comforter ; but not so, our LORD Himself will send Him. And He is "another Comforter ;" for our LORD Himself is called by the same name of "Comforter:"(*o*) and yet He is not another, but it is He Himself that is to come ; and again, He will not send Him, but He Himself will come. All these things to us are not contradictions, but Christian verities. Humanely speaking, they are such things as cannot be ; but Divinely speaking, such as cannot be otherwise."(*p*)

19 Yet a little while, and the World seeth Me no more : but ye see Me : because I live, ye shall live also.

Perhaps it should rather be,—"Because as I live, so shall ye live." "We are adopted sons of GOD to Eternal Life," (says Hooker) "by participation of the Only-Begotten SON of GOD, whose Life is the well-spring and cause of ours."

The meaning of the entire passage seems therefore to be,—Pass a few hours, and I shall be withdrawn from the gaze of the World. Men will see Me no longer. But ye shall see Me,— not with your bodily organs indeed, (except at intervals during the great Forty Days,) but with that inner vision of which I have already spoken, and which will result from My indwelling presence with you.(*q*) Thus will ye behold Me, in Time ; and throughout Eternity, ye will behold Me, not as in a glass darkly, but face to face. For, by virtue of that well-spring of Life which is in Myself, ye shall be raised from Death, and live also.(*r*) "Doth any man doubt," (asks pious Hooker,) "but that even from the Flesh of CHRIST our very bodies do receive that life which shall make them glorious at the latter day, and for which they are presently accounted parts of His blessed Body ?"

(*h*) St. John xv. 26.   (*i*) See below ver. 26.   (*j*) 2 St. Pet. L. 3.
(*k*) St. John xvi. 13, and 1 St. John ii. 27.   Contrast with this 1 Tim. iv. 1.
(*l*) See below, ver. 26.   Also St. John xvi. 13.   1 St. John ii. 20, 27.   Consider St. John xii. 16, and the note there.
(*m*) 1 Cor. ii. 12, 14.   (*n*) St. John xiii. 33.
(*o*) 1 St. John ii. 1.   (*p*) Williams.
(*q*) Consider ver. 17.   (*r*) Compare St. John v. 26.

20 At that day ye shall know that I *am* in My FATHER, and ye in Me, and I in you.

This seems rather to mean.—"In that day ye shall know that as I am in My FATHER, [and My FATHER in Me,](*s*) even so ye are in Me, and I in you." The former of these sublime truths has been made the subject of remark already.(*t*) The latter demands special notice at our hands now.

"We are by nature the sons of Adam. When GOD created Adam, He created us, and as many as are descended from Adam have in themselves the root out of which they spring. The sons of GOD have GOD's own natural SON as a second Adam(*u*) from Heaven, whose race and progeny they are by spiritual and heavenly birth." "In Him we actually are, by our actual incorporation into that society which hath Him for their Head,(*x*) and doth make together with Him One Body, (He and they having in that respect one Name ;(*y*) for which cause by virtue of this mystical conjunction, we are of Him and in Him, even as though our very flesh and bones should be made continuate with His.(*z*) No man actually is in Him, but they in whom he actually is. For " he which hath not the SON of GOD hath not life,"(*a*) " I am the Vine, ye are the branches : he that abideth in Me, and I in him, the same bringeth forth much fruit ;"(*b*) but the branch severed from the Vine withereth.

"It is too cold an interpretation, whereby some men expound our being 'in CHRIST' to import nothing else, but only that the selfsame nature which maketh us to be men, is in Him, and maketh Him man, as we are. For what man in the World is there which hath not so far forth communion with JESUS CHRIST? It is not this that can sustain the weight of such sentences as speak of the mystery of our coherence(*c*) with JESUS CHRIST. The Church is in CHRIST as Eve was in Adam. Yea, by Grace we are every of us in CHRIST and in His Church, as by Nature we are in these our first Parents. GOD made Eve of the rib of Adam. And His Church He frameth out of the very flesh, the very wounded and bleeding side, of the Son of Man. His Body crucified and His Blood shed for the life of the World, are the true Elements of that Heavenly Being, which maketh us such as Himself is of whom we come.(*d*) For which cause, the words of Adam may be fitly the words of CHRIST concerning His Church, 'flesh of My flesh and bone of My bones,' a true native extract out of Mine own Body. So that in Him even according to His Manhood, we according to our heavenly being are as branches in that root out of which they grow."(*e*)—And this must suffice on this great subject; but the reader is invited to consider, in connection with it, St. John vi. 53 to 57 ; particularly ver. 56 ; and to read the notes thereon. He is also referred to chapters xv. 4, 5, and iv. 15, 16.

21 He that hath My commandments, and keepeth them, he it is that loveth Me : and he that loveth Me shall be loved of My FATHER, and I will love him, and will manifest Myself to him.

This amounts to a declaration that the sad hearts and weeping eyes of the Apostles would not be accepted by their LORD as any proof of their Love. *Obedience* was the test He chose, and which He now, once more insists upon. — He intimates, at the same time, that the manifestation of Himself which He had already promised to the Eleven would not be confined to themselves alone ; but should prove the common reward of "all them that love our LORD JESUS CHRIST in sincerity :"(*f*) of every one, that is, who besides "holding" the commandments of CHRIST in theory, "keeps" them in practice, also.

All such "shall be loved of the FATHER." What is implied thereby, may be gathered from those words of the Evangelist: "Behold, what manner of love the FATHER hath bestowed upon us that we should be called the Sons of GOD."(*g*)

(*s*) Consider well St. John xvii. 21
(*t*) See above, the note on the first words of ver. 10.
(*u*) 1 Cor. xv. 47
(*y*) 1 Cor. xii. 12.
(*a*) 1 St. John v. 12.
(*c*) St. John xiv. 20 : xv. 4.
(*e*) Hooker.
(*g*) 1 St. John iii. 1.

(*x*) Col. ii. 10.
(*z*) Ephes. v. 30.
(*b*) St. John xv. 5.
(*d*) 1 Cor. xv. 48.
(*f*) Eph. vi. 24.

Now, "*to be called*," in Scripture language, is "*to be.*" " Like as a Father pitieth his children," therefore, " so the LORD pitieth them that fear Him."(*h*) Every such obedient disciple, moreover, the Son of Man, who is sitting at the Right Hand of GOD, will love also. The words, " and will manifest Myself to him," seem equivalent to the promise which our SAVIOUR made to His Apostles, in verse 19, that they should " see" Him: words, which He will be found to explain presently, in verse 23.

22 Judas saith unto Him, (not Iscariot,) LORD, how is it that Thou wilt manifest Thyself unto us, and not unto the World?

St. John testifies singular anxiety to preclude the supposition that it was the Traitor, (the only " Judas" whom he has hitherto named,) who asked this question. The speaker was " Judas", the brother of James ;" called by St. Matthew, " Lebbæus, whose surname was Thaddæus." He was one of our LORD's cousins, (" brethren," as they are called in the Gospels,) and author of the Epistle which bears his name.(*i*) . . . His surprise seems to have arisen out of the deep-rooted belief, (which St. Jude will have entertained with the rest of his nation,) that the manifestation of MESSIAH was to be something of a wholly different nature from that which He here, for the second time, intimates. Our SAVIOUR's renewed allusion to what He had more fully stated in ver. 19, suggests the inquiry which St. Jude had probably desired to make ever since those words were spoken ; but which, after the promise of a " manifestation," (in ver. 21,) he could suppress no longer.

23 JESUS answered and said unto him, If a man love Me, he will keep My words: and My FATHER will love him, and We will come unto him, and make our abode with him.

In these words, our LORD very nearly repeats what He said in verse 21: but it will be felt that His reply to the inquiry of St. Jude was well fitted to dispel any carnal notion of the manner of His future presence with His Disciples, which they might have conceived from verses 18, 19, and 21. "*We* will come and make *our* abode with him,"—can only indicate a spiritual presence : real indeed, yet not visible ; personal indeed, yet not corporeal.

" Here is the soul of man made the habitation of GOD the FATHER, and GOD the SON ; and the presence of the SPIRIT cannot be wanting where these two are inhabiting ; for " if any man have not the SPIRIT of CHRIST, he is none of His."(*k*) In other words, the indwelling of the SPIRIT, by virtue of the mystery of the Divine Nature, procures the presence of the FATHER also, and of the SON : for "since they all are but One GOD in number, one indivisible Essence, or Substance, their distinction cannot possibly admit separation." " Dare any man," (asks Hooker,) " unless he be ignorant altogether how inseparable the Persons of the Trinity are, persuade himself that every of them may have their sole and several possessions ; or that we being *not partakers of all, can have fellowship with any One* ?" . . . . See above, on verse 11.

Our SAVIOUR's promise of " coming," and " abiding"(*l*) with the believer, recalls that striking declaration in the Book of Revelation : " Behold, I stand at the door, and knock : if any Man hear My voice and open the door, I will come in to him, and sup with him, and he with Me."(*m*)

On the saying which immediately follows, the reader is referred to the note above, on verse 15.

24 He that loveth Me not, keepeth not My sayings: and the word which ye hear is not Mine, but the FATHER's which sent Me.

In other words, the precepts of the SON(*n*) are the precepts *also* of the FATHER ; as so often explained elsewhere.—The reader is particularly requested to read here the notes on St. John vii. 16, and xii. 49. — " The full sense of this clause is as follows: As those who show their love to Me by keeping My words will be loved

(*h*) Ps. ciii. 13.   (*i*) See the note on St. Mark iii. 18.
(*k*) Bp. Pearson, quoting Rom. viii. 9.
(*l*) See above, the note on ver. 2. Compare St. John i. 38, 39.
(*m*) Rev. iii. 20.   (*n*) See above, ver. 21.

both by Me and My FATHER,(o) so, on the other hand, they who, loving Me not, do not keep My sayings, will be excluded as well from My FATHER's love, as from Mine; since the Word which ye hear from Me, is not Mine only, but My FATHER's also who sent Me."(p)

25, 26 These things have I spoken unto you, being *yet* present with you. But the Comforter,

"The connection is as follows:—But since, of the things which I have spoken to you during My presence with you, some are imperfectly understood, and some will be forgotten by you, the Comforter,"(q)

which is the HOLY GHOST, whom the FATHER will send in My Name, He shall teach you all things, and bring all things to your remembrance, whatsoever I have said unto you.

"The HOLY GHOST *whom the FATHER will send."* The lofty Doctrine which is implied by this right of Mission, will be found largely commented on in the notes on St. John xv. 26.

So much has been already offered above on ver. 16, concerning the meaning of *Paraclete,* (which we here again translate "Comforter,") that in this place, where one great office of that Divine Person is described, it shall only be added that the Name embraces an allusion to every function of the Ministry to which the Apostles were set apart;—not only the office of Consolation,(r) and of Intercession or Entreaty,(s) but of Exhortation,(t) and of *Teaching*(u) likewise.

Our SAVIOUR is therefore here supplying a fresh ground of consolation to His sorrowing Apostles. He renews the promise "of the Paraclete," whom He now, for the first time, tells them is "the HOLY GHOST;" and intimates that it will be His two-fold office to "teach" them, (that is, *to explain* to them the meaning of,) everything which He had Himself ever said to them; and to recall to their memories all the precious words which He had ever spoken,—"being yet present with them." The HOLY GHOST was therefore to prove the instructor of the Apostles; guiding them "into all the Truth" of those many things which CHRIST desired to explain to them; but which at present they were "not able to bear."(v) He was to teach them "all things;" not as though CHRIST's Teaching was incomplete, but inasmuch as it was imperfectly understood. He was to bring all things to their remembrance, not merely as enabling their memories to retain the actual words and matter of their LORD's teaching; but as illuminating their minds to see and hold fast all that was contained within it: to clear up its difficulties; to carry it out to its consequences; to apply its principles to all particular cases; to expand and connect all its separate oracles into one consistent and complete body and system of Heavenly wisdom. Thus, when our LORD said, "Destroy this Temple, and in three days I will raise it up,"—speaking not of the Temple on Mount Moriah, but of the Temple of His own Body,—His Disciples evidently did not understand His meaning much more clearly than the unbelieving Jews: for the Evangelist adds, "When therefore He was risen from the dead, His Disciples remembered that He had said this unto them; and they believed the Scriptures and the word which JESUS had said."(x) That is, the Comforter brought to their remembrance not the mere words, but the deep, solemn, and mysterious truth, which, in His mouth, they contained. So again, when our LORD fulfilled the prophecy of Zechariah by His entering into Jerusalem, we are told that "these things understood not His Disciples at the first: but when JESUS was glorified, then remembered they that these things were written of Him, and that they had done these things unto Him."(y)

"Thus then is seen the difference between the teaching of CHRIST, and of the HOLY GHOST; and, at the same time, its sameness. The teaching was the same, but in a different way. CHRIST taught them: the HOLY GHOST made them understand. The WORD gave the Doctrine: the SPIRIT gave the capacity. The SAVIOUR

(o) See ver. 23.
(q) Lonsdale and Hale.
(s) Acts xiv. 22.
(u) Acts xiii. 15.
(x) St. John ii. 22. See the note on St. John ii. 17.
(y) St. John xii. 16,—where see the note.

(p) Lonsdale and Hale.
(r) Acts xv. 31: xvi. 40.   2 Cor. L 3 to 7.
(t) Acts xi. 23: xv. 32.
(v) See St. John xvi. 12, 13.

was with them: the COMFORTER was within them. The change, therefore, was not in the teaching, but in themselves; as when a man's eyes are dim, and you give him a Bible, and he can hardly read it. The Word is GOD's Word; and so, perfect: but its use to him is small. Let his eyes be healed, however, and what a change comes over his use of it. It is the same; but to him how different! . . . . Such is the teaching of the SPIRIT; making to mankind available the teaching of the Son of Man."(z)

In passing, we would ask those writers who are prone to suspect the Apostles and Evangelists of inaccurate memories, how they reconcile their notion of Inspiration with this promise of our LORD?(a)

The sending of the HOLY GHOST "in the Name" of JESUS CHRIST implies that His office would be to carry forward and complete the gracious work which CHRIST had effectually begun. Thus, He would add the great work of Sanctification to the work of Redemption; would recall to the Apostles our SAVIOUR's teaching, and guide them into all the Truth of it; for he who comes "in the name" of another, comes to do the work of that other. Consider, and compare the language of St. John v. 43.

27 Peace I leave with you, My peace I give unto you: not as the World giveth, give I unto you.

Friends are ever wont to use words of Peace at parting; and by saying, "Peace I leave with you," the Prince of Peace(b) here shows that He is about to be parted by Death from His Disciples,—to whom these words convey His prevailing Benediction, and Divine legacy,—their large inheritance. But it is more than "Peace" that He "leaves" them. "My Peace," (He says,) "I give unto you." The nature of it, St. Paul declares in a familiar place;(c) and twice calls it "the Peace of GOD."(d) For this Peace, the Church prays daily in her second Collect at Evening Prayer: in her Litany also; and herein she bestows her parting Benediction.(f) —It is interesting to find these words of our LORD prefixed to the Confession, or Creed, of the 630 Bishops who met at Chalcedon, about A.D. 451; as the Divine warrant for uniformity of Doctrine.

Take notice that our LORD goes on to contrast His gifts with those unreal goods which the World gives; as well as His manner, with the World's manner of giving. Those, eternal, and "without repentance;"(g) these, temporal, and altogether insecure: those, proceeding from Him to whom all things of right belong; these, conferred by persons who are not their true possessors. . . . . The Blessed Speaker may have observed His Disciples growing sorrowful as well as afraid at the prospect which these sayings, ominous of His near departure, disclosed. He therefore, "whose words had cast down their hearts, raises them presently again with chosen sentences of sweet encouragement;"(h) repeating, first, the soothing exhortation.

28 Let not your heart be troubled, neither let it be afraid. Ye have heard how I said unto you, I go away, and come again unto you. If ye loved Me, ye would rejoice, because I said, I go unto the FATHER:

Alluding to what is found above, in verses 2 and 3; also, 12, 18, and 23: and "teaching us," (observes Cyprian,) "that we must rejoice rather than grieve at the departure out of this World of those we love."—The knowledge whither our SAVIOUR was going should have caused His Disciples to rejoice. He saith:

for My FATHER is greater than I.

In order to understand what made this a season for such rejoicing, consider Phil. ii. 5 to 11. Read also St. John xvii. 1, 2, and 5: Eph. i. 20 to 22: Hebr. i. 3, 4: ii. 9: xii. 2, &c.—For a kindred saying, see St. John x. 29, and the Commentary

---

(z) These valuable remarks are from a MS. Sermon by the Rev. Robert Scott, D.D., Master of Balliol.

(a) See the note on St. John xii. 15.   (b) Is. ix. 6: compare xxvi. 3.
(c) Phil. iv. 7.   (d) Col. iii. 15.
(f) At the end of the Communion Service; availing herself of St. Paul's allusion to the words in Phil. iv. 7.
(g) Rom. xi. 21.   (h) Hooker.

on that place: taking note of the emphatic statement which immediately follows in verse 30,—namely, "I and [the] FATHER are One."

It remains, then, to offer a few words on the remarkable declaration before us: concerning which, it is perhaps not enough to suggest that our LORD here declares Himself "inferior to the FATHER *as touching His Manhood:*" for, (as Gregory of Nazianzus points out,) however *true*, this would have been a very trifling statement for our LORD to make: so perfectly obvious is it that GOD is greater than Man. In the opinion of the most learned of the Fathers, a loftier doctrine is here conveyed; and the subject may be fitly introduced by a reference to what has been already offered in the notes on St. John v. 20. Because the SON received His essence from the FATHER, He which was equal, even in that equality, is considered here to confess a priority; saying, "the FATHER is greater than I:" the SON, equal in respect of His Nature; the FATHER, greater in regard to the communication of the Godhead.

"I know Him," (saith the Holy One,) "for I am from Him."(*i*) "And because He is from the FATHER, therefore He is called by those of the Nicene Council, in their Creed, 'GOD of GOD, LIGHT of LIGHT, Very GOD of very GOD.' The FATHER is GOD, but not *of* GOD; LIGHT, but not *of* LIGHT: CHRIST is GOD, but *of* GOD; LIGHT, but *of* LIGHT. There is no difference or inequality in the Nature or Essence, because the same in both; both the FATHER of our LORD JESUS CHRIST hath that Essence of Himself, from none; CHRIST hath the same not of Himself, but from Him." This, then, hath been thought by many Doctors of the Church to be the ground of the superiority ascribed to the FATHER by the SON, in the text. "And the privilege or priority of the First Person, (say they,) consisteth not in this,—that the Essence or attributes of the One are greater than the Essence or attributes of the Other; (for they are the same in both;) but only in this,—that the FATHER hath that Essence of Himself; the SON, by communication from the FATHER."(*j*) And this is certainly what those 250 Bishops, who met at Sardica in A.D. 347, meant, when they said,—"No one ever denies that the FATHER is greater than the SON; not because their Substance is different, nor indeed because of any other disparity whatsoever: but because the very Name 'FATHER' is greater than the Name 'SON.' "

It may yet be a satisfaction to those who are inclined to think that it was only because He had taken "the form of a servant," that the Eternal SON said, "My FATHER is greater than I,"—to know that Augustine, in eighteen out of nineteen places in his writings, advocates their view; and that even Cyril himself, when he wrote his Commentary on St. John, was of the same opinion. Let better men decide whether the true account of the matter may not possibly be *this:*—that, however certain *the Doctrine* laid down in the former part of the present note may be, yet that, *in the actual context of the words under consideration*, they are to be explained otherwise. So, at least, thought all those Patriarchs and Metropolitans who discussed the saying "My FATHER is greater than I," in a Synod held at Constantinople, A.D. 1166.(*k*)

29 And now I have told you before it come to pass, that, when it is come to pass, ye might believe.

With the same design with which He here foretells His approaching departure to the FATHER, the Blessed Speaker had before predicted the treachery of Judas Iscariot, in St. John xiii. 19; and, with the same design, He will foretell the sufferings of the Apostles in chap. xvi. 4. Consider what is stated in St. John ii. 22. Our SAVIOUR next intimates that His time for intercourse with His Apostles is now drawing to a close. He had yet much to tell them;(*l*) and they were hanging on every word with intense interest and wonder. But the night was already wearing fast away. He says therefore:

30 Hereafter I will not talk much with you: for the Prince of this World cometh, and hath nothing in Me.

(*i*) St. John vii. 29: where see the note.
(*j*) So Bp. Pearson: also Bp. Bull, following therein Athanasius, his predecessor Alexander, Hilary, and many others.
(*k*) The acts of that Synod have lately been found in the Vatican.
(*l*) St. John xvi. 12.

already called Satan "the Prince of this World" in St. John xii. 31,
note should be referred to. See also St. John xvi. 11 : and consider how
the intimation here given of the actual *approach* of that Old Serpent at
it juncture,—which may not be explained away, as if the instruments of
ias and the rest, were all that is meant. After the Temptation, he had
from the Holy One "until a season,"—which season had now at last
)

aing searcher hath pried narrowly into every corner of His Life ; and, if
been anything amiss, would have been sure to have spied it, and pro-
;; but he could find nothing."(*n*) From Sin, CHRIST "was clearly void,
is Flesh, and in His Spirit."(*o*) It is not therefore because Satan, (to
LORD had never "given place"(*p*) for a moment,) had any power over
urt Him, that He was about to suffer Death, (which is "the wages of
but,—

it that the World may know that I love the FATHER ; and as
IER gave Me commandment, even so I do.

,—But I will submit to Death, (and thus slay Satan with his own wea-
hat I may redeem the World ; and that thereby the World may know that
FATHER ; and do, even as He gave Me commandment. This verse should
lly compared with the latter portion of St. John xv. 10 ; where see the
rry. See also St. John x. 18 ; and the notes on the place. The Blessed
dds,—

let us go hence.

hich, we picture to ourselves the Eleven Apostles, amazed at all they had
heard during the last few hours, sorrowfully rising from table ; quitting
a upper-chamber" where they had been partaking of the last Jewish Pass-
irst LORD's Supper ; and preparing to follow the Holy One through the
Jerusalem to their customy place of resort,—the Garden of Gethsemane,
: of the Mount of Olives.

CHAPTER XV.

ssolation *and mutual love between* CHRIST *and His members, under the*
of the Vine. 18 *A comfort in the hatred and persecution of the World.* 26
s of the HOLY GHOST, *and of the Apostles.*

rmer chapter ended with the words,—"Arise, let us go hence." It is to
red that the blessed Company rose at that saying, and followed our SA-
·ough the streets of Jerusalem in the direction of the Mount of Olives.
y will have led them past the Temple ; above the gates of which, and just
he coping, a golden Vine was constructed of surprising size and very
rkmanship. Its depending clusters were of the height of a man. How
we forbear suspecting that the words which follow were spoken with spe-
mce to that symbol ; which may have all the while hung mantling above
e Speaker, and the little band of mournful Disciples which surrounded
hey reposed in one of the porches of the sacred edifice ?

the true Vine, and My FATHER is the Husbandman.

the note on St. Luke iv. 13.   (*n*) Bp. Sanderson.
XV.
iv. 27.   (*q*) Rom. vi. 23. See Heb. ii. 14.
io-Fell on Heb. ii. 14, 15,—which see.

The sense in which our LORD here calls Himself "the *true* Vine," and elsewhere
"the *true* Bread ;"(*a*) in which also the Evangelist St. John styles Him "the *true*
Light ;"(*b*) is much to be noted. It is not implied that the noble Vine(*c*) which He
had brought out of Egypt, casting out the heathen in order to plant it ;(*d*) the
"Angels' food" with which He had fed His people in the Wilderness ; or the Light
which He pronounced, "in the beginning," "very good,"— were all otherwise than
true : but only, that every thing implied in those titles, when bestowed on any of
His creatures, was *fulfilled* in Himself alone. They were but shadows ; He, the
very substance. They, the signs ; He, the very thing signified. They, the type ;
He, the antitype.(*e*) Wiclif translates, "I am the *verri* Vine." CHRIST is therefore not only "the Lord of the Vineyard :"(*f*) not only is He "the Son" of "the
Lord of the Vineyard ;"(*g*) but He is also the "Vine" itself. And this, His universal character, has been already pointed out in the note on St. John x. 11. Having
thus styled *Himself* the Vine, it became necessary, in order to pursue the Parable,
to speak of the FATHER as the Husbandman ; in which, moreover, there will be felt
to be an exceeding propriety. Let us, however, instead of perplexing ourselves
with such minor details, bear in mind a remark which has been already elsewhere
offered ; namely, that in interpreting each of our LORD's parables, the *great purpose* for which it was delivered is to be ever borne in mind, if we would understand
it rightly.(*h*) Thus, in the present instance, our LORD is chiefly bent on showing
that it is only by abiding in Him, like branches in the Vine, that we can become
fruitful ; or indeed, that we can live. The remark is also true, that "what is principally to be regarded in this place is,— that hitherto indeed *Israel* had been *the
Vine*, into which every one that would betake himself to the worship of the true
GOD, was to be set and grafted in. But from henceforward they were to be planted
no more into the Jewish Religion, but into the profession of CHRIST. Hence the
Disciples were no longer called 'Jews' or 'Israelites,' but '*Christians*.'"(*i*)

Of all the fruit-trees, then, why does our LORD here resemble Himself to a "*Vine?*"
Doubtless, the immediate reason was in order thereby to interpret and illumine many
a dark place of Psalm and ancient prophecy, where the image of the Vine was found
already. But this is only to postpone our answer. The Prophets, speaking by
"the Spirit of CHRIST which was in them,"(*l*) had been moved to discourse of a
Vine, in preference to any other fruit-tree, because it was foreseen that our SAVIOUR
would have occasion hereafter to refer, (as He does here,) to the image of a very
fruitful tree with many branches ;(*m*) a tree which not only admits of pruning ; but
whose very productiveness depends on the judicious use of the pruning-knife. It
needs, in truth, very slender powers of fancy, or a very limited acquaintance with
the sacred writings, to discover a multitude of additional reasons why CHRIST should
compare Himself to a Vine. Its fruit is a type of spiritual gifts, as our LORD testified both by His acts and by His sayings.(*n*) The use of the juice of the grape in
the Holy Eucharist imparts a solemn meaning to the Psalmist's declaration, that
it is this which "maketh glad the heart of man."(*o*) The very phrase, "*blood* of
grapes,"(*p*) prepares us, from the first, for something mysterious in connection
with the Vine.

Delightful is it to find writers about the Grape-Vine, who had nothing less in view
than the illustration of the Gospel, becoming our instructors in such passages as the
following :—" It is hardly possible to plant a Vine in any situation in which it will
not thrive. . . . The truth is that the roots of the Vine possess an extraordinary
power of adapting themselves to any situation in which they may be planted, provided it be a dry one. They will ramble in every direction in search of food, and
extract nourishment from sources apparently the most barren. In short, they are
the best caterers that can possibly be imagined ; for they will grow, and even thrive
luxuriantly, where almost every other description of plant or tree would inevitably
starve."

(*a*) St. John vi. 32.   (*b*) St. John i. 9.
(*c*) Jer. ii. 21.   (*d*) Ps. lxxx. 8.
(*e*) Consider Heb. viii. 2, and ix. 24. Also the note on St. John x. 11.
(*f*) St. Matth. xx. 8.   (*g*) St. Matth. xxi. 37, 40.
(*h*) See the note on St. Luke xvi. 8.   (*i*) Lightfoot, referring to Acts xi. 26.
(*l*) 1 St. Pet. i. 11.
(*m*) Ps. lxxx. 11. See the note on St. Mark iv. 32.
(*n*) St. John ii. 11, (where see the note ;) and St. Matth. ix. 17.
(*o*) Ps. civ. 15. Compare Judges ix. 13.   (*p*) Gen. xlix. 11. Deut. xxxii. 14.

The author of the same treatise seems to be discoursing in a parable when he adds :—" Pruning and Training are so closely connected together, that they almost constitute one operation. In pruning a Vine, regard must be had to the manner in which it is afterwards to be trained; and, in training it, the position of the branches must, in a great measure, be regulated by the mode in which it has previously been pruned."

" The *old wood* of a Vine is not only of no use, but is a positive injury to the fertility of the plant."

" The sole object in view in pruning a Vine is to increase its fertility." But it is added, (and there is something affecting in the remark:)—" Although by pruning a Vine its fertility is increased, its existence is no doubt thereby shortened. The severing of a healthy branch from any tree is, without doubt, doing an act of violence to it; the effects of which are only overcome by the superior strength of the vegetative powers of its roots."(q)

To understand our SAVIOUR'S next words, we must anticipate His declaration in ver. 5 : — " I am the Vine, *ye are the branches.*"

2 Every branch in Me that beareth not fruit He taketh away: and every *branch* that beareth fruit, He purgeth it, that it may bring forth more fruit.

Nothing is here said about unbelievers. Our SAVIOUR is talking only of Christian men,— (" Every branch *in Me*," He says: and He distinguishes believers into two classes; those who bear not, and those who bear fruit. The former, " He taketh away,"—" like Judas, who was even now gone forth, and severed from the Church. The latter class, ' He purgeth,' (' or cleanseth,') — by His Word, by His Spirit, by His Providence, by trials and afflictions; as He was about to do with these His beloved Apostles: not willingly, but that they might ' bear more fruit.'"(r)

Under one of these two classes, all perforce are comprised; and take notice, that the words of Solomon, adopted by the Apostle in his exhortation, (" My son despise not thou the chastening of the LORD," &c.,)(s) must, by our LORD'S showing, be applicable to *all* who are not reprobates.

3 Now ye are clean through the Word which I have spoken unto you.

" Ye are already sanctified" (He says) " by the operation of My Doctrine and Spirit upon you,(t) though ye may need further pruning in order to a greater degree of fruitfulness."(u) This saying should be thoughtfully compared with what is found in St. John xiii. 10: and let the learned reader decide whether there is not an allusion here to the precept contained in Levit. xix. 23.

There is a slight play of sound in the original, (which disappears in the translation,) between the words " taketh away," " purgeth," and " clean." Observe that here, our SAVIOUR claims to Himself the Husbandman's Office; since it is *His* Word which cleanseth the branches. " And thus, throughout these Discourses, He departs from them, yet He continues with them. He is One with the FATHER, yet different. He is One with the Comforter, yet another. He is the Vine, and His FATHER is the Husbandman; and yet, He and the FATHER are One. He is the Vine, and yet the Vine are His Disciples."(x)

4 Abide in Me, and I in you.

That is, — " And I will abide in you :" or, " that I also may abide in you." . . . " How is this communion, but by prayer; by keeping His word; by good works; by His Sacraments; by His sanctifying Grace; by the Peace of GOD keeping the heart; by Faith exercised in Love ?"(y) Lastly, from a comparison of this place with 1 St. John ii. 6, it must be added, — By walking even *as He* walked.

As the branch cannot bear fruit of itself, except it abide in the Vine; no more can ye, except ye abide in Me.

(q) Clement on the Cultivation of the Grape-Vine, 1837.
(r) Williams.　　　　　　(s) Heb. xii. 5, — quoting Prov. iii. 11, 12.
(t) Compare Eph. v. 26.　　(u) Hammond.
(x) Williams.　　　　　　(y) Williams.

To understand the meaning of these words, it must be remembered that "except it abide," "except ye abide," in this place signify,—"*but must* abide." See the note on the next verse.

5 I am the Vine, ye *are* the branches: He that abideth in Me, and I in him, the same bringeth forth much fruit: for without Me ye can do nothing.

Rather, — "severed," or "apart from" Me. . . . The teaching of these words is not to be mistaken. Only while in CHRIST, (into whose body we were "grafted" at our Baptism,) can we bring forth the fruit of good works,—as branches can only produce grapes while they abide in the Vine. Yet are those works not ours, but *His;* being done solely by virtue of that life which we enjoy because we are in Him. *His* infused grace it is which makes us productive; without whom, we can do nothing.

He says not, "For without Me ye can bring forth but *little* fruit;" not, "There are some things ye cannot do without Me;" or, "There are many things ye cannot do without Me;" but, "Without," (or "Apart from) Me, *ye can do nothing:*" nothing good, nothing pleasing and acceptable unto GOD: whereas if we could either prepare ourselves to turn, or turn ourselves when prepared, without him, we could do much. And to put it out of doubt, the same Spirit tells us elsewhere, "For it is GOD which worketh in you both to will and to do of His good pleasure."(z)

On the doctrine implied by that saying,—"He that abideth in Me, and I in him," (that is, "and in whom I abide,")—see the notes on St. John xiv. 20. The branch bears fruit, not because it abideth in the Vine, but because in it the Vine abideth.

6 If a man abide not in Me, he is cast forth as a branch, and is withered;

"O wonderful and mysterious life-giving union! He is still a branch, but a dead branch. No longer, by prayer and communion with GOD doth he draw life; and then, he is cut off from the Body." "*Cast out*" is he, — according to the constant language of Holy Scripture: compare St. Matth. viii. 12: xxii. 13: xxv. 30; and read the latter part of the note on St. John xiii. 30. — "But the end is yet to come.(a)

and men gather them, and cast *them* into the fire, and they are burned.

There is no word for "men" in the original.(b). "The fire spoken of is, doubtless, that fire into which the soul is cast; the soul that can never die, and the fire that can never be quenched."(c) . . . . Consider, in connection with this place of Scripture, St. Matth xiii. 30: and see the next note.

7 If ye abide in Me, and My words abide in you, ye shall ask what ye will, and it shall be done unto you.

Thus is set forth, (in verses 6 and 7,) in a few words of awful contrast, the blessed consequence of "abiding" in CHRIST, — like the Eleven: and the terrible result of "abiding not" in Him,—like Judas. "If a man abide not," his "end is to be burned," as speaks the Apostle.(d) This is the fate of "every tree which bringeth not forth good fruit," — proclaimed in the self-same words both by our SAVIOUR CHRIST, and by His Forerunner.(e) But the result of "abiding" in CHRIST, is, that the Believer asketh what he will, "and it *shall be done* unto" him :(f) for *he* will not "ask amiss." Consider Romans viii. 26, and St. James iv. 3. In connection with the phrase, "My words abide in you," the reader is invited to consider attentively the language of St. Peter and St. John in the two places referred to at foot.(g) "If ye keep My commandments," (saith our SAVIOUR,

(z) Bp. Beveridge, quoting Phil. ii. 13.   Consider Art. X.
(a) Williams.   (b) See note on St. Luke vi. 38.
(c) Williams.   (d) Heb. vi. 8.
(e) St. Matth. vii. 19 and iii. 10.   (f) See also St. John xiv. 13, 14: xvi. 23.
(g) 1 St. Pet. i. 23, and 1 St. John iii. 9, — where, what is here called the *Word*, is spoken of as *Seed*.

in verse 10,) "ye shall abide in My love:" and, as if in allusion to these sayings, the beloved Disciple declares in his first Epistle, "Whatsoever we ask, we receive of Him, because we keep His Commandments, and do those things that are pleasing in His sight."(*h*)   "This is the confidence that we have in Him, that if we ask any thing according to His will, He heareth us."(*i*)   See below, the latter part of ver. 16.

8 Herein is My FATHER glorified, that ye bear much fruit; so shall ye be My Disciples.

Our SAVIOUR declares that the Eternal FATHER will be glorified by the fruits of Faith which the Apostles should hereafter exhibit; doubtless, alluding chiefly to the time when they should "be endued with power from on high."(*k*)   The conversion of the nations to the knowledge of "the Truth as it is in CHRIST JESUS," is of course the result chiefly intended; as appears from verse 16, — where see the note: but take notice how it is declared that the fruit of good works, as shown in the life and conversation of the humblest believer, is the glorifying of our FATHER which is in Heaven.   See St. Matthew v. 16: 1 Cor. vi. 20. — "What unspeakable condescension is it that even GOD Himself should deign to receive glory from His creatures, and be glorified in their obedience!"(*l*)
The meaning of the last clause is uncertain.   It seems probable that our SAVIOUR is here declaring two respects wherein the FATHER will be glorified; — namely, by the Apostles' bearing "*much fruit*;" and by their becoming His "*Disciples indeed*;" which title, as He once told the Jews, belongs only to as many as "*continue in His Word*."(*m*)

9 As the FATHER hath loved Me, so have I loved you: continue ye in My love.

The words are plain; and the saying seems at first to present no difficulty.   But, on examination, *all* the discourses of Him who spake as "never man spake"(*n*) are found to present doubts, if not difficulties.   In what respect, (for example,) had our LORD so loved His Disciples as the FATHER had loved *Him?* . . . . Again, — Does He here exhort them to continue in His love towards *them?* that is, not to forfeit His gracious friendship: or to persevere in their love towards *Him?* that is, to be faithful unto death.   For, (as Augustine remarks,) "the words themselves do not make it evident which love He means; His to us, or ours to Him."   The latter sense will be found to be fully established by a reference to the places indicated at foot.(*o*)   See the note on the next verse. . . . . Lastly, — Is that brief concluding sentence, "Continue ye in My love," to be taken by itself? or is it to be taken with what goes before? making the meaning of the whole verse, this: — "As the FATHER hath loved Me, and I have loved you, [so] continue ye in My love."(*p*) . . . . It follows:

10 If ye keep My Commandments, ye shall abide in My love; even as I have kept My FATHER'S Commandments, and abide in His love.

As already hinted, the meaning certainly is, that the keeping of CHRIST'S Commandments would be the best evidence that the Disciples persevered in their love of CHRIST; (according to those sayings of their Divine Master, — "If ye love Me, keep My commandments."(*q*)   "This is My commandment, That ye love one another as I have loved you."(*r*)   "By this shall all men know that ye are My Disciples, if ye have love one to another."(*s*)   Consider also St. John xiv. 24; and especially 1 St. John ii. 3 to 6.)   And the concluding clause means, — Even as the evidence that I love the FATHER, is, that I keep His commandments. — In illustration of which last words, it will suffice to refer the reader to the Commentary on

---

(*h*) 1 St. John iii. 22.
(*k*) St. Luke xxiv. 49.
(*m*) St. John viii. 31.
(*o*) Consider St. Luke xi. 42.   St. John v. 42.
sider especially 1 St. John ii. 3 to 6, not only as an allusion, but also as a commentary, on verses 4, 5, 9, 10, of the present chapter.
(*p*) Compare verse 4, above: also vi. 57.
(*r*) St. John xv. 12.

(*i*) 1 St. John v. 14.
(*l*) Williams.
(*n*) St. John vii. 46.
1 St. John ii. 5, and 15: also iii. 17.   Con-
(*q*) St. John xiv. 15.
(*s*) St. John xiii. 35.

St. John iv. 34, v. 30, and vi. 38.   Let him consider also St. John xiv. 31, and read the note on that place.

11 These things have I spoken unto you, that My joy might remain in you, and *that* your joy might be full.

The meaning of these few difficult words seems to be, — I have been thus earnestly exhorting you to persevere in love towards Me, and obedience to my commands, in order that, when I am away, ye may have an abiding sense of that joy which my presence inspired ; and not only so, but, this life ended, that ye may find in Me a full measure of Bliss.(*t*)   Consolation in this World, amid hardships and trials : and in the World to come, an inheritance of perfect joy.   For, as it is written, "Eye hath not seen, nor ear heard, neither have entered into the heart of man the things which GOD hath prepared for them that love Him."(*u*)

12 This is My Commandment, That ye love one another, as I have loved you.

Observe how our SAVIOUR takes occasion here to repeat that self-same "new Commandment" which he had already delivered in chap. xiii. 34 ; and which He here distinguishes from all other commands, by calling it *His own*.   So much has been already offered on this subject, that it must suffice, on this occasion, to refer the reader to the note on St. John xiii. 34.

The largeness of the love wherewith CHRIST hath loved us, was not alluded to before.   Here, it is distinctly specified.   He seems to say, — Love ye one another even unto Death, as even unto Death I have loved you.

13 Greater love hath no man than this, that a man·lay down his life for his friends.

"But GOD commendeth His Love towards us, in that, while we were yet sinners, CHRIST died for us." If then, "when we were *enemies*, we were reconciled to GOD by the death of His SON, much more being reconciled, we shall be saved by His Life!"(*x*) "This is the love which has been shown to us ; and it was exhibited for those who were *not* "friends ;" who were *unreconciled ;* aye, who were *enemies*.   When we had neither the power nor the will to make ourselves friends of GOD, did He first redeem us, and then adopt us for his own ; reveal Himself to us, and take us to His own bosom as the Disciples whom He loved."(*y*)

Take notice that in the expression "lay down His life," it is implied that by His own free will CHRIST would submit to death.

Most interesting, however, is it that we should have our attention directed to the plain and repeated allusions in St. John's first Epistle, to the present and the preceding verse.   "In this was manifested the love of GOD toward us, because that GOD sent His Only Begotten SON(*z*) into the World, that we might live through Him. . . . Beloved, if GOD so loved us, we ought also to love one another."(*a*) "Herein perceive we Love, because He laid down His life for us : and we ought to lay down our lives for the brethren."(*b*)

Upon the last word of the verse before us ("friends,") the Divine Speaker proceeds to engraft a further gracious statement :

14 Ye are My friends, if ye do whatsoever I command you.

That is, — Ye *will be* My friends.   The present verse is therefore exactly equivalent to the former half of verse 10, as we have already explained it.   Take notice of the largeness of the Love, which anticipates the obedience of the Apostles, in the ensuing verse bestows upon them, in advance, the very title of endearment which He here promises !

Obvious must it be to an attentive reader, that the word "friends" occurs in a

---

(*t*) Compare for the expression St. John iii. 29 : xvii. 13.   Phil. ii. 2.   1 John i. 4, and 3 John 12.

(*u*) 1 Cor. ii. 9, quoting Is. lxiv. 4.   (*x*) Rom. v. 8, 10.

(*y*) From a MS. Sermon by Rev. Robert Scott, D.D., Master of Balliol.

(*z*) A few words here seem intended to recall our SAVIOUR'S discourse to Nicodemus.   St. John iii. 16.

(*a*) 1 St. John iv. 9, 11.   (*b*) 1 St. John iii. 16.

somewhat different sense here, and in verses 13 and 15. *Here*, the conduct of men shows that *they* love *CHRIST: there*, the treatment which they experience at CHRIST's hands, proves that *He* loves *them.* . . . In verse 17, our LORD will explain what He specially means by "whatsoever I command you." In the meantime, He proceeds to show why He will henceforth call His Disciples "friends:"

15 Henceforth I call you not servants; for the servant knoweth not what His LORD doeth : but I have called you friends;

Rather,—"I call you servants *no longer*." Not but what he may still, by implication, sometimes call His Disciples by the name of "servants;" as He had done in time past.(c) But He here declares that He will henceforth regard them as standing towards Himself in a new and more endearing relation : that, namely, of "friends."

This glorious appellation had been already bestowed by GOD on faithful Abraham :(d) "and striking it is to observe that unto this day, all those on the face of the earth who call upon the GOD of Israel,—not Christians and Jews only, but even the followers of the false prophet,—so glory in this title of the Patriarch, that Mamre or Hebron, where Abraham dwelt, is no longer called by either of those names ; but by one which signifies simply, '*the Friend*;'(e)—a reverent and mysterious expression of the name of Abraham,—' the friend of GOD.' "

The title thus bestowed by our SAVIOUR upon His Disciples, (be it observed,) "was an advance and promotion even of those who had been of His company from the beginning:" "I call you servants *no longer*:" that is, "I have hitherto called you so;" but will call you so no more. "Now, here is a two-fold blessing. First, that we should be servants, or even *bondmen* of GOD at all, is the work of His infinite mercy, who hath redeemed us out of the power of the evil One to whom we were in bondage. But the Love which sought us out in the House of our Captivity, and brought us into the household and family of GOD, giving us that service which is perfect freedom, in exchange for the grinding drudgery and noisome dungeons of the Adversary's prison-house, has not even stopped short there. Having begun to love those whom He had made His own, He loved them unto the end.(f) "No longer do I call you servants, . . . but I have called you friends." This is the spirit of Adoption, which replaces the Spirit of bondage unto fear. For this purpose CHRIST came into the World, and took upon Him the form of *a Servant*, being made in the likeness of man ; that He might not only speak to us, but be with us, as a man with his friend. And that this bond of Friendship, begun through this humiliation of His, might remain firm and ratified eternally, in the truth of that Human Nature which He hath united with the Godhead for ever. Thus, our citizenship is in Heaven : *there* is He who is our friend, and who calls us His friends,—the "friend that sticketh closer than a brother !"(g)

The particular distinction between the "Servant" and the "Friend," which is here drawn by our Blessed LORD, demands our attention:—"The servant knoweth not what his LORD doeth." "It is not necessary that he should ! The common soldier is neither expected nor permitted to know the plans of the commander. *His* part is simply to do that which is appointed him : to keep watch and guard; to march hither or thither ; in faith that his work is part of a large plan, but still without knowing the end, without understanding what he does. Thus was it with the Jews, through whom GOD was working even from the time when He called Abraham His friend, in preparation for the Advent of the REDEEMER. Their whole Law and its disposition were designed and adapted for that end ;(h) and yet, how entirely ignorant were they of it, even when the end came ! 'Ye know nothing at all,' said Caiaphas. How true of all those to whom he said it, while they were the instruments of GOD's work ! How true, above all, of Himself ! They 'knew nothing at all.'(i) . . . This is to be *a servant*, in the sense in which CHRIST uses the word here ; not as it is often used in Holy Writ, of that 'service which is perfect freedom ;' our 'reasonable service ;' the ministrations of a dedicated life to GOD and His Son ; but in contrast to the higher gift and more intimate relation of those

(c) Compare ver. 20 of the present chapter with St. John xiii. 16.
(d) Is. xli. 8.   See St. James ii. 22.
(f) St. John xiii. 1.   (e) Al Khalil.
(h) Consider Eph. iii. 5.   (g) Prov. xviii. 24.
                                                        (i) Col. i. 26.

whom the Son, having made free, has made. friends. 'I have called you *friends:'"*(k)

for all things that I have heard of My FATHER I have made known unto you.

"All things, (that is,) which were within their grasp ;(*l*) . . . which were within the sphere of their own work and position :(*m*)— for it need hardly be remarked that we must not understand it of the deep things of GOD, which are known only to the FATHER, the SON and the HOLY SPIRIT, who searcheth the depths of the Godhead. These are things which our nature makes it impossible for us to know: so that it is not so much that GOD withholds them from man, as that man cannot take them in. But all the work in which they have their part; all the living organisation and body of which they are lively members; all His own work, will, affections, His whole self as the Mediator between GOD and Man,—all this, He reveals to them, in proportion to the truth of their friendship.(*n*)   In short, He says in the text, that *He has no secrets from His friends.*

" So it is said of Moses, (though, in a more strict sense, GOD calls him His '*servant*,') 'the LORD spake unto Him *face to face, as a man speaketh unto his friend.*'(*o*) And this was the reward of a servant ; that, for his faithfulness, he should be treated *confidentially ;* and, so far, raised above a servant's place.' Accordingly, it is worth observing that where it is said 'My servant Moses . . . is faithful in all Mine House. With Him will I speak mouth to mouth, even apparently, and not in dark speeches,'(*p*)— the Greek rendering of the word 'servant' is peculiar : a term of milder import than usual being employed, which St. Paul is careful to repeat when he alludes to this place of Scripture, in Hebrews iii. 5.— Still more clearly is all this seen, as we might expect, in the case of him who was by pre-eminence called 'the friend of GOD.'(*q*)   'And the LORD said, *Shall I hide from Abraham* that thing which I do ?'(*r*)—Accordingly, long before the time of this His last discourse, our LORD had made a marked distinction between those who came to hear Him, in general ; and the inmost circle of His Disciples."   Consider St. Matthew xiii. 10 to 17.(*s*)

It might be thought that the past tense is used above, as so often elsewhere, with reference to an act yet future : since it was to be the office of the HOLY GHOST, on the ensuing Day of Pentecost, to teach the Disciples "all things," and to guide them "into all the Truth."(*t*)   But in what sense this was spoken, has been fully explained in the notes on St. John xiv. 26,—to which the reader is referred. The office of the HOLY GHOST was *to explain* to the Disciples those many things which CHRIST Himself had *taught* them.

With reference to the words, "all things that I have heard of My FATHER," the reader is requested to read the note on St. John v. 20: also the extract from Hooker in the note on St. John xvi. 15.

16 Ye have not chosen Me, but I have chosen you,

" The whole blessing, then, is *a gift, a grace, a mercy;* and, in this respect, differing from the character of earthly friendships ; for at the very beginning and root of these there lies a notion of equality and mutual choice, and of liking for one another. But here, the notion of equality is preposterous ; and therefore, we could not have chosen Him, though it lay in His sovereign power to choose us, as of His sovereign power He hath done, *making* us His friends, and thereby giving us the power, which but for that gift we could not have had, of making Him our friend also.(*u*)   "I have chosen you,"(*x*) He says ; (commending thereby His undeserved affection towards our fallen race :)—

(*k*) From a valuable MS. Sermon by the Rev. Robert Scott, D.D., Master of Balliol.
(*l*) Consider St. John xvi. 12.   (*m*) Compare Acts xx. 27.
(*n*) Consider Ps. xxv. 14 : Prov. iii. 32.
(*o*) Exod. xxxiii. 11.   Compare Deut. xxxiv. 10.
(*p*) Numb. xii. 7, 8.   Consider what is implied by the reference to this place in 1 Cor. xiii. 12.
(*q*) See above, the beginning of the note on verse 15.
(*r*) Gen. xviii. 17.   (*s*) From the MS. Sermon last quoted.
(*t*) See St. John xiv. 26, and xvi. 13.   (*u*) From the same MS. Sermon.
(*x*) See St. John xiii. 18.

and ordained you, that ye should go and bring forth fruit, and *that* your fruit should remain :

That is, — It was not ye, in the first instance, who made choice of Me; but, in order that I might send you forth as Apostles, I made choice of you, and ordained(y) you to this office; that ye should " *go* into all the World, and preach the Gospel to every creature."(z) " This his choice, however, laid no constraint on their will, that they should not fall ; for He had said before, " Have I not chosen you Twelve, and one of you is a devil ?"(a) Nor had he chosen them for sensible assurances, but for bearing fruit.(b) . . , Consider St. Paul's language to the Romans i. 13 ;(c) and refer back to what has been already offered above, on verse 8. The allusion here to "fruit," (that is, to works,) which "should remain," or "abide" the trial, recalls that striking passage in 1 Cor. iii. 12 to 15,—to which, (especially to the language of verse 14,) it must suffice simply to refer. Or we may understand the allusion more definitely as referring to that setting up of the Church of CHRIST, which shall never be destroyed,(d) and which was to be the great and abiding work of the Apostles of the LAMB. Consider Rev. xxi. 14: Ephes. ii. 20 ; and St. Matth. xvi. 18.—Our SAVIOUR adds:

that whatsoever ye shall ask of the FATHER in My Name, He may give it you.

This should be compared with verse 7, above.—It will be found that there is the same connection of thought traceable in verses 7 and 8, as throughout the present verse. See chap. xiv. 13, and 14. Consider also, chap. ix. 31.

17 These things I command you, that ye love one another.

Take notice that our SAVIOUR here recurs to what He was saying in verse 14. " Ye are My friends," (we heard Him say,) " if ye do whatsoever I command you." Accordingly, having, in verse 15, enlarged on that gracious appellation, "friends," He here repeats His " new commandment:" " These things I command you," (or " These [are the things which] I command you," namely,)—" *that ye love one another*." He reverts continually to this His heavenly requirement. . . . And now the Discourse takes a fresh turn. Our SAVIOUR fortifies His Disciples against the World's hate and unkindness.

18 If the World hate you, ye know that it hated Me before *it hated* you.

" Marvel not," therefore,—it seems to be implied. See 1 St. John iii. 13.

19 If ye were of the World, the World would love his own : but because ye are not of the World, but I have chosen ye out of the World, therefore the World hateth you.

Twofold, therefore, was to be the consolation of the Disciples under the World's hatred : first, the thought of what their Divine Master had experienced at its hands : next, the evidence which would thus be afforded them that they were not of the World, but the chosen of CHRIST. " For if I yet pleased men," (exclaims the great Apostle,) " I should not be the servant of CHRIST."(e) Compare St. John xvii. 14, and 1 St. John iv. 5. Consider also the saying, (addressed to those who " did not believe in Him,") in St. John vii. 7, — where " the World" is used in the same sense as here.

" The godly," (says Bishop Sanderson,) " are in this World ' as strangers and pilgrims'(f) in a foreign, yea, in the enemy's country ; and they look upon the World, and are looked upon by it, as strangers ; and are used by it accordingly. If they were of the World, the World would own them, and love them, as her own ; and they would also love the World again, as their own home. But because

---

(y) " The original word is similarly used in Acts xx. 28. 1 Cor. xii. 28: 1 Tim. i. 12: ii. 7. 2 Tim. i. 11."—Lonsdale and Hale.

(z) St. Mark xvi. 15.
(b) Williams.
(d) Lonsdale and Hale.

(a) St. John vi. 70.
(c) Compare Phil. i. 11, and Col. i. 6.
(e) Gal. i. 10.   (f) 1 St. Pet. ii. 11.

they are not of the World, though they be in it, but are denizens of Heaven,(*g*) therefore the World hateth them; and they, on the other side, are weary of the World, and long after Heaven, their own country, where their treasure is laid up, and where their hearts and affections also are."

, 20 Remember the Word that I said unto you, The servant is not greater than his lord.

How full of solemn interest becomes any saying of our LORD which He could in so marked a manner recall to the minds of His Disciples! He reminds them of what He had said an hour or two before, after washing their feet. See St. John xiii. 16, and the note on the place. Take notice, however, that His present allusion is not to that occasion; but to the charge which He had delivered to them about a year and a half before, when He sent them out by two and two; and when, in order to arm them for the strife on which they were that day to enter, He said, —"The Disciple is not above his Master, *nor the Servant above his Lord.* It is enough for the Disciple that he be as his Master, and the Servant as his Lord. If they have called the Master of the house Beelzebub, how much more shall they call them of his household?"(*h*)   And so it follows here:

If they have persecuted Me, they will also persecute you; if they have kept My saying, they will keep yours' also.

But they *did* persecute Me, (it is implied;) therefore, will they also persecute you. And they did not keep My word; therefore, neither will they keep yours. . . . "Keeping" CHRIST's "Word" obviously denotes holding fast His Doctrine, and obeying His precepts; as in so many other places.(*i*)

21 But all these things will they do unto you for My Name's sake, because they know not Him that sent Me.

"For My Name's sake" seems to be a prophetic allusion to the future appellation of Christians. "Do not they blaspheme *that worthy Name by which ye are called?*"—asks St. James.(*j*) Compare St. Matthew xxiv. 9, and St. Mark xiii. 13; and the note on the latter place. "If any man suffer as *a Christian,*" (writes St. Peter,) "let him not be ashamed; but let him glorify GOD on this behalf."(*k*) And we know that the Apostles did so; departing from the presence of Councils, "rejoicing that they were counted worthy to suffer shame for His Name."(*l*)

The reason of the enmity of the Jews follows:—"because they know not Him that sent Me." Ever marvelous, or at least unexpected, are the reasons which CHRIST assigns. Thus, He here ascribes the Jews' hostility not to their ignorance of Himself, but of the FATHER who sent Him,(*m*) whom they yet professed to know.(*n*) It will be found suggested in the note on verse 23, that the Doctrine which our LORD states openly on so many other occasions, is here implied; namely, that every act of despite which the Jews had committed against the Son of Man, had been, in effect, a proof that they hated the FATHER also. For take notice, that the point of this accusation rests in the words, "they *know not;* that is, they *refuse to know,* they *will not know.*(*o*) In short, "they *hate:*" even as CHRIST is said to "know" those only whom He *loves.*(*p*) As it is elsewhere written,—"They have blinded their eyes, and hardened their heart; that they should not see with *their* eyes, nor understand with *their* heart, and be converted, and I should heal them."(*q*)   Hence, it follows:

(*g*) Phil. iii. 20.   (*h*) St. Matth. x. 25.
(*i*) They are as follows: St. John viii. 51, 52, 55: xiv. 23, 24: xvii. 6.   1 St. John ii. 5.   Rev. iii. 8, 10: xxii. 7, 9.   Compare above, verse 10.
(*j*) St. James ii. 7.   Compare Acts xi. 26: xxvi. 28.
(*k*) 1 St. Peter iv. 16.   (*l*) Acts v. 41.
(*m*) Compare St. John xiv. 24: xvi. 3: xvii. 25.
(*n*) St. John viii. 41, 42, 54, 55.
(*o*) Compare St. Luke xix. 42, 44.   1 Sam. ii. 12.   Ps. lxxix. 6.   Is. l. 3: v. 13: xlv. 5.   Jer. ix. 3, 6.   Hos. iv. 6.   2 Thess. i. 8.   2 St. Pet. iii. 5.
(*p*) See St. Matth. vi. 23, and xxv. 12, (and the notes;) also St. Luke xiii. 25.   Compare St. John ii. 4 and 5.
(*q*) St. John xii. 40, where see the note.

22 If I had not come and spoken unto them, they had not had sin: but now they have no cloak for their sin.

"He meaneth, they had no colour of plea; nothing to pretend by way of excuse."(r)

He had before, (in verse 21,) declared that the enmity of the Jews proceeded from their not knowing the FATHER. He here explains that their ignorance was nevertheless inexcusable; the result of a depraved will. He "had come and spoken unto them," "as never man spake;"(s) and it rested with themselves to hear, or to forbear.

Prophetically of this very matter had it been written:—"Wisdom crieth without: she uttereth her voice in the streets: she crieth in the chief place of concourse, in the openings of the gates: in the city she uttereth her words, saying, How long, ye simple ones, will ye love simplicity? and the scorners delight in their scorning, and fools hate knowledge? Turn you at My reproof: behold I will pour out My Spirit unto you, I will make known My words unto you." But "they hated knowledge, and did not choose the fear of the LORD. They would none of My counsel: they despised all My reproof. Therefore they shall eat the fruit of their own way."(t)

When our LORD says that if He had not "come and spoken unto them, they had not had sin,"—He can, of course, but mean that the Jewish nation would, in that case, have been guiltless of the special sin of not knowing by whom He had been sent; and of rejecting Him. This is explained in chap. xvi. 9. Men sin as often as they resist the guidance of conscience,—however imperfectly informed that conscience may happen to be. Hence it is that the most degraded among the heathen are capable of Virtue and of Vice.(u) All those on whom the glorious light of the Gospel hath not yet shined, are nevertheless secure from the Sin of rejecting the blessed offer of Salvation; even as (alas!) they are excluded from the opportunity of embracing it.

Some of the most striking occasions when, by His words and by His works, CHRIST spoke to this nation, and was rejected, will be recalled with advantage in this place.(v)

23 He that hateth Me, hateth My FATHER also.

This seems to belong to what our SAVIOUR was saying above, in ver. 21, to complete its sense, and to be, as it were, explanatory of it. He there declared that His Disciples would have to endure persecution at the hands of the Jews, because that nation had not known the FATHER that sent Him. "These things will they do unto you," (we shall hear Him presently declare,) "because they have not known the FATHER, nor Me."(w) "If ye had known Me," (we have heard Him say on two former occasions,) "ye should have known My FATHER also."(x) Here it is, plainly,—"He that hateth Me, hateth My FATHER also."

24 If I had not done among them the works which none other man did, they had not had sin: but now have they both seen and hated both Me and My FATHER.

As verse 23 corresponds in a manner with verse 21, so does the present verse correspond with verse 22; showing what was meant thereby. The works of CHRIST, so far exceeding any which were ever wrought by mere man :(y) those many wonderful works so often elsewhere alluded to,(z) and concerning which the Evangelist himself says such striking things, in chapter xii. 27 to 41; the miracles, in short, which our SAVIOUR had so freely wrought in the presence of his countrymen, were what rendered their hardness of heart inexcusable.

(r) Sanderson.
(s) St. John vii. 46. Consider below, verse 24.
(t) Prov. i. 20 to 23, 29 to 31.   (u) See Rom. ii. 12, 14, 15.
(v) As, St. Matthew ix. 32 to 34: xii. 22 to 24. St. John v. 8 to 16: viii. 43 to 59: ix. 13 to 22: x. 29 to 39: xi. 43 to 53. See also St. John v. 36: x. 25, 37, 38,—where see the references at foot of the page.
(w) St. John xvi. 3.   (x) St. John viii. 19, and xiv. 7.
(y) Consider St. John iii. 2: vii. 31: ix. 32.
(z) See St. John x. 37, 38, and the notes there.

By saying, "the works which none other man did," it is not meant that *every* single miracle which our LORD performed surpassed in wonder *any* single miracle recorded of Moses, or Elijah, or Elisha; for that would not be true. But the works were made so great by the way He wrought them. Without effort, by a mere word, He showed that all Creation was obedient to His will. From Him, as from an inexhaustible fountain,(*a*) flowed forth healing virtue equal to the needs of all.

In illustration of the concluding words, "Now have they both *seen* and hated both Me and My FATHER," see above, St. John xii. 45, and xiv. 9.

25 But *this cometh to pass*, that the word might be fulfilled that is written in their Law, They hated Me without a cause.

The meaning is this, as in so many other places of the Gospel,(*b*) is not that the Jews hated CHRIST in order that the words of David might be fulfilled; but that, from their hatred, resulted the fulfillment of certain words, spoken prophetically by the inspired Psalmist; and which the Evangelist here adduces as having reference to the sacred person of our LORD.—The "Law" here stands for the whole volume of the ancient Scriptures;(*c*) and it is emphatically called "theirs," (as in other places,)(*d*) to convey a tacit reproof of that wickedness which, "one of themselves, *even a Prophet of their own*,"(*e*) had foreseen and denounced.

That the present reference is to the Book of Psalms, is certain; but it seems impossible to declare precisely to which place in the Psalter our SAVIOUR alludes: whether to Ps. xxxv. 19,—or to lxix. 4,—or to cix. 3.(*f*) The sentence, exactly as it stands in the Gospel, is not found in any part of the sacred writings. Some will infer, (and perhaps rightly,) that the reference here, like that in St. Matth. ii. 23, is to *no particular* Psalm, but to the repeated witness of the SPIRIT, in three or more places.

A very important text follows. Our LORD has been alleging the unbelief and the hatred of the nation. He adds:

26 But when the Comforter is come, whom I will send unto you from the FATHER, *even* the Spirit of Truth, which proceedeth from the FATHER, He shall testify of Me:

The "Comforter" is thus, for the second time, identified with the HOLY GHOST; (*i*) who is also now, for the second time, called "the Spirit of Truth." Concerning that appellation, see the note on St. John xiv. 17.

Here, and here only, is it expressly declared in Scripture that the HOLY GHOST "*proceedeth from*" the FATHER.(*j*) And this is that great truth concerning the Third Person in the Blessed Trinity, which we proclaim in the two Creeds incorrectly called the Nicene Creed and the Creed of St. Athanasius. Incorrectly: for the Creed of the Council of Nice (A.D. 325,) does not contain this doctrine. It was added to that Creed by the Council of Constantinople, in A.D. 380. The Athanasian Creed is of later date than the famous Father whose name it bears; and is clearly of Western, not Eastern, origin.

But in both the Creeds above alluded to, (as well as in the Litany,) we declare, not only that the HOLY GHOST proceedeth from the FATHER, but also "*from the* SON." The Church's warrant for so doing is chiefly the verse of St. John now under discussion, added to the following place of St. John's Gospel,—chap. xvi. 7, 14, 15. She argues, that "though it be not expressly spoken in Scripture that the HOLY GHOST proceedeth from the SON, yet the substance of the same truth is virtually contained there: because those very expressions which are spoken of the HOLY SPIRIT in relation to the FATHER, for that reason because He proceedeth from the FATHER, are also spoken of the same SPIRIT in relation to the SON; and therefore there must be the same reason presupposed in reference to the SON, which is expressed in reference to the FATHER." Thus, "since the HOLY SPIRIT is called

(*a*) St. Mark vi. 56.
(*b*) See the note on St. John xii. 38.
(*c*) As in St. John x. 34; where see the note.
(*d*) St. John viii. 17 : x. 34.   (*e*) Titus i. 12.
(*f*) The marginal reference in the Vulgate is (unreasonably enough,) to Ps. xxv. 19.
(*i*) See St. John xiv. 26.   (*j*) Consider also 1 Cor. ii. 12.

the Spirit of God,(k) and the Spirit of the FATHER,(l) because He proceedeth from
the FATHER, it followeth that being called also [the Spirit of CHRIST,(m) and] the
Spirit of the SON,(n) He proceedeth also from the SON."(o)   "The Spirit of both,
as *sent* and *proceeding from* both."(p)

   "The HOLY GHOST," writes an Eastern Bishop,(q) "is expressly declared to
be from the FATHER; and is moreover witnessed to as being from the SON. For,
(saith the Scripture,) ' If any man have not the Spirit of CHRIST, he is none of
His.'(r) Thus, the Spirit, which is from God, is the Spirit of CHRIST also. On
the other hand the SON, though He is from God, neither is, nor is anywhere
declared to be, from the SPIRIT."(s)

   Again : Because the HOLY GHOST "proceedeth from" the FATHER, He is therefore " sent by" the FATHER ; as from Him who hath by the original communication
a right of mission: as, — " The Comforter, which is the HOLY GHOST whom the
FATHER *will send*." But the same SPIRIT which is sent by the FATHER is also sent
by the SON ; as He saith, — " When the Comforter is come, whom *I will send* unto
you."(t) Therefore the SON hath the same right of mission with the FATHER, and
consequently must be acknowledged to have communicated the same essence. The
FATHER is never sent by the SON, because He received not the Godhead from Him ;
but the FATHER sendeth the SON, because He communicated the Godhead to Him.
In the same manner, neither the FATHER nor the SON is ever sent by the HOLY
SPIRIT ; because neither of them received the Divine Nature from the SPIRIT: but
both the FATHER and the SON sendeth the HOLY GHOST, because the Divine Nature,
common to both the FATHER and the SON, was communicated by them both to the
HOLY GHOST. As therefore, the Scriptures declare expressly that the SPIRIT proceedeth from the FATHER, so do they also virtually teach that He proceedeth from
the SON.

   "From whence it came to pass in the primitive times, that the Latin Fathers
taught expressly the procession of the SPIRIT from the FATHER and the SON ;
because, by good consequence, they did collect so much from those passages of the
Scripture which we have used to prove that truth. And the Greek Fathers, though
they stuck more closely to the phrase and language of Scripture,—(saying, that the
SPIRIT proceedeth from the FATHER, and not saying, that He proceedeth from the
SON,)—yet they acknowledge under another Scripture expression the same thing
which the Latins understand by " Procession," viz., that the SPIRIT is of or from
the SON,(u) as He is of and from the FATHER; and therefore, usually, when they
said He "proceedeth from the FATHER," they also added, He "received of the
SON."(v) The interpretation of which words, according to the Latins, inferred a
Procession ; and that which the Greeks did understand thereby, was the same
which the Latins meant by the Procession from the SON ; that is, the receiving of
His Essence from Him : that, as the SON is GOD of GOD by being of the FATHER,
so the HOLY GHOST is GOD of GOD by being of the FATHER and the SON ; as receiving that infinite and eternal essence from both."

   From a difference of language concerning this great Doctrine, the Eastern Church
proceeded to its express and open *denial*. This led to many disputes ; until at last,
the Latins (in A. D. 858), thrust the words " and from the SON" into the Creed of
Constantinople, — in open defiance of the General Council of Ephesus, A. D. 431,
"which had prohibited all additions: and that, without the least pretence of the
authority of another Council." "And being admonished by the Greeks of that, as
of an unlawful addition, and refusing to erase it out of the Creed again, it became
an occasion of the vast schism between the Eastern and the Western Churches;"
a schism, "never to be ended, until those words, (' and from the SON,') are taken

(k) 1 Cor. ii. 11, 12.   (l) St. Matth. x. 20.
(m) Rom. viii. 9 ; Phil. i. 19 ; and 1 St. Pet. i. 11.
(n) Gal. iv. 6.   (o) Bp. Pearson.
(p) Bp. Andrewes.
(q) Gregory, Bp. of Nyssa in Cappadocia. A. D., 375.
(r) Rom. viii. 9.
   (s) From a newly-discovered fragment of this Father: in the margin of which, an ancient
critic has written, — "Nobly said, great Gregory."
   (t) Above, ver. 26: also St. John xvi. 7. Compare Acts ii. 33, and Eph. iv. 8, (quoting Ps.
lxviii. 18.)
   (u) See the passage from a Greek Father, quoted above; in which, take notice that the word
rendered "from," may be rendered "of," throughout, at pleasure.
   (v) From St. John xvi. 14, 15.

out of the Creed."(x)   In the year 1043, the Eastern Church proceeded to excommunicate the Western, on this account, as heretical.

"This, therefore, is much to be lamented," (says Bp. Pearson, summing up the question,) "that the Greeks should not acknowledge the truth, which was acknowledged by their ancestors, in the substance of it; and that the Latins should force the Greeks to make an addition to the Creed, without as great an authority as hath prohibited it; and to use that language in the expression of this doctrine which never was used by any of the Greek Fathers."   The Doctrine itself is certain; for it "may be proved by most certain warrants of Holy Scripture:"(y) the addition of words to the formal Creed without consent, and against the protestation of the Oriental Church, was unjustifiable.

The connection of ver. 26 with what goes before, has already been briefly noticed. Our SAVIOUR said, (in verses 24, 25,) that the Jewish nation had seen, and disbelieved, and hated, both Himself and His FATHER: "but when the Paraclete(z) is come," (He proceeds,) "He shall testify of Me;" that is, "He shall bear witness to you and to the World that I came forth from GOD, and that My doctrine is true. In other words, He shall bear witness of the injustice of the World's hatred,"(a) and the sinfulness of its unbelief.   Consider, in passing, what striking "witness" to the Divine Mind the HOLY SPIRIT is related occasionally to have borne: as in Acts viii. 29: x. 19: xi. 12: xiii. 2.   Reasonably, therefore, is it added concerning this Divine Witness,—"even *the Spirit of Truth*, which *proceedeth from the* FATHER." "The Spirit of Truth," — and therefore, (it seems to be implied,) *a sure Witness.* More than "an Angel from Heaven."(b)   One that actually "proceedeth from the FATHER,"—and therefore, (it seems to be hinted,) the very fittest Person *to testify concerning the* SON. . . .   As for the testimony here spoken of, the SPIRIT sent down upon the Apostles, did even thereby testify that CHRIST was risen; because it was CHRIST who sent that SPIRIT from the FATHER; and, (as He frequently declared,) He could not send Him, until He was Himself "gone away."(c)   Then further, the miracles which the Apostles were enabled to perform, wrought conviction in every beholder;(d) while "the wisdom and the spirit by which they spake,"(e) (according to their LORD's true promise,) were such as all their adversaries were "not able to gainsay or resist;"(f) for "*with great power* gave the Apostles witness of the Resurrection."(g) — It follows:

27 And ye also shall bear witness, because ye have been with Me from the beginning.

"The Apostles witnessed together with that SPIRIT, because they were enlightened, comforted, confirmed, and strengthened in their testimony by the same SPIRIT."(h)   They were enabled, moreover, to bear their unaided human testimony to our SAVIOUR,—as eye-witnesses of His miracles, "from the beginning;" and as men who had listened to that Divine teaching, which it was to be the office of the HOLY GHOST to bring back to their memories, and to explain.   Accordingly, we frequently hear them bearing witness of CHRIST, and urging the very plea here put into their mouths, as the ground of their claim to attention:—"*We beheld His glory!*" exclaims St. John in the first chapter of his Gospel.   And again: "That which was from the beginning, which *we have heard*, which *we have seen with our eyes*, which *we have looked upon, and our hands have handled* of the WORD of Life; ... that which we have *seen* and *heard* declare we unto you."(i)   St. Peter relates concerning St. John, St. James, and himself: "This voice which came from Heaven *we heard*, when we were with Him in the Holy Mount;" and this he says to show that he and the rest "had not followed cunningly devised fables," when they made known to the Church "the Power and Coming of our LORD JESUS CHRIST, but *were eye-witnesses of His Majesty*."(j)   The same S. Peter, when one had to be chosen into the place of the traitor Judas, addressed the Disciples to much the same effect,

---

(x) Bp. Pearson.   (y) Article VIII.
(z) The sense of "Comforter" seems less applicable here than in St. John xiv. 16,—where see the latter part of the note.
(a) Lonsdale and Hale.   (b) Gal. i. 8.
(c) See St. John xvi. 7; and the note on the last words of vii. 39.
(d) Consider Acts iv. 14: viii. 18, 19.   (e) Acts vi. 10.
(f) St. Luke xxi. 15.   Consider Acts ii. 37.
(g) Acts iv. 33.   (h) Bp. Pearson.
(i) St. John i. 1, 3.   (j) 2. St. Peter i. 16, 18.

in these familiar words: "Wherefore of these men which have companied with us all the time that the LORD JESUS went in and out among us, beginning from the baptism of John, unto the same day that He was taken up from us, must one be ordained to be a witness with us of His resurrection. And they appointed two, Joseph called Barsabas, who was surnamed Justus, and Matthias."(k) Consider further St. Luke xxiv. 48; Acts i. 8: ii. 32: iv. 20, 33: and x. 41. But, above all, Acts v. 32 is worth referring to; for there we hear the Apostles say, — "And we are His witnesses of these things; *and so is the* HOLY GHOST, whom GOD hath given to them that obey Him."

CHAPTER XVI.

1 CHRIST *comforteth His Disciples against tribulation by the promise of the* HOLY GHOST, *and by His Resurrection and Ascension:* 23 *Assureth their prayers made in His Name to be acceptable to His* FATHER. 33 *Peace in* CHRIST, *and in the World affliction.*

THE connection of what follows with what went before, seems to be of the closest kind. The scene will therefore have been the same which was indicated in the note prefixed to chap. xv.—The first words contain an allusion to what the Blessed Speaker was saying in verse 18 of the former chapter.

THESE things have I spoken unto you, that ye should not be offended.

The purpose, then, with which our LORD had been forewarning His Disciples(a) was not to sadden them ; but that when assailed by the storm of persecution, they might not be shaken from their steadfastness. Somewhat similar was the object of all that follows, — as we shall be reminded in verse 33. A few instances of what the Apostles would have to expect at the hands of their countrymen, are specified :

2 They shall put you out of the synagogues : yea, the time cometh, that whosoever killeth you will think that he doth GOD service.

More than "doing service" is here meant. The original expression amounts very nearly to "*offering sacrifice.*" And so it came to pass: "as it is written," (said the great Apostle, applying to the early Christians a prophecy of David,) "For Thy sake are we killed all the day long; we are accounted as sheep for the slaughter."(b) . . . . Instances of such treatment are found in Acts viii. 1 : ix. 1, &c. : and the confession of one who had been a persecutor is preserved; namely, that he regarded every act of violence against the Christians, as the mere discharge of his duty.(c)

We have already seen, (in the case of the man born blind,) how prompt the Pharisees were to pass sentence of excommunication :(d) which sentence, though it could not *harm* the Apostles, was yet a convincing proof of the hate with which they would be regarded by the rest of the Jews.

3 And these things will they do unto you, because they have not known the FATHER, nor Me.

This should be compared with what is read in chap. xv. 21; and the note on that place may be referred to. Compare also the last words of chap. xv. 24.

(k) Acts i. 21 to 23.
(b) Rom. viii. 36, quoting Ps. xliv. 22.
(d) See St. John ix. 22, 34. Compare xii. 42.

(a) See St. John xv. 20, 21.
(c) Acts xxvi. 9 to 11.

4 But these things have I told you, that when the time shall come, ye may remember that I told you of them.

And the thought that all had been fully foreseen by Me, (it is implied,) will prove your comfort and your stay. Compare verse 1, and consider St. Matthew xxiv. 25.

And these things I said not unto you at the beginning, because I was with you.

The allusion seems to be no longer to the hardships which should hereafter befall the Disciples. It may well be thought, in fact, by any one reading the Charge with which our LORD originally sent His Disciples forth,(e) that He had, even from the very beginning, "said these things" unto them. Our LORD here seems to speak rather of His departure to the FATHER; concerning which He had hitherto said so little, for the reason which He here assigns.

5 But now I go My way to Him that sent Me; and none of you asketh Me, Whither goest Thou?

He contrasts the demeanor of His Disciples, as they now hang upon His words, sad and silent, — with that impatience and importunity which had before characterized their inquiries; namely, in chap. xiii. 36 and xiv. 5. There may even be a slight reproof implied: as if He had said, — When I spoke before of departure, there was no lack of inquiry as to whither I went. I exclaimed, in reply, that I depart to Him who sent Me; and lo, ye ask no further questions:

6 But because I have said these things unto you, sorrow hath filled your heart.

My words have made you sad, and therefore silent. . . . "He was indeed about to leave them as to His visible presence, but not in Spirit. Without Him they could do nothing; all their life must be from Him. As GOD, He would be ever with them. The change was to be this: He was to go away from them as Man, and in future to hold communion with them as such not by visible actions and by word of mouth, but by sending to them the HOLY SPIRIT from the presence of the FATHER, whose throne He shares."(f)—Accordingly, (still pursuing the same train of thought,) our SAVIOUR adds:

7 Nevertheless I tell you the truth: It is expedient for you that I go away: for if I go not away, the Comforter will not come unto you; if I depart, I will send Him unto you.

By this tender assurance that it was for *their* good that He must soon depart, our SAVIOUR seeks to reconcile His little band of faithful followers to the prospect of His loss: but "it was a hard saying, (and who could endure it?) that it should be expedient for them, or for any, to have CHRIST go from them, or forsake them."(g) Verily, it required to be supported by the assurance that it was "*the truth*" which He told them! . . . Consider only what must be the value of that great blessing which was given to them, which is given to us, to compensate for the loss of His visible presence!

"And sure, the proposition is not so hard, but the reason that induceth it is as hard, or harder. 'The Comforter will not come.' Be it so. Let Him not come. Stay you! We desire no other Comforter! And the condition moveth not, neither: 'If I go not away.' Why may CHRIST not stay, and the HOLY GHOST come notwithstanding? What hinders it but we may enjoy both together?"—So writes pious Bp. Andrewes in his quaint, but beautiful sermon on this text.

"We shall never see the absolute necessity of the HOLY GHOST's coming," (he proceeds,) "until we see the inconvenience of His *not* coming; that it may by no means be admitted. We cannot be without Him. For first, in both the principal works of the DEITY,"—as in the Old Creation, so in the New,—"all three Persons

(e) St. Matth. x. 16 to the end.   See also St. Matth. v. 11, 12: xxiv. 9.
(f) Rev. C. Marriott.   (g) Bp. Andrewes.

must co-operate. It was the counsel of GOD that every Person in the Trinity should have His part in both.—And secondly, the work of our Salvation must not be left half undone, but be brought to full perfection. CHRIST's Coming, however, can do us no good, if the HOLY GHOST come not. When all is done, nothing is done. Our SAVIOUR could say truly, 'It is finished,' in respect of the work itself: but in regard of us, and making it ours, it is *not* finished if the HOLY GHOST come not too. The deed is not valid till the seal is set. . . . And as nothing is done for us, so can nothing be done by us, if He come not: no means on our part avail us aught, neither Sacraments, nor Preaching, nor Prayer, if the SPIRIT be away."(*h*)

Then further, the Disciples " were to know more of CHRIST's Power and Glory, more of His Goodness and Love, even by not seeing Him for awhile; when they beheld Him extend His care and kindness to all the ends of the Earth, by sending His HOLY SPIRIT on all that believe, and by manifesting His presence with them everywhere, although unseen.—It was well also that the Church of GOD should be exercised in walking by Faith and not by sight: that He should make trial of His servants in a few things, before placing in their hands the whole of the inheritance He intended for them."—" *That*, in short, is best for us now, which is best calculated to fit us for meeting Him in judgment, and for living with Him in glory."

" But the language of the text seems plainly to speak of another, and *that* the principal reason, why it was better that our LORD should leave His people upon Earth for awhile: namely, that He might present Himself before the FATHER on their behalf; and sitting down on His Right Hand, might send the HOLY GHOST to supply His place on Earth."(*i*) The mission of the HOLY GHOST, by GOD's inscrutable decree, was made *dependent* on our LORD's return to the bosom of His FATHER. This has been already noticed in the note on the latter part of St. John vii. 39. The entire subject is manifestly above us. CHRIST is here declaring as much as it is good for men to know of so great a mystery; proclaiming in the ears of His Church one of the relations in which the persons in the Blessed Trinity stand to one another: *necessary* relations, indeed: yet not as men understand Necessity. The writer last quoted has said:—" We cannot so scan the Law which GOD hath set Himself to work by as that we should know how it is that one of His acts requires and implies another; as the sending the HOLY SPIRIT required that our LORD should leave His flock for a time. But we can see much connection and mutual fitness in these things. Had our LORD remained visibly present, many things could not have been done which have since been done by the HOLY SPIRIT. Our very duties to Him, as visibly before us on Earth, would have been entirely different from what they are now. Our relation to the World would have been different, and our whole state so entirely another thing than it has been, that we cannot tell at all what it would have been. Only thus much we seem to gather from the scattered intimations of Holy Writ, that it is because of the exceeding glory of that which is to come, that we need this time of preparation."

" If I depart," (saith our LORD,) " *I will send Him unto you.*" From this right of Mission on the part of the SON, as already so largely explained in the Commentary on St. John xv. 26, is argued the Procession of the HOLY GHOST *from the SON* as well as from the FATHER.

8 And when He is come, He will reprove the World of Sin, and of Righteousness, and of Judgment:

Verses 8 to 11 comprise a passage of considerable difficulty, yet of prime importance, and of unusual interest: for our SAVIOUR is here describing nothing less than the work of the HOLY GHOST in the World; giving a brief summary of what was the object, and what would be the end, of His Mission. He declares that the HOLY GHOST, at His coming, would " convince" the World; for the term employed is far stronger than " reprove." The Divine meaning is,—" He who shall come in My Name shall so bring home to the World its own " Sin," My perfect " Righteousness," GOD's coming " Judgment;" shall so " convince it of these, that it shall be obliged itself to acknowledge them."(*j*) And this was to be a pledge of what would take place in that great day, yet future, when " Sin, which we now see but witnessed against, shall be condemned in the eyes of men and Angels: when that Righteousness which we now see but feebly proclaimed, and set forth in a few faint examples, shall shine forth in the Royal and priestly Glory of CHRIST our King and

---

(*h*) Abridged from Bp. Andrewes.   (*i*) Rev. C. Marriott.   (*j*) Trench.

SAVIOUR: and that Judgment which men hear of and forget, shall be seen and felt in the fullness of eternal joy, and the terrors of eternal fire."(k) In this announcement, take notice, was contained a ground of real consolation to the Apostles; warned, as they had already been, of the hostility they would have to encounter at the World's hands. The were promised a powerful ally, who should "convince the gainsayers,"(l) and therefore convict their common Enemy.

The HOLY GHOST "was to convince the World of *Sin*, of *Righteousness*, and of *Judgment*. In these three things are summed up the chief truths concerning Man in his present state. The great distinction between Sin and Righteousness, and how the one is to be avoided and the other attained; how they are to be known, and where they are to be seen: this, the HOLY SPIRIT was about to make manifest. And He was also to give warning to man of the righteous Judgment of GOD; and to prove to those who would learn, that it should be executed in due time, and by Him who was now despised and rejected of men."(m) "However easy or difficult it may prove to interpret the reasons of the HOLY GHOST, the three doctrines themselves, seem to form so plain and intelligible a series, as to require to be interpreted connectedly. They appear to comprise the History of Man, from his fall to his glory. Sin,—the sin of mankind: Righteousness,—the state or condition of being restored out of Sin, in CHRIST," (who is declared by the prophet to be "*our Righteousness:*")(n) "Judgment,—the final retribution, in which GOD will reward those who, in CHRIST, obey His Law, and punish those who are impenitent."(o) But a clue to the Divine meaning is supplied by the words which follow, without which it would have been dark indeed. First, then, the HODY GHOST would convince the World of SIN :—

9 of Sin, because they believe not on Me ;

The Blessed Speaker "names Sin first, because Sin is the present state of the World."(p) Now, throughout His Ministry, CHRIST had been condemning the World. But the World, in turn, had accused Him of being a Sinner; and had even put Him to death as such. He therefore here declares that the HOLY GHOST would, like an umpire, decide between their respective claims; and convict *the World* of Sin. That is, He would cause it to confess not only that it is generally sinful, but that it had specially sinned in respect of its unbelief and rejection of MESSIAH: in the words of CHRIST Himself,—"*Because they believe not on Me.*" And with this should be compared the language of St. John viii. 24.

In illustration of the promise thus delivered to the Apostles, consider the conscience-stricken cry of the multitude, at the end of St. Peter's first Pentecostal Sermon : "Men and brethren, what shall we do?"(q) On being called upon to "repent and be baptized in the name of JESUS CHRIST for the remission of sins," three thousand were obedient to the exhortation. Consider again, the conduct of the jailor of Philippi: "Sirs, what must I do to be saved? And they said, Believe on the LORD JESUS CHRIST, and thou shalt be saved, and thine house. . . . And he . . . . was baptized, he and all his, straightway."(r) Such also, (St. Paul declares,) would be the confession of an individual unbeliever on entering the Church, and beholding the spiritual gifts which abounded at Corinth.(s) "Men were *convinced* by the reproof of the HOLY SPIRIT, and the wicked World was *convicted*. True, the World resists and will resist the clearest evidence. But the SPIRIT in the Apostles bore witness; and the same HOLY SPIRIT, by the Scriptures, and in the Church of GOD, does still bear witness against the Sin of the World, whether in disbelieving or in disobeying our LORD."(t) In the words of another excellent writer, "When the Spirit of Truth came, His first province was to convince the World of Sin, because they believed not in their LORD. And since that Heavenly witness is perpetual, since unbelief still characterizes the World as such, therefore it is that the World is yet held an enemy by the Church, which, though in, is not of, the World."(u)

Take notice, then, that under one great head of *Unbelief*, the guilt of the World is gathered up and comprised. Unbelief is therefore a sin of the heart, not a mere error of the understanding: *a fault*, not a *misfortune*.

But the HOLY GHOST "was also to reprove the World, that is, to give proof in the face of the World, and against its false judgments, concerning RIGHTEOUSNESS."

(k) Rev. C. Marriott.   (l) Tit. i. 9.   (m) Rev. C. Marriott.
(n) Jer. xxiii. 6, and xxxiii. 16.   (o) Dr. Moverly.   (p) 1 St. John v. 19.
(q) Acts ii. 37.   (r) Acts xvi. 30, 31, 33.   (s) Consider 1 Cor. xiv. 24,25.
(t) Rev. C. Marriott.   (u) Dr. W. H. Mill.

10 of Righteousness, because I go to My FATHER, and ye see Me no more;

" He was to make it manifest that CHRIST was indeed the Righteous One ; and that through Him, and in Him alone, man could either attain to Righteousness, or be accepted before GOD, as righteous.　He was to do this, because our LORD was going to the FATHER, and because for a time the World was to see Him no more."(x) While He was on Earth, men had stumbled, (been offended,) at the lowly aspect of One who had been described in Prophecy as " a worm and no man :"(y) but this cause of offence was now about to be removed.　CHRIST was to be withdrawn from the sight of men ; and straightway the work of convincing the World of His " Righteousness" would be found to begin.　Thus, no sooner had our LORD commended His Spirit into the Hands of His FATHER, than the Centurion who " saw what was done," was heard to glorify GOD, saying, "*Certainly this was a righteous Man !*"(z)　Still more apparent did our LORD's Righteousness become when, at the end of three days, He rose from death ; and when, at the end of forty days more, He ascended up into Heaven. . . . As He had declared long before by the mouth of His Prophet,—" He is near that justifieth Me !"(a)

But it would not be enough that the Righteousness of CHRIST should in this manner be made to appear.　" The HOLY SPIRIT was further to give proof before all men that the Righteousness of our LORD JESUS CHRIST was approved and accepted of the FATHER.　And of this indeed He gave the strongest proof that could be given. For our LORD was taken up to Heaven : having promised that He would send the HOLY SPIRIT from the FATHER to His Disciples.　When therefore the promised gift was sent, it was the proper token that His work was accomplished, and His Righteousness accepted of the FATHER in behalf of His Church, as well as of Himself : so that St. Peter, when he would prove that He was indeed glorified, had but to say, " He hath shed forth *this*, which ye now see and hear."(b)　And as the HOLY SPIRIT came to teach men that CHRIST is indeed the only source of Righteousness, and the only means of our being accepted as righteous ; (for as our LORD says in ver. 14, " He shall glorify me, for He shall receive of Mine and shall show it unto you ;") so He also came to teach men Righteousness, in the place of our LORD ; and this He has done ever since, both by inward and secret influences, and by outward means."(c)

The third great office of the Comforter remains.　He was to convince the World,

11 of Judgment, because the Prince of this World is judged.

Lastly, the HOLY GHOST would " convince the World of JUDGMENT ;" (that is, *of its own* Judgment :) when it found itself judged, and beheld itself condemned, in the person of the Devil, " its Prince,"—by which name Satan is repeatedly spoken of.(d)　The great Legal type of this mighty event was exhibited at the time of the Exodus from Egypt, when " Israel saw the Egyptians dead upon the sea-shore ;"(e) a proof that GOD had "*judged*" the nation whom they had served.(f)　An Evangelical prelude to the same transaction took place when Satan was seen to fall, like Lightning from Heaven.(g)　But it did not actually take place until the great Captain of our Salvation, ascending up on High, " led Captivity captive,"(h) that is, the Devil, Sin, and Death :) for we know that " having spoiled Powers and Principalities," (the Rulers of Darkness,)(i) and the Princes of this World,(k) " He made a show of them openly, triumphing over them by" His Cross.(l)　For the Cross of CHRIST, as St. Paul elsewhere a second time assures us,(m) was the very instrument of His Victory, and as it were the chariot on which He was borne aloft in Triumph. . . . Concerning this mighty transaction, however, so much has been already offered on that previous saying of our LORD, " Now is the Judgment of this World : now shall the Prince of this world be cast out," that it must suffice to refer the reader to the note on St. John xii. 31.

(x) Rev. C. Marriott.

(a) Is. l. 8.

(d) St. John xii. 31, where see the note ; and xiv. 30.

(e) Exod. xiv. 30.

(g) St. Luke x. 18, where see the note.

(h) Eph. iv. 8, quoting Ps. lxviii. 18.

(i) Eph. vi. 12.

(l) Col. ii. 15.

(y) Ps. xxii. 6.

(b) Acts ii. 33.

(f) Gen. xv. 14.

Compare Judges v. 12.

(k) 1 Cor. ii. 6.

(m) Heb. ii. 14.

(z) St. Luke xxiii. 46, 47.

(c) Rev. C. Marriott.

Take notice that the World could in no better way be convinced of its own condemnation than by beholding the condemnation of its Chief. Moreover, his downfall was the virtual overthrow of his empire; even as the slaying of Goliath was a pledge to Israel, and more than a pledge, of the conquest of the Philistines. "And that Satan was indeed judged, was clearly shown by the power exercised over him by the believers of old, who cast out devils from numbers that were possessed, and trod underfoot "all the power of the enemy."(n)   St. Paul was sent to turn the Gentiles "*from the power of Satan* unto God :"(o) while our Lord Himself repeatedly intimates that, by His miracles of Healing, He was "spoiling the house" of the "strong man armed," who had so long been "keeping his goods in peace." Consider St. Luke xiii. 16, and see the latter part of the note on the place. "Nor was Satan driven only from his dominion over men's persons, and over the minds of thousands, but the very "Kingdoms of the World" became "the Kingdoms of the Lord and of His Christ."(p)   The altars where the Devils used to receive the erring homage of the multitudes whom they deceived, were razed to the ground ; and the fairest portion of the Earth is wrested from the hand of him who boasted that he could dispose of its Kingdoms as he would, and adjudged to his righteous Conqueror."(q)

Such then was to be, — such is, — such will be to the end, the office of the Holy Spirit in the World : — (1st) to convince Man of his sinfulness, and to incline his heart to Faith in the Lord Jesus Christ : (2ndly) to convince him that Christ, who now sitteth at the Right Hand of God, "is made unto us Wisdom, and Righteousness, and Sanctification, and Redemption :(r) (3rdly) to convince him that Judgment on Sin hath begun already, and will be duly executed on all sinners, in the end; including Satan himself, the Prince of Sinners, and all his evil angels. . . . . May we, without presumption, point out that the awful details of this vast threefold picture, as they may be supposed to have presented themselves, in overwhelming majesty, to the mind of the Divine Speaker, naturally led to the words which follow ?

12 I have yet many things to say unto you, but ye cannot bear them now.

In these words, there is nothing inconsistent with our Lord's declaration that all things that He had heard of the Father, He had made known unto the Twelve.(s) This has been already pointed out at p. 844. All those Divine things which perfect Wisdom had decreed to communicate to the Apostles, must needs be conveyed to them, either now or hereafter. As many of those things as they were "able to bear,"(t) our Lord had communicated with His own lips. Even those things, however, He had but *taught* them ; leaving it to the Holy Ghost fully *to explain* their meaning at some future time.(u) There still remained, (as we learn from the present place,) many things which the Apostles must needs be taught; but which they were not in a fit condition yet to receive. The mysterious method by which a knowledge of these things was to be imparted, is explained in the next verse.

13 Howbeit, when He the Spirit of Truth is come, He will guide you into all truth :

" He,"—namely, "the Comforter," spoken of above, in ver. 7 : and to which the present verse, in a manner, refers. For the third time, the Holy Ghost is here called "the Spirit of Truth ;" concerning which appellation, see the note on St. John xiv. 17 : and for the Gospel notion of "Truth," see on xviii. 38. "Let us but observe how the whole World at this time lay in falsehood and error : the Gentiles, under a Spirit of delusion ; the Jews, under the cheat of traditions ; and then it will appear how seasonable and necessary a thing it was that ' the Spirit *of Truth*,' should be sent into the World."(v) And it is here declared of Him, that, at His coming, He should lead the Apostles "into *all the truth*" of the many things which Christ had yet to say, but which at present the Apostles could not bear. "By this means it came to pass that ' all Scripture was given by inspiration of God ;'"(x)

(n) St. Luke x. 19.   (o) Acts xxvi. 18.   (p) Rev. xi. 15
(q) Rev. C. Marriott. -   (r) 1 Cor. i. 30.   (s) St. John xv. 15.
(t) Consider St. Matth. ix. 17, &c. (u) See the note on St. John xiv. 26.
(v) Lightfoot.   (x) 2 Tim. iii. 16.

that is, by the motion and operation of the SPIRIT of GOD; and so, whatsoever is necessary for us to know and believe, was delivered by Revelation."(y) Hence the dignified declaration of the first Council that their decree was the expression of what *seemed good to the* HOLY GHOST,(z) and to them. The statement in the text so nearly resembles what is met with in St. John xiv. 26, that the reader must be invited to refer thither, as well as to the note on the place. The reason why the HOLY SPIRIT would guide the Apostles "into all the truth" of the things which CHRIST had spoken, follows:

for He shall not speak of Himself; but whatsoever He shall hear, *that* shall He speak.

This is to be compared with those well-known sayings of our SAVIOUR concerning Himself:—" He that sent Me is true; and I speak to the world those things which I have heard of Him. . . . I do nothing of Myself; but as My FATHER hath taught Me, I speak these things."(a) " My Doctrine is not Mine, but His that sent Me." (b) " The words that I speak unto you, I speak not of Myself."(c) " I can of Mine own self do nothing: as I hear, I judge."(d) " Whatsoever I speak, therefore, even as the FATHER said unto Me, so I speak."(e) In the Commentary on these places, it will be found suggested that our SAVIOUR, when He used such words, spoke *not* as He was the Son of Man, but as He was the Only-Begotten SON of the Eternal FATHER: and the application of similar expressions to the HOLY GHOST, in this place, will be felt to be fully confirmatory of that view. The third Person in the Blessed Trinity, because He derives His essence eternally from the other two Persons, is said not to " speak *of Himself*,"—to save the necessity of a prolonged discussion on this subject, the reader may be at once invited to read what has been already offered at pp. 711, 804, 681. He is requested to observe, however, (and the remark will be found of importance towards the right understanding of the connection of what follows in verses 14, 15,) that what our SAVIOUR is here specially asserting, at least by implication, is the Procession of the HOLY GHOST *from the SON*. He adds:

and He will show you things to come.

But why is this added? Is it simply a promise that among other lofty gifts, the early Church would possess the faculty of foreseeing future events?(f) A few instances of this gift in operation are indeed met with in the Acts: as when Agabus prophesied an approaching famine,(g) and warned St. Paul of the danger that awaited him at Jerusalem;(h) and St. Paul himself foresaw(i) what should befall the Church of Ephesus(k) after his departure;(l) as well as that, in the last days, there would be a departure from the Faith;(m) and that perilous times would come. (n) . . . An allusion to such a power generally residing in the Church seems, however, to have little to do with the matter in hand. Is not the reference rather to those prophetic intimations of the future destiny and prospects of *the Church* with which the Apostolic Age was favoured? The complement, as it were, of that Divine Knowledge which our SAVIOUR was even now desirous of imparting to His Apostles, but which they were as yet unable to receive. Shall we be thought rash if we venture more particularly to suggest that a promise is here specially given of that "*Revelation of* JESUS CHRIST, *which* GOD *gave unto Him, to show unto His servants things which must come to pass shortly:* and He sent and signified it by His Angel to His servant John; who bare testimony to the Word of GOD, and to the profession of JESUS CHRIST, and [bare witness of] all things that He saw ?"(o)

14 He shall glorify Me: for He shall receive of Mine, and shall show *it* unto you.

(y) Bishop Pearson.
(a) St. John viii. 26, 28.
(c) St. John xiv. 10.
(e) St. John xii. 50.
(g) Acts xi. 28.
(h) Acts xxi. 10, 11. Agabus seems to have been one of many who uttered this prophecy; Acts xx. 22, 23.
(i) Acts xx. 29.
(l) Consider also 1 Cor. ii. 10
(n) 2 Tim. iii. 1.

(z) Acts xv. 28.
(b) St. John vii. 16.
(d) St. John v. 30.
(f) Acts xiii. 1. Eph. iv. 11.

(k) Rev. ii. 1 to 6.
(m) 1 Tim. iv. 1.
(o) Rev. i. 1, 2.

"Of Mine," (or, "Of that which is Mine,") does not seem to be quite the same thing as "Of *Me:*" neither, perhaps, is it enough to say that, "He shall receive of Mine," signifies "He proceedeth from Me." We nothing doubt, indeed, that it is only because the HOLY GHOST derives His Essence eternally from the SON no less than from the FATHER, that He is here said *to "receive* of" that which is CHRIST's. We humbly accept the decision of our predecessors in the Faith, that the SPIRIT is "GOD of GOD"(*p*) the FATHER, *and of* GOD *the* SON; and that this doctrine is to be gathered from the declarations in the present and the next verse, ("He shall take," or "receive of Mine,")(*q*) joined to the famous declaration in chapter xv. 26, that He "*proceedeth from the* FATHER." Moreover, with the Latin Church, we fully believe that this assertion amounts to a declaration that the HOLY GHOST *proceedeth from* the SON as well as from the FATHER.(*r*) All these momentous truths seem, however, to be *implied* in the text, rather than *enunciated* by it. They are incidentally conveyed by what was asserted; not the especial thing asserted, or at least chiefly meant.

The design of the Divine Speaker seems to have been to prosecute what He was saying in ver. 12, and the beginning of ver. 13. When the Spirit of Truth should come, it would be His office to instruct the Apostles in all the Truth of what had been delivered, or left unspoken, by CHRIST Himself; to reveal, in Apocalyptic vision, the future destinies of CHRIST's Church; and to glorify MESSIAH, by taking of that which was His, and proclaiming it to mankind. This is, by delivering to mankind, and enforcing, His Doctrine; by explaining, (like an ambassador,) His Mind and Will; and by teaching the application of His precepts to every fresh requirement of His Church. Manifestly would the HOLY GHOST be glorifying CHRIST, if none but Christian mysteries formed the subject of His teaching; none but works like those of CHRIST were wrought at His suggestion! . . It follows:

15 All things that the FATHER hath, are Mine: therefore said I, that He shall take of Mine, and shall show *it* unto you.

Every step, here, brings with it increase of Divine knowledge. Every word reveals something more of the proportions of Eternal Truth.—The SPIRIT was known to be the SPIRIT *of the FATHER.* But because "all things that the FATHER hath," those the SON hath likewise; therefore could the SON say that the HOLY GHOST would take *of His;* which amounted to a declaration that the HOLY GHOST is the Spirit of the SON,(*s*) no less than of the FATHER. . . . Out of this statement directly arises the lofty Doctrine that the FATHER and the SON are One in respect of Essence. "All things that the FATHER hath are Mine," saith CHRIST; because in Him is the same fullness of the Godhead.(*t*)

Let us hear our own Hooker on this grand theme,—the Law of subordination in the most Holy Trinity. "Our GOD is one, or rather very Oneness, and mere Unity having nothing but itself in itself, and not consisting (as all things do besides GOD) of many things. In which essential Unity of GOD, a Trinity personal nevertheless subsisteth, after a manner far exceeding the possibility of man's conceit. The works which outwardly are of GOD, they are in such sort of Him being One, that each Person [in the Divine Unity] hath in them somewhat peculiar and proper. For being Three, and they all subsisting in the essence of One Deity; from the FATHER, by the SON, through the SPIRIT, all things are.(*u*) That which the SON doth hear of the FATHER, and which the SPIRIT doth receive of the FATHER and the SON, the same we have at the hands of the SPIRIT as being the last, and therefore the nearest unto us in order, although in power the same with the second and the first."

16 A little while, and ye shall not see Me: and again, a little while, and ye shall see Me, because I go to the FATHER.

(*p*) Alluding to the expression in the Nicene Creed, already remarked upon.
(*q*) The same word is repeated in the Original, in verse 15.
(*r*) The Greek Fathers, "sticking more closely to the phrase and language of the Scripture," (says Bishop Pearson,) "yet acknowledge, under another Scripture expression, the same thing which the Latins understand by 'Procession;' namely, That the SPIRIT is of or from the SON, as He is of and from the FATHER."
(*s*) See Rom. viii. 9. Gal. iv. 6. Phil. i. 19. 1 St. Pet. i. 11.
(*t*) Bp. Pearson.
(*u*) Consider Ephes. iv. 6,—which Hippolytus (A.D. 230) seems to allude to when he says, "The FATHER is above all, and the SON through all, and the HOLY GHOST in all." Compare 1 Cor. viii. 6, and Romans xi. 36.

" Because I go to the FATHER ;" and, (it seems to be further implied,) will send down the HOLY GHOST to enlighten your eyes, whereby ye shall see Me indeed.

He shows that on His departure depended His mysterious presence: " Ye shall see Me, *because* I go to the FATHER ;" but in verse 10, we read, " because I go to the FATHER, and ye see Me no more." Thus, because He went to His FATHER, they should both see Him, and not see Him. They should not see Him in the flesh, but they should see Him in the Spirit ;(*x*) no longer with their bodily organs, but with that inner vision which results from CHRIST's indwelling presence, and which best deserves the name of Sight. . . . . Such seems to be the true meaning of this difficult passage ; as the reader will probably be inclined to admit if he will ponder carefully our LORD's words in chap. xiv. 18 to 20.

A similar promise had been already made to the Apostles, in St. John xiv. 19 :— " Yet a little while, and the World seeth Me no more, *but ye see Me*." The same mysterious reason also which is here assigned in explanation of the Apostles' faculty of supernatural vision, is elsewhere given to explain why the believer in CHRIST should do greater works than CHRIST Himself had wrought: namely,— "*Because I go to My* FATHER." See the notes on St. John xiv. 12, where the words are briefly explained. For the self-same reason, Mary Magdalene was forbidden to touch her risen LORD in the garden. " Touch Me not," (He said,) "*for* I am not yet ascended." See St. John xx. 17, and the note on the place.

The first words of the verse before us(*z*) may either mean, Pass a few hours, and ye shall not see Me ; because I shall be crucified, dead, and buried ; and so, hidden from the eyes of men : — or, Pass forty days, and ye shall not see Me ; because I shall have ascended up into Heaven. If the reader considers only the three places indicated at the foot of the page.(*a*) he will probably incline to the former view as the more probable. We would humbly suggest, however, that since the promise delivered here, and in chap. xiv 19, that the Disciples should hereafter " see " CHRIST, seems clearly connected with the Day of Pentecost,—when the promise was further given that *He* would return,(*b*) and see *them*,(*c*) — it is better to regard the Death and the Ascension of our LORD, as parts of one event; the beginning and the end of that *departure* to the FATHER which he had so often announced to His Disciples.

17, 18 Then said *some* of His Disciples among themselves, What is this that He saith unto us, A little while, and ye shall not see Me ; and again, a little while, and ye shall see Me ; and, Because I go to the FATHER ? They said therefore, What is this that He saith, A little while ? we cannot tell what He saith.

Rather, "of what He is talking." — Something very similar, our LORD had said repeatedly before ;(*d*) but never in so pointed and enigmatic a manner as now. It need excite the surprise of none that the Disciples found the saying a hard one, since the meaning of it is not understood with certainty even at the present day. Our LORD's explanation has been before the world for eighteen hundred years ; and the most learned doctors and fathers of the Church are not yet agreed as to the precise signification of what was spoken. What must have been its obscurity prior to the " glorious Resurrection and Ascension" of CHRIST, and to the Coming of the HOLY GHOST !

But the Disciples had to do with One "unto whom all hearts be open, all desires known, and from whom no secrets are hid." Accordingly, it follows:

19, 20 Now JESUS knew that they were desirous to ask Him ; and said unto them, Do ye inquire of yourselves of that I said, A little while, and ye shall not see Me : and again, a little while, and ye shall see Me ? Verily, verily, I say unto you, That ye shall weep and lament, but the World shall rejoice : and ye shall be sorrowful, but your sorrow shall be turned into joy.

(*x*) Dr. Moberly.
(*z*) Compare for the expression St. John vii. 33 : xii. 35.
(*a*) Verse 22 of the present chapter, compared with St. John xx. 20, and Acts i. 3.
(*b*) St. John xiv. 18.   (*c*) See below, ver. 22.
(*d*) See St. John vii. 33 : xiv. 2, 4, 12, 28 : xvi. 5, 7, &c.

"Whereas the World's joy," (it is implied,) "shall be turned into sorrow."

Take notice that, by this reply, our Blessed LORD does not explain the proposed difficulty. Only indirectly do His words bear upon the doubt which the Disciples had expressed. May it be thereby intimated that it is not for Disciples "to know the times or the seasons which the FATHER hath put in His own power?"(e) that it is better for Faith to be exercised, than for curiosity to be appeased? and that the Divine Counsels must ever be interpreted by *the result?*

Let us however observe what our SAVIOUR's reply really does amount to: even this,—the events were at hand which would affect His faithful followers, and the wicked World, very differently. Sorrow awaited the one: joy, the other. But the sorrow of the Disciples was not to be abiding. It was to be turned into joy. Here, therefore, two distinct periods are indicated: and it is obviously implied that the period of sorrow would begin when, after a little while, the Disciples should no longer see CHRIST; the season of Joy, when again, after a little while, they *should* see Him. Take notice, that the present discourse extends down to the end of ver. 28, where the same two periods are again marked, and the two events indicated which would occasion successively the Sorrow and the Joy. "I leave the World;" hence, the Sorrow:—"I go unto the FATHER;" hence, the Joy. Sorrow,—because with our LORD's leaving the World, came bereavement: Joy, — because with our LORD's going to the FATHER, was mysteriously connected the promise of His return. Consider, by all means, ver. 22 of the present chapter; also chap. xiv. 18.

But the words of CHRIST are ever high as Heaven; and he who seeks to limit their meaning, (as we have been just now doing,) speedily becomes reminded of his error. "*In the World ye shall have tribulation,*" our LORD is found to say below, in ver. 33. The periods of sorrow and of Joy of which He speaks must therefore be extended beyond the limits of the first Easter and Whitsuntide. Nay, His words are the property of all believers, to the end of Time. Whatever may have been their immediate force, they have a yet broader application, holding true of man's entire journey through this Vale of tears; which stands in the same relation to a Heaven of bliss, as the Sorrow which may endure for a night to the Joy which cometh in the morning.(*f*) The Saints of GOD are taught to expect tribulation here below,(*g*) but they have the promise of abiding blessedness hereafter:(*h*) while earthly prosperity is often the short-lived inheritance of the wicked.(*i*)

21, 22 A woman when she is in travail hath sorrow, because her hour is come: but as soon as she is delivered of the child, she remembereth no more the anguish, for joy that a man is born into the World. And ye now therefore have sorrow; but I will see you again, and your heart shall rejoice, and your joy no man taketh from you.

When the Disciples heard our Blessed LORD so expound His own words, they will have naturally thought that by this image of maternal anguish suddenly exchanged for maternal rapture, He had but intended to set forth the contrast between the weeping and lamentation which awaited themselves at His approaching departure, and the joy into which that sorrow of theirs was, in a little while to be turned.

Is it not pretty evident however, that, besides this, His Divine words had a profounder meaning? and may we not reverently suppose that when the HOLY SPIRIT brought to the Disciples' remembrance all things which CHRIST had ever said unto them,(*k*) He may have also guided them to perceive that by this image of a travailing woman was conveyed a sublime hint of the relation in which this present Life stands to the Glory which shall be revealed?(*l*) "For we know," (says the great Apostle,) "that the whole Creation groaneth and travaileth in pain together until now. And not only they, but ourselves also, which have the first fruits of the Spirit, even we ourselves groan within ourselves, waiting for the adoption, to wit, the redemption of our body:"(*m*) meaning by that word "redemption,"

(*e*) Acts i. 7.   (*f*) Ps. xxx. 5.
(*g*) 2 Tim. iii. 12.   1 St. Peter iv. 12.
(*h*) Consider St. Luke vi. 20 to 23.   Rom. viii. 18.   2 Cor. iv. 17.
(*i*) Consider Ps. lxxiii. 2 to 5, and 12.   Job xxi. 7 to 9.   Jer. xii. 1.
(*k*) St. John xiv. 26, and the note there.   (*l*) Rom. viii. 18.
(*m*) Rom. viii. 22, 23.

the final vindication of the body from corruption,(n) which will take place at the time of the general Resurrection, — hence called " the *Regeneration*."(o)

" When these things begin to come to pass," (said our SAVIOUR, speaking of the calamities which were to come upon Jerusalem, and which He had already described as " the beginning of *birth-pangs*,"(p) " then look up, and lift up your heads; for your *Redemption* draweth nigh."(q)   Accordingly, as the first-born of the New Creation, His own Resurrection from Death is spoken of under the same remarkable image; — " as it is written in the second Psalm, Thou art My SON, *this day have I begotten Thee*."(r) — Do not these several intimations of the SPIRIT guide us, therefore, to the full meaning of our LORD's words on the present occasion?   In a certain sense, the travailing Mother's "hour had come,"(s) already; and she was to "have sorrow." Already also was she to forget her anguish; for on Easter-morning, her sorrow was to be turned into Joy.   In a far higher and truer sense, however, she travails still: nor, till the consummation of all things, will her heart rejoice with that Joy which no man taketh from her. . . . . And thus, the same breadth of meaning is vindicated for verses 21 and 22, which we claimed above, for verses 19 and 20.

It will appear, therefore, that we understand our LORD's promise, "I will see you again, and your heart shall rejoice," to have had a primary fulfillment on that memorable occasion, (the evening of the first Easter-Day,) when He stood in the midst of the Disciples, "and saith unto them, Peace be unto you:" for "then," (we read,) "*were the Disciples glad, when they saw the* LORD."(t)   A yet higher fulfillment will His Divine words have received when the Day of Pentecost arrived ; as we have already elsewhere endeavoured to explain.(u)   Not until the last Day, however, when, having prepared a place for them, He "will come again" and receive His Disciples unto Himself; that where He is, there they may be also :(v) not until *then* will that fullness of Joy of which our SAVIOUR here speaks, become the abiding portion of His Saints.

Our SAVIOUR concludes as follows :

23 And in that day ye shall ask Me nothing.

Words which evidently require the same largeness of interpretation as the rest of our LORD's discourse.   In a primary sense, doubtless, the "Day" spoken of was the Day of Pentecost: when there would be no more such questions asked as the Disciples had been asking throughout this mournful evening.(w)   Our LORD had already alluded thereto by the phrase "In that day," in a kindred passage.(x) The great Day, however, is evidently yet future when Faith will be swallowed up in Enjoyment; and when there will be no more room for any kind of doubt or question.

Take notice that the word translated "ask" in what follows, is a wholly different word from that which is used in the place before us.   *Here*, "asking questions" is meant: *there*, "making petitions."

Verily, verily, I say unto you, Whatsoever ye shall ask the FATHER in My Name, He will give *it* you.

Or, (as it is expressed in chap. xiv. 13,) "Whatsoever ye shall ask in My name, that will *I* do."   Doubtless, from that day forward, the Church learned to conclude all her prayers, (as now,) with the Divine formula "*Through* JESUS CHRIST *our* LORD." . . . . In this verse then, there is "no contrast drawn between asking THE SON, which shall cease; and asking THE FATHER, which shall begin. But the first half of the verse closes the declaration of one blessing, namely, that hereafter they shall be so taught by the SPIRIT as to have nothing further to inquire: the second half of the verse begins the declaration of altogether a new

(n) Eph. i. 14: iv. 30.   (o) St. Matth. xix. 28, where see the note.
(p) St. Matth. xxiv. 8.   (q) St. Luke xxi. 28.
(r) Acts xiii. 33.
(s) Compare the language of St. John xvii. 1: see the latter part of the note on St. John xii. 23.
(t) St. John xx. 19, 20 : compare St. Luke xxiv. 41 ; not losing sight of ver. 52.   See also Acts ii. 46: xiii. 52.
(u) See the note on ver. 16.   (v) St. John xiv. 3.
(w) See above, ver. 5.   (x) St. John xiv. 20.

blessing; that whatever they shall ask from the FATHER in the SON's Name, He will give it them."(z)

24 Hitherto have ye asked nothing in My Name: ask, and ye shall receive, that your joy may be full.

"Ye have hitherto indeed been accustomed to pray to the FATHER, but not in My Name, — as ye shall hereafter pray to Him."(a)   "Ask, and ye shall receive, that your joy may be perfect."

25 These things have I spoken unto you in proverbs:

"These things in dark speeches have I spoken unto you" saith our LORD; alluding first, to His saying in ver. 16; next, to His reply, in ver. 20, and still more in ver. 21, to the Disciples' question in ver. 17.   Nay, verse 22 itself is "a dark speech," even to ourselves: how much more to the men to whom the words were originally addressed! . . . It follows:

but the time cometh, when I shall no more speak unto you in proverbs, but I shall shew you plainly of the FATHER.

"Shall show you plainly in what relation the FATHER stands to Me, and to you."(b)   The allusion here is certainly to the Day of Pentecost; as already suggested above, on ver. 23.   The Divine doctrine conveyed seems to be, that by the descent of the HOLY SPIRIT, the Apostles would become enlightened to such a degree, as to need no other instruction.   At that time, our SAVIOUR promises that He will teach them more openly than now; meaning thereby, that it will be the office of the HOLY GHOST to teach them.   For the HOLY GHOST was to be sent by Himself, and to come in His Name.(c)   Whatsoever therefore, He did,—inasmuch as He received of CHRIST's, and showed it unto the Disciples,(d) — might truly be said to be the work of CHRIST Himself.

26, 27 At that day ye shall ask in My Name: and I say not unto you, that I will pray the FATHER for you: for the FATHER Himself loveth you.

"In that Day," still indicates the season which followed the Day of Pentecost: and our Blessed LORD is comforting His Disciples concerning it.   They had been hitherto blessed with His own prevailing prayers on their behalf.   Henceforth they will have to pray for themselves.   But, in the meantime, He encourages them to believe that they will be unconscious of any lack.   "He speaks of those who love Him being brought into such close communion with the FATHER, that they may pray to the FATHER in His Name, and not need Him to pray for them, but be at once accepted and answered for His sake.   They are still accepted for His sake; and therefore His not praying for them separately must be, because they are brought so near to Him, so made one with Him, that in their very prayer He prays."(e) So abundantly, in short, are they blessed with the love of the Eternal FATHER, that He will freely give them whatsoever things they need. — And wherefore! The reason follows:

Because ye have loved Me, and have believed that I came out from GOD.

Our SAVIOUR says not simply, "and have believed in Me." He designed to show wherein belief in CHRIST consists: namely, in a belief that He "came out from GOD;" that He is His true and natural SON; and that, for us men and for our Salvation, He was by Him sent into the World.(f)   Consider chap. xvi. 8.
Bishop Pearson handles this great subject in his usual lofty way.   "Though CHRIST saith ' the FATHER is in Me, and I in Him ;'(g) yet withal He saith, ' I came out from the FATHER:' by the former, showing the Divinity of His Essence; by the

(z) Trench.
(b) Lonsdale and Hale.
(d) See above, verses 14, 15.
(f) Maldonatus.

(a) Lonsdale and Hale.
(c) St. John xiv. 26: xv. 26: xvi. 7.
(e) Rev. C. Marriott.
(g) St. John x. 38.

latter, the origination of Himself. We must not look upon the Divine Nature as sterile, but rather acknowledge and admire the fecundity and communicability of itself, upon which the Creation of the World dependeth ; God making all things by His Word, to whom He first communicated that Omnipotency which is the cause of all things."—Such remarks as these do not indeed help us to understand the passage of Scripture to which they relate, *in its actual connection.* But they are important, if they bring before us the depth and fullness of the inspired Word ; and remind us that it is " profitable for *Doctrine,*" as well as " for instruction in Righteousness."(*h*) Take notice that in what follows, the phrase, " I came forth from God," is exchanged for another :—

28 I came forth from the FATHER, and am come into the World : again, I leave the World, and go to the FATHER.

Availing Himself of the last words He had spoken, our SAVIOUR makes this fuller and more formal statement concerning Himself ; a statement, (let it be observed in passing,) which conveys by implication the important assurance of the pre-existence of our LORD's Divine Nature. He had already, (in verses 5 and 16,) declared that He was about to " leave the World, and go unto the FATHER." By the form of speech which He here uses, He seems to imply that in that very statement · is contained and implied that He had first " come forth from the FATHER," and was " come into the World."(*i*) " Now, that He ascended," (saith His Apostle,) " what is it but that He also descended first ? . . . He that descended is the same also that ascended up far above all heavens."(*k*)

Let us hear Augustine concerning this mysterious statement. " Our belief hath altogether been, nor should it seem an incredible account of the matter to any, that when CHRIST came forth from the FATHER, He so *came into the World,* as never to leave the FATHER: so *left the World* and went unto the FATHER, as never to leave the World. He ' came forth from the FATHER,' because He is ' of the FATHER :' He came into the World, because He displayed to the World that Body which He had taken of the substance of the Virgin. He left the World, by withdrawing from it His Human Body ; but He did not leave the World by withdrawing from it His governing presence."

29, 30 His Disciples said unto Him, Lo, now speakest Thou plainly, and speakest no proverb. Now are we sure that Thou knowest all things, and needest not that any man should ask Thee : by this we believe that Thou camest forth from God.

Had not our LORD indeed spoken as plainly with reference to their difficulty, before ?(*l*) Was He really speaking no " proverb ;" that is, uttering no difficult saying, now ? What then is the meaning of His words in verse 25 ? The latter part of this reply of the Disciples is perhaps our best guide to the meaning of the earlier portion of it. Our LORD had shown by His entire discourse from ver. 19 to ver. 28, that unto Him the hearts of the Disciples were open ; the question they desired to ask Him, known ; that, in short, from Him no secrets are hid : and this astounding discovery drew from those guileless men their present prompt and hearty confession of His Divinity. Their entire reply, therefore, will have perhaps amounted to this : —" Lo, now Thou declarest Thy Divine Original quite plainly. We have now heard Thee even more emphatically than ever we heard Thee before, proclaim whence Thou camest and whither Thou goest. We recall the many occasions on which Thou hast spoken of Thyself as the very and Eternal SON of GOD ;(*m*) as of the same Nature with the FATHER ;(*n*) as One with the FATHER ;(*o*) entitled to the same Faith(*p*) and Love(*q*) as Himself. And *now*, because Thou connectest with

(*h*) 2 Tim. iii. 16.
(*i*) Compare St. John viii. 42, (where see the note,) and xvii. 8.
(*k*) Ephes. iv. 9, 10. Compare St. John iii. 13.
(*l*) Consider the following expressions : "I proceeded forth and came from GOD :" (St. John viii. 42,) " and now I go My way to Him that sent Me," (xvi. 5.) " I go to My FATHER, and ye see Me no more," (ver. 10.)—Grotius, with his usual acuteness, points out that the words " I leave the world," occur here for the first time. But are they not *fully* implied by St. John xiv. 18 to 31?

(*m*) St. John vii. 29, &c.   (*n*) St. John x. 38 : xiv. 9, 10, 20, &c.
(*o*) St. John x. 30.   (*p*) St. John xiv. 1.
(*q*) St. John xv. 23, 24.

all this a convincing *proof* that Thou art indeed the Searcher of Hearts, we believe all that is implied by that mysterious saying, 'I came forth from GOD!'"

Take notice that, because the particular circumstance which wrought conviction in the Disciples was the discovery that when they wished to ask our LORD a question, His words had shown that for them to ask was superfluous,— they ground their confession on this circumstance. Else, the natural form of words for them to have used would have been,—" and *needest not to ask* any man."

It is not, of course, to be thought that the Disciples did not believe before:(r) or that they so believed now, that their Faith could receive no future increase. Faith admits of degrees;(s) and one of the periods is here marked when the Disciples, (even Nathaniel,(t) and Simon Peter,)(u) made a clear advance in this heavenly grace. Their emphatic "Now," twice repeated, suggests the form of our LORD's reply.

31, 32 JESUS answered them, Do ye now believe? Behold, the hour cometh, yea, is now come, that ye shall be scattered, every man to his own, and shall leave Me alone: and yet I am not alone, because the FATHER is with Me.

As if He said,—" Do ye think yourselves now at length, 'grounded and settled' in the Faith?"(x) (for our LORD is probably asking a question here, as in chap. xiii. 38.) "Behold, the hour cometh, yea, is now come, that ye shall be scattered"— like sheep when their Shepherd is smitten. Consider St. Matthew xxvi. 31. The allusion is obviously to that hour, now so very close at hand, when, at sight of the treachery of Judas and its consequences, "all the disciples forsook Him, and fled."(y)

Take notice, that even while delivering this mournful prophecy, our SAVIOUR proclaimed a great truth concerning His own Divinity; thus administering twofold support to that very Faith which He yet foresaw would fail. He was so "One" with GOD the FATHER, by the sameness of His Essence, that He could not be separated from the FATHER; nor be, in a divine sense, "alone." Consider chap. viii. 16, 29. A good man has said, "There is something inexpressively touching in these simple words, when we remember the relation between the Speaker and those whom He addressed . . . We cannot read them without having our thoughts led to the misery and woe which for our sakes He endured; to the mightiness of that struggle for which He resigned the presence, and the aid and the comfort of the Everlasting FATHER."(z)

Our SAVIOUR with two short sentences brings His Heavenly discourse to a close:

33 These things I have spoken unto you, that in Me ye might have Peace.

Referring to all that He had been lately saying; but especially, as it would seem, to what is found in verses 5, 7, 8, and 13 to 16;— as, the expediency of His departure, the comfort and aid of the HOLY GHOST, the mysterious promise of His return. The purpose with which all this had been spoken, is declared briefly; namely, that in CHRIST the Apostles "might have Peace." And here it may be well to remind the reader that we had a similar form of expression, and announcement of a purpose, in ver. 1. It is thought that the places referred to at foot of the page, will be also found to merit attention.(a)

It was not the object of the present Divine Discourse, therefore, to gratify curiosity, or to solve doubts; (for *that* was reserved for the HOLY GHOST;(b) but to administer heavenly consolation. All that is implied by that largest word of blessedness,—" the Peace of GOD,"—would largely flow into the Disciples' hearts when the COMFORTER should bring this farewell discourse of their LORD and Master to their remembrance.

In the World ye shall have tribulation: but be of good cheer; I have overcome the World.

(r) Consider St. John ii. 11, and vi. 69.
(t) St. John i. 48 to 50.
(x) Col. i. 23.
(z) Rev. Hugh James Rose.
(b) See the note on St. John.

(s) St. Luke xvii. 5.
(u) St. Matth. xvi. 15 to 17.
(y) St. Matth. xxvi. 56.
(a) St. John xiii. 19: xiv. 29: xv. 11: xvi. 1, 4.

Thus He foretells the World's Enmity; but, at the same time, promises His own mightier aid. "*I have overcome* the World," He says; because His Victory, to be obtained over the Prince of this World, was already close at hand: and though His Death was to be the price of it, it was to be complete, and it was altogether certain.(*t*) Thus, in a former chapter, He had said, "Now is the judgment of this World; now shall the Prince of this World be cast out."(*u*)

And this encouragement to cheerful confidence is addressed to all believers in CHRIST to the end of Time. Moreover the successful warfare of the great Captain of our Salvation is to be imitated by His faithful soldiers and servants,—as every baptized Christian is called at the very font, when he is exhorted "manfully to fight under His banner, against Sin, the World, and the Devil." It was the confession of an Apostle that "we wrestle not against flesh and blood; but against Principalities and Powers; against the Rulers of the darkness of this World; against spiritual wickedness in high places."(*v*) "But," (it was his boast,) "thanks be to GOD which giveth us the victory through our LORD JESUS CHRIST!" (*x*) And so, in many striking places, says St. John,(*y*)—once, with apparent reference to the present occasion.(*z*)

CHAPTER XVII.

1 CHRIST *prayeth to His* FATHER *to glorify Him,* 6 *to preserve His Apostles.* 11 *in Unity,* 17 *and Truth,* 20 *to glorify them, and all other believers with Him in Heaven.*

THE Discourse which the SAVIOUR of the World held to His sorrowful Disciples on the evening before His Passion having extended through three chapters, and reached its close in the preceding chapter, His great Intercession follows. In order to approach it intelligently, we must consider that our Eternal High-Priest, by solemn prayer, is here consecrating Himself as the great Sacrifice to GOD the FATHER. Now, the office of the Priesthood consisted of two parts, *Sacrifice* and *Intercession.* The first was fulfilled by our LORD's "one oblation of Himself once offered;" the second, which continues still, (for "He ever liveth to make intercession,")(*a*) and gives efficacy to the other, is in the present chapter set before us. "It was with reference to this part of the office, which He still sustains, that He showed Himself to St. John in Patmos, in "a garment down to the feet,"(*b*)—the sacerdotal robe: and, afterwards, as an Angel, mixing in a "golden censer the prayers of all the Saints,(*c*) with the incense,—which represents His own prevailing Intercession."(*d*)

We seem to require no better reason for the introduction of this prayer in this place. Speculation is in fact swallowed up in a sense of gratitude and wonder at the Divine condescension, which here presents us with a specimen of the mysterious intercourse which the Son of Man held with the Eternal FATHER in the days of His Humiliation. "We can never thank GOD enough that He has permitted us to hear such words; to come, as it were, into the Council of Heaven; and to hear what CHRIST our LORD says concerning us to the Almighty FATHER. Not that He speaks in His invisible Godhead, of things that are too deep for us to hear; but as Man, in our own nature, of things that much concern us."(*e*) . . . "Plain and artless as this address sounds, it is so deep, rich, and wide, that no one can find its bottom or extent."(*f*) A celebrated foreign Divine declared that he never ventured to preach on this Prayer of CHRIST; humbly confessing that "the right understanding of it surpasses the measure of faith which the LORD usually imparts to His people during their earthly pilgrimage."(*g*) Need it be stated that from countless

---

(*t*) St. John xiv. 30.
(*v*) Ephesians vi. 12.
(*y*) 1 St. John ii. 13, 14: v. 4. Rev. xii. 11.
(*a*) Hebrews vii. 25.
(*c*) Rev. viii. 3.   (*d*) Dr. Macbride. See Ps. cxli. 2.
(*e*) Rev. C. Marriott
(*g*) Quoted from Spener by Olshausen.

(*u*) St. John xii. 31.
(*x*) 1 Cor. xv. 57.
(*s*) 1 St. John iv. 4.
(*b*) Rev. i. 13.
Rev. v. 8: viii. 3, 4.
(*f*) Luther.

passages in the Gospel the Commentator also would fain turn aside, if he might, with the ejaculation of Simon Peter on his lips,—"Depart from me; for I am a sinful man, O LORD!"(h) .. The scene of all that is contained in the present chapter was doubtless still the same as that indicated in the note prefixed to chap. xv. Our great High Priest makes His prayer for Himself and for His people within the very precincts of His Holy Temple.

These words spake JESUS, and lifted up His eyes to Heaven, and said,

Take notice of the precious indication of the gesture with which our SAVIOUR pronounced the words which follow. Compare chap. xi. 41, and St. Mark vi. 41. If the Publican, in the parable, did not presume to do the like,(i) it was because he was overwhelmed by the sense of Sin,—which in CHRIST had not the slightest place. . . . There are far more indications in our LORD's manner and gesture contained in the Gospels than a careless reader would suppose.

FATHER, the hour is come; glorify Thy SON, that Thy SON also may glorify Thee;

That " Hour," thrice mysteriously hinted at in the beginning of the Gospel, as " not yet come,"(k) and now, for the third, almost for the fourth time, declared to have at length arrived,(l)—is twice called the hour " that the Son of Man should be glorified."(m) By that expression we find is denoted our LORD's Triumph over Death, His Ascension into Heaven, and exaltation to the right hand of GOD ;(n) which were all preliminary steps to that outpouring of the SPIRIT,(o) whereby the Eternal SON was to be yet further " glorified,"—as we have heard Himself so recently declare.(p) But the reader must be referred on this subject to what has been already so largely offered in another part of the present Commentary."(q)

The sense of the passage will therefore be, that the Son of Man, having reached the close of His Ministry, prays the Eternal FATHER, (who wills that men should pray for those very things which He hath yet pledged Himself to grant,(r) to glorify Him,—even by raising Him from the dead, and receiving Him up into Glory; in order that He may in turn glorify the FATHER,—even by causing the knowledge of the FATHER to spread throughout the World, and by thus bringing many unto Salvation. Consider St. John xv. 8. Augustine explains the passage,—" Raise Me from the dead, that by Me Thou mayest be known to the whole World." See more on ver. 5. CHRIST speaks here in His Mediatorial character. So also in the next verse. The fulfillment of all that is here prayed for is described in Ephesians i. 20 to 23.

" Some things," (says Hooker,) " He knew should come to pass, and notwithstanding prayed for them; because He also knew that the necessay means to effect them were His prayers. As in the Psalm it is said, 'Ask of Me, and I shall give Thee the heathen for Thine inheritance, and the uttermost parts of the Earth for Thy possession.'(s) Wherefore, that which GOD there promiseth His SON, the same He here prayeth for." . . . The pious writer goes on to show that our SAVIOUR had not the like promise concerning every thing for which He prayed : observing,— " We know in what sort He prayed for removal of that bitter cup, which cup He tasted, notwithstanding His prayer."(t)

2 As Thou hast given Him power over all flesh, that He should give eternal life to as many as Thou hast given Him.

That is,—" Even as Thou hast already given Him authority over all human creatures ;(u) and so effectually given it, that He is able to impart Eternal Life to as many as Thou hast given Him." . . . . The connection of this with what precedes,

(h) St. Luke v. 8.
(k) St. John ii. 4 : vii. 30: viii. 20.
(l) St. John xii. 23, and xiii. 1.   Consider xiii. 31.
(m) St. John xii. 23 : xiii. 31.
(o) St. John vii. 39 : xvi. 7. Acts ii. 33.
(q) See the notes on St. John xiii. 31 and 32: on vii. 39 : on xii. 28.
(r) See St. John xii. 28.
(t) St. Matthew xxvi. 39. St. Mark xiv. 36. St. Luke xxii. 42.
(u) Compare St. Luke iii. 6.

(i) St. Luke xviii. 13.

(n) St. John xii. 16.
(p) St. John xvi. 14.

(s) Psalm ii. 8.

seems to be somewhat of the following nature. The Divine Speaker has been anticipating the work whereby He is shortly to "glorify" the FATHER. Here, therefore, He enlarges slightly on that subject; hinting, both at the vastness of the field of Mercy which lies before Him; and at the earnest of what is to follow, which He possesses in the Divine gift which the FATHER has already bestowed. "For being set down at the Right Hand of GOD, 'all authority hath been committed to Him both in Heaven and Earth;'(x) and the end of this power which He hath received is, to confer Salvation upon those which believe in Him. For 'we look for the SAVIOUR, the LORD JESUS CHRIST, who shall change our vile body that it may be fashioned like unto His glorious Body.'"(y) A thoughtful study of St. John v. 22 to 27, inclusive, and of chap. vi. 37 to 40, will be found to furnish a valuable commentary on the present verse. Consider also chap. iii. 35.

"The following verse shows, in a precise manner, how the communication of Eternal Life is a glorification of the FATHER, this life consisting in the knowledge of GOD Himself."(z)

3 And this is Life Eternal, that they might know Thee the only true GOD, and JESUS CHRIST, whom Thou hast sent.

Rather,—"*To know* Thee the only true GOD," &c. Who that reads this, does not exclaim with the Psalmist of old, "Thy thoughts are very deep?" . . "Of course we are not to take our LORD'S words so far out of their proper meaning as to suppose that He means a mere barren knowledge, such as Balaam had."(a) Nor may we explain them away, by advancing such an obvious truism concerning them as that the knowledge of GOD is *the condition* of our entrance into Life Eternal. Far more is implied; even *this*,—that "to *know* GOD," (according to the mind of the SPIRIT,) is to have become a partaker of His Nature: so that none can be said to know Him, save those to whom GOD imparts Himself. Consider 1 St. John v. 12. Hence, one of the ancients,(b) after declaring that "Life results from the participating of GOD, remarks that 'to know Him, and to have experience of His graciousness, *is* the very participation of Him.' . . . . The mysterious depth of the Divine language on such occasions is much to be noted, as supplying a clue to the meaning of many kindred passages, of which we might else little suspect the wondrous fullness. Thus, our LORD says—"He that believeth on Me hath everlasting Life:"(c) and elsewhere, "He that heareth My Word, and believeth on Him that sent Me, hath everlasting Life."(d) Again, "Whosoever liveth and believeth in Me, shall never die."(e) It is evident that a clue to the right understanding of all these passages is to be sought for in the true notion of "*belief;*" just as the true notion of "*knowing* GOD" furnishes us with a clue to the meaning of the text. It results from all, that "GOD is the life of the soul, as much as the soul is the life of the body: and that we must not think of Eternal Life as a thing to be begun *hereafter*; but as something to be begun *now*. The Life of Glory is, in fact, the Life of Grace continued."(f) See more on this subject in the notes on St. John v. 24: vi. 47, and xi. 26.

"Life Eternal," then, consists in the "knowledge" of the FATHER, who alone of all gods is very GOD;(g) in saying which, take notice that the Son of Man is speaking *as* the Son of Man. Yet, even so, He straightway represents Himself as co-ordinate with GOD the FATHER; by adding, "*and* JESUS CHRIST *whom Thou hast sent.*" The meaning of this is put out of all doubt by the passages alluded to at foot; where our Divine LORD plainly represents *Himself* as the proper object of human Faith.(h) Especially should reference be made to 1 St. John v. 11, 12, 20,—in which last verse the very language here applied to the FATHER will be found used of the SON.

4 I have glorified Thee on the Earth: I have finished the work which Thou gavest Me to do.

(x) St. Matth. xxviii. 18.
(z) Olshausen.
(b) Irenæus.
(d) St. John v. 24: see the whole verse.
(f) Rev. C. Marriott.
(g) Such is the meaning of the expression "the only true GOD."
(h) St. John iii. 15, 16, 36: vi. 47: xi. 25, 26.

(y) Bp. Pearson, quoting Phil. iii. 20, 21.
(a) Rev. C. Marriott.
(c) St. John vi. 47: compare iii. 36.
(e) St. John xi. 26.

The latter part of this sentence explains the former part. By performing the great work which the FATHER had given Him to do.—by His miracles,(i) by His Doctrine,(k) by His pure and spotless Life, by the call of the Twelve, and by laying the foundation of the Church,— the SON had glorified the FATHER upon the Earth. See more on verse 6.

Thus, on that memorable occasion, so largely treated of in a former part of the Commentary, where our SAVIOUR was entering on the first portion of His earthly inheritance, in reply to the request of His Disciples that He would "eat," we heard Him declare,—"My meat is to do the will of Him that sent Me, *and to finish His work* :(m) and of His miracles generally, He afterwards said,—" *The works which the* FATHER *gave Me to finish*, the very works which I do, bear witness concerning Me that the FATHER hath sent Me."(n) . . . If the Holy One asserted that He had already finished the great Work for which He came into the World, although the final triumph over Satan remained yet to be won, it may well be thought that inasmuch as a few hours of conflict alone remained, He spoke by anticipation of what was now so certain. Polycarp, (a disciple of St. John the Evangelist,) is thought to have written as follows :—" How doth He say that He hath finished the Work of Man's Salvation, since He hath not yet climbed the standard of the Cross? Nay, but, by the determination of His Will, whereby He had resolved to endure every article of His mysterious Passion, He may truly proclaim that He hath finished the Work." Shall St. Paul say concerning himself, in his old age, "I have fought a good fight, *I have finished my course* :"(o) and shall not the Incarnate SON anticipate, by some seventeen hours, the triumphant cry—" *It is finished?*"(p)

5 And now, O FATHER, glorify Thou Me with Thine own self with the Glory which I had with Thee before the World was.

The Holy One here prays His FATHER to confer on Himself, as GOD *and Man* that Glory which, as GOD, He had from all Eternity with the FATHER. " Bring My Human Nature into a participation of the Glory, which I, the WORD, had with Thee before the beginning of the World."(q) . . . A more splendid assertion of the pre-existence of our SAVIOUR CHRIST, could not be desired.(r) " The LORD possessed Me in the beginning of His Way, before His works of old," saith Wisdom. " I was set up from Everlasting, from the beginning, or ever the World was :"(s) (" before the foundation of the World," as it is said below in v. 24.) " And the same Wisdom of GOD, being made Man, reflecteth upon the same priority, saying, ' Now, O FATHER, glorify Thou Me with Thine own self,' (that is, ' in Thine own presence,') ' with the glory which I had with Thee before the World was.' "(t)

The Very and Eternal GOD, who was of one Substance with the FATHER, having taken Man's nature in the womb of the Blessed Virgin, of her substance, two whole and perfect Natures, that is to say, the Godhead and Manhood, became joined together in one Person *never to be divided*.(u) And it is for the Divine glorification of this new Being, very GOD and very Man, that the Eternal SON is thought here to pray. This was He who, " being in the form of GOD, thought it not robbery to be equal with GOD: but made Himself of no reputation, and took upon Him the form of a servant, and was made in the likeness of men : and being found in fashion as a man, He humbled Himself, and became obedient unto death, even the death of the Cross. Wherefore GOD also *hath highly exalted Him*."(x) Consider the latter part of ver. 24.

6 I have manifested Thy Name unto the men which Thou gavest Me out of the World :

It was in this manner, in part, that our SAVIOUR had glorified His FATHER on the Earth, (as we heard Him declare in ver. 4,) and finished the Work which the FATHER had given Him to do.—But *how* did He " manifest," that is, make plain

(i) See St. John ii. 11: xi. 4, 40.
(m) St. John iv. 34.
(o) 2 Tim. iv. 7.
(q) Theophylact.
(r) Consider St. John i. 1, 2: vi. 62: viii. 58. Col. i. 17. 1 St. John i. 1, 2, &c.
(s) Prov. viii. 22, 23.
(u) Article II.

(k) See St. John vii. 16, 18.
(n) St. John v. 36. Compare also ix. 4.
(p) St. John xix. 30,—where see the note.

(t) Bp. Pearson.
(x) Phil. ii. 6 to 9.

and manifest, ("make *known*," as it is said in ver. 26,) GOD's "Name" upon Earth? Doubtless, the word "Name" is here used in that large signification, so well known to the readers of Holy Scripture, whereby it is made to stand for GOD Himself. "The Name of the GOD of Jacob defend thee!"(y) exclaims the Psalmist: and the author of the Book of Proverbs declares that "the Name of the LORD is a strong tower; the righteous runneth into it and is safe."(z) "They shall call His Name Emmanuel," says the Evangelist, quoting the prophet Isaiah,(a) and implying that our SAVIOUR Himself would be, what the Name "Emmanuel" means,—namely, "GOD with us."(b) As often therefore as our LORD made known to men the mind and will of the Eternal FATHER,—(as when He declared that "GOD so loved the World that He gave His Only-Begotten SON, to the end that whosoever believeth in Him should not perish, but have everlasting Life,")(c)—or work miracles in token of His Divine Mission,(d) —so often did He "*manifest His Name.*"

This manifestation, then, is said to have been made to the men whom GOD the FATHER "gave" the SON. By which, it is not meant that there were any of the Jewish nation to whom the REDEEMER did *not* preach the Gospel; much less is it implied that He had kept from any the knowledge of the FATHER,—whom to know is Everlasting Life:(e) but only, that not all who heard believed. And those believed whom GOD had given Him,—and none others: for "no man can come to Me," (saith our LORD,) "except the FATHER which hath sent Me draw him."(f) This may seem to open the hard question of Predestination and Election; into which we have neither the ability, nor the leisure, nor the inclination here to enter. *This* at least is certain, that unbelief is represented to us throughout the Bible *as a Sin.* See St. John xvi. 9.—What else we desire to offer on this deep subject will be found below, in the note on the latter part of ver. 12.

Thine they were, and Thou gavest them Me: and they have kept Thy Word.

"'Thine they were,'—in Thy secret Predestination unknown to Man and inscrutable;"(g) "and Thou gavest them Me." Thus, for the second time, the "gift" of the FATHER is mentioned. It will be found alluded to further, below, in verses 11, 12, and 24. "As One with the FATHER, our SAVIOUR had before said, 'I have chosen you out of the World;'(h) but here, as Son of Man, He attributes it, not to His own election of them, but to the gift of the FATHER!"(i)

7 Now they have known that all things whatsoever Thou hast given Me are of Thee.

"For having obeyed the Word, they have come to know the Doctrine, whether it be of GOD, or whether I speak of Myself."(k) Take notice how constantly the Eternal SON refers everything He has—even His very essence,—to the Eternal FATHER. This has been already largely dwelt upon in the Commentary on St. John v. 20, and on the latter part of xiv. 28. It appears, however, from ver. 8, that what is here printed "things," should rather have been "*words.*"

8 For I have given unto them the words which Thou gavest Me;

"Therefore CHRIST hath revealed the perfect Will of GOD."(l) He had before said, "The Word which ye hear is not Mine, but the FATHER's which sent Me."(m) The present statement should in fact be connected and compared with what is found in chap. vii. 16, 17: viii. 28: xii. 49, and xiv. 10. See also chap. v. 19, 30.

and they have received *them*, and have known surely that I came out from Thee, and they have believed that Thou didst send Me.

"*This* also our LORD often alludes to; namely, that by keeping His words men

(y) Ps. xx. 1.
(a) St. Matth. i. 23, quoting Is. vii. 14.
(c) St. John iii. 16.
(e) See above ver. 3.
(g) Williams.
(h) St. John xv. 19: See also xiii. 18: xv. 16.
(i) Williams.
(l) Bp. Pearson.

(z) Prov. xviii. 10.
(b) Consider further, Exod. vi. 3.
(d) St. John x. 25.
(f) St. John vi. 44.

(k) Williams,—quoting St. John vii. 17.
(m) St. John xiv. 24.

come to know the FATHER: for He says, 'Whosoever shall receive Me receiveth Him that sent Me.' "(*n*)   Refer to verses 27 and 30 of the preceding chapter, and see the note there.   See also below, ver. 25.(*o*)

Having, up to this place, prayed for Himself, and specified the grounds of His own right to that Glory for which He prayed,—our SAVIOUR now makes the Disciples the subject of His request:—

9 I pray for them: I pray not for the World, but for them which Thou hast given Me; for they are Thine.

Take notice that the word in the original is not so much "I *pray*," as, "I *ask*," or "*make request;*" and so, in ver. 20. . . . CHRIST died for all; He willed the Salvation of all men.   Yet, inasmuch as it depended on the will of others whether those gracious intentions should be frustrated or not, and He foresaw the obduracy of many, He says, "I pray not for the World:" meaning thereby the hardened and impenitent. . . . "In that prayer for Eternal Life," (says Hooker,) "which our SAVIOUR knew could not be made without effect, He excepteth them for whom He knew His sufferings would be frustrate, and commendeth unto GOD His own. They are the blessed of GOD, for whom He ordained His Kingdom:(*p*) to their charge nothing can be laid:(*q*) of them, those words of the wise man are meant, that 'none can hinder, when He will save.' "(*r*)   "For this is that great prayer of Intercession on which the Salvation of the Church depended, and the prayer of CHRIST cannot but be availing to the attainment of that for which He prays. Thus, when He prayed for His murderers, the Centurion, (who was one of them,) on that day believed: and when St. Stephen prayed for his persecutors, St. Paul, the chief of them, was pardoned."(*s*)

The plea, or reason, follows: — "Because *they are Thine.*"   In ver. 6, we heard Him say,—"Thine *they were,* and Thou gavest them Me."   Very naturally therefore does it follow:

10 And all Mine are Thine, and Thine are Mine; and I am glorified in them.

"'Thine are Mine;' therefore they belonged unto CHRIST before they were given by the FATHER.   'And all Mine are Thine;' therefore, after they were given unto CHRIST, they belonged unto the FATHER."(*t*)   "As if to imply, — Let no one, on hearing Me say, 'them which Thou hast given Me,' suppose that they are separated from the FATHER; for all things that are Mine are His.   Nor, because I said, 'they are Thine,' suppose that they are separate from Me: for all things that are His, are Mine."(*u*)   "All things that the FATHER hath are Mine,"(*x*) our LORD had already declared:—by virtue of the Divine Unity, claiming such participation in the things of the FATHER. . . . But this is parenthetical.   The words "and I am glorified in them," cohere closely with the last words of ver. 9.   We are reminded thereby that CHRIST is glorified in His Saints, — by their life,(*y*) and by their death.(*z*)

11 And now I am no more in the World, but these are in the World, and I come to Thee.

Because He was so soon to leave the World, our LORD says, "Now *I am no more* in the World."   His allusion to the forlorn state of His Disciples recalls what we met with in chap. xiii. 1,—where see the note, on p. 541. . . . "I come to Thee" reminds us of the fuller statement we met with in ver. 28 of the former chapter.

Holy FATHER, keep through Thine own Name those whom Thou hast given Me, that they may be one, as We *are.*

The Eternal SON here used the epithet "Holy" in addressing the FATHER, (whom

(*n*) Williams,—quoting St. Luke ix. 48.   (*o*) Consider also St. John viii. 42.
(*p*) St. Matth. xxv. 34.   (*q*) Rom. viii. 33.
(*r*) Eccles. xxxix. 18.   (*s*) Williams.
(*t*) Williams.   (*u*) Chrysostom.
(*x*) St. John xvi. 15.   (*y*) 1 Cor. x. 31.
(*z*) St. John xxi. 19.

He calls "Just," in ver. 25,) perhaps because it was the sanctifying influence of the FATHER to which He chiefly alludes in the words, "*Keep* through Thine own Name those whom Thou hast given Me." Consider ver. 17 ; and take notice that St. Jude addresses His Epistle "to them that are sanctified by GOD the FATHER, and preserved in JESUS CHRIST."(*a*) The "Name" of GOD is here used in the same large signification as in verses 6, 12, and 26.

It might seem, to a careless reader, that the language of the present verse favors the error of those who deny the Divinity of the SON. If believers may be "one," as CHRIST and the FATHER are "One," then, (it may be thought,) there can be no such mystery in the Divine Unity as the Church teaches. But quite of a contrary kind is the direct and only lawful inference from the present passage. The Disciples of CHRIST being all of one nature, (and that, *Human*,) as GOD the FATHER and GOD the SON are both of One Nature, (and that, *Divine*,) our SAVIOUR here prays that the Disciples may all be of one mind and will likewise, even as Himself and the FATHER are of One Mind and Will. Take notice, however, that the word "as," here and in ver. 21, does not denote strict correspondence, but only general resemblance ; as in the Athanasian Creed, where the union of two Natures in the One Person of CHRIST is popularly illustrated by the union of "the reasonable soul and flesh" in man. Consider also in St. Matthew v. 48, St. Luke vi. 36, and the note on the former place. . . . . *Unity*, therefore, is what CHRIST and His Apostles(*b*) desire to behold in the Church. See more on ver. 21.

12 While I was with them in the World, I kept them in Thy Name:

The Divine Speaker says, "in *Thy* Name,"(*c*) because, throughout the period of His Humiliation and the days of His Ministry, He had referred all things, as the Son of Man, to the Eternal FATHER who had "sent" Him. But the repeated mention of the FATHER's "*Name*" in verses 6, 11, 12, and 26 of the present chapter, is remarkable.

those that Thou gavest Me I have kept, and none of them is lost, but the son of perdition ; that the Scripture might be fulfilled.

Thus does the Great Shepherd of the sheep give an account of His shepherding, in language which recalls the speech of one of His special types.(*e*) Our great Ministerial example is able to boast that He has not lost one of that little flock which the FATHER had committed to Him, — Judas Iscariot only excepted, whose designation, ("the son of perdition,") St. Paul applies to the "Man of Sin ;"(*f*) and who had fallen through his own determined wickedness, in defiance of checks, and helps, and warnings innumerable, — as we have elsewhere shown. "None of them is lost," (saith our LORD;) that is, As far as *I* am concerned : for, as He declares elsewhere more clearly, — "Him that cometh unto Me, I will in no wise cast out."(*h*) "But when they cast themselves out, I will not draw them to Myself by compulsion." So writes Chrysostom.

The ordinary reader will perhaps be grateful for a few words on the subject thus opened to his notice, — one of the deepest in the whole domain of speculative Theology. — "That Judas was *converted*, and, as far as concerned the present state, (abstracted from Perseverance,) *effectually converted*, I offer but this one testimony, —the words of CHRIST to His FATHER : "Of those that Thou gavest Me none is lost but the son of perdition." That whosoever is by the FATHER "given" to CHRIST, is *converted*, and that *effectually*, is concluded from CHRIST's universal proposition : "All that the FATHER giveth Me shall come to Me."(*i*) And here it is expressly said that Judas, though by his apostasy now become "the son of perdition," was by GOD given to CHRIST, and therefore he came to CHRIST; that is, he was converted : which also his being lost, his very apostasy, testifies ; for how could he apostatize from CHRIST, that was never come to Him ?" . . . . . . Of two persons therefore, (as two of the Apostles,) "supposing that the outward means are accompanied to both with a sufficient measure of inward Grace, the discrimination comes immediately from one man's *resisting* sufficient grace ; which the other doth *not* resist, but, *makes use of*. And as it is from corruption, and liberty to do evil, that

(*a*) St. Jude ver. 1.   (*b*) See 1 Cor. i. 10.
(*c*) The same Greek phrase is translated in the previous verse, "through Thine own Name."
(*e*) See Gen. xxxi. 38, 39.   (*f*) 2 Thess. ii. 3.
(*h*) St. John vi. 37.   (*i*) St. John vi. 37.

one resists it; so it is likely from the work of Grace upon an obedient heart, that the other is converted. Thus we ascribe all the good to the Work of Grace; that is, to that power which by supernatural Grace is given to man; and all the ill to man and his liberty, or ability to resist.

"But from what hath been said, there is yet more to be added; namely, that the obedience of the one to the call of Grace, when the other, (supposed to have sufficient, if not an equal measure,) obeys not, — may reasonably be imputed to the humble, malleable, melting temper which the other wanted; and that, again, owing to the preventing Graces of GOD, and not to the natural probity, or Free-Will of Man. Whereas the other, having resisted those preparing Graces, or not made use of them, lieth under some degree of obduration, pride, sloth, voluptuousness, &c., and that makes the discrimination on this side; that is, renders him unqualified and incapable to be wrought on by sufficient Grace. And so still, if it be attentively weighed, this attributes nothing to Free Will, considered by itself, but *the power of resisting and frustrating* GOD's *method;* yielding the glory of all the work of Conversion, and all the first preparations to it, to His sole Grace, by which the will is first set free; then, fitted and cultivated; and then, the seed of Eternal Life is successfully sowed in it."*(j)*

The place of Scripture specially intended by our LORD, seems to be that passage in Psalm cix., which St. Peter quoted on a memorable occasion, — "Let his days be few, and let another take his office."*(k)* If any could be so perverse as to suppose from the manner in which Holy Scripture is here referred to, that it was the intention of the Divine Speaker to imply that Judas was *under the necessity* of proving a Traitor, let him notice how effectually the suspicion is repelled by ver. 9 of the ensuing chapter; where the Apostles are said to have retired from the Garden of Gethsemane in safety, "that the saying might be fulfilled which He spake, Of them which Thou gavest Me have I lost none." The allusion of our LORD on that occasion is to the words before us.

13 And now come I to Thee; and these things I speak in the World, that they might have my Joy fulfilled in themselves.

An attentive reader of the Gospel will observe that our SAVIOUR has specified *the purpose* with which He delivered many of His recorded sayings, on this the last day of His earthly Ministry. Consider the following places,—St. John xiii. 19: xiv. 29: xv. 11: xvi. 1, 4, 33, &c. . . . . It seems to be here implied that one object of the present Intercession was, that when our LORD should be withdrawn from His Disciples' eyes, they might be filled, in full measure, with that joy which they had hitherto derived from His presence. Such seems to be the meaning of the expression, "that they may have my joy fulfilled in themselves:" with which, compare St. John xv. 11, and see the note on that place.

14 I have given them Thy Word; and the World hath hated them, because they are not of the World, even as I am not of the World.

His Doctrine, like every other thing which is His, the Eternal SON refers to the FATHER, as already pointed out in the note on ver. 7; and explained in the notes on chap. vii. 16, and xii. 49. . . . . Already, doubtless, the Apostles of the LAMB had had a foretaste of the treatment which they were to expect at the World's hands. It was especially, however, with reference to what was to follow, that our Blessed LORD thus proclaimed the World's hostility, and traced it to its source,— which He again notices, and in the selfsame words in ver. 16. This topic has been already urged in chap. xv. 19, where see the note. Compare the concluding words with chap. viii. 23.

15 I pray not that Thou shouldest take them out of the World, but that Thou shouldest keep them from the Evil.

Rather,—"from *the Evil One;*" that is, the Devil, who is repeatedly called "the Prince of this World."*(l)* The same meaning is doubtless intended by our LORD in St. Matthew v. 37; and by His Apostle, in St. John v. 19. . . . Hence we learn,

(*j*) From Dr. Hammond's Letter to Dr. Sanderson, concerning GOD's Grace and Decrees.
(*k*) Ver. 8, quoted in Acts i. 20. See also Ps. lxix. 25.
(*l*) See the note on St. John xii. 31.

that until our appointed earthly work is completed, Divine Love is concerned only to keep us from the power of the Enemy; *not to take us out of the World.*

16 They are not of the World, even as I am not of the World.

Why are these words, already met with in ver. 14, thus repeated? Is it in order to imply that the Disciples, however liable to harm from "the crafts and assaults of the Devil," (referred to in verse 15,) were in their disposition guileless and unworldly men?

17 Sanctify them through Thy Truth: Thy Word is Truth.

Simple words; yet full of difficulty, as usual. Their meaning seems to be as follows. It will be perceived that, from this place, our SAVIOUR is speaking of the *Ministry* of His Apostles. As a preliminary step therefore, He prays that they may be sanctified, — that is, duly set apart for the Ministerial Office, for the work of preaching the Gospel. "Separate them for the Ministry of the Word, and preaching," — as Chrysostom explains the place. Thus, St. Paul describes himself as "called to be an Apostle, separated unto the Gospel of GOD;"(*m*) even as Jeremiah from the womb was "sanctified," and ordained "a prophet unto the nations."(*n*) This thought, so familiar to persons living under the Law, the Divine Author of the Gospel here transfers to the new Dispensation. And because the Religion of CHRIST consists not of types and shadows, nor has any such ceremonial initiatory rites as attended the ordination of the Jewish priesthood, it is spoken of as approached through the sanctification of the Eternal WORD, who is the Truth itself. Consider St. John i. 14, 17: xiv. 6; and below, ver. 19. This is to "have an unction from the Holy One;" which anointing, as St. John elsewhere declares, is Truth itself.(*o*) The reader is invited to read what will be offered on this great subject, (the Gospel notion of *Truth,*) in the notes on chap. xviii. 37 and 38. . . . Our LORD, proceeds:

18 As Thou hast sent Me into the World, even so have I also sent them into the World.

Even as CHRIST was the Apostle, or Sent(*p*) of the FATHER, ("*the Apostle* and High Priest *of our profession,*"(*q*) as St. Paul calls Him,) so were the Twelve, the Apostles or Sent of CHRIST; (for take notice that "*Apostle*" means "one *sent*:") and our LORD speaks of Himself in a certain place, as "Him whom the FATHER *hath sanctified, and sent into the World.*"(*r*)—He uses here the past tense, ("I *have* sent them,") as in St. John iv. 58, for the reason specified in the note on that place. The mission of the Apostles "into the World" was yet future; dating its commencement partly from the moment when the words recorded in St. John xx. 21 were spoken, (the self-same words almost, as are found here;) and yet more strikingly from the Day of Pentecost, — until which time the Apostles were forbidden to leave Jerusalem.(*s*)

Two things seem to be especially intended by the parallel here established between the mission of CHRIST, and the mission of His Apostles. First, both were anointed in a similar manner; namely, not with material oil, but *with the* HOLY GHOST. Next,—both were sent forth with *the right of delegating authority* to others. But the reader must be referred on this head to the note on St. John xx. 21,— where the subject will be more fitly introduced.

19 And for their sakes I sanctify Myself, that they also might be sanctified through the Truth.

All is for our sakes! . . . . The Holy One continues His allusion to the Ceremonial Law, pointed out in the note on verse 17. Thus, because He was about to offer Himself up to the Eternal FATHER; and because whatsoever was dedicated or set apart for GOD's service, was said, in legal language, to be "sanctified;"(*t*) He

(*m*) Rom. i. 1: and see Gal. i. 15.   (*n*) Jer. i. 5.
(*o*) 1 St. John ii. 20, 27. Perhaps St. John viii. 31, 32 should also be compared.
(*p*) The reader is referred to the note on St. John ix. 7.
(*q*) Heb. iii. 1.   (*r*) St. John x. 36.
(*s*) Acts i. 4, 5.
(*t*) See Ex. xiii. 2. (Compare Numb. xviii. 15, 16, 17,) xxix. 36, 44: xxx. 29, &c. Joel i. 14: ii. 15.

declares that, for the Apostles' sake, He "*sanctifies Himself.*" Not meaning that He could be *made more holy* than He was already, — in whom "dwelt all the fullness of the Godhead bodily ;"(*u*) but saying of Himself the same thing which is said in Heb. ix. 14 ; and announced in St. John x. 11 and 15 : namely, "And for their sakes, I offer Myself as a sacrifice unto Thee."(*v*)

And this "sanctification," in a legal sense, we find had for its object the *actual* sanctification of the Apostles to their Ministerial Office. At the Consecration of Priests, under the Mosaic Law, a sacrifice was prescribed,(*x*) with many singular ceremonies ; but now, the great Sacrifice for the sins of the whole World was about to be offered up. It is, therefore, as if our LORD had said, — In the room of that sacrifice, and of all those other ceremonies which were practised at the consecration and sanctification of the Ministers of the Old Testament, lo, I am about to offer up Myself on the Altar of the Cross. And since this Mighty Sacrifice of Myself is the very substance of which all those others were but shadows, the Truth of which all those were but Types, My Apostles being thereby sanctified will be *sanctified through the Truth.*(*y*)

With reference to His words in ver. 9, (" I pray for them,") our SAVIOUR proceeds :

20 Neither pray I for these alone, but for them also which shall believe on Me through their word :

" The Apostles believed in CHRIST through His own Word ; and the primitive Christians believed on the same CHRIST through the Apostles' word ; and this distinction our SAVIOUR Himself hath clearly made. Not that the word of the Apostles was really distinct from the word of CHRIST ; but only it was called theirs, because delivered by their Ministry : otherwise it was the same word which they had heard from Him, and upon which they themselves believed."(*z*)

21 that they all may be one ; as Thou, FATHER, *art* in Me, and I in Thee, that they also may be one in us :

Rather, "As Thou, FATHER in Me, and I in Thee,(*a*) [are One,] — that they also may in us be one."(*b*) . . . "We must particularly observe that our LORD did not say, " that *We* may all be one ;" but " that *they* may all be one." For the FATHER is so in the SON that they are One because they are of one substance. We can be one *in* Them, but not *with* Them ; because we and They are not of one substance. They are in us, and we in Them, so as that They are one in Their nature ; we, in ours. They are in us, as GOD is in the Temple ; we in Them, as the creature is in its Creator. Wherefore, He adds " *in us*," to show that our being made one by charity is to be attributed to the grace of GOD, not to ourselves."(*c*)

Thus does the SAVIOUR's prevailing Prayer extend as far as to ourselves, and embrace the men of the present generation in its span of Mercy and Love : for the prayer is unto us, and to our "children, and to all that are afar off, even as many as the LORD our GOD shall call."(*d*) Let us well observe that the thing which CHRIST especially desires for the Church, is *Unity*, — here for the second time mentioned ; from which the guilt of Schism, the offence of "division,"(*e*) appears in the strongest light.(*f*) On this occasion it is not merely said " that they may be one, *as we are ;*" but by a striking enlargement of phrase, the nature and manner of the unity of believers is described. For men can only be " one" in GOD the FATHER and GOD the SON, by believing in " One LORD," professing " one Faith," being made partakers of " one Baptism :"(*g*) being, in short, one *in Spirit ;* " having," (as the Apostle says,) " the same love, being of one accord, of one mind."(*h*) As often, moreover, as " with a true penitent heart and lively faith" we receive the Sacrament of CHRIST's Body and Blood, do we not "dwell in CHRIST, and CHRIST in us ?" are we not "*one with* CHRIST, *and* CHRIST *with us ?*"

The consequence foreseen by the Divine Speaker of such Unity in His Church, follows :

(*u*) Col. ii. 9.
(*x*) Exod. xxix. 10, 15, 19, 25, &c.
(*z*) Bp. Pearson.
(*b*) See Gal. iii. 28.
(*d*) Acts ii. 39.
(*f*) See above, ver. 11 ; also below, ver. 22.
(*h*) Phil. ii. 2.—Consider Rom. xii. 5. Ephes. iv. 3.

(*v*) Chrysostom.
(*y*) So Maldonatus.
(*a*) Compare St. John xiv. 10, 11, &c.
(*c*) Augustine.
(*e*) 1 Cor. i. 10, &c.
(*g*) Eph. iv. 5.

That the World may believe that Thou hast sent Me.

The meaning must be, that the sight of unanimity among Disciples, the discovery that "the multitude of them that believed were of one heart and one soul,"(i) would so impress beholders, as to convince them that the Author of Christianity must have been sent from Heaven; that the Gospel can have been no human invention, but must have come from GOD.—Very similar to these were the words which our SAVIOUR addressed to His Disciples in chap. xiii. 35,—where see the note.

22 And the Glory which Thou gavest Me I have given them; that they may be one, even as We are One:

By "the Glory" thus derived from the FATHER,(k) it has been thought that the Eternal SON refers to that glorious Spirit, which the FATHER "giveth not by measure unto Him."(l) He must be understood therefore here to say that He had made His Disciples "partakers of the Divine Nature,"(m) and surely this was pre-eminently done by the gift of the Sacrament of His Body and Blood, which He had just instituted. Consider, by all means, 1 Cor. x. 16, 17; where the participation of CHRIST in the LORD's Supper is noticed as the very condition of that oneness of believers of which our SAVIOUR here, for the third time, speaks.(n) . . . The power of working *Miracles*,(o) seems to have been rather the consequence of the gift here spoken of, than the gift itself.

23 I in them, and Thou in Me, that they may be made perfect in one;

Is the meaning perhaps to be made out thus,—"[Inasmuch as] I [am] in them, and Thou [art] in Me, that they may be made perfectly one?" For it is evidently implied that since the FATHER and His CHRIST are One, and since CHRIST and His Disciples are one,—the Disciples must be one with the FATHER: according to that of the Apostle,— "all things are yours: and ye are CHRIST's; and CHRIST is GOD's."(p) "This communion of the Saints with the SON of GOD," (says Bishop Pearson,) "is, as most evident, so most remarkable."

And that the World may know that Thou hast sent Me, and hast loved them, as Thou hast loved Me.

From the FATHER's love, thus declared in the Disciples, the Divine Speaker anticipates the same blessed result which has been already remarked upon in the note on the latter part of ver. 21.

In what follows, the requests of the SON of Man extend beyond this World: stretching out into the far and glorious Future of the blessed.

24 FATHER, I will that they also, whom Thou hast given Me, be with Me where I am;

Rather, "I *wish;*" that is, "I request."(q) And O the unspeakable condescension of that wish on the lips of the Eternal SON!—even that He may be united throughout the ages of Eternity to the men whom the FATHER had given Him; that is, to as many as being called according to GOD's purpose by His SPIRIT working in due season, shall by grace obey the calling.(r) For take notice, that more is said here than in St. John xii. 26, and xiv. 3. CHRIST's faithful servants shall be throughout Eternity not only "where" CHRIST is, but "*with*" Him(s) likewise. "If we suffer we shall also reign with Him," says the great Apostle, writing to Timothy.(t) . . . He wishes, therefore, that His own may be with Him,—

(i) Acts iv. 32.
(k) Consider St. John i. 14, (in the original,) and 2 St. Pet. i. 17.
(l) St. John iii. 34.   Consider 2 Cor. iii. 18.
(m) 2 St. Pet. i. 4.
(o) Consider St. John ii. 11 : xi. 40.
(q) See verses 9 and 20.
(s) See 1 Thess. iv. 17.

(n) See verses 11 and 21.
(p) 1 Cor. iii. 22, 23.
(r) Article XVII.
(t) 2 Tim. ii. 12.

That they may behold My Glory, which Thou hast given Me : for
Thou lovest Me before the foundation of the World.

The reception of His Glory, (as of His Essence,)(u) the Eternal SON again refers
to the Almighty FATHER.(v) But in this place we are perhaps to consider that He
speaks of the Glory which He was to receive *as Man;* a subject already alluded to
in ver. 5, (where the mode of expression is very similar,) and explained in the note
thereon. . . . *To behold,* in this place, is doubtless *to be made a partaker of,*— as in
St. John iii. 3, (compared with ver. 5,) and 36 : also viii. 51, compared with ver. 52.
Irenæus calls attention to the gracious manner in which our LORD adverts to the
subject of His Glory ; namely, only in order to make request that His faithful
Disciples may share it with Him.

25 O righteous FATHER, the World hath not known Thee : but I
have known Thee, and these have known that Thou hast sent Me.

The Eternal FATHER is here addressed as "righteous," or "just," because it is in
virtue of this Divine attribute that none but believers in CHRIST will be admitted
to be where CHRIST eternally is.—Concerning the "knowledge" here spoken of, see
what has been already offered in the note on ver. 3.—The great truth concerning
the Son of Man which the Disciples are declared to have "known" has been made
the subject of comment already, in the note on the latter part of ver. 8.

26 And I have declared unto them Thy Name, and will declare *it :*

The largeness of the signification in which the *Name* of GOD is here spoken of,
has been sufficiently explained above, in the note on ver. 6.—The first words of the
verse before us marks the difference of our LORD's knowledge from that of His
Disciples, (alluded to in ver. 25 ;) for, "no man hath seen GOD at any time ; the
only-begotten SON, which is in the bosom of the FATHER, He hath declared Him."(x)

How CHRIST had hitherto "declared," or "made known," the FATHER's "Name,"
has been shown in the note on ver. 6. He was to make it yet better known, as He
here asserts,— referring probably to the great Pentecostal effusion of the SPIRIT
which was to do so much for the illumination of His Church. He may also allude
to that accession of knowledge in Divine things which the Apostles were to enjoy
during the great Forty days.(y)

that the love wherewith Thou hast loved Me may be in them, and I
in them.

This seems to mean, "that being made One with Me, by Faith and Love, Thou
mayest love them, with the same love, wherewith Thou lovest Me." The concluding clause, ("and I in them,") might almost be rendered, "Even as I am in them :"
and implies, that CHRIST being in His Disciples as the head is in the body, and
therefore *One* with them, it could not but be that the Love of the FATHER, which
was poured out upon the SON, must be poured out upon the Disciples likewise.
Consider St. John xiv. 23.

We cheerfully adopt the language of a pious Commentator at the close of his
notes on the present chapter. "After all our endeavours to explain it, we must
allow that our thoughts are swallowed up in those depths of Wisdom and Love, and
in those mysteries of the Godhead, with which it is replete ; and that the light of
Heaven alone can fully clear it up to us."(z)

On reviewing this solemn Address, it will be found that in the first five verses,
the Divine Speaker makes request for Himself : in the next three,(a) He introduces
the subject of His Apostles ; and then, prays for them.(b) Next, He prays for all
believers.(c) Lastly, looking beyond this World, He makes request that the men
whom His FATHER had given Him, might behold His future Glory, and be made
partakers of His Heavenly Joy. . . . "It may be observed that almost all the expressions of CHRIST to the FATHER, in the presence of the Disciples, seem to have a

(u) See above, on ver. 7.
(x) St. John i. 18.
(z) Rev. Thomas Scott.
(b) Verses 9 to 19.

(v) See above, ver. 22, and the note.
(y) See St. Luke xxiv. 45. Acts i. 3.
(a) Verses 6 to 8.
(c) Verses 20 to 23.

reference to things spoken in His previous discourse with them. In both alike He speaks of His Departure,—and of His being One with the FATHER,—of His union of Will with the FATHER,—of their union with Him,—of the World not knowing GOD, —of their love to each other, and sanctification in Him,—of the FATHER abiding with them in their love to each other. As if, in this twofold expression of the same things, first to Man and then to the FATHER, were contained some mysterious manifestation flowing from the ineffable union of CHRIST with GOD, and with Man : so that what He says to Man as their SAVIOUR and their Judge, He says also unto GOD, as their Intercessor and High Priest. But when He speaks to Man, it is for the Glory of GOD: and when He speaks to GOD, it is for the edification of Man."(d)

We imagine the little company, in attendance on their Divine LORD, now withdrawing solemnly from the precincts of the Temple where we conceive the fifteenth, sixteenth, and seventeenth chapters to have been spoken. They move in the direction of what is now called St. Stephen's gate ; and are soon seen descending by the path which will conduct them, across Cedron, to the Garden at the foot of the Mount of Olives.

CHAPTER XVIII.

1 *Judas betrayeth* JESUS. 6 *The officers fall to the ground.* 10 *Peter smiteth off Malchus' ear.* 12 JESUS *is taken, and led unto Annas and Caiaphas.* 15 *Peter's denial.* 19 JESUS *examined before Caiaphas.* 28 *His arraignment before Pilate.* 36 *His Kingdom.* 40 *The Jews ask Barabbas to be let loose.*

THE preceding chapter ended with the great Intercession of the SAVIOUR for His Church. Our High Priest is now bent on nothing so much as completing His great Sacrifice also. Accordingly,

When JESUS had spoken these words, He went forth with His Disciples over the brook Cedron, where was a Garden, into the which He entered, and His Disciples.

" He " went forth," or " out," of the Gate of Jerusalem. A slight declivity conducts to the brook Kidron, — which the Son of David now crosses, as His father David had done a thousand years before, in bitterness of spirit: flying from persecution and treachery. And it was in order to guide the reader to the typical bearing of that ancient history, that the Evangelist was divinely guided to introduce the mention of " Kidron" in this place. "All the country wept with a loud voice, and all the people passed over: the King also himself passed over *the brook Kidron*. . . . And David went up by the ascent of the Mount Olivet, and wept as he went up."(a) CHRIST also now " went, as He was wont, to the Mount of Olives."(b)

The word thus repeatedly translated "brook" means, in fact, a "winter-torrent ;" and such, precisely, " Cedron" is described to be by modern travellers. "The channel of the Valley of Jehoshaphat," (writes Dr. Robinson,) " the ' brook Kidron' of the Scriptures, is nothing more than the dry bed of a wintry torrent, bearing marks of being occasionally swept over by a large volume of water. No stream flows here now except during the heavy rains of winter, when the waters descend into it from the neighboring hills. Yet, even in winter, there is no constant flow ; and our friends, who had resided several years in the city, had never seen a stream running through the valley. Nor is there any evidence that there was anciently more water in it than at present." From the manner in which St. John writes the word, we discover that the Greek population of his day, overlooking the Hebrew original of Kidron, (which is derived from a root signifying to be

(d) Williams.   (a) 2 Sam. xv. 23, 30.   (b) St. Luke xxii. 39.

"dark" or "turbid," pronounced the name as if it were of Greek derivation, and meant "the brook *of Cedars.*"(c) Such perversions of words are common in all languages; remarkably, in our own.

St. John is also the only Evangelist who mentions that Gethsemane, the scene of our SAVIOUR's Passion, was *a Garden;* as well as that "in the place where he was crucified there was *a Garden;* and in the Garden a new sepulchre;" and that "there laid they JESUS."(d) Was not this said in order to recall a yet earlier page in sacred History? to remind us that as a Garden was the scene of MAN's Fall in the person of Adam, so was a Garden also the scene of Man's recovery in the person of CHRIST? "He chose that place for His Agony and satisfactory pains," (says Bp. Taylor,) "in which the first scene of Human misery was represented; and where He might best attend the offices of devotion preparatory to His Death."

2 And Judas also, which betrayed Him, knew the place; for JESUS ofttimes resorted thither with His Disciples.

Our SAVIOUR was not seeking to escape from His enemies therefore, by withdrawing to the Garden of Gethsemane; but knowing that "the hour was come," He repaired to his accustomed haunt, in meek submission to the Will of His Eternal FATHER.

That Judas "knew the place," the Evangelist mentions to prepare us for the history of the apprehension of the Holy One, which immediately follows; but he reveals thereby the interesting circumstance that Gethsemane was a favourite haunt of our SAVIOUR and His Disciples during the time of their sojourn at Jerusalem. Perhaps ever since His arrival in the Capital, on this last occasion, though His nights were spent at Bethany,(e) the first hours of every evening may have been passed in soothing converse or in mysterious prayer amid the shades of this very garden.(f) How must it have aggravated the bitterness of what followed, that Judas should have availed himself of the knowledge which his Discipleship supplied to betray our SAVIOUR into the hands of His Enemies! "For it was not an enemy that reproached Me; then I could have borne it: neither was it he that hated Me that did magnify himself against me; then I would have hid Myself from him; but it was thou, a man Mine equal, My guide, and Mine acquaintance. We took sweet counsel together, and walked unto the house of GOD in company."(g) . . . . . . Here, where His Divine Master had taught him how to pray, the traitor comes to apprehend Him; and it would seem from the narrative of the other three Evangelists, as if he had even selected the moment of prayer itself as the fittest for the execution of his infernal purpose.

It is worthy of remark how entirely St. John passes over that period of Agony, concerning which the other Evangelists have supplied us with such an affecting record.(h) He had nothing to add to the narratives of St. Matthew and St. Mark; above all, of St. Luke. From the account of our LORD's Intercession, he passes at once to the history of His Sacrifice. The wicked agent whose disappearance from the guest-chamber had been the signal(i) for the free and unrestrained discourse of the Son of Man, now re-appears. As it follows:

3 Judas then, having received a band *of men* and officers from the chief priests and Pharisees, cometh thither with lanterns and torches and weapons.

Rather,—"having obtained the band, and [armed] servants, at the hands of the chief priests and Pharisees." Mention is here made of well-known officials:—First, the cohort of Roman soldiers, which on great festivals like the present the Procurator put at the disposal of the Sanhedrin, to protect the Temple, and to keep order in the City. Their Præfect is mentioned below, in ver. 12. Next, the armed servants of the Sanhedrin, who guarded the Temple, and were under the command of a Jewish Captain.(k) . . . . The word "Officers" is apt to convey a notion of rank,

(c) So also in the ancient Greek version of 2 Sam. xv. 23.
(d) St. John xix. 41, 42.
(f) See St. Luke xxi. 37: xxiii. 39.
(h) St. Matth. xxvi. 36 to 46. St. Mark xiv. 32 to 42. St. Luke xxii. 39 to 46.
(i) See St. John xii. 31, and the note there.
(k) Acts iv. 1: v. 26, &c.

(e) See the note on St. John xi. 1.
(g) Ps. lv. 12 to 14.

which belonged to only a few of their number ;(*l*) while "Servants,"(*m*) is too vague a term. From the violence of their conduct,(*n*) and the nature of the service on which they are found employed,(*o*) they would appear to have been a species of soldiery.

With this band of Roman soldiers, therefore, (or some part of it,) and the armed officials which the chief priests and Pharisees supplied, Judas drew near. The present mention of "lanterns and torches" at a time when the moon was at full, while it marks the eagerness of the Traitor to effect his sinful purpose, suggests also the gloom of the Garden where our SAVIOUR loved to pray; an olive-grove,— if the venerable trees which stand on the site of Gethsemane, may be supposed to recall in any way the ancient aspect of the place. The "weapons" may have been a precaution against any attempt of the Disciples to rescue their LORD by an appeal to arms. That certain of their number carried swords, the Traitor will have certainly known; though he had left the apartment, probably, before those "two swords" were produced,(*p*) — of which Simon Peter is found to have carried one.

4 JESUS therefore, knowing all things that should come upon Him, went forth, and said unto them, Whom seek ye?

Rather, "all things that were coming upon Him."—The present Evangelist, who is careful on many occasions to declare that his LORD "knew all things,"(*q*) fails not to prefix the same statement to his History of the Passion; that it may be clearly borne in mind that whatever happened was duly foreseen in the Divine counsels. His Gospel was written, (as he declared,) that men might "believe that JESUS is the CHRIST the SON of GOD."(*r*) ... Our SAVIOUR "went forth," (or "out,") of the Garden where He had been passing the last hour or two, and accosted the rabble and soldiery who had now assembled at the gate, with the question, "Whom seek ye?"

5 They answered Him, JESUS of Nazareth. JESUS saith unto them, I am *He*. And Judas also, which betrayed Him, stood with them.

It has been already elsewhere remarked,(*s*) that by the very idiom of the language, our SAVIOUR proclaimed Himself on this, and many other occasions, by the self-same Name, (I AM,) whereby He made Himself known to Moses. . . . . The statement concerning Judas, (introduced by St. John, so much in the manner of one who was an eye-witness of the scene he describes!) suggests that the Traitor, inasmuch as he walked *in advance* of the rest,(*t*) shared the overthrow of his companions, described in the next verse: according to that of the Psalmist, "Let them be confounded and put to shame that seek after my soul: let them be turned back and brought to confusion that devise my hurt."(*u*)

6 As soon then as He had said unto them, I am *He*, they went backward, and fell to the ground.

An incident which recalls those prophetic words of the Psalmist,—"When the wicked, even Mine enemies and My foes, came upon Me to eat up My flesh, they stumbled and fell."(*x*) And thus was exhibited in emblem the fate of the wicked in the presence of the Most High: "By the blast of GOD they perish, and by the breath of His nostrils are they consumed."(*y*) Would it not seem as if Judas had anticipated some such possible contingency, (remembering perhaps what had taken place before, on similar occasions,)(*z*) when he charged the soldiers to notice whom he should kiss and "*hold Him fast!*"(*a*)

By thus causing His Divinity to break forth upon His enemies(*b*) to their utter

(*l*) St. Luke xxii. 4.   (*m*) St. Matth. xxvi. 58.
(*n*) St. Mark xiv. 65.   St. John xviii. 22.
(*o*) St. John vii. 32, 45 : xviii. 3, 12 : xix. 6.   Acts v. 22, 26.
(*p*) St. Luke xxii. 38.
(*q*) Consider the following places : chap. ii. 24, 25 : vi. 64, 65 : xiii. 11 : xvi. 30 : xxi. 17.
(*r*) St. John xx. 31.   (*s*) See the note on chap. vi. 20.
(*t*) St. Luke xxii. 47.   (*u*) Ps. xxxv. 4.
(*x*) Ps. xxvii. 2.   (*y*) Job iv. 9.
(*z*) Consider St. Luke iv. 30.   St John vii. 30, 44 : viii. 59 : x. 39.
(*a*) St. Matth. xxvii. 48.   *   (*b*) Compare Exod. xix. 22, 24.

discomfiture, in the very moment when they were about to apprehend Him, our
LORD showed in the clearest manner that it was by His own express permission that
these wicked men afterwards prevailed : else could they have had no power against
Him at all.   He lifts up for an instant the mantle which screened His Divinity
from the eyes of men ; and lo, they are unable even to stand in His presence ! . . . .
Let us not fail to observe that an opportunity was thus afforded them for reflection,
as well as an argument for repentance ; for here was a plain "sign" that He with
whom they had to do was not mere Man. And take notice, that besides this miracle
of Power, a miracle *of Mercy* follows in verses 10 and 11.

7 Then asked He them again, Whom seek ye?   And they said,
JESUS of Nazareth.

It is obvious to imagine this inquiry repeated in the same firm voice, and with
the same calm Majesty, as before ; but the reply of the soldiers, faltered forth in a
very different manner from at first.   This time, however, no such miraculous exercise of Divine power ensues as on the former occasion.

8 JESUS answered, I have told you that I am *He :* if therefore ye
seek Me, let these go their way :

Meaning the Eleven Apostles, who will have followed our LORD to the entrance
of the Garden, and now stood by His side.   The first part of this reply must have
at once confounded and perplexed the men to whom it was addressed,—reminding
them that they had been before *withheld*,(c) from laying hands on the Divine Speaker.
Taking them at their word, however, in the concluding sentence, our SAVIOUR
merely claims for His followers license to depart, since it was Himself whom the
soldiers said they sought.   And this was because He must needs tread the wine-
press alone, and of the people there must be none with Him :(d) lest it should even
enter into the dreams of any that the price of Man's Salvation was paid by some
other sacrifice besides that of CHRIST only.   Whereas Caiaphas, without intending
it, had divinely declared that it was "expedient for us that *one Man* should die for
the people."(e)

In one respect, our LORD's saying on this occasion recalls that of His great type,
and ancestor after the flesh, King David.(f)   Truly has it been pointed out,(g)
however, that by these powerful words,—(which conveyed a command rather than
expressed a petition,) — He divinely diverted from His Disciples the wrath of the
man whom He addressed.   So large was His love, in the hour of danger and of
Death, that to screen *them* from fiery trial was all His care.

9 That the saying might be fulfilled, which He spake, Of them which
Thou gavest Me have I lost none.

This is a somewhat surprising statement: for our SAVIOUR, when He uttered the
words referred to,(h) was speaking of eternal, not temporal Death ; and certainly
He cannot be thought to have been alluding to the mere *apprehension* of His Apostles.   What, however, if the faith of those men was as yet so imperfect and insecure,
that their apprehension *now* would have infallibly resulted in their ultimate fall?
Simon Peter, no prisoner, but a voluntary intruder into the scene of danger, thrice
denied that he so much as knew CHRIST.   What might have been the conduct, what
would have been the fate, of the others, if they had now been separated from their
LORD, and dragged away to a terrible death?

"When they which were about Him saw what would follow, they said unto Him,
LORD, shall we smite with the sword?   And one of them,"(i)—or, as St. John more
particularly says,—

10 Then Simon Peter having a sword drew it, and smote the High
Priest's servant, and cut off his right ear.

Simon, when he drew his sword, (probably, with the intention of cleaving

(c) Consider St. John vii. 30, 44.
(e) St. John xi. 50.
(g) By Chrysostom.
(i) St. Luke xxii. 49,-50.

(d) Is. lxiii. 3.
(f) 1 Chron. xxi. 17
(h) St. John xvii. 12.

Malchus through the skull,) will have thought that the moment had arrived for which His Divine Master's Discourse at the Paschal Supper had prepared him.(*k*) —We need not discuss the morality of his act. If he struck the blow in alarm, under the impulse of sudden anger, zealous for the safety of his LORD,—(whose leave to shed blood he was careful to ask,(*l*) although he did not wait to obtain His permission,)—the deed was at least excusable. We are neither invited to dwell upon its sinfulness, nor to exalt its heroism.(*m*)

The servant's name was Malchus.

Thus, the latest Evangelist not only tells us who struck this famous blow, but supplies us with a name which all his predecessors had omitted. St. John, as being "known to the High-priest," was very naturally acquainted with the High-priest's household. Hence, he knew the maid who kept the door,(*n*)—the name of the servant who encountered Simon's sword,—nay, he knew that it was a kinsman of this man who charged Simon, as he stood by the fire, with having been with CHRIST in the Garden.(*o*) . . . Let us only beware, when we make such remarks, of the spirit in which we make them. However clever they may sound, however interesting they may prove, they are the shallowest remarks of all, and belong to the lowest style of criticism. Far worse than worthless are they, if their tendency be to obscure our apprehension of the Divinity of these precious Narratives,—where every word was weighed in a heavenly balance; and Almighty Wisdom held the scale; and nothing was set down without a lofty purpose. There were eternal reasons, not only why it should be recorded that "the servant's name was Malchus ;" but also why St. John, and no one but he, was selected to record that fact. It may be a true, but it is only a very partial account of the matter, to say that St. John knew the High-priest, and therefore knew Malchus, and therefore preserved his name. This is to reason about the Gospel as if it were a common book of History. Nay, when Piety has suggested (1st) that St. John hereby challenges inquiry into the exactness of his narrative ; (2d) that the family of Malchus,—and, indeed, the High-priest's entire household,—were hereby made witnesses of one of our LORD's miracles ; (3d) that when St. John's Gospel was written, St. Peter, and Malchus himself, being probably dead, no mischief could any longer result from a mention of the Apostle's name in conjunction with that of the High-priest's servant; and hence that St. John mentions what the other Evangelists omit:—when Piety has suggested all this, and more, we are probably as far as ever from knowing all the reasons why it was set down that "the servant's name was Malchus." . . . May we humbly suggest, as a better reason than any we have ever met with, why such things are so recorded, that it was in order to be *a trial of Faith?* to expose the men of this generation to the self-same trial as those who beheld the WORD made flesh ; and who were therefore tempted to think Him *mere* Man ?(*p*)

11 Then said JESUS unto Peter, Put up thy sword into the sheath :

"For all they that take the sword, shall perish by the sword."

the cup which the FATHER hath given Me, shall I not drink it ?

"Thinkest thou that I cannot now pray to My FATHER, and He shall presently give Me more than twelve legions of Angels? But how, then, shall the Scriptures be fulfilled, that thus it must be ?"(*q*) . . . Such were the Divine sayings of the SAVIOUR of the World on this memorable occasion, as collected from an earlier Gospel. In St. John's narrative we meet with a second allusion to that "Cup," the bitterness of which has been already shown us in the way of foretaste in the Garden.(*r*)

But we must turn to the Gospel of "Luke, the beloved physician,"(*s*) for the affecting Miracle of healing which now took place. The reader is referred to the place at foot for some remarks on this subject.(*t*)

(*k*) See St. Luke xxii. 36, 37.   (*l*) St. Luke xxii. 49.
(*m*) With the Papists,—who seem to consider themselves at liberty to identify St. Peter with the Church of Rome, on all occasions.
(*n*) See above, verse 16.   (*o*) See above, verse 26.
(*p*) See the second note on St. John xii. 48.
(*q*) St. Matthew xxvi. 52 to 54.   (*r*) See St. Matth. xxvi. 39, &c.
(*s*) Colossians iv. 14.
(*t*) St. Luke xxii. 51.   See also St. Matthew xxvi. 51 to 53.

12 Then the band and the captain and officers of the Jews took JESUS, and bound Him,

For some remarks on the several personages here named, see above, on verse 3. Concerning the phrase, "*the Jews*," (instead of "the Chief Priests and Pharisees," as in verse 3,) see the note on St. John v. 15.—These various officials "took JESUS and bound Him," in conformity with the Traitor's instructions not only to "hold Him fast,"(u) but also to "lead Him away safely."(x) See above, on ver. 6.

It is hard to conceive after two such recent "signs,"—so unequivocal a proof of Divine power,(y) superadded to this last extraordinary miracle of *Mercy*,—how these miscreants can have dared to prosecute their wicked purpose. Certain it is that those terrors which our SAVIOUR had suddenly put forth, and with which He had for a moment smitten them to the ground, must have been by Him withdrawn, to facilitate their purpose; or they never could have proceeded to the actual apprehension of the Holy JESUS.

Augustine remarks in his peculiar way,—"Unless our LORD had suffered Himself to be apprehended by them, they certainly could never have done that which they came to do: but then, on the other hand, neither could He himself have done that for which *He* came. For they, in their rage, sought His destruction; while He, by His Death, sought our Life."

13 And led Him away to Annas first; for he was father-in-law to Caiaphas, which was the High Priest that same year.

Thus the Evangelist assigns *the reason* why our LORD was first conveyed to the house of Annas. It has been thought that this house was, perhaps, near at hand, and that the multitude may have been at a loss to know how to proceed. But it seems to be implied that Caiaphas would wish for the sanction, advice, and assistance of his father-in-law, in what was to follow. And indeed, on a careful review of the whole transaction, does it not seem something more than possible that it was in consequence of *this* man's counsel that the Jews persisted in requiring *Pilate* to execute their sentence? May not the old man's advice to Caiaphas have been that he must by all means transfer the odium of the death of their Great Prisoner to *the Roman power?*

St. John repeats no less than three times that Caiaphas was "the High Priest that same year."(z)

14 Now Caiaphas was he which gave counsel to the Jews, that it was expedient that one man should die for the people.

Alluding to the remarkable incident recorded in chap. xi. 49 to 52,—where the reader is invited to read the notes. St. John's manner of identifying persons by some single circumstance in their history, has already been the subject of comment in the note on chapter iv. 46: but the prophecy of Caiaphas is here referred to for the additional purpose of reminding the reader of the Divine purpose of the sacrifice of the Death of CHRIST.

15 And Simon Peter followed JESUS, and *so did* another Disciple:

Rather, "And so did *the* other Disciple,"—by which phrase the present writer designates *himself*. The expression is found to recur in chap. xx. 2, 3, 4, and 8; where St. John is spoken of (as here) in connection with Simon. So intimate a friendship is known to have subsisted between these two Apostles,(a) that it is not hard to understand how, in the primitive Church after mention had been made of St. Peter, it was obvious to infer, that by the phrase "*the other* Disciple," no person could be intended but St. John. And this has been remarked by others. May it not be further suggested however, and with even better reason, that besides the tie of personal friendship which distinguished these two Saints from every other pair of Apostles, they two had clearly enjoyed marks of personal favour at the hands of their Divine LORD,(b) to which the rest of the Twelve were utter strang-

---

(u) St. Matthew xxvi. 48.   (x) St. Mark xiv. 44.   (y) See above, on verse 6.
(z) See St. John xi. 49 and 51, and the notes on 50. Compare St. Luke iii. 2.
(a) St. John xx. 2 to 4: xxi. 7, also 20 and 21. Acts iii. 1: iv. 13.
(b) On this subject, see the notes on St. Mark iii. 16 and 17.

ers? To say nothing of the occasions when their names are found associated,—think of the great promise to St. Peter recorded in St. Matt. xvi. 18, 19! of his walking on the water to CHRIST! of his paying tribute with his LORD! Think, on the other hand, of the place which St. John occupied near his Master's person! above all, of the place, which he held in his Master's heart,—(the heart of CHRIST!): and of the affecting pledge of Love which he received from the lips of his dying LORD! Such favours are found to have produced debate and rivalry among the Apostles, at the time ;(c) and St. Peter must have been deeply conscious that " the Disciple whom JESUS loved" was even the more important person of the twain. His question concerning St. John in chap. xxi. 21, is very remarkable. By tacit consent therefore, among the Apostolic body, St. Peter and St. John seem to have enjoyed a kind of precedence of rank over their fellows : — so that of *two* Apostles mentioned, when Simon Peter was *one*, St. John was understood to be designated by the mention of " *the other.*"

that Disciple was known unto the High Priest, and went in with JESUS into the palace of the High Priest.

Rather, " into the Hall :" from which it appears, that in what follows, we are presented with the narrative of an eye-witness of all that occurred. Take notice also that St. John thus *accounts* for his own admission to the scene of danger, as well as for St. Peter's exclusion from it. He lays no claim to superior personal boldness, (though he evidently possessed that quality in a very eminent degree ;)(d) nor insinuates any lack of it in his friend.

16 But Peter stood at the door without. Then went out that other Disciple, which was known unto the High Priest, and spake unto her that kept the door, and brought in Peter.

It was usual to commit the care of the door, or porch, to a female servant. See Acts xii. 13.

17 Then saith the damsel that kept the door unto Peter, Art not thou also *one* of this Man's Disciples ? He saith, I am not.

When St. John missed Simon Peter, it was natural that he should suspect what had been the cause of his exclusion. He therefore speaks to the female servant who kept the door and brings in his friend. The damsel scrutinizes the person so admitted, somewhat closely ; and recognizes a follower of JESUS of Galilee.

To reconcile this denial of St. Peter with the others recorded by the earlier Evangelists, is the province of a Harmony of the Gospels. It may suffice to refer the reader, concerning the entire transaction, to the notes on St. Mark xiv. 66 to 72 : also on St. Matthew xxvi. 73, 74.

18 And the servants and officers stood there, who had made a fire of coals ; for it was cold : and they warmed themselves : and Peter stood with them, and warmed himself.

These were the private " servants" of the High Priest, and the public " officers" who were employed in the service of the Temple ; as explained in the note on verse 3. — Travellers admit that the nights in Palestine at the Paschal season are often intensely cold. Frost and snow are not unknown ; and these men had been exposed, besides, to the heavy dews. They therefore heaped together a fire of charcoal ashes, and assembled round it. . . . Connect this, with St. Luke xxii. 44,—where see the note.

Peter first stood, then sat,(e) then went out into the porch,(f) — changing his posture through uneasiness at the near prospect of detection.

19 The High Priest then asked JESUS of His Disciples, and of His Doctrine.

(c) St. Mark ix. 34 : St. Luke ix. 46 : xxii. 24.
(d) This appears also from St. John xix. 26.
(e) St. Luke xxii. 55, 56.　　　　　　　　　　(f) St. Matth. xxvi. 71.

What may have been the purport of those questions? Was it perhaps implied by the Speaker that the Calling of Disciples indicated a design to become the Leader of a party; and that our LORD's Doctrine was of a seditious tendency? What is certain, the High Priest affected to inquire what His Doctrine actually was.

20, 21 JESUS answered him, I spake openly to the World, I ever taught in the Synagogue, and in the Temple, whither the Jews always resort; and in secret have I said nothing. Why askest thou Me? ask them which heard Me, what I have said unto them: behold, they know what I have said.

Rather,—"Behold, *these persons:*" pointing probably to some of the bystanders as He spoke. . . . A more sinister course than that pursued by Caiaphas, — a more triumphant reply than that of our LORD,—cannot be imagined. The former, instead of bringing a charge against his Prisoner, (if he had any to bring,) proceeds to ask questions about the Disciples and the Doctrine of the Holy JESUS. For all reply, our SAVIOUR refers him to the persons present, adherents of his own. They had many a time been in the Temple during our SAVIOUR's Discourses to the people. Let *them* satisfy the curiosity of the High Priest; and bear witness against Himself, if they are able.

22 And when He had thus spoken, one of the officers which stood by struck JESUS with the palm of his hand, saying, Answerest Thou the High Priest so?

Consider the terrible indignity which was thus offered to the CREATOR of the World,—the brightness of the FATHER's Glory, and the express image of His Person!(g)   Consider next the monstrous wickedness of the menial who could strike such a blow at such a time; and of the High Priest who, sitting on the judgment seat, could suffer it to be inflicted. Above all, consider the meek bearing of Him, who "was brought as a lamb to the slaughter." "As a sheep before her shearers is dumb, so He opened not His mouth."(h) . . . A prelude to this act of cruelty and injustice is found in the history of the Kings:(i) but still more striking is the parallel afforded by the treatment of St. Paul by the High Priest Ananias.(k)

23 JESUS answered him, If I have spoken evil, bear witness of the evil: but if well, why smitest thou Me?

The allusion is clearly to that command in Exod. xxii. 28, — "Thou shalt not revile the gods, nor curse the ruler of thy people." If I have done this thing, saith our LORD, charge Me openly with My offence!

24 Now Annas had sent Him bound unto Caiaphas the High Priest.

This is said in order to recall the subject which has been suspended since ver. 13. Similar instances of the Divine method are discoverable in other parts of Scripture.(l)   In like manner the words which follow next are intended to recall what was stated in ver. 18.

25 And Simon Peter stood and warmed himself.

They said therefore unto him, Art not thou also *one* of His Disciples? He denied *it*, and said, I am not.

26 One of the servants of the High Priest, being *his* kinsman whose ear Peter cut off, saith, Did not I see thee in the garden with Him?

The charge which this person, Malchus's kinsman, brought against Simon Peter, is recorded by no other Evangelist except St. John. See above, the note on the last words of ver. 10. . . . . . Thus, for the third time questioned, the Apostle's

(g) Heb. i. 3.   (h) Is. liii. 7.
(i) 1 Kings xxii. 24.   (k) Acts xxiii. 2 to 4.
(l) e. g. Exod. vi. 29, 30, recalls ver. 10, 11, 12, of the same chapter.

perplexity became extreme. St. Matthew and St. Mark say, "Then began he to curse and to swear." St. John says simply,—

27 Peter then denied again: and immediately the cock crew.

Whereby the Divine prophecy was fulfilled,—as all the four Evangelists conspire in recording. "And the LORD turned, and looked upon Peter. And Peter remembered the word of the LORD, how He had said unto him, Before the cock crow, thou shalt deny Me thrice. And Peter went out and wept bitterly." This bitter repentance of Simon Peter is not noticed by the Disciple whom JESUS loved. See, concerning it, the note on St. Matthew xxvi. 75.

A fresh scene of indignity and suffering,—a new phase in our SAVIOUR's Passion, —is now presented to us. We behold Him next dragged before Pontius Pilate the governor; whose Judgment-hall, (*Prætorium*, as it is called in the original,) is the scene of all that follows.

28 Then led they JESUS from Caiaphas unto the Hall of judgment: and it was early; and they themselves went not into the judgment-hall, lest they should be defiled; but that they might eat the Passover.

That is,—"but [remained without,] in order that they might eat the Passover:" which occasions a well-known difficulty; for the Passover supper, as we have seen, had been already eaten. It is obvious to suggest, either that some portion of the repast which might be called by the same name of "the Passover," yet remained to be partaken of; (which is known to have been the case:) or else that these miscreants, who proved so unscrupulous in their violation of the most sacred principles of justice, resolved still to sit down to their Paschal Supper, although the season appointed for that purpose by the Divine Law had fully elapsed. Unforeseen events had *compelled* them, in fact, to postpone their evening meal until the morning.

The chief priests then, and others, who brought our SAVIOUR to the Prætorium, remained in the street till Pilate came out to speak to them. Their Prisoner, however, they sent within. This appears from the subsequent narrative. . . . . Take notice also, in passing, that the terrible repentance of Judas is related by St. Matthew in this place.(*m*)

29 Pilate then went out unto them, and said, What accusation bring ye against this man?

"'Pilate *therefore* went out unto them,'—because their fear of contracting uncleanness prevented them from going into the judgment-hall."(*n*)

30 They answered and said unto him, If He were not a malefactor, we would not have delivered Him up unto thee.

Implying that they had satisfied themselves of our SAVIOUR's guilt, and that nothing but a formal sentence was wanting.

31 Then said Pilate unto them, Take ye Him, and judge Him according to your law.

Rather, "and condemn Him,"—"adjudge Him to punishment."—Pilate's first words fully set before us the character of the man,—the very model of a weak temporizing politician. Evidently impressed by the mysterious majesty of his Prisoner, and heartily desiring His acquittal, he is found to be yet more anxious for his own personal safety. If CHRIST must needs die, let it at least be by the hands of others; not by his own. He has not the courage to order His instant release,—which was the requirement of justice, and the plain dictate of conscience.

The Jews therefore said unto him, It is not lawful for us to put any man to death:

It has been thought that they thereby meant that during "the days of unlea-

(*m*) St. Matth. xxvii. 3 to 10.   (*n*) Lonsdale and Hale.

vened bread," and especially on the Feast-day itself, it was unlawful for them to order the execution of a criminal. But it is far more likely that this speech of theirs is to be taken in its plain signification, and that the power of life and death was no longer in any Court of the Jews, but in the Roman Governor alone as supreme.

" Pilate had told the Jews to take Jesus and judge Him according to their Law. The force of their answer is, It will be to no purpose that we should judge Him according to our Law ; for His is an offence deserving of *Death :*(o) and, in such a case, we have no longer the power of carrying our sentence into execution against any man. . . . This answer agrees entirely with what we read elsewhere ;(p) for we find the Jewish High Priest and Council bearing evidence against Jesus, and condemning Him to Death, but obliged to have recourse to the authority of the Roman Governor, in order that the condemnation might be carried into effect."(q) These wicked men were evidently bent on proceeding with all the forms of Law; else would they at once have had recourse to *stoning,*— as on so many other occasions.(r) It may very well be that the fear of a disturbance among the people was what mainly deterred them from pursuing that violent and irregular course. Their object had been, (as we know,) to effect our Lord's apprehension " *not* on the feast-day ;(s) inasmuch however as their intentions had been frustrated, it remained to procure that the cruel punishment of *Crucifixion* should terminate the sufferings of their great prisoner,— what to do with whom was probably a source of no small perplexity to them, now that He was actually in their power. And thus it came to pass that the prophecy which our Lord had so often delivered concerning the manner of His own death, unexpectedly found fulfillment. This is what the Evangelist means, when he adds,—

32 that the saying of JESUS might be fulfilled, which He spake, signifying what death He should die.

The allusion is evidently to those many occasions on which our Lord, more or less openly, had predicted His Crucifixion.(t) Especially might the Evangelist be thought to allude to the minute and extraordinary prophecy in St. Matthew xx. 18, 19 ; but that the recurrence of *the very phrase* which St. John here uses, in an earlier chapter of the present Gospel,(u) seems to prove that the allusion is to a different and more recent occasion.

" If the Jews had sought from Pilate permission to put Jesus to Death according to their own Law, they would probably have obtained it ; in which case, He would have died by stoning as a blasphemer;(v) but then His prophecy that He should die by Crucifixion, which was a Roman, not a Jewish punishment, would not have been fulfilled."(x) See above, what was offered on ver. 13.

Take notice, however, that it was at this juncture, the multitude brought a specific charge against the Holy One. "They began to accuse Him, saying, We found this fellow perverting the nation, and forbidding to give tribute to Cæsar, saying that He Himself is Christ a King."(y) Unless this is attended to, Pilate's question, which immediately follows, is scarcely intelligible.

33 Then Pilate entered into the judgment-hall again, and called JESUS, and said unto Him, Art Thou the King of the Jews?

A momentous question, doubtless ; for it is recorded by all the four Evangelists, and in the self-same words.(z) Take notice that the Roman Governor does not ask our Lord whether it be true that He has said this thing concerning Himself? but simply requires Him to declare Whether He *be* " the King of the Jews," or not? And this was divinely ordained ; for thus it came to pass that our Lord's true title was eventually affixed to His Cross,—to the infinite annoyance of His enemies, who wished His accusation to be set forth in different language. See St. John xix. 19 to 22.

(o) St. John xix. 7.   St. Matth. xxvi. 66.
(p) St. Matth. xxvi. 59 to 66: xxvii. 1, 2.
(q) Lonsdale and Hale, quoting St. Matth. xx. 18, 19 : xxvii. 3.
(r) St. John viii. 59 : x. 31 : (xi. 8 :) also Acts vii. 57 to 59.
(s) St. Matth. xxvi. 5.   (t) St. John iii. 14: viii. 28.
(u) St. John xii. 32, 33.   (v) Levit. xxiv. 16.
(x) Lonsdale and Hale.   (y) St. Luke xxiii. 2.
(z) St. Matth. xxvii. 11.   St. Mark xv. 2.   St. Luke xxiii. 3.

Pontius Pilate having entered the Prætorium, (from which he had issued on learning that the multitude were at his gate,)(a) ordered our SAVIOUR to be summoned into his presence. Our SAVIOUR and the Roman Governor now stood face to face ;(b) when the latter, with a miserable apprehension (which all that followed must have conspired to heighten,) that he had to do with more than mortal Man, asked our SAVIOUR the question recorded in the text. The answer which the three earlier Evangelists record, is found not to have been immediate : for it follows.

34 JESUS answered him, Sayest thou this thing of thyself, or did others tell it thee of Me ?

Tell thee, (that is,) that I had declared Myself to be "the King of the Jews." For, as we have elsewhere shown, the charge of claiming to be a King was brought against our SAVIOUR while he was within the Judgment-hall, by His enemies, who were then assembled without. Full well indeed did the Holy One " perceive in Spirit"(c) all that had taken place on this occasion ; but He asks a question of Pilate,—as He asked a question of Adam,(d) and of Cain ;(e) of Abraham,(f) and of Moses,(g)—the object of which seems to have been to arouse Pilate to a speedy sense of the shameful injustice of the charge. It is, perhaps, as if He had said,— Thou hast been the Governor of this Country for five years. Did any rumour ever reach thee that I have been guilty of the class of crimes which Mine enemies lay to My charge? Sayest thou this therefore of thyself? or is the question altogether prompted by the accusation of the multitude at thy gate?

Now, it is not to be supposed that Pilate can have been unaware of the general belief which prevailed at this time throughout the World that a King was about to appear. He will have inevitably discovered, during his residence in Judæa, that such an expectation was very prevalent among the Jewish nation ; and that this hope was in some mysterious manner connected with their religious profession, he will have also certainly known. Hence his rejoinder, which follows.

35 Pilate answered, Am I a Jew ?

This seems to mean, What should I, a Roman, know of such superstitions? "Am I a Jew,—that I should of myself know what Thy pretensions among Thy countrymen are?"(h)

Thine own nation and the chief priests have delivered Thee unto me : what hast Thou done ?

For all reply, our SAVIOUR proceeds to answer Pilate's question in ver. 33.

36 JESUS answered, My Kingdom is not of this World: if My Kingdom were of this World, then would My servants fight, that I should not be delivered to the Jews: but now is my Kingdom not from hence.

Rather, " *would have fought,* that I should not have been delivered." . . . . Our SAVIOUR does not say that He has no earthly Kingdom ; but that His Kingdom is not of *earthly origin.* "As for repugnancy between ecclesiastical and civil power, or any inconvenience that these two powers should be united, it doth not appear that this was the cause of His resistance either to reign, or to judge."(i)

It is related that in the time of Domitian, certain descendants of St. Jude, our LORD'S cousin, were brought before the Emperor, on a charge of being of the royal line of David. "The Emperor questioned them concerning CHRIST, and the nature of His Kingdom ; where and when it was to appear. The peasants, (for they were no more,) made answer that it was *not of this World, neither was it earthly in its nature,* but heavenly and angelic,—and that it would not be revealed until the Last Day."(j) The entire anecdote is related by one who lived in the middle of the second century, and is full of affecting interest.

The English reader should be told that there is a marked emphasis, both in Pilate's reply, and our Blessed LORD'S rejoinder, which it is difficult to convey

---

(a) See above, ver. 29.　　　　　　　　　(b) St. Matth. xxvii. 11.
(c) Compare St. Mark ii. 8.　　　　　　　(d) Gen. iii. 9.
(e) Gen. iv. 9.　　　　　　　　　　　　　(f) Gen. xviii. 9.
(g) Exod. iv. 2.　　　　　　　　　　　　(h) Lonsdale and Hale.
(i) Hooker,—referring to St. John viii. 11, and St. Luke xii. 14.　　　(j) Hegesippus.

exactly in English,—except perhaps by the use of italics. "*Thy* nation, and the High Priest," says Pilate. "*My* Kingdom is not of this World," (says the Divine Speaker). If of this World were *My* Kingdom, then would *My* servants have fought," &c.,—the word for "servants" being the same which is translated "officers" in verses 3 and 12.

37 Pilate therefore said unto Him, Art Thou a King then ?

The exact rendering of the words would perhaps rather be,—" Thou art a King, then; art Thou not?" . . . Inasmuch as our SAVIOUR had thrice made mention of His "Kingdom," it followed that, in some sense, He claimed to be a King. Pilate seems to have had a very correct notion of our LORD's meaning,—namely, that He spoke with reference to things spiritual. Otherwise, it is incredible that he would have hesitated to put his Prisoner to death. The Roman cannot but have had a general knowledge of the singular religion of the people over whose affairs he had come to preside; and the present accusation being urged by the chief priests, he may have easily had a suspicion that it partook of a religious character. What is certain, Pilate persisted in bestowing this obnoxious title upon our LORD to the very last. He is recorded to have used it no less than five time.(*k*) In reply to the present question,

JESUS answered, Thou sayest that I am a King.

Witnessing by those words, (which amount, in Hebrew, to an affirmation,) that "good confession before Pontius Pilate," to which the great Apostle directs the attention of his son Timothy ;(*l*) and through him, of the Church for ever. The particulars of this dialogue St. John will be found to give far more in detail than the other three Evangelists. He also presents us with the remainder of our LORD's reply : as it follows,—

To this end was I born, and for this cause came I into the World, that I should bear witness unto the Truth.

Pilate will not, or rather cannot have known the full sublimity of this declaration. The pre-existence of CHRIST in His Divine Nature ; the mystery of His Holy Incarnation ; the gracious purpose of His Coming into the World, — of all this he can scarcely have had so much as a remote conception. Yet had he seen and heard enough to be fully convinced of our LORD's Innocence ;(*m*) to be aware that the chief priests had delivered Him for envy ;(*n*) and heartily to desire His release.(*o*)

So emphatic a mention of " Truth," in connection with the very purpose of our SAVIOUR's Advent in the flesh, suggests a few remarks in addition to what has been already offered on this subject in the note on St. John xiv. 17. It is not enough then, to speak of " Truth," as (1st) " the body of the Gospel Doctrines conveyed in our Blessed LORD's Lessons, and the Apostle's inspired teaching :"(*p*) nor yet (2nd) as " a principle of good, a holy influence, affecting the personal character, producing certain fruits and blessed with certain privileges attached to it :"(*q*) nor even (3rd) as that which really exists, in contradistinction to that which is false and unreal,—all true Being, as contrasted with all Falsehood, Vanity, and Sin."(*r*) "The full idea of the Apostle is not reached ; for (4th) his conception of Truth mounts still higher, and identifies it with GOD Himself. He is the only reality, the only absolute Truth. He is the source and limit of all that is ; and in Him, all that is good and all that exists are united. Whatever was the thought in Pilate's mind, when he inquired, "What is Truth ?" the only adequate answer which Scripture gives, in its absolute sense, is that which JESUS addressed to His Disciples, "I am the Truth and the Life."(*s*) He thus claimed Deity to Himself ; and St. John no less assigned it to the HOLY SPIRIT, when he declared that "the SPIRIT is Truth."(*t*)

(*k*) St. John xv. ii. 39.   St. Mark xv. 12.   St. John xix. 14, 15, 19.
(*l*) 1 Tim. vi. 13.
(*m*) See ver. 38 : also St. Luke xxiii. 4 and 22.
(*n*) St. Mark xv. 10.   (*o*) St. Luke xxiii. 20.
(*p*) As in Gal. iii. 1.   2 Tim. iii. 7.   Rom. i. 18.
(*q*) As in St. John viii. 32, 44 : xvii. 17.   2 St. John ver. 2, 4.   So in the Old Testament, 2 Kings xx. 3.   2 Sam. xv. 20.
(*r*) As Rom. i. 25.   Nahum iii. 1.   St. John i. 17.
(*s*) St. John xiv. 6.   (*t*) 1 St. John v. 6.

All the other ideas of the Truth are summed up, and find their home and source, in this first principle; for, from this one fount, all Existence, all that really is, proceeded in the beginning, and has its continuance. From Him flows that holy influence of Truth as it dwells in Man, working in him manifold graces; and it is knowledge of Him, veiled in His works, unveiled by His Word, and applied by the Spirit, which constitutes that true Doctrine, whether of Science or of Grace, which informs Man's understanding, and enlightens his reason."(u)

"To this end was I born," (saith our LORD,) "and for this cause came I into the World, that I should bear witness unto the Truth." In connection with this remarkable saying, the thoughtful reader of the Bible will perhaps be glad to be reminded of the many proofs which the Old Testament Scriptures afford that under the Law the perfect obligation of Truth is not found declared and enforced as under the Gospel. The strict duty of Truthfulness was not acknowledged when Isaac bade his wife Rebekah,(x) (as Abram had before bade his wife Sarai,)(y) say she was his sister: when Rebekah taught Jacob to deceive his father,(z) and personate Esau:(a) when Jacob told his brother that he was on his way to Seir, when in reality he intended nothing less than going into the country of Edom:(b) when Simeon and Levi spake falsely to the men of Shechem ;(c) and Rachel covered her theft by an untruth ;(d) and Jael, in order to slay Sisera, was at once treacherous and cruel ;(e) and David gave Achish a false account of his expedition against the Amalekites.(f) All these passages in the history of persons who lived under the Law, we find it hard to reconcile with our notions of Truth derived from the Gospel. Will it not help us, to consider that "the Law was given by Moses, but Grace and Truth came by JESUS CHRIST."(g)

Every one that is of the Truth heareth My voice.

"Now, being of the Truth" implies belonging to it; being mastered by it; taken up into it. It implies the being possessed by a principle which moulds that wherein it dwells to itself, as the weaker is held by the stronger; even a possession of the soul by the very Essence of Being and of Life, manifested in the person of the SON, and administered by the HOLY GHOST. We cannot attach a lesser meaning than this to our LORD's words, in their first sense. But, in a subordinate sense, the "being of the Truth" will imply the being under an influence and temper of heart and of mind; a virtue peculiarly practical; an honesty and sincerity affecting the whole character, and shown in the conduct of daily life. Holy Scripture frequently presents the idea of Truth in this practical aspect: as when it speaks of "walking in the Truth;" of those who "do not the Truth ;" and when it classes amongst those who are shut out from the River and the Tree of Life, "whatsoever loveth or maketh a lie."

"It is this truth of character which may be understood in our SAVIOUR's saying in the verse before us: that virtue which in words is Veracity; in heart is Sincerity; in conduct is Honesty. And though it be classed among the moral rather than the spiritual qualities of heart, yet it is not therefore to be cut off from the great first source of Truth, as though it were not an emanation from GOD Himself. On the contrary; like the life, or reason, or conscience, it forms one of those lesser, yet good and perfect gifts, with which He has endowed His rational creatures, and which the Fall has marred but not destroyed."(h)

38 Pilate saith unto Him, What is Truth?

It cannot be thought that Pilate was "jesting" when he asked this question; although it seems to be indeed the fact that he "would not stay for an answer."(i) In the language of a thoughtful writer, already largely quoted,—"he was too much impressed by our SAVIOUR's presence, too much alarmed by the sanguinary cry of the multitude, and the remonstrances of his own conscience, to indulge a scoff or a sneer. Rather, in the very sadness of his heart he uttered what had long been to him a subject of hopeless inquiry. Like so many of the higher intellects of his time, Pilate had fallen into the depths of scepticism; and after ranging through the

(u) From a MS. Sermon by the Ven. Archdeacon Grant, preached before the University, May 13th, 1855.

(x) Gen. xxvi. 6, 7.
(z) Gen. xxvii. 11 — 19.
(b) Gen. xxxiii. 14, 16, 17.
(d) Gen. xxxi. 34, 35.
(f) 1 Sam. xxvii. 8 — 12.
(h) From the same MS. Sermon.

(y) Gen. xii. 10 — 13.
(a) Gen. xxvii. 24.
(c) Gen. xxxiv.
(e) Judges iv. 18 — 21.
(g) St. John i. 17: compare 14.
(i) Lord Bacon.

many systems of men,—their attempts to solve the mysteries of our nature, and to satisfy the understanding and the heart with some object on which they might lay hold, — regarded the attainment of Truth in anything as an impossibility, and the promise of it as a snare. Probably he thought that Jesus professed only to add one more to the list of philosophies, or systems of ideas, and turned away from it in sickness of heart."(k)

Did Pilate then not wait for an answer, for the reason already suggested? or was it because he spurned the notion of learning philosophy at the hands of such an One as Christ? or was it because Time pressed, and because it was impossible at such a moment to pursue such an inquiry? or was it not rather because he was terrified at the prospect of having to condemn so mysterious a Being; and eager to procure His acquittal on a plea which had suddenly occurred to him, and which is embodied in the words which follow?

39 And when he had said this, he went out again unto the Jews, and saith unto them, I find in Him no fault *at all*. But ye have a custom, that I should release unto you one at the Passover; will ye therefore that I release unto you the King of the Jews?

Thus, Pilate at once witnesses to our Lord's Innocence, and proposes to act towards Him as if He were guilty. He has neither the courage to condemn nor to release Him, on the ground of His accusation; but thinks that by promising to the Jews that they should avail themselves of a practice recently established of setting a malefactor free at the Paschal season, the ends of either party may be attained. Neither will Pilate do violence to his own conscience; nor will the honor of the High Priest be compromised. In such crooked policy, the Roman governor was signally and deservedly defeated.

It will be discovered however, by a reference to St. Luke's Gospel, that between verses 38 and 39 comes the judicial interview between Herod and our Lord. Pilate, catching eagerly at the mention of Galilee in a second charge which the chief priests and people brought against Christ, and finding "that He belonged unto Herod's jurisdiction," sent Jacob's remote Descendant to suffer indignity and insult at the hands of the remote descendant of Esau. It was on our Saviour's return from that interview, that Pilate made the proposition recorded in the text.

40 Then cried they all again, saying, Not this Man, but Barabbas. Now Barabbas was a robber.

"Who, for a certain sedition made in the City, and for murder, was cast into prison."(l)—This was that denial "in the presence of Pilate, when he was determined to let Him go," with which St. Peter reproached the Jews at a later period:(m) adding, "But ye denied the Holy One and the Just, and desired a murderer to be granted unto you." . . . . "His own, they among whom He had gone about all His life-long, healing them, teaching them, feeding them, doing them all the good He could; it is they that cry, 'Not this Man, but Barabbas!' "(n)

CHAPTER XIX.

1 Christ *is scourged, crowned with thorns, and beaten.* 4 *Pilate is desirous to release Him, but being overcome with the outcries of the Jews, he delivered Him to be crucified.* 23 *They cast lots for His garments.* 26 *He commendeth His Mother to John.* 28 *He dieth.* 31 *His side is pierced.* 38 *He is buried by Joseph and Nicodemus.*

Then Pilate therefore took Jesus, and scourged *Him*.

(k) From the same MS. Sermon. ·
(l) St. Luke xxiii. 19, — and see what follows down to ver. 24.
(m) Acts iii. 13.   (n) Bp. Andrewes.

Concerning this awful outrage, it must suffice to refer the reader to the commentary on St. Matthew xxvii. 26: but we may well repeat the Prophet's assurance, (reminded of it as we are by an Apostle,) that "with His stripes we are healed."(a) It follows in St. Matthew's Gospel,—"Then the soldiers of the Governor took Jesus into the Prætorium, and gathered unto Him the whole band; and they stripped Him:"

2 And the soldiers platted a crown of thorns, and put *it* on His Head,

"A most unquestionable token this, that CHRIST'S Kingdom was not of this World, when He was crowned only with thorns and briars, which are the curse of the Earth."(b) But the reader is requested to read what has been already offered concerning this mysterious incident, in the commentary on St. Matth. xxvii. 29.— Besides the thorny crown, other mock insignia of Royalty were not wanting; as, " a reed in His Right Hand:"

and they put on Him a purple robe,

" and they bowed the knee before Him, and mocked Him."

3 And said, Hail, King of the Jews; and they smote Him with their hands.

"And they spit upon Him, and took the reed, and smote Him on the Head."(c) Take notice how intensely, by this last act of cruelty, the torture of the thorny crown must have been aggravated.

4 Pilate therefore went forth again, and saith unto them, Behold, I bring Him forth to you, that ye may know that I find no fault in Him.

Thus, passing sentence of condemnation on himself, even while pronouncing, nor yet for the first time,(d) our LORD's acquittal. "Behold, I bring Him forth unto you, that ye may know:"—for had Pilate judged that our LORD was in any sense guilty, he would have passed sentence upon Him *within* the Prætorium.

The Roman governor, notwithstanding that he was himself "a man of an high, rough, untractable spirit,"(e) melted by the sight of so much meek endurance on the part of One whom he knew to be perfectly innocent of the crimes laid to His charge, had stepped out before his Prisoner, in order to address the multitude on His behalf. Our LORD is found to have followed Pilate:

5 Then came JESUS forth, wearing the crown of thorns, and the purple robe. And *Pilate* saith unto them, Behold the Man!

Take notice that, this time, Pilate, in addressing the Jews, does not, as heretofore, call our LORD their "*King*." He knew that they were exasperated by his use of that title;(f) and *now*, he desires to move their pity, and if possible to persuade them to consent to our LORD's release. . . . . "Behold the Man!" As if he said,—Behold the afflicted and tortured object of your malice and cruelty; " a worm, and no man." If ye have human hearts, ye cannot behold such a dismal spectacle without commiseration! . . . . These miscreants, on the contrary, are only the more exasperated at the sight: for, "*when they saw Him,*" (as it follows:)

6 When the chief Priests therefore and officers saw Him, they cried out, saying, Crucify *Him*, crucify *Him*.

Pilate was little prepared to see his expedient answer so ill,—to find that showing CHRIST to His enemies was but heaping fuel on the flame. These instruments of Satan, in fact, spake the language of *him* who was urging them on. Truly was it their " hour, and the power of Darkness."(g)

Pilate saith unto them, Take ye Him, and crucify *Him*: for I find no fault in Him.

(a) Is. liii. 5, quoted in 1 St. Pet. ii. 24.   (b) Lightfoot.
(c) St. Matth. xxvii. 29, 30, — on which places see the notes.
(d) St. John xviii. 38.   St. Luke xxiii. 14, 15, 22.
(e) Bp. Pearson from Philo.   (f) See the note on St. John xviii. 37.
(g) St. Luke xxii. 53.

Monstrous, that a heathen should have had thus to remonstrate with the chief Priests of a nation taught of GOD! Desiring above all things our LORD's release, but determined at all events that he will not become himself the author of His Death, Pilate tells our LORD's accusers that if they will crucify his Prisoner, they must do it themselves; for that he does not find Him guilty of the pretensions to Royalty which they had brought against Him. Hence, they invent an entirely new ground of accusation: as it follows,—

7 The Jews answered Him, We have a law, and by our law He ought to die, because He made Himself the SON of GOD.

They allude to the law contained in Levit. xxiv. 16,—"He that blasphemeth the name of the LORD, he shall surely be put to death, and all the congregation shall certainly stone him." But of the *manner* of death thus prescribed, these hypocrites say nothing; because they desire our LORD's *Crucifixion*. Some think that the reference is rather to Deuteronomy xviii. 20.

Let those who deny or doubt the true Divinity of our SAVIOUR CHRIST, notice well the charge here brought against Him by His enemies; and learn, even from those wicked men, a lesson. Full well were they aware of the nature of the claim which our LORD advanced, on many occasions; namely, of being "very GOD of very GOD," and "of one Substance with the FATHER." Consider St. John v. 18, together with what follows; also chap. viii. 58, and x. 30 to 38: and see the notes there.

As Pilate had miscalculated on the effect which the sight of the Holy One, when "His visage was so marred more than any man, and His form more than the sons of men,"(h) would produce on His enemies, so are *they* found to have very wrongly conceived the effect which their accusation would have on Pilate. Already over-awed by the unearthly bearing of our SAVIOUR, and rendered uneasy by the unexpected message which he had in the meantime received from his Wife,(k) this last intimation that his mysterious Prisoner claimed to be of Divine extraction, seems to have completed his embarrassment. Pilate had been shocked, before, to find himself urged to the commission of an act of such flagrant injustice: but now, there were superadded the terrors of the unseen World.

8, 9 When Pilate therefore heard that saying, he was the more afraid; and went again into the judgment-hall, and saith unto JESUS, Whence art Thou?

The form of this inquiry sufficiently shows what was passing through the mind of Pilate. He desires to know the *origin* of his Prisoner. *Whence* does He come? in other words, *Who was His Father?*"(l) His Kingdom, (Pilate had heard Him say,) is "not of this World." Is *He* also "not of this World?" . . . The heathen Procurator again puts the descendants of Abraham to shame. Like Gamaliel in the Acts, he is seized with a salutary apprehension "lest haply he be found even to fight against GOD."(m)

But JESUS gave him no answer.

Perhaps, because the inquiry was made in such a spirit that Pilate could not have been profited by our LORD's reply; even had our LORD seen fit to give him all the information he asked for. The arrogant tone of the words which follow, which convey an imperious threat, seems to prove the truth of this conjecture.

10 Then saith Pilate unto Him, Speakest Thou not unto me? knowest Thou not that I have power to crucify Thee, and have power to release Thee?

"*Power* to crucify, and *power* to release." . . . "By this very saying, thou dost condemn thyself, O Pilate!" (exclaims Ambrose). "It is thy consciousness of *thine own power*, therefore, not thy conviction of *His guilt*, which moves thee to deliver up the Holy One to crucifixion!"—A modern critic observes, with truth,

(h) Is. lii. 14. See above, on the first words of ver. 6.
(k) St. Matth. xxvii. 19. (l) See the notes on St. John vii. 27.
(m) Acts v. 59.

that Pilate further condemns himself in servilely yielding to a popular clamour, after so plainly declaring his own absolute unfettered authority.(*n*)

11 JESUS answered, Thou couldst have no power *at all* against Me, except it were given thee from above: therefore he that delivered Me unto thee hath the greater sin.

That is, This boasted power of thine against Me, thou never wouldest have had, "were it not that GOD, who is My FATHER, hath, in His Divine counsels, for the good of the World, determined to deliver Me up to suffer death under thee. And this is a great aggravation of the sin of Judas, and the Jewish Sanhedrin: he, to deliver Me up to them; they, to make thee the instrument of their malice in cruci-fying Me, not only an innocent person, but even the SON of GOD Himself. This, they have had means to know better than thou; and therefore, though thy sin be great, yet theirs, being against more light, is much more criminal, and shall be more severely punished."(*o*)

12 And from thenceforth Pilate sought to release Him:

It is evidently implied that the Roman here came forward, addressed the chief Priests and multitude, and tried again to persuade them to consent to our SAVIOUR's acquittal.

but the Jews cried out, saying, If thou let this Man go, thou art not Cæsar's friend: whosoever maketh Himself a King speaketh against Cæsar.

Thus, the enemies of the Holy JESUS again shift the ground of their accusation; and, having discovered that Pilate is heedless of their charge of blasphemy, assail him on his weakest side, by appealing to his political fears; at the same time pre-ferring against our SAVIOUR the favourite and most prevalent, because the most successful, charge of those times. They give Pilate to understand that if he perse-veres in advocating the release of JESUS CHRIST, they will accuse him at Rome before his Imperial master, of disloyalty and supineness in the discharge of his duties as Procurator of Judæa. Pilate's scruples vanish, at once, under so formida-ble a threat. He knows the suspicious and irritable temper of Tiberius; and he fears less to put the SON of GOD to death, than to incur the Roman Emperor's dis-pleasure. Accordingly,

13 When Pilate therefore heard that saying, he brought JESUS forth, and sat down in the judgment-seat in a place that is called the Pave-ment, but in the Hebrew, Gabbatha.

"The word is Syriac or Chaldee; called Hebrew here, according to the custom of the new Testament, which calls the Syriac language, (being at that time the vulgar tongue of the Jews,) *Hebrew*."(*p*) Thus Golgotha, in ver. 17, and one of the in-scriptions on the Cross, in ver. 20, are spoken of as belonging to the Hebrew tongue. On the Cross, Hammond says the words were Syriac in Hebrew letters.
Pilate is thus related to have passed sentence on our LORD in the place appointed for the trial and condemnation of criminals. What is here called "the Pavement" is supposed to have been a piece of mosaic or tesselated work, whereon the judgment-seat stood. Julius Cæsar, in his military expeditions, carried about with him a "pavement" of this description. The Jews called the locality "Gabbatha," (which means *raised* or *elevated*,) with reference, seemingly, to the lofty place where the Roman Governor sat.

14 And it was the preparation of the Passover, and about the sixth hour: and he saith unto the Jews, Behold your King!

Before, it was "Behold the Man!" See ver. 5, and the note there. Pilate now grows reckless, and bestows upon our SAVIOUR the title which he knows is most obnoxious. How maddened with senseless rage they had by this time become, their rejoinder, in ver. 15, sufficiently shows.

(*n*) Grotius.   (*o*) Hammond.   (*p*) Hammond.

Thus does St. John fix the day, and the hour of the day, when the Roman Governor delivered up our SAVIOUR into the hands of His Enemies. See the note on St. John i. 39. "The Preparation of the Passover" signifies the Friday in Passover-Week: "the sixth hour," in St. John's Gospel, is not Twelve at noon, but *Six o'clock in the morning.* This has been explained more than once, in a previous part of the commentary.(q)

15 But they cried out, Away with *Him,* away with *Him,* crucify Him. Pilate saith unto them, Shall I crucify your King?

Take notice how Pilate persists in bestowing the title of "King." upon our SAVIOUR. Ever since his inquiry, in chap. xviii. 33, ("Art Thou the King of the Jews?") until he inscribes it on the title over His Cross, the Roman perseveres in this appellation;(r) which he may have felt a growing conviction, in some way, *belonged* to CHRIST; while it was evidently most distasteful to His enemies. There may have been bitter irony also in this: for Pilate was addressing a people whom he and his countrymen despised; a people now in utter subjection to the Roman Power. And it seems to be implied that the scorned and outraged Being who stood before him, was a fit person to be styled the King of such a race. At the same time, who sees not that, (as in the case of Caiaphas,)(s) what was spoken in cruelty, was overruled by a Higher Power to a lofty issue: that there was Divinest Truth in what was meant for mockery and insult? See the note on St. Matth. xxvi. 65.

"But with whatever view Pilate thus expressed himself, he thereby drew forth from the Rulers of the Jews that public rejection of JESUS as their King, which led to the rejection of their nation by GOD. They were so blinded by their eagerness to accomplish the destruction of JESUS, that they did not scruple to make such an acknowledgment of Cæsar's sovereignty over them, as was at variance with all their national principles and feelings."(t)

The chief Priests answered, We have no King but Cæsar.

As if they had said,—We have never acknowledged Him by any such title. It is thou, not we, who favour these pretensions. "We have no king but Cæsar!" (whereas their Fathers used to exclaim, "*We have no King but* GOD!") . . . And the miserable men who by such an argument urge Pilate to the commission of a crime which he dreads, but has no longer the courage to refuse, thereby convict themselves of rebellion, when they subsequently resist their Roman masters; and seal their own subjection to that cruel Power which in a few years will destroy them root and branch, overthrow their Temple and City, and inflict greater misery upon them than is recorded in the annals of any other nation, since the beginning of the world. See the note on St. Mark xiii. 19.

16 Then delivered he Him therefore unto them to be crucified. And they took JESUS and led *Him* away.

"And when they had mocked Him, they took off the purple from Him, and put His own clothes on Him, and led Him out to crucify Him."(u) . . . All the Evangelists, in this way, pass straight from Pilate's condemnation, or rather surrender of our LORD, to His Crucifixion. But we find that it was not until "the third hour,"(x) (that is, not until nine o'clock in the forenoon,) that "they crucified Him." Three hours had therefore elapsed, during which the hideous preparations for Death were in progress:— a severe aggravation doubtless of our SAVIOUR's sufferings; prolonging, as it did, His pains, and exposing Him to the brutality of an infuriated populace, and ruffianly soldiery. Satan was not inactive at such a time; and his agents were all about him. An important statement follows:

17 And He bearing His Cross went forth

That is, the SAVIOUR "went forth" or "out" *of the City-gate;* being there relieved of His awful burthen by "a man of Cyrene, Simon by name,"(y) who was even then "coming out of the country" and about to enter Jerusalem,—as the Evange-

(q) See the notes on St. John i. 39: iv. 6, and 52.
(r) See the notes on St. John xviii. 37.   (s) See the notes on St. John xi. 49 to 52.
(t) Lonsdale and Hale.
(u) St. Mark xv. 20: compare St. Matth. xxvii. 31.
(x) St. Mark xv. 25.   (y) St. Matth. xxvii. 32.

lists are careful to explain.(z)   St. John, omitting this incident, alone relates that the REDEEMER at first, (in conformity with the established custom of the Romans,) was made to bear His own Cross.   But what was a mere aggravation of bodily suffering in the case of others, was in the case of the Incarnate WORD, much more. He thereby showed that JEHOVAH had "laid on Him the iniquity of us all ;" and that "surely He hath borne our griefs, and carried our sorrows !"(a) . . . Hereby, too, was fulfilled a famous type ; for that "Isaac bearing the wood did presignify CHRIST bearing the Cross,"(b) is observed not only by Christians.   Pearson shows the " the Jews themselves have referred this type unto that custom : for upon the words, "And Abraham took the wood of the burnt-offering, and laid it upon Isaac his son,"(c) they have this note,—"as a man *carries his Cross upon his shoulders.*" —The true Isaac, therefore, went forth :

into a place called *the place* of a skull, which is called in the Hebrew Golgotha :

A place outside the city-gate,(d) set apart for the execution of criminals, and which doubtless derived its Syriac(e) appellation from the hideous insignia of death which may well have abounded there.   Close to it, however, as we shall be presently reminded, there was a garden ;(f) one, indeed, which seems to have been kept with care.(g) . . . In the mean time they have reached this awful spot :

18 Where they crucified Him, and two others with Him, on either side one, and JESUS in the midst.

These two were robbers, as we learn from the other Gospels : whereby, doubtless, it was craftily intended to draw as thick a veil as malice could devise over the Righteousness of CHRIST.   Not vainly, however, does the Psalmist counsel,—"Commit thy way unto the LORD, . . . and He shall bring forth thy righteousness as the light."(h)   Hereby, it came to pass, (1st) that a prophecy of Isaiah was fulfilled : (i) (2dly) that CHRIST found a Confessor upon the very Cross.   "Then said JESUS, FATHER, forgive them ; for they know not what they do :"(k)—which is the first of His seven last sayings !

The present Evangelist, until he has to describe the breaking of the legs of the malefactors, notices in no other way the fate of the two men who were thus crucified with CHRIST.   St. Luke it is who relates the striking circumstance that they bore in a manner the image of those who shall stand at His Right and at His Left in Judgment,—"the elect of GOD, and the reprobate :"(l) and to St. Luke's Gospel the reader must be referred on this most important, and very instructive subject.(m)

19 And Pilate wrote a title, and put *it* on the Cross.   And the writing was, JESUS OF NAZARETH, THE KING OF THE JEWS.

The inscription upon the Cross of CHRIST, (concerning which, see the note on St. Luke xxiii. 38,(n) is recorded, with slight and unimportant variations, by all the four Evangelists ;(o) but St. John alone relates the name of its author, and the circumstances under which it was written, in the verses which follow.

20 This title then read many of the Jews : for the place where JESUS was crucified was nigh to the city : and it was written in Hebrew, *and* Greek, *and* Latin.

(z) See the notes on St. Matthew xxvii. 31, 32 : also, on St. Mark xv. 21.
(a) Isaiah liii. 4, 6.
(c) Genesis xxii. 6.
(e) See above, on verse 18.
(g) Consider St. John xx. 15.
(i) Isaiah liii. 12.   See the note on St. Mark xv. 28.
(k) St. Luke xxiii. 34,—where see the note.
(l) Dr. W. H. Mill.
(m) See St. Luke xxiii. 38 to 43, and the notes there.
(n) See also on St. Matth. xxvii. 37.
(o) St. Matth. xxvii. 37.   St. Mark xv. 26.   St. Luke xxiii. 38.

(b) Bishop Pearson.
(d) Consider Hebrews xiii. 12.
(f) See below, verse 41.
(h) Psalm xxxvii. 5, 6.

21 Then said the chief Priests of the Jews to Pilate, Write not, The
King of the Jews; but that He said, I am King of the Jews.
22 Pilate answered, What I have written, I have written.

See above, the notes at pp. 886 and 888. . . . How remarkable was the firmness
of Pilate in this particular! The Chief Priests have had their own way in every
thing else: but in *this* respect, at least, the Roman will not yield. "He doth act
the Prophet almost as well as Caiaphas. 'What I have written, I have written;'
and it shall stand and obtain. They shall have no other King MESSIAH than this
for ever!"(*p*) . . May he have had an awful consciousness all the while upon him,
that what he had written was *the Truth?* or was he simply bent on indulging the
naturally obstinacy and inflexibility of his own disposition,—wholly unconscious
of everything beside?

"It was not for nothing," (says Pearson, beautifully,) "that Pilate suddenly
wrote, and resolutely maintained what he had written. That title on the Cross did
signify no less than that His Royal power was active even there: for ' having spoiled
Principalities and Powers, He made a show of them openly, triumphing over them
in it ;'(*q*) and, 'through His Death, destroyed him that had the power of Death,
that is, the Devil.' "(*x*)

23 Then the soldiers, when they had crucified JESUS, took His garments, and made four parts, to every soldier a part;

"Casting lots upon them," (says St. Mark,) "what every man should take."(*s*)
And thus, at the very foot of the Cross of CHRIST, was enacted the emblem of that
triumph over our SAVIOUR which the Powers of Darkness, it may well be supposed,
by this time thought secure! They had slain their great Enemy, (the Devils will
have already assumed;) and their wicked agents may now be instigated to "*divide
the spoil.*" See the references on St. Luke xi. 22. . . . Little can it have been imagined by those accursed ones that the Cross of CHRIST was to be the very instrument of MESSIAH's final Triumph: that Satan had indeed succeeded in "bruising
the heel" of the Son of Man; but that, in return, the Seed of the Woman, the Incarnate WORD, was about to fulfil the primœval prophecy, and to "bruise his
head:"(*t*) that One stronger than "the strong Man armed" had at last appeared;
had already overcome him, and taken from him the armour wherein he trusted;
and was even now about to spoil his goods.(*u*) . . . . All this has been so fully discussed on more than one previous occasion, that it shall suffice here simply to refer
the reader to an earlier page of the present Commentary.(*w*) Let it only be further suggested that the paltry evidence of success which was actually discernible,
—as contrasted with the signal and utter, but *unseen*, defeat which was in reality
going on,—affords no unapt image of the relation which Earthly persecution bears
to Heavenly Glory; the slender and hollow triumph which attends the best directed
endeavours of the wicked against the Church of CHRIST, and His accepted servants,
—compared with the glorious Victory which is in store alike for *it*, and for *them;*
but which is revealed, on this side of Eternity, to the eye of Faith alone. . . . They
"took His garments," therefore,—

and also *His* coat: now the coat was without seam, woven from the
top throughout.   ·

The word here translated "coat" denotes an *inner* garment. . . . St. John alone
mentions the mysterious circumstance here recorded: for it doubtless *is* a mysterious circumstance. In other words, this apparently trivial statement is full of sacred import, which yet does not strike the common reader.(*y*) Was the seamless
coat allusive to the lofty *Priesthood* of the Divine Wearer? for it seems to correspond

(*p*) Lightfoot.   (*q*) Col. ii. 15.
(*r*) Heb. ii. 14.   (*s*) St. Mark xv. 24.
(*t*) Genesis iii. 15.
(*u*) Consider St. Luke xi. 22, and the note there; also St. Luke xiii. 16, and the latter part
of the note on the place. See also St. Mark iii. 27.
(*w*) See especially St. John xii. 31: also chap. xvi. 11. The reader is also requested to read
what has been offered on St. Matth. xxvii. 35.
(*y*) Consider what was offered on the last words of St. John xviii. 10.

in description with what is related(z) of the High Priest's tunic. Cyprian says,—
"Because CHRIST'S people cannot be rent and torn by divisions, His tunic, seamless
and woven throughout, was not rent by them into whose hands it fell. Single,—
united,—connected,—it shows the concord which should subsist among as many of
ourselves as put on CHRIST. That vest of His declares to us, in a sacrament, the
Unity of the Church." Chrysostom, in like manner, (speaking of the sin of Division,) says that it is to do that which even those men did not dare to do,—namely,
to rend into many pieces the seamless garment of our LORD. For, (as it follows,)

24 They said therefore among themselves, Let us not rend it, but
cast lots for it, whose it shall be: that the Scripture might be fulfilled,
which saith, They parted My raiment among them, and for My vesture
they did cast lots.

The fullest, and by far the most interesting account of what befell the garments
of the Holy JESUS is given by St. John. But the reader is referred to the note on
the latter part of St. Matth. xxvii. 35,—where the present remarkable quotation
from Psalm xxii. 18 is also found. How little can the author of that Psalm, so full
of a suffering MESSIAH, have suspected the awful and literal sense which his words
were destined hereafter to receive!... "These Divine garments," (says a pious
writer,) "from the very hem of which 'virtue went forth and healed them all,'(a)
we may well suppose were, of all things that hand of man had ever formed, the
most worthy of being expressly spoken of by all of the Four Evangelists, and by
the Prophet beforehand. . . . . CHRIST, like Joseph, was about to flee from this
evil and adulterous World; and leave His garment in its hands."(b)

Such then was the rapacity of the four miscreants, (the quarternion of Soldiers,)
who were appointed to superintend the Sacrifice of CHRIST, that His poor outer
garments must be divided among them; and even His tunic is not spared! Thus
it came to pass that our SAVIOUR was crucified in nakedness, — whereby He undid
the shame of our first father Adam: for consider Gen. iii. 10.

These things therefore the soldiers did.

Does that mean, — Such was the part which the soldiers played in this terrible
Tragedy? Uninfluenced by the Jews, — without any directions from Pilate, —
"these things the soldiers did."

25 Now there stood by the Cross of JESUS His Mother, and His
Mother's Sister, Mary the *wife* of Cleophas, and Mary Magdalene.

The three Marys!... that the Virgin should not have forsaken the side of her
adorable Son at this fearful moment, no one who knows the nature of a Mother's
love will at all wonder. The surprise would have been if she had been away.
Meantime, what *she felt*,—aged Simon had long before described by that mysterious
prediction, "Yea, a sword shall *pierce through thy own soul* also!"(c) She, who
had known no pang at the Birth of CHRIST, is tortured to extremity at His Death!

But it excites both surprise and admiration to read that "Mary the [wife] of
Cleophas,(d) and Mary Magedelene," should have had the courage to press up to the
very Cross of our Blessed LORD at such a time. The second of our SAVIOUR'S sayings on the Cross, follows. It suggests the remark, (sufficiently probable on other
grounds,) that Joseph, the Blessed Virgin's husband, was now dead.

26, 27 When JESUS therefore saw His Mother, and the Disciple
standing by whom He loved, He saith unto His Mother, Woman,
behold thy Son! Then saith He to the Disciple, Behold thy Mother!

Besides the three Marys the Evangelist himself is found to have remained faithful to our SAVIOUR to the very last; and to have stood by the Cross of his Divine
Master until it was "finished." . . . . O amazing privilege! thus to have been
appointed by the Incarnate WORD Himself to supply His place towards His

(z) By Josephus.   (a) St. Luke vi. 19.
(b) Williams.   (c) St. Luke ii. 35.
(d) "Cleophas," our translators have erroneously retained from the Vulgate.

bereaved Mother! How stupendous a legacy was this for Divine Piety to bequeath, and for adoring Love to inherit! . . . The Blessed Virgin was henceforth to regard St. John with maternal affection: while the Disciple himself was "to love, honour, and succour" that holy Woman, as though he had been in reality her son. " It is clear then that the presence of the Godhead in our LORD's person did not efface and outshine the essential feelings of a Human heart. It did but quicken and strengthen all those affections and sympathies which are still left us as remnants of the Heavenly image, and the groundwork of its renewal within us. As GOD, our SAVIOUR might have removed His human Mother to the best of those "many mansions" which are prepared for those that love Him. But it was *as* GOD He willed that she should stay awhile on earth: while, *as Man*, He both provided a home for her such as He could never give her while He lived; and called the human feelings of a friend into play in her behalf, while He did so."(*f*) Do we need the assurance which follows?

And from that hour that Disciple took her unto his own *home.*

The abode, namely, of St. John, and St. James, and their Mother Salome, (who was even now beholding the scene from a little distance;)(*g*) for Zebedee was probably now dead. — The word "*home*" is not found in the original; and yet, the phrase "took her home," would probably have exactly conveyed the meaning of an expression which recurs in St. John i. 11: xvi. 32; and Acts xxi. 6.

Truly has it been observed that "there is no incident in St. John's life more touching than this; none, which in a few words conveys more fully his nearness and dearness to his LORD's human affections."(*h*) It is as obvious, as it is delightful, to imagine the tender care of the beloved Disciple, henceforth, towards his adopted Mother. How will they, evermore, have discoursed together of their SAVIOUR and their GOD!—the reverence of either towards the other increasing, as the vastness of their respective privileges became more and more apparent to themselves. "Imagination and thought are overwhelmed when we look into that home, where CHRIST's beloved Disciple and CHRIST's Mother were. Surely that place must have been the resort of holy Angels, if any habitation on Earth has been meet to be so."(*i*) St. John will at last have closed her eyes, — at Ephesus perhaps; himself calmly tarrying for the fulfillment of his LORD's mysterious promise to " come" to him, after many days. But, from this place in the history, all is left to conjecture. The Blessed Virgin emerges but once(*j*) from the secrecy and shelter of that roof which St. John was careful henceforth to provide for her bereaved and widowed head.

" It is remarkable," (observes a pious writer,)(*k*) " how Holy Scripture seems to have thrown around her a sort of Holy silence. There appears, also, to be a sort of mysterious reserve in what is recorded of our LORD's expressions towards her. It was, as we may venture to suppose, out of tender consideration for our weakness; and from His foreseeing that great heresy which should arise in the Church, under the plea of doing her honor. And this will account for the circumstance, that on the very few occasions when our LORD is mentioned as addressing His Mother, there is something different from what we should have been, perhaps, inclined to expect." On the present occasion, what chiefly strikes us is the purely *human* character of the incident recorded; and indeed it is the very aspect of our LORD's words which makes them so exceedingly affecting.

Do any inquire what Divine lesson this transaction conveys? " Learn from it, first, that the Grace of GOD is designed to deepen and strengthen all the better feelings of our Human Nature. — Learn next, to seek to supply in the Church of GOD those relationships of which our Heavenly FATHER, year by year, is pleased to bereave us. The tie of Christian Brotherhood, if truly realized, will both incite us to become to the bereaved of human friends, a substitute, in some degree, (as St. John was,) for the departed; and it will bid us also seek, if we be ourselves the bereaved, (like the Virgin Mother,) the solace of our lost joys in drawing closer to those who love their LORD, and dwell in the same Household of Faith."(*l*)

(*f*) From a MS. Sermon by the Rev. Edm. Hobhouse.
(*g*) St. Matth. xxvii. 55, 56.
(*i*) Williams.
(*k*) Williams.
(*l*) From a MS. Sermon by the Rev. Edm. Hobhouse.

(*h*) From the same MS. Sermon.
(*j*) See Acts i. 14.

28 After this, JESUS knowing that all things were now accomplished,

Literally,—"that all things are now *finished.*" The word is the self-same as in ver. 30, and suggests some striking considerations. "Behold, we are going up to Jerusalem," (our LORD had said on a previous occasion ;) "and all things that are written by the Prophets concerning the Son of Man *must be finished.*"(*m*) There yet remained one article of the Passion, which had been foretold. It follows, therefore, that our SAVIOUR,—

that the Scripture might be fulfilled, saith, I thirst.

The reader is invited to refer to the note on St. Luke xxii. 37.—This was the fifth of the Seven last sayings of CHRIST. It had been said prophetically, in a Psalm which is full of His Passion,—"My strength is dried up like a potsherd ; and My tongue cleaveth to My jaws." But a more striking fulfillment than this, is here alluded to: for David elsewhere says,—"They gave Me also gall for My meat; and in My thirst they gave Me vinegar to drink."(*o*) Accordingly, besides the very literal fulfillment which these words had already received,(*p*) it is found that in reply to our LORD's express declaration that He *thirsted,* the bystanders proceeded to offer Him vinegar to drink. This seems to have been no longer done in cruelty and insult as before :(*q*) but the beverage was furnished from the provision which the soldiers had made for their own use. As it follows:

29 Now there was set a vessel full of vinegar: and they filled a sponge with vinegar, and put *it* upon hyssop, and put *it* to His mouth.

St. Matthew and St. Mark write of a sponge filled with vinegar, put "*upon a reed.*"(*r*) St. John, by his further mention of "hyssop," leaves us to the conjecture, that the reed which was employed on the present occasion for conveying a moistened sponge to the lips of our expiring REDEEMER, was none other than the instrument used for the purpose of sprinkling the people ; a use to which we know that a bunch of hyssop, (fastened, as we may reasonably conjecture, to the extremity of a reed,) was largely applied under the Law.(*s*) . . . . . And thus, for the last time, (for of every such "shadow of good things to come, '(*t*) it was now said, " It is finished,") a type will have been exhibited, even beside the very Cross of CHRIST, of the work of Him who, (in the words of the Evangelical prophet,) came *to " sprinkle many nations.*"(*u*) . . . . . Consider by all means, in connection with this great subject, the ixth chapter of the Epistle to the Hebrews, verse 11 to the end.

30 When JESUS therefore had received the vinegar, He said, It is finished :

The sixth of our LORD's sayings on the Cross ! . . . Do any inquire, *What was* then finished ? In truth, so many things are contained in that single word that it were hard to enumerate them all. "The sorrows of His Life were finished: the griefs, and sufferings, and humiliations which were crowded into His Youth and Ministry: the watchings and weariness, the toils and strivings. So also, the fickleness and ingratitude of the multitude ; the revilings and blasphemies of the Scribes and Pharisees ; the cruel revenge of the Priests ; all had done their work. They could do no more. There is a point at which cruelty exhausts, and hatred overreaches itself. Torture could go no further, because life could no longer sustain it. It was finished !

" It was, in truth, 'finished' " in another sense: finished, fulfilled, accomplished, *in them.* They had shown themselves the children of those who killed the Prophets: they had filled up the measure of their fathers. This was finished and fulfilled, that all the righteous blood which had been shed from the foundation of the World should

(*m*) St. Luke xviii. 31. Consider also xxii. 37.
(*n*) Ps. xxii. 15.
(*p*) See St. Matth. xxvii. 34.
(*r*) St. Matth. xxvii. 48. St. Mark xv. 36.
(*s*) See Ex. xii. 22. Levit. xiv. 4, 6, 49, 51, 52.
(*t*) Heb. x. 1.
(*o*) Ps. lxix. 21.
(*q*) St. Luke xxiii. 36.
Numb. xix. 6, 18. See Hebr. ix. 11 to 28.
(*u*) Is. lii. 15.

be required of that generation. The trial of their nation was at an end. Their destiny was completed and sealed up. It was finished!

" Then further, the life and power of the Old Covenant had come to an end. The brightness of Moses' face had passed away. Age after age had their Temple-worship gone on, and notwithstanding all their sins and all its imperfections, GOD was in it, and among *them*. But their Priesthood and their Ritual had now come to an end. Their sacrifice had ceased. The Glory had departed which had made this latter House more glorious than the former.(x) The Veil of the Temple was rent in twain, from the top to the bottom ;(y) and—It was finished!

" Once more, The long line of legal types and figures ; together with all those many predictions which ' the glorious fellowship of the Prophets,' moved by ' the Spirit of CHRIST,(z) had from time to time delivered : all things, in short, which had ever been ' written by the Prophets concerning the Son of Man,' were now ' finished.'(a) This last and greatest indignity of all, to which He had Himself referred, as still requiring ' to be accomplished,' (literally ' to be finished,') in His own person,(b)—namely, that He should be ' numbered with the transgressors,'—*this* also was now ' finished.' He may therefore bow His Holy Head,— bow it, as if in meek submission to the Will of the Eternal FATHER, and exclaim, concerning it all, ' It is finished !'

" Once more : ' Old things are passed away. Behold, all things are become new !'(c) All that had gone before was a preparation for this. The stones of the arch had been laid : the key-stone alone had been wanting. But now, the key-stone *was* laid : the arch was *finished :* and what more ado was there with the scaffolding? '*Old* things' go before the Crucifixion of CHRIST, and are ' finished.' ' *New* things' spring from His Cross. . . . ' Behold, I make all things new,' (said ' He that sat upon the throne.') And He straightway added,—' *It is done !*'(d)—' The Will of GOD is fulfilled : the scene of His dispensations is perfected : the Prophecy is sealed up : the Revelation is completed : the Atonement is made : the Victory is accomplished : the Kingdom of GOD is come ! . . . It was *the work of the New Creation ;* and CHRIST as on this day entered into His rest, and kept the Sabbath in the Grave. It was ' finished,' then ; not only in so far as ' old things' were finished and done away with ; not only as the Void was finished when the Universe was called into existence ; but it was finished also, inasmuch as new things were accomplished, and brought to perfection ; finished, as the new order of things in the Creation was finished, after the evening and the morning were the sixth day, when ' GOD saw everything that He had made ; and behold, it was very good !'(e) . . . . CHRIST had come to do the will of the FATHER that sent Him, and to finish His Work :(f) and Lo, as He had already said,—' I have glorified Thee on the Earth : *I have finished* the Work which Thou gavest Me to do ;"(g)— as, before that exclamation in ver. 28, ' I thirst,' He is declared to have known that, ' now, *all things were finished ;*"— so, finally, with His dying breath, He is careful to repeat and to affirm, that, " *It is finished !*"

It follows in St. Luke,—"And when JESUS had cried with a loud voice ;" (a memorable epithet, which is found in all the three first Gospels, and which contains the record of a miracle, as will be found explained in the note on St. Mark xv. 39 ;) " He said, FATHER, into Thy Hands I commend My Spirit."(h) . . . It was the seventh and last of the REDEEMER's sayings on the Cross !

and He bowed His Head and gave up the Ghost.

" Gave His Spirit up,"— namely, into the Hands of the Eternal FATHER :(i) whereby " a separation was made between His Soul and Body, but no disunion of them and His Deity. They were disjoined one from another ; but not from Him that took them both together. Rather, by virtue of that remaining conjunction, they were again united after their separation. . . . . The WORD was once indeed without either Soul or Body : but after it was ' made flesh,' it was never again parted from the one or from the other."(j)

(x) Haggai ii. 9.   (y) See the note on St. Matth. xxvii. 51.
(z) 1 St. Peter i. 11.   (a) St. Luke xviii. 31.
(b) St. Luke xxii. 37,—where read the note.
(c) 2 Cor. v. 17.   (d) Rev. xxi. 6.
(e) Abridged from a MS. Sermon, by the Rev. Robert Scott, D.D., Master of Balliol.
(f) St. John iv. 34. Compare chap. v. 36.
(g) St. John xvii. 4.   (h) St. Luke xxiii. 46.
(i) St. Luke xxiii. 46. Eccl. xii. 7.   (j) Bp. Pearson.

"He bowed His Head, and gave up the Ghost." "Not," (observes Chrysostom,) "that He then bowed His Head, *because* He expired; but He then expired, because He bowed His Head. By the mention of all which things, the Evangelist shows that He was the LORD of all." ... On the bowing of His Head, Origen beautifully says, that He was "reclining His Head as on His FATHER'S BOSOM."(k) Death dared not to draw nigh, (says another of the ancients,) till by bowing His Head, our SAVIOUR invited his approach. The Fathers abound in such remarks on the manner of our LORD's departure. . . . . Verily these men handled the Gospel in a very different spirit from ourselves!

"O wonderful exhibition of the goodness and severity of GOD! It is the ninth hour; and JESUS, strong to the last in suffering, commending His Spirit to the FATHER with a loud voice, bows His anointed Head, and renders up the Ghost. Nature is convulsed. Earth trembles. The Sanctuary, that type of the Heaven of Heavens, is suddenly and forcibly thrown open. The tombs are burst.(l) JESUS hangs upon the Cross, a corpse. And lo! the fountain which, according to the Prophet, was this day to be set open for Sin and pollution, is seen suddenly springing from His wound!(m) . . . Who, contemplating only in imagination the mysterious, awful scene, exclaims not with the Centurion, 'Truly, this *was* the SON of GOD!'"(n)

And here the reader is invited to notice the very marvellous and unexpected course of GOD's Providence;—a Providence, which is, "the same yesterday, to-day, and forever." "As many as were sentenced by the Romans to die upon the Cross, had not the favour of a sepulchre; but their bodies were exposed to the fowls of the air, and the beasts of the field: or, if they escape their voracity, to the longer injury of the air and weather. A guard was also usually set about them, lest any pitying hand should take the body from the cursed tree, and cover it with earth. Under that custom of the Roman law was now the Body of our SAVIOUR on the Cross, and the guard was set. There was "the Centurion, and they that were with him, watching JESUS."(o) "How then can the ancient predictions be fulfilled?" (asks learned Bishop Pearson.) "How can this Jonas be conveyed into the belly of the whale?(p) Where shall He 'make His Grave with the wicked,' or 'with the rich, — in this His death' of Crucifixion? By the Providence of Him who did foretell it, it shall be fulfilled. They who petitioned that He might be crucified, *shall petition that He might be interred.*" As it follows:

31 The Jews therefore, because it was the Preparation, that the bodies should not remain upon the Cross on the Sabbath-day, (for that Sabbath-day was an high day,) besought Pilate that their legs might be broken, and *that* they might be taken away.

It was commanded in Moses' Law,—"if a man have committed a sin worthy of death, and he be put to death, and thou hang him on a tree: his body shall not remain all night upon the tree, but thou shalt in any wise *bury him that day.*"(q) Inasmuch, however, as it was now near sunset, and a Sabbath of more than usual solemnity, (namely, the Sabbath in Paschal week,) would then begin, (throughout which, it would be unlawful to touch the bodies of the dead,)—it became necessary to act with unusual promptitude, and to remove them, all three, at once. If Death had not already put an end to the sufferings of our REDEEMER, and His companions in suffering, dissolution must therefore be accelerated by an aggravation of torture; and to break the legs of those that were crucified was a common Roman practice. It follows therefore:

32, 33 Then came the soldiers, and brake the legs of the first, and of the other which was crucified with Him. But when they came to JESUS, and saw that He was dead already, they brake not His legs:

Our SAVIOUR then, "was dead already:" dead, — because He had seen fit to die. It is however, in addition, a plain fact, and allowable that we should point out, that He had submitted to an infinitely larger amount of suffering than the two

---

(k) Quoted by Williams.
(m) See below, ver. 34.
(o) St. Matth. xxvii. 54.
(q) Deut. xxi. 22, 23. Take notice that "*to be* put to death," as in our Version, is a mistranslation. *Death* was the punishment. Hanging was an indignity offered to the dead body.

(l) St. Matth. xxvii. 51 to 54.
(n) Bp. Horsley.
(p) See St. Matth. xii. 40.

malefactors who were crucified with Him. Bp. Pearson remarks in a certain place,
that "although the Human Nature was conjoined to the Divine, in our LORD's
person, yet it suffered as much as if it had been alone; and the Divine as little suffered as if it had not been conjoined; because each kept their respective proper-
ties distinct, without the least confusion in their most intimate conjunction." That
the Divine Nature can suffer *nothing*, admits of no manner of doubt: but does not
the pious writer understate the truth, when he declares the case of our LORD's
Humanity? Its perfect texture doubtless rendered its Possessor sensible, to an
unknown extent, of outward violence: while its union with GODhead may well
have added intensity to every description of suffering.

**34 But one of the soldiers with a spear pierced His side, and forth-
with came there out Blood and Water.**

"It was not out of compassion that the merciless soldiers brake not His legs,"
(says Pearson,) "but because they found Him dead whom they came to dispatch,
and being enraged that their cruelty should be thus prevented, with an impertinent
villany they pierced His side; thereby becoming stronger witnesses than they would,
by being less the authors than they desired, of His Death."—Whether this was indeed the sentiment with which the soldier committed the outrage described in the
text, and which was overruled to so marvellous a result, may perhaps be doubted.
But the question is unimportant. The statement which follows, however, yields
perhaps to none in the whole Book of Life for august dignity, and mysterious interest: and we should endeavor to ascertain its true value and import.

That one great purpose of it was to furnish a convincing proof of the reality of
CHRIST's Death, we nothing doubt: but we turn away, with sorrow and concern,
not to say with amazement, from those who can really believe that this is a full account of the matter; that no miracle is here recorded; and that the solemn attestation of the Evangelist, contained in the next verse, means so little, — or rather,
means nothing at all.(r) . . . . A little attention to what has been written on this
subject, will not be misspent here.

"These are the two blessed Sacraments of the Spouse of CHRIST," (says Bishop
Pearson,) "each assuring her of the Death of her Beloved." By those words, he
clearly adopts a favorite interpretation of many of the ancient Fathers; an interpretation which Chrysostom repeats four or five times, and Augustine nearly thrice as
often, in his writings.(s) The latter delights in drawing it out in detail; and, (as
Ambrose had done before him,) connecting it with that prophetic saying in the
third Psalm,—"I laid Me down *and slept; I* awaked; for the LORD sustained Me."
"CHRIST *slept*," (he says,) "upon the Cross: and *there* exhibited in figure, nay,
there He fulfilled in reality, what Adam had foreshown in the Garden. For, while
Adam slept, Eve was formed out of his side: and so, while our LORD slept," (but
it was the sleep of Death,) "out of His pierced and wounded side the Sacraments
flowed," — from which the Church receives life and spiritual nutriment. "Thus,
the Spouse of CHRIST was fashioned out of the side of CHRIST; even as Eve was
fashioned out of the side of Adam." . . . . In the words of our own Hooker: "GOD
made Eve of the rib of Adam; and His Church, He frameth out of the very wounded and bleeding side of the Son of Man. His Body crucified, and His Blood shed
for the life of the World are the true elements of that heavenly being, which maketh
us such as Himself is, of whom we come. For which cause the words of Adam
may be fitly the Words of CHRIST concerning His Church, 'flesh of My flesh, and
bone of My bones;'(t) a true native extract out of Mine own Body." Augustine
beautifully points out how, in strictness, it is said in Genesis ii. 22, that, of Adam's
rib, GOD "*builded* a woman:"(u) and reminds us that St. Paul accordingly speaks
of "*edifying*," (that is "*building*,") the Body of CHRIST."(x) We know indeed
that St. Paul is there speaking of "*the Church*, — which is *His Body*."(y) We
know too that Adam "is the figure of Him that was to come;"(z) and that "as in
Adam all die, even so in CHRIST shall all be made alive."(a) . . . . The very *day* on

(r) See the note on ver. 35. — Those who talk of "the pericardium," and "a serous matter
resembling water," know not what they say.
(s) A remarkable testimony, by the way, to the answer in our Catechism, which follows the
question, — "How many Sacraments hath CHRIST ordained in His Church?"

(t) Gen. ii. 23: consider Ephes. v. 20.   (u) See the margin of Gen. ii. 22.
(x) Eph. iv. 12.   (y) Ephes. i. 23.
(s) Rom. v. 14.   (a) 1 Cor. xv. 22.

which all this happened is not without meaning. It was on the sixth day that Man was created "in the beginning:" and lo, on the sixth day, Man is created anew in Christ!

It would be difficult, indeed, to believe that so beautiful and apt a specimen of allegorical interpretation, adopted as it has been by so many judicious Divines of our own Communion, is other than trustworthy. We gratefully accept it, and recommend it to our reader's acceptance; with the humble suggestion that, perhaps, it will be safer not to *insist*, (with good Bp. Andrewes, in a certain place,)(b) that these are none other than "the twin-sacraments of the Church: Baptism, and the Cup of the New Testament,"—the one precisely signified by the Water; the other, precisely by the Blood. There is a great consent of the Fathers as to the *general* reference of the present miracle to the Sacraments: and we shall be safest if we do not attempt to define over closely. CHRIST,—(says a Bishop of Hierapolis who was born about fifty years after St. John wrote his Gospel,)—CHRIST "shed out of His side the two renewed [instruments of Man's] cleansing,—Water and Blood." (c) And what is this but the very language of our own Baptismal service; whereby, in effect, the Church connects with Holy Baptism the fountain which gushed forth from our REDEEMER's side? Because He was the SON of GOD, (remarks a great expositor of Scripture,) "by His Divine Power infused into both, He gave the Water such a piercing force, and the Blood so inestimably high a value, as was able to put an end to that which neither the Washings nor Sacrifices, of Nature or of the Law, could rid us of."(d) The first,—was that "Fountain opened to the House of David and to the inhabitants of Jerusalem for Sin and for uncleanness," which had been predicted long before by the Prophet Zechariah:(e) the second,— that "Blood of His Testament, whereby He set His guilty prisoners free;" so mysteriously noticed by the same prophet.(f) .. "The flowing of this Water and this Blood, immediately upon our LORD's Death, from the wound opened in His side, was a notification to the surrounding multitudes, though at the time understood by few, that the real expiation was now complete, and the cleansing fount set open."(g)

"This is He that came by Water and Blood,"(h)—saith the SPIRIT; with clear reference to the present place of the Gospel. .. Bp. Andrewes observes upon those words,—"Thus did CHRIST come: did, and doth still. And that He means *His coming to us*, the order showeth. For when it came *from Him*, it came in another order: Blood came first, *then* Water. See the Gospel. But here, in the Epistle, when He comes to us, Water is first, then Blood. 'Blood and Water,' the order on *His* side: 'Water and Blood,' the order on *ours*. Even to us, in Water first!"

Yet a few words, and we pass on. "This is He that came by Water and Blood," (saith the SPIRIT,) "even JESUS CHRIST; *not by Water only*," (it is straightway added,) "*but by Water and Blood*."(i) Doubtless, another aspect of this great mystery is here opened to our view, and St. John is the interpreter of his own words. JESUS, (he implies,) "was proved to be the CHRIST,—not by the Water only, but by the Water *and the Blood*."(k) And when the entire passage is taken with its context; when it is considered that the Apostle is engaged in confuting those who denied that JESUS is the CHRIST,—the Cerinthian heretics on the one hand, who denied His Divinity; the sect of the Docetæ, on the other, who denied His Manhood; —how is it possible to avoid suspecting that what He means, by appealing to the miracle before us is, that our SAVIOUR CHRIST came with those two as witnesses(l) that He was very *Man* as well as very GOD? that He came not only in the Divine Nature,—which was symbolized by the *Water;* but in the Human,—which was symbolized by the *Blood?* ... Traces of this interpretation are to be found in some of the early commentators, as Gregory of Nazianzus and Theophylact; and it is advocated by one of the most learned of modern Doctors,—the late venerable President of Magdalen College; a Divine whose remarks on such subjects were ever

---

(b) Serm. xiii., "Of the sending of the HOLY GHOST." Andrewes is there adopting an expression of Augustine,—which, however, the present writer cannot find anywhere in the writings of that Father.

(c) Apollinaris. He seems to mean that these correspond with the legal means of Purification. Consider Hebr. ix. 18 to 22.

(d) Bishop Andrewes.

(f) Bp. Andrewes, quoting Zech. ix. 11.

(h) 1 St. John v. 6.

(k) Bishop Horsley.

(e) Zech. xiii. 1.

(g) Bp. Horsley.

(i) 1 St. John v. 6.

(l) Consider Deut. xvii. 6, and xix. 15.

singularly cautious and well-weighed. He calls attention to the following places, which, in his judgment, illustrate the matter in hand:—St. John i. 13: iv. 14: xix. 34. St. Matth. xvi. 17. Rom. i. 3, 4. Heb. ii. 14. 1 St. John iv. 2, 3: 2 St. John 7. Acts v. 32.(*m*)
"If the Jews that stood by said truly of Him at Lazarus' grave, Behold how He loved him! when He shed a few tears out of His eyes; much more truly may we say, Behold how He loved. *us!* seeing Him shed both Blood and Water in great plenty out of His heart:"(*n*) "which He ministered in so great abundance, that all His blood did stream over us, until He made the fountain dry; and reserved nothing of that by which He knew His Church was to 'live and move and have her being.' "(*o*)
These are many words: but he who will be at the pains to consider the immense dignity of the subject, will not think them superfluous. "It was with prophetic reference to this wound in CHRIST's side," (writes Augustine,) "that Noah was commanded to make a door in the side of the Ark, by which every creature might enter, which was to be saved from perishing in the waters of the Flood." The Rock which, when smitten by Moses' rod, sent forth a stream of water for the parched assembly of the people, presented a lively image of the same transaction "That Rock," (we know,) "was CHRIST;"(*p*) and, what is strange, the Targum of Jonathan(*q*) records a tradition, that when Moses first struck it, "it dropped *blood:* at the second time, came out much *water.*" . . Thus foreshadowed by many a type, and discoursed of in many a prophecy.(*r*)—represented in emblem, even while it was being inflicted,(*s*)—and appealed to by St. Thomas, and by CHRIST,— the wound in our SAVIOUR's side is connected by the beloved Disciple with the mention of the great and terrible Day itself:—"Every eye shall see Him, and *they also which pierced Him!*"(*t*) . . . It follows:

35 And he that saw *it* bare record, and his record is true: and he knoweth that he saith truth, that ye might believe.

"St. John dwells upon it with earnest, reiterated asseveration, as a thing so wonderful that the explicit testimony of an eye-witness was requisite to make it credible; and yet of great importance to be accredited, as a main foundation of the Faith." When a man so speaks, "he certainly speaks of something extraordinary, and hard to be believed; and yet, in his judgment, of great importance." Moreover, "he must be supposed to speak with the most scrupulous precision, and to call everything by its name. The Water, therefore, which he says he saw streaming from the wound, was as truly water, as the Blood was blood; and herein consists the miracle. This pure Water and this pure Blood coming forth together, are two of those three earthly witnesses, whose testimony is so efficacious for the confirmation of the Faith."(*u*)
"*He that saw it* bare record." "From this one sentence we discover what was St. John's special work among the Evangelists of his LORD. It was to bear record, as eye-witness and ear-witness, of those things which he had seen and heard; and that he might bear record, he was privileged to see more than all the rest." Take notice how he rejoices in his office, and speaks ever of his own experience as the proof of his record:—"That which was from the beginning, which we have heard, which we have seen with our eyes, which we have looked upon, and our hands have handled, of the WORD of Life: . . . that which we have heard and seen declare we unto you."(*x*) With such language he opens his Epistle: while his Gospel begins and ends(*y*) with a similar declaration.(*z*)
"That *ye* might believe." Is not St. John the only Evangelist who in this manner addresses his Christian readers?(*a*)

(*m*) The learned reader is referred to the first volume of the *Reliquiæ,* pp. 170, 171, 487.
(*n*) Bp. Andrewes.   (*o*) Bp. Taylor.
(*p*) 1 Cor. x. 4.
(*q*) On Numb. xx. 11. However worthless the tradition, its existence in a Jewish Commentary of the Apostolic age is surely a marvellous circumstance.
(*r*) Zech. xii. 10: xiii. 1.
(*s*) Consider St. Matth. xxvii. 51, in connection with Heb. x. 19, 20.
(*t*) Rev. i. 7.   (*u*) Bp. Horsley.
(*x*) 1 St. John i. 1, 3.   (*y*) St. John i. 14: xxi. 24.
(*z*) Abridged from a MS. Sermon by the Rev. Edm. Hobhouse.
(*a*) Here, and in chap. xx. 31.

36 For these things were done, that the Scripture should be fulfilled, A bone of Him shall not be broken.

The Scripture alluded to, is found to be partly Exodus xii. 46, partly Psalm xxxiv. 20; a blended quotation, and therefore intended doubtless as well to recall the prophetical bearing of the place in the Psalms, as of the Paschal type.

37 And again another Scripture saith, They shall look on Him whom they pierced.

This should be printed "They shall look on *Me*, whom they pierced;" as the learned reader, with a Greek Gospel before him, will perceive at a glance. The prophet Zechariah so writes in the remarkable place from which the text is quoted, —chap. xii. 10; where it will be perceived that JEHOVAH is the Speaker. CHRIST is therefore JEHOVAH. . . . In the ensuing chapter, Zechariah notices the wounds in our SAVIOUR's *Hands*."(b)

There seems to be truth in the suggestion that this prophecy embraces a distinct reference to both the Advents of CHRIST. "They *pierced" Him*,—now: "they **shall** *look on Him*,"— then. For, (as the same St. John by Revelation elsewhere writes,)—"Behold, He cometh with clouds; and every eye shall see Him,(c) *and they also which pierced Him*."(d) . . . . Take notice, also, that the prophecy of Zechariah proceeds, — "and they *shall mourn for Him*, as one mourneth for his only son." While St. John's next words in the same Book of Revelation,—"and all kindreds of the Earth *shall wail because of Him*."

38 And after this, Joseph of Arimathæa, being a Disciple of JESUS, but secretly for fear of the Jews, besought Pilate that he might take away the Body of JESUS:

What evidence have we here of a noble nature! The sight of the ignominious death to which his LORD had submitted, instead of quenching his zeal or his love, only caused the dull embers to burst into a flame. The transition, in the case of the Divine Sufferer, from exceeding degradation to some slight foretaste of the glory which awaited Him, is instantaneous. . . . It follows:

and Pilate gave *him* leave. He came therefore, and took the Body of JESUS.

Holy, and thrice happy man: though, as yet, little conscious of his happiness! Least of all, when he planted for himself a garden, and dug in the rock a new grave for himself, can he have suspected what was in store for that garden and that grave! . . . . Surely, this entire history has consecrated expensive funerals, and given a solemn sanction to care bestowed on burial-places, for ever! The reader is referred to a few remarks which have been already offered on this transaction, in the commentary on St. Matth. xxvii. 58 and 60: on St. Mark xv. 42 to 46; and on St. Luke xxiii. 51.—Augustine points out that He who died for the sake of others, might well rest in the tomb of another: that the Prince of Life could require no sepulchral chamber of His own: nay, that it was but for three days that He needed the rich man's tomb, at all; during which brief period, He "laid Him down and slept" "*a deep sleep*."(e)

39 And there came also Nicodemus, which at the first came to JESUS by night, and brought a mixture of myrrh and aloes, about an hundred pound *weight*.

Thus, even in death, it may be said of Him, "All Thy garments smell of myrrh, aloes, and cassia!"(g) . . . "There had been an interpreted,(h) and an intended,(i) unction of our SAVIOUR; but really and actually He was interred with the spices which Nicodemus brought."(k) The large quantity specified indicates alike the opulence and the love of this disciple; and indeed, from what we read of the man-

---

(b) Zech. xiii. 6.　　　　　(c) Compare St. Matth. xxvi. 64.
(d) Rev. i. 7.　　　　　　　(e) Gen. ii. 31.
(g) Ps. xlv. 8.　　　　　　　(h) St. Mark xiv. 8.
(i) St. Mark xvi. 1.　　　　　(k) Bp. Pearson.

ner of King Asa's burial,(*l*) it may be thought that the present was a far costlier method of interment than was within the reach of our LORD's female followers, or was intended by them.

St. John is the only Evangelist who records the share of Nicodemus in the Burial of CHRIST. The progressive boldness of this good man in the cause of CHRIST, has been fully noticed elsewhere.(*m*) St. John's manner of identifying the persons of whom he writes, by some single remarkable passage in their past history, (as Nicodemus, by his visit to CHRIST,) has been also elsewhere commented on.(*n*)

40 Then took they the Body of JESUS, and wound it in linen clothes with the spices, as the manner of the Jews is to bury.

Rather, "to prepare for burial." Compare chap. xi. 44. The last few words, (together with many other similar expressions in the present Gospel,) remind us that St. John wrote at a distance from Judea.(*o*) . . . . Joseph and Nicodemus,—members of the High Court of Sanhedrin, who yet had not been partakers in the guilt of their fellow-counsellors,—knew not as yet that this was He of whom it is written in the xvith. Psalm, "Thou wilt not leave My soul in Hell: *neither wilt Thou suffer Thine* HOLY ONE *to see Corruption.*" Nor was it fitting, as yet, that they should know it. Everything that was customary in the case of human burials, must in *His* case be transacted; who verily and indeed, "died, *and was buried;*" as well as, "on the third day rose again." It follows:

41 Now in the place where He was crucified there was a Garden: and in the Garden a new Sepulchre, wherein was never man yet laid.

Observe the prominence which the inspired Evangelist gives to the fact that it was in *a Garden* that the Second Adam "laid Him down in peace and took His rest."(*p*) The reason of this has been already mentioned in the note on St. John xviii. 1. Take notice, also, that now was done literally that thing which our SAVIOUR had discoursed of, long before, in parable: for this was none other than that "grain of Mustard seed, which a Man took, and cast *into his Garden;* and it grew, and waxed a great Tree."(*q*) This was that "corn of Wheat," which, except it "fall into the ground and die, abideth alone: but if it die, bringeth forth much fruit!"(*r*) . . . . The writer supposed, for a moment, that the idea of connecting St. Luke xiii. 19 with the present verse, might be novel: but he found that Gregory the Great had anticipated him; and that Ambrose had anticipated Gregory. Such thoughts have probably occurred to believers in every age.

A *new* sepulchre was surely the only fitting resting-place for One whose Death was to "make all things new:"(*s*) for One, who, as the Author of Life and Immortality, could have no intercourse, even in Death, with corruption: for One, about whose Resurrection there must be no room for doubt or cavil: for One, lastly, who, (as the CREATOR of the World,) must ever find honor, at the hands of some of His creatures, amid the very depth of that dishonor, to which, for our sakes, He submitted. See the note on St. Matthew ii. 2.

42 There laid they JESUS therefore because of the Jews' preparation *day;* for the Sepulchre was nigh at hand.

In other words, the Garden closely adjoined the scene of the Crucifixion.—"Preparation" was the ancient name for "Friday," or the eve of the Sabbath; "therefore called the *Preparation,* because on that day they did prepare whatever was necessary for the celebration of the following festival."(*t*) See above, verses 14 and 31.

(*l*) 2 Chron. xvi. 14.
(*m*) See the note on St. John iii. 1.
(*n*) See the notes on St. John iv. 46, and xviii. 14.
(*o*) See the note on St. John vi. 1.
(*q*) St. Luke xiii. 19.
(*r*) St. John xii. 24. Compare 1 Cor. xv. 36.
(*s*) See the notes on St. John xiii. 34.

(*p*) Ps. iv. 8.

(*t*) Bp. Pearson.

CHAPTER XX.

1 *Mary cometh to the Sepulchre:* 3 *so do Peter and John, ignorant of the Resurrection.* 11 JESUS *appeareth to Mary Magdalene,* 19 *and to His Disciples.* 24 *The incredulity, and confession of Thomas.* 30 *The Scripture is sufficient to Salvation.*

BETWEEN the last verse of chapter xix. and the words which follow, there is an interval of one entire day; which, with the concluding portion of Friday, (the day of Death and Burial,) and the beginning of Sunday, (the day of Resurrection,) makes, according to the idiom of the Sacred writings, the well-known space of "three days" after which CHRIST "rose from the dead." And during this entire period, (the space probably of nearly thirty-six hours,) our SAVIOUR's human Body lay in the Grave, while His human Soul went to the place of departed spirits. The reader is requested to read what has been already offered on this great subject in the note on St. Luke xxiv. 3, as well as in the note prefixed to St. Mark xvi. . . . In the words of the prophet Jonah, — "The waters compassed me about, even to the soul: the depth closed me round about, the weeds were wrapped about my head. I went down to the bottoms of the mountains; the earth with her bars was about me for ever: yet hast Thou brought my life from corruption, O LORD my GOD."(a) —Consider St. Matthew xii. 40; and observe the fulfilment of our SAVIOUR's prophecy in the words which follow.

1 THE first *day* of the week cometh Mary Magdalene early, when it was yet dark, unto the Sepulchre, and seeth the stone taken away from the Sepulchre.

St. John, like the first two Evangelists, sets the name of Mary Magdalene, (who is not to be confounded with the sister of Lazarus,) in the very forefront of his account of the Resurrection; marking thereby, doubtless, the eagerness of her love, as well as preparing us for the amazing privilege which was in reserve for her of beholding, before any one else, her risen LORD.(b) "Good proof gave she of that love," says Bp. Andrewes. "She was last at His Cross, and first at His Grave: staid longest *there*, was soonest *here:* could not rest till she were up to seek Him: sought Him while it was yet dark, before she had light to seek Him by." . . . . . Is it not written in a certain place, "I love them that love Me; and those that seek Me early shall find me?"(c)

To show how entirely consistent with one another are the four inspired accounts of our Blessed SAVIOUR's Resurrection, is the province of a Harmony, rather than of a Commentary on the Gospels. It shall but be observed in this place that if men would but approach the Word of GOD with the same fairness, and apply to it the same principles of Interpretation, which are so readily applied to the writings of uninspired authors, we should have heard less of the difficulties which are supposed to beset this subject.

The moment indicated by the beloved Disciple, is that which immediately precedes the dawn. The Jewish Sabbath, which had begun on Friday evening, had come to a close at the sunset of the previous day; and the prescribed period of sacred rest having then ceased, it would have been lawful for the party of holy Women of whom we read in the other three Gospels, and who had "rested the Sabbath-day, according to the commandment,"(d) now at length to approach the Sepulchre. But, for their purpose of anointing our LORD's Body,(e) they required light; and they knew that in a few moments the Sun would rise upon the Earth. They set out, therefore, "while it was yet dark," for their love would not suffer them to wait any longer, and reached the Sepulchre, (as they had intended,) "at the rising of the Sun."(f) . . . They knew not, that He of whom the Sun is a faint emblem or shadow,(g) had already come forth "as a Bridegroom out of His Chamber,"

(a) Jonah ii. 5, 6.   (b) St. Mark xvi. 9.
(c) Prov. viii. 17.   (d) St. Luke xxiii. 56.
(e) See the note on St. Luke xxiv. 1.   (f) St. Mark xvi. 2.
(g) Ps. xix. 5.

rejoicing " as a Giant(h) to run His course ;" nor yet that the last Jewish Sabbath had already reached its close, and that the first LORD's Day was about to begin,— the birthday of the New Creation ! . . . . See the note prefixed to St. Matthew xxviii.—In the meantime, Mary Magdalene, (who had not come alone,) " seeth the stone taken away from the Sepulchre." The *manner* of its removal is described by St. Matthew.(i)

2 Then she runneth, and cometh to Simon Peter, and to the other Disciple, whom JESUS loved,

It seems fair to infer from this statement, both that Mary Magdalene knew where St. Peter and St. John were to be found, and that they were already living *together*. Consider what has been already offered concerning this noble pair of Disciples, in the commentary on St. John xviii. 15. Were they perhaps engaged, at this time, in administering consolation to the bereaved Mother of our Blessed LORD?(k) . . . How little Mary understood, as yet, what had taken place, appears from her words which follow :

and saith unto them, They have taken away the LORD out of the Sepulchre, and we know not where they have laid Him.

" They have *taken away !*"—the very thing, (though she knew it not,) which the band of soldiers had been stationed there in order to prevent ;(l) the very thing which, afterwards, the high Priests would have had the World believe.(m) So possessed was she by the belief that our LORD's Body had been carried off by some one, that she repeats her conviction, as if it were an established fact, no less than three times.(n) " *We* know not," — because she was one of a company of many women, as we learn from St. Mark xvi. 1.

3, 4, 5 Peter therefore went forth, and that other Disciple, and came to the Sepulchre. So they ran both together : and the other Disciple did outrun Peter, and came first to the Sepulchre. And he stooping down, *and looking in*, saw the linen clothes lying ; yet went he not in.

Rather, he " saw the linen *cloths.*" Not apparel, but that wherewith the corpse had been swathed, is spoken of.(o)

6, 7 Then cometh Simon Peter following him, and went into the Sepulchre, and seeth the linen clothes lie, and the napkin, that was about His head, not lying with the linen clothes, but wrapped together in a place by itself.

Everything which St. Peter saw indicated Divine calmness and perfect order. There had been no hurried rising, — still less had there been any hostile intrusion into the chamber of Death. Our SAVIOUR CHRIST having laid Him down in peace and taken His rest, awoke on the morning of the third day ; for GOD,—who would not leave His soul in Hell, neither would suffer His Holy One to see Corruption,(p) —GOD Himself sustained Him.(q) The linen clothes in which the Body had been shrouded, lay together, and the napkin which had covered His sacred Head, was discovered carefully folded, and deposited in a place apart, — the work, it may be, of ministering Angels, who waited upon His Rising.

 · Let it only be remarked in passing that when, in conformity with the express word of Scripture,) we speak of our SAVIOUR as " sustained ;" as not left in Hell, nor suffered to see Corruption : as " raised from Death, and ministered to by Angels, — we do not forget that we speak of Him who even then sustained Creation ; who *raised Himself* from Death, — as He pleased, and when He pleased ;(r) and quitted the Holy Sepulchre in the manner which to Himself seemed good, without the help of any, — much less of His own created Angels. No ; the stone

(h) Consider Judges xvi. 3.
(k) For consider St. John xix. 27.
(m) See St. Matth. xxviii. 11 to 15.
(o) See St. John xix. 40.
(q) Ps. iii. 5.

(i) St. Matth. xxviii. 2.
(l) See St. Matth. xxvii. 63 to 66.
(u) In verses 2, 13, 15.
(p) Ps. xvi. 10.
(r) See the note on the last half of St. John x. 18.

rolled away was the work of one of these heavenly ministers, indeed; but only as
a sign to the soldiers and the rest that CHRIST was risen already.

**8 Then went in also that other Disciple, which came first to the
Sepulchre, and he saw, and believed.**

"Believed," (that is,) in *the Resurrection.* St. John knew how Nicodemus and
Joseph had swathed the Body of his LORD; — the Hands and Feet fettered, as it
were, with grave-clothes;(*s*) which must have been compacted together by the
glutinous nature of the myrrh so profusely employed on this occasion;(*t*) while
the sacred Face had been bound about with a napkin. He knew too of the soldiers
who had been stationed to guard the Sepulchre; and of the seal which had been
set upon the stone. When, therefore, he beheld those soldiers dispersed, and that
seal broken, and that stone removed; those linen clothes deposited in order, and
that napkin folded together in a place apart;— the truth flashed upon him in an
instant. Many a dark saying of his LORD as to what was to befall Himself grew
bright; and he believed that the crowning marvel of all must have taken place,—
even that the Holy One had raised Himself from Death! . . . Take notice, therefore, that the Disciple whom JESUS loved, was *the first of all mankind to believe and
to know the truth of His Resurrection!*

What is recorded of the two Disciples on this occasion, (and which St. Luke
relates so concisely,(*u*) that even the identity of the narratives has been doubted,)
is remarkably illustrative of the characters of St. Peter and St. John, respectively.
Both of an eager disposition, they are both found to "run" towards the Sepulchre.
St. John, — was it because he was the more youthful, and therefore perhaps the
more vigorous? — reaches the goal first; but he is withheld by reverence and awe
from entering. He stoops, and only gazes in. So was it afterwards upon the
Lake. The Disciple whom JESUS loved reached the goal first, in heart and by
Faith, then, as it was he who reached the Sepulchre first, in bodily presence, now.
By throwing himself into the Water, he might have come to our LORD; yet, for
whatever reason, "went he not in." He remained in the ship. Not so Simon
Peter, on that occasion: not so Simon Peter now. On reaching the spot, he enters
immediately. St. John at last overcomes his hesitation. He enters,—and at once
believes. . . . What is implied by this last announcement is shown by the words
which follow; which also explain the reason why the Apostles were so slow to
admit the fact of their LORD's Resurrection.

**9 For as yet they knew not the Scripture, that He must rise again
from the dead.**

Marvellous declaration!—and we have it from the pen of St. John himself. The
Apostles knew many things which Moses and the prophets had announced concerning MESSIAH; but "the Scripture that He must rise again from the dead,"—
that they knew not. They had heard their LORD say this thing many times; but
they had not understood Him. See St. John xii. 16, and the beginning of the note
on the place. They had heard Him not only darkly intimate the period of His
own Resurrection,(*x*) but even plainly declare that "*on the third Day,* He should
rise again;"(*y*) yet had those words, as it seems, hitherto conveyed no clear signification to their minds. Nay, they had "kept that saying with themselves,
questioning one with another *what the rising from the dead should mean:*"(*z*) for
"they understood not that saying, and were afraid to ask Him."(*a*) What is
truly astonishing, the *enemies* of CHRIST seem to have understood its import perfectly well: for see St. Matthew xxvii. 63, 64.

What St. John here asserts of himself and his fellow-disciples, however, is, that
"as yet they *knew not,*" that is, "*did not understand the Scripture.*"(*b*) To what
"Scripture," then, may he be supposed to allude? The only texts expressly *quoted*
in this behalf, in the Book of the Acts, are Psalms ii. 7,(*c*) and xvi. 10;(*d*) yet is it

(*s*) See St. John xi. 44.
(*t*) St. John xix. 39, 40.   Chrysostom says that the myrrh was glutinous.
(*u*) St. Luke xxiv. 12.   (*x*) St. John ii. 19, and St. Matth. xii. 40.
(*y*) See St. Matth. xvi. 21: xvii. 9 and 23: xx. 19.
(*z*) St. Mark ix. 10.   (*a*) St. Mark ix. 32.
(*b*) Consider St. Luke xxiv. 45.   (*c*) Acts xiii. 33.
(*d*) See Acts ii. 25, &c., and xiii. 34, 35.

reasonable to suppose from the emphatic words of our LORD on two other occasions.(e) as well as from the language of St. Paul,(f) that this stupendous truth is
contained, in one form or other, throughout "Moses, and the Prophets, and the
Psalms," also: not only darkly,—as in Ps. cx. 7; but plainly,—as in the histories
of Isaac, of Joseph, and of Jonah: indeed, in many other ways, in many other
places.   It has been well remarked, that "as the number *seven* is of special use in
Scripture, because of the Sabbath-day,(g) so *three* is a mystical number, because
of CHRIST's rising from the dead on the third day."(h)   The reader will do well to
consider the several references indicated at foot.(i)   "Unto which we may add a
Jew's testimony, commenting on Gen. xxii. 4, that "there are many a three days in
the Holy Scripture, *of which one is the Resurrection of* MESSIAS."(j)
    May we, without fear of offence, humbly suggest that something more than we
have in any way even alluded to, may possibly lie concealed beneath the surface of
the narrative contained in the last seven verses? . . . *Why* are we told so minutely
what was the conduct and bearing of the two Disciples on this occasion? . . . But
to have said these few words shall suffice.   There is surely a third course open to
us, besides being either fanciful in assigning interpretations on every occasion, and
presumptuous in assuming that we know *all* that is contained in the words of the
SPIRIT.

10 Then the Disciples went away again unto their own home.

    And if that home, as above suggested,(k) was already the home of the Blessed
Virgin,—O the rapture of the intelligence which St. John will have had to convey
to her bruised and almost broken heart! . . . . .   The reader is invited to consider
that one only incident is recorded of our Blessed LORD, from His Infancy to His
Manhood,—*that* visit, namely, to Jerusalem, when His Parents missed Him; and
"*after three days* found Him" in His FATHER's House.(l)   "The circumstance
itself creates an apprehension that there is more in the matter than appears.   The
whole transaction seems calculated to train His Mother to a trust and reliance in
Him, when He should be out of her sight; and when, for "three days," she should
be in vain seeking for Him, sorrowing.   If this incident, and the instruction conveyed by it, had not the effect of schooling her beforehand for her great trial,—
will not His Divine Teaching on that occasion have appeared to her now, in the
retrospect, after His Resurrection?"(m)
    In the meanwhile, what is expressly revealed to us is, that the two Disciples,
leaving Mary Magdalene behind, went home: St. John, in faith; St. Peter *in wonder*.(n)   And this last circumstance, by the way, may possibly explain why a special appearance was vouchsafed to Simon.(o)   Is it not remarkable, when St. Peter's
share in St. Mark's Gospel is considered, that we should discover an explanation of
this slowness of heart on his own part, *twice* inserted there? namely, in St. Mark
ix. 10 and 32,(p)—where the words have evident reference, by anticipation, to the
present hour.

11 But Mary stood without at the Sepulchre weeping:

    For she had, of course, hastened back to the spot in company with the two Dis-
ciples.—The indications of her love are many and affecting.   So late at the Cross,
—so early at the Grave,—so impatient for sympathy and help when she found the

---

    (e) See St. Luke xxiv. 25, 26: 45, 46, and the notes.
    (f) 1 Cor. xv. 4.   (g) Gen. ii. 2.
    (h) St. Matth. xvii. 23: 1 Cor. xv. 4.
    (i) Gen. xxii. 4: xl. 12, 13: xlii. 17, 18.   Exod. v. 3: xv. 22: xix. 11.   Numb. x. 33: xix.
12.   Josh. i. 11: ii. 16.   Esther v. 1.   Jonah i. 17.   Hos. vi. 2.   St. Mark xv. 25.   St. Luke
xiii. 32, &c.   Threefold is the division of St. Matthew's genealogy: and threefold the temptation
of our LORD.   Thrice did our SAVIOUR repeat His mysterious prayer in the Garden of Gethsemane,—St. Matthew xxvi. 44: and thrice command St. Peter to feed His sheep,—St. John xxi.
17.   And see ver. 14.   St. Peter declares concerning his vision, "*This was done three times*,"—
Acts ix. 10.
    (j) Ainsworth, quoting *Bereshith Rabba.*
    (k) See the note on ver. 2.   (l) St. Luke ii. 46.
    (m) Williams.   (n) St. Luke xxiv. 12.
    (o) St. Luke xxiv. 34, and 1 Cor. xv. 5.
    (p) Compare, (for it is delightful to have one's attention called to such things,) the language
of St. Mark ix. 6, and xiv. 40.

sacred Body missing,—so faithful to the spot, when not only the other woman, but even St. Peter and St. John, had left it! We shall presently learn that as she stood weeping, (she *stood*, for she could not rest,) her tears were so abundant, that the first inquiry of the Angels, yea, of CHRIST Himself, was "Woman, why weepest thou?" It follows, that not satisfied with her former inspection of the chamber of Death, nor with the experience of St. Peter and St. John, she cannot help gazing through her streaming eyes into the vacant Sepulchre, yet once more.

12 And as she wept, she stooped down, *and looked* into the Sepulchre, and seeth two Angels in white sitting, the one at the Head, and the other at the feet, where the body of JESUS had lain.

"And yet, these two Angels had not been seen there by others, nor by herself before: like vast spiritual truths, of which, at one moment, we have a full and distinct perception; but, at another, lose sight of them; and which one sees, and another does not."(q) For it is not to be supposed that these Angels now repaired to the place of our SAVIOUR'S Burial for the first time. They had been there from the very first.
At His Transfiguration, at His Resurrection, and at His Ascension, He is waited on by *two*.(r) . . . "In white,"—"their Easter-Day color, for it is the color of the Resurrection." . . . . "In white," and "sitting,"—a sufficient proof that He was no longer there! "As the color, of joy; so the situation, of rest." . . . . . "The one at the head, and the other at the feet, where the Body of JESUS had lain." For CHRIST'S Body was the true Ark, in which it pleased "the Godhead to dwell bodily."(s) His resting-place is therefore between two Angels, like the mercy-seat, of old. Even in His Death, He is found to have dwelt, as in ancient days, "between the Cherubim."(t)

13 And they say unto her, Woman, why weepest thou?

"They mean," (remarks good Bp. Andrewes,) "that she had no cause to weep. She weeps, because she found the grave empty,—which GOD forbid that she should have found full! for then CHRIST must have been dead still, and so, no Resurrection. And this case of Mary Magdalene is our case oftentimes: in the error of our conceit, to weep where we have no cause; to joy, where we have as little. Where we have cause to joy, we weep; and where to weep, we joy. False joys, and false sorrows, false hopes and false fears, this life of ours is full of. GOD help us!"

She saith unto them, Because they have taken away my LORD, and I know not where they have laid Him.

Like the Spouse in the Canticles, "by night she sought Him whom her soul loved; she sought Him but she found Him not."(u) . . . . "The suddenness, the strangeness, the gloriousness of the sight of two Angels, moves her not at all. She seems to have no sense of it; and so, to be in a kind of ecstacy all the while. She had rather find *His* dead Body, than behold *them* in all their Glory. Until she find Him again, her soul refuses all manner of comfort; yea, even from Heaven; even from the Angels themselves."(x)
"Now when JESUS was risen early the first day of the week, He appeared first to Mary Magdalene, out of whom He had cast seven devils."(y) Accordingly, it follows:

14 And when she had thus said, she turned herself back, and saw JESUS standing, and knew not that it was JESUS.

Augustine remarks that "CHRIST is never long absent from those who seek Him." But how did it happen that Mary Magdalene "turned herself back," thus opportunely? Was she not gazing intently into the Sepulchre? and must not the sight of those two radiant beings, (notwithstanding the pious remark of Bp. An-

---

(q) Williams.
(s) Col. ii. 9.
(t) Exod. xxv. 17 to 21, and the marginal references against ver. 22.
(u) Solomon's Song iii. 1.   (x) Bp. Andrewes.
(y) St. Mark xvi. 9.

(r) See the note on St. Luke ix. 30.

drewes,) have sufficiently occupied her attention? Yes, doubtless. But at the sight of their CREATOR, the Angels will have expressed awe, perhaps adoration. They will have risen from their seats, and bowed their heads, or prostrated their bodies. And Mary, amazed, will have turned to see what was passing behind her. . . . She beholds her risen LORD, but she does not recognize Him. Her eyes are holden, — as in the case of the two going to Emmaus,(z) and of the Disciples by the Lake in the next chapter."(a)

15 JESUS saith unto her, Woman, why weepest thou? whom seekest thou?

"It is the voice of her Beloved,"—whose "head is filled with dew, and his locks with the drops of the Night;"(b) but she knows Him not. . . . Our LORD begins as the Angels had begun.(c) See above on verse 11. It is to teach us, (remarks Ambrose,) that the words of Angels are spoken by command of GOD. A great Father of our own Church, observes upon it,—"Now, seeing CHRIST asks it again a second time, we will think there is something in it, and stay a little at it. The rather, for that it is the very opening of His mouth; *the very first words that ever came from Him*, and that He spake first of all, after His rising again from death. There is sure some more than ordinary matter in this, 'Why weepest thou?' if it be put even for that!" . . . (How keen and true a sense of the dignity of the Gospel had the Man who could so write! He proceeds;) — "Thus say the Fathers; that Mary Magdalene standing by the Grave's side, and there weeping, is thus brought in to represent unto us the state of all mankind before this Day, the Day of CHRIST's rising again; weeping over the dead as do the heathen, who have no hope.(d) But CHRIST comes and asks 'Why weepest thou?' as much as to say, 'Weep not! There is no cause of weeping now.' Henceforth, none shall need to stand by the grave to weep there any more. . . . . . So that this, 'Why weepest thou?' of CHRIST's, (a question very proper for the day of the Resurrection,) wipes away tears from all eyes; puts off our mourning weeds, girds us with gladness, and robes us all 'in white,' with the Angels."(e)

The further inquiry "Whom seekest thou?" seems to have reference to Mary's brief conversation with the two Angels, which our LORD will have overheard, as He stood behind her.

She, supposing Him to be the Gardener, saith unto Him, Sir, if thou have borne Him hence, tell me, where thou hast laid Him, and I will take Him away.

The second ADAM is seen standing in the Garden, and straightway he is mistaken for "the Gardener!" . . . Can we suppose that any single word is set down idly here? If Mary's surmise had had no reasonableness in it, — think you, that the HOLY SPIRIT would have suffered St. John to write her surmise down? Not so, there is deep Divinity in the circumstance. "She mistook Him," (observes Gregory the Great,) "without being in reality mistaken." "A Gardener He is," (adds pious Bp. Andrewes;) "the first, the fairest Garden that ever was, was of His planting!" — alluding to Genesis ii. 8.

"If thou have borne *Him* hence,"—are her first words: but she has not, as yet, mentioned of whom she speaks. "The soul, transported with love, seems at first to express her affection without declaring its object, as thinking all the world must know who is the person intended."(f) "An irregular speech, but Love's own dialect," exclaims Bp. Andrewes. "*Him* is enough with Love. Who knows not *who* it is, though we never tell His name, nor say a word more!"(g)

Observe further her intention to "take Him away." A weak woman to think of accomplishing such a task alone! And yet, the Body "had more than a hundred pounds weight of myrrh and other odours upon it!" But Love is stronger than the Grave. . . . She suspected that the Gardener had removed beyond the limits of his Garden, our LORD's Body; and if she may but know where those sacred limbs have been laid, she promises to convey them away to some other place.

(z) St. Luke xxiv. 16. Compare St. Mark xvi. 12.
(a) St. John xxi. 4.
(b) Song of Solomon v. 2.
(c) See ver. 13.
(d) 1 Thess. iv. 13.
(e) Bp. Andrewes.
(f) Bp. Horne on Ps. cxvi. 1.
(g) So also Gregory the Great. Rarely indeed does it happen that a *true* remark of a modern Divine is not to be found in the pages of an ancient Father.

It seems that in accosting the Gardener, she called him "*Sir,*" in order to conciliate his favour. Unconsciously, she bestows upon the Stranger His right title. The word is literally "Lord," in the original. Nay, every word she now utters, bears a lofty and an unsuspected meaning: for *who* but CHRIST Himself, whom she addressed had borne away that body of which she was in search?

Having spoken such words to the supposed Gardener, Mary turns away from Him to gaze again into the Sepulchre,—as we learn from the next verse. Was it perhaps because,.for a few moments, our SAVIOUR made her no reply?

16 JESUS saith unto her, Mary.

"It should seem that before, with His shape, He had changed His voice also. But now, He speaks to her in His known voice, in the wonted accent. He does but name her name, ' Mary;' and that is enough." . . . Call to mind, here, what is said in so many places of Scripture about CHRIST "calling," "knowing," His sheep and His people "*by Name.*"(h) Consider further, that "till He knows us, we shall never know Him aright."

"And with this, all is turned out and in," (proceeds the pious commentator from whom we have quoted so largely.) "A new World, now! For, in very deed, a kind of Resurrection it was which was wrought in her; revived, as it were, and raised from a dead and drooping, to a lively and cheerful state. The Gardener has done his part: made her all green on the sudden. And all by a word of His mouth. Such power is there in every word of His! So easily are they called whom CHRIST will but speak to!"

She turned herself, and saith unto Him, Rabboni; which is to say, Master.

O the rapture, the joy unspeakable which must have found expression, in that single word! . . . "We see that He chose to be made known by the ear, rather than by the eye. He opens her ears first, and her eyes after. Hearing is the sense of Faith: and so, most meet; for CHRIST is THE WORD. In matters of faith, the ear is of more use, and to be trusted before the eye: for in many cases, Faith holdeth where Sight faileth.(i) . . . . Concerning the title by which she addressed our SAVIOUR, see the note on St. John xi. 28.

It would seem, that, at the sound of the well-known voice, Mary fell prostrate at the feet of Him whom she so desired, and sought to embrace His feet. She has "found Him whom her soul loveth: she holds Him and will not let Him go."(k) For it follows,—

17 JESUS saith unto her, Touch Me not; for I am not yet ascended to My FATHER.

Strange that both the old World and the new should have begun with the same prohibition,—"Touch not!"(l) In the words before us, there are two difficulties which require explaining. (1st.) Why may not Mary Magdalene touch her risen LORD, if the other woman may "hold Him by the feet;"(m) if St. Thomas may thrust his hand into His side; and all the assembled Disciples may be even *invited* to "handle" Him, and see that it is He indeed?—The true answer is probably supplied by Chrysostom. "To touch, would not have cured her disease, but made it worse. *They* touched, because they believed not: *she* touched not because she believed not of Him aright. *They* touched, that they might know He was risen: *she* touched not, that she might know He was not so risen as she wrongly imagined; that is, that He was no longer as in former times she had known Him."(n)—The reader is invited to refer to the notes on St. Luke viii. 39, and St. Mark v. 19: also to the end of the note on St. Matthew xi. 5.

(2nd.) What is the force of that reason assigned: "Touch Me not, *for* I am not yet ascended?" Doubtless, Augustine has rightly suggested that, in these words, CHRIST's meaning was to wean her from all sensual and fleshly touching: to teach her a new and a truer touch,— truer than that which she intended. The form of His prohibition clearly conveys a promise that *after* His Ascension she *may,*

(h) See the note on the latter part of St. John x. 3.
(i) Bp. Andrewes.   (k) Song of Solomon iii. 4.   (l) Gen. iii. 3.
(m) St. Matth. xxviii. 9.   (n) Bishop Andrewes.

nay, that she *must*, touch Him. This *touch of Faith* could not begin till then. He had hinted as much, indeed, to the men of Capernaum, when He asked, 'Doth this offend you? What, and if ye shall see the SON of MAN ascend up where He was before?"(c) . . . This touching, therefore, is ours and our children's, forever. A loftier privilege we find, a more real "touching," than Mary could have enjoyed in the Garden, or the Twelve in the upper chamber at Jerusalem! . . . Consider, in illustration of what has been thus offered concerning the spiritual touch, the note on St. Mark v. 31.—Let us then send up our Faith, (says Andrewes after Augustine,) and *that* shall touch Him; and there will come forth virtue out of Him. Yea, it shall take such hold on Him, that it shall raise us up to where He is; bring us to the end of all our desires,—a joyful Ascension to our FATHER and to His; to Himself, and to the Unity of the Blessed SPIRIT. "Here, then, is the doctrine, which detached from the particular case and character of Mary, (who herein stood in the place of the Church,) seems to fill up the great doctrine of CHRIST's presence in the Church. It could not be until, in the flesh, He had ascended to the FATHER."(p) Consider St. John xvi. 7.

"Shall she then be quite cast off, in the meantime? Denied touching, and nothing to comfort her, in lieu of it? No. CHRIST is not unrighteous that He should forget the work and labour of her Love, which she, this day, made so many ways to appear. Somewhat He deviseth to comfort her. He will employ her in a message," —and thus make her an Apostle; yea, make her the very Apostle of the Apostles! send her to preach the very Gospel of the Gospel! . . . He says:

But go to My Brethren,

"There is nothing here that savours of anger or of pride. He calls them *Brethren*,"— an endearing title which He had never bestowed upon His Disciples till now. "Even as Joseph, in the top of his honour, so He, in this the day of His glorious exaltation, claims kindred with them,—a sort of poor forlorn men; and, (as the Apostle expresseth it,) He is not "ashamed" of them that were ashamed of Him.(q) Poor as they are, unkind as they were, He vouchsafes to call them "Brethren:" which word implies two things. First, that His Nature is not changed by Death; but, He rises again in the same Nature He died in. Secondly, He is risen with the same love and affection He had before. He hath not changed *that*, either."(r) . . . . How remarkable is the discovery that inasmuch as the twenty-second Psalm, (which the Church hath appointed to be used on Good Friday,) consisteth of two parts,—whereof the former, (ver. 1 to 21,) is prophetical of CHRIST's Passion, and the latter, (verse 22 to 31,) celebrateth His Resurrection,(s)—the strain changes to a hymn of triumph in the mouth of the REDEEMER with the words, "I will declare Thy Name unto *My Brethren!*" Nay, can we doubt that our risen LORD, by the use of this word here, and in St. Matthew xxviii. 10, lays his finger on that very place in ancient Prophecy? . . . "Go to *My Brethren*," (saith He,)—

and say unto them, I ascend unto My FATHER, and your FATHER; and *to* My GOD, and your GOD.

He sends not word to His "Brethren" that He is "risen." Of *this*, Mary needs no assurance; nor, very soon, will *they*. But, lest they should simply think of Him as returned to Earth,—restored to them eternally on the same terms as before, —He sends them a message of His approaching departure from them, and *Ascension* into Heaven; as if He had said, Look not any more for My bodily presence among you. Learn, at last, to "lift up your hearts!" . . . Then, further, because "He is no sooner risen than He makes ready for His ascending,— so, with us, *Rising* and *Ascending* are to follow straight one upon the other."

"And out of what CHRIST did, we learn what we are to do. Seeing CHRIST staid not here, we are not to set up our stay here neither: not to make Earth our Heaven, nor to place our felicity here below."

Take notice that our LORD makes mention of *ascending*, twice; of *rising*, not at all. And it is to teach us, (observes the same pious writer,) that *Resurrection* is nothing, nor is any account to be made of it, if *Ascension* go not with it. . . . . . . "Never take care for Resurrection! *That* will come of itself, without any thought-taking of thine. Take thought for Ascension! set your minds there! Better lie still in our graves, better never rise, than *rise*, and rising not *ascend*."

(o) St. John vi. 61, 62.   (p) Dr. Moberly.   (q) Heb. ii. 11.
(r) Bp. Andrewes.   (s) See Bp. Horne on that Psalm.

"Where then, or what, is their comfort, or ours, in these tidings? To deal plainly, when we seek it in the announcement of our LORD's Ascension to His FATHER and His GOD, we find it not: but in the assurance that it is 'our FATHER,' and 'our GOD,' as well, to whom He ascended, *there* we find it! CHRIST implied as much, indeed, when He called the Disciples His 'Brethren;' but He would not deliver so blessed a truth only by implication,—but explicitly and plainly: and not once, but twice. And it is happy for us He did so; for this point cannot be too plainly or too often repeated. All the joy of this morning is in this. Tell them that if I go to Him thus because He is MY FATHER, they also shall come after Me, because He is theirs. Moreover, by virtue hereof, if we cry Abba, FATHER, He is ready to hear our prayers; and when we go hence, ready to receive our persons. If at any time we repent, and say, 'I will arise and go to my FATHER,'(t) He is ready to receive us to Grace; and when we go hence, we may say with CHRIST, 'I ascend unto My FATHER,' for he is ready to receive us to Glory. So useful to us is this blessed assurance both here and there!"(u)

"Now, that CHRIST should speak of His 'FATHER,' is natural; but how should He speak of His 'GOD?' And again, though it needs no explanation that He should speak of our GOD, what propriety is there in His calling that same GOD our FATHER? In exact propriety of speech, then, 'Father' here refers to CHRIST; GOD, to us. But observe, that *His* Father becomes *our* Father by *His* means : our GOD becomes *His* GOD, by ours. In order to effect this, He that doth here 'ascend' did first 'descend,' even to be one of us; and so, being one of us, to be a creature as well as we. What He was, such He is, — for the Soul and Body of CHRIST are in the rank of creatures; and when He speaks with relation to His human Soul and Body, a creature He is, a GOD He hath,—the same that we have; for there is but One. And so, He may truly say that *our* GOD is *His* GOD. That *we* might cry 'Abba, Father,' He was content to cry that strange cry 'ELI, ELI,' on the Cross.(x) So CHRIST might truly say 'My GOD,' no less than 'My FATHER.' His FATHER, as GOD : His GOD as Man. As the SON of GOD, a GOD He hath not, — a FATHER He hath. As the Son of Man, a Father He hath not, — a GOD He hath. A GOD then He hath; but never till then : yet what He then had, He hath ever since. And thus, He that was ours and not His, is now *His* as well as ours." St. Paul accordingly, in a certain place, makes mention of '*the* GOD *of our* LORD JESUS CHRIST :'(y) and our SAVIOUR Himself, speaking by Revelation to 'His servant John,' four times in one verse uses the expression 'My GOD.'(z)

"In like manner, though He alone can properly say 'My FATHER,' yet, by becoming one of us, by becoming our *Brother*, we also become partakers of His SON-ship. And this explains why, at His rising from the Grave, and ascending into Heaven, He is careful to speak of us as '*His Brethren*:' for thereby He adopts us; and, by adopting, makes us for ever *Children of His* FATHER. He, GOD's Only SON by Nature and Eternal Generation: we, 'the sons of God'(a) by Adoption and Grace. For, a Brotherhood, we grant, was begun at Christmas, by His Birth; but His Resurrection is a second Birth, — Easter, a second Christmas. 'This day,' (saith GOD,) 'I have begotten Thee!'(b) And if there was a new begetting, so was there a new Paternity and Fraternity both. Indeed, the Brotherhood of Christmas would have been dissolved by His Death, but for this day's rising. Accordingly, as soon as He was born again of the womb of the Grave, He begins a new Brotherhood straight: adopts us, we see, over again; whereby He that was 'the First-born from the dead,'(c) becomes 'the First-born among many brethren.'(d) Before, by the Mother's side, He was ours : now, by the FATHER's side, we are His. Brethren at Christmas, because our GOD was His GOD; brethren at Easter, because His FATHER is our FATHER. But half-brothers before; never of the whole blood till now. Now, by FATHER and Mother, very Brethren. We cannot be more!"

So full of meaning were the first words which proceeded from the lips of our risen LORD! So important was the first message He sent to a World which He had renewed! So much of doctrine, so much of exhortation, did His short speech to Mary Magdalene comprise! He teaches her therein (1st) His Resurrection; (2nd)

(t) St. Luke xv. 18.
(u) Altered from Bp. Andrewes, who also supplies what follows.
(x) St. Matth. xxvii. 46, quoting Ps. xxii. 1.
(y) Ephes. i. 17.　　　　　　　　　　　　　　　　(z) Rev. iii. 12.
(a) 1 St. John iii. 1.
(b) Ps. ii 7, — explained in Acts xiii. 33, and adopted by the Church as a Proper Psalm for Easter-day.
(c) Col. i. 18. Rev. i. 5.　　　　　　　　　　　(d) Rom. viii. 29.

wherein He was the same, and wherein He differed, from what He was before; (3rd) His approaching Ascension; (4th) what would be the fruit thereof to the whole Human Family; (5th) the mystery of His Godhead and of His Manhood; (6th) our adoption to be sons: (7th and lastly,) He conveys a message of Peace and Love to all! . . . If any one is of opinion that our remarks have been too many, let him consider that we are here unfolding the first page in the History of the New Creation. *What* is worthy of our attention, if it be not such a History as this?

18 Mary Magdalene came and told the Disciples that she had seen the LORD, and *that* He had spoken these things unto her.

Thus at once, arresting the tide of sorrow in those "who had been with Him, as they mourned and wept,"(e) and setting a seal on the faith of St. John, as well as fulfilling his loftiest anticipations. Take notice that thus, "as by a Woman came the first news of Death, so, by a Woman came also the first notice of the Resurrection of the dead. And the place fits well; for, in a Garden they came, both." The words are Bp. Andrewes's, but the remark is common to all the Fathers. . . . . Consider how that announcement "I ascend unto My FATHER," must have struck a chord in the Disciples' memories which could hardly yet have ceased to vibrate! See chap. xiv. 28: xvi. 10, 16, 28.

Passing over the next three appearances of our LORD on the first Easter,(f) St. John proceeds to describe what occurred at evening, when the Disciples were assembled.

19 Then the same day at evening, being the first *day* of the week,

Take notice how emphatically St. John marks on which day this happened. He told us in ver. 1, and here he repeats, that it was now *the first day of the week,*— a day ever since dedicated to the special service of Him who on this day rose from death! See the note prefixed to St. Matthew xxviii. This was, then, the first time the Church had ever met; and lo, JESUS CHRIST was found to be there, in the midst of them! Consider the repeated sanction which His presence gave to the next "LORD's Day,"(g) (as St. John elsewhere calls Sunday;)(h) whereby the Great Architect taught Mankind,

"Sundays the pillars are
On which Heaven's palace arched lies."

Observe, too, the many indications that the first day of the week became regarded henceforth as the Christian Sabbath.(i) . . . "The fear of the Jews," which St. John proceeds to mention, explains as well why the Disciples assembled together "*at evening,*" as why "*the doors were shut.*"

when the doors were shut where the Disciples were assembled for fear of the Jews, came JESUS and stood in the midst,

By mentioning that "the doors were shut," St. John teaches us that our LORD entered the chamber by virtue of the altered nature of His risen Body, — even as He had already risen from the closed tomb.(k) Consider also St. Luke xxiv. 31. "He stood in the midst of them," as if suddenly, and without a sound or step being heard, or any approach or passing by being noticed; noiseless as a shadow, and sightless in His coming as a dream. . . . Here then was the promise visibly fulfilled, "where two or three are gathered together in My Name, there am I in the midst of them."(l) — Hooker observes that the question at Capernaum was, "Rabbi, how camest Thou hither?" "The Disciples, when CHRIST appeared to them in a far more strange and miraculous manner, moved no question, but rejoiced greatly in that they saw. For why? The one sort beheld only *that* in CHRIST which they knew was more than natural, but yet their affection was not rapt therewith through any great extraordinary gladness; the other, when they looked on CHRIST, were not ignorant that they saw the well-spring of their own everlasting felicity. The one, because they enjoyed not, disputed: the other disputed not, because they enjoyed." —JESUS, then, "stood in the midst:"

(e) St. Mark xvi. 10.
(f) St. Matt. xxviii. 9. St. Luke xxiv. 34, and 13, &c.
(g) See ver. 26. Consider also Acts ii. 1. (h) Rev. i. 10.
(i) See Acts xx. 7, — (an assembly *at evening*, observe, still:) also 1 Cor. xvi. 2.
(k) See above, the note on ver. 7. (l) Williams, quoting St. Matth. xviii. 20.

and saith unto them, Peace *be* unto you.

"Why weepest thou?" had been our Saviour's first words to Mary Magdalene. He asked the two going to Emmaus. Why they were sad?(*m*) To the women, He exclaimed, "Hail!" that is, "Rejoice!"(*n*) "Peace be unto you!" are His first words to the assembled Disciples. "There was therefore to be no 'weeping,' no 'being sad,' now. Nothing, on this day, but 'Peace' and 'Joy.'"(*o*) "By this declaration of Peace, our Lord showed the efficacy of His Cross."(*p*)

Nor can we forget that this was the salutation of Shiloh, (that is, "Peace,"(*q*) even the "Prince of Peace" Himself?(*r*) of Him who is declared to be "our Peace:" (*s*) who bequeathed His Peace to the Disciples ;(*t*) and promised that Peace should be their abiding portion :(*u*) and directed them to salute with "Peace" every house into which they entered.(*x*) Peace was the subject of the Angel's carol on the night of the Lord's Nativity :(*y*) behold, Peace is the first word He pronounces in the hearing of His Disciples now that He is risen from Death !(*z*) . . . "I know well," (says Bp. Cosin,) "that by many frigid and common expositors, 'Peace be unto you,' is taken for no more than an ordinary salutation among the Jews; but, by the best and most ancient, for a higher and deeper mystery: as being well assured that His coming was to leave that Peace, first, which He had so lately purchased betwixt God and Man, among men themselves ; and then, to leave that Power which God had conferred upon Him for the benefit of His Church forever."

Notwithstanding this comfortable greeting, we learn from St. Luke's Gospel that "they were terrified and affrighted, and supposed that they had seen a Spirit. And He said unto them, Why are ye troubled? and why do thoughts arise in your hearts? Behold My hands and My feet, that it is I Myself: handle Me, and see ; for a Spirit hath not flesh and bones, as ye see Me have."(*a*)

20 And when He had so said, He showed unto them *His* hands and His side.

His risen body retained, and yet retains, the marks of its wounds. They are the tokens of His victory over Sin and Death,—His trophy when He returned from the conquest of the Enemy of our Race. Consider Zechariah xiii. 6. With these, He will at last return to Judgment !(*b*)

It is a terrible subject to dwell on; but the reader will take notice that these were as yet *open* wounds,—not *scars :* for see below, ver. 27.

Then were the Disciples glad, when they saw the Lord.

The same who "liveth, and was dead ; and behold, He is alive evermore !"(*c*)— Brief and simple, yet most important record ! Thus did the promise which our Saviour had made to His Disciples on the night before He suffered, receive its first fulfillment : "I will see you again, and *your heart shall rejoice.*"(*d*) Surely, no words can describe "what a deluge of joy was in their hearts"(*e*) when they beheld Him ! To know what followed, refer to the xxiv. chapter of St. Luke, and read from ver. 41 to 49.

21 Then said Jesus to them again, Peace *be* unto you ! as My Father hath sent Me, even so I send you.

Words almost identical with these are found in the Great Intercession, in St. John xvii. 18,—to which the reader is referred. It was there remarked that in the parallel thus established between the sending of Christ and the sending of the Apostles, two circumstances seem to be chiefly intended. First,—both Messiah and the Twelve were anointed not with natural oil, but with the Holy Ghost. Thus, Messiah was "anointed with the Holy Ghost and with power,"(*f*) both at

(*m*) St. Luke xxiv. 17.   (*n*) St. Matth. xxviii. 9.
(*o*) Bp. Andrewes.   (*p*) Chrysostom.
(*q*) Gen. xlix. 10.   That text was wrongly explained in vol. i. p. 100; and above, at p. 743, note(*g*).   Doctors are much divided, indeed: but the best-informed modern Hebrew scholars, (as Dr. McCaul,) say that "Shiloh" certainly means "Peace."
(*r*) Is. ix. 6.   Compare Hebr. vii. 2.   (*s*) Ephes. ii. 14.
(*t*) St. John xiv. 27.   (*u*) St. John xvi. 33.
(*x*) St. Luke x. 5.   (*y*) St. Luke ii. 14.
(*z*) Consider Rom. v. 1.   Col. i. 20.   Is. xxvi. 3: lvii. 19.   Ps. lxxxv. 8.
(*a*) St. Luke xxiv. 37 to 39.   (*b*) Rev. i. 7.
(*c*) Rev. i. 18.   (*d*) St. John xvi. 22.
(*e*) Abp. Leighton.   (*f*) Acts x. 38.

the time of His miraculous Conception,(g) and in the hour of His Baptism.(h) Twofold, in like manner, was the unction of the Apostles: for "He breathed on them, and saith unto them, Receive ye the HOLY GHOST,"(i) on the present occasion; and fifty days after, on the Day of Pentecost, they were "baptized with the HOLY GHOST and with fire."(j)

Secondly,—Besides being commissioned to teach the same Doctrines which our SAVIOUR CHRIST Himself had taught, the Apostles must have been armed with the like general *powers*. "If, then, CHRIST sent the Apostles *as* His FATHER had sent Him,—sent them, that is to say, to do His work after He had departed from the World; if by that very act He showed that, in His ministerial character, He had the power of delegating and continuing His authority,—could they, to whom He promised the same power as He possessed, conceive that that essential part of it, *the right of delegation*, was withheld, when *the Religion* was to be continued forever?"(k) Not so. "Lo! I am with you always," (said He,) "even to the end of the World."(l) Why was such a promise given, except to imply that they and their successors forever would need His perpetual presence at the execution of every function of the Apostolic office; of which Ordination hath ever been accounted the very chief? . . As CHRIST had been sent to establish the Church upon Earth, even so were the Apostles of CHRIST now sent,—with the like authority and for the same end. "And, as the SON sent the Apostles, so did they send others by virtue of the same Spirit. Thus, by virtue of an Apostolic Ordination, there is forever to be continued a Ministerial Succession."(m)

22 And when He had said this, He breathed on *them*, and saith unto them, Receive ye the Holy Ghost:

" 'He *breathed* on them.' Another proof of the reality of His risen Body! a proof whereby the blind, and deaf, and benumbed, (without touching,) may be convinced of the reality of a living bodily presence near them !"(n)

O most solemn and mysterious incident, as well as most awful and prevailing words! The action of our SAVIOUR here described may have shown emblematically (as Augustine suggests) that the HOLY GHOST *proceedeth also from the* SON. It may further have served to show that this was He by the breath of whose mouth all the Host of Heaven were made ;(o) and especially, (as Cyril supposes,) that CHRIST was the same who, after creating Man in the beginning, "breathed into his nostrils the breath of life, and he became a living soul."(p) But more than that is here intended. For it is to be thought that, at the time of Man's Creation, "together with his soul, or the principle of his natural life, he received also the Grace of the HOLY SPIRIT as a principle of the Divine Life to which he was also designed."(q) That is, the soul of Man received from the very first "the peculiar impress of the HOLY SPIRIT superadded," as Clement of Alexandria writes. And Basil, expressly comparing the Divine insufflation upon Adam with that of CHRIST upon the Apostles, tells us that it was the same SON of GOD "by whom GOD gave the insufflation: then indeed, *together with* the soul; but now, *into* the soul."—Eusebius is even more explicit. "The LORD," (he says,) "renews Mankind. That Grace which Man enjoyed at first, because GOD breathed into his nostrils,—that same Grace did CHRIST restore when He breathed into the face of the Apostles, and said, Receive the HOLY GHOST."(r) . . Is it not written in a certain place, "When Thou lettest Thy breath go forth, Thou shalt renew the face of the Earth ?"(s)

We have elsewhere pointed out that at the first institution of certain mysteries of the Faith, there was not wanting the outward emblem of an inward grace; which grace was afterwards conveyed without any such visible demonstration. Thus, at the Baptism of CHRIST, "the HOLY GHOST descended *in a bodily shape like a dove* upon Him."(t) And now, at the Ordination of His Apostles, our LORD is found to have "breathed into" their faces, when He would convey to them the gift of the same Blessed SPIRIT "to confirm them in their Apostolical Commission. The gift which they received from Him soon after, on the Day of Pentecost, was to enable

(g) See St. Luke i. 35.
(h) St. Luke iii. 22: with which compare iv. 1, 14, 18, 21.
(i) St. John xx. 22.
(j) St. Matth. iii. 11.
(k) Rev. Hugh James Rose.
(l) See St. Matth. xxviii. 20.
(m) Bp. Pearson, quoting 1 Tim. v. 22. Tit. i. 5.
(n) From a MS. Sermon by the Rev. Edm. Hobhouse.
(o) Psalm xxxiii. 6.
(p) Genesis ii. 7.
(q) Bishop Bull.
(r) From a newly-discovered fragment of this Father.
(s) Psalm civ. 30.
(t) St. Luke iii. 22: see the note on St. Matth. iii. 17.

them, by the possession of miraculous power, to carry that Commission into effect."(*u*) The self-same form of words is retained in Ordination, at the present day; but the Heavenly gift is sent unseen. How apt the emblem was which our LORD employed on this occasion, we are at no loss to perceive, from such places of Scripture as St. John ii. 8, and Acts ii. 2.—Our great High-Priest proceeds:

23 Whose soever sins ye remit, they are remitted unto them; *and* whose soever *sins* ye retain, they are retained.

A further illustration is thus presented to us of our LORD's meaning in ver. 21. It was discovered, from an earlier page of the Gospel, that "the power of forgiveness on the Earth was delegated to CHRIST as the Son of Man,"(*x*)—*that* Son of Man to whom the SPIRIT was given without measure. "This power He now gives to the Apostles, the successors of the Son of Man upon the Earth, by the gift of the same HOLY GHOST by whom it was in Himself."(*y*) The words before us are accordingly used by the Bishop at the present day, in the Church of CHRIST, on admitting a Deacon to the Order of Priesthood.

But, "the very largeness of this grant startles many, from their reverence for the Word of GOD, into an unwillingness to receive in their plain sense its explicit declarations,—nay, the very words, full of Grace and Truth, of Him who was the Truth itself. "What!" (they object,) "The incommunicable power of GOD made over to miserable, sinful man! the destiny of immortal souls placed in the keeping of mere mortal worms!"

"No such thing. It is an utter misconception of the grant that prompts the just objection.

"Forgiveness of sins is revealed to us as exclusively conditional. Not even GOD Himself, (we may reverently say,) can forgive the impenitent and unbelieving; because He has declared that He will not, and it is impossible that He should lie. Forgiveness of sins, declared or conveyed by whomsoever or howsoever it may be, can be the boon only of the repentant believer. Faith must exist, to receive it,— whether declared by Revelation, proved by Miracle, imparted by official Absolution, or sealed in a Sacramental Ordinance. . . . . Faith then; Faith in JESUS; shown, on the believer's part, by laying hold on the promises in the Sacraments,(*z*)— 'washing away his sins in Baptism,' and eating the 'flesh' and drinking the 'blood' which are 'meat' and 'drink indeed,' in the Supper of the LORD,—is the pre-requisite to that forgiveness of Sin, which the SAVIOUR gave His Apostles and their successors power to minister, when He sent them in His Name even as He had been sent forth of the FATHER."(*a*) See the notes on St. Matthew xvi. 19.

"The power of remitting sins, then, is originally in GOD, and in GOD alone; in CHRIST our SAVIOUR, by means of the union of the Godhead and Manhood in one Person, by virtue whereof the Son of Man hath power to forgive sins upon Earth. This of the Apostles is nothing else but a branch out of His, which He Himself, as Man, had here upon Earth. For, as Man, He Himself was sent; was anointed with the SPIRIT; and proceeded by Commission."(*b*)

From a comparison of the three places in the Gospel, which relate to Absolution, "the general result is this: that the power of binding and loosing is a solemn privilege or prerogative of the Church of CHRIST, thrice insisted upon by our SAVIOUR:—First, by way of prediction that He would confer it.(*c*) Secondly, by way of more particular description of the manner, and direction for the end and use of it.(*d*) And thirdly, by a preparatory kind of instating them in his power, an initial investing them with this sacred ghostly authority,(*e*) immediately before His final departure from the World; which seemeth to have been thoroughly perfected and completed, when after His Ascension, the HOLY GHOST did visibly descend upon those to whom these words where by CHRIST then delivered."(*f*)

The Evangelist proceeds to relate what occured, perhaps, at a later hour on the same evening; when ALMIGHTY GOD, "for the more confirmation of the Faith, suffered His holy Apostle Thomas to be doubtful in His SON's Resurrection."(*g*)—

(*u*) Lonsdale and Hale,—quoting St. Luke xxiv. 49. Acts i. 4, 5, 8: ii. 1 to 4, and 33.
(*x*) Consider St. Matth. ix. 6.   (*y*) Dr. Moberly.
(*z*) Acts xxii. 16. St. John vi. 55.
(*a*) From the first of two valuable Discourses (on "The Priesthood in the Church,") by Bp. Whittingham, the learned Bishop of Maryland,—printed at Baltimore, 1843.
(*b*) Bp. Andrewes.   (*c*) St. Matth. xvi. 19   (*d*) St. Matth. xviii. 18.
(*e*) St. John xx. 23.   (*f*) Dr. Hammond.   (*g*) Collect for St. Thomas' Day.

Take notice that the absence of St. Thomas from the scene above described finds a remarkable parallel in the Old Testament, where the absence of two of the seventy Elders, Eldad and Medad, from the Tabernacle, is recorded, at the time when the LORD gave His Spirit to the rest; and yet, " *the Spirit rested upon them* like-wise."(*h*)

24 But Thomas, one of the Twelve, called Didymus, was not with them when JESUS came.

Not to repeat what has been already so fully offered concerning the character of this eminent Apostle of THE LAMB, the reader is particularly requested, before he proceeds any further, to read the note on St. John xi. 16. He may also refer to St. John xiv. 5, and the comment on the place. That St. Thomas presents us with an example of the desponding temperament, is pretty clearly established. " When therefore the hour of darkness came, realizing apparently in its worst form the me-lancholy anticipation of Thomas ; and when a despair of the redemption of Israel through JESUS of Nazareth fell not on him only, but on them all, — can we wonder that this Apostle was the last to receive the new hope awakened by the unexpected news of the LORD's Resurrection from the grave ? Unexpected it ought not to have been: the LORD's prediction to that effect, the knowledge of which had reached, as we find, even the counsels of the enemies, ought never to have been absent from the faithful recollection of his chosen ones ; yet so it was. The reports of the holy women who found the Body gone, and heard the Angel's assu rance that the LORD yet lived, were regarded by them as idle tales, and they be lieved them not. But this culpable incredulity and dullness of heart, for which our LORD upbraided them all, (as we are told by St. Mark,)(*i*) proceeded in Thomas one step further. By accident, as we may well conceive, though not without a Divine Providence overruling the accident, he was not with the rest when JESUS, on the evening of the first Easter-Sunday, appeared in the midst of them."(*k*)

25 The other Disciples therefore said unto him, We have seen the LORD.

Any one who considers the matter will perceive that "the other Disciples" must have said much more than this to St. Thomas. They must have related how our SAVIOUR had "showed them His Hands and His Feet ;"(*l*) and how, not only those sacred extremities bore the impress of their recent wounds, but how the SAVIOUR's gaping side proclaimed the further outrage of the soldier who had "pierced Him." Accordingly, it follows concerning St. Thomas :

But He said unto them, Except I shall see in His hands the print of the nails, and put my finger into the print of the nails, and thrust my hand into His side, I will not believe.

He refuses to admit any proof of the Resurrection of our LORD, arising from the testimony of others, "unless the fact of its being a real and not a fantastic body were made evident to the sense that alone could determine that question. Let us not exaggerate the feeling, blameworthy as it is, which dictated this deter-mined refusal. There is not the least reason for thinking that Thomas suspected his companions either of fraud or of a deluded vision ; but, without better proof than their assurances or arguments could afford to his questioning spirit, he could not believe but that this was a mere spectral apparation, such as common belief and tradition affirmed as not unusual with the ghosts of the departed ; and that his LORD might be yet in Hades, His body still lifeless, either in the grave where He was laid, or elsewhere. And his gracious LORD, who saw in this too wilful oblivion of His own promised resuscitation, only an extension of the same unbelief that had existed and had been forgiven in the other Apostles,—an extension proceeding less from any greater moral evil in him, then from a peculiarity in mental constitu-tion, — does not refuse to St. Thomas that proof which He had in mere mercy afforded to them, the sensible proof that He was risen."

It must have been a gaping and a ghastly wound,—*that* wound in our SAVIOUR's side, — that St. Thomas should have proposed to "thrust his hand" therein !

26 And after eight days again His Disciples were within, and

(*h*) Numb. xi. 24 to 26.
(*k*) Dr. W. H. Mill.

(*i*) St. Mark xvi. 14.
(*l*) St. Luke xxiv. 40.

Thomas with them: *then* came JESUS, the doors being shut, and stood in the midst, and said, Peace *be* unto you.

Take notice that the salutation is thus repeated for the *third* time, see above, the concluding part of the note on verse 9. — It will be perceived that our SAVIOUR did not silence His servant's doubts immediately; but suffered him to remain in a state of suspense, and even of unbelief, until the following Sunday; "as if to teach us that, during the six days of this world, we are to walk by faith and not by sight; and that on the last, which will be the first day of the new World, and the coming in of His heavenly Kingdom, He will reveal Himself to us; but not till then."(m) No incident whatever is related by any of the Evangelists as having occurred during the interval. "On the Sunday following that of the Resurrection, — (for such honor did he to that holy day, which was to be the standing LORD'S DAY of the Christian Church, as to mark it by this very expressive token, a weekly recurring festival of His rising again,)—on this Sunday after Easter, He appears to Thomas as well as to the other Ten."(n) And it is worth observing that he now repeats every circumstance of His former manifestation, — bearing the infirmities of the weak,"(o) and making Himself therein an example to ourselves.

But when He thus appeared for the second time, we may be well assured that He designed *more* than the removal of unbelief from the mind of a single Disciple. He vouchsafed this appearance for the sake of confirming the faith of all the others,—and of ourselves.

27 Then saith He to Thomas, Reach hither thy finger, and behold My Hands; and reach hither thy hand, and thrust *it* into My Side: and be not faithless but believing.

Literally, "Be," (or rather, "Become,") "not unbelieving, but believing."— "Not content with the proof of sight which He renews to them, He invites the doubting Disciple specially to prove by touch that it was no mere spectre or phantom of a body, but the same body which was pierced with the nails and spear, now revived and incorruptible."(p) Whereby, take notice that our LORD not only affords evidence of the truth of the Resurrection of His human Body, but gives proof of His Divine knowledge as well. For His invitation to St. Thomas showed that He knew what had been the thoughts of his heart, and what the words of his lips, on the previous Sunday. Having thus "convinced" the Disciple, He proceeds to "rebuke" him,(q) — which now He may do with good effect; whereas before, rebuke would have been fruitless.

28 And Thomas answered and said unto Him, My LORD, and my GOD.

It is usual, in pictures, to represent St. Thomas as *touching* our LORD'S side: but, in the Gospel, it is not related that he did so. Our SAVIOUR'S words to him are, "Because thou hast *seen* Me, thou hast believed." "However produced and confirmed, we find that his conviction was complete; and that it embraced not the bare fact of a man risen from the dead, but the saving truth of the Christian creed, — the Resurrection of the Incarnate LORD: that, with the Humanity, it embraced also the inherent Divinity concerned in this fact; the Divinity and Humanity of Him who had power to lay down His life, and had power to take it again, — who was One with the FATHER that raised Him from the tomb; One with the SPIRIT that quickened His human remains to new life. This confession, the foundation of the Christian's hope for time and for eternity, is expressed by the convinced Apostle in the exclamation, 'My LORD and my GOD.'"(r) .... Take notice that this is the first place in the Gospel where our SAVIOUR CHRIST *is addressed as God!*

"The first instruction which his case appears to suggest is this; that minds of every natural complexion are called to the exercise of Christian faith. The principle of Faith,—the disposition to receive the Word of GOD as such, to embrace and to walk by it,—is not indeed the gift of Nature, but of Grace: but its operation in each individual mind is modified by that mind's peculiar cast or temperament; and to every class of mind there are sufficient motives presented for the willing admission of the Truth whereby we are sanctified and saved." Let us beware, above all, that we partake not of the thoughtless irreverence which can venture to

(m) Williams.　　　(n) Dr. W. H. Mill.　See above, the note on the first words of ver. 19.
(o) Rom. xv. 1.　　　(p) Dr. W. H. Mill.　　　(q) 2 Tim. iv. 2.　　　(r) Dr. W. H. Mill.

speak of "*unbelieving* Thomas;" as if unbelief were indeed the characteristic feature of this holy man. "We cannot doubt the exemplary fidelity, and earnest self-devotion, of one who bore the name of his LORD to remote regions of Asia, and sealed his testimony with a glorious martyrdom: nor can we but feel a singular interest in that Apostle to whom ecclesiastical tradition assigns the first implantation of the Christian faith in India; a country in which the Church, planted by him and subsequent Apostolical labourers, has never ceased to exist after a manner; while yet, in the great body of its inhabitants, the dominion of its ancient idolatry remains unshaken, even to the time when Divine Providence has brought it under British rule."(*s*)

"But the great lesson of this example, — that which raises it above all merely local or personal considerations, and gives to all in every age an intimate concern in this doubt and its removal,—lies in the Divine address which follows:"

29 JESUS saith unto him, Thomas, because thou hast seen Me, thou hast believed: blessed *are* they that have not seen and *yet* have believed.

Mighty indeed was the privilege of those who heard, saw with their eyes, who had looked upon, and whose hands had handled, of the WORD of Life;(*t*) yet are not these the persons who are here pronounced "blessed." The blessedness of Faith without the evidence of sense, —*this* it is of which our LORD here assures us; and of this, St. John, (concerning whom it is expressly related that "*he saw, and believed*,")(*u*) St. Peter, St. Thomas, and all the rest, were perforce destitute. . . . "Never can we sufficiently estimate the value of this assurance to distant ages of the Church. Here, men are no longer tested by the fiery trial of persecution, urging them to forsake their LORD, as was the case when the proofs of Divine presence in the Church were more conspicuous; a different, and to some dispositions a far more severe trial is afforded by the speculative difficulties which arise in the absence of such plain tokens; the temptation thence presented to insincere, or fluctuating minds, to abandon all practical regard to the unseen objects of Faith; and to live the life of sense and of the World."

"Blessed are they who have not seen, and yet have believed: who, against the things of sense, the temptations of the World and Satan, against the perplexities of the natural mind, the misgivings of a fearful, and the lacerations of a wounded heart, have opposed a firm faith in facts remote in Time, but indelible and eternal in effect: who have admitted to their hearts and understandings the purifying truth, that He whom the Church now contemplates, He who was once born in the manger of Bethlehem, is indeed their LORD and their GOD. He truly died for their sins: He is truly risen for their justification. He is their SAVIOUR, and will be their Judge!"(*v*)

30 And many other signs truly did JESUS in the presence of His Disciples, which are not written in this Book;

It does not seem quite certain whether the Evangelist alludes here to our SAVIOUR's miracles in general, — the "signs" of His Divine Mission, which He displayed both before and after His Resurrection; or only to those various appearances of CHRIST which the other Evangelists record, — and which were "signs" of the reality of His Resurrection. Ten of our LORD's appearances are recorded, in all; of which St. John describes but four. In this place, therefore, he probably alludes to the accounts of the Great Forty Days which are contained in the earlier Gospels; as well as to those "many" convincing marvels,—those unrecorded manifestations of Himself, it may be,—which seem glanced at by St. Luke in Acts i. 3. And, at the close of the ensuing chapter, he will allude to the multitudinous transactions of our LORD's entire Ministry, which nowhere find any record at all.

31 but these are written, that ye might believe that JESUS is the CHRIST, the SON of GOD; and that believing ye might have life through His Name.

That is, "Eternal Life through *Him*."—On the Evangelist's form of address, see the note on chapter xix. 35. — "These things have I written unto you that ye believe on the Name of the SON of GOD," (declares the same St. John in another place;)

(*s*) Dr. W. H. Mill.　　(*t*) St. John i. 1.　　(*u*) See above, ver. 8.　　(*v*) Dr. W. H. Mill.

" that ye may know that ye have Eternal Life, and that ye may believe on the name of the SON of GOD."(*w*)

" The main drift of the whole New Testament, is that which St. John setteth down as the purpose of his history," says our own thoughtful Hooker. To adopt the weighty observations of a great modern writer : " It is the real Incarnation of the Eternal WORD,—the actual coming in the flesh of the SON of GOD, born, dead, and risen for our Salvation,— which is the sole basis of our Religion ; and this, through the divinely-appointed means by which its belief and salutary influence is propagated, becomes the principle of Christian faith and righteousness. This great fact, and not any particular proposition concerning it, however true or useful in its place, which men may consider as containing the whole idea, or all that is essential to its purpose ; this great fact, I say, in the totality of its objective character, and in the consequent totality of its applicable virtue and influence ; this is the real *Article of a standing or falling Church.*"(*x*)

With the words before us, St. John's Gospel seems to come to a close. His twenty-first chapter has a supplementary air. Many have not hesitated to apply to it the name of *an after-thought.* . . . We make wondrous free with the Gospels ! Are they mere human works, then ? and do they stand on the same footing as the Annals of Tacitus, or the Commentaries of Cæsar ? Or are they the work of the SPIRIT ; the inspired oracles of the Eternal GOD ? . . . We humbly suspect, (with many of our Fathers in the Faith,) that it is because the transactions of the ensuing chapter have a distinct character of their own,—are prophetic in their details, and stretch out their shadows even unto the end of the World,— that the Evangelist thus severs them from all that went before. By two verses of like character and import,(*y*) he seems to put a wall on this side and on that of the solemn narrative which follows ; and which he thereby emphatically commends to the devout attention of the Church to the end of Time.

CHAPTER XXI.

1. CHRIST *appearing again to His Disciples was known of them by the great draught of fishes.* 12. *He dineth with them :* 15 *earnestly commandeth Peter to feed His lambs and sheep:* 18 *foretelleth him of his death :* 22 *rebuketh his curiosity touching John.* 25. *The conclusion.*

THE reader is invited to read the remark which was offered at the close of the Commentary on the preceding chapter. It has been already there suggested, that the concluding chapter of the present Gospel has a prophetic character of its own,— shadowing forth, in symbolic outline, the ultimate fortunes of the Church. We turn with amazement from those who, from making over-free with the wondrous details which follow, have presumed even to question the authenticity of the chapter in which they are found.(*a*) To ourselves, every word of the record seems to glow with mysterious meaning ; every trivial feature of the history seems pregnant with momentous interest. Be sure that nothing here is set down in vain. It is the last page of the Eternal Gospel ! We are going to read the last words which " the Disciple whom JESUS loved" was instructed to write for the eternal edification of the Church. Immediately after which, his task will be completed, and the record of MESSIAH's First Advent will be sealed up for ever !

" One feels a reluctance," (as Isaac Williams truly remarks,) " to dwell much on spiritual significations, from the objections which some persons feel to entertain them: objections, partly arising from a natural inability to enter into cases of analogy, and from finding nothing to satisfy their minds in such resemblances,—of which, indeed, they have but a faint perception. But even those who are most averse to speculations of this class, do feel constrained, in this instance, to admit that there are indications of most pregnant significancy, breaking forth throughout, and rising to the very surface of the narrative." . . . Let the reader beware, then, how he reads,—at least this, the last page of the Gospel,— lest he miss its solemn

---

(*w*) 1 St. John v. 13.   (*x*) Dr. W. H. Mill.   (*y*) Chap. xx. 30 and xxi. 25.
(*a*) As Grotius. The reader may refer to the Preface.

meaning, while he is laudably anxious not to substitute his own imaginations for the Truth. Let the exceeding minuteness of the narrative be first considered, together with every possible explanation of which that minuteness will admit. Then, let that similar miracle to the present, which St. Luke records,(b) be compared throughout with what is related here. Next, let the parable of the Draw-net be studied attentively, and our LORD'S Divine interpretation thereof be devoutly read.(c) When, in conclusion, the analogy of Scripture language is considered;(d) and the rebuke which our SAVIOUR administered to His Disciples on a certain occasion for their dullness in not understanding what He *meant* when He spoke of "leaven,"(e) is borne in mind; as well as the many occasions on which He intimated to them that His words and actions had a profounder meaning than met their ear or their eye;(f)—when all this has been duly weighed, we cannot understand why any one should hesitate to admit that *here* at least, the narrative is of that kind which is called *mystical :* that, in this place, the SPIRIT is teaching us by signs "things which shall be hereafter."

> After these things JESUS showed Himself again to the Disciples at the sea of Tiberias; and on this wise showed He *Himself.*

St. John has already mentioned the two occasions on which our SAVIOUR "showed Himself to His Disciples," collectively. He proceeds here to describe the third. To what period of the great Forty days, the appearance at the Sea of Galilee, (or, as St. John calls it, "of Tiberias,")(g) belongs, cannot be ascertained: but the discovery that the Apostles have left Jerusalem,—wandered back to their ancient locality, and resumed their former trade of fishermen,—seems to suggest that a considerable interval of time has elapsed since the octave of the first Easter.

They had returned to Galilee, doubtless in obedience to the command conveyed by the Angel to the woman on the morning of the Resurrection. "Go your way, tell His Disciples and Peter that He goeth before you *into Galilee :* there shall ye see Him, as He said unto you."(h) They will have also doubtless remembered our SAVIOUR'S words,—"After I am risen again, I will go before you *into Galilee.*"(i) And this we say, remembering well that the appearance specially promised on the occasion referred to, is that which St. Matthew describes in the five last verses of his Gospel, and concerning which the reader is invited to read the note on St. Matthew xxviii. 16.—And now, "they are again among their former haunts and abodes; in a spot already hallowed by so many endearing and sacred associations, and presenting so great a contrast with the turbulent Jerusalem; amidst scenes of nature, and the quiet waters of their own beautiful sea. They are again on that very place and shore which had probably been their home from childhood, and where they had been since trained to things Divine, by miracle, and precept, and parable; the place where they had been first called."(k)

> 2 There were together Simon Peter, and Thomas called Didymus, and Nathanael of Cana in Galilee, and the *sons* of Zebedee, and two other of His Disciples.

"*First,* Simon ;"(l) but Thomas, who so late was doubtful, is mentioned next. Never more will it be said that "Thomas, one of the Twelve, called Didymus, was not with them when JESUS came !"(m) Nathanael, (that is Bartholomew,) of whom we have heard nothing since the day of his first call to Apostleship,(n) is found in the third place; and we learn that he was "of Cana in Galilee,"—by which intimation, the record of this, our LORD'S last miracle, is connected with the "beginning of miracles." St. James and St. John come next; and by the "two other of His Disciples" are doubtless meant St. Andrew and St. Philip;—whose names are always recorded among the first five of the Twelve. They were both from the same city,(o) and their names are found connected on two,(p) indeed on three(q) occa-

---

(b) St. Luke v. 1 to 8.   (c) St. Matth. xiii. 47 to 50.
(d) See St. John vi. 51, &c.   St. Luke v. 10.
(e) St. Matth. xvi. 11, 12.   Consider also St. John xii. 16.
(f) See St. John xiii. 7, and the note there: also xiv. 26, and the long note on the place.
(g) Concerning it, see the note on St. Mark i. 16. See especially St. John vi. 1, and the note there.
(h) St. Mark xvi. 7.   Compare St. Matth. xxviii. 7.   (i) St. Matth. xxvi. 32.
(k) Williams.   (l) St. Matth. x. 2.   (m) St. John xx. 24.
(n) See St. John i. 45 to 50.   (o) St. John i. 44.
(p) St. John vi. 5, 8, and xii. 21, 22.   (q) St. Mark iii. 18.

sions. To *seven* of His Disciples, therefore, on this occasion our LORD revealed Himself. . . . "Wisdom," (that is CHRIST,) is about to "build her House :" wherefore "she hath hewn out her seven pillars."(r)

3 Simon Peter saith unto them, I go a fishing. They say unto him, We also go with thee.

The Disciples have therefore returned to their nets, as at the beginning! In fact, the whole of the present miraculous narrative exhibits parallel features of resemblance and of contrast with that earlier one, recorded in St. Luke's Gospel, chap. v. 1 to 11, which would be extraordinary indeed were those features not, every one, intentional, and full of mysterious meaning.

Here, then, *seven* Disciples go forth to fish on the Sea of Galilee, as *four* had gone forth in the first days of the Gospel. Simon Peter is foremost on both occasions, and his partners are still with him. We felt something akin to surprise, when we last beheld these fishermen gone forth; for we said to ourselves, Are not these the men whom CHRIST hath so recently brought to the knowledge of Himself?(s) and a like feeling of surprise awaits us now. These men were so lately assembled at Jerusalem, and CHRIST was among them : — what do they here on the waters of their familiar lake, and engaged in their ancient trade?

One thing, at least, is certain ; and the circumstance is full of affecting interest : it must have been *their necessities* which sent the Apostles forth on their present lowly errand. And yet, these were they on whom the Church was to be built! These were the names which were to be written on the twelve foundations of the Heavenly Jerusalem !(t) . . . Verily, the discovery that their LORD and their GOD could suffer the men He loved to remain in such a low estate and precarious condition, should teach Christians for evermore to submit cheerfully to poverty, as well as to behold with a feeling akin to reverence, the brother of low degree. . . . The Seven Apostles seem to have been sitting together in-doors, and it was the time of evening: a Sabbath-evening perhaps,—so that the manifestation which follows may have taken place, like the former two, on a Sunday.

They went forth, and entered into a ship immediately; and that night they caught nothing.

Rather, "into *the* ship," — as on so many other occasions. . . . A point of contrast between the miracle in St. Luke v., and *that* here recorded, at once presents itself: namely, that *one* vessel, not *two* are employed.(u)

The night, (as we were once before reminded,) was the season when fishermen were accustomed to pursue their trade: but on this, (as on that other night,) the Disciples "caught nothing."(x) And it was to convince them,—and through them to instruct *us*,—that, without CHRIST, we "can do nothing."(y) The "ministers and stewards of His mysteries," in particular, are hereby taught that "except the LORD build the House, their labour is but lost that build it."(z)

4 But when the morning was now come, JESUS stood on the shore :

"There appears a Stranger in the dim twilight, drawing the attention as it were to Himself, though they knew not who it was."(a) . . . "When the morning was now come,—JESUS stood on the shore." How prophetic is the sound of every word! It was a symbol of the Eternal Morning, when JESUS (who is "the hope of them that remain in the broad Sea!")(b) will at last appear: for the Church as yet waiteth, "until the day break and the shadows flee away."(c) No longer in the ship with His Disciples, — as on the occasion of the former miraculous draught of fishes,(d) when He was like one crossing "the waves of this troublesome World," — He is seen standing on the fixed immovable shore! Thither "they shall go to Him, but thence He shall not return to them."(e) Consider how that word (" the shore,") is introduced in the parable of the draw-net, which our LORD Himself explained to be symbolical of what "shall be at the end of the World."(f)

but the Disciples knew not that it was JESUS.

Not because they were a long way off from where He stood, (" for they were not

(r) Prov. ix. 1. Compare Gal. ii. 9.   (s) See the note on St. Matth. iv. 18.
(t) Rev. xxi. 14.   (u) See St. Luke v. 7.
(x) Compare St. Luke v. 5.   (y) St. John xv. 5.   (z) Ps. cxxvii. 1.   (a) Williams.
(b) Ps. lxv. 5.   (c) Song of Solomon ii. 17 : iv. 6.   (d) St. Luke. v. 3.
(e) 2 Sam. xii. 23.   (f) St. Matth. xiii. 48, 49.

far from land:")(*g*) nor yet because the morning was grey and misty. "The Dis ciples knew not that it was JESUS" for the same reason that Mary Magdalene "knew not that it was JESUS,"(*h*) when she saw Him standing close beside her: for the same reason that the two who walked with Him to Emmaus knew not that it was He. The eyes of all "*were holden* that they should not know Him."(*i*) So enveloped was His risen Body with something that was Divine, something which He brought from the grave, — that it allowed not of human affection, but Divine Love, to discern it."(*j*) And it was done in order to accustom them to walk by *Faith*, and not by *Sight*. For thus it was that our SAVIOUR was recognized by St. John *now*. The *miracle* was to be the evidence that it was He.

5 Then JESUS saith unto them, Children, have ye any meat? They answered Him, No.

The word for "Children" here, is not the same which our SAVIOUR had applied to His Disciples in chap. xiii. 33, (where see the note;) but rather, as in the margin, —"Sirs."(*k*) . . . Chrysostom says that He accosted them in the manner of one who was desirous to buy fish of them. Such a remark, from one whose native lan guage was Greek, is entitled to attention. The word rendered "meat" perhaps especially implied that *fish* was the food inquired for. . . . The SAVIOUR, (as so often pointed out elsewhere,)(*l*) did not *need* to be informed how unsuccessfully the Dis ciples had been toiling; but His inquiry was to remind them of the fact, as well as to draw from them an admission of their forlorn and unprovided state.

6 And He said unto them, Cast the net on the right side of the ship, and ye shall find.

The season for fishing prescribed by Nature, had already expired: it was now the season appointed by Grace. In truth, Man's extremity is ever found to be GOD's opportunity. So was it at Cana's Feast; and so, on many other occasions recorded in the Gospels,—as the reader will find pointed out, if he will refer to the places in the commentary, indicated at foot.(*m*) In the meantime, take notice that the neces sity of human exertion is not to be *superseded* by the promise of Divine help. Paul must plant and Apollos water, though GOD must give all the increase.

"Nothing better brings to light the import of the present mystery than the com parison of this miracle with that recorded in St. Luke v.: and already, there is a marked difference between them. In the former miraculous draught of fishes, it had been simply said, 'Let down your net for a draught.' Neither right nor left was specified; for, on the former occasion, there was set forth in figure the Church visible,—the net spoken of in the parable as 'gathering of every kind,' and being 'filled with bad and good.' The net, therefore, was then thrown, as it were, at random, neither to the right nor left. But here, where the Church invisible of the Elect is represented, — such as is filled only with those that are finally saved, and come to the land of everlasting life, — ('*great* fishes, an hundred and fifty, and three,')—it is said, 'Cast ye on the right side.' Here is choice and election as de signed in secret knowledge by CHRIST Himself."(*n*)

Not only *when* GOD commands, therefore, but *as* GOD directs, must the net be thrown, if we would secure the prize we long for. By commanding the Disciples now to shift the position of their net, and to cast it on the right side of the ship, our SAVIOUR teaches them that the draught of fishes which they presently capture is no chance transaction, but takes place by His own Providential ordinance. . . . At the same time, He inclines the hearts of the men in the ship to obedience; or their own unyielding wills would have marred the gracious designs of His Provi dence towards them.

Many are the occasions in Holy Scripture where "the *right* side" is designated with special honour. Not to insist on the session of the Eternal SON "at the Right Hand of GOD,"(*o*) we know that the "Right Hand" is given to "the sheep" in the

(*g*) See ver. 8.   (*h*) St. John xx. 14.   (*i*) St. Luke xxiv. 16.   (*j*) Williams.
(*k*) It is often, however, a term of kindness, — as in St. John ii. 13, 18.
(*l*) See the notes on St. Mark v. 9 and 30: viii. 24: ix. 21. Also on St. John xi. 34,—where see the references.
(*m*) See the notes on St. Matth. xiv. 26. St. Mark v. 24 and 35: St. Luke v. 17, and St. John iv. 47: ix. 6.
(*n*) Williams.
(*o*) Ps. cx. 1, quoted in St. Luke xx. 42. Acts ii. 34. Heb. i. 13. Consider St. Mark xiv. 62, and St. Luke xxii. 69: also St. Mark xvi. 19, Acts vii. 55, &c.

Kingdom ;(*p*) that "the Cherubim stood on the right side of the House" in Ezekiel's vision ;(*q*) and that Zacharias saw the Angel "standing on the right side of the altar of incense."(*r*) . . In the meantime, the Disciples comply with the Stranger's injunction, and marvellous is the result.

They cast, therefore, and now they were not able to draw it for the multitude of fishes.

It is manifest that the only difference between the right and the left side of the ship, in this instance, consisted in the fact that the one side had been preferred by God before the other. A net will capture the same prey precisely, on whichever side of the ship it is let down, if a shoal of fish are swimming past the ship: and yet, *who* doubts that on the present occasion, success, or failure, depended entirely on the Disciples' obedience, their strict compliance with the required condition ? . . It may teach us that, in things to all appearance indifferent, a Divine command, (a *positive precept*, as it is called,) overcomes all other considerations, and must be implicitly obeyed, if we would inherit a blessing.

Applied to the matter immediately before us, we are reminded, (as we were in the Evangelical account of the former miraculous draught of fishes, (that Ministerial labour must of necessity be fruitless, until it is conducted in obedience to a Divine call,(*s*) and in conformity with a Divine command. Throughout the long night, the Disciples have been toiling fruitlessly. Once thrown in the morning, the prey which their net captures is so large as to be even unmanageable.

7 Therefore that Disciple whom Jesus loved saith unto Peter, It is the Lord. Now when Simon Peter heard that it was the Lord, he girt *his* fisher's coat *unto him*, (for he was naked,) and did cast himself into the sea.

St. Peter had nothing on him but his inner garment,(*t*)—as was natural in one engaged in toil. . . . Strange, that he should have been slower than his friend and fellow-disciple to discover that it was the Lord! The prominent part which he played at both the miraculous draughts of fishes,—being the chief speaker, and, as it would seem, the most conspicuous agent on the latter as well as on the former occasion,—would prepare us naturally to expect that the recognition of their Divine Master would have first taken place on the side of *St. Peter*. But it was not so. St. John, who reached the Sepulchre before St. Peter by speed of limb, and "believed," now reaches his risen Saviour first, by Faith, and informs the other, that "it is the Lord!" To St. John, on both occasions, the statement is applicable,—"Yet went he not in:" even as, on both occasions, St. Peter is the one to press farthest forward afterwards,—casting himself now into the water with a noble instinct of love which we cannot too much admire; and wading through the shallows in the direction of the Figure upon the strand. . . There was nothing whatever to be gained by this proceeding on his part,—which makes it the more interesting, as an exhibition probably of the personal character of the Apostle: for this was he who must needs walk to Christ upon the water,—follow Him into the High-priest's palace, —and press eagerly into the Holy Sepulchre, after His Resurrection, while St. John was gazing without.

A great Doctor of our own writes as follows concerning the transaction in the text : " It is St. John whose instinct of love penetrates the disguise, and tells Peter that it is the Lord. It might strike the recollection of both, how a few short years before, the same Lord had, in His mortal days, given a similar direction,—a like miraculous draught following: though, then, they drew the net; but now, they could not: then, the net brake; but now, for all the greater multitude of fishes, when it was drawn to land, the net was unbroken: then, the ship began to sink, and Simon Peter, affrighted, besought the Lord to depart from him, a sinful man ; whereas now, as soon as he heard that it was the Lord, and believed it was so, he plunged into the water to go to Him. These circumstances, symbolizing the greater power of the risen Lord,—or rather the greater power He obtained for the fishers of men when the mysteries of His Redemption were accomplished,—were not lost on St. John ; who, ever calmer than St. Peter, while his emotions were the

---

(*p*) St. Matth. xxv. 33.　　　　　　　　　　(*q*) Ezek. x. 3.
(*r*) St. Luke i. 11.　Compare Lev. i. 11.　　(*s*) Consider St. Luke v. 5.
(*t*) The word "naked," in the original, implies this.　Compare St. Mark xiv. 52.

deepest, tranquilly remained with the rest in the vessel, till it was brought to the shore."(*u*)

8 And the other Disciples came in a little ship; (for they were not far from land, but as it were two hundred cubits,) dragging the net with fishes.

Rather, "the other Disciples came in *the boat*." Their fishing-vessel drew too much water to approach any closer to the edge of the Lake, from which they were about a hundred yards distant: the Disciples accordingly lowered the boat, and rowed for land,—dragging the net with them. Take notice, that this time the fish are not emptied *into the boats*.—as on the former occasion ; but drawn *to shore*.

"Two hundred cubits." "So near are we, even in this troublous World, to the land of Everlasting Rest," and to Him who there abideth ; "though He be not far from every one of us, for in Him we live, and move, and have our being."(*v*)

9 As soon then as they were come to land, they saw a fire of coals there, and fish laid thereon, and bread.

Fish and Bread :—the very materials out of which, a year before, their LORD had fed five thousand, on one of the mountains hard by ! The food may have been symbolical ; but we will not presume to divine of *what*.

A charcoal fire, miraculously prepared,—a supply of food also, miraculously provided,—awaits the arrival of the seven wondering Apostles. "A fire already made upon the shore, to welcome them in the cold of the early morning : fish already baked thereon ; and bread by itself. Then, surely, no needy suppliant for their hospitality had accosted them a few moments since : but the same who says,—" If I be hungry, I will not tell thee ; for the whole World is Mine, and all that is therein !"(*x*) The circumstance is the more mysterious, because our LORD never appears to have worked miracles for no purpose ; and, humanly speaking, there was no need for this bread and this fish,—not of the fish, certainly ; for the Disciples were already abundantly supplied. Something, no doubt, very great and Divine must be contained in all this !"(*y*)

10 JESUS saith unto them, Bring of the fish which ye have now caught.

It was *they* indeed who had *caught* the fish ; "yet, how true was it of these, 'All things come of Thee ; and of Thine own have we given Thee !' "(*z*)

Twofold, it may be, was the purpose with which this command was given. Our risen LORD probably willed that the attention of the seven Disciples should be drawn to the extent of the prey they had recently captured,—the size, and the number of the fishes ;—as well as to the circumstance that, "for all there were so many, yet was not the net broken." The Divine command seems to have a further gracious intention, which the reader will find indicated at the conclusion of the note on verse 13,—the suggestion being there offered, not without distrust, to his indulgent consideration.

11 Simon Peter went up, and drew the net to land full of great fishes, an hundred and fifty and three :

A moment since, and we were told that "they were *not able to draw it* for the multitude of fishes." Simon Peter now goes up, and draws the net to land, alone ! (*a*) Did our LORD perhaps command him to take upon himself this office ? or do we only behold here another example of St. Peter's forwardness and zeal ?

Take notice that it is declared that the fishes were all "great." Their number is also specified ;—a circumstance which suggests that the Disciples were instructed to ascertain the exact sum of them. But how singular does it seem that their attention should have been directed to such a circumstance, at such a time ! and how strange that the circumstance should be recorded ! Is it, perhaps, done, (among other reasons,) with allusion to "*the number* of the elect,"—certainly fixed in the eternal counsels of the Most High, though to Man a thing ever unknown ? Or may there be some real connection between this place of Scripture, and that place

(*u*) Dr. W. H. Mill.   (*v*) Acts xvii. 27, 28.   (*x*) Ps. l. 12.
(*y*) Williams.   (*z*) Williams, quoting 1 Chron. xxix. 14.
(*a*) Consider the conduct of Jacob, as related in Gen. xxix. 2, 3, 7, 8, 10.

where it is mentioned that " all the strangers that were in the land of Israel were found *an hundred and fifty thousand, and three thousand,* and six hundred !"(*c*) The reasons which Augustine gives for the number, (" an hundred and fifty and three,") seem fanciful and insufficient. Hereby, however, we are reminded of the sum, which is also recorded, of those who were saved in the ship which conveyed St. Paul,—" two hundred, three score, and sixteen souls;"(*d*) as well as of the doings of Him who " doeth all things in measure, and *number,* and weight."(*e*)

and for all there were so many, yet was not the net broken.

A mysterious circumstance, which seems to be noticed with special reference to that former occasion when, because the Disciples " enclosed a great multitude of fishes," St. Luke relates that *"their net brake."*(*f*) . . . If the rents and divisions in the Church of CHRIST during these, the days of her warfare, are signified by the broken net, the net unbroken must represent symbolically the Church's altered fortune, when her " Prayer for Unity" will at last be granted.

12 JESUS said unto them, Come *and* dine.

Rather,—"Come, breakfast."(*g*) . . . . . The tender love of Him whose mercies are over all His works is apparent in this invitation; for the Disciples had toiled long, were cold, and wet, and weary, and had hitherto eaten nothing. Yet, through reverence and awe, they kept aloof from the simple banquet which their Divine Master had provided for them; nor, till they were specially invited, did they presume to approach the place where He stood.

Meantime, beneath these lowly symbols was transacted the image of a lofty mystery; for what did this meal signify but that Heavenly banquet, of which it is promised that the redeemed shall partake hereafter, when they shall " *sit down* with Abraham, and Isaac, and Jacob, in the Kingdom of Heaven ?"(*h*) " Blessed are they which are called into the Marriage Supper of the LAMB !"(*i*) . . . The seven Disciples exhibited in a figure the blissful estate of those who shall *eat bread* in the Kingdom of GOD :"(*j*) while the true Joseph,—(speedily to be revealed in his other character of " the Shepherd,"(*k*)— displayed an emblem of that spiritual repast which He will then provide for the perfect refreshment of His Brethren. Consider further St. John xii. 2.—Our LORD may have Himself partaken of the present meal, in order to convince His Disciples of the truth of His Resurrection,— as He had done once before:(*l*) for in this interval between His Resurrection and Ascension, " as He had risen Himself, so He is raising them from their unbelief."(*m*) But the fact is assumed, in the heading of the chapter; where we read, —"*He dineth with them.*"

And none of the Disciples durst ask Him, Who art Thou? knowing that it was the LORD.

" No one dared to ask Him, for they had no longer the same freedom of speech and boldness as heretofore." A change seems to have passed upon His aspect: He was another,—yet the same: And the Disciples, " beholding His form altered, and replete with something exceedingly astonishing, were stricken with very great fear; being desirous to make some inquiry concerning it, but awe, and the consciousness that it was not another, but He Himself, restrained the question; and they only ate those things which He had created with great power."(*n*)

13 JESUS then cometh, and taketh bread, and giveth them, and fish likewise.

" On this occasion," (as Chrysostom points out,) " He no longer looks up to Heaven," blessing and giving thanks, as He had invariably done before His Resurrection; " showing that those acts had formerly taken place by condescension." "All power," (He seems to say,) "is given unto Me in Heaven and in Earth."(*o*)
Is it meant, in the verse before us, that He " came" to the spot where the Disciples were,—the spot, comparatively a remote one, where they had timidly seated

(*c*) 2 Chron. ii. 17.   (*d*) Acts xxvii. 37.   (*e*) Wisdom xi. 20.   (*f*) St. Luke v. 6.
(*g*) Compare St. Matth. xxv. 34.   (*h*) St. Matth. viii. 11, where see the note.
(*i*) Rev. xix. 9.   (*j*) St. Luke xiv. 15,—where see the note.   (*k*) Gen. xlix. 34.
(*l*) See St. Luke xxiv. 41 to 43.   (*m*) Abp. Leighton.
(*n*) Chrysostom.   (*o*) St. Matth. xxviii. 18.

themselves? Or is it simply that, after the Disciples had sat down, our SAVIOUR
Himself approached the spot,—"came" and sat down likewise? . . . . . Observe,
that the Disciples do not *help themselves* to food. It is still CHRIST that taketh,—
CHRIST that giveth! All the spiritual refreshment of Heaven will still be *His* gift!
The very Bliss of the Saints will be altogether from *Him!* . . . . And yet, besides
the fish miraculously provided for the refreshment of the Disciples, we find that
they were fed with some of the fish which they had themselves recently caught.
This we gather from the special statement in verse 10. But those fishes, as we
certainly know,(p) symbolize the successful result with which the Apostles should
hereafter preach the Gospel. Are we not at liberty, then, to connect with the present passage that remarkable declaration of St. Paul,—"For what is our hope, or
joy, or crown of rejoicing? *Are not even ye, in the presence of our* LORD JESUS
CHRIST, *at His Coming?"*(q) . . . . . O mystery of Divine Love, in reserve for
those who have faithfully fed the flock of CHRIST committed to their care; if,
throughout the ages, they shall be conscious of an augmentation of Bliss from the
souls of those to whom in life it was their privilege to minister!

14 This is now the third time that JESUS showed Himself to His
Disciples, after that He was risen from the dead.

Not, His third *appearance*, or manifestation of Himself; for no less than five
appearances, (as already remarked elsewhere,) are recorded to have taken place on
the day of His Resurrection; and this is the fourth appearance which St. John
himself describes. But this is "the third time that JESUS *showed Himself to His
Disciples*," collectively.

Throughout the Bible, "the *third* time," (a number ever divinely allusive to the
mystery of the Blessed Trinity!) is either for confirmation or consummation. If
the present is an example of "the third time" being used in this latter sense, we
shall be presented, further on, with an example of its use in the former. The
reader may be referred, on this head, to the note on chapter xx. . . . . . And here,
a new subject as it were begins,—a new scene is disclosed. It is no longer fishermen, and their nets, and the salt lake; but shepherds, with their flocks, and a green
pasture which comes to view. Above all, our LORD JESUS CHRIST, now newly
risen from the dead, comes before us, (as St. Paul not obscurely intimates,) in the
character of "*the Great Shepherd of the sheep*,"(r)—(His ancient character;)(s)—
even as "the Shepherd and Bishop of our souls."

"Some part of the great Pastoral Office to which He had been designated by
ancient Prophecy, and His own Divine words, our Blessed LORD discharged while
He remained on Earth in the flesh; pitying, tending, feeding, loving those who had
been "as sheep having no shepherd;" and above all exhibiting that greatest token
of the Good Shepherd, the laying down of His life for the sheep. But when He
had done this, and having now risen from the grave, was about to ascend where
He was before, He left behind Him in the great saying which follows, ("FEED MY
SHEEP,") the institution of Pastoral Succession to the end of the World."(t)

15 So when they had dined, JESUS saith to Simon Peter, Simon,
son of Jonas, lovest thou Me more than these?

This very form of address recalls that former occasion when our LORD pronounced
Simon Peter "blessed" for his glorious confession of His Divinity, and bestowed
upon him a mysterious promise concerning His future Church. "Blessed art thou,
Simon *Bar jona*,"—He began.(u)

"Lovest thou Me more than these [love Me]?" asks our LORD. The inquiry has
clear reference to that recent occasion when Simon had declared that his attach-
ment to our LORD's person was stronger than that of any of the other Apostles.
See St. Matthew xxvi. 33. Thrice, on the very night of his confident boasting, as
our SAVIOUR proceeded immediately to predict,(v) Simon did nevertheless deny

(p) Consider St. Matth. xiii. 47–49; and see St. Luke v. 10.
(q) 1 Thess. ii. 19.   (r) Heb. xiii. 20.
(s) Ps. xxiii. 2: lxxvii. 20: lxxviii. 52: cxix. 176. Is. xl. 11. Ezek. xxxiv. 11 to 23:
xxxvii. 24. Jer. iii. 15: xxiii. 3, 4. See the notes on St. Luke xv. 3 to 6; but, above all, St.
John x. 1 to 16.
(t) Dr. Moberly.   (u) St. Matth. xvi. 17,—where see the note.
(v) St. John xiii. 38. St. Matth. xxvi. 34.

Him. And so, *thrice*, at the present time, His risen LORD repeats His inquiry,— "Simon son of Jonas, lovest thou Me?"

A remarkable variety, however, is discoverable in the terms of our SAVIOUR's repeated question, and St. Peter's repeated answer, which is lost to the English reader. Two words differing in their intensity, are employed for "to love," where we possess but one. Our SAVIOUR, using first the word expressive of less strong personal affection, asks,— "Lovest thou Me?" "At this moment, when all the pulses in the heart of the now penitent Apostle are beating with an earnest affection toward his LORD, this word on that LORD's lips sounds too cold. Besides the question itself, which grieves and hurts Peter, there is an additional pang in the form which the question takes, sounding as though it were intended to put him at a comparative distance from his LORD, and to keep him there; or at least, as not permitting him to approach so near to Him as he fain would. He therefore in his answer substitutes for it the word of a more personal love,—"Thou knowest that I love Thee dearly." When CHRIST repeats the question in the same words as at the first, Peter in his reply again substitutes his "love Thee dearly" for the "lovest thou" of his LORD. And now at length he has conquered; for when his Master puts the question to him for the third time, He does it with the word which Peter feels will alone express all that is in his heart; and instead of the twice repeated "Lovest thou Me?" His word is, "Dost thou *love Me Dearly?*" . . . . The question, grievous in itself to Peter, as seeming to imply a doubt in his love, is not any longer made more grievous still, by the peculiar shape which it assumes."(*w*)

> He saith unto him, Yea, LORD; Thou knowest that I love Thee.

"Dearly." Take notice that Simon, in his reply, presumes not to speak, (as he did before,)(*x*) of the love of his fellow-disciples,—concerning which he *can* know nothing. Humbled by his fall,(*y*) he does but make profession of his own love; appealing, in proof thereof, to the perfect knowledge of Him by whom he is addressed. "*Thou* knowest!"—knowest that I do *more* than "love" Thee.

> He saith unto him, Feed My Lambs.

That is,—If thou truly lovest Me, then,—"Feed My lambs!" Prepare thyself, for their sakes, even to lay down that life which thou didst once so boastfully profess thyself willing to lay down for Mine:(*z*) remembering that "the good shepherd *giveth his life* for the sheep.(*a*) . . . Does not St. John allude to all this in his first Epistle, when he writes,—"Hereby perceive we the love of GOD, because He laid down His life for us: and we ought to lay down our lives for the brethren?"(*b*)

This rejoinder of our LORD is surely full of precious teaching to the Ministers of CHRIST forever. The *test* of their love towards their Divine Master,—the only test which He Himself proposes, the only proof which He will Himself accept,—is *their care of His flock;* and first, of *the lambs* of the flock. Consider Isaiah xl. 11. Now the "lambs" are those little ones, — (whether in respect of age, or abilities, or station,) — who, as "babes in CHRIST," require to be fed "with milk and not with meat;" and "have need that one teach them which be the first principles of the oracles of GOD." "For every one that useth milk is unskilful in the word of righteousness: for he is a babe. But strong meat belongeth to them that are of full age."(*c*) So far, St. Paul. How remarkable is it to find the self-same image in the writings of St. Peter also!(*d*)

Every word here is, in fact, a Homily. The lambs are to be *fed*. Their daily portion of *food* (all that is needed for the soul's health and strength, all that is included in that petition "Give us this day *our daily bread*,") is here specially spoken of. And those "lambs," saith "the Great Shepherd of the sheep,"(*e*) are "*Mine.*" . . . . O salutary thought for the pastor of souls, that the "sheep" and the "lambs" are not *his*, but CHRIST's! Not *his;* — therefore, like Jacob with the flock of Laban, should he be prepared to give account for all!(*f*) Not *his;* — therefore must there be One above him, to whom they are a care as well as to

(*w*) Trench, "on the Synonyms of the New Testament," — a delightful little work.
(*x*) St. Matth. xxvi. 33.   (*y*) See the note on St. Matth. xxvi. 75.
(*z*) St. John xiii. 37.   (*a*) St. John x. 11.   (*b*) 1 St. John iii. 16.
(*c*) Heb. v. 13, 14. Abp. Laud supplies these two references.   (*d*) 1 St. Pet. ii. 2.
(*e*) Heb. xiii. 20. Consider the whole verse.   (*f*) Gen. xxxi. 39.

himself; even "the Chief Shepherd,"(*g*) who careth alike for *him* and for *them!* the Same who saith, "I will seek that which was lost, and bring again that which was driven away, and will bind up that which was broken, and will strengthen that which was sick."(*h*) — But "Woe be to the shepherds of Israel that do feed themselves! Should not the shepherds feed the flocks?"(*i*) . . . . See below, on ver. 17.

16 He saith to him again the second time, Simon, *son* of Jonas, lovest thou Me? He saith unto Him, Yea, LORD; Thou knowest that I love Thee. He saith unto him, Feed My sheep.

Rather, "*Tend* My sheep." . . . . Before, it was "Feed;" now, it is "Tend" or "Shepherd:" that is, "Perform all a shepherd's duties" by them; "Feed the flock, *like a shepherd;*"(*j*) do all that should be done by a "*shepherd of the sheep.*"(*k*) Call thine own sheep by name, and lead them out; and when thou puttest forth thine own sheep, go before them, that the sheep (knowing thy voice) may follow thee. Consider St. John x. 3, 4.—Before, also, the little "lambs" were specified as the prime object of pastoral solicitude. Now, it is the grown "sheep." But of both alike, "the Good Shepherd" says — They are "*Mine.*"

17 He saith unto him the third time, Simon, *son* of Jonas, lovest thou Me?

As Peter had thrice repeated his denial, so does our LORD give him the opportunity of thrice repeating the declaration of his love; — thereby conveying to him forgiveness, and restoring the afflicted Apostle to favour. Not once, however, now, does CHRIST address him by his name of strength;(*l*) but repeats, on every occasion, an allusion to his humble parentage. . . . . . Concerning the altered form of the present inquiry, see above, the note on ver. 15.

A practical lesson also is surely to be derived by ourselves from this repeated question. The Divine Speaker "seems to say that, in a Pastor, the first, the second, the third requisite, is *love of* CHRIST."(*m*)

Peter was grieved because He said unto him the third time, Lovest thou Me? And he said unto Him, LORD, Thou knowest all things; Thou knowest that I love Thee.

He was perhaps "grieved," because the sad remembrance of the past suggested the possibility that his present confidence was only the prelude to a second fall. He appeals, therefore, to his LORD's Omniscience,(*n*) and humbly repeats the assurance of his personal affection.

JESUS saith unto him, Feed My sheep.

This is not, by any means, the same injunction as the last. It is no longer "*Tend,*" or "*Shepherd,*" My sheep, — as in ver. 16; but "*Feed*" them, — the same word which was used above, in ver. 15, with reference to the little lambs. . . . The same catechetical training therefore, — the same careful attention to the soul's natural cravings and acquired needs, which was enjoined on behalf of the "lambs" of the fold, — is here enjoined on behalf of the "sheep," also.

Thus earnestly did our LORD, for the third time, commend "the people of His pasture and the sheep of His Hand," to the care of *all* the Bishops and Pastors of His Church, — as Augustine truly observes. For, though the Blessed Speaker directed His words to St. Peter in particular, it is not to be imagined that He entrusted His "lambs" and His "sheep" to him *alone.* So obvious a circumstance would not require even passing notice, but for the profane and ridiculous pretensions of the Church of Rome, which are based, in great part, on the words of our SAVIOUR here recorded. The Papists assume,—(1st) that He hereby appointed St. Peter His Vicar upon Earth; (2ndly) that St. Peter was the first Bishop of Rome; (3rdly) that St. Peter transmitted to the Bishops of the same see in endless succes-

(*g*) St. Pet. v. 4.
(*i*) Ezek. xxxiv. 2.
(*k*) St. John x. 3.
(*m*) Williams.

(*h*) Ezek. xxxiv 16.
(*j*) Is. xl. 11.
(*l*) See St. Luke xxii. 34.
(*n*) See St. John xvi. 30.

sion, his own (supposed) authority over the rest of Christendom. Each one of these assumptions is simply unfounded and untrue; opposed alike to Scripture and to Reason; to the records of the early Church, and the opinions of the primitive Fathers. With such fictions, nevertheless, do Romish writers distort the true image of Christianity: disfiguring their commentaries therewith; and betraying, by a restless eagerness to obtrude their ambitious and unscriptural theory on all occasions, their secret misgivings as to its real value.

But *why*, (it will perhaps be asked,) did our LORD deliver this charge to *one*, if He designed it equally for the rest? — We begin by observing that a certain *precedence in Rank*, though no kind of *superiority in Authority*, was certainly enjoyed by St. Peter over the rest of the Apostles.(*o*) It is only necessary to take a careful review of the entire Gospel History to be fully convinced of this. To St. Peter, therefore, chief of the Apostles,—(*chief* in *rank*, where all were *equal* in *power*,)— what is more natural than that our SAVIOUR should address that instruction which He designed for the acceptance of the whole body?(*p*) When He conveyed the power of binding and loosing, He addressed His words, in the first instance, to St. Peter alone ;(*q*) "and yet we certainly know that they were not intended for St. Peter, exclusively of the other Apostles; for in the eighteenth chapter of the same Gospel, they are repeated in a promise to the Church; and in the twentieth of St. John, the promised power is given to the Twelve without distinction or difference."(*r*) The gracious intention of thus restoring the Great Apostle to his half-forfeited Apostleship, is suggested by Cyril as another reason why our LORD should have now addressed him singly. Cyprian declares that " the other Apostles were what Peter was, — endowed with an equal participation of honor and power; but the beginning [of Pastoral authority] proceeds from unity, that the Church may be shown to be *one*." . . . . Whatever may be thought of these suggestions, (which are as old as Christianity itself,) the modern *Church of Rome*, at all events, can lay no exclusive claim to any single privilege which our LORD may be supposed, at any time, to have bestowed on *Simon Peter*. This has been already shown in the notes on St. Matthew xvi. 19,—and a careful examination of the writings of the Fathers of the first three centuries does but serve " to confirm the ancient tradition of the entire equality in all powers and rights, not excluding the pastoral, of the whole Apostolic college."(*s*)

But *did* our LORD convey to St. Peter any special privilege on this occasion? Is there any reason for supposing that the Pastoral Office belongs to him alone,—and was derived from him to the others? We are conducted to the very opposite conclusion: First, because, being equal in all other Apostolic powers, the Apostles cannot be conceived to be unequal in the power which is conveyed in the Pastoral Commission. "But the real answer to the proposed question, is this: when we turn to the Apostolic commentary upon these sacred sayings contained in the latter Scriptures, — a commentary from which we derive the undeniable and inspired record of the meaning in which the LORD spake them; and the holy Apostles, under the Spirit of Knowledge and Power understood and administered them, — we find a complete and final proof of the equality of the Apostles in all Apostolic powers; and a disproof of any personal superiority of St. Peter, even in any such peculiar powers as may be esteemed specifically pastoral. It is impossible that this argument can be stated too strongly. There is not, from one end to the other of the Apostolical Epistles, a verse or word that can be tortured into proving or supporting the pastoral supremacy of St. Peter. There are, meanwhile, many words and passages, and recorded acts, which do most distinctly disprove it."(*t*) But it must suffice to refer the reader, for the partial proof of these statements, to the references at the foot of the page.(*u*)

A matter of deep and affecting interest it is, with the scene before us fresh in our recollection, to notice in what terms the same St. Peter afterwards exhorted the elders of the Church. "The elders which are among you I exhort, who am also an elder, and a witness of the sufferings of CHRIST, . . . Feed the flock of GOD which is among you, taking the oversight thereof, not by constraint, but willingly; not for filthy lucre, but of a ready mind; neither as being lords over GOD's heritage, but

(*o*) See vol. i. p. 155
(*q*) St. Matth. xvi. 19.
(*s*) Dr. Moberly.
(*p*) See Acts xx. 28. 1 St. Pet. v. 1 to 4.
(*r*) Dr. Moberly.
(*t*) Dr. Moberly.
(*u*) Consider Acts xv. 6 to 21. Gal. i. 1: ii. 6 to 9, and 11 to 14. 2 Cor. xi. 5: xii. 11, 12. St. Matth. xix. 28.

being ensamples to the flock. And when the chief Shepherd shall appear, ye shall
receive a crown of glory that fadeth not away."(z) It is worth observing also
that in this exhortation of St. Peter to the elders of the Church, he has a few words
of address to the "younger" also. St. John, in like manner, writes as well to the
"little children," and "young men," as to the "fathers" of his flock.(y)—The reader is here invited to call to mind a passage in St. Paul's charge to the elders of
Ephesus,—Acts xx. 28.

Whatever the nature of St. Peter's "grief" may have been at the repeated inquiry
of our LORD, most instructive surely is it to observe in what terms his anxieties
are dispelled: even by the announcement of the bloody baptism which was in store
for him! It follows:

18 Verily, verily, I say unto thee, When thou wast young, thou girdedst
thyself, and walkest whither thou wouldest: but when thou shalt be old,
thou shalt stretch forth thy hands, and another shall gird thee, and
carry *thee* whither thou wouldest not.

19 This spake HE, signifying by what death HE should glorify GOD.

Compare with these last words, the language of St. John xii. 32, 33,—where the
terms are recorded in which our Blessed LORD signified that He should Himself
die; should Himself "glorify GOD." See the note on St. John xiii. 31.

By such sayings, then, our SAVIOUR CHRIST intimated to Simon Peter, (obscurely,
as it seems to *us*,) that death by crucifixion would be his portion in his age; and the
Apostle grew old in the anticipation, (to *him* a blissful one!) of thus treading in his
Master's footsteps, and "following Him" in His mysterious pathway of pain.
"Knowing that shortly I must put off this my tabernacle, even as our LORD JESUS
CHRIST hath showed me." See 2 St. Peter i. 14.

"When thou wast young, thou girdedst thyself," &c.,—the action of one who prepares for bodily exertion.(a) But the words, here, seem to have been spoken with
special reference to the act which St. Peter had so lately performed; when he
yielded to the impulse of his love, and walked through the water whither he
would, — even unto CHRIST! . . . . *That* is perhaps why, (or one of the reasons
why,) the circumstance contained in the latter part of ver. 7, finds so distinct a
record.

"Thou shalt stretch forth thy hands." "The words are descriptive of the practice, mentioned by ancient authors, of stretching out the hands of criminals upon
the two extremities of a yoke placed across the neck, and so carrying them out to
crucifixion."(b) That St. Peter was crucified at Rome, we learn from Church History; and the affecting circumstance is recorded that he suffered by his own request,
with his head downwards,—as unworthy even to be agonized with the same agony
as his LORD.

In illustration of being "girded by another," refer to Acts xxi. 10, 11. It was
perhaps usual *to bind* criminals, by the loins, to the Cross whereon they suffered;
or at least, through decency, to gird them. Consider Psalm cxviii. 27.

"Whither thou wouldest not," by no means implies that St. Peter would be *unwilling* to suffer martyrdom for his Master's sake. The expression does but indicate
that the death by which "he should glorify GOD" would be one from which all the
blameless instincts of his Nature would recoil, — a violent and a torturing death.

And when HE had spoken this, HE saith unto him, Follow Me.

After the Paschal Supper was ended, it will be remembered that Simon Peter
said "LORD, whither goest Thou? JESUS answered Him, Whither I go, thou canst
not follow Me now; but thou shalt follow Me afterwards."(c) The season which
the Blessed Speaker then alluded to, had now at last arrived; and the solemn prophecy which goes before, sufficiently shows along *which* pathway, in particular, it
was intended that St. Peter should tread in his beloved Master's footsteps. That
same Master had indeed, long before, declared,—"If any man will come after Me,

(z) 1 St. Pet. v. 1 to 4.
(y) 1 St. Pet. v. 5, and 1 St. John ii. 12, 13, 14.
(a) See St. Luke xii. 35, and Exod. xii. 11.
(c) St. John xiii. 36, where see the note.

(b) Lonsdale and Hale.

let him deny himself, and take up his Cross, and follow Me."(*d*) (How far-reaching and many-sided are the sayings of our LORD!) To complete by symbol, therefore, the instruction which it was His gracious pleasure on this occasion to deliver to His highly-favoured servant, our SAVIOUR seems to have next moved to a little distance from the band of wondering Apostles; delivering to the foremost of the seven, as He went, the invitation,—"Follow Me!" . . . We do not need the assurance that the man so addressed was prompt to obey the summons; separating himself from his brethren, and proceeding a few paces in the same direction as his retiring LORD. · St. John is found to have followed,—(it must have been in silent adoring love!)—at a distance: for we read,

20 Then Peter, turning about, seeth the Disciple whom JESUS loved following; which also leaned on His breast at supper, and said, LORD, which is he that betrayeth Thee?

21 Peter seeing him saith to JESUS, LORD, and what *shall* this man *do?*

Take notice here, first, of the method by which the blessed writer of the present Gospel identifies himself. Enough has been already offered on this subject in the note on St. John iv. 46,—to which the reader is requested to refer. See also the note on St. John xiii. 25. It should however perhaps be suggested that there may have been a distinct reason why St. John, on the present occasion, refers in so pointed a manner to a certain incident in the history of the Paschal Supper. The three tokens of his Master's special favour which he enumerates, may have been the very considerations which now so weighed with St. Peter, (and of this, St. Peter himself may have afterwards informed St. John,) as to draw from his lips the memorable inquiry which follows.

The suggestion thus offered leads naturally to our next remark,—namely, that the solicitude of St. Peter to know what St. John was to do, deserves attention; and here the reader must be invited to consider what has been already written on chap. xviii. 15. So deeply must Simon by this time have become convinced of the lofty pinnacle which St. John occupied in their Master's love,—(was not St. John His chosen friend? yea, His adopted Brother?)—that on hearing the summons, "Follow Me!" addressed to himself, the natural instincts of an honest and good heart may well have caused St. Peter to turn about in quest of St. John. He beheld that favoured Apostle of THE LAMB, "following;" and he could not repress his loving desire, (for mere curiosity it was not,) to know what should be done by *him*. "LORD:" (he says,) "and *this* man,—what?" as if he would have added,—Is not *he* to follow Thee as well? Thou mysterious Risen One, who, moving away from us, dost graciously bid *me* to follow Thee,—may not this man, who hath never denied Thee, never forsaken Thee: may not *this man* follow Thee too? . . . He presumes not, however, to say all this. A broken sentence conveys all his timid inquiry: and our Divine LORD, by the form of His rejoinder, teaches him how much deeper had been the meaning of His command than either St. John, or himself, as yet, suspected. He also repeats the summons for the second, yea, rather for *the third*(*e*) time; and it becomes apparent that He uses the words figuratively,—as St. Peter now perceives full well.(*f*)

22 JESUS saith unto him, If I will that he tarry till I come, what *is that* to thee? follow thou Me.

This reply has been thought very difficult; but the most obvious interpretation of our LORD's meaning is probably also the correct one. He is intimating what shall be the portion of St. John; and His words seem to imply that the beloved Disciple should not "*follow*" Him,—should not *come* to Him through the gate of Martyrdom,—like Simon Peter: but that he should "*tarry*" behind; tarry for the coming of His LORD *to him*. . . . . This Divine method of speaking of Life and Death derives illustration from the following places of Scripture:—St. Mark xiii. 35, 36, (where see the note:) also Philipp. i. 23, 24, and 1 Cor. xv. 6; also St. Matthew xvi. 27, 28; and xxiv. 30.(*g*)

(*d*) St. Matth. xvi. 24. See also x. 38.
(*e*) See St. Matth. iv. 19, 20,   (*f*) Consider 1 St. Pet. ii. 21, &c.
(*g*) 2 Thess. iii. 5 is perhaps not a case in point: 1 Cor. i. 7 is not, certainly.

This, then, we regard as the Divine announcement of *the manner* of St. John's departure; (an event which, as we learn from this place, depended altogether on the *Will* of Him who is at once GOD and CHRIST;) and most instructive, as well as most comfortable, the language may well prove to every Christian heart. It is most instructive; for we cannot but call to remembrance the prophetic promise made by our SAVIOUR, long before, to St. James and St. John, that they should indeed drink of His bitter cup, and be made partakers of His Baptism and Blood.(*h*) St. James, the first Apostolic Martyr,(*i*) fulfilled our SAVIOUR's prophecy to the very letter: but how different in circumstance was the verification of that prophecy in the case of St. John! He was to "tarry" till CHRIST "came;" patiently to "linger on, year after year, in loneliness and weariness of spirit;"(*k*) to abide persecution,(*l*) oppression, and wrong; to endure the enmity of the wicked,(*m*) and the sight of heresies abounding in the Church:(*n*) "as if to exemplify all classes of the faithful, that there are *various modes* of drinking the cup of CHRIST, and being baptized even with that baptism with which He was finally baptized."(*o*) The reader is invited to read the note on St. Matthew xx. 23.

Our SAVIOUR's language is most comfortable,—for it recalls those many places in the Gospel where Death is spoken of as disarmed of its terrors. Thus,—"When ye *fail*," said our LORD, in a certain place;(*p*) meaning "When ye *die*." As if to teach us that the death of His Saints is, in His sight, but like the fainting of a strong man at the end of a long race; a mere failure of bodily vigour. Nay, Death is "*abolished*,"(*q*) according to the Gospel view. This subject will be found to be touched upon above, at page 446. . . . The Divine Speaker's intention, then, seems to have been, not so much to intimate that St. John was *to die*, as that he was *to wait*: to imply, not so much that *he* was to *go*, as that CHRIST was to *come*. "Surely I *come quickly*. Amen," are accordingly the last words addressed by Revelation to the Evangelist; and he closes the inspired Canon with his own devout reply,— "Even so, *come*, LORD JESUS!"(*r*)

Besides what this memorable reply may be considered to reveal, as well concerning the future destiny of St. John, as concerning our own state in Life and in Death, the rebuke thus administered to St. Peter is surely full of practical teaching, also. The words seem to have an abiding force, and to be of universal application; yet not because they are *ambiguous*, (like the oracles of old,) but because they are *Divine*. They are made up of rebuke and counsel. "What is that to thee?"— which of us has not deserved the rebuke? "Follow thou Me!"—which of us does not require the counsel? The heart and eye are thus called away from the problem which perplexes, the prospect which discourages, the thoughts which distract and paralyze; and a plain duty is proposed instead. Not Speculation is enjoined, but Practice; not knowledge, but Goodness; not another man's matters, but *our own*. Let the reader consider the places indicated at foot;(*s*) and decide whether St. Peter may not have learned *now* the lesson which he afterwards conveyed to the Church in the precept that no one should be "*a busybody in other men's matters*."(*t*) . . . Nay, our LORD's rebuke may well silence over-anxiety also about our own future fate: as "what thoughtful, forecasting Christian has not felt a desire to know how long he shall live? what shall be the manner of his life, and what of his death? Such inquiries are sure to arise, more or less, in every breast: but He who alone could make answer, will not. Ask Him, and He will say,—"If I will that thou tarry till I come, what is that to thee?"(*u*)

Leighton says,—"This was a transient stumbling in one who, but lately recovered of a great disease, did not walk firmly. But it is the common track of most, to wear out their days with impertinent inquiries. There is a natural desire in men to know the things of others, and to neglect their own; and to be more concerned about things to come, than about things present."

(*h*) St. Matth. xx. 23, and St. Mark x. 39.
(*i*) Acts xii. 2.
(*l*) Rev. i. 9.
(*k*) Rev. A. P. Stanley.
(*m*) 1 St. John iii. 13: 2 St. John ver. 9, 10.
(*n*) 1 St. John ii. 18, 19, 26: iv. 1, 3. 2 St. John ver. 7.
(*o*) Dr. W. H. Mill.
(*p*) St. Luke xvi. 9,—where see the beginning of the note.
(*q*) 2 Tim. i. 10.
(*r*) Rev. xxii. 20.
(*s*) St. Luke xiii. 1 to 3; and 23 to 24. St. Matth. vi. 31 to 33. Exod. xxxiii. 18, 19. Deut. xxix. 29. Ps. cxxxi. 1, 2.
(*t*) 1 St. Pet. iv. 15. Compare 1 Tim. v. 13.
(*u*) From a MS. Sermon by the Rev. Edm. Hobhouse.

23 Then went this saying abroad among the brethren, that that Disciple should not die :

Would it not seem to be a fair inference from the present verse, that the Evangelist St. John, at the time when he wrote his Gospel, was a very aged person ?

The literal sense in which, (as we gather from this passage,) the primitive Church was accustomed to understand the words of her LORD, is striking and instructive. No quaint improbable notion that the Blessed Speaker referred, in the words before us, to the Destruction of Jerusalem, found place in the minds of these simple men. The event alluded to was over long before the date at which St. John wrote his Gospel ; but the "saying" that " the Disciple whom JESUS loved" " should not die," still prevailed in the Church. These early believers reasoned thus :—CHRIST spake of St. John's tarrying till Himself *came ;* but CHRIST is in Heaven, — from whence He shall *come(x)* to " judge the quick and the dead,(*y*) at the Last Day. St. John is therefore one of those who will " be alive and remain unto the coming of the LORD,"(*z*)—(a season, be it observed, which some of the first believers incorrectly supposed to be very near at hand. See 2 Thess. ii. 2 to 6.) . . . The simple manner, meanwhile, in which the Evangelist himself, without either denying or admitting the possible correctness of the inference, effectually shows that the thing itself had not been by his Divine Master foretold, — is much to be noticed. He says,

yet JESUS said not unto him, He shall not die ; but, If I will that he tarry till I come, what *is* that to thee ?

O faithful witness ! Verily, the man who could so write, was a fit person to be an Evangelist. St. John here teaches us in what way we should deal with Divine Truth when its features come to us concealed under a dark saying. It must be our part to accept every statement of our LORD even as *He* hath been pleased to deliver it to our acceptance : not to gloss it with fancies of our own. Do but consider how applicable to the supposed equivalent of many a controverted saying in Divinity, the words of the text would be !

24 This is the Disciple which testifieth of these things, and wrote these things : and we know that his testimony is true.

"*We* know," — as in 1 St. John i. 1 to 5, and 3 St. John ver. 12. Consider also 1 Thess. ii. 18. In such terms does St. John indicate *himself;* explaining to the Church *who* was the author of the last of the Four Gospels, — and certainly not excepting this, the concluding chapter of all. The expressions may be compared with what are found in chap. xix. 35, where the reader is invited to peruse the note. " The emphatic singularity of his designation as ' the Disciple whom JESUS loved,'— the mystery which encompassed, and in some degree still seems to overshadow the Divine announcement of his destiny to his fellow Apostle, — are made yet more striking and significant to us by the circumstance that the subject of these mysterious words is also their recorder. It cannot but be so when we perceive what the narrative itself impresses irresistibly on every reader, that it is dictated by no self-exalting, no self-reflecting spirit, but by a deep devotion of the author's whole mind and thoughts to the Speaker, the Incarnate WORD ; whose special love to himself inspires awe as well as gratitude : — an awe that suffers him not to name himself beside others apparently less favoured ; while every word that fell from his LORD, is, on that account, treasured up with reverence, as full of weighty meaning ; fraught with the mysteries of an Eternal Life."(*a*)

25 And there are also many other things which JESUS did ; the which, if they should be written every one, I suppose that even the World itself could not contain the books that should be written. Amen.

"Great and many were the miracles which Moses and the rest of the Prophets wrought for the ratification of the Law, and the demonstration of God's constant presence with His people ; and yet, all those wrought by so many several persons, in the space of above three thousand years, are far short of those which our LORD

(*x*) St. Matth. xvi. 27 : xxiv. 30.   (*y*) 2 Tim. iv. 1.
(*z*) 1 Thess. iv. 15.   (*a*) Dr. W. H. Mill.

Jesus Christ did perform within the compass of three years;"—concerning which, (adds Bishop Pearson,) " St. John testifieth *with as great certainty of truth as height of hyperbole."*

"Amen," he adds, (like his three predecessors,) in confirmation of every sentence which has gone before; and doubtless of the sentence with which he concludes. Let us not prate, then, about " the hyperbolical language of the East," in order to dwarf this majestic statement of the faithful witness, — this " record" of him " that saw it." Let not our last words be words of cold, paltry criticism ; but rather of adoration, and wonder, and admiring love. The blessed Writer seems to have been transported, at last, by the recollection of the many things he had been divinely guided to leave unsaid : — those many mighty Miracles, which neither in this, nor in any other Gospel, find the slightest record ;(b) — those many Discourses, so full of unutterable Majesty and sweetness, to which we scarcely anywhere find so much as an allusion ;(c)—and he challenges the World itself to find room for the written history of His beloved Master's acts and sayings, even could historians be found to commit each several particular to writing. Surely, at such words, our part should only be to wonder and admire ! " Blessed be the Lord God, the God of Israel, who only doeth wondrous things ! And blessed be His glorious Name for ever : and let the whole Earth be filled with His Glory ; Amen, and Amen !"(d)

(b) Consider St. Matth. xi. 20, 21, 23 : iv. 24. St. Mark i. 32, &c.
(c) Consider St. Matth. iv. 23 : ix. 35. St. Mark vi. 6. St. Luke xiii. 22 : xxi. 37 : xxiv. 27, &c.
(d) Ps. lxxii. 18, 19.

Teque deprecor, bone JESU, ut cui propitius donasti verba Tuæ Scientiæ dulciter haurire, dones etiam benignus aliquando ad Te, fontem omnis sapientiæ pervenire, et parere semper ante faciem Tuam ! Ven. Beda, ad calcem Hist. Eccl.